SMOKESCREEN

DICK FRANCIS wrote more than forty international bestsellers and was widely acclaimed as one of the world's finest thriller writers. His awards included the Crime Writers' Association's Cartier Diamond Dagger for his outstanding contribution to the genre, and an honorary Doctorate of Humane Letters from Tufts University of Boston. In 1996 Dick Francis was made a Mystery Writers of America Grand Master for a lifetime's achievement and in 2000 he was awarded the CBE in the Queen's Birthday Honours list. Sadly he died in 2010.

Also by Dick Francis

Dead Cert   Nerve   For Kicks
Odds Against   Flying Finish   Blood Sport
Forfeit   Enquiry   Rat Race
Bonecrack   Slay-Ride   Knock Down
High Stakes   Longshot   Decider
In the Frame   Risk   Trial Run
Whip Hand   Reflex   Twice Shy
Banker   The Danger   Proof
Break In   Bolt   Hot Money
The Edge   Straight   Comeback
Driving Force   Wild Horses   Come to Grief
To the Hilt   10lb Penalty   Field of 13
Second Wind   Shattered   Under Orders

With Felix Francis

Dead Heat   Silks

Autobiography

The Sport of Queens

Biography

Lester: the Official Biography

Dick Francis

SMOKESCREEN

PAN BOOKS

First published 1972 by Michael Joseph Ltd

This edition published 2009 by Pan Books
an imprint of Pan Macmillan, a division of Macmillan Publishers Limited
Pan Macmillan, 20 New Wharf Road, London N1 9RR
Basingstoke and Oxford
Associated companies throughout the world
www.panmacmillan.com

ISBN 978-0-330-51917-5

1 3 5 7 9 8 6 4 2

A CIP catalogue record for this book is available from
the British Library.

Typeset by SetSystems Ltd, Saffron Walden, Essex
Printed and bound by CPI Group (UK) Ltd, Croydon, CR0 4YY

With thanks to

Jane and Christoper Coldrey

CHAPTER ONE

Sweating, thirsty, hot, uncomfortable, and tired to the point of explosion.

Cynically, I counted my woes.

Considerable, they were. Considerable, one way and another.

I sat in the driving seat of a custom-built aerodynamic sports car, the cast-off toy of an oil sheik's son. I had been sitting there for the best part of three days. Ahead, the sun dried plain spread gently away to some distant brown and purple hills, and hour by hour their hunched shapes remained exactly where they were on the horizon, because the 150 mph Special was not moving.

Nor was I. I looked morosely at the solid untarnishable handcuffs locked round my wrists. One of my arms led through the steering wheel, and the other was outside it, so that in total effect I was locked on to the wheel, and in consequence firmly attached to the car.

There was also the small matter of seat belts. The Special would not start until the safety harness was fastened. Despite the fact that the key was missing from the ignition, the harness was securely fastened: one strap over my stomach, one diagonally across my chest.

I could not bring my legs up from their stretched forward sports car position in order to break the steering wheel with my feet. I had tried it. I was too tall, and couldn't bend my knees far enough. And apart from that, the steering wheel was not of possibly breakable plastic. People who built spectacularly expensive cars like the Special didn't mess around with plastic steering wheels. This was one of the small diameter leather-covered metal type, as durable as Mont Blanc.

I was thoroughly fed up with sitting in the car. Every muscle in my legs, up my spine and down my arms protested energetically against the constraint. A hard band of heaviness behind my eyes was tightening into a perceptible ache.

It was time to make another determined effort to get free, though I knew from countless similar attempts that it couldn't be done.

I tugged, strained, used all my strength against the straps and the handcuffs: struggled until fresh sweat rolled down my face; and couldn't, as before, progress even a millimetre towards freedom.

I put my head back against the padded headrest, and rolled my face around towards the open window beside me, on my right.

I shut my eyes. I could feel the slash of sunlight cut across my cheek and neck and shoulder with all the vigour of 15.00 hours in July at 37° North. I could feel the heat on my left eyelid. I let lines of frustration and pain develop across my forehead, put a certain grimness into my mouth, twitched a muscle along my jaw, and swallowed with an abandonment of hope.

After that I sat still, and waited.

The desert plain was very quiet.

I waited.

Then Evan Pentelow shouted 'Cut' with detectable reluctance, and the cameramen removed their eyes from the view-finders. No whisper of wind fluttered the large bright-coloured umbrellas which shielded them and their apparatus. Evan fanned himself vigorously with his shooting schedule, creating the breeze that nature had neglected, and others in the small group in the shade of portable green polystyrene sun-shelters came languidly to life, the relentless heat having hours ago drained their energy. The sound mixer took off his ear-phones, hung them over the back of his chair, and fiddled slowly with the knobs on his Nagra recorder, and the electricians kindly switched off the clutch of minibrute lamps which had been ruthlessly reinforcing the sun.

I looked into the lens of the Arriflex which had been recording every sweating pore at a distance of six feet from my right shoulder. Terry, behind his camera, mopped his neck with a dusty handkerchief, and Simon added to his Picture Negative Report for the processing laboratory.

Further back, from a different angle, the Mitchell with its thousand feet magazine had shot the same scene. Lucky, who operated it, was busily not meeting my eye, as he had been since breakfast. He believed I was angry with him, because, although he swore it was not his fault, the last lot of film he had shot the day before had turned out to be fogged. I had asked him quite mildly in the circumstances just to be sure that today there should be no more mishaps, as I reckoned I couldn't stand many more retakes of Scene 623.

Since then, we had retaken it six times. With, I grant you, a short break for lunch.

Evan Pentelow had apologized to everyone, loudly and often, that we would just have to go on and on shooting the scene until I got it right. He changed his mind about how it should go after every second take, and although I followed a good many of his minutely detailed directions, he had not yet once pronounced himself satisfied.

Every single member of the team who had come to southern Spain to complete the location shots was aware of the animosity behind the tight-reined politeness with which he spoke to me, and behind that with which I answered him. The unit, I had heard, had opened a book on how long I would hang on to my temper.

The girl who carried the precious key to the handcuffs walked slowly over from the furthest green shelter, where the continuity, make-up, and wardrobe girls sat exhaustedly on spread out towels. Tendrils of damp hair clung to the girl's neck as she opened the door of the car and fitted the key into the hole. They were regulation British police handcuffs, fastening with a stiffish screw instead of a ratchet, and she always had some difficulty in pushing the key round its last few all-important turns.

She looked at me apprehensively, knowing that I couldn't be far from erupting. I achieved at least the muscle movements of a smile, and relief at not being bawled at gave her impetus to finish taking off the handcuffs smoothly and quickly.

I unfastened the seat harness and stood up stiffly outside in the sun. It was a good ten degrees cooler than inside the Special.

'Get back in,' Evan said. 'We'll have to take it again.'

I inhaled a lungful straight from the Sahara, and counted five in my mind. Then I said, 'I'm going over to the caravan for a beer and a pee, and we'll shoot it again when I come back.'

They wouldn't pay out the pool on that, I thought in amusement. That might be a crack in the volcano, but it wasn't Krakatoa. I wondered if they would let me take a bet on the flashpoint myself.

No one had bothered to put the canvas over the Minimoke, to shield it from the sun. I climbed into the little buggy where it was parked behind the largest shelter, and swore as the seat leather scorched through my thin cotton trousers. The steering wheel was hot enough to fry eggs.

The legs of my trousers were rolled up to the knee, and on my feet were flip-flops. They contrasted oddly with the formal white shirt and dark tie which I wore above, but then the Arriflex angle cut me off at the knee, and the Mitchell higher still, above the waist.

I drove the Moke without haste to where the semicircle of caravans was parked, two hundred yards away in a hollow. An apology for a tree cast a patch of thinnish shade that was better than nothing for the Moke, so I stopped it there and walked over to the caravan assigned to me as a dressing-room.

The air-conditioning inside hit like a cold shower, and felt marvellous. I loosened my tie, undid the top button of my shirt, fetched a can of beer from the refrigerator, and sat wearily down on the divan to drink it.

Evan Pentelow was busy paying off an old resentment, and unfortunately there was no way I could stop him. I had worked with him only once before, on his first major film and my seventh, and by the end of it we had detested each other. Nothing had improved by my subsequently refusing to sign for films if he were to direct, a circumstance which had cut him off from at least two smash hits he might otherwise have collared.

Evan was the darling of those critics who believed that actors couldn't act unless the director told them inch by inch what to do. Evan never gave directions by halves: he liked to see his films called 'Evan Pentelow's latest', and he achieved that by making the gullible believe that step by tiny step the whole thing stemmed from his talent, and his alone. Never mind how old a hand an actor was, Evan remorselessly taught him his business. Evan never *discussed* how a scene should be played, how a word should be inflected. He dictated.

He had cut some great names down to size, down to notices like 'Pentelow has drawn a sympathetic performance from Miss Five-Star Blank . . .' He resented everyone, like me, who wouldn't give him the chance.

There was no doubt that he was an outstanding director in that he had a visual imagination of a very high quality. Most actors positively liked to work with him, as their salaries were generous and his films never went unsung. Only uncompromising bloody asses like myself believed that at least nine-tenths of a performance should be the actor's own work.

I sighed, finished the beer, visited the loo, and went out to the Moke. Apollo still raged away in the brazen sky, as one might say if one had a taste for that sort of thing.

The original director of the glossy action thriller on which we were engaged had been a quiet-spoken sophisticate who usually lifted the first elbow before breakfast and had died on his feet at 10 a.m., from a surfeit of Scotch. It happened during a free weekend which I had spent alone in Yorkshire, walking on the hills, and I had returned to the set on Tuesday to find Evan already ensconsed and making his stranglehold felt.

There was about an eighth of the film still to do. The sly smile that he had put on when he saw me arrive had been pure clotted malice.

Protestations to the management had brought soothing noises but no joy.

'No one else of that calibre was free . . . can't take risks with the backers' money, can we, not as things are these days . . . got to look at it realistically . . . sure, Link, I know you won't work with him ordinarily, but this is a *crisis*, dammit . . . it isn't actually in your contract in black and white this time, you know, because I checked . . . well, actually, we were relying on your good nature, I suppose . . .'

I interrupted dryly, 'And on the fact that I'll be collecting four per cent of the gross?'

The management cleared its throat. 'Er, we wouldn't ourselves have made the mistake of reminding you . . . but since you mention it . . . yes.'

Amused, I had finally given in, but with foreboding, as the location scenes of the car all lay ahead. I had known Evan would be difficult: hadn't reckoned, though, that he would be the next best thing to sadistic.

I stopped the Moke with a jerk behind the shelter and pulled the canvas cover over it to stop it sizzling. I had been away exactly twelve minutes, but when I walked round into the shelter Evan was apologizing to the camera crews for my keeping them hanging around in this heat. Terry made a disclaiming gesture, as I could see perfectly well that he had barely finished loading the Arriflex with a fresh mazagine out of the ice box. No one bothered to argue. At a hundred degrees in the shade, no one but Evan had any energy.

'Right,' he said briskly, 'Get into the car, Link. Scene 623, Take 10. And let's for hell's sake get this one right.'

I said nothing. Of the nine previous takes, three had been fogged: that left today's six; and I knew, as everyone else knew, that Evan could have used any one of them.

I got into the car. We retook the scene twice more.

Evan managed to shake his head dubiously even after that, but the head cameraman told him the light was getting too yellow, and even if they took any more it would be no good, as they wouldn't be able to match it to the scene which went before. Evan gave in only because he could come up with no possible reason for going on, for which Apollo had my thanks.

The unit packed up. The girl came limply across and undid the handcuffs. Two general duty men began to wrap up the Special in dust-sheets and pegged-down tarpaulins, and Terry and Lucky began to dismantle their cameras and pack them in cases, to take them away for the night.

In twos and threes everyone straggled across to the caravans, with me driving Evan in the Moke and saying not a word to him on the way. The coach had arrived from the small nearby town of Madroledo, bringing the two nightwatchmen. Coach was a flattering word for it; an old airport runabout bus with a lot of room for equipment and minimum comfort for passengers. The company said they had stipulated a luxury touring coach with air-conditioning, but the bone-shaker was what had actually turned up.

The hotel in Madroledo where the whole unit was staying was in much the same category. The small inland town, far from the tourist beat, offered amenities that package holiday operators would have blanched at; but the management had had to install us there, they said, because the best hotels on the coast at Almeria were booked solid by hundreds of Americans engaged on making an epic Western in the next bit of desert to ours.

In fact I much preferred even the rough bits of this film to the last little caper I had been engaged on, a misty rock-climbing affair in which I had spent days and days clinging to the ledges while the effects men showered buckets of artificial rainstorm over my head. It was never much good my complaining about the occasional wringers I got put through: I'd started out as a sort of stunt man, they said, so what was a little cold, a little heat? Get out there on the ledges, they said. Get out there in the car. And just concentrate on how much lolly you're stacking away to comfort you later through arthritis. Never fear, they said, we won't let you come to any real harm, not so long as the insurance premiums are so high, and not so long as almost every film you make covers its production costs in the first month of showing. Such charming people, those managements, with dollar signs for eyes, cash registers for hearts.

Cooler and cleaner, the entire unit met for before-dinner drinks in Madroledo's idea of an American Bar. Away out on the plain in the warm night the Special sat under its guarding floodlights, a shrouded hump, done with for the day. By tomorrow night, I thought, or at least the day after, we would have completed all the scenes which needed me stuck in the driving seat. Provided Evan could think of no reason for re-shooting Scene 623 yet again, we only had 624 and 625 to do, the cavalry-to-the-rescue bits. We had done Scenes 622 and 621, which showed the man waking from a drugged sleep, and assessing his predicament, and the helicopter shots were also in the can; the wide-circling and then narrowing aerial views which established the Special in its bare lonely terrain, and gave glimpses of the man slumped inside. Those were to be the opening shots of the film and the background to the credits, the bulk of the story being told afterwards in one long flashback to explain why the car and the man were where they were.

In the bar Terry and the Director of Photography were holding a desultory discussion about focal lengths, punctuating every wise thought with draughts of sangria. The Director, otherwise known professionally as the lighting cameraman, and personally as Conrad, patted me gently on the shoulder and pressed an almost cold glass into my hand. We had all grown to like this indigenous thirst quencher, a rough red local wine diluted by ice and a touch of the fruit salads.

'There you are, dear boy, it does wonders for the dehydration,' he said, and then in the same breath finished his broken-off sentence to Terry. 'So he used an eighteen millimetre wide angle and of course every scrap of tension evaporated from the scene.'

Conrad spoke from the strength of an Oscar on the sideboard, and called everyone 'dear boy' from chairmen downwards. Aided by a naturally resonant bass voice and a droopy cultivated moustache, he had achieved the notable status of 'a character' in a business which specialized in them, but behind the flamboyance there was a sharp technician's mind which saw life analytically at twenty-four frames per second and thought in Eastman-colour.

Terry said, 'Beale Films won't use him now because of the time he shot two thousand feet one day at Ascot without an 85 filter, and there wasn't another race meeting due there until a month after they ran into compensation time . . .'

Terry was fat, bald, forty, and had given up earlier aspirations to climb to Director of Photography with his name writ large in credits. He had settled instead for being a steady, reliable, experienced, and continually in-work craftsman, and Conrad always liked to have him on his team.

Simon joined us and Conrad gave him, too, a glass of Sangria. Simon, the clapper/loader of Terry's crew, had less assurance than he ought to have had at twenty-three, and was sometimes naïve to the point where one speculated about arrested development. His job entailed operating the clapper board before every shot, keeping careful records of the type and footage of film used, and loading the raw film into the magazines which were used in the cameras.

Terry himself had taught him how to load the magazines, a job which meant winding unexposed film on to reels, in total darkness and by feel only. Everyone, to begin with, learned how to do it with unwanted exposed film in a well-lit room, and practised it over and over until they could do it with their eyes shut. When Simon could do this faultlessly, Terry sent him to load some magazines in earnest, and it was not until after a long day's shooting that the laboratory discovered all the film to be completely black.

Simon, it appeared, had done exactly what he had been taught: gone into the loading room and threaded the film on to the magazine with his eyes shut. And left the electric light on while he did it.

He took a sip of his pink restorer, looked at the others in bewilderment, and said, 'Evan told me to write "print" against every one of those shots we took today.' He searched their faces for astonishment and found none. 'But, I say,' he protested, 'if all the first takes were good enough to print, why on earth did he go on doing so many?'

No one answered except Conrad, who looked at him with pity and said, 'Work it out, dear boy. Work it out.' But Simon hadn't the equipment.

The bar room was large and cool, with thick white-painted walls and a brown tiled floor: pleasant in the daytime, when we were seldom there, but too stark at night because of the glaring striplighting some insensitive soul had installed on the ceiling. The four girls, sitting languidly round a table with half empty glasses of lime juice and Bacardi and soda, took on a greenish tinge as the sunlight faded outside, and aged ten years. The pouches beneath Conrad's eyes developed shadows, and Simon's chin receded too far for flattery.

Another long evening stretched ahead, exactly like the nine that had gone before: several hours of shop and gossip punctuated by occasional brandies, cigars and a Spanish-type dinner. I hadn't even any lines to learn for the next day, as my entire vocal contribution to Scenes 624 and 625 was to be a variety of grunts and mumbles. I would be glad, I thought, by God I would be glad, to get back home.

We went in to eat in a private dining-room as uninviting as the bar. I found myself between Simon and the handcuffs' girl, two-thirds of the way along one side of the long table at which we all sat together haphazardly. About twenty-five of us, there were: all technicians of some sort except me and the actor due to amble to the rescue as a Mexican peasant. The group had been cut to a minimum, and our stay scheduled for as short a time as possible: the management had wanted even the desert scenes shot at Pinewood like the rest of the film, or at least on some dried up bit of England, but the original director had stuck out for the authentic shimmer of real heat, damn and bless his departed spirit.

There was an empty space around the far side of the table.

No Evan.

'He's telephoning,' the handcuffs' girl said. 'I think he's been telephoning ever since we came back.'

I nodded. Evan telephoned the management most evenings, though not normally at great length. He was probably having difficulty getting through.

'I'll be glad to go home,' the girl said, sighing. Her first location job, which she had looked forward to, was proving disappointing; boring, too hot and no fun. Jill – her real name was Jill, though Evan had started calling her Handcuffs, and most of the unit had copied him – slid a speculative look sideways at my face, and added, 'Won't you?'

'Yes,' I said neutrally.

Conrad, sitting opposite, snorted loudly. 'Handcuffs, dear girl, that's cheating. Anyone who prods him has her bet cancelled.'

'It wasn't a prod,' she said defensively.

'Next best thing.'

'Just how many of you are in this pool?' I asked sarcastically.

'Everyone except Evan,' Conrad admitted cheerfully. 'Quite a healthy little jackpot it is.'

'And has anyone lost their money yet?'

Conrad chuckled. 'Most of them, dear boy. This afternoon.'

'And you,' I said, 'have you?'

He narrowed his eyes at me and put his head on one side. 'You've a temper that blows the roof off, but usually on behalf of someone else.'

'He can't answer your question, you see,' Jill explained to me. 'That's against the rules too.'

But I had worked with Conrad on three previous films, and he had indeed told me where he had placed his bet.

Evan came back from telephoning, walked purposefully to his empty chair, and splashed busily into his turtle soup. Intent, concentrated, he stared at the table and either didn't hear or didn't wish to hear, Terry's tentative generalities.

I looked at Even thoughtfully. At forty he was wiry, of medium height and packed with aggressive energy. He had undisciplined black curling hair, a face in which even the bones looked determined, and fierce hot brown eyes. That evening the eyes were looking inwards, seeing visions in his head; and the tumultuous activity going on in there showed unmistakably in the tension in his muscles. His spoon was held in rigid ringers, and his neck and back were as stiff as stakes.

I didn't like his intensity, not at any time or in any circumstances. It always set up in me the unreasonable reaction of wanting to avoid doing what he was pressing for, even when his ideas made good sense. That evening he was building up a good head of steam, and my own antipathy rose to match.

He shovelled his way briskly through the anglicized *paella* which followed, and pushed his empty plate away decisively.

'Now . . .' he said: and everybody listened. His voice sounded loud and high, strung up with his inner urgency. It would have been impossible to sit in that room and ignore him.

'As you know, this film we are making is called *Man in a Car*.'

We knew.

'And as you know, the car has figured in at least half the scenes that have been shot.'

We knew that too, better than he did, as we had been with it all through.

'Well . . .' he paused, looking round the table, collecting eyes. 'I have been talking to the producer, and he agrees . . . I want to change the emphasis . . . change the whole shape of the film. There are going to be a number of flashbacks now, and not just one. The story will jump back every time from the desert scene and each desert shot will give an impression of the days passing, and show the man growing weaker. There is to be no rescue, as such. This means, I'm afraid, Stephen . . .' He looked directly at the other actor, '. . . that your part is out entirely, but you will of course be paid what was agreed.' He turned back to the unit in general. 'We are going to scrap those cool witty scenes of reunion with the girl that you did at Pinewood. Instead, we will end the film with the reverse of the opening. That is to say, a helicopter shot that starts with the car in close-up and gradually recedes from it until it is merely a dot on the plain. The view will widen just at the end to indicate a peasant walking along a ridge of hill, leading a donkey, and everyone who sees the film can decide for himself whether the peasant rescues the man, or passes by without seeing him.'

He cleared his throat into a wholly attentive silence. 'This of course means that we shall have to do much more work here on location. I estimate that we will here for at least another two weeks, as there will have to be many more scenes of Link in the car.'

Someone groaned. Evan looked fiercely in the direction of the protest, and silenced it effectively. Only Conrad made any actual comment.

'I'm glad I'm behind the camera, and not in front of it,' he said slowly. 'Link's showing wear and tear already.'

I pushed the last two bits of chicken around with my fork, not really seeing my plate. Conrad was staring across at me: I could feel his eyes. And all the others', too. It was the actor in me, I knew, which kept them waiting while I ate a mouthful, drank some wine, and finally looked up again at Evan.

'All right,' I said.

A sort of quiver ran through the unit, and I realized they had all been holding their breath for the explosion of the century. But setting my own feelings aside, I had to admit that what Evan had suggested made excellent film sense, and I trusted to that instinct, if not to his humanity. There was a lot I would do, to make a good film.

He was surprised at my unconditional agreement, but also excited by it. Visions poured out of him, faster than his tongue.

'There will be tears . . . and skin cracks, and sun blisters . . . and terrible thirst . . . and muscles and tendons quivering with strain like violin strings, and hands curled with cramp . . . and agony and frightful despair . . . and the scorching, inexorable, thunderous silence . . . and towards the end, the gradual disintegration of a human soul . . . so that even if he is rescued he will be different . . . and there won't be a single person who sees the film who doesn't leave exhausted and wrung out and filled with pictures he'll never forget.'

The camera crews listened with an air of we've-seen-all-this-before and the make-up girl began looking particularly thoughtful. It was only I who seemed to see it from the inside looking out, and I felt a shudder go through my gut as if it had been a real dying I was to do, and not pretence. It was foolish. I shook myself; shook off the illusion of personal involvement. To be any good, acting had to be deliberate, not emotional.

He paused in his harangue, waiting with fixed gaze for me to answer him, and I reckoned that if I were not to let him stampede all over me it was time to contribute something myself.

'Noise,' I said calmly.

What . . .?'

'Noise,' I repeated. 'He would make a noise, too, at first. Shouting for help. Shouting from fury, and hunger, and terror. Shouting his bloody head off.'

Evan's eyes widened and embraced the truth of it.

'Yes,' he said. He took a deep ecstatic breath at the thought of his idea taking actual shape. '. . . Yes.'

Some of the inner furnace died down to a saner, more calculating heat.

'Will you do it?' he said.

I knew he meant not would I just get through the scenes

somehow, but would I put into them the best I could. And he might well ask, after his behaviour to me that day. I would, I thought; I would make it bloody marvellous; but I answered him flippantly.

'There won't be a dry eye in the house.'

He looked irritated and disappointed, which would do no harm. The others relaxed and began talking, but some undercurrent of excitement had awoken, and it was the best evening we had had since we arrived.

So we went back to the desert plain for another two weeks, and it was lousy, but the glossy little adventure turned into an eventual box-office blockbuster which even the critics seemed to like.

I got through the whole fortnight with my temper intact; and in consequence Conrad, who had guessed right, won his bet and scooped the pool.

CHAPTER TWO

England in August seemed green and cool in comparison when I got back. At Heathrow I collected my car, a production line BMW, darkish blue, ordinarily jumbled registration number, nothing Special about it, and drove westwards into Berkshire with a feeling of ease.

Four o'clock in the afternoon.

Going home.

I found myself grinning at nothing in particular. Like a kid out of school, I thought. Going home to a summer evening.

The house was middle-sized, part old, part new, built on a gentle slope outside a village far up the Thames. There was a view down over the river, and lots of evening sun, and an unsignposted lane to approach by, that most people missed.

There was a boy's bicycle lying half on the grass, half on the drive, and some gardening tools near a half weeded flowerbed. I stopped the car outside the garage, looked at the shut front door, and walked round the house to the back.

I saw all four of them before they saw me; like looking in through a window. Two small boys splashing in the pool with a black and white beach ball. A slightly faded sun umbrella nearby, with a little girl lying on an air bed in its shade. A young woman with short chestnut hair, sitting on a rug in the sun, hugging her knees.

One of the boys looked up and saw me standing watching them from across the lawn.

'Hey,' he shouted. 'Dad's home,' and ducked his brother.

I walked towards them, smiling. Charlie unstuck herself from the rug and came unhurriedly to meet me.

'Hi,' she said. 'I'm covered in oil.' She put her mouth forward for a kiss and held my face between the insides of her wrists.

'What on earth have you been doing with yourself?' she asked. 'You look terribly thin.'

'It was hot in Spain,' I said. I walked back to the pool beside her, stripping off my loosened tie, and then my shirt.

'You didn't get very sunburned.'

'No . . . Sat in the car most of the time . . .'

'Did it go all right?'

I made a face. 'Time will tell . . . How are the kids?'

'Fine.'

I had been away a month. It might have been a day. Any father coming home to his family after a day's work.

Peter levered himself out of the pool via his stomach and splashed across the grass.

'What did you bring us?' he demanded.

'Pete, I've *told* you . . .' Charlie said, exasperated. 'If you ask, you won't *get*.'

'You won't get much this time anyway,' I told him. 'We were miles from any decent shops. And go and pick your bike up off the drive.'

'Oh honestly,' he said. 'The minute you're home, we've done something wrong.' He retreated round the house, his backview stiff with protest.

Charlie laughed. 'I'm glad you're back . . .'

'Me too.'

'Dad, look at me. Look at me do this, Dad.'

I obediently watched while Chris turned some complicated sort of somersault over the beach ball and came up with a triumphant smile, shaking water out of his eyes and waiting for praise.

'Jolly good,' I said.

'Watch me again, Dad . . .'

'In a minute.'

Charlie and I walked over to the umbrella, and looked down at our daughter. She was five years old, brown-haired, and pretty. I sat down beside the air bed and tickled her tummy. She chuckled, and smiled at me deliriously.

'How's she been?'

'Same as usual.'

'Shall I take her in the pool?'

'She came in with me this morning . . . but she loves it. It wouldn't do her any harm to go again.'

Charlie squatted down beside her. 'Daddy's home, little

one,' she said. But to Libby, our little one, the words themselves meant almost nothing. Her mental development had slowed to a snail's pace after the age of ten months, when her skull had been fractured. Peter, who had been five then, had lifted her out of her pram, wanting to be helpful and bring her indoors for lunch. But Charlie, going out to fetch her, had seen him trip and fall and it had been Libby's head which struck the stone step on the terrace of the flat we then occupied in London. The baby had been stunned, but after an hour or two the doctors could find nothing wrong with her.

It was only two or three weeks later that she felt sick, and later still, when she was surviving a desperate illness, that the hospital doctors told us she had had a hair-line fracture at the base of the brain, which had become infected and given her meningitis. We were so relieved that she was alive that we scarcely took notice of the cautiously phrased warnings . . . 'We must not be surprised if she were a little late in developing . . .' Of course she would be a little late after being so ill. But she would soon catch up, wouldn't she? And we dismissed the dubious expression, and that unfamiliar word 'retarded'.

During the next year we learned what it meant, and in facing such a mammoth disaster had also discovered much about ourselves. Before the accident, our marriage had been shaking towards disintegration under the onslaughts of prosperity and success: after it, we had gradually cemented ourselves together again, with a much clearer view of what was really important, and what was not.

We had left the bright lights, the adulation, and the whoopee, and gone to live in the country, where anyway both of us had our original roots. Better for the kids, we said; and knew it was better for us, too.

Libby's state no longer caused us any acute grief. It was just part of life, accepted and accustomed. She was treated with good humour by the boys, with love by Charlie, and with gentleness by me; and as she was seldom ill and seemed to be happy enough, it could have been a lot worse.

It had proved harder in the end to grow skins against the reactions of strangers, but after all these years neither Charlie nor I gave a damn what anyone said. So maybe Libby couldn't talk yet, couldn't walk steadily, fed herself messily, and was not reliably continent: but she was our daughter, and that was that.

I went into the house, changed into swimming trunks, and took her with me into the pool. She was slowly learning to swim, and had no fear of the water. She splashed around happily in my grasp, patted my face with wet palms and called me 'Dada', and wound her arms round my neck and clung to me like a little limpet.

After a bit I handed her over to Charlie to dry, and played water polo (of sorts) with Peter and Chris, and after twenty minutes of that decided that even Evan Pentelow was a lesser task master.

'More, Dad,' they said, and, 'I *say*, Dad, you aren't getting out already, are you?'

'Yes,' I said firmly, and dried myself sitting beside Charlie on the rug.

She put the kids to bed while I unpacked, and I read them stories while she cooked, and we spent the evening by ourselves, eating chicken and watching an old movie (from before my days) on television. After that we stacked the dishes in the washer and went to bed.

We had no one else living in the house with us. On four mornings a week a woman walked up from the village to help with the chores, and there was also a retired nurse there who would always come to look after Libby and the boys if we wanted to go out. These arrangements were Charlie's own choice: I had married a quiet, intelligent girl who had grown into a practical, down-to-earth, and to her own surprise, domesticated woman. Since we had left London she had developed an added strength which one could only call serenity, and although she could on occasions lose her temper as furiously as I could, her foundations were now built on rock.

A lot of people in the film world, I knew, thought my wife unexciting and my home life a drag, and expected me to break out in blondes and red-heads, like a rash. But I had very little in common with the sort of larger-than-life action man I played in film after film. They were my work, and I worked hard at them, but I didn't take them home.

Charlie snuggled beside me under the duvet and put her head on my chest. I smoothed my hands over her bare skin, feeling the ripple deep in her abdomen and the faint tremble in her legs.

'OK?' I asked, kissing her hair.

'Very . . .'

We made love in the simple, ordinary way, as we always did; but because I had been away a month it was one of the best times, one of the breathtaking, fundamental, indescribable times which became a base to live from. Certainty begins here, I thought. With this, what else did one need?

'Fantastic,' Charlie sighed. 'That was *fantastic*.'

'Remind us to do it less often.'

She laughed. 'It does improve with keeping . . .'

'Mm.' I yawned.

'I say,' she said, 'I was reading a magazine in the dentist's waiting-room this morning while Chris was having his teeth done, and there was a letter in it on the sob-stuff page, from a woman who had a bald fat middle-aged husband she didn't fancy, and she was asking for advice on her sex life. And do you know what advice they gave her?' There was a smile in her voice. 'It was, "Imagine you are sleeping with Edward Lincoln".'

'That's silly.' I yawned again.

'Yeah . . . Actually, I thought of writing up and asking what advice they would give *me*.'

'Probably tell you to imagine you're sleeping with some fat bald middle-aged man you don't fancy.'

She chuckled. 'Maybe I will be, in twenty years' time.'

'You are so kind.'

'Think nothing of it.'

We drifted contentedly to sleep.

*

I had a racehorse, a steeplechaser, in training with a thriving stable about five miles away, and I used to go over when I was not working and ride out with the string at morning exercise. Bill Tracker, the energetic trainer, did not in general like to have owners who wanted to ride their own horses, but he put up with my intermittent presence on the same two counts as his stable lads did, namely that my father had once been a head lad along in Lambourn, and that I had also at one time earned my living by riding, even if not in races.

There wasn't much doing in August, but I went over, a couple of days after my return, and rode out on the Downs. The new jumping season had barely begun, and most of the horses, including my own, were still plodding round the roads to strengthen their legs. Bill generously let me take out one of the more forward hurdlers which was due to have its first run in two weeks or so, and as usual I much appreciated the chance he gave me to ride to some useful purpose, and to shake the dust off the one skill I had been born with.

I had learned to ride before I could walk, and had grown up intending to be a jockey. But the fates weren't kind: I was six feet tall when I was seventeen, and whatever special something it took to be a racer, I hadn't got. The realization had been painful. The switch to jigging along in films, a wretched second best.

Ironic, to remember that.

The Downs were wide and windy and covered in

breathable air: nice and primaeval still, except for the power station on the horizon and the distant slash of the motorway. We walked and trotted up to the gallops, cantered, galloped where and when bidden, and walked down again, cooling the horses off; and it was absolutely great.

I stayed to breakfast with the Trackers and rode my own horse afterwards with the second lot round the roads, cursing like the rest of the lads at the cars which didn't slow down to pass. I relaxed easily in the saddle and smiled as I remembered how my father had yelled himself hoarse at me – 'Sit *up*, you bloody boy. And keep your elbows *in*.'

Evan Pentelow and Madroledo were in another world.

When I got back the boys were squabbling noisily over whose turn it was with the unbroken roller skates, and Charlie was making a cake.

'Hi,' she said. 'Did you have a good ride?'

'Great.'

'Fine . . . Well there weren't any calls, except Nerissa rang . . . Will you two be *quiet*, we can't hear ourselves think . . .'

'It's *my* turn,' Peter yelled.

'If you two don't both shut up I'll twist your ears,' I said.

They shut up. I'd never carried out the often repeated

threat, but they didn't like the idea of it. Chris immediately pinched the disputed skates and disappeared out of the kitchen, and Peter gave chase with muted yells.

'Kids!' Charlie said disgustedly.

I scooped out a fingerful of raw cake mixture and got my wrist slapped.

'What did Nerissa want?'

'She wants us to go to lunch.' Charlie paused, with the wooden spoon dropping gouts of chocolate goo into the bowl. 'She was a bit . . . well . . . odd, in a way. Not her usual brisk self. Anyway, she wanted us to go today . . .'

'Today!' I said, looking at the clock.

'Oh, I told her we couldn't, that you wouldn't be back until twelve. So she asked if we could make it tomorrow.'

'Why the rush?'

'Well, I don't know, darling. She just said, could we come as soon as poss. Before you got tied up in another film, she said.'

'I don't start the next one until November.'

'Yes, I told her that. Still, she was pretty insistent. So I said we'd love to go tomorrow unless you couldn't, in which case I'd ring back this lunch time.'

'I wonder what she wants,' I said. 'We haven't seen her for ages. We'd better go, don't you think?'

'Oh yes, of course.'

So we went.

It is just as well one can never foresee the future.

*

Nerissa was a sort of cross between an aunt, a godmother, and a guardian, none of which I had ever actually had. I had had a stepmother who loved her two previous children exclusively, and a busy father nagged by her to distraction. Nerissa, who had owned three horses in the yard where my father reigned, had given me first sweets, then pound notes, then encouragement, and then, as the years passed, friendship. It had never been a close relationship, but always a warmth in the background.

She was waiting for us, primed with crystal glasses and a decanter of dry sherry on a silver tray, in the summer sitting-room of her Cotswold house, and she rose to meet us when she heard her manservant bringing us through the hall.

'Come in, my dears, come in,' she said. 'How lovely to see you. Charlotte, I love you in yellow . . . and Edward, how very thin you are . . .'

She had her back to the sunlight which poured in through the window framing the best view in Gloucestershire, and it was only when we each in turn kissed her offered cheek that we could see the pitiful change in her.

The last time I had seen her she had been an attractive woman of fifty plus, with young blue eyes and an apparently indestructible vitality. Her walk seemed to be on the edge of dancing, and her voice held a wise sense of humour. She came from the blue-blooded end of the Stud Book and had what my father had succinctly described as 'class'.

But now, within three months, her strength had vanished and her eyes were dull. The gloss on her hair, the spring in her step, the laugh in her voice: all were gone. She looked nearer seventy than fifty, and her hands trembled.

'Nerissa,' Charlie exclaimed in a sort of anguish, for she like me held her in much more than affection.

'Yes, dear. Yes,' Nerissa said comfortingly. 'Now sit down, dear, and Edward shall pour you some sherry.'

I poured all three of us some of the fine pale liquid, but Nerissa hardly sipped hers at all. She sat in a gold brocade chair in a long-sleeved blue linen dress, with her back to the sun and her face in shadow.

'How are those two little monkeys?' she asked. 'And how is dear little Libby? And Edward, my dear, being so thin doesn't suit you . . .' She talked on, making practised conversation and looking interested in our answers, and gave us no opening to ask what was the matter with her.

When she went into the dining-room it was with the help of a walking stick and my arm, and the feather-light lunch which had been geared to her needs did nothing to restore my lost pounds. Afterwards, we went slowly back to the summer-room for coffee.

'Do smoke, Edward dear . . . There are some cigars in the cupboard. You know how I love the smell . . . and so few people smoke here, nowadays.'

I imagined they didn't because of her condition, but if she wanted it, I would, even though I rarely did, and only in the evening. They were Coronas, but a little dry from old age. I lit one, and she inhaled the smoke deeply, and smiled with real pleasure.

'That's so good,' she said.

Charlie poured the coffee but again Nerissa hardly drank. She settled back gently into the same chair as before, and crossed her elegant ankles.

'Now, my dears,' she said calmly, 'I shall be dead by Christmas.'

We didn't even make any contradictory noises. It was all too easy to believe.

She smiled at us. 'So sensible, you two are. No silly swooning, or making a fuss.' She paused. 'It appears I have some stupid ailment, and they tell me there isn't much to be done. As a matter of fact, it's what they *do* do which is making me feel so ill. Before, it wasn't so bad . . . but I have had to have X-rays so often . . . and now all these horrid cytotoxic drugs, and really, they make me most unwell.' She managed another smile. 'I've asked them to stop, but you know what it's like . . . if they can, they say they must. Quite an unreasonable view to take, don't you think? Anyway, my dears, that need not trouble you . . .'

'But you would like us to do something for you?' Charlie suggested.

Nerissa looked surprised. 'How did you know I had anything like that in mind?'

'Oh . . . Because you wanted us in a hurry . . . and you must have known for weeks how ill you were.'

'Edward, how clever your Charlotte is,' she said. 'Yes, I do want something . . . want Edward to do something for me, if he will.'

'Of course,' I said.

A dry amusement crept back into her voice. 'Wait until you hear what it is, before you promise so glibly.'

'OK.'

'It is to do with my horses.' She paused to consider, her head inclined to one side. 'They are running so badly.'

'But,' I said, in bewilderment, 'they haven't been out yet, this season.'

She still had two steeplechasers trained in the yard where I had grown up, and although since my father's death I had had no direct contact with them, I knew they had won a couple of races each the season before.

She shook her head. 'Not the jumpers, Edward. My other horses. Five colts and six fillies, running on the flat.'

'On the flat? I'm sorry . . . I didn't realize you had any.'

'In South Africa.'

'Oh.' I looked at her a bit blankly. 'I don't know anything about South African racing. I'm awfully sorry. I'd love to be of use to you . . . but I don't know enough to begin to suggest why your horses there are running badly.'

'It's nice of you, Edward dear, to look disappointed. But you really can help me, you know. If you will.'

'Just tell him how,' Charlie said, 'and he'll do it. He'll do anything for you, Nerissa.'

At that time, and in those circumstances, she was right. The finality of Nerissa's condition made me sharply aware of how much I had always owed her: not in concrete terms as much as in the feeling that she was *there*, interested and caring about what I did. In my motherless teens, that had meant a lot.

She sighed. 'I've been writing to my trainer out there about it, and he seems very puzzled. He doesn't know why my horses are running badly, because all the others he trains are doing all right. But it takes so long for letters to pass . . . the postal services at both ends seem to be so erratic these days. And I wondered, Edward, my dear, if you could possibly . . . I mean, I know it's a good deal to ask . . . but could you possibly give me a week of your time, and go out there and find out what's happening?'

There was a small silence. Even Charlie did not rush to say that of course I would go, although it was clear already that it would have to be a matter of how, not of whether.

Nerissa went on persuasively, 'You see, Edward, you do know about racing. You know what goes on in a stable, and things like that. You could see, couldn't you, if there is something wrong with their training? And then of course you are so good at investigating things . . .'

'I'm what?' I asked. 'I've never investigated anything in my life.'

She fluttered a hand. 'You know how to find things out, and nothing ever deflects you.'

'Nerissa,' I said suspiciously, 'you've been seeing my films.'

'Well, of course. I've seen nearly all of them.'

'Yes, but that's not me. Those investigating supermen, they're just acting.'

'Don't be silly, Edward dear. You couldn't do all the things you do in films without being brave and determined and very clever at finding things out.'

I looked at her in a mixture of affection and exasperation. So many people mistook the image for the man, but that she should . . .

'You've known me since I was eight,' I protested. 'You know I'm not brave or particularly determined. I'm ordinary. I'm me. I'm the boy you gave sweets to, when I was crying because I'd fallen off a pony, and said "never mind" to, when I didn't have the nerve to be a jockey.'

She smiled indulgently. 'But since then you've learned to fight. And look at that last picture, when you were clinging to a ledge by one hand with a thousand foot drop just below you . . .'

'Nerissa, dear Nerissa,' I interrupted her. 'I'll go to South Africa for you. I really will. But those fights in films . . . most of the time that isn't me, it's someone my size and shape who really does know judo. I don't. I can't fight at all. It's just my face in close-ups. And those ledges I was clinging to . . . certainly they were on a real rock face, but I was in no danger. I wouldn't have fallen a thousand feet, but only about ten, into one of those nets they use under trapeze acts in circuses. I did fall, two or three times. And there wasn't really a thousand feet below me; not sheer anyway. We filmed it in the Valley of Rocks in North Devon, where there are a lot of little plateaux among the rock faces, to stand the cameras on.'

She listened with an air of being completely unconvinced. I reckoned it was useless to go on: to tell her that I was not a crack shot, couldn't fly an aeroplane or beat Olympic skiers downhill, couldn't speak Russian or build a radio transmitter or dismantle bombs, and would tell all at the first threat of torture. She knew different, she'd seen it with her own eyes. Her expression told me so.

'Well, all right,' I said, capitulating. 'I do know what should and should not go on in a racing stable. In England, anyway.'

'And,' she said complacently, 'you can't say it wasn't you who did all that trick riding when you first went into films.'

I couldn't. It was. But it had been nothing unique.

'I'll go and look at your horses, and see what your trainer says,' I said; and thought that if he had no reasons to offer, I would be most unlikely to find any.

'Dear Edward, so kind . . .' She seemed suddenly weaker, as if the effort of persuading me had been too much. But when she saw the alarm on Charlie's face, and on mine, she raised a reassuring smile.

'Not yet, my dears. Another two months, perhaps . . . Two months at least, I think.'

Charlie shook her head in protest, but Nerissa patted her hand. 'It's all right, my dear. I've come to terms with it. But I want to arrange things . . . which is why I want Edward to see about the horses, and I really ought to explain . . .'

'Don't tire yourself,' I said.

'I'm not . . . tired,' she said, obviously untruthfully. 'And I want to tell you. The horses used to belong to my sister, Portia, who married and went to live in South Africa thirty years ago. After she was widowed she stayed there because all her friends were there, and I've been out to visit her several times over the years. I know I've told you about her.'

We nodded.

'She died last winter,' I said.

'Yes . . . a great sorrow.' Nerissa looked a good deal more upset about her sister's death than about her own. 'She had no close relatives except me, and she left me nearly everything she had inherited from her husband. And all her horses, too. She paused, as much to gather her forces as her thoughts. 'They were yearlings. Expensive ones. And her trainer wrote to me to ask if I wanted to sell them, as of course owing to the African horsesickness quarantine laws we cannot bring South African horses to England. But I thought it might be fun . . . interesting . . . to run them in South Africa, and then sell them for stud. But now . . . well, now I won't be here when they are old enough for stud, and meanwhile their value has dropped disastrously.'

'Dearest Nerissa,' Charlie said. 'Does it matter?'

'Oh yes. Yes, my dear, it does,' she said positively.

'Because I'm leaving them to my nephew, Danilo, and I don't like the idea of leaving him something worthless.'

She looked from one of us to the other. 'I can't remember – have you ever met Danilo?'

Charlie said, 'No,' and I said, 'Once or twice, when he was a small boy. You used to bring him to the stables.'

'That's right, so I did. And then of course my brother-in-law divorced that frightful woman, Danilo's mother, and took him to live in California with him. Well . . . Danilo has been back in England recently, and he has grown into such a nice young man. And isn't that lucky, my dears? Because, you see, I have so few relatives. In fact, really, Danilo is the only one, and even he is not a blood relative, his father being dear John's youngest brother, do you see?'

We saw. John Cavesey, dead sixteen years or more, had been a country gent with four hunters and a sense of humour. He had also had Nerissa, no children, one brother, one nephew, and five square miles of Merrie England.

After a pause Nerissa said, I'll cable to Mr Arknold . . . that's my trainer . . . to tell him you're coming to look into things, and to book some rooms for you.'

'No, don't do that. He might resent your sending anyone, and I'd get no cooperation from him at all. I'll fix the rooms, and so on. And if you cable him, just say I might be calling in, out of interest, while I'm in South Africa on a short visit.'

She smiled slowly and sweetly, and said, 'You see, my dear, you do know how to investigate, after all.'

CHAPTER THREE

I flew to Johannesburg five days later, equipped with a lot of facts and no faith in my ability to disentangle them.

Charlie and I had driven home from Nerissa's in a double state of depression. Poor Nerissa, we said. And poor us, losing her.

'And you've only just come home,' Charlie added.

'Yes,' I sighed. 'Still . . . I couldn't have said no.'

No.'

'Not that it'll do much good.'

'You never know, you might spot something.'

'Very doubtful.'

'But,' she said with a touch of anxiety, 'you will do your best?'

'Of course, love.'

She shook her head. 'You're cleverer than you think.'

'Yeah,' I said. 'Sure.'

She made a face, and we went some way in silence. Then she said, 'When you went out to look at those two young chasers in her paddock, Nerissa told me what is the matter with her.'

'Did she?'

Charlie nodded. 'Some ghastly thing called Hodgkin's disease, which makes her glands swell, or something, and turn cellular, whatever that really means. She didn't know very clearly herself, I don't think. Except that it is absolutely fatal.'

Poor Nerissa.

'She also told me,' Charlie went on, 'that she has left us a keepsake each in her will.'

'Has she really?' I turned my head to look at Charlie. 'How kind of her. Did she say what?'

'Keep your eyes on the road, for heaven's sake. No, she didn't say what. Just something to remember her by. She said she had quite enjoyed herself, drawing up her new will and giving people presents in it. Isn't she amazing?'

'She is.'

'She really meant it. And she is so pleased that her nephew has turned out well. I've never seen anyone like that before . . . dying, and quite calm about it . . . and even enjoying things, like making a will . . . and knowing . . . knowing . . .'

I glanced at her sideways. Tears on Charlie's cheeks. She seldom cried, and didn't like to be watched.

I kept my eyes on the road.

I telephoned my agent and stunned him.

'But,' he stuttered, 'you never go anywhere, you always refuse . . . you thumped my table and shouted about it . . .'

'Quite,' I agreed. 'But now I want a good reason for

going to South Africa, so are any of my films due to open there soon, or are they not?'

'Well . . .' he sounded thoroughly disorganized. 'Well, I'll have to look it up. And are you sure,' he added in disbelief, 'that if one of them is due to open, you really and truly want me to tell them you'll turn up in person?'

'That's what I said.'

'Yes. I just don't believe it.'

He rang back an hour later.

'There are two coming up. They are showing *One Way to Moscow* in Cape Town, starting Monday week. That's the first in a series of six revivals, so although *Moscow* itself is pretty old, you could turn up to give the whole lot a boost. Or there's the opening of *Rocks* in Johannesburg. But that's not until September 14th. Three weeks off. Is that soon enough?'

'Not really.' I pondered. 'It will have to be the Johannesburg one, though.'

'All right. I'll fix it. And . . . er . . . does the sudden change of heart extend to chat shows and newspaper interviews?'

'No, it does not.'

'I was afraid of that.'

I had taken home from Nerissa's house all her trainer's letters, all the South African Racing Calendars, newspaper cuttings and magazines she had been sent, and all the details of breeding and racing form of her eleven non-winning youngsters. A formidable bulk of paper, it had proved; and not miraculously easy to understand.

The picture which emerged, though, was enough to make anyone think, let alone the owner of the horses in question. Nine of the eleven had run nicely when they began their racing careers, and between December and May had clocked up a joint total of fourteen wins. Since the middle of May, none of them had finished nearer than fourth.

As far as I could judge from a limited squint at the leading-sires tables and the breeding notes section of the South African *Horse and Hound*, all of them were of impeccable pedigree, and certainly, from the amounts she had laid out, Nerissa's sister Portia had bought no bargains. None of them had so far won enough prize money to cover their purchase price, and with every resounding defeat their future stud value, too, slid a notch towards zero.

As a bequest, the South African horses were a lump of lead. Charlie came with me to Heathrow to see me off, as I had been home only nine days, which hadn't been long enough for either of us. While we were waiting at the check-in counter half a dozen ladies asked for my autograph for their daughters – nephews – grandchildren – and a few eyes swivelled our way; and presently a dark-uniformed airline official appeared at our side and offered a small private room for waiting in. They were pretty good about that sort of thing, as I came through the airport fairly often, and we accepted gratefully.

'It's like being married to two people,' Charlie sighed, sitting down. 'The public you, and the private you. Quite separate. Do you know, if I see one of the films, or even a clip of one on the box, I look at the pictures of you, and I think, I slept with that man last night. And it seems extraordinary, because that public you doesn't really belong to me at all, but to all the people who pay to see you. And then you come home again, and you're just you, my familiar husband, and the public you is some other fellow . . .'

I looked at her affectionately. 'The private me has forgotten to pay the telephone bill.'

'Well, damn it, I reminded you sixteen times . . .'

'Will you pay it, then?'

'Well, I suppose so. But the telephone bill is one of your jobs. Checking all those cables, and those phone calls to America – I don't know what they should be. We're probably being overcharged, if you don't check it.'

'Have to risk it.'

'Honestly!'

'It will be set off against tax, anyway.'

'I suppose so.'

I sat down beside her. The unpaid telephone bill was as good as anything else to talk about: we no longer needed to say aloud what we were saying to each other underneath. In all our life together we had taken good-byes casually, and hellos, too. A lot of people mistook it for not caring. It was perhaps too much the opposite. We needed each other like bees and honey.

When I landed at Jan Smuts International Airport sixteen hours later, I was met by a nervous man with damp palms who introduced himself as the South African Distribution Manager for Worldic Cinemas.

'Wenkins,' he said. 'Clifford Wenkins. So nice to see you.'

He had restless eyes and a clipped South African accent. About forty. Never going to be successful. Talking a little too loudly, a little too familiarly, with the sort of uneasy bonhomie I found hardest to take.

As politely as possible I removed my sleeve from his grasp.

'Nice of you to come,' I said; and wished he hadn't.

'Couldn't let Edward Lincoln arrive without a reception, you know.' He laughed loudly, out of nerves. I wondered idly why he should be so painfully self-conscious: as Distribution Manager he surely met film actors before breakfast every month of the year.

'Car over here.' He walked crabwise in front of me with his arms extended fore and aft, as if to push a path for me with the one and usher me along it with the other. There were not enough people around for it to be remotely necessary.

I followed him, carrying my suitcase and making an effort to suffer his attentions gladly.

'Not far,' he said anxiously, looking up placatingly at my face.

'Fine,' I said.

There was a group of about ten people just inside the main doors. I looked at them in disillusion: their clothes and the way they stood had 'media' stamped all over them, and it was without surprise that I saw the tape-recorders and cameras sprout all over as soon as we drew near.

'Mr Lincoln, what do you think of South Africa?'

'Hey, Link, how about a big smile . . . ?'

'Is there any truth in the rumour . . . ?'

'Our readers would like your views on . . .'

'Give us a smile . . .'

I tried not to stop walking, but they slowed us down to a crawl. I smiled at them collectively and said soothing things like 'I'm glad to be here. This is my first visit. I am looking forward to it very much,' and eventually we persevered into the open air.

Clifford Wenkins's dampness extended to his brow, though the sunshine at 6,000 feet above sea level was decidedly chilly.

'Sorry,' he said, 'but they would come.'

'Marvellous how they knew the right day and the right time, when my flight was only booked yesterday morning.'

'Er . . . yes,' he agreed weakly.

'I expect they are often willing to arrange publicity for people, when you want them to.'

'Oh yes indeed,' he agreed warmly.

I smiled at him. One could hardly blame him for using me as payment for past and future services, and I knew it was widely considered irrational that I preferred to avoid interviews. In many countries the media gave you a rough passage if you wouldn't let them milk you for copy, and the South Africans had been more civil than most.

Wenkins rubbed his beaded forehead with one of the damp palms, and said, 'Let me take your suitcase.'

I shook my head. 'It isn't heavy,' I said, and besides, I was a good deal bigger than he was.

We walked across the car park to his car, and I experienced for the first time the extraordinary smell of Africa. A blend of hot sweet odours with a kink of mustiness; a strong disturbing smell which stayed in my nostrils for three or four days, until my scenting nerves got used to it and disregarded it. But my first overriding impression of South Africa was the way it smelt.

Smiling too much, sweating too much, talking too much, Clifford Wenkins drove me down the road to Johannesburg. The airport lay east of the city, out on the bare expanses of the Transvaal, and we were a good half hour reaching our destination.

'I hope everything will be all right for you,' Wenkins said. 'We don't often get . . . I mean, well . . .' He laughed jerkily. 'Your agent was telling me on the telephone not to arrange any receptions or parties or radio shows or anything . . . I mean, we usually put on that sort of show for visiting stars . . . that is, er, of course, if Worldic are handling their films . . . but, er, we haven't done anything like that for you, and it seems all wrong to me . . . but then, your agent insisted . . . and then, your room . . . not in the city, he said. Not in the city itself, and not in a private house, he said, so I hope you will like . . . I mean, we were shattered . . . er, that is, honoured . . . to hear you were coming . . .'

Mr Wenkins, I thought, you would get a lot further on in life if you didn't chatter so much. And aloud I said, 'I'm sure everything will be fine.'

'Yes, well . . . Er, if you don't want the usual round of things, though, what am I to arrange for you? I mean, there is a fortnight before the premiere of *Rocks*, don't you see? So what . . .?'

I didn't answer that one straight away. Instead I said, 'This premiere . . . How much of a thing are you making of it?'

'Oh.' He laughed again at nothing funny. 'Er, well, big, of course. Invitations. Tickets in aid of charity. All the glitter, old boy . . . er, I mean . . . sorry . . . er, well, Worldic said to push the boat right out, you see, once they'd got over the shock, that is.'

'I do see.' I sighed slightly. I had chosen to do the damn thing, I thought. So I ought, in all fairness, to give them value for their trouble.

'Look,' I said, 'if you want to, and if you think anyone would want to come, go ahead and arrange some sort of drinks and canapés affair either before or after the showing of the film, and I'll go to that. And one morning soon, if you'd like to, you could ask all those good friends of yours at the airport, and any others in their trade that you want to include, to meet us somewhere for coffee or a drink or something. How would that do?'

For once he was dumb. I looked across at him. His mouth was opening and shutting like a fish.

I laughed in my throat. Nerissa had a lot to answer for.

'The rest of the time, don't worry about me. I'll amuse myself all right. For one thing, I'll go to the races.'

'Oh.' He finally overcame the jaw problem and got the two halves into proper working order. 'Er . . . I could get someone to take you there, if you like.'

'We'll see,' I said noncommittally.

The journey ended at the Iguana Rock, a very pleasant country hotel on the northern edge of the city. The management gave me a civil greeting and a luxurious room and indicated that a clap of the hands would bring anything from iced water to dancing girls, as required.

'I would like to hire a car,' I said, and Wenkins gushed forth to say it was all arranged, he had arranged it, a chauffeur-driven pumpkin would be constantly on call, courtesy of Worldic.

I shook my head. 'Courtesy of me,' I said. 'Didn't my agent tell you that I intended to pay all the expenses of my trip myself?'

'Well, he did, yes, but . . . Worldic say they'd like to pick up the tab . . .'

'No,' I said.

He laughed nervously. 'No . . . well, I see, er, I mean . . . yes.' He spluttered to a stop. The eyes darted around restlessly, the hands gestured vaguely, the meaningless smile twitched his mouth convulsively, and he couldn't stand still on his two feet. I didn't usually throw people into such a tizzy, and I wondered what on earth my agent could have said to him, to bring him to such a state.

He managed eventually to get himself out of the Iguana Rock and back to his car, and his departure was a great relief. Within an hour, however, he was on the telephone.

'Would tomorrow, er, morning . . . suit you for, er, I mean, the Press?'

'Yes,' I said.

'Then, er, would you ask your driver to take you to, er, Randfontein House, er . . . the Dettrick Room . . . that's a reception room, you see, which we hire for this, well, sort of thing.'

'What time?'

'Oh . . . say eleven thirty. Could you . . . er . . . get there at about eleven thirty?'

'Yes,' I said briefly again, and after a few further squirms he said he would look forward . . . er . . . to seeing me then.

I put the receiver down, finished unpacking, drank some coffee, summoned up the pumpkin, and went briskly off to the races.

CHAPTER FOUR

Flat racing in South Africa took place on Wednesdays and Saturdays throughout the year, but only occasionally on other days. Accordingly it had seemed good sense to arrive in Johannesburg on Wednesday morning and go to the only race-meeting in South Africa that day, at Newmarket.

I paid to go in and bought a race-card. One of Nerissa's constant failures, I saw, was due to have another go later in the afternoon.

Newmarket was Newmarket the world over. Stands, cards, horses, bookmakers; atmosphere of bustle and purpose; air of tradition and order. All were much the same. I wandered across to the parade ring, where the runners for the first race were already walking round. Same little clumps of owners and trainers standing in hopeful conversations in the middle. Same earnest race-goers leaning on the rails and studying the wares.

Differences were small. The horses, to English eyes, looked slightly smaller-framed and had very upright fetlocks, and they were led round, not by white stable lads in their own darkish clothes, but by black stable-boys in long white coats.

On the principle of only backing horses I knew something about, I kept my hands in my pockets. The jockeys in their bright silks came out and mounted, the runners went away down the track and scurried back, hooves rattling on the bone-dry ground, and I strolled down from the stands to search for and identify Nerissa's trainer, Greville Arknold. He had a runner in the following race, and somewhere he would be found, saddling it up.

In the event, I hardly had to look. On my way to the saddling boxes, a young man touched me on the arm.

'I say,' he said. 'Aren't you Edward Lincoln?'

I nodded and half smiled, and kept on walking.

'Guess I'd better introduce myself. Danilo Cavesey. I believe you know my aunt.'

That stopped me, all right. I put out my hand, and he shook it warmly.

'I heard you were coming, of course. Aunt Nerissa cabled Greville you were on your way out here for some film premiere, and would he look out for you at the races. So I was kind of expecting you, you see.'

His accent was a slow Californian drawl full of lazy warmth. It was instantly clear why Nerissa had liked him: his sun-tanned, good-looking face, his open, pleasant expression, his clean, casual, blond-brown hair, all were in the best tradition of American youth.

'She didn't say you were in South Africa,' I commented, surprised.

'Well, no.' He wrinkled his nose disarmingly. 'I don't believe she knows. I only flew out here a few days ago, on a vacation. Say, how is the old girl? She wasn't all that sprightly when I last visited with her.'

He was smiling happily. He didn't know.

I said, 'She's pretty ill, I'm afraid.'

'Is that so? I'm sure sorry to hear that. I must write her, tell her I'm out here, tell her I'm taking a look-see into the state of the horses.'

'The state of the horses?' I echoed.

'Oh sure. Aunt Nerissa's horses out here are not running good. Stinking bad, to be accurate.' He grinned cheerfully. 'I shouldn't bet on number eight in the fourth race, if you want to die rich.'

'Thanks,' I said. 'She did mention to me that they were not doing so well just now.'

'I'll bet she did. They wouldn't win if you gave them ten minutes start and nobbled the others.'

'Is there any reason for it, do you know?'

'Search me,' he shrugged. 'Greville's real chewed up about it. Says he hasn't had anything like this happen before.'

'Not a virus?' I suggested.

'Can't be. Otherwise all the others would get it too, not just Aunt Nerissa's. We've been talking it over, you see, Greville just hasn't an idea.'

'I'd like to meet him,' I said casually.

'Oh sure. Yes, indeed. But say, why don't we get out of this wind and have ourselves a beer or something?

Greville has this starter now, but he'll be happy to see us later on.'

'All right,' I agreed, and we went and had ourselves the beer. Danilo was right: the south wind was cold and spring was still a hint and a memory.

Danilo, I judged, was about twenty years old. He had bright blue eyes and blond-brown eyelashes, and his teeth were California-straight. He had the untouched air of one to whom the rigours of life had not yet happened; a boy not necessarily spoilt, but to whom much had been given.

He was at Berkeley University studying Political Science, he said, with one more year to do. 'This time next summer I'll be all through with college . . .'

'What do you plan to do after that?' I asked, making conversation.

There was a flash of amusement in the blue eyes. 'Oh, I guess I'll have to think of something, but I've nothing lined up right now.'

The future could take care of itself, I thought, and reflected that for golden boys like Danilo it usually did.

We watched the next race together. Greville's starter finished third, close up.

'Too bad,' Danilo sighed. 'I just had it on the nose, not across the boards.'

'Did you lose much?' I asked sympathetically.

'I guess not. Just a few rand.'

Rands came just under two to the pound sterling, or a little over one to the dollar. He couldn't have done himself much harm.

We walked down from the stands and over towards the unsaddling enclosures. 'Do you know something?' he said. 'You're not a bit what I expected.'

'In what way?' I asked, smiling.

'Oh, I guess . . . For a big movie star, I expected some sort of, well, *presence*. You know?'

'Off the screen, movie actors are as dim as anyone else.'

He glanced at me suspiciously, but I wasn't laughing at him. I meant it. He had a much more naturally luminous personality than I had. I might have been an inch or two taller, an inch or two broader across the shoulders, but the plus factor has nothing to do with size.

The man stalking round the horse which had finished third, peering judiciously at its legs and running a probing hand along its loins, was a burly thickset man with an air of dissatisfaction.

'That's Greville,' Danilo nodded, following my gaze.

The trainer spoke briefly to a woman Danilo identified to me as the horse's owner. His manner, from twenty feet away, looked brusque and far from conciliatory. I knew trainers had to grow hard skins if they were to stay sane: one could not for ever be apologizing to owners if their horses got beaten, one had to make them realize that regardless of the oats and exercise crammed into them, maybe other people's horses could actually run faster: but Greville Arknold appeared plainly disagreeable.

After a while the horses were led away and the crowd thinned out. Arknold listened, with a pinched mouth and a stubborn backward tilt of the head, to what looked almost like apologies from the woman owner. She came to a stop, got no melting response from him, shrugged, turned slowly, and walked away.

Arknold's gaze rose from down his nose and fastened on Danilo. He stared for a moment, then raised his eyebrows questioningly. Danilo very slightly jerked his head in my direction, and Arknold transferred his attention to me.

Again the slow appraisal. Then he came across.

Danilo introduced us with an air of what fun it was for us to know each other. A mutual privilege.

Great.

I didn't take to Greville Arknold, neither then nor ever after. Yet he was pleasant enough to me: smiled, shook hands, said he was glad to meet me, said that Mrs Cavesey had cabled to say I might be coming to the races, and to look after me if I did.

He had a flat-sounding Afrikaaner accent, and like many South Africans he was, I discovered later, trilingual in English, Afrikaans and Zulu. He had a face formed of thick slabs of flesh, lips so thin that they hardly existed, the scars of old acne over his chin and down his neck, and a bristly ginger moustache one inch by two below his nose. And for all the smiling and the welcoming chat, he had cold eyes.

'Your horse ran well just then,' I suggested conversationally.

The recent anger reappeared at once in his manner.

'That stupid woman insisted that her horse ran today when I wanted to run it Saturday instead. He had a hard race at Turffontein last Saturday. He needed another three days' rest.'

'She looked as if she were apologizing,' I said.

'*Ja*. She was. Too late, of course. She should have had more sense. Decent colt, that. Would have won on Saturday. No sense. Owners always ought to do what a trainer says. They pay for expert knowledge, don't they? So they always ought to do what the experts say.'

I smiled vaguely, non-committally. As an owner myself, even of only one moderate steeplechasing gelding, I disagreed with him about always. Sometimes, even usually, yes. But always, no. I knew of at least one Grand National winner which would never have gone to the start if the owner had paid attention to the trainer's advice.

'I see Mrs Cavesey has a runner in the fourth,' I said.

The dogmatic look faded to be replaced by a slight frown.

'*Ja*,' Arknold said. 'I expect she may have mentioned to you that her horses are not doing well.'

'She told me you had no idea why,' I nodded.

He shook his head. 'I cannot understand it. They get the same treatment as all the others. Same food, same exercise, everything. They are not ill. I have had a veterinarian examine them, several times. It is worrying. Very.'

'It must be,' I agreed sympathetically.

'And dope tests!' he said. 'We must have had a hundred dope tests. All negative, the whole lot.'

'Do they look fit?' I asked. 'I mean, would you expect them to do better, from the way they look?'

'See for yourself.' He shrugged. 'That is . . . I don't know how much of a judge of a horse you are . . .'

'Bound to be a pretty good one, I'd say,' said Danilo positively. 'After all, it's no secret his old man was a stable hand.'

'Is that so?' he said. 'Then perhaps you would like to see round the stables? Maybe you could even come up with some suggestion about Mrs Cavesey's string, you never know.'

The irony in his voice made it clear that he thought that impossible. Which meant that either he really did not know what was the matter with the horses, or he did know, but was absolutely certain that I would not find out.

'I'd like to see the stables very much,' I said.

'Good. Then you shall. How about tomorrow evening? Walk round with me, at evening stables. Four thirty?'

I nodded.

'That's fixed then. And you, Danilo. Do you want to come as well?'

'That would be just fine, Greville. I sure would like that.'

So it was settled; and Danilo said he would come and pick me up at the Iguana Rock himself.

Chink, Nerissa's runner in the fourth race, looked good enough in the parade ring, with a healthy bloom on his coat and muscles looking strong and free and loose. There wasn't a great deal of substance about him, but he had an intelligent head and strong, well-placed shoulders. Nerissa's sister Portia had given twenty-five thousand rand for him as a yearling on the strength of his breeding, and he had won only one race, his first, way back in April.

'What do you think of him, Link?' Danilo asked, leaning his hip against the parade ring rail.

'He looks fit enough,' I said.

'Yeah. They all do, Greville says.'

Chink was being led round by two stable lads, one each side. Nothing wrong with Arknold's security arrangements.

Because of the upright fetlocks I found it hard to judge the degree of spring in Chink's stride. All the horses looked to me as if they were standing on their toes, a condition I imagined was caused by living from birth on hard dry ground. Certainly he went down to the post moving no more scratchily than the others, and he lined up in the stalls and bounded out of them with no trouble. I watched every step of his journey through my Zeiss eight by fifties.

He took the first half mile without apparent effort, lying about sixth, nice and handy, just behind the leading bunch. When they turned into the straight for home, the leaders quickened, but Chink didn't. I saw the head of the jockey bob and the rest of his body become energetically busy trying to keep the horse going: but when a jockey has to work like that on a horse a long way out, he might as well not bother. Chink had run out of steam, and the best rider in the world could have done nothing about that.

I put down my race glasses. The winner fought a ding-dong, the crowd roared, and Chink returned unsung, unbacked, unwatched, and a good thirty lengths later.

With Danilo I went down to where he was being unsaddled, and joined Greville Arknold in his aura of perplexed gloom.

'There you are,' he said. 'You saw for yourself.'

'I did,' I agreed.

Chink was sweating and looked tired. He stood still, with drooping head, as if he felt the disgrace.

'What do you think?' Arknold asked.

I silently shook my head. He had in fact looked plainly like a slow horse, yet on his breeding, and the fast time of the race he had won, he should not be.

He and the other ten could not all have bad hearts, or bad teeth, or blood disorders, all undetected. Not after those thorough veterinary investigations. And not *all* of them. It was impossible.

They had not all been ridden every time by the same jockey. There were, I had discovered from Nerissa's racing papers, very few jockeys in South Africa compared with England: only thirteen jockeys and twenty-two apprentices riding on the Natal tracks near Durban, the supposed centre of the sport.

There were four main racing areas; the Johannesburg tracks in the Transvaal, the Pietermaritzburg-Durban tracks in Natal, the Port Elizabeth tracks in the Eastern Cape, and the Cape Town tracks in Cape Province. Various ones of Nerissa's horses had been to all four areas, had been ridden by the local bunch of jockeys, and had turned in the same results.

Fast until May, dead slow from June onwards.

The fact that they moved around meant that it probably could not be attributed to something in their base quarters.

No illness. No dope. No fixed address. No common jockey.

All of which pointed to one solution. One source of disaster.

The trainer himself.

It was easy enough for a trainer to make sure a horse of his didn't win, if he had a mind to. He merely had to give it too severe an exercise gallop too soon before a race. Enough races had in sober fact been lost that way by accident for it to be impossible to prove that anyone had done it on purpose.

Trainers seldom nobbled their own horses because they had demonstrably more to gain if they won. But it looked to me as if it had to be Arknold who was responsible, even if the method he was using turned out to be the simplest in the world.

I thought the solution to Nerissa's problem lay in transferring her string to a different trainer.

I thought I might just as well go straight home and tell her so.

Two nasty snags.

I was committed to a premiere two weeks off.

And I might guess who and how, about the horses.

But I had no idea *why*.

CHAPTER FIVE

The ladies and gentlemen of the Press (or in other words a partially shaven, polo-neck sweatered, elaborately casual and uninformed mob) yawned to their feet when I reached the Dettrick Room in Randfontein House within ticking distance of half past eleven.

Clifford Wenkins had met me in the hall, twittering as before, and with wetter than ever palms. We rode up in the lift together, with him explaining to me exactly whom he had asked, and who had come. Interviewers from two radio programmes. He hoped I wouldn't mind? They would be happy just to tape my answers to their questions. Just into a microphone. If I didn't mind? And then there were the dailies, the weeklies, the ladies' magazines, and one or two people who had flown up especially from Cape Town and Durban.

I wished I hadn't suggested it. Too late to run away.

The only thing to do, I thought, as the lift hissed to a halt and the doors slid open, was to put on a sort of performance. To act.

'Wait a minute,' I said to Wenkins.

He stopped with me outside the lift as the doors shut again behind us.

'What is it?' he asked anxiously.

'Nothing. I just need a few seconds, before we go in.'

He didn't understand, though what I was doing was not a process by any means confined to professional actors. Girding up the loins, the Bible called it. Getting the adrenalin on the move. Making the heart beat faster. Shifting the mental gears into top. Politicians could do it in three seconds flat.

'OK,' I said.

He sighed with relief, walked across the hallway, and opened a heavy polished door opposite.

We went in.

They unfolded themselves from sofas and carpet, pushed themselves tiredly off the walls, stubbed out one or two cigarettes and went on puffing at others.

'Hi,' said one of the men: and the others, like a sort of jungle pack, watched and waited. He was one of those who had been at the airport. He had no reason, as none of them had, to believe I would now be any different.

'Hullo,' I said.

Well, I could always do it, if I really wanted to. Almost every well trained actor can.

I watched them loosen, saw the tiredness go out of their manner and the smile creep into their eyes. They wouldn't now chew me to bits in their columns, even if they still came across with those carefully sharpened questions they all had ready in their notebooks.

The man who had said hi, their apparently natural leader, put out his hand to be shaken, and said, 'I'm Roderick Hodge of the *Rand Daily Star*. Features Editor.'

Late thirties, but trying to ignore the passage of time: young haircut, young clothes, young affectation of speech. A certain *panache* about him, but also some of the ruthless cynicism of experienced journalists.

I shook his hand and smiled at him as a friend. I needed him to be one.

'Look,' I said. 'Unless you are all in a hurry, why don't we sit down again, and then you can all ask whatever you like, perhaps in groups, maybe I can move around a bit, and then everyone might have more time for things than if I just sort of stand here in front of you.'

They thought that was all right. No one was in much of a hurry, they said. Roderick said dryly that no one would go before the booze started flowing, and the atmosphere started mellowing nicely into an all-pals-together trade meeting.

They mostly asked the personal questions first.

According to their calculations, I was thirty-three. Was that right?'

It was.

And married? Yes. Happily? Yes. My first or second marriage? First. And her first? Yes.

They wanted to know how many children I had, with their names and ages. They asked how many rooms my house had, and what it had cost. How many cars, dogs, horses, yachts I had. How much I earned in a year, how much I had been paid for *Rocks*.

How much did I give my wife to buy clothes with? Did I think a woman's place was in the home?

'In the heart,' I said flippantly, which pleased the women's mag girl who had asked, but was slightly sick-making to all the others.

Why didn't I go to live in a tax haven? I liked England. An expensive luxury? Very. And was I a millionaire? Perhaps some days, on paper, when share prices went up: If I was as rich as that, why did I work? To pay taxes, I said.

Clifford Wenkins had summoned up some caterers who brought coffee and cheese biscuits and bottles of Scotch. The Press poured the whiskey into the coffee and sighed contentedly. I kept mine separate, but had great difficulty in explaining to the waiter that I did not like my liquor diluted in nine times as much water. In South Africa, I had already discovered, they tended to fill up the tumblers; and I supposed it made sense as a long drink in a hot climate, but while it was so cold it merely ruined good Scotch.

Clifford Wenkins eyed my small drink in its large glass.

'Let me get you some water.'

'I've got some. I prefer it like this . . .'

'Oh . . . really?'

He scuttled busily away and came back with an earnestly bearded man trailing a hand microphone and a long lead. There was no sense of humour behind the beard, which made, I thought, for a fairly stodgy interview, but he assured me that what I had said was just right, just perfect for a five minute slot in his Saturday evening show. He took back the microphone which I had been holding, shook me earnestly by the hand, and disappeared into a large array of recording equipment in one corner.

After that I was supposed to do a second interview, this time for a woman's programme, but some technical hitches had developed in the gear.

I moved, in time, right round the room, sitting on the floor, on the arms of chairs, leaning on the window-sills, or just plain standing.

Loosened by the Scotch, they asked the other questions.

What did I think of South Africa? I liked it.

What were my opinions of their political scene? I hadn't any, I said. I had been in their country only one day. One couldn't form opinions in that time.

Most people arrived with them already formed, they observed. I said I didn't think that was sensible.

Well, what were my views on racial discrimination? I said without heat that I thought any form of discrimination was bound to give rise to some injustice. I said I thought it a pity that various people found it necessary to discriminate against women, Jews, Aborigines, American Indians and a friend of mine in Nairobi who couldn't get promotion in a job he excelled at because he was white.

I also said I couldn't answer any more of that sort of question, and could we please get off politics and civil rights unless they would like me to explain the differences between the economic theories of the Tory and Labour parties.

They laughed. No, they said. They wouldn't.

They reverted to films and asked questions I felt better able to answer.

Was it true I had started as a stunt man? Sort of, I said. I rode horses across everything from Robin Hood via Bosworth Field to the Charge of the Light Brigade. Until one day when I was doing a bit of solo stuff a director called me over, gave me some words to say, and told me I was in. Good clean romantic stuff, for which I apologized. It did happen sometimes like that though.

And then? Oh then I got given a better part in his next film. And how old was I at the time? Twenty-two, just married, living on baked beans in a basement flat in Hammersmith, and still attending part-time speech and drama classes, as I had for three years.

I was standing more or less in the centre of the room when the door opened behind me. Clifford Wenkins turned his head to see who it was, frowned with puzzlement and went busily across to deal with the situation.

'I'm afraid you can't come in here,' he was saying bossily. 'This is a private room. Private reception. I'm sorry, but would you mind . . . I say, you can't . . . this is a private room . . . I say . . .'

I gathered Wenkins was losing. Not surprising, really.

Then I felt the clump on the shoulder and heard the familiar fruity voice.

'Link, dear boy. Do tell this . . . er . . . person, that we are old buddy buddies. He doesn't seem to want me to come in. Now, I asked you . . .'

I turned round. Stared in surprise. Said to Wenkins, 'Perhaps you would let him stay. I do know him. He's a cameraman.'

Conrad raised his eyebrows sharply. 'Director of Photography, dear boy. A cameraman indeed!'

'Sorry,' I said ironically. 'Have a Scotch?'

'Now that, dear boy, is more like it.'

Wenkins gave up the struggle and went off to get Conrad a drink. Conrad surveyed the relaxed atmosphere, the hovering smoke, the empty cups and half empty glasses, and the gentle communicators chatting in seated groups.

'My God,' he said. 'My great God. I don't believe it. I didn't, in fact, believe it when they told me Edward Lincoln was giving a press conference right here in Johannesburg at this very moment. I bet on it not being true. So they told me where. In that ritzy room at the top of the Randfontein, they said. Go and see for yourself. So I did.'

A laugh began rumbling somewhere down in his belly and erupted in a coughing guffaw.

'Shut up,' I said.

He spread his arms wide, embracing the room. 'They

don't know, they just don't know what they're seeing, do they? They've just no idea.'

'Be quiet, Conrad, damn it,' I said.

He went on wheezing away in uncontainable chuckles. 'My dear boy. I didn't know you could do it. Off the set, that is. Talk about a lot of tame tigers eating out of your hand . . . Just wait until Evan hears.'

'He isn't likely to,' I said comfortably. 'Not from five thousand or so miles away.'

He shook with amusement. 'Oh no, dear boy. He's right here in Johannesburg. Practically in the next street.'

'He can't be!'

'We've been here since Sunday.' He choked off the last of his laughter and wiped his eyes with his thumb. 'Come and have some lunch, dear boy, and I'll tell you all about it.'

I looked at my watch. Twelve thirty.

'In a while, then. I've still got one more bit of taping to do, when they get hold of a spare microphone.'

Roderick Hodge detached himself from a group by one of the windows and brought a decorative female over with him, and Clifford Wenkins dead-heated with Conrad's drink.

The girl, the would-be interviewer from the woman's radio programme, had the sort of face that would have been plain on a different personality: but she also had a bushy mop of curly brown hair, enormous yellow-rimmed sunglasses, and a sticklike figure clad in an orange and tan checked trouser suit. The spontaneous friendliness in her manner saved her from any impression of caricature. Conrad took in her colour temperature with an appreciative eye, while explaining he had been engaged on four films with me in the recent past.

Roderick's attention sharpened like an adjusted focus.

'What is he like to work with?' he demanded.

'That's not fair,' I said.

Neither Roderick nor Conrad paid any attention. Conrad looked at me judiciously, pursed his lips, lifted up a hand, and bent the fingers over one by one as he rolled his tongue lovingly around the words.

'Patient, powerful, punctual, professional, and puritanical.' And aside to me he stage-whispered, 'How's that?'

'Ham,' I said.

Roderick predictably pounced on the last one. 'Puritanical. How do you mean?'

Conrad was enjoying himself. 'All his leading ladies complain that he kisses them with art, not heart.'

I could see the headlines writing themselves in Roderick's head. His eye was bright.

'My sons don't like it,' I said.

'What?'

'When the elder one saw me in a film kissing someone who wasn't his mother, he wouldn't speak to me for a week.'

They laughed.

But at the time it had been far from funny. Peter had

also started wetting his bed again at five years old and had cried a lot, and a child psychiatrist had told us it was because he felt insecure: he felt his foundations were slipping away, because Daddy kissed other ladies, and quarrelled with Mummy at home. It had happened so soon after Libby's accident that we wondered whether he was also worrying about that: but we had never told him Libby had been ill because he had dropped her, and never intended to. One couldn't burden a child with that sort of knowledge, because a pointless, unnecessary feeling of guilt could have distorted the whole of his development.

'What did you do about that?' the girl asked sympathetically.

'Took him to some good clean horror films instead.'

'Oh, yeah,' Conrad said.

Clifford Wenkins came twittering back from another of his darting foraging expeditions. Sweat still lay in pearl-sized beads in the furrows of his forehead. How did he cope, I vaguely wondered, when summer came.

He thrust a stick microphone triumphantly into my hands. Its lead ran back to the corner where the radio apparatus stood. 'There we are . . . er . . . all fixed, I mean.' He looked in unnecessary confusion from me to the girl. 'There we are, Katya dear. Er . . . all ready, I think.'

I looked at Conrad. I said, 'I learned just one word of Afrikaans at the races yesterday, and you can do it while I tape this interview.'

Conrad said suspiciously, 'What word?'

'*Voetsek*,' I said conversationally.

They all split themselves politely. *Voetsek* meant bugger off.

Conrad's chuckles broke out again like a recurring infection, when they explained.

'If only Evan could see this . . .' he wheezed.

'Let's forget Evan,' I suggested.

Conrad put his hand on Roderick's arm and took him away, each of them enjoying a separate joke.

Katya's smallish eyes were laughing behind the enormous yellow specs. 'And to think they said that at the airport you were the chilliest of cold fish . . .'

I gave her a sideways smile. 'Maybe I was tired . . .' I eyed the notebook she clutched in one hand. 'What sort of things are you going to ask?'

'Oh, only the same as the others, I should think.' But there was a mischievous glint of teeth that boded no good.

'All set, Katya,' a man called from the row of electronic boxes and dials. 'Any time you say.'

'Right.' She looked down at the notebook and then up at me. I was about three feet away from her, holding my glass in one hand and the microphone in the other. She considered this with her curly head on one side, then took a large step closer. Almost touching.

'That's better, I think. There will be too much background noise if either of us is too far from that microphone. It's an old one, by the looks of it. Oh, and maybe I'd better hold it. You look a bit awkward . . .' She took the microphone and called across the room. 'OK, Joe, switch on.'

Joe switched on.

Katya jerked appallingly from head to foot, arched backwards through the air and fell to the floor.

The murmuring peaceful faces turned, gasped, cried out, screwed themselves up in horror.

'Switch off,' I shouted urgently. 'Switch everything off. At once.'

Roderick took two strides and bent over Katya with outstretched hands to help her, and I pulled him back.

'Get Joe to switch that bloody microphone off first, or you will take the shock as well.'

The Joe in question ran over, looking ill.

'I have,' he said. 'It's off now.'

I thought that all, that any of them would know what to do, and do it. But they all just stood and knelt around looking at me, as if it were up to me to know, to do, to be the resourceful man in all those films who always took the lead, always . . .

Oh God, I thought.

Just look at them, I thought. And there was no time to waste. No time at all. She was no longer breathing.

I knelt down beside her and took her glasses off. Pulled open the neck of her shirt. Stretched her head back. Put my mouth on hers, and blew my breath into her lungs.

'Get a doctor,' Roderick said. 'And an ambulance . . . Oh Christ . . . Hurry. Hurry . . .'

I breathed into her. Not too hard. Just with the force of breath. But over and over, heaving her chest up and down.

A lethal electric voltage stops the heart.

I tried to feel a pulse beating in her neck, but couldn't find one. Roderick interpreted my fingers and picked up her wrist, but it was no good there, either. His face was agonized. Katya was a great deal more, it seemed, than just a colleague.

Two thousand years passed like two more minutes. Roderick put his ear down on Katya's left breast. I went on breathing air into her, feeling as the seconds passed that it was no good, that she was dead. Her flesh was the colour of death, and very cold.

He heard the first thud before I felt it. I saw it in his face. Then there were two separate jolts in the blood vessel I had my fingers on under her jaw, and then some uneven, jerky little bumps, and then at last, unbelievably, slow, rhythmic, and strengthening, the life-giving ba-boom ba-boom ba-boom of a heart back in business.

Roderick's mouth tightened and twisted as he raised his head, and the cords in his neck stood out with the effort he was putting into not weeping. But the tears of relief ran for all that down his cheeks, and he tried to get rid of them with his fingers.

I pretended not to see, if that was what he wanted. But I knew, Heaven forgive me, that one day I would put that face, that reaction, into a film. Whatever one learned, whatever one saw, and however private it was, in the end, if one were an actor, one used it.

She breathed in, convulsively, on her own, while I was still breathing in myself, through my nose. It felt extraordinary, as if she were sucking the air out of me.

I took my mouth away from hers, and stopped holding her jaws open with my hands. She went on breathing: a bit sketchily at first, but then quite regularly, in shallow body-shaking, audible gasps.

'She ought to be warmer,' I said to Roderick. 'She needs blankets.'

He looked at me dazedly. 'Yes. Blankets.'

'I'll get some,' someone said, and the breath-held quietness in the room erupted with sudden bustle. Frozen shock turned to worried shock, and that to relieved shock, and from that to revival via the whiskey bottle.

I saw Clifford Wenkins looking down at Katya's still unconscious form. His face was grey and looked like putty oozing, as the sweat had not had time to dry. For once, however, he had been reduced to speechlessness.

Conrad, too, seemed temporarily to have run out of 'dear boys'. But I guessed sharply that the blankness in his face as he watched the proceedings was not the result of shock. He was at his business, as I had been at mine, seeing an electrocution in terms of camera angles, atmospheric shadows, impact-making colours. And at what point, I wondered, did making use of other people's agonies become a spiritual sin.

Someone reappeared with some blankets, and with shaking hands Roderick wrapped Katya up in them, and put a cushion under her head.

I said to him, 'Don't expect too much when she wakes up. She'll be confused, I think.'

He nodded. Colour was coming back to her cheeks. She seemed securely alive. The time of fiercest anxiety was over.

He looked suddenly up at me, then down at her, then up at me again. The first thought that was not raw emotion was taking root.

As if it were a sudden discovery, he slowly said, 'You're Edward Lincoln.'

For him too the dilemma of conscience arose: whether or not to make professional copy out of the near-death of his girlfriend.

I looked round the room, and so did he. There had been a noticeable thinning of the ranks. I met Roderick's eyes and knew what he was thinking: the Press had made for the telephones, and he was the only one there from the *Rand Daily Star*.

He looked down again at the girl. 'She'll be all right, now, won't she?' he said.

I made an inconclusive gesture with my hands and didn't directly answer. I didn't know whether or not she would be all right. I thought her heart had probably not been stopped for much over three minutes, so with a bit of luck her brain would not be irreparably damaged. But my knowledge was only the sketchy remains of a long past first-aid course.

The journalist in Roderick won the day. He stood up abruptly and said, 'Do me a favour . . . ? Don't let them take her to hospital or anywhere before I get back.'

'I'll do my best,' I said; and he made a highly rapid exit.

Joe, the radio equipment man, was coiling up the lead of the faulty microphone, having disconnected it gingerly from its power socket. He looked at it dubiously and said, 'It's such an old one I didn't know we had it. It was just there, in the box . . . I wish to God I hadn't decided to use it. It just seemed quicker than waiting any longer for the replacement from the studio. I'll make sure it'll do no more damage, anyway. I'll dismantle it and throw it away.'

Conrad returned to my side and stood looking down at Katya, who began showing signs of returning consciousness. Her eyelids fluttered. She moved under the blankets.

Conrad said, 'You do realize, dear boy, that until very shortly before the accident you were holding that microphone yourself.'

'Yes,' I said neutrally. 'I do.'

'And,' said Conrad, 'just how many people in this room showed the slightest sign of knowing that the only hope for the electrocuted is artificial respiration, instantly applied?'

I looked at him straightly.

'Did you know?'

He sighed. 'You are so cynical, dear boy. But no, I didn't.'

CHAPTER SIX

Damilo arrived at the Iguana Rock at four o'clock with a hired Triumph, a scarlet open-necked shirt and a sun-tanned grin.

I had been back there less than an hour myself, Conrad and I having dawdled over a beer and sandwich lunch in an unobtrusive bar. Katya had gone to hospital, with Roderick in frantic tow, and the other journalists were currently stubbing their fingernails on their typewriters. Clifford Wenkins had twittered off at some unmarked point in the proceedings, and when Conrad and I left we saw him, too, engaged in earnest conversation on the telephone. Reporting to Worldic, no doubt. I stifled a despairing sigh. Not a butterfly's chance in a blizzard that anyone would ignore the whole thing as uninteresting.

Danilo chatted in his carefree way, navigating us round the elevated Sir de Villiers Graaf ring road, that God's gift to the city's inhabitants which took the through traffic out of their way, over their heads.

'I can't imagine what Johannesburg was like before they built this highway,' Danilo commented. 'They still have a big traffic problem downtown, and as for parking . . . there's more cars parked along the streets down there than one-armed bandits in Nevada . . .'

'You've been here quite a time, then?'

'Hell, no,' he grinned. 'Only a few days. But I've been here before, once, and anyway it sure only takes twenty minutes of searching around to teach you that all the car parks are permanently full and that you can never park within a quarter mile of where you want to be.'

He drove expertly and coolly on what was to him the wrong side of the road.

'Greville lives down near Turffontein,' he said. 'We drop down off this elevated part soon now . . . did that sign say Eloff Street Extension?'

'It did,' I confirmed.

'Great.' He took the turn and we left the South African Ml and presently passed some football fields and a skating rink.

'They call this "Wembley",' Danilo said. 'And over there is a lake called Wemmer Pan for boating. And say, they have a water organ there which shoots coloured fountains up into the air in time to the music'

'Have you been there?'

'No . . . Greville told me, I guess. He also says it's a great place for fishing out rotting corpses and headless torsos.'

'Nice,' I said.

He grinned.

Before we reached Turffontein he turned off down a

side road which presently became hard impacted earth covered with a layer of dust.

'They've had no rain here for four-five months,' Danilo said. 'Everything's sure looking dry.'

The grass was certainly brownish, but that was what I expected. I was surprised to learn from Danilo that in a month's time, when the rain came and the days were warmer, the whole area would be lush, colourful, and green.

'It's sure sad you won't be here to see the jacarandas,' Danilo said. 'They'll flower all over, after you've gone.'

'You've seen them before?'

He hesitated. 'Well no, not exactly. Last time I was here, they weren't flowering. It's just that Greville says.'

'I see,' I said.

'Here it is. This is Greville's place, right in here.' He pointed, then turned in between some severe-looking brick pillars and drove up a gravel drive into a stable which looked as if it had been transplanted straight from England.

Arknold himself was already out in the yard talking to a black African whom he introduced as his head boy, Barty. Arknold's head lad looked as tough as himself: a solid strong-looking man of about thirty, with a short thick neck and unsmiling cold eyes. He was the first black African I had seen, I thought in mild surprise, whose natural expression had not been good-natured.

There was nothing in his manner, however, but civility, and he nodded to Danilo's greeting with the ordinary acknowledgment of people who meet each other fairly often.

Arknold said that everything was ready, and we started looking round the boxes without more ado. The horses were all like those I had seen on the track; up on their toes, with slightly less bone all round than those at home.

There was nothing at all to distinguish Nerissa's horses from their stable-mates. They looked as well, had legs as firm, eyes as bright; and they were not all stabled in one block, but were scattered among the rest. Colts in one quadrangle, fillies in another. Everything as it should be, as it normally would be in England.

The lads – the boys – were all young and all black. Like lads the world over they were possessively proud of the horses they cared for, though alongside this pride there emerged a second, quite definite, pattern of behaviour.

They responded to me with smiles, to Arknold with respect, and to Barty with unmistakable fear.

I had no knowledge of what sort of tribal hold he had over them, and I never did find out, but in their wary eyes and their shrinking away at his approach, one could see he held them in a bondage far severer than any British head lad could have imposed.

I thought back to the iron hand my father had once wielded. The lads had jumped to what he said, the apprentices had scurried, and indeed I had wasted no time, but I could not remember that anyone had held him in actual physical fear.

I looked at Barty and faintly shivered. I wouldn't have liked to work under him, any more than Arknold's lads did.

'This is Tables Turned,' Arknold was saying, approaching the box door of a dark chestnut colt. 'One of Mrs Cavesey's. Running at Germiston on Saturday.'

'I thought I might go to Germiston,' I said.

'Great,' Danilo said with enthusiasm.

Arknold nodded more moderately, and said he would arrange for me to pick up free entrance tickets at the gate.

We went into the box and stood in the usual sort of appreciative pause, looking Tables Turned over from head to foot while Arknold noted how he was looking compared with the day before and I thought of something not too uncomplimentary to say about him.

'Good neck,' I said. 'Good strong shoulders.' And a bit ratlike about the head, I thought to myself.

Arknold shrugged heavily. 'I took him down to Natal for the winter season, along with all the others. Had nearly the whole string down there for getting on for three months, like we do every year. We keep them at Summerveld, do you see?'

'Where is Summerveld?' I asked.

'More like what is Summerveld,' he said. 'It's a large area with stabling for about eight hundred horses, at Shongweni, near Durban. We book a block of stables there for the season. They have everything in the area one could need – practice track, restaurants, hostels for the boys, everything. And the school for jockeys and apprentices is there, as well.'

'But you didn't do much good, this year?' I said sympathetically.

'We won a few races with the others, but Mrs Cavesey's string . . . Well, to be frank, there are so many of hers that I can't afford to have them all go wrong. Does my reputation no good, do you see?'

I did see. I also thought he spoke with less passion than he might have done.

'This Tables Turned,' he said, slapping the horse's rump, 'on his breeding and his early form he looked a pretty good prospect for the Hollis Memorial Plate in June . . . that's one of the top two-year-old races . . . and he ran just like you saw Chink do at Newmarket. Blew up five hundred metres from home and finished exhausted, though I'd have sworn he was as fit as any of them.'

He nodded to the boy holding the horse's head, turned on his heel, and strode out of the box. Further down the line we reached another of Nerissa's, who evoked an even deeper display of disgust.

'Now this colt, Medic, he should have been a proper world-beater. I thought once that he'd win the Natal Free Handicap in July, but in the end I never sent him to Clairwood at all. His four races before that were too shameful.'

I had a strong feeling that his anger was half genuine. It puzzled me. He certainly did seem to care that the horses had all failed, yet I was still sure that he not only knew why they had but had engineered it himself.

With Barty in attendance, pointing out omissions with a stabbing black forefinger to every intimidated stable-boy, we finished inspecting every one of the string, and afterwards went across to the house for a drink.

'All of Mrs Cavesey's lot are now counted as three-year-olds, of course,' Arknold said. 'The date for the age-change out here is August 1st, not January 1st as with you.'

'Yes,' I said.

'There isn't much good racing here on Rand tracks during August. Nothing much to interest you, I dare say.'

'I find it all extremely interesting,' I said truthfully. 'Will you go on running Mrs Cavesey's string as three-year-olds?'

'As long as she cares to go on paying their training fees,' he said gloomily.

'And if she decides to sell?'

'She'd get very little for them now.'

'If she sold them, would you buy any of them?' I asked.

He didn't answer immediately as he was showing us the way into his office, a square room full of papers, form books, filing cabinets and hard upright chairs. Arknold's guests were not, it seemed, to be made so comfortable that they outstayed their limited welcome.

I repeated my question unwisely, and received the full glare of the Arknold displeasure.

'Look, Mister,' he said fiercely. 'I don't like what you're suggesting. You are saying that maybe I lose races so I can buy the horses cheap, then win races when I have them myself, and then sell them well for stud. That's what you're saying, Mister.'

'I didn't say anything of the sort,' I protested mildly.

'It's what you were thinking.'

'Well,' I agreed 'It was a possibility. Looking at it from outside, objectively, wouldn't that have occurred to you, too?'

He still glowered, but the antagonism slowly subsided. I wished I could decide whether he had been angry because I had insulted him, or because I had come too near the truth.

Danilo, who had been tagging along all the way making sunny comments to no one in particular, tried to smooth his ruffled friend.

'Aw, c'mon Greville, he meant no harm.'

Arknold gave me a sour look.

'Hey, c'mon. Aunt Nerissa probably told him to poke around for reasons, if he got the chance. You can't blame her, when she's pouring all that money into bad horses, now can you, Greville?'

Arknold made a fair pretence at being pacified and offered us a drink. Danilo smiled hugely in relief and said it wouldn't do, it wouldn't do at all, for us to quarrel.

I sipped my drink and looked at the two of them. Glossy young golden boy. Square surly middle-aged man. They both drank, and watched me over the rims of the glasses.

I couldn't see an inch into either of their souls.

Back at the Iguana Rock there was a hand-delivered letter waiting for me. I read it upstairs in my room, standing by the window which looked out over the gardens, the tennis courts, and the great African outdoors. The light had begun fading and would soon go quickly, but the positive handwriting was still easy to see.

Dear Mr Lincoln,

I have received a cable from Nerissa Cavesey asking me to invite you to dinner. My wife and I would be pleased to entertain you during your visit, if you would care to accept.

Nerissa is the sister of my late brother's wife, Portia, and has become close to us through her visits to our country. I explain this, as Mr Clifford Wenkins of Worldic Cinemas, who very reluctantly informed me of your whereabouts, was most insistent that you would not welcome any private invitations.

Yours sincerely,

Quentin van Huren

Behind the stiffly polite sentences, one could feel the irritation with which he had written that note. It was not only I, it seemed, who would do things slightly against their will, for Nerissa's sake: and Clifford Wenkins, with his fussing misjudgement of his responsibilities, had clearly not improved the situation.

I went over to the telephone beside the bed and put a call through to the number printed alongside the address on the writing-paper.

The call was answered by a black voice who said she would see if Mr van Huren was home.

Mr van Huren decided he was.

'I called to thank you for your letter,' I said. 'And to say that I would very much like to accept your invitation to dine with you, during my stay.' Two, I reckoned, could be ultra polite.

His voice was as firm as his handwriting, and equally reserved.

'Good.' He didn't sound overjoyed, however. 'It is always a pleasure to please Nerissa.'

'Yes,' I said.

There was a pause. The conversation could hardly be said to be rocketing along at a scintillating rate.

I said helpfully, 'I shall be here until a week next Wednesday.'

'I see. Yes. However, I shall be away from home all next week, and we are already engaged this Saturday and Sunday . . .'

'Then please don't worry,' I said.

He cleared his throat. 'I suppose,' he suggested doubtfully, 'that you would not be free tomorrow? Or, indeed, this evening? My house is not far from the Iguana Rock . . . but of course I expect you are fully engaged.'

Tomorrow morning, I thought, all the newspapers would be flourishing a paragraph or two about Roderick Hodge's girlfriend. By tomorrow night, Mrs van Huren, if she felt like it, could fill her house with the sort of party I didn't like to go to. And tomorrow night I had agreed to have dinner with Conrad, though I could change that if I had to.

I said, 'If it is not too short notice, tonight would be fine.'

'Very well, then. Shall we say eight o'clock? I'll send my car to fetch you.'

I put down the receiver half regretting that I had said I would go, as his pleasure in my acceptance was about as intense as a rice-pudding. However, the alternatives seemed to be the same as the night before: either dine in the Iguana Rock restaurant with the sideways glances reaching me from the other tables, or upstairs alone in my room, wishing I was home with Charlie.

The house to which the van Hurens' car took me was big, old, and spelled money from the marble doorstep onwards. The hall was large, with the ceiling soaring away into invisibility, and round all four sides there was a graceful colonnade of pillars and arches: it looked like a small, splendid Italian piazza, with a roof somewhere over the top.

In the hall, from a door under the colonnade on the far side, came a man and a woman.

'I am Quentin van Huren,' he said. 'And this is my wife Vivi.'

'How do you do?' I said politely, and shook their hands. There was a small hiatus.

'Yes . . . well,' he said, making a gesture which was very nearly a shrug. 'Come along in.'

I followed them into the room they had come from. In the clearer light there, Quentin van Huren was instantly identifiable as a serious man of substance, since about him clung that unmistakable aura of know-how, experience, and ability that constitutes true authority. As solidity and professionalism were qualities I felt at home with, I was immediately prepared to like him more than it seemed probable he would like me.

His wife Vivi was not the same: elegant-looking, but not in the same league intellectually.

She said, 'Do sit down, Mr Lincoln. We are so pleased you could come. Nerissa is such a very dear friend . . .'

She had cool eyes and a highly practised social manner. There was less warmth in her voice than in her words.

'Whiskey?' van Huren asked, and I said 'Thank you,' and got the tumbler full of water with the tablespoon of Scotch.

'I'm afraid I haven't seen any of your films,' van Huren said, without sounding in the least sorry about it, and his wife added, 'We seldom go to the cinema.'

'Very wise,' I said without inflection, and neither of them knew quite how to take it.

I found it easier on the whole to deal with people intent on taking me down a peg rather than with the sycophantically over-flattering. Towards the snubbers I felt no obligation.

I sat down on the gold-brocaded sofa which she had indicated, and sipped my enervated drink.

'Has Nerissa told you she is . . . ill?' I asked.

They both sat without haste. Van Huren shifted a small cushion out of his way, twisting in his armchair to see what he was doing, and answered over his shoulder.

'She wrote a little while ago. She said she had something wrong with her glands.'

'She's dying,' I said flatly, and got from them their first genuine response. They stopped thinking about me. Thought about Nerissa. About themselves. The shock and regret in their faces was real.

Van Huren still held the cushion in his hand.

'Are you sure?' he said.

I nodded. 'She told me herself. A month or two, she says, is all she has.'

'Oh no,' Vivi said, her grief showing through the social gloss like a thistle among orchids.

'I can't believe it,' van Huren exclaimed. 'She is always so full of life. So gay. So vital.'

I thought of Nerissa as I had left her: vitality gone and life itself draining away.

'She is worried about her racehorses,' I said. 'The ones Portia left her.'

Neither of them was ready to think about racehorses. Van Huren shook his head, finished putting the cushion comfortably in his chair, and stared into space. He was a well-built man, at a guess in his fifties, with hair going neatly grey in distinguished wings above his ears. Seen in profile his nose was strongly rounded outwards from the bridge, but stopped straight and short with no impression of a hook. He had a firm, full-lipped, well-defined mouth, hands with square well-manicured nails, and a dark grey suit over which someone had taken a lot of trouble.

The door from the hall opened suddenly and a boy and

a girl, quite remarkably alike, came in. He, about twenty, had the slightly sullen air of one whose feelings of rebellion had not carried him as far as actually leaving his palatial home. She, about fifteen, had the uncomplicated directness of one to whom the idea of rebellion had not yet occurred.

'Oh sorry,' she said. 'Didn't know we had anyone for dinner.' She came across the room in her jeans and a pale yellow tee-shirt, with her brother behind her dressed very much the same.

Van Huren said, 'This is my son Jonathan, and my daughter Sally . . .'

I stood up to shake hands with the girl, which seemed to amuse her.

'I say,' she said. 'Did anyone ever tell you you look like Edward Lincoln?'

'Yes,' I said. 'I am.'

'You are what?'

'Edward Lincoln.'

'Oh yeah.' She took a closer look. 'Oh golly. Good heavens. So you are.' Then doubtfully, afraid I was making a fool of her. 'Are you really?'

Her father said, 'Mr Lincoln is a friend of Mrs Cavesey . . .'

'Aunt Nerissa! Oh yes. She told us once that she knew you well . . . She's such a darling, isn't she?'

'She is,' I agreed, sitting down again.

Jonathan looked at me steadily with a cold and unimpressed eye.

'I never go to see your sort of film,' he stated.

I smiled mildly and made no answer: it was typical of the putting-down brand of remark made to me with varying degrees of aggression almost every week of my life. Experience had long ago shown that the only unprovocative reply was silence.

'Well, I do,' Sally said. 'I've seen quite a few of them. Was it really you riding that horse in *Spy Across Country*, like the posters said?'

I nodded, 'Mm.'

She looked at me consideringly. 'Wouldn't you have found it easier in a hackamore?'

I laughed involuntarily. 'Well, no. I know the script said the horse had a very light mouth, but the one they actually gave me to ride had a hard one.'

'Sally is a great little horsewoman,' her mother said unnecessarily. 'She won the big pony class at the Rand Easter Show.'

'On Rojedda Reef,' Sally added.

The name meant nothing to me. But the others clearly thought it would. They looked at me expectantly, and in the end it was Jonathan who said with superiority, 'It's the name of our gold mine.'

'Really? I didn't know you had a gold mine.' I half deliberately said it with the same inflection that father and son had said they didn't see my films, and Quentin van Huren heard it. He turned his head quite sharply towards me, and I could feel the internal smile coming out of my eyes.

'Yes,' he said thoughtfully, holding my gaze. 'I see.' His lips twitched. 'Would you care to go down one? To see what goes on?'

From the surprised expressions on the rest of his family, I gathered that what he had offered was more or less the equivalent of my suggesting a press conference.

'I'd like it enormously,' I assured him. 'I really would.'

'I'm flying down to Welkom on Monday morning,' he said. 'That's the town where Rojedda is . . . I'll be there the whole week, but if you care to come down with me Monday, you can fly back again the same evening.'

I said that would be great.

By the end of dinner the van Huren-Lincoln *entente* had progressed to the point where three of the family decided to go to Germiston that Saturday to watch Nerissa's horses run. Jonathan said he had more important things to do.

'Like what?' Sally demanded.

Jonathan didn't really know.

CHAPTER SEVEN

Friday turned out to be a meagre day for world news, which left a lot too much space for the perils of Katya. Seldom had the Press been invited in advance to such a spectacle, and in most papers it seemed to have made the front page.

One of them first unkindly suggested that it had all been a publicity stunt which had gone wrong, and then denied it most unconvincingly in the following paragraph.

I wondered, reading it, how many people would believe just that. I wondered, remembering that mischievous smile, whether Katya could possibly even have set it up herself. She and Roderick, between them.

But she wouldn't have risked her life. Not unless she hadn't realized she was risking it.

I picked up the *Rand Daily Star*, to see what they had made of Roderick's information, and found that he had written the piece himself. 'By our own *Rand Daily Star* eye-witness, Roderick Hodge' it announced at the top. Considering his emotional involvement it was not too highly coloured, but it was he, more than any of the others, who stressed, as Conrad had done, that if Katya had not taken the microphone away from me, it would have been I who got the shock.

I wondered how much Roderick wished I had done. For one thing, it would have made a better story.

With a twisting smile I read on to the end. Katya, he reported finally, was being detained in hospital overnight, her condition described as 'comfortable'.

I shoved the papers aside, and while I showered and shaved came to two conclusions. One was that what I had done was not particularly remarkable and certainly not worth the coverage, and the other was that after this I was going to have even more trouble explaining to Nerissa why all I could bring her were guesses, not proof.

Down at the reception desk I asked if they could get me a packed lunch and hire me a horse for the day out in some decent riding country. Certainly, they said, and waved a few magic wands: by mid-morning I was twenty-five miles north of Johannesburg setting out along a dirt road in brilliant sunshine on a pensioned off race-horse who had seen better days. I took a deep contented breath of the sweet smell of Africa and padded along with a great feeling of freedom. The people who owned the horse had gently insisted on sending their head boy along with me so that I shouldn't get lost, but as he spoke little English and I no Bantu, I found him a most peaceful companion. George was small, rode well, and had a great line in banana-shaped smiles.

We passed a cross-roads where there was a large stall,

all by itself, loaded with bright orange fruit and festooned with pineapples, with one man beaming beside them.

'*Naartjies*,' George said, pointing.

I made signs that I didn't understand. One thing about being an actor, it occasionally came in useful.

'*Naartjies.*' George repeated, dismounting from his horse and leading it towards the stall. I grasped the fact that George wanted to buy, so I called to him and fished out a five rand note. George smiled, negotiated rapidly, and returned with a huge string bag of *naartjies*, two ripe pineapples, and most of the money.

In easy undemanding companionship we rode further, dismounted in some shade, ate a pineapple each, and cold chicken from the Iguana Rock, and drank some refreshing unsweet apple juice from tins George had been given to bring along. The *naartjies* turned out to be like large lumpy tangerines with green patches on the skin: they also tasted like tangerine, but better.

George ate his lunch thirty feet away from me. I beckoned to him to come closer, but he wouldn't.

In the afternoon we trotted and cantered a long way over tough scrubby brown dried grass, and finally, walking to cool the horses, found ourselves approaching the home stables from the opposite direction to the way we set out.

They asked ten rand for the hire of the horse, though the day I had had was worth a thousand, and I gave George five rand for himself, which his employers whispered was too much. George with a last dazzling smile handed me the bag of *naartjies* and they all gave me friendly waves when I left. If only life were all so natural, so undemanding, so unfettered.

Five miles down the road I reflected that if it were, I would be bored to death.

Conrad was before me at the Iguana.

He met me as I came into the hall and surveyed me from head to foot, dust, sweat, *naartjies* and all.

'What on earth have you been doing, dear boy?'

'Riding.'

'What a pity I haven't an Arriflex with me,' he exclaimed. 'What a shot . . . you standing there looking like a gypsy with your back to the light . . . and those oranges . . . have to work it into our next film together, can't waste a shot like that . . .'

'You're early,' I remarked.

'Might as well wait here as anywhere else.'

'Come upstairs, then, while I change.'

He came up to my room and with unfailing instinct chose the most comfortable chair.

'Have a *naartjie*,' I said.

'I'd rather have a Martini, dear boy.'

'Order one, then.'

He rang for his drink and it came while I was in the shower. I towelled dry and went back into the bedroom in underpants to find him equipped also with a Churchill-sized cigar, wreathed in smoke and smelling of London clubs and plutocracy. He was looking through the pile of newspapers which still lay tidily on the table, but in the end left them undisturbed.

'I've seen all those,' he said. 'How do you like being a real hero, for a change?'

'Don't be nutty. What's so heroic about first aid?'

He grinned. Changed the subject.

'What in hell's name made you come out here for a premiere after all those years of refusing to show your face off the screen?'

'I came to see some horses,' I said, and explained about Nerissa.

'Oh, well, then, dear boy, that does make more sense, I agree. And have you found out what's wrong?'

I shrugged. 'Not really. Don't see how I can.' I fished out a clean shirt and buttoned it on. 'I'm going to Germiston races tomorrow, and I'll keep my eyes open again, but I doubt if anyone could ever prove anything against Greville Arknold.' I put on some socks and dark blue trousers, and some slip-on shoes. 'What are you and Evan doing here, anyway?'

'Film making. What else?'

'What film?'

'Some goddam awful story about elephants that Evan took it into his head to do. It was all set up before he got roped in to finish *Man in a Car*, and since he chose to ponce around in Spain for all that time, we were late getting out here. Should be down in the Kruger Game Park by now.'

I brushed my hair.

'Who's playing the lead?'

'Drix Goddart.'

I glanced at Conrad over my shoulder. He smiled sardonically.

'Wax in Evan's hands, dear boy. Laps up direction like a well patted puppy.'

'Nice for you all.'

'He's so neurotic that if someone doesn't tell him every five minutes that he's brilliant, he thinks everyone hates him.'

'Is he here with you?'

'No, thank God. He was supposed to be, but now he comes out with all the rest of the team after Evan and I have sorted out which locations we want to use.'

I put down the brushes and fastened my watch round my wrist. Keys, change, handkerchief into trouser pockets.

'Did you see the rushes of the desert scenes while you were in England?' Conrad asked.

'No,' I said. 'Evan didn't invite me.'

'Just like him.' He took a long swallow and rolled the Martini round his teeth. He squinted at the long ash on the end of his mini-torpedo. He said, 'They were good.'

'So they damn well ought to be. We did them enough times.'

He smiled without looking at me. 'You won't like the finished film.'

After a pause, as he didn't explain, I said, 'Why not?'

'There's something in it besides and beyond acting.' He paused again, considering his words. 'Even to a jaundiced eye like mine, dear boy, the quality of suffering is shattering.'

I didn't say anything. He swivelled his eyes in my direction.

'Usually you do not reveal much of yourself, do you? Well, this time, dear boy, this time . . .'

I compressed my lips. I knew what I'd done. I'd known while I did it. I had just hoped that no one would be perceptive enough to notice.

'Will the critics see what you saw?' I asked. He smiled lopsidedly. 'Bound to, aren't they? The best ones, anyway.'

I stared despondently at the carpet. The trouble with interpreting scenes too well, with taking an emotion and making the audience feel it sharply, was that it meant stripping oneself naked in public. Nothing as simple as naked skin, but letting the whole world peer into one's mind, one's beliefs, one's experience.

To be able to reproduce a feeling so that others could recognize it, and perhaps understand it for the first time, one had to have some idea of what it felt like in reality. To show that one knew, meant revealing what one had felt. Revealing oneself too nakedly did not come easily to a private man, and if one did not reveal oneself, one never became a great actor.

I was not a great actor. I was competent and popular, but unless I whole-heartedly took the step into frightening personal exposure, I would never do anything great. There was always for me, in acting beyond a certain limit, an element of mental distress. But I had thought, when I risked doing it in the car, that my own self would be merged indiscernibly with the trials the fictional character was enduring.

I had done it because of Evan: to spite him, more than to please him. There was a point beyond which no director could claim credit for an actor's performance, and I had gone a long way beyond that point.

'What are you thinking?' Conrad demanded.

'I was deciding to stick exclusively in future to unreal entertaining escapades, as in the past.'

'You're a coward, dear boy.'

'Yes.'

He tapped the ash off his cigar.

'No one is going to be satisfied, if you do.'

'Of course they are.'

'Uhuh.' He shook his head. 'No one will settle for paste after they see they could have the real thing.'

'Stop drinking Martinis,' I said. 'They give you rotten ideas.'

I walked across the room, picked up my jacket, put it on, and stowed wallet and diary inside it.

'Let's go down to the bar,' I said.

He levered himself obediendy out of the chair.

'You can't run away from yourself for ever, dear boy.'

'I'm not the man you think I am.'

'Oh yes,' Conrad said. 'Dear boy, you are.'

*

At Germiston races the next day I found waiting for me at the gate not only the free entrance tickets promised by Greville Arknold, but also a racecourse official with a duplicate set and instructions to take me up to lunch with the Chairman of the Race Club.

I meekly followed where he led, and was presently shown into a large dining-room where about a hundred people were already eating at long tables. The whole van Huren family, including a sulky Jonathan, occupied chairs near the end of the table closest to the door, and when he saw me come in, van Huren himself rose to his feet.

'Mr Klugvoigt, this is Edward Lincoln,' he said to the man sitting at the end of the table: and to me added, 'Mr Klugvoigt is the Chairman.'

Klugvoigt stood up, shook hands, indicated the empty chair on his left, and we all sat down.

Vivi van Huren in a sweeping green hat sat opposite me, on the Chairman's right, with her husband beside her. Sally van Huren was on my left, with her brother beyond. They all seemed to know Klugvoigt well, and as a personality he had much in common with van Huren: same air of wealth and substance, same self confidence, same bulk of body and acuity of mind.

Once past the preliminaries and the politeness (how did I like South Africa: nowhere so comfortable as the Iguana Rock: how long was I staying) the conversation veered naturally back to the chief matter in hand.

Horses.

The van Hurens owned a four-year-old which had finished third in the Dunlop Gold Cup a month earlier, but they were giving it a breather during these less important months. Klugvoigt owned two three-year-olds running that afternoon with nothing much expected.

I steered the conversation round to Nerissa's horses without much difficulty, and from there to Greville Arknold, asking, but not pointedly, how he was in general regarded, both as man and trainer.

Neither van Huren nor Klugvoigt were of the kind to come straight out with what they thought. It was Jonathan who leant forward and let out the jet of truth.

'He's a rude bloody bastard with hands as heavy as a gold brick.'

'I have to advise Nerissa, when I get home,' I commented.

'Aunt Portia always said he had a way with horses,' Sally objected, in defence.

'Yeah. Backwards,' said Jonathan.

Van Huren gave him a flickering glance in which humour was by no means lacking, but he changed the subject immediately with the expertise of one thoroughly awake to the risk of slander.

'Your Clifford Wenkins, Link, telephoned to me yesterday afternoon to offer us all some tickets to your premiere.' He looked amused. I gratefully accepted that he had loosened with me to the point of dropping the meticulous 'Mr' and thought that in an hour or two I might get around to Quentin.

'Apparently he had had second thoughts about his abruptness to me when I asked for your address.'

'Probably been doing some belated homework,' agreed Klugvoigt, who seemed to know all about it.

'It's only a . . . an adventure film,' I said. 'You might not enjoy it.'

He gave me a dry sardonic smile. 'You won't accuse me again of condemning what I haven't seen.'

I smiled back. I considerably liked Nerissa's sister's husband's brother.

We finished the excellent lunch and wandered out for the first race. Horses were already being mounted, and Vivi and Sally hurried off to upset the odds with a couple of rand.

'Your friend Wenkins said he would be here today,' van Huren remarked.

'Oh dear.'

He chuckled.

Arknold, in the parade ring, was throwing his magenta-shirted jockey up into the saddle.

'How heavy is a gold brick?' I asked.

Van Huren followed my gaze. 'Seventy-two pounds, usually. You can't lift them as easily, though, as seventy-two pounds of jockey.'

Danilo was standing by the rails, watching. He turned as the mounted horses walked away, caught sight of us, and came straight across.

'Hi, Link, I've been looking out for you. How's about a beer?'

I said, 'Quentin,' (not two hours: ten minutes) 'this is Danilo Cavesey, Nerissa's nephew. And Danilo, this is Quentin van Huren, whose sister-in-law, Portia van Huren, was Nerissa's sister.'

'Gee,' Danilo said. His eyes widened and stayed wide, without blinking. He was more than ordinarily surprised.

'Good heavens,' van Huren exclaimed. 'I didn't even know she had a nephew.'

'I kinda dropped out of her life when I was about six, I guess,' Danilo said. 'I only saw her again this summer, when I was over in England from the States.'

Van Huren said he had only twice met Nerissa's husband, and never his brother, Danilo's father. Danilo said he had never met Portia. The two of them sorted out the family ramifications to their own content and seemed to meet in understanding in a very short time.

'Well, what do you know?' Danilo said, evidently pleased to the roots. 'Say, isn't that just too much?'

When Vivi and Sally and Jonathan rejoined us after the race they chattered about it like birds, waving their arms about and lifting their voices in little whoops.

'He's a sort of cousin,' said Sally positively. 'Isn't it the greatest fun?'

Even Jonathan seemed to brighten up at the idea of receiving the sunshine kid into the family, and the two of them presently bore him away on their own. I saw him looking back over his shoulder with a glance for me that was a lot older than anything Jonathan or Sally could produce.

'What a nice boy,' Vivi said.

'Nerissa is very fond of him,' I agreed.

'We must ask him over, while he is here, don't you think, Quentin? Oh look, do you see who's down there . . . Janet Frankenloots . . . haven't seen her for ages. Oh, do excuse me, Link . . .' The great hat swooped off to meet the long-lost friend.

Van Huren was too depressingly right about Clifford Wenkins being at the races. To say that the Distribution Manager approached as directly as Danilo had done would be inaccurate: he made a crabwise deprecating semicircle, tripping over his feet, and ended damply by my side.

'Er . . . Link, good to see you . . . er, would you be Mr van Huren? Pleased . . . er . . . to meet you, sir.'

He shook hands with van Huren, who from long social practice managed not to wipe his palm on his trousers afterwards.

'Now. Er . . . Link. I've tried to reach you a couple of times, but you never seem, er . . . I mean . . . I haven't called you when you are . . . er . . . in. So I thought . . . well, I mean, er . . . I would be certain to see you here.'

I waited without much patience. He pulled a batch of papers hastily out of an inside pocket.

'Now, we want . . . that is to say, Worldic have arranged . . . er . . . since you did the press interviews, I mean . . . they want you to go to . . . let's see . . . there's a beauty competition to judge next Wednesday for Miss Jo'burg . . . and er . . . guest of honour at the Ladies' Kinema Luncheon Club on Thursday . . . and on Friday a fund-raising charity reception given by . . . er . . . our sponsors for the premiere . . . er, that is Bow-Miouw Pet-food, of course . . . and er . . . well . . . Saturday's . . . the official opening of er . . . the Modern Homes' Exhibition . . . all good publicity . . . er . . .'

'No,' I said. And for hell's sake don't lose your temper here, I told myself severely.

'Er,' Wenkins said, seeing no danger signals. 'We . . . er . . . that is, Worldic, do think . . . I mean . . . that you really ought to cooperate . . .'

'Oh they do.' I slowed my breathing deliberately. 'Why do you think I won't let Worldic pay my expenses? Why do you think I pay for everything myself?'

He was extremely unhappy. Worldic must have been putting on the pressure from one side, and now I was resisting him from the other. The beads sprang out on his forehead.

'Yes, but . . .' He swallowed. 'Well . . . I expect . . . I mean . . . the various organizations might be prepared to offer . . . er . . . I mean . . . well, *fees*.'

I counted five. Squeezed my eyes shut and open. Said, when I was sure it would come out moderately, 'Mr Wenkins, you can tell Worldic that I do not wish to accept any of those invitations. In fact, I will go only to the premiere itself and a simple reception before or after, as I said.'

'But . . . We have told everybody that you will.'

'You know that my agent particularly asked you, right at the beginning, not to fix anything at all.'

'Yes, but Worldic say . . . I mean . . .'

Stuff Worldic, I thought violently. I said, 'I'm not going to those things.'

'But . . . you can't . . . I mean . . . *disappoint* them all . . . not now . . . they will not go to your films, if you don't turn up when . . . er . . . we've . . . er . . . well . . . promised you will.'

'You will have to tell them that you committed me without asking me first.'

'Worldic won't like it . . .'

'They won't like it because it will hurt their own takings, if it hurts anything at all. But it's their own fault. If they thought they could make me go to those functions by a species of blackmail, they were wrong.'

Clifford Wenkins was looking at me anxiously and van Huren with some curiosity, and I knew that despite my best intentions the anger was showing through.

I took pity on Clifford Wenkins and a grip on myself. 'Tell Worldic I will not be in Johannesburg at all next week. Tell them that if they had had the commonsense to check with me first, I could have told them I am committed elsewhere, until the premiere.'

He swallowed again and looked even unhappier.

'They said I must persuade you . . .'

'I'm sorry.'

'They might even fire me . . .'

'Even for you, Mr Wenkins, I can't do it. I won't be here.'

He gave me a spanked-spaniel look which I didn't find

endearing, and when I said no more he turned disgustedly away and walked off, stuffing the papers roughly into the side pocket of his jacket.

Van Huren turned his handsome head and gave me an assessing look.

'Why did you refuse him?' he asked. No blame in his voice; simply interest.

I took a deep breath: got the rueful smile out, and stifled the irritation which Clifford Wenkins had raised like an allergic rash.

'I never do those things . . . beauty contests and lunches and opening things.'

'Yes. But why not?'

'I haven't the stamina.'

'You're big enough,' he said.

I smiled and shook my head. It would have sounded pretentious to tell him that so-called 'personal appearances' left me feeling invaded, battered, and devoured, and that complimentary introductory speeches gave me nothing in return. The only compliment I truly appreciated was the money plonked down at the box-office.

'Where are you off to, next week, then?' he asked.

'Africa is huge,' I said, and he laughed.

We wandered back to look at the next batch of hopefuls in the parade ring, and identified number eight as Nerissa's filly, Lebona.

'She looks perfectly all right,' van Huren commented.

'She will start all right,' I agreed. 'And run well for three-quarters of the way. Then she'll tire suddenly within a few strides and drop right out, and when she comes back her sides will be heaving and she'll look exhausted.'

He was startled. 'You sound as if you know all about it.'

'Only guessing. I saw Chink run like that at Newmarket on Wednesday.'

'But you think they are all running to the same pattern?'

'The form book confirms it.'

'What will you tell Nerissa, then?'

I shrugged. 'I don't know . . . Probably to change her trainer.'

In due course we returned to the stands and watched Lebona run as expected. Van Huren seeming in no haste to jettison me for more stimulating company, and I well content to have him as a buffer state, the two of us, passing the cluster of tables and chairs under sun umbrellas, decided to sit down there and order refreshers.

For the first day since I had arrived, the sunshine had grown hot. No breeze stirred the fringes round the flowered umbrellas, and ladies in all directions were shedding their coats.

Van Huren, however, sighed when I commented on the good weather.

'I like winter best,' he said. 'When it's cold, dry, and sunny. The summers are wet, and far too hot, even up here on the highveld.'

'One thinks of South Africa as always being hot.'

'It is, of course. Once you get down near to sea level, it can be scorching even as early as this.'

The shadows of two men fell across the table, and we both looked up.

Two men I knew. Conrad: and Evan Pentelow.

I made introductions, and they pulled up chairs and joined us; Conrad his usual flamboyant self, scattering dear boys with abandon, and Evan, hair as unruly as ever, and eyes as hot.

Evan weighed straight in. 'You won't now refuse to turn up at the premiere of my *Man in a Car*, I hope.'

'You sound very proprietary,' I said mildly. 'It isn't altogether yours.'

'My name will come first in the credits,' he asserted aggressively.

'Before mine?'

Posters of Evan's films were apt to have Evan Pentelow in large letters at the top, followed by the name of the film, followed, in the last third of the space, by the actors' names all squashed closely together. Piracy, it was, or little short.

Evan glared, and I guessed he had checked my contract for the film, and found, as I had done, that in the matter of billing my agent had made no mistakes.

'Before the other director,' he said grudgingly.

I supposed that was fair. Although he had directed less than a quarter, the shape of the finished film would be his idea.

Van Huren followed the sparring with amusement and attention.

'So billing does matter as much as they say.'

'It depends,' I smiled, 'on who is sticking knives into whose back.'

Evan had no sense of humour and was not amused. He began instead to talk about the film he was going to make next.

'It's an allegory . . . every human scene is balanced by a similar one involving elephants. They were supposed to be the good guys of the action, originally, but I've been learning a thing or two about elephants. Did you know they are more dangerous to man than any other animal in Africa? Did you know that nothing preys on them except ivory hunters, and as ivory hunting is banned in the Kruger Park, the elephants are in the middle of a population explosion? They are increasing by a thousand a year, which means that in ten years there will be no room for any other animals, and probably no trees in the park, as the elephants uproot them by the hundred.'

Evan, as usual on any subject which took his attention, was dogmatic and intense.

'And do you know,' he went on, 'that elephants don't like Volkswagens? Those small ones, I mean. Elephants seldom attack cars ordinarily, but they seem to make a bee-line for Volkswagens.'

Van Huren gave a disbelieving smile which naturally stirred Evan to further passion.

'It's true! I might even incorporate it in the film.'

'Should be interesting,' Conrad said with more than a touch of dryness. 'Leaving a car around as bait at least makes a change from goats and tigers.'

Evan glanced at him sharply, but nodded. 'We go down to the park on Wednesday.'

Van Huren turned to me with a look of regret,

'What a pity you can't go down there too, Link, next week. You want somewhere to go, and you'd have liked it there. The game reserves are about all that's left of the old natural Africa, and the Kruger is big and open and still pretty wild. But I know the accommodation there is always booked up months ahead.'

I didn't think Evan would have wanted me in the least, but to my surprise he slowly said, 'Well, as it happens, we made reservations for Drix Goddart to be down there with us, but now he's not coming for a week or two. We haven't cancelled . . . there will be an empty bed, if you want to come.'

I looked at Conrad in amazement but found no clue in his raised eyebrows and sardonic mouth.

If it hadn't been for Evan himself I would have leapt at it; but I supposed that even he was a great deal preferable to Clifford Wenkins's programme. And if I didn't go to the Kruger, which very much appealed to me, where else?

'I'd like to,' I said. 'And thanks.'

CHAPTER EIGHT

Danilo fetched up at the sun-shade flanked by his two van Huren satellites.

Sally waited for no introductions to Conrad and Evan. She looked to see that she was not actually interrupting anyone in mid-sentence, and then spoke directly to her father.

'We told Danilo you were taking Link down the gold mine on Monday, and he wants to know if he could go too.'

Danilo looked slightly embarrassed to have his request put so baldly, but after only a fraction's hesitation van Huren said, 'Why, of course, Danilo, if you would like to.'

'I sure would,' he said earnestly.

'Gold mine?' said Evan intently, pouncing on the words.

'The family business,' explained van Huren, and scattered introductions all round.

'There could be great background material . . . a gold mine . . . something I could use one day.' He looked expectantly at van Huren who was thus landed unfairly with the choice of being coerced or ungracious. He took it in his stride.

'By all means join us on Monday, if you would care to.'

Evan gave him no chance to retract and included Conrad in the deal.

When they and the three young ones had all gone off to place their bets, I apologized to van Huren that his generosity should have been stretched.

He shook his head. 'It will be all right. We seldom take large parties of visitors down the mine as it slows or stops production too much, but we can manage four of you without a break in work, if you are all sensible, as I am sure you will be.'

By the end of the afternoon the number had grown to five, as Roderick Hodge also turned up at Germiston, and having learnt of the expedition begged van Huren privately to be allowed to tag along with a view to a feature article in the *Rand Daily Star*.

I would have thought that gold mines were a stale topic in Johannesburg, but Roderick had his way.

I found him unexpectedly at my elbow while I was watching Tables Turned amble round the parade ring looking the prize colt he was not. Danilo and all the van Hurens had gone to take tea with the Chairman, a meal I preferred to do without, and Conrad and Evan were away in the distance being accosted by the ever perspiring Clifford.

Roderick touched me on the arm, and said tentatively, 'Link?'

I turned. His fortyish face had grown new lines in the last few days and looked much too old for the length of his trendy hair and the boyish cut of his clothes.

'How is Katya?' I asked.

'She's fine. Remarkable, really,'

I said I was glad, and then asked if he often went to the races.

'No . . . actually I came to see you. I tried to get you at the Iguana Rock but they said you were at the races . . .'

'Did they indeed,' I murmured.

'Er . . .' he explained. 'I have what you might call a *source* there. Keeps me informed, you see.'

I saw. All over the world there was a grey little army which tipped off the Press and got tipped in return: hotel porters, railway porters, hospital porters, and anyone within earshot of VIP lounges at airports.

'I live this side of the city, so I thought I might just as well drift along.'

'A nice day,' I said.

He looked up at the sky as if it would have been all one to him if it had been snowing.

'I suppose so . . . Look, I got a call this morning from Joe . . . that's the chap who was setting up the radio equipment at Randfontein House.'

'I remember,' I said.

'He said he had taken that microphone to pieces, and

there was nothing wrong with it. The outer wire of the coaxial cable was of course connected to the metal casing, though . . .'

'Ah,' I interrupted. 'And what exactly is a coaxial cable?'

'Don't you know? It's an electric cable made of two wires, but one wire goes up the centre like a core, and the other wire is circular, outside it. Television aerial cables are coaxial . . . you can see that by the ends, where you plug them into the sets.'

'Oh yes,' I agreed. 'I see.'

'Joe says he found the earth wire and the live wire had been fastened to the wrong terminals in the power plug of the recorder he was using for Katya. He says people are warned over and over again about the dangers of doing that, but they still do it. The current would go straight through the mike's casing, and earth itself through whoever was holding it.'

I thought. 'Wouldn't the whole recorder have been live too?'

He blinked. 'Yes. Joe says that inside it must have been. But no one would have got a shock from it. The casing of the recorder was plastic, the knobs were plastic, and Joe himself was wearing rubber soled shoes, which he says he always does anyway, as a precaution.'

'But he must have used that recorder before,' I protested.

'He says not. He says he plugged it in because it was

just standing there when something went wrong with his own. He didn't know whose it was, and no one seems to have claimed it since.'

Arknold gave his jockey a leg up on to Tables Turned and the horses began to move out for the race.

I said, 'It was all very bad luck.'

'Joe thinks so,' he agreed. There was however a shade of doubt in his voice and I looked at him enquiringly. 'Well . . . it's an appalling thing to say, but Joe wondered whether it could possibly have been a publicity stunt that went too far. He says that Clifford Wenkins was fussing round the electronic equipment after your first broadcast, and that you yourself set up the conference, and you did get the most fantastic press coverage for saving Katya . . .'

'I agree it's an appalling thing to say,' I said cheerfully. 'Consider me appalled. Consider also that I have already wondered whether it was a publicity stunt set up by you and Katya . . . which went too far.'

He stared. Then relaxed. Then ruefully smiled.

'All right,' he said. 'Neither of us fixed it. How about our Clifford?'

'You know him better than I do,' I said. 'But although he seems to have sold his soul to Worldic Cinemas, he doesn't strike me as having the nerve or the ingenuity to fix it all up.'

'You fluster him,' Roderick observed. 'He isn't always as futile-seeming as he's been since you arrived.'

Further along the rails from us stood Danilo, watching Nerissa's colt with a smile on his frank and bonny face.

I thought that if he had known he was so soon to inherit them, he would have been anxious instead.

Arknold joined him, and together they walked on to the stands to watch. Roderick and I tailed along after. We all watched Tables Turned set off at a great rate, run out of puff two furlongs from home, and finish a spent force.

Arknold, muttering under his breath and looking like thunder, bumped into me as he made his way down the stands' steps to hold a post-mortem with the jockey.

He focused on me and said abruptly, 'It's too much, Mister. It's too much. That's a bloody good colt and he should have won by a mile in that company.' He shut his mouth like a trap, brushed past me, and thrust his way down through the crowd.

'Whatever's all that about?' Roderick asked casually; so casually that I remembered the *Rand Daily Star*, and didn't tell him.

'No idea,' I said, putting on a bit of puzzle: but Roderick's sceptical expression said that he similarly was remembering where I worked.

We walked down from the stands. I considered ways and means, and decided Klugvoigt was the best bet for what I wanted. So I drifted Roderick gently to where Conrad and Evan were discussing adjourning to the bar, inserted him into their notice, and left as he began telling Conrad the theories of Joe and the coaxial cable.

The Chairman was in his private box surrounded by ladies in decorative hats. He saw me hovering alone, beckoned to me to come up the adjacent stairs, and when I reached his side, pressed into my hand some drowned whiskey in a warmish glass.

'How are you doing?' he asked. 'Winning, I hope.'

'Not losing, anyway.' I smiled.

'What do you fancy in the next?'

'I'd have to see them in the parade ring first.'

'Wise fellow,' he agreed.

I admired the facilities. 'The stands look new,' I commented.

'Not long built,' he agreed. 'Very much needed, of course.'

'And the weighing room . . . from the outside it looks so comfortable.'

'Oh, it is, my dear chap.' A thought struck him. 'Would you care to see round inside it?'

'How very kind of you,' I said warmly and made ready-to-go-at-once movements so that he shouldn't forget. After a moment or two we parked our unfinished drinks and strolled easily across to the large square administrative block which housed the weighing and changing rooms on the ground floor and the racecourse offices upstairs.

The whole thing was modern and comfortable, a long way from all too many English equivalents. There was a large room furnished with easy-chairs where owners and trainers could sit in comfort to plan their coups and dissect their flops, but Klugvoigt whisked me past it into the inner recesses.

The jockeys themselves shared in the bonanza, being supplied with man-sized wire lockers for their clothes (instead of a peg), a sauna bath (as well as showers) and upholstered daybeds to rest on (instead of a hard narrow wooden bench).

The man I had hoped to see was lying on one of the black leather-covered beds supporting himself on one elbow. He was known to me via the number boards as K. L. Fahrden. He was Greville Arknold's jockey.

I told Klugvoigt I would be interested to speak to him, and he said sure, go ahead, he would wait for me in the reception room by the door, as there was someone there he too wanted to speak with.

Fahrden had the usual sharp fine bones with the usual lack of fatty tissue between them and the skin. His wary, narrow-eyed manner changed a shade for the better when Klugvoigt told him my name, but underwent a relapse when I said I was a friend of Mrs Cavesey.

'You can't blame me for her horses running so stinking,' he said defensively.

'I don't,' I said patiently. 'I only wanted to ask you how they felt to you personally, so that I could tell Mrs Cavesey what you said.'

'Oh. Oh, well, then.' He considered, and came across. 'They give you a good feel, see, at the start. Full of running, and revelling in it. Then you go pick 'em up, see, and there's bloody nothing there. Put on the pressure, see, and they blow up instant like.'

'You must have given them a lot of thought,' I said. 'What do you think is wrong with them?'

He gave me a sideways look. 'Search me,' he said.

'You must have a theory,' I urged.

'Only the same as anyone would,' he agreed reluctantly. 'And I'm not saying more than that.'

'Mm . . . Well, what do you think of Mr Arknold's head lad?'

'Barty? That great brute. Can't say as I've ever thought much about him. Wouldn't want to meet him alone on a dark night, if that's what you mean.'

It wasn't entirely what I meant, but I let it go. I asked him instead how he got on with Danilo.

'A real nice guy, that,' he said, with the first sign of friendliness. 'Always takes a great interest in Arknold's horses, of course, seeing as how so many of them are his aunt's.'

'Did you meet him when he was over here before?' I asked.

'Oh sure. He stayed in the hotel down in Summerveld, for a couple of weeks. A great guy. Always good for a laugh. He said he'd just been staying with his aunt, and she was a great girl. He was the only cheerful thing around, when the horses started running badly.'

'When was that?' I asked with sympathy in my voice.

'Oh, way back in June sometime. Since then there's been every investigation you could think of, into why they flop. Dope tests, vets, the lot.'

'Is Arknold a good man to ride for?' I asked.

He closed up at once. 'More than my job's worth to say different.'

I fielded Klugvoigt from the reception room, thanked him, and walked back with him towards the parade ring. Someone button-holed him on the way, so I wandered by myself right across the course to the simple stand of plain wooden steps on the far side. From there one had a comprehensive view of the whole lay-out; the long sweep of stands, the small patch of sun umbrellas, the block of private boxes. Behind them all, the parade ring and the weighing room.

And round and about, mingling, chatting, exchanging information and sipping at cooling glasses, went Danilo and Arknold, Conrad and Evan, Roderick and Clifford Wenkins, and Quentin, Vivi, Jonathan and Sally van Huren.

I booked a telephone call to Charlie when I got back to the Iguana Rock that evening, and it came through punctually the next morning, Sunday, at ten o'clock.

We could hear each other as clearly as if we had been six miles apart instead of six thousand. She said she was glad I had called and glad that I wasn't electrocuted: yes, she said, it had been in all the papers at home yesterday, and one or two disgustedly hinted that it had all been a put-up job.

'It wasn't,' I said. 'I'll tell you all about it when I get home. How are the kids?'

'Oh, fine. Chris says he's going to be an astronaut, and Libby has managed to say "pool" when she wants to go in the water.'

'That's great,' said, meaning Libby's advance, and Charlie said yes, it was great, it really was.

'I do miss you,' I said lightly, and she answered with equal lack of intensity, 'It seems a lot longer than four days since you went away.'

'I'll be back straight after the premiere,' I said. 'Before that I'm taking a look round a gold mine and then going to the Kruger National Park for a few days.'

'Lucky sod.'

'After the kids have gone back to school, we'll have a holiday somewhere, just by ourselves,' I said.

'I'll hold you to it.'

'You can choose, so start planning.'

'OK,' she said it casually, but sounded pleased.

'Look . . . I really rang about Nerissa's horses.'

'Have you found out what's wrong with them?'

'I don't know,' I said. 'But I have had a fairly cataclysmic idea. I can't be sure I'm right, though, until, or in fact unless, you can do something for me in England.'

'Shoot,' she said economically.

'I want you to take a look at Nerissa's will.'

'Wow.' She drew in a sharp breath. 'How on earth do I do that?'

'Ask her. I don't know how you'll manage it, but if she's had fun drawing it up, she might not mind talking about it.'

'Well . . . what exactly do you want me to look for if she lets me see it?'

'I want to know particularly if besides the horses she has left the residue of her estate to Danilo.'

'All right,' she said doubtfully. 'Is it very important?'

'Yes and no.' I half laughed. 'Young Danilo is out here in South Africa at this moment.'

'Is he?' she exclaimed. 'Nerissa didn't tell us that.'

'Nerissa doesn't know,' I said. I described the golden Danilo to her, and also Arknold, and explained how the horses all lost to the same pattern.

'Sounds like the trainer nobbling them,' she commented.

'Yes. I thought so too, at first. But now . . . well, I think it's the Californian kid, our Danilo.'

'But it can't be,' she objected. 'Whatever could he have to gain?'

'Death duties,' I said.

After a pause Charlie said doubtfully, 'You can't mean it.'

'I do mean it. It's a theory, anyway. But I can't begin to prove it.'

'I don't really see . . .'

'Imagine,' I said, 'that when Danilo went to see Nerissa in the early summer, their first reunion after all those years, she told him she had Hodgkin's disease. He had only to look it up in a medical directory . . . he would find out it is always fatal.'

'Oh dear,' she sighed. 'Go on.'

'Nerissa liked him very much,' I said. 'Well . . . he's an attractive boy in many ways. Supposing that, after she'd decided to, she told Danilo she was leaving him her horses, and some money as well.'

'It's an awful lot of supposing.'

'Yes,' I agreed. 'Would you ask Nerissa? Ask her if she told Danilo what illness she had, and also if she told him what she was leaving him.'

'Darling, she'd be terribly distressed, at this stage, to find she was wrong about him.' Charlie herself sounded upset. 'She is so very pleased to have him to leave things to.'

'Just get her chatting on the subject, if you can, and ask her casually. I agree that it's important not to distress her. It might actually be better to let Danilo get away with it. In fact, I've been thinking about that for most of the night. He has been defrauding her of the prize money she might have won. How much would she mind?'

'She might even laugh. Like you did just now. She might even think it was a pretty bright idea.'

'Yes . . . Of course he has also been defrauding the South African betting public, but I suppose it's up to the racing authorities here to deal with it, if they catch him.'

'What makes you think it is Danilo?'

'It's so insubstantial,' I said with frustration. 'Mostly a matter of chance remarks and impressions, and terribly few facts. Well . . . for one thing, Danilo was around the horses when they started doing badly. Their jockey told me Danilo was in Africa then, in June, for a fortnight, which must have been just after he had stayed with Nerissa, because he talked about having seen her. After that he presumably went back to the States for a while, but the horses went on losing, so obviously he was not doing the actual stopping himself. It's difficult to see how he could ever have the opportunity of doing it himself, anyway, but he seems to have an understanding with Arknold's head lad: and I'll admit that all I have to go on *there*, is the way they look at each other. Danilo never guards his face, by the way. He guards his tongue, but not his face. So suppose it is Barty, the head boy, who is arranging the actual fixing, with suitable rewards from Danilo.'

'Well . . . if you are right . . . how?'

'There are only two completely undetectable ways which can go on safely for a long time . . . over-exercising, which loses the race on the gallops at home (though in that case it is always the trainer who's guilty, and people notice and talk) . . . and the way I think Barty must be using, the plain old simple bucket of water.'

Charlie said, 'Keep a horse thirsty, maybe even put lashings of salt in its feed, and then give it a bucket or two of water before the race?'

'Absolutely. The poor things can't last the distance with three or four gallons sloshing around in their stomachs. And as for Barty . . . even if he were not always around to supply the water at the right time, he has all the other lads intimidated to such an extent that they'd probably cut off their own ears if he told them to.'

'But,' she objected, 'if the head lad has been doing this for weeks and weeks surely the trainer would have cottoned on?'

'I think he has,' I agreed. 'I don't think he likes it, but he's letting it pass. He said it was "too much" when one of Nerissa's best colts got beaten out of sight yesterday in a poor class race. And then he himself gave me a version of what might be going on, and what may happen in the future. He accused me of implying that he was losing with the horses so that Nerissa would sell them: he would then buy them cheap, start winning, and sell them at a vast profit for stud. I had only vaguely been thinking along those lines, but he crystallized it as though the thought were by no means new to him. It was that, really, which set me wondering about Danilo. That, and the way he was smiling while he watched one of the horses go out to race. That smile was all wrong. Anyway . . . if he can reduce the value of the horses to nearly nil by Nerissa's death, there will be a great deal less duty to pay on them than if they were all winning. The difference would run into many thousands, considering there are eleven horses. That would be a profit well worth the outlay on a couple of trips to South Africa and payola for the head lad. I think they are going to change the system, but as the tax laws stand at present he would have to be in line for the residue of the estate, for there to be any point in his doing it.'

'Unscramble my brains,' Charlie said.

I laughed. 'Well. Estate duty will be paid on everything Nerissa owns. Then the separate bequests will be handed out. Then what is left will be the residue. Even though the horses are in South Africa, estate duty on them will be levied in England, because Nerissa lives there. So if the estate has to pay out all those thousands in death duties on the horses, there will be that many thousands less in the residue for Danilo to inherit.'

'Gotcha,' she said. 'And wow again.'

'Then, after they are safely his, he stops the watering lark, lets them win, sells them or puts them to stud, and collects some more lolly.'

'Oh, neat. Very neat.'

'Pretty simple, too.'

'I say,' she said. 'Isn't there anything we could try along the same lines? All that mountain of surtax we pay . . . and then when one of us dies we lose another terrific chunk of what we've paid tax on once already.'

I smiled. 'Can't think of anything which fluctuates in value so easily as a horse.'

'Let's buy some more, then.'

'And of course you have to know, pretty well to a month, exactly when you are going to die.'

'Oh damn it,' Charlie said laughing. 'Life is a lot of little green apples and pains in the neck.'

'I wonder if "a pain in the neck" originated from the axe.'

'The axeman cometh,' she said. 'Or for axe, read tax.'

'I'll bring you back a nugget or two from the gold mine,' I promised.

'Oh thanks.'

'And I'll telephone again on ... say ... Thursday evening. I'll be down in the Kruger Park by then. Would Thursday be OK for you?'

'Yes,' she said soberly, the fun vanishing like mist. 'I'll go over to Nerissa's before then, and see what I can find out.'

CHAPTER NINE

You can't keep a good Dakota down.

There were two of them waiting at the small Rand Airport near Germiston racecourse, sitting on their tail wheels and pointing their dolphin snouts hopefully to the sky.

We onloaded one of them at eight on Monday morning, along with several other passengers and a sizeable amount of freight. Day and time were unkind to Roderick, making it clearer than ever that letting go of a semblance of youth was long overdue. The mature man, I reflected, was in danger of wasting altogether the period when he could look most impressive: if Roderick were not careful he would slip straight from ageing youth to obvious old age, a mistake more often found in show business than journalism.

He was wearing a brown long-sleeved suede jacket with fringes hanging from every possible edge. Under that, an open-necked shirt in an orange-tan colour, trousers which were cut to prove masculinity, and the latest thing in desert boots.

Van Huren, at the other end of the scale in dark city suit, arrived last, took control easily, and shunted us all aboard. The Dakota trip took an hour, and landed one hundred and sixty miles south, at an isolated mining town which had Welkom on the mat and on practically everything else.

The van Huren mine was on the far side from the airport, and a small bus had come to fetch us. The town was neat, modern, geometrical, with straight bright rows of little square houses and acres of glass-walled supermarkets. A town of hygienic packaging, with its life blood deep underground.

Our destination looked at first sight to be a collection of huge whitish grey tips, one with its railway track climbing to the top. Closer acquaintance revealed the wheel-in-scaffolding at the top of the shaft, masses of administration buildings and miners' hostels, and dozens of decorative date palms. The short frondy trees, their sunlit leaf-branches chattering gently in the light breeze, did a fair job at beating the starkness, like gift-wrapping on a shovel.

Van Huren apologized with a smile for not being able to go down the mine with us himself: he had meetings all morning which could not be switched.

'But we'll meet for lunch,' he promised, 'and for that drink which you will all need!'

The guide someone a couple of rungs down the hierarchy had detailed to show us round, was a grumpy young Afrikaaner who announced that he was Pieter Losenwoldt and a mining engineer, and more or less explicitly added that his present task was a nuisance, an interruption of his work, and beneath his dignity.

He showed us into a changing room where we were to sink all differences in white overalls, heavy boots, and high-domed helmets.

'Don't take anything of your own down the mine except your underpants and a handkerchief,' he said dogmatically. 'No cameras.' He glowered at the equipment Conrad had lugged along. 'Camera flashes are not safe. And no matches. No lighters. When I say nothing, I mean nothing.'

'How about wallets?' Danilo demanded, antagonized and showing it.

Losenwoldt inspected him, saw a better looking, richer, more obviously likeable person than himself, and reacted with an even worse display of chips on shoulder.

'Leave everything,' he said impatiently. 'The room will be locked. Everything will be quite safe until you get back.'

He went away while we changed, and came back in similar togs.

'Ready? Right. Now, we are going four thousand feet down. The lift descends at 2,800 feet a minute. It will be hot in places underground. Anyone who feels claustrophobic or ill in any way is to ask to return to the surface straight away. Understand?'

He got five nods and no affection.

He peered suddenly at me, speculating, then dismissed

the thought with pursed lips and a shake of the head. No one enlightened him.

'Your light packs are on the table. Please put them on.'

The light packs consisted of a flat power pack which one wore slung over the lumbar region, and a light which clipped on to the front of the helmet. A lead led from one to the other. The power packs fastened round one's waist with webbing, and were noticeably heavy.

Much like the seven dwarfs we tramped forth to the mine. The cage we went down in had half-sides only, so that the realities of rock burrowing hit at once. No comfort. A lot of noise. The nasty thought of all that space below one's booted feet.

It presumably took less than two minutes to complete the trip, but as I was jammed tight between Evan, whose hot eyes looked for once apprehensive, and a six-foot-four twenty-stone miner who had joined with several cronies at the top, I couldn't exactly check it by stop-watch.

We landed with a clang at the bottom and disembarked. Another contingent were waiting to go up, and as soon as we were out, they loaded and operated the system of buzzers which got them clanking on their way.

'Get into the trucks,' said Losenwoldt bossily. 'They hold twelve people in each.'

Conrad surveyed the two trucks, which looked like wire cages on wheels with accommodation for one large dog if he curled himself up, and said sideways to me: 'Sardines have struck for less.'

I laughed. But the trucks did hold twelve; just. The last

man in had to sit in the hole that did duty as doorway, and trust to what he could find to hang on to that he didn't fall out. Evan was last in. He hung on to Losenwoldt's overalls. Losenwoldt didn't like it.

Loaded to the gunnels, the trucks trundled off along the tunnel which stretched straight ahead for as far as one could see. The walls were painted white to about four feet: then there was a two inch deep bright red line, then above that the natural grey rock.

Conrad asked Losenwoldt why the red line was there: he had to shout to be heard, and he had to shout twice, as Losenwoldt was in no hurry to answer.

Finally he crossly shouted back. 'It is a guide to the tunnellers. When the tunnel is painted like this, they can see that they are making it straight and level. The red line is an eye-line.'

Conversation lapsed. The trucks covered about two miles at a fast trot and stopped abruptly at nowhere in particular. It was suddenly possible to hear oneself speak again, and Losenwoldt said, 'We get out here, and walk.'

Everyone unsqueezed themselves and climbed out. The miners strode purposefully away down the tunnel, but there was, it seemed, a set pattern for instructing visitors. Losenwoldt said ungraciously (but at least he said it), 'Along the roof of the tunnel you can see the cables from which we have the electric lights.' The lights were spaced overhead at regular intervals so that the whole tunnel was evenly lit. 'Beside it there is a live electric rail.' He pointed. 'That provides power for the trucks which take the rock along to the surface. The rock goes up in a faster lift, at more than 3,000 feet a minute. That big round pipe up there carries air. The mine is ventilated by blowing compressed air into it at many points.'

We all looked at him like kids round a teacher, but he had come to the end of that bit of official spiel, so he turned his back on us and trudged away down the tunnel.

We followed.

We met a large party of black Africans walking the other way. They were dressed as we were except that they were wearing sports jackets on top of their overalls.

Roderick asked, 'Why the jackets?'

Losenwoldt said, 'It is hot down here. The body gets accustomed. Without a jacket, it feels cold on reaching the surface. You can catch chills.'

Evan nodded wisely. We went on walking. Eventually we came to a wider space where a second tunnel branched off to the right. Another party of Africans was collecting there, putting on jackets and being checked against a list.

'They have finished their shift,' Losenwoldt said, in his clipped way, hating us. 'They are being checked to make sure none of them is still underground when blasting takes place.'

'Blasting, dear boy?' said Conrad vaguely.

The expert eyed him with disfavour. 'The rock has to be blasted. One cannot remove it with pickaxes.'

'But I thought this was a gold mine, dear boy. Surely

one does not need blasting to remove gold? Surely one digs out gravel and sifts the gold from it.'

Losenwoldt looked at him with near contempt. 'In California and Alaska, and in some other places, this may be so. In South Africa the gold is not visible. It is in minute particles in rock. One has to blast out the gold-bearing rock, take it to the surface, and put it through many processes, to remove the gold. In this mine, one has to take three tons of rock to the surface to obtain one ounce of pure gold.'

I think we were all struck dumb. Danilo's mouth actually dropped open.

'In some mines here in the Odendaalsrus gold field,' Losenwoldt went on, seeming not to notice the stunned reaction, 'it is necessary to remove only one and a half tons to get one ounce. These mines are of course the richest. Some need more than this one: three and a half or four tons.'

Roderick looked around him. 'And all the gold has been taken from here? And from where we came?'

His turn for the look of pity-contempt.

'This tunnel is not made through gold-bearing rock. This tunnel is just to enable us to get to the gold-bearing rock, which is in this part of the mine. It can only be reached at more than 4,000 feet underground.'

'Good God,' Conrad said, and spoke for us all.

Losenwoldt plodded grudgingly on with his lecture, but his audience were riveted.

'The reef . . . that is to say, the gold-bearing rock . . . is only a thin layer. It slopes underground from the north, being deepest beyond Welkom, further south. It extends for about eight miles from east to west, and about fourteen miles from north to south, but its limits are irregular. It is nowhere more than three feet in depth, and in this mine it is on average thirteen inches.'

He collected a lot of truly astonished glances, but only Danilo had a question.

'I suppose it must be worth it,' he said doubtfully. 'All this work and equipment, just to get so little gold.'

'It must be worth it or we would not be here,' said Losenwoldt squelchingly, which I at least interpreted as ignorance of the profit and loss figures of the business. But it must be worth it, I reflected, or van Huren would not live in a sub-palace.

No one else said anything. Seldom had cheerful casual conversation been more actively discouraged. Even Evan's natural inclination to put himself in charge of everything was being severely inhibited; and in fact, after looking apprehensive in the lift he now seemed the most oppressed of us all at the thought of millions of tons of rocks pressing down directly above our heads.

'Right,' said Losenwoldt with heavy satisfaction at having reduced the ranks to pulped silence. 'Now, switch on your helmet lights. There are no electric lights further along there.' He pointed up the branch tunnel. 'We will go to see the tunnelling in progress.'

He strode off without checking to see that we all

followed, but we did, though Evan gave a backward glance in the direction of the shaft which would have warned a more careful guide not to take too much for granted.

The tunnel ran straight for a while and then curved to the right. As we approached the corner we could hear a constantly increasing roaring noise, and round on the new tack it noticeably increased.

'What's that noise?' Evan asked in a voice still the safe side of active anxiety.

Losenwoldt said over his shoulder, 'Partly the air-conditioning, partly the drilling,' and kept on going. The spaced electric light bulbs came to an end. The lights on our helmets picked the way.

Suddenly, far ahead, we could discern a separate glimmer of light beyond the beams we were ourselves throwing. Closer contact divided the glimmer into three individual helmet lights pointing in the same direction as ours: but these lit only solid rock. We were coming to the end of the tunnel.

The walls at this point were no longer painted a comforting white with a red line, but became the uniform dark grey of the basic rock, which somehow emphasized the fanaticism of burrowing so deep in the earth's undisturbed crust, in search of invisible yellow dust.

The air pipe stopped abruptly, the compressed air roaring out from its open mouth. Beyond that the noise of the drilling took over, as aggressive to the eardrums as six fortissimo discotheques.

There were three miners standing on a wooden platform,

drilling a hole into the rock up near the eight-foot-high roof. Our lights shone on the sweat on their dark skins and reflected on the vests and thin trousers they wore in place of everyone else's thick white overalls.

The racket came from a compressor standing on the ground, as much as from the drill itself. We watched for a while. Evan tried to ask something, but it would have taken a lip reader to get anywhere.

Finally Losenwoldt, with a tight mouth and tired eyelids, jerked his head for us to go back. We followed him, glad about the lessening load on our ears. Walking last, I turned round where the air pipe ended, switched off my helmet light for a moment, and looked back. Three men on their scaffolding, intent on their task, enveloped in noise, and lit only by the glow-worms on their heads. When I had turned and gone, they would be alone with the primaeval darkness closing in behind them. I was left with a fanciful impression of a busy team of devils moleing along towards Inferno.

Once back in the wider section Losenwoldt continued our instruction.

'They were drilling holes about six feet deep, with tungsten drills. That,' he pointed, 'is a pile of drills.'

We looked where he pointed. The horizontal stack of six-foot rods by the tunnel wall had looked more like a heap of unused piping before: but they were solid metal rods about two inches in diameter with a blade of tungsten shining at the end of each.

'The rods have to be taken to the surface every day, to be sharpened.'

We nodded like wise owls.

'Those three men have nearly finished drilling for today. They have drilled many holes in the face of the tunnel. Each hole will receive its charge of explosive, and after the blasting the broken rock will be removed. Then the drillers return and start the process again.'

'How much tunnel can you make in one day?' Roderick asked.

'Eight feet a shift.'

Evan leant against the rock wall and passed a hand over a forehead that Clifford Wenkins could not have bettered.

'Don't you ever use pit-props?' he said.

Losenwoldt answered the face of the question and didn't see the fear behind it.

'Of course not. We are tunnelling not through earth, but through bedrock. There is no danger of the tunnel collapsing inwards. Occasionally, loosened slabs of rock fall from the roof or the wall. This usually happens in areas recently blasted. Where we see such loosened rocks, we pull them down, if we can, so that there is no danger of them falling on anyone later.'

Evan failed to look comforted. He dug out his handkerchief and mopped up.

'What sort of explosive do you use,' Danilo asked, 'for blasting?'

Losenwoldt still didn't like him, and didn't answer. Roderick, who was also interested, repeated the same question.

Losenwoldt ostentatiously stifled a sigh and replied in more staccato sentences than ever.

'It is dynagel. It is a black powder. It is kept in locked red boxes fastened to the tunnel wall.'

He pointed to one of them a little further on. I had walked past two or three of them, padlocks and all, without wondering what they were for.

Danilo, with sarcasm, said to Roderick, 'Ask him what happens when they blast,' and Roderick did.

Losenwoldt shrugged. 'What would you expect? But no one sees the blasting. Everyone is out of the mine before the charges are detonated. No one returns down the mine for four hours after blasting.'

'Why not, dear boy?' drawled Conrad.

'Dust,' Losenwoldt said succinctly.

'When do we get to see this gold rock . . . this reef?' asked Danilo.

'Now.' Losenwoldt pointed along the continuation of the main tunnel. 'Further down there it will be very hot. There is a stretch with no air conditioning. Beyond that there is air again. Leave your helmet lights on, you will need them. Take care where you walk. The floor of the tunnel is rough in places.'

He finished with a snap and as before set off with his back to us.

Again we followed.

I said to Evan, 'Are you OK?' which irritated him into straightening his spine and flashing the eyes and saying of course he damn well was, did I think he was a fool.

'No,' I said.

'Right then.' He strode purposefully past me to get nearer to the pearls spat from Losenwoldt's lips and I again brought up the rear.

The heat further on was intense but dry, so that although one felt it, it produced no feeling of sweat. The tunnel at this point grew rough, with uneven walls, no painted lines, no lights, and a broken-up floor: it also sloped gradually downhill. We trudged on, boots crunching on the gritty surface.

The further we went, the more activity we came across. Men in white overalls were everywhere, busy, carrying equipment, with their helmet lights shining on other people's concentrated faces. The peak of each helmet tended to throw a dark band of shadow across every man's eyes, and once or twice I had to touch Roderick, who was in front of me, so that he would turn and reassure me that I was still following the right man.

At the end of the hot stretch it felt like stepping straight into the Arctic. Losenwoldt stopped there and consulted briefly with two other young miners he found talking to each other.

'We will split up here,' he said finally. 'You two with me.' He pointed to Roderick and Evan. 'You two with Mr Anders. He assigned Conrad and Danilo to a larger version of himself. 'You,' he pointed at me, 'with Mr Yates.'

Yates, younger than the others, appeared unhelpfully subservient to them, and spoke with a slight speech impediment in the order of a cleft palate. He gave me a twitchy smile and said he hoped I wouldn't mind, he wasn't used to showing people round, it wasn't usually his job.

'It's kind of you to do so,' I said soothingly.

The others were moving off in their little groups and were soon lost in the general crowd of white overalls.

'Come along then.'

We continued down the tunnel. I asked my new guide what the gradient was.

'About one in twenty,' he said. But after that he lapsed into silence, and I reckoned if I wanted to know any more I would have to ask. Yates did not know the conducted tour script like Losenwoldt, who in retrospect did not seem too bad.

Holes appeared from time to time in the left-hand wall, with apparently a big emptiness behind them.

'I thought this tunnel was through solid rock,' I observed. 'So what are those holes?'

'Oh . . . we are now in the reef. The reef has been removed from much of that portion behind that wall. In a minute I'll be able to show you better.'

'Does the reef slope at one in twenty, then?' I asked.

He thought it a surprising question. 'Of course,' he said.

'That tunnel which is still being drilled, back there, where is that going?'

'To reach another area of reef.'

Yes. Silly question. The reef spread laterally for miles. Quite. Removing the reef must be rather like chipping a thin slice of ham out of a thick bread sandwich.

'What happens when all the reef is removed?' I asked. 'There must be enormous areas with nothing holding up the layers of rock above.'

He answered willingly enough. 'We do not remove all supports. For instance, the wall of the tunnel is thick, despite the holes, which are for blasting and ventilation purposes. It will hold the roof up in all this area. Eventually, of course, when this tunnel is worked out and disused, the layers will gradually close together. I believe that most of Johannesburg sank about three feet, as the layers below it closed together, after all the reef was out.'

'Not recently?' I said, surprised.

'Oh, no. Long ago. The Rand gold fields are shallower and mining began there first.'

People were carrying tungsten rods up the tunnel and others were passing us down it.

'We are getting ready to blast,' Yates said without being asked. 'All the drilling is finished and the engineers are setting the charges.'

'We haven't very long, then,' I said.

'Probably not.'

'I'd like to see how they actually work the reef.'

'Oh . . . yes. Just down here a bit further, then. I will take you to the nearest part. There are others further down.'

We came to a larger than usual hole in the wall. It stretched from the floor to about five feet up, but one could not walk straight through it, as it sloped sharply upwards inside.

He said, 'You will have to mind your head. It is very shallow in here.'

'OK,' I said.

He gestured to me to crawl in ahead of him, which I did. The space was about three feet high but extended out of sight in two directions. A good deal of ham had already gone from this part of the sandwich.

Instead of a firm rock floor, we were now scrambling over a bed of sharp-edged chips of rock, which rattled away as one tried to climb up over them. I went some way into the flat cavern and then waited for Yates. He was close behind, looking across to our right where several men lower down were working along a curving thirty-foot stretch of the far wall.

'They are making final checks on the explosive charges,' he said. 'Soon everyone will begin to leave.'

'This loose stuff we are lying on,' I said. 'Is this the reef?'

'Oh . . . no, not exactly. These are just chips of rock. See, the reef used to lie about midway up the stope.'

'What is the stope?'

'Sorry . . . the stope is what we are now in. The place we take the reef from.'

'Well . . . down there, in the part which is not blasted yet, how do you tell which is the reef?'

The whole thing looked the same to me. Dark grey from top to bottom. Dark grey uneven roof curving down in dark grey uneven walls, merging into dark grey shingle floor.

'I'll get you a piece,' he said obligingly, and crawled crab-wise on his stomach over to where his colleagues were working. It was barely possible to sit up in the stope. Just about possible to rise to hands and knees, if one kept one's head down. I supported myself on one elbow and watched him borrow a small hand pick and lever a sliver of rock out of the far wall.

He scrambled back.

'There you are . . . This is a piece of reef.'

We focused both our lights on it. A two-inch-long grey sharp-edged lump with darker grey slightly light-reflecting spots and streaks on its surface.

'What are those dark spots?' I said.

'That's the ore,' he said. 'The paler part is just ordinary rock. The more of those dark bits there are in the reef, the better the yield of gold per ton of rock.'

'Then is this dark stuff . . . gold?' I asked dubiously.

'It has gold in it,' he nodded. 'Actually it is made up of four elements: gold, silver, uranium and chrome. When the reef is milled and treated, they are separated out. There is more gold than silver or uranium.'

'Can I keep this piece?' I asked.

'Certainly.' He cleared his throat. 'I am sorry, but they have a job for me to do down there. Could you possibly find your own way back up the tunnel? You cannot get lost.'

'That's all right,' I said. 'You go on, I don't want to interfere with your job.'

'Thank you,' he said, and scrambled away in haste to please the people who really mattered to him.

I stayed where I was, for a while, watching the engineers and peering into the interminable dug-out space uphill. The light of my helmet couldn't reach its limits: it stretched away into impenetrable blackness.

The workers below me were thinning out, returning to the tunnel to make their way back towards the shaft. I put the tiny piece of reef in my pocket, took a last look round, and began to inch my way back to the hole where I had come in. I turned round to go into the tunnel feet first, but as I started to shuffle backwards I heard someone begin to climb into the stope behind me, the light from his helmet flashing on my overalls. I stopped, to let him go by. He made a little forward progress and I glanced briefly over my shoulder to see who it was. I could see only the peak of his helmet, and shadow beneath.

Then my own helmet tipped off forward and a large chunk of old Africa clobbered me forcefully on the back of the head.

Stunned, it seemed to me that consciousness ebbed away slowly: I fell dizzily down endless mine shafts with flashing dots before my eyes.

I had blacked out completely long before I had hit the bottom.

CHAPTER TEN

Blackness.

Nothing.

I opened my eyes. Couldn't see. Put my hand to my face to feel if my eyelids were open.

They were.

Thought was entirely disconnected. I didn't know where I was, or why I was there, or why I couldn't see. Time seemed suspended. I couldn't decide whether I was asleep or not, and for a while I couldn't remember my own name.

Drifted away again. Came back. Snapped suddenly into consciousness. Knew I was awake. Knew I was me.

Still couldn't see.

I moved; tried to sit up. Discovered I was lying on my side. When I moved, I heard the crunching noise and felt the sharp rock chips shifting against my pressure.

In the stope.

Cautiously I put up a hand. The rock ceiling was a couple of feet above my head.

No helmet on my head. A tender lump on the back of it and a thumping pain inside it.

Bloody hell, I thought. I must have bashed my head. I'm in the stope. I can't see because there isn't any light. Everyone has left the mine. And the blasting charges will go off at any minute.

For a paralysing age I couldn't think beyond the fact that I was going to be blown to bits before I had even finished realizing it. After that I thought it might have been better if I'd been blown to bits before I woke up. At least I wouldn't now be awake worrying. After that, and not before time, I began wondering what to do.

Light, first.

I felt around to my back, found the lead from the power pack and gently pulled it. The other end scraped towards me over the choppy shingle, but when I picked up the torch I knew I wasn't going to get any light. The glass and the bulb were both smashed.

The light unit had come off the bracket on the helmet. I felt around with an outstretched hand, but couldn't find the helmet.

Must get out, I thought urgently, and in the same split second wondered . . . which way was out.

I made myself stay still. The last thing I remembered was agreeing with Yates that I could find my own way back. I must have been stupid enough to try to raise my head too high. Must literally have hit the roof. I couldn't remember doing it. The only thing that seemed clear was that I had smashed my helmet light when I fell, and that no one had seen me lying there in the dark.

Bloody fool, I cursed myself. Clumsy bloody fool, getting into this mess.

Gingerly, with one arm outstretched, I shifted myself a foot forward. My fingers found nothing to touch except stone chips.

I had to know which way I was going. Otherwise, I thought, I may be crawling away from safety, not towards it. I had to find the hole in the tunnel.

I picked up a handful of the flinty pebbles and began throwing them methodically round in a circle, starting on my right. It was an erratic process, as some hit the roof and some the ground, but enough went far enough before they fell to assure me that there was a small space all around me in front.

I rolled over on to my back and the power pack dug into me. I unfastened the webbing and pulled it off. Then I threw another lot of stones in an arc round my legs.

The wall of the tunnel was there. A lot of the stones hit it.

My heart by then was thudding so much it was deafening me. Shut up, shut up, I said to myself. Don't be so bloody scared, it isn't of any practical use.

I threw more stones, this time not to find the wall, but the hole in it. I found it almost at once. Threw more stones to make sure: but there it had to be, just to the left of where my feet were pointing, because all the stones that went over there were falling further away, and clattering after they landed. They weren't round enough to roll, but heavy enough to continue downhill when they fell. Downhill . . . on the steep little slope from the stope into the tunnel.

More stones. I moved my feet, then my whole body, until the hole was straight in front over my toes. Then on my elbows and my bottom, keeping my head well back, I shuffled forwards.

More stones. Hole still there.

More shuffling. Another check.

It couldn't have been more than ten feet. Felt like ten miles.

I tentatively swept my arms around in the air. Could feel the roof, nothing else.

Went forward another two or three feet. Felt around with my arms. Touched solid rock. Ahead, to the right.

Another foot forward. Felt my feet turn abruptly downwards, bending my knees. Put both my hands out sideways and forwards and felt rock on both sides. Halfway out of the hole . . . and gingerly, lying flat, I inched forward until my feet scrunched on the tunnel floor. Even then I bent my knees and continued slithering without raising my head, all too aware of the hard sharpness of the rock above the vulnerability of my unhelmeted skull.

I ended on my knees in the tunnel, gasping and feeling as frightened as ever.

Think.

The holes had been in the left-hand wall, as we came down. Once in the tunnel, Yates had said, I couldn't get lost.

OK. Turn right. Straight forward. Dead simple.

I stood up carefully, and with the hole at my back, turned left. Put my hand on the rough rock wall. Took a step forward.

The scrunch of my boot on the rock floor made me realize for the first time how quiet it was. Before, I had had both the stones and my own heart to fill my ears. Now, there was nothing. The silence was as absolute as the darkness.

I didn't waste time brooding about it. Scrunched ahead as fast as I dared, step by careful step. No sound . . . that meant that the air-conditioning had been switched off . . . which hardly mattered, there was a mineful still to breathe . . . even if it were hot.

My hand lost the wall suddenly, and my heart set up a fresh chorus. Taking a grip on my breath I took a step backwards. Right hand back on wall. OK. Breathe out. Now, kneel down, grope along floor, keep in contact with wall on right . . . navigate past another of the holes which led through to the stope.

Holes which would let the blast out of the stope, when the charges exploded.

Blast travelled far when confined in a long narrow space. Blast was a killing force, as deadly as flying rocks.

Oh God, I thought. Oh hell's bloody bells. What did one think about if one were probably going to die at any minute?

I thought about getting as far back up the mine as quickly as I could. I thought about not losing contact with the right-hand wall when I passed the holes in it, because if I did I might turn round in the darkness and find the other wall instead, and go straight back towards the explosion. I didn't think about anything else at all. Not even about Charlie.

I went on. The air became hotter and hotter. The stretch that had been hot coming down was now an assault on the nerve endings.

Struggling on, I couldn't tell how fast I was going. Very slowly, I imagined. Like in a nightmare, trying to flee from a terror at one's heels, and not being able to run.

I got back in the end to the wider space, and the explosion still hadn't happened. Another explosion was due to take place down the branch tunnel also . . . but the bend in the tunnel should disperse some of the blast.

Beginning at last to let hope creep in, and keeping my hand on the right-hand wall literally for dear life, I trudged slowly on. Two miles to go, maybe, to the bottom of the shaft . . . but every step taking me nearer to safety.

Those lethal pockets of dynagel never did explode; or not while I was down the mine.

One minute I was taking another step into darkness. The next, I was blinded by light.

I shut my eyes, wincing against the brightness, and I stopped walking and leaned against the wall instead. When I opened my eyes again, the electric lights were blazing in all their glory, and the tunnel looked as solid, safe, and reassuringly painted, as it had done on the way in.

Weakened by relief, I shifted off the wall and went on again, with knees that were suddenly trembling, and a head that was back to aching like a hangover.

There was a background hum now again in the mine, and from far away up the tunnel a separate noise detached itself and grew louder: the rattle of the wire cage trucks making the outward journey. Eventually it stopped and then there was the sound of several boots, and then finally, round a shallow curve, came four men in white overalls.

Hurrying.

They spotted me, and began to run. Slowed and stopped just before they reached me, with relief that I was mobile showing on their faces. Losenwoldt was one of them: I didn't know the others.

'Mr Lincoln . . . are you all right?' one of them asked anxiously.

'Sure,' I said. It didn't sound right. I said it again. 'Sure.' Much better.

'How did you get left behind?' Losenwoldt said reprovingly, shifting all possible blame from himself. Not that I would have allotted him any: he was just forestalling it.

I said, 'I'm sorry to have been such a nuisance . . . I think I must have hit my head and knocked myself out, but I can't actually remember how . . .' I wrinkled my forehead. 'So damned stupid of me.'

One them said, 'Where were you, exactly?'

'In the stope,' I said.

'Good grief ... You probably lifted your head too sharply ... or maybe a piece of rock fell from the roof and caught you.'

'Yes,' I said.

Another of them said, 'If you were unconscious in the stope, however did you get back here?'

I told them about the stones. They didn't say anything. Just looked at each other.

One of them walked round my back and after a moment said, 'There's some blood on your hair and down your neck, but it looks dry ... I don't think you're still bleeding.' He came round to my side. 'Do you feel all right to walk to the trucks? We brought a stretcher ... just in case.'

I smiled. 'Guess I can walk.'

We walked. I asked, 'How did you discover I was down here?'

One of them said ruefully, 'Our system of checking everyone is out of the mine before blasting is supposed to be infallible. And so it is, as far as the miners are concerned. But visitors ... you see, we don't often have small groups of unofficial visitors, like today. Mr van Huren seldom invites anyone, and no one else is allowed to. Nearly all the visitors we have here are official tourist groups, of about twenty people, and the mine more or less stops while we show them round, but we only do that every six weeks or so. We don't usually blast at all, on those days. Today, though, one of your party felt ill and went back before the others, and I think everyone took it for granted that you had gone with him. Tim Yates said when he last saw you, you were just about to return up the tunnel.'

'Yes . . .' I agreed. 'I remember that.'

'The other three visitors went up together, and the checkers accounted for every miner, so we assumed everyone was out, and were all set to detonate . . .'

A tall thin man took up the story. 'Then one of the men who counts the numbers going up and down in the lift said that one more had gone down than had come up. The shift checkers said it was impossible, each group had been checked out by name. The lift man said he was sure. Well . . . that only left the visitors. So we checked them. The three in the changing room said you hadn't changed yet, your clothes were still there, so you must be in the first-aid room with one called Conrad, who had not felt well.'

'Conrad,' I exclaimed. I had thought they meant Evan. 'What was wrong with him?'

'I think they said he had an attack of asthma. Anyway, we went and asked him, and he said you hadn't come up with him.'

'Oh,' I said blankly. Certainly, if I had been with him I would have gone up, but I hadn't seen him at all after we had separated at the beginning of the reef.

We came to the trucks and climbed in. A lot of space with only five people instead of twelve.

'The one who was ill,' Losenwoldt stated virtuously, 'the stout onc with thc droopy moustache, he was not with me. If he had been, of course I would have escorted him back to the trucks, and of course I would have known you were not with him.'

'Of course,' I said dryly.

We clattered back along the tunnel to the bottom of the shaft, and from there, after the exchange of signal buzzes, rose in the cage through three-quarters of a mile of rock up to the sunlight. Its brilliance was momentarily painful, and it was also cold enough to start me shivering.

'Jacket,' exclaimed one of my escorts. 'We took down a blanket . . . should have put it round you.' He hurried off into a small building by the shaft and came back with a much used tweed sports coat, which he held for me to put on.

There was an anxious looking reception committee hovering around: Evan, Roderick, Danilo, and van Huren himself.

'My dear fellow,' he said, peering at me as if to reassure himself that I was real. 'What can I say?'

'For heaven's sake,' I said, 'it was my own fault and I'm terribly sorry to have caused all this fuss . . .' Van Huren looked relieved and smiled, and so did Evan, Roderick and Danilo. I turned back to the three strangers who had come down for me: Losenwoldt had already gone. 'Thank you,' I said. 'Thank you very much.'

They all grinned. 'We want payment,' one said.

I must have looked bewildered. I was wondering what was right. How much.

'Your autograph,' one of them explained.

'Oh . . .' I laughed. 'OK.'

One of them produced a notebook, and I wrote a thank-you to each of them, on three separate pages. And cheap at the price, I thought.

The mine's doctor swabbed stone dust from the cut on my head, said it wasn't deep, nothing serious, didn't need stitching, didn't need a plaster, even, unless I wanted one . . .

'I don't,' I said.

'Good, good. Swallow these, then. In case you develop a headache.'

I swallowed obediently. Collected Conrad, now breathing normally again, from a rest room next door, and followed directions to the bar and dining-room for lunch. On the way, we swopped operations, so to speak. Neither of us felt much pleased with himself.

The five of us sat at a table with Quentin van Huren, plus two other senior executives whose names I never learned. My narrow escape was chewed over by everyone all over again, and I said with feeling to Roderick that I would be much obliged if he would keep my embarrassment out of his inky columns.

He grinned. 'Yeah . . . Much better copy if you'd been blown up. Not much news value in a checker doing his job properly.'

'Thank God for that,' I said.

Conrad looked at me sideways. 'There must be a jinx

on you in South Africa, dear boy. That's the second time you've been close to extinction within a week.'

I shook my head. 'No jinx. Just the opposite. I've survived twice. Look at it that way.'

'Only seven lives left,' Conrad said.

The talk worked back to gold. I suspected that in Welkom it always did, like Newmarket and horses.

'Say, how do you get it out of the rock?' Danilo demanded. 'You can't even see it.'

Van Huren smiled indulgently. 'Danilo, it is simple. You crush the rock in mills until it is powdered. You add cyanide of potassium, which holds the gold particles in solution. You add zinc, to which the gold particles stick. You then wash out the acid. You then separate the zinc from the gold again, using aqua regia, and finally you retrieve the gold.'

'Oh simple,' Conrad agreed. 'Dear boy.'

Van Huren warmed to him, and smiled with pleasure. 'That is not exactly all. One still has to refine the gold . . . to remove impurities by melting it to white heat in giant crucibles, and pouring it out into bricks. The residue flows away, and you are left with the pure gold.'

Danilo did a rapid calculation. 'You'll have gotten around three thousand five hundred tons of reef out of the mine, for one little old brick.'

'That's so,' agreed van Huren, smiling. 'Give or take a ton or two.'

'How much do you bring out in a week?' Danilo asked.

'Just over forty thousand metric tons.'

Danilo's eyes flickered as he did the mental arithmetic. 'That means . . . er . . . about eleven and a half gold bricks every week.'

'Do you want a job in the accounting department, Danilo?' asked van Huren, much amused.

But Danilo hadn't finished. 'Each brick weighs 72 lbs, right? So that makes . . . let's see . . . around 800 lbs of gold a week. Say, what's the price of gold per ounce? Gee, this is sure the right business to be in. What a gas!' He was deeply stimulated, as he had been by the whole trip, with a strong inner excitement shining out of his eyes. An attraction towards money-making, and the calculations needed to work out estate-duty dodging, seemed to me to be all of a piece.

Van Huren, still smiling, said, 'You're forgetting the wages, the maintenance, and the shareholders. There are only a few grains of dust left after they've all taken their cut.'

Danilo's curving mouth showed he didn't believe it. Roderick shot an orange cuff out of the brown suede sleeve to reveal half a ton of tiger's eye doing duty as a cufflink.

'Don't you own the mine altogether, then, Quentin?' he asked.

The executives and van Huren himself both smiled indulgently at Roderick for his naïvety.

'No,' van Huren said. 'My family own the land and the

mineral rights. Technically, I suppose, we do own the gold. But it takes an enormous amount of capital, many millions of rands, to sink a shaft and build all the surface plant needed. About twenty-five years ago my brother and I floated a company to raise capital to start drilling, so the company has hundreds of private shareholders.'

'That mine doesn't look twenty-five years old,' I objected amiably.

Van Huren shifted his smiling eyes in my direction and went on explaining.

'The part you saw this morning is the newest tunnel, and the deepest. There are other tunnels at higher levels . . . in past years we have taken out all the up-slope areas of the reef.'

'And there's still a lot left?'

Van Huren's smile had the ease of one who would never be short of a thousand. 'It will see Jonathan out,' he said.

Evan chose to find the mechanics and economics less interesting than the purpose, and waved his arms about as he pinned every gaze down in turn with the fierce eyes and declaimed with his usual intensity.

'What is gold for, though? This is what we should be asking. What everyone should be asking. What is the *point*? Everyone goes to so much trouble to get it, and pays so much for it, and it has no real *use*.'

'Gold plated lunar bugs,' I murmured.

Evan glared at me. 'Everyone digs it out of the ground here and puts it back underground at Fort Knox, where it never sees daylight again . . . Don't you see . . . the whole thing is *artificial*? Why should the whole world's wealth be based on a yellow metal which has no *use*?'

'Good for filling teeth,' I said conversationally.

'And for pure radio contacts in transistor units,' Roderick added, joining the game.

Van Huren listened and watched as if he found the entertainment a nice change for a Monday. I stopped baiting Evan, though, because after seeing the mine I half held his views.

I travelled back to Johannesburg in the Dakota that evening sitting next to Roderick and feeling a trifle worn. A hot afternoon spent walking round the surface buildings of a mine, watching gold being poured from a crucible, seeing (and hearing) the ore being crushed, and visiting one of the miners' hostels, had done no good at all to a throbbing head. Half a dozen times I had almost dropped out, but, especially with Roderick's ready typewriter in the background, I hadn't wanted to make a fuss.

The visit to the hostel had been best: lunch was being cooked for the next surface shift off work, and we tasted it in the kitchen. Vast vats of thick broth with a splendid flavour, vegetables I couldn't identify and hadn't the energy to ask about, and thick wads of cream-coloured mealie bread, a sort of fat-less version of pastry.

From there we went next door into the hostel's bar, where the first of the returning shift were settling down to the serious business of drinking what looked like half gallon plastic tubs of milky cocoa.

'That's Bantu beer,' said our afternoon guide, who had proved as sweet as Losenwoldt was sour.

We drank some. It had a pleasant dry flavour but tasted nothing like beer.

'Is it alcoholic, dear boy?' Conrad asked.

The dear boy said it was, but weak. Considering that we saw one man dispatch his whole tubful in two great draughts, the weakness was just as well.

Our guide beckoned to one of the men sitting at a table with his colleagues, and he got to his feet and came over. He was tall and not young, and he had a wide white grin which I found infectious.

The guide said, 'This is Piano Nyembezi. He is the checker who insisted we had left someone down the mine.'

'Was it you?' I asked with interest.

'*Yebo*,' he said, which I later learnt meant yes in Zulu. ('No' turned out to consist of a click, a glottal stop, and an 'aa' sound. As far as a European was concerned, it was impossible to say no in a hurry.)

'Well, Piano,' I said. 'Thank you very much.' I put out my hand and he shook it, an event which drew large smiles from his friends, an indrawn breath from our guide, a shake of the head from Roderick and no reaction whatsoever from Evan, Conrad or Danilo.

There was a certain amount of scuffling in the background, and then one of the others brought forward a well thumbed copy of a film magazine.

'It is Piano's paper,' the newcomer said, and thrust it into his hands. Nyembezi looked embarrassed, but showed me what it was. Full page, and as boring-looking as usual.

Wrinkling my nose I took the magazine from him and wrote across the bottom of my picture, 'I owe my life to Piano Nyembezi', and signed my name.

'He'll keep that for ever,' the guide said.

Until tomorrow, perhaps, I thought.

The Dakota droned on. The evening sun fell heavily across my eyelids as we banked round on to a new course, and I gingerly lifted my head off the seat-back to put it down the other way. The cut on my head, though not deep, was sore.

For some reason the small movement triggered off a few sleepy nerve cells, and in a quiet fashion I remembered that there had been someone with me in the stope.

I remembered I had been turning round to leave feet first, and had stopped to let someone else in. I remembered that I hadn't seen his face: didn't know who he was.

If he had been there when I bashed my head, why on earth hadn't he helped me?

Such was my fuzzy state of mind that it took me a whole minute more to move on to the conclusion that he hadn't helped me because he'd applied the rock himself.

I opened my eyes with a jolt. Roderick's face was turned towards mine. I opened my mouth to tell him. Then I shut it again, firmly. I did not in the least want to tell the *Rand Daily Star*.

CHAPTER ELEVEN

I used a lot of the time I could have more profitably spent sleeping that night in coming to terms with the thought that someone might have tried to kill me.

Didn't know who. Couldn't guess why. And still was not certain whether my memory was complete: perhaps the other man in the stope had gone away again, and I had forgotten it.

Also, even if I had been a hundred per cent certain, I didn't know what I should do about it.

Telephone van Huren? Start an investigation? But there had been so many people down the mine, all dressed alike, and half in darkness. Any investigation was going to produce more talk and doubt than results, and 'Lincoln complains of attempted murder' were gossip-column snippets I could do without.

Twice within a week, Conrad had said, 'Close to extinction.'

It didn't make sense. It was only in films that the chaps I played got threatened and attacked, and made miraculous escapes.

Yet if I did nothing about it, what then? If someone really had been trying to kill me, there was nothing to stop him trying again. How could I possibly protect myself every minute of every day . . . especially against unforeseen things like microphones and rocks in gold mines?

If . . . and I wasn't altogther convinced . . . two murder attempts had been made, they had both been arranged to look like accidents. So it was of little use taking future precautions against things like poison and bullets and knives-in-the-back down dark alleys. One would have to beware instead of cars with no brakes, deadly insects in one's shoes, and disintegrating balconies.

I shied away for a long time from thinking about *who*, for it had to be someone who had been down in the mine.

A miner who didn't hke my films taking steps to avoid sitting through any others? He wouldn't have to kill me: could simply vote with his feet.

Someone smouldering from ungovernable professional jealousy? The only person I knew of who regularly swore undying hatred was Drix Goddart, but he was not yet in South Africa, let alone 4,000 feet under Welkom.

None of the people working in the mine had known I was going to be there, and before the incident, none of them had used my name.

That left . . . Oh hell, I thought. Well . . . it left Evan . . . and Conrad . . . and Danilo . . . and Roderick. And also van Huren, who owned a lot of souls and could have things done by proxy.

As for *why* . . . Evan's professional resentment was

surely not obsessive enough, and Danilo didn't know my guess of what he was up to with the horses; and in any case, even if he did, he wouldn't try to cover up such a minor crime with murder. More likely to confess and laugh, I would have thought, and meet a warning-off with a what-the-hell shrug.

Motives for Conrad, Roderick and van Huren took even less cogitation. I couldn't rake up a decent one between them.

They had all (except Conrad who had been in the surgery) looked relieved when I stepped safely out of the mine . . . could they possibly have looked relieved just because I said I couldn't remember how I got knocked out?

It all seemed so improbable. I couldn't imagine any of them plotting away in murky labyrinths of villainy. It didn't make sense. I must, I concluded, be imagining things. I had been involved in too much fiction, and I had begun to project it on to reality.

I sighed. Realized that my head had stopped aching and that the unsettled feeling of concussion was subsiding, and presently, imperceptibly, went to sleep.

In the morning the night thoughts seemed even more preposterous. It was Conrad who had suggested a connection between the mike and the mine; and Conrad had got it wrong.

*

Roderick telephoned at breakfast time. Would I care to have dinner at his flat, with Katya, just the three of us and no fuss: and when I hesitated for a few seconds over replying, he added quickly that it would all be strictly off the record, anything I said would not be taken down and used against me.

'OK,' I agreed, with a smile in my voice and reservations in my mind. 'Where do I find you?'

He told me the address, and said, 'That chauffeur of yours will know where to find it.'

'Oh. Yes,' I agreed.

I put the receiver down slowly: but there was no reason why he shouldn't know about the hired car-and-driver, and there was of course his source at the Iguana. Roderick had all along known where I was going, what I was doing, and how often I brushed my teeth.

Almost before I had taken my hand off it, the telephone rang again.

Clifford Wenkins. Could he, er, that was to say, would it be convenient for him to come to the club that morning to discuss, er, details, for the, er, premiere?

Er yes, I said.

After that, Conrad rang. Was I going to travel down to the Kruger Park with him and Evan?

'How long are you staying there?' I asked.

'About ten days, I should think.'

'No, then. I'll have to come back by next Tuesday, at the latest. I'll drive down separately. It will be better anyway to have two cars, with you and Evan concentrating on locations.'

'Yeah,' he said, sounding relieved: hadn't wanted to spend a week at close quarters keeping Evan and me off each other's throats, I imagined.

They would come around for a drink before lunch, he said. Evan, it appeared, was bursting with inspirations for his new film. (When was he not?)

After that, Arknold.

'Look, Mister Lincoln. About Mrs Cavesey's horses . . . Look . . .' He petered heavily out.

After waiting in vain for him to start up again I said, 'I'll be here all morning, if you'd care to come over.'

Three heavy breaths. Then he said, 'Perhaps. Might be as well. Yes. All right. About eleven, then, after I've watched the horses work.'

'See you,' I said.

Hot sunshine, blue sky.

I went downstairs and drank my coffee out on the terrace, and read the newspaper. Close columns filled with local issues, all assuming a background of common knowledge which I didn't have. Reading them was like going into a film halfway through.

A man had been murdered in Johannesburg: found two days ago, with a wire twisted round his neck.

With a shiver I put down the paper. No one was trying to murder me. I had decided it was nonsense. Another man's death had no business to be raising hairs on my skin. The trouble was, no one had told my subconscious that we were all through with red alerts.

'Morning,' said a fresh young voice in my ear. 'What are you doing?'

'Watching the flowers grow.'

She sat down opposite me, grinning all over her fifteen-year-old face.

'I've come to play tennis.'

She wore a short white dress, white socks, white shoes, and carried two racquets in zipped waterproof covers. Her dark shoulder length hair was held back by a green head-band, and the van Huren wealth spoke as eloquently as ever in her natural confidence and poise.

'Coffee?' I suggested.

'Rather have orange juice.'

I ordered it.

'Didn't you just love the gold mine?' she demanded.

'I just did,' I agreed, imitating Danilo's accent, as she had done his turn of phrase.

She wrinkled her nose, amused. 'You never miss a damn thing, do you? Dad says you have an intuitive mind, whatever the hell that is.'

'It means I jump to conclusions,' I said.

She shook her head dubiously. 'Uhuh. He seemed to think it was good.'

The orange juice came and she drank some, clinking the ice. She had long dark eyelashes and more cream than peaches. I stifled as always the inner lurch of regret that young girls like Sally gave me: my own daughter might grow up as pretty, but the zest and the flash would be missing.

She put down the glass and her eyes searched the hotel buildings behind me.

'Have you see Danilo anywhere?' she said. 'The swine said he'd be here at ten, and it's a quarter after already.'

'He was busy doing sums all yesterday,' I said gravely. 'I expect they wore him out.'

'What sums?' she said suspiciously.

I told her.

She laughed. 'He can't help doing sums, then, I shouldn't think. All Saturday at the races, he was doing it. A living computer, I called him.' She took another orange sip. 'I say, did you know he's a terrific gambler? He had ten rand on one of those horses. *Ten rand!*'

I thought van Huren had made a sensible job of her, if a ten-rand bet still seemed excessive.

'Mind you,' she added, 'The horse won. I went with him to collect the winnings. Twenty-five rand, would you believe it? He says he often wins. He was all sort of gay and laughing about it.'

'Everyone loses in the end,' I said.

'Oh, don't be such a downpour,' she exploded. 'Just like Dad.'

Her eyes suddenly opened wider, and she transferred her attention to somewhere behind me.

Danilo joined us. White shorts, sturdy sunburned legs, light blue windcheater hanging open.

'Hi,' he said happily, including us both.

'Hi,' echoed Sally, looking smitten.

She left me and the half finished orange juice without a backward glance, and went off with the bright boy as girls have been going off since Eve. But this girl's father had a gold mine; and Danilo had done his sums.

Arknold came, and the reception desk directed him to the garden. He shook hands, sat down, huffed and puffed, and agreed to a beer. Away in the distance Danilo and Sally belted the ball sporadically over the net and laughed a lot in between.

Arknold followed my gaze, recognized Danilo, and consolidated his indecision in a heavy frown.

'I didn't know Danilo would be here,' he said.

'He can't hear you.'

'No . . . but . . . Look, Mister . . . Do you mind if we go indoors?'

'If you like,' I agreed; so we transferred to the lounge, where he was again too apprehensive to come to the boil, and finally up to my room. One could still see the tennis courts; but the tennis courts couldn't see us.

He sat, like Conrad, in the larger of the two armchairs, seeing himself as a dominant character. The slab-like features made no provision for subtle nuances of feeling to show in changing muscle tensions round eyes, mouth or jaw line, so that I found it as nearly impossible as always to guess what he was thinking. The overall impression was of aggression and worry having a ding-dong: the result, apparent indecision about whether to attack or placate.

'Look,' he said in the end. 'What are you going to tell Mrs Cavesey when you get back to England?'

I considered. 'I haven't decided.'

He thrust his face forward like a bulldog. 'Don't you go telling her to change her trainer.'

'Why precisely not?'

'There's nothing wrong with the way I train them.'

'They look well,' I agreed. 'And they run stinking. Most owners would have sent them to someone else long ago.'

'It's not my fault they don't win,' he asserted heavily. 'You tell her that. That's what I came to say. You tell her it's not my fault.'

'You would lose their training fees, if they went,' I said. 'And you would lose face, perhaps. But you would gain freedom from the fear of being prosecuted for fraud.'

'See here, Mister,' he began angrily, but I interrupted him.

'Alternatively, you could sack your head boy, Barty.'

Whatever he had been going to say remained unsaid. His trap-like mouth dropped open.

'Should you decide to sack Barty,' I said conversationally, 'I could advise Mrs Cavesey to leave the horses where they are.'

He shut his mouth. There was a long pause while most of the aggression oozed away and a tired sort of defeatism took its place.

'I can't do that,' he said sullenly, not denying the need for it.

'Because of a threat that you will be warned off?' I suggested. 'Or because of the profit to come?'

'Look, Mister . . .'

'See that Barty leaves before I go home,' I said pleasantly.

He stood heavily up, and gave me a hard stare which got him nowhere very much. Breathing loudly through his nose, he was inarticulate; and I couldn't guess from his expression whether what hung fire on his tongue was a stream of invective, a defence in mitigation, or even a plea for help.

He checked through the window that his buddy Danilo was still on the courts, then turned away abruptly and departed from my room without another word: a man on a three-pronged toasting fork if ever I saw one.

I returned to the terrace: found Clifford Wenkins walking indecisively about peering at strangers behind their newspapers.

'Mr Wenkins,' I called.

He looked up, nodded nervously, and scuttled around tables and chairs to reach me.

'Good morning . . . er . . . Link,' he began and half-held out one hand, too far away for me to shake, it. I sketched an equally noncommittal welcome. His best friend must have been telling him, I thought.

We sat at one of the small tables in the shade of a yellow and white sun awning, and he agreed that . . . er . . . yes . . . a beer would be fine. He pulled another untidy wad of papers out of an inner pocket. Consulting them seemed to give him strength.

'Er . . . Worldic have decided . . . er . . . they think it would be best, I mean, to hold the reception before . . . er . . . the film, you see.'

I saw. They were afraid I would vanish during the showing, if they arranged things the other way round.

'Here . . . er . . . is a list of people . . . er . . . invited by Worldic . . . and here . . . somewhere here . . . ah, yes, here is the Press list and . . . er . . . a list of people who have bought tickets to the reception . . . We limited the . . . er . . . numbers, but we have . . . er . . . had . . . I mean . . . it may be . . . perhaps . . . just a bit of a *crush*, if you see what I mean.'

He sweated. Mopped up with a neatly folded white square. Waited, apparently, for me to burn. But what could I say? I'd arranged it myself; and I supposed I was grateful that people actually wanted to come.

'Er . . . if that's all right . . . I mean . . . well . . . there are still some tickets left . . . er . . . for the premiere itself, you see . . . er . . . some at twenty rand . . .'

'Twenty rand?' I said. 'Surely that's too much?'

'It's for charity,' he said quickly. 'Charity.'

'What charity?'

'Oh . . . er . . . let's see . . . I've got it here somewhere . . .' But he couldn't find it. 'Anyway . . . for charity

. . . so Worldic want you to . . . I mean, because there are still some tickets, you see, to . . . er . . . well, some sort of publicity stunt . . .'

'No,' I said.

He looked unhappy. 'I told them . . . but they said . . . er . . . well . . .' He faded away like a pop song, and didn't say that Worldic's attitude to actors had made the KGB seem paternal.

'Where is the reception to be?' I asked.

'Oh . . . er . . . opposite the Wideworld Cinema, in the Klipspringer Heights Hotel. I . . . er . . . I think you will like it . . . I mean . . . it is one of the best . . . er . . . hotels in Johannesburg.'

'Fine,' I said. 'I'll be back here by, say, six o'clock next Tuesday evening. You could ring me here for final arrangements.'

'Oh yes . . . er,' he said, 'but . . . er . . . Worldic said they would like . . . er . . . to know where you are staying . . . er . . . in the Kruger Park.'

'I don't know,' I said.

'Well, er . . . could you find out?' He looked unhappy. 'Worldic said . . . er . . . on no account . . . should I not find out . . .'

'Oh. Very well,' I said. I'll let you know.'

'Thank you,' he gasped. 'Now . . . er . . . well . . . I mean . . . er . . .' He was working himself into a worse lather than ever over what he was trying to say next. My mind had framed one large *No* before the thought of Worldic on his tail had goaded him to get it out.

'We . . . well, that is to say . . . Worldic . . . have fixed a . . . er . . . photographic . . . session for you . . . I mean . . . well, this afternoon, in fact.'

'What photographic session?' I asked ominously.

He had another mop. 'Just . . . well . . . photographs.'

He had a terrible time explaining, and a worse time when I got it straight, that what Worldic wanted were some pictures of me reclining in bathing trunks under a sun umbrella beside a bosomy model in a bikini.

'You just run along and tell Worldic that their promotion ideas are fifty years out of date, if they think cheese-cake will sell twenty-rand seats.'

He sweated.

'And furthermore you can tell Worldic that one more damn fool suggestion and I'll never again turn up at anything they handle.'

'But . . .' he stuttered. 'You see . . . after those pics in the newspapers . . . of you giving Katya the kiss of life . . . after that . . . see . . . we were flooded . . . simply flooded . . . with inquiries . . . and all the cheaper seats went in a flash . . . and the reception tickets, too . . . all went . . .'

'But that,' I said slowly and positively, 'was not a publicity stunt.'

'Oh no.' He gulped. 'Oh no. Of course not. Oh no. Oh no . . .' He rocked to his feet, knocking his chair over. The beads were running down his forehead and his eyes looked wild. He was on the point, the very point of panic flight, when Danilo and Sally came breezily back from the courts.

'Hullo, Mr Wenkins,' Sally said in her adolescent unperceptive way. 'I say, you look almost as hot and sweaty as we do.'

Wenkins gave her a glazed, mesmerized look and fumbled around with his handkerchief. Danilo looked at him piercingly and thoughtfully and made no remark at all.

'Well . . . I'll . . . er, tell them . . . but they won't . . . like it.'

'You tell them.' I agreed. 'No stunts.'

'No stunts,' he echoed weakly; but I doubted whether he would ever have the nerve to pass on the message.

Sally watched his backview weave unsteadily into the club, as she sprawled exhaustedly in her garden chair.

'I say, he does get himself into a fuss, don't you think? Were you bullying the poor lamb, Link?'

'He's a sheep, not a lamb.'

'A silly sheep,' Danilo said vaguely, as if his thoughts were somewhere else.

'Could I have some orange juice?' Sally said.

Evan and Conrad arrived before the waiter, and the drinks order expanded. Evan was at his most insistent, waving his arms about and laying down the law to Conrad in the usual dominating I-am-the-director-and-the-rest-of-you-are-scum manner. Conrad looked half patient, half irritated: lighting cameramen were outranked by directors, but they didn't have to like it.

'Symbolism,' Evan was saying fiercely. 'Symbolism is what the film is all about. And Post Office Towers are the new phallic symbol of national strength. Every virile country has to have its revolving restaurant . . .'

'It might be just because every country has one, that the one in Johannesburg is not news,' Conrad murmured, in a tone a little too carefully unargumentative.

'The tower is *in*,' stated Evan with finality.

'Even if you can't find an elephant that shape,' I said, nodding.

Conrad choked and Evan glared.

Sally said, 'What is a phallic symbol?' And Danilo told her kindly to look it up in the dictionary.

I asked Evan where exactly we would be staying in the Kruger Park, so that I could be found if necessary.

'Don't expect me to help,' he said unhelpfully. 'The production department made the bookings months ago. Several different camps, starting in the south and working north, I believe.'

Conrad added casually, 'We do have a list, back at the hotel . . . I could copy it out for you, dear boy.'

'It isn't important,' I said. 'It was only Worldic who wanted it.'

'Not important!' Evans exclaimed. 'If Worldic wants it, of course they must have it.' Evan had no reservations towards companies that might screen his masterpieces. 'Conrad can copy the list and send it to them direct.'

I looked at Conrad in amusement. 'To Clifford Wenkins, then,' I suggested. 'It was he who asked.'

Conrad nodded shortly. Copying the list from friendliness was one thing and on Evan's orders another: I knew exactly how he felt.

'I don't suppose you are intending to bring the chauffeur Worldic gave you,' Evan said bossily to me. 'There won't be any rooms for him.'

I shook my head. 'No,' I said mildly. 'I'm hiring a car to drive myself.'

'All right, then.'

Even on a fine Tuesday morning with a healthy gin half drunk and no pressure on him at all, he still flourished the hot eyes like lances and curled his fingers so that the tendons snowed tight. The unruly curly hair sprang out vigorously like Medusa's snakes, and the very air around him seemed to quiver from his energy output.

Sally thought him fascinating. 'You'll love it in the game park,' she told him earnestly. 'The animals are so sweet.'

Evan only knew how to deal with girls that young if he could bully them in front of a camera: and the idea that animals could be sweet instead of symbolic seemed to nonplus him.

'Er . . .' he said uncertainly, and sounded exactly like Wenkins.

Conrad cheered up perceptibly: smoothed his moustache and looked on Sally benignly. She gave him an uncomplicated smile and turned to Danilo.

'You'd love it too,' she said. 'Next time you come to South Africa, we must take you down there.'

Danilo could scarcely wait. Conrad asked him how much longer he was staying this time, and Danilo said a week or so, he guessed, and Sally insisted anxiously that he was staying until after Link's premiere, surely he remembered he was going to the reception with the van Hurens. Danilo remembered: he sure was.

He grinned at her. She blossomed. I hoped that the sun kid dealt in compassion alongside the mathematics.

Evan and Conrad stayed for lunch, endlessly discussing the locations they had picked throughout the city. They were, it appeared, going to incorporate a lot of *cinéma vérité*, with Conrad humping around a hand-held Arriflex to film life as it was lived. By the end of the cheese, the whole film, symbolism, elephants, and all, seemed to me doomed to be a crashing bore.

Conrad's interest was principally technical. Mine was nonexistent. Evan's, as usual, inexhaustible.

'So we'll take the Arriflex with us, of course,' he was telling Conrad. 'We may see unrepeatable shots . . . it would be stupid not to be equipped.'

Conrad agreed. They also discussed sound-recording equipment and decided to take that too. The production department had fixed up for a park ranger to show them round in a Land Rover, so there would be room to use everything comfortably.

Anything which they could not cram into their hired station wagon for the journey down, they said, could go in my car, couldn't it? It could. I agreed to drive to their hotel first thing in the morning to embark the surplus.

When they had gone I paid off the car and chauffeur Worldic had arranged, and hired a modest self-drive saloon instead. A man from the hiring company brought it to the Iguana, showed me the gear system, said it was a new car only just run-in and that I should have no trouble with it, and departed with the chauffeur.

I went for a practice drive, got lost, bought a map, and found my way back. The car was short on power uphill, but very stable on corners; a car for Sunday afternoons, airing Grandma in a hat.

CHAPTER TWELVE

The map and the car took me to Roderick's flat just as it was getting dark.

I tested the brakes before I set off, the car having stood alone in the car park for hours. Nothing wrong with them, of course. I sneered inwardly at myself for being so silly.

Roderick's flat was on the sixth floor.

It had a balcony.

Roderick invited me out first thing to look at the view.

'It looks marvellous at this time of night,' he said, 'with the lights springing up in every direction. In the daytime there are too many factories and roads and mining tips, unless of course you find the sinews of trade stimulating . . . and soon it will be too dark to see the shape of things in the dusk . . .'

I hovered, despite myself, on the threshold.

'Come on,' he said. 'Are you afraid of heights?'

'No.'

I stepped out there, and the view lived up to his commercial. The balcony faced south, with the kite-shaped Southern Cross flying on its side in the sky straight ahead;

and orange lights stretching like a chain away towards Durban down the motorway.

Roderick was not leaning on the pierced ironwork which edged the balcony. With part of my mind shivering and the rest telling me not to be such an ass, I kept my weight nearer the building than his: I felt guilty of mistrust and yet couldn't trust, and saw that suspicion was a wrecker.

We went in. Of course, we went in. Safely. I could feel muscles relax in my jaw and abdomen that I hadn't known were tense. Silly fool, I thought: and tried to shut out the fact that for both mike and mine, Roderick had been there.

His flat was small but predictably full of impact. A black sack chair flopped on a pale olive carpet: khaki-coloured walls sprouted huge brass lamp brackets between large canvasses of ultra simple abstracts in brash challenging colours: a low glass-topped table stood before an imitation tiger skin sofa of stark square construction; and an Andy Warholish imitation can of beer stood waist high in one corner. Desperately trendy, the whole thing; giving, like its incumbent, the impression that way out was where it was all at, man, and if you weren't out there as far as you could go you might as well be dead. It seemed a foregone conclusion that he smoked pot.

Naturally, he had an expensive stereo. The music he chose was less underground than could be got in London, but the mix of anarchy and self-pity came across strongly in the nasal voices. I wondered whether it was just part of the image, or whether he sincerely enjoyed it.

'Drink?' he offered, and I said yes, please.

Campari and soda, bitter-sweet pink stuff. He took it for granted I would like it.

'Katya won't be long. She had some recording session or other.'

'Is she all right now?'

'Sure,' he said. 'A hundred per cent.' He underplayed the relief, but I remembered his tormented tears: real emotions still lived down there under the with-it front.

He was wearing another pair of pasted-on trousers, and a blue ruffled close-fitting shirt with lacing instead of buttons. As casual clothes, they were as deliberate as signposts: the rugged male in his sexual finery. I supposed my own clothes too made a statement, as indeed everyone's did, always.

Katya's statement was as clear as a trumpet, and said 'look at me'.

She arrived like a gust of bright and breezy showbiz, wearing an eye-stunning yellow catsuit which flared widely from the knees in black-edged ruffles. She looked like a flamenco dancer split up the middle, and she topped up the impression with a high tortoise-shell mantilla comb pegged like a tiara into her mop of hair.

Stretching out her arms she advanced on me with life positively spurting from every pore, as if instead of harming her the input of electric current had doubled her vitality.

'Link, darling, how marvellous,' she said extravagantly. And she had brought someone with her.

The barriers in my mind rose immediately like a hedge and prickled away all evening. Roderick and Katya had planted a bombshell to lead me astray, and were betraying their intention through the heightened mischief in Katya's manner. I didn't like the game, but I was an old hand at it, and nowadays I never lost. I sighed regretfully for the quiet no-fuss dinner which Roderick had promised. Too much ever to hope for, I supposed.

The girl was ravishing, with cloudy dark hair and enormous slightly myopic-looking eyes. She wore a soft floaty garment, floor length and green, which swirled and lay against her as she moved, outlining now a hip, now a breast, and all parts in quite clearly good shape.

Roderick was watching my reactions sideways, while pretending to pour out more Camparis.

'This is Melanie,' Katya said as if inventing Venus from the waves; and there was perhaps a touch of the Botticellis in the graceful neck.

Christened Mabel, no doubt, I said to myself uncharitably, and greeted her with a lukewarm smile and a conventional handshake. Melanie was not a girl to be put off by a cool reception. She gave me a gentle flutter of lengthy lashes, a sweet curve of soft pink lips, and a smouldering promise in the smoky eyes. I thought: she's done this sort of thing before, and she is as aware of her power as I am when I act.

Melanie just happened to sit beside me on the tiger skin sofa, stretching out languorously so that the green material revealed the whole slender shape. Just happened to have no lighter of her own, so that I had to help her with Roderick's orange globe table model. Just happened to have to cup my hand in both of her own to guide the flame to the end of her cigarette. Just happened to steady herself with a hand on my arm as she leant forward to flick off ash.

Katya gaily sparkled and Roderick filled my glass with gin when he thought I wasn't looking, and I began to wonder where he had hidden the tape-recorder. If this little lot was to be off the record, I was the plumber's mate.

Dinner was laid with candles on a square black table in a mustard-painted dining alcove. The food was great and the talk provocative, but mostly the three of them tossed the ball among themselves while I replied when essential with murmurs and smiles, which couldn't be picked on as quotes.

Melanie's scent was as subtle as Joy, and Roderick had laced my wine with brandy. He watched and spoke and attended to me with friendly eyes, and waited for me to deliver myself up. Go stuff the *Rand Daily Star*, I thought: my friend Roderick is a bastard and my tongue is my own.

Something of my awareness must have shown in my eyes, for a thoughtful look suddenly crossed his forehead and he changed his tack in two sentences from sexual innuendo to meaningful social comment.

He said, 'What do you think of apartheid, now that you've been here a week?'

'What do you?' I replied. 'Tell me about it. You three who live here . . . you tell *me*.'

Roderick shook his head and Katya said it was what visitors thought that mattered, and only Melanie, who was playing different rules, came across with the goods.

'Apartheid,' she said earnestly, 'is necessary.'

Roderick made a negative movement, and I asked, 'In what way?'

'It means living separately,' she said. 'It doesn't mean that one race is better than the other, just that they are different, and should remain so. All the world seems to think that white South Africans hate the blacks and try to repress them, but it is not true. We care for them . . . and the phrase, "black is beautiful" was thought up by white Africans to give black Africans a sense of being important as individuals.'

I was intensely surprised, but Roderick reluctantly nodded. 'That's true. The Black Power Movement have adopted it as their own, but they didn't invent it. You might say, I suppose, that the phrase has achieved everything it was intended to, and a bit more besides.'

'To read foreign papers,' said Melanie indignantly, warming to her subject, 'you would think the blacks are a lot of illiterate cheap labour. And it isn't true. Schooling is compulsory for both races, and factories pay the rate for the job, regardless of skin colour. And that,' she added, 'was negotiated by the white trade unionists.'

I liked her a lot better since she'd forgotten the sexpot role. The dark eyes held fire as well as smoke, and it was a change to hear someone passionately defending her country.

'Tell me more,' I said flippantly.

'Oh . . .' She looked confused for a moment, then took a fresh hold on enthusiasm, like a horse getting its second wind. 'Black people have everything the same as white people. Everything that they want to have. Only a minority have big houses because the majority don't like them: they like to live out of doors, and only go into shelters to sleep. But they have cars and businesses and holidays and hospitals and hotels and cinemas . . . everything like that.'

The white people on the whole had more money, I thought; and undoubtedly more freedom of action. I opened my mouth to make some innocuous remark about the many entrance doors marked 'non-whites' and 'whites only', but Melanie jumped right in to forestall any adverse comment, which was not in the least what Roderick wanted. He frowned at her. She was too busy to notice.

'I know what you're going to say,' she said inaccurately. 'You're going to talk about injustice. Everyone from England always does. Well, certainly, of course, there are injustices. There are in every country in the world, including yours. Injustices make the headlines. Justice is not news. People come here purposely seeking for injustice, and of course they find it. But they never report on the good things, they just shut their eyes and pretend there aren't any.'

I looked at her thoughtfully. There was truth in what she said.

'Every time a country like England attacks our way of life,' she said, 'they do more harm than good. You can feel the people here close their ranks and harden their attitude. It is stupid. It slows down the progress our country is gradually making towards partnership between the races. The old rigid type of apartheid is dying out, you know . . . and in five or ten years' time it will only be the militants and extremists on both sides who take it seriously. They shout and thump, and the foreign press listens and pays attention, like they always do to crackpots, and they don't see, or at any rate they never mention, the slow quiet change for the better which is going on here.'

I wondered how she would feel about it if she were black: even if things were changing, there was still no overall equality of opportunity. Blacks could be teachers, doctors, lawyers, priests. They couldn't be jockeys. Unfair, unfair.

Roderick, waiting in vain for me to jump in with both feet, was driven again to a direct question.

'What are your views, Link?'

I smiled at him.

'I belong to a profession,' I said, 'which never discriminates against blacks or Jews or women or Catholics or Protestants or bug-eyed monsters, but only against non-members of Equity.'

Melanie looked blank about Equity but she had a word to say about Jews.

'Whatever white South Africans may be accused of,' she contended, 'we have never sent six million blacks to the gas chamber.'

Which was rather like saying, I thought frivolously,

that one might have measles, but had never infected anyone with whooping-cough.

Roderick gave up angling for a quotable political commitment and tried to bounce Melanie back into sultry seduction. Her own instincts were telling her she would get further with me if she laid off the sex, because the doubt showed clearly in her manner as she attempted to do as he wanted. But evidently it was important to them both that she should persevere, and she refused to be discouraged by my lack of answering spark. She smiled a meek feminine smile to deprecate every opinion she had uttered, and bashfully lowered the thick black lashes.

Katya and Roderick exchanged eye-signals as blinding as lighthouses on a dark night, and Katya said she was going to make coffee. Roderick said he would help: and why didn't Melanie and Link move over to the sofa, it was more comfortable than sitting round the table.

Melanie smiled shyly. I admired the achievement: she was as shy underneath as a sergeant-major. She draped herself beautifully over the sofa with the green material swirling closely across the perfect bosom which rose and fell gently with every breath. She noted the direction of my eyes and smiled with pussy-cat satisfaction.

Premature, dearest Melanie, premature, I thought.

Roderick carried in a tray of coffee cups and Katya went out on to the balcony. When she came in, she shook her head. Roderick poured out the coffee and Katya handed it round: the suppressed inner excitement, absent during dinner, was fizzing away again in the corners of her smile.

I looked at my watch. A quarter past ten.

I said, 'I must be going soon. Early start tomorrow morning, I'm afraid.'

Katya said quickly, 'Oh no, you can't go yet, Link,' and Roderick handed me a bulbous glass with enough brandy to sink a battleship. I took a sip but made it look like a swallow, and reflected that if I'd drunk everything he'd given me I would have been in no state to drive away.

Melanie kicked off her golden slippers and flexed her toes. On them she wore pearly pink nail varnish and nothing else: and with a quick flash of bare ankle and calf she managed to plant the idea in my mind that under the green shift there were no other clothes.

The coffee was as good as the dinner: Katya was more expert a cook than conspirator. Within twenty minutes she again strolled out on to the balcony, and this time, when she came back, the message was a nod.

I looked at all three of them, wondering. Roderick with his old-young face, Katya yellow-frilly and irresponsible, Melanie conscientiously weaving her web. They had laid some sort of trap. The only thing was . . . what?

Twenty to eleven. I finished my coffee, stood up, and said, 'I really must go now . . .'

This time there was no resistance. They all three uncurled themselves to their feet.

'Thank you,' I said, 'for a great evening.'

They smiled.

'Marvellous food,' I said to Katya.

She smiled.

'Splendid drinks,' I said to Roderick.

He smiled.

'Superb company,' I said to Melanie.

She smiled.

Not a really genuine smile among them. They had watchful, expectant eyes. My mouth, for all the available liquid, felt dry.

We moved towards the lobby, which was an extension of the sitting-room.

Melanie said, 'Time I was going too . . . Roderick, would you order me a taxi?'

'Sure, love,' he said easily, and then, as if the thought was just striking, 'but you go the same way as Link . . . I'm sure he would give you a lift.'

They all looked at me, smiling.

'Of course,' I said. What else. What else could I say?

The smiles went on and on.

Melanie scooped up a tiny wrap from beside the front door, and Roderick and Katya saw us down the hall and into the lift, and were still waving farewell as the doors closed between us. The lift sank. One of those automatic lifts which stopped at every floor one had pre-selected. I pressed G for ground, and at G for ground it stopped.

Politely I let Melanie out first. Then I said, 'I say . . . terribly sorry . . . I've left my signet ring on the wash basin in Roderick's bathroom. I'll just dash back for it. You wait there, I won't be a second.'

The doors were closing before she could demur. I pressed the buttons for floors 2 and 6. Got out at 2. Watched the pointer begin to slide towards Roderick's floor at 6, and skipped quickly through the doors of the service stairs at the back of the hall.

The unadorned concrete and ironwork steps wound down round a small steep well and let me out into an area full of stacked laundry baskets, central-heating boilers, and rows of garbage cans. Out in the narrow street behind the covered yard I turned left, skirted the whole of the next door block at a fast pace, and finally, more slowly, inconspicuously walked in the shadows back towards Roderick's.

I stopped in a doorway a hundred yards away, and watched.

There were four men in the street, waiting. Two opposite the front entrance of Roderick's apartment block. Two others patiently standing near my hired car. All of them carried objects which gleamed in the street lamps, and whose shapes I knew all too well.

Melanie came out of the apartment block and hurried across the road to talk to two of the men. The green dress clung to her body and appeared diaphanous to the point of transparency in the quality of light in the street. She and the men conferred agitatedly, and there was a great deal of shaking of heads.

All three of them suddenly looked up, and I followed

the direction of their gaze. Roderick and Katya were standing out on the balcony, calling down. I was too far away to hear the exact words, but the gist was entirely guessable. The quarry had got away, and none of them was pleased.

Melanie and the two men turned and walked in my direction, but only as far as the other two beside my car. They all five went into a huddle which could produce no happiness, and in the end Melanie walked back alone and disappeared into the flats.

I sighed wryly. Roderick was no murderer. He was a newspaperman. The four men had come armed with cameras. Not knives. Not guns.

Not my life they were after; just my picture.

Just my picture outside a block of flats at night alone with a beautiful girl in a totally revealing dress.

I looked thoughtfully at the four men beside my car, decided the odds were against it, turned on my heel, and quietly walked away.

Back at the Iguana Rock (by taxi), I telephoned Roderick.

He sounded subdued.

I said, 'Damn your bloody eyes.'

'Yes.'

'Have you got this telephone bugged?'

A pause. Then on a sigh again he said, 'Yes.'

'Too late for honesty, my friend.'

'Link . . .'

'Forget it,' I said. 'Just tell me why.'

'My paper . . .'

'No,' I said. 'Newspapers don't get up to such tricks. That was a spot of private enterprise.'

A longer pause.

'I guess I owe it to you,' he said slowly. 'We did it for Clifford Wenkins. The little runt is scared silly by Worldic, and he begged us, in return for favours he has done us from time to time, to set you up for him. He said Worldic would sack him if he couldn't persuade you to do a girly session to sell their twenty-rand seats, and he had asked you, and you had absolutely refused. Melanie is our top model girl, and he got her to help in a good cause.'

'That Wenkins,' I said bitterly, 'would sell his soul for publicity stunts.'

'I'm sorry, Link . . .'

'Not as sorry as he will be,' I said ominously.

'I promised him I wouldn't tell you . . .'

'Stuff both of you,' I said violently, and rattled the receiver into its cradle.

CHAPTER THIRTEEN

The next morning, the Iguana management having kindly sent someone with the keys to fetch my hired car from outside Roderick's flat, I packed what little I would need for the Kruger Park, and chuntered round to Evan and Conrad's hotel.

The loading of their station wagon was in process of being directed by Evan as if it were the key scene in a prestige production, and performed by Conrad at his most eccentric. Boxes, bags, and black zipped equipment littered the ground for a radius of ten yards.

'Dear boy,' Conrad said as I approached, 'for God's sake get some ice.'

'Ice?' I echoed vaguely.

'Ice.' He pointed to a yellow plastic box about two feet by one. 'In there. For the film.'

'What about beer?'

He gave me a sorrowful, withering glance. 'Beer in the red one, dear boy.'

The red thermal box had had priority; had already been clipped tight shut and lifted on to the car. Smiling, I went into the hotel on the errand and returned with a large plastic bagful. Conrad laid the ice-pack in the yellow box and carefully stacked his raw stock on top. The yellow box joined the red one and Evan said that at this rate we wouldn't reach the Kruger by nightfall.

At eleven the station wagon was full to the gunnels but the ground was still littered with that extraordinary collection of wires, boxes, tripods and clips which seem to accompany cameramen everywhere.

Evan waved his arms as if by magic wand the whole lot would leap into order. Conrad pulled his moustache dubiously. I opened the boot of my saloon, shovelled the whole lot in unceremoniously, and told him he could sort it all out when we arrived.

After that we adjourned for thirst quenchers, and finally got the wheels on the road at noon. We drove east by north for several hours and descended from the high Johannesburg plateau down to a few hundred feet above sea level. The air grew noticeably warmer on every long downhill stretch, which gave rise to three or four more stops for sustenance. Conrad's cubic capacity rivalled the Bantus'.

By five we arrived at the Numbi gate, the nearest way into the park. The Kruger itself stretched a further two hundred miles north and fifty east with nothing to keep the animals in except their own wish to stay. The Numbi gate consisted of a simple swinging barrier guarded by two khaki-uniformed black Africans and a small office. Evan produced passes for two cars and reservations for staying in the camps, and with grins and salutes the passes were stamped and the gates swung open.

Brilliant scarlet and magenta bougainvillaea just inside proved misleading: the park itself was tinder dry and thorny brown after months of sun and no rain. The narrow road stretched ahead into a baked wilderness where the only manmade thing in sight was the tarmac itself.

'Zebras,' shouted Evan, winding down his window and screaming out of it.

I followed his pointing finger, and saw the dusty herd of them standing patiently under bare-branched trees, slowly swinging their tails and merging uncannily into the striped shade.

Conrad had a map, which was just as well. We were headed for the nearest camp, Pretoriuskop, but roads wound and crisscrossed as we approached it, unmade-up dry earth roads leading off at tangents to vast areas inhabited believably by lion, rhinoceros, buffalo and crocodile.

And, of course, elephant.

The camp turned out to be an area of several dozen acres, enclosed by a stout wire fence, and containing nothing so camplike as tents. Rather like Butlins gone native, I thought: clusters of round, brick-walled, thatched-roofed cabins like pink-coloured drums with wide-brimmed hats on.

'*Rondavels*,' Evan said in his best dogmatic manner, waving a hand at them. He checked in at the big reception office and drove off to search for the huts with the right numbers. There were three of them: one each. Inside, two beds, a table, two chairs, fitted cupboard, shower room, and air-conditioning. Every mod con in the middle of the jungle.

Evan banged on my door and said come out, we were going for a drive. The camp locked its gates for the night at six thirty, he said, which gave us forty minutes to go and look at baboons.

'It will take too long to unpack the station wagon,' he said. 'So we will all go in your car.'

I drove and they gazed steadfastly out of the windows. There were some distant baboons scratching themselves in the evening sunlight on a rocky hill, and a herd of impala munching away at almost leafless bushes, but not an elephant in sight.

'We'd better go back before we get lost,' I said, but even then we only whizzed through the gates seconds before closing time.

'What happens if you're late?' I asked.

'You have to spend the night outside,' Evan said positively. 'Once the gate is closed, it's closed.'

Evan, as usual, seemed to be drawing information out of the air, though he gave the game away later by producing an information booklet he had been given in reception. The booklet also said not to wind down windows and scream 'zebra' out of them, as the animals didn't like it. Wild animals, it appeared, thought cars were harmless and left them alone, but were liable to bite any bits of humans sticking out.

Conrad had had to unpack the whole station wagon to unload the red beer box, which was likely to reverse his priorities. We sat round a table outside the huts, cooling our throats in the warm air and watching the dark creep closer between the *rondavels*. Even with Evan there it was peaceful enough to unjangle the screwiest nerves . . . and lull the wariest mind into a sense of security.

Thursday, the following day, we set off at daybreak and breakfasted at the next camp, Skukuza, where we were to stay that night.

Skukuza was larger and boasted executive-status *rondavels*, which Evan's production company had naturally latched on to. They had also engaged the full-time attendance of a park ranger for the day, which would have been splendid had he not been an Afrikaaner with incomplete English. He was big, slow moving, quiet, and unemotional, the complete antithesis of Evan's fiery zeal for allegory.

Evan shot questions and had to wait through silences for his answers: no doubt Haagner was merely translating the one into Afrikaans in his head, formulating the other and translating that into English, but the delay irritated Evan from the start. Haagner treated Evan with detachment and refused to be hurried, which gave Conrad the (decently concealed) satisfaction of an underdog seeing his master slip on a banana skin.

We set off in Haagner's Range Rover, accompanied by

the Arriflex, a tape recorder, half a dozen smaller cameras, and the red thermal box loaded with a mixed cargo of film, beer, fruit, and sandwiches in plastic bags. Evan had brought sketch pads, maps and notebooks, and six times remarked that the company should have equipped him with a secretary. Conrad murmured that we should be glad that we weren't equipped with Drix Goddart, but from the sour look Evan slid me he didn't necessarily agree.

'*Olifant*,' Haagner said, pointing, having been three times told of the aim of the expedition.

He stopped the van. 'There, in the valley.'

We looked. A lot of trees, a patch of green, a winding river.

'There, man,' he said.

Eventually our untrained eyes saw them; three dark hunched shapes made small by distance, flapping a lazy ear behind a bush.

'Not near enough,' Evan said disgustedly. 'We must get nearer.'

'Not here,' said Haagner. 'They are across the river. The Sabie river. *Sabie* is Bantu word: it means Fear.'

I looked at him suspiciously but he was not provoking Evan in any way; simply imparting information. The slow peaceful-looking water wound through the valley and looked as unfearful as the Thames.

Evan had no eyes for the various antelope-like species Haagner pointed out, nor for the blue jays or turkey buzzards or vervet monkeys or wildebeest, and particularly not for the herds of gentle impala. Only the implicitly violent took his attention: the vultures, the hyena, the wart-hog, the possibility of lion and the scarcity of cheetah.

And, of course, *olifants*. Evan adopted the Afrikaans word as his own and rolled it round his tongue as if he alone had invented it. *Olifant* droppings on the road (fresh, said Haagner) excited him almost to orgasm. He insisted on us stopping there and reversing for a better view, and on Conrad sticking the Arriflex lens out of the window and exposing about fifty feet of film from different angles and with several focal lengths.

Haagner, patiently positioning the van for every shot, watched these antics and clearly thought Evan unhinged, and I laughed internally until my throat ached. Had the obliging elephant returned Evan would no doubt have directed *him* to defecate again for Scene I, Take II. He would have seen nothing odd in it.

Evan left the heap reluctantly and was working out how to symbolize it in an utterly meaningful way. Conrad said he could do with a beer but Haagner pointed ahead and said 'Onder-Sabie', which turned out to be another rest camp like the others.

'*Olifant* in Saliji river,' said Haagner coming back from a chat with some colleagues. 'If we go now, you see them perhaps.'

Evan swept us away from the shady table and our half empty glasses and scurried forth again into the increasing noonday heat. All around us, more sensible mortals were fanning themselves and contemplating siesta, but *olifants*, with Evan, came before sense.

The Range Rover was as hot as an oven.

'It is hot, today,' Haagner said. 'Hotter tomorrow. Summer is coming. Soon we will have the rain, and all the park will be green.'

Evan, alarmed, said, 'No, no. The park must be burned up, just like this. Inhospitable land, bare, hungry, predatory, aggressive and cruel. Certainly not soft and lush.'

Haagner understood less than a tenth. After a long pause he merely repeated the bad news: 'In one month, after the rains start, the park will be all green. Then, much water. Now, not much. All small rivers are dry. We find *olifant* near bigger rivers. In Saliji.'

He drove several miles and stopped beside a large wooden sun shelter built high at the end of a valley. Below, the Saliji river stretched away straight ahead, and the *olifants* had done Evan proud. A large family of them were playing in the water, squirting each other through their trunks and taking care of their kids.

As it was an official picnic place especially built in an area of cleared ground, we were all allowed out of the car. I stretched myself thankfully and dug into the red box for a spot of irrigation. Conrad had a camera in one hand and a beer in the other and Evan brandished his enthusiasm over us all like a whip.

Haagner and I sat in ninety degrees in the shade at one of the small scattered tables and ate some of the packed sandwiches. He had warned Evan not to go too far from the shelter while filming as it presented an open invitation to a hungry lion, but Evan naturally believed that he would not meet one: and he didn't. He took Conrad plus Arrifiex fifty yards downhill into the bush for some closer shots and Haagner called him urgently to come back, telling me his job would be lost if Evan were.

Conrad soon climbed up again, mopping drops from his brow which were not all heat, and reported that 'something' was grunting down there behind some rocks.

'There are twelve hundred lion in the park,' Haagner said. 'When hungry, they kill. Lions alone kill thirty thousand animals in the park every year.'

'God,' said Conrad, visibly losing interest in Evan's whole project.

Eventually Evan returned unscathed, but Haagner regarded him with disfavour.

'More *olifant* in the north,' he said. 'For *olifant*, you go north.' Out of his district, his tone said.

Evan nodded briskly and set his mind at rest.

'Tomorrow. We set off northwards tomorrow, and tomorrow night we stay in a camp called Satara.'

Reassured, Haagner drove us slowly back towards Skukuza, conscientiously pointing out animals all the way.

'Could you cross the park on a horse?' I asked.

He shook his head decisively. 'Very dangerous. More dangerous than walking, and walking is not safe.' He looked directly at Evan. 'If your car break down, wait for next car, and ask people to tell rangers at the next camp. Do not leave your car. Do not walk in the park. Especially do not walk in the park at night. Stay in car all night.'

Evan listened to the lecture with every symptom of ignoring it. He pointed instead to one of the several unmetalled side roads we had passed with 'no entry' signs on them, and asked where they led.

'Some go to the many Bantu ranger stations,' said Haagner after the pause for translation. 'Some to water holes. Some are fire breaks. They are roads for rangers. Not roads for visitors. Do not go down those roads.' He looked at Evan, clearly seeing that Evan would not necessarily obey. 'It is not allowed.'

'Why not?'

'The park is 8,000 square miles . . . visitors can get lost.'

'We have a map,' Evan argued.

'The service roads,' Haagner said stolidly, 'are not on the maps.'

Evan ate a packet of sandwiches mutinously and rolled down the window to throw out the plastic bag.

'Do not do that,' Haagner said sharply enough to stop him.

'Why not?'

'The animals eat them, and choke. No litter must be thrown. It kills the animals.'

'Oh very well,' said Evan ungraciously, and handed me the screwed up bag to return to the red box. The box was clipped shut and tidy, so I shoved it in my pocket. Evan polished off the job of being a nuisance by throwing out instead the half eaten crust of his cheese-and-tomato.

'Do not feed the animals,' said Haagner automatically.

'Why not?' Evan, belligerent, putting on an RSPCA face.

'It is unwise to teach animals that cars contain food.'

That silenced him flat. Conrad twitched an eyebrow at me and I arranged my face into as near impassiveness as one can get while falling about inside.

Owing to an *olifant* waving its ears at us within cricket ball distance we did not get back to Skukuza before the gates shut. Evan, oblivious to the fast setting sun, saw allegories all over the place and had Conrad wasting film by the mile, taking shots through glass. He had wanted Conrad to set up a tripod in the road to get steadier than hand-held pictures, but even he was slightly damped by the frantic quality in Haagner's voice as he told him not to.

'*Olifant* is the most dangerous of all the animals,' he said earnestly, and Conrad equally earnestly assured him that for nothing on earth would he, Conrad, leave the safety of the Range Rover. Haagner wouldn't even have the window open and wanted to drive away at once. It appeared that when *olifants* waved their ears like that they were expressing annoyance, and since they weighed seven tons and could charge at 25 mph, it didn't do to hang about.

Evan didn't believe that any animal would have the

gall to attack such important humans as E. Pentelow, director, and E. Lincoln, actor. He persuaded Conrad to get clicking, and Haagner sat there with the engine running and his foot on the clutch. When the elephant finally took one step in our direction we were off down the road with a jolt that threw Conrad, camera and all, to the floor.

I helped him up, while Evan complained about it to Haagner. The ranger, nearing the end of his patience, stopped the car with an equal jerk and hauled on the hand brake.

'Very well,' he said. 'We wait.'

The elephant came out on to the road, a hundred yards behind us. The big ears were flapping like flags.

Conrad looked back. 'Do drive on, dear boy,' he said with anxiety in his voice.

Haagner folded his lips. The elephant decided to follow us. He was also accelerating to a trot.

It took more seconds than I cared before Evan cracked. He was saying 'For God's sake, where is the Arriflex?' to Conrad, when it seemed at last to dawn on him that there might be some real danger.

'Drive away,' he said to Haagner urgently. 'Can't you see that that animal is charging?'

And it had tusks, I observed.

Haagner too decided that enough was enough. He had the hand brake off and the gears in mesh in one slick movement, and the elephant got a trunkful of dust.

'What about the next car coming along?' I asked. 'They'll meet it head on.'

Haagner shook his head. 'No cars will come this way any more today. It is too late. They will all be near the camps now. And that *olifant*, he will go straight away into the bush. He will not stay on the road.'

Conrad looked at his watch. 'How long will it take us to get back to Skukuza?'

'With no more stops,' Haagner said with bite, 'about half an hour.'

'But it is six fifteen already!' Conrad said.

Haagner made a noncommittal movement of his head and didn't answer. Evan appeared subdued into silence and a look of peaceful satisfaction awoke on the Afrikaaner's face. For the whole of the rest of the way it stayed there, first in the quick dust, then in the reflected glow of the headlights. Before we reached Skukuza he swung the Range Rover down one of the no entry side roads, a detour which brought us after a mile or two suddenly and unexpectedly into a village of modern bungalows with tiny little flower gardens and street lighting.

We stared in amazement. A suburb, no less, set down greenly in the brown dry veldt.

'This is the ranger village,' Haagner said. 'My house is over there, the third down that road. All the whites who work in the camp, and the white rangers, we live here. The Bantu rangers and workers also have villages in the park.'

'But the lions,' I said. 'Are the villages safe, isolated like this?'

He smiled. 'It is not isolated.' The Range Rover came to the end of the houses, crossed about fifty unlit yards of road and sped straight into the back regions of Skukuza camp. 'But also, no, it is not entirely safe. One must not walk far from the houses at night. Lions do not normally come near the gardens . . . and we have fences round them . . . but a young Bantu was taken by a lion one night on that short piece of road between our village and the camp. I knew him well. He had been told never to walk . . . it was truly sad.'

'Are people often . . . taken . . . by lions?' I asked, as he pulled up by our *rondavels*, and we unloaded ourselves, the cameras, and the red box.

'No. Sometimes. Not often. People who work in the park; never visitors. It is safe in cars.' He gave Evan one last meaningful stare. 'Do not leave your car. To do so is not safe.'

Before dinner in the camp restaurant I put a call through to England. Two hours' delay, they said, but by nine o'clock I was talking to Charlie.

Everything was fine, she said, the children were little hooligans, and she had been to see Nerissa.

'I spent the whole day with her yesterday . . . Most of the time we just sat, because she felt awfully tired, but she didn't seem to want me to go. I asked her the things you wanted . . . not all at once, but spread over . . .'

'What did she say?'

'Well . . . You were right about some things. She did tell Danilo she had Hodgkin's disease. She said she didn't know herself that it was fatal when she told him, but she doesn't think he took much notice, because all he said was that he thought only young people got it.'

If he knew that, I thought, he knew a lot more.

'Apparently he stayed with her for about ten days, and they became firm friends. That was how she described it. So she told him, before he went back to America, that she would be leaving him the horses as a personal gift, and also, as he was all the family she had, all the rest of her money after other bequests had been met.'

'Lucky old Danilo.'

'Yes . . . Well, he came to see her again, a few weeks ago, late July or early August. While you were in Spain, anyway. She knew by then that she was dying, but she didn't mention it to Danilo. She did show him her will, though, as he seemed interested in it. She said he was so sweet when he had read it, and hoped not to be inheriting for twenty years.'

'Little hypocrite.'

'I don't know,' said Charlie doubtfully, 'because although you were right about so much, there is a distinct fly in the wood pile.'

'What's that?'

'It can't be Danilo who is making the horses lose. It simply cannot.'

'It must be,' I said. 'And why not?'

'Because when Nerissa told him she was worried about the way they were running, and wished she could find out what was wrong, it was Danilo himself who came up with the idea of sending *you*.'

'It can't have been,' I exclaimed.

'It definitely was,' Charlie said. 'She was positive about it. It was Danilo's own suggestion.'

'Blast,' I said.

'He wouldn't have suggested she send someone to investigate, if he'd been nobbling them himself.'

'No . . . I suppose not.'

'You sound depressed,' she said.

'I haven't any other answers for Nerissa.'

'Don't worry. You weren't anyway going to tell her her nephew was up to no good.'

'That's true,' I agreed.

'And it wasn't difficult for Danilo to read her will. She leaves it lying around all the time on that marquetry table in the corner of the sitting-room. She showed it to me immediately, as soon as I mentioned it, because it interests her a lot. And I saw what keepsakes she is leaving us, if you're interested.'

'What are they?' I asked idly, thinking about Danilo.

'She's leaving you her holding in something called Rojedda, and she's leaving me a diamond pendant and some earrings. She showed them to me . . . they are absolutely beautiful and I told her they were far too much, but she made me try them on so she would see how I looked. She seemed to be so pleased . . . so happy . . . isn't she incredible? I can hardly bear . . . oh . . . oh dear . . .'

'Don't cry, darling,' I said.

There were some swallowing noises.

'I . . . can't . . . help it. She is already much worse than when we saw her before, and she's very uncomfortable. One of her swollen glands is pressing on things in her chest.'

'We'll go and see her as soon as I get back.'

'Yes.' She sniffed away the tears. 'God, I do miss you.'

'Me too,' I said. 'Only one more week. I'll be home a week today, and we'll take the kids down to Cornwall.'

After the call I went outside and walked slowly past our *rondavels* and out on to the rough grassy area beyond. The African night was very quiet. No roar of traffic from any distant city, just the faint steady hum of the generator supplying Skukuza with electricity, and the energetic music of cicadas.

Nerissa had given me my answers.

I saw what they meant, and I didn't want to believe it.

A gamble. No more, no less.

With my life as the stake.

I went back to the telephone and made one more call. Van Huren's manservant said he would see, and Quentin came on the line. I said I knew it was an odd thing to ask, and I would explain why when next I saw him, but could he possibly tell me what size Nerissa's holding in Rojedda was likely to be.

'The same as my own,' he said without hesitation. 'She has my brother's holding, passed to her by Portia.'

I thanked him numbly.

'See you at the premiere,' he said. 'We are looking forward to it very much.'

For hours, I couldn't go to sleep. Yet where could I be safer than inside a guarded camp, with Evan and Conrad snoring their heads off in the huts next door?

But when I woke up, I was no longer in bed.

I was in the car I had hired in Johannesburg.

The car was surrounded by early daylight in the Kruger National Park. Trees, scrub, and dry grass. Not a *rondavel* in sight.

Remnants of an ether smell blurred my senses, but one fact was sharp and self-evident.

One of my arms lay through the steering wheel, and my wrists were locked together in a pair of handcuffs.

CHAPTER FOURTEEN

This had to be some ghastly practical joke. Evan, being malicious.

This had to be Clifford Wenkins thinking up some frightful publicity stunt.

This had to be anything but real.

But I knew, deep down in some deathly cold core, that this time there was no girl called Jill coming to set me free.

This time the dying was there to be done. Staring me in the face. Straining already across my shoulders and down my arms.

Danilo was playing for his gold mine.

I felt sick and ill. Whatever anaesthetic had been used on me had been given crudely. Probably far too much for the purpose. Not that that was likely to worry anyone but me.

For an age I could think no further. The dizziness kept coming back in clammy pea-green waves. My physical wretchedness blocked any other thought; took up all my attention. Bouts of semi-consciousness brought me each time to a fresh awakening, to renewed awareness of my plight, to malaise and misery.

The first objective observation which pierced the fog was that I had gone to bed wearing shorts, and now had clothes on. The trousers I had worn the day before, and the shirt. Also, upon investigation, socks and slip-on shoes.

The next discovery, which had been knocking at the door of consciousness for some time but had been shut out as unwelcome, was that the car's seat belts were fastened. Across my chest and over my lap, just as in the Special.

They weren't tightly fastened, but I couldn't reach the clip.

I tried. The first of many tries at many things. The first of many frustrations.

I tried to slide my hands out of the handcuffs: but, as before, they were the regulation British police model, designed precisely not to let people slide their hands out. My bones, as before, were too big.

I tried with all my strength to break the steering wheel, but although this one looked flimsy compared with the one in the Special, I still couldn't do it.

I could move a shade more than in the film. The straps were not so tight and there was more room round my legs. Apart from that, there was little in it.

For the first of many times I wondered how long it would be before anyone set out to look for me.

Evan and Conrad, when they found me missing, would surely start a search. Haagner, surely, would alert every ranger in the park. Someone would come along very soon. Of course they would. And set me free.

The day began to warm up, the sun in a cloudless sky

shining brightly through the window on my right. The car was therefore facing north . . . and I groaned at the thought, because in the Southern Hemisphere the sun shone at midday from the north, and I should have its heat and light full in the face.

Perhaps someone would come before midday.

Perhaps.

The worst of the sickness passed in an hour or two, though the tides of unease ebbed and flowed for much longer. Gradually however I began to think again, and to lose the feeling that even if death were already perched on my elbow I was too bilious to care.

Clear thought number one was that Danilo had locked me in this car so that I should die and he would inherit Nerissa's half share in the van Huren gold mine.

Nerissa was leaving her Rojedda holding to me in her will, and Danilo, having read the will, knew.

Danilo was to inherit the residue. Should I die before Nerissa, the Rojedda bequest would be void, and the holding would become part of his residue. Should I live, he stood to lose not only a share of the mine, but hundreds of thousands of pounds besides.

As the law stood then, and would still stand when Nerissa died, estate duty on everything she possessed would be paid out of the residue. Danilo personally stood to lose every penny of the estate duty paid on the inheritance which Nerissa was leaving to me.

If only, I thought uselessly, she had told me what she was doing: I could have explained why she shouldn't.

Perhaps she hadn't realized how immensely valuable the Rojedda holding was: she had only recently received it from her sister. Perhaps she hadn't understood how estate duty worked. Certainly, in view of the enjoyment she had found in her long-lost nephew, she had not intended me to prosper out of all proportion at Danilo's expense.

Any accountant would have told her, but wills were usually drawn up by solicitors, not accountants, and solicitors didn't give financial advice.

Danilo, with his mathematical mind, had read the will and seen the barbs in it, as I would have done. Danilo must have begun plotting my death from that very moment.

He had only had to tell me what she had written. But how could he know that? If he himself in reversed positions would have stuck two fingers up in my face, perhaps he thought that I, that anyone, would do that too.

Nerissa, I thought. Dear, dear Nerissa. Meaning good to everyone, and happily leaving them presents, and landing me in consequence in the most unholy bloody mess.

Danilo the gambler. Danilo the bright lad who knew that Hodgkin's disease was fatal. Danilo the little schemer who started by lowering the value of a string of racehorses to pay less estate duty on them, and who, when he found that the real stakes were much higher, had the nerve to move at once into the senior league.

I remembered his fascination down the mine, his questions about quantities at lunch, and his tennis game with Sally. He was after the whole works, not just half. Inherit one half and marry the other. No matter that she was only fifteen: in two more years it would be a highly suitable alliance.

Danilo . . .

I tugged uselessly, in sudden shaking fury, at the obstinate steering wheel. Such cruelty was impossible. How could he . . . how could anyone . . . lock a man in a car and leave him to die of heat and thirst and exhaustion? It only happened in films . . . in one film . . . in *Man in a Car*.

Don't get out of the car, Haagner had said. It is not safe to get out of the car. And a right bloody laugh that was. If I could get out of this car I would take my chance with the lions.

All that screaming and shouting I had done in the film. I remembered it coldly. The agony of spirit I had imagined and acted. The disintegration of a soul, a process I had dissected into a series of pictures to be presented one by one until the progression led inexorably to the empty shell of a man too far gone to recover his mind, even if his body were saved.

The man in the Special had been a fictional character. The man had been shown as reacting to every situation throughout the story with impulsive emotion, which was why his weeping fits *in extremis* had been valid. But I was not like the man: in many respects, diametrically opposite. I saw the present problem in mainly practical terms, and intended to go on doing so.

Someone, sometime, would find me. I would just have

to try, in any way I could, to be alive – and sane – when they did so.

The sun rose high and the car grew hot; but this was only a secondary discomfort.

My bladder was full to bursting.

I could stretch my hands round the wheel to reach and undo the fly zip fastener, which I did. But I couldn't move far on the seat and even if I managed to open the door with my elbow, there would be no chance of clearing the car. Although there was no sense in it, I postponed the inevitable moment until continence was nearer a pain than a nuisance. But reluctance had its limits. When in the end I had to let go, a lot went as far as the floor, but a lot of it didn't, and I could feel the wetness soaking into my trousers from crutch to knee.

Sitting in a puddle made me extremely angry. Quite unreasonably, forcing me to mess myself seemed a more callous act than putting me in the car in the first place. In the film, we had glossed over this problem as being secondary to the mental state. We had been wrong. It was part of it.

The net result on me was to make me more resolved than ever not to be defeated. It made me mean and revengeful.

It made me hate Danilo.

*

The morning wore on. The heat became a trial and I got tired of sitting still. I had however, I told myself, spent three weeks in Spain in precisely this position. There, in fact, it had been much hotter. I wilfully ignored the thought that in Spain we had knocked off for lunch.

Lunchtime was pretty near, by my watch. Well . . . maybe someone would come . . .

And how would they get there, I wondered. Ahead of me there was no road, just small trees, dry grass and scrubby undergrowth. To each side, just the same. But the car must have been driven there, not dropped by passing eagle . . . Twisting my neck, and consulting the reflection in the mirror, I saw that the road, such as it was, lay directly at my back. It was an earth road showing no sign of upkeep and all too many of desertion, and it petered out completely twenty yards or so from where I sat. My car had been driven straight off the end of it into the bush.

In less than a month it would rain: the trees and the grass would grow thick and green, and the road turn to mud. No one would find the car, if it were still there when the rains came.

If I . . . were still there when the rains came.

I shook myself. That way led straight towards the mental state of the Man in the film, and of course I had decided to steer clear of it.

Of course.

Perhaps they would send a helicopter . . .

It was a grey car; nondescript. But surely any car would show up, from the air. There was a small aerodrome near

Skukuza, I'd seen it marked on the map. Surely Evan would send a helicopter . . .

But where to? I was facing north, off the end of an abandoned track. I could be anywhere.

Maybe if I did after all make a noise, someone would hear . . . All those people driving along miles away in their safe little cars with the engines droning and the windows securely shut.

The car's horn . . . Useless. It was one of those cars which had to have the ignition on before the horn would sound.

In the ignition . . . no keys.

Lunchtime came and went. I could have done with a nice cold beer.

A heavy swishing in the bush behind me sent my head twisting hopefully in its direction. Someone had come . . . Well, hadn't I known they would?

No human voices, though, exclaimed over me, bringing freedom. My visitor, in fact, had no voice at all, as he was a giraffe.

The great fawn sky-scraper with paler patches rolled rhythmically past the car and began pulling at the sparse leaves scattering the top of the tree straight ahead. He was so close that his bulk shut out the sun, giving me a welcome oasis of shade. Huge and graceful, he stayed for a while, munching peacefully and pausing now and then to bend his great horned head towards the car, peering at it from eyes fringed by outrageously long lashes. The most seductive lady would be reduced to despair by a giraffe's eyelashes.

I found myself talking to him aloud. 'Just buzz off over to Skukuza, will you, and get our friend Haagner to come here in his Range Rover at the bloody double.'

The sound of my voice startled me, because in it I heard my own conviction. I might hope that Evan or Conrad or Haagner or the merest passing stranger would soon find me, but I didn't believe it. Unconsciously, because of the film, I was already geared to a long wait.

But what I did believe was that in the end someone would come. The peasant would ride by on his donkey, and see the car, and rescue the man. That was the only tolerable ending. The one I had to cling to, and work for.

For in the end, people would search.

If I didn't turn up at the premiere, there would be questions and checks, and finally a search.

The premiere was next Wednesday.

Today, I supposed, was Friday.

People could live only six or seven days without water.

I stared sombrely at the giraffe. He batted the fantastic eyelashes, shook his head gently as if in sorrow, and ambled elegantly away.

By Wednesday night I would have spent six whole days without water. No one would find me as soon as the Thursday.

Friday or Saturday, perhaps, if they were clever.

*

It couldn't be done.

It had to be.

When the giraffe took away with him his patch of shade I realized how fierce the sun had grown. If I did nothing about it, I thought, I would have me a nasty case of sunburn.

The parts of me most relentlessly in the sun were oddly enough my hands. As in most hot-country cars, the top third of the windscreen was tinted green against glare, and if I rolled my head back I could get my face out of the direct rays; but they fell unimpeded on to my lap. I solved the worst of that by unbuttoning my shirt cuffs and tucking my hands in the opposite sleeves, like a muff.

After that I debated the wisdom of taking my shoes and socks off, and of opening a window to let in some fresh and cooler air. I could get my feet, one at a time, up to my hands to get my socks off. I could also swivel enough in my seat to wind the left-hand window handle with my toes.

It wasn't the thought of invasion by animals that stopped me doing it at once, but the niggling subject of humidity.

The only water available to me for the whole of the time I sat there would be what was contained at that moment in my own body. With every movement and every breath I was depleting the stock, releasing water into the air about me in the form of invisible water vapour. If I kept the windows shut, the water vapour would mostly stay inside the car. If I opened them, it would instantly be lost.

The outside air, after all those rainless months, was as dry as Prohibition. It seemed to me that though I couldn't stop my body losing a lot of moisture, I could to some extent re-use it. It would take longer, in damper air, for my skin to crack in dehydration. Re-breathing water vapour would go some small way to postponing the time when the mucous linings of nose and throat would dry raw.

So what with one thing and another, I didn't open the window.

Like a man with an obsession I turned back again and again to the hope-despair see-saw of rescue, one minute convinced that Evan and Conrad would have sent out sorties the moment they found me gone, the next that they would simply have cursed my rudeness and set off by themselves towards the north, where Evan would become so engrossed with *olifant* that E. Lincoln would fade from his mind like yesterday's news.

No one else would miss me. Everyone back in Johannesburg – the van Hurens, Roderick, Clifford Wenkins – knew I had gone down to the game reserve for the rest of the week. None of them would expect to hear from me. None of them would expect me back before Tuesday.

The only hope I had lay in Evan and Conrad . . . and the peasant passing by with his donkey.

*

At some point during the long afternoon I thought of seeing if I still had in my trouser pockets the things I had had there the day before. I hadn't emptied the pockets when I undressed, I had just laid my clothes on the second bed.

Investigation showed that my wallet was still buttoned into my rear pocket, because I could feel its shape if I pushed back against the seat. But money, in these circumstances, was useless.

By twisting, lifting myself an inch off the seat, and tugging, I managed to get my right-hand pocket round to centre front, and, carefully exploring, brought forth a total prize of a packet of Iguana Rock book matches, with four matches left, a blue rubber band, and a three-inch stub of pencil with no point.

I put all these carefully back where they came from, and reversed the tugging until I could reach into the left-hand pocket.

Two things only in there. A handkerchief . . . and the forgotten screwed-up plastic bag from Evan's sandwiches.

'Don't throw plastic bags out of car windows,' Haagner had said. 'They can kill the animals.'

And save the lives of men.

Precious, precious plastic bag.

Never cross a desert without one.

I knew how to get half a cup of water every twenty-four hours from a sheet of plastic in a hot climate, but it couldn't be done by someone strapped into a sitting position inside a car. It needed a hole dug in the ground, a small weight, and something to catch the water in.

All the same, the principle was there, if I could make it work.

Condensation.

The hole in the ground method worked during the night. In the heat of the day one dug a hole, making it about eighteen inches deep, and in diameter slightly smaller than the available piece of plastic. One placed a cup in the hole, in the centre. One spread the sheet of plastic over the hole, and sealed it down round the edges with the dug out earth or sand. And finally one placed a small stone or some coins on the centre of the plastic, weighing it down at a spot directly over the cup.

After that, one waited.

Cooled by the night, the water vapour in the hot air trapped in the hole condensed into visible water droplets, which formed on the cold unporous plastic, trickled downhill to the weighted point, and dripped from there into the cup.

A plastic bagful of hot air should produce a teaspoonful of water by dawn.

*

It wasn't much.

After a while I pulled one hand towards me as far as it would go, and leaned forward hard against the seat belt, and found I could reach far enough to blow into the bag if I held its gathered neck loosely with an O of forefinger and thumb.

For probably half an hour I breathed in through my nose, and out through my mouth, into the plastic bag. At the end of that time there were hundreds of small water droplets sticking to the inside of the bag . . . the water vapour out of my lungs, trapped there instead of escaping into the air.

I turned the bag inside out and licked it. It was wet. When I'd sucked off as much as I could, I laid the cool damp surface against my face, and perhaps because of the paltriness of what I had achieved, felt the first deep stab of desolation.

I fished out the blue rubber band again, and while the sunlit air was still hot, filled the bag with it, twisting the neck tight and fastening it with the band to one side of the steering wheel. It hung there like a fool's balloon, bobbing lightly away if I touched it.

I had been thirsty all day, but not unbearably.

After dark some hovering internal rumbles identified themselvcs as hunger. Again, not unbearably.

The bladder problem reappeared and was again a disaster. But time, I supposed, would lessen the difficulty: no input, less output.

Hope had to be filed under 'Pending', after dark. Twelve hours to be lived before one could climb on to the will-they-won't-they treadmill again. I found them long, lonely, and dreadful.

The cramps which I had so imaginatively constructed for the film began to afflict my own body in earnest, once the heat of the day drained away and let my muscles grow stiff.

At first I warmed up by another dozen wrenching attempts to break the steering wheel off the control column, the net result of which was considerable wear and tear on me, and none on the car. After that I tried to plan a sensible series of isometric exercises which would keep everything warm and working, but I only got about half of them done.

Against all the odds, I went to sleep.

The nightmare was still there when I woke up.

I was shivering with cold, creakingly stiff, and perceptibly hungrier.

I had nothing to eat but four matches, a handkerchief, and a blunt pencil.

After a small amount of thought I dug out the pencil,

and chewed that. Not exactly for the food value, but to bare the lead. With that pencil, I decided, I could bring Danilo down.

Before dawn the realization crept slowly in that Danilo could not have abandoned me in the car without help. He would have needed someone to drive him away when he had finished locking me in. He wouldn't have walked through the game reserve, not only because of the danger from animals, but because a man on foot would have been as conspicuous as gallantry.

So someone had helped him.

Who?

Arknold . . .

He had shut his eyes to Danilo's fraud, when he had discovered it: had kept silent, because by not arranging better security he had put his licence at risk. But would he step deep into murder to save himself a suspension?

No. He wouldn't.

Barty, for money?

I didn't know.

*

One . . . any . . . of the van Hurens, for any reason at all?

No.

Roderick, for news? Or Katya, or Melanie?

No.

Clifford Wenkins, for publicity?

If it was him, I was safe, because he wouldn't leave me there much longer. He wouldn't dare. Worldic, for a start, wouldn't want the merchandise turning up in a damaged state. I wished I believed it was Wenkins, but I didn't.

Evan? Conrad?

I couldn't face it.

They had both been there. On the spot. Sleeping next door. Handy for breaking in in the night and smothering me with ether.

One of them could have done it while the other slept. But which? And why?

If it were either Evan or Conrad I was going to die, because only they could save me.

*

The dawn came up on this bleakest of thoughts and showed me that my theories on water vapour were correct. I could see nothing of the Kruger National Park, because all the windows were fogged and beaded with condensation.

I could reach the glass beside me, and I licked it. It felt great. The dryness of my tongue and throat became instantly less aggravating, though I could still have done with a pint of draught.

I looked through the licked patch. Same old wilderness. Same old no one there.

My spoonful of water had formed all right inside the now cold plastic bag. Carefully I loosened its neck in the rubber band and squeezed the shrunken air out, to prevent it expanding again when the day grew hot, and reabsorbing the precious liquid. I wouldn't drink it until later, I decided. Until things got worse.

With all the precious humidity clinging to the inside of the windows, it was safe to embark on a change of air. I took off my sock and turned the handle with my toes, and opened the left-hand window a scant inch. Couldn't risk not being able to shut it again: but when the sun came up I got it shut without much trouble. When the growing heat cleared the windows by re-evaporating the water, at least I had such comfort as there was in knowing it was all still inside the car, doing its best.

*

The pencil I had chewed in the night (and stowed for safe storage under my watch strap) was showing signs of usefulness. One more session with the incisors, and it had enough bare lead at the tip to write with.

The only thing to write on that I had in my pockets was the inside of the book of matches, which was room enough for 'Danilo did it', but not for my whole purpose. There were maps and car documents, however, in the glove compartment in front of the passenger seat, and after a long struggle, tying my toes in knots and using up a great deal too much precious energy, I collected into my hands a large brown envelope, and a book of maps with nice blank end papers.

There was a lot to write.

CHAPTER FIFTEEN

Danilo had suggested to Nerissa that I go to South Africa because there, far from home, he could take or make any opportunity that offered to bring me to an accidental looking death. He had lured me to the killing ground with a bait he knew I would take – a near-dying request from a woman I liked and was grateful to.

A death which was clearly a murder would have left him too dangerously exposed as a suspect. An obvious accident would be less suspiciously investigated . . . like a live microphone.

Danilo hadn't been there, in Randfontein House.

Roderick had been there, and Clifford Wenkins, and Conrad. And fifty others besides. If Danilo had provided the live mike, someone at the press interview must have steered it into my hands. Luck alone had taken it out again.

Down the mine, at the suddenly opportune moment . . . bash.

Except for the steadfastness of a checker called Nyembezi, that attempt would have come off.

This wouldn't look like a natural accident, though. The handcuffs couldn't be called accidental.

Perhaps Danilo intended to come back, after I was dead, and take them away. Perhaps people would believe then that I had lost my way in the park and had died in the car rather than risk walking.

But the time span was tight. He couldn't wait a week to make sure I was dead before coming back, because by then everyone would be searching for me, and someone might have reached me before he did.

I sighed dispiritedly.

None of it made any sense.

The day proved an inferno compared with the one before. Much worse even than Spain. The scorching fury of the heat stunned me to the point where thought became impossible, and cramps wracked my shoulders, arms and stomach.

I tucked my hands into my sleeves and rolled my head back out of the direct rays and just sat there enduring it, because there was nothing else to do.

So much for my pathetic little attempts at water management. The brutal sun was shrivelling me minute by minute, and I knew that a week was wildly optimistic. In this heat, a day or two would be enough.

My throat burned with thirst and saliva was a thing of the past.

A gallon of water in the car's radiator . . . as out of reach as a mirage.

When I couldn't swallow without wincing or breathe without feeling the intaken air cut like a knife, I untied the plastic bag and poured the contents into my mouth. I made the divine H_2O last as long as possible; rolled it round my teeth and gums, and under my tongue. There was hardly enough left to swallow, and when it was gone I felt wretched. There was nothing, now, between me and nightfall.

I turned the bag inside out and sucked it, and held it against my mouth until the heat had dried it entirely, and then I filled it again with hot air, and with trembling fingers fumbled it back into the rubber band on the steering wheel.

I remembered that the boot of the car still held, as far as I knew, a lot of oddments of Conrad's equipment. Surely he would need it, would come looking for that, if not for me.

Evan, I thought, for God's sake come and find me.

But Evan had gone north in the park which stretched two hundred miles to the boundary on the great grey green greasy Limpopo river. Evan was searching there for his Elephant's Child.

And I . . . I was sitting in a car, dying for a gold mine I didn't want.

*

Night came, and hunger.

People paid to be starved in health farms, and people went on hunger strikes to protest about this or that, so what was so special about hunger?

Nothing. It was just a pain.

The night was cool, was blessed. In the morning, when I had licked as much of the window as I could reach, I went on with the writing. I wrote every thing I could think of which would help an investigation into my death.

The heat started up before I had finished. I wrote 'give my love to Charlie', and signed my name, because I wasn't certain that by that evening I would be able to write any more. Then I slid the written papers under my left thigh so that they wouldn't slip out of reach on the floor, and tucked the little pencil under my watch strap, and collapsed the air out of the plastic bag to keep the next teaspoonful safe, and wondered how long, how long I would last.

By midday I didn't want to last.

I held out until then for my sip of water, but when it was gone I would have been happy to die. After the bag had dried against my face it took a very long time, and a great effort of will, for me to balloon it out and fix it again to the steering wheel. Tomorrow, I thought, the thimbleful would form again, but I would be past drinking it.

We had been wrong in the film, I thought. We had focused on the mental state of the Man too much, to the neglect of the physical. We hadn't known about legs like lead and ankles swollen to giant puffballs. I had long ago shed my socks, and would have had as much chance of forcing my shoes on again as of flying.

We hadn't known the abdomen would become agonizingly distended with gas, or that the seat belts would strain across it like hawsers. We hadn't guessed that the eyes would feel like sand paper when the lachrymal glands dried up. We had underestimated what dehydration did to the throat.

The overwhelming heat battered all emotions into numbness. There was nothing anywhere but pain, and no prospect that it would stop.

Except, of course, in death.

In the late afternoon an elephant came and uprooted the tree the giraffe had browsed from.

That should be allegorical enough for Evan, I thought confusedly. Elephants were the indestructible destroyers of the wilderness.

But Evan was miles away.

Evan, I thought, Evan . . . Oh God, Evan . . . come . . . and find me.

The elephant ate a few succulent leaves off the tree and went away and left it with its roots in the air, dying for lack of water.

Before dark I did write a few more sentences. My hands trembled continually, and folded into tight cramps, and were in the end too weak to hold the pencil.

It fell down on the floor and rolled beneath my seat I couldn't see it, or pick it up with my swollen toes.

Weeping would have been a waste of water.

Night came again and time began to blur.

I couldn't remember how long I had been there, or how long it was until Wednesday.

Wednesday was as far away as Charlie, and I wouldn't see either of them. I had a vision of the pool in the garden with the kids splashing in it, and it was the car that seemed unreal, not the pool.

Tremors shook my limbs for hours on end.

The night was cold. Muscles stiffened. Teeth chattered. Stomach shrieked to be fed.

In the morning, the condensation on the windows was so heavy that water trickled in rivulets down the glass. I could only, as ever, reach the small area near my head. I licked it weakly. It wasn't enough.

I hadn't the energy any more to open the window for a change of air: but cars were never entirely airtight, and it wouldn't be asphyxiation which saw me off.

The inevitable sun came back in an innocent rosy dawn, gentle prelude to the terrifying day ahead.

I no longer believed that anyone would come.

All that remained was to suffer into unconsciousness, because after that there would be peace. Even delirium would be a sort of peace, because the worst torment was to be aware, to understand. I would welcome a clouded mind, when it came. That, for me, would be the real death. The only one that mattered. I wouldn't know or care when my heart finally stopped.

Heat bullied into the car like a battering ram.

I burned.

I burned.

CHAPTER SIXTEEN

They did come.

When the sun was high, Evan and Conrad came in the station wagon. Evan stampeding about in a frenzy of energy, waving his arms about, with his hair sticking out crazily and his eyes too hot for comfort. Conrad, puffing slightly under the droopy moustache, mopping his forehead with a handkerchief.

They simply walked up to the car and opened the door. Then they stood still. And stared.

I thought they were unreal; the onset of delusion. I stared back, waiting for them to vanish.

Then Evan said, 'Where the hell have you been? We've been searching the whole bloody park for you since yesterday morning.'

I didn't answer him. I couldn't.

Conrad was saying, 'My God, my God, dear boy, my God . . .' as if the needle had stuck.

Evan went back to the station wagon, drove it across the grass, and parked it alongside the car I was in. Then he scrambled into the back and unclipped the red ice box.

'Will beer do?' he shouted. 'We didn't bring any water.'

Beer would do.

He poured it from a can into a plastic cup and held it to my mouth. It was cold; alive; incredible. I only drank half, because it hurt to swallow.

Conrad opened the left-hand door and sat on the seat beside me.

'We haven't a key for the handcuffs,' he said apologetically.

A laugh twitched somewhere inside me, the first for a long time.

'Phew,' Evan said, 'You do stink.'

They saw I couldn't talk. Evan poured more beer into the cup and held it for me, and Conrad got out of the car and rummaged about in the boot. He came back with four short lengths of strong wire and a roll of insulating tape, and with these he proceeded to set me free.

He stuck the four wires into the barrel of the handcuff lock, bound the protruding ends tightly together to give a handle for leverage, and began to turn. The makeshift key did a grand job. With a lot of swearing and a couple of fresh starts when the wires slipped out, Conrad got the ratchet on my right wrist opened.

And who cared about the other? It could wait.

They unclipped the seat belts and tried to help me out of the car, but I had been sitting in the same restricted position for over eighty hours, and like concrete my body seemed to have set in the mould.

Evan said doubtfully, 'I think one of us should go and find a doctor.'

I shook my head decidedly. There were things I wanted to tell them before the outside world broke in. I felt jerkily under my thigh for the papers I had written, and made writing motions with my hands. Conrad silently produced the gold ballpoint he always carried, and I shakily wrote on an unused corner of brown envelope, '*If you do not tell anyone you have found me, we can catch the man who put me here.*' And as an afterthought, I added, '*I want to do that.*'

They read the uneven words and stood wondering, almost literally scratching their heads.

I wrote a bit more. '*Please put something over the windscreen.*'

That at least made sense to them. Conrad draped the front of the car with a heavy groundsheet which effectively brought the temperature down by ten degrees.

Evan saw the plastic bag hanging from the steering wheel and pulled it off its rubber band.

'What the hell is this?' he said.

I pointed to the still undrunk mouthful of water lurking in one corner. Evan understood, and looked completely appalled.

He took the written pages out of my hand, and read them. I drank some more beer, holding the cup with trembly fingers but feeling life flowing back through all the dying channels with every difficult swallow.

He read right to the end and handed the pages to

Conrad. He stared at me with stunned speechlessness. An unaccustomed state for Evan. After a long time he said slowly, 'Did you really think Conrad or I had helped to leave you here?'

I shook my head.

'And you can cross off poor old Clifford Wenkins, too, because he's dead. They fished him out of the Wemmer Pan on Saturday afternoon. He went boating, and drowned.'

The news took a while to percolate. I thought, no more stuttering, no more damp palms, no more nervous little man . . . poor little nervous man . . .

I lifted Conrad's golden pen, and Evan gave me one of his ubiquitous notebooks to write on.

'*I'd like to lie down. In the station wagon?*'

'Sure,' he said, seeming to be glad of an excuse for activity. 'We'll make you a bed.'

He hopped into the estate car again and hauled all their equipment to one side. In the cleared space he constructed a mattress from the back seats of both cars, and made a thick pillow out of coats and sweaters.

'The Ritz,' he said, 'is at your service.'

I tried a smile and caught sight of it in the driving mirror.

Ghastly. I had a four day beard and sunken pinkish eyes and looked as grey and red as a sunburned ghost.

With more gentleness than I would have thought either of them had in their natures, they helped me out of the car and carried more than supported me over to the station wagon. Bent double, creaking in every muscle, and feeling that my lumbar vertebrae were breaking, I completed the journey, and once lying on the makeshift bed began the luxuriously painful process of straightening myself out. Evan took the groundsheet off my car and spread it over the roof of the station wagon, as much to shut out the heat as for shade.

I wrote again. '*Stay here, Evan*,' because I thought they might start my car with a jump lead, and drive off for help. He looked doubtful, so I added with a fair amount of desperation, '*Please don't leave me.*'

'Christ,' he said, when he read that. 'Christ, mate, we won't leave you.' He was clearly emotionally upset, which surprised me. He didn't even like me, and in the Special had heaped on the discomfort without mercy.

I drank some more beer, mouthful by separate mouthful. My throat still beat a raging case of tonsillitis out of sight, but the lubrication was slowly taking effect. I could move my tongue better, and it was beginning to feel less like a swollen lump of liver.

Evan and Conrad sat in the front seats of the estate car and began discussing where to go. They had no accommodation reserved at Skukuza, which it appeared was still the nearest camp, and it was two hours drive to the beds booked at Satara.

Satara and the beds won, which seemed good enough for me.

Evan said, 'We might as well get going, then. It's too bloody hot here. I've had enough of it. We'll find a patch of decent shade along the road, and stop for lunch. It's after two, already, and I'm hungry.'

That was a lot more like the Evan I knew and detested. With an inward smile I had another go with the pen.

'*Remember how to get back here.*'

'Someone else can fetch the car,' said Evan impatiently. 'Later.'

I shook my head. '*We must come back.*'

'Why?'

'*To catch Danilo Cavesey.*'

They looked from the pad to my face. Then Evan merely said, 'How?'

I wrote down how. They read it. The air of excited intensity reawoke in Evan, and rapid professional calculations furrowed Conrad's forehead, for what I was asking them to do was much to their liking. Then a separate, secondary thought struck both of them, and they looked at me doubtfully.

'You can't mean it, dear boy,' Conrad said.

I nodded.

'What about the person who helped him?' Evan asked. 'What are you going to do about him?'

'*He's dead, now.*'

'Dead?' He looked incredulous. 'You don't mean . . . Clifford Wenkins?'

I nodded. I was tired. I wrote '*Tell you when I can talk.*'

They agreed to that. They shut the doors of my car, climbed into the front seats of the station wagon, turned it, and set off along the dirt road which had for so long for me been just a reflection in a three-by-six inch looking glass.

Conrad drove, and Evan made a map. They seemed to have found me by the merest chance, as I had been a mile up a side branch of an equally unkempt road leading to a now dry water hole. The water hole road joined into another, which led finally back to the roads used by visitors. Evan said he could find the way straight back to my car: it was easy. They had searched, he added, every side road they could find between Skukuza and Numbi, and that had been yesterday. Today, they had tried the dry sparse land to the south of the Sabie river, and they had found me on the fifth no-entry they had explored.

After five or six miles we came to a small group of trees throwing some dappled shade: Conrad at once pulled in and stopped the car, and Evan without more ado started burrowing into the red box. They had brought more sandwiches, more fruit, more beer.

I thought I would postpone sandwiches and fruit. Beer was doing wonders. I drank some more.

The other two munched away as if the whole picnic were routine. They opened the windows wide, reckoning that any sensible animal would be sleeping in this heat, not looking out for unwary humans.

No cars passed. Every sensible human, too, was busy at siesta in the air-conditioned camps. Evan, of course, was impervious to heat, and Conrad had to lump it.

I wrote again, '*What made you start looking for me?*'

Evan spoke round bits of ham sandwich. 'We kept wanting the things of Conrad's which were in your car. It became most annoying not to have them. So yesterday morning we telephoned the Iguana to tell you how selfish you had been to take them away with you.'

'They said you weren't there,' Conrad said. 'They said they understood you were going to the Kruger Park for several days.'

'We couldn't understand it,' Evan nodded. 'In view of your note.'

'What note?' I tried automatically to say the words, but my throat still wouldn't have it. I wrote them instead.

'The note you left,' Evan said impatiently. 'Saying you had gone back to Johannesburg.'

'*I left no note.*'

He stopped chewing and sat with his mouth full as if in suspended animation. Then he took up chewing again, and said, 'No. That's right. You couldn't have.'

'We thought you had, anyway,' Conrad said. 'It was just a piece of paper, written in capital letters, saying, "*Gone back to Johannesburg. Link.*" Bloody rude and ungrateful, dear boy, we thought it. Packing all your gear and buzzing off at the crack of dawn without even bothering to say goodbye.'

'*Sorry.*'

Conrad laughed. 'After that we tried to reach Clifford Wenkins, because we thought he might know where you were, but all we got at his number was some hysterical woman saying he'd been drowned in the Wemmer Pan.'

'We tried one or two other people,' Evan went on. 'The van Hurens, and so on.'

'*Danilo?*' I wrote.

'No.' Evan shook his head. 'Didn't think of him. Wouldn't know where he's staying, for a start.' He ate a mouthful, reflecting. 'We thought it a bit unhelpful of you to go off without letting anyone know where you could be found, and then we thought perhaps you'd been damn bloody careless and got lost in the park, and never got back to Johannesburg at all. So after a bit of argy-bargy we persuaded the reception office at Satara to check what time you went out of the Numbi gate on Friday morning, and the gate keeper said that according to their records you hadn't gone out at all.'

'We telephoned Haagner, dear boy,' Conrad said, 'and explained the situation, but he didn't seem to be much worried. He said people often talked their way out of Numbi without papers, even though one was supposed to produce receipts to show one had paid for staying in camps. Mr Lincoln would only have to say, Haagner said, that Evan and Conrad were still in the park, and had paid for him. The Numbi men would check with Skukuza, and then let Mr Lincoln go. He also said you couldn't be lost in the park. You were too sensible, he said, and only fools got lost. People who drove miles down no-entry roads and then had their cars break down.'

And that, I presumed, was what they thought had happened. But I wouldn't grumble.

They opened cans of beer and gulped. I went on sipping.

'We had sure enough paid for you at Skukuza,' Evan said accusingly. 'Including the window you broke.'

I only had to pick up the pen.

'My God,' Evan said, before I got it to the paper. 'Danilo Cavesey broke the window . . . to get into your *rondavel*.'

I supposed so. He had got past the locked door without waking me.

'You're a fairly valuable property, dear boy,' Conrad said, finishing the saga. 'So we decided we ought perhaps to spend a day or so looking for you.'

'We saw a splendid herd of elephants yesterday afternoon,' said Evan, pointing out that the delay to their original plans had not been an entire waste. 'And we might see some more today,' he said.

They helped me into the *rondavel* in Satara and I asked them to turn the air-conditioning off, as to me the hut felt cold. If I got cold again I would get stiff again, which would only add to my aches . . . I lay on one of the beds with three blankets over me and felt lousy,

Conrad fetched a glass of water and he and Evan stood around looking helpless.

Evan said, 'Let's take your stinking clothes off. You'd embarrass a pig, as you are.' I shook my head.

'If we bring you some water, would you like to wash?' No, again.

Evan wrinkled his nose. 'Well, you won't mind if neither of us sleeps in here with you?'

I shook my head. My smell was offensive to myself as well, now that I'd breathed so much clean fresh air.

Conrad went off to the camp shop to find something I could swallow and presently came back with a pint of milk and a tin of chicken soup. The only opener they had was the beer can opener, but they got the soup out into a jug in the end. There was nothing to heat the soup with, so they tipped in half the milk and stirred it around until it was runny. Then they poured out a glassful, and, grateful for their clumsy care, I drank it bit by bit.

'Now,' said Evan briskly, satisfied that they had done the best possible for me, 'let's get on with planning the trap.'

This time, when I tried, some semblance of speech came out.

'Danilo is staying at the Vaal Majestic,' I said.

'What did you say?' Evan demanded. 'Thank God you can talk again, but I couldn't understand a word of it.'

I wrote it down.

'Oh. Right.'

I said, 'Telephone in the morning, and tell him . . .' It was a croak, rough and cracked.

'Look,' Evan interrupted. 'We'll get along quicker if you write it.'

I nodded. Much easier on my throat, if he preferred it that way.

'At breakfast time, tell Danilo you are trying to find out where I am, because I have Conrad's equipment in my car. Tell him I also have Conrad's gold pencil in my pocket, and he especially wants it back. Tell him I also have one of your notebooks, and you need your notes. Tell him you are worried because I had some theory that someone I knew had been trying to kill me.'

Evan read, and looked dubious. 'Are you sure that will bring him?'

I wrote: '*Would you risk my being able to write down that theory, if you knew I had pencil and paper within reach?*'

He considered. He said, 'No. I wouldn't.'

'*I did do it.*'

'So you did.'

Conrad sat heavily down in the armchair, nodding.

'What next, dear boy?'

I wrote: '*This evening, telephone Quentin van Huren. Tell him where and in what state you found me. Say I wrote some notes. Read them to him. Tell him about the trap for Danilo. Ask him to tell the police. With his authority, he can arrange it properly.*'

'Sure. Sure.' Evan with undaunted wiry energy collected up my writings from the car and his notebook with all our plans, and strode off at once to the telephone in the main buildings.

Conrad stayed behind and lit a cigar, no doubt to fend off evil odours.

'It was Evan who insisted on looking for you, dear

boy,' he said. 'Absolutely fanatical, he was. You know how he never lets up when he gets an idea. We went up every unlikely track . . . bloody silly, I thought . . . until we found you.'

'Who,' I said slowly, trying to speak clearly, 'told Danilo about the film . . . *Man in the Car*?'

He shrugged a little uncomfortably. 'Maybe I did. At Germiston. They were all asking about your latest work . . . the van Hurens, Clifford Wenkins, Danilo . . . everybody.'

It didn't matter. Wenkins could have got hold of the film's plot easily enough, through Worldic.

'Dear boy,' Conrad said thoughtfully. 'The make-up is all wrong in the film.' He puffed the cigar. 'Mind you,' he said, 'what you actually look like would be pretty poor box-office.'

'Thanks.'

He smiled. 'Have some more soup?'

Evan was gone a long time and came back looking earnest and intense.

'He wants me to ring back later. He was pretty incoherent when I'd finished.' Evan raised his eyebrows, surprised that anyone should need time to assimilate so many unwelcome facts. 'He said he would think over what ought to be done. And oh yes, he said to ask you why you now thought it was Clifford Wenkins who helped Danilo.'

I said, 'Clifford Wenkins would have helped . . .'

'Write it down,' said Evan impatiendy. 'You sound like a crow with laryngitis.'

I wrote: '*Clifford Wenkins would do anything for*

publicity stunts. He would exchange recording gear and microphones, for instance. I do not believe he thought anyone would be killed, but if I got an electric shock at a press conference, it would put my name and the purpose of my visit in the papers. I believe Danilo put it all into his head, and gave him the live equipment. Wenkins was terrified when Katya was so badly shocked, and afterwards I saw him telephoning, looking very worried. I thought he was calling Worldic, but he might have been telling Danilo that the stunt had gone wrong.'

'It went better, dear boy, from Worldic's point of view,' Conrad commented.

'*Worldic drove Clifford Wenkins unmercifully to arrange publicity stunts . . . so if Danilo suggested to him that they should kidnap me and lock me in a car, just like in my new film, he would have been foolish enough to agree.*

'*When I'd been in the car for three days, I did not think it could be Wenkins who'd been helping Danilo because I knew Wenkins would not leave me there very long. But once Wenkins was dead, no one but Danilo knew where I was. He had only to leave me there . . .*

'*After my body was discovered, people would work out that it had been a publicity stunt planned by Wenkins and myself, which went wrong because he drowned and could not set in motion the necessary search.*

'*I expect it was in Wenkins's car that he and Danilo drove into the park, so that the Numbi gate office would have it on record that he had been there.*'

Evan practically tore the notebook out of my hands, as

he had been striding around with impatience while I wrote. He read to the end and handed the notebook to Conrad.

'Do you realize,' he demanded, 'that you are practically accusing Danilo of killing Clifford Wenkins, so that you shouldn't be found?'

I nodded.

'I think he did,' I croaked. 'For a gold mine.'

They left me with water and soup to hand and went off to dinner in the restaurant. When they came back, Evan had telephoned again to van Huren.

'He'd grasped everything a bit better,' Evan allowed condescendingly. 'I read him what you wrote about Wenkins, and he said he thought you could be right. He said he was upset about Danilo, because he had liked him, but he would do as you asked. He said that he himself would come down here . . . he's flying down to the Skukuza airstrip first thing in the morning. The police will be properly genned up. Conrad and I will meet them and van Huren at Skukuza, and go on from there, if it looks likely that Danilo has taken the bait.'

We were going to call Danilo in the morning. Even if he, too, flew down as fast as possible, everyone should be in position before he came.

The night was paradise compared with its predecessors, but still far short of heaven. In the morning I felt a good deal stronger; there were no more cramps and the fire in my throat would no longer frighten Celsius. I got myself to the bathroom looking as bent as old Adam the gardener, but I got there; and I ate the banana which Conrad brought me for breakfast.

Evan had gone to telephone Danilo, Conrad said, and Evan came later with a satisfied smile.

'He was there,' he said. 'And I'd say there was no doubt he swallowed it. He sounded pretty worried . . . sharp voice, that sort of thing. He asked why I was so sure about the gold pencil. Can you believe it? I said Conrad had lent it to you Thursday evening and I'd seen you put it in your pocket. Then, Friday morning, you went off to Johannesburg without giving it back.'

CHAPTER SEVENTEEN

The hardest thing I ever did was to get back into that car.

We reached it at half past ten, and Evan and Conrad busily rigged up various bits and pieces, including a warning buzzer which would tell me when Danilo was approaching.

Half an hour later, when they had finished, the day was stoking up to another roaster. I drank the whole of the bottle of water we had brought from Satara and ate another banana.

Evan danced up and down. 'Come on. Come on. We haven't got all day. We've got to hurry to Skukuza to meet van Huren.'

I left the station wagon, hobbled across to the car, sat in the front seat, and fastened the seat belts.

The dying aches flared up at once.

Conrad approached with the handcuffs, and my throat closed. I couldn't look at him, couldn't look at Evan . . . at anything. Couldn't do it . . . all my nerves and muscles revolted.

Couldn't.

Conrad, watching me, said practically, 'You haven't got to, Link. It's your own idea, dear boy. He will come, whether you are here or not.'

'Don't try and dissuade him,' Evan said crossly. 'Not now we've gone to all this trouble. And as Link pointed out himself, if he isn't in the car when Danilo comes, nothing will be conclusive.'

Conrad still hesitated. My fault.

'Get on with it,' Evan said.

I put my arm through the steering wheel. It was trembling. Conrad clicked the handcuffs shut first on one wrist and then the other, and I shuddered from head to foot.

'Dear boy . . .' Conrad said doubtfully.

'Come on,' Evan urged.

I didn't say anything. I thought that whatever I might start to say, it would come out as a screaming plea that they wouldn't leave me. Leave me, however, they must.

Evan shut the car door brusquely, and jerked his head for Conrad to follow him into the estate car. Conrad went with his head turned backwards, looking to see if I were calling him.

They climbed into the front seat, reversed, turned, drove away. The silence of the tinder-dry park settled around me.

I wished I had never suggested this plan. The car seemed hotter than ever, the heat more intolerable. Within an hour, and in spite of the quantities of water I had drunk that morning, fierce thirst returned.

Cramps began again in my legs. My spine protested. My shoulders pulled with strain.

I cursed myself.

Supposing he took all day, I thought. Supposing he didn't fly down, but drove. Eight o'clock, when Evan telephoned him. At least five hours' drive to Numbi, another hour and a half to reach me . . . He might not come until three or four . . . which meant five hours in the car . . .

I tucked my hands into my shirt sleeves and rolled my head back out of the sun.

There was no water vapour, no plastic bag, to keep my mind occupied. The pencil-written sheets lay on my knees, with Conrad's gold pencil, companion to his pen, clipping them together. There was no leaping from hope to despair and back again, which was certainly a blessed relief, but unexpectedly left too much time free for pure feeling.

Every minute dragged.

The premiere, I thought, was due to be held the following night. I wondered who would be arranging everything, with poor Clifford Wenkins in his watery grave. I wondered if I would get to the Klipspringer Heights Hotel on time. In another twenty-four hours, shaved, bathed, rested, watered and fed, perhaps I might just make it. All those people paying twenty rand for a seat . . . unfair not to turn up, if I could . . .

*

Time crawled. I looked at my watch. It wasn't trying.

One o'clock came. One o'clock went.

Conrad had fixed a radio transmitter with a button for me to press if I simply could not stand any more. But if I pressed it, the whole of today's effort would be wasted. If I pressed it, the cohorts would rush to my rescue, but Danilo would see the activity, and would never come near.

I wished Conrad hadn't insisted on that button. Evan said it was necessary, so that he and van Huren and the police would know for certain that Danilo had come, if they should by some mischance miss him on the road.

One buzz was to mean that Danilo had come.

Two buzzes that he had left again.

A series of short buzzes would bring them instantly at any time to set me free.

I would wait another ten minutes before I gave up, I thought.

Then another ten.

Then another.

Ten minutes was always possible. Conrad's warning buzzer sounded like a wasp in my ear and jerked me into action.

Danilo drove up beside me and stopped where the station wagon had been.

I pressed the buttons taped within reach on the steering column.

I put all the actor's art I had into looking not far from death: and didn't have to elaborate all that much on what I knew of the real thing. A couple of vultures had conveniently flapped and spiralled down, and now perched on a nearby tree like brooding anarchists awaiting the revolution. I eyed them sourly, but Danilo was reassured.

He opened the door and through slit eyes I saw him draw back when the unmitigated heat-stoked stench met his nostrils. It had been worth not washing, not changing my clothes. There was nothing about me to show I hadn't sat in that spot continuously since he had left me there, and a great deal to prove I had.

He looked at my lolling head, my flaccid hands, my bare swollen feet. He showed no remorse whatever. The sun blazed on the bright blond head, giving him a halo. The clean-featured all-American boy, as shiny, cold and ruthless as ice.

He bent down and practically snatched the papers off my lap. Unclipped the pencil and threw it on the back seat of the car. Read what I had written, right to the end.

'So you did guess . . . you did write . . .' he said. 'Clever Ed Lincoln, too clever by half. Too bad no one will ever read this . . .' He peered down into my half shut eyes to make sure I could hear him, could see him. Then he took out a cigarette lighter, flicked the flint, and set the corners of the papers into the flame.

I shook feebly in my seat, in mute protest. It pleased him.

He smiled.

He turned the papers, burning them all up, and then ground the ashes into just more dust in the dusty grass.

'There,' he said cheerfully.

I made a small croak. He paid attention.

I said, 'Let . . . me . . . go.'

'Not a chance.' He put his hand in his pocket and brought out a bunch of keys. 'Keys to the car.' He held them up, jingling. 'Key to the handcuffs.' He waved it in front of my eyes.

'Please . . .' I said.

'You're worth too much to me dead, pal. Sorry and all that. But there it is.'

He put the keys in his pocket, shut the door on me, and without another glance, drove heartlessly away.

Poor Nerissa, I thought. I hoped she would die before she found out about Danilo; but life was not always kind.

In time, four cars rolled back into the reflection in the driving mirror, and stopped in a cluster round my car. Evan and Conrad's estate wagon. A chauffeur-driven car with van Huren. Two police cars; the first containing, I later discovered, their photographer and their surgeon;

the second, three senior police officers . . . and Danilo Cavesey.

They all stood up outside the cars; a meal and a half for any passing pride of lion. Wild animals, however, kept decently out of sight. Danilo outdid them all for savagery.

Conrad bustled over and pulled open the door.

'You all right, dear boy?' he said anxiously.

I nodded.

Danilo was saying loudly and virtuously, 'I told you, I'd just found him, and I was driving away to get help.'

'Oh yeah,' Conrad muttered, digging out his bits of wire.

'He has the key of the handcuffs in his pocket,' I said.

'You don't mean it, dear boy?' He saw I did mean it. He went over and told the police, and after a short scuffle they found the key. Also the car keys. And now, perhaps Mr Cavesey would explain why he was driving away, when he had in his pocket the means of freeing Mr Lincoln?

Mr Cavesey glowered and declined. He had been going for help, he said.

Evan, enjoying himself immensely, walked over to the tree the elephant had uprooted, and from its withering foliage disentangled the Arriflex on its tripod.

'Everything you did here, we filmed,' he told Danilo. 'Link had a cable to the car. He started the camera when you arrived.'

Conrad fished his best tape-recorder out from under the car and unhitched the sensitive microphone from just inside the door frame.

'Everything you said here,' he echoed, with equal satisfaction, 'we recorded. Link switched on the recorder, when you came.'

The police produced a pair of handcuffs of their own, and put them on Danilo, who had gone blue-white under the suntan.

Quentin van Huren walked over to the car and looked down at me. Conrad had forgotten the small detail of bringing back the key to free me. I still sat, locked and helpless, where I had begun.

'For God's sake . . .' van Huren looked appalled.

I smiled lop-sidedly and shook my head. 'For gold's sake,' I said.

His mouth moved, but no words came out.

Gold, greed and gilded boys . . . a thoroughly bad mixture.

Evan was strutting around looking important, intense, and satisfied, as if he had stage-managed and directed the entire performance. But he saw that I was still tethered, and for once some twitch of compassion reached him. He went to fetch the handcuffs' key and brought it over.

He stood beside van Huren for a second, staring down at me as if seeing something new. For the first time ever he smiled with a hint of friendship.

'Cut,' he said. 'No re-takes, today.'

PRAISE FOR DAVID BALDACCI AND HIS NOVELS

LAST MAN STANDING

'Baldacci grabs you by the balls and squeezes steadily until you don't know whether to scream out in pain or pass out with pleasure'
Punch

'Baldacci's most accomplished thriller. The action . . . is nonstop and expertly drawn'
Publishers Weekly

WISH YOU WELL

'Reveals his talent as a storyteller of the highest merit'
Punch

'Abounds with affection for the state he makes his home'
USA Today

'Succeeds as a departure for Baldacci . . . a tender . . . inspirational story . . . some wonderfully lyric prose'
Denver Post

ABSOLUTE POWER

'A brilliant thriller'
Guardian

'Accomplished and amazing – one of the hottest reads around'
Daily Mail

'Baldacci's prose is fluent and racy . . . This book is sure to make a killing'
The Times

'First rate . . . Baldacci cuts everyone's grass – Grisham's, Ludlum's, even Patricia Cornwell's – and more than gets away with it'
People

THE WINNER

'Yet another winner . . . The excitement builds . . . The plot's many planted bombs explode unpredictably'
New York Times

THE SIMPLE TRUTH

'A plot strong enough to make the bath go cold around you'
Independent on Sunday

SAVING FAITH

'An adrenaline-pumping plot that could, once again, make you late for work'
Heat

TOTAL CONTROL

'Wonderfully tricky. His genius is to keep readers guessing, and reading while he's tossing out twists like confetti . . . David Baldacci is a superb storyteller, and even better writer . . . he compels you to read, and read, and read. You won't argue'
Literary Review Service

saving faith

David Baldacci is the internationally acclaimed author of more than 20 bestselling novels. With his books published in at least 45 languages, and with over 90 million copies in print, he is one of the world's favourite storytellers. His family foundation, the Wish You Well Foundation, a non-profit organization, works to eliminate illiteracy across America. Still a resident of his native Virginia, he invites you to visit him at www.DavidBaldacci.com, and his foundation at www.WishYouWellFoundation.org, and to look into its programme to spread books across America at www.FeedingBodyandMind.com.

Also by David Baldacci

The Camel Club series

The Camel Club
The Collectors
Stone Cold
Divine Justice
Hell's Corner

Sean King and Michelle Maxwell series

Split Second
Hour Game
Simple Genius
First Family
The Sixth Man

Shaw series

The Whole Truth
Deliver Us From Evil

Other novels

True Blue
Absolute Power
Total Control
The Winner
The Simple Truth
Wish You Well
Last Man Standing
The Christmas Train

DAVID BALDACCI

saving faith

PAN BOOKS

First published 1999 by Warner Books, USA

First published in Great Britain 1999 by Simon & Schuster UK Ltd

This edition published 2003 by Pan Books
an imprint of Pan Macmillan, a division of Macmillan Publishers Limited
Pan Macmillan, 20 New Wharf Road, London N1 9RR
Basingstoke and Oxford
Associated companies throughout the world
www.panmacmillan.com

ISBN 978-0-330-51849-9

1 3 5 7 9 8 6 4 2

A CIP catalogue record for this book is available from
the British Library.

Printed and bound in the UK by CPI Mackays, Chatham ME5 8TD

To Aaron Priest,
my friend

ONE

The somber group of men sat in a large room that rested far belowground, accessed by only a single, high-speed elevator. The chamber had been secretly built during the early 1960s under the guise of renovating the private building that squatted over it. The original plan, of course, was to use this "super-bunker" as a refuge during a nuclear attack. This facility was not for the top leaders of American government, it was for those whose level of relative "unimportance" dictated that they probably wouldn't be able to get out in time but who still rated protection afforded no ordinary citizen. Politically, even in the context of total destruction, there must be order.

The bunker was built at a time when people believed it possible to survive a direct nuclear hit by burrowing into the earth inside a steel cocoon. After the holocaust that would annihilate the rest of the country, leaders would emerge from the rubble with absolutely nothing left to lead, unless you counted vapor.

The original, aboveground building had been leveled long ago, but the subterranean room remained under what was now a small strip mall that had been vacant for years. Forgotten by virtually all, the chamber was now used as a meeting place for certain people in the country's primary intelligence-gathering agency. There was some risk involved, since the meetings were not related to the men's official duties. The matters discussed at these gatherings were illegal, and tonight even murderous. Thus additional precautions had been necessary.

The super-thick steel walls had been supplemented by a copper coating. That measure, along with tons of dirt overhead, protected against prying electronic ears lurking in space and elsewhere. These men didn't particularly like coming to this underground room. It was inconvenient, and ironically, it seemed a little too James Bondish even for their admittedly cloak-and-dagger tastes. However, the truth was the earth was now encircled with so much advanced surveillance technology that virtually no conversation taking place on its surface was safe from interception. One had to dig into the dirt to escape his enemies, and if there was a place where people could meet with reasonable confidence that their conversations would not be overheard even in their world of ultrasophisticated peekaboo, this was it.

The gray-headed people present at the meeting were all white males, and most were nearing their agency's mandatory retirement age of sixty. Dressed quietly and professionally, they could have been doctors, lawyers or investment bankers. One would probably not remember any of the group a day after seeing them. This anonymity was their stock-in-trade. These sorts of people lived and died, sometimes violently, over such details.

Collectively, this cabal possessed thousands of secrets that could never be known by the general public because the public would certainly condemn rather than applaud the actions giving rise to these secrets. However, America often demanded results – economic, political, social and otherwise – that could be obtained only by smashing certain parts of the world to a bloody pulp. It was the job of these men to figure out how to do so in a clandestine manner that would not reflect poorly on the United States, yet would still keep the country safe from the pesky, international terrorists and other foreigners unhappy with these global developments.

The purpose of tonight's gathering was to plot the killing of Faith Lockhart. Technically, the CIA was prohibited by presidential executive order from engaging in assassination. However, these men, though employed by the Agency, were not representing the CIA tonight. This was their private agenda, and there was little disagreement that the woman had to die, and soon; it was critical for the well-being of the country. These men knew this, even if American presidents did not. However, because of another life that was involved, the meeting had become acrimonious, the group resembling a cadre of posturing members fighting on Capitol Hill over billion-dollar slices of pork.

"What you're saying, then," one of the white-haired men said as he poked the smoke-filled air with a slender finger, "is that along with Lockhart we have to kill a federal agent." This man shook his head incredulously. "Why kill one of our own? It can only lead to disaster."

The gentleman at the head of the table nodded thoughtfully. Robert Thornhill was the CIA's most distinguished Cold War soldier, a man whose status at the Agency was unique. His reputation was unassailable, his compilation of professional victories unmatched. As associate deputy director of Operations, he was the Agency's ultimate free safety. The DDO, or deputy director of operations, was responsible for running the field operations that undertook the secret collection of foreign intelligence. The operations directorate of the CIA was also unofficially known as the "spy shop," and the deputy director was still not even publicly identified. It was the perfect place to get meaningful work done.

Thornhill had organized this select group, who were as upset as he about the state of affairs at the CIA. It was he who had remembered that this bloated underground time capsule existed. And it was Thornhill who had found the money to secretly bring the chamber back to working condition and upgrade its facilities. There were thousands of little taxpayer-funded toys like that sprinkled around the country, many of them gone to complete waste. Thornhill joked to himself, *Well, if governments didn't waste their citizens' hard-earned money, then what would be left for governments to do?*

Even now, as he ran his hand over the stainless steel console with its quaint built-in ashtrays, sniffed the filtered air and felt the protective coolness of the earth all around, Thornhill's mind wandered back for a moment to the Cold War period. At least there was a measure of certainty with the hammer and sickle. In truth, Thornhill would take the lumbering Russian bull over the agile sand snake that you never knew was out there until it flung its venom into you. There were many who wanted nothing more in life than to topple the United States. It was his job to ensure that never happened.

Gazing around the table, Thornhill gauged each man's devotion to his country and was satisfied. He had wanted to serve America for as long as he could remember. His father had been with the OSS, the World War II-era predecessor to the CIA. He had known little of what his father did at the time, but the man had instilled in his son the philosophy that there was no greater thing to do with one's life than to serve one's country. Thornhill had joined the Agency right out of Yale. Right up until the day he died, his father had been proud of his son. But no prouder than the son had been of the old man.

Thornhill's hair was a shining silver, which lent him a distinguished air. His eyes were gray and active, the angle of his chin blunt. His voice was deep, cultured; technical jargon and the poetry of Longfellow flowed from his mouth with equal ease. The man still wore three-piece suits and favored pipe smoking over cigarettes. The fifty-eight-year-old Thornhill could have quietly finished out his time at the CIA and led the pleasant life of a former public servant, well traveled, erudite. He had no thought of going out quietly, and the reason was very clear.

For the last ten years, the CIA's responsibilities and budgets had been decimated. It was a disastrous development, for the firestorms that were popping up across the world now often involved fanatical minds accountable to no political body and possessing the capability to obtain weapons of mass destruction. And while just about everyone thought high-tech was the answer for all the ills of the world, the best satellites in the world couldn't stroll down alleys in Baghdad, Seoul or Belgrade and take the emotional temperature of the people there. Computers in space could never capture what people were thinking, what devilish thoughts were lurking in their hearts. Thornhill would always choose a smart field operative willing to risk his or her life over the best hardware money could buy.

Thornhill had just such a small group of skilled operatives within the CIA, completely loyal to him and his private agenda. They had all worked hard to regain for the Agency its former prominence. Now Thornhill finally had the vehicle to do that. He would very soon have under his thumb powerful congressmen, senators, even the vice president himself, and enough high-ranking bureaucrats to choke an independent counsel. Thornhill would see his budgets revive, his manpower skyrocket, his agency's scope of responsibility in the world return to its rightful place.

The strategy had worked for J. Edgar Hoover and the FBI. It was no coincidence, Thornhill believed, that the Bureau's budget and influence had flourished under the late director and his allegedly "secret" files on powerful politicians. If there was one organization in the world that Robert Thornhill hated with all his soul, it was the FBI. But he would use whatever tactics he could to bring his agency back to the forefront, even if it meant stealing a page from his most bitter foe. *Well, watch me do you one better, Ed.*

Thornhill focused again on the men clustered around him. "Not having to kill one of our own would, of course, be ideal," he said. "However, the fact is, the FBI have her under 'round-the-clock stealth security. The only time she's truly vulnerable is when she goes to the cottage. They may place her in Witness Protection without warning, so we have to hit them at the cottage."

Another man spoke up. "Okay, we kill Lockhart, but let the FBI agent live, for God's sake, Bob."

Thornhill shook his head. "The risk is too great. I know that killing a fellow agent is deplorable. But to shirk our duty now would be a catastrophic mistake. You know what we've invested in this operation. We cannot fail."

"Dammit, Bob," the first man to protest said, "do you know what will happen if the FBI learns we took out one of their people?"

"If we can't keep a secret like that, we have no business doing what we do," Thornhill snapped. "This is not the first time lives have been sacrificed."

Another member of the group leaned forward in his chair. He was the youngest of them. He had, however, earned the respect of the group with his intelligence and his ability to exercise extreme, focused ruthlessness.

"We've only really looked at the scenario of killing Lockhart to forestall the FBI's investigation into Buchanan. Why not appeal to the FBI director and have him order his team to give up the investigation? Then no one has to die."

Thornhill gave his younger colleague a disappointed look. "And how would you propose going about explaining to the FBI director why we wish him to do so?"

"How about some semblance of the truth?" the younger man said. "Even in the intelligence business there's sometimes room for that, isn't there?"

Thornhill smiled warmly. "So I should say to the FBI director – who, by the way, would love to see us all permanently interred in a museum – that we wish him to call off his potentially blockbuster investigation so that the CIA can use illegal means to trump his agency. Brilliant. Why didn't I think of that? And where would you like to serve *your* prison term?"

"For chrissakes, Bob, we *work* with the FBI now. This isn't 1960 anymore. Don't forget about CTC."

CTC stood for the Counter Terrorism Center, a cooperative effort between the CIA and the FBI to fight terrorism by sharing intelligence and resources. It had been generally deemed a success by those involved. To Thornhill, it was simply another way for the FBI to stick its greedy fingers into his business.

"I happen to be involved in CTC in a modest way," Thornhill said. "I find it an ideal perch on which to keep tabs on the Bureau and what they're up to, which is usually no good, as far as we're concerned."

"Come on, we're all on the same team, Bob."

Thornhill's eyes focused on the younger man in such a way that everyone in the room froze. "I request that you never say those words in my presence again," Thornhill said.

The man paled and sat back in his chair.

Thornhill clenched his pipe between his teeth. "Would you like me to give you concrete examples of the FBI taking the credit, the glory for work done by our agency? For the blood spilled by our field agents? For the countless times we've saved the world from annihilation? How they manipulate investigations in order to crush everyone else, to beef up their already bloated budget? Would you like me to give you instances in my thirty-six-year career where the FBI did all it could to discredit our mission, our people? Would you?" The man slowly shook his head as Thornhill's gaze bored into him. "I don't give a damn if the FBI director himself came down here and kissed my shoes and swore his undying allegiance to me – I will not be swayed. Ever! Have I made my position clear?"

"I understand." As he said this, the younger man managed not to shake his head in bewilderment. Everyone in this room other than Robert Thornhill knew that the FBI and CIA actually got along well. Though they could be ham-handed at times in joint investigations because they had more resources than anyone else, the FBI was not on a witch hunt to bring down the Agency. But the men in this room also understood quite clearly that Robert Thornhill believed the FBI was their worst enemy. And they also knew that Thornhill had, decades ago, orchestrated a number of Agency-authorized assassinations with cunning and zeal. Why cross such a man?

Another colleague said, "But if we kill the agent, don't you think the FBI will go on a crusade to find out the truth? They have the resources to scorch the earth. No matter how good we are, we can't match their strength. Then where are we?"

Some grumbling rose from the others. Thornhill looked around warily. The collection of men here represented an uneasy alliance. They were paranoid, inscrutable fellows long used to keeping their own counsel. It had truly been a miracle to forge them together in the first place.

"The FBI *will* do everything they can to solve the murder of one of their agents and the chief witness to one of their most ambitious investigations ever. So what I would propose doing is to give them the solution we desire them to have." They looked curiously at him. He sipped water from his glass and then took a minute to prime his pipe.

"After years of helping Buchanan run his operation, Faith Lockhart's conscience or good sense or paranoia got the better of her. She went to the FBI and has now begun telling them everything she knows. Through a little foresight on my part, we were able to discover this development. Buchanan, however, is completely unaware that his partner has turned against him. He also doesn't know that we intend to kill her. Only we know." Thornhill inwardly congratulated himself for this last remark. It felt good, omniscience; it was the business he was in, after all.

"The FBI, however, may suspect that he does know about her betrayal or may find out at some point. Thus, to the outside observer, no one in the world has greater motivation to kill Faith Lockhart than Danny Buchanan."

"And your point?" the questioner persisted.

"My point," said Thornhill tersely, "is quite

simple. Instead of allowing Buchanan to disappear, we tip off the FBI that he and his clients discovered Lockhart's duplicity and had her and the agent murdered."

"But once they get hold of Buchanan, he'll tell them everything," the man quickly responded.

Thornhill looked at him as a disappointed teacher to pupil. Over the last year, Buchanan had given them everything they needed; he was now officially expendable.

The truth slowly dawned on the group. "So we tip the FBI about Buchanan *posthumously*. Three deaths. Correction, three murders," another man said.

Thornhill looked around the room, silently gauging the reaction of the others to this exchange, to his plan. Despite their protestations about killing an FBI agent he knew that three deaths meant nothing to these men. They were from the old school, which quite clearly understood that sacrifices of that nature were sometimes necessary. Certainly what they did for a living sometimes cost people their lives; however, their operations had also avoided open war. Kill three to save three million, who could possibly argue with that? Even if the victims were relatively innocent. Every soldier who ever died in battle was innocent too. Covert action, quaintly referred to as the "third option" in intelligence circles, the one between diplomacy and open war, was where the CIA could really prove its worth, Thornhill believed. Although it was also at the heart of some of the Agency's worst disasters. Well, without risk there was never the possibility for glory. That epitaph could be put on his tombstone.

No formal vote was taken by Thornhill; none was needed.

"Thank you, gentlemen," Thornhill said. "I'll take care of everything." He adjourned the meeting.

TWO

The small, wood-shingled cottage stood alone at the end of a short, hard-packed gravel road, its dirt shoulders laced with the tangled sprawl of dandelion, curly dock and chickweed. The ramshackle structure rested on an acre of cleared flat land, but was surrounded on three sides by woods where each tree struggled to find sunlight at the expense of its neighbor. Because of wetlands and other development problems, the eighty-year-old home had never had any neighbors. The nearest community was about three miles away by car, but less than half that distance if one had the backbone to challenge the dense woods.

For much of the last twenty years the rustic cottage had been used for impromptu teen parties, and on occasion by the wandering homeless looking for the comfort and relative safety of four walls and a roof, however porous. The cottage's discouraged current owner, who had recently inherited the beast, had finally opted to rent it out. He had found a willing tenant who had paid the full year's rent in advance, in cash.

Tonight the calf-high grass in the front yard was pushed low and then straightened in the face of a strengthening wind. Behind the house a line of thick oaks seemed to mimic the movements of the grass as they swayed back and forth. It hardly seemed possible, yet except for the wind, there were no other sounds.

Save one.

In the woods, several hundred yards directly behind the house, a pair of feet splashed through a shallow creek bed. The man's dirty trousers and soaked boots attested to the difficulty with which he had navigated the congested terrain in the dark, even with the aid of a three-quarters-full moon. He paused to scrape his muddy boots against the trunk of a fallen tree.

Lee Adams was both sweaty and chilled after the punishing trek. At forty-one years of age, his six-foot-two body was exceptionally strong. He worked out regularly, and his biceps and delts showed it. Keeping in reasonably good shape was a necessity in his line of work. While he was often required to sit in a car for days on end, or in a library or courthouse reviewing microfiche records, he also, on occasion, had to climb trees, subdue men even larger than he was or, like now, slog through gully-filled woods in the dead of night. A little extra muscle never hurt. However, he wasn't twenty anymore either, and his body was letting him know it.

Lee had thick, wavy brown hair that seemed perpetually in his face, a quick, infectious smile, pronounced cheekbones and an engaging set of blue eyes that had caused female hearts spontaneously to flutter from fifth grade onward. He had suffered enough broken bones during his career, though, and other assorted injuries, that his body felt far older than it looked. And that's what hit him every morning when he rose. The creaks, the little pains. Cancerous tumor or merely arthritis? he sometimes wondered. What the hell did it really matter? When God punched your ticket, He did so with authority. A good diet and messing around with weights or pitter-pattering on the treadmill wasn't going to change the Man's decision to pull your string.

Lee looked up ahead. He couldn't see the cottage just yet; the forest clutter was too thick. He fussed with the controls of the camera he had pulled from his knapsack while he took a series of replenishing breaths. Lee had made this same trek several times before but had never gone inside the cottage. He had seen things, though – peculiar things. That's why he was back. It was time to learn the secret of this place.

His wind having returned, Lee trudged on, his only companions the scurrying wildlife. Deer, rabbit, squirrel and even beaver were plentiful in this still-rural part of northern Virginia. As he walked along, Lee listened to the flit of flying creatures. All he could envision were rabid, foaming bats blindly cleaving the air around his head. And it seemed that every few steps he would run straight into a twister of mosquitoes. Though he had been paid a large amount of cash up front, he was seriously considering increasing his daily fee on this one.

When he approached the edge of the woods, Lee stopped. He had a great deal of experience spying on the haunts of people and their activities. Slow and methodical was the best way, like a pilot's checklist. You just had to hope nothing happened to make you improvise.

Lee's bent nose was a permanent badge of honor from his time as an amateur boxer in the Navy, where he had taken out his youthful aggression in a square of roped canvas against an opponent of like weight and ability. A pair of stout gloves, quick hands and nimble feet, cagey mind and a strong heart had constituted his arsenal of weapons. The majority of the time, they had been enough for victory.

After his military stint, things had worked out mostly okay for him. Never rich, never actually poor despite being mostly self-employed over the years, usually free; never quite alone, though he had been divorced for almost fifteen years. The only good thing from that marriage had just turned twenty. His daughter was tall, blond and brainy, as well as the proud bearer of a full academic scholarship to the University of Virginia and a star on the women's soccer team. And for the last ten years, Renee Adams had no interest whatsoever in having anything to do with her old man. A decision that had her mother's full blessing, if not her insistence, Lee well knew. And his ex had seemed so kind on those first few dates, so infatuated with his Navy uniform, so enthusiastic in tearing up his bed.

His ex-wife, a former stripper named Trish Bardoe, had married on the rebound a fellow by the name of Eddie Stipowicz, an unemployed engineer with a drinking problem. Lee thought she was heading for disaster and had tried to get custody of Renee on the grounds that her mom and stepfather could not provide for her. Well, about that time, Eddie, a sneaky runt Lee despised, invented, mostly by accident, some microchip piece of crap that had made him a gazillionaire. Lee's custody battle had lost its juice after that. To add insult to injury, there had been stories on Eddie in the *Wall Street Journal*, *Time*, *Newsweek* and a number of other publications. He was famous. Their house had even been featured in *Architectural Digest*.

Lee had gotten that issue of the *Digest*. Trish's new home was grossly huge, mostly crimson red or eggplant so dark it made Lee think of the inside of a coffin. The windows were cathedral-size, the furniture large enough to become lost in and there were enough wood moldings, paneling and staircases to heat a typical midwestern town for an entire year. There were also stone fountains sculpted with naked people. What a kicker! A photo of the happy couple was included in the spread. In Lee's opinion they might as well have captioned it "The Nerd and the Bombshell strike it rich in poor taste."

One photo had captured Lee's complete attention, however. Renee had been poised on the most magnificent stallion Lee had ever seen, on a field of grass that was so green and perfectly trimmed that it looked like a pond of sea glass. Lee had carefully cut that photo out and put it away in a safe spot – his family album of sorts. The article, of course, made no mention of him; no reason that it should. The one thing that had ticked him off, though, was the reference to Renee as Ed's daughter.

"Stepdaughter," Lee had said out loud when he read that line. "Stepdaughter. That one you can't take away, Trish." Most of the time he felt no envy for the wealth his ex-wife now had, for it meant that his daughter would never want. But it still hurt.

When you had something for all those years, something you had made with a part of yourself, and loved more than it was probably good to love anything, and then lost it – well, Lee tried never to dwell for long on that loss. Big tough guy that he was, when he did let himself think about the massive hole dead center in his chest, he ended up blubbering like a baby.

Life was so funny sometimes. Funny like when you get a clean bill of health one day and drop dead the next.

Lee looked down at his muddy pants and worked a painful cramp out of his weary leg at the same time he swatted a mosquito out of his eye. Hotel-size house. Servants. Fountains. Big horses. Sleek private jet. . . . Probably all a real pain in the ass.

Lee hugged the camera to his chest. It was loaded with 400-speed film that Lee was "turbocharging" by setting the camera's ISO speed to 1600. Fast film required less light, and with the shutter opening for shorter periods of time, there was far less likelihood that camera wobble or vibration would distort any photos. He slipped on a 600mm telephoto lens and flipped down the lens' attached tripod.

Peering between the branches of a wild dogwood, Lee focused on the rear of the cottage. Scattered clouds drifted past the moon and deepened the darkness around him. He took a series of shots and then put the camera away.

As he stared at the house, the problem was he couldn't tell from here if the place was occupied or not. It was true he couldn't see a light on, but the place might have an interior room not visible from here. Added to that, he couldn't see the front of the house, and there might be a car parked there, for all he knew. He had observed the traffic and foot patterns on his other trips here. There hadn't been much to see. Few cars came down this road, and no walkers or joggers did. All the cars he had seen had turned around, obviously having made a wrong turn. All, that is, except one.

He glanced up at the sky. The wind had died down. Lee roughly calculated that the clouds would obscure the moonlight for a few minutes more. He slung the pack across his back, tensed for a moment, as though marshaling all of his energy, and then slid out of the woods.

Lee glided noiselessly until he reached a spot where he could squat behind a copse of overgrown bushes and still observe the front and back of the house. While he watched the house, the shades of darkness grew lighter as the moon reappeared. It seemed to be lazily watching him, curious as to what he was doing here.

Though isolated, the cottage was only a forty-minute drive from downtown D.C. That made it very convenient for any number of things. Lee had made inquiries about the owner and found him to be squeaky clean. The renter, however, had been a little tougher to pin down.

Lee pulled out a device that looked like a cassette recorder but was actually a battery-powered lock-pick gun, along with a zippered case, which he opened. He felt the different lock picks inside, then selected the one he wanted. Using an Allen wrench, he secured the pick into the machine. Lee's fingers moved quickly, confidently, even as another bank of cloud passed over, deepening the darkness once more. Lee had done this so many times that he could have closed his eyes and his fingers would carry on, manipulating his tools of felony with enviable precision.

Lee had already checked out the locks on the cottage with his spotting scope during daylight. That had also disturbed him. Deadbolt locks on all the exterior doors. Sash locks on both the first- *and* second-story windows. All the hardware looked new too. On a falling-down rental in the middle of nowhere.

Despite the cool weather, a bead of nervous sweat surfaced on Lee's forehead as he thought about this. He touched the 9mm in his belt clip holster; the metal was comforting. He took a moment to put the single-action pistol in a cocked-and-locked position – a round in the firing chamber, the hammer cocked and the safety set.

The cottage also had a security system. That had been a real stunner. If he was smart, Lee would pack his tools of criminality and go home, reporting failure to his employer. However, he took pride in his work. He would see it through at least until something happened to make him change his mind. And Lee could run very fast when he needed to.

Getting into the house wouldn't be all that difficult, particularly since Lee had the pass-code. He'd managed to get it the third time he'd been there, when the two people had come to the cottage. He had already confirmed the place was wired, so he had come prepared. He had beat the couple here and waited while they did whatever they were doing inside. When they had come out, the woman had entered the pass-code to arm the system. Lee, hiding in the same copse he was in now, just happened to have a bit of electronic wizardry that snatched that code right out of the air like a fly ball neatly falling into a glove. All electrical current produces a magnetic field, like a little transmitter. When the tall woman had punched in the numbers, the security system had thrown off a discrete signal for each digit, right into Lee's electronic mitt.

Lee checked the cloud cover once more, slapped on a pair of latex gloves with reinforced fingertip and palm pads, readied his flashlight and took another deep breath. A minute later he moved out from the cover of the bushes and made it quietly to the back door. He slipped off his muddy boots and set them next to the door. He didn't want to leave traces of his visit. Good private investigators were invisible. Lee held the light under his arm while he inserted the pick in the door lock and activated the device.

He used the pick gun partly for speed and partly because he didn't crack enough locks to be that proficient at it. A pick and tension tool required constant use to allow the fingers the level of sensitivity required to detect the proximity of the shear line, the subtle descent of the tension tool as the lock's tumblers began to do their little jig. Using a pick and tension tool, an experienced locksmith could pick the lock faster than Lee could with his pick gun. It was a true art and Lee knew his limitations. Soon, he felt the dead bolt sliding back.

When he eased open the door, the silence was broken by the low beeping sound of the security system. He quickly found the control pad, punched in six numbers and the beeping sound immediately stopped. As Lee closed the door softly behind him, he knew he was now a felon.

The man lowered his rifle and the red dot emanating from the weapon's laser scope disappeared from the wide back of an unsuspecting Lee Adams. The man holding the rifle was Leonid Serov, a former KGB officer specializing in assassination. Serov had found himself without gainful employment after the breakup of the Soviet Union. However, his ability to efficiently kill human beings was much in demand in the "civilized" world. Fairly well pampered as a communist for many years, with his own apartment and car, Serov had grown wealthy literally overnight as a capitalist. If he had only known.

Serov didn't know Lee Adams and had no idea why he was here. He had not noticed him until Lee had made his break for the bushes near the house, because Lee had come through the woods on the side farthest from the Russian. The sounds of his presence, Serov correctly surmised, had been covered by the wind.

Serov checked his watch. They would be coming soon. He inspected the elongated suppressor attached to the rifle. He rubbed its long snout gently, like a favorite pet, as though bestowing the notion of infallibility on to the polished metal. The rifle's stock was a special composite of Kevlar, fiberglass and graphite that provided remarkable stability. And the weapon's bore was not rifled in the conventional way. Instead it had a rounded rectangular profile, known as polygonal boring, with a right-hand twist. This type of rifling was supposed to increase muzzle velocity by upward of eight percent, and, more important, a ballistics match on a bullet fired from this gun was virtually impossible because there were no lands or grooves in the barrel that would make distinctive markings on the bullet as it exploded from the weapon. Success really was all in the details. Serov had built his entire career on that one philosophy.

The place was so isolated that Serov had mulled over perhaps removing the suppressor and relying on his skill as a marksman, his high-tech scope and his well-conceived exit plan. His confidence was justified, he believed. Just like the tree falling, when you kill someone in the middle of nowhere, who can hear him die? And he had known some suppressors to greatly distort the flight path of a bullet, with the unacceptable result that no one had died, except for the would-be assassin once his client had learned of the failure. Still, Serov had personally supervised this device's construction and was confident it would perform as designed.

The Russian shifted quietly, working out a cramp in his shoulder. He had been here since nightfall but was used to lengthy vigils. He never tired during these assignments. He took life seriously enough that preparing to extinguish another's kept his adrenaline high. With risk always came invigoration, it seemed. Whether you were mountain climbing or contemplating murder, it ironically made you feel more alive to have the possibility of death so close.

His escape route through the woods would take him to a quiet road where a car would be waiting to whisk him to nearby Dulles Airport. He would go on to other assignments, other places probably far more exotic than this. However, for his particular purpose, this setting had its virtues.

Killing someone in the city was the most difficult. Setting up where you would shoot, pulling the trigger and then escaping, all were vastly complicated by the fact that witnesses and the police were only a few anxious steps away in any direction. Give him the country, the isolation of the rural life, the cover of trees, the separation of homes, and like a tiger in a cattle pen he would kill with numbing efficiency every day of the week.

Serov sat on a stump a few feet from the tree line and only about thirty yards from the house. Despite the thickness of the woods, this spot allowed a clear field of fire: A bullet only needed an inch or so of free space. The man and woman, he had been told, would enter the house from the rear door. Only they would never make it that far. Whatever the laser touched, the bullet would destroy. He was confident he could hit a lightning bug from twice the distance he was confronted with here.

Things were set up so perfectly that Serov's instincts told him to be on high alert. Now he had an excellent reason not to fall into that trap: the man in the house. He was not the police. Law enforcement types didn't slink through the bushes and break into people's homes. Since he had not been made aware beforehand of the man's presence tonight, he concluded that the man was not on his side. However, Serov did not like to deviate from an established plan. He decided that if the man remained in the house after the bodies fell, he would follow through on his original plan and escape through the woods. If the man interfered in any way or came outside after the shots were fired – well, Serov had plenty of ammo, and the result would be three bodies instead of two.

THREE

Daniel Buchanan sat in his darkened office and sipped black coffee of such strength that he could almost feel his pulse rise with each swallow. After another long day of trying to convince legislators that his causes were worthy of their attention, the level of exhaustion was intense, and enormous amounts of caffeine were increasingly becoming the only remedy. A full night of sleep was not typically an option. A catnap here or there, closing his eyes while being driven around to the next meeting, the next flight, occasionally blanking out during an interminably long congressional hearing, even an hour or two in his bed at home – that was his official rest. Otherwise, he was working the Hill in all its near-mystical facets.

Sitting in the chambers of various congressmen, Buchanan would hear the voting buzzer go off and watch the TV every member had in his or her office. The monitor gave them the current bill up for vote, the tally for and against and the time they had left to scurry like ants to the floor and cast their ballot. With about five minutes remaining on a vote, Buchanan would conclude his meeting and hurry down the corridors looking for other members he needed to talk to, the Whip Wind-up Report clutched in his hand. It gave the daily voting schedules, which helped Buchanan determine where certain members might be – critical information when you were tracking dozens of moving targets who probably didn't want to talk to you.

Today Buchanan had managed to grab the ear of an important senator by riding the private underground subway to the Capitol for a floor vote. Buchanan left the man feeling fairly confident of help. He wasn't one of Buchanan's "special" people, but Buchanan was aware that you never knew where help could come from. He didn't care that his clients weren't popular or that they lacked a constituency that would hook a member's attention. He would just keep hammering away. The cause was a virtuous one; the means were therefore susceptible to a lower standard of conduct.

Buchanan's office was sparsely furnished and lacked many of the normal accoutrements of a busy lobbyist. Danny, as he liked to be called, kept no computer, no diskettes, no files, no records of anything of importance here. Paper files could be stolen, computers could be hacked into. Telephone conversations were bugged all the time. Spies were listening with everything from drinking glasses pressed to walls, to the latest gadgets that a year before hadn't even been invented but that could suck up streams of valuable information right out of the air. A typical organization bled confidential information the way a torpedoed ship shed its sailors. And Buchanan had a lot to hide.

For over two decades Buchanan had been the top influence peddler of them all. In some important ways he had laid the groundwork for lobbying in Washington. It had evolved from highly paid lawyers dozing at congressional hearings to a world of numbing complexity where the stakes couldn't possibly be higher. As a Capitol Hill hired gun, he had successfully represented environmental polluters in battles with the EPA, allowing them to spread death to an unsuspecting public; he had been the lead political strategist for pharmaceutical giants who had killed moms and their kids; next a passionate advocate for gun makers who didn't care if their weapons were safe; then a behind-the-scenes player for automobile manufacturers who would rather fight than admit they were wrong on safety issues; and finally, in the mother of all cash cows, he had spearheaded the efforts of tobacco companies in bloody wars with everyone. Back then Washington could not afford to ignore him or his clients. And Buchanan had earned an enormous fortune.

Many of the strategies he had concocted during that time had become staples of current legislative manipulation. He had had congressmen float bills on the House floor he knew would be defeated, in order to rip away platforms for change later. Buchanan's clients hated change. He had constantly fought rearguard actions as those who wanted what his clients had nipped at his heels. How many times had he avoided outright political disaster by flooding members' offices with letters, propaganda, thinly veiled threats to drop financial support. "My client will support you for reelection, Senator, because we know you'll do right by us. And, by the way, the contribution check is already in your campaign account." How many times had he said those words.

Ironically, it was the spoils of lobbying for the powerful that had led to a dramatic change in Buchanan's life over ten years ago. His original plan had been to build his career first and then settle down with a wife and raise a family. Deciding to see the world before he took on the responsibilities of marriage and family, Buchanan had driven through western Africa in a sixty-thousand-dollar Range Rover on a photography safari. In addition to the beautiful animals, he had seen squalor and human suffering of unmatched depth. On another trip, to a remote region of the Sudan, he had witnessed a mass burial of children. An epidemic had swept the village earlier, he was told. It was one of the devastating diseases that routinely afflicted the area, killing off the young and elderly. What was the disease? Buchanan had asked. Something like measles, he was told.

Another trip he had watched as billions of American-produced cigarettes were unloaded on Chinese docks, to be consumed by people who already spent their lives wearing masks because of abysmal air pollution. He was witness to birth-control devices that had been banned in the United States being dumped by the hundreds of thousands in South America with one set of instructions written only in English. He had viewed shacks next to skyscrapers in Mexico City, starvation next to crooked capitalists in Russia. Though he had never been able to go there, North Korea, he knew, was a certified gangster state where it was believed that ten percent of the population had starved to death in the last five years. Every country had its schizophrenic story to tell.

After two years of this "pilgrimage," Buchanan's passion for marriage, having a family of his own, had evaporated. All the dying children he had seen became his children, his family. Fresh graves would still come by the millions for the young, the old, the starving of the world, but not without a fight that had become his. And he brought to it all that he had, more than he had ever given to the tobacco, chemical and gun behemoths. To this day he recalled in precise detail how this revelation of sorts had come: returning from a trip to South America, an airplane lavatory, him on his knees, his stomach sickened. It was as though he had personally murdered every dying child he had seen on that continent.

With eyes freshly opened, Buchanan started marching to these places to see precisely how he could help. He had personally brought a shipment of food and medicine to one country, only to discover there was no way to transport it to the interior regions. He had watched, helpless, as looters stripped his "care" package clean. Then he started working as an unpaid fund-raiser for humanitarian organizations ranging from CARE to Catholic Relief Services. He had done well, but the dollars amounted to a drip into a bottomless bucket. The numbers were not in their favor; the problem was only getting worse.

That's when Buchanan turned to his mastery of Washington. He had left the firm he had founded, taking only one person with him: Faith Lockhart. For the last decade his clients, his wards, were the most impoverished countries in the world. In truth, it was difficult for Buchanan to regard them as geopolitical units; he saw them as fragile clusters of devastated people under various flags who had no voice. He had dedicated the remainder of his life to solving the unsolvable problem of the global have-nots.

He had used all of his immense lobbying skills and contacts in Washington, only to find that these new causes paled in popularity to those he had represented before. When he had gone to Capitol Hill as an advocate of the powerful, the politicians had greeted him with smiles, no doubt with visions of campaign contributions and PAC dollars dancing in their heads. Now they gave him nothing. Some members of Congress bragged that they didn't even have passports, that the United States already spent far too much on foreign aid. Charity starts at home, they had said, and let's damn well keep it there.

But by far the most common retort was, "Where's the constituency, Danny? How does feeding the Ethiopians get me reelected in Illinois?" As he was quickly ushered from office after office, he sensed that they all looked at him with pity: Danny Buchanan, perhaps the greatest lobbyist ever, was now muddled, senile. It was so sad. Sure, it was a good cause and all, who can doubt that, but get real. Africa? Starving babies in Latin America? I've got my own problems right here.

"Look, if it ain't trade, troops or oil, Danny, why the hell are you here wasting my time?" one highly regarded senator had told him. That could be the quintessential statement on America foreign policy.

Could they be that blind? Buchanan had asked himself over and over. Or was he the utter fool?

Finally, Buchanan decided he had only one option. It was completely illegal, but a man pushed to the precipice could not afford allegiance to pristine ethics. Using the fortune he had amassed over the years, he had taken to bribing, in very special ways, certain key politicians for their assistance. It had worked wonderfully. The aid to his clients had grown, in so many different ways. Even as his own wealth was dissipated, things were looking up, Buchanan believed. Or at least things were not getting worse; he would count holding of precious, hard-won ground as a success. It had all worked well, until about a year ago.

As if on cue, the knock on his office door startled him from his reverie. The building was closed, supposedly secure, the cleaning crews long since departed. He didn't get up from his desk. He simply watched as the door swung inward, the silhouette of a tall man framed against the opening. The man's hand reached out and flicked on the light.

Buchanan squinted as the glare of the overheads

hit him. When his eyes adjusted to the brightness, he watched as Robert Thornhill took off his trench coat, smoothed down his jacket and shirt and sat down across from him. The man's movements were graceful, unhurried, as though he had plopped down for a leisurely drink at his country club.

"How did you get in here?" Buchanan asked sharply. "The building is supposed to be secure." For some reason Buchanan could sense that others lurked right outside the door.

"And it is, Danny. It is. For *most* people."

"I don't like you coming here, Thornhill."

"I'm courteous enough to use your given name. I'd appreciate reciprocity on that point. A small thing, to be sure, but at least I'm not demanding that you address me as *Mister* Thornhill. That's the norm between master and servant, isn't it, Danny? You see, I'm not so bad to work for."

The man's smug look was designed, Buchanan knew, to drive him to such distraction that he couldn't think clearly. Instead he leaned back in his chair and settled his hands across his middle.

"To what do I owe the pleasure of your visit, *Bob*?"

"Your meeting with Senator Milstead."

"I could easily have met him in town. I'm not sure why you insisted that I go to Pennsylvania."

"But this way you get one more opportunity to make your pitch for all those starving masses. You see, I do have a heart."

"Does it even make a dent in whatever you call a conscience that you're using the plight of millions of men, women and children who consider it a miracle to see the sun rise, to further your own selfish agenda?"

"I'm not paid to have a conscience. I'm paid to protect the interests of this country. *Your* interests. Besides, if having a conscience were the criteria, there would be no one left in this town. In fact, I applaud your efforts. I have nothing against the poor and helpless. Good for you, Danny!"

"Sorry if I don't buy that."

Thornhill smiled. "Every country in the world has people like me. That is, they do if they're smart. We get the results everybody wants, because most 'everybody' lacks the courage to do it himself."

"So you play God? Interesting line of work."

"God is conceptual. I deal in facts. Speaking of which, you powered your agenda by illegal means; who are you to deny me the same right?"

In truth, Buchanan had no response to this statement. And Thornhill's intractably calm demeanor only reinforced the helplessness he felt.

"Any questions about the meeting with Milstead?" Thornhill asked.

"You have enough on Harvey Milstead to put him away for three lives. What are you really after?"

Thornhill chuckled. "I hope you're not accusing me of having a hidden agenda."

"You can tell me, Bob, we're partners."

"Maybe it's as simple as wanting you to jump when I snap my fingers."

"Fine, but a year from now, if you pop up like this, you may not leave under your own power."

"Threats from a solitary lobbyist to *me*." Thornhill sighed. "But not so solitary. You have an army of one. How is Faith? Doing well?"

"Faith is not a part of this. Faith will never be a part of this."

Thornhill nodded. "You're the only one in the crosshairs. You and your fine group of felonious politicians. America's best and brightest."

Buchanan stared coldly at his antagonist and said nothing.

"Things are coming to a head, Danny. As you said,

the show will be coming to a close soon. I hope you're ready to exit cleanly."

"When I leave, my trail will be so clean, not even your spy satellites will be able to pick it up."

"Confidence is inspiring. Yet so often misplaced."

"Is that all you wanted to tell me? Be prepared to escape? I've been ready to do that since the first minute I met you."

Thornhill stood. "You focus on Senator Milstead. Get us some good, juicy stuff. Get him to talk about the income he'll have when he retires, the nominal tasks he'll have to perform as window dressing. The more specific, the better."

"It heartens me to see you enjoying this so much. Probably a lot more fun than the Bay of Pigs."

"Before my time."

"Well, I'm sure you've made your mark in other ways."

Thornhill bristled for a moment and then his calm returned. "You'd make a fine poker player, Danny. But try to remember that a bluff when one is holding no face cards is still a bluff." Thornhill put on his trench coat. "Don't trouble yourself, I can find my way out."

In the next instant Thornhill was gone. The man appeared and disappeared at will, it seemed. Buchanan leaned back in his chair and let out a quick breath. His hands were trembling and he pressed them hard against the desk until the quivering stopped.

Thornhill had thundered into his life like an exploding torpedo. Buchanan had become, essentially, a lackey, now spying on those he had been bribing for years with his own money, now collecting a wealth of material for this ogre to use as blackmail. And Buchanan was powerless to stop the man.

Ironically, this decline in his material assets and now his work in the service of another had brought Buchanan directly back from whence he had come. He had grown up on the illustrious Philadelphia Main Line. He had lived on one of the most magnificent estates in that area. Stacked fieldstone walls – like thick gray brushstrokes of paint – outlined the grass perimeters of the vast, perfect lawns, on which was situated a sprawling twelve-thousand-square-foot house with broad, covered porches, and a detached quadruple-car garage with an apartment overhead. The house had more bedrooms than a dormitory, and lavish baths with costly tile and the luster of gold on something as commonplace as a faucet.

It was the world of the American blue bloods, where pampered lifestyles and crushing expectations existed side by side. Buchanan had observed this complex universe from an intimate perspective, yet he was not one of its privileged inhabitants. Buchanan's family had been the chauffeurs and maids and gardeners, the handymen, nannies and cooks to these blue bloods. Having survived the Canadian border winters, the Buchanans had migrated south, en masse, to a gentler climate, to less demanding work than that required by ax and spade, boat and hook. Up there they had hunted for food and cut wood for warmth, only to watch helplessly as nature mercilessly culled their ranks in a natural process that had made the survivors stronger, their descendants stronger still. And Danny Buchanan was perhaps the strongest of them all.

Young Danny Buchanan had watered the lawn and cleaned the pool, swept and repainted the tennis court, picked the flowers and vegetables and played, in a properly respectful manner, with the children.

As he had gotten older, Buchanan had huddled with the younger generation of the spoiled rich, deep in the privacy of the complex flower gardens, smoking, drinking and exploring each other sexually. Buchanan had even acted as pallbearer, weeping sincerely as he bore two of the young and the rich who had wasted their privileged lives, mixing too much whisky with a racing sports car, driving too fast for impaired motor skills. When you lived life that fast, often you died fast as well. Right now Buchanan could see his own end rushing headlong at him.

Buchanan had never felt comfortable in either group – the rich or the poor – since then. The rich he would never be a part of, no matter how much his bank account swelled. He had played with the wealthy heirs, but when mealtime came, they went to the formal dining room while he trudged to the kitchen to break his bread with the other servants. The baby blues had attended Harvard, Yale and Princeton; he had worked his way through night school at an institution his betters would openly mock.

Buchanan's own family was now equally foreign to him. He sent his relatives money. They sent it back. When he went to visit, he had found they had nothing to talk about. They neither understood nor cared about what he did. However, they made him feel that there was nothing honest about his life's occupation; he could see that in their tightly drawn faces, their mumbled words. Washington was as foreign as hell itself to all that they believed in. He lied for money, large sums of it. Better he had followed in their tread; honest if simple work. By rising above them, he had fallen far below what they represented: fairness, integrity, character.

The path he had chosen during the last ten years

had only deepened this solitary confinement. He had few friends. Nevertheless, he did have millions of strangers across the world who deeply depended on him for something as basic as survival. Even Buchanan had to admit, it was a bizarre existence.

And now, with the coming of Thornhill, Buchanan's foothold had dropped another rung on the ladder leading to the abyss. Now he could no longer even confide in his one indisputable soul mate, Faith Lockhart. She knew nothing about Thornhill, and she never would know of the man from the CIA; this was all that was keeping her safe. It had cost him his last thread of real human contact.

Danny Buchanan was now truly alone.

He stepped to the window of his office and looked out at majestic monuments known around the world. Some might argue that their beautiful facades were just that: Like the magician's hand, they were designed to guide the eyes away from the truly important business of this city, transacted usually for the benefit of a select few.

Buchanan had learned that effective, long-term power came essentially from the gentle force of rule of the few over the many, for most people were not political beasts. A delicate balance was called for, the few over the many, *gently*, civilly; and Buchanan knew that the most perfect example of it in the history of the world existed right here.

Closing his eyes, he let the darkness envelop him, let new energy spill into his body for the fight tomorrow. It promised to be a very long night, however, for in truth, his life had now become one long tunnel to nowhere. If he could only ensure Thornhill's destruction as well, it would all be worth it. One small crack in the darkness, that would be all Buchanan needed. If only it could be so.

FOUR

The car moved down the highway at precisely the speed limit. The man was driving, the woman next to him. Both sat rigidly, as though one feared a sudden attack from the other.

As a jet, landing gear down, roared over them like a swooping hawk on its way in to Dulles Airport, Faith Lockhart closed her eyes and pretended for a moment that she was on that plane, and instead of landing, it was beginning some far-flung journey. As she slowly opened her eyes, the car took an exit off the highway and they left the unsettling glare of sodium lights behind. They were soon sailing past jagged rows of trees on both sides of the road, the wide, grassy ditches deep and soggy; the dull pulse of flat-looking stars was now their only source of light other than the car's twin beams stabbing the darkness.

"I don't understand why Agent Reynolds couldn't come tonight," she said.

"The simple answer is, you're not the only investigation she has going, Faith," Special Agent Ken Newman replied. "But I'm not exactly a stranger, am I? We're just going to talk, like the other times. Pretend I'm Brooke Reynolds. We're all on the same team."

The car turned on to another, even more isolated road. On this stretch the trees were replaced by denuded fields awaiting the final scrape of the bulldozers. In a year's time there would be almost as many homes here as there had been trees before, as suburban sprawl continued its push. Now the land simply looked ravaged, naked. And bleak, perhaps because of what was to come. In that regard, the land and Faith Lockhart were as one.

Newman glanced over at her. Although he didn't like to admit it, he felt uneasy around Faith Lockhart, as though he were seated next to a ball of wired C-4 with no idea when it might explode. He shifted in his seat. His skin was a little raw where the leather of his shoulder holster usually rubbed against his skin. Most people developed a callus at that spot, but his skin just kept blistering and then peeling off. Ironically, he felt that the twinge of pain gave him an edge because he never relaxed; it was a clear warning that if he let down his guard, that small discomfort could become a fatal one. Tonight, however, because he was wearing body armor, the holster wasn't scraping his skin; the pain and heightened sense of awareness were not nearly as strong.

Faith could feel the blood rush through her ears, all senses elevated, the way they were when you were lying in bed late at night and hearing a strange, troubling sound. When you were a child and that happened, you raced to your parents' bed and climbed in, to be wrapped up, consoled by loving, understanding arms. Her parents were dead and she was now thirty-six years old. Who was out there for Faith Lockhart?

"And after tonight, it'll be Agent Reynolds instead of me," Newman said. "You're comfortable with her, aren't you?"

"I'm not sure 'comfort' applies to situations like this."

"Sure it does. It's very important, in fact. Reynolds is a straight shooter. Believe me, if it weren't for her, this thing would be going nowhere. You haven't exactly given us much to go on. But she believes in you. So long as you don't do anything to destroy that confidence, you have a powerful ally in Brooke Reynolds. She cares about you."

Faith crossed her legs and folded her arms across her chest. She was about five-five, and her torso was short. Her bosom was flatter than she would have liked, but her legs were long and well shaped. If nothing else, she could always count on her legs to get attention. The defined muscles in her calves and thighs, visible through her sheer stockings, were enough to cause Newman's gaze to flicker over them several times with what appeared to be mild interest, she noted.

Faith swatted her long auburn hair out of her face and rested her hand on the bridge of her nose. A few white strands of hair floated among the darker. They were not yet noticeable, but that would change with time. In fact, the pressure she was under would undoubtedly accelerate the aging process. Besides her hard work, agile wits and poise, Faith's good looks, she knew, had helped her career. It was shallow to believe that one's features made a difference. Yet the truth was they did, particularly when one dealt with an overwhelmingly male audience, as she had for her entire career.

The broad smiles she received when entering a senator's office were not so much due to her gray matter, she knew, as to the above-the-knee skirts she favored. Sometimes it was as simple as dangling a shoe. She was talking about children dying, families living in sewers in far-off lands, and these men were fixated on toe cleavage. God, testosterone was a man's greatest weakness and a woman's most powerful advantage. At least it helped to level a playing field that had always been tilted in favor of the males.

"It's nice to be so well loved," said Faith. "But picking me up in an alley. Coming out here in the middle of nowhere in the dead of night. That's a little much, don't you think?"

"Your walking into the Washington Field Office just wasn't an option. You're the star witness in what could be a very important investigation. This place is safe."

"You mean it's perfect for an ambush. How do you know we haven't been followed?"

"We've been followed, all right. By our people. If anyone else had been around, believe me, our people would've noticed it before sending us on. We had a tail car until we turned off the highway. There's nobody back there."

"So your people are infallible. I wish I had that kind of people working for me. Where do you find them?"

"Look, we know what we're doing, okay? Relax." Even as he said this, though, he checked the mirror again.

He glanced at the cell phone lying on the front seat, and Faith could easily read his thoughts. "Suddenly wanting backup?" Newman glanced sharply at her but said nothing. "Okay, so let's get to the principal terms," she said. "What do I really get out of all this? We've never quite nailed it down." When Newman still didn't respond, she studied his profile for a minute, sizing up his nerve. She reached over and touched his arm.

"I took a lot of risk to do what I'm doing," she said. She felt him tense through his suit jacket where her fingers rested. She kept her fingers there, applied slightly more pressure. Her fingertips could now distinguish the material of his jacket from that of his shirt. As he turned slightly toward her, Faith was able to see the bulletproof vest he was wearing. The saliva in her mouth suddenly evaporated, along with her composure.

Newman glanced at her. "I'll give it to you straight. What exactly your deal will be, that's not up to me. So far, you haven't really given us anything. But play by the rules and everything will be okay. You'll cut your deal, you'll give us what we need and pretty soon you'll have a new identity selling seashells on Fiji, while your partner and his playmates become long-term guests of the government. Don't revel in it, don't think too much about it, just try to survive it. Remember, we're on your side here. We're the only friends you have."

Faith sat back, finally drawing her gaze from the body armor. She decided it was time to drop her bombshell. She may as well try it out on Newman instead of Reynolds. In some ways, Reynolds and she had hit it off. Two women in a sea of men. In many subtle ways, the female agent had understood things a man never would have. In other ways, however, they had been like two alley cats circling around fish bones.

"I want to bring in Buchanan. I know I can get him to do it. If we work together, your case will be much stronger." She said all of this quickly, vastly relieved to have it finally out.

Newman's face betrayed his astonishment. "Faith, we're pretty flexible, but we're not cutting a deal with the guy who, according to you, masterminded this whole thing."

"You don't understand all the facts. Why he did it. He's not the bad person in all this. He's a good guy."

"He broke the law. According to you, he corrupted government officials. That's enough for me."

"When you understand why he did it, you won't think that way."

"Don't pin your hopes on that strategy, Faith. Don't do that to yourself."

"What if I say it's both or none?"

"Then you're making the biggest mistake of your life."

"So it's either me or him?"

"And it shouldn't be that tough a choice."

"I'll just have to talk to Reynolds, then."

"She'll tell you the same thing I just did."

"Don't be so sure. I can be pretty persuasive. And I also happen to be right."

"Faith, you have no idea what's involved here. FBI agents don't decide who to prosecute. The U.S. Attorney's Office does. Even if Reynolds sided with you, and I doubt she will, I can tell you there's no way in hell the lawyers will go along. If they try to take down all these powerful politicos and cut a sweetheart deal with the guy who got them into it in the first place, they're gonna lose their asses, and then their jobs. This is Washington, these are eight-hundred-pound gorillas we're dealing with here. There'll be phones ringing off the hook, a media frenzy, behind-the-scenes deals going a mile a minute, and at the end of the day, we'll all be toast. Trust me, I've been doing this for twenty years. It's Buchanan or nothing."

Faith sat back and stared at the sky. For a moment, amid the clouds, she envisioned Danny Buchanan slumped over in a dark, hopeless prison cell. She could never let it come to that. She would have to talk to Reynolds and the attorneys, make them see that Buchanan had to be given immunity too. That was the only way it could work. But Newman sounded so sure of himself. What he had just said made perfect sense. This was Washington. As suddenly as the strike of a match, her confidence completely deserted her. Had she, the consummate lobbyist, who had been tallying political scorecards for God knew how long, failed to account for the political situation here?

"I need a bathroom," Faith said.

"We'll be at the cottage in about fifteen minutes."

"Actually, if you take the next left, there's a twenty-four-hour gas station about a mile down the road."

He looked at her in surprise. "How do you know that?"

She looked back with a look of confidence that masked a rising panic. "I like to know what I'm getting into. That includes the people and the geography."

He didn't answer, but hung the left, and they were soon at the well-lit Exxon, which had a convenience store component. The highway had to be nearby, despite the isolation of the surroundings, because semis were parked up and down the lot. The Exxon obviously catered to open-road truckers. Men in boots and cowboy hats, Wrangler jeans and windbreakers, with trucking- and automotive-parts' logos stenciled across them, strode across the lot. Some patiently filled their rigs with fuel; others sipped hot coffee, tiny wisps of steam heat rising past tired, leathery faces. No one paid attention to the sedan as it pulled up next to the rest room located on the far side of the building.

Faith locked the bathroom door behind her, put the toilet lid down and sat on it. She didn't need to use the facilities; she needed time to think, to control the panic hitting her from all sides. She looked around, her eyes absently taking in the handwritten scribbles on the chipping yellow paint covering the block walls. Some of the obscene language almost made her blush. Some of the writings were witty – belly-rocking funny, even – in their crudeness. They probably surpassed anything the men had composed to decorate their rest room next door, although most males would never concede this possibility. Men were always underestimating women.

She stood, splashed cold tap water on her face and dried it with a paper towel. About that time her knees decided to give, and she locked them, her fingers curling tightly around the stained porcelain of the sink. She had had nightmares about doing that at her wedding: locking her knees and then passing out because of it. Well, one less thing to worry about now. She'd never had a lasting relationship in her life, unless one counted a certain young man in fifth grade whose name she couldn't remember but whose sky-blue eyes she would never forget.

Danny Buchanan had given her lasting friendship. He'd been her mentor and substitute father for the last fifteen years. He had seen potential in her where no one else had. He had given her a chance when she so desperately needed one. She had come to Washington with boundless ambition and enthusiasm and absolutely no focus. Lobbying? She knew nothing about it, but it sounded exciting. And lucrative. Her father had been a good-natured if aimless wanderer, dragging his wife and daughter from one get-rich scheme to the next. He was one of nature's cruelest concoctions: a visionary lacking the skills to implement that vision. He measured gainful employment in days instead of years. They all lived one nervous week to the next. When his plans went awry and he was losing other people's money, he would pack up Faith and her mother and flee. They'd been homeless on occasion, hungry more often than not; still, her father had always gotten back on his feet, however totteringly. Until the day he died. Poverty was a lasting, powerful memory for her.

Faith wanted a good, stable life, and she wanted to be dependent on no one for it. Buchanan had given her the opportunity, the skills to accomplish her dream, and much more than that. He had not only vision, but also the tools to execute his sweeping ideas. She could never betray him. She was in breathless awe of what he had done and was still trying so hard to do. He was the rock she needed at that stage of her life. In the last year their relationship had changed. Ever more reclusive, he had stopped talking to her. Danny was irritable, snapping for little reason. When she pressed him to tell her what was troubling him, he withdrew even more. Their relationship had been so close that the change had been even harder for her to accept. He became stealthy, stopped inviting her to travel with him; they no longer even engaged in their lengthy strategy sessions.

And then he had done something entirely original and personally devastating: He had lied to her. The matter had been purely trivial, but the implications were serious. If he spun lies in small areas, what was he holding from her of importance? They had one final confrontation and Buchanan had told her that no possible good could come from him sharing what troubled him. And then he dropped the real stunner.

If she wanted to leave his employ, she was free to do so, and maybe it was time she did, he had strongly intimated. His employ! The father telling his precocious daughter to get the hell out of the house was more the effect upon her.

Why did he want her to go away? And then it finally dawned on her. How could she have been so blind? They were on to Danny. Somebody was on to him, and he didn't want her to share his fate. She had point-blank confronted him on that issue. And he had point-blank denied it. And then insisted that she leave. Noble to the end.

And yet if he wouldn't confide in her, she would map a separate course for them. After much deliberation she had gone to the FBI. She knew there was a chance it was the FBI that had somehow discovered Danny's secret, but this might make it easier, Faith had thought. Now a thousand doubts assailed her for the decision to approach the Bureau. Did she really believe the Bureau would just fall all over themselves inviting Buchanan into the prosecution's fold? She cursed herself for giving them Danny's name, although he was very famous in a town of famous people; the FBI would not have failed to make the connection. They wanted Danny to go to prison. Her for Danny. That was supposed to be her choice? She had never felt more alone.

She looked at herself in the cracked mirror. The bones of her face seemed to be pushing through her skin, her eye sockets hollowing right in front of her. A centimeter of skin between her and nothing. Her grand vision, the way out for them both, had suddenly become a free fall of insane, dizzying proportion. Her father would have just packed up and fled into the night. What was his daughter supposed to do?

FIVE

Lee pulled out his pistol and pointed it ahead of him as he moved through the hallway. With his other hand he swung the flashlight in slow, steady arcs.

The first room he peered into was the kitchen, containing a small 1950s-era refrigerator, GE electric range and tattered black-and-yellow-checked linoleum flooring. The walls were discolored in places by water damage. The ceiling was unfinished, the joists and the subfloor above clearly visible. Lee gazed at the old copper pipes and the newer grafts of PVC as they made a series of right angles through the exposed, darkened wall studs.

There was no aroma of food here, only a smell of grease, presumably hardened in the stove-top burners and in the bowels of the vent, along with probably a few trillion bacteria. A chipped Formica table and four bent-metal, vinyl-backed chairs stood in the center of the kitchen. The counters were barren, no dishes visible. There were also no towels, coffeemaker or condiment canisters, nor any other item or personal touch that might have suggested the kitchen had been used in the last decade or so. It was as though he had stepped back in time, or happened upon a bomb shelter put into service during the hysteria of the fifties.

The small dining room was across the hallway from the kitchen. Lee looked at the waist-high wood paneling, darkened and cracked over the years. He had a sudden chill, though the air was stale and oppressive inside. The house apparently had no central heating, nor had Lee seen any wall-mounted air conditioners. There had been no heating oil tank outside either, at least aboveground. Lee eyed the chill-chasers bolted along the bottom of the walls, their power cords plugged into electrical outlets. As in the kitchen, the ceiling here was unfinished. The electrical line to the dust-ridden chandelier ran through holes bored in the exposed joists. Electricity, Lee deduced, must have come to the home after it was first built.

As he moved down the hallway toward the front of the house, Lee was unable to see the invisible trip beam, positioned at knee height, that stretched across the hall. He pierced this security perimeter, and from somewhere in the house a barely audible click was heard. Lee jerked for a moment, pointing his gun in wide circles, and then relaxed. It was an old house, and old houses made lots of noises. He was just being jumpy, yet he had a right to be. The cottage and its location were right the hell out of a *Friday the 13th* movie.

Lee entered one of the front rooms. There, under the sweep of his flashlight, he saw that the furniture had been moved up against the walls, and there were footprints and drag patterns in the layers of dust on the floor. In the center of the room were a number of folding chairs and a rectangular-shaped table. A stack of Styrofoam coffee cups rested at one end of the table next to a coffeemaker. Packets of coffee, creamer and sugar lay next to the coffeemaker.

Lee took all this in and jerked when he saw the windows. Not only were the heavy drapes drawn tight, but also the windows had been boarded over with big sheets of plywood, the drapes dangling from underneath the wood.

"Shit," Lee muttered. He quickly discovered that the small square windows set in the front door had been covered over with cardboard. He pulled out his camera and snapped some shots of all these puzzling items.

Wanting to complete his search as soon as possible, Lee hurried up the stairs to the second floor. He cautiously opened the door to the first bedroom and peered in. The bed was small and made, and its smell of mildew hit him immediately. The walls here were unfinished as well. Lee put his hand against the exposed wall and immediately felt air from the outside coming through the cracks. He was startled for a moment when he saw a slender line of light coming from the top of the wall. Then he realized it was the moonlight coming through a gap where wall was supposed to meet roof.

Lee carefully nudged open the closet door. It still let out a prolonged squeak that made him catch a breath. No clothes, not even a single hanger. He shook his head and went into the small connecting bathroom. Here, there was a more modern, drop-down ceiling, linoleum floor with pebble design and plasterboard walls covered with peeling flower-patterned wallpaper. The shower was a one-piece fiberglass unit. However, there were no towels, toilet paper or soap. No way to shower or even freshen up.

He went through into the other, adjoining bedroom. Here, the smell of mildew on the bedcovers was so strong he almost had to hold his nose. The closet here was empty as well.

None of this was making sense. He stood in the pool of moonlight coming through the window, felt his neck tickled by the drafts of air pushing through the cracks in the walls and shook his head. What was Faith Lockhart doing here if not using it as some kind of love nest? That was what his initial conclusion had been, even though he had only seen her with the tall woman. People swung lots of ways. But not even with concrete up their noses could they have been having sex on these sheets.

Returning downstairs, he went across the hallway and into the other front space, which Lee assumed was the living room. The windows here had been boarded over as well. There was a bookshelf notched into one of the walls, although no books were on it. As in the kitchen, the ceiling was unfinished. As Lee swung his light upward, he spied the short pieces of wood tacked between the joists at forty-five-degree angles, forming a line of X's across the ceiling. The wood was clearly different from that used for the original construction; it was lighter and of a different grain. Additional support? Why had that been necessary?

He shook his head in the manner of a man resigned to his fate. Now added to Lee's list of worries was the possibility that the damn second floor would collapse at any minute on his head. He envisioned his obit headlined something like: LUCKLESS PI FELLED BY BATHTUB/SHOWER COMBO; WEALTHY EX-WIFE REFUSES COMMENT.

As Lee shone his light around, he froze. Set into one wall was a door. A closet, most likely. Nothing unusual about that, except that this door was secured by a deadbolt. He went over and examined the lock more closely, glancing at the small pile of wood dust on the floor directly under the lock. Lee knew it had been left over when the person installing the lock had drilled the hole through the wooden door. Exterior deadbolts. A security system. A deadbolt recently installed on an *interior* closet door in a crappy rental in the boonies. What could be so valuable here to go to all this trouble?

"Shit," Lee said again. He wanted to leave this

place, but he could not take his eyes off the lock. If Lee Adams had one fault – and it could hardly be considered a fault for someone in his line of work – it was that he was a very curious man. Secrets plagued him. People attempting to hide things came close to infuriating him. As a "lunch pail" kind of guy utterly convinced that great monied forces stalked the earth creating all kinds of havoc for ordinary folk like him, Lee believed in the principle of full and fair disclosure with all his substantial heart. Putting action to that belief, he wedged the flashlight under his armpit, holstered his gun and pulled out his lock-pick kit. His fingers worked nimbly as he slipped a fresh pick into the lock-pick gun. He took a deep breath, inserted the pick in the lock and turned on the machine.

When the deadbolt slid back, Lee took another deep breath, pulled his pistol and pointed it at the door as he turned the knob. He didn't really believe that anyone had locked himself in a closet and was about to jump him, but then again, he had seen stranger things happen. Someone might be on the other side of this door.

When he saw what was in the closet, a part of him wished the problem were as simple as someone preparing to ambush him. He swore under his breath, holstered his pistol and ran.

In the closet the blink of red lights from the stacks of electronic equipment shone forth now in the open doorway.

Lee raced into the other front room and shone his light around the walls in even patterns, moving higher and higher. Then he saw it. There was a camera lens in the wall next to the molding. Probably a pinhole lens, designed specifically for covert surveillance. It was impossible to see in the poor lighting, but the beam from the flashlight was reflecting off it. As he moved the beam around, he hit a total of four camera lenses.

Holy shit. The sound he had heard earlier. He must have tripped some device that had triggered the cameras. He raced back to the living room closet, flashed his light on the front of the video machine.

Eject! Where the hell was eject? He found the button, hit it and nothing happened. He punched it again and again. He hit the other buttons. Nothing. Then Lee's gaze closed on the *second* small infrared portal in the front of the machine, and the answer hit him. The machine was controlled by a special remote, its function buttons overridden. His blood ran cold with the possibilities this sort of arrangement suggested. He thought about putting a bullet into the thing, to make it cough up the precious tape. But for all he knew, the damn thing was armored and he'd end up eating his own slug off the ricochet. And what if it had a real-time satellite link and the tape was only a backup? Was there a camera in here? People could be looking at him right now. For one ridiculous second, he thought about giving them the finger.

Lee was about to run again but then had a sudden inspiration. He fumbled in his knapsack, his usually steady fingers now not quite so dexterous. His hands closed around the small case. He whipped it out, fought with the lid for an instant and then managed to pull out the small but powerful magnet.

Magnets were a popular burglary tool because they were ideal for locating and popping window pins once you had cut through the glass. Otherwise, the pins would defeat the most accomplished burglar. Now the magnet would play the reverse role: not helping him break in, but rather assisting him in making what he hoped would be an invisible exit.

He palmed the magnet and then ran it in front of the video machine and then over the top. He did it as many times as he could in the one minute he had allowed himself before fleeing for his life. He prayed that the magnetic field would obliterate the images on the tape. *His* images.

He threw the magnet back in his bag, turned and ran for the door. God only knew who might be on their way here. Lee suddenly stopped. Should he go back to the closet, rip the VCR out and take it with him? The next sound Lee heard drove all thoughts of the VCR from his mind.

A car was coming.

"Sonofabitch!" hissed Lee. Was it Lockhart and her escort? They had come here every *other* evening. So much for a pattern. He raced back down the hall, threw open the back door, burst through and hurdled the concrete stoop. He landed heavily in the slick grass, his shoeless feet slipped and he fell hard. The impact knocked the breath out of him and he felt a sharp pain where his elbow had struck at an odd angle. But fear was a great painkiller. Within a few seconds he was up and chugging for the tree line.

He was halfway to the woods when the car pulled into the driveway, its light beams bouncing a little as the car moved from flat road to uneven ground. Lee took another few strides, hit the tree line and dove under cover.

The red dot had lingered for a few moments on Lee's chest. Serov could have taken the man so easily. But that would warn the people in the car. The former KGB man aimed the rifle at the driver's-side door. He hoped the man who had now made it to the woods would not be stupid enough to try anything. He had been very lucky up until now. He had escaped death not once, but twice. One should not waste that much luck. It would be in such poor taste, Serov thought as he once more sighted through the laser scope.

Lee should have kept running, but he stopped, his chest heaving, and crept back to the tree line. His curiosity had always been his strongest trait, sometimes too strong. Besides, the people behind all the electronic equipment probably had already identified him. Hell, they probably knew the dentist he used and his preference for Coke over Pepsi, so he might as well stick around and see what was coming next. If the people in the car started for the woods, he would do his best impersonation of an Olympic marathoner, shoeless feet and all, and dare anyone to catch him.

He crouched down and took out his night-vision monocular. It utilized forward-looking infrared, or FLIR, technology, which was a vast improvement over the ambient light intensifier, or I-squareds, Lee had used in the past. FLIR worked by detecting, in essence, heat. It needed no light to operate, and unlike the I-squareds, it could distinguish dark images against dark backgrounds, with the heat transferred into crystal-clear video images.

As Lee focused the contraption, his field of vision was now a green screen with red images. The car appeared so close that Lee had the sense that he could reach out and touch it. The engine area glowed particularly brightly, since it was still very hot. He watched the man as he climbed out of the driver's side. Lee didn't recognize him, but the private investigator tensed as he watched Faith Lockhart climb out of the car and join the man. They were side by side at this point. The man hesitated as though he had forgotten something.

"Damn," Lee hissed between clenched teeth. "The

door." Lee focused for a moment on the back door to the cottage. It was standing wide open.

The man had obviously seen this. He turned, facing the woman, and reached inside his coat.

*

In the woods, Serov fixed his laser point on the base of the man's neck. He smiled contentedly. The man and woman were lined up nicely. The ammo the Russian was chambering was highly customized, military-style ordnance with full metal jackets. Serov was a careful student of both weapons and the wounds they caused. With its high velocity, the bullet would have minimal projectile deformity as it passed through its target. However, it would still cause devastating injury when the kinetic energy the bullet carried was released and then rapidly lost in the body. The initial wound track and cavity would be many times larger than the size of the bullet before it partially closed. And the destruction to tissue and bone would occur radially, akin to the epicenter of an earthquake, with terrible damage resulting a great distance away. It was quite beautiful, in its own way, Serov felt.

Velocity was the key to kinetic energy levels – the Russian was well aware – which, in turn, determined damage force on the target. Double the weight of a bullet and it doubled the kinetic energy. However, Serov had long ago learned that when you doubled the velocity at which the bullet was fired, the kinetic energy was *quadrupled*. And Serov's weapon and ammo were at the top end of the scale on velocity. Yes, beautiful indeed.

However, because of its full metal jacket, the bullet could also easily pass through one person and then strike and kill another. This was not an unpopular result for soldiers who were going at it in combat. And for hired killers with two targets.

However, if another bullet was required to kill the woman, so be it. Ammo was relatively cheap. Consequently, so were humans.

Serov took a slight breath, became absolutely still and lightly squeezed the trigger.

"Omigod!" Lee shouted as he watched the man's body twist and then pitch violently against the woman. They both dropped to the ground as though sewn together.

Lee instinctively started to race out of the woods to help. A shot hit the tree right next to his head. Lee instantly dropped to the ground and sought cover as another shot hit near him. Lying on his back, his body shaking so hard he could barely focus the damn monocular, Lee scanned the area where he thought the shots had come from.

Another shot hit close to him, kicking up wet dirt in his face, stinging his eyes. Whoever was out there knew what he was doing and was loaded for dinosaur. Lee could sense the shooter methodically closing in on him grid by grid.

Lee could tell that the shooter was using a suppressor, because each shot sounded like someone slapping a wall hard with the palm of his hand. *Splat. Splat. Splat.* They could have been balloons exploding at a children's party, not cone-shaped pieces of metal flying at a million Mach seeking to wipe out a certain PI.

Other than the hand holding his monocular, Lee tried not to move, tried not to breathe. For one terrifying instant he saw the red line of the laser dart near his leg like a curious snake, and then it was gone. He didn't have much time. If he just stayed here, he was a dead man.

Laying his gun on his chest, Lee stretched his fingers out and carefully groped for a moment in the dirt until his hand closed around a stone. Using just the flick of his wrist, he tossed the stone about five feet away, waited; and when it hit a tree, a bullet struck the same spot a few seconds later.

With his infrared eye, Lee instantly zeroed in on the heat of this last muzzle flash, as oxygen-deprived, super-hot gas escaping from the rifle barrel collided with the outside air. This simple reaction of physical elements had cost many a soldier his life as it revealed his position. Lee could only hope for the same result now.

Lee used the muzzle flash to fix on the man's thermal image amid the cover of trees. The shooter wasn't that far away, well within range of Lee's SIG. Realizing he would probably get only one attempt, Lee slowly gripped his gun and raised his arm, trying to locate a clear line of fire. Keeping his gaze on his target through the monocular, Lee clicked off the safety, said a silent prayer and fired eight shots from his fifteen-round mag. They were all aimed fairly close together, increasing his chances of a hit. His pistol shots were much louder than the rifle's suppressed ones. On all sides of him wildlife fled the human conflict.

One of Lee's shots miraculously found its mark, mainly because Serov had moved right into the path of the shot as he was attempting to shift to a closer position. The Russian grunted in pain as the bullet entered his left forearm. For a split second it stung, then the dull throbbing came as the bullet ripped through soft tissue and veins, shattered his humerus and finally came to rest in his clavicle. His left arm immediately became heavy and useless. After killing a dozen people in his career, always with a gun, Leonid Serov finally knew what it felt like to be shot. Clutching the rifle in his good hand, the ex-KGB agent took the professional way out. He turned and ran, blood splattering on the ground with each step.

Through the FLIR, Lee watched him run for a few moments. From the way the man was retreating, Lee was pretty certain that at least one of his shots had scored a hit. He decided it would be both stupid and unnecessary to chase an armed and wounded man. Besides, he had something else to do. He grabbed his bag and ran toward the cottage.

SIX

While Lee and Serov were exchanging fire, Faith struggled to get her breath back. The collision with Newman had taken most of her wind and left a throbbing pain in her shoulder. With convulsive strength she was able to roll him off. She felt a warm and sticky substance on her dress. For a terrifying moment she thought she had been shot. Faith couldn't have known it, but the agent's Glock had acted as a mini-shield, deflecting the bullet as it left his body. It was the only reason she was still alive. For a moment she stared at what was left of Newman's face and felt herself growing sick.

Pulling her gaze away, Faith managed to squat low in the driveway and slide her hand into Newman's pocket, then pulled out his car keys. Faith's heart was pumping so frantically that it was difficult for her mind to focus. She could barely hold the damn car keys. Still crouching, she eased open the driver's-side door.

Her body was shaking so hard she didn't even know if she could drive the car once she got in it. Then she was inside, slammed the door shut and locked it. When the engine caught, she put the car in gear, hit the gas and the engine flooded and died on her. Swearing loudly, she turned the key again; the engine caught. She made a more cautious movement on the gas pedal and the engine remained purring.

She was about to hit the gas when her breath

caught in her throat. A man stood at the driver's-side window. He was breathing heavily and looked as scared as she felt. What really held her attention, though, was the gun pointed directly at her. He motioned for her to roll the window down. She contemplated hitting the gas.

"Don't try it," he said, seemingly reading her thoughts. "I'm not the one who shot at you," he said through the glass. He added, "If I were, you'd already be dead."

Finally Faith edged down the window.

"Unlock the door," he said, "and move over."

"Who are you?"

"Let's go, lady. I don't know about you, but I don't want to be here when someone else shows up. They might be a better shot."

Faith unlocked the door and slid over. Lee holstered his gun, threw his bag in the back, got in, slammed the door shut and backed out. Right at that instant the cell phone rang, causing them to both jump. He stopped the car and they looked down at the phone and then at each other.

"It's not my phone," he said.

"It's not mine either," replied Faith.

When the ringing stopped, he asked, "Who's the dead guy?"

"I'm not telling you anything."

The car hit the road and he shifted to drive and punched the gas. "You might regret that decision."

"I don't think so."

He appeared confused by her confident tone.

She slipped her seat belt on as he took a curve a little fast. "If you shot that man back there, then you'll shoot me regardless of what I tell you or not. If you're telling the truth and you didn't shoot him, then I don't think you'll kill me simply because I won't talk."

"You have a very naive perspective of good and bad. Even good guys have to kill on occasion," he said.

"Are you speaking from experience?" Faith edged closer against the door.

He hit the auto door lock. "Now, don't go and throw yourself out the car. I just want to know what's going on. Starting with who's the dead guy."

Faith stared at him, her nerves completely shattered. When she finally spoke, her voice was very weak. "Do you mind if we just go somewhere, anywhere, so I can just sit and think for a bit?" She curled her fingers and added hoarsely, "I've never seen anyone killed before. I've never almost been . . ." Her voice rose as she said this last part and she started to tremble. "Please pull over. For God's sake, pull over! I'm going to be sick."

He skidded the car to a stop on the shoulder and hit the auto unlock button. Faith threw open the door, leaned out and vomited.

He reached across and put his hand on her shoulder, squeezing tightly until she stopped shaking. He spoke in a slow, steady tone. "You're gonna be okay." He paused and waited until she was able to sit back up and close the door before continuing. "First we need to ditch this car. Mine's on the other side of the woods. It'll only take a few minutes to get there. Then I know a place where you can be safe. Okay?"

"Okay," Faith managed to say.

SEVEN

Barely twenty minutes later, a sedan pulled into the cottage's driveway and a man and woman got out. The metal of their weapons reflected off the light thrown from the car's headlights. Approaching the dead man, the woman knelt down and looked at the body. If she hadn't known Ken Newman very well, she might not have recognized him. She had seen human death before, yet she still felt something rising from her stomach to her throat. She quickly stood and turned away. The pair searched the cottage thoroughly and then did a quick sweep of the tree line before coming back to the body.

The large, barrel-chested fellow looked down at Ken Newman's body and uttered a curse. Howard Constantinople was "Connie" to all who knew him. A veteran FBI agent, he had seen just about everything in his career. However, tonight was new territory even for him. Ken Newman was a good friend of his. Connie looked as though he might burst into sobs.

The woman stood next to him. At six feet one, she matched Connie's height. Her brunette hair was cut very short, curving over her ears. Her face was long, narrow and intelligent, and she was dressed in a stylishly fitting pantsuit. Both the years and the stress of her occupation had hammered fine lines around her mouth and around her dark, sad eyes. Her gaze swept the surrounding area with the ease of someone accustomed not only to observing but also to making accurate deductions from what she observed. There was an edge to her features that clearly demonstrated a powerful internal anger.

At age thirty-nine, Brooke Reynolds's attractive features and tall, lean physique would make her appealing to men for as long as she desired the attention. However, immersed as she was in the middle of a bitter divorce that had wreaked havoc on her two young children, she questioned whether she would ever again want the companionship of a man.

Reynolds had been christened, over the objections of her mother, Brooklyn Dodgers Reynolds by her overzealous baseball-fan father. Her old man had never been the same when his beloved ball club went to California. Almost from day one, her mother had insisted she be called Brooke.

"My God," Reynolds finally said, her gaze fixed on her dead colleague.

Connie looked over at her. "So what do we do now?"

She shook off the net of despair that had settled over her. Action was called for, swift but methodical. "We have a crime scene, Connie. We don't have much choice."

"Locals?"

"This is an AFO," she said, referring to an assault on a federal officer, "so the Bureau will be in the lead." She found she couldn't take her gaze from the body. "But we'll still have to work with the county and state people. I have contacts with them, so I'm reasonably sure we can control the information flow."

"With an AFO we have the Bureau's Violent Crime Unit. That breaks our Chinese wall."

Reynolds took a deep breath to quell the tears she felt rising to her eyes. "We'll do the best we can. The first thing we have to do is secure the crime scene, not that it's going to be too difficult out here. I'll call Paul Fisher at HQ and fill him in." Reynolds mentally went up her chain of command at the Bureau's Washington Field Office, or WFO. The ASAC, SAC and ADIC would have to be notified; the ADIC, or assistant director in charge, was the head of the WFO, really only a notch below the director of the FBI himself. Soon, she thought, there would be enough abbreviations here to sink a battleship.

"Dollars to donuts the director himself will be out here too," Connie added.

The walls of Reynolds's stomach started to burn. An agent being killed was a shock. An agent losing his life on her watch was a nightmare she would never wake up from.

An hour later, forces had converged on the scene, fortunately without any media. The state medical examiner verified what everyone who had even remotely seen the devastating wound already knew: namely, that Special Agent Ken Newman had died from a distant gunshot entry wound to the upper neck, exiting from his face. While the local police stood guard, the VCU, or Violent Crime Unit, agents methodically collected evidence.

Reynolds, Connie and their superiors gathered around her car. The ADIC was Fred Massey, the ranking agent at the scene. He was a small, humorless man who kept shaking his head in exaggerated motions. His white shirt collar was loose around a skinny neck, his bald head seeming to glow under the moonlight.

A VCU agent appeared with a videotape from the cottage and a pair of muddy boots. Reynolds and

Connie had noted the boots when they had searched the cottage, but had wisely opted against disturbing any evidence.

"Someone was in the house," he reported. "These boots were on the back stoop. No forced entry. The alarm was deactivated and the equipment closet was open. Looks like we maybe got the person on tape. They tripped the laser."

He handed the tape to Massey, who promptly handed it over to Reynolds. The act was far from subtle. All this was her responsibility. She would either get the credit or take the fall. The VCU agent put the boots in an evidence bag and went back into the house to continue searching.

Massey said, "Give me your observations, Agent Reynolds." His tone was curt, and everyone understood why.

Some of the other agents had openly shed tears and cursed loudly when they saw their colleague's body. As the only woman here, and Newman's squad supervisor to boot, Reynolds didn't feel she had the luxury of dissolving into tears in front of them. The vast majority of FBI agents went through their entire careers without ever even drawing their sidearms except for weapons recertification. Reynolds had sometimes wondered how she would react if such a catastrophe ever hit home. Now she knew: Not very well.

This was probably the most important case Reynolds would ever handle. A while back, she had been assigned to the Bureau's Public Corruption Unit, a component of the illustrious Criminal Investigation Division. After receiving a phone call from Faith Lockhart one night and secretly meeting the woman on several occasions, Reynolds had been named the squad supervisor of a unit detailed to a special. That "special" had the opportunity, if

Lockhart was telling the truth, to topple some of the biggest names in the United States government. Most agents would die for such a case during their careers. Well, one had tonight.

Reynolds held up the tape. "I'm hoping this tape will tell us something of what happened here. And what happened to Faith Lockhart."

"You think it's likely she shot Ken? If so, a nationwide APB goes out in about two seconds," Massey said.

Reynolds shook her head. "My gut tells me she had nothing to do with it. But the fact is we don't know enough. We'll check the blood type and other residue. If it only matches Ken's, then we know she wasn't hit as well. We know Ken hadn't fired his gun. And he had on his vest. Something took a chunk out of his Glock, though."

Connie nodded. "The bullet that killed him. Through the back of the neck and out the front. He had his weapon out, probably eye-height, the slug hit and deflected off it." Connie swallowed with difficulty. "The residue on Ken's pistol supports that conclusion."

Reynolds stared sadly at the man and continued the analysis. "So Ken might have been between Lockhart and the shooter?"

Connie slowly shook her head. "Human shield. I thought only the Secret Service did that crap."

Reynolds said, "I spoke with the ME. We won't know anything until the post and we can see the wound track, but I think it was most likely a rifle shot. Not the sort of weapon a woman ordinarily carries in her purse."

"So another person waiting for them?" Massey ventured.

"And why would that person kill and then go inside the house?" Connie asked.

"Maybe it was Newman and Lockhart who went in the house," Massey surmised.

Reynolds knew it had been years since Massey had worked a field investigation, but he was still her ADIC and she couldn't very well ignore him. She didn't have to agree with him, though.

Reynolds shook her head decisively. "If they had gone in the house, Ken wouldn't have been killed in the driveway. They'd still be in the house. We interview Lockhart for at least two hours each time. We got here a half hour after they would have, tops. And those weren't Ken's boots. But they are men's boots, about a size twelve. Odds are a big guy."

"If Newman and Lockhart didn't go in the house, and there are no signs of forced entry, then this third party had the passcode to the alarm." Massey's tone was clearly accusatory.

Reynolds looked miserable, but she had to keep going. "From where Ken fell, it looked like he had just gotten out of the car. Then something must have spooked Ken. He pulls his Glock and then takes the round."

Reynolds led them over to the driveway. "Look at the rut marks here. The ground around here is reasonably dry, but the tires really gouged the dirt. I think somebody was getting out of here in a hurry. Hell, fast enough that he ran out of his boots."

"And Lockhart?"

"Maybe the shooter took her with him," Connie said.

Reynolds thought about this. "It's possible, but I don't see why. They'd want her dead too."

"In the first place, how would a shooter know to come here?" Massey asked, and then answered his own question. "A leak?"

Reynolds had been considering this possibility from the moment she had seen Newman's body.

"With all due respect, sir, I don't see how that could be the case."

Massey coldly ticked off the points on his fingers. "We've got one dead man, a missing woman and a pair of boots. Put it all together and I'm looking at a third party being involved. Tell me how that third party got here without inside information."

Reynolds spoke in a very low tone. "It could be a random thing. Lonely place, possible armed robbery. It happens." She took a quick breath. "But if you're right and there is a leak, it's not complete." They all looked at her curiously. "The shooter obviously didn't know about our last-second change of plan. That Connie and I would be here tonight," Reynolds explained. "Ordinarily, I would've been with Faith, but I was working another case. It didn't pan out and I decided at the last minute to hook up with Connie and come out here."

Connie glanced over at the van. "You're right, no one could have known about that. Ken didn't even know."

"I *tried* to call Ken about twenty minutes before we got here. I didn't want to just suddenly appear. If he heard a car pull up to the safe house without prior warning, he might have gotten spooked, shot first and asked questions later. He must have already been dead when I tried to reach him."

Massey stepped toward her. "Agent Reynolds, I know you've been handling this investigation from the beginning. I know that your use of this safe house and the closed-circuit TV surveillance of Ms. Lockhart were all approved by the appropriate parties. I understand your difficulties in pursuing this case and gaining this witness's trust." Massey paused for a moment, seeming to select his words with great care. Newman's death had stunned them all, although agents were often in harm's way. Still, there would be definite blame assessed in this case, and everyone knew it.

Massey continued, "However, your approach was hardly textbook. And the fact is, an agent is dead."

Reynolds plunged right in. "We had to do this very quietly. We couldn't exactly have surrounded Lockhart with agents. Buchanan would've been gone before we had enough evidence for prosecution." She took a long breath. "Sir, you asked for my observations. Here they are. I don't think Lockhart killed Ken. I think Buchanan is behind it. We have to find her. But we have to do it quietly. If we put out an APB, then Ken Newman has probably died in vain. And if Lockhart is alive, she won't be for long if we go public."

Reynolds looked over at the van just as its doors closed on Newman's body. If she had been escorting Faith Lockhart instead of Ken, the odds were that she would have lost her life tonight. For any FBI agent, death was always a possibility, however remote. If she were killed, would Brooklyn Dodgers Reynolds fade in her children's memory? She was certain her six-year-old daughter would always remember "Mommy." She had doubts about three-year-old David, though. If she were killed, would David, years from now, only refer to Reynolds as his "birth" mother? The thought itself was nearly paralyzing.

One day she had actually taken the ridiculous step of having her palm read. The palm reader had warmly welcomed Reynolds, given her a cup of herbal tea, and chatted with her, asking her questions that tried to sound casual. These queries, Reynolds knew, were designed to gather background information to which the woman could add appropriate mumbo-jumbo as she "saw" into Reynolds's past, as well as her future.

After examining Reynolds's hand, the palm reader had told her that her life line was short. Significantly so, in fact. The worst she'd ever seen. The woman said this as she stared at what appeared to be a scar on Reynolds's palm. Reynolds knew it was the result of falling on a broken Coke bottle in her backyard when she was eight.

The reader had picked up her cup of tea, apparently waiting for Reynolds to plead for more information, presumably at an appropriate premium over the initial fee. Reynolds had informed her that she was strong as a horse with years in between even a simple bout of flu.

Death needn't be by natural causes, the palm reader had replied, her painted eyebrows rising to emphasize the obvious point.

On that, Reynolds had paid her five dollars and walked out the door.

Now she wondered.

Connie scuffed the dirt with his toe. "If Buchanan is behind this, he's probably long gone by now anyway."

"I don't think so," Reynolds replied. "If he runs right after this, then he's as good as admitting guilt. No, he'll play it cool."

"I don't like this," Massey said. "I say we APB Lockhart and bring her in, assuming she's still living."

"Sir," Reynolds said, her voice tight, edgy, "we can't name her as a subject in a homicide when we have reason to believe she wasn't involved in the murder, but may well be a victim herself. That opens the Bureau to a whole civil-action can of worms if she does turn up. You know that."

"Material witness, then. She damn well qualifies for that," said Massey.

Reynolds looked directly at him. "An APB is not

the answer. It's going to do more harm than good. For everybody involved."

"Buchanan has no reason to keep her alive."

"Lockhart is a smart woman," Reynolds said. "I spent time with her, got to know her. She's a survivor. If she can hang on for a few days, we have a shot. Buchanan can't possibly know what she's been telling us. But we do an APB naming her as a material witness, we just sign her death notice."

They were all silent for a bit. "All right, I see your point," Massey finally said. "You really think you can find her on the Q.T.?"

"Yes." What else could she say?

"Is that your gut talking, or your brain?"

"Both."

Massey studied her for a long moment. "For now, Agent Reynolds, you focus on finding Lockhart. The VCU people will investigate Newman's murder."

"I'd have them lockstep the yard looking for the slug that killed Ken. Then I'd search the woods," Reynolds said.

"Why the woods? The boots were on the stoop."

She glanced over at the tree line. "If I were here to ambush someone, that" – she pointed toward the woods – "would be my first tactical choice. Good cover, excellent line of fire and a hidden escape route. Car waiting, gun disposed of, a quick trip to Dulles Airport. In an hour the shooter's in another time zone. The shot that killed Ken entered the back of his neck. He's facing away from the woods. Ken must not have seen his attacker, or else he wouldn't have turned his back." She eyed the thick woods. "It all points there."

Another car pulled up and the director of the FBI himself climbed out. Massey and his aides hurried over, leaving Connie and Reynolds alone.

"So what's our plan of action?" Connie asked.

"Maybe I'll try to match those boots to my Cinderella," Reynolds said as she watched Massey talking to the director. The director was a former field agent who, Reynolds knew, would take this catastrophe extremely personally. Everybody and everything associated with it would be subject to intense scrutiny.

"We'll cover all the usual bases." She tapped her finger against the tape. "But this is really all we have. Whoever's on this tape we hit hard, like there's no tomorrow."

"Depending on how this turns out, we might not have many tomorrows left, Brooke," said Connie.

EIGHT

Lee gripped the steering wheel so hard his fingers were turning white. As the police car, lights blazing, raced past him going in the opposite direction, he let out an enormous breath and then pushed hard on the accelerator. They were in Lee's car after having ditched the other. He had scrubbed down the inside of the dead man's car, but he could have easily missed something. And nowadays equipment existed that could find things completely invisible to the naked eye. Not good.

As she watched the swirling lights disappear into the darkness, Faith wondered if the police were heading to the cottage. Did Ken Newman have a wife and kids? she wondered. There had been no wedding band on his finger. Like many women, Faith had the habit of making that quick observation. Yet he'd seemed like the fatherly type.

As Lee maneuvered the car through the back roads, Faith's hand moved up, down and then drew a vertical line across her chest as she finished crossing herself. The near-automatic movement conveyed a subtle sense of surprise to her. She added a silent prayer for the dead man. She whispered another prayer for any family he might have. "I'm so sorry you're dead," she said out loud, to help assuage her mounting feelings of guilt for simply having survived.

Lee looked over at her. "Friend of yours?"

She shook her head. "He was killed because of me. Isn't that enough?"

Faith was surprised at how easily the words of prayer and remorse had come back to her. Because of her nomadic father, her attendance at mass over the years had been sporadic. But her mother had insisted on Catholic schools wherever the family happened to venture, and her father had followed this rule after his wife had died. Catholic school must have ingrained something in her other than the constant bite of the ruler on her knuckles from Sister Something-or-other. The summer before her senior year, she had become an orphan, her travels with her father abruptly cut short by a heart attack. She was sent to live with a relative who did not want her and who took pains to show no attention to her. Faith had rebelled however she could. She smoked, she drank, she ceased to become virgin Faith long before it was fashionable to do so. At school the daily tugging down of her skirt to below her knees by the nuns only made her want to pull the damn thing up to her crotch. All in all, it was a truly forgettable year in her life, followed by several more as she struggled through college, tried to gain some direction in her life. Then for the past fifteen years she had thought her rudder was flawless, the grand movements of her life fluid. Now she was floundering, speeding toward the rocks.

Faith looked at Lee. "We need to call the police, tell somebody that he's back there."

Lee shook his head. "That opens a whole other can of worms. That is definitely not a good idea."

"We can't just leave him back there. It's not right."

"Do you suggest we go to the local precinct and try to explain this thing? They'll put us in strait-jackets."

"Dammit! If you won't do it, I will. I am *not* leaving him back there for the squirrels."

"All right, all right. Calm down." He sighed. "I guess we could place an anonymous call in a little while, get the cops to check it out."

"Fine," said Faith.

A few minutes later, Lee noticed that Faith was fidgeting.

"I have another request," she said.

The woman's demanding style was really starting to annoy him. Lee tried not to think about the hurt in his elbow, the irritating specks of cold dirt in his eyes, the unknown dangers that lay ahead.

"Like what?" he said wearily.

"There's a gas station near her. I'd like to wash up." She added quietly, "If that's okay."

Lee looked down at the stains on her clothes and his expression softened. "No problem," he said.

"It's down this road—"

"I know where it is," Lee said. "I like to get the lay of the land where I'm working."

Faith simply stared at him.

In the bathroom Faith tried not to focus on what she was doing as she painstakingly cleaned the blood off her clothing. Still, every couple of minutes she felt like ripping off all her clothes and scrubbing herself down using the soap from the dispenser and the stack of paper towels on the dirty sink.

When she climbed back in the car, her companion's look said what his mouth didn't.

"I'll make it, for now," she said.

"By the way, my name's Lee. Lee Adams."

Faith said nothing. He started the car and they left the gas station.

"You don't have to tell me your name," he said. "I

was hired to follow you, Ms. Lockhart."

She eyed him suspiciously. "Who hired you to do that?"

"Don't know."

"How could you possibly not know who hired you?"

"I admit it's a little unusual, but it happens, on occasion. Some people are embarrassed about hiring a private detective."

"So that's what you are, a private eye?" Her tone was one of contempt.

"It can be a very legit way of earning a buck. And I'm as legit as they come."

"And how did this person come to hire you?"

"Other than the fact that I've got a killer Yellow Pages ad, I don't have a clue."

"Do you have any idea what you're mixed up in, Mr. Adams?"

"Let's just say I have a better idea now than I did a little bit ago. Getting shot at is the one thing that has always captured my undivided attention."

"And who shot at you?"

"The same guy who nailed your friend. I think I winged him, but he got away."

Faith rubbed her temples and looked out into the darkness. His next words startled her.

"What are you, Witness Protection?" Lee waited. When she didn't answer, he continued. "I did a ten-second down-and-dirty on your friend while you were busy choking out the car. He had a Glock nine-millimeter and a Kevlar vest, for all the good it did him. The shield on his belt said FBI. I didn't have time to check for ID. So what was his name?"

"Does it matter?"

"It might."

"Why Witness Protection?" she asked.

"The cottage. Special locks, security system. It's a

safe house, of sorts. Nobody's living there, that's for sure."

"So you've been inside."

He nodded. "At first I thought you were having an affair. A couple minutes inside told me it wasn't a love nest. Strange house, though. Hidden cameras, tape-recording system. Did you know you were on stage, by the way?"

The astonished look on her face answered his question.

"If you didn't know who hired you, how were you engaged to follow me?"

"Easy enough. Phone message said a packet of information on you and an advance on my fee would be delivered to my office. They were. A file on you, and a big chunk of cash. It said to follow your movements, and I did."

"I was told I wasn't being followed."

"I've gotten pretty good at it."

"Apparently."

"Once I knew where you were going, I just got here ahead of you. Pretty simple."

"Was the voice a man's or woman's?"

"Couldn't tell; it was scrambled."

"Didn't that make you suspicious?"

"Everything makes me suspicious. One thing's for sure, whoever's after you, they ain't playing around. The ammo the guy was using back there could have wasted an elephant. I got to see it up close and personal."

He fell silent and Faith could not bring herself to say anything else. She had several credit cards in her purse, all with virtually limitless spending power. And they were all useless to her, because as soon as one went through the swipe machine, they would know where she was. She put her hand in her purse and touched the Tiffany pewter ring holding the keys to her beautiful home and her luxury car. Useless as well. In her wallet was the grand sum of fifty-five dollars and a few pennies. She had been stripped bare except for this cash and the clothes on her back. Her impoverished childhood had come roaring back in all its tarnished, hopeless memory.

She did have a large sum of cash, but it was in a safe-deposit box at her bank in D.C. The bank would not be open until tomorrow morning. And there were two other items she kept in that box that were even more critical to her: a driver's license and another credit card. They were both under a fake name. They had been relatively easy to set up, but she had hoped she would never have to use them. So much so that she had kept them in her bank instead of a more accessible place. Now she shook her head at such stupidity.

With those two cards she could go just about anywhere. If everything collapsed on top of her, she had often reminded herself, this would be her way out. *Well*, she thought now, *the roof's gone, the walls are creaking, the killer tornado's at the window and the fat lady is in the limo on the way back to the hotel. It's time to pull the tent and call it a life.*

She looked at Lee. What would she do with him? Faith knew that her most pressing challenge was surviving the rest of the night. Maybe he could help her do that. He seemed to know what he was doing, and he had a gun. If she could just get in and out of her bank without too much trouble, she would be okay. There were about seven hours between now and the bank's opening. They might as well have been seven years.

NINE

Thornhill sat in the small study of his lovely ivy-draped old home in a much-sought-after neighborhood in McLean, Virginia. His wife's family had money, and he enjoyed the luxuries that money could buy, as well as the freedom it gave him to be a public servant his entire career. Right now, though, he was not feeling much comfort.

The message he had just received was unbelievable to him, and yet all the plans had the potential for failure. He looked at the man sitting across from him. This person was also a veteran at the Agency, and a member of Thornhill's secret group. Philip Winslow shared Thornhill's ideals and concerns. They had spent many a night in Thornhill's study, both reminiscing about past glories and devising plans that would ensure there would be many future triumphs as well. They were both Yale graduates, two of the best and brightest. They had come along at a time when it was considered honorable to serve one's country. And the CIA had gotten its share of the Ivy League's best back then. They had also come from a generation in which a man did whatever it took to protect his country's interests. A man with vision, Thornhill believed with all his heart, had to be willing to take risks to achieve that vision.

"The FBI agent was killed," Thornhill said to his friend and colleague.

"And Lockhart?" Winslow asked.

Thornhill gave one brief shake of his head. "She's disappeared."

Winslow summed it up. "So we take out one of the Bureau's finest and let the real target get away." He clinked the ice in his drink. "Not good, Bob. The others won't be happy to hear that."

"Just to get all the good news out, our man was also shot in the process."

"By the agent?"

Thornhill shook his head. "No. There was someone else there tonight. Unknown as yet. Serov has been debriefed. He gave a description of the man who was at the cottage. We're doing computer generations of him right now. We should know his identity shortly."

"Could he tell us anything else?"

"Not at present. Mr. Serov is being detained, for now, in safe quarters."

"You know the Bureau will go after this tooth and nail, Bob."

"More precisely," Thornhill said, "they will do everything in their power to find Faith Lockhart."

"Who do they suspect?"

"Buchanan, of course. It's logical," Thornhill replied.

"So what do we do with Buchanan?"

"For now, nothing. We'll keep him informed. Of at least our version of the truth, that is. We'll keep him busy at the same time we keep close tabs on the FBI. He has a trip out of town this morning, so we're covered there. However, if the FBI's investigation gets too close to Buchanan, we'll provide him with an early death and provide our professional brethren with all the sordid facts of how Buchanan tried to have Lockhart murdered."

"And Lockhart?" Winslow asked.

"Oh, the FBI will find her. They're quite good at that sort of thing, in their limited way."

"I don't see how that helps us. She talks, and Buchanan goes down and takes us with him."

"I hardly think that," Thornhill said. "When the FBI finds her, we will be there as well, if we don't find her first. And this time we won't miss her. With Lockhart gone, Buchanan will soon follow. Then we can move forward with our original plan."

"God, if it could only work."

"Oh, it will work," said Thornhill with his usual optimism. To last as long as he had in this business, one had to have a positive attitude.

TEN

Lee pulled the car into the alleyway and stopped. His gaze swept over the darkened landscape. They had driven around for over two hours until he felt reasonably sure they had not been followed, and then he had made the phone call to the police from a pay phone. Although they seemed relatively safe now, Lee still kept one hand resting on the grip of his pistol, ready to pull it in an instant, to terminate their enemies with the salvos from his deadly SIG. That was a joke.

These days you could kill from a sky away, with a bomb smarter than a man, taking the most important thing men had without so much as a "Hello, you're dead." Lee wondered if, during the millisecond it took to cremate the poor bastards, the brain moved fast enough to spark the thought that the Hand of God had struck them down instead of something manufactured by man, the idiot. For a crazy moment, Lee scanned the sky looking for a guided missile. And depending on who was involved in all this, maybe it wasn't so crazy after all.

"What did you tell the police?" Faith asked.

"Short and sweet. The location of the place and what happened."

"And?"

"And the dispatcher was skeptical but did his best to keep me on the line."

Faith looked around the alley. "Is *this* the safe

place you mentioned?" She took in the darkness, the hidden crevices, the garbage can and the distant tap of footsteps on pavement.

"No, we leave the car here and walk to the safe place. Which, by the way, is my apartment."

"Where are we?"

"North Arlington. It's being yuppified, but it can still be dangerous, especially this time of night."

She stayed right next to him as they made their way down the alley and out on to the next street, which was an avenue of old but nicely kept-up attached rowhouses.

"Which one's yours?"

"The big one at the end there. Owner's retired, lives in Florida. He's got a couple of other properties. I troubleshoot for him, and he gives me a break on the rent."

Faith started to walk out of the alley, but Lee stopped her. "Give me a sec, I want to check things first."

She clutched his jacket. "You are not leaving me here alone."

"I'm just making sure there's nobody there waiting to throw us a surprise party. Anything looks weird, give a shout and I'm back in two shakes."

He disappeared and Faith edged into the crevice of the alley. Her heart was beating so loud, she half expected a window to open and a shoe to come sailing out at her. When she thought she could not take being alone anymore, Lee reappeared.

"Okay, it looks good. Let's go."

The outer door to the building was locked, but Lee opened it with his key. Faith noted the video camera bolted to the wall above her head.

Lee looked at her. "My idea. I like to know who's coming to see me."

They went up four flights of stairs to the top floor

and down the hallway to the last door on the right. Faith eyed the three locks on the door. Lee opened each of them with the same special key.

When the door opened, she heard a beeping sound. They went inside the apartment. On the wall was an alarm panel. Screwed into the wall above it was a piece of shiny copper on a hinge. Lee flipped the copper shield down so that it covered the alarm panel. He reached his hand underneath the copper plate and hit some buttons on the panel and the beeping sound stopped.

He looked over at Faith, who was watching him closely.

"Van Eck radiation. You probably wouldn't understand."

She hiked her eyebrows. "You're probably right."

Next to the alarm panel was a small video screen built into the wall. On the screen Faith could see the front stoop of the building. It was obviously the video link to the surveillance camera outside.

Lee locked the front door and then put his hand on it. "It's steel, set in a special metal frame I built myself. It doesn't matter how strong the lock is. What usually gives is the frame. A lousy two-by-four if you're lucky. A crook's Christmas present handed out by the building industry. I've also got pick-proof window locks, outside motion detectors, piggyback cellular on the alarm system's phone link. We'll be okay."

"I take it you're somewhat security-minded?" she said.

"No, I'm paranoid."

Faith heard something approaching from down the hall. She flinched, but relaxed when she saw Lee smile and move toward the sound. A second later an old German shepherd wandered around the corner. Lee squatted and played with the big dog, who rolled over on his back. Lee accommodated the animal with a belly rub.

"Hey, Max, how you doing, boy?" Lee patted Max's head and the dog affectionately licked his owner's hand.

"Now, this thing is the best security device ever invented. Don't have to worry about electrical outages, batteries going dead or somebody turning his loyalties."

"So your plan is that we stay here?"

Lee looked up at her. "You want something to eat or drink? We might as well work on this over a full stomach."

"Hot tea would be nice. I couldn't really look at food right now."

A few minutes later they were sitting at the kitchen table. Faith sipped on herbal tea while Lee worked on a cup of coffee. Max dozed under the table.

"We have a problem," Lee began. "When I went in the cottage I tripped something. So I'm on the videotape."

Faith looked stricken. "My God, they could be on their way here right now."

"Maybe that's a good thing." Lee looked at her sharply.

"And why is that?"

"I'm not into helping criminals."

"So you think I'm a criminal?"

"Are you?"

Faith fingered her teacup. "I was working with the FBI, not against them."

"Okay, what were they doing with you?"

"I can't answer that."

"Then I can't help you. Come on, I'll give you a ride to your place." Lee started to rise from his chair.

She gripped his arm. "Wait, please wait." The thought of being left alone now was paralyzing.

He sat back down and waited expectantly.

"How much do I have to tell you before you'll help me?"

"Depends on what sort of help you want. I'm not doing anything against the law."

"I wouldn't ask you to."

"Then you've got no problem, other than somebody wanting to kill you."

Faith took a nervous sip of her tea while Lee watched her.

"If they know who you are from the video, should we be just sitting here?" she asked.

"I messed with the tape. Ran my magnet over it."

Faith looked at him, a glint of hope in her eyes. "You think you were able to erase it?"

"I can't tell for sure. I'm not an expert in that stuff."

"But at the very least it might take some time for them to reconstruct it?"

"That's what I'm hoping. But we're not exactly dealing with the Campfire Girls here. The recording equipment also had a security system built in. Chances are if the police try to force the tape out, it might self-destruct. Personally, I'd give the forty-seven bucks I have in the bank if that did happen. I'm a man who likes his privacy. But you still need to fill me in."

Faith didn't say anything. She just stared at him, like he had just made an unwanted pass at her.

Lee cocked his head at her. "I tell you what. I'm the detective, okay? I'll make some deductions and you tell me if I'm right or not, how's that?" When Faith still said nothing, he continued. "The cameras I saw were only in the living room. And the table, chairs, coffee and stuff were set up in the living room only. Now, I tripped the laser or whatever it was going in. That apparently set off the cameras."

"I guess that would make sense," Faith said.

"No, it doesn't. I had the access code to the alarm system," said Lee.

"So?"

"So I put in the code and disarmed the security system. So why have the trip device still operating? The way it was set up, even when the guy you were with disarmed the security system, he would still have engaged the cameras. Why would he want to record himself?"

Faith looked deeply confused. "I don't know."

"Hello, so they'd have you on film without you knowing it. Now the out-of-the-way place with the CIA-level security in place, the Feds, the cameras and taping equipment, all point to one thing." Lee paused as he thought about exactly how he was going to phrase this. "They brought you there to interrogate you. But maybe they're not sure of your level of cooperation, or they think somebody might try to pop you, so they film the interrogations just in case you turn up missing later on."

Faith looked at him with a resigned smile. "Terribly prescient of them, don't you think? The 'turning up missing' thing."

Lee stood and stared out the window as he thought things through. Something very important had just occurred to him. Something that he should have thought about a lot sooner. And even though he didn't know the woman, he was feeling kind of crappy about what he had to say. "I've got some bad news for you."

Faith looked startled. "What do you mean?"

"You're under interrogation by the FBI. Presumably you're also in their protective custody. One of their guys gets popped protecting you and I probably wounded the guy who killed him. The Feds have my face on their tape." He paused for a moment. "I've got to turn you in."

Faith jumped up. "You can't do that! You can't! You said you'd help me."

"If I don't, then I'm looking at some serious time in a place where guys get way too friendly with other guys. At the very least I lose my PI license. I'm sure if I knew you better I'd feel even worse about doing this, but at the end of the day I'm not sure even my grandma would be worth that much trouble." He slipped on his jacket. "Who's your principal handler?"

"I don't know his name," Faith said coldly.

"Do you have a phone number?"

"It wouldn't do any good. I doubt he'd be able to take the call now."

Lee eyed her dubiously. "Are you telling me the dead guy back there is your only contact?"

"That's it." Faith told this lie with a completely straight face.

"The guy was your handler and he never bothered to tell you his name? That's not exactly textbook FBI."

"Sorry, that's all I know."

"Is that right? Well, let me tell you what I know. I saw you at that cottage three other times with a woman. A tall brunette. What, did you sit around calling her Agent X?" He leaned right into her face. "Bullshit Rule Number One: Make damn sure the person you're lying to can't prove same." He hooked an arm around hers. "Let's go."

"You know, Mr. Adams, *you* have a problem you may not have thought about."

"Is that right? Care to share it?"

"What exactly are you going to tell the FBI when you bring me in?"

"I don't know, how about the truth?"

"Okay. Let's look at the truth. You were following

me because someone you don't know and can't identify instructed you to. Which means we only have your word for that. You were able to follow me even though the FBI assured me no one could. You were in that house tonight. Your face is on the tape. An FBI agent is dead. You fired your gun. You say you shot the other man, but you have no way to prove another man was even there. So the proven facts are we have you at the house and me at the house. You fired your gun and an FBI agent is dead."

"The ammo that killed that guy is not something my pistol happens to chamber," he said angrily, releasing her arm.

"So you threw the other gun away."

"Why would I snatch you from the place, then? If I was the shooter, why wouldn't I have killed you back there?"

"I'm not saying what *I* think, Mr. Adams. I'm just suggesting to you that the FBI might suspect you. I suppose if there's nothing in your past to make them suspicious, the FBI might believe you." She added offhandedly. "They'll probably just investigate you for a year and then drop it if nothing turns up."

Lee scowled at her. His recent past was squeaky clean. Going back a little further, the waters got a little murkier. When he was first starting out as a PI, he had done some things he would never even consider doing now. Not illegal, but still hard to explain to straightlaced federal agents.

And then there was the restraining order his ex had gotten right before Lucky Eddie had struck patent gold. Claimed Lee was stalking her, was perhaps violent. Lee would have become violent if he had gotten hold of the little shit. Every time Lee thought about the bruises on his daughter's arms and cheek when he had made an unexpected visit to their rat-trap apartment he almost had a stroke. Trish claimed Renee had fallen down the stairs. Stood there and lied to his face, when Lee could see the imprint of what he knew was a knuckle against his daughter's soft skin. He had taken a crowbar to Eddie's car and would've taken one to Eddie if the guy hadn't locked himself in the bathroom and called the cops.

So did he really want the FBI snooping around his life for the next twelve months? On the other hand, if he let the woman walk away and the Feds tracked him down, then where would he be? Everywhere he turned, he ran into a nest of snakes.

Faith spoke in a pleasant tone. "Do you want to drop me at the Washington Field Office? They're at Fourth and F Streets."

"Okay, okay, you've made your point," Lee said hotly. "But I didn't ask for this crap to be dropped in my lap."

"And I didn't ask for you to become involved in this either. But . . ."

"But what?"

"But if you weren't there tonight, I wouldn't be alive right now. I'm sorry I haven't thanked you before. I'm thanking you now."

Despite his suspicions, Lee felt his anger slowly receding. Either the woman was sincere or she was one of the slickest operators he'd come across. Or maybe it was a little slice of both. This was Washington, after all.

"Always glad to help a lady," he said dryly. "Okay, supposing I decide not to turn you in. What do you have in mind to pass the night away?"

"I need to get away from here. I need some time to think things through."

"The FBI is not going to just let you walk away. I'm assuming you've cut some sort of deal."

"Not yet. And even if I had, don't you think I have good grounds to declare them in default?"

"What about the people who tried to kill you?"

"Once I have some space, I can decide what to do. I'll probably end up just going back to the FBI. But I don't want to die. I don't want anyone else associated with me to die." She stared very deliberately at him.

"I appreciate your concern, but I can take care of myself. So where do you plan to run, and how do you plan to get there?"

Faith started to say something and then stopped. She looked down, suddenly wary.

"If you don't trust me, Faith, none of this works," Lee prodded gently. "If I let you walk, that means I'm going to bat for you big-time. But I haven't made that decision yet. A lot depends on what you're thinking. If the Feds need you to bring down some powerful people – and what I've seen so far clearly rules out this being shoplifting material – then I'm going to have to side with the Feds."

"What if I agreed to come back as long as they could give guarantees as to my safety?"

"I guess that sounds reasonable. But what guarantee is there that you'll come back at all?"

"What if you come with me?" she said quickly.

Lee stiffened so much that he accidentally kicked Max, who came out from under the table and looked at him pitifully.

Faith rushed on. "You said yourself that it's only a matter of time before they identify you on the tape. The person you shot, what if he identifies you to whoever hired him? It's obvious that you're in danger too."

"I'm not sure—"

"Lee," Faith said excitedly, "did it ever occur to you that the person who hired you to follow me had you trailed as well? You could very well have been used to set up the shooting."

"Well, if they could follow me, they could follow you," he countered.

"But what if they wanted to frame you for all this somehow?"

Lee blew the air from his cheeks as the hopelessness of his situation set in. Sonofabitch, what a night. How the hell hadn't he seen it coming? Anonymous client. Bag full of cash. Mystery target. Lonely cottage. Had he been in a frigging coma or what? "I'm listening."

"I have a safe-deposit box in a bank in D.C. In that box I have cash, and some pieces of plastic with another name on them that'll let us go about as far as we need to. The only problem is they might be watching my bank. I need your help."

"*I* can't access your safe-deposit box."

"But you can help me scope the place out, see if anyone's watching. You're obviously better at that than I am. I go in, clean out the box and get out as fast as possible while you cover me. Anything looks suspicious, we run like hell."

"It sounds like we're planning to rob the place," he said angrily.

"I swear to God all the things in that box are mine."

Lee put a hand through his hair. "Okay, maybe that works. Then what?"

"Then we head south."

"South where?"

"The Carolina shore. Outer Banks. I have a place there."

"Are you listed as the owner? They can check that."

"I bought it in the name of a corporation and signed the papers under my other name, as an officer. But what about you? You can't travel under your own name."

"Don't worry about me. I've been more people in my life than Shirley MacLaine, and I've got the papers to prove it."

"Then we're all set."

Lee looked down at Max, who had settled his big head in his lap. Lee gently stroked the dog's nose.

"How long?"

Faith shook her head. "I don't know. A week, maybe."

Lee sighed. "I guess I can have the lady downstairs take care of Max."

"Then you'll do it?"

"Just so long as you understand that while I don't mind helping somebody who needs it, I'm not playing the world's greatest sucker either."

"You don't strike me as someone who would ever play that role."

"If you really want a laugh, tell my ex-wife that."

ELEVEN

Old Town Alexandria was located in northern Virginia next to the Potomac River, about a fifteen-minute drive south of Washington, D.C. The waters had been the primary reason the city had been established, and it had flourished as a seaport for a very long time. It was still an affluent and desirable place to live, although the river no longer played a prominent role in the town's economic future.

It was a setting of both old wealth and freshly monied families nestled within the graceful brick, stone and wood-frame structures of late eighteenth and early nineteenth century architecture. A few of the streets were covered in the very same rolling cobblestone that had supported the treads of Washington and Jefferson. And of the young Robert E. Lee at his two boyhood homes, which were set across from each other on Oronoco Street, itself named after a particular brand of long-ago Virginia-grown tobacco. Many of the town's sidewalks were brick and had buckled up around the numerous trees that had shaded the homes, streets and inhabitants for so long. A number of the wrought-iron fences that encircled the courtyards and gardens of the homes were painted the color of gold on their European-inspired spikes and finials.

At this early hour the streets of Old Town were quiet except for the drizzle of rain and the rush of wind among the branches of the aged, knobby trees whose shallow roots clutched at the hard Virginia clay. The street names reflected the colonial origins of the place. Driving through town, one would pass King, Queen, Duke and Prince Streets. Off-road parking was scarce here, so the narrow avenues were lined with virtually every make and model of vehicle. Placed against the two-hundred-year-old homes, the chrome, rubber and metal hulls seemed oddly out of place, as though a time warp had whisked the automobile back to the era of horse and buggy.

The narrow four-story brick townhouse that was wedged among a line of others along Duke Street was by no means the grandest in the area. There was a lone, tilting maple in the small front yard, its split trunk covered with leafy suckers. The wrought-iron fencing was in good but not superb condition. The home had a garden and courtyard out back, yet the plantings, dripping fountain and brickwork there were unremarkable when compared with others located but a few steps away.

Inside the home, the furnishings were far more elegant than the outside of the place would have led the observer to expect. There was a simple reason for this: The outside of the home was something Danny Buchanan could not hide from curious eyes.

The first traces of the pink dawn were just starting to nudge at the edges of the horizon as Buchanan sat, fully dressed, in the small oval-shaped library off the dining room. A car was waiting to take him to Reagan National Airport.

The senator he was meeting with was on the Appropriations Committee, arguably the Senate's most important committee, since it (and its subcommittees) controlled the government's purse strings. More importantly for Buchanan's purposes, the man also chaired the Subcommittee on Foreign

Operations, which determined where most foreign aid dollars went. The tall, distinguished senator with the smooth manners and confident tones was a longtime associate of Buchanan's. The man had always enjoyed the power that came with his position and he had consistently lived beyond his means. The retirement package he had waiting from Buchanan would be almost impossible for a human being to exhaust.

Buchanan's bribery scheme had started out cautiously at first. He had analyzed all the players in Washington who even remotely might further his goals, and whether they could be bribed. Many members of Congress were wealthy, but many others were not. It was often both a financial and familial nightmare for people to serve in Congress. Members had to maintain two residences, and the Washington metro area was not cheap. And their families often did not come with them. Buchanan approached the ones he figured he could corrupt and began a long process of feeling them out on possible involvement. The carrots he dangled were small at first but quickly grew in size if the targets showed any enthusiasm. Buchanan had selected well, because he had never had a target not agree to exchange votes and influence for rewards down the road. Perhaps they felt that the difference between what he proposed and what occurred in Washington every day was marginal at best. He didn't know if they cared that the goal was a worthy one. However, they hadn't gone out of their way to increase foreign aid to any of Buchanan's clients on their own.

And they had all seen colleagues leave office and grab the gold of lobbydom. But who wanted to work that hard then? Buchanan's experience was that ex-members made terrible lobbyists anyway. Going back hat in hand to lobby former colleagues over whom you no longer had any leverage was not appealing to these overly proud folk. Much smarter to use them when they were the most powerful they would ever be. Work them hard first. And then pay them grandly later. What could be better?

Buchanan wondered if he could really hold it together during the meeting with a man he had already betrayed. But then, betrayal was doled out in large doses in this town. Everyone was constantly scrambling for a chair before the music stopped. The senator would be understandably upset. Well, he would have to stand in line with the rest.

Buchanan suddenly felt tired. He didn't want to get in the car or climb on another plane, but he had no say in the matter. *Still a member of the Philadelphia servant class?*

The lobbyist focused his attention on the man who was standing before him.

"He sends his compliments," the burly man said. To the outside world he was Buchanan's driver. In reality he was one of Thornhill's men keeping close tabs on their most important charge.

"And please send Mr. Thornhill my sincerest wishes that God should decree he not grow one day older," said Buchanan.

"There have been important developments of which he would like you to be aware," the man said impassively.

"Such as?"

"Lockhart is working with the FBI to bring you down."

For a brief, dizzying moment Buchanan thought he would vomit all over himself. "What in the hell are you talking about?"

"This information was just discovered by our operative inside the Bureau."

"You mean they entrapped her? Made her work

for them?" *Just like you did to me.*

"She voluntarily went to them."

Buchanan slowly regained his composure. "Tell me everything," he said.

The man responded with a series of truths, half-truths and outright lies. He told them all with equal, practiced sincerity.

"Where is Faith now?"

"She's gone underground. The FBI is looking for her."

"How much has she told them? Should I be making plans to leave the country?"

"No. It's very early in the game. What she's told them thus far would not warrant prosecution of any kind. She's told them more of the process of how it was done, but not who was involved. However, that's not to say they can't follow up what she's told them. But they have to be careful. The targets aren't exactly flipping burgers at McDonald's."

"And the vaunted Mr. Thornhill doesn't know where Faith is? I hope his omniscience isn't failing him now."

"I have no information about that," said the man.

"A poor state of affairs for an intelligence-gathering agency," Buchanan said, even managing a smile. A log in the fireplace let out a loud pop, and a fat wad of sap shot out and hit the screen. Buchanan watched it dripping down the mesh face, its escape halted, its existence over. Why did he suddenly feel the remainder of his life had just been symbolically played out?

"Perhaps I should try to find her."

"It's really not your concern."

Buchanan stared at him. Had the idiot really said that? "*You* won't be the one going to prison."

"It'll work out. You just continue right on."

"I want to be kept informed. Clear?" Buchanan

turned to the window. In its reflection he studied the man's reaction to his sharply spoken words. But what were they really worth? Buchanan had clearly lost this round; he had no way of winning it, actually.

The street was dark, no visible movement, just the familiar sounds of squirrels corkscrewing up the trees and then leaping from branch to branch in their never-ending game of survival. Buchanan was engaged in a similar contest, but even more dangerous than hopping across the slippery bark of thirty-foot-tall trees. The wind had picked up some; the beginnings of a low howling sound could be heard in the chimney. A bit of smoke from the fire drifted into the room with the backdraft of air.

The man looked at his watch. "We need to leave in fifteen minutes to make your flight." He picked up Buchanan's briefcase, turned and left.

Robert Thornhill had always been careful in how he contacted Buchanan. No phone calls to the house or office. Face-to-face meetings only under conditions such as these where it would not raise suspicions, where surveillance by others could not be maintained. The first meeting between the two had been one of the few times in Buchanan's life that he had felt inadequate in the face of an opponent. Thornhill had calmly presented stark evidence of Buchanan's illegal dealings with members of Congress, high-ranking bureaucrats, even reaching inside the White House. Tapes of them going over voting schemes, strategies to defeat legislation, frank discussions of what their fake duties would be once they left office, how the payoffs would occur. The CIA man had uncovered Buchanan's web of slush funds and corporations designed to funnel money to his public officials.

"You now work for me," Thornhill had said

bluntly. "And you will go right on doing what you are doing until my net is as strong as steel. And then you will stand clear, and I will take over."

Buchanan had refused. "I'll go to prison," he had said. "I'll take that over indentured servitude."

Thornhill, Buchanan recalled, had looked slightly impatient. "I'm sorry if I wasn't clear. Prison isn't an option. You either work for me or you cease to live."

Buchanan had paled in the face of this threat, but still held firm. "A public servant embroiled in murder?"

"I'm a special type of public servant. I work in extremes. It tends to justify what I do."

"My answer's the same."

"Do you also speak for Faith Lockhart? Or should I consult her personally on the matter?"

That remark had struck Buchanan like a bullet to the brain. It was quite clear to Buchanan that Robert Thornhill was no bully. There was not a hint of bluster in the man. If he said something as innocuous as, "I'm sorry it's come to this," you would probably be dead the next day. Thornhill was a careful, deliberate, focused person, Buchanan had thought at the time. Not unlike himself. Buchanan had gone along. To save Faith.

Now Buchanan understood the relevance of Thornhill's safeguards. The FBI was watching him. Well, they had their work cut out for them, for Buchanan doubted they were in Thornhill's league when it came to clandestine operations. But everyone had an Achilles' heel. Thornhill had easily found his in Faith Lockhart. Buchanan had long wondered what Thornhill's weakness was.

Buchanan slumped in a chair and studied the painting hanging on the library wall. It was a portrait of a mother and child. It had hung in a private museum for almost eighty years. It was by one of the acknowledged – but lesser known – masters of the Renaissance period. The mother was clearly the protector, the infant boy unable to defend himself. The wondrous colors, the exquisitely painted profiles, the subtle brilliance of the hand that had invented this image so clearly evident in every brushstroke, never failed to enrapture anyone who saw it. The gentle curl of finger, the luminosity of the eyes, each detail still so vibrant almost four hundred years after the paint had hardened.

It was perfect love on both sides, uncomplicated by silent, corrosive agendas. As one level it was the simple thread of biological function. At another it was a phenomenon enhanced by the touch of God. This painting was his most prized possession. Unfortunately, it would soon have to be sold, and perhaps his home as well. He was running out of money to fund the "retirements" of his people. Indeed, he felt guilty for still owning the painting. The funds it could generate, the help it could bring to so many. And yet just to sit and gaze at it was so soothing, so uplifting. It was the height of selfishness, and brought him more pleasure than just about anything else.

But maybe it was all moot at this point. The end was coming for Buchanan. He knew that Thornhill would never let him walk away from all of this. And he had no illusions that he would let Buchanan's people enjoy any retirement whatsoever. They were his slaves-in-waiting. The CIA man, despite his refinement and pedigree, was a spy. What were spies but living lies? However, Buchanan would honor his agreement with his politicians. What he had promised them in return for helping him would be there, whether they would be able to enjoy it or not.

As the light of the fire played over the painting,

the woman's face, it seemed to Buchanan, took on the characteristics of Faith Lockhart – not the first time he had observed this. His gaze traced the set of full lips that could turn petulant or sensual without warning. As his eye ran down the long, gracefully formed face, the hair golden, not auburn, in just the right splash of angled light, he always thought of Faith. She had a pair of eyes that held you; the left pupil slightly off center added depth to make Faith's countenance truly remarkable. And it was as though this flaw of nature had empowered her to see right through anyone.

He remembered every detail of their very first meeting. Fresh out of college, she had bounded into his life with the enthusiasm of a newly minted missionary, ready to take on the world. She was raw, immature at certain levels, largely ignorant of the ways of Washington, astonishingly naive in various respects. And yet she could also command a room like a movie star. She could be funny and then turn serious on a dime. She could stroke egos with the best of them and still get her message across, without overtly pushing the issue. After five minutes talking to her, Buchanan knew she had what it took to flourish in his world. After her first month on the job, his intuition proved correct. She did her homework, worked tirelessly, learned the issues, dissected the players down to the level needed to do the job and then went deeper. She understood what everyone needed in order to walk away a winner. Burning bridges in this town meant you didn't survive. Sooner or later, you needed help from everyone, and memories were exceptionally long in the capital city. As tenacious as a wolverine, she had endured defeat after defeat on a number of fronts, but continued to pound away until she was victorious. He had never met anyone like her before or since. They had been through more together in fifteen years than couples married a lifetime. She was really all the family he had. The precocious daughter he was destined never to have. And now? How did he protect his little girl?

As the rain drifted across the roof and the wind strummed its peculiar sounds down the aged firebrick of his Old Town chimney, Buchanan forgot about his car and his flight and the dilemmas confronting him. The man continued to stare at the painting in the soft glow of the quietly crackling fire. And it was clearly not the work of the grand master that fascinated him so.

Faith had not betrayed him. Nothing Thornhill could ever tell him would change that belief. But now she was in Thornhill's way, which meant she was in mortal danger. He stared at the painting. "Run, Faith, run just as fast as you can," he said under his breath, with all the anguish of a desperate father seeing violent death racing after his child. In the face of the protector mother in the painting, Buchanan felt even more powerless.

TWELVE

Brooke Reynolds sat in rented office space about ten blocks from the Washington Field Office. The Bureau sometimes took off-site space for agents engaged in sensitive investigations, where something overheard even in the cafeteria or hallway could have disastrous effects. Virtually everything the Public Corruption Unit did was of a sensitive nature. The usual targets of the unit's investigation were not bank robbers wearing masks and waving guns. They were often people one read about on the front pages of the newspapers or saw being interviewed on the TV news.

Reynolds leaned forward and slipped out of her flats, rubbing her aching feet against the legs of her chair. Everything about her was tight, raw and hurting: Her sinuses were almost completely closed, her skin feverish, her throat scratchy. But at least she was alive. Unlike Ken Newman. She had driven straight to his home after first calling ahead to let his wife know she had to see her. Reynolds hadn't said why, but Anne Newman had known that her husband was dead. Reynolds had heard it in the tone of the few words the woman had managed to speak.

Normally, a person of a higher level than Reynolds would accompany her to the home of a bereaved spouse, to show that the Bureau did care, from top to bottom, when it lost one of its own. However, Reynolds had not waited for anyone else to volunteer to come with her. Ken was her responsibility, including telling his family that he was dead.

When she had arrived at the house, Reynolds had gotten right down to it, figuring a drawn-out monologue would only prolong the woman's obvious agony. Reynolds's compassion and empathy for the bereaved woman had been unhurried, however, and sincere. She had held Anne, consoled her as best she could, broken down in tears with her. Anne had taken the absence of information well, Reynolds had thought, far better than she probably would were the roles reversed.

Anne would be allowed to see her husband's body. Then it would be autopsied by the state's chief medical examiner. Connie and Reynolds would attend the post along with representatives from the Virginia State Police and the commonwealth's attorney office, all of whom were under strict confidentiality orders.

They would also have to count on Anne Newman to help keep angry and confused family members under control. It was a potentially weak link in the chain, expecting a woman in personal agony to help a government agency that couldn't even tell her all the circumstances of her husband's death. But it was all they had.

As she had left the stricken woman's home – the kids had been away with friends – Reynolds had the distinct feeling that Anne blamed her for Ken's death. And as Reynolds had walked back to her car she couldn't really disagree with that. The guilt Reynolds was feeling right now was like a crusty barnacle sunk into her skin, a free radical roaming inside her body, seeking a place to nest, grow and eventually kill her.

Outside the Newmans' home she had run into the

director of the FBI as he had come to offer his own condolences. He conveyed heartfelt sympathy to Reynolds for the loss of one of her men. He told her that he had been briefed on her conversation with Massey and that he concurred in her judgment. However, he made it clear that results had better be both quick and substantial.

As Reynolds now eyed the considerable clutter of her office, it occurred to her that the mess well symbolized the disorganization, some would say dysfunction, of her personal life. Matters of importance from many open cases lay across her desk and small conference table. They were wedged on to her shelves, had mutated into piles on her floor and even found their way on to the couch where she often slept, far away from her children.

But for her live-in nanny and the nanny's teenage daughter, Reynolds didn't know how should could possibly keep a halfway normal life for her kids. Rosemary, a wonderful woman from Central America who loved the children nearly as much as Reynolds did and was fanatical about keeping the house clean, the meals cooked and the clothes laundered, was costing Reynolds over a quarter of her entire salary and was more than worth every penny. But after the divorce was final it would be very tight. And Reynolds's ex would not be paying any alimony. His work as a fashion photographer, though lucrative, came in quick bursts followed by long periods of deliberate inactivity. Reynolds would be lucky if she didn't end up paying *him* alimony. And child support from him, while she would seek it, would be a joke. The man may as well have had "dead-beat dad" engraved on his forehead.

She looked at her watch. The FBI lab was working on the videotape right now. Because the existence of her "special" was unknown within the FBI except for very select personnel, any lab work that was required was supposed to be sent over under a dummy case name and file number. It would be nice to have separate laboratory facilities and personnel, but that would entail enormous expense that just didn't figure in the Bureau's budget. Even elite crime fighters had to live within the allowance Uncle Sam gave them. Normally a liaison agent at the main agency would work with Reynolds's team to coordinate any lab submissions and findings with Reynolds. However, Reynolds didn't have time for normal channels. She had personally delivered the tape to the lab and with her superior's blessing it had received a very high priority.

After meeting with Anne Newman she had gone home, cuddled for as long as she could with her sleeping kids, showered, changed and driven right back to work. All the time she had been thinking of that damn tape. As if in response to her thoughts, the phone rang.

"Yes?"

"You better come over," said the man. "And just so you know, it's not good news."

THIRTEEN

Faith awoke with a start. She looked at her watch. It was nearly seven. Lee had insisted that she get some rest, but she hadn't expected to be out so long. She sat up, feeling thickheaded. Her body was aching and when she swung her legs over the side of the bed, she felt a little sick to her stomach. She still had her suit on, but she had slipped off her shoes and pantyhose before lying down.

She got off the bed, padded into the adjoining bathroom and looked at herself in the mirror. "God," was all she could manage to say. Her hair was matted flat, her face a mess, her clothes filthy and her brain felt like cement. Such a pleasant way to begin the day.

She turned on the shower and stepped back into the bedroom to undress. She had taken off her clothes and was standing naked in the middle of the bedroom when Lee knocked on the door.

"Yes?" she said anxiously.

"Before you get in the shower, we need to do something," Lee said through the door.

"Is that right?" The odd tone of his words sent a chill up her spine. She quickly put her clothes back on and stood rigidly in the middle of the room.

"Can I come in?" He sounded impatient.

She went over and edged open the door. "What is—" Faith almost screamed when she saw him.

The man looking at her was not Lee Adams. This

man had a buzz cut, the hair dyed blond and damp, a matching short beard and mustache, and he wore glasses. And instead of dazzling blue, his eyes were brown.

The man smiled as he watched her reaction. "Good, it passed the test."

"Lee?"

"We can't exactly walk past the FBI as ourselves."

Lee held out his hands. Faith saw the scissors and a box of hair coloring.

"Short hair is easier to take care of, and personally I think it's a myth that blondes have more fun."

She looked at him dully. "You want me to cut my hair? And then color it?"

"No, I'll cut it. And if you want, I can color it for you too."

"I can't do that."

"You have to do that."

"I know it seems silly under the circumstances—"

"You're right, it does seem silly under the circumstances. Hair grows back, but once you're dead, you're dead," he said bluntly.

She started to protest but then realized he was right.

"How short?"

He cocked his head, examining her hair from different angles. "How about a short, Joan of Arc do? Boyish, but cute."

Faith just stared at him. "Wonderful. Boyish, but cute – my lifetime ambitions realized with a few snips and a bottle of hair color."

They went into the bathroom. Lee sat her down on the toilet and began to cut while Faith kept her eyes tightly shut.

"Want me to do the color too?" Lee asked when he was done.

"Please. I'm not sure I can look at it right now."

It took some time under the sink, and the smell of chemicals contained in the coloring mix was tough to take on an empty stomach, but when Faith finally managed to look in the mirror she was pleasantly surprised. It didn't look as bad as she would have thought. The outline of her head, now more fully revealed, was actually a nice shape. And the dark color went well with her skin tones.

"Now grab a shower," Lee said. "You can get your hair wet. Blow dryer's under the sink. There'll be some clean clothes on the bed."

She eyed his big frame. "I'm not your size."

"Not to worry. I run a full-service resort."

Thirty minutes later, Faith emerged from the bedroom in jeans and a flannel shirt, jacket and low-heeled boots that Lee had left for her. From power suit to college student. She felt years younger. The short black hair encircled her face, which she left au naturel. Faith had decided to forgo her usual makeup routine. Fresh start all around.

Lee sat at the kitchen table. He studied her new appearance. "Looks good," he said approvingly.

"You did it." She looked at his wet hair and a thought struck her. "Do you have a second bathroom?"

"Nope, just the one. I showered while you were sleeping. I didn't use the hair dryer because I was afraid it would wake you. You'll find I'm a very considerate soul."

She recoiled slightly. It was a creepy revelation, that he had been lurking around while she was asleep in his bed. She got this sudden image of a maniacal, scissors-toting Lee Adams leering while she lay there tied to the bed, naked and helpless.

"God, I must have really been out," she said as casually as she could.

"You were. I actually grabbed some shut-eye too."

He continued to study her appearance. "You know, you look better without makeup."

Faith smiled. "Your lies are very much appreciated." She smoothed down her shirt. "By the way, do you always keep women's clothes around your apartment?"

Lee pulled on a pair of socks and then some tennis shoes. He wore jeans and a white T-shirt that was spread taut across his chest. The veins in his biceps and smooth forearms rippled, and Faith hadn't really noticed before how thick his neck was. His torso narrowed dramatically at his waist, the pants slightly loose there, giving him a hard V-shape. His thighs looked ready to burst through the denim. He caught her staring and Faith quickly looked away.

"My niece Rachel," he said. "She goes to law school at Michigan. She clerked at the law firm here last year and stayed with me, rent-free. Only she earned more money in one summer than I do in about a year. She left some of her stuff. Lucky you're about the same size. She'll probably be back next summer."

"Tell her to be careful. This town has a way of destroying people."

"I don't think she'll have your problems. She wants to be a judge one day. No felons need apply."

Faith's face flushed. She took a mug from the sink rack and poured a cup of coffee.

Lee stood. "Look, that was out of line. I'm sorry."

"I deserve a lot worse than that, actually."

"Fine, I'll let other people do the honors."

Faith poured a cup of coffee for him and sat down at the table. Max came into the kitchen and nudged her hand. She smiled and petted the dog's broad head.

"Max taken care of?"

"All set." He checked his watch. "The bank opens

shortly. We'll have just enough time to pack. We'll get your stuff, head to the airport, get our tickets and fly, fly away."

"I can call down and arrange for the house from the airport. Or should I try from here?"

"No. Phone logs can be checked."

"I didn't think of that."

"You're going to have to start to." He took a sip of coffee. "Hope the place is available."

"It will be. I happen to own it. Or at least my other identity does."

"Small place?"

"Depends on what you call small. I think you'll be comfortable."

"I'm easy." He carried his coffee into the bedroom and came out a few minutes later wearing a navy blue sweater over his T-shirt. His mustache and beard were gone and he had a baseball cap on. He was carrying a small plastic bag.

"The evidence of our makeovers," he explained.

"And no disguise?"

"Mrs. Carter's used to me keeping odd hours, but if I barge in looking like somebody else, it'll be a little much for her this early in the morning. And I don't want her being able to give anyone a description later on."

"You are good at this," said Faith. "That's reassuring."

He called Max. The big dog obediently padded from the small living room into the kitchen, stretched his body and then sat next to Lee. "If the phone rings, don't answer it. And stay away from the windows."

Faith nodded and then he and Max were gone. She took her coffee and walked around the small apartment. It was a curious cross between a messy college dorm and a more mature person's home. In what should have been the dining room, Faith found a home gym. Nothing fancy, no high-dollar, high-tech machines, just barbells, a weight bench and squat rack that were set up throughout the space. In one corner was a heavy punching bag and next to it a speed bag. Boxing and weight gloves, hand wraps and towels were neatly arranged on a small wooden table next to a box of white powder. A medicine ball sat in another corner.

On the walls were some photos of men in Navy whites. Faith picked out Lee quite easily. He looked pretty much the same at eighteen as he did now. However, the years had weathered his face, cut in lines and angles that made him even more attractive, even more seductive. Why was aging so damn tilted in favor of men? There were black and white photos of Lee in the boxing ring, and one of him with his hand raised in victory, a medal resting against his wide chest. His expression was calm, as though he had expected to win; in fact, as though he would not accept losing.

Faith gave the heavy bag a small punch with a loosely made fist, and her hand and wrist instantly throbbed. In that moment she recalled how big and thick Lee's hands were, the knuckles resembling a miniature mountain range. A very strong, resourceful, tough man. A man who could take punishment. She just hoped he would remain on her side.

She went into the bedroom. On the nightstand next to his bed was a cell phone and next to that a portable panic-button device. Faith had been too exhausted to notice them last night. She wondered if he slept with his pistol under his pillow. Was he really just paranoid or did he know something the rest of the world didn't?

It suddenly occurred to her: Wasn't he afraid she might make a run for it? She went back into the hallway. The front was covered; he would see her leave that way. But there was a back door off the kitchen that went down a fire escape. She went over to the door and tried to open it. It was locked. Deadbolted. The kind you could only open with a key even from inside. The windows also had key locks. It angered Faith, being trapped like this, but the truth was she had been trapped long before Lee Adams popped up in her life.

She continued looking through the apartment. Faith smiled at the collection of record albums housed in their original covers, and a framed poster from the movie *The Sting*. She doubted if the man had a CD player or even cable TV. She opened another door and went into the room. She started to turn on the light and then paused as a sound caught her attention. She stepped to the window, inched back the blinds and looked out. It was fully light outside now, although the sky was still gray and gloomy. She didn't see anyone, but that meant nothing. She could be encircled by an army and she'd never know it.

She turned the light on and looked around, surprised. A desk, file cabinets, a sophisticated phone system and shelves filled with manuals surrounded her. There were large pegboards on the wall with memo cards tacked to them. On the desk were neatly arranged files, a calendar and the usual desktop accessories. Apparently, Lee's home also served as his place of business.

If this was his office, maybe the file on her was here. Lee would probably be gone for a few more minutes. She started to sift carefully through the papers on his desk. Then she went through the desk drawers and then moved on to the file cabinets. Lee was very organized and he had a lot of clients – mostly business and law firms, from the file labels she was seeing. Defense lawyers, she assumed, since prosecutors had their own detective force.

The ringing phone made her almost leap out of her shoes. Trembling, she went over to it. The base unit had an LCD readout. Lee obviously had caller ID, because the number of the person calling him was displayed on the readout. It was long distance, with a 215 area code. Philadelphia, she recalled. Lee's voice came on and told the caller to leave a message after the beep. When that person started talking, Faith froze.

"Where is Faith Lockhart?" asked the voice of Danny Buchanan. Danny sounded very distressed as he fired more questions: What had Lee found out? He wanted answers and he wanted them immediately. Buchanan left a phone number, then hung up. Faith felt herself backing away from the phone. She stopped and stood still, transfixed by what she had just heard. A full minute passed as numbing thoughts of betrayal swirled through her mind like confetti in a parade. Then she heard a sound behind her and whirled around. Her scream was short, sharp, leaving her momentarily breathless. Lee was staring at her.

FOURTEEN

Buchanan looked around the crowded airport. He had taken a risk in calling Lee Adams directly, but his options now were few. As his eyes roamed the area, he wondered which of the people it was. The old lady in the corner with her big purse and hair in a bun? She had been on Buchanan's flight. A tall, middle-aged man had been pacing the aisle while Buchanan had been on the phone. He too had been on the flight from National.

The truth was Thornhill's people could be anywhere, anyone. It was like being attacked by nerve gas. You never saw the enemy. A sense of profound hopelessness gripped Buchanan.

Buchanan's greatest fear had been that Thornhill would either try to get Faith involved in his scheme, or suddenly find her a liability. He might have pushed Faith away, but would never abandon her. This was why he had hired Adams to follow her. As the end drew near, he had to make sure she remained safe.

Buchanan had looked in the phone book, of all places, and used the simplest logic he could think of. Lee Adams had been the first person listed under private investigators. Buchanan almost laughed out loud now at what he had done. But unlike Thornhill, he didn't have an army at his beck and call. For all he knew, Adams hadn't reported in because he was dead.

He paused for a moment. Should he just flee to the

ticket counter, book the first flight available to anywhere remote and then lose himself? Easy to fantasize about, quite another thing to implement. He envisioned trying to escape: Thornhill's heretofore invisible army would suddenly materialize and descend upon him from the shadows, displaying official-looking badges to anyone bold enough to intervene. Then Buchanan would be taken to a quiet room in the bowels of the Philadelphia airport. There Robert Thornhill would be calmly waiting with his pipe and his three-piece suit and his casual arrogance. He would calmly ask Buchanan, did he want to die right this very minute? Because Thornhill would certainly accommodate him if he did. And Buchanan would have absolutely no response.

Finally Danny Buchanan did the only thing he could do. He left the airport, climbed in his waiting car and drove to see his friend the senator, to put another nail in the man's coffin with his smiling, disarming manner and the listening device he was wearing, which looked exactly like skin and hair follicles and was so advanced that it wouldn't set off the most sophisticated of metal detectors. A surveillance van would follow him to his destination and record every word said by Buchanan and the senator.

As a backup, in case the transmission from his listening device was somehow interfered with, Buchanan's briefcase had a tape recorder built in to its frame. A slight twist on the briefcase handle activated the recorder. It too was undetectable by even the most sophisticated airport security. Thornhill really had thought of everything. *Damn the man.*

On the drive over, Buchanan comforted himself with a deliriously inspiring fantasy involving a pleading, broken Thornhill, an assortment of poisonous snakes, boiling oil and a rusted machete.

If only dreams could come true.

The person sitting in the airport was clean-cut, mid-thirties, dressed in a dark, conservatively cut suit and working on a laptop computer – meaning he mirrored about a thousand other business travelers all around him. He seemed busy and focused, even talking to himself at times. He gave the appearance, to the casual passersby, of a man preparing for a sales pitch or compiling a marketing report. He was actually quietly talking into the tiny microphone embedded in his necktie. What looked like infrared data ports on the backside of his computer were really sensors. One was designed to capture electronic signals. The other was a sound wand that collected words and posted them on to the screen. The first sensor quite easily snagged the phone number Buchanan had just called and automatically transmitted it to the screen. The voice sensor had been a little garbled, what with so many conversations going on at the airport; but enough had come through to make the man excited. The words "Where is Faith Lockhart?" stared back at him from the screen.

The man conveyed the telephone number and other information to his colleagues back in Washington. Within seconds a computer at Langley had produced the account holder of the phone and the address to which the phone number was registered. Within minutes a very experienced team of professionals completely in the allegiance of Robert Thornhill – who had been waiting for just such a mission – was dispatched to Lee Adams's apartment.

Thornhill's instructions were simple. If Faith

Lockhart was there, they were to "terminate" her, as it was so benignly termed in official espionage parlance, as though she would simply be fired and asked to collect her personal belongings and leave the building, instead of a bullet fired into her head. Anyone with her would suffer the same fate. For the good of the country.

FIFTEEN

"You scared the hell out of me." Faith couldn't stop trembling.

Lee moved into the room and looked around. "What are you doing in my office?"

"Nothing! I was just wandering. I didn't even know you had your office here."

"That's because you didn't need to know that."

"I thought I heard a sound outside the window when I came in here."

"You did hear a sound, but it didn't come from the window." He pointed to the doorjamb.

Faith noted the rectangular piece of white plastic attached to the wood there.

"It's a sensor. Anybody opens the door to my office, it trips the sensor and triggers my beeper." He took the device out of his pocket. "If I hadn't had Max to calm down at Mrs. Carter's, I would've been up here a lot sooner." He scowled at her. "I don't appreciate this, Faith."

"Hey, I was just looking around, killing time."

"Interesting choice of words: 'killing.'"

"Lee, I'm not plotting against you. I swear it."

"Let's finish packing. Don't want to keep your bankers waiting."

Faith avoided looking at the phone again. Lee must not have heard the message. He had been hired by Buchanan to follow her. Had he killed the agent last night? When they got on the plane, would he somehow manage to push her out at thirty thousand feet and laugh riotously while she plummeted screaming through the clouds?

But he could have killed her at any point from last night to now. Leaving her dead at the cottage would have been the easiest move. That's when it hit her: It would have been the easiest move unless Danny wanted to know how much she had told the FBI. That would explain why she was still alive. And also why Lee was so eager to get her to talk. Once she did, then he would kill her. And here they were flying off together to a North Carolina beach community that would be largely deserted this time of year. She slowly walked out of the room, a condemned woman on the way to her execution.

Twenty minutes later, Faith closed the small travel bag and slid her purse strap over her head and on to her shoulder. Lee came into the bedroom. He had put back on the mustache and beard, and the baseball cap was gone. In his right hand was his pistol, two boxes of ammo and his belt holster.

Faith watched as he loaded the items into a special hard-sided container. "You can't take a gun on a plane," she said.

"You're kidding, really? When did they start that shit?" He closed the container and locked it, pocketing the keys before looking at her. "You *can* take a gun on a plane if you disclose the weapon when you check in and fill out a declaration form. They ensure that the weapon is unloaded and in an approved case." He rapped his knuckles against the hard-sided aluminum case. "Which it is. They check that the ammo is a hundred rounds or fewer and is in the manufacturer's original or otherwise FAA-approved packaging. Again, I'm cool. Then they mark the bag with a special tag and it goes to the cargo bay, where it would be real hard for me to get to if I was thinking about skyjacking the plane, wouldn't you agree?"

"Thanks for the explanation," Faith said curtly.

"I'm not a damn amateur," he said hotly.

"I never said you were."

"Right."

"Okay, I'm sorry." She hesitated, intensely desiring to establish some sort of truce, for a number of reasons, her survival being chief among them. "Would you do me a favor?"

He looked at her suspiciously.

"Call me Faith."

The door buzzer startled them both.

Lee checked his watch. "Little early for visitors."

Faith watched in amazement as his hands moved like a machine. Within twenty seconds the pistol was out of the container and fully loaded. He put the container and the ammo boxes in his small travel bag and hoisted it over his shoulder. "Get your bag."

"Who do you think it is?" Faith felt her pulse throbbing in her ears.

"Let's go find out."

They stepped quietly into the hallway and Faith followed Lee to the front door.

He checked the TV screen. They both saw the man standing there on the front stoop of the building, a couple of packages in his arms. The familiar brown uniform was clearly visible. As they watched, he hit the buzzer once more.

"It's just the UPS man," Faith said, letting out a relieved breath.

Lee didn't take his eyes off the screen. "Is that right?" He hit a button on the screen that obviously moved the camera, as Faith found herself now staring at the street in front of the building. Something that should have been there wasn't.

"Where's his truck?" she said, her fear abruptly returning.

"Excellent question. And the fact is I know the UPS guy on this route real well, and that's not him."

"Maybe he's on vacation."

"Actually, he just got back from a week in the islands with his new bride. And he never comes at this time of the morning. Which means we've got a big problem."

"Maybe we can get out through the back."

"Yeah, I'm sure they forgot to cover the rear."

"There's only the one man."

"No, he's the only one we can see. He's got the front. They probably want to flush us out the back right into their arms."

"So we're trapped," she managed to whisper.

The buzzer rang again and Lee reached out his finger to hit the intercom button.

Faith grabbed his hand. "What the hell are you doing?"

"I'm going to ask what he wants: He'll say UPS and I'm going to let him in."

"You're going to let him in," Faith repeated dully. She glanced at his pistol. "What, and have a shoot-out in your apartment building?"

Lee's face hardened. "When I tell you to move, you move your ass like a T-Rex is breathing down your neck."

"Move? Move where?"

"Just follow me. And no more questions."

Lee hit the intercom button, the man identified himself and Lee touched the door release. As soon as he did, he activated the apartment's alarm system, whipped open the front door, grabbed Faith by the arm and pulled her out into the hallway. There was a door across from Lee's apartment. It had no apartment number on it. As Faith listened to the UPS man's footsteps echoing in the building down below, Lee already had unlocked the door. They were through it in an instant and he quietly closed and locked the door behind them. The place was very dark, but Lee obviously knew his way around here. He led her to the back, through another door that opened up into what looked like a back bedroom, from the little Faith could see.

Lee opened another door in the room and motioned Faith in. She stepped through and almost immediately felt a wall against her. When Lee joined her, it was a very tight fit, like a telephone booth. He closed the door and the darkness became blacker than anything Faith had ever experienced before.

He startled her when he spoke, his breath tickling her ear. "Right in front of you there's a ladder. Here are the rungs." He gripped her hand and guided it until her fingers touched the rungs. "Okay?" She nodded. Lee continued whispering. "Give me your bag and start climbing. Take it slow. I'll sacrifice speed for silence right now. I'll be right behind you. When you get to the top, just stop. I'll take it from there."

As she began to climb, Faith started feeling severely claustrophobic. And, because she had lost her bearings, she was becoming queasy. Now would be such a perfect time to lose the contents of her stomach, little though it was.

She moved her hands and feet slowly as she went up. Then, gaining confidence, she started to pick up her pace. That was a mistake because her foot missed a rung, she slipped and her chin painfully clipped one of the rungs. But then Lee's strong arm was round her in an instant, holding her up. She took a moment to steady herself, tried to ignore the pain in her chin and kept climbing until she felt the ceiling above her head and then stopped.

Lee was still on the rung right below her. Then he

suddenly moved up on the same rung she was on, his legs on either side of hers so that her legs were pinched between his. He leaned against her with increasing force, and she wasn't sure what he was trying to do. It was becoming painful to breathe with her chest pushed up hard against the ladder rungs. For one terrifying moment she thought he had lured her in here to rape her. Suddenly a blast of light hit her from above and he moved away from her. She looked up, blinking rapidly. The view of the blue sky was so wonderful after the terror of the darkness that she felt like screaming in relief.

"Go up and on to the roof, but keep low. As low as you can," Lee whispered urgently into her ear.

She went up and through, dropping to her belly and looking around. The roof of the old building was flat, with a gravel and tar base. Bulky old heating units and newer air-conditioning machinery dotted the roof in various places. They made for good hiding places and Faith slid over and squatted next to the nearest one.

Lee was still on the ladder. He listened intently and then checked his watch. The guy would be at his door right about now. He would buzz, wait for Lee to answer. They had thirty seconds at most before the guy realized no one was coming to the door. It would be nice to have a little more time than that, and also a way to draw in the other forces Lee knew were out there. He pulled his cell phone from his pocket and hit a speed-dial number.

When the person answered, he said, "Mrs. Carter, it's Lee Adams. Listen to me, I want you to let Max out in the hallway. Right, I know I just dropped him off. I know he'll head up to my apartment. That's what I want. I, uh, I forgot to give him a shot he needs. Please hurry, I really need to get out of here."

He pocketed the phone and pushed the bags up

and out, then he hoisted himself through the opening and closed the hatch behind him. He scanned the roof and spotted Faith. Grabbing the bags, he slid over to her.

"Okay, we got a little time."

Down below they heard a dog start to bark loudly and Lee smiled. "Follow me." Squatting low, they made their way to the edge of the roof. The building attached to Lee's was a little shorter so that the roof was about five feet lower. Lee motioned for Faith to take his hands. She did so and he lowered her over the edge, holding tightly until her feet touched the roof. As soon as Lee joined her, they both heard shouts coming from Lee's building.

"Okay, they've made their all-out assault. They'll go through the door and that'll trip the alarm. I don't have a call-back option with the alarm company, so there's no delay in sending the cops. A few minutes and it'll be a big mess."

"What do we do in the meantime?" Faith asked.

"Three more buildings and then down the fire escape. Move!"

Five minutes later they were running through a back alley and then out on to another quiet suburban street flanked by a number of low-rise apartment buildings. The street was lined on both sides with parked cars. In the background Faith could hear the thump of a tennis ball being hit. She could make out a tennis court surrounded by several tall pine trees in a small park across from the apartment building.

She watched as Lee eyed a line of cars parked at the curb. Then he jogged across to the park area and bent down. When he straightened up, he was holding a tennis ball – one of many that had landed there from years of errant shots on the court. He walked back over to Faith. She could see that he was working a hole in the tennis ball with his pocketknife.

"What are you doing?" she asked.

"Go up on the sidewalk and walk as calmly as you can. And keep your eyes open."

"Lee—"

"Just do it, Faith!"

She spun around and went up on the sidewalk, paralleling his movements as he walked on the other side of the parked cars, his eyes scanning each of the vehicles. He finally stopped at a new-looking luxury model.

"See anybody watching us?" Lee asked.

Faith shook her head.

He walked over to the car and held the tennis ball against the key lock, the hole in the ball facing the lock's opening.

Faith looked at him as if he were insane. "What are you doing?"

In response, he slammed his fist against the tennis ball, driving all the air out of the ball and into the key lock. Faith watched in amazement as all four door locks popped open.

"How did you do that?"

"Get in."

Lee slid into the car, and Faith did the same.

He poked his head under the steering column and found the wires he needed.

"You can't hot-wire these new cars. The technology—" Faith stopped talking when the car started.

Lee sat up, put the car in gear and pulled away from the curb. He looked at Faith. "What?"

"All right, so how did the tennis ball unlock the car?"

"I've got my professional secrets."

Faith stared forward while he drove.

While Lee waited in the car with his eyes sharply on

the lookout, Faith entered her bank, explained what she wanted to the assistant manager and managed to sign her name, all without falling over in a dead faint. *Steady girl, one step at a time.* Fortunately, she knew the man.

The assistant manager looked curiously at her new appearance.

"Midlife crisis," she said, responding to his stare. "Decided to go for the youthful, streamlined look."

"It's very becoming, Ms. Lockhart," he said gallantly.

She closely watched him as he took her key, inserted it and the bank's duplicate key into the lock and pulled out her box. They left the vault and he set the box inside the private booth across from the vault reserved for safe-deposit box tenants. As he walked away, Faith continued to watch him.

Was he one of them? Was he going to slip away and call the police or the FBI or whoever was running around killing people? Instead he sat down at his desk, opened a white bag, extracted a glazed donut and proceeded to devour it.

Satisfied for the moment, Faith closed and locked the door. She opened the box and stared at the contents for a moment. Then she swept it all into her bag and closed the box. The young man put the safe-deposit box back in the vault and Faith walked out as calmly as she could.

Back in the car, Faith and Lee headed down Interstate 395, where they exited on to the GW Parkway and headed south to Reagan National Airport. Going against the morning rush hour, they made good time.

Faith looked over at Lee, who stared straight ahead, lost in thought.

"You did really well back there," she said.

"Actually, we cut it closer than I would have

liked." He paused and shook his head. "I'm really worried about Max, as stupid as that sounds under the circumstances."

"It doesn't sound stupid."

"Max and I have been together a long time. For years it's been only me and that old dog."

"I doubt they would have done anything to him with all those people around."

"Yeah, you'd like to think so, wouldn't you? But the fact is if they'll kill a man, a dog doesn't stand a chance."

"I'm sorry you had to do that for me."

He sat up straight. "Well, a dog is still a dog, Faith. And we've got other things to worry about, don't we?"

Faith found herself nodding. "Yes."

"I guess my magnet trick didn't work so well. They must have identified me through the video. Still, that was awfully fast." He shook his head, his expression a mix of admiration and fear. "Like scary fast."

Faith felt her spirits sink. If Lee was scared, at what level of sheer terror should she be operating? "Not very encouraging, is it?" she said.

"I might be a little better prepared if you tell me what's going on."

After the man's heroics, Faith found herself wanting to confide in him. But then the phone call from Buchanan came flashing back, ringing in her ears, like the shots last night.

"When we get to North Carolina, we'll have it all out. *Both* sides," Faith said.

SIXTEEN

Thornhill replaced the phone receiver and looked around his office, a disturbed expression on his face. His men had found the nest empty, and one of them had even been bitten by a dog. There had been reports of a man and woman running down the street. This was all just a little too much. Thornhill was a patient man, used to working on projects for many years, but still, there were limits to what he could tolerate. His men had listened to the message Buchanan had left on Lee's answering machine. They had taken the tape and played it back for Thornhill over his secure phone line.

"So you've hired a private investigator, Danny," Thornhill muttered to himself. "You'll pay for that one." He nodded thoughtfully. "I'll make you pay."

The police had responded to the burglar alarm, but when Thornhill's men had flashed official-looking IDs they had quickly backed off. Legally, the CIA had no authority to operate within the United States. Thus, Thornhill's team routinely carried several types of identification and would select one depending on who confronted them.

The patrolmen had been sent off with instructions to bury deeply all that they had seen. Still, Thornhill didn't like it. It was all too close to the edge. There were holes there, ways for people to gain an advantage over him.

He went to the window and looked outside. It was

a beautiful fall day, the colors starting to turn. As he studied the pleasing foliage, he primed his pipe, but unfortunately that was all he could do. CIA headquarters was a nonsmoking building. The deputy director had a balcony outside his office where Thornhill could sit and smoke, but it was not the same. During the Cold War, the CIA offices had been as foggy as steam baths. Tobacco helped one think, Thornhill believed. It was a minor thing, yet it symbolized all that had gone wrong with the place.

In Thornhill's opinion, the CIA's downfall had accelerated in 1994 with the Aldrich Ames' debacle. Thornhill still winced every time he thought of the former CIA counterintelligence officer being arrested for spying for the Soviets and later the Russians. And of course, as fate would have it, the FBI had broken the case. After that, the president had issued a directive ordering an FBI agent to be made a permanent employee of the CIA. From then on, this FBI agent oversaw the agency's counterespionage efforts and had access to all CIA files. An FBI agent on the premises! His nose in all their secrets! Not to be outdone by the executive branch, the idiotic Congress had followed with a law requiring all government agencies, including the CIA, to notify the FBI whenever there was evidence that classified information might have been improperly disclosed to foreign powers. The result: The CIA took all the risk and gave the prize to the FBI. Thornhill seethed. It was a direct usurpation of the CIA's mission.

Thornhill's rage was building. The CIA could no longer even put people under surveillance or wiretap. If it had suspicions of someone, it had to go to the FBI and request surveillance, electronic or otherwise. If electronic surveillance was desired, then the FBI had to go to FISC, the Foreign Intelligence

Surveillance Court, and obtain authorization. The CIA couldn't even approach FISC on its own. It had to have its hand held by Big Brother. Everything was stacked in the FBI's favor.

Thornhill's thoughts went into a tailspin as he reminded himself that the shackles on the CIA weren't just domestic; the Agency had to get authorization from the president before commencing any covert operations overseas. The congressional oversight committees had to be told of any such operations in a timely fashion. And with the world of espionage becoming more and more complicated, the CIA and FBI found themselves continually running into each other over jurisdictional squabbles, use of witnesses and informants and the like. Though it was supposed to be a domestic agency only, the FBI, in reality, did considerable work abroad, where it focused on antiterrorism and anti-drug operations, including the collection and analysis of information. Again, that hit right at the CIA's home turf.

Was it any wonder Thornhill hated his federal counterparts? Like a cancer, the bastards were everywhere. And to drive the nail a little farther into the CIA's coffin, a former FBI agent now headed up the Center for CIA Security, which conducted internal background checks on all current and prospective personnel. And all CIA employees had to file annual financial disclosure forms that were damn well exhaustive in their current requirements.

Before he suffered a stroke thinking any more on this sore subject, Thornhill forced himself to turn his attention to other matters. If Buchanan had hired this PI person to follow Lockhart, then he very well could have been the man at the cottage last night and the person who had shot Serov. There had been permanent nerve damage to the man's arm from the gunshot wound, and Thornhill had ordered the Russian to be finished off. A hired killer who could no longer hold a weapon steady enough to kill would look for other ways to make money and could pose a small threat. It was Serov's own fault, and if there was one thing Thornhill demanded from his people, it was accountability.

So this Lee Adams was now in the mix of things, he mused. Thornhill had already ordered a complete background search on the man. In these days of computerized files, he would have a full dossier in half an hour, if not sooner. Thornhill did have Adams's file on Faith Lockhart; his men had taken that from the apartment. The notes showed that the man was thorough, logical in his approach to investigation. That was both good and bad for Thornhill's purposes. Adams had also given Thornhill's men the slip. That was not an easy thing to do. On the good side, if Adams was logical, he should be amenable to a reasonable offer, meaning one that would allow him to live.

Presumably Adams had also escaped from the cottage with Faith Lockhart. He had not reported in to Buchanan about this, which was why Buchanan had left that phone message. Buchanan was obviously unaware of what had happened last night. Thornhill would do all he could to make sure this state of affairs continued.

How would they run? A train? Thornhill doubted it. Trains were slow. And you couldn't take a train overseas. Now, a train to an airport was a more intriguing possibility. Or a cab. That seemed certainly more likely.

Thornhill eased back into his chair as an assistant entered with some files he had requested. While everything at the CIA was computerized these days, Thornhill still liked the feel of paper in his hand. He could think much more clearly with paper than when he was simply staring at the pixeled screen.

So all the usual bases were covered. What about the unusual? With the added element of a professional investigator, Adams and Lockhart might be fleeing under false identities, even disguises. He had men at all three airports and the train stations. That would only go so far. The pair could easily rent a car and drive to New York and take a plane there. Or they could go south and do the same thing. It certainly was problematic.

Thornhill hated these sorts of chases. There were too many places to cover and he had limited manpower for these "extracurricular" activities of his. At least he had the advantage of operating more or less autonomously. No one from the director of central intelligence on down really questioned him as to what he was up to. Or if they did, he was able to dance around any issue they threw at him. He got results that made them all look good, and that was his biggest weapon.

It was much better to coax the runners out, bring them to you, which was certainly possible with the right sort of bait. Thornhill just had to come up with that bait. That would take some thinking. Lockhart had no family, no elderly parents or young children. He didn't know enough about Adams yet, but he would. If the man had just hooked up with the woman, he couldn't possibly be willing to sacrifice everything for her. Not just yet. Other things being equal, Adams was the one to focus on. And they had a communication link to him by virtue of knowing where he lived. If they needed to get a discreet message to him, they could.

Now Thornhill's thoughts turned to Buchanan. He was currently in Philadelphia meeting with a prominent senator on how best to further the agenda of one of Buchanan's clients. They had this particular fellow on enough felonious activity to make the man literally break down and plead for his miserable life. He had been a special pain in the ass to the CIA, nickle-and-diming them to death from the high perch of his Appropriations Committee seat. The payback would be so gratifying.

Thornhill envisioned walking into all these mighty politicians' offices and showing them the videos, the audiotapes, the paper trails. Of them and Buchanan plotting their little conspiracies, all the details of the future payoffs; they so eager to do Buchanan's bidding in return for all that money. How greedy they looked!

Good Senator, would you mind very much licking my boots, you whiny, squealing excuse for a human being. And then you will do exactly as I say, no more, no less, or I will crush you underfoot faster than you can say "vote for me."

Of course, Thornhill would never say that. These men demanded your respect even if they didn't deserve it. He would tell them that Danny Buchanan had disappeared and left these tapes with them. They weren't quite sure what to do with the evidence, but it appeared that the tapes should be turned over to the FBI. It seemed an awful thing to do; these fine men couldn't possibly be guilty of these sorts of things, but once the FBI started its feeding frenzy, they all knew where that would end: prison. And how could that possibly help the country? The world would laugh at us. Terrorists would be emboldened in the face of a supposedly weakened foe. And resources were so tight. Why, the CIA itself was understaffed and underfunded, it's responsibility unfairly curtailed. And could you fine people perhaps do something to change that? And would you please do so at the expense of the

FBI, the very bastards who would love to get their hands on these tapes so they could destroy you? Starting with getting them the hell off our backs? And we thank you very much, you fine public leaders. We knew you'd understand.

The first move in Thornhill's grand plan would be to have his new allies find a way to completely remove the FBI presence from the Agency. Next, the operations budget for the CIA would be increased by fifty percent. To start. In the next fiscal year he would get serious about the dollars. In the future, the CIA would only report to a joint intelligence committee instead of the separate House and Senate committees it was confronted with now. It was far easier to co-opt one committee. Then the hierarchy of the U.S. intelligence-gathering agencies needed to be straightened out once and for all. And the director of Central Intelligence would be at the very top of that pyramid. The FBI would be as far down the totem pole as Thornhill could bury it. And the tools of the CIA would be considerably strengthened. Domestic surveillance, the covert funding and arming of insurgency groups to overthrow enemies of the United States, even selective assassination, all would come back as weapons of choice for him and his colleagues. Right that minute Thornhill could think of five heads of state whose immediate deaths would leave the world a better, safer, more humane place. It was time to take the shackles off the best and brightest and let them do their jobs again. God, he was so close.

"Keep up the good work, Danny," Thornhill said out loud. "Pour it on until the end. That's a good man. Let them almost taste victory right before I take their lives away."

Grim-faced, he looked at his watch and rose from behind his desk. Thornhill was a man who loathed the press. He had, of course, never granted an interview in all his years at the Agency. But as senior as he was now, he occasionally had to undertake another sort of appearance, one that he equally detested. He had to testify before the House and Senate Select Committees on Intelligence on a series of matters involving the Agency.

In these "enlightened" times, CIA personnel gave more than one thousand substantive reports to Congress in a year's time. So much for covert operations. Thornhill was able to get through these briefings only by focusing on how easily he could manipulate the idiots who were supposed to be overseeing his agency. With their smug looks, they posed to him questions formulated by their very diligent staffs, who were more knowledgeable about most intelligence matters than the elected officials they served.

At least the hearing would be in camera, no public or press allowed. To Thornhill the First Amendment's rights to an unfettered press had been the biggest mistake the Founding Fathers had ever made. You had to be damn careful around the scribes; they looked for every advantage, any chance to put words in your mouth, trip you up, make the Agency look bad. It deeply hurt Thornhill that no one seemed to really trust them. Of course they lied about things; that was their job.

In Thornhill's mind the CIA was clearly the Hill's favorite whipping boy. The members loved to look tough in facing down the super-secret organization. That really played well back home: FARMER-TURNED-CONGRESSMAN STARES DOWN SPOOKS. By now Thornhill could write the headlines himself.

However, today's hearing actually promised to be positive because the Agency had scored some serious PR points lately in the most recent Middle

East peace talks. Indeed, largely through Thornhill's behind-the-scenes work, the Agency had overall fashioned a more benign, upstanding image, an image he would seek to bolster today.

Thornhill snapped his briefcase shut and put his pipe in his pocket. *Off to lie to a bunch of liars, and we both know it and we both win*, he thought. *Only in America.*

SEVENTEEN

"Senator," Buchanan said, shaking hands with the tall, elegant-looking gentleman. Senator Harvey Milstead was a proven leader with high morals and strong political instincts who offered thoughtful insight on the issues. A true statesman. That was the public perception. The reality was that Milstead was a womanizer of the first order and was addicted to painkillers for a chronically bad back, medications that sometimes left him incoherent. He also had a worsening drinking problem. It was years since he had sponsored any meaningful legislation of his own, although in his prime he had helped enact laws from which every American now benefited. These days when he spoke, it was in gobbledygook that no one ever bothered to check up on because he said it with such authority. Besides, the press loved the charming guy with such genteel manners, and he held a very powerful leadership position. He also fed the media machine with a flow of appropriately timed juicy leaks, and he was quotable to a fault. They loved him, Buchanan knew. How could they not?

There were five hundred and thirty-five members of Congress – a hundred senators plus the representatives in the House. Well over three-quarters of them, Buchanan estimated perhaps a little generously, were decent, hardworking, genuinely caring men and women who believed strongly in what they were doing both in Washington and for the people. Buchanan termed them, collectively, the "Believers." Buchanan stayed away from the Believers. Touching those folk would only have earned him a quick trip to prison.

The rest of the Washington leadership were like Harvey Milstead. Most were not drunks or womanizers or shells of their former selves, but, for various reasons, they were ripe for manipulation, easy targets for the lures Buchanan was tossing overboard.

There were two such groups that Buchanan had successfully recruited over the years. Forget Republicans and Democrats. The parties Buchanan was interested in were the members of the venerable "Townies," and the group Buchanan had labeled, only somewhat tongue-in-cheek, the "Zombies."

The Townies knew the system better than anyone. They *were* the system. Washington was their town, hence the nickname. They had all been here longer than God. If you cut them, their blood would run red, white and blue, or so they liked to tell you. There was another color Buchanan had added to that mix: green.

By contrast, the Zombies had come to Congress with nary a stitch of moral fiber or whiff of a political philosophy. They had won their place of leadership with the finest campaigns that media dollars could buy. They were fabulous on sound bite TV and in the confines of tightly controlled debates. They were, at best, mediocre in intellect and ability and yet delivered the sales pitch with the verve and enthusiasm of a JFK at his oratorical best. And when they were elected, they arrived in Washington with absolutely no idea what to do. Their only goal had already been achieved: They had won their campaign.

However, despite this, the Zombies tended to stay in Congress because they loved the power and access that came with being an incumbent. And with the cost of elections going through the stratosphere, it was still possible to defeat an entrenched incumbent . . . in the same way that it was still theoretically possible to climb Mount Everest without oxygen. One only had to hold his breath for several days.

Buchanan and Milstead sat down on a comfortable leather couch in the senator's spacious office. The shelves were filled with the usual spoils of a longtime politician: plaques and medals of appreciation, silver cups, awards made of crystal, hundreds of photographs of the senator standing with people even more famous than he; inscribed ceremonial gavels and bronzed miniature shovels symbolizing political pork brought to his state. As Buchanan looked around, it occurred to him that he had spent his entire professional life coming to places such as this, hat in hand, essentially begging.

It was early yet, but the man's staff was busy in the outer suite preparing for a hectic day with Keystone State constituents, a day laced with lunches, speeches, appearances and pop-in-and-out dinners, meet-and-greets, drinks and parties. The senator was not up for reelection, but it was always nice to put on a good show for the people back home.

"I appreciate your meeting with me on such short notice, Harvey."

"Hard to refuse you, Danny."

"I'll get right to it. Pickens's bill is looking to knock out my funding, along with about twenty other aid packages. We can't let that happen. The results speak for themselves. The infant mortality rate has been cut seventy percent. My God, the wonders of vaccine and antibiotics. Jobs are being created, the economy is moving from thuggery to legitimate business. Exports are up by a third, and imports from us are up twenty percent. So you see it's creating jobs here too. We can't let the plug be pulled now. Not only is it morally wrong, it's stupid from our side. If we can get countries like this on their feet, we won't have a trade imbalance. But you need reliable sources of electricity first. You need an educated population."

"AID has accomplished a lot," the senator pointed out.

Buchanan was intimately familiar with AID, or the Agency for International Development. Formerly an independent agency, it now reported to the Secretary of State, who also more or less controlled its very substantial budget. AID was the flagship of American foreign aid, with the vast majority of funds flowing through its long-standing programs. Every year it was like musical chairs to see where AID's limited budget dollars would end up. Buchanan had been caught without a seat many times, and he was so weary of it. The grant process was intensive and highly competitive, and unless you fit the template set up by AID for the programs it wanted to sponsor, you were out of luck.

"AID can't do it all. And my clients are too small a bite for IMF and the World Bank. Besides, now all I hear is 'sustainable development.' No dollars unless it goes for sustainable development. Hell, last time I looked, food and medicine were necessary for life. Doesn't that qualify?"

"You're preaching to the choir, Danny. But people count pennies around here too. The days of fat are over," Milstead said solemnly.

"My clients will take gristle. Just don't cut them off."

"Look, I just won't schedule the bill."

In the Senate, if a chairman didn't want a bill to get out of committee, he simply didn't schedule it for hearing, as Milstead was now suggesting. Buchanan had played that game many times before.

"But Pickens could end-run you on that," Buchanan said. "Word is he's dead set on getting this thing heard one way or another. And he might get a more sympathetic audience on the floor than he would in committee. Why not put a hold on the bill and run it out of session?" Buchanan suggested.

Danny Buchanan was the master at this technique. A hold was simply one senator objecting to a pending bill. The legislation would be in complete limbo until the hold was removed. Years ago, Buchanan and his allies on the Hill had used it to stunning effect in representing the most powerful special interests in the country. It took real power in Washington to make things not happen. And for Buchanan, that had always been the most fascinating aspect of the city. Why health care reform legislation or the tobacco settlement bills, propelled by intense media coverage and public clamor, simply disappeared into the yawning gulf of the Congress. And it was very often the case that special interests wanted to maintain the status quo they had worked so hard to erect. For them change was not good. Hence, a good deal of Buchanan's previous lobbying work had focused on burying any legislation that would harm his powerful clients.

The hold maneuver was also known as the "blind rolling" hold because, like the passing of the baton on a relay team, a different senator could place a new hold when the previous one had been released, and only the leadership knew who had placed the restriction. There was a lot more to it, but at the end of the day the blind rolling hold was an enormous waste of time, and hugely effective, which explained much of politics in a nutshell, Buchanan well knew.

The senator shook his head. "I found out Pickens has holds on two of my pieces, and I'm close to cutting a deal that'll make him let go. I hit him with another hold and the sonofabitch'll clamp down on my ass like a ferret on a cobra."

Buchanan sat back and sipped his coffee as a number of potential strategies rolled through his mind. "Look, let's go back to square one. If you have the votes to knock it out, schedule it and let the committee vote on it and kill the bastard for good. Then if he takes it to the floor I can't believe he'll have the support to carry it. Hell, once it's on the floor we can hold it up forever, ask for amendments, hit it in the cloak room, cut the crap out of it pretending to want to deal for some juice on one of your bills. In fact, we're so close to the elections now we can even play the quorum call game until he yells uncle."

Milstead nodded thoughtfully. "You know Archer and Simms are giving me a little trouble."

"Harvey, you've sent enough highway construction dollars to both those bastards' states to choke every man and woman and child there. Call them on it! They don't give a damn about this bill. They probably haven't even read the staff briefing materials."

Milstead looked suddenly confident. "One way or another, we'll get it done for you. In a one-point-seven-trillion-dollar budget, it's not that big a deal."

"It is for my client. A lot of people are counting on this one, Harvey. And most of them can't even walk yet."

"I hear you."

"You should take a fact-finding trip over there. I'll go with you. It's really beautiful country, you just can't use the land for shit. God might have blessed

America, but he forgot about a lot of the rest of the world. But they keep going. If you ever think you're having a bad day, it's a good memory to have."

Milstead coughed. "My schedule is really full, Danny. And you know I'm not running for re-election. Two more years and I'm out of here."

Okay, shop talk and humanitarian plea time is over, Buchanan thought. *Now let's play traitor.*

He leaned forward and casually moved his briefcase out of the way. One twist on the handle activated the recording device secreted inside. *This one's for you, Thornhill, you smug bastard.*

Buchanan cleared his throat. "Well, I guess it's never too early to talk about replacements. I need some people on Foreign Aid and Ops who'll participate in my little retirement program. I can promise them as good as I'll be paying you. They'll want for nothing. They just have to get my agenda done. I'm at the point now where I can't afford defeat on anything. They have to come through for me. That's the only way I can guarantee the payoff at the end. Just like you. You always come through for me, Harvey. Almost ten years and counting, and you always get it done. By hook or crook."

Milstead glanced at the door and then spoke in a very low voice, as though that made it all better. "I do have some people you might want to talk to." He looked nervous, uncomfortable. "About taking over some of my *duties*. I haven't broached the issue with them directly, of course, but I'd be surprised if they weren't amenable to some sort of arrangement."

"That's real good to hear."

"And you're right to plan ahead. The two years will go quickly."

"Hell, in two years I might not be here, Harvey."

The senator smiled warmly. "I didn't think you'd ever retire." He paused. "But I guess you have your heir apparent. How is Faith, by the way? Vivacious as ever, I'm sure."

"Faith is Faith. You know that."

"Lucky to have someone like her backing you up."

"Very lucky," Buchanan said, frowning slightly.

"Give her my best when you see her. Tell her to come up and see old Harvey. Best mind and legs in the place," he added with a wink.

To this, Buchanan said nothing.

The senator sat back against the couch. "I've been in public service half my life. The pay is ridiculous – chickenshit, really, for somebody of my ability and stature. You know what I could earn on the outside. That's the trade-off when you serve your country."

"Absolutely, Harvey. Of course it is." *The bribe money is only your due. You earned it.*

"But I don't regret it. Any of it."

"No reason you should."

Milstead smiled wearily. "The dollars I've spent over the years rebuilding this country, shaping it for the future, for the next generation. And the next."

Now it was *his* money. *He* saved the country. "People never appreciate that," said Buchanan. "The media only goes after the dirt."

"Guess I'm just making up for it in my golden years."

After all these years a little humility, a little guilt remain. "You deserve it. You served your country well. It's all waiting for you. Just like we discussed. Better than we discussed. You and Louise will want for nothing. You'll live like a king and queen. You did your job, and you'll reap the rewards. The American way."

"I'm tired, Danny. Weary to the bones. Between you and me, I'm not sure I can last two more minutes, much less two more years. This place has sucked the life right out of me."

"You're a true statesman. A hero to us all."

Buchanan took a deep breath and wondered if Thornhill's boys parked in the van outside were enjoying this sappy exchange. In truth, Buchanan too was looking forward to getting out. He looked at his old friend. An expression of giddiness was on the man's features as he no doubt thought of a truly glorious retirement with his wife of thirty-five years, a woman he had cheated on many times, who had always allowed him back. And kept silent about it. The psychology of political wives would be a worthy college course, Buchanan believed.

In truth, Buchanan had a soft spot for his Townies. They actually had accomplished a lot, and in their own way were some of the most honorable people Buchanan had ever met. And yet the senator had no problem being bought.

Very soon Harvey Milstead would have a new master. The Thirteenth Amendment to the Constitution had outlawed slavery, but apparently no one had bothered telling Robert Thornhill that. He was turning his friends over to the Devil. That's what troubled Buchanan most of all. Thornhill, always Thornhill.

The men rose and Buchanan and the senator shook hands. "Thank you, Danny. Thank you for everything."

"Please, don't mention it," Buchanan said. "Please don't." He grabbed his spy briefcase and fled the room.

EIGHTEEN

"Degaussed?" Reynolds stared at the two technicians.

"My tape has been degaussed? Will someone please explain that to me?" She had watched the video twenty times now. From every angle possible. Or rather, she had watched jagged lines and dots swarm across the screen like a World War I aerial dogfight with heavy doses of ground flack thrown in. She had been sitting here for a very long time and knew no more than when she had first walked in.

"Without getting too technical—" one of the men started to say.

"Please don't," Reynolds interjected. Her head was pounding. If the tape was useless? Good God, it can't be.

"'Degaussing' is the reference term used for the erasure of a magnetic media. It's done for many reasons, some of the most common being so that the media can be used again, or to eliminate confidential information that was recorded on the media. A videotape is a form of magnetic media. What happened to the tape you gave us was an unwanted intrusional influence that has distorted and/or corrupted the media, preventing its proper utilization."

Reynolds stared in wonder at the man. What the hell would his technical answer have been?

"So you're saying someone intentionally screwed with the tape?" she said.

"That's right."

"But couldn't it be a problem with the tape itself? How can you be sure someone 'intruded' upon it?"

The other technician spoke up. "The level of corruption we've seen in the images so far would preclude that conclusion. We can't be one hundred percent sure, of course, but it really does look like third party interference. From what I understand, the surveillance system used was very sophisticated. A multiplexer with three or four cameras on line, so there was no dwell time gap. How were the units activated? Motion or trip?"

"Trip."

"Motion is better. The systems these days are so sensitive they can pick up a hand reaching for something on a desk in a one-foot-square-zone. Trips are obsolete."

"Thanks, I'll keep that in mind," she said dryly.

"We did a pixel zoom for detail enhancement, but still nothing. Definitely interference."

Reynolds remembered that the closet at the cottage containing the video equipment had been found open.

"Okay, how could they have done it?"

"Well, there's a wide variety of specialized equipment available."

Reynolds shook her head. "No, we're not talking a lab setting. We're looking at doing it on site, where the equipment was set up. And maybe whoever did it wouldn't have even known there was video recording equipment there. So assume that whatever they happened to have with them would have been what they used."

The techs thought for a moment. "Well," one of them said, "if the person had a powerful magnet and passed it over the recorder a number of times, that could distort the tape by rearranging the metallic particles, which would, in turn, remove the previously recorded signals."

Reynolds took a deep, troubled breath. A simple magnet could have blown away her only clue. "Is there any way to get it back, the images on the tape?"

"It's possible, but it will take some time. We can't make any guarantees until we get in there."

"Do it. But let me make this real clear." She stood, towering over the two men. "I need to be able to see what's on that tape. I need to be able to see who was in that house. You have no higher priority than that. Check with the AD if you have a conflict, but whatever it takes, twenty-four hours a day. I need it. Understand?"

The men looked at each other briefly before nodding.

When Reynolds got back to her office, a man was waiting to see her.

"Paul." She nodded at him as she sat down.

Paul Fisher rose and closed the door to Reynolds's office. He was her liaison at Headquarters. He stepped over a pile of documents as he sat back down. "You look like you're overworked, Brooke. You always look like you're overworked. I guess that's what I love about you."

He smiled and Brooke caught herself smiling back.

Fisher was one of the few people at the FBI whom Reynolds looked up to, literally, as he was easily six-foot-five. They were about the same age, although Fisher was her superior in the chain of command and had been at the Bureau two years longer. He was competent and assured. He was also handsome, having retained the tousled blond hair and trim figure of his California days at UCLA. After her marriage had started to disintegrate, Reynolds had imagined having an affair with the divorced Fisher.

Even now, his unexpected visit made Reynolds feel fortunate she'd had the opportunity to go home, shower and change her clothes.

Fisher's jacket was off, his shirt draped gracefully over his long torso. He had just come on duty, she knew, although he tended to be around at all hours.

"I'm sorry about Ken," he said. "I was out of town, or I would've been there last night."

Reynolds played with a letter opener on her desk. "Not as sorry as I am. And neither of us is anywhere near where Anne Newman is on the sorry meter."

"I've talked to the SAC," Fisher said, referring to the special agent in charge, "but I want you to tell me about it."

After she told him what she knew, he rubbed his chin. "Obviously the targets know you're on to them."

"It would seem so."

"You're not that far along in the investigation, are you?"

"Nowhere near referring it to the U.S. attorney for indictment, if that's what you mean."

"So Ken's dead and your chief and only witness is MIA. Tell me about Faith Lockhart."

She glanced up sharply, being equally disturbed by his choice of words and the blunt tone he had used to say them.

He stared back at her, his hazel eyes holding a definable measure of unfriendliness, Reynolds concluded. But right now, she knew, he was not supposed to be her friend. He represented Headquarters.

"Is there something you want to tell *me*, Paul?"

"Brooke, we've always shot straight with each other." He paused and tapped his fingers against the arm of the chair as though trying to communicate with her in Morse code. "I know Massey authorized some leeway for you last night, but they're all very concerned about you. You need to know that."

"I know that in light of recent developments—"

"They were concerned *before* this. Recent developments have only heightened that level of concern."

"Do they want me to just drop it? Christ, it could implicate people who have government buildings named after them."

"It's a question of proof. Without Lockhart what do you have?"

"It's there, Paul."

"What names has she given you, other than Buchanan?"

Reynolds looked momentarily flustered. The problem was Lockhart hadn't given them any names. Yet. She had been too smart for that. She was saving that for when her deal was completed.

"Nothing specific yet. But we'll get it. Buchanan didn't do business with local school board members. And she told us some of his scheme. They work for him while in power, and when they leave office he lines up jobs for them with no real duties and megadollars in compensation and other perks. It's simple. Simply brilliant. The level of detail she's provided us could not be made up."

"I'm not disputing her credibility. But again, can you prove your case? Right now?"

"We're doing everything we can to prove it. I was going to ask her to wear a wire for us when all this happened, but you can't rush these things, you know that. If I pushed too hard, or lost her confidence, we'd end up with nothing."

"Do you want my coldly reasoned analysis?" Fisher took her silence as assent. "You've got all these nameless but very powerful people, many of whom may have things lined up in the future or currently have nice post-public service careers. What's so unusual about that? It happens all the time. They get on the phone, have lunches, whisper in ears, call in some favors. That's America. So where are we?"

"This is more than that, Paul. A lot more."

"Are you saying you can trace the actual illegal activity, how the legislation was manipulated?"

"Not exactly."

"'Not exactly' is right. It's really like trying to prove a negative."

Reynolds knew he was right on that point. How did you prove someone *didn't* do something? Many of the tools Buchanan's people would have used to further his agenda were probably tools every politician used, legitimately. They were talking motivation here. *Why* somebody was doing something, not *how* they were doing it. The why was illegal, the how wasn't. Like a basketball player not trying his best because he'd been paid off.

"Is Buchanan a director in these unknown firms where the former, unknown politicians get jobs? A stockholder? Did he put up the money? Does he have any ongoing business with any of them?"

"You sound like a defense lawyer," she said hotly.

"That's exactly my intent. Because those are the sort of questions you'll need answers for."

"We have not been able to uncover evidence directly tying Buchanan to any of it."

"Then what are you basing your conclusion on? What's your evidence that there is a connection at all?"

Reynolds started to speak and then stopped. Her face flushed and in her agitation she broke in half the pencil she was holding.

"Let me answer that for you," said Fisher. "Faith Lockhart, your missing witness."

"We'll find her, Paul. And then we're back in business."

"And if you don't find her? What then?"

"We'll find another way."

"Can you determine the identities of the bribed officials independently?"

Reynolds desperately wanted to say yes to that question, but she couldn't. Buchanan had been in Washington for decades. He'd probably had dealings with just about every politician and bureaucrat in the city. It would be impossible to narrow down the list without Lockhart.

"Anything's possible," she said gamely.

He shook his head. "Actually, it's not, Brooke."

Reynolds erupted. "Buchanan and his cronies have broken the law. Doesn't that count for anything?"

"In a court of law it counts for zero without proof," he shot back.

She slammed her fist down on the desk. "I damn well refuse to believe that. Besides, the evidence is there; we just have to keep digging."

"You see, that's the problem. It would be one thing if you could do it in complete secrecy. But an investigation of this magnitude, with the sort of important targets we're talking about, can never remain completely secret. And now we have a homicide investigation to deal with as well."

"Meaning there will be leaks," Reynolds said, wondering if Fisher suspected that those leaks might have already occurred.

"Meaning that when you go after important people, you better be damn sure of your case before any leaks do occur. You can't target people like that unless you're loaded for bear. Right now, your gun's empty and I'm not sure where you go to reload. It pretty much says in the Bureau manual, you can't hunt down public officials based on rumor and innuendo."

She looked at him coolly when he finished saying this. "Okay, Paul, would you like to tell me exactly what it is you want me to do?"

"The Violent Crime Unit will keep you informed on its investigation. You have to find Lockhart. Since the two cases are inextricably connected, I suggest cooperation."

"I can't tell them anything about our investigation."

"I'm not asking you to. Just work with them to help clear Newman's murder. And find Lockhart."

"And beyond that? If we can't find her? What happens to my investigation?"

"I don't know, Brooke. The tea leaves are very hard to read right now."

Reynolds stood and looked out the window. Thick, dark clouds had turned day almost into night. She could see both her reflection and Fisher's in the window. He never took his eyes off her, and she doubted if he was all that interested at the moment in how her backside and long legs looked in the black knee-length skirt and matching stockings she was wearing.

As she stood there her ears picked up on a sound they usually didn't: the "white noise." At sensitive government facilities windows were potential outlets for valuable information, namely speech. To plug this leak, speakers were mounted at the windows in these facilities to filter out the sound of voices such that anyone lurking outside with the fanciest in surveillance equipment would end up with zip. The speakers accomplished this by emitting a sound akin to a small waterfall, hence the term "white noise." Reynolds, like most employees in such buildings, had tuned out the background noise; it was such a daily part of her life. Now she noticed it with stunning clarity. Was that a signal to her to notice other things as well? Things, people she saw every day and then thought no more of, accepting them for what they proclaimed to be? She turned to face Fisher.

"Thanks for the ringing vote of confidence, Paul."

"Your career has been nothing short of spectacular. But the public sector is often like the private in one regard: It's the 'what have you done for me lately?' syndrome. I'm not going to sugarcoat this, Brooke. I've already started to hear the rumblings."

She folded her arms across her chest. "I appreciate your complete bluntness," she said coldly. "If you'll excuse me, I'll see what I can do for you lately, Agent Fisher."

As Fisher rose to leave, he moved next to her, touching her lightly on the shoulder. Reynolds recoiled slightly from this, the bite of his words still weighing heavily upon her.

"I've always supported you, and I will continue to support you, Brooke. Don't read this as though I'm throwing you to the wolves. I'm not. I respect the hell out of you. I just didn't want you to be blindsided on this. You don't deserve that. This messenger is friendly."

"That's good to know, Paul," she said unenthusiastically.

When he reached the door, he turned back. "We're handling the media relations from WFO. We've already had inquiries from the press. For now, an agent was killed during an undercover operation. No other details were provided, including his identity. That won't last long. And when the dam breaks, I'm not sure who can keep dry."

As soon as the door closed behind him, a cold shudder hit Reynolds. She felt as though she were being suspended over a vat of boiling something. Was it her old paranoia kicking in? Or was it simply her reasoned judgment? She kicked her shoes off and paced her office, stepping over the paper land mines as she did so. She rocked on the balls of her feet, trying to guide the massive tension she was feeling throughout her body toward the floor. It didn't come close to working.

NINETEEN

The recently named Ronald Reagan Washington National Airport, which everyone in the area still simply called "National," was very busy this morning. It was loved for its convenience to the city and its numerous daily flights, and hated for its congestion, short runways and stomach-jolting tight left turns to avoid restricted airspace. However, the airport's new sparkling terminal with its row of Jeffersonian-inspired domes and hulking, multi-tiered parking garages with skywalks to the terminal were very welcome to the hassled air traveler.

Lee and Faith entered the new terminal, where Lee eyed a police officer patrolling the corridor. They had left the car in one of the parking lots.

Faith watched the policeman's movements too. She was wearing "eyeglasses" that Lee had given her. The lenses were ordinary glass, but they helped to further change her look. She touched Lee's arm. "Nervous?"

"Always. It kind of gives me an edge. Makes up for a serious lack of formal schooling." He put their bags over his shoulder. "Let's grab a cup of coffee and let the line at the ticket counter die down a little, scope the place out." As they looked for a coffee shop, he asked, "Any idea of when we can get a flight out of here?"

"We fly through Norfolk and then take a commuter to Pine Island, off the Outer Banks of North

Carolina. Flights to Norfolk are pretty frequent. The commuter to Pine Island you have to call ahead and schedule. Once we get the Norfolk flight scheduled, I'll call down and arrange that. They only fly during daylight."

"Why's that?"

"Because we won't be landing on a regular runway; it's more like a little road. No lights or tower or anything. Just a wind sock."

"That's comforting."

"Let me call down and check on the house."

They went over to the phone bank and Lee listened while Faith confirmed their arrival. She hung up. "All set. We can get a rental car once we get down there."

"So far, so good."

"It's a nice place to relax. You don't need to see or talk to anybody else if you don't want to."

"I don't want to," said Lee firmly.

"I'd like to ask you a question," Faith said as they walked toward a café.

"Shoot."

"How long had you been following me?"

"Six days," he promptly answered, "during which you made three trips to the cottage, including last night."

Last night, Faith thought. Was that all it had been? "And you haven't reported back to your employer yet?"

"No."

"Why not?"

"I like to do weekly reports, unless something really extraordinary happens. Believe me, if I'd had time, last night would have qualified for the mother of all reports."

"How were you to make these reports if you don't know who hired you?"

"I was given a phone number."

"And you never checked up on it?"

He looked at her with annoyance. "Nah, why should I care? Take the money and run."

She looked chastened. "I didn't mean it like that."

"Uh-huh, sure." He shifted the bags slightly and continued, "There's a special crisscross directory that'll give you the corresponding address if you have the phone number."

"And?"

"And in these days of satellite phones and nationwide cell networks and crap like that, nothing came up. I called the number. It must have been set up just to receive calls from me because it told Mr. Adams to leave any information on the tape. It also gave a P.O. box in D.C. Being the ever curious type I checked that out too, but it was listed in the name of a corporation I'd never heard of, with an address that turned out to be phony. Dead end." He looked down at her. "I take my work seriously, Faith. I don't like walking into traps. Famous last words, right?"

They stopped at the small café, bought their coffee and a couple of bagels and sat down in a vacant corner of the place.

Faith took a troubled breath as she sipped her coffee and nibbled on a poppyseed bagel oozing butter. Maybe he was being straight with her, but he still had a connection to Danny Buchanan. It was such a strange feeling suddenly being fearful of a man she had idolized. If things had not changed so much between them the last year, she would have been tempted to call Danny. But she was confused now, the horror of last night so crystal clear in her mind. Besides, what was she supposed to ask him: *Danny, did you try and have me killed last night? If you did, please stop, I'm working with the FBI to help you, really. And why did you hire Lee to follow me, Danny?* Yes, she had to part company with Lee, and soon.

"The report you were given, tell me what it said about me," Faith said.

"You're a lobbyist. You used to be with a big outfit, represented Fortune 500s. About ten years ago, you and a man named Daniel Buchanan started your own firm."

"Did it mention any of our current clients?"

He cocked his head. "No, is that important?"

"What do you know about Buchanan?"

"The report didn't say much about him, but I did some digging on my own, nothing you won't know. Buchanan is a legend on the Hill. Knows everybody and everybody knows him. Fought all the big battles, made a ton of money doing it. I assume you didn't do so badly yourself."

"I did well. What else?"

He stared at her strangely. "Why do you want to hear something you already know? Is Buchanan somehow mixed up in all this?"

Now it was Faith's turn to scrutinize Lee. If he was playing dumb, he was doing an exceptional job, she thought.

"Danny Buchanan is an honorable man. I owe him everything I have."

"Sounds like a good friend. But you didn't answer my question."

"People like Danny are rare. A true visionary."

"And you?"

"Me? I just help implement his vision. People like me are a dime a dozen."

"You don't strike me as so ordinary." Faith took a sip of coffee and didn't respond. "So how does one become a lobbyist?"

Faith stifled a yawn and sipped her coffee again. Her head was starting to pound. She had never needed much rest, galloping the globe, catching only plane catnaps. But right now she felt like curling up under the table and sleeping for the next ten years. Maybe her body was reacting to the last twelve hours of horror by shutting itself down, throwing in the towel. *Please don't hurt me.*

"I could lie and say I wanted to change the world. That's what everyone says, isn't it?" She pulled a bottle of aspirin from her bag, popped two and washed them down with coffee. "Actually, I remember watching the Watergate hearings when I was a kid. All those very serious people in that room. All these middle-aged men with wide ugly ties, puffy faces, over-easy hair, talking into these clunky microphones, and all the lawyers whispering into their ears. All the media, the whole world focused right there. What the rest of the country apparently found appalling, I found extremely cool. All that power!" She smiled weakly into her coffee cup. "My demented soul. The nuns were right about me. One in particular, Sister Audrey Ann, truly believed my name was a blasphemy. 'Dear Faith,' she would say, 'live up to your Christian name, not down to your devilish urges.'"

"So you were a rabble rouser?"

"It's like if I saw a habit coming my way I just turned evil. My dad moved us around a lot, but I did well enough in school, even if I raised hell outside it. I went to a good college, ended up in Washington with all those memories of absolute power dancing in my head. I didn't have the faintest idea what to do with myself, but I knew desperately I wanted to get into the game. I did a stint on Capitol Hill for a freshman congressman and caught the eye of Danny Buchanan. He snatched me up, saw something in me, I guess. I think he liked my spirit – I was running the office with all of two months' experience behind me. The way I sort of refused to back down from anyone, even the Speaker of the House."

"I guess that is impressive for somebody right out of college."

"My philosophy was, after the nuns, politicians weren't much of a challenge."

Lee cracked a smile. "Makes me glad I went to public school." He glanced away for a second. "Don't look now, but the FBI is circling."

"What?" She whipped her head around, looking everywhere.

Lee rolled his eyes. "Oh, that was good."

"Where are they?"

He lightly smacked the tabletop. "They're nowhere. And they're everywhere. The Feds don't walk around with their badges pinned to their foreheads. You won't see them."

"So why the hell did you say they were circling?"

"It was a little test. And you failed. *I* can spot the Feds, sometimes, not always. If I ever say that to you again, I won't be kidding. They will be there. And you can't react the way you just did. Normal, slow movements. Just a pretty woman on a holiday with her boyfriend. Understand?"

"Okay, fine. But just don't pull that crap on me again. My nerves aren't well rested."

"How are you paying for the tickets?"

"How should I pay for them?"

"Your credit card. Under your other name. Don't want to flash a bunch of cash around. You buy a one-way ticket with cash leaving today, that might be a red flag for the airline. Right now, the less attention, the better. What is it, by the way? Your other name?"

"Suzanne Blake."

"Nice name."

"Suzanne was my mother's name."

"Was? Passed on?"

"Both my parents. My mother when I was eleven. My dad six years later. No brothers or sisters. I was a seventeen-year-old orphan."

"That must've been tough."

Faith didn't say anything for a long moment. Talking about her past was always hard, so she rarely did so. And she really didn't know this man. Still, there was something about Lee Adams that was comforting, solid. "I really loved my mother," she began. "She was a good woman, and long-suffering, because of my dad. He was a good person too, but one of those souls who always have an angle, a way to make a quick buck with these crazy ideas. And when his plan blew up, and it always did, we'd have to pack up and move on."

"Why was that?"

"Because other people always lost their money with my dad's grand schemes too. And they were understandably upset about it. We moved four times before my mother died. Five more times after that. We prayed for my dad every day, my mom and I. Right before she died, she told me to take care of him, and me all of eleven."

Lee shook his head. "I can't even relate to that. My parents have lived in the same house for fifty years. How did you manage to keep it together after your mother died?"

The words somehow came easier for Faith now. "It wasn't as tough as you'd think. Mom loved my dad, hated how he lived, his schemes, all the moving. But he wasn't going to change, so they weren't the happiest couple to live with. There were times I really thought she was going to kill him. When she died, it sort of became my dad and me against the world. He'd dress me up in the one nice outfit I had and show me off to all his prospective partners. I guess people would think, how can this guy be so bad, what with his little girl right there and all? When I got to be sixteen I'd even help him pitch his deals. I grew up fast. I guess that's where I got my motor mouth and my backbone. I learned to think on my feet."

"Quite an alternative education," Lee commented. "But I can see how it would serve you well as a lobbyist."

Her eyes grew moist. "On the way to every meeting, he'd say, 'This is the one, Faith, darling. I can feel it right here,' and he'd put his hand over his heart. 'It's all for you, baby girl. Daddy loves his Faith.' And I believed him every single damn time."

"Sounds like he really ended up hurting you," Lee said quietly.

Faith shook her head stubbornly. "It wasn't like he was trying to rip people off. We're not talking Ponzi schemes or anything. He sincerely believed his ideas would work. But they never did and we'd move on. And it wasn't like we ever made any money. God, we slept in our car enough times. How many times do I remember my dad strolling into the back door of restaurants and walking out a little later with dinner he had talked them into giving him. We'd sit in the backseat and eat. He'd stare at the sky, pointing out the constellations to me. He never even finished high school, but he knew all about the stars. Said he'd been chasing enough of them his whole life. We'd just sit there far into the night, and my dad would tell me things would get better. Just down the road."

"Sounds like a man who could talk his way into anywhere. Probably would've made a good PI."

Faith smiled as she thought back. "I'd walk into a bank with him, and within five minutes he'd know everybody by name, drinking coffee, talking with the bank manager like he'd known him all his whole life. And we'd walk out with a letter of recommendation and a list of local high-net-worth individuals for my dad to solicit. He just had that way about him. Everyone liked him. Until they lost their money. And we always lost what little we had too. Dad was a stickler about that. His money went in too. He was actually very honest."

"You sound like you still miss him."

"I do," she said proudly. "He named me Faith because he said with Faith beside him, how could he ever fail?" On this Faith closed her eyes, tears trickling down her cheeks.

Lee pulled a napkin out of the holder and slipped it into her hand. She wiped her eyes.

"I'm sorry," she said. "I've never really talked about this with anyone before."

"It's okay, Faith. I'm a good listener."

"I found my dad again in Danny," she said, clearing her throat, her eyes wide. "He has the same way about him. The pluck of the Irishman. He can talk his way into seeing anybody. Knows every angle, every issue. Refuses to back down from anyone. He's taught me a lot. And not just about lobbying. About life. He didn't have it easy growing up either. We had a lot in common."

Lee smiled. "So from scams with your dad to lobbying in D.C.?"

"And some would say my job description hasn't changed." Faith smiled at her own remark.

"And some would say that the nut didn't fall far from the tree."

She bit into her bagel. "Since we're into true confessions, how about your family?"

Lee settled back. "Four of each. I'm number six."

"God! Eight kids. Your mother must be a saint."

"We gave them both enough heartache to last ten lifetimes."

"So they're both still around."

"Going strong. We're all pretty close now, although we had some rough times growing up. Good support groups when things go haywire. Help's only a phone call away. Usually, that is. Not this time, though."

"That sounds nice. Real nice." Faith looked away.

Lee eyed her keenly, easily reading her thoughts. "Families have their problems too, Faith. Divorces, serious illnesses, depression, hard times, we've seen it all. I have to say sometimes I'd rather be an only child."

"No, you wouldn't," she said with authority. "You might think you would, but trust me, you wouldn't."

"I do."

She looked confused. "You do what?"

"Trust you."

She said slowly, "You know, for a paranoid PI, you sure make friends fast. I could be a mass murderer, for all you know."

"If you were really bad, the Feds would've had you in custody."

She put down her coffee and leaned toward him, her expression very serious. "I appreciate the observation. But just so we're very clear on this, I've never physically harmed even an ant in my entire life, and I still don't consider myself a criminal, but I guess if the FBI wanted to put me in jail, they could. Just so we're clear," she said again. "Now, you still want to get on that plane with me?"

"Absolutely. You've really got my curiosity up now."

She sighed and sat back, glancing down the terminal's corridor. "Don't look now, but here come a pair who look an awful lot like the FBI."

"Seriously?"

"Unlike you, I wouldn't even attempt to joke about something like that." She bent over and fiddled with something in her bag. After a few anxious moments, she sat back up as the pair passed by without looking at them.

"Lee, depending on what they've found out, they may be looking for a man and a woman. Why don't you stay here while I go buy the tickets? I'll meet you at the security gate."

Lee looked uncertain. "Let me think about that."

"I thought you said you trusted me."

"I do." For a moment he envisioned Faith's dad standing in front of him, asking for money. And damn if Lee wasn't reaching in his pocket for his wallet.

"But even trust has its limits, right? I tell you what, you keep the bags. I need to take my purse. If you're really worried, you have a clear view of the security entrance from here. If I try to give you the slip, you've got me dead on. And I'm sure you can run much faster than I can." She stood. "And you know I can't call in the FBI, now, can I?"

She eyed him for a moment longer, apparently daring him to challenge her logic.

"Okay."

"What's your new name? I'll need it for your ticket."

"Charles Wright."

She winked at him. "And your friends call you Chuck?"

He gave her an uneasy smile and then Faith turned and disappeared into the crowd.

As soon as she was gone, Lee regretted his decision. Sure she had left her bag, but it only had a few clothes in it, the ones he had given her! She had her purse with her, which meant she had what she really needed: her fake ID and her money. Yes, he could see the security gate from here, but what if she just walked out the front door? What if that's what she was doing right now? Without her, he had nothing. Except some really dangerous people who now knew where he lived. People who would take great pleasure in breaking his bones one by one until he told them what he knew, which was nothing. They wouldn't be thrilled to hear that. Next stop: your standard landfill burial. That did it. Lee jumped up, grabbed the bags and headed after her.

TWENTY

There was a knock on Reynolds's door. Connie popped his head in. Reynolds was on the phone but she waved him in.

Connie had two cups of coffee. He put one in front of Reynolds, together with two cream packets, a sugar and a swizzle stick. She thanked him with an appreciative smile. He sat down and sipped on his coffee while she finished her call.

Reynolds put down the phone and started mixing her coffee. "I would absolutely love some good news, Connie." She noted that he also had gone home, showered and changed. Rambling through the woods in the dark had probably done a real number on his suit, she assumed. His hair was still damp and the wetness made it seem more gray than usual. Reynolds kept forgetting that he was in his fifties. Connie just never seemed to change, always big, always craggy, the weatherbeaten rock upon which she clung when the riptide came calling. As it was right now.

"Do you want lies or the truth?"

Reynolds took a sip of the coffee, sighed and leaned back in her chair. "Right now, I'm not sure."

He sat forward, perching his coffee on her desk. "I worked the scene with the VCU boys. That's where I started at the Bureau, you know. Just like old times." He put his palms flat on his knees and flexed his thick neck to work out a kink. "Damn, my back feels like Reggie White's been doing jumping jacks on it. I'm getting too old for this kind of work."

"You can't retire. I can't function without you."

Connie picked up his coffee cup. "The hell you say." It was obvious, though, that the remark had pleased him. He sat back, unbuttoned his jacket and let his belly push through. He let a minute or so pass as he presumably collected his thoughts.

Reynolds waited patiently. She knew Connie had not come down here to shoot the breeze with her. He rarely did that with anyone. Reynolds had learned that just about everything the man did had a specific purpose. Connie was a true veteran of the ways of bureaucracy and, consequently, he carried an agenda with him everywhere. While she thoroughly relied on him for his field expertise and his instincts, Reynolds never quite lost sight of the fact that she was younger, less experienced, yet was still his boss; it had to be a sore point with the man. And she was a woman, to boot, in a field that still didn't have many at her level of responsibility. She could not really blame Connie if he felt resentment toward her. And yet he had never said a negative word about her, nor had he ever dragged his feet on an assignment in order to make her look bad. On the contrary, he was methodical to a fault, and reliable as the sunrise. Still, she had to watch herself.

"I saw Anne Newman this morning. She appreciated your coming over last night. She said you were a real comfort."

This surprised Reynolds. Maybe the woman *didn't* blame her. "She took it about as well as anyone could."

"I understand the director went too. That was good of him. You know Ken and I go way back." The look on Connie's face was easily read. If the man caught up to the killer before the VCU did, there might not be any need for a trial.

"I know. I never stopped to think how hard this must be for you."

"You have enough on your mind. Besides, I'm the last person you need to worry about." Connie took a swallow of coffee. "The shooter was hit. Least it looks that way."

Reynolds immediately sat forward. "Let me have everything."

Connie momentarily smiled. "Don't want to wait for the written report from VCU?" He crossed one thick leg over the other, hitching up his cuffed trousers as he did so. "You were right about the shooter's location. We found blood, a fair amount of it in the woods behind the house. Did a rough trajectory. The location jells with where the shot probably came from. We followed the trail as best we could, but lost it in the woods after a few hundred feet."

"Exactly how much blood? Life-threatening?"

"Hard to say. It was dark. A team's over there right now continuing the search. They're lock-stepping the lawn, looking for the slug that killed Ken. They're also canvassing the neighborhood, but the place was so isolated, I'm not sure that'll pay off."

Reynolds took a deep breath. "If we find a body, that would both simplify and complicate things."

Connie nodded thoughtfully. "I see where you're going with that."

"You got a blood sample?"

"Lab's running it as we speak. Don't know what it'll be worth."

"At the very least it'll confirm whether it's human or not."

"That's true. Maybe all we'll find is a deer carcass. But I don't think so." Reynolds perked up. "Nothing concrete," he said in response to her look, "just call it my gut."

"If the guy's wounded, that should make it a little easier to track him down."

"Maybe. If he required medical attention, he wouldn't be so stupid as to go to the local emergency room. They have to report gunshot wounds. And we don't know how badly he was hurt. Might have just been a flesh wound that bled like a bitch. If so, he bandages it up, gets on a plane and poof. Gone. I mean we've got all the bases covered, but if the guy was leaving on a private plane, then we got problems. The truth is he's probably already long gone."

"Or maybe dead. Apparently he missed his primary target. Whoever hired him won't be happy about that."

"Right."

Reynolds folded her hands in front of her as she thought of the next topic she wanted to discuss. "Connie, Ken's gun was unfired."

Connie had obviously given this line of inquiry some thought because he said, "Which means, if the blood is confirmed as human, we definitely have a *fourth* person at the cottage last night. And that party shot the shooter." He shook his head wearily. "Shit, listen to us, it all sounds crazy."

"Crazy but apparently true under the facts as we know them. Think about this: Could this fourth person have killed Ken? And not the guy who was wounded?"

"Don't think so. The VCUs are looking for shell cartridges in the woods where we think the other shot came from, as confirmation. If there was a gun battle between two unknown parties, then maybe we'll find another set of ejected shells as well."

"Well, this fourth person being present may

explain the door being unlocked and the cameras being tripped."

He sat up straight. "Anything on the tape yet? We had to get some faces or something."

"To put it simply, we have been degaussed."

"What?"

"Don't ask. For right now we can't count on the tape."

"Well, shit. That doesn't leave us with much."

"Specifically, it leaves us with Faith Lockhart."

"We've got all the airports, train and bus stations, rental car agencies covered. Her firm too, although I can't believe she'd go there."

"Agreed. Actually, that may be where the bullet came from," Reynolds said slowly.

"Buchanan?"

"Wish we could prove it."

"If we find Lockhart, we still may be able to. We'll have some leverage there."

"Don't count on it. Almost getting your head blown off can make you rethink loyalties," Reynolds said dryly.

"If Buchanan and his people are on to Lockhart, then they must be on to us as well."

"You said that before. A leak? From here?"

"A leak from somewhere. Here or at Lockhart's end. Maybe she did something to make Buchanan suspicious. From all accounts, the guy's cagey as hell. He had her followed somehow. They saw her meeting with you at the house. He dug a little more, hit the truth and contracted to take her out."

"I'd like to believe *that* more than someone here selling us down the river."

"So would I. But the fact is every law enforcement agency has some bad apples."

Reynolds briefly wondered for a moment if Connie was suspicious of her. Everyone who worked at the FBI, from special agents to support staff, had top-secret security clearance. When you applied for a job at the Bureau, teams of agents would show up investigating every single piece of your past, no matter how insignificant, talking to everyone who ever knew you. Every five years a full field investigation was conducted on on-board Bureau employees. In the interim any suspicious activity involving a bureau employee or any complaints of persons asking suspicious questions of an employee were to be reported to the security officer in the employee's division. That had never happened to Reynolds, thank God. Her record was clean.

If there were suspicions of a leak or other type of security breach, it might very well be investigated by the Office of Professional Responsibility, and a polygraph exam might be ordered for the suspect employee. Other than that, the Bureau was always on the lookout for any signs that an employee was having undue personal or professional problems that might make him or her susceptible to bribes or influence by third parties.

Reynolds knew Connie was doing okay financially. His wife had died years ago from a lengthy illness that had sapped their resources, but he lived in a nice house that was worth a lot more than he had paid for it. His kids' college educations were done, and he had his pension locked in. All in all, he had a nice retirement to look forward to.

On the other hand, Reynolds knew her personal life and finances were in abysmal shape. College funds? Hell, she'd be lucky if she could continue to afford the private school tuition for first grade. And pretty soon, she wouldn't have a house to call her own. That was being sold as part of the divorce. The condo she was eyeing was about the size of the one she had rented when she had finished college. It had seemed cozy with one person. An adult and two energetic kids would quickly turn cozy into cramped. And could she afford to keep her nanny? With her hours, how could she not? She couldn't leave the kids alone at night.

In any other occupation she would probably be on the top ten soon-to-crash-and-burn list. But in the FBI, the divorce rate was such that her mess of a marriage would not create a blip on the Bureau radar. A career in the FBI was often simply not conducive to a happy personal life.

She blinked for a moment as she found Connie's gaze still upon her. Did he really suspect her of being the leak? Of causing Ken Newman to die? She knew it looked bad. On the very night when she'd had Newman substitute for her with Lockhart, he was killed. She knew Paul Fisher had been thinking that, and she was reasonably sure Connie was right now.

She composed herself and said, "There's really nothing we can do about this theory of a leak right now. Let's concentrate on what we can do."

"Fine. So what's our next move?"

"Hit all our lines of investigation as hard as we can. Find Lockhart. Let's hope she uses a credit card for plane or train tickets. If she does that, we've got her. We need to at least make an effort to find the shooter. Shadow Buchanan. Unscramble that tape and see who was in the house. I want you to act as liaison with the VCU. We have a lot of threads, if we can only grab one or two of them and hold on."

"Hey, isn't that always the case?"

"We're in a *really* tight spot here, Connie."

He nodded thoughtfully. "I heard Fisher was here. Figured he'd been by to see you."

Reynolds didn't respond to this, and Connie plunged on.

"Thirteen years ago, I was heading up a joint undercover drug operation with the DEA in Brownsville, Texas." He paused for a moment as if deciding whether to go forward or not. "Our official goal was to disrupt the flow of cocaine over the Mexican border. Our unofficial goal was to accomplish our mission without making the Mexican government look bad. For that reason, we had open lines of communication with our counterparts in Mexico City. Perhaps too open, since there was rampant corruption south of the border at all levels. But it was done that way so the Mexican authorities could share in the glory after we did all the work and scored the perps heading up the cartel. After two years of work, a huge bust was planned. But our plans got leaked and my guys walked into an ambush that left two of them dead."

"Omigod. I heard about that case, but I didn't know you were involved in it."

"Hell, you were probably still cutting your teeth at Quantico."

Reynolds didn't know if this was a backdoor barb or not, but she chose not to respond.

"Anyway, after all that went down, I got a visit from one of the young ladder climbers at HQ who wouldn't know which end of his pistol to hold, and who politely informed me that if I didn't make things right, my ass was cooked. But there was one stipulation. If I found out our friends in Mexico sent us down the river, I couldn't use that as an excuse. International relations, I was told. I'd just have to fall on the sword for the good of the world." Connie's voice trembled a little as he said this last part.

Reynolds found she was holding her breath. It was not like Connie to talk this much. In the dictionary, the man's picture could well be found next to the word "taciturn."

He took a gulp of coffee and took a moment to wipe his lips with the back of his hand. "Well, you know what? I traced the leak right to the top of the Mexican police department and I put a big X on the bastards' foreheads and walked away from it. If my superiors didn't want to do anything about it, fine. But damn if I was going to take the fall for somebody else's shit." He eyed her steadily. "'International relations,'" he said, a bitter smile spreading across his lips as he did so. He rested his elbows on her desk.

Was this a challenge he was laying before her? Reynolds wondered. Was he expecting to leave an X on her forehead, or daring her to pin one on his?

"That's been my official motto ever since," he said.

"What's that?"

"Screw 'international relations.'"

TWENTY-ONE

Through the airport terminal drifted members of both the FBI and Central Intelligence, with the former group completely unaware of the latter's presence. Thornhill's men had the advantage of knowing that Lee Adams was probably traveling with Faith Lockhart. The FBI agents were only looking for the woman.

Lee unknowingly passed a couple of the FBI agents dressed as businessmen with briefcases and *Wall Street Journals*. They were equally oblivious to him. Faith had passed by the agents a moment earlier.

Lee slowed when he got near to the main ticket counter. Faith was up there speaking with a clerk. This was starting to look okay. He had a sudden feeling of guilt for not having trusted her. He edged over to a corner and waited.

At the counter, Faith displayed her new ID and purchased three tickets. Two tickets were in the name of Suzanne Blake and Charles Wright. The woman barely looked at her photo. Thank God for that, although Faith supposed people rarely looked like their ID photos anyway. The flight to Norfolk International left in about forty-five minutes. The third ticket she purchased was in the name of Faith Lockhart. It was a flight heading to San Francisco with a stopover in Chicago. It left in forty minutes. She had spotted it on the monitors. West Coast, big city. She could lose herself, drive down the coast, maybe even sneak into Mexico. She wasn't sure how she would accomplish that, but she just had to take it one step at a time.

Faith had explained that she was buying the ticket to San Francisco for her boss, who would arrive shortly.

"She'll have to hurry," the clerk said. "She still has to check in. And they're going to begin boarding in about ten minutes."

"It won't be a problem," Faith assured her. "She doesn't have any luggage, so she can check in at the gate."

The clerk handed her the ticket. Faith figured she was safe using her real name on the ticket because she paid for all of them with her Suzanne Blake credit card. And the only other ID she had to check in with was her real one. It was Faith Lockhart or nothing. Everything would be okay.

She could not have been any more wrong.

As Lee watched Faith, a thought jolted him. His gun! He had to check it before going through security or all hell would break lose. He shot across to the counter and next to a startled Faith.

He put his arm around her and gave her a quick kiss on the cheek. "Hey, babe. Sorry, the phone call took longer than I thought." He looked at the ticket agent and said casually, "I have a pistol I need to check."

The ticket agent raised her eyes slightly at this.

"You're Mr. Wright?"

Lee nodded. She went about processing the necessary documents. He showed her his fake ID and she stamped his passenger ticket appropriately and entered the information in the computer. He turned over the gun and ammo, and filled out the declaration form. The agent tagged the container and they left the ticket counter.

"Sorry, I forgot about the gun." Lee looked up ahead to the security gate. "Okay, they're going to have people posted at the gate. We'll go through separately. Be cool; you don't look anything like Faith Lockhart."

Although Faith felt her heart in her throat the entire time, they went through the security gate without incident.

As they passed the flight information monitors, Lee spotted their gate. "Down this way."

Faith nodded as she noted how the gates were configured here. The departure gate for the San Francisco flight was close enough to easily get to, but far enough away from the Norfolk gate. She hid a smile. Perfect.

As they walked along, she looked over at Lee. He had done a lot for her. She wasn't feeling good about what she was about to do, but had convinced herself it was for the best. For both of them.

They reached the gate for the flight to Norfolk. The plane would be boarding in about ten minutes, they were told. There was a good crowd waiting.

Lee looked at her. "You better call that commuter service for the flight to Pine Island."

Lee and Faith walked over to the phone bank and she made that call.

"All set," Faith said. "Now we can relax."

"Right," Lee said dryly.

Faith looked around. "I need to use the rest room."

"Better hurry."

She hustled off while Lee looked after her thoughtfully.

TWENTY-TWO

"Bingo!" The man sitting in front of the computer screen said. He was in a van outside of the airport. The FBI had a designated liaison with the airlines to monitor the travel of persons the Bureau was looking for. With more than one airline sharing reservation systems and data and the advent of code-sharing, the FBI's job had been made a little easier. The Bureau had requested that the name Faith Lockhart be marked with a tag in the major airlines' reservation systems. That request had just paid an enormous dividend.

"She just made a reservation for a flight to San Francisco that leaves in about half an hour," he said into his headset microphone. "United Airlines." He passed along the flight number and gate information. "Hit it," he ordered the men inside the terminal. He picked up the phone to notify Brooke Reynolds.

Lee was leafing through a magazine someone had left on the seat next to his when two men dressed in suits flew past. A few moments later, a pair of gents in jeans and windbreakers hurried past, heading in the same direction.

Lee immediately jumped up, looked around for anyone else hustling by, saw no one moving fast and then followed after the group.

The FBI agents, followed by the men in jeans, hurried past the women's room a minute before

Faith came out. The men had disappeared into the crowds by the time she emerged.

Lee slowed as he saw Faith come out from the women's room. Another false alarm? When she turned away from him and went in the opposite direction, he knew his fears were justified. As he kept his gaze on her, she looked at her watch and picked up her pace. Shit, he knew exactly what she was doing: going for another flight. And from the way she had checked her watch and started walking faster, it must be close to leaving. As he pushed through the crowds, he scanned the aisle ahead. There were ten gates remaining down here. He stopped for a second at the monitors, his gaze flying down the listings, checking the gates off one by one until he stopped at the flashing "boarding" message for a United flight to San Francisco. As his eye drifted farther, he saw that a flight to Toledo was also boarding. Which one was it? Well, there was one definite way to find out.

He sprinted ahead, cut through a waiting area and managed to get past Faith without her seeing him. He abruptly stopped within sight of the gate for the San Francisco flight. The men in suits who had sprinted past him were standing at the departure door talking to a nervous-looking United employee. Then the stone-faced men moved off and stood behind a partition, their gaze fixed on the crowd and departure area. FBI for sure. The San Francisco flight had to be the one Faith was going for.

But something didn't make sense. If Faith had used her phony name, how . . .? Then it hit Lee. She couldn't use her phony name for both tickets for flights leaving a few minutes apart. That would have been a big red flag for the ticket agent. She had used her real name because she needed ID to get on the flight. Shit! She was heading right for them. She'd show her ticket, the agent would signal the FBI and then it would be over.

Just as he was about to turn, he spotted the two men in windbreakers and jeans who had rushed past him earlier. To Lee's experienced eyes, they were watching the Feds intently, without seeming to do so. He edged closer, and with the gloomy weather outside he managed to catch their reflection in the window. One man held something in his hand. A chill went down Lee's back as he maneuvered some more and managed to spot what it was. Or what he thought it was. This case suddenly took on a whole other dimension.

Lee fought his way back down the aisle; seemingly everyone who lived in the Washington metropolitan area had decided to fly today. He saw Faith across the aisle. In another moment she'd be past him. He made a lunge across the wall of people and tripped over a garment bag someone had set down. He fell to the floor hard, his knee taking the brunt of the collision. When he sprang up, Faith was past him. He had a few seconds, if that.

"Suzanne? Suzanne Blake?" he called out.

At first it didn't register. But then she stopped, looked around. If she saw him, Lee knew she might run. But her stopping had given him the few seconds he needed. He circled and came up behind her.

Faith almost collapsed when he gripped her arm. "Turn around and walk with me," he said.

She pulled at his fingers. "Lee, you don't understand. Please, let me go."

"No, *you* don't understand. The FBI is waiting for you at the San Francisco gate."

The words made her freeze.

"You messed up bad. You made the second reservation in your name. They monitor stuff like that, Faith. They know you're here now."

They headed as quickly as they could back down the aisle to the original departure gate. The plane was boarding. Lee grabbed their bags, but instead of getting on the plane, Lee veered off, pulling Faith along with him. They went back through security and headed toward the elevator.

"Where are we going?" Faith said. "The plane to Norfolk is leaving."

"We're getting the hell out of here before they shut the whole terminal down looking for us."

They took the elevator down to the lower level, went outside and Lee signaled for a taxi. They got in one, Lee gave the man an address in Virginia and the cab pulled off. Only then did Lee look at her.

"We couldn't get on the plane to Norfolk."

"Why not? That ticket was in my other name."

Lee glanced at the driver, an old guy slumped down in his seat listening to country western on the radio.

Satisfied, Lee still spoke in low tones. "Because the first thing they'll do is check at the ticket counter to see who purchased the ticket for Faith Lockhart. Then they'll know Suzanne Blake did. And they'll know Charles Wright is traveling with you. And they'll be given descriptions of us both. And they'll check the reservations for Blake and Wright and the FBI will be waiting for us when we get off the plane in Norfolk."

Faith paled. "They move that fast?"

Lee trembled with rage. "Who the hell do you think you're dealing with here? Larry, Moe and Curly Joe?" He slapped his thigh in sudden anger. "Sonofabitch!"

"What?" Faith said frantically. "What?"

"They have my gun. It's registered in my name. My *real* name. Dammit! Now I've aided and abetted, and the Feds right on our ass." In his despair he rested his head in his hands. "This must be my birthday, things are going so good for me."

Faith started to touch him on the shoulder, but pulled her hand back. She looked out the window instead. "I'm sorry. I'm really, really sorry." She put a hand against the car window, letting the cold from the glass seep into her skin. "Look, just take me to the FBI. I'll tell them the truth."

"That would be great except the FBI's not going to take your word for it. And there's another thing."

"What?" Faith wondered if he was going to tell her about working for Buchanan.

"Not now." Lee was actually thinking of the other men at the gate, what he had seen in one of the men's hands. "Right now I'd like you to tell me what that was all about back there."

She stared out the window at the choppy gray Potomac. "I'm not sure I can," she said so softly he could barely hear her.

"Well, I'd like you to try," he said very firmly. "I'd like you to try very, very hard."

"I don't think you'd understand."

"I can understand with the best of them."

She finally turned to him, her face flushed, her gaze refusing to catch his. She nervously played with the edge of her jacket. "I just thought it would be better if you weren't with me. You see, I thought you'd be safer that way."

Lee looked away in disgust. "Bullshit!"

"It's true!"

He whirled back around and clutched her shoulder so tightly she winced in pain. "Listen, Faith, they were at my apartment, whoever *they* are. They know I'm involved. Whether I'm with you or not, the danger level really doesn't change for me, it actually gets worse. And you running around trying to ditch me isn't damn well helping."

"But they knew you were involved. Remember back at your apartment."

Lee shook his head. "Those weren't the Feds."

She looked stunned. "Who, then?"

"I don't know. But the Feds don't show up disguised as UPS men. FBI Rule Number One: Overwhelming force trumps all. They would've come with about a hundred guys and the Hostage Rescue Team and the dogs and body armor and shit like that. And they just come in and take your ass, case closed." Lee's voice grew calmer as he thought things through. "Now, the guys waiting for you at the gate were FBI." He nodded thoughtfully. "They weren't trying to hide who they were." The other two men at the departure gate? All bets were off. But he knew Faith was very lucky to be alive.

"Oh, and by the way, you're welcome for me saving your butt again. Another few seconds and you're back in FBI land with more questions than you have answers for. Maybe I should've just let them take you," he added wearily.

"Why didn't you?" she asked quietly.

Lee almost felt like laughing. The whole experience was like a dream. *But where do I go to wake up?*

"Right now, lunacy seems to be at the top of the list."

Faith attempted a smile. "Thank God for lunatics."

Lee didn't smile back. "From now on, we are Siamese twins. You better get used to seeing a man take a piss because, lady, we are inseparable from here on."

"Lee—"

"I don't want to hear it! Just don't say a damn thing." His voice was trembling. "I'm so close to punching the shit out of you, I swear to God." He made a big show of reaching over and clamping one big hand over her wrist, as though a living handcuff. Then he sat back, staring at nothing.

Faith didn't try to pull her hand away, not that she could have. And she was really terrified he might take a swing at her. This was probably about as angry as Lee Adams had ever gotten in his entire life, she thought. She finally sat back and tried to calm down. Her heart was beating so fast it seemed impossible for her blood vessels to survive the pressure. Maybe she'd save everyone a lot of trouble and just drop from a coronary.

In Washington you could lie about sex, money, power, loyalties. You could spin falsehoods into truths and simple facts into lies. She had seen it all. It was one of the most frustrating and cruelest places on earth, where one relied on old alliances and quick feet for survival and where every new day, every fresh relationship, could be the one that made you or destroyed you. And Faith had thrived in that world, loved it, in fact. Until now.

Faith could not look at Lee Adams, for fear of what she would see in his eyes. He was all she had. Although she barely knew the man, for some reason she craved his respect, his understanding. She knew she would get neither. She didn't deserve them.

Out of the car window she stared at a plane quickly gaining altitude. In another few seconds it would disappear into the clouds. Soon the passengers would only be able to see that layer of puffy cumulus beneath them, as though the world below had suddenly disappeared. Why couldn't she be on that plane and just keep climbing, to a place where she could start over? Why couldn't a place like that exist? Why?

TWENTY-THREE

Brooke Reynolds sat glumly at the small table, chin resting on her palm, and wondered if anything ever was going to go right on this case. They had found Ken Newman's car. It had been professionally cleansed such that her team of "experts" were unable to provide her with any real clues. She had just checked with the lab. They were still messing around with the tape. Worst of all, Faith Lockhart had slipped right through her fingers. At this rate she'd be FBI director in no time. She was certain there would be a stream of messages from the ADIC on down when she returned to her office, and none of them complimentary, she imagined.

Reynolds and Connie were in a private area at Reagan National. They had thoroughly questioned the airline employee who had sold Faith Lockhart her tickets. They had reviewed all the surveillance tapes and the agent had readily picked out Lockhart. Reynolds assumed the woman was Faith Lockhart. The ticket agent had been shown a picture of Lockhart and was reasonably sure she was the same woman.

If it was Lockhart, she had changed her appearance considerably: a haircut and dye job, from what Reynolds had seen on the airport surveillance tape. And now Lockhart had help. For also captured on the video was a tall, well-built man leaving with Lockhart. Reynolds had initiated the obvious inquiries including checking taxi pickups at the airport during that time. They also had colleagues checking in Norfolk in case the pair had made additional travel arrangements there. So far nothing had turned up. They did, however, have one very promising lead.

Reynolds opened the metal gun case and looked at the SIG-Sauer 9mm while Connie leaned against the wall and scowled at nothing. The gun had already been checked for prints, and they were running the results through the Bureau's databases, but they had something even better: The gun was registered. They had quickly gotten the name and address of the owner from the Virginia State Police.

Reynolds said, "Okay, so the gun's registered to this Lee Adams. We're getting a photo of the guy from DMV. I'm assuming he's the one with Lockhart. What do we know about him so far?"

Connie took a mouthful of Coke from the cup he was holding and popped two Advil. "PI. Been around awhile. Seems very legit. Some of the guys at the Bureau know him in fact. Say he's a good guy. We'll get his picture to the ticket agent. See if she can positive-ID him. That's all for right now. We'll have more soon." He glanced at the gun. "We found shell casings in the woods behind the cottage. They'd been fired from a pistol. Nine-millimeter. From the number we found, the person emptied half his mag at something."

"Think this is the pistol?"

"We haven't found any slugs to match it to, but ballistics will tell us if the pinprick on the shell casings we found match ones fired from that gun," Connie said, referring to the indentation a gun's firing pin makes on the bottom of the shell casing, a mark about as unique as a fingerprint. "And since we've got his ammo, we can test-fire from the source, which is ideal, you know. And we're running a print check on the casings. That won't definitely confirm if Adams was there, since he could've loaded the pistol earlier and someone else could have fired it at the cottage, but it's still something."

They both knew that shell casings were much better surfaces for getting usable prints than a pistol grip.

"It'd be nice if we could get his prints inside the cottage."

"VCU found nothing. Adams obviously knows how to do this stuff. Had to be wearing gloves."

"If ballistics does match, then Adams looks to be the one who wounded the shooter."

"He didn't fire all those times at Ken, that's for sure, and a SIG is for shit long-distance. If Adams was able to hit Ken with a pistol shot from that distance in the dark, then we've got to get him a job at Quantico on the firing range."

Reynolds looked unconvinced.

Connie went on. "And the lab confirmed that the blood in the woods is definitely human. We also found a slug near the spot where all the pistol shell casings were. Struck a tree and stayed there. We also turned up a number of shell casings near the blood. Rifle ordnance. Full metal jacket, heavy-caliber stuff. And customized, no manufacturer's code or caliber stamp on the casings. But the lab did say the ammo used a Berdan primer instead of an American Boxer."

Reynolds looked at him sharply. "Berdan? So European manufacture?"

"There are so many freaky variations these days, but it looks that way."

Reynolds was very familiar with the Berdan primer. It differed from the American version principally in that it had no integral anvil. The anvil was constructed right into the cartridge case, forming a miniature T-shaped projection in the primer pocket with two flash holes to allow the exploded primer to get to the powder. It was a clever, efficient design, Reynolds thought.

When you pulled the trigger of a weapon, Brooke had learned when she joined the Bureau, the firing pin hit the primer cup, compressing the primer between the cup and anvil and causing the primer to explode. This mini-explosion, in turn, shot through the flash holes and ignited the powder to temperatures in excess of five thousand degrees. A millisecond later the bullet went roaring down the gun barrel, and before you could blink, a human being was probably dead. Guns were by far the weapon of choice for murder in America, and Brooke knew that homicide events happened at the rate of fifty-five times a day in the United States. Consequently, Reynolds and her colleagues would never lack for work.

"European-manufactured shells might tie in to the foreign interest angle Lockhart was telling us about," Reynolds said almost to herself. "So Adams and the shooter were going at it and Adams gets the better of it." Reynolds stared thoughtfully at her partner. "Any connection between Adams and Lockhart?"

"None that we can see right now, but we've just started digging."

"Here's another theory, Connie: Adams came out of the woods, killed Ken and then went back through the woods. He could've fallen on something and cut himself. That would account for the blood. I know that doesn't explain the rifle slug, but it's a possibility we can't ignore. For all we know, he was carrying a rifle as well. Or it could have been from a hunter's gun. They hunt in those woods, I bet."

"Come on, Brooke. The guy can't have a gun battle with himself. Remember the two separate piles of different shell casings. And no hunter I know is going to stand there and pump shot after shot at something. They'll kill their buddy or maybe themselves. Most states require plugs in a rifle's magazine to limit shots for that very reason. And those shell casings hadn't been there very long."

"Okay, okay, but I'm just not willing to trust Adams at this point."

"And you think I am? I don't trust my own mother, God rest her soul. But I can't ignore facts either. Lockhart drives away in Ken's car? And Adams just leaves his boots behind before he takes his jaunt through the woods? Come on, you don't believe that."

"Look, Connie, I'm just pointing out the possibilities. I'm not saying I'm sold on any of them. The thing that keeps bugging me is, what spooked Ken? If the shooter's in the woods, it wasn't *him*."

Connie rubbed his jaw. "Now, that's true."

Reynolds suddenly snapped her fingers. "Dammit, the door. How could I have been so blind? When we got to the cottage the screen door was wide open. I remember it clearly. It opens out, so Ken would have seen it when he turned that way. What would he have done? Pull his gun."

"And he might have seen the boots too. It was dark, but the cottage's back porch isn't that big." Connie took another swallow of Coke and rubbed his left temple. "Come on, Advil, do your magic. Well, we'll know for certain if Adams was even there when the lab guys unscramble the video."

"*If* they unscramble it. But why would Adams have been at the cottage in the first place?"

"Maybe someone hired him to shadow Lockhart."

"Buchanan?"

"Probably first on my list."

"But if Buchanan hired the shooter to take out Lockhart, why have Adams there to witness it?"

Connie bunched up his thick shoulders and then let them collapse, like a bear scratching itself against a tree. "That for sure doesn't make a helluva lot of sense."

"Well, let me complicate things further for you. Two tickets were purchased by Lockhart for a trip to Norfolk. But only *one* in her real name for the trip to San Francisco."

"And you got Adams running after our guys on the airport surveillance video."

"Think Lockhart tried to give him the slip?"

"Ticket agent said Adams didn't come up to the counter until after Lockhart had purchased the tickets. And the video shows Adams leading her back from the vicinity of the San Francisco gate."

"So maybe an involuntary partnership of sorts," Reynolds said. She had a sudden thought as she looked at Connie. *Like ours, perhaps?* "You know what I'd really like?" Reynolds said. Connie raised his eyebrows. "I'd like to return Mr. Adams's boots. We have his home address?"

"North Arlington. Twenty minutes from here, tops."

Reynolds rose. "Let's go."

TWENTY-FOUR

While Connie parked the car at the curb, Reynolds stared up at the old brownstone. "Adams must do pretty well. This isn't a cheap area."

Connie looked around and said, "Maybe I should sell my house and buy an apartment around here. Stroll around the street, sit in the park, enjoy life."

"Thoughts of retirement creeping in?"

"Seeing Ken in a body bag isn't making me want to do this forever."

They walked up to the front door. Each of them noted the video camera, and then Connie rang the door buzzer.

"Who is it?" a voice fiercely demanded.

"FBI," Reynolds said. "Agents Reynolds and Constantinople."

The door didn't buzz open as they had expected.

"Show me your badges," the elderly voice proclaimed. "Hold them up to the camera."

The two agents looked at each other.

Reynolds smiled. "Let's play nice and do as we're told, Connie."

The pair held up their credentials, or "creds," to the camera. They both carried them the same way: gold badge pinned to the outside of the ID case, so you got the shield first and the picture ID card last. It was intended to be intimidating. And it was. A minute later they heard a door open from inside the building and a woman's face appeared at the glass of the old-fashioned double doors.

"Let me see them again," she said. "My eyes aren't all that good anymore."

"Ma'am—" Connie began hotly until Reynolds elbowed him. They held up their creds again.

The woman scrutinized them and then opened the door.

"I'm sorry," she said as they came in. "But after all the goings-on this morning, I'm about ready to pack my bags and leave for good. And this has been my home for twenty years."

"What goings-on?" Reynolds asked sharply.

The woman eyed her warily. "Who did you come here to see?"

"Lee Adams," Reynolds said.

"I thought so. Well, he's not here."

"Any idea where he might be, Mrs. . . .?"

"Carter. Angie Carter. And no, I don't have any idea where he's got to. Left this morning and I haven't seen him since."

"So what happened this morning?" Connie said. "It was this morning, right?"

Carter nodded. "Fairly early. Just having my coffee when Lee called down and said he wanted me to watch Max because he was going away." They looked at her curiously. "Max is Lee's German shepherd." Her mouth quivered for a moment. "Poor animal."

Reynolds said, "What happened to the dog?"

"They hit him. He'll be okay, but they hurt him."

Connie edged closer to the old woman. "Who hurt him?"

"Ms. Carter, why don't we go into your apartment and sit down?" Reynolds suggested.

The apartment contained old, comfortable furniture, tiny shelves with odd knickknacks placed just so and the aroma of burnt kale and onions.

After they were seated, Reynolds said, "Maybe it would be better if you just started at the beginning, and we'll ask questions along the way."

Carter told of how she had agreed to keep Lee's dog. "I do it a lot, Lee's gone a lot. He's a private investigator, you know."

"We know. So he didn't say where he was going? Nothing at all?" Connie prompted.

"Never does. *Private* investigator is just what it means, and Lee was a stickler for that."

"Does he have a separate office somewhere?"

"No, he uses his spare bedroom for an office. He also looks after the building. He's the one who put in the camera outside, sturdy locks on the doors, things like that. Never accepted one penny for it either. Anybody has a problem in the building – the tenants are mostly old, like me – they go to Lee, and he takes care of it."

Reynolds smiled warmly. "Sounds like a nice guy. Go on with your story."

"Well, I had just gotten Max settled when the UPS man came. Saw him out the window. And then Lee called me and said to let Max out."

Reynolds interrupted. "Did he call from the building?"

"Don't know. The connection was a little scratchy, like one of those cellular phones, maybe. But the thing is, I didn't see him leave the building. Guess he could have gone out the back and down the fire escape, though."

"How did he sound?"

Mrs. Carter patted her hands together while she thought. "Well, I guess I have to say he was agitated about something. I was surprised he wanted me to let Max back out. I mean, I had just gotten him settled, like I told you. Lee said he needed to give the dog a shot or something. Now that didn't make any sense to me, but I did what Lee told me and then all hell broke loose after that."

"This UPS man, did you see him?"

Mrs. Carter snorted. "He wasn't the UPS man. I mean, he had on the uniform and everything, but he wasn't our regular UPS person."

"Maybe a replacement. A substitute."

"I've never seen a UPS man carrying a gun before, have you?"

"So you saw a gun?"

She nodded. "When he came running back down the steps. He had a gun in one hand, and his other hand was bleeding. But I'm getting ahead of myself. Before that I heard Max barking like I've never heard him bark before. Then there was a scuffle, could hear it clear as day. Feet stomping, a man yelling, Max's claws on the wood floor. Then I heard a thud and then I heard poor old Max howl. Then somebody started beating on Lee's door. The next thing I know, I hear a bunch of feet going up the fire escape. I looked out the window of my kitchen and saw all these men running up the fire escape. It was like I was watching a TV show. I went back to the front door and looked out my peephole. That's when I saw the UPS man go out the front door. Guess he went around back and joined the others. I'm not sure."

Connie leaned forward in his chair. "Did these other men have any type of uniforms on?"

Mrs. Carter looked at him strangely. "Well, you of all people should know."

Reynolds looked at her, confused. "What do you mean?"

But Mrs. Carter hurried on with her story. "When they knocked the back door in, the alarm went off. The police came right off."

"What happened when the police came?"

"The men were still here. At least some of them were."

"Did the police arrest them?"

"Of course not. The police took Max away and let them keep searching the place."

Reynolds exclaimed, "Do you have any idea why the police let them stay?"

"Same reason I let you in the door."

Reynolds looked in shock at Connie and then back at Carter and said, "You mean—"

"I mean," Carter broke in testily, "they were the FBI."

TWENTY-FIVE

"What exactly are we doing here, Lee?" Faith asked. They had taken two other cabs after the one from the airport. The last taxi had dropped them off in what seemed like the middle of nowhere, and they had been walking along back streets now for what seemed like several miles.

Lee glanced at her. "Rule number one when running from the law: Assume they'll find the cabbie or cabbies who dropped you off. So you never let a cabbie drop you off at your real destination." He pointed up ahead. "We're almost there." As he walked along, Lee put his hands up to his eyes and popped out the contact lenses, returning his eyes to their normal blue. He put the lenses away in a special case in his bag. "Those suckers kill my eyes."

Faith stared ahead but saw nothing other than run-down homes, cracked sidewalks and sickly-looking trees and lawns. They were traveling parallel to U.S. Route 1 in Virginia, also known as Jefferson Davis Highway after the president of the Confederacy. It was ironic they were here, Faith thought, since Davis himself knew very well about being chased. In fact he had been chased all over the South after the war until the boys in blue had finally caught up with him and Davis had served a long prison term. Faith knew the history, she just didn't want the same result.

She didn't ordinarily come to this part of northern

Virginia. It was heavily industrialized, speckled with on-the-fringe small businesses, truck and boat repair shops, shady-looking car dealerships working out of rusted trailers, and a flea market housed in a decrepit building one failing support beam from condemnation. She was a little surprised when Lee turned and headed for Jeff Davis. She hurried to stay up with him.

"Shouldn't we be getting out of town? I mean, according to you, the FBI can do anything. And then there's the other people you refused to name who are on our track. I'm sure they're incredibly deadly in their own right. And here we are strolling through the suburbs." Lee said nothing and she finally grabbed his arm. "Lee, will you please tell me what's going on?"

He stopped so abruptly she bumped into him. It was like hitting a wall.

Lee glared at her. "Call me stupid, but I just can't shake the feeling that the more information you have, the more likely you'll get another harebrained idea in your head that'll end up getting us both checked into coffins."

"Look, I'm sorry about the airport. You're right, it was stupid. But I had my reasons."

"Your reasons are bullshit. Your whole life is bullshit," he said angrily, and started walking again.

She hurried up next to him, jerked on his arm and they squared off.

"Okay, if you really feel like that, what do you say we just go our separate ways? Here and now. Each take our chances."

He put his hands on his hips. "Because of you I can't go home and I can't use my credit card. I don't have my gun, the Feds are right on my butt and I've got four bucks in my wallet. Let me just jump right on that offer, lady."

"You can have half my cash."

"And where exactly are you going to go?"

"My whole life might be bullshit, and this may shock you, but I *can* take care of myself."

He shook his head. "We stick together. For a lot of reasons. Number one being when and if the Feds pick us up, I want you right there next to me swearing on your mother's grave that yours truly is just an innocent babe stuck in the middle of *your* nightmare."

"Lee!"

"Discussion closed."

He started walking fast and Faith decided against saying anything else. The truth was she didn't *want* to go it alone. She jogged up to him as they turned on to Route 1. At the light they hurried across the street.

"I want you to wait here," Lee said, putting the bags down. "There's a chance I might get recognized where I'm going, and I don't want you with me."

Faith looked around. Behind her was an eight-foot-high chain-link fence with barbed wire on the top. It housed a boat repair facility. Inside the fence a Doberman patrolled the area. Did boats really require that much security? she wondered. Maybe in this area everything did. The business on the next corner was located inside an ugly cinder-block building with big red banners across the windows proclaiming the best deals in town on new and used motorcycles. The parking lot was filled with the two-wheeled machines.

"Do I *have* to stay here by myself?" she said.

Lee pulled out a baseball cap from his bag and put on his sunglasses. "Yes," he said curtly. "Or was that a ghost back there telling me she can take care of herself?"

With no snappy reply coming to mind, Faith had to content herself with angrily watching as Lee hurried across the street and into the motorcycle shop. As she waited, she suddenly sensed a presence behind her. When she turned, she was staring directly at the large Doberman. It had wandered out of the yard. Apparently the boat yard's tight security didn't include closing the damn gate! When the animal showed its teeth and uttered a low, terrifying growl, Faith slowly reached down and gripped the bags. Holding them in front of her, she backed across the street and into the parking lot of the motorcycle shop. The Dobie lost interest in her and went back inside the boat yard.

Faith breathed a sigh of relief and put down the bags. She noted a couple of fleshy teenagers sporting sparse goatees checking out a used Yamaha at the same time they were ogling her. She pulled her baseball cap down farther, turned away and pretended to examine a shiny red Kawasaki that was, surprise, on sale. Across Jeff Davis was a business that leased heavy construction equipment. She looked at a crane that rose a good thirty feet in the air. Dangling from its cable was a small forklift that had a sign painted across it that read, RENT ME. Everywhere she looked was a world she no longer knew much about. She had traveled a much different circuit: capital cities of the world, high political stakes, demanding clients, enormous amounts of power and money, all perpetually shifting like the continental plates. Things got crushed in between these masses all the time, and no one even knew it. She suddenly realized that the *real* world was a two-ton forklift dangling like a guppy on a string. Rent me. Employ people. Build something.

But Danny had given her a shot at redemption. She was a dime a dozen, yet she had been doing some good in the world. For ten years now she had been helping people who desperately needed it. Perhaps also these ten years she'd been atoning for the vicarious guilt she'd felt growing up, watching her father's shenanigans, however well intentioned, and all the pain they had caused. She had actually been afraid to ever analyze that part of her life too deeply.

Faith heard footsteps behind her and turned around. The man was dressed in jeans, black boots and a sweatshirt with the logo of the motorcycle shop printed across it. He was young, early twenties, big, sleepy eyes, tall, slender and good-looking. And he knew it, she could readily tell, by his cocky manner. His expression clearly evidenced that his interest in Faith was deeper than her choice in two-wheeled transportation.

"Can I help you with anything, ma'am? Anything at all?"

"Just browsing. I'm waiting for my boyfriend."

"Hey, this is a pretty machine over here." He pointed to a BMW cycle that just reeked, even to Faith's untrained eye, of money. Wasted money, in her opinion. But then again, wasn't she the proud owner of a big BMW sedan, which sat in the garage of her very expensive digs in McLean?

He rubbed one hand slowly across the Beemer's gas tank. "Purrs like a kitten. You take care of beautiful things, they take good care of you. Real good." A big smile broke across his features as he said this. He looked her over and winked.

Faith wondered if this was his best pickup line.

"I don't drive them, I just ride on them," she said casually, and then regretted her choice of words.

He smiled broadly. "Well, that's the best news I've heard all day. In fact, you just made my whole year. Just ride 'em, huh?" The young man laughed and clapped his hands together. "Well, how about we go for a spin, sweet thing? You can check out *my* equipment. Just climb on."

Her face flashed. "I don't appreciate your—"

"Now, don't go getting mad. If you need anything, my name's Rick." He held out his card and winked at her again. He added in a low voice, "Home phone's on the back, babe."

She looked at the card in his hand with distaste. "Okay, Rick, but I like full disclosure. My boyfriend is inside. Are you man enough to meet him?"

Rick didn't look so comfortable now. "I'm man enough for anything, babe."

"Good to hear. My boyfriend is inside. He's about your height, but he's got a real man's body."

The hand holding the card dropped to Rick's side as he scowled at her. Faith easily sensed that his pat lines had been forgotten and his mind was too slow to think of new ones.

Faith eyed him closely. "Yeah, his shoulders are about the size of Nebraska, and did I mention he's an ex-Navy boxing champ?"

"Is that right?" Rick pocketed his card.

"Don't take my word for it; he's right there. Go ahead and ask him." She pointed behind him.

Rick whirled around and watched as Lee came out of the building carrying two helmets and two one-piece riding suits. A map was stuffed into his front jacket pocket. Even under the bulky clothes he was wearing, Lee's impressive build was very apparent. He glared suspiciously at Rick.

"Do I know you?" Lee asked him gruffly.

Rick smiled uneasily and then swallowed with difficulty as he looked Lee over. "N-no, sir," he stammered.

"Then what the hell do you want, kid?"

Faith piped in, "Oh, he was just asking me the sorts of things I liked in my riding equipment, right,

Ricky?" She smiled at the young salesman.

"That's right. Yep. Well, see ya." Rick practically ran toward the shop.

"Bye-bye, sweet thing," Faith called after him.

Lee scowled at her. "I told you to wait across the street. Can I not leave you alone for one damn minute?"

"I had an encounter with a Dobie. Retreat seemed the wisest course."

"Right. What, were you negotiating with the guy to jump me so you can get away?"

"Don't get crazy on me, Lee."

"I kind of wished you had. It'd give me an excuse to kick the shit out of somebody. What'd he really want?"

"Junior wanted to sell me something, and it wasn't a motorcycle. What's that?" she asked, pointing at what he was carrying.

"Necessary equipment for motorcycle riders this time of year. At sixty miles an hour, there's a tiny bite in the air."

"We don't have a motorcycle."

"We do now."

She followed him around back to where an enormous Honda Gold Wing SE road bike sat. With its slick chrome and futuristic design, high-tech equipment and full windshield, the motorcycle looked like something Batman might tool around on. It was painted pearl-gray-green with dark gray green trim and had a king and queen seat with a padded backrest. The passenger would fit snugly there, like a ball in a glove. It was so big and elaborately equipped that it looked like an open-air recreational vehicle.

Lee stuck a key in the ignition and started putting on his suit. He handed the other outfit to Faith.

"Just where are we going on this thing?"

Lee zipped up his suit. "*We* are going to your little place in North Carolina."

"All that way on a motorcycle?"

"We can't rent a car without a credit card and ID. Your car and mine are useless. We can't take a train, plane or bus. They'll cover all those places. Unless you can sprout wings, this is it."

"I've never even been on a motorcycle."

He took off his shades. "You don't have to drive it. That's what I'm here for. So what do you say? Want to go for a ride?" He flashed a grin at her.

Faith felt as though a brick had hit her in the head when he said those words. Her skin was afire as she looked at him perched on that machine. And at that exact moment, as though by the will of God, the sun broke through the gloom. A shaft of light came down and ignited those already dazzling blue eyes into flame-filled sapphires. She found she couldn't move. Lord, she could barely breathe; her knees began to quiver.

It was fifth grade, recess. The boy with the man-size eyes the exact color of Lee's had ridden his bike with the banana seat up to where she sat on the swing reading a book.

"Want to go for a ride?" he had asked her. "No," she had said, and then immediately dropped her book and climbed on back. They were an "item" for two months, planning their lives together, vowing their undying love for each other, even though they never exchanged so much as a peck on the lips. Then her mother died, and Faith's father moved them away. She briefly wondered if Lee and he could be one and the same. She had banished the memory so completely from her subconscious that she couldn't even remember the boy's name. It could be Lee, couldn't it? She thought this because the only other time in her entire life when her knees had gone weak was on that playground. The boy had said what Lee had just said, and the sun had hit those eyes just as it had smacked Lee's, and her heart felt as though it would explode if she didn't do exactly as he said. Just how it felt right now.

"Are you okay?" Lee asked.

Faith gripped one of the handlebars to steady herself, and said as calmly as she could, "And they're just going to let you drive off with it?"

"My brother runs the place. It's a demo. We're officially taking it for an extended test drive."

"I can't believe I'm doing this." Just like fifth grade, there was no way she could not get on that bike.

"Consider the alternative, and then the idea of your butt on this Honda starts looking beautiful." He slid his shades on and flipped his helmet's shield down as though putting an exclamation point on this statement.

Faith slipped on the suit, and with Lee's help managed to get the helmet on snugly. He loaded their bags into the Honda's spacious trunk and saddle pouches, and Faith climbed on behind him. He started the engine, gunned it for a moment or so and then hit the gas. When he released the clutch, the power of the Honda threw Faith back against the padded bar and she found herself clamping her arms and legs around Lee and the eight-hundred-pound motorcycle, respectively, as they rocketed on to Jeff Davis heading south.

She almost jumped off the bike when she heard the voice in her ear.

"Okay, calm down, it's a Chatterbox helmet-to-helmet audio link," Lee's voice said. He'd obviously felt her shock. "You ever driven down to your beach house?"

"No, I always flew."

"That's okay. I've got a map. We'll take 95 down and pick up Interstate 64 at Richmond. That'll get us to Norfolk. We'll figure out the best way from there. We'll grab something to eat on the way. We should make it before it gets too dark. Okay?"

She found herself nodding and then remembered to say, "Okay."

"Now, just sit back and relax. You're in good hands."

Instead, she leaned into him, circled her arms around his waist and held tightly. She was suddenly immersed in the recollection of those divine two months in fifth grade. This had to be an omen. Maybe they could drive off and never come back. Start at the Outer Banks, hire a boat and end up on a patch of soil somewhere in the Caribbean no one had ever been before, a place no one would ever see except for them. She could learn to keep a hut, cook with coconut milk or whatever they had there, be a good little homemaker while Lee was off catching fish. They could make love every night under the moonlight and there would be no one to complain. Or watch. She leaned farther into him. None of that sounded bad. Or too far-fetched, under the circumstances. None of it.

"Oh, and Faith?" Lee said into her ear.

She touched her helmet to his, felt the solid breadth of his torso against her breasts. She was twenty again, the wind was delicious, the warmth of the sun inspiring, her greatest worry a midterm exam. A sudden vision of them lying naked under the sky, skin brown, hair wet, limbs intertwined, made her wish they weren't in body suits with thick zippers, going sixty miles an hour over hard pavement.

"Yes?"

"If you even think about trying to pull another

stunt on me like at the airport, I'll use those good hands to wring your neck. Understand?"

She leaned away from him and rested her back against the sissy bar, pushing herself deep into the leather. And away from him. Her shining white knight with the bedeviling blue eyes.

So much for memories. So much for dreams.

TWENTY-SIX

The event was typical of Washington: A political fund-raising dinner at a downtown hotel. The chicken was stringy and cold, the wine cheap, the conversation high-powered, the stakes enormous, the protocol tricky, the egos often impossible. The attendees were either wealthy and/or well connected, or underpaid political staffers who worked long, frantic hours during the day and were rewarded for these prodigious efforts by being compelled to work these sorts of events at night. The Secretary of the Treasury was supposed to have attended, along with some other political heavyweights; even since he had become engaged to a well-known Hollywood actress with a thing about exhibiting her cleavage at the drop of an intern, the secretary had been more in demand than the keeper of the cash normally was. Then, at the last minute, he had gotten a better offer to speak at another event, which was often the case in the endless game of "where is the political grass greener?" An underling had been sent in his place, a gawky, nervous person no one really knew or cared about.

The event was another opportunity to see and be seen, to check the ever-changing pecking order of a certain subgroup of the political hierarchy. Most never even sat down to eat. They just dropped off their check and then it was off to another fund-raiser. Networking flowed through the room as though from a well-fed spring. Or open wound, depending on how one looked at it.

Danny Buchanan surveyed the room. How many of these events had he attended over the years? During the frenzy of key fund-raising periods when he used to represent Big Business, Buchanan would attend breakfasts, luncheons, dinners and assorted parties nonstop for weeks. Exhausted, he had sometimes shown up at the wrong event – a reception for the senator from North Dakota instead of a dinner for the South Dakota congressman. After taking over for the world's poor, he had no such problems, for the simple fact that he now had no money to give members. However, Buchanan was well aware that if there was one truism in political fund-raising, it was that there was never enough money. And that meant that there would *always* be the opportunity for influence peddling. Always.

After he got back from Philly, his day had really started. He had met with half a dozen different members on the Hill and their staff on a myriad of matters, and set up appointments for future meetings. Staffs were important, particularly committee staff, especially appropriations committee staff. Members came and went. The staff tended to stay forever; they knew the issues and process cold. And Danny knew that you never wanted to surprise a member by trying to dodge the staff. You might be successful once, but you were dead after that, as the angry aides took their revenge by shutting you completely out.

A late luncheon followed, with a paying client whom Faith had typically taken care of. Buchanan had had to make excuses for her absence, and he did so with his usual aplomb and humor. "Sorry, you get the second string today," he told the client. "But I'll try not to mess things up too badly for you."

Though there was no need to bolster Faith's

excellent reputation, Buchanan had recounted to this client the story of how Faith had once personally hand-delivered – in a gift box with a big red ribbon, no less – to all five hundred and thirty-five members of Congress detailed polling data that showed the American public was fully in support of funding for global vaccination of all children. She'd included in the gift box accompanying briefing materials and before-and-after photos of vaccinated children from distant lands. Sometimes pictures were the most important weapons Danny and she had. Then she had worked the phone for thirty-six hours straight enlisting support here and overseas and made exhaustive presentations with several of the larger international relief organizations over a two-week period on three continents to show just how such a thing could be accomplished. How important it was. The result: passage of a bill in Congress that supported a study to determine if such an endeavor could work. Now consultants would rack up millions of dollars in fees and kill several forests of trees for the mountains of paper the study would generate (to justify the enormous consulting fees, of course), with no assurances that a single child would receive a single dose of vaccine.

"A small success, to be sure, but a step forward," Buchanan had told the client. "When Faith goes after something, stay out of her way." The client already knew this about Faith, Buchanan was aware. Perhaps he was just saying it to bolster his own spirits. Perhaps he just wanted to talk about Faith. He had been hard on her the last year, very hard. Terrified that she would be drawn into his Thornhillian nightmare, he had outright pushed her away. Well, he had succeeded in driving her right into the arms of the FBI, it seemed. *I'm sorry, Faith.*

After the luncheon it was back to the Hill, where

Buchanan waited with a handful of Rolaids on a series of floor votes. He sent in his cards to the floor asking for time from some of the members. He would buttonhole others as they came off the elevator.

"Foreign debt relief is essential, Senator," he individually told more than a dozen members, hustling along beside them and their overly protective entourage. "They're spending more on debt payments than on health and education," Danny would plead. "What good is a strong balance sheet when the population is dying at the rate of ten percent a year? They'll have great credit and not a damn person left to use it. Let's spread the wealth here."

"Right, right, Danny, we'll get back to you. Send me some materials." Like the petals of a flower closing up for the night, the entourage would close ranks around the member, and Danny the bee would be off to gather other nectar.

Congress was an ecosystem just as complicated as the one existing in the oceans. As Danny trolled the corridors, he looked at the activity swirling all around. True to their titles, whips were everywhere prodding members to follow party line. Back in the whip's chamber, Buchanan knew the phones were constantly being worked with the same goal in mind. Gofers scurried down the corridors in search of people more important than themselves. Small groups of people huddled in pockets of the broad hallways, discussing matters of importance with solemn, downcast expressions. Men and women pushed on to crowded elevators with the hope of snaring a few precious seconds with a member whose support they desperately needed. Members talked with each other, laying the groundwork for future deals or reaffirming agreements already struck. It was all chaotic and yet possessed a certain order, as people coupled and uncoupled like robotic arms around hunks of metal on an assembly line. Give a touch here and on to the next one. Danny dared to think that his work might be as exhausting as childbirth; and he would swear it was more exhilarating than skydiving. Buchanan was thoroughly addicted to it. As crazy as it sounded, he would miss it.

"Get back to me?" was his typical closing to each member's aide.

"Of course, you can count on it," would be each aide's typical response.

And, of course, he'd never hear back. But they would hear from him. Again and again, until they got it. You just fired your shotgun pellets and hoped one stuck somewhere.

Next, Buchanan had spent a few minutes with one of his "chosen few," going over the language Buchanan wanted to insert in a line amendment in a bill's report. Almost no one ever read the report language, but it was in the monotonous details that important actions were accomplished. In this case, the language would tell the managers at AID precisely how funding approved by the underlying bill was to be spent.

With the verbiage in good shape, Buchanan mentally checked that off his list and went prowling again for other members. From years of practice, Buchanan navigated with ease the labyrinths of the Senate and House office buildings where even veterans of the Hill sometimes became lost. The only other place where he spent as much time was the Capitol itself. His eyes darted left and right, picking up on everyone he saw, staff members or other lobbyists, swiftly making a calculation as to whether a particular person could help the cause or not. And when you went into chambers with members or caught them in the halls, you had better be ready to roll. They were busy, often harassed, and thinking of five hundred things at once.

Fortunately, Buchanan could summarize the most complex issues in a matter of sentences, a talent for which he was legendary; members, besieged on all sides by special interests of every kind, absolutely demanded this skill. And he could pitch his client's position with passion. All in two minutes while walking down a crowded corridor or while packed inside an elevator or, if he was very lucky, on a long plane flight. Catching the really powerful members was important. If he could get the Speaker of the House to voice support for one of his bills, even informally, Buchanan would use that to leverage other members on the fence. Sometimes that was enough.

"He in, Doris?" Buchanan asked as he popped his head into a member's chambers and eyed the matronly appointments secretary, a veteran of the place.

"He's leaving in five minutes to catch a flight, Danny."

"That's great because I only need two minutes. I can use the other three to catch up with you. I like talking to you better anyway. And God bless Steve, but you're far easier on the eye, my dear."

Doris's heavy face crinkled into a smile. "You smoothie, you."

And he got his two minutes with Congressman Steve.

Buchanan next had stopped at the cloakroom and found out which Senate committees had been assigned to a series of bills he was interested in. There were committees of primary and sequential and, in rare cases, concurrent jurisdiction, depending on what was in a particular bill. Simply determining who had what bill and in what priority of importance was a huge, ever-changing jigsaw puzzle that lobbyists had to constantly figure out. It was often a maddening challenge, and there was no one better at it than Danny Buchanan.

In the course of this day Buchanan had, as always, plied members' offices with his "leave behinds," information and summaries the staff would need to educate their members on the issues. If they had a question or concern, he would find an answer or an expert, promptly. And Buchanan had concluded every single meeting with the all-important question: "When can I follow up?" Without getting a date certain, he would never hear back from any of them. He would be forgotten, his place taken by a hundred others clamoring just as passionately for their clients.

Then he had spent the late afternoon covering other clients normally handled by Faith. He gave apologies and vague explanations for her absence. What else could he do?

After that he gave remarks at a think-tank-sponsored seminar on world hunger, and then it was back to his office to make phone calls ranging from reminding members' staffs of a variety of issues coming up for vote, to drumming up coalition support from other charitable organizations. A couple of dinners were arranged, future overseas travel booked, along with a visit in January to the White House, where he would personally introduce the President to the new head of an international children's right organization. It was a real coup that Buchanan and the organizations he supported hoped would generate some good publicity. They were constantly on the lookout for celebrity support. Faith had been particularly good at that. Journalists were rarely interested in the poor from faraway lands, but throw in a Hollywood superstar and the media room would be bustling with scribes. Such was life.

Then Buchanan had spent some time doing his FARA – or Foreign Agent Registration Act – quarterly reports, which were a real pain in the ass, particularly since you had to stamp every page filed with Congress with the ominous label "foreign propaganda," as if you were Tokyo Rose calling for the overthrow of the U.S. government, instead of, in Danny's case, selling his soul to get crop seeds and powdered milk.

After bending a few more ears on the phone, then studying a few hundred pages of briefing materials, he had decided to call it a day. A glamorous day in the life of a typical Washington lobbyist, which usually ended with him collapsing into bed, except that today he did not have that luxury. Instead, he was here in this downtown hotel, attending yet another political fund-raiser, and the reason was standing in the far corner of the room sipping a glass of white wine and looking extremely bored. Buchanan headed over.

"You look like you could use something stronger than white wine."

Senator Russell Ward turned and a smile broke across his face as he looked at Buchanan. "It's good to see an honest face in this sea of iniquity, Danny."

"How about we trade this place for the Monocle?"

Ward put his glass down on a table. "Best offer I've had all day."

TWENTY-SEVEN

The Monocle was a restaurant of longstanding on Capitol Hill's Senate side. The restaurant, and the U.S. Capitol Police building, which itself used to be an Immigration and Naturalization building, were the only two structures left in this location that formerly housed a long row of buildings. The Monocle was a favorite place for politicians, lobbyists and VIPs to gather for lunch, dinner and drinks.

The maître d' welcomed Buchanan and Ward by name and ushered the pair to a private corner table. The decor was conservative, the walls adorned with enough photographs of past and present politicians to fill the Washington Monument. The food was good, yet people didn't come for the delights of the menus; they came to be seen, do business and talk shop. Ward and Buchanan were regulars here.

They ordered drinks and perused the menu for a moment.

As Ward studied his menu, Buchanan studied him.

Russell Ward had been called Rusty for as long as Buchanan could remember. And that was a long time, since the two had grown up together. As chairman of the Senate Select Committee on Intelligence, Ward was a powerful influence on the well-being – or not – of all the country's intelligence agencies. He was smart, politically savvy, honest, hard-working, and he came from a very wealthy northeast family that had lost its fortune when Ward was a young man. He had gone south to Raleigh and methodically built himself a career in public service. He was North Carolina's senior senator and worshipped by the entire state. Under Buchanan's classification system, Rusty Ward would be absolutely labeled a "Believer." He was familiar with every political game ever played. Ward knew all the inside stories on everyone in this town. He knew people's strengths and, more important, their weaknesses. Physically, the man was a wreck, Buchanan knew, with problems ranging from diabetes to the prostate. Yet mentally, Ward was sharp as ever. Those who underestimated the man's massive intellect because of the physical ailments had all lived to regret it.

Ward looked up from his menu. "Anything interesting on your plate these days, Danny?"

Ward's voice was deep and sonorous, and so wonderfully southern, all traces of clipped Yankee long gone. Buchanan could sit and listen to the man for hours. And he had done so on many occasions.

Buchanan replied, "Same old, same old. You?"

"Had an interesting hearing this morning. Senate Intelligence. CIA."

"Is that right?"

"You ever hear of a gentleman by the name of Thornhill? Robert Thornhill?"

Buchanan's features were impassive. "Can't say that I know the man at all. Tell me about him."

"He's one of the old powers there. Associate DDO. Smart, cunning, lies his ass off with the best of them. I don't trust him."

"Doesn't sound like you should."

"I have to give the man his due though. He's done terrific work, outlasted numerous CIA directors. Really served his country extraordinarily well. He's actually a legend over there. They let him do more or less what he wants because of that. Such a policy, however, is dangerous."

"Really? He sounds like a real patriot."

"That's what worries me. People who believe themselves to be true patriots tend to be zealots. Zealots, in my opinion, are one short step from lunatics. History has given us enough examples of that." Ward grinned. "I remember this one time he came in to deliver the usual bullshit. He looked so smug I decided I had to tweak him a little."

Buchanan looked very interested. "How'd you do that?"

"I asked him about death squads." Ward paused and looked around for a moment. "We've had problems with the CIA over that in the past. They fund these little insurgency groups, outfit and train 'em, then turn 'em loose, like an old coon dog. Then, unlike a good coon dog, they go and do things they weren't supposed to be doing. At least according to the official agency rules."

"What'd he say to that?"

"Well, it wasn't part of his little script. He looked through his briefing book like he was attempting to shake out a small band of armed men." Ward laughed deeply. "Then he threw me some gobbledygook that really amounted to nothing. Said that the 'new' CIA was merely a collector and analyzer of information. When I asked him if he was conceding that there was something wrong with the 'old' CIA, I thought he might come over the table at me." Ward laughed again. "Same old, same old."

"So what's he up to now that's got you ticked off?"

Ward smiled. "Trying to get me to reveal confidences?"

"Of course."

Ward glanced around again and then leaned

growing up in the mansion with all that money while my family waited on yours. Now which of us sounds drunk?"

"You're the best friend I ever had."

"And you know that sentiment is reciprocated, Senator."

"It's even more remarkable that you've never asked me for a damn thing. You damn well know I sit on a couple committees that could help your causes."

"I like to avoid the appearance of impropriety."

"You must be the only one in this town." Ward chuckled.

"Let's just say our friendship is more important to me than even that."

Ward spoke softly. "I never told you, but what you said at my mother's funeral touched me deeply. I swear, I think you knew the woman better than I did."

"She was a class act. Taught me all I ever needed to know about everything. She deserved a grand sendoff. What I said didn't come close by half."

Ward stared into his glass. "If my stepfather could have only lived off my family's inheritance and not tried to play businessman we might have kept the estate, and he wouldn't have taken his head off with a shotgun. But then maybe I wouldn't have gotten to play senator all these years if I'd had a trust fund to blow."

"If more people played the game the way you do, Rusty, the country would be far better off."

"I wasn't fishing for a compliment, but I appreciate you saying it."

Buchanan drummed his fingers against the table. "I drove out to the old place the other day."

Ward looked up, surprised. "Why?"

Buchanan shrugged. "Not really sure. I was close

by, I had some time. It hasn't changed much. Still beautiful."

"I haven't been there since I left for college. Don't even know who owns it now."

"A young couple. I saw the wife and kids through the gate, playing on the front lawn. Investment banker or Internet mogul, probably. An idea and ten bucks in his pocket yesterday, a red-hot company and a hundred million in stock today."

Ward lifted his glass. "God bless America."

"If I had had the money back then, your mother wouldn't have lost that house."

"I know that, Danny."

"But everything happens for a reason, Rusty. Like you said, you might not have gone into politics. You've had a grand career. You're a Believer."

Ward smiled. "Your little classification system has always intrigued me. You have it all written down somewhere? I'd like to compare it with my own conclusions about my distinguished colleagues."

Buchanan tapped his forehead. "It's all up here."

"All that gold, stored in one man's brain. What a pity."

"You know everything about everybody in this town too." Buchanan paused and then added quietly, "So what do you know about me?"

Ward seemed surprised by the question.

"Don't tell me the world's greatest lobbyist is having self-doubt? I thought the book on Daniel J. Buchanan was unshakable confidence, encyclopedic mind and a keen insight into the psychology of windbag politicians and their innate weaknesses, which could fill the Pacific, by the way."

"Everybody has doubts, Rusty, even people like you and me. That's why we last so long. One inch from the edge. Death at any minute if you let down your guard."

The way he said this made Ward drop his amused look. "You got something you'd like to talk about?"

"Not in a million years," Buchanan said with a sudden smile. "If I start telling the sorry likes of you all my secrets, then I'll have to take my lemonade stand somewhere else and start over. And I'm way too old for that."

Ward leaned back against the soft cushion and looked his friend over. "What makes you do it, Danny? Not money, surely."

Buchanan slowly nodded in agreement. "If I did it solely for the dollars, I would've been gone ten years ago." He swallowed the rest of his drink and looked over at the doorway, where the ambassador from Italy and his substantial entourage stood, along with several senior Hill staffers, a couple of senators and three women in short black dresses who looked like they had been rented for the evening, and very well might have been. The Monocle was filling up with so many VIPs now you could hardly spit without nailing some leader of something. And they all wanted the world. And they all wanted you to get it for them. Eat you up and leave nothing and then call you a friend. Buchanan knew all the lyrics to that song.

He looked up at an old photograph on the wall. A bald-headed man with a beak nose, dour look and ferocious eyes peered down at him. Long dead now, he had once been one of the most powerful men in Washington for decades. And most feared. Power and fear seemed to go hand in hand here. Now Buchanan couldn't even remember the man's name. Didn't that speak volumes.

Ward put down his glass. "I think I know. Your causes have become much more benevolent over the years. You're out to save a world few even care about. You're really the only lobbyist I know who does it."

Buchanan shook his head. "A poor Irish lad who brought himself up by the bootstraps and made a fortune sees the light and then uses his golden years helping the less fortunate? Hell, Rusty, I'm driven more by fear than altruism."

Ward looked at him curiously. "How's that?"

Buchanan sat up very straight, put his palms together and cleared his throat. He had never told anyone this. Not even Faith. Maybe it was time. He would look insane, of course, but at least Rusty would keep it to himself.

"I have this recurring dream, you see. In my dream America keeps getting richer and richer, fatter and fatter. Where an athlete gets a hundred million dollars to bounce a ball, a movie star earns twenty million to act in trash and a model gets ten million to walk around in her underwear. Where a nineteen-year-old can make a billion dollars in stock options by using the Internet to sell us more things we don't need faster than ever." Buchanan stopped and smiled grimly at his bread plate. "And where a lobbyist can earn enough to buy his own plane. We keep hoarding the wealth of the world. Anybody gets in the way, we crush them, in a hundred different ways, while selling them the message of America the Beautiful. The world's remaining superpower, right?

"Then, little by little, the rest of the world wakes up and sees us for what we are: a fraud. And they start coming for us. In log boats and propeller planes and God knows how else. First by the thousands, then by the millions and then by the billions. And they wipe us out. Stuff us all down some pipe and flush us for good. You, me, the ballplayers, the movie stars, the supermodels, Wall Street,

Hollywood and Washington. The true land of make believe."

Ward stared at him wide eyed. "My God, a dream or a nightmare?"

Buchanan shot him a stern glance. "You tell me."

"Your country, love it or leave it, Danny. There's an element of truth in that slogan. We're not so bad."

"We also suck up a disproportionate share of the wealth and energy in the world. We pollute more than any other country. We trash foreign economies and never look back. But still, for a lot of big and small reasons that I really can't explain, I do love my country. That's why this nightmare disturbs me so much. *I don't want it to happen.* But it's getting harder and harder to feel any hope."

"If that's the case, why *do* you do it?"

Buchanan stared at the old photograph again and said, "Do you want something pithy or philosophical?"

"How about the truth?"

Buchanan looked at his old friend. "I deeply regret never having children," he began slowly, then paused. "A good friend of mine has a dozen grandchildren. He was telling me about a PTA meeting he had attended at his granddaughter's elementary school. I asked him why he was bothering with doing that. Wasn't that the parents' job? I said. You know what he told me? He said that with the way the world is now, we all have to think about things beyond our lifetime. Beyond our children's lifetime, in fact. It's our right. It's our duty, my good friend told me."

Buchanan smoothed out his napkin. "So maybe I do what I do because the sum of the world's tragedies outweighs its happiness.

"Other than that, I haven't the faintest idea."

TWENTY-EIGHT

Brooke Reynolds was just finished saying grace, and they all started on their meals. She had burst through the door ten minutes earlier, determined to eat dinner with her family. Her regular hours at the Bureau were eight-fifteen A.M. to five P.M. That was the funniest joke at the Bureau: regular hours. She had changed into jeans and a sweatshirt and exchanged her suede flats for Reeboks. Reynolds took much pleasure in scooping out spoonfuls of peas and mashed potatoes for all their plates. Rosemary poured out milk for the kids while her teenage daughter Theresa helped three-year-old David cut up his meat. It was a nice, quiet family gathering, which Reynolds had come to cherish and which she did everything possible to make each evening, even if it meant going back to work later.

Reynolds rose from the table and poured herself a glass of white wine. While half her brain focused on finding Faith Lockhart and her new confederate, Lee Adams, the other part was looking ahead with much anticipation to Halloween, less than a week away. Sydney, her six-year-old daughter, was dead set on being Eeyore, for the second year in a row. David would be the bouncy Tigger, a character that fit the perpetual-motion child perfectly. After that, Thanksgiving, perhaps a trip to her parents' in Florida, if she could find the time. Then Christmas. This year Reynolds was taking the kids to see Santa

Claus. She had missed last year because of – what else? – Bureau business. This year she would pull her 9mm on anyone who tried to stop her appointment with Kris Kringle. All in all, a good plan, if she could just make it work. Conception was easy; execution was the key that so often fell out of the lock.

As she put the cork back in the bottle, she looked sadly around a home that would not be hers much longer. Her son and daughter sensed that the change was coming. David hadn't slept through the night in over a week. Reynolds, home after working fifteen-hour days, would hold the quivering, wailing little boy, trying to calm him, rock him back to sleep. She tried to tell him that things would be just fine, when she was as uncertain as anyone whether they would be. It was sometimes terrifying being a parent, particularly in the midst of a divorce and all the pain it caused, which you saw every day etched into the faces of your children. More than once Reynolds had thought about calling off the divorce for that reason alone. But hanging on for the sake of the children wasn't the answer, she felt. At least not for her. They would have a better life without the man than they'd had with him. And her ex, she thought, might be a better father after the divorce than he had been before. Well, at least she could hope. Reynolds simply did not want to let her children down.

When Reynolds caught her daughter Sydney looking apprehensively at her, she smiled as naturally as she could. Sydney was six going on sixteen, so mature beyond her years that it scared Reynolds to death. She picked up on everything, missed nothing of significance. Reynolds had never in her career interrogated a suspect as thoroughly as Sydney did her mother nearly every day. The child dug deep, trying to understand what was going on, what their future would hold, and Reynolds had no ready answers for any of it.

More than once, she had found Sydney holding her crying brother in his bed late at night, attempting to soothe him, relieve his fears. Reynolds had recently told her daughter that she didn't need to assume the responsibility too, that her mother would always be there. Her statement had a hollow ring, and Sydney's face plainly showed a lack of belief. The fact that her daughter had not accepted this statement as dead, solid truth had aged Reynolds several years in several seconds. The memory of the palm reader and her predictions of premature death had come back to roost with a vengeance.

"Rosemary's chicken is awesome, isn't it, honey?" Reynolds said to Sydney.

The little girl nodded.

"Thank you, ma'am," Rosemary said, pleased.

"Are you okay, Mom?" Sydney asked. At the same time, she moved her little brother's milk away from the edge of the table. David had a propensity for spilling any liquid within his reach.

That subtle act of motherhood and her daughter's earnest question moved Reynolds almost to tears. She had been on such an emotional roller coaster of late that it didn't take much to set her off. She took a sip of wine, hoping it would prevent her from actually collapsing into a crying fit. It was like being pregnant again. The littlest thing affected her as if it were life or death. But then her common sense kicked in. She was a mom, things would work out. She had the luxury of a devoted live-in nanny. Sitting around whining, feeling sorry for yourself, wasn't the answer. So their life wasn't perfect. Whose was? She thought of what Anne Newman was going through right now. Suddenly Reynolds's problems didn't seem so bad.

"Everything's really good, Syd. Really good. Congratulations on your spelling test. Ms. Betack said you were the star of the day."

"I like school a lot."

"And it shows, young lady."

Reynolds was about to sit back down when the phone rang. She had caller ID and checked the readout screen. The ID screen came up blank. The caller must have ID block or his number was unlisted. She debated whether to answer it or not. The problem was that every FBI agent she knew had unlisted numbers. Ordinarily, though, anyone from the Bureau would call her on her pager or cell phone, both of which numbers she closely guarded; and calls to those two she would always answer. It was probably a random computer dialer and she would be told to wait until a real person came on and tried to sell her a time-share in Disney World. Still, something made her reach out and pick up the phone.

"Hello?"

"Brooke?"

Anne Newman sounded distressed. And as she listened to the woman, Reynolds sensed that there was something in addition to her husband's violent death – poor Anne, what worse could there be?

"I'll be there in thirty minutes," Reynolds said.

She grabbed her coat and car keys, took a bite out of a slice of the bread on her plate and kissed her children.

"Will you be back in time to read us a story, Mom?" Sydney asked.

"Three bears, three pigs, three goats." David promptly recited his favorite nighttime storytelling ritual to Brooke, his favorite story reader. His sister Sydney favored reading the stories herself, every night, sounding out each word along the way. Little David now took a big gulp of milk, loudly burped and then excused himself in a fit of laughter.

Reynolds smiled. Sometimes when she was tired she would tell the stories so fast they almost blurred together. The pigs built their houses, the bears went for their walk while Goldilocks burglarized the joint and the three billy goats gruff trounced the evil troll and lived happily ever after in their new pasture of grass. Sounded nice. Where could she buy some? And then, undressing for bed, Reynolds would endure spasms of crushing guilt. The reality was that her kids would be grown and gone before she blinked her eyes twice, and she routinely short-changed them on three short fairy tales because she wanted to do something so unimportant as sleep. Sometimes it was better not to think too much. Reynolds was a classic over-achiever and a perfectionist, to boot, while a "perfect parent" was the world's greatest oxymoron.

"I'll try my best. I promise."

The disappointed look on her daughter's face made Reynolds turn and flee the room. She stopped at the small room on the first floor that served as her study. From the top of a cabinet she removed a squat, heavy metal box, which she unlocked. Removing her SIG 9mm, she loaded in a fresh mag, pulled the slide back to chamber a round, clicked the safety on, slid the weapon in her clip holster and was out the door before she could think any more about another interrupted meal in a long string of disappointments for her children. Superwoman: career, kids, she had it all. Now, if she could only clone herself. Twice.

TWENTY-NINE

Lee and Faith had made two stops on the way to North Carolina, once for a late lunch at a Cracker Barrel and another at a large strip mall in southern Virginia. Lee had seen a billboard off the highway advertising a week-long gun show. The parking lot was packed with pickup trucks, RVs and cars with fat tires and engines erupting through their hoods. Some of the men were dressed in Polo and Chaps, and others in Grateful Dead T-shirts and ragged jeans. Americans of all backgrounds apparently loved their guns.

"Why here?" Faith asked as Lee got off the bike.

"Virginia law requires that licensed gun dealers conduct on-the-spot background checks on people trying to buy weapons," he explained. "You have to fill out a form, have your gun permit and two forms of identification. But the law doesn't apply to gun shows. All they want is your money. Which, by the way, I need."

"Do you *really* have to have a gun?"

He stared at her as though she had just hatched from an egg. "Everybody coming after *us* has them."

Unable to dispute this devastating logic, she said nothing more, gave him the cash and huddled on the bike as he went inside. Leave it to the man to say something that would paralyze her very soul.

Inside, Lee purchased a Smith & Wesson double-action autopistol with a fifteen-round mag, chambering 9mm Parabellums. The autopistol tag was misleading. You had to pull the trigger each time to fire. The "auto" term referred to the fact that the pistol automatically loaded a new round with each pull of the trigger. He also bought a box of ammo and a cleaning kit and then returned to the parking lot.

Faith watched closely as he packed the gun and ammo away in the motorcycle's storage compartment.

"Feel safer now?" she asked dryly.

"Right now I wouldn't feel safe sitting in the Hoover Building with a hundred FBI agents staring at me. Gee, I wonder why."

They made Duck, North Carolina, by nightfall, and Faith gave Lee directions to the house in the Pine Island community.

When they pulled up in front, Lee stared at the immense structure, tugged off his helmet and turned to her. "I thought you said it was small."

"Actually, I think you referred to it as small. I said it was comfortable."

She climbed off the Honda and stretched out her body. Every bit of her, especially her butt, was one solid knot.

"It must be at least six thousand square feet." Lee continued to stare at the three-story, wooden-shingle-siding house that had dual stone chimneys and a cedar shake roof. Two broad veranda-style porches ran across the second and third floors, which gave it a plantation feel. There were gabled turrets and walls of lattice and glass; and immense displays of fountain grass erupted from the ground. Lee watched as the automatic sprinklers came on, along with the exterior landscape lighting. Behind the house he could hear the pounding surf. The house was situated at the end of a quiet cul-de-sac, although there were similar monster homes painted yellow, blue, green and gray lined up on the beach side in both directions as far as the eye could see. Although the air was warm and slightly humid, they were approaching November, and virtually all the other homes were dark.

Faith said, "I've never really bothered to add up the square footage. I rent it out April through September. It covers the mortgage and nets me about thirty thousand a year – just in case you're interested." Taking off her helmet and running her hands through her sweaty hair, she said, "I need a shower and some food. The kitchen should be stocked. You can put the bike in the carport."

Faith unlocked the front door and went inside while Lee parked the Honda in one of two bays of the carport and then carried in the bags. The inside of the house was even more beautiful than the outside. Lee was also grateful to see that the place had a security system. As he looked around, he took in the soaring ceilings, pickled wood beams and paneling, an enormous kitchen, Italian tile floors in some places, high-dollar Berber carpeting elsewhere. He counted six bedrooms, seven bathrooms and discovered an outdoor Jacuzzi on the back porch big enough for at least six drunken adults to flop around in. There were also three fireplaces, including a gas one in the master suite. The furniture was overstuffed rattan and wicker, all seemingly designed to beckon one to catnap.

Lee opened a set of French doors off the kitchen, stepped on to the deck and looked down into the enclosed courtyard. A kidney-shaped pool was situated down there. The chlorinated water sparkled under the glow of the pool lights. A Creepy Crawly made its way through the water, sucking up bugs and debris.

Faith joined him on the deck. "I had the people

come out this morning and get everything going. They maintain the pool all year 'round anyway. I've skinny-dipped down here in December. It's gloriously peaceful."

"There doesn't seem to be anybody else in the other houses."

"Certain parts of the Outer Banks are pretty full about nine or even ten months out of the year now, what with the nice weather. But you always have the chance of hurricanes this time of year, and this area is pretty expensive. The houses rent out for a small fortune, even in the off season. Unless you can get a big group together to rent them, your average family isn't going to be staying here. Mostly, you see the owners come down this time of year. But with kids in school, it's tough to do that during the week. So empty we have."

"Empty I like."

"The pool's heated, if you want to take a dip."

"I didn't bring my trunks."

"Not into skinny-dipping, huh?" She smiled and was very relieved that it was too dark for her to really see his eyes. If his baby blues had hit her just right, she might have pushed him in the pool, dived after him and everything else be damned.

"There are plenty of places in town to get some swimming stuff. I keep clothes down here, so I'm okay. We'll buy you some things tomorrow."

"I think I'm fine with what I brought."

"You don't want to stick out here, do you?"

"I'm not sure we'll be here long enough for that."

Faith looked out toward the wooden walkways leading past the sand dunes to where the Atlantic Ocean pitched and bellowed. "You never know. I don't think there's a better place to sleep than at the beach. There's nothing like the sound of waves crashing in your ears to drive you into unconsciousness. Back in D.C. I never sleep well. Too many things to worry about."

"Funny, I sleep just fine there."

She glared at him. "To each his own."

"What's for dinner?"

"First, a shower. You can have the master suite."

"It's your place. I'm fine on a couch."

"With six bedrooms, I don't think that would make much sense. Take the one at the end of the hall upstairs. It opens out on to the back porch. The Jacuzzi's out there. Feel free. Even without trunks. Don't worry, I won't peek."

They went inside. Lee grabbed his bag and followed her upstairs. He showered and put on a clean pair of khakis, a sweatshirt and sneakers without socks, since he had forgotten to bring the latter. He didn't bother to dry his new buzz cut. He caught himself looking in the mirror. The haircut didn't look so bad on him. In fact, it had taken a few years off. He slapped his hard gut, even did an exaggerated flex in the mirror.

"Yeah, right," he said to his reflection. "Even if she were your type, which she sure as hell ain't." He left his room and was about to head downstairs when he stopped in the hallway.

Faith's bedroom was at the other end of the corridor. He could still hear her shower running. She was probably taking her time under the hot water after the long ride. She had held up well, he had to admit, hadn't complained too much. He was edging down the hallway the whole time he was thinking this, because it just occurred to him that Faith might at this very minute be escaping out the back door while using the running shower as a ruse. For all he knew, she had arranged for a rental car that was parked down the street, and she was about to drive off, leaving him with not much of a life. Was she just like her old man? Running away into the night when things got tough?

He knocked on her door. "Faith?" There was no answer, so he knocked louder. "Faith? Faith!" The water was still running. "Faith!" he yelled. He tried the door. It was locked. He pounded on the door again and yelled her name.

Lee was about to hustle down the stairs when he heard footsteps and the door was flung open. Faith stood there, her hair soaked and hanging in her face, water dripping down her legs, a towel covering, barely, the front of her.

"What?" she demanded. "What's wrong?"

Lee found himself staring at the elegant bone development of her shoulders, the now fully revealed Audrey Hepburn neck, the tightness of her arms. Then his gaze slid down to her upper thighs and he quickly concluded that her arms had nothing on her legs.

"What the hell is it, Lee?" she said loudly.

He snapped back. "Oh. I was just wondering, um, how about I make dinner?" He smiled weakly.

She stared incredulously at him as a puddle of water collected on the carpet at her feet. As she wrapped the mostly wet towel around her, Faith's small, firm breasts were now fully outlined against the thin wet fabric. That's when Lee began thinking seriously about taking another shower, only this time with water cold enough to turn certain parts of his anatomy the same color as his eyes.

"Fine." She slammed the door in his face.

"Very fine," Lee said quietly to the door.

He went downstairs and examined the contents of the refrigerator. He decided on a menu and started pulling food and pans. He had been living alone for so long that he had finally decided, after years of

Golden Arches food, that he had better learn how to cook properly. He actually found it therapeutic, and he fully expected to live an extra twenty years now that he had cleaned his arteries of all the grease. At least until he met Faith Lockhart. Now all bets on a long life were off.

Lee laid out talapia on a baking sheet, brushed the fish with butter he had melted in a pan and let it soak in. Then he added garlic, lemon juice and some other secret spices handed down to him through generations of Adamses and put the fish in the wall oven to broil. He sliced up tomatoes and a slab of mozzarella, arranged them nicely on a serving plate and doused them with olive oil and seasoning. Next he prepared a salad and then slit a length of French bread, buttered it, added garlic and placed it in the lower oven. He got out two plates, silverware and cloth napkins he found in a drawer and set the table. There were candles on the table, but lighting them seemed like a cheesy idea. This wasn't a honeymoon, and they still had that nationwide manhunt thing to consider.

He opened a small, built-in wine cooler next to the fridge and selected a chilled bottle of white. As he was pouring out two glasses of wine, Faith came down the stairs. She wore an unbuttoned blue denim shirt with a white T-shirt underneath, a pair of loose-fitting white slacks and red sandals. He noted she still wore no makeup, at least that he could detect. A silver bangle bracelet dangled at her wrist. She also wore turquoise earrings done in a loopy southwestern design.

She looked surprised at the kitchen activity. "A man who can shoot a gun, lose the Feds and cook too. You just never cease to amaze me."

He handed her a wine glass. "A good meal, a quiet evening and then we get down to serious business."

She glanced coolly at him as he clinked his glass against hers. "You clean up well," she said.

"Another one of my talents." He went to check the fish while Faith went over to the wall of windows and stared out.

They ate quietly, both of them apparently feeling a little awkward now that they had arrived at their destination. Getting here, ironically enough, seemed to be the easy part.

Faith insisted on cleaning up the kitchen while Lee turned on the TV.

"Did we make the news?" Faith asked.

"Not that I can see. But there must have been reports of the FBI agent being found. A murdered Fed is still pretty damn rare even in this day and age, thank God. I'll get a newspaper tomorrow."

Faith finished cleaning up, poured herself another glass of wine and joined him.

"Okay, our bellies are full, the booze has us about as mellow as we're ever going to get, so now's the time to talk," Lee said. "I need to hear the whole story, Faith. As sweet and simple as that."

"So you feed a girl a nice meal, fill her with wine and you think she's yours for the asking?" She smiled coyly.

He frowned. "I'm serious, Faith."

Her smile disappeared, along with her coyness. "Let's go for a walk on the beach."

Lee started to protest but then stopped. "Okay. It's your turf, home rules apply." He headed up the stairs.

"Where are you going?"

"Be right back."

When Lee came back down, he had on a windbreaker.

"You didn't need a jacket, it's still pretty warm."

He spread open the front of the jacket, revealing

the clip holster and the Smith & Wesson in it. "Didn't want to spook any sand crabs we come across."

"Guns frighten me to death."

"Guns also prevent death, when *properly* used. Usually sudden, violent death."

"No one could have followed us. No one knows we're here."

His reply chilled her to the bone.

"I hope to God you're right."

THIRTY

Reynolds didn't use her bubble light but would have if a patrol car had tried to pull her over, as she was exceeding the speed limit by more than twenty miles per hour on the few open stretches of the Beltway before having to slow down in a sea of red brake lights. She checked her watch: seven-thirty. When wasn't there a rush hour in this damn area? People got up earlier and earlier to go to work, or stayed later and later before going home to avoid the traffic. Pretty soon the two groups would smack right into each other and the twenty-four-hour-a-day highway parking lot would officially begin. Luckily Anne Newman's house was only a few exits down from hers.

As she drove, Reynolds thought about her visit to Adams's apartment building. Reynolds had thought she had seen and heard everything by now, but Angie Carter's statement about the FBI had stunned her, and the shock of it had moved her and Connie into hyperspeed. They'd notified their superiors at the Bureau and quickly determined that no FBI operations had been conducted at Adams's address. Then the shit had really hit the fan. The impersonation of FBI agents got the attention of the director himself, and he had personally issued orders on the case. Even though the back door to Adams's apartment had been knocked off its hinges and they could have walked right in, a search warrant was fast-tracked and executed, again with the director's personal blessing. Reynolds was actually relieved about that because she didn't want to have any slip-ups on this one. Any mistakes would come home to roost right on her head.

The apartment was thoroughly searched by one of the Bureau's crack forensics teams, pulled off another high-profile case. In the end they didn't find much. There was no tape in the answering machine. That had really ticked Reynolds off. If the phony FBI people had taken the tape, there must have been something important on it. Her search team had continued to strike out. There were no travel documents, maps consulted, nothing that would hint as to where Adams and Lockhart were going. They had found fingerprints matching Faith Lockhart's, so that was something. They were checking into Adams's background. He had family in the area; maybe they knew something.

They had discovered the roof hatch in the empty apartment next door to Adams's. Clever. Reynolds had also noted the extra locks, video surveillance, steel door and frame and the copper shield over the alarm panel. Lee Adams knew what he was doing.

They had retrieved the bag of hair and hair coloring from one of the trash cans behind the apartment. That, together with the snips they had seen of the airport surveillance tapes, showed that Adams was now a blond, Lockhart a brunette. Not that this helped much. They were checking into whether either of them had other residences listed in their names elsewhere in the country. That was a needle in a haystack, she knew, even if they had used their real names. She doubted they would be that stupid. And even if they had used their aliases, the names Suzanne Blake and Charles Wright were too common to aid Reynolds very much.

The police officers who responded to the call at

Adams's apartment were pulled in and questioned. The men posing as FBI agents had fed them a story that Lee Adams was wanted in connection with a kidnapping ring across state lines. The FBI posers' credentials looked real, both police officers were quick to point out. And they carried the firepower and the professional swagger one normally associated with federal law enforcement. They were searching the place expertly and had made no move to run when the cruiser had shown up. The imposters talked the talk and walked the walk in all respects, said the two police officers, who were both veterans on the street. They had been given the name of the supposed special agent in charge. It was run through the FBI personnel database and came up negative. No surprise there. The police officers had given descriptions of the men they had seen, and a Bureau technician was creating computer images of them. Still, all in all, it was a dead end, with frightening implications. Implications that struck very close to home for Reynolds.

She had received another visit from Paul Fisher. He came with orders right from Massey, as he was quick to point out. Reynolds was to proceed with all due speed, but with the utmost caution, to find Faith Lockhart, and she could be assured of all the support she needed.

"Just don't make any more mistakes," he had said.

"I wasn't aware I had made any mistakes, Paul."

"An agent killed. Faith Lockhart falls into your lap and you let her get away. What would you call those?"

"Leaked information caused Ken to die," she had fired back. "I fail to see how that was my fault."

"Brooke," Fisher had said, "if you really believe that, then you might want to request reassignment right now. The buck stops with you. As far as the

Bureau is concerned, if there is a leak, every member of your squad, including you, is at the top of the list. And that's how the Bureau's following that up."

As soon as he left her office, Reynolds had thrown her shoe against the closed door. Then she had thrown the other one, just to be sure he was aware of her extreme displeasure. Paul Fisher was officially off her sexual fantasy list.

Reynolds raced down the exit ramp, hung a left on Braddock Road and fought through some late traffic backup until she turned off and entered the quiet residential neighborhood of the slain FBI agent. She slowed when she reached the Newmans' street. The house was dark, a single car in the driveway. Reynolds parked her government-issue sedan at the curb, got out and hustled up to the door.

Anne Newman must have been watching for her, because the door opened before Reynolds could ring the bell.

Anne Newman didn't attempt to make small talk or ask Reynolds if she wanted anything to drink. She led the FBI agent directly to a small back room that had been set up as an office with a desk, metal file cabinet, computer and fax machine. On the wall were framed baseball cards and other sports memorabilia. On the desk were stacks of silver dollars encased in hard plastic and neatly labeled.

"I was looking through Ken's office. I don't know why. It just seemed . . ."

"You don't have to explain, Anne. There are no set rules for what you're going through."

Anne Newman wiped away a tear as Reynolds studied her. Clearly the woman was near the breaking point, on all fronts. She was dressed in an old robe, her hair unwashed, eyes red and puffy. Yesterday afternoon, the most pressing decision she probably had to make was what to have for dinner,

Reynolds assumed. God, it could all turn on a dime. Ken Newman wasn't the only one being buried. Anne was right there beside him. The only catch was she still had to go on living.

"I found these photo albums. I didn't even know they were back here. They were in a box with some other things. I know this might look bad, but . . . but if it helps in finding out what happened to Ken . . ." She faded out for a moment as more tears plunked down on to the photo album with its tattered, seventies-style psychedelic cover.

"Calling you was the right thing to do," Anne finally said with a bluntness that was both painful and gratifying for Reynolds to hear.

"I know this is terribly difficult for you." Reynolds eyed the album, not wanting to prolong this any more than absolutely necessary. "Can I see what you found?"

Anne Newman sat down on a small sofa and opened the album and pulled up the clear plastic sheet that kept the photos securely inside. On the page she had opened to was an eight-by-ten photo of a group of men in hunting garb holding rifles. Ken Newman was one of the men. She pulled out the photo, revealing a piece of paper and a small key pressed into the album page. She handed Reynolds both and watched her closely as the FBI agent examined them.

The piece of paper was an account statement for a safe-deposit box at a local bank. The key, presumably, fit that box.

Reynolds looked at her. "You didn't know about this?"

Anne Newman shook her head. "We have a safe-deposit box. But not at that bank. And of course that's not all."

Reynolds looked back at the bank statement and

she jerked involuntarily. The name of the boxholder was not Ken Newman. Nor was the billing address for the house she was in. "Who's Frank Andrews?"

Anne Newman looked like she would burst into tears again. "God, I have no idea."

"Did Ken ever mention that name to you?" Newman shook her head.

Reynolds took a deep breath. If Newman had a safe-deposit box under a false name, he would have needed one thing to set up the account.

She sat on the sofa next to Anne and took her hand. "Have you found any identification around here that might match the name Frank Andrews?"

The tears welled in the stricken woman's eyes and Reynolds truly felt for her.

"You mean with Ken's picture on it? Showing that he was this Frank Andrews person?"

"Yes, that's what I mean," Reynolds said softly.

Anne Newman put her hand in her robe and pulled out a Virginia driver's license. The name on it was Frank Andrews. The license number, which in Virginia was the person's Social Security number, was on there. And in the small accompanying photo Ken Newman was staring back at her.

"I thought about going to open the safe-deposit box myself, but then I realized they wouldn't let me. I'm not on the account. And I wouldn't be able to explain that it was my husband, but just under a false name."

"I know, Anne. I know. You were right to bring me in. Now, where exactly did you find the fake ID?"

"In another one of the photo albums. They weren't family albums, of course. I keep those, been through them a zillion times. These albums were pictures of Ken and his hunting and fishing buddies. They took trips every year. Ken was good about taking pictures. I never knew he kept them in albums. I wasn't all that interested in looking at those pictures, you see." She stared wistfully at the far wall. "Sometimes it seemed Ken was happier with his buddies shooting at ducks or at his coin and card shows than he was at home." She caught a quick breath, put a hand over her mouth and looked down.

Reynolds could sense Anne had never meant to share that personal bit of information with her, a semi-stranger. She said nothing. Experience told her to allow Anne Newman to work her way through this. A minute later the woman started speaking again.

"I never would have found it, I suppose, unless . . . what happened to Ken . . . you know. I guess life is funny sometimes."

Or terribly cruel. "Anne, I need to check this out. I'm going to take these items, and I don't want you to mention it to anyone. Not friends, family . . ." She paused, choosing her words as carefully as she could. "Or anyone else at the Bureau. Not until I dig a little bit."

Anne Newman looked up at her with frightened eyes. "What do you think Ken was involved in, Brooke?"

"I don't know yet. Let's not jump to conclusions on this. The safe-deposit box might be empty. Ken might have leased it a long time ago and then forgotten about it."

"And the fake ID?"

Reynolds licked her dry lips. "Ken worked some undercover over the years. This might be a souvenir of those days." Reynolds knew this was a lie, and Anne Newman probably did too, she thought. The license had a recent issue date on it. And those working undercover in the FBI didn't usually take home the props with their secret identities on them once their tasks were completed. The fake license, she was fairly certain, was unrelated to his FBI duties. It was her job to discover what it *was* connected to.

"Anne, not a word to anyone. It's for your own safety as much as anything."

Anne Newman clutched her arm as Reynolds stood. "Brooke, I've got three kids. If Ken was mixed up in something . . ."

"I'll put the house under twenty-four-hour surveillance. Anything remotely suspicious catches your eye, you call me." She handed her a card with her direct-dial numbers on it. "Day or night."

"I didn't know where else to turn. Ken thought a lot of you, he really did."

"He was a damn good agent and he had a terrific career." If she discovered that Ken Newman had been a sell-out, however, the Bureau would crush his memory, his reputation, everything about his professional life. That would, of course, destroy his private side as well, including the woman Reynolds was looking at, and her children. But that was life. Reynolds didn't make the rules, didn't always agree with the rules, but she lived by them. However, she would check out the safe-deposit box by herself. If there was nothing suspicious in there, she would tell no one. She would continue to investigate why Newman was using an alias, but that would be done on her own time. She wasn't going to destroy his memory without a very compelling reason. She owed the man that.

She left Anne Newman sitting on the sofa, the photo album open in her lap. The ironic thing was, if Newman was the leak on the Lockhart case, he had probably helped himself to an early death. Now that Reynolds thought about it, whoever might have hired him had probably hoped to eliminate the mole and the main target in one efficient thrust. Only a slug deflecting off a pistol barrel had saved Faith Lockhart from joining Ken Newman on a slab. And perhaps the assistance of Lee Adams as well?

Whoever had orchestrated it clearly knew what he was doing. Which was bad for Reynolds. Contrary to popular fiction and film, most criminals weren't that accomplished and couldn't so easily outmaneuver the police at every turn. The majority of murderers, rapists, burglars, robbers, drug dealers and other felons were usually uneducated or scared; or drugged-out punks or drunks terrified of their own shadows when off the needle or bottle, yet demons when high. They left many clues behind and were usually caught, or turned themselves in, or were ratted on by their "friends." They were prosecuted and did jail time or, in rare cases, were executed. They were in no sense of the word professionals.

Reynolds knew that this was not the case here. Amateurs didn't find ways to pay off veteran FBI agents. They didn't hire hit men who lurked in the woods waiting for their prey. They didn't impersonate FBI agents with credentials so authentic they had scared off the cops. Sinister theories of conspiracy swirled in her head, sending a shiver of fear down her back. No matter how long you did this, the fear was always there. To be alive was to be afraid. To not be afraid was to be dead.

As she walked out, Reynolds passed under a blinking fire detector that was in the hallway. There were three other such devices in the house, including one in Ken Newman's office. While they were plugged into the home's electrical wiring and did function as designed, they all also housed sophisticated surveillance cameras with pinhole lenses. Two of the wall outlets on each level were similarly "modified." The modifications had taken place two weeks ago when the Newmans had taken a rare three-day vacation. This type of surveillance mode was based upon PLCs, power line carrier technology favored by the FBI. And the Central Intelligence Agency.

Robert Thornhill was on the prowl. And his attention would now turn to Brooke Reynolds.

As she climbed in her car, Reynolds understood very clearly that she was perhaps at the crossroads of her career. She would probably need every bit of ingenuity and inner strength she could muster to survive this. And yet the only thing she really wanted to do right now was drive home and tell her two beautiful children the story of the three pigs, just as slowly, accurately and colorfully as she possibly could.

THIRTY-ONE

The wind, it turned out, was blowing hard along the beach, and the temperature had dropped drastically. Faith buttoned her overshirt; then, despite the cold, she took off her sandals and held them in one hand.

"I like to feel the sand," she explained to Lee. The tide was low, so they had a broad beach on which to meander. The sky held scattered clouds, the moon almost full, the stars winks of light staring down upon them. Far out on the water they saw the blink of what was probably a ship's light or stationary buoy. Except for the wind, it was completely quiet. No cars, no blaring TVs, no planes, no other people.

"It's really nice out here," Lee finally said as he watched a sand crab do its funny sideways scuttle into its tiny home. Stuck in the sand was a piece of PVC pipe. Lee knew that fishermen would stick their poles in the hollow tube when they were fishing from the beach.

"I've thought of moving here permanently," said Faith. She broke ranks with him and ventured into the water up to her ankles. Lee slipped off his shoes, rolled up his pants legs and joined her.

"Colder than I thought it would be," he said. "No swimming out here."

"You wouldn't believe how invigorating a swim in cold water can be."

"You're right, I wouldn't."

"I'm sure you've been asked this a million times,

but how did you become a private investigator?"

He shrugged and looked out toward the ocean. "Sort of fell into it. My dad was an engineer and I was a gadget guy, like him. But I never had the book smarts he did. I was sort of a rebel too, like you. But I didn't go to college. I joined the Navy."

"Please tell me you were a Navy SEAL. I'd sleep better."

Lee smiled. "I can barely shoot straight. I can't build a nuclear device out of toothpicks and gum wrappers, and the last time I checked, I couldn't disable a man simply by pressing my thumb against his head."

"I guess I'll keep you anyway. Sorry to interrupt."

"Not much more to it. I studied telephony, communications, that sort of thing in the Navy. Got married, had a kid. Worked at the phone company as a repairman. Then I lost my daughter in a messy divorce. I quit my job, answered an ad at a private security firm for someone experienced in electronic surveillance. I figured with my technical background I could learn what I needed to know. The job really got into my blood. I started my own private investigation firm, got some decent clients, made mistakes along the way but then got a firm footing. Now you see me today as the head of a mighty empire."

"How long have you been divorced?"

"A long time." He looked at her. "Why?"

"Just curious. Ever gotten close to the altar since then?"

"No. I guess I'm terrified of making the same mistakes." He stuffed his hands into his pockets. "Quite honestly, the problems came from both ends. I'm not easy to live with." He smiled. "I think God makes two kinds of people: those who should marry and procreate and those who should remain alone and have sex only for fun. I think I'm in the latter group."

Faith looked down. "Save some room for me."

"Not to worry. There's plenty of space left."

He touched her elbow. "Let's talk. We're running out of time."

Faith led him back up on to the beach and plopped down cross-legged on a patch of dry sand. He sat next to her.

"Where would you like to begin?" she asked.

"How about the beginnings?"

"No, I mean do you want me to tell you all first, or do you want to spill *your* secrets first?"

He looked startled. "*My* secrets? Sorry, I'm fresh out."

She picked up a stick, drew the letters *d* and *b* in the sand and then glanced at him. "Danny Buchanan. What do you really know about him?"

"Just what I told you. He's your partner."

"He's also the man who hired you."

Lee couldn't find his voice for a few seconds. "I told you I didn't know who had hired me."

"That's right. That's what you *told* me."

"How do you know he hired me?"

"While I was in your office, I listened to a message from Danny, and he sounded quite anxious to know where I was and what you had found out. He left his phone number for you to call him back. He was more distressed than I've ever heard him. I guess I would be too if someone I had arranged to have killed was still alive and kicking."

"You're sure it was him on the phone?"

"After fifteen years of working with him I think I know his voice. So you didn't know?"

"No, I didn't."

"You know that's really hard to believe."

"I guess it is," he agreed. "But it happens to be the

truth." He scooped up some sand and let it run through his fingers. "So I take it that phone call is why you tried to give me the slip at the airport? You don't trust me."

She licked her dry lips and glanced at the holstered gun, which was visible as the wind whipped Lee's jacket around. "I *do* trust you, Lee. Otherwise I wouldn't be sitting on a lonely beach in the dark with an armed man who's still pretty much a stranger to me."

Lee let his shoulders slump. "I was hired to follow you, Faith. That's all."

"Don't you first find out if the client or his intentions are legitimate?"

Lee started to say something and then stopped. That was a reasonable question. The fact was business had been slow recently and the assignment and cash had been timely. And the file he had been given had a photo of Faith. And then he had seen her in person. Well, what the hell could he say? Most of his targets weren't as attractive as Faith Lockhart. In the photo her face had suggested vulnerability. After meeting her, he knew that impression wasn't necessarily true. But it was a very potent combination for him. For any man.

"Normally, I like to meet with a client, get to know him and his agenda before I agree to accept a job."

"But not here?"

"It was a little difficult, since I didn't know who had hired me."

"So instead of returning the cash, you accepted the offer and started following me – blindly, as it were."

"I didn't see any harm in just following you."

"But they could have been using you to get to me."

"It's not exactly like you were in hiding. Like I said, I thought you might be having some sort of affair. When I went inside the cottage, I knew that wasn't the case. The rest of the night's events damn sure reinforced that conclusion. That's all I really know."

Faith stared out toward the ocean, to the horizon, where water met sky. It was a visual collision of sorts that happened every day and was comforting for some reason. It gave her hope when she probably had no other reason to feel it. Other than the man sitting beside her, perhaps.

"Let's go back to the house," she said.

THIRTY-TWO

They sat in the spacious family room. Faith picked up a remote control, hit a button and the flames in the gas fireplace crept to life. She poured another glass of wine, offered one to Lee, but he declined. They sat on the overstuffed couch.

Faith took a sip of wine and stared out the window, her eyes focusing on nothing. "Washington represents the richest, most enormous pie in the history of mankind. And everyone in the whole world wants a slice of it. There are certain people who hold the knife that portions out that pie. If you want a slice, you have to go through them."

"That's where you and Buchanan come in?"

"I lived, breathed and ate my career. Sometimes I worked more than twenty-four hours in a day because I'd cross the International Date Line. I can't tell you the hundreds of details, nuances, mind-reading, gut checks and sheer nerve and perseverance that lobbying on the scale we did requires." She put down her wine glass and focused on him. "I had a great teacher in Danny Buchanan. He almost never lost. That's remarkable, don't you think?"

"I guess never losing at anything is pretty remarkable. We can't all be Michael Jordan."

"In your line of work can you guarantee to your client that a certain result will occur?"

Lee smiled. "If I could foresee the future, I'd start playing the lottery."

"Danny Buchanan could guarantee the future."

Lee stopped smiling. "How?"

"He who controls the gatekeepers controls the future."

Lee slowly nodded in understanding. "So he was paying off people in government?"

"On a more sophisticated scale than anyone's done before."

"Congressmen on the payroll? That sort of thing?"

"Actually, they did it for free."

"What—"

"Until they left office. Then Danny had a whole world of goodies lined up for them. Lucrative do-nothing jobs in companies he had set up. Income from private portfolios of stocks and bonds, and cash funneled through legitimate businesses under the cover of services rendered. They could play golf all day, make a couple of sham phone calls to the Hill, take a few meetings and live like Kings. Hell, it's like a super 401(k). You know how Americans are so into their stocks. Danny worked them hard while they were on the Hill, but he would give them the best golden years money could buy."

"How many of them have 'retired'?"

"None, as yet. But everything is set up for when they do. Danny's been doing this only about ten years."

"He's been in D.C. a lot longer than ten years."

"I mean he's been bribing people for only ten years. Before then, he was a much more successful lobbyist. Since the start of his private company, he's made a lot less money."

"I thought guaranteeing results would bring him a lot *more* money."

"The last ten years have been pretty much a charitable decade for him."

"The man must have deep pockets."

"Danny has pretty much gone through his money. We started representing paying clients again so we could continue what we were doing. And the longer his people do what they are told, the more they will receive later. And by waiting until they're out of office to be paid, the chances any of them will be caught go down considerably."

"They must really trust Buchanan's word."

"I'm sure he's had to show them proof of what's waiting for them. But he's also an honorable man."

"All crooks are, aren't they? Who are some of the people on his retirement plan?"

She looked at him suspiciously. "Why?"

"Just humor me."

Faith named two of the men.

"Correct me if I'm mistaken, but aren't they the current vice president of the United States and the Speaker of the House?"

"Danny doesn't work with middle management. He actually started working with the vice president before he rose to that office, back when he was a House whip. But when Danny needs the man to pick up the phone and put the screws to someone, the man does."

"Holy shit, Faith. What the hell did you need that kind of firepower for? Are we talking military secrets?"

"Actually, something much more valuable." She picked up her wine glass. "We represent the poorest of the world's poor. African nations, in issues of humanitarian aid, food, medicine, clothing, farm equipment, crop seed, desalinization systems. In Latin America, money for vaccines and other medical supplies. The export of legal birth control devices, sterile needles and health information in the poorest countries."

Lee looked skeptical. "You're saying you were

bribing government officials to help third world countries?"

She set down her wine glass and looked directly at him. "Actually, the official lexicon has changed. The rich nations have developed very politically correct terminology for their destitute neighbors. The CIA publishes a manual on them, in fact. So instead of 'third world,' you have new categories: LDCs are 'less-developed countries,' meaning they're in the bottom group of the hierarchy of developed countries. There are officially one hundred and seventy-two LDCs, or the vast majority of countries in the world. Then there are the LLDCs. They're the 'least developed countries.' They're the bottom of the barrel, dead in the water. There are *only* forty-two of them. This may surprise you, but about half of the people on this planet live in abject poverty."

"And that makes it right?" Lee said. "That makes bribery and cheating right?"

"I'm not asking you to condone any of it. I don't really care if you agree with it or not. You wanted the facts, I'm giving them to you."

"America gives lots of foreign aid. And we don't *have* to give a dime."

She gave him a fierce look, one he had never seen from her before. "If you talk facts with me, you lose," she said sharply.

"Come again?"

"I've been researching this – hell, living this – for more than ten years! We pay farmers in this country more *not* to grow crops than we do on humanitarian relief overseas. Of the total federal budget, foreign aid represents about one percent, with the majority of that going to two countries, Egypt and Israel. Americans spend a hundred times as much money on makeup or fast food or video rentals in a year's time than we do on feeding starving children in third world countries in a decade. We could wipe out a dozen serious childhood diseases in undeveloped countries around the world with less money than we spend on Beanie Babies."

"You're naïve, Faith. You and Buchanan are probably just filling the lining of some dictator's pockets."

"No! That's an easy excuse, and one that I'm sick of. The money we do manage to get goes directly to legitimate humanitarian relief organizations, and never to the government directly. I've personally seen enough health ministers in African countries wearing Armani and driving a Mercedes while babies starve at their feet."

"And there aren't starving children in this country?"

"They get a lot of aid, and rightfully so. All I'm saying is that Danny and I had our agenda, and ours involved the *foreign* poor. Human beings are dying, Lee, by the millions. Children all over the world are perishing for no reason other than neglect. Every day, every hour, every minute."

"And do you really expect me to believe you two did this out of the goodness of your hearts?" He looked around the house. "This isn't exactly a soup kitchen, Faith."

"The first five years I worked with Danny I did my job, represented the big clients and I made a lot of money. A *lot* of money. I'll be the first to admit I'm one materialistic hardass. I like the money, and I loved what the money could buy."

"And then what happened? You found God?"

"No, he found me." Lee looked bewildered, and Faith quickly continued. "Danny had begun lobbying on behalf of the foreign poor. He was getting nowhere. No one cared, he kept telling me. The other partners at our firm were getting tired of

Danny's charitable endeavors. They wanted to represent IBM and Philip Morris, not Sudan's starving masses. Danny came to my office one day, said he was forming his own firm and wanted me to go with him. We weren't taking any clients, but Danny told me not to worry, that he'd take care of me."

Lee appeared mollified. "That much I can believe: You didn't know he was bribing people, or at least planning to."

"Of course I knew about it! He told me everything. He wanted me to go into this with eyes wide open. That's how he is. He's not some crook."

"Faith, do you know what you're saying? You *went along*, even though you knew you'd be breaking the law?"

She fixed a cold gaze upon him. "If I could fix it so that cigarette companies could keep selling cancer on a stick to anybody with a fresh set of lungs and gun manufacturers could roll out machine guns to anyone with a heartbeat, I guess I felt nothing was beneath me. And the goal here was something I could actually be proud of."

"Materialistic hardass goes soft?" Lee said with contempt.

"It's been known to happen," she shot back.

"How did you two work it?" Lee said in a baiting tone.

"I was Mister Outside, working all the people we didn't have in our back pockets. I was also good at getting celebrities to appear at some events, even travel to some of the countries. Photo ops, meet-and-greets with members." She sipped her wine. "Danny was Mister Inside. He worked all the people on the take while I pushed from the outside."

"And you kept this up for ten years?"

Faith nodded. "About a year ago Danny started

running out of money. A lot of our lobbying expenses he paid out of his own pocket. It wasn't like our clients could afford to pay us anything. And he had to invest a lot of his own money into these 'trust' funds, as he called them, for the members we were bribing. Danny took that part very seriously. He was their trustee. Every cent he promised would be there."

"Honor among thieves."

Faith ignored the barb. "That's when he told me to concentrate on paying clients while he carried the torch on the other matters. I offered to sell my house, and this house, to help raise money. He refused. He said I'd done enough." She shook her head. "Maybe I should still sell it – believe me, no one could ever do enough."

She fell silent for a bit and Lee chose not to break it. She stared across at him. "We really were accomplishing a lot of good."

"What do you want, Faith? You want me to break out in applause?"

Her eyes flashed at him. "Why don't you get on that stupid motorcycle and get the hell out of my life?"

"All right," Lee said calmly, "if you thought so highly of what you were doing, how did you turn out to be a witness for the FBI?"

Faith covered her face with her hands, as though she were about to start bawling. When Faith finally looked at him she seemed so distressed, Lee felt his anger slip away.

"For some time Danny had been acting strangely. I suspected that maybe someone was on to him. That scared the hell out of me. I didn't want to go to prison. I kept asking him what was wrong, but he wouldn't talk to me about it. He kept withdrawing, became more and more paranoid, finally even asking me to leave the firm. I felt so alone, for the first time in a long time. It was like I had lost my father again."

"So you went to the FBI, tried to cut a deal. You for Buchanan."

"No!" she exclaimed. "Never!"

"What, then?"

"About three months ago there was a lot of news coverage about the FBI breaking a major public corruption case, involving a defense contractor bribing several congressmen to help it win a large federal contract. A couple of employees at the defense contractor contacted the FBI and revealed what was going on. They were actually part of the conspiracy early on, but were granted immunity in exchange for their testimony and assistance. That sounded like a good deal to me. Maybe I could get a deal too. Since Danny wouldn't confide in me, I decided to go for it. The lead agent was named in the article: Brooke Reynolds. I called her.

"I didn't know what to expect from the FBI but I knew one thing: I wouldn't tell them much right away, no names or anything, not until I saw what the lay of the land was. And I had leverage. They needed a live witness with a head full of dates, times, names, meetings, records of votes and agendas to make this work."

"And Buchanan was ignorant of all this?"

"I guess not, considering he hired someone to kill me."

"We don't know that he did."

"Oh, come on, Lee, who else could it be?"

Lee thought back to the other men he had seen at the airport. The device in the man's hand was a high-tech blowgun of sorts. Lee had seen a demonstration of one at a seminar on counterterrorism. The gun and ammo were constructed solely from plastic to allow passage through metal detectors. You hit the palm trigger and the air compression fired a tiny needle either tipped or filled with a deadly toxin, like thallium or ricin, or the all-time favorite of assassins, curare, because it reacted so damn fast in the body that there was no known antidote. In a crowd, the act could be carried out and the assassin gone before the victim fell dead.

"Go on," he said.

"I offered to bring Danny into the fold."

"And how did they react to that?"

"They made it very clear that Danny was going down."

"I'm not following your logic. If you *and* Buchanan were going to turn witness, who were the Feds going to prosecute: the foreign countries?"

"No. Their representatives didn't know what we were doing. As I said, the money didn't go directly to the governments. And it's not like CARE or the Catholic Relief Services or UNICEF would ever condone bribery. Danny was their unofficial and unpaid lobbyist-in-residence but they had no idea what he was doing. He represented about fifteen such organizations. It was tough going. They all had their agendas, took a scattergun approach. They typically proposed hundreds of single-issue bills, instead of a few comprehensive ones. Danny got them organized, working together, sponsoring a small number of bills containing more comprehensive legislation. He taught them what they had to do to be more effective."

"So tell me exactly who were you going to testify against, then?"

"The politicians we paid off," she said simply. "They did it just for the money. It's not like they gave a damn about children with dead eyes living in Hepatitis Heaven. I saw it every day in their greedy faces. They just expected a rich reward – thought it was their due."

"Don't you think you're coming down a little heavy on these guys?"

"Why don't *you* stop being so naïve? How do you think people get elected in this country? They get elected by the groups who *organize* the voters, who shape citizens' decisions on who and what to vote for. And do you know who those groups are? They're big business and special interests, and the wealthy who fill the coffers of political candidates every year. Do you really think ordinary people attend five-thousand-dollar-a-plate dinners? And then do you really think these groups give all that money out of the goodness of *their* collective hearts? When the politicians get into office, you better believe they're expected to deliver."

"So you're saying all politicians in this country are corrupt. That still doesn't make what you did right."

"No? What congressman from the state of Michigan would vote to do anything to seriously hurt the automobile industry? How long do you think she'd be in office? Or high-tech in California? Or farmers in the Midwest? Or tobacco in the South? It's like a self-fulfilling prophecy in a way. Business and labor and other special interests have a lot at stake. They're focused, they have big dollars, they have PACs and lobbyists blasting their messages to Washington nonstop. Big and small business employ just about everybody. Those same people vote in elections. They vote their pocketbooks. Voilà, there's your big, dark conspiracy of American politics. I see Danny as the first visionary ever to outsmart greed and selfishness."

"But what about the foreign aid? If this story came out, wouldn't that kill the pipeline?"

"That's the thing! Can you imagine all the positive

attention it would get? The poorest countries on earth forced to bribe greedy American politicians to get the help they so desperately needed because it was unavailable any other way. You get stories like that in the media, then maybe some real, substantive changes would be made."

"That all sounds pretty far-fetched. I mean, come on."

"Maybe so, but my options weren't exactly flowing over. It's real damn easy to second-guess, Lee."

Lee sat back as he muddled this over. "Okay, okay. Do you *really* think Buchanan would try to kill you?"

"We were partners, friends. Actually, more than that. In many ways he was like a father to me. I . . . I just don't know. Maybe he found out I went to the FBI. He would think I betrayed him. That could have driven him over the edge."

"There's a major problem with the theory that Buchanan is behind all this."

She looked over at him curiously.

"I *hadn't reported back* to Buchanan, remember? So unless he has someone else working for him, he doesn't know you're dealing with the FBI. And it takes time to set up a professional-caliber hit. You can't just call your local shooter and ask him to pop somebody for you and charge it to your Visa."

"But he might have known a hired killer already, and then he planned to somehow set you up for the murder."

Lee was shaking his head before she finished. "He would have had no idea I would be there that night. And if you had been killed, he'd have the problem of me finding out about it and maybe going to the police with the result that everything gets traced back to him. Why bring all that misery on himself?

Think about it, Faith, if Buchanan was planning to kill you, he would not have hired me."

She slumped in a chair. "My God, what you're saying makes perfect sense." Terror seeped into Faith's eyes as she thought about what all this meant. "Then you're saying . . .?"

"I'm saying that somebody else wants you dead."

"Who? Who?" She almost shouted this at him.

"I don't know," he said.

Faith abruptly stood and stared into the fire. The shadows of the flames lapped against her face. When she spoke her voice was calm, almost resigned. "Do you see your daughter much?"

"Not much. Why?"

"I thought marriage and kids could wait. And then months turned to years and years to decades. And now this."

"You're not in your golden years yet."

She looked at him. "Can you tell me I'll be alive tomorrow, a week from tomorrow?"

"Nobody has that guarantee. We can always go to the FBI, and now maybe we should."

"I can't do that. Not after what you've just told me."

He stood and gripped her shoulder. "What are you talking about?"

She moved away from him. "The FBI won't let me bring Danny in. Either he goes to jail or I do. When I thought he was behind trying to have me killed, I probably would have gone back and testified. But I can't do that now. I can't be part of him going to prison."

"If there hadn't been an attempt on your life, what were you going to do?"

"I was going to give them an ultimatum. If they wanted my cooperation, then Danny would have to be given immunity."

"And if they turned you down, like they did?"

"Then Danny and I would have been long gone. Somehow." She stared directly at him. "I'm not going back. For a lot of reasons. Not wanting to die being right at the top."

"And exactly where the hell does that leave me?"

"This isn't such a bad place, is it?" Faith said weakly.

"Are you crazy? We can't stay here forever."

"Then we better think of another place to run to."

"And what about my home? My life? I *do* have a family. Do you expect me to just kiss it all goodbye?"

"Whoever wants me dead will assume you know everything I do. You won't be safe."

"That's *my* decision, not yours."

"I'm sorry, Lee. I never thought anyone else would be dragged into this. Especially not someone like you."

"There has to be another way."

She headed for the stairs. "I'm very, very tired. And what else is there to talk about?"

"Dammit, I can't just walk away and start over."

Faith was halfway up the stairs. She stopped, turned and looked down at him.

"Do you think things will look better in the morning?" she asked.

"No," said Lee frankly.

"Which is why there's nothing left for us to talk about. Good night."

"Why do I think you made your decision not to go back a long time ago? Like the minute you met me."

"Lee—"

"You sucker me into going with you, pull that stupid stunt at the airport and now I'm trapped too. Thanks a helluva lot, lady."

"I didn't plan it like this! You're wrong."

"And you really expect me to believe you?"

"What do you want me to say?"

Lee stared up at her. "Granted it's not much, but I like my life, Faith."

"I'm sorry." She fled upstairs.

THIRTY-THREE

Lee grabbed a six-pack of Red Dog from the refrigerator and slammed the side door on his way out. He stopped at the Honda, wondering whether he should just climb on the big machine and run until his gas, money or sanity were gone. Then another possibility occurred to him. He could go to the Feds alone. Turn Faith in and claim ignorance about all of this. And he *was* ignorant. He hadn't done anything wrong. And he owed the woman nothing. In fact, she had been a source of misery, terror and near-death experiences. Turning her in should be an easy decision. So why the hell wasn't it?

He went out the rear gate and on to the walkway leading past the dunes. Lee intended to go down to the sand, watch the ocean and drink beer until either his mind ceased to function or he came up with a brilliant plan that would save them both. Or at least him. For some reason, he turned to look back at the house for a moment. The light was on in Faith's bedroom. The mini-blinds were down but not closed.

As Faith came into view, Lee stiffened. She didn't close the blinds. She moved through the room, disappeared into the bathroom for a minute and then reappeared. As she started to undress, Lee looked around to see if anyone was watching him watching her. The police responding to a Peeping-Tom call would put the finishing touches on a spectacular day in the charmed life of Lee Adams. The other homes were dark, however; he could safely continue his voyeurism. Her shirt came off first, then her pants. She kept shedding clothes until all the window was filled with skin. And she didn't slip into any pajamas or even a T-shirt. Apparently this highly paid lobbyist-turned-Joan-of-Arc slept in the raw. Lee had a fairly clear view of things the towel had only hinted at. Maybe she knew he was out here and was putting on a peep show for him. What, as compensation for destroying his life? The bedroom light went out and Lee popped a beer, turned and headed for the beach. The show was over.

He had finished the first beer by the time he hit the sand. The tide was starting to roll in, and he didn't have to venture far to be in water past his ankles. He cracked another beer and went in farther, up to his knees. The water was freezing, but he went in farther still, almost to his crotch, and then stopped, for a practical reason: A wet pistol wasn't particularly useful.

He sloughed back to the sand, dropped the beer, slipped off his waterlogged sneakers and started to run. He was tired, but his legs moved seemingly of their own accord, his limbs scissoring, his breath coming in great chunks of foggy air. He did a quick mile, one of his fastest ever, it seemed to him. Then he dropped to the sand, sucking oxygen from the damp air. He felt hot and then chilled. He thought about his mother and father, his siblings. He envisioned his daughter Renee when she was young, falling off her great horse and calling for Daddy, her cries finally dying away to nothing when he did not come. It was as though his flow of blood had been reversed; it was all backing up, not knowing where to go. He felt the walls of his body giving way, unable to hold everything inside.

He stood on shaky legs, jogged unsteadily back to the beer and his shoes. He sat on the sand for a while, listened to the ocean scream at him and downed another two cans of Red Dog. He squinted into the darkness. It was funny. A few beers and he could see clearly the end of his life at the edge of the horizon. Always wondered when it was going to happen. Now he knew. Forty-one years, three months and fourteen days and the Man upstairs had pulled his ticket. He looked to the sky, waved. *Thanks a lot, God.*

He rose and moved on to the house but didn't go inside. Instead he went to the enclosed courtyard, put his pistol on the table, stripped off all his clothes and dived into the pool. The water temperature, he figured, hovered around eighty-five degrees. His chills quickly disappeared and he went under, touched bottom, did an awkward handstand, blowing freshly chlorinated water out his nostrils, and then floated on the surface, staring at a sky smeared with clouds. He swam some more, practiced his crawl and breast strokes and then drifted over to the side and downed another beer.

He crawled up on the pool deck and thought of his ruined life and of the woman who had done it to him. He dove back in, did another few laps and then climbed out of the pool for good. He looked down, surprised. That was a real kicker. He looked up at the dark window. Was she asleep? How could she be? How in hell could she be, after all this?

Lee decided he would find out for certain. No one could screw up his life and then fall into peaceful sleep. He looked down at himself again. Shit! He glanced at his soggy, sandy clothes and then up at the window. He finished another can of beer in quick gulps, his pulse seemingly spiking with each swallow. He wouldn't need the threads. He'd leave his pistol down here too. If things got out of hand, he didn't want lead to start flying. He pitched the last can of Red Dog over the fence, unopened. Let the birds pry it open and get a buzz. Why should he have all the fun?

He opened the side door quietly and took the stairs two at a time. He thought about kicking her bedroom door in but found it unlocked. He pushed the door open, peered in, letting his eyes adjust to the darkness here. He could make her out on the bed, one long hump. *One long hump.* To his alcohol-saturated mind, that phrase was immensely funny. He took three quick strides and was next to the bed.

Faith stared up at him. "Lee." It wasn't a question, how she said it. It was a simple statement that he didn't know the meaning of.

He knew she could see he was naked. Even in the darkness he trusted she could see he was fully aroused. With a sudden thrust of his arm he stripped the cover off her.

"Lee?" she said again, this time a question.

He looked down at the fine curves and softness of her naked body. His pulse rose, the blood rocketed through his veins, delivering a devilish potency to a man severely wronged. He roughly bulled between her legs, flopped down chest-to-chest. She made no move to resist, her body limp. He started to kiss her on the neck and then stopped. It was not that sort of thing. No tenderness. He clenched her wrists hard.

She just lay there, saying nothing, not telling him to stop. This angered him. He breathed heavily in her face. He wanted her to know it was the beer, not her. He wanted her to feel, to know this was not about her or how she looked or how he felt about her or anything else. He was a red-eyed drunken sonofabitch and she was easy meat. That was all. He loosened his grip. He wanted her to scream, to slug him as hard as she could. Then he would stop. But not before.

Her voice broke through the sounds of what he was doing. "I'd appreciate if you'd get your elbows off my chest."

He wouldn't stop, however, kept going. Hard elbow against soft tissue. The king and the peasant. *Give it to me, Faith. Clean my clock.*

"You don't have to do it like this."

"Whad'cha have in mind?" he slurred back. Navy shore leave in New York City was the last time he had even come close to being this drunk. Intense pain clacked against his temples. Five beers and a few glasses of wine and he was pretty damn well blitzed. God, he was getting old.

"Me on top. You're obviously too intoxicated to know what you're even doing." Her tone was blunt, reproachful.

"On top? Always the boss, even between the sheets? The hell with you." He squeezed her wrists so tightly his thumbs and index fingers touched together. To her credit she didn't even make a whimper, though he could sense the pain coursing through her in how her body tensed under him. He pawed her breasts and buttocks, roughly pummeled her legs and torso. He made no move, though, to enter her. And it wasn't because he was too drunk to accomplish the mechanics; it was because not even alcohol could make him do that to a woman. He kept his eyes closed, didn't want to look at her. But he dipped his face to hers. Lee wanted Faith to smell the stink of his sweat, to soak in the barley and hops base of his lust.

"I just thought you might enjoy it more, that's all," she said.

"Dammit!" he roared. "Are you just gonna let me do this?"

"Would you have me call the police?"

Her voice was like a twirling drill bit against his already throbbing skull. He hovered over her, arms locked, the cords of his triceps bulging.

He felt a tear escape his eye, touch his cheeks, like a single wandering snowflake – homeless, just like him. "Why aren't you kicking the shit out of me, Faith?"

"Because it's not your fault."

Lee started to feel sick to his stomach, his arms weakening. She moved her arm, and he let it go, releasing her without Faith having to say a word. She touched his face, very gently, like a feather dropped from the sky. With a simple motion she rubbed the single tear away. When she spoke, her voice was hoarse. "Because I took your life."

He nodded in understanding. "So if I run with you, do I get this every night? My little dog biscuit?"

"If that's what you want." She suddenly took her hand away, let it drop to the bedding.

He made no move to take it again.

He finally opened his eyes and stared down at the numbing sadness in her gaze, the lingering pain in the tightness of her neck and face; pain he had inflicted and she had taken, silently; the outline of her own hopeless tears against pale cheeks. They all were like searing heat that somehow flashed right past his skin, collided with his heart, vaporizing it.

He pulled himself off her, staggered into the bathroom. He barely made it to the toilet, where the beer and dinner came out much faster than it had gone in. Then Lee passed out on the very expensive Italian tile floor.

The tingle of the cold washcloth against his forehead brought him around. Faith was behind him, cradling him. She seemed to be wearing some kind of long-sleeved T-shirt. He could make out her long, muscular calves and her skinny, curved toes. Lee felt a thick towel across his middle. He was still nauseous, and cold, his teeth chattering. She helped him sit up and then stand, her arm around his waist. He was wearing a pair of Jockeys. She must have done it; he wouldn't have been capable. As it was, he felt like he'd been hog-tied to a whirlybird for about two days. Together they made it back to the bed and she helped him in, covering him with the sheet and comforter.

"I'll sleep in another room," she said softly.

He said nothing, refusing to open his eyes once more.

He could hear her move to the door. Right before she left, he said, "I'm sorry, Faith." He swallowed; his tongue felt big as a damn pineapple.

Before she closed the door, he heard her say so very quietly, "You won't believe this, Lee, but I'm more sorry than you."

THIRTY-FOUR

Brooke Reynolds looked calmly around the interior of the bank. It had just opened and there were no other customers in the branch. In another life she might have been casing the place for future robbery. The thought actually brought a rare smile to her face. She had several scenarios she could have played out, but the very young man sitting behind the desk, with the title of assistant branch manager on a name plate in front of him, had decided the matter.

He looked up as she approached. "Can I help you?"

His eyes grew appreciably larger when the FBI creds came out, and he sat up much straighter, as though attempting to show her that he indeed had a backbone beneath the boyish facade. "Is there a problem?"

"I need your assistance, Mr. Sobel," Reynolds said, eyeing the name on the brass plate. "It has to do with an ongoing Bureau investigation."

"Of course, certainly, whatever I can do," he said.

Reynolds sat down across from him and spoke in a quiet, direct manner. "I have a key here that fits a safe-deposit box at this branch. It was obtained during the investigation. We think whatever's in the box might lead to serious consequences. I need to get inside that box."

"I see. Well, um—"

"I have the account statement with me, if that'll help."

Bankers loved paper, she knew; and the more numbers and statistics, the better. She handed it across to him.

He looked down at the statement.

"Do you recognize the name Frank Andrews?" she asked.

"No," he said. "But I've only been at this branch for a week. Bank consolidation, it never ends."

"I'm sure; even the government is cutting way back."

"I hope not with you people. Lot of crime out there."

"I guess, being in bank management, you see a lot."

The young man looked smug and sipped his coffee. "Oh, the stories I could tell you."

"I bet. Is there any way to tell how often Mr. Andrews visited the box?"

"Absolutely. We transfer those logs to the computer now." He punched in the account number on his computer and waited while it crunched the data. "Would you like some coffee, Agent Reynolds?"

"Thanks, no. How large a box is it?"

He glanced at the statement. "From the monthly fee, it's our deluxe, double width."

"I guess it can hold a lot."

"They're very roomy." He leaned forward and spoke in a low voice. "I bet this has to do with drugs, doesn't it? Laundering, that sort of thing? I've taken a class on the subject."

"I'm sorry, Mr. Sobel, it's an ongoing investigation, and I really can't comment. You understand."

He quickly leaned back. "Absolutely. Sure. We all have rules – you wouldn't believe what we have to deal with at this place."

"I'm sure. Anything come up on the computer?"

"Oh, right." Sobel looked at the screen. "He's actually been in here quite a bit. I can print the log out for you, if you'd like."

"That would be a big help."

As they walked toward the vault a minute later, Sobel started looking nervous. "I'm just wondering if I should check upstairs first. I mean, I'm sure they'd have no problem and all, but still, they're incredibly strict with safe-deposit box access."

"I understand, but I thought the assistant branch manager would have the authority. I won't be taking anything out, just reviewing the contents. And depending on what I find, the box may have to be impounded. It's not the first time the Bureau's had to do this. I'll take full responsibility. Don't worry."

That seemed to relieve the young man and they proceeded into the vault. He took Reynolds's key and his own master and pulled out the large box.

"We have a private room where you can look at it."

He showed her into the small room and Reynolds closed the door. She took a deep breath and noticed that her palms were sweaty. In this box might be something that could shatter any number of lives and perhaps careers. She slowly raised the lid. What she saw made her swear under her breath.

The cash was neatly bundled with thick rubber bands, old, not new bills. She did a quick count. Tens of thousands. She put the lid back down.

Sobel was standing outside the booth when she opened the door. He returned the box to the vault.

"Can I see the sign-in register for this box?"

He showed her the signature log. It was Ken Newman's handwriting; she knew it well. A murdered FBI agent and a box full of cash under an alias. God help them.

"Did you find anything helpful?" Sobel asked.

"I need this box impounded. Anyone shows up wanting to get inside, you're to call me immediately at these numbers." She handed him her card.

"This is serious, isn't it?" Sobel suddenly looked very unhappy that he had been assigned to this branch.

"I appreciate your help, Mr. Sobel. I'll be in touch."

Reynolds returned to her car and drove as quickly as possible toward Anne Newman's house. She called from her car and confirmed the woman would be home. The funeral was scheduled to take place in three days. It would be a big affair, with top officials from the Bureau as well as law enforcement agencies from across the country attending. The funeral motorcade would be especially long and would pass between columns of somber, respectful federal agents and men and women in blue. The FBI buried its agents who died in the line of duty with the great honor and dignity they deserved.

"What did you find out, Brooke?" Anne Newman wore a black dress, her hair was nicely styled, and there was a touch of makeup on her face. Reynolds could hear talk coming from the kitchen. There were two cars parked out front when she had arrived. Probably family or friends offering condolences. She also noted platters of food on the dining room table. Cooking and condolences seemed, ironically, to go hand in hand; grief was better digested on a full stomach, apparently.

"I need to see records of your and Ken's bank accounts. Do you know where they are?"

"Well, Ken always handled the finances, but I'm sure they're in his office." She led Reynolds down the hallway and they went into Ken Newman's home office.

"Do you have more than one bank you deal with?"

"No. That much I do know. I always get the mail. It's just the one bank. And we only have a checking account, no savings. Ken said the interest they paid was a joke. He was really good about money. We own some good stocks, and the kids have their college accounts."

While Anne looked for the records, Reynolds idly glanced around the room. Stacked on one bookshelf were numerous hard plastic containers in various colors. While she had noted the coins encased in clear plastic on her previous visit, she hadn't really focused on these.

"What's in those containers?"

Anne looked at where she was pointing. "Oh, those are Ken's sports cards. Coins too. He was really good at it. He even took a course and became certified to grade both cards and coins. Just about every weekend he was at some show or another." She pointed up to the ceiling. "That's why there's a fire detector in here. Ken was really afraid of fire, in this room especially. All that paper and plastic. It could go up in a minute."

"I'm surprised he found the time for collecting."

"Well, he made the time. He really loved it."

"Did you or the kids ever go with him?"

"No. He never asked us to."

Her tone made Reynolds drop that line of inquiry. "I hate to ask this, but did Ken have life insurance?"

"Yes. A lot."

"At least you won't have to worry about that. I know it's little enough consolation, but so many people never think about those things. Ken obviously wanted you all to be taken care of if anything happened to him. Acts of love often speak louder than words." Reynolds was sincere, yet that last statement had sounded so incredibly lame that she decided to shut her mouth on the subject.

Anne pulled out a three-inch red notebook and handed it to Reynolds.

"I think this is what you're looking for. There are more in the drawer. This is the most current one."

Reynolds looked down at the binder. There was a laminated label affixed to the front flap of the notebook indicating that it contained checking account statements for the current year. She flipped it open. The statements were neatly labeled and organized chronologically by month, the most recent month on top.

"The canceled checks are in the other drawer. Ken kept them divided by year."

Damn! Reynolds kept her financial records stuffed in an assortment of drawers in her bedroom and even in the garage. Tax time at the Reynolds household was an accountant's worst nightmare.

"Anne, I know you have company. I can look through these by myself."

"You can take them with you if you want."

"If you don't mind, I'll look at them here."

"Okay. Would you like something to drink or eat? Lord knows we've got plenty of food. And I just put on a fresh pot of coffee."

"Actually, coffee would be great, thanks. Just a little cream and sugar."

Anne suddenly looked nervous. "You still haven't told me if you found out anything."

"I want to make absolutely sure before I say anything. I don't want to be wrong." As Reynolds looked into the poor woman's face, she felt tremendous guilt. Here she was letting the man's wife unknowingly assist her in possibly tarnishing her husband's memory.

"How are the kids holding up?" Reynolds asked, doing her best to shake this traitorous feeling.

"How any children would be, I suppose. They're sixteen and seventeen, so they understand things better than a five-year-old would. But it's still hard. For all of us. Only reason I'm not still bawling is that I ran out of tears this morning. I sent them to school. I decided it couldn't be any worse than sitting around here while a parade of people came through talking about their dad."

"You're probably right."

"You can only do the best you can. I knew there was always the possibility. God, Ken was an agent for twenty years. The only time he ever got hurt on duty was when his car got a flat and he wrenched his back changing the tire." Anne smiled briefly at this memory. "He was even talking about retirement. Maybe moving away when the kids were both at college. His mother lives in South Carolina. She's getting to the age where she needs some family close by."

Anne looked like she might start crying again. If she did, Reynolds wasn't sure she wouldn't join her, given her own mental state right now.

"You have children?"

"Boy and girl. Three and six."

Anne smiled. "Oh, still babies."

"I understand it gets tougher as they get older."

"Well, let's put it this way, it gets more complex. You go from spitting, biting, potty-training, to battles over clothes, boys, money. About age thirteen they suddenly can't stand being around Mom and Dad. That one was tough, but they finally came back. Then you worry yourself sick over alcohol and cars and sex and drugs."

Reynolds managed a weak smile. "Gee, I can't wait."

"How long have you been with the Bureau?"

"Thirteen years. Joined after one incredibly boring

year as a corporate lawyer."

"It can be a dangerous business."

Reynolds stared at her. "It certainly can be."

"You're married?"

"Technically, yes, but in a couple of months, no."

"Sorry to hear that."

"Believe me, it's best all around."

"You're keeping the children?"

"Absolutely."

"That's good. Children belong with their mothers, I don't care what the politically correct folk say."

"In my case, I wonder – I work long, unpredictable hours. All I know is that my children belong with me."

"You say you have a law degree?"

"From Georgetown."

"Lawyers make good money. And it's not nearly as dangerous as being an FBI agent."

"I suppose not." Reynolds finally realized where this was going.

"You might want to think about a career change. Too many nuts out there now. And too many guns. When Ken started at the Bureau, there weren't kids just out of diapers running around with machine guns shooting people down like they were in some damn cartoon."

Reynolds had no answer for that. She just stood there hugging the notebook to her chest, thinking of her kids.

"I'll bring your coffee."

Anne closed the door behind her and Reynolds sank into the nearest chair. She was having a sudden vision of her body being put inside a black pouch while the palm reader delivered the bad news to her bereaved children. *I told your mother so.* Shit! She shook off these thoughts and opened the notebook. Anne returned with her coffee, and then, left to herself, Reynolds made considerable progress. What she found out was very disturbing.

For at least the last three years, Ken Newman had made deposits, all in cash, to his checking account. The amounts were small – a hundred dollars here, fifty there – and they were made at random times. She pulled out the log Sobel had given her and ran her eye down the dates Newman had visited the safe-deposit box. Most of them corresponded with the dates he had also deposited cash into his checking account. Visit the box, put fresh cash in, take some old cash out and deposit it in the family bank account, she surmised.

It all added up to a significant amount of money, yet not a vast fortune. The thing was, the total balance of the checking account was never very large because there were always checks written on the account that depleted this balance. Newman's FBI payroll checks were on direct deposit, she noted. And there were numerous checks written to a stock brokerage firm. Reynolds found those records in another drawer and quickly determined that while Newman was far from wealthy, he'd had a nice stock portfolio going, and the records showed he religiously added to it. With the long bull market still steaming along, his investments had grown considerably.

Except for the cash deposits, what she was looking at wasn't really that unusual. He had saved money and invested it well. He wasn't wealthy, but he was comfortable. Dividends from the investment account were also deposited to the Newmans' checking account, further muddling the income picture. Simply put, it would be difficult to conclude that there was anything suspicious about the agent's finances unless one really took a very close look. And unless one knew about the safe-deposit box cash, the amount of money seemingly at issue just didn't warrant that level of scrutiny.

The confusing thing was the amount of cash she had seen in the safe-deposit box. Why keep that much in the box where it was earning no interest? What puzzled her almost as much as the cash was what she *wasn't* finding. When Anne came to check on her, she decided to ask her directly.

"I'm not finding any mortgage or credit card payments recorded here."

"We don't have a mortgage. That is, we did, a thirty-year one, but Ken made extra payments and finally paid it off early."

"Good for him. When was that?"

"About three or four years ago, I think."

"What about credit cards?"

"Ken didn't believe in them. What we bought, we bought with cash. Appliances, clothes, even cars. We never bought new, only used."

"Well, that's smart. Saves a ton in finance charges."

"Like I said, Ken was really good with the money."

"If I'd known how good, I would've had him help me."

"Do you need to look at anything else?"

"One more thing, I'm afraid. Your tax returns for the last couple of years, if you have them."

The large amount of cash in the box made sense now to Reynolds. If Newman paid cash for everything, then he would have no need to deposit it in his checking account. Of course, for things like the mortgage, the utilities and the phone bill, he needed to write a check, so he would have to deposit cash to cover those checks. And this also meant that for the money he didn't deposit into his checking account there was no record that he ever had the money in the box at all. Cash was cash, after all. And that meant that the IRS would have no way of knowing Newman ever had it either.

He wisely hadn't changed his lifestyle. Same house, no fancy cars, and he hadn't gone on insane shopping binges that had toppled so many thieves. And with no mortgage or credit card payments, he had a lot of free cash flow; on a cursory examination, this would seem to explain the ability to make the regular stock investments. Someone would have to really dig as Reynolds had to uncover the truth.

Anne found tax returns for the last six years in the metal filing cabinet standing against one wall. These were as well organized as the rest of the man's financial records. A quick look at the returns for the last three years confirmed Reynolds's suspicions. The only income listed was Newman's FBI salary and some miscellaneous investment interest and dividends and bank interest.

Reynolds put the files back and slipped on her coat. "Anne, I'm so sorry I had to come and do all this in the middle of everything you're having to deal with."

"I asked *you* for help, Brooke."

Reynolds felt another stab of guilt. "Well, I don't know how much help I've been."

Anne gripped her arm. "Now can you tell me what's going on? Has Ken done anything wrong?"

"All I can tell you right now is that I found some things I can't explain. I won't lie to you, they are very troubling."

Anne slowly took her hand away. "I guess you'll have to report what you've found."

Reynolds stared at the woman. Technically what she should do was go directly to OPR and tell them everything. The Office of Professional Responsibility was officially under the umbrella of the Bureau but was actually run by the Department of Justice. OPR investigated allegations of misconduct by Bureau personnel. They had a reputation for being very thorough. An OPR investigation could put a scare into even the toughest FBI agent.

Yes, from a simple technical point of view, it was a no-brainer. If life could only be so simple. The devastated woman standing before Reynolds made her decision much less simple. In the end she went with her human side and put aside the Bureau manual for now. Ken Newman would be buried a hero. The man had been an agent for two decades; he at least deserved that.

"At some point, yes, I'll have to report my findings. But not right now." She paused and gripped the woman's hand. "I know when the funeral is. I'll be there with everyone else, paying our respects to Ken."

Reynolds gave Anne a reassuring hug and then walked out, her mind whirling so fast she felt a little dizzy.

If Ken Newman was on the take, he had been doing it for a while. Was he the leak on Reynolds's investigation? Had he sold out other investigations as well? Was he just a freelancing mole selling to the highest bidder? Or was he a regular snitch working for the same party? If so, why was such a party interested in Faith Lockhart? There were foreign interests involved. Lockhart had told them that much. Was that the key? Was Newman working for a foreign government all this time, a foreign government that was also coincidentally caught up in Buchanan's scheme?

She sighed. The whole thing was snowballing into something so big, she halfway felt like running home and pulling the covers over her head. Instead she would get in her car, drive to the office and continue chipping away at this case, as she had hundreds of others over the years. She had won more than she had lost. And that was the best anyone in her line of work could ever hope for.

THIRTY-FIVE

Lee had awoken very late with the mother of all hangovers and decided to run it off. At first, each of his strides on the sand sent lethal darts through his brain. Then, as he loosened up, breathed the chilly air, felt the salty wind on his face, at about the one-mile point in his run, the effects of his crushed grape and Red Dog shooters disappeared. When he got back to the beach house, he went around to the pool and retrieved his clothes and his gun. He sat in a sling chair for a while, letting the sun warm him. When he went back inside, he smelled coffee and eggs.

Faith was in the kitchen, pouring a cup of coffee. She had on jeans and a short-sleeved shirt and was barefoot. When she saw him come in, she pulled out another mug and filled it. For a moment, this simple act of companionship pleased him. And then his actions of the night before washed that feeling away, like ocean waves brutally wiping out sand castles.

"I figured you'd sleep all day," she said. Her tone was excessively casual, he thought, and she didn't look at him when she spoke.

This qualified for the most awkward moment in Lee's entire life. What was he supposed to say? *Hey, sorry about that little sexual assault thing last night.*

He came into the kitchen area, fingered the mug, half hoping the large lump in his throat would end up strangling him to death. "Sometimes the best remedy for doing something incredibly stupid and inexcusable is to run until you drop." He glanced at the eggs. "Smells good."

"Doesn't compare to the meal you made last night. But then again, I'm no whiz in the kitchen. I guess I'm a room-service kind of girl. But I'm sure you already figured that out." As she moved over to the stove, he noted she walked with a slight limp. He also couldn't fail to notice the bruises on her uncovered wrists. He laid the pistol down on the counter before he could impulsively use it to blow his brains out.

"Faith?"

She didn't turn around, just kept scrambling the eggs around in the pan.

"If you want me to leave, I'll leave," said Lee.

While she seemed to consider this, he decided to say what he had been thinking during his run. "What happened last night, what I *did* to you last night, there's no excuse for. I've never, ever done anything like that in my life. That's not who I am. I can't blame you if you don't believe that. But it's the truth."

She suddenly turned to him, her eyes glistening. "Well, I can't say I hadn't imagined something happening between us, even in the nightmare we're in. I just didn't think it would be like that. . . ." Her voice broke off and she just as quickly turned away from him.

He looked down and nodded slightly, her words doubly devastating to him. "You see, I'm in a bit of a dilemma here. My gut and my conscience tell me to get out of your life so you won't have to be reminded of what happened last night every time you see me. But I don't want to leave you alone with all this. Not when someone's out to kill you."

She turned the burner off and set out two plates, shoveled the eggs on them, buttered two pieces of toast and put everything on the table. Lee didn't move. He just watched her, moving slowly, her cheeks wet from her tears. The bruises on her wrists were like permanent shackles around his soul.

He sat down across from her and picked at his eggs.

"I could have stopped you last night," she said bluntly. The tears slid down her cheeks and she made no attempt to wipe them away.

Lee felt his own eyes begin to burn with the beginnings of tears. "I wish to God you had."

"You were drunk. I'm not saying that's an excuse for what you did, but I also know you wouldn't have done it if you had been sober. And you also didn't go all the way. I choose to believe you would never sink so low as that. In fact, if I weren't absolutely sure of that, I would've shot you with your gun when you passed out." She paused, seemed to be searching for the right combination of words. "But maybe what I've done to you is much more awful than what you could have done to me last night." She pushed her plate away and looked out the window at what was shaping up to be a beautiful day.

When she next spoke, it was in a wistful, faraway tone that was curiously both hopeful and tragic. "When I was a little girl, I had my whole life planned out. I was going to be a nurse. And then a doctor. And I was going to get married and have ten kids. Dr. Faith Lockhart was going to save lives during the day and then come home to a wonderful man who loved her and be the perfect mother to her perfect children. After moving around all those years with my father, I just wanted *one* home. I'd live there the rest of my life. My children would always, always know where to find me. It seemed so simple, so . . . achievable, when I was only eight years old." She finally used her paper napkin to dab at her eyes, only then seeming to feel the wetness on her face.

She looked back at Lee. "But I have this life instead." Her gaze roamed the lovely room. "I actually had a pretty good run. Made a lot of money. What do I have to complain about? That's the American dream, isn't it? Money? Power? Owning beautiful things? Hell, I even ended up doing a little good, even if I did it illegally. But then I went and ruined everything. The best of intentions, but I struck out in the end. Just like my father. You're right, the nut didn't fall far from the tree." She paused again, played with her silverware, precisely placing the fork and butter knife perpendicular to one another.

"I don't want you to leave." On this she rose, quickly crossed the room and then raced up the stairs.

Lee heard her bedroom door slam shut.

Lee took a deep breath, stood and was surprised to find his legs so rubbery. It wasn't from the run, he knew. He showered, changed and came back downstairs. Faith's door was still closed and he had no intention of interrupting whatever she was doing in there. With his nerves unraveling, he decided to spend an hour with the mundane task of thoroughly cleaning his gun. The downside to salt and water was that they were tough on weapons, and automatic pistols were notoriously finicky anyway. If the ammo wasn't of a very high quality, you could count on the thing misfiring and then jamming – or a little sand and grit could cause the same malfunction. And you couldn't clear a pistol by simply pulling the trigger and bringing up a clean cylinder, as you would a revolver. By the time you got your pistol all straightened out, you'd be dead. And with Lee's luck to date, it would happen right when he absolutely needed the thing to fire true and straight. However, on the plus side, the 9mm Parabellums fired by the compact Smith & Wesson had excellent stopping power. Whatever they hit would drop. He prayed he wouldn't have to use the gun, however. Because that would probably mean someone was shooting at him.

He reloaded the fifteen-shot magazine, inserted it in the grip and chambered a round. He clicked the safety on and holstered the gun. He thought about taking the Honda down to the store for a newspaper but decided he didn't quite have the energy or desire to undertake even such a simple task. He also didn't want to leave Faith alone. When she came downstairs, he wanted to be here.

When Lee went to get a drink of water at the kitchen sink, he glanced out the window and almost had a heart attack. Across the road, above a tall hedge that ran about as far as the eye could see, suddenly exploding into his line of vision was a small plane! That's when Lee remembered the runway Faith had told him about. It was across from the house and shielded by the tall hedge.

Lee hurried to the front door to watch the landing. By the time he got outside, the plane had already disappeared. Then whizzing above the top of the hedge was the tail of the plane. It flashed in front of him and then continued past at a fast clip.

He went up on the second-story front porch and watched as the plane taxied to a stop and the passengers deplaned. A car was waiting to pick them up. Bags were off-loaded and stored in the car, which left with the passengers. The pilot got out of the twin-prop plane, checked a few things and then climbed back in. A few minutes later the plane taxied to the other end of the runway and turned around. The pilot opened the throttle and came roaring down the runway in the same direction he had landed, and then lifted gracefully into the air.

The plane headed out toward the water, made a turn and quickly disappeared into the horizon.

Lee went back inside and tried to watch some TV, while at the same time listening for Faith. After roaming through about a thousand channels, he concluded there was absolutely nothing worth watching, and he played a game of solitaire. He enjoyed losing so much, he played another dozen games, with the same result. He wandered downstairs and shot some pool in the game room. When lunchtime came around, he fixed a tuna sandwich and some beef barley soup and ate out on the deck overlooking the pool. He watched the same plane land once more around one o'clock. It shed its passengers and soared once more. He thought about knocking on Faith's door to see if she was hungry and then decided against it. He went for a swim in the pool and then lay on the cool concrete and caught some rays from the intense sun. He felt guilty every minute for enjoying it.

The hours passed and when it started to grow dark, he began contemplating cooking dinner. He would go and get Faith this time, and make her eat. He was just about to head up the stairs when her door opened and she came out.

The first thing that caught his eye was what she was wearing: a white cotton dress, knee-length and clingy, paired with a light blue cotton sweater. Her legs were bare, and she wore simple sandals that managed to look very classy. Her hair was nicely styled; a touch of makeup highlighted her features and pale red lipstick completed the look. She held a small clutch purse. The sweater covered the bruises on her wrists. Probably why she had picked it, he thought. He was thankful that her limp seemed to be gone.

"Going out?" Lee asked.

"Dinner. I'm starving."

"I was going to make something."

"I'd rather eat out. I'm getting cabin fever."

"So where are you going?"

"Well, actually I thought *we* might go."

Lee looked down at his faded khakis, deck shoes and short-sleeved Polo shirt. "I look sort of ragged next to you."

"You look fine." She glanced at the holstered gun. "I'd leave the six-shooter behind, though."

He looked at her dress. "Faith, I'm not sure how comfortable you'll be on the Honda in that."

"The country club's only a half mile up the road. It has a public restaurant. I thought we could walk. Looks to be a beautiful evening."

Lee finally nodded, understanding that getting out made perfect sense, for a lot of reasons. "Sounds good. Give me a sec." He ran upstairs, slipped off his gun and put it in a drawer in his room. He splashed water on his face, wet down his hair a little, grabbed his jacket and joined Faith at the front door, where she was activating the alarm. They left the house and crossed the service road. Reaching the sidewalk, which ran parallel to the main road, they strolled along under a sky that had changed to pink from blue as the sun sank. Landscape lighting had come on in the common areas and so had the underground sprinklers. The sound of the pressurized water was soothing to Lee. The lighting lent a nice mood to the walk, he thought. The whole place seemed to possess almost an ethereal glow, as though they were in a perfectly lit scene from a movie.

Lee looked up in time to see the same twin-prop airplane coming in for a landing. He shook his head. "Scared the hell out of me the first time I saw that thing this morning."

"It would have scared me too, except the first time

I came here I was flying on it. That's the last flight for the evening. It's getting too dark now."

They reached the restaurant, which was decorated with a distinctly nautical theme: a big ship's wheel at the front entrance, diving helmets hung on the wall, fish netting suspended from the ceiling, knotty pine walls, rope banisters and hand rails and an enormous aquarium filled with castles, plant life and an odd assortment of fish peeking out here and there. The servers were young, energetic and attired in cruise line uniforms. The one attending Faith and Lee's table was particularly bubbly. She took their drink orders. Lee opted for iced tea. Faith ordered a wine spritzer. That done, the waitress proceeded to sing the specials of the day in a pleasant if wavering alto. After she left, Faith and Lee looked at each other and had to laugh.

While they waited for their drinks, Faith looked around the room.

Lee shot her a glance. "See anybody you recognize?"

"No. I never really went out when I came down here. I was afraid I'd run into someone I knew."

"Stay cool. You look very different from Faith Lockhart." He looked her over. "And I should have said this before, but you look really . . . well, you really look pretty tonight. I mean really fine." He suddenly looked embarrassed. "Not that you don't look good all the time. I meant . . ." Thoroughly tongue-tied, Lee lapsed into silence, sat back and perused his menu.

Faith looked over at him, feeling just as awkward as he did, she was sure, but a smile still eased across her lips. "Thank you."

They were there for two pleasant stolen hours, discussing innocuous subjects, telling stories of times past and learning more about each other. Since it was the off-season and a weekday, there were few other patrons. They finished their meal, then had coffee and shared a thick slice of coconut cream pie. They paid in cash and left a very generous tip, which would probably make their waitress sing all the way home.

Faith and Lee walked slowly back, enjoying the crisp night air and digesting their meals. Instead of going to the house, though, Faith led Lee down to the beach after dropping her purse off by the back door of the beach house. She slipped off her sandals and they continued their stroll on the sand. It was completely dark now, the wind light and refreshing, and they had the beach entirely to themselves.

Lee looked over at her. "Going out was a good idea. I really enjoyed myself."

"You can be very charming when you want to be."

He looked annoyed for a moment until he realized she was kidding him. "I guess going out together made for a fresh start of sorts too."

"That did cross my mind." She stopped and sat down on the beach, sinking her feet into the sand. Lee remained standing, looking out to the ocean.

"So what do we do now, Lee?"

He sat next to her, slipped off his shoes and curled his toes under the sand. "It would be great if we could stay here, but I don't think we can."

"Then where? I'm fresh out of houses."

"I've been thinking about that. I've got some good buddies in San Diego. Private investigators like me. They know everybody. If I ask, I'm sure they'll help us slip across the border into Mexico."

Faith didn't look very enthusiastic about that idea. "Mexico? And from there?"

Lee shrugged. "I don't know. We can maybe get some fake documents and use them to get to South America."

"South America? And you work the cocaine fields while I labor in a brothel?"

"Look, I've been there. It's not just drugs and prostitutes. We'll have lots of options."

"Two fugitives from justice with God knows who else after them?" Faith looked down at the sand and shook her head doubtfully.

"If you have a better idea, I'm listening," said Lee.

"I've got money. A lot of it in a numbered account in Switzerland."

He looked skeptical. "They really have those things?"

"Oh, yes. And all those global conspiracies you've probably heard about? Secret organizations ruling the planet? Well, they're all true." She smiled and tossed sand on him.

"Well, if the Feds search your home or office, will they find records for it? If they know the account numbers, they can put a tag on it. Trace the money."

"The whole purpose of a Swiss numbered account is to ensure absolute confidentiality. If Swiss bankers ran around giving out that information to anyone who asked for it, their whole system sort of topples."

"The FBI isn't just anyone."

"Not to worry, I didn't keep any records. I have the access information with me."

Lee looked unconvinced. "So do you have to go to Switzerland to get the money? Because that would be, you know, sort of impossible."

"I went there to open the account. The bank appointed a fiduciary, a bank employee, with a power of attorney to handle the transaction in person. It's pretty elaborate. You have to show your access numbers, give positive ID, then provide your signature, which they compare with the one they have on file."

"So from then on you call the fiduciary and he

does all that for you?"

"Right. I've done small transactions in the past, just to make sure it works. It's the same guy. He knows me and my voice. I give him the numbers and where I want the money to go. And it happens."

"You know you can't deposit it in Faith Lockhart's checking account."

"No, but I have a bank account down here under the name of SLC Corporation."

"And you're a signatory as an officer?"

"Yes, as Suzanne Blake."

"The problem is, the Feds know that name. Remember, from the airport."

"Do you know how many Suzanne Blakes there are in this country?"

Lee shrugged. "That's true."

"So at least we'll have money to live off. It won't last us forever, but it's something."

"Something is good."

They fell silent for a bit. Faith alternated between nervously looking at him and then out toward the ocean.

He glanced at her, having noticed her scrutiny. "What is it? Do I have coconut pie on my chin?"

"Lee, when the money comes, you can take half and leave. You don't have to come with me."

"Faith, we've already been through this."

"No, we haven't. I practically ordered you to come with me. I know it would be difficult to go back without me, but at least you'll have the money to go somewhere. Look, I can even call the FBI. I'll tell them you had no involvement. You were just blindly helping me. And that I gave you the slip. Then you can go back home."

"Thanks, Faith, but let's take it one step at a time. And I can't leave until I know you're safe."

"Are you sure?"

"Yes, I'm really sure. I won't go unless you tell me to. And then even if you do, I'll still stalk you, to make sure you're okay."

She reached out and took his arm. "Lee, I can never thank you enough for all you've done for me."

"Just consider me the big brother you never had."

The look they shared, though, held more than sibling affection. He looked down at the sand, trying to get his head straight. Faith looked back out at the water. When Lee looked over at her a minute later, Faith was moving her head from side to side and smiling.

"What are you thinking?" he asked.

She stood and looked down at him. "I'm thinking that I'd like to dance."

He stared up at her in amazement. "Dancing? How much *did* you have to drink?"

"How many nights do we have left here? Two? Three? Then it's off to play fugitive for the rest of our lives? Come on, Lee, last chance to party." She slipped off her sweater and let it fall to the sand. The white dress had spaghetti straps. She slipped them off her shoulders, gave him a heart-stopping wink and held out her hands for Lee to take. "Let's go, big boy."

"You're crazy, you truly are." However, Lee gripped her hands and stood. "Fair warning, I haven't danced in a long time."

"You're a boxer, right? Your footwork is probably better than mine. I'll lead first, and then you take over."

Lee took a few halting steps and dropped his hands. "This is silly, Faith. What if somebody's watching? They'll think we're nuts."

She looked at him stubbornly. "I've spent the last fifteen years of my life worrying about what everybody thought about everything. So right now, I don't give a damn about what anybody thinks about anything."

"But we don't even have any music."

"Hum a tune. Listen to the wind, it'll come."

And surprisingly it did. They started slowly at first, Lee feeling clumsy and Faith unused to leading. Then, as they started to get more familiar with each other's movements, they began making wider circles in the sand. After about ten minutes, Lee's right hand was perched comfortably on Faith's hip, hers was around his waist, their other pair of hands were interlocked and held chest high.

Then they grew noticeably braver and started doing some spins and twirls and other moves reminiscent of Big Band swing and Lindy hop. It was difficult, even in the hard-packed sand, but they gave it an inspired effort. Anyone watching would have thought them either intoxicated or reliving their youth and having the time of their lives. And, in a way, both observations would have been true.

"I haven't done this since high school," Lee said, smiling. "Although Three Dog Night was the big thing back then, not Benny Goodman."

Faith said nothing as she twirled and dipped around him, her moves growing more and more daring, more and more seductive; a flamenco dancer in white flaming heat.

She hiked her skirt up to give herself more freedom of movement, and Lee felt his heart race at the sight of her pale thighs.

They even ventured out into the water, splashing mightily as they went about their increasingly intricate dance steps. They had some tumbles into the sand and even into the salty, chilly water, but they got back up and kept going. Occasionally a truly spectacular combination, perfectly executed, left them both breathless and grinning like schoolkids at a prom.

They finally reached the point where they both grew silent, their smiles faded and they drew closer to each other. The spins and twirls stopped, their heavy breaths eased and they found their bodies touching as their dance circles grew smaller. Finally they stopped altogether and simply stood there rocking slightly side to side, the last dance of the evening, arms around each other, faces close, eyes directly on one another as the wind whistled around them, the waves pitched and crashed hard, the stars and the moon watched from above.

Faith finally stepped away from him, her eyelids heavy, her limbs starting to once again erotically move to a silent tune.

Lee reached out to take her back. "I don't feel like dancing anymore, Faith." His meaning was crystal clear.

She reached out to him too, and then, quick as the snap of a whip, she shoved him hard in the chest and he flopped backward into the sand. She turned and ran, her peals of laughter descending over him as he looked after her, stunned. He grinned, jumped up and raced after her, catching her at the stairs going up to the beach house. He slung her over his shoulder and carried her the rest of the way, her legs and arms flailing in mock protest. They had forgotten the house alarm was set and went in the back door. Faith had to race like mad to the front door to disarm it in time.

"God, that was close. Like we really want the police coming by," she said.

"I don't want anybody coming by."

Gripping his hand tightly, Faith led Lee up to her bedroom. They sat on the bed in the darkness for a few minutes holding one another, gently rocking back and forth as though extending their movements on the beach to this more intimate place.

Finally she eased back from him, cupped his chin with her hand. "It's been a while, Lee. It's been a long time, in fact." Her tone was almost one of embarrassment, and Faith did feel embarrassed at this admission. She didn't want to disappoint him.

He stroked her fingers gently, held her gaze with his as the sounds of the waves reached them through the open window. It was comforting, she thought, the water, the wind, the touches of skin; a moment she may not experience again for a very long time, if ever.

"It'll never be easier for you, Faith."

This surprised her. "Why do you say that?"

Even in the darkness the glow of his eyes surrounded her, held her – protectively, she felt. The fifth-grade romance finally consummated? And yet she was with a man, not a boy. A very unique man, in his own right. She looked him over. No, definitely not a boy.

"Because I can't believe you've ever been with a man who feels the way I do about you."

"Easy to say," she murmured, though in fact his words had touched her deeply.

"Not for me," Lee said.

These few words were spoken with such depth of sincerity, with not a trace of the glibness, the self-servedness of the world she had thrived in for the last fifteen years, that Faith honestly didn't know how to react. But the time for talk had passed. She found herself sliding Lee's clothes off, and then he disrobed her. He massaged her shoulders and neck as he did so. Lee's big fingers were surprisingly gentle. She would've expected them to be rough.

All of their movements were unhurried, natural, as though they had done this thousands of times over the course of a long, happy marriage, seeking just the right spots to work, to please the other.

They slid under the covers. Ten minutes later Lee slumped down, breathing heavy. Faith was under him, gasping for air as well. She kissed his face, his chest, his arms. Their sweat mingled, their limbs intertwined, they lay there talking and slowly kissing for another two hours, falling in and out of sleep as they did so. About three in the morning they made love again. And then both collapsed into deep, exhausted sleep.

THIRTY-SIX

Reynolds was sitting at her desk when the phone call came. It was Joyce Bennett, the lawyer representing Reynolds in her divorce.

"We have a problem, Brooke. Your husband's attorney just called, ranting and raving about you hiding assets."

Brooke's face collapsed in disbelief. "Are you serious? Well, tell him to let me in on it. I could use the extra money."

"This isn't a joke. He faxed me some account statements he says he just discovered. Under the children's names."

"For God's sake, Joyce, those are the kids' college accounts. Steve knew about those. That's why I didn't list them with my assets. Besides, they only have a few hundred dollars in them."

"Actually, the statements I'm looking at show a balance of fifty thousand dollars in each."

Reynolds's mouth went dry. "That's not possible. There must be some mistake."

"The other troubling thing is that the accounts are set up as Uniform Transfer to Minor's Act accounts. That means they're revocable at the discretion of the donor and trustee. You're the listed trustee, and I'm assuming you would be the donor of the funds as well. In essence, it's your money. You should have told me about these, Brooke."

"Joyce, there was nothing to tell. I have no idea

where that money came from. What do the statements show as the origin of funds?"

"Several wire transfers of roughly equal amounts. It doesn't show where they came from. Steve's attorney is threatening to go to court and claim fraud. Brooke, he also says he's called the Bureau."

Reynolds squeezed the phone and sat rigidly. "The Bureau?"

"You're sure you don't know where the money came from? How about your parents?"

"They don't have that kind of money. Can we trace the funds?"

"It's *your* account. I think you better do something. Keep me posted."

Reynolds hung up the phone and stared blankly at the papers on her desk, her mind reeling from this latest development. When the phone rang again a few minutes later, she almost didn't answer it. She knew who it was.

Paul Fisher spoke more coldly than ever to her. She was to come to the Hoover Building immediately. That was all he would tell her. As she walked down the stairs to the parking garage, her legs threatened to collapse under her several times. Every instinct she had told her she had just been summoned to her own professional execution.

The conference room at the Hoover Building was small and windowless. Paul Fisher was there, along with the ADIC, Fred Massey. Massey sat at the head of the table, twirling a pen between his fingers, his gaze locked on her. She recognized the two other people in the room: a Bureau lawyer and a senior investigator from OPR.

"Sit down, Agent Reynolds," Massey said firmly.

Reynolds sat. She wasn't guilty of anything, so why did she feel like Charlie Manson with a bloody knife in his sock?

"We have some things to discuss with you." He glanced at the Bureau lawyer. "I have to advise you, however, that you have the right to have counsel present, if you so wish."

She tried to act surprised, but couldn't really, not after the phone call from Joyce Bennett. Her forced reaction certainly increased her guilt in their eyes, she felt sure. She wondered about the timing of that phone call from Bennett. Not a big believer in conspiracies, Reynolds suddenly began to reconsider that stance.

"And why would I need counsel?"

Massey eyed Fisher, who turned to Reynolds. "We received a phone call from the attorney representing your husband in the divorce."

"I see. Well, I just received a call from my attorney, and I can assure you I'm as much in the dark as anyone else about how that money got into those accounts."

"Really?" Massey looked at her skeptically. "So you're saying it's a mistake that someone very recently dumped a hundred thousand dollars into accounts under your children's names, monies which are solely controlled by you?"

"I'm saying I don't know what to think. But I will find out, I can assure you."

"The timing, as you can understand, has us deeply troubled," Massey said.

"Not as troubled as me. It's my reputation at stake."

"Actually, it's the reputation of the Bureau we're concerned about," Fisher bluntly pointed out.

Reynolds gave him a cold stare and then looked back at Massey. "I don't know what's going on. Feel free to investigate; I've got nothing to hide."

Massey glanced down at a file in front of him. "Are you quite certain of that?"

Reynolds looked at the file. This was a classic interrogation technique. She had used it herself. Bluff the subject by suggesting you had incriminating evidence that would catch him in a lie and hope he'd cave. The only thing was, she didn't know if Massey was really bluffing or not. She suddenly knew what it was like to be on the other side of the interrogation. It wasn't fun.

"Am I quite certain of what?" she said, buying time.

"That you have nothing to hide?"

"I really resent that question, sir."

He tapped the file with his index finger. "You know what has deeply distressed me about Ken Newman's death? The fact that on the night he was murdered, he had taken your place. At your instruction. But for that order, he would be alive today. Would you?"

Reynolds's face turned red and she stood, towering over Massey. "Are you accusing me of being involved in Ken's murder?"

"Please sit down, Agent Reynolds."

"Are you?"

"I'm saying the coincidence, if it is one, has me concerned."

"It *was* a coincidence, since I didn't happen to know there was someone waiting there to kill him. If you recall, I showed up almost in time to stop it."

"Almost in time. That was convenient. Almost like a built-in alibi. A coincidence, or perfect timing? Perhaps too perfect timing?" Massey's gaze burned into her.

"I was working another case and finished sooner than I thought I would. Howard Constantinople can corroborate that."

"Oh, we plan to talk to Connie. You and he are friends, aren't you?"

"We're professional colleagues."

"I'm sure he wouldn't want to say anything that would implicate you in any way."

"I'm *sure* he'll tell you the truth if you just ask him."

"So you're saying there is no connection between Ken Newman's murder and the money showing up in your account?"

"Let me put it a little more strongly than that. I'm saying it's all bullshit! If I were guilty, why would I have anyone put a hundred grand into one of my accounts so close to the time Ken was killed? Don't you think that's a little obvious?"

"But it wasn't really your account, was it? It was in your children's names. And according to your personnel records, you're not due for a Bureau five-year check for another two years. I rather doubt the money would be in the account at that time, and by then I'm sure you'd have a good answer in case anyone did discover that money had once been there. The point is, if your husband's attorney hadn't dug it up, no one would know. That hardly qualifies as obvious."

"Okay, if it's not a mistake, then someone is setting me up."

"And who exactly would be doing that?"

"The person who killed Ken, and who tried to kill Faith Lockhart. Maybe he's afraid I'm getting too close."

"So Danny Buchanan is trying to set you up, is that what you're saying?"

Reynolds glanced at the Bureau lawyer and the representative from OPR. "Do they have clearance to hear this?"

"Your investigation has taken a backseat to these more recent charges," Fisher said.

Reynolds glared at him with rising anger. "Charges! They're unsubstantiated garbage."

Massey opened the file. "So are you saying that your *private* investigation into Ken Newman's finances is garbage?"

On this Reynolds froze and then abruptly sat down. She pressed sweaty palms against the table and tried to get her emotions under control. Her temper was not doing her any good. She was playing right into their hands. Indeed, Fisher and Massey exchanged what she saw as pleased glances at her obvious distress.

"We talked to Anne Newman. She told us everything you've done," Fisher said. "I can't even begin to tell you how many Bureau rules you've broken."

"I was trying to protect Ken and his family."

"Oh, please!" Fisher exclaimed.

"It's true! I was going to go to OPR, but not until after the funeral."

"That was so very considerate of you," Fisher said sarcastically.

"Why don't you go to hell, Paul."

"Agent Reynolds, keep a civil tongue in your head," Massey commanded.

Reynolds sat back and rubbed her forehead. "May I ask how you found out about what I was doing? Did Anne Newman come to you?"

"If you don't mind, we'll ask the questions." Massey leaned forward and made a pyramid with his fingers. "What exactly did you find in the safe-deposit box?"

"Cash. A lot. Thousands."

"And Newman's financial records?"

"A lot of unexplained income."

"We've also talked to the bank branch you visited. You told them not to allow access to the box to anyone except yourself. And you told Anne Newman not to tell anyone about it, not even anyone at the Bureau."

"I didn't want anybody getting to that money. It was material evidence. And I told Anne to keep quiet until I had a chance to dig further. It was for her own protection, until I found out who was behind it."

"Or did you want the time to get the money for yourself? With Ken dead and Anne Newman apparently not even aware her husband had the safe-deposit box, you would be the only one who knew the money was there." Massey stared directly at her; his tiny eyes resembled twin bullets coming for her.

Fisher piped in: "It's curious that when Newman dies you access a box with thousands of dollars in it that he had under a fake name, and about the same time, accounts controlled by you fill up with a hundred thousand dollars."

"If you're somehow trying to say I had Ken killed because of the money in the box, you're way off base. Anne called and asked for my help. I never knew Ken had a safe-deposit box until she told me about it. I had no idea what was in the box until after Ken was already dead."

"So you say," Fisher said.

"So I know," Reynolds replied hotly. She looked at Massey. "Am I being formally charged with anything?"

Massey sat back and put his hands behind his head. "You must realize how very, very bad this all looks. If you were sitting in my chair, what would your conclusions be?"

"I can see how you might have your suspicions. But if you just give me the chance—"

Massey closed his file and stood. "You're suspended, Agent Reynolds, effective immediately."

Reynolds was stunned. "Suspended? I haven't

even been formally charged. You don't even have any specific evidence that I've done anything wrong. And you're suspending me?"

"You should be grateful it's not worse," Fisher said.

"Fred," Reynolds said, half rising from her chair, "I can understand your taking me off this assignment. You can transfer me somewhere else while you investigate, but don't suspend me. Everybody in the Bureau will assume I'm guilty. It's not right."

Massey's face did not soften at all. "Please turn in your credentials and sidearm to Agent Fisher. You are not to return to your office. And you are not to leave the area for any reason."

The blood drained from Reynolds's face and she fell back into her chair.

Massey went to the door. "Your highly suspicious actions, coupled with the murder of an agent and reports of unknown people impersonating FBI agents, does not allow me the option of merely reassigning you, Reynolds. If you're innocent as you claim, then you'll be reinstated with no loss in pay, seniority or responsibility. And I'll make absolutely certain there's no permanent damage to your reputation. If you're guilty, well, you know better than most what awaits you." Massey closed the door behind him.

Reynolds stood to leave, but Fisher blocked her way.

"Creds and gun. Now."

Reynolds slipped them out and handed them over. It was as though she were giving up one of her children. She looked at Fisher's triumphant features. "Gee, Paul, try not to enjoy it so much. You'll look like less of a fool when I'm exonerated."

"Exonerated? You'll be lucky if you're not under arrest by day's end. But we want this case to be airtight. And if you're thinking of running, we'll be watching. So don't even try."

"I wouldn't dream of it. I want to be here to see your face when I come and get my gun and badge back. Don't worry, I won't ask you to kiss my ass."

Reynolds walked down the hallway and out of the building, feeling as though every pair of eyes in the entire Bureau were fully upon her.

THIRTY-SEVEN

Lee got up before Faith, showered, changed his clothes and then stood next to the bed, watching her as she slept. For a few seconds he allowed himself to forget about everything except the wonderful night the two had spent together. He knew it had changed his life forever, and that thought scared him to death.

He went downstairs, moving a little slowly. Parts of him were aching that hadn't in a long time. And it wasn't just from the dancing. He went into the kitchen and made coffee. While it was brewing, he thought about last night. In his mind, Lee had made a very strong commitment to Faith Lockhart. Perhaps an old-fashioned sentiment to some, but sleeping with a woman meant you had deep feelings for her, at least as far as Lee was concerned.

He poured a cup of coffee and went out to sit on the deck off the kitchen. It was a warm day, sunny, but off in the distance, Lee could see darkening clouds approaching. Ahead of the storm was the twin-prop plane as it floated in for a landing with another load of passengers. Faith had told him that during the summer months, the planes might make ten or so trips a day. Now it was down to three; morning, noon and early evening. And so far none of the plane passengers had remained on this street. They had driven off to other places, which suited Lee just fine.

As he sipped his coffee, Lee concluded that he did

have such feelings for Faith, even though he had only known her a few days. Stranger things had happened. Did he love Faith Lockhart? He knew that right now he didn't want to be away from her. He wanted to protect her from harm. He wanted to hold her, spend every minute with her and, yes, have incredibly energetic sex with her as often as his body could manage. Did that constitute love?

On the other hand, she had participated in a bribery scheme involving government officials and was wanted by the FBI, among others. Yes, he thought with a sigh, things had gotten very complicated indeed. Right before they were taking off to God knew where. It wasn't like they could go to a church or even a justice of the peace and get married. *That's right, Father, we're the fugitive couple. Could you please hurry it up?*

Lee rolled his eyes and slapped his forehead hard. Marriage! Good God, was he nuts? Maybe that was how he felt, but what about Faith? Maybe she was into one-night stands, although everything he had observed about the woman argued against such a conclusion. Did she love him? Maybe she was infatuated, caught up in his role as her protector. Last night could be explained away by alcohol, the intoxication of the danger swirling around them or perhaps just simple lust. And he wasn't going to ask her how she felt. She had enough going on.

He focused on the immediate future. Was traveling cross-country on the Honda to San Diego the best plan? Mexico and then South America? He felt a pang of guilt when he thought of the family he would be leaving behind. Then he thought about something else: what everybody would think. His reputation. If he ran, he would be admitting guilt of sorts. And if they did get caught while running, who would believe them?

He slumped back in his chair and suddenly pondered a very different strategy. A few minutes before, flight seemed the wisest choice. Faith, understandably, didn't want to go back and help send Buchanan to prison. Lee really didn't have much interest in doing that either, not after hearing why the man had been bribing the politicians. Danny Buchanan probably should be sainted instead. That's when an idea started to form in his head.

Lee went back inside and picked up his cell phone from the coffee table. He had one of those mega-minute deals with no long distance or roaming charges, so that he rarely even used his hard-line phone anymore. It had voice mail, text mail, caller ID. It even had a news banner where you could check out late-breaking stories, or how your stocks were doing, not that he had any.

When he had first started out as a private investigator, Lee had used an IBM typewriter; touch-tone phones were cutting edge; and fax machines spit out curly thermal paper and were the domain of only the largest companies. That was less than fifteen years ago. Now he was holding a global communications command center in the palm of his hand. Change that fast just couldn't be healthy. But still, who could live without these damn things now?

He plopped down on the couch and stared at the slowly revolving ceiling fan's rattan blades, contemplating the pros and cons of what he was thinking about doing. Then he made up his mind, and slipped his wallet out of his back pocket. The piece of paper was in there with the number his client, Danny Buchanan, had originally given him. The one he had been unable to trace. Then doubt seized him. What if he was wrong about Buchanan's not being involved in the attempt on Faith's life? He stood and paced. When he looked out the window at the blue sky, he saw only possible disaster looming in the approaching storm clouds. Still, Buchanan had hired him. He was technically working for the man. Maybe it was time to report in. He said a silent prayer, picked up his cell phone and punched in the numbers from the piece of paper.

THIRTY-EIGHT

Connie did not look happy as Paul Fisher leaned toward him and addressed him in a conspiratorial tone.

"We have every reason to believe that she's in on it, Connie. Despite what you've told us."

Connie glared at the man. He hated everything about Fisher, from his perfect hair and rocky-ledge chin down to his ramrod-straight posture and wrinkle-free shirts. He had been sitting in here for half an hour. He had told Fisher and Massey his side of the story, and they had told him theirs. They were not going to find any middle ground.

"That's bullshit with a capital *B*, Paul."

Fisher sat back and looked at Massey. "You heard the facts. How can you sit there and defend her?"

"Because I know she's innocent, how about that?"

"Do you have any facts to back that up, Connie?" Massey wanted to know.

"I've been sitting here telling you the facts, Fred. We had a hot lead at Agriculture on another case. Brooke didn't even want Ken to go with Lockhart that night. She wanted to go."

"Or so she told you," Massey replied.

"Look, I've got twenty-five years' worth of experience that says Brooke Reynolds is as clean as they come."

"She investigated Ken Newman's finances without telling anyone."

"Come on, it's not the first time an agent's gone off

the manual. She gets a hot one and wants to follow it up. But she doesn't want to bury Ken's reputation along with the body. Not until she's sure."

"And the hundred thousand dollars in her kids' accounts?"

"Planted."

"By whom?"

"That's what we have to figure out."

Fisher shook his head in frustration. "We're going to have her followed. Every minute until we break this."

Connie leaned forward and did his best to keep his big hands from flying to Fisher's neck. "What you should be doing, Paul, is following up the leads from Ken's murder. And trying to track down Faith Lockhart."

"If you don't mind, Connie, we'll run the investigation."

Connie looked over at Fred Massey. "You want a tail on Reynolds, I'm your guy."

"You! No way!" Fisher protested.

"Hear me out, Fred," Connie said, his gaze locked on Massey. "I admit, things look bad for Brooke. But I also know there's not a finer agent in the Bureau. And I don't want to see a good agent's career go down the toilet because somebody made the wrong call. I've been down that road myself. Right, Fred?"

Massey looked intensely troubled at this last statement. He seemed to shrink in his chair under Connie's withering gaze.

"Fred," Fisher said, "we need an independent source—"

Connie interrupted, "I can be independent. If I'm wrong, then Brooke goes down, and I'll be the first one to break the news to her. But I'm betting she's going to come back and pick up her badge and gun.

In fact, in ten years I see her running this whole damn place."

"I don't know, Connie," Massey began.

"I think *somebody* owes me that opportunity, Fred," Connie said very quietly. "What do you think?"

There was a long moment of silence while Fisher looked back and forth between the two men.

"All right, Connie, you follow her," Massey said. "And you report back to me at regular intervals. Exactly what you see. No more. No less. I'm counting on you. For old times' sake."

Connie rose from the table and flicked a victorious glance at Fisher. "Thanks for the vote of confidence, gentlemen. I won't disappoint."

Fisher followed Connie out into the hallway.

"I don't know what you just pulled in there, but remember this: Your career already has one black mark against it, Connie. It can't afford another. And anything you report to Massey, I want to know about."

Connie crowded the much taller Fisher back against the wall.

"Listen up, Paul." He paused, ostensibly to pick a piece of lint off Fisher's shirt. "I understand that, technically, you're my superior here. Don't confuse that, though, with reality."

"You're treading a dangerous line, Connie."

"I like danger, Paul, that's why I joined the Bureau. That's why I carry a gun. I've killed somebody with mine. How about you?"

"You're not making sense. You're throwing your career away." Fisher felt the wall behind him; his face was growing red as Connie continued to lean into him like a listing oak against a picket fence.

"Is that right? Well, let me make some sense of this for you. Somebody is setting Brooke up. Now, who could that be? It's got to be the leak here at the Bureau. Somebody wants to discredit her, bring her down. And if you ask me, Paul, you're trying awfully hard to do just that."

"Me? You're accusing me of being the leak?"

"I'm not accusing anybody of anything. I'm just reminding you that until we do find that leak, nobody, and I mean nobody, from the director down to the guys who clean the johns here, is above suspicion in my book."

Connie moved away from Fisher. "Have a nice day, Paul. I'm off to catch some bad guys."

Fisher stared after him, slowly shaking his head, something close to fear in his eyes.

THIRTY-NINE

The phone number Lee called was linked to a pager, so that Buchanan would know the instant the number was called. When the pager went off, Buchanan was at home packing his briefcase for a meeting at a downtown law firm that was doing pro bono work for one of Buchanan's clients. He had given up hope of the damn beeper ever sounding. When it did, he thought he would suffer a stroke.

Now Buchanan's dilemma was apparent. How to check the message and call back without Thornhill knowing about it. Then he thought of a plan. He called his driver. It was Thornhill's man, of course. It always was. They drove downtown to the law firm.

"I'll be a couple of hours. I'll phone when I'm done," he told the driver.

Buchanan went into the building. He had been here before, knew the layout well. He didn't go to the elevator bank, but instead went through the main lobby and passed through a door in the back that also served as a rear entrance to the parking garage. He took the elevator down two levels and stepped off. He went through the underground lobby area and out into the parking level. Right next to the door leading out from the lobby was a pay phone. He put in his coins and dialed the number that would allow him to check the message. His reasoning was clear: If Thornhill could intercept a random hard-line call under a thousand tons of concrete, he was the devil himself and Buchanan had no chance of beating him anyway.

On the message Lee's voice was tight, his words few. And the impact on Buchanan was enormous. He had left a number. Buchanan dialed it. A man answered the phone immediately.

"Mr. Buchanan?" Lee asked.

"Is Faith all right?"

Lee gave a sigh of relief. He was hoping that would be the man's first question. That told him a lot. But still, he had to be cautious. "Just to verify it's really you: You sent me a package of information. How did you send it, and what was in it? And let me have the answers fast."

"Personal courier. I use Dash Services. The packet had a photo of Faith, five pages of background information on her and my firm, the contact phone number, a summary of my concerns and what I wanted you to do. It also had five thousand dollars in cash in denominations of fifties and twenties. I also called you three days ago at your office and left a message on your machine. Now please tell me that Faith is all right."

"She's fine, for now. But we have some problems."

"Yes, we do. For starters, how do I know you're Adams?"

Lee thought quickly. "I have a great Yellow Pages ad with a corny magnifying glass and everything. I have three brothers. The youngest works at a motorcycle shop in south Alexandria. He goes by Scotty, but his nickname in college was Scooter because he played football and could run so damn fast. If you want you can call him, check it out and call me back."

"Not necessary. I'm convinced. What happened? Why did you run?"

"Well, you would have too if someone tried to kill you."

"Tell me everything, Mr. Adams. Leave nothing out."

"Well, I know *who* you are, but I'm not sure I trust *you*. What can you do about that?"

"You tell me *why* Faith went to the FBI. That much I do know. And then I'll tell you who you're really up against. And it's not me. When I tell you who it is, you'll wish it were me."

Lee debated this for a moment. He could hear Faith getting up and heading probably to the shower. *Well, here goes.* "She was scared. She said you had been acting strangely, jumpy for a while. She had tried to talk to you about it, but you blew her off, even asked her to leave the firm. That made her even more fearful. She was afraid the authorities were on to you. She went to the FBI with the idea of bringing you in to testify too. Against the people you were bribing. You both cut a deal and walk."

"That would never have worked."

"Well, as she's fond of telling me, it's easy to second-guess."

"So she's told you everything?"

"Pretty much. She thought maybe you were the one who tried to kill her. But I put that notion to rest." *I hope I was right.*

"I had no idea Faith had even gone to the FBI until after she disappeared."

"It's not just the FBI after her. There are some other people too. They were at the airport. And they were carrying something I've only seen at a seminar on counterterrorism."

"Who sponsored the seminar?"

This question puzzled Lee. "The counterterrorism stuff was put on by the official spooks. You know, I guess the guys at CIA."

Buchanan said, "Well, at least you have encountered the enemy and you're still alive. That's good."

"What are you talking . . ." The blood suddenly seemed to pool over Lee's temples. "Are you saying what I think you're saying?"

"Let's just put it this way, Mr. Adams: Faith is not the only one working for a prominent federal agency. At least her involvement was voluntarily. Mine wasn't."

"Oh, shit."

"To put it mildly, yes. Where are you?"

"Why?"

"Because I need to get to you."

"And how can you do that without bringing the ACME assassin squad down on us? I assume you're under surveillance."

"Unbelievably, astonishingly tight surveillance."

"Okay, so you're not coming anywhere near us."

"Mr. Adams, the only chance we have is to work together. That can't be done from a distance. I have to come to you, because I don't think it wise for you to come here."

"You're not convincing me."

"I won't come if I can't lose them."

"Lose them? Look, who do you think you are, Houdini reincarnated? Well, let me tell you, not even Houdini could lose *both* the FBI *and* the CIA."

"I'm neither a spy nor a magician. I'm a humble lobbyist, but I have one advantage: I know this city better than anyone alive. And I have friends in both high and low places. And right now, they are equally valuable to me. Rest assured, I will get to you alone. And then we might be able to survive this. Now I want to speak to Faith."

"I'm not sure that's a good idea, Mr. Buchanan."

"Yes, it is."

Lee whirled around and saw Faith standing on the stairs in a T-shirt. "It's time, Lee. In fact, it's way past time."

He took a deep breath and held out the phone.

"Hello, Danny," she said into the phone.

"God, Faith, I'm sorry. For all of this." Buchanan's voice cracked in midsentence.

"I should be apologizing. I started this whole nightmare by going to the FBI."

"Well, we have to finish it. We may as well do it together. How is Adams? Is he capable? We're going to need some support."

Faith glanced over at Lee, who was anxiously watching her. "In my informed opinion, we have no problems there. In fact, that's probably our one ace in the hole."

"Tell me where you are, and I'll be down as quickly as possible."

She did. She also told Buchanan everything she and Lee knew. When she hung up, she looked over at Lee.

He shrugged. "I figured it was our only shot. Either that or we spend the rest of our lives running."

She sat on his lap, curled her legs up and laid her head against his chest. "You did the right thing. Whoever's involved in this, they'll find a tough opponent in Danny."

Lee's hopes, however, had plummeted. The CIA. Hired assassins, legions of people expert in all sorts of nasty things: computers, satellites, covert operations, air guns with poisoned bullets, all coming for him. If he was smart, he'd throw Faith on the Honda and run like hell.

"I'm going to grab a shower," Faith said. "Danny said he'd be down as soon as he could."

"Right," Lee said, a faraway look in his eyes.

As Faith headed up the stairs, Lee picked up his phone, glanced at it and froze. Lee Adams had never been more stunned in his life. And with the events of the last few days, the bar on what surprised him had risen to about the level of the sun. The text message on the cell phone's screen was concise. And it came close to stopping even Lee's very strong heart.

Faith Lockhart for Renee Adams, it said. There was a phone number to call. They wanted Faith in exchange for his daughter.

FORTY

Reynolds sat in her living room cradling a cup of tea and staring into a fire that was slowly dying. The last time she could remember being home at this time of the day was when she had been on maternity leave with David. Her son had been as surprised to see her come through the door as Rosemary. David was now napping, and Rosemary was busy doing laundry. Just another normal day for them. Reynolds simply stared into the embers of the fire, wishing that something, anything about her life could be normal.

It had started to rain hard, which fit in perfectly with her deep depression. Suspended. She felt naked without her gun and credentials. All those years at the Bureau, never a blemish, and now she was a step away from a ruined career. Then what would she do? Where could she go? Without her job, would her husband try to take the kids? Could she stop him if he did?

She put her cup down, kicked off her shoes and sank back on the couch. The tears started to come fast and heavy, and she put an arm across her face both to soak them up and muffle her sobs. The ringing doorbell made her sit up, wipe at her face and head to the door. She looked through the peephole and found herself staring at Howard Constantinople.

Connie stood in front of the fire he had just stoked,

warming his hands. An embarrassed Reynolds quickly dabbed at her eyes with a tissue. He could not have missed her red eyes and splotchy cheeks, she knew, but he had tactfully said nothing.

"Did they talk to you?" she asked.

Connie turned and dropped into a chair, nodding as he did so. "And I came damn close to being suspended myself. I was about two seconds from punching out Fisher, that shit-faced excuse for an agent."

"Don't go and crater your career for me, Connie."

"If I had sugged the guy, believe me, it would've been for me, not you." He popped a big knuckle, as though emphasizing the point, and then looked across at her. "The thing that kills me is, they actually believe you're somehow involved in this. I told them the truth. Something came up, we were working another case. You wanted to go with Lockhart because you had the relationship with her, but we had this potential whistleblower over at Agriculture we were committed to. I told them you were fretting like all get-out because you didn't know if Ken going with Lockhart out there was the right thing to do."

"And?"

"And they weren't listening. They've already made up their minds."

"Because of the money? Did they tell you about that?"

Connie nodded slowly and suddenly hunched forward. For a big man his movements could be quick, agile. "I don't like kicking you while you're down, but why in hell did you go sniffing around Newman's accounts without telling somebody? Like me, for instance? You know detectives go in pairs for lots of reasons, not the least of which is to cover the other's ass. Now you've got nobody to corroborate shit for you, except Anne Newman. And as far as they're concerned, she doesn't count."

Reynolds threw up her hands. "I never in a million years thought this would happen. I was trying to do right by Ken and his family."

"Well, if he was being paid off, maybe Ken doesn't deserve that sort of consideration. And that's coming from a good friend of his."

"We don't know that he was bad yet."

"Cash in a safe-deposit box under a fake name? Yeah, I guess everybody does that, don't they?"

"Connie, how did they know I was investigating Ken's finances? I can't believe Anne would have called the Bureau. She asked me for help."

"I asked Massey, but he's a clam. Figures I'm the enemy too. I nosed around a bit, though, and I think they got a phone tip. Anonymous, of course. Massey told me you were screaming frame-up. And you know what, I think you're right, even if they don't."

The sight of Connie at the door had been welcome. The fact that he was still loyal meant a lot to her. And she wanted to do right by him too. Especially him. "Look, this isn't going to help your career, being seen with me, Connie. I'm sure Fisher has a tail on me."

"Actually, I'm your tail."

"You're kidding."

"No, the hell I am not. I talked the ADIC into it. Called in a few markers. For old times' sake, Massey said. In case you didn't know, Fred Massey was the guy who asked me to take the dive on the Brownsville case all those years ago. If he thinks this evens us up, he's brain-dead. But don't get all excited. They know I have every incentive to cover *my* ass on this. And that means if you fall, they don't have to go putting blame anywhere else.

Including on yours truly." Connie paused and made a mock show of surprise. "ADIC? Come to think of it, that acronym really fits. Massey's a little shit too."

"You don't have much respect for your chain of command." Reynolds smiled. "What do you think of me, Agent Constantinople?"

"I think you screwed up big-time, and you just gave the Bureau a face-saving scapegoat," he said bluntly.

Reynolds's face grew serious. "You don't sugar-coat."

"Do you want me to waste time doing that?" Connie stood. "Or do you want to clear your name?"

"I *have* to clear my name. If I don't, I could lose it all, Connie. My kids, my career. All of it." Reynolds could feel herself trembling again and she took several deep breaths to counteract the panic she was feeling. She felt like a high schooler who had just learned she was pregnant. "But I'm suspended. No creds, no gun. No authority."

In answer Connie pulled on his overcoat. "Well, you've got me. I've got creds, a gun and, while I'm only a humble field agent after two and a half decades of doing this crap, I can do authority with the best of them. So get your coat and let's try to track down Lockhart."

"Lockhart?"

"I figure we deliver her, the pieces start to fall into place. The more they do, the more the blame gets shifted off you. I've talked to the VCU boys. They're spinning their wheels waiting on lab results and crap like that. And now Massey has them going hot and heavy on your angle and to hell with Lockhart for now. You know nobody's even gone to her house looking for clues?"

Reynolds looked miserable. "We were so reactive

on the whole thing. Ken killed. Lockhart gone. The fiasco at the airport. Then people calling themselves the FBI at Adams's apartment. We never really had a chance to take the proper investigative steps."

"So I figure we follow up some leads while they're still hot. Like checking out Adams's family in the area. I've got the list of names and addresses. If he went on the run, he might have gotten one of them to help."

"You could get into deep trouble for this, Connie."

He shrugged. "Not for the first time. Besides, we don't have a squad supervisor anymore. I don't know if you heard, but she was suspended for being stupid."

They exchanged smiles.

Connie continued. "So, as second-in-command, I'm entitled to investigate an active case I happened to be assigned to. My instructions are to find Faith Lockhart, so that's what I'm going to do. They just don't know I'm doing it with you. And I talked to the VCU guys. They know what I'm up to, so we won't run into another team going through Adams's relatives."

"I need to tell Rosemary I might be gone overnight."

"Then go." He looked at his watch. "I guess Sydney's still in school. Where's your boy?"

"Sleeping."

"Whisper in his ear that Mommy's gonna kick some butt."

When Reynolds returned, she went straight to the closet and got her coat. She hustled toward her study and then stopped.

"What's wrong?" Connie asked.

She looked at him, slightly embarrassed. "I was going to get my gun. Old habits die hard."

"Not to worry. You'll get yours back soon enough.

But you have to make me a promise. When you go to get your gun and creds, take me with you. I want to see their faces."

She opened the door for him. "Deal."

FORTY-ONE

Buchanan made a number of other phone calls from the parking garage as he worked out his arrangements. He then went up to the law firm and spent time on an important matter he suddenly cared nothing about. He was driven home, his mind working the whole time as he devised his plan against Robert Thornhill. That was one area of his being that the CIA man could never penetrate or control: Buchanan's mind. That fact was enormously comforting. Buchanan was slowly regaining his confidence. Maybe he could give the man a run for his money.

Buchanan unlocked the front door to his home and went inside. He lay his briefcase down on a chair and passed the darkened library. He turned on the light to gaze at his beloved painting, to give him strength for what lay ahead. As the light came on, Buchanan stared in disbelief at the empty frame. He staggered over to it, put his hands through the frame and touched the wall. He had been robbed. Yet he had a very good security system, and it had not been tripped.

He raced across to the phone to call the police. As his hand touched the receiver, it rang. He picked it up.

"Your car will be around in a couple of minutes, sir. Going to the office?"

At first Buchanan's mind didn't register.

"To the office, sir?"

"Yes," Buchanan was finally able to say.

He put the phone down and stared over at where his painting had hung. First Faith, and now his painting. All Thornhill's doing. *All right, Bob, first point to you. Now it's my turn.*

He went upstairs, washed his face and changed his clothes, carefully selecting what he needed to wear. He had a custom-built entertainment system in his bedroom housing a TV, stereo, VCR and DVD player. It was relatively safe from burglars since one couldn't take the components out without unscrewing numerous wooden pieces, a very time-consuming process. Buchanan did not watch TV or movies. And when he wanted music, he put a 33 platter on his old phonograph.

Sticking his hand in the slot of the VCR, Buchanan pulled out his passport, credit card and ID, all under an alias, and a slim bundle of hundred-dollar bills and put it all in a zippered inner pocket of his coat. Coming back downstairs, he looked outside and saw his car waiting. He would let him wait for a few more minutes, just for the hell of it.

When that time had passed, Buchanan picked up his briefcase and walked out to the car. He climbed in and the car drove off.

"Hello, Bob," Buchanan said as calmly as he could.

Thornhill glanced down at the briefcase.

Buchanan nodded his head toward the tinted window.

"I'm going to the office. The FBI will expect me to take my briefcase. Unless you assume they haven't tapped my phone line by now."

Thornhill nodded. "You have the makings of a good field operative in you, Danny."

"Where is the painting?"

"In a very safe place, which is far more than you deserve under the circumstances."

"What exactly does that mean?"

"That exactly means Lee Adams, private investigator. Hired by you to follow Faith Lockhart."

Buchanan feigned being taken aback for a minute. As a young man he'd had notions of being an actor. Not in the movies, but on the stage. For him, lobbying was the next best thing. "I didn't know she had gone to the FBI when I did that. I was only concerned for her safety."

"And why was that?"

"I think you know the answer."

Thornhill looked offended. "Why in the world would I want to harm Faith Lockhart? I don't even know the woman."

"Do you have to know someone before you destroy her?"

Thornhill's tone was mocking. "You were wrong to have done it, Danny. The painting will probably be returned to you. But for now, learn to live without it."

"How did you get into my house, Thornhill? I have a security system."

Thornhill looked as though he might burst out laughing. "A *home* security system? Oh, dear."

It was all Buchanan could do not to fling himself on the man.

"You amuse me, Danny, you really do. Running around trying to save the have-nots. Don't you understand? That's what makes the world go 'round. The rich and the poor. The powerful and the powerless. We'll always have them, until the world ends. And nothing you do will change that. Just as people will always hate each other, will betray each other. If it weren't for the evil qualities in humanity, I wouldn't have a job."

"I was just thinking that you missed your calling as a psychiatrist," said Buchanan. "For the criminally insane. You'd have so much in common with your patients."

Thornhill smiled. "That's how I got on to you, you know. Someone you tried to help ended up betraying you. Jealous of your success, your wanting to do good, I suppose. He didn't know about your little scheme, but he aroused my curiosity. And when I focus on someone's life, well, kept secrets are not an option. I tapped your home, your office, even your clothing, and found myself a treasure trove. We so enjoyed listening to you."

"Fascinating. Now tell me where Faith is."

"I was hoping you could tell me that."

"What do you want with her?"

"I want her to come and work for me. There is a friendly competition between the two agencies, but between the FBI and my agency, I would have to say that we play much fairer with our people. I've been working on this project longer than the Bureau. I don't want all my efforts to be in vain."

Buchanan chose his words carefully. He knew he was in great personal danger here. "What can Faith possibly give you that I haven't already?"

"In my line of work, two is always better than one."

"Would your math include the FBI agent you had killed, Bob?"

Thornhill took out his pipe and fiddled with it.

"You know, Danny, you would be well advised to keep yourself focused on your part of this puzzle only."

"I consider *every* part my part. I read the newspapers. You told me Faith had gone to the FBI. An FBI agent is killed working on an undisclosed case. Faith disappears at the same time. You're right, I hired Lee Adams to find out what was going on. I haven't heard from him. Did you have him killed too?"

"I'm a public servant. I don't have people killed."

"The FBI got on to Faith somehow, and you couldn't allow that, because your whole plan goes down the tubes if they find out the truth. And did you really think I believed you'd let me walk away with a slap on the back for a job well done? I didn't survive this long in the business by being a damned idiot."

Thornhill put his pipe away. "Survival, interesting concept. You consider yourself a survivor, and yet you come to me and make all these sorts of unfounded accusations—"

Buchanan leaned forward and placed his face right next to Thornhill's. "I've forgotten more about the subject of survival than you ever knew. I don't have armies of people with guns running around doing my bidding while I sit safely behind the walls of Langley analyzing the field of battle like it was a chess game. The minute you came into my life, I made contingency plans that will absolutely *destroy* you if anything happens to me. Didn't you ever consider the possibility that someone might be half as agile as yourself? Or have all your successes really gone to your head?"

Thornhill simply stared at him, so Buchanan kept going. "Now, I consider myself a partner of sorts with you, no matter how loathsome that thought is. And I want to know if you killed the FBI agent, because I want to know exactly what I have to do to get out of this nightmare. And I want to know if you killed Faith and Adams as well. And if you don't tell me, the minute I leave this car, my next stop will be the FBI. And if you think yourself so invincible as to try and kill me while the Feds are back there, then go ahead. However, if I die, you go down too."

Buchanan leaned back and allowed himself a

smile. "You know the old story of the frog and the scorpion, don't you? The scorpion needs a ride across the water and tells the frog he won't sting it if the frog will provide that ride. And the frog knows that if the scorpion does sting it, that the scorpion will drown, so he gives it the ride. Halfway across the water, the scorpion, against all reason, does sting the frog. As it's dying, the frog cries out, 'Why did you do it? Now you'll die too.' And the scorpion simply tells him, 'It's my nature.'" Buchanan made a mock show of waving. "Hello, Mr. Frog."

The two men sat staring at each other for the next mile until Thornhill broke the silence.

"Lockhart needed to be eliminated. The FBI agent was with her. So he had to die too."

"But you missed Faith?"

"With your private investigator's help. But for your blunder, this crisis would never have happened."

"It never *occurred* to me that you would be planning to kill anyone. So you have no idea where she is?"

"It's only a matter of time. I have a number of irons in the fire. And where there's bait, there's always hope."

"Meaning what?"

"Meaning I'm done talking with you."

The next fifteen minutes passed in complete silence. The car drove into the underground parking garage of Buchanan's building. A gray sedan waited on the lower level, its engine running. Before Thornhill got out, he gripped Buchanan's arm.

"You claim to have the ability to destroy me if anything happens to you. Well, here's my side. If your colleague and her new 'friend' bring all that I've worked for crashing down, you will all be eliminated. Immediately." He removed his hand.

"Just so we understand one another, Mr. Scorpion," Thornhill added scornfully.

A minute later, the gray sedan pulled out of the parking garage. Thornhill was already on the phone.

"Buchanan is not to be out of sight for even one second." He clicked off and began to think of how to attack this new development.

FORTY-TWO

"This is the last place," Connie said as they pulled up to the motorcycle shop in his sedan.

They got out and Reynolds looked around. "His younger brother?"

Connie nodded as he checked his list. "Scott Adams. Manages the place."

"Well, let's hope he's a little more helpful than the others."

They had covered all of Lee's relatives in the area. None had seen or heard from him in the last week. Or at least that's what they said. Scott Adams might be their last chance. However, when they got inside they were told he was out of town for a friend's wedding and wouldn't be back for a couple of days.

Connie handed the young man behind the counter his card. "Tell him to call me when he gets in."

Rick, the salesman who had obnoxiously flirted with Faith, looked down at the card. "Does this have anything to do with his brother?"

Connie and Reynolds eyed him. "Do you know Lee Adams?" Reynolds asked.

"Can't say I know him. He don't know my name or nothing. But he's come by a few times. Just a couple of days ago, in fact."

The two agents looked Rick up and down, gauging his credibility.

"Was he alone?" Reynolds asked.

"No. He had some chick with him."

Reynolds took out a photo of Lockhart and handed it over to him. "Think short hair, not long, black, not auburn."

Rick nodded as he stared at the photograph. "Yep, that's her. And Lee's hair was different too. Short and blond. And he had a beard and mustache too, but I'm real good at noticing things."

Reynolds and Connie looked at each other, trying hard to hide their excitement.

"Any idea where they might have gone?" Connie asked.

"Maybe. But I sure know why they came here."

"Really? Why's that?"

"They needed wheels. Took a bike. One of the big Gold Wings."

"Gold Wing?" Reynolds repeated.

"Yeah." Rick rifled through a stack of color brochures on the counter and flipped one around so Reynolds could see. "This one here. The Honda Gold Wing SE. If you're going long distance, nothing beats this baby. Trust me."

"And you say Adams took one. Got a color, license plate number?"

"I can look the plate up. The color's the same as on the brochure. That was a demo. Scotty let him take it."

"You said you might have an idea where they went," Reynolds prompted.

"What do you want with Lee?"

"We want to talk with him. And the lady he's with," she said amiably.

"They do something wrong?"

"Won't know until we talk to them," Connie replied. He stepped forward a little. "It's an ongoing FBI investigation. You a friend of theirs or something?"

Rick paled at the suggestion. "Hell, no, that chick

is bad news. A real attitude. While Lee was inside, I went out to the sales lot and tried to help her. Real professional-like, and she jumped all over me. And Lee's no better. When he came out, he gave me some lip. I came close to kicking his ass, in fact."

As Connie looked at the beanpole Rick, he recalled the surveillance tape of the physically imposing Lee Adams. "Kick his ass? Is that right?"

Rick looked defensive. "He's got some weight on me, but he's an old guy. And I'm into tae kwon do."

Reynolds studied Rick closely. "So you're saying that Lee Adams was inside for a while, and the woman was out in the lot by herself?"

"That's right."

Reynolds and Connie traded a quick glance. "If you have information as to where they went, the Bureau would greatly appreciate it," Reynolds said, growing impatient. "That and the plate number on the bike. Like right now, if you don't mind. We're sort of in a hurry."

"Sure. Lee also got a map for North Carolina. We sell 'em here, but Scotty just gave it to him. That's what Shirley, the girl who usually works the desk, said."

"Is she in today?"

"Nope. Sick. I'm it."

"Can I get one of those Carolina maps?"

Rick pulled one out and handed it to her. "How much?"

He smiled. "Hey, it's on the house. Just being a good citizen. You know, I'm thinking about joining the FBI."

"Well, we could always use a good man," Connie said with a blank expression, his gaze averted.

Rick looked up the plate number on the demo and gave it to Connie. "You guys let me know what happens," Rick said as they started to leave.

"You'll be the first," Connie called back over his shoulder.

The two agents settled back in the car.

Reynolds looked at her partner. "Well, Lockhart isn't being held by Adams against her will. He left her outside by herself. She could've taken off."

"They sure look to be a team of sorts. At least right now."

"North Carolina," Reynolds said almost to herself.

"Big state," Connie said back.

Reynolds looked at him with a wry expression. "Well, let's see if we can cut it down some. At the airport, Lockhart bought two tickets for a flight to Norfolk International."

"So why the map for North Carolina?"

"They couldn't take the plane. We'd have been waiting for them in Norfolk. At least Adams seemed to know that. He was probably aware we have an arrangement with the airlines, and that's how we scored Lockhart at the airport."

"Lockhart screwed up by using her real name for the second ticket. But that was probably all she could do, unless she had a third fake ID," Connie added.

"So no plane. Can't use a credit card, so no rental car. Adams figures we have the bus and railroad terminals covered. So they get the Honda from his brother and a map for their true destination: North Carolina."

"Meaning that when they got to Norfolk by plane they were either going to drive or hop another plane to someplace in Carolina."

Reynolds shook her head. "But that doesn't make sense. If they were going to North Carolina, why not just take a plane directly there? There are tons of flights to Raleigh and Charlotte out of National. Why go through Norfolk?"

"Well, maybe you'd go through Norfolk if you

weren't going to Charlotte or Raleigh or anyplace near them," Connie ventured, "but still wanted to go to someplace in North Carolina."

"But why not still go through one of those two major airports?"

"Well, what if Norfolk is a lot closer to where they wanted to go than Charlotte or Raleigh are?"

Reynolds thought a moment. "Raleigh's roughly in the middle of the state. Charlotte is west."

Connie snapped his fingers. "East! The coast. The Outer Banks?"

Reynolds found herself nodding in agreement. "Maybe. The Outer Banks has thousands of beach houses where one could hide."

Connie suddenly looked less hopeful. "Thousands of beach houses," he muttered.

"Well, the first thing you can do is call the Bureau's airline liaison and find out what flights run out of Norfolk for the Outer Banks. And we have some times to work with. Their flight was scheduled to get into Norfolk at noon. I don't see them cooling their heels any longer than necessary at a public place, so the flight out had to be relatively close to noon or so. Maybe one of the commuters has regular service. We already checked with the major airlines. They didn't reserve with any of them out of Norfolk."

Connie picked up the car phone and placed the call. It didn't take long before they got an answer.

Connie's features looked hopeful again. "You're not going to believe this, but there's only one commuter service to the Outer Banks from Norfolk International."

Reynolds smiled broadly and shook her head. "Finally, some luck in this damn case. Talk to me."

"Tarheel Airways. They fly out of Norfolk to five places in Carolina: Kill Devil Hills, Manteo,

Ocracoke, Hatteras and a place called Pine Island, near Duck. There're no regular departures. You call ahead and the plane is waiting for you."

Reynolds spread open the map and scanned it. "Okay, there are Hatteras and Ocracoke. They're the farthest south." She put a finger on the map. "Kill Devil Hills is here. Manteo south of that. And Duck is here, to the north."

Connie looked at where she was pointing. "I've been down there on vacation. You cross the bridge over the sound and head north for Duck. South for Kill Devil. They're fairly equidistant from each other at that point."

"So what do you think? North or south?"

"Well, if they were going to North Carolina, it was probably at Lockhart's prompting." Reynolds looked at him curiously. "Because Adams took the map," Connie explained. "If he knew the area, he wouldn't have done that."

"Nice, Sherlock, what else?"

"Well, Lockhart has some serious money. One look at her house in McLean will tell you that. If I were her, I'd have a safe house under my phony name in case the roof caved in."

"But we're still at square one: north or south?"

They sat there stewing over this until Reynolds suddenly slapped her forehead. "God, how stupid. Connie, if you have to call Tarheel to arrange for a flight, our answer's right there."

Connie's eyes grew wide. "Damn, talk about blind." He picked up the phone, got the number for Tarheel and placed the call, relaying the date and approximate time and the name Suzanne Blake.

He hung up and looked at her. "A reservation for two people with Tarheel was made by our Ms. Blake two days ago to fly out of Norfolk around two P.M. They were pissed because she never showed. They normally take a credit card, but she'd flown with them before, and so they just took her on her word."

"And their destination?"

"Pine Island."

Reynolds couldn't help but smile. "God, Connie, we might actually pull this off."

Connie put the car in gear. "Only bad thing is, I don't rate one of the Bureau's planes. We're stuck with the old Crown Vic here. I figure six hours or so, not counting stops." He checked his watch. "With stops, that'll put us there about one in the morning."

"I'm not supposed to leave the area."

"Bureau Rule Number One: You can go anywhere so long as you have your guardian angel along."

Reynolds looked troubled. "What do you think about calling in reinforcements?"

He eyed her quizzically. "Well, I guess we could call Massey and Fisher and let them take all the credit."

Reynolds suddenly smiled. "Like you said, screw international relations. Give me a minute to call home and then let's roll."

FORTY-THREE

It had taken Lee several agonizing hours, but he had finally tracked down Renee. Her mother had flatly refused to give him her phone number at college, but in a series of calls to the admissions office, among others, Lee had lied, begged and threatened until the number had been given up. It figured. He hadn't called his daughter for a long time, and when he did, it had to be for something like this. Boy, she was really going to cherish her old man now.

Renee's roommate at UVA swore on her grave that Renee had left for class accompanied by two members of the football team, one of whom she was dating. After telling the young woman who he was and leaving a number for Renee to call, Lee had hung up the phone and then gotten the telephone number for the Albermarle County Sheriff's office. He talked his way to a deputy sheriff and told the woman that someone had made threats against Renee Adams, a student at UVA. Would they please send someone to check on her? The woman asked questions that Lee could not answer, including wanting to know who the hell he was. *Just check the latest most-wanted list*, he wanted to tell her. Sick with worry, he tried his best to impress upon her the sincerity of what he was saying. Then he hung up and stared down at the digital missive once more: "Renee for Faith," he slowly said to himself.

"What?"

He jerked around and stared at Faith, there on the stairs, her eyes wide, her mouth open.

"Lee, what is it?"

Lee was out of ideas at the moment. He simply held up the phone for Faith, his face an anguished mess.

She looked at the message and then stared at him. "We have to call the police."

"She's okay, I just talked to her roommate. And I called the police. Somebody's blowing smoke at us. Trying to spook us."

"You don't know that."

"You're right, I don't," he said miserably.

"Are you going to call the number back?"

"That's probably what they want me to do."

"You mean so they can trace the call? Can you trace a cellular call?"

"It's possible, if you have the right equipment. Phone carriers have to be able to trace a cell call to determine the location of a 911 caller. It uses a time difference of arrival method by measuring signal distances between cell towers and kicks out a string of possible locations. . . . Shit, my daughter's head might be in the guillotine and I sound like a damn walking science magazine."

"But not an exact location."

"No, at least I don't think so. It's not as precise as satellite positioning, that's for certain. But who the hell really knows? Some geeky asshole invents some new piece of shit every second that rips away a little bit more of your privacy. I know, my ex-wife married one."

"You should call, Lee."

"And what the hell am I supposed to say? They want to trade you for her."

She put one hand on his shoulder, rubbed his neck and then leaned against him. "Call them. And then we'll see what we can do. Nothing is going to happen to your daughter."

He looked at her. "You can't guarantee that."

"I *can* guarantee that I will do everything I can to make sure she's not harmed."

"Including walking into their hands?"

"If it comes to that, yes. I'm not going to let an innocent person get hurt because of me."

Lee slumped back against the couch. "I'm supposed to be so good under pressure too and I can't even think straight."

"Call them," Faith said very firmly.

Lee took a long breath and punched in the numbers. With Faith sitting beside him and listening in, they waited as the phone rang once and then was answered.

"Mr. Adams?" Neither of them recognized the voice. It had a mechanical quality to it, making them both think it was being altered somehow. It sounded inhuman enough to make their skin tingle with absolute dread.

"This is Lee Adams."

"Nice of you to leave your cell phone number at your apartment. It made contacting you much more convenient."

"I just checked on my daughter. She's fine. And the cops are on the scene. So your little kidnapping plan—"

"I have no need to kidnap your daughter, Mr. Adams."

"Then I'm not sure why I'm talking to you."

"You needn't abduct someone to kill her. Your daughter can be eliminated today, tomorrow, next month, next year. While going to class, lacrosse practice, driving on holiday, even while she's sleeping. Her bed is right next to a window, first floor. She often stays late at the library. It couldn't be easier, really."

"You sick bastard! You sonofabitch!" Lee looked like he wanted to break the phone in two.

Faith gripped his shoulders, trying to calm him down.

The voice continued with irritating calm. "Histrionics won't help your daughter. Where is Faith Lockhart, Mr. Adams? That's all we want. Give her up and all your problems go away."

"And I'm supposed to just accept that as gospel?"

"You really don't have a choice."

"How do you know I've even got the woman?"

"Do you want your daughter to die?"

"I'm telling the truth, Lockhart got away."

"Fine, next week you can bury Renee."

Faith jerked at Lee's arm and pointed at the phone.

"Wait, wait!" Lee said. "Okay, okay, if I have Faith, what do you propose?"

"A meeting."

"She's not going to come voluntarily."

"I don't really care how you get her there. That's your responsibility. We'll be waiting."

"And you'll just let me walk away?"

"Drop her off and drive away. We'll take care of the rest. You don't interest us."

"Where?"

Lee was given an address outside of Washington D.C., on the Maryland side. He knew it well: very isolated.

"I have to drive it. And the cops are everywhere. I need a few days."

"Tomorrow night. Twelve sharp."

"Dammit, that's not a lot of time."

"Then I suggest you start right now."

"Listen, if you lay a hand on my daughter, I'll find you, somehow I will. I swear it. First I'll break every bone in your body, and then I'll really hurt you."

"Mr. Adams, consider yourself the luckiest human being on the face of the earth that we don't see you as a threat. And do yourself a favor. When you walk away don't ever, ever look back. You won't turn to salt, but it still won't be pretty." The line went dead.

Lee put the phone down. For a few minutes he and Faith just sat there without speaking. "Now what do we do?" Lee finally managed to say.

"Danny said he'd be here as soon as he could."

"Great. I've got a deadline: tomorrow, midnight."

"If Danny's not here in time we'll drive to the place they gave you. But first we'll call in some reinforcements."

"Like who, the FBI?" Faith nodded. "Faith, I'm not sure we could explain all this to the Feds in one year, much less one day."

"It's all we have, Lee. If Danny gets here in time and has a better plan, so be it. Otherwise I'll call Agent Reynolds. She'll help us. I'll make it work." She squeezed his arm. "Nothing is going to happen to your daughter. I promise."

Lee gripped her hand, hoping with all his heart that the woman was right.

FORTY-FOUR

Buchanan had a number of meetings on Capitol Hill scheduled for the early evening, pitching to an audience that didn't want to hear him. It was like throwing a ball at a wave. It would either be kicked back in your face or lost at sea. Well, today was the end. No more.

His car dropped him off near the Capitol. He went up the front steps and over to the Senate side of the building, where he climbed the broad staircase to the second floor, which was mostly restricted space, and continued to the third floor, where people could freely wander.

Buchanan knew he was being followed by more people now. While there were lots of dark suits around, he had trekked these halls long enough to sense who should be here as opposed to those who looked out of place. He assumed they were the FBI and Thornhill's men. After the encounter in the car, the Frog would have deployed more resources. Good. Buchanan smiled. He would, from now on, refer to the CIA man as the Frog. Spies liked code names. And he couldn't think of a more appropriate one for Thornhill. Buchanan just hoped that his stinger was ready, filled to the hilt with poison, and that the Frog's shiny, inviting back wouldn't prove too slippery.

The door was the first one a person would come to upon reaching the third floor and turning left. A middle-aged man in a suit stood next to it. There was no brass plate to identify whose office this was. Right next door was the office of Franklin Graham, the Senate sergeant-at-arms. The sergeant-at-arms was the Senate's principal law enforcement, administrative support and protocol officer. Graham was a good friend of Buchanan's.

"Good to see you, Danny," the man in the suit said.

"Hello, Phil, how's that back of yours?"

"Doc says I should have the surgery."

"Listen to me, don't let them cut you. When you're feeling the pain, have a nice, pleasing shot of Scotch, sing a song at the top of your lungs and then make love to your wife."

"Drinking, dancing and loving – sounds like good advice to me," Phil said.

"What'd you expect from an Irishman?"

Phil laughed. "You're a good man, Danny Buchanan."

"You know why I'm here?"

Phil nodded. "Mr. Graham told me. You can go right in."

He unlocked the door and Buchanan passed through, and then Phil closed the door and stood guard. He didn't notice the two pairs of people who had idly watched this exchange.

The agents reasonably figured they could wait for Buchanan to come out and then take up their surveillance once more. They were on the third floor, after all. It wasn't like the man could fly away.

Inside the room, Buchanan grabbed a raincoat off the hook on the wall. Lucky for him it was drizzly outside. There was also a yellow hard hat on another wall hook. He slipped this on as well. Then he pulled Coke-bottle glasses and work gloves from his briefcase. At least from a distance, with his briefcase under the raincoat, he would change from lobbyist to laborer.

Going to another door at the end of the room, Buchanan removed the chain locking this door and opened it. He went up the stairs and then opened a hatchlike door, which revealed a ladder leading up. Buchanan put his feet on the rungs and started climbing. At the top, he popped another hatch and found himself on the roof of the Capitol.

The attic room was how the pages accessed the roof to change the flags that flew over the Capitol. The inside joke was that the flags were constantly changed, some flying only for seconds, so that members could send generous constituents back home a continuous supply of Stars and Stripes that had "flown" over the Capitol. Buchanan rubbed his brow. God, what a town.

Buchanan looked down at the front grounds of the Capitol. People were scurrying here and there, running for meetings with people they desperately needed help from. And with all the egos, factions, agendas, crisis upon crisis and stakes greater than anything that had come before in the world's history, everything somehow seemed to work out. A large anthill came to mind as Buchanan looked down upon this well-oiled machine of democracy. At least the ants did it for survival. But maybe in a way, we did too, he thought.

He looked up at Lady Liberty on her century-and a-half perch atop the Capitol's dome. She had recently been removed via helicopter and stout cable, and the grime of a hundred fifty years had been thoroughly cleaned away. Too bad the sins of people weren't as easy to scrape off.

For one insane moment, Buchanan contemplated jumping. He might have, too, except the desire to beat Thornhill was simply too strong. And that would be the coward's way out anyway. Buchanan was many things, but a coward was not one of them.

There was a catwalk that ran across the roof of the Capitol, and it would take Buchanan to the second part of his journey. Or, more accurately, his escape. The House wing of the Capitol building had a similar attic room, which its pages used to raise and lower its flags. Buchanan quickly went across the catwalk and through the hatch on the House side. He climbed down the ladder and into the attic room, where he removed the hard hat and gloves, but kept on the glasses. He pulled a snap-brim hat from his briefcase and put it on. Pulling up the collar on the raincoat, he took a deep breath, opened the door to the attic room and passed through. People milled here and there, but no one really gave him a second glance.

In another minute he had left the Capitol through a rear doorway known only to the few veterans of the place. A car was waiting for him there. A half hour later he was at National Airport, where a private plane, its twin engines revving, awaited its sole passenger. Here was where the friend in *high* places earned his money. The plane received clearance for takeoff a few minutes later. Soon thereafter Buchanan looked out the window of the plane as the capital city slowly disappeared from view. How many times had he seen that sight from the air?

"Good riddance," he said under his breath.

FORTY-FIVE

Thornhill was heading home early after a very productive day. With Adams now in the fold, they would soon have Faith Lockhart. The man might try to dupe them, but Thornhill didn't think so. He had heard the very real fear in Adams's voice. Thank God for families. Yes, all in all, a productive day. The ringing phone would soon change all that.

"Yes?" Thornhill's confident look vanished as the man reported to him that somehow, some way, Danny Buchanan had utterly vanished, from the very top floor of the Capitol, no less.

"Find him!" Thornhill roared into the phone before slamming it down. What could the man's game be? Had he decided to begin his escape a little early? Or was it for another reason? Had he contacted Lockhart somehow? That was intensely troubling. Shared information between the two was not good for Thornhill. He thought back to their meeting in the car. Buchanan had displayed his usual temper, his little word games – empty bluster, really – but had otherwise been fairly subdued. What could have precipitated this latest development?

In his agitation, Thornhill drummed his fingers on the briefcase, he had in his lap. As he looked down at the hard leather, his mouth dropped open. The briefcase! The damn briefcase! He had provided one for Buchanan. It had a backup recorder in it. The conversation in the car. Thornhill admitting he had

had the FBI agent killed. Buchanan had tricked him into betraying himself and then taped him. Taped him with CIA-issue equipment. That two-faced sonofabitch!

Thornhill grabbed the phone; his fingers were shaking so badly he misdialed twice. "His briefcase, the tape in it. Find it. And him. You must get it. You *have* to get it."

He dropped the phone and slumped back in the seat. The master strategist of over a thousand clandestine operations spanning nearly four decades was absolutely stunned by this development. Buchanan could take him down with this. He was running loose with the evidence to crush him. But Buchanan would go down too, had to, there was no way around it.

Wait. The scorpion! The frog! Now it all made sense. Buchanan was going to go down and take Thornhill with him. The CIA man loosened his tie, wedged himself into the seat and fought the panic he felt flooding his body.

This is not how it will end, Robert, he told himself. *After thirty-five years this is not damn well how it's going to end. Calm down. Now is when you need to think. Now is where you earn your place in history. This man will not beat you.* Slowly, steadily, Thornhill's breathing returned to normal.

It could be that Buchanan would simply use the tape as insurance. Why spend the rest of his life in prison when he could quietly disappear? No, it made no sense that he would take the tape to the authorities. He had as much to lose as Thornhill, and he couldn't possibly be that vindictive. Thornhill had a sudden thought: Perhaps it was the painting, the idiotic painting. Maybe that was what had started this whole thing. Thornhill should never have taken the damned thing. He would leave a message on Buchanan's machine at once, telling him his precious object had been returned. Thornhill left the message and arranged for the painting to be returned.

As Thornhill sat back and looked out the window, his confidence returned. He had one ace in the hole. A good commander always held something in reserve. Thornhill made another phone call and received some positive news, a piece of intelligence that had just come in. His face brightened, the visions of doom receding. It would be all right after all. His mouth eased into a smile. The snatch of victory from the jaws of defeat; it could either age a man several decades overnight or give him bronze balls. Or sometimes both.

In another few minutes Thornhill was getting out of his car and walking up the sidewalk to his lovely house. His impeccably dressed wife met him at the door and gave him a perfunctory peck on the cheek. She had just come back from a country club function. In fact, she was always coming back from a country club function, he thought, muttering to himself. While he agonized over terrorists sneaking into the country with nuclear-bomb-making materials, she lounged at fashion shows where young, vacuous women with legs stretching to their inflated bosoms pranced about in outfits that didn't even bother to cover their derrieres. He was out every day saving the world, and his spouse ate finger sandwiches and drank champagne in the afternoon with other ladies of considerable means. The idle rich were as stupid as the uneducated poor – more brainless than cows, in fact, was Thornhill's opinion. At least cows had a reasonable understanding that they were the slaves. *I'm an underpaid civil servant*, Thornhill mused, *and if I ever let my defenses down, the only thing left of the wealthy and powerful in this country would be the echoes of their screams*. It was a powerful, mesmerizing thought.

He barely heard his wife's inconsequential ramblings on "her day" as he put down his briefcase, mixed a drink and escaped to his study and closed the door. He never told the woman about *his* day. She'd chat about it to her one-name, oh-so-chic glorified barber, who would tell another client, who would let it slip to someone else and the world would stop tomorrow. No, he never talked shop with the wife. But he did indulge her in just about everything else. But finger sandwiches indeed!

Ironically, Thornhill's home office was much like Buchanan's. There were no plaques, testimonials or souvenirs of his long career on display. He was a spy, after all. Was he supposed to act like the idiotic FBI and wear T-shirts and hats emblazoned with CIA? He almost choked on his whiskey at the thought. No, his career had been invisible to the public, but highly visible to those who mattered. The country was far better off because of him, though the ordinary folk would never know it. That was all right. To seek accolades from the great and ignorant public was the vice of a fool. He did what he did because of pride. Pride in himself, in his devotion to his country.

Thornhill thought back to his beloved father, a patriot who carried his secrets, his distinguished triumphs to the grave. Service and honor. That was what it was all about.

Soon, with a little luck, the son would notch another triumph in his own career. When Faith showed up, she would be dead within an hour. And Adams? Well, he would have to die too. Certainly Thornhill had lied to the man on the phone. Thornhill understood quite clearly that deceit was nothing more nor less than a highly effective tool of the trade. One just had to make sure that lies at work didn't interfere with one's personal life. But Thornhill had always been good with compartmentalization. Just ask his country club wife. He could initiate a covert action in Central America in the morning and play, and win, at bridge at the Congressional Country Club in the evening. Now, dammit, *that* was compartmentalization!

And whatever anyone said about him within the confines of the Agency, he had always been good with his people. He pulled them out of situations when they needed to be pulled. He had never left an agent or case officer spinning in the wind, helpless. But he also kept them in the field when he knew they could carry it home. He had developed an instinct for such things, and it had hardly ever proved wrong. He also didn't play political games with intelligence collection. He had never told the politicians simply what they wanted to hear, as others at the Agency had – sometimes with disastrous consequences. Well, he could only do what he could. In two years it would be someone else's problem. He would leave the organization in as strong a state as he could. His parting gift. There was no need to thank him. Service and honor. He lifted his drink in memory of his late father.

FORTY-SIX

"Stay low, Faith," Lee said as he edged close to a window overlooking the street. He had his gun out and was watching a car drop a man off out front. "Is that Buchanan?" he asked.

Faith anxiously peered over the windowsill and then immediately relaxed.

"Yes."

"Okay, answer the front door. I'll cover you."

"I told you it was Danny."

"Great, then go let *Danny* in. I'm not taking any unnecessary chances."

Frowning at this remark, Faith went to the front door and opened it. Buchanan slipped through and she closed and locked the door behind him. They exchanged a prolonged hug as Lee watched from the stairs, his gun in plain sight in his belt clip. He felt a pang of jealousy at this embrace. It quickly passed, though, as he sensed the exchange of affection was clearly that of a father and his daughter.

"You must be Lee Adams," Buchanan said, extending his hand. "I'm sure you regret the day you ever took on this assignment."

Lee came down and shook his hand. "Nah. This one's been a piece of cake. I'm actually thinking about specializing in this area, especially considering no one else would be stupid enough to do it."

"I thank God you were there to protect Faith."

"Actually, I've gotten pretty good at saving Faith." Lee and Faith exchanged smiles, then Lee looked back at Buchanan. "But the fact is we have one additional complication. A very important one," Lee added. "Let's go to the kitchen. You might want to hear it over a drink."

As they sat at the kitchen table, Lee filled Buchanan in on the situation with his daughter.

Buchanan looked furious. "That bastard."

Lee eyed him keenly. "This bastard have a name? I'd love to know it, for future reference."

Buchanan eyed him keenly and then shook his head. "Trust me, you don't want to go down that route."

"Who is behind all this, Danny?" Faith touched his arm. "I think I have a right to know."

Buchanan looked at Lee.

"Sorry," Lee said, putting up his hands, "that's your call."

Buchanan gripped Faith's arm. "They're very powerful people and they happen to work for this country. That's all I can really say without endangering you even more."

Faith sat back astonished. "*Our* own government is trying to kill us?"

"The gentleman I've been dealing with tends to go his own way. But he does have resources, lots of them."

"So Lee's daughter is in real danger?"

"Yes. This man will usually say rather less than what he actually intends."

"Why'd you come here, Buchanan?" Lee wanted to know. "You got away from the guy. At least for our sakes I hope you did. You could've lost yourself in a million different places. Why come here?"

"I got you both into this. I intend to get you out."

"Well, whatever plan you have better include

saving my daughter or else you can count me out. I'll park myself inside her skin for the next twenty years if I have to."

Faith said, "I thought I could call the FBI agent I was working with, Brooke Reynolds. We can tell her what's going on. She could place Lee's daughter in protective custody."

"For the rest of her life?" Buchanan shook his head. "No, that won't work. We have to cut the hydra's head off and then burn the stub. Otherwise we're just wasting time."

"And exactly how do we do that?" Lee asked.

Buchanan opened his briefcase and pulled out the tiny cassette tape from a hidden crevice. "With this. I was able to record the gentleman I've been talking about. On this tape he admits that he had the FBI agent killed, among other incriminating things."

For the first time Lee looked hopeful. "Are you serious?"

"Trust me, I would never joke about this man."

"So we use this tape to keep the hound at bay. He hurts us, we destroy him? He knows that. Then we've pulled his fangs."

Buchanan slowly nodded. "Exactly."

"And you know how to contact him?" asked Lee.

Buchanan nodded. "I'm sure that he's figured out what I did and is right now trying to deduce what my intention is."

"Well, *my* intention is that you call up this asshole right this second and tell him to stay the hell away from my daughter. I want it in blood. And I don't trust the sonofabitch, so I still want something like a company of SEALs outside her dorm room for good measure. And I still plan on heading up there myself. Just in case. They want Renee? They go through me."

"I'm not sure that's a good idea," Buchanan said.

"I don't remember asking for your permission," Lee fired back.

"Lee, please," Faith said. "Danny's just trying to help."

"I wouldn't be in this nightmare if this guy had been straight with me up front. So excuse the hell out of me if I don't treat him like he's my best buddy."

"I don't blame you for feeling that way," Buchanan said. "But you called me for help, and I'll do whatever I can to help you. And your daughter. That I swear."

Lee's guarded manner relaxed somewhat in the face of this seemingly frank declaration.

"Okay," he said grudgingly. "I admit you get points for coming here. You'll get more points when you call off the assassins. And then after that we should get the hell out of here. I've already called this psycho once on my cell phone. I'm assuming that at some point he'll be able to narrow our location down from that. When you call him, it'll give them even more info to work with."

"Understood. I have a plane at my disposal at a private airstrip not too far from here."

"Your friends in high places?"

"*Friend*. Senior senator from this state, Russell Ward."

"Good old Rusty," Faith said, smiling.

"You're sure you weren't followed?" Lee glanced at the front door.

"No one could have followed me. I'm not sure of much anymore, but I am certain of that."

"If this guy is as good as you seem to think he is, I wouldn't feel too certain of anything." Lee held out his cell phone. "Now please make the call."

FORTY-SEVEN

Thornhill was in his study at home when Buchanan's phone call came in. His communication link was such that the call was not traceable to Thornhill, if Buchanan was perhaps sitting at FBI headquarters. And Thornhill's phone also had a voice scrambler that would make voice ID impossible. On the other hand, Thornhill's people were working on tracing Buchanan's location, but as yet they hadn't been successful. Even the CIA had its limits, what with the explosion in the field of communications technology. There were so many electronic signals flying through the air, it made it damn near impossible to trace a wireless call to a precise location.

The National Security Agency would be able to trace the call with its stadium-size circular antennas. The super-secret NSA possessed technological might that made anything the CIA had pale by comparison, Thornhill well knew. It was said that the intelligence the NSA perpetually swept out of the air could fill the Library of Congress every *three* hours, gobbling up information in avalanche-byte mouthfuls. Thornhill had availed himself of the NSA's services before. However, the NSA (the inside joke was that the acronym stood for "no such agency") was often difficult for anyone to control. Thus Thornhill didn't want to involve them in this highly sensitive matter. He would handle it himself.

"You know why I'm calling?" Buchanan said.

"A tape. A highly personal one."

"It's good doing business with someone who considers himself omniscient."

"I would appreciate some small bit of evidence, if it's not too much trouble," Thornhill said placidly.

Buchanan played a snatch of the earlier conversation between the two men.

"Thank you, Danny. Now, your terms?"

"Point one, you don't go near Lee Adams's daughter. That is called off. Now and forever."

"Do you happen to be with Mr. Adams and Ms. Lockhart right now?"

"Second, all three of us are off limits as well. If anything remotely suspicious happens, then the tape goes directly to the FBI."

"During our last conversation you said you already had the means to destroy me."

"I lied."

"Do Adams and Lockhart know of my involvement?"

"No."

"How can I trust you?"

"It would only have put them in more danger to tell them. All they want to do is survive. It seems a common enough goal these days. And I'm afraid you'll just have to take my word for it."

"Even though you just admitted lying to me?"

"Exactly. Tell me, how does it feel?"

"And my long-term plan?"

"I really don't give a damn at this point."

"Why did you run?"

"Put yourself in my place; what would you have done?"

"I would never have allowed myself to be put in your place," said Thornhill.

"Thank God we can't all be like you. Do we have an agreement?"

"I don't have much choice, do I?"

"Join the club," said Buchanan. "However, you can be absolutely certain that if anything happens to any of us, it's over for you. But if you play fair, you accomplish your goal. Everyone lives to celebrate."

"Good doing business with you too, Danny."

Thornhill clicked off and sat there seething for a few moments. Then he made another call but came away disappointed. The trace had not been made. Well, that was all right. He hardly expected it to be so easy. He still had his ace in the hole. He made one more phone call and this time the information brought a broad smile to his lips. As Danny had said, Thornhill did know all there was to know, and he thanked God for his omniscience. When you planned for every possible contingency you were difficult to beat.

Buchanan was with Lockhart, of that he was almost certain. His two golden birds were occupying the same nest. That made his task infinitely simpler. Buchanan had outsmarted himself.

He was just about to refill his scotch when his wife popped her head in. Would he like to go to the club with her? There was a bridge tournament going on. She had just gotten a call. A couple had canceled and wanted to know if the Thornhills could take their place.

"Actually," he said, "I'm very much engaged in a game of chess." His wife looked around the empty room. "Oh, it's long-distance, dear," Thornhill explained, nodding at his desktop computer. "You know the things one can do with technology these days. You can do battle and never even see your opponent."

"Well, don't stay up too late," she said. "You've

been working very hard and you're not a young man anymore."

"I see light at the end of the tunnel," Thornhill replied. And this time he was telling the absolute truth.

FORTY-EIGHT

Reynolds and Connie reached Duck, North Carolina, around one in the morning after only a single stop for fuel and food and reached Pine Island a short while later. The streets were dark, the businesses closed. They were fortunate in finding an all-night gas station, however. While Reynolds got two coffees and some pastries, Connie found out from the clerk on duty where the airplane runway was located. They sat in the gas station lot, ate, and mulled things over.

"I checked in at WFO," Connie told Reynolds as he stirred sugar into his coffee. "Interesting twist. Buchanan's disappeared."

She swallowed a bite of her pastry and stared at him. "How the hell did that happen?"

"Nobody knows. That's why so many people are catching grief over it."

"Well, at least they can't blame that one on us."

"Don't be too sure of that. Laying blame is a fine art in D.C., and the Bureau ain't no exception."

Reynolds had a sudden thought. "Connie, do you think Buchanan could be trying to rendezvous with Lockhart? That may be why he disappeared."

"If we could nail them both at the same time, you might get appointed director."

Reynolds smiled. "I'll settle for having my suspension lifted. But Buchanan might be on his way here. What time did they say they lost the tail?"

"Late this afternoon."

"Then he could already be here, if he took a plane."

Connie sipped his coffee, while he thought this over. "Why would Buchanan and Lockhart be doing anything together?" he asked slowly.

"Don't forget, if we're right about Buchanan hiring Adams, then maybe Adams called Buchanan and they hooked up that way."

"*If* Adams is innocent in all this. But he sure as hell wouldn't call Buchanan if he thought the guy had anything to do with trying to knock off Lockhart. After all we've found out, I'm gauging the guy as her protector, of sorts."

"I think you're right about that. But maybe Adams found out something that made him believe Buchanan didn't order the hit. If that was the case, he might try to team with Buchanan to figure out together what the hell was going on and who else was out there trying to kill Lockhart."

"Somebody else behind this? One of the foreign governments Buchanan was working with, maybe? If the truth came out, they'd be sitting out there with world-class egg on their face. That's plenty of incentive to kill somebody," Connie said.

"I wonder," Reynolds began, as Connie watched her closely. "There's just been something about this case that's never added up," she said. "We've got somebody impersonating FBI agents. Somebody who seems to know our every move."

"Ken Newman?"

"Maybe. But that doesn't seem to make sense either. Ken's had cash coming in for a long time. Has he been somebody's mole for that long a period of time? Or is it somebody else?"

"And don't forget about whoever's trying to frame you. Moving money around accounts like that takes some expertise."

"Exactly. But I just don't see operatives of a

foreign government being able to do all that, and no one the wiser."

"Brooke, countries conduct industrial espionage against us every day. Shit, our staunchest allies even do it, ripping off our technology because they're not smart enough to do it on their own. And our borders are so open it doesn't take much to get in. You know that."

Reynolds let out a deep sigh as she stared into the darkness lying right outside the gas station's harsh ring of lights. "I suppose you're right. I guess instead of trying to figure out who's behind this, we should try to find Lockhart and company and just ask them."

"Now, that's a plan I can relate to." Connie put the car in gear and they sped off into the darkness.

After locating the runway, Reynolds and Connie cruised the dark streets looking for the Honda Gold Wing. Virtually all of the beach houses appeared vacant now, which made their search both easier and more difficult. It cut down the number of places they had to focus on, but it also made the agents stand out more.

Connie finally spotted the Honda in the carport of one of the beach houses. Reynolds eased out of the car and got a close enough look to confirm that the license tag matched the bike Lee Adams had borrowed from his brother's shop. Then they drove to the other end of the street, hit the lights and talked it over.

"Maybe it's as simple as me going in the front and you going in the back," Reynolds said as she studied the dark house. Her skin was tingling with the thought that a bare fifty feet away were two or possibly the three key people in this whole investigation.

Connie shook his head. "I don't like that. The Honda being there means Adams is in there too."

"We've got his gun."

"A guy like that, first thing he would've done is get another one. And we go in, even if we surprise him, he knows the lay of the land better than we do. He might get one of us." He added, "And you don't even have a gun, so we're not splitting up."

"You're the one who said you thought Adams wasn't a bad guy."

"Thinking something and being absolutely certain of it are two different things. And that difference is not something I'm willing to risk anybody's life over. And rushing in on anybody, good or bad, in the middle of the night, mistakes can happen. I intend on getting you back to your kids in one piece. And I wouldn't mind doing the same."

"So how do we play it? Wait for daylight and call in reinforcements?"

"Calling in the locals will probably mean every TV station down here will be on the block an hour after we do. That won't earn us many points at HQ."

"Well, I guess we can wait for them to ride off on the Honda and then pull them."

"Other things being equal, I'm inclined to watch the place and see what happens. If they come out, we move in. If we get real lucky, Lockhart will surface without Adams and we can take her. After that, I'm figuring we can bait Adams out pretty easy."

"And if they don't come out, together or singly?"

"Then we'll cross that bridge when we come to it."

"I don't want to lose them again, Connie."

"It's not like they can just take off down the beach or swim to England. Adams went to a lot of trouble to get those wheels. He's not going to abandon the bike because he doesn't have another way to replace it. Where he goes, that Honda goes. And that Honda ain't going anywhere without us seeing it."

They settled down and waited.

FORTY-NINE

His pistol resting on his belly, Lee had spent a few fitful hours on the couch downstairs. Every few minutes he thought he heard someone breaking in, and each time it proved to be nothing more than his very tired imagination doing its best to drive him crazy. Since he couldn't sleep, he had finally decided to get ready to leave for Charlottesville. He grabbed a quick shower and changed his clothes. He was packing his bag when a soft knock came on his door.

Faith was dressed in a long white robe; her puffy cheeks and tired-looking eyes were stark testaments to her inability to sleep.

"Where's Buchanan?" he asked.

"Actually dozing, I think. I never came close."

"Tell me about it." He finished packing and closed his bag.

"Are you sure you don't want me to come with you?" she asked.

He shook his head. "I don't want you anywhere near this guy and his goons if they show up. I got through to Renee last night. First time I've talked to her in I don't know how long and I have to tell her she might be the target of some psycho because of something her stupid dad did."

"How did she take it?"

On this Lee brightened. "Actually, she seemed happy to hear from me. I didn't tell her everything that was going on. I didn't want to panic her, but I think she's looking forward to seeing me."

"I'm glad to hear that. I'm really happy for you, Lee."

"The cops at least took my call seriously. Renee said a patrolman came by and a marked car's been cruising the area."

He put his bag down, took her hand. "I don't feel good about leaving you."

"It's your daughter. We'll be fine. You heard Danny. He's got this person over a barrel."

Lee looked unconvinced. "The last thing you should do right now is let down your guard. The car will be here at eight to take you and Buchanan to the plane. You head back to D.C."

"And then what?"

"Go to a motel in the suburbs. Register under a false name and then call me on my cell phone. As soon as things are okay with Renee I'll head back. I already talked it over with Buchanan. He's in agreement."

"And then?" Faith persisted.

"Let's just take it a step at a time. I told you there are no guarantees in this."

"I was actually talking about *us*."

Lee played with the strap on his bag. "Oh," was all that came out, and it sounded idiotic.

"I see."

"You see what?" Lee demanded.

"Wham, bam, thank you, ma'am."

"Where do you get off thinking like that? Don't you know what kind of a man I am by now?"

"Actually, I thought I did. But I guess I forgot. You're in the loner group: sex only for fun. Right?"

"Why are we doing this? Like we don't have enough going on. We can talk about it later. It's not like I'm not coming back."

Lee didn't mean to put her off, but – hell, why

couldn't she see there was no time for this right now?

Faith sat down on the bed.

"Like you said, no guarantees," she said.

He put a hand on her shoulder. "I am coming back, Faith. I didn't come this far to desert you now."

"Okay," was all she said. She stood, wiped her face and gave him a quick hug. "Please, please, be careful."

Faith let him out the rear door. As she turned to go back in, Lee's gaze was riveted on her. He took in everything, from the bare feet to the short dark hair and all points in between. For one troubling moment, he wondered if this was the last time he would ever see her.

Lee climbed on the Honda and quickly started up the bike.

As Lee roared out the driveway and hit the street, Brooke Reynolds raced back to the Crown Vic and threw open the door. Breathless, she looked inside.

"Shit, I knew the minute I left the car to get a closer look at the house this would happen. He must have come out a rear door. He didn't even turn on the carport light. I never saw him until the bike cranked up. So what do we do? House or the bike?"

Connie looked down the road. "Adams is already out of sight. And that bike is a lot more agile than this tank."

"I guess that leaves the house and Lockhart."

Connie suddenly looked worried. "We're presuming she's still inside. In fact, we don't even know if she was ever inside."

"Shit, I knew you were going to say that. She damn well better be. If we just let Adams go and Lockhart isn't in that house, *I* will swim to England. And you're going to have to be right beside me.

Come on, Connie, we have to go in the house."

Connie climbed out of the car, pulled his gun and looked around nervously. "Shit, I don't like this. It could be a setup. We could be walking right into an ambush. And we've got no backup."

"We don't have much choice, do we?"

"All right, but dammit, stay behind me."

They headed for the house.

FIFTY

Dressed in black sweats and tennis shoes, the three men raced along the beach, keeping low to the sand. Although the dawn was fast approaching, they were virtually invisible in their dark clothing against the backdrop of the ocean, and the pounding surf covered all sounds of their movements.

They had arrived in the area barely an hour ago and had just received some very disturbing news. Lee Adams had left the house. Lockhart wasn't with him. She must still be in the house. Or at least they hoped she was. Buchanan, they had been told, might be there as well. They would take those two over Adams. He could wait. They would eventually get him. In fact, they would not stop until they got him.

Each team member was equipped with an automatic pistol and a knife specially designed to take out the carotid in one efficient stroke. Each man was well skilled in exactly how to execute just such a lethal blow. Their orders were clear. Everyone in the house had to die. Perfectly executed, it could be a clean operation. They could be back in Washington by late morning.

They were proud men, professionals in their own right and long in the service of Robert Thornhill. As a team they had survived some dangerous times in the last twenty years with their wit, skill, physical strength and stamina. They had saved lives, made certain parts of the world safer, helped to ensure that the United States would become the world's sole remaining superpower. This would mean a fairer, more just world for many. Like Robert Thornhill, they had joined the Agency to perform a service, to engage in a public trust. To them, there was no higher calling.

All three men were also part of the group Lee and Faith had eluded at Adams's apartment. The episode had embarrassed them, tarnishing their reputation for near perfection. They had been hoping for a shot at redemption, and now they did not intend to waste it.

One man stayed near the top of the stairs to keep watch, while the other two hurried down the boardwalk to the rear of the house. The plan was simple, direct, unencumbered by layers of detail. They would hit the house hard and fast, starting on the ground floor and moving up. When they ran into anyone, they wouldn't ask questions or seek identification. Their suppressor-equipped pistols would fire one time for each victim, and then they would move on until every living thing in the house no longer was. Yes, it was definitely conceivable they could be back in Washington before lunch.

FIFTY-ONE

Lee slowed down the Honda and then stopped in the middle of the road, his feet coming down lightly on the asphalt. He looked back over his shoulder. The street was long, black and empty. The dawn would be coming soon, though. He could see it in the softening edges of the sky, like the streaked edges of a Polaroid slowly lapping to vibrancy.

So why couldn't he have waited? He could have waited until the car came to take Faith and Buchanan to the airstrip. It would only delay his trip to Charlottesville by a couple of hours at most. And it would certainly increase his peace of mind. Why the hell was he running away so fast? Renee was protected. What about Faith?

His gloved hand tapped against the Honda's throttle. It would also give him a chance to talk to the woman, to let Faith know that he cared very much for her.

He turned the Honda around and headed back. When he reached the street, he slowed the bike. The car was parked at the far end of the street. It was a big sedan that just screamed federal government. True, it was at the opposite end of the street and he wouldn't have passed it heading to the main road, but how the hell had his "expert" eyes missed that? God, was he really getting that old?

He drove directly at the car, figuring that if it was the Feds, he could cut off easily enough and lose them. As he drew closer, however, it was clear the car was empty. Starting to panic, he swung the Honda around, drove up into the driveway of the beach house two lots down from Faith's and jumped off. Throwing down his helmet and pulling his pistol, Lee raced around to the rear courtyard of the house and then on to the boardwalk that criss-crossed the rear common areas connecting all the houses to the main steps going to the beach, like human veins leading to the heart's arteries. His own heart was pumping at a feverishly high pace.

He jumped off the boardwalk, squatted low behind some sawgrass and peered at the back of Faith's beach house. What he saw chilled him to the bone. The two men were dressed all in black and were sliding over the rear wall of Faith's courtyard. Were they the Feds? Or were they the men who had been prepared to assassinate Faith at the airport? *Please, God, don't let it be them.* The two men had already disappeared over the wall. In seconds they would be in the house. Had Faith reset the alarm system after she let him out? No, he thought, she probably hadn't.

Lee jumped up and dashed toward the house. As he crossed the boardwalk, he sensed something coming at him from the left as the darkness began to lift even more. That sensation was probably the only thing that saved his life.

The knife plunged into his arm instead of his neck as he ducked and rolled. He came up bleeding, but the rigid material of the bike suit had absorbed a good deal of the blow. His attacker didn't hesitate but leaped straight at him.

However, Lee timed it just right, managed to raise his good arm, pushed hard, levered the man over him, throwing him into the sawgrass, which was about as unpleasant as having a sharp knife driven into your flesh. Lee lunged for his gun, which he had lost when the guy had slammed into him. Lee had no qualms about shooting the guy down and raising a ruckus. Right now he would welcome any assistance the local police cared to provide.

His opponent made a stunning recovery, however, bursting out of the sawgrass with startling velocity and colliding with Lee before he could retrieve his pistol. The two men landed at the edge of the steps. Lee saw the knife thrust coming again but was able to grip the man's wrist before the blade hit him. The guy was strong; Lee could feel the steely tendons in the man's forearm and in the rocklike triceps as he grabbed the man's upper arm in an attempt to force the knife out of his hand. But Lee wasn't exactly a weakling either. He hadn't shoved tons of barbells around for years for nothing.

The guy he was battling was an experienced fighter as well because he had managed to get in two or three efficient gut punches with his free hand. After the first one, though, Lee tightened his abdominals and obliques and felt little pain from the other jabs. He had spent over two decades doing stomach crunches and having medicine balls slammed into his belly. After that punishment, the human fist offered very little difficulty for him, no matter how hard it was thrown.

Thinking that two could play at that game, Lee let go of the man's upper arm and landed a body uppercut to the diaphragm. He felt the wind go out of the guy, but the grip on the knife remained unbroken. Then Lee landed three successful kidney punches, about the most painful ones you could throw and still leave your opponent conscious. The knife fell from the man's hand, clattering down the steps.

Then both men rose to their feet, breathing hard, still clinging one to the other. Like a burst of wind, the man executed a nifty loopkick that knocked Lee's legs from under him. He went down with a grunt but popped right back up when he saw the guy go for his pistol. Being seconds from death gave Lee's body resiliency he could never summon in less dangerous times. He hit the guy low and hard, linebacker to running back in a textbook impact, and they both went over the edge of the steps, bouncing painfully down each pressure-treated plank and landing in a pile of twisted arms, legs and torsos in the sand and then eating mouthfuls of salty water as they rolled into the water, the rising tide being almost up to the steps.

Lee had seen the pistol tumble away during the fall, so he kicked himself free and stood in ankle-deep water. The guy rose too, but not as swiftly. Lee, however, was tightly on guard. The guy knew karate; Lee had felt it in the kick at the top of the stairs; he was seeing it in the defensive posture the man now assumed, making himself into a little ball, leaving no angles, nothing of much width to hit. His brain working faster than conscious thought, Lee figured he had about four inches and fifty pounds on the guy, but if the man nailed him with a lethal foot to the head, Lee would go down. And then he and Faith and Buchanan were all dead. But if he didn't finish the guy within the next minute, Faith and Buchanan would be dead anyway.

The man aimed a crushing side kick to Lee's torso; however, his having to slosh through water to deliver the kick gave Lee the little extra time he needed. Lee had to get in close, grab what he could and not give Chuck Norris Jr. enough space to do his martial arts magic. Lee was a boxer; in-close fighting, where whipping legs couldn't do much damage, was where he could be absolutely devastating. Lee braced himself and absorbed the rib-rattling leg shot to the body but then held on to the limb with his bloodied arm, clinching it to his side in a viselike grip. With his free hand, he landed a cartilage-shattering blow to the guy's knee, driving it backward to a degree knees were not designed to go. The man screamed. Then Lee delivered a crunching straight jab to the guy's face, feeling the nose flatten under the impact. Finally, in a flash of almost choreographed movement, Lee dropped the leg, curled low and then erupted out of that position with a cannonball left hook that carried all two hundred and twenty pounds of his bulk plus whatever multiplying factor pure fury brought to the table. When his fist hit facial bone, which promptly yielded under the terrible impact, Lee knew he had won. Nobody short of a professional heavyweight had a jaw that hard.

The man went down as though shot through the head. Lee instantly flipped him on his stomach and pushed his head under the water. He didn't have time to actually drown the guy, so he brought his elbow down with all his might dead center on the back of the man's neck. The resulting sound was unmistakable, even with the water lapping all over them, as though God wanted Lee to damn well know what he'd done, and didn't want him to ever forget it.

The body went limp and Lee rose over the dead man. Lee had been in more than his share of fights both in and out of the boxing ring, but he had never killed anyone before. As he looked down at the body, he knew it was nothing to be proud of. Lee was just grateful it wasn't him lying dead.

Sick to his stomach, suddenly feeling the full force of the pain in his wounded arm, Lee looked up the steps leading to the beach houses. He had only two other beasts to conquer and then he could call it a day. And it was clear they weren't the FBI. FBI agents didn't run around trying to kill people with fancy knives and karate kicks; they pulled their shield and guns and told you to stop right in your tracks. And if you were smart, you did.

No, they were the other guys. The CIA robokillers. He raced up the steps, found his pistol and hustled as fast as he could to the beach house, hoping with every labored breath that he was not too late.

FIFTY-TWO

Faith had changed into jeans and a sweatshirt and now sat on her bed staring at her bare feet. The sounds of the motorcycle had disappeared as though into an enormous vacuum. As she looked around the room, it was as though Lee Adams had never even been here, had never been real. She had spent so much time and energy trying to lose the man, and now that he was gone, all of her spirit seemed to have been swept into the void Lee had left behind.

At first she thought the sound she heard in the stillness of the house was Buchanan stirring. Then she thought it might actually be Lee returning. It had sounded like the back door. As she rose from the bed, it suddenly occurred to her that it couldn't be Lee because she hadn't heard the motorcycle pull into the carport; as this thought hit her, her heartbeat went through the roof.

Had she locked the door? She couldn't remember. She knew she hadn't set the alarm. Could it be just Danny stumbling around? For some reason Faith knew it wasn't.

She eased over to the doorway and peered out, her ears straining to hear any sound. She knew she hadn't imagined the noise. Someone had come in the house, she was sure of it. Someone was in the house right now. She looked down the hallway. There was another alarm control panel in the bedroom Lee had used. Could she reach it, activate the system, the motion detector? She dropped to her knees and crawled out into the hallway.

Connie and Reynolds had gone in the side door and made their way down the lower-floor hallway. Connie had his gun pointed ahead. Reynolds was behind him, feeling naked and useless without her own pistol. They eased open each door on the lower level and found each room empty.

"They must be upstairs," Reynolds whispered into Connie's ear.

"I hope there's somebody here," he whispered back, his voice carrying an ominous tone.

They both froze when a sound came from somewhere within the house. Connie motioned upstairs with his finger and Reynolds nodded in agreement. They approached the stairs and headed up. Fortunately, the stairs were carpeted and absorbed the sounds of their footsteps. They reached the first landing and paused, listening intently. Silence. They moved forward again.

The family area was empty, as far as they could see. They moved along one wall, their heads swiveling in near-synchronized motion.

Right above them, in the upstairs hallway, Faith was flat on her stomach on the floor. She peered over the edge and relaxed slightly as she saw that it was Agents Reynolds and Constantinople. When she saw the two other men moving up the stairs from the lower level, her fear instantly returned.

"Look out," Faith yelled.

Connie and Reynolds turned back to look at her and saw where she was pointing. Connie swung his gun in the direction of the two men, who also had their guns out, pointed directly at the two agents.

"FBI," Reynolds barked out to the men in black.

"Drop your weapons." Usually when she said that, she felt fairly confident of the response. Now, with two guns against one, she was not nearly as confident.

The two men didn't drop their weapons. They moved forward as Connie swung his gun back and forth between the two.

One of the men looked up at Faith. "Come down here, Ms. Lockhart."

"Stay up there, Faith," Reynolds called out, her gaze finding Faith's and holding on it. "Go to your room and lock the door."

"Faith?" Buchanan appeared in the hallway, his hair disheveled, his eyes blinking.

"You too, Buchanan. Now," the same man commanded. "Down here."

"No!" Reynolds said, moving forward. "Listen up, an HRT unit is on its way here right now. We're looking at an ETA of about two minutes. If you won't put your weapons down, then I suggest you run like hell unless you want to go up against those guys."

The man looked at her and smiled. "There's no HRT unit coming, Agent Reynolds."

Reynolds could not hide her astonishment. That astonishment immeasurably increased with the man's next words.

"Agent Constantinople," the man said, looking over at Connie, "you can leave now. We have it under control, but we appreciate your assistance."

Slowly, Reynolds turned and looked at her partner, her mouth open in absolute shock.

Connie stared back at her, both extreme discomfort and a profound sense of resignation on his features.

"Connie?" Reynolds took a quick breath. "It can't be, Connie. Please tell me it's not."

Connie fingered his pistol and he shrugged. Gradually his taut posture relaxed. "My plan was to get you out of this alive *and* get your suspension lifted." He looked over at the two men. One of them shook his head decisively.

"You're the leak?" Reynolds said. "Not Ken?"

"Ken was no leak," Connie said.

"But the money in the safe-deposit box?"

"That came from his card and coin trading. He operated all in cash. I actually did some shows with him. I knew. He was cheating the tax guys. So who the hell cared? More power to him. Most of it was going to college funds for his kids anyway."

"You let me think he was the leak."

"Well, I didn't want you to think it was me. Obviously, that would not have been good."

One of the men ran upstairs and disappeared into one of the bedrooms. A minute later he emerged carrying Buchanan's briefcase. He escorted Faith and Buchanan down the stairs. The man popped open the briefcase and took out the cassette. He played a little of the tape to confirm what was on it. Then he cracked open the cassette, pulled out the tape and threw the long strands into the gas fireplace and hit the remote switch. They all watched in silence as the tape was quickly reduced to a gooey mess.

As Reynolds watched the tape disappear, she couldn't help but think she was being shown the next few minutes of her life. The *last* few minutes of her life.

Reynolds looked at the two men and then at Connie. "So they just tailed us all the way down? I didn't see anybody," she said bitterly.

Connie shook his head. "There was a transmitter in my car. They've been listening in. They let us find the right house and then followed."

"Why, Connie? Why turn traitor?"

Connie's tone was reflective. "I put in twenty-five years at the Bureau. Twenty-five damn good years, and I'm still at square one, still a grunt in the field. I got a dozen years on you and you're my boss. Because I wouldn't play the political game south of the border. Because I wouldn't lie and just go along, they tanked my career." He shook his head and looked down. When he stared back up at her, he looked apologetic. "Understand, I got nothing against you, Brooke. Nothing. You're a damn fine agent. I didn't want it to end like this. The plan was for us to stay outside and let these guys do their thing. When I got the all-clear, we'd go in and find the bodies. Your name would be cleared, everything would work out fine. Adams taking off like that blew our plan apart." Connie stared with unfriendly eyes at the man in black who had identified him by name. "But if this guy hadn't said anything, maybe I still could have figured out a way for you to walk away with me."

The man shrugged. "Sorry, I didn't know that was important to you. But you'd better get going. It's getting light outside. Give us half an hour. Then you can call the cops. Make up any cover story you want."

Reynolds never took her eyes off Connie. "Let me make up a cover story for you, Connie. It goes like this: We found the house. I go in the front while you cover the rear. I don't come out. You hear shots, you go in. Find us all dead." Reynolds's voice broke as she thought of her children, of never seeing them again. "You see someone leaving, empty your pistol at him. But you miss, give chase, are almost killed, but luckily barely survive. You call the cops. They get here. You call HQ, fill them in. They send people down. You get bitched at a little for coming down here with me, but you were just standing by your boss. Loyalty. Who could really blame you? They investigate and never reach a satisfactory answer. Probably think I'm the leak for sure, came down for a payoff. You can tell them it was my idea to come here, that I knew exactly where to go. I go in the house, get popped. And you, a poor innocent dupe, almost lost your life too. Case closed. How's that sound, Agent Constantinople?" She almost spat this last part out.

One of Thornhill's men looked over at Connie and smiled. "Sounds good to me."

Connie never took his eyes off Reynolds. "I'm sorry, Brooke, I really am."

Reynolds's eyes filled with tears and her voice cracked again when she spoke. "Tell Anne Newman that. Tell *my* kids that, you bastard!"

His eyes downcast, Connie moved past them and started to head down the stairs.

"We'll do them here, one by one," the first man said.

He looked at Buchanan. "You first."

"I take it that was a special request from your boss," Buchanan said.

"Who? I want a name," Reynolds demanded.

"What does it matter?" the second man said. "It's not like you're going to be around to testify—"

The instant he said this, the bullet hit him in the back of the head and he went down instantly.

The other man whirled, trying to aim his gun, but was too late and took a blast right in the face. He dropped, dead, next to his partner.

Connie came back up the stairs, a wisp of smoke still trailing from his pistol's muzzle. He looked down at the two dead men. "That was for Ken Newman, you assholes." He looked up at Reynolds. "I didn't know they were going to kill Ken, Brooke. I swear that on a stack of Bibles. But after it happened, there was nothing I could do but bide my time and see what happened."

"And let me chase a wild goose? Watch me get suspended. My career ruined."

"There wasn't much I could do about that. Like I said, my intent was to get you out of this, get you reinstated. Let you be the hero. Let Ken take the charge as snitch. He was dead, what did it matter?"

"It would matter to his family, Connie."

Connie's features turned angry. "Look, I don't have to stand here and explain shit to you or anybody else. I'm not proud of what I did, but I had my reasons. You don't have to agree with them, and I'm not asking you to, but don't stand there and lecture me about something you know nothing about, lady. You want'a talk pain and bitterness? I got about fifteen years of it on you."

Reynolds blinked and stepped back, eyeing the pistol.

"Okay, Connie, you just saved our lives. That'll count for a lot."

"You think so, do you?"

She pulled out her cell phone. "I'm going to call Massey and get a team down here."

"Put the phone away, Brooke."

"Connie—"

"Put the damn phone down. Now!"

Reynolds let the phone drop to the floor. "Connie, it's over."

"It's never over, Brooke, you know that. Stuff that happened years ago will always come back to bite you in the ass. People find out stuff and look you up and suddenly your life is over."

"Is that why you're involved in this? Somebody was blackmailing you?"

He slowly gazed about. "What the hell does it matter?"

"It matters to me!" said Reynolds.

Connie let out a deep sigh. "When my wife got cancer, our insurance wouldn't cover all the specialized treatments. The doctors thought the treatments might give her a chance, a few more months. I mortgaged the house to the hilt. I cleaned out our bank accounts. It still wasn't enough. What was I supposed to do? Just let her die?" Connie angrily shook his head. "So some coke and other stuff turned up missing from the Bureau evidence room. Some people found out about it later. And suddenly I had a new employer." He paused and looked down for a moment. "And the most damnable thing is June died anyway."

"I can help you, Connie. You can end this right now."

Connie smiled grimly. "Nobody can help me, Brooke. I made my deal with the devil."

"Connie, let them go. It's over."

He shook his head. "I came here to do a job. And you know me well enough to know that I always finish what I start."

"Then what? How will you talk yourself out of these?" She looked at the two dead men. "And now you're going to kill three *more* people? That's crazy. Please."

"Not as crazy as giving up and spending the rest of my life in prison. Or maybe getting the chair." He shrugged his big shoulders. "I'll think of something."

"Please, Connie. Don't do this. You can't do this. I know you. You can't."

Connie looked at his pistol and then knelt down and picked up one of the dead men's guns that had a suppressor attached. "I've got to. And I am sorry, Brooke."

They all heard the click. Connie and Reynolds

instantly recognized it as the cock of a semi-automatic pistol.

Lee barked, "Drop the pistol. Now! Or I put a tunnel in your head."

Connie froze and let the gun fall to the floor.

Lee came up the stairs and put the muzzle of his pistol against the agent's head. "I'm real tempted to shoot you anyway, but you did save me the trouble of tangling with two more gorillas." Lee looked at Reynolds. "Agent Reynolds, I'd appreciate if you'd pick up the pistol and keep it trained on your boy here."

Reynolds did so, her eyes burning into her partner's. "Sit down, Connie. Now!" she ordered.

Lee went over and put his arms around Faith.

"Lee," was all she said, leaning into him.

"Thank God I decided to come back."

"Can someone tell me what the hell this is all about?" Reynolds said.

Buchanan stepped forward. "I can, but it may not do any good. The proof I had was on that tape. I was planning on making copies, but I didn't have the chance to before I left Washington."

Reynolds looked down at Connie. "You obviously know what's going on. If you cooperate, it'll help your sentencing."

"I might as well strap myself in the chair," Connie said.

"Who? Dammit, who is behind this that everybody's so scared to death of?"

"Agent Reynolds," Buchanan said, "I'm sure that particular gentleman is waiting to hear the outcome of all this. If he doesn't get it soon, he'll send out more men. I suggest we stop that from happening."

Reynolds looked at him. "Why should I trust you? What I should do is call the cops."

Faith said, "The night Agent Newman was killed,

I told him I wanted Danny to come in and testify with me. Newman told me that would never happen."

"Well, he told you right."

"But I think if you know all the facts, you won't think that way. What we did was wrong, but there was *no other way*. . . ."

"Well, that makes it all perfectly clear," Reynolds replied.

"That can wait," Buchanan said with urgency. "Right now we have to take care of the man behind these people." He looked down at the dead men.

"You can add one more to that count," Lee said. "He's outside taking a dip in the ocean."

Reynolds looked exasperated. "Everybody except for me seems to know everything." She turned to Buchanan with a scowl. "Okay, I'm listening. What's your suggestion?"

Buchanan started to answer when they all heard the sound of a plane coming in. Their eyes went to the window, where the dawn had broken.

"It's just the commuter service. It's daylight. First flight in. The runway's across the street," Faith explained.

"That I *do* know," Reynolds said.

"I suggest we use your friend there," Buchanan said, nodding at Connie, "to communicate with this person."

"And tell him what?"

"That his operation was a total success, except that his men were killed in the ensuing battle. He'll understand that, of course. Losses happen. But that Faith and I were killed and the tape was destroyed. That way he'll feel safe."

"And me?" Lee said.

Buchanan glanced at him. "We'll let you be our wild card."

"And why exactly should I do that?" Reynolds wanted to know. "When I could take you and Faith, and him" – she flicked her pistol at Connie – "to the WFO, get my job back and walk away a hero."

"Because if you do that, the man who has caused all of this will go free. Free to do something like this again."

Reynolds looked confused and troubled.

Buchanan watched her closely. "It's up to you."

Reynolds looked at each of them and then her gaze came to rest on Lee. She noted the blood on his sleeve, the cuts and bruises on his face.

"You saved all of our lives. You're probably the most innocent person in this room. What do you think?"

Lee looked at Faith and then at Buchanan before coming back to Reynolds. "I don't think I can give you a great reason to do it, but if you want my gut, I'd say to go along with them."

Reynolds sighed and looked over at Connie. "You have a way of contacting this monster?" Connie said nothing. "Connie, you work with us on this, it'll help you. I know you were just prepared to kill all of us, and I shouldn't give a damn about what happens to you." She paused and looked down for a moment. "But I do. Last chance, Connie, what do you say?"

Connie's big hands clenched and unclenched nervously. He looked at Buchanan. "What exactly do you want me to say?"

Buchanan told him precisely, and Connie sat down on the couch, picked up the phone and dialed. When the line was answered, he said, "This is . . ." – Connie looked embarrassed for a moment – "this is Ace-in-the-Hole." Ten minutes later Connie put down the phone and looked at each of them. "Okay, it's done."

"Did he seem to buy it?" Lee asked.

"Yes, but you can never be sure with these guys."

"Good, enough; that gives us some time," Buchanan said.

"Well, right now we have some things to tend to," Reynolds said. "Like a number of dead bodies. And I've got to report in. And get you" – she looked at Connie – "into a cell."

Connie glared at her. "So much for loyalty," he said.

She glared back. "You made your choices. What you did for us *will* help you. But you're going to be in prison a long time, Connie. At least you get to live. That's more of a choice than Ken had."

She looked at Buchanan. "Now what?"

"I suggest we leave here immediately. Once we're out of the area, you can call the police. When we get back to Washington, Faith and I will meet with the FBI, tell them what we know. We must keep everything completely secret. If he knows we're working with the FBI, we'll never get the proof we need."

"This guy had Ken killed?"

"Yes."

"Is he with a foreign interest?"

"Actually, you both have the same employer."

Reynolds looked at him, stunned. "Uncle Sam?" she said slowly.

Buchanan nodded. "If you trust me, I will do my best to bring him to you. I have my own personal score to settle with him."

"And what exactly do you expect in return?"

"For me? Nothing. If I go to prison, I go to prison. But Faith goes free. Unless you can guarantee me that, you can just call the police right now."

Faith grabbed his arm. "Danny, you're not taking the fall for this."

"Why not? It was my doing."

"But your reasons—"

"Reasons are no defense. I knew I was taking a chance when I broke the law."

"Well, so did I, dammit!"

Buchanan turned back to Reynolds. "Do we have a deal? Faith does not go to prison."

"I'm really not in a position to offer you anything." She pondered the issue for a moment. "But I can promise you this: If you are shooting straight with me, I'll do everything in my power to see that Faith goes free."

Connie stood up, suddenly looking pale. "Brooke, I need to hit the john, like quick." He was wobbly on his feet; one hand slid to his chest.

She glanced at him suspiciously. "What's the matter?" She scrutinized his pallid features. "Are you all right?"

"To tell the truth, I've been better," he mumbled, his head rolling to one side, his left side drooping.

"I'll go with him," Lee said.

As the pair started to the stairs, Connie seemed to lose his balance and he pressed his hand hard against the center of his chest, his face contorted in pain. "Shit. Oh, God!" He dropped to one knee, moaning, saliva dripping out of his mouth; he started gurgling.

"Connie!" Reynolds started toward him.

"He's having a heart attack," Faith cried out.

"Connie!" Reynolds said again as she stared at her stricken partner, who was fast sinking to the floor, his body twitching uncontrollably.

The movement was fast. It seemed too fast for a man in his fifties, but then again, desperation could mix with adrenaline in a flash.

Connie's hand dipped to his ankle. A compact pistol was in a holster there. The gun was out and aimed before anyone could react. Connie had multiple targets, but he chose Danny Buchanan and fired.

The only one who reacted as fast as Connie did was Faith Lockhart.

From where she was standing next to Buchanan, she saw the pistol come out before anyone else. She saw the barrel pointed at her friend. In her mind she could hear the explosion that would launch the bullet that would kill Buchanan. How she moved that fast was inexplicable.

The bullet hit Faith in the chest; she gasped once and then dropped at Buchanan's feet.

"Faith!" Lee screamed. Instead of tackling Connie, he lunged for her.

Reynolds's gun was trained on Connie. As he swung the pistol around in her direction, the image of the palm reader flashed through her mind. That all-too-short life line. MOTHER OF TWO, FEDERAL AGENT DEAD. She saw the headline fully and boldly in her mind. The whole thing was almost paralyzing. Almost.

She and Connie locked gazes. He was bringing up his pistol, lining it up with her. He would pull the trigger, she had no doubt. He clearly had the nerve, the balls to kill. Did she? Her finger tightened on her own trigger as the entire world seemed to slow to the pace of an underwater world, where gravity was either suspended or magnified. Her partner. An FBI agent. A traitor. Her children. Her own life. Now or never.

Reynolds pulled the trigger once and then a second time. The recoil was short, her aim perfect. As the bullets entered Connie's body, his bulk quivered, his mind perhaps still sending messages, not yet realizing that it was dead.

Reynolds thought she saw Connie stare searchingly at her as he started to go down, the gun falling from his hand. That image would haunt her forever. Only when Agent Howard Constantinople hit the floor and didn't move again did Brooke Reynolds take a breath.

"Faith, Faith!" Lee was tearing at her shirt, exposing the horribly bloody wound in her chest. "Omigod. Faith." She was unconscious, her breathing barely detectable.

Buchanan stared down in blank horror.

Reynolds knelt beside Lee. "How bad?"

Lee looked up in anguish. He couldn't speak.

Reynolds assessed the wound. "Bad," she said. "Slug's still in her. The hole's right near her heart."

Lee looked at Faith. Her skin was already beginning to pale. He could feel the warmth of life spilling out from her with each shallow breath she took. "Oh, God. No. Please!" he cried out.

"We've got to get her to a hospital. Fast," Reynolds said. She had no idea where the closest hospital was, let alone a trauma center, which was what Faith really needed. And searching the local area by car would be akin to signing the woman's death warrant. She could call the paramedics, but who knew how long it would take for them to get here? The roar of the plane engine outside made Reynolds glance at the window. The plan formed in her head within seconds. She raced back to Connie and lifted his FBI credentials from his body. For one brief moment she gazed at her former colleague. She shouldn't feel bad for what she had done. He had been well prepared to kill her. So why did she feel crushed by remorse? But Connie was dead. Faith Lockhart wasn't. At least not yet. Reynolds hustled back over to where Faith lay. "Lee, we're taking the plane. Hurry!"

The group raced outside, Reynolds in the lead. They could hear the plane's engines revving up as it prepared to take off. Reynolds sprinted ahead, tore her way through the hedge and found herself on the runway. She looked down at the opposite end. The plane was turning, getting ready to roar down the tarmac, lift into the air; their only hope would be gone in seconds. She ran down the asphalt, directly at the aircraft, waving the pistol, the badge, screaming, "FBI!" at the top of her lungs. The plane came racing at her, as Buchanan, holding clear an opening in the hedge, helped Lee carry Faith through. They burst on to the runway.

The pilot finally focused on the woman waving a pistol and coming at him. He pulled back on the throttle and the aircraft stopped its roll, the engines whined down.

Reynolds reached the plane, held up the badge and the pilot slid open his window.

"FBI," she said hoarsely. "I have a badly wounded person. I need your aircraft. You're going to fly us to the nearest hospital. Now."

The pilot looked at the badge, the gun and nodded dumbly. "Okay."

They all climbed on the plane, Lee cradling Faith against his chest. The pilot turned the aircraft around again, went back to the end of the runway and started his takeoff roll once more. A minute later the plane lifted into the air and rushed toward the embrace of the quickly lightening sky.

FIFTY-THREE

The pilot radioed ahead and a life-support ambulance was waiting on the tarmac at the airstrip in Manteo, which was thankfully only a few minutes of flight time away. Reynolds and Lee had used some bandages from the first-aid kit on the plane to try to stop the bleeding, and Lee had given Faith oxygen from the small canister on board, but none of it seemed to have any effect. She had not yet regained consciousness; they could barely get a pulse now. Her limbs were beginning to grow cold, even as Lee clung to her, tried to give her heat from his own body, as though that would do any good.

Lee rode in the ambulance with Faith over to Beach Medical Center, which had an emergency and trauma center. Reynolds and Buchanan were driven there in a car. On the way to the hospital, Reynolds called Fred Massey in Washington. She told him just enough that he was already running to catch a Bureau plane. Just him, Reynolds had insisted; no one else could come. Massey had accepted this condition without comment. Perhaps it had been the tone of her voice, or simply the stunning content of her very few words.

Faith was immediately taken to the emergency room, where doctors labored over her for almost two hours, trying to get her vitals up, her heart regulated, the internal bleeding stopped. None of it looked good. Once, the crash cart even had to be called.

Through the doors Lee had watched in the

numbest horror as Faith repeatedly jerked under the impact of the electrical current surging through the paddles. Only when he saw the heart monitor go from flat line to its regular peaks and valleys did he find he could even move.

Barely two hours later they had to cut her chest open, spread her ribs wide and massage her heart to get it going. Every hour seemed to bring a new crisis as she barely clung to life.

Lee paced the floor incessantly, hands shoved in his pockets, head down, talking to no one. He had said every prayer he could remember. He had made up some new ones. He was helpless to do anything for the woman, and that's what tore at him. How could he have let this happen? How could Connie, that old, bulky sonofabitch, have gotten that shot off? And him right beside the guy? And Faith, why had she taken the round? Why? Buchanan should be the guy lying on that gurney with people swarming over him, trying desperately to push life back into his wrecked body.

Lee slumped against the wall and slid down to the floor, covering his face with both hands as his big body shook.

In a private room, Reynolds waited with Buchanan, who had barely spoken a word since Faith had been shot. He just sat there and stared at the wall. To look at Buchanan, no one would have guessed that anger was building in him: the absolute hatred he was holding for Robert Thornhill, a man who had destroyed everything he had cared about.

About the time Fred Massey arrived, Faith was taken to the ICU. She was stabilized for the time being, the doctor told them. The bullet was one of those vicious dum-dums, he said. It had tumbled through her body like a runaway bowling ball, doing considerable damage to organs, and the internal hemorrhaging had been severe. She was strong and for now she was alive. She had a chance, that was all, he cautioned. They would know more soon.

As the doctor walked away, Reynolds put a hand on Lee's shoulder and handed him a fresh cup of coffee.

"Lee, if she survived until now, I have to believe she's going to make it."

"No guarantees," he mumbled to himself, unable to look at the woman.

They went to the private room, where Reynolds introduced Buchanan and Lee to Fred Massey.

"I think Mr. Buchanan should start telling you his story," Reynolds said to Massey.

"And he's willing to do that?" Massey asked skeptically.

At this Buchanan perked up. "Something more than willing. But before I do, tell me one thing. What's more important to you? What I did, or arresting the person who killed your agent?"

Massey leaned forward. "I'm not sure I'm prepared to discuss any sort of deal with you."

Buchanan put his elbows on the table. "When I tell you my story, you will be. But I'll do so on only one condition. You let me deal with this man. In my own way."

"Agent Reynolds informed me this person works for the federal government."

"That's right."

"Well, that's pretty damn unbelievable. Do you have proof?"

"You let me do this my way, and you'll have your proof."

Massey looked over at Reynolds. "The bodies at

the house. Do we know who they are yet?"

She shook her head. "I just checked in. The police and agents from D.C., Raleigh and Norfolk are on the scene. But it's too early yet to have that info. But everything's on the QT. The locals have been told nothing. We're controlling all flows of information. You won't see anything on the news about the bodies or about Faith being alive and in this hospital."

Massey nodded. "Good work." As though suddenly remembering something, he opened his briefcase, pulled out two objects and handed them to her.

Reynolds looked down at her pistol and creds.

"I'm sorry any of this happened, Brooke," Massey said. "I should have trusted you and I didn't. Maybe I've been out of the field too damn long. Pushing too many papers and not listening to my instincts anymore."

Reynolds holstered her gun and put the creds in her purse. She once more felt complete. "Maybe I wouldn't have either, in your position. But it's in the past, Fred, let's move on. We don't have much time."

"Rest assured, Mr. Massey," Buchanan said, "you'll never identify those men. Or if you do, they'll have no ties to the person I'm talking about."

"How can you be so sure of that?" Massey demanded.

"Trust me, I know how this man operates."

"Look, why don't you just tell me who it is and I'll handle it from there?"

"No," Buchanan said firmly.

"What do you mean no? We're the FBI, mister, we do this for a living. If you want any sort of deal—"

"You will listen to me." Buchanan hardly raised his voice, but his eyes bored into Massey with such overwhelming force that the ADIC lost his train of thought and fell silent. "We have one chance to bring him in. One! He's already infiltrated the FBI. Constantinople may not be the only mole. There may be others."

"I highly doubt that—" Massey began.

Now Buchanan raised his voice. "Can you guarantee me that there aren't? Can you?"

Massey sat back, looking uncomfortable. He glanced at Reynolds, who shrugged.

"If they could turn Connie, they could turn anybody," she said.

Massey looked miserable, shaking his head slowly. "Connie . . . I still can't believe it."

Buchanan tapped the tabletop. "And if there is another spy in your ranks and you try to trap this man on your own, you will absolutely fail. And your chance will be gone. Forever. Do you really want to risk that?"

Massey rubbed his smooth chin, thinking it over. When he looked up at Buchanan, his expression was wary but interested.

"Do you really think you can nail this guy?"

"I'm prepared to die trying. And I need to work the phones. Call in some very special help." Buchanan smiled to himself. A lobbyist to the very end. He turned to Lee. "And I need your help, Lee. If you're willing."

Lee looked surprised. "Me? What can I do to help anybody?"

"I spoke with Faith about you last night. She told me about your 'special' abilities. She said you were a good man to have in a bad situation."

"I guess she was wrong about that. Otherwise she wouldn't be lying up there with a hole in her chest."

Buchanan put a hand on Lee's arm. "I can barely function with the guilt I have, for her having stepped in front of that bullet. But I can't change that now.

What I can do is try to make sure she didn't risk her life for nothing. There's great danger for you. Even if we get this man, he has many at his back. There'll always be some out there."

Buchanan settled back in his chair and watched Lee closely. Massey and Reynolds stared at the PI too. Lee's muscular arms and broad shoulders were in stark contrast to the fragility of the look deep within his eyes.

Lee Adams took a deep breath. What he really wanted to do was stand next to Faith's bed and never leave until she woke up, saw him, smiled, said she'd be okay. And then, so would he. But, Lee knew, one rarely got what one wished for in this life. So instead, he looked at Buchanan and said, "I guess I'm your man."

FIFTY-FOUR

The black sedan pulled up to the front of the house. Robert Thornhill and his wife, dressed in formal evening clothes, came out the front door. Thornhill locked the house, then the two got in the car and were driven away. The Thornhills were attending an official dinner at the White House.

The sedan passed the phone-line control pedestal belonging to the community where the Thornhills lived. The metal box was large, bulky and painted light green. It had been placed there about two years ago when the phone company had upgraded the communications lines for this old neighborhood. The metal box had been a sudden eyesore in an area that prided itself on splendid homes and high-dollar landscaping. Thus, the residents had paid for a number of large bushes to be planted around the aboveground pedestal. These bushes now hid the box completely from the road, which meant that the telephone servicemen had to approach it from the rear side, which faced the woods. Aesthetically pleasing, the bushes were also very welcome to the man who had watched the sedan pass by and then had opened the box and begun delicately picking his way through its electronic guts.

Lee Adams identified the line going to the Thornhills' residence with a special piece of his own customized equipment. His background in communications hardware was serving him well. The Thornhills' home had a good security system.

However, every security system had an Achilles' heel: the phone line. Always the phone line. Thank you, Mr Bell.

Lee went through the steps in his head. When an intruder broke into someone's home, the alarm went off and the computer dialed the central monitoring station to inform them of the break-in. Then the security person at the monitoring station called the home to see if everything was okay. If the owner answered, he had to give his special code or else the police would be sent. If no one answered the phone, the police would be sent automatically.

Simply put, Lee was making sure that the home's computer would never reach the monitoring station, yet would let it think that it had. He was accomplishing this by building an in-line component or phone simulator. He had dropped the Thornhill home from the landline feed, effectively severing outside phone communication. Now he had to trick the alarm computer into thinking it had phone service. To do this, he installed the in-line component and threw the switch, effectively giving the Thornhills' home a dial tone and phone line that went absolutely nowhere.

He had also found out that the Thornhills' alarm system had no cellular backup, just the regular landline. That was a big hole. A cellular backup was incapable of being fooled, since it was a wireless system with no way for Lee to access its feed line. Virtually all alarm systems in the country had the very same backbone land- and data-lines. And, thus, they all had back doors in. Lee had just completed his.

He packed up his tools and made his way through the woods to the rear of the Thornhills' home. He located a window that was not visible from the street. He had a copy of the Thornhills' floor plan and alarm layout. It had been provided to him by Fred Massey. By accessing this window, he could reach the upstairs alarm panel without passing any motion detector points.

He pulled a stun gun from his backpack and held it flush against the window. The windows were all wired, even the second-floor ones, he knew. And both top and bottom window components had contacts. Most homes only had contacts at the bottom window casement; if that had been the case here, Lee would have simply picked the window lock and slid down the top window, without breaking any contacts.

He pulled the trigger on the stun gun and then moved it to another position on the window where he thought the contact elements were probably located. In all, he fired eight shots into the window frame from the stun gun. The electrical charge from the gun would melt the contacts, fusing them together and rendering them inoperable.

He picked the sash lock, held his breath and slid the window up. No alarm sounded. He quickly climbed through the window and closed it. Pulling a small flashlight from his pocket, he found the stairs and headed up. The Thornhills, he quickly observed, lived in extremely comfortable luxury. The furnishings were mostly antique; real oil paintings hung on the walls; and his feet melted into the thick and, he assumed, expensive carpet.

The alarm panel was where all such alarm panels were located; on the upper floor in the master bedroom. He unscrewed the plate and found the wire for the sound cannon. Two snips and the alarm system had suddenly developed laryngitis. Now he was free to roam. He went downstairs and passed in front of the motion detector, waving his arms in defiance, even giving it the finger, pretending it was

Thornhill there scowling at him, helpless to do anything about the intrusion. The red light came on and the alarm system was activated, although the system no longer could scream its warning. The computer would soon be dialing the central station, only its call would never get there. It would dial the number eight times, get no answer and then it would stop trying and go back to sleep. At the central station, everything would seem perfectly normal: a burglar's dream.

Lee watched as the red light on the motion detector disappeared. Each time he passed in front of it, though, it would go through the same routine, with the same result. Call eight times and then stop. Lee smiled. So far, so good. Before the Thornhills came home he would reattach the wires for the sound cannons: Thornhill would be suspicious if the normal beeping sound didn't occur when he opened the door. But for now, Lee had work to do.

FIFTY-FIVE

The White House dinner was very memorable for Mrs. Thornhill. Her husband, on the other hand, was working. He sat at the long table and made inconsequential conversation when called upon, but spent most of his time listening intently to the guests. There were a number of foreign visitors tonight, and Thornhill knew that good intelligence might come from unusual sources, even a White House dinner. Whether the foreign guests knew he was with the CIA, he wasn't sure. That was certainly not public knowledge. The guest list that would be printed in the *Washington Post* the next morning would identify them only as Mr. and Mrs. Robert Thornhill.

Ironically, the invitation to the dinner had not come because of Thornhill's position at the Agency. Who was invited to White House functions such as this, and why, were the greatest of mysteries in the capital city. However, the Thornhills' invitation had been extended because of his wife's well-known philanthropic work for the District of Columbia poor – a charitable endeavor in which the first lady herself was much involved as well. And Thornhill had to admit, his wife was dedicated to this cause. When she wasn't at the country club, of course.

The ride home was uneventful; the couple talked of mundane things while most of Thornhill's mind was focused on the phone call from Howard Constantinople. Losing his men had been a blow to

Thornhill, both personally and professionally. He had worked with them for years. How all three had been killed was beyond his comprehension. He had people down in North Carolina right now finding out as much as possible.

He had not heard anything further from Constantinople. Whether the man had run was unknown. But Faith and Buchanan were dead. And so was the other FBI agent, Reynolds. At least he was almost certain they were dead. The fact that no newspaper reports had come out regarding at least six dead bodies at a beach house in an affluent area in the Outer Banks was particularly troubling. It had been over a week, and nothing. It might be the Bureau's doing, covering up what was quickly building to a PR nightmare for them. Yes, he could see them doing that. Unfortunately, without Constantinople he had lost his eyes and ears at the Bureau. He would have to do something about that soon. It would take time to cultivate a new mole, yet nothing was impossible.

Well, the trail could never lead back to him. His three operatives had cover buried so deeply that the authorities would be incredibly fortunate if they managed to dig through even the surface layer. They would find nothing after that. Well, the three had died heroes. He and his colleagues had toasted their memory in the underground chamber upon learning of their deaths.

There was one more troubling loose end: Lee Adams. He had gone off on his motorcycle, presumably to Charlottesville to make sure his daughter was safe. He had never arrived in Charlottesville, that Thornhill knew for a fact. So where was he? Had he come back and managed to kill Thornhill's men? And yet one man taking out all three of them was incomprehensible. But

Constantinople had not mentioned Adams in the call.

As the car drove along, Thornhill felt much less confident than he had at the beginning of the evening. He would have to watch the situation very carefully. Perhaps there would be some message waiting for him at home.

As the car pulled into their driveway, Thornhill glanced at his watch. It was late, and he had an early morning. He had to testify tomorrow before Rusty Ward's committee. He had finally tracked down the answers the senator wanted, meaning he was prepared to throw out so much bullshit that the room would have to be fumigated after he had finished.

Thornhill disarmed the security system, kissed his wife good night and watched as she went up the stairs to her bedroom. She was still a very attractive woman, slender, fine-boned. Retirement would be coming soon. Perhaps it wouldn't be so bad. He'd had nightmares about it; his sitting in agony at interminable bridge games, country club dinners, fund-raisers; or hacking his way through infinite rounds of golf, his insufferably perky wife at his side for all of it.

However, as he watched the woman's nicely shaped backside gliding up the stairs, Thornhill suddenly saw more enticing possibilities for his golden years. They were relatively young, wealthy; they could travel the world. He even thought he might turn in early tonight, and take advantage of the physical urges he was suddenly feeling as he watched Mrs. Thornhill gracefully ascend the stairs to their bedroom. He liked the way she slid her high heels off, exposing black-hosed feet; moved a hand along her curvy hip; let her hair down her back, her shoulder muscles tensing with each movement.

Those hours at the country club certainly hadn't all been wasted. He would just pop in his study to check his messages and then head upstairs.

He clicked on the light in his study and went over to his desk. He was about to check for any messages on his secure phone when he heard a noise. He turned to the French doors that opened out on to the garden. The doors were opening and a man was stepping through.

Lee put a finger to his lips and smiled, his gun pointed directly at Thornhill. The CIA man stiffened, his eyes darting left and right, looking for escape, but there was none to be had. If he ran or screamed, he would be dead; he could see that in the man's eyes. Lee crossed the room and closed, then locked the door to the study. Thornhill watched him silently.

Thornhill received a second shock when another man stepped through the French doors, closing and locking them too.

Danny Buchanan looked so calm as to be almost asleep, yet a high level of energy danced behind his eyes.

"Who are you? What are you doing in my house?" Thornhill demanded.

"I expected something a little more original, Bob," said Buchanan. "How often is it that you see a ghost from the very recent past?"

"Sit," Lee ordered Thornhill.

Thornhill eyed the gun one more time, then went over and sat on the leather couch facing the two men. He undid his bow tie and dropped it on the couch, trying, with some difficulty, to assess the situation and decide on a course of action.

"I thought we had a deal, Bob," Buchanan said. "Why did you send your team of killers down? A lot of people lost their lives unnecessarily. Why?"

Thornhill looked at him suspiciously and then at Lee.

"I don't know what you're talking about. I don't even know who the hell you are."

It was clear what Thornhill was thinking: Lee and Buchanan were wired. Perhaps they were working with the FBI. And they were in his house. His wife was upstairs undressing, and these two men were in his house asking him these sorts of questions. Well, they would get nothing for their troubles.

"I" – Buchanan stopped and glanced at Lee – "we came here, as the sole survivors, to see what sort of arrangement we can work out. I don't want to keep looking over my shoulder for the rest of my life."

"Arrangement? How about I yell up to my wife to call the police? You like that arrangement?" Thornhill eyed Buchanan closely and then pretended recognition. "I know I've seen you somewhere before. In the newspapers?"

Buchanan smiled. "That certain tape Agent Constantinople told you was destroyed?" He slid his hand in his coat pocket and pulled out a cassette. "Well, he didn't get it exactly right."

Thornhill stared at the cassette as if it were plutonium about to be shoved down his throat. He reached into his own jacket.

Lee raised the pistol.

Thornhill gave him a disappointed look and slowly edged out his pipe and lighter, taking a moment to light it. Several soothing puffs later, he eyed Buchanan.

"Since I don't even know what you're talking about, why don't you play the tape? I'd be interested to know what's on it. It might explain why two complete strangers have broken into my house." *And if that tape had me talking about killing an FBI agent, neither of you would be here, and I'd already be under arrest. Bluff, bluff, bluff, Danny.*

Buchanan slowly tapped the cassette against his palm, while Lee looked nervous.

"Come now, don't tease me with something and then pull it away," said Thornhill.

Buchanan dropped the cassette on the desk. "Maybe later. Right now I want to know what you're going to do for us. Something that will make us not go to the FBI and tell them what we know."

"And what might that be? You talked about people getting killed. Are you insinuating that I might have killed somebody? I'm assuming that you know I'm employed by the CIA. Are you foreign agents attempting some sort of bizarre blackmail scheme? The problem with that is, you need to have something to blackmail me with."

Lee said, "We know enough to bury you."

"Well, then I suggest you go get your shovel and start digging, Mr. . . .?"

"Adams, Lee Adams," Lee said with a fierce scowl.

"Faith is dead, you know, Bob," Buchanan said. As he said this, Lee looked down. "She almost made it. Constantinople killed her. He also killed two of your men. Payback for your killing the FBI agent."

Thornhill looked suitably bewildered. "Faith? Constantinople? What the hell are you talking about?"

Lee came and stood directly in front of Thornhill. "You bastard! You kill people like stepping on ants. A game. That's all it is to you."

"Please put the gun away and leave my house. Now!"

"Damn you!" Lee aimed his pistol directly at Thornhill's head.

Buchanan was next to him in an instant. "Lee, please don't. That won't do any good."

"I would listen to your friend if I were you," Thornhill said as calmly as he could. He had had a gun pulled on him once before, when his cover had been blown in Istanbul many years ago. He had been lucky to get out alive. He wondered if his luck would hold tonight.

"Why should I listen to anybody?" Lee growled.

"Lee, please," Buchanan said.

Lee's finger hovered on the trigger for an instant, his gaze locked with Thornhill's. Finally, he lowered the gun, slowly.

"Well, I guess we'll have to go to the Feds with what we have," Lee said.

"I just want you out of my house."

"And all I want," Buchanan said, "is your personal assurances that no one else will be killed. You've got what you want. You don't have to harm anyone else."

"Right. Right, whatever you say. I won't kill anybody else," Thornhill said sarcastically. "Now if you'll please leave my house. I don't want to upset my wife. She has no idea she's married to a mass murderer."

"This is no joke," Buchanan said angrily.

"No, it really isn't, and I hope you get the help you so obviously need," said Thornhill. "And please take care that your gun-toting friend doesn't hurt anyone." *That should sound very nice on the tape. I am actually caring about others.*

Buchanan picked up the cassette.

"Not leaving the evidence of my crimes?"

Buchanan swiveled around and eyed him severely. "Under the circumstances, I don't think it will be necessary."

He looks like he wants to kill me, Thornhill thought. *Good, very good.*

Thornhill watched as the two men hurried down

his driveway and disappeared on to the darkened street. A minute later he heard a car start up. He raced to the phone and then stopped. Was it tapped? Was this whole thing a charade to trick him into a mistake? He stared at the window. Yes, they could be out there right now. He hit a button under his desk. All the drapes in the room descended and then a small whooshing sound commenced at each of the windows: white noise. He slid open his drawer and pulled out his secure phone. It had so many security and scrambling features that not even the NSA jocks could lift it from the air. Like the technology used on military aircraft, the phone threw out electronic chaff that jammed attempts to intercept its signal. *So much for electronic eavesdropping, you amateurs.*

"Buchanan and Lee Adams were in my study," he said into the phone. "Yes. In my home, dammit! They just left. I want all the men we can spare. We're only minutes from Langley. You should be able to find them." He paused to relight his pipe. "They sang some bullshit song about the cassette tape where I admitted to having the FBI agent killed. But Buchanan was just bluffing. The tape is gone. I figured they were wired, and I played dumb with everything. It almost cost me my life. That idiot Adams was two seconds away from blowing my head off. Buchanan said Lockhart was dead, which is good for us, if it's true. But I don't know if they're somehow working with the FBI. But without that tape they've got no evidence of what we've done. What? No, Buchanan was begging for us to leave him alone. We could go ahead with the blackmail plan, just let him live. It was pitiful, actually. When I first saw them, I thought they had come to kill me. That Adams is dangerous. And they told me Constantinople killed two of our men. Constantinople must be dead, so we need to get another spy at the FBI. But whatever you do, you find them. And this time no mistakes. They are dead. And after that, it's time to execute the plan. I can't wait to see those pitiful faces on Capitol Hill when I hit them with this."

Thornhill clicked off and sat at his desk. It was funny, their coming here that way. A desperate act. From desperate men. Did they really think they could bluff a man such as himself? It was rather insulting. But he had won in the end. The reality was that tomorrow or soon thereafter they would be dead and he wouldn't be.

He rose from behind the desk. Having survived that little scare had actually made him feel quite invigorated. He had been brave, cool under pressure. It was rather intoxicating, primal. He bounded up the stairs. To see Mrs. Thornhill. To demonstrate for her quite clearly who the man of the house was.

FIFTY-SIX

The Dirksen Senate Office Building was bustling as usual on this crisp morning. Robert Thornhill walked with special purpose down the long hallway, swinging his briefcase cavalierly at his side. Last night had been quite something, a success in many ways. The only downside was that they had failed to find Buchanan and Adams.

The rest of the night had been simply marvelous. Mrs. Thornhill had been impressed with his animalistic zeal. The woman had even gotten up early and made him breakfast, dressed in a sheer, clingy black outfit. That hadn't happened in years: making his breakfast or the clingy number.

The hearing room was at the far end of the hallway. Rusty Ward's little fiefdom, Thornhill thought with a snort. He ruled with a Southern fist, meaning velvet-gloved, yet with granite knuckles underneath. Ward would lull you to sleep with his ridiculously syrupy drawl and when you least expected it, he would pounce and shred you, his intense gaze and oh-so-precise words melting the unsuspecting foe right in his uncomfortable, government-issue hot seat.

Everything about Rusty Ward painfully assaulted Thornhill's old-school, Ivy-League sensibilities. But this morning he was ready. He would talk death squads and redactions until the cows came home, to borrow one of Ward's favorite lines; and the senator would be left with no more information at the end of the day than when he had started.

Before entering the hearing room, Thornhill took one energizing deep breath. He envisioned the setting that he was about to confront: Ward and company behind their little bench, the chairman pulling at his suspenders, his fat face looking here and there as he rustled through his briefing papers, missing nothing in the confines of his pathetic kingdom. When Thornhill entered, Ward would look at him, smile, nod, give him some little innocent greeting intended to disarm Thornhill's defenses, as if that were even a possibility. *But I guess he has to go through the motions. Teaching an old dog new tricks indeed.* That was another of Ward's stupid little sayings. How dreary.

Thornhill pulled open the door and strode confidently down the aisle of the hearing room. About halfway down, he realized that the room held many more people than usual. The small space was literally bursting with bodies. And as he looked around, he noted numerous faces he did not recognize. As he approached the witness table, he received another shock. There were already people sitting there, their backs to him.

He looked up at the committee. Ward stared back at him. There was no smile, no inane greeting from the portly chairman.

"Mr. Thornhill, take a seat in the front row, will you? We have one person testifying before you."

Thornhill looked dazed. "Excuse me?"

"Just sit down, Mr. Thornhill," Ward said again.

Thornhill looked at his watch. "I'm afraid I have limited time today, Mr. Chairman. And I wasn't told about anyone else testifying." Thornhill glanced at the witness table. He didn't recognize the men sitting there. "Perhaps we should just reschedule."

Ward looked past Thornhill. The latter turned and followed his gaze. The uniformed Capitol Hill police officer ceremoniously closed the door to the hearing room and then stood with his broad back against it, as though daring anyone to try to get past him.

Thornhill looked back around at Ward. "Am I missing something here?"

"If you are, it will be made crystal clear in a minute," Ward replied ominously. Then he looked over at one of his aides and nodded.

The aide disappeared through a small doorway behind the committee. He was back in a few seconds. And then Thornhill received what amounted to the greatest shock of his life, as Danny Buchanan walked through the doorway and made his way to the witness table. He never even looked at Thornhill, who just stood there in the middle of the aisle, his briefcase now resting motionless against his leg. The men rose from the witness table and took seats in the audience.

Buchanan stood in front of the witness table, raised his right hand, was sworn in and then sat down.

Ward glanced over at Thornhill, who still hadn't moved.

"Mr. Thornhill, will you please sit down so we can get started here?"

Thornhill couldn't take his eyes off Buchanan. He shuffled sideways toward the one remaining empty seat in the front row. The large man sitting at the end of the row moved aside so Thornhill could pass by. As Thornhill sat, he glanced over at the man and found himself staring at Lee Adams.

"Good to see you again," Lee said with a smile before settling back in his chair and turning his attention toward the front of the room.

"Mr. Buchanan," Ward began. "Can you tell us why you're here today, sir?"

"To provide testimony regarding a shocking conspiracy at the Central Intelligence Agency," Buchanan replied in a calm, assured tone. Over the years he had testified before more committees than all the Watergate folk combined. He was on familiar ground, his best friend in the world doing the questioning. This was his time. Finally.

"Then I guess you should start at the beginning, sir."

Buchanan placed his hands neatly in front of him, leaned forward and spoke into the microphone.

"Approximately fifteen months ago I was approached by a high-level official at the CIA. The gentleman was quite familiar with my lobbying practice. He was aware that I knew many of the members on the Hill intimately. He wanted me to help him with a very special project."

"What sort of project?" Ward prompted.

"He wanted me to help him gather evidence against congressmen that could be used to blackmail them."

"Blackmail? How?"

"He knew of my efforts to lobby on behalf of impoverished countries and world humanitarian organizations."

"We all are aware of your efforts in that regard," Ward said magnanimously.

"As you can imagine, it's a tough sell up here. I've used most of my own money in that crusade. The man knew that too. He felt I was desperate. An easy mark, I believe is what he said."

"Precisely how would this blackmail scheme work?"

"I would approach certain congressmen and bureaucrats who could help influence foreign-aid dollars and other overseas relief. I would only approach those who needed money. I would tell them that in return for their help, they would be compensated after they left office. They didn't know it, of course, but the CIA would finance these 'retirement' packages. If they agreed to help, then I would wear a wire provided by the CIA and record incriminating conversations with these men and women. They would also be placed under surveillance by the CIA. All this 'illegal' activity would be captured and subsequently used against them by the man at the CIA."

"How so?"

"Many of the people I was supposed to bribe for foreign aid also serve on committees overseeing the CIA. For example, two of the members of this very committee, Senators Johnson and McNamara, also sit on the appropriations committee for foreign operations. The gentleman from CIA gave me a list of names of all the people he wanted to target. Senators Johnson and McNamara were on that list. The plan was to blackmail them and others into using their committee positions to help the CIA. Increased budgets for the CIA, greater responsibilities, less congressional oversight. That sort of thing. In return, I would be paid a large sum of money."

Buchanan looked at Johnson and McNamara, men he had recruited so easily ten years ago. They stared back at him with exactly the proper look of shock and anger. Over the last week Buchanan had met with every single one of his bribees and had explained what was happening. If they wanted to survive, they would back up every word of the lie he was now telling. What choice did they have? They would also continue to support Buchanan's causes, and they wouldn't be getting a dime from him for doing so. Their efforts would really turn out to be "charitable." Praise God.

And he had confided in Ward as well. His friend had taken it better than Buchanan had thought possible. He had not condemned Buchanan's actions, but he had decided to stand by his old friend. There were greater crimes to punish.

"This is all the truth, Mr. Buchanan?"

"Yes sir," Buchanan said, with the look of a saint.

Thornhill sat impassively in his seat. The man's expression was akin to the condemned walking alone to the gas chamber – a mixture of bitterness, terror and disbelief. Buchanan had obviously cut a deal. The politicians were backing his story. He could see it in Johnson's and McNamara's faces. How could Thornhill attack their claims without revealing his own participation? He could hardly jump up and say, "That's not how it happened. Buchanan was already bribing them, I just caught him and used him for my own blackmail purposes." His Achilles' heel. It had never occurred to him. The frog and the scorpion, only the scorpion was going to survive.

"What did you do?" Ward asked Buchanan.

"I immediately went to the people on the list and told them what had happened, including Senators Johnson and McNamara. I'm sorry we were unable to bring you into the loop at the time, Mr. Chairman, but absolute confidentiality was the key. We collectively decided to set up a sting of sorts. I would pretend to go along with the CIA's plan, and the targets would pretend to be part of the plan. Then, while the CIA was gathering its blackmail material, I would secretly gather evidence against the CIA. When we felt the case was strong enough, we planned to go to the FBI with what we had."

Ward took off his glasses and dangled them in

front of his face. "Damn risky business, Mr. Buchanan. Was this blackmail operation officially sanctioned by the CIA, do you know?"

Buchanan shook his head. "It was clearly the work of one official there, and not the CIA."

"What happened then?"

"I gathered my evidence, but then my associate, Faith Lockhart, who was unaware of any of this, became suspicious of me. She thought, I suppose, that I was actually involved in a blackmail scheme. I, of course, couldn't confide in her. She went to the FBI with her story. They commenced an investigation. The man from the CIA found out about this development and arranged to have Ms. Lockhart killed. Thankfully, she escaped, but an FBI agent was killed."

The entire room began buzzing at this.

Ward looked pointedly at Buchanan. "Are you telling me that an official from the CIA was responsible for the murder of an FBI agent?"

Buchanan nodded. "Several other deaths have also occurred, including" – Buchanan looked down for a moment, his lips trembling – "Faith Lockhart. That is what has prompted my appearance here today. To stop the killing."

"Who is this man, Mr. Buchanan?" Ward said with as much indignity and curiosity as he could feign.

Buchanan turned and pointed directly at Robert Thornhill.

"Associate Deputy Director of Operations Robert Thornhill."

Thornhill erupted from his chair, waving an angry fist in the air, and roared, "This is a damnable lie! This entire event is a circus, an abomination the likes of which I have never witnessed in all my years in government. You bring me here under false pretenses and then subject me to the preposterous, outrageous accusations of this person. They – they were in my home last night. This Buchanan person, and this man!" Thornhill pointed an angry finger at Lee. "This man held a gun to my head. They threatened me with this same insane story. They claimed to have evidence of this nonsense, but when I called their bluff, they ran off. I demand that you place them under immediate arrest. I intend to press full charges. And now, if you'll excuse me, I have legitimate business elsewhere."

Thornhill tried to get past Lee, but the PI stood up and blocked his way.

Thornhill looked at Ward. "Unless you do something right this instant, Mr. Chairman, I will be forced to call the police on my portable phone. I doubt if it would look very good on the evening news."

"I have proof of all that I've said," Buchanan said.

"What," Thornhill cried out, "the silly tape you threatened me with last night? If you have it, produce it. But whatever's on it is obviously forged."

Buchanan opened a briefcase, which rested on the table in front of him. Instead of an audiocassette, he took out a videocassette and handed it to an aide of Ward's.

Everyone in the room watched as another aide wheeled a television, with a VCR attached, out into a corner of the room where everyone could see the screen. The aide took the tape and inserted it in the VCR, hit the remote, stepped back. Everyone in the room watched breathlessly as the screen came to life.

On the TV Lee and Buchanan were just leaving Thornhill's study. Then Thornhill was at his desk, picking up his phone. He spoke into it anxiously. His conversation of the night before was played out before the entire room. His blackmail scheme, the killing of the FBI agent, his ordering the murders of Buchanan and Lee Adams. The look of triumph on his face as he put down the phone was in monumental contrast to the look the man wore now.

As the screen went to black, Thornhill continued to stare at the TV, his mouth slightly open, his lips moving but no words coming out. His briefcase, with all its important papers, fell to the floor, forgotten.

Ward tapped his pen against the microphone, his eyes squarely on Thornhill. There was some satisfaction in the Senator's features, but it could not overcome the horror there as well. Ward was sickened by what he had just seen; he was ready to pitch his political career and go sit on his back porch and watch his grandchildren play games of complete innocence. He didn't want to do this anymore.

"I suppose that since you've admitted that these men were in your home last night, then you won't claim this piece of evidence is a forgery, Mr. Thornhill?" Ward said.

Danny Buchanan sat quietly at the table, his eyes downcast. On his features were relief, sadness, hope; and uneasiness for what lay ahead. He too had clearly had enough.

Lee watched Thornhill intently. The other task he had performed at the Thornhill residence last night had been a relatively simple one. The underlying technology was known as PLC, or power line carrier technology. It was a wireless system with a 2.4-gigahertz transmitter, covert camera and antenna installed in a device that looked just like the smoke alarm in Thornhill's study and actually performed the functions of a smoke detector while it simultaneously conducted surveillance. It was powered by the home's regular electrical current and produced clear, crisp video and audio of everything in its range. Thornhill had stopped his incriminating conversation from leaving his house, but it had never occurred to him that there was a miniature Trojan horse *inside* his house.

"I will be available to testify at the trial," said Danny Buchanan. He rose, turned and started to walk up the aisle.

Lee put a hand on Thornhill's shoulder. "Excuse me," he said politely. He made his way past the frozen Thornhill and joined Buchanan. The two men quietly walked out together.

FIFTY-SEVEN

One month to the day after Buchanan's testimony to Ward's committee, Robert Thornhill bounded down the steps of the federal courthouse in Washington, leaving his lawyers in his liberated, if anxious, wake. The car was waiting for him. He slid inside. He had been granted bail, after four weeks of sitting behind bars. Now it was time to get to work. Now it was damn well time for revenge.

"Have they all been contacted?" Thornhill asked the driver.

The man nodded. "They're already there. Waiting for you."

"Buchanan and Adams? Status?"

"Buchanan is in Witness Protection, but we have some leads. Adams is right out in the open. Available anytime to take out."

"Lockhart?"

"Dead."

"You're certain?"

"We haven't actually dug up her body, but everything else points to her having died from her wounds at the hospital in North Carolina."

Thornhill leaned back against his seat with a sigh. "Lucky her."

The car entered a public garage, where Thornhill left the vehicle. He stepped directly into a van waiting there for him, which then pulled out from the garage and headed in the opposite direction. So much for any tail the FBI had.

Within forty-five minutes he was at the small abandoned strip mall. He stepped into the elevator and was zipping several hundred feet down into the earth. The lower he was carried, the better Thornhill felt. This thought deeply amused him.

The doors parted and he literally burst out of the confines of the elevator. The men, his colleagues, were all there. His chair at the head of the table was empty. His trusty comrade Phil Winslow was in the seat to the immediate right. Thornhill allowed himself a grateful smile. Back in business, ready to go.

He sat down, looked around.

"Congratulations on getting bail, Bob," Winslow said.

"Four weeks later," Thornhill said bitterly. "I think the Agency needs to upgrade its legal counsel."

"Well, that video was very damaging," said Aaron Royce, the younger man who had butted heads with Thornhill at the previous meeting here. "I'm actually surprised you were able to get bail at all. And, quite frankly, I'm a little stunned that the Agency even saw fit to provide counsel."

"Of course it was damaging," Thornhill said scornfully. "And the Agency provided counsel because of loyalty. It doesn't forget its people. Unfortunately, however, it means I have to disappear. The lawyers think we have a shot at suppressing the video, but I think all would agree that, despite having technical legal deficiencies, the subject matter of the tape was a little too detailed to allow me to continue in my present capacity." Thornhill looked saddened for a moment. His career over, and not in the way he had planned. But then his features reassumed their usual steeliness; his resolve flooded back into him like an oil gusher. He looked around the room in triumph. "But I will lead the battle from a distance. And we will win the war. Now, I understand Buchanan went underground. But Adams didn't. We'll go the path of least resistance. Adams first. Then Buchanan. I want someone at the U.S. marshal's service. We have people there. We locate good old Danny and make his life disappear. Next, I want to make damn *sure* Faith Lockhart is no more." He looked at Winslow. "Are my travel documents ready, Phil?"

"Actually, no, Bob," Winslow said slowly.

Royce stared at Thornhill. "This operation has cost us too much," he said. "Three operatives dead. You indicted. The Agency's turned upside down. The FBI is all over us. It's a total and complete disaster. This makes Aldrich Ames seem like a bounced check."

Thornhill noticed that every man in the room, Winslow included, was looking at him with a very unfriendly face. "We will survive this, make no mistake about that," Thornhill said in an encouraging tone.

"I'm quite sure *we* will survive it," Royce said forcefully.

Royce was definitely beginning to bother Thornhill. He was showing backbone in a way that had to be quickly quashed. But for now Thornhill decided to ignore him. "The damn FBI," complained Thornhill. "Bugging my house. Is the Constitution not applicable to them?"

"Thank God you didn't mention my name during the phone call that night," Winslow said.

Thornhill looked at him again, struck by the curious tone in his friend's voice. "About my documents . . . I should prepare to leave the country as soon as possible."

"That won't be necessary, Bob," Royce said. "And

frankly, despite your constant outbursts to the contrary, until you screwed everything up, we had quite a good working relationship with the FBI. Cooperation is the key these days. Turf battles make losers of everyone. You made us into dinosaurs and you're dragging us down into the mud with you."

Thornhill gave him an exasperated look and then glanced at Winslow. "Phil, I don't have time for this. You deal with him."

Winslow coughed nervously. "I'm afraid he's right, Bob."

Thornhill froze for a moment and then looked around the table before settling back on Winslow. "Phil, I want my documents and my cover, and I want them right now."

Winslow looked at Royce and gave a slight nod of the head.

Aaron Royce rose from his chair. He didn't smile; he showed no signs of triumph. Just as he had been trained.

"Bob," he said, "there's been a change in plan. We won't be needing your assistance in this matter any further."

Thornhill's face flushed with anger. "What the hell are you talking about? I'm running this operation. And I want Buchanan and Adams dead. Now!"

"There will be no more killing," Winslow said fiercely. "No more killing of innocent people," he added quietly.

He stood. "I'm sorry, Bob. I truly am."

Thornhill stared at him, the first tremors of the truth hitting him. Phil Winslow had been his classmate at Yale, his fraternity brother. The two men were members of Skull & Bones. Winslow had been his best man. They'd been lifelong friends. Lifelong.

"Phil?" Thornhill said cautiously.

Winslow motioned to the other men, who rose too. They all headed for the elevator.

"Phil?" Thornhill said again, his mouth going dry.

When the group reached the elevator, Winslow looked back. "We can't let this matter go any further. We can't let it go to trial. And we can't let you steal away. They'll never stop looking for you. We need closure, Bob."

Thornhill half rose from his chair. "Then we can fake my death. My suicide."

"I'm sorry, Bob. We need complete and *honest* closure."

"Phil!" Thornhill screamed out. "Please!"

When all the men were inside the elevator, Winslow looked at his friend one last time. "Sacrifices are sometimes necessary, Bob. You know that better than anyone. For the good of the country."

The elevator doors closed.

FIFTY-EIGHT

Lee carefully held the basket of flowers in both hands as he walked down the hospital corridor. Once she'd regained enough strength, Faith had been transferred to a hospital outside of Richmond, Virginia. There she was listed under an alias, though, and an armed guard was stationed outside her room at all times. The hospital was considered far enough away from Washington to maintain absolute secrecy on her whereabouts, yet close enough for Brooke Reynolds to keep a close watch on her.

This was the first time Lee had been allowed in to see her, despite his frantic pleas to Reynolds. At least she was alive. And getting better every day, he had been told.

Thus he was very surprised when he approached her room and there was no guard outside. He knocked on the door, waited, then pushed it open. The room was empty, the bed stripped. He walked around the room in a daze for a few seconds and then ran back out into the hallway where he nearly collided with a nurse. He grabbed the woman's arm.

"The patient in 212? Where is she?" he asked.

The nurse glanced at the empty room and then back at him, her expression a sad one. "Are you family?"

"Yes," he lied.

She looked at the flowers and her expression grew even more distressed. "Didn't anyone call you?"

"Call me? About what?"

"She passed away last night."

Lee's face paled. "Passed away," he said numbly. "But she was out of danger. She was going to make it. What the hell are you talking about – passing away?"

"Please, sir, there are other patients here." She took his arm and steered him away from the room. "I don't know the exact details. I wasn't on duty. I can refer you to someone here who can answer your questions."

Lee pulled his arm free. "Look, she can't be dead, okay? That was just a story. To keep her safe."

"What?" The woman looked puzzled.

"I'll take it from here," a voice said.

They both turned and looked at Brooke Reynolds standing there. She held out her badge for the nurse to see. "I'll take it from here," she said again. The nurse nodded and walked quickly away.

"What the hell is going on?" Lee demanded.

"Let's go to a quiet place and talk this over."

"Where is Faith?"

"Lee, not here! Dammit, do you want to ruin everything?" She pulled on his arm, but he wasn't budging, and she knew she couldn't physically make him.

"Why should I go with you?"

"Because I'm going to tell you the truth."

They got in Reynolds's car and she pulled out of the parking lot.

"I knew you were coming today, and I was planning on being at the hospital ahead of you, waiting. I didn't quite make it. I'm sorry you had to hear about it from a nurse: that's not what I intended." Reynolds looked down at the flowers he still held tightly, and her heart went out to him. She wasn't an FBI agent for this moment – she was simply a fellow human being sitting next to someone whose heart, she knew, was being torn apart. And what she had to tell him would only make it worse.

"Faith has been placed in Witness Protection. Buchanan too."

"*What?* Buchanan I can understand! But Faith isn't a witness to anything!" Lee's relief was matched only by his outrage. This was all wrong.

"But she is in need of protection. If certain people knew she was still alive – well, you know what could happen."

"When's the damn trial?"

"Actually, there isn't going to be a trial."

He stared over at her. "Don't tell me that sonofabitch Thornhill copped some sort of sweetheart deal. Don't tell me that."

"He didn't."

"So why no trial?"

"A trial needs a defendant." Reynolds tapped her fingers against the steering wheel and then slid on a pair of sunglasses. She proceeded to fiddle with the heating control.

"I'm waiting," Lee said. "Or don't I qualify for an explanation?"

Reynolds sighed and straightened up. "Thornhill is dead. He was found in his car on a back-country road with a single gunshot wound to the head. Suicide."

Lee was stunned into silence. After a minute he was able to mutter, "The coward's way out."

"I think everyone's relieved, actually. I know the people at CIA are. To say this whole thing rocked them to their super-secretive bones is an understatement. I guess for the good of the country, it's better to be spared a lengthy, embarrassing trial."

"Right, dirty laundry and all," Lee said acidly.

"Hooray for the country." Lee gave a mock salute to a flag flying in front of a post office they passed. "So if Thornhill's out of the way, why does Faith need Witness Protection?"

"You know the answer to that. When Thornhill died, he took the identity of everyone else involved in this with him to the grave. But they're out there, we know they are. Remember the videotape you orchestrated? Thornhill was talking to somebody on that phone, and that somebody is still out there. The CIA is doing an internal investigation to try to ferret them out, but I'm not holding my breath. And you know these people will do their best to get to Faith and Buchanan. For pure revenge, if nothing else." She touched his arm. "And you too, Lee."

He glanced over at her, read her mind. "No. There is no way I'm going into Witness Protection. I can't deal with a new name. I have a hard enough time remembering my real one. Might as well wait for Thornhill's sidekicks. Least I'll have some fun before I die."

"Lee, this is no joke. If you don't go underground, you'll be in great danger. And we can't follow you around twenty-four hours a day."

"No? After all I did for the Bureau? Does this also mean I don't get the FBI decoder ring and free T-shirt?"

"Why are you being such a smartass about this?"

"Maybe I don't give a shit anymore, Brooke. You're a smart lady, didn't that one ever occur to you?"

Neither said a word for the next couple of miles.

"If it were up to me, you'd get anything you wanted, including your own island somewhere with servants, but it's not up to me," Reynolds finally said.

He shrugged. "I'll take my chances. If they want to

come after me, so be it. They'll find me a little tougher bite than they think."

"Isn't there anything I can say to change your mind?"

He held up the flowers. "You can tell me where Faith is."

"I can't do that. You know I can't do that."

"Oh, come on, sure you can. You just have to *say* it."

"Lee, please—"

He smashed his big fist against the dashboard, cracking it. "Dammit, Brooke, you don't understand. I have to see Faith. I have to!"

"You're wrong, Lee, I do understand. And that's why this is so hard for me. But if I tell you and you go to her, that puts her in danger. And you too. You know that. That breaks all the rules. And I'm not going to do that. I'm sorry. You don't know how terrible I feel about all this."

Lee laid his head against the back of the seat and the two remained silent for another several minutes as Reynolds drove aimlessly.

"How is she?" he finally asked quietly.

"I won't lie to you. That bullet did a lot of damage. She's recovering, but slowly. They almost lost her a couple more times along the way."

Lee put his hand over his face, slowly shook his head.

"If it's any consolation, she was as upset as you are about this arrangement."

"Boy," Lee said, "that just makes everything wonderful. I'm the friggin' king of the world."

"That's not how I meant it."

"You're really not going to let me see her, are you?"

"No, I'm really not."

"Then you can drop me at the corner."

"But your car's back at the hospital."

He opened the car door before she came to a stop. "I'll walk."

"It's miles," Reynolds said, her voice strained. "And it's freezing outside. Lee, let me drive you. Let's go get some coffee. Talk about this some more."

"I need the fresh air. And what's there to talk about? I'm all talked out. I may never talk again." He climbed out and then leaned back in. "You *can* do something for me."

"Just name it."

He handed her the flowers. "Could you see that Faith gets these? I'd appreciate it." Lee shut the door and walked off.

Reynolds gripped the flowers and looked at Lee as he trudged away, head down, hands stuffed in his pockets. She saw his shoulders quiver. And then Brooke Reynolds lay back against the seat as the tears trickled down her face.

FIFTY-NINE

Nine months later Lee was staking out the hideaway townhouse of a man soon to be involved in an acrimonious divorce proceeding with his many-times-cheated-on wife. Lee had been hired by the very suspicious spouse to collect dirt on her hubby, and it hadn't taken him long to fill up bag after bag, as Lee watched a parade of pretty young things flounce through the premises. The wife wanted a nice-size financial settlement from the guy, who had about five hundred million bucks worth of stock options at some high-tech Internet outfit he had cofounded. And Lee was very happy to help her get it. The adulterous husband reminded him of Eddie Stipowicz, his ex-wife's billion-dollar man. Collecting evidence on this guy was a little bit like hurling rocks at little Eddie's bloated head.

Lee took out his camera and shot some pictures of a tall, blond, miniskirted number sauntering up to the townhouse. The photo of the bare-chested guy standing at the door awaiting her, beer can in hand, a goofy, lascivious smile on his fat face, would be exhibit numero uno for the wife's lawyers. No-fault divorce laws had seriously depressed the business of PIs running around digging up dirt, but when it came time to split the marriage loot, the slimy ooze still carried weight. Nobody liked being embarrassed with that stuff. Especially when there were kids involved, as there were here.

The long-legged blond couldn't have been more than twenty, about his daughter Renee's age, while the hubby was pushing fifty. God, those stock options. Must be nice. Or maybe it was the man's bald head, diminutive stature and soft pooch. You couldn't figure some women. *Nah, must be the dough,* Lee told himself. He put the camera away.

It was August in Washington, which meant just about everybody, other than cheating husbands and their bimbos, and PIs who spied on them, was out of town. It was hot, muggy, miserable. Lee had his window rolled down, praying for even the slightest movement of air, as he munched on trail mix and bottled water. The hardest thing with this type of surveillance was the lack of pee-pee breaks. That's why he preferred bottled water. The empty plastic containers had come in handy more than once for him.

He checked his watch; it was close on midnight. Most lights in the apartments and townhouses in the area had long since gone out. He was thinking about heading on, himself. He had gotten enough stuff in the last few days, including some embarrassing shots of a late-night romp in the townhouse's outdoor hot tub, to make the guy easily fork up half his net worth. Two naked girls who looked young enough to be thinking about the senior prom, frolicking in the bubbly water with a guy old enough to know better this probably wouldn't sit too well with the upstanding stockholders of the husband's nice little high-tech concern, Lee imagined.

His own life had taken on a routine bordering on obsessive monotony, or so he had dubbed it. He got up early, worked out hard, pounding the bag, crunching the stomach and hoisting the weights until he thought his body would raise the white flag and then present him with an aneurysm. Then he went to work and kept at it nonstop until he barely made it to dinner at the McDonald's late-night drive-through near his apartment. Then he went home, alone, and tried to sleep, but found that he was never able to actually accomplish total unconsciousness. So he would prowl the apartment, look out the window, wonder about a whole bunch of things he couldn't do a damn thing about. His life's "what if" book was filled up. He'd have to go buy another one.

There had been some positives. Brooke Reynolds had made it her mission to send as much business his way as possible, and it had been quality, good-paying stuff. She had also had a number of ex-FBI agent buddies now in corporate security offer him full-time employment with, of course, stock options. He had turned them all down. The gesture was appreciated, he had told Reynolds, but he worked alone. He was not a suit type. He didn't like eating the kinds of lunches that required silverware. Traditional elements of success would undoubtedly be hazardous to his health.

He had seen Renee a great deal, and each time, things had gotten better between them. For about a month after everything had shaken out, he had barely left her side, making sure that nothing would happen to her because of Robert Thornhill and company. After Thornhill had killed himself his concerns had faded, although he was always on her to stay alert. She was going to come and visit him before school started up again. Maybe he'd drop Trish and Eddie a postcard, telling them what a fabulous job they'd done raising her. Or maybe he wouldn't.

Life was good, he kept telling himself. Business was good, he was in good health, his daughter was back in his life. He wasn't six feet under helping to fertilize grass. And he had served his country. All good shit. Which made him wonder why he was so unhappy, so out-and-out miserable. Actually, he knew, but there was absolutely nothing he could do about it. Wasn't that a kicker? Story of his life. Know the blues, but just can't change them.

A car's headlights flicked across his side mirror. His gaze immediately went to the car that had just pulled up behind him. It wasn't a cop wondering why he had parked here for several hours. He frowned and looked over at the townhouse. He wondered if his naughty tech mogul had noticed him and called in some reinforcements to help teach the curious PI a little lesson. Lee hoped that was the case. He had his crowbar in the seat next to him. This might actually be fun. Kicking the crap out of somebody might be the depression antidote he needed; get those endorphins going. At least it might get him through the night.

He was surprised when only one person emerged from the passenger side and headed his way. The person was small, slender, hidden inside an ankle-length coat with a hood, not exactly your recommended attire for a ninety-degree thermometer and one hundred percent humidity. His hand tightened on the crowbar. As the figure came up to his passenger door, he hit the door lock. The next moment, his lungs had locked up and he was gasping for air.

The face looking in at him was very pale and very thin. And very Faith Lockhart. He unlocked the door and she slid in.

He looked at her, finally found his voice down near his knees. "God, is it really you?"

She smiled, and suddenly she didn't seem so pale, so drawn, so frail. She slid off her long, hooded coat. Underneath she had on a short-sleeved shirt and khaki shorts. Her feet were in sandals. Her legs were very pale and thinner than he remembered; all of her was. Months in a hospital had decimated her, he realized. Her hair had grown out and was longer, though far from its original length. She looked better with her real hair color, he thought. Actually, he would have taken the woman bald.

"It's me," she said quietly. "At least, what's left."

"Is that Reynolds back there?"

"Nervous and upset that I talked her into it."

"You look beautiful, Faith."

She smiled in a resigned fashion. "Liar. I look like hell. I can't even bear to look at my chest. God!" She said the words in a joking manner, but Lee could sense the anguish behind the light tone.

He very gently touched her face with his hand. "I'm not lying, and you know it."

She put her hand around his and gripped it with amazing strength. "Thank you."

"How are you really doing? I want facts, nothing but."

She stretched her arm slowly, the pain in her face so evident from such a simple movement. "I'm officially retired from the aerobics circuit, but I'm hanging in there. Actually, each day it gets better. The doctors expect a full recovery. Well, in the ninety percentile anyway."

"I never thought I'd see you again."

"I couldn't let that happen."

He slid over to her, put his arm around her. She winced a little as he did this, and he quickly backed off.

"I'm sorry, Faith, I'm sorry."

She smiled and put his arm back around her, patting his hand as she did so. "I'm not that fragile. And the day you can't put your arm around me is the day I call it a life."

"I'd ask you where you're living, but I don't want

to do anything that could put you in danger."

"Helluva way to have to live, don't you think?" Faith asked.

"Yes."

She leaned against him, resting her head against his chest. "I saw Danny right after I got out of the hospital. When they told us Thornhill had killed himself, I didn't think he was ever going to stop smiling."

"Can't say I felt any different."

She looked at him. "How are *you*, Lee?"

"Me! Nothing happened to me. Nobody shot me. Nobody tells me where I have to live. I'm doing fine. I got the best deal of all."

"Lie or the truth?"

"Lie," he said softly.

They exchanged a quick kiss and then a longer one. The movements were so easy, Lee thought, their heads turning at just the right angle, their arms going around each other with no wasted motion, like pieces in a puzzle someone was sliding together. They could be waking up at the beach house, the morning after. The nightmare never having occurred. How was it possible that one could know another person for such a short period of time and have it feel like several lifetimes? God would only let that happen once, if ever. And in Lee's case, he had taken it away. It wasn't fair, it wasn't right. He pressed his face into her hair, soaking up every particle of her scent.

"How long are you here?" he asked.

"What did you have in mind?"

"Nothing fancy. Dinner at my place, a quiet talk. Letting me hold you all night."

"As wonderful as that sounds, I'm not sure I'm up to that last part just yet."

He looked at her. "I'm being literal, Faith. I just

want to hold you. That's all. That's all I've been thinking about all these months. Just holding you."

Faith looked as though she might start crying. Instead she brushed away the lone tear that had tumbled down Lee's face.

Lee glanced in the rearview mirror. "But I guess that's not in Reynolds's agenda, is it?"

"I doubt it."

He looked back at her. "Faith," he said softly, "why did you step in front of that bullet? I know you care for Buchanan and all, but why?"

She took a shallow breath. "Like I said, he's unique, I'm ordinary. I couldn't let him die."

"I wouldn't have done it."

"Would you have done it for me?" she asked.

"Yes."

"You sacrifice for people you care about. And I care a great deal about Danny."

"I guess the fact that you had all the means to disappear – fake ID, Swiss bank account, safe house – and instead went to the FBI to try and save Buchanan should have clued me in on that."

She clutched his arm. "But I survived. I made it. Maybe that makes me just a little extraordinary, in a way?"

He cupped her face with his hand. "Now that you're here, I really don't want you to go, Faith. Like I would give everything I have, do anything I can, if you wouldn't leave me."

She traced his mouth with her fingers, kissed his lips, stared at his eyes, which even in the darkness seemed to have the blinding heat of the sun behind them. She never thought she would ever see those eyes again; maybe the fact that she might, if she were to survive, had been the only thing that had saved her, had not let her die. Right now she wasn't sure what else she had to live for. Other than the apparently depthless love of this man.

"Start the car," she said.

Puzzled, he looked at her but said nothing. He turned the key in the ignition, put the car in gear.

"Go ahead," Faith said.

He pulled the car away from the curb and the vehicle behind them immediately did the same.

They drove along, the car following them.

"Reynolds must be pulling her hair out," Lee said.

"She'll get over it."

"Where to?" he said.

"How much gas do you have in the car?" Faith asked.

He looked surprised. "I was on a stakeout. Full tank."

She was settled against him, her arm curling around his middle, her hair tickling his nose; she smelled so wonderful he felt dizzy.

"Let's go get some takeout Chinese. We can drive to the lookout spot off the GW Parkway." She looked at the star-filled sky. "I can show you the constellations."

He looked at her. "Been chasing stars lately?"

She smiled at him. "Always."

"And after that?"

"They can't keep me in Witness Protection against my will, can they?"

"No. But you'd be in danger."

"How about *we'd* be in danger?"

"In a second, Faith. In a second. But what happens when we run out of gas?"

"For now, just drive."

And that's exactly what he did.

ACKNOWLEDGMENTS

To my dear friend Jennifer Steinberg, for tracking down so much information for me. You'd make a great PI!

To my wife, Michelle, for always telling me the truth about the books.

To Neal Schiff at the FBI for his continued help and cooperation with my novels.

A very special thanks to FBI Special Agent Shawn Henry, who was very generous with his time, expertise, and enthusiasm, and who helped me avoid some serious gaffes in the story. Shawn, your comments made the book much better.

To Martha Pope for her valuable, insightful knowledge on Capitol Hill matters, and her patience with a political neophyte. Martha, you'd make a great teacher!

To Bobby Rosen, Diane Dewhirst, and Marty Paone for sharing their experiences and institutional memories with me.

To Tom DePont, Dawn Bailey, and Charles Nelson of NationsBank for assistance on financial and tax matters.

To Joe Duffy for enlightening me on foreign aid policy and procedures. And to his wife, Anne Wexler, for sharing her valuable time and insight with me.

A very, very special thanks to my friend Bob Schule for going above and beyond the call of duty in helping me on this book, by not only providing fascinating details about his long and distinguished career in Washington, but also for casting a wide net among his friends and colleagues in order to help me better understand politics, lobbying, and how Washington really works. Bob, you're a wonderful friend and a true professional.

To Congressman Rod Blagojevich (D. Ill) for allowing me a glimpse into the life of a member of Congress.

To Congressman Tony Hall (D. Ohio) for helping me better understand the plight of the world's poor, and how that issue plays out (or doesn't) in Washington.

To my good friend and family member Congressman John Baldacci (D. Maine) for his support and assistance with this project. If everyone in Washington were like John, the plot of this book would seem totally implausible.

To Larry Benoit and Bob Beene for their help on everything from lobbying to the nuts and bolts of governing, to all the little nooks and crannies in the U.S. Capitol building. To them I owe one of the best scenes in the book.

To John Deutch for his generous assistance in helping me to better understand the Central Intelligence Agency.

To Mark Jordan of Baldino's Lock and Key for educating me on the ways of security and phone systems and how to crack them. Mark, you're the best.

To Steve Jennings for reading every word as usual and helping to make them better.

To my dear friends David and Catherine Broome for exposing me to the North Carolina settings and for their continued encouragement and support.

To all those other people who contributed to this novel but for various reasons wish to remain anonymous. I couldn't have done it without all of you.

To my editor and my friend Frances Jalet-Miller. Her skill, encouragement, and gentle persuasion are all that any writer could ever want in an editor. To many more books together, Francie.

Last, but absolutely not least, to Larry, Maureen, Jamie, Tina, Emi, Jonathan, Karen Torres, Martha Otis, Jackie Joiner, and Jackie Meyer, Bruce Paonessa and Peter Mauceri, and all the rest of the Warner Books family. It takes *all* of us to make this happen. Friends for life.

All the people listed above gave me the knowledge and help I needed to write this novel. How I used all of that assistance to conjure up all sorts of shenanigans, misdeeds, outright crimes, and depictions of felonious and conspiratorial souls in *Saving Faith*, however, is my responsibility alone.

EYE OF THE NEEDLE

Ken Follett was only twenty-seven when he wrote the award-winning *Eye of the Needle,* which became an international bestseller. He has since written several equally successful novels, including *World Without End,* the long-awaited sequel to the worldwide bestselling *The Pillars of the Earth,* an epic of family drama, violent conflict and vaulting ambition set around the building of a great cathedral. Ken Follett is also the author of the non-fiction bestseller *On Wings of Eagles.* He lives with his family in London and Hertfordshire.

www.ken-follett.com

Also by Ken Follett

The Modigliani Scandal

Paper Money

Triple

The Key to Rebecca

The Man from St Petersburg

On Wings of Eagles

Lie Down with Lions

Night Over Water

A Dangerous Fortune

A Place Called Freedom

The Third Twin

The Hammer of Eden

Code to Zero

Jackdaws

Hornet Flight

Whiteout

World Without End

The Pillars of the Earth

KEN FOLLETT

EYE OF THE NEEDLE

PAN BOOKS

First published in Great Britain 1978 by Futura Publications Ltd

This edition published 2009 by Pan Books
an imprint of Pan Macmillan, a division of Macmillan Publishers Limited
Pan Macmillan, 20 New Wharf Road, London N1 9RR
Basingstoke and Oxford
Associated companies throughout the world
www.panmacmillan.com

ISBN 978-1-4472-0877-8

1 3 5 7 9 8 6 4 2

A CIP catalogue record for this book is available from
the British Library.

Typeset by SetSystems Ltd, Saffron Walden, Essex
Printed in the UK by CPI Mackays, Chatham ME5 8TD

The Germans were almost completely deceived – only Hitler guessed right, and he hesitated to back his hunch . . .

A. J. P. Taylor
English History 1914–1945

My thanks to Malcolm Hulke

for invaluable help, generously given.

Preface

Early in 1944 German Intelligence was piecing together evidence of a huge army in south-eastern England. Reconnaissance planes brought back photographs of barracks and airfields and fleets of ships in the Wash; General George S. Patton was seen in his unmistakable pink jodhpurs walking his white bulldog; there were bursts of wireless activity, signals between regiments, in the area; confirming signs were reported by German spies in Britain.

There was no army, of course. The ships were rubber-and-timber fakes, the barracks no more real than a movie set; Patton did not have a single man under his command; the radio signals were meaningless; the spies were double agents.

The object was to fool the enemy into preparing for an invasion via the Pas de Calais, so that on D-Day the Normandy assault would have the advantage of surprise.

It was a huge, near-impossible deception. Literally thousands of people were involved in perpetrating the trick. It would have been a miracle if none of Hitler's spies ever got to know about it.

Were there any spies? At the time people thought

they were surrounded by what were then called Fifth Columnists. After the war a myth grew up that MI5 had rounded up the lot by Christmas 1939. The truth seems to be that there were very few: MI5 did capture nearly all of them.

But it only needs one . . .

We know that the Germans saw the signs they were meant to see in East Anglia. We also know that they suspected a trick. And we know that they tried very hard to discover the truth.

That much is history, and I have discovered no facts that aren't already in history books. What follows is fiction.

Still and all, I think something like this must have happened . . .

Camberley, Surrey

PART ONE

ONE

It was the coldest winter for forty-five years. Villages in the English countryside were cut off by the snow, and the Thames froze over. One day in January the Glasgow to London train arrived at Euston twenty-four hours late. The snow and the blackout combined to make motoring perilous: road accidents doubled, and people told jokes about how it was more risky to drive an Austin Seven along Piccadilly at night than to take a tank across the Siegfried Line.

Then, when the spring came, it was glorious. Barrage balloons floated majestically in bright blue skies, and soldiers on leave flirted with girls in sleeveless dresses on the streets of London.

The city did not look much like the capital of a nation at war. There were signs, of course; and Henry Faber, cycling from Waterloo Station toward Highgate, noted them: piles of sandbags outside important public buildings, Anderson shelters in suburban gardens, propaganda posters about evacuation and Air Raid Precautions. Faber watched such things – he was considerably more observant than the average railway clerk. He saw crowds of children in the parks, and concluded that evacuation had been a failure. He marked the number of motor cars on the road, despite petrol rationing; and he read about the new models announced by the motor manufacturers. He knew the significance of night-shift workers pouring into factories where, only months previously, there had been hardly enough work for the day shift. Most of all he monitored the movement of troops around Britain's railway network: all the paperwork passed through his office. One could learn a lot from that paperwork. Today, for example, he had rubber-stamped a batch of forms which led him to believe that a new Expeditionary Force was being gathered. He was fairly sure that it would have a complement of about 100,000 men, and that it was for Finland.

There were signs, yes; but there was something jokey about it all. Radio shows satirised the red tape of wartime regulations, there was community singing in the air-raid shelters, and fashionable women carried their gas masks in couturier-designed containers. They talked about the Bore War. It was at once larger-than-life and trivial, like a moving-picture show. All the air-raid warnings, without exception, had been false alarms.

Faber had a different point of view – but then, he was a different kind of person.

He steered his cycle into Archway Road and leaned forward a little to take the uphill slope, his long legs pumping as tirelessly as the pistons of a railway engine. He was very fit for his age, which was thirty-nine, although he lied about it: he lied about most things, as a safety precaution.

He began to perspire as he climbed the hill into Highgate. The building in which he lived was one of the highest in London, which was why he chose to live there. It was a Victorian brick house at one end of a terrace of six. The houses were high, narrow and dark, like the minds of the men for whom they had been built. Each had three storeys plus a basement with a servants' entrance – the English middle class of the nineteenth century insisted on a servants' entrance, even if they had no servants. Faber was a cynic about the English.

Number six had been owned by Mr Harold Garden, of Garden's Tea And Coffee, a small company which went broke in the Slump. Having lived by the principle that insolvency is a mortal sin, the bankrupt Mr Garden had no option but to die. The house was all he bequeathed to his widow, who was then obliged to take in lodgers. She enjoyed being a landlady, although the etiquette of her social circle demanded that she pretend to be a little ashamed of it. Faber had a room on the top floor with a dormer window. He lived there from Monday to Friday, and told Mrs Garden that he spent weekends with his mother in Erith. In fact he had another landlady in Blackheath who called him Mr Baker and believed he was a travelling salesman for a stationery manufacturer and spent all week on the road.

He wheeled his cycle up the garden path under the disapproving frown of the tall front-room windows. He put it in the shed and padlocked it to the lawn-mower – it was against the law to leave a vehicle unlocked. The seed potatoes in boxes all around the shed were sprouting. Mrs Garden had turned her flower beds over to vegetables for the war effort.

Faber entered the house, hung his hat on the hall-stand, washed his hands and went in to tea.

Three of the other lodgers were already eating: a pimply boy from Yorkshire who was trying to get into the Army; a confectionery salesman with receding sandy hair; and a retired naval officer who, Faber was convinced, was a degenerate. Faber nodded to them and sat down.

The salesman was telling a joke. 'So the Squadron-Leader says, "You're back early!" and the pilot turns round and says, "Yes, I dropped my leaflets in bundles, wasn't that right?" so the Squadron-Leader says, "Good God! You might've hurt somebody!" '

The naval officer cackled and Faber smiled. Mrs Garden came in with a teapot. 'Good evening, Mr Faber. We started without you – I hope you don't mind.'

Faber spread margarine thinly on a slice of whole-meal bread, and momentarily yearned for a fat sausage. 'Your seed potatoes are ready to plant,' he told her.

Faber hurried through his tea. The others were arguing over whether Chamberlain should be sacked and replaced by Churchill. Mrs Garden kept voicing opinions then looking at Faber for a reaction. She was a blowsy woman, a little overweight. About Faber's age, she wore the clothes of a woman of thirty, and he guessed she wanted another husband. He kept out of the discussion.

Mrs Garden turned on the radio. It hummed for a while, then an announcer said: 'This is the BBC Home Service. *It's That Man Again*!'

Faber had heard the show. It regularly featured a German spy called Funf. He excused himself and went up to his room.

Mrs Garden was left alone after *It's That Man Again*: the naval officer went to the pub with the salesman, and the boy from Yorkshire, who was religious, went to a prayer meeting. She sat in the parlour with a small glass of gin, looking at the blackout curtains and thinking about Mr Faber. She wished he wouldn't spend so much time in his room. She needed company, and he was the kind of company she needed.

Such thoughts made her feel guilty. To assuage the guilt she thought of Mr Garden. Her memories were familiar but blurred, like an old print of a movie with worn sprocket-holes and an indistinct soundtrack; so that, although she could easily remember what it was like to have him here in the room with her, it was difficult to imagine his face, or the clothes he might be wearing, or the comment he would make on the day's war news. He had been a small, dapper man, successful in business when he was lucky and unsuccessful when he was not, undemonstrative in public and insatiably affectionate in bed. She had loved him a lot. There would be many women in her position if this war ever got going properly. She poured another drink.

Mr Faber was a quiet one – that was the trouble. He didn't seem to have any vices. He didn't smoke, she had never smelled drink on his breath, and he spent every evening in his room, listening to classical music on his radio. He read a lot of newspapers and went for long walks. She suspected he was quite clever, despite his humble job: his contributions to the conversation in the dining-room were always a shade more thoughtful than anyone else's. He surely could get a better job if he tried. He seemed not to give himself the chance he deserved.

It was the same with his appearance. He was a fine figure of a man: tall, quite heavy around the neck and shoulders, not a bit fat, with long legs. And he had a strong face, with a high forehead and a long jaw and bright blue eyes; not pretty, like a film star, but the kind of face that appealed to a woman. Except for the mouth – that was small and thin, and she could imagine him being cruel. Mr Garden had been incapable of cruelty.

And yet at first sight he was not the kind of man a woman would look at twice. The trousers of his old worn suit were never pressed – she would have done that for him, and gladly, but he never asked – and he always wore a shabby raincoat and a flat docker's cap. He had no moustache, and his hair was trimmed short every fortnight. It was as if he wanted to look like a nonentity.

He needed a woman, there was no doubt of that. She wondered for a moment whether he might be what people called effeminate, but she dismissed the idea quickly. He needed a wife to smarten him up and give him ambition. She needed a man to keep her company and for – well, love.

Yet he never made a move. Sometimes she could scream with frustration. She was sure she was attractive. She looked in a mirror as she poured another gin. She had a nice face, and fair curly hair, and there was something for a man to get hold of . . . She giggled at that thought. She must be getting tiddly.

She sipped her drink and considered whether *she* ought to make the first move. Mr Faber was obviously shy – chronically shy. He wasn't sexless – she could tell by the look in his eyes on the two occasions he had seen her in her nightdress. Perhaps she could overcome his shyness by being brazen. What did she have to lose? She tried imagining the worst, just to see what it felt like. Suppose he rejected her. Well, it would be embarrassing – even humiliating. It would be a blow to her pride. But nobody else need know it had happened. He would just have to leave.

The thought of rejection had put her off the whole idea. She got to her feet slowly, thinking: I'm just not the brazen type. It was bedtime. If she had one more gin in bed she would be able to sleep. She took the bottle upstairs.

Her bedroom was below Mr Faber's, and she could hear violin music from his radio as she undressed. She put on a new nightdress – pink, with an embroidered neckline, and no one to see it! – and made her last drink. She wondered what Mr Faber looked like undressed. He would have a flat stomach, and hairs on his nipples, and you would be able to see his ribs, because he was slim. He probably had a small bottom. She giggled again, thinking: I'm a disgrace.

She took her drink to bed and picked up her book, but it was too much effort to focus on the print. Besides, she was bored with vicarious romance. Stories about dangerous love affairs were fine when you yourself had a perfectly safe love affair with your husband, but a woman needed more than Barbara Cartland. She sipped her gin, and wished Mr Faber would turn the radio off. It was like trying to sleep at a tea-dance!

She could, of course, ask him to turn it off. She looked at her bedside clock: it was past ten. She could put on her dressing-gown, which matched the nightdress, and just comb her hair a little, then step into her slippers – quite dainty, with a pattern of roses – and just pop up the stairs to the next landing, and just, well, tap on his door. He would open it, perhaps wearing his trousers and singlet, and then he would *look* at her the way he had *looked* when he saw her in her nightdress on the way to the bathroom . . .

'Silly old fool,' she said to herself aloud. 'You're just making excuses to go up there.'

And then she wondered why she needed excuses. She was a mature adult, and it was her house, and in ten years she had not met another man who was just right for her, and what the *hell*, she needed to feel someone strong and hard and hairy on top of her, squeezing her breasts and panting in her ear and parting her thighs with his broad flat hands, for tomorrow the gas bombs might come over from Germany and they would all die choking and gasping and poisoned and she would have lost her last chance.

So she drained her glass, and got out of bed, and put on her dressing-gown, and just combed her hair a little, and stepped into her slippers, and picked up her bunch of keys in case he had locked the door and couldn't hear her knock above the sound of the radio.

There was nobody on the landing. She found the stairs in the darkness. She intended to step over the stair that creaked, but she stumbled on the loose carpet and trod on it heavily; but it seemed that nobody heard, so she went on up and tapped on the door at the top. She tried it gently. It was locked.

The radio was turned down, and Mr Faber called out: 'Yes?'

He was well-spoken: not cockney, or foreign – not anything, really, just a pleasantly neutral voice.

She said: 'Can I have a word with you?'

He seemed to hesitate, then he said: 'I'm undressed.'

'So am I,' she giggled, and she opened the door with her duplicate key. He was standing in front of the radio with some kind of screwdriver in his hand. He wore his trousers and *no* singlet. His face was white and he looked scared to death.

She stepped inside and closed the door behind her, not knowing what to say. Suddenly she remembered a line from an American film, and she said: 'Would you buy a lonely girl a drink?' It was silly, really, because she knew he had no drink in his room, and she certainly wasn't dressed to go out; but it sounded vampish.

It seemed to have the desired effect. Without speaking, he came slowly toward her. He *did* have hair on his nipples. She took a step forward, and then his arms went around her, and she closed her eyes and turned up her face, and he kissed her, and she moved slightly in his arms, and then there was a terrible, awful, unbearable *sharp* pain in her back and she opened her mouth to scream.

He had heard her stumble on the stairs. If she'd waited another minute he would have had the radio transmitter back in its case and the code books in the drawer and there would have been no need for her to die. But before he could conceal the evidence he had heard her key in the lock, and when she opened the door the stiletto had been in his hand.

Because she moved slightly in his arms, Faber missed her heart with the first jab of the weapon, and he had to thrust his fingers down her throat to stop her crying out. He jabbed again, but she moved again and the blade struck a rib and merely slashed her superficially. Then the blood was spurting and he knew it would not be a clean kill, it never was when you missed with the first stroke.

She was wriggling too much to be killed with a jab now. Keeping his fingers in her mouth, he gripped her jaw with his thumb and pushed her back against the door. Her head hit the woodwork with a loud bump, and he wished he had not turned the radio down, but how could he have expected this?

He hesitated before killing her, because it would be much better if she died on the bed – better for the cover-up which was already taking shape in his mind – but he could not be sure of getting her that far in silence. He tightened his hold on her jaw, kept her head still by jamming it against the door, and brought the stiletto around in a wide slashing arc that ripped away most of her throat, for the stiletto was not a slashing knife and the throat was not Faber's favoured target.

He jumped back to avoid the first horrible gush of blood, then stepped forward again to catch her before she hit the floor. He dragged her to the bed, trying not to look at her neck, and laid her down.

He had killed before, so he expected the reaction: it always came as soon as he felt safe. He went over to the sink in the corner of the room and waited for it. He could see his face in the little shaving mirror. He was white, and his eyes were staring. He looked at himself and thought: *Killer*. Then he threw up.

When that was over he felt better. He could go to work now. He knew what he had to do: the details had come to him even while he was killing her.

He washed his face, brushed his teeth, and cleaned the washbasin. Then he sat down at the table beside his radio. He looked at his notebook, found his place, and began tapping the key. It was a long message, about the mustering of an army for Finland, and he had been half way through when he was interrupted. It was written down in cipher on the pad. When he had completed it he signed off with: 'Regards to Willi.'

The transmitter packed away neatly into a specially designed suitcase. Faber put the rest of his possessions into a second case. He took off his trousers and sponged the bloodstains, then washed himself all over.

At last he looked at the corpse.

He was able to be cold about her now. It was wartime; they were enemies: if he had not killed her, she would have caused his death. She had been a threat, and all he felt now was relief that the threat had been nullified. She should not have frightened him.

Nevertheless, his last task was distasteful. He opened her robe and lifted her nightdress, pulling it up around her waist. She was wearing knickers. He tore them, so that the hair of her pubis was visible. Poor woman: she had wanted only to seduce him. But he could not have got her out of the room without her seeing the transmitter; and the British propaganda had made these people alert for spies – ridiculously so: if the Abwehr had as many agents as the newspapers made out then the British would have lost the war already.

He stepped back and looked at her with his head on one side. There was something wrong. He tried to think like a sex maniac. If I were crazed with lust for a woman like Una Garden, and I killed her just so that I could have my way with her, what would I then do?

Of course: that kind of lunatic would want to look at her breasts. Faber leaned over the body, gripped the neckline of the nightdress, and ripped it to the waist. Her large breasts sagged sideways.

The police doctor would soon discover that she had not been raped, but Faber did not think that mattered. He had taken a criminology course at Heidelberg, and he knew that many sexual assaults were not consummated. Besides, he could not have carried the deception that far, not even for the Fatherland. He was not in the SS. Some of *them* would queue up to rape the corpse . . . He put the thought out of his mind.

He washed his hands again and got dressed. It was almost midnight. He would wait an hour before leaving: it would be safer later.

He sat down to think about how he had gone wrong.

There was no question that he had made a mistake. If his cover were perfect, he would be totally secure. If he were totally secure no one could discover his secret. Mrs Garden had discovered his secret – or rather, she would have if she had lived a few seconds longer – therefore he had not been totally secure, therefore his cover was not perfect, therefore he had made a mistake.

He should have put a bolt on the door. Better to be thought chronically shy than to have landladies with duplicate keys sneaking in at night in their bedwear.

That was the surface error. The deep flaw was that he was too eligible to be a bachelor. He thought this with irritation, not conceit. He knew that he was a pleasant, attractive man, and that there was no apparent reason why he should be single. He turned his mind to thinking up a cover that would explain this without inviting advances from the Mrs Gardens of this world.

He ought to be able to find inspiration in his real personality. Why *was* he single? He stirred uneasily: he did not like mirrors. The answer was simple. He was single because of his profession. If there were deeper reasons, he did not want to know them.

He would have to spend tonight in the open. Highgate Wood would do. In the morning he would take his suitcases to a railway station left-luggage office, then tomorrow evening he would go to his room in Blackheath.

He would shift to his second identity. He had little fear of being caught by the police. The commercial traveller who occupied the room at Blackheath on weekends looked rather different from the railway clerk who had killed his landlady. The Blackheath persona was expansive, vulgar and flashy. He wore loud ties, bought rounds of drinks, and combed his hair differently. The police would circulate a description of a shabby little pervert who would not say boo to a goose until he was inflamed with lust, and no one would look twice at the handsome salesman in the striped suit who was obviously the type that was more or less permanently inflamed with lust and did not have to kill women to get them to show him their breasts.

He would have to set up another identity – he always kept at least two. He needed a new job, fresh papers – passport, identity card, ration book, birth certificate. It was all so *risky*. Damn Mrs Garden. Why couldn't she have drunk herself to sleep as usual?

It was one o'clock. Faber took a last look around the room. He was not concerned about leaving clues – his fingerprints were obviously all over the house, and there would be no doubt in anyone's mind about who was the murderer. Nor did he feel any sentiment about leaving the place that had been his home for two years: he had never thought of it as home. He had never thought of anywhere as home.

He would always think of this as the place where he had learned to put a bolt on a door.

He turned out the light, picked up his cases, and crept down the stairs and out of the door into the night.

TWO

Henry II was a remarkable king. In an age when the term 'flying visit' had not yet been coined, he flitted between England and France with such rapidity that he was credited with magical powers; a rumour which, understandably, he did nothing to suppress. In 1173 – either the June or the September, depending upon which secondary source one favours – he arrived in England and left for France again so quickly that no contemporary writer ever found out about it. Later historians discovered the record of his expenditure in the Pipe Rolls. At the time his kingdom was under attack by his sons at its northern and southern extremes – the Scottish border and the South of France. But what, precisely, was the purpose of his visit? Whom did he see? Why was it secret, when the myth of his magical speed was worth an army? What did he accomplish?

This was the problem that taxed Percival Godliman in the summer of 1940, when Hitler's armies swept across the French cornfields like a scythe, and the British poured out of the Dunkirk bottleneck in bloody disarray.

Professor Godliman knew more about the Middle

Ages than any man alive. His book on the Black Death had upended every convention of medievalism; it had also been a bestseller and published as a Penguin. With that behind him he had turned to a slightly earlier and even more intractable period.

At 12.30 on a splendid June day in London, a secretary found Godliman hunched over an illuminated manuscript, laboriously translating its medieval Latin, making notes in his own even less legible handwriting. The secretary, who was planning to eat her lunch in the garden of Gordon Square, did not like the manuscript room because it smelled dead. You needed so many keys to get in there, it might as well have been a tomb.

Godliman stood at a lectern, perched on one leg like a bird, his face lit bleakly by a spotlight above: he might have been the ghost of the monk who wrote the book, standing a cold vigil over his precious chronicle. The girl cleared her throat and waited for him to notice her. She saw a short man in his fifties, with round shoulders and weak eyesight, wearing a tweed suit. She knew he could be perfectly sensible once you dragged him out of the Middle Ages. She coughed again and said: 'Professor Godliman?'

He looked up, and when he saw her he smiled, and then he did not look like a ghost, more like someone's dotty father. 'Hello!' he said, in an astonished tone, as if he had just met his next door neighbour in the middle of the Sahara Desert.

'You asked me to remind you that you have lunch at the Savoy with Colonel Terry.'

'Oh, yes.' He took his watch out of his waistcoat

pocket and peered at it. 'If I'm going to walk it, I'd better leave now.'

She nodded. 'I brought your gas mask.'

'You are thoughtful!' He smiled again, and she decided he looked quite nice. He took the mask from her and said: 'Do I need my coat?'

'You didn't wear one this morning. It's quite warm. Shall I lock up after you?'

'Thank you, thank you.' He jammed his notebook into his jacket pocket and went out.

The secretary looked around, shivered, and followed him.

Colonel Andrew Terry was a red-faced Scot, pauper-thin from a lifetime of heavy smoking, with sparse dark-blond hair thickly brilliantined. Godliman found him at a corner table in the Savoy Grill, wearing civilian clothes. There were three cigarette stubs in the ashtray. He stood up to shake hands.

Godliman said: 'Morning, Uncle Andrew.' Terry was his mother's baby brother.

'How are you, Percy?'

'I'm writing a book about the Plantagenets.' Godliman sat down.

'Are your manuscripts still in London? I'm surprised.'

'Why?'

Terry lit another cigarette. 'Move them to the country in case of bombing.'

'Should I?'

'Half the National Gallery has been shoved into a bloody big hole in the ground somewhere up in Wales. Young Kenneth Clark is quicker off the mark than you. Might be sensible to take yourself off out of it too, while you're about it. I don't suppose you've many students left.'

'That's true.' Godliman took a menu from a waiter and said: 'I don't want a drink.'

Terry did not look at his menu. 'Seriously, Percy, why are you still in Town?'

Godliman's eyes seemed to clear, like the image on a screen when the projector is focused, as if he had to think for the first time since he walked in. 'It's all right for children to leave, and national institutions like Bertrand Russell. But for me – well, it's a bit like running away and letting other people fight for you. I realize that's not a strictly logical argument. It's a matter of sentiment, not logic.'

Terry smiled the smile of one whose expectations have been fulfilled. But he dropped the subject and looked at the menu. After a moment he said: 'Good God. *Le Lord Woolton Pie.*'

Godliman grinned. 'I'm sure it's still just potatoes and vegetables.'

When they had ordered, Terry said: 'What do you think of our new Prime Minister?'

'The man's an ass. But then, Hitler's a fool, and look how well he's doing. You?'

'We can live with Winston. At least he's bellicose.'

Godliman raised his eyebrows. '"We?" Are you back in the game?'

'I never really left it, you know.'

'But you said—'

'Percy. Can't you think of a department whose staff all say they don't work for the Army?'

'Well, I'm damned. All this time . . .'

Their first course came, and they started a bottle of white Bordeaux. Godliman ate potted salmon and looked pensive.

Eventually Terry said: 'Thinking about the last lot?'

Godliman nodded. 'Young days, you know. Terrible time.' But his tone was wistful.

'This war isn't the same at all. My chaps don't go behind enemy lines and count bivouacs like you did. Well, they do, but that side of things is much less important this time. Nowadays we just listen to the wireless.'

'Don't they broadcast in code?'

Terry shrugged. 'Codes can be broken. Candidly, we get to know just about everything we need these days.'

Godliman glanced around, but there was no one within earshot, and it was not for him to tell Terry that careless talk costs lives.

Terry went on: 'In fact my job is to make sure *they* don't have the information they need about *us*.'

They both had chicken pie to follow. There was no beef on the menu. Godliman fell silent, but Terry talked on.

'Canaris is a funny chap, you know. Admiral Wilhelm Canaris, head of the Abwehr. I met him before this lot started. Likes England. My guess is he's none too fond of Hitler. Anyway, we know he's been told to mount a major intelligence operation against us, in preparation for the invasion – but he's not doing much. We arrested their best man in England the day after war broke out. He's in Wandsworth prison now. Useless people, Canaris's spies. Old ladies in boarding-houses, mad Fascists, petty criminals—'

Godliman said: 'Look here, old boy, this is too much.' He trembled slightly with a mixture of anger and incomprehension. 'All this stuff is secret. I don't want to know!'

Terry was unperturbed. 'Would you like something else?' he offered. 'I'm having chocolate ice-cream.'

Godliman stood up. 'I don't think so. I'm going to go back to my work, if you don't mind.'

Terry looked up at him coolly. 'The world can wait for your reappraisal of the Plantagenets, Percy. There's a war on, dear boy. I want you to work for me.'

Godliman stared down at him for a long moment. 'What on earth would I do?'

Terry smiled wolfishly. 'Catch spies.'

Walking back to the college, Godliman felt depressed despite the weather. He would accept Colonel Terry's offer: no doubt about that. His country was at war; it was a just war; and if he was too old to fight, he was still young enough to help.

But the thought of leaving his work – and for how many years? – depressed him. He loved history, and he had been totally absorbed in medieval England since the death of his wife ten years ago. He liked the unravelling of mysteries, the discovery of faint clues, the resolution of contradictions, the unmasking of lies and propaganda and myth. His new book would be the best on its subject written in the last hundred years, and there would not be one to equal it for another century. It had ruled his life for so long that the thought of abandoning it was almost unreal, as difficult to digest as the discovery that one is an orphan and no relation at all to the people one has always called Mother and Father.

An air-raid warning stridently interrupted his thoughts. He contemplated ignoring it: so many people did now, and he was only ten minutes' walk from the college. But he had no real reason to return to his study – he knew he would do no more work today. So he hurried into a Tube station and joined the solid mass of Londoners crowding down the staircases and on to the grimy platform. He stood close to the wall, staring at a Bovril poster, and thought: But it's not just the things I'm leaving behind.

Going back into the game depressed him, too. There were some things he liked about it: the importance of *little* things, the value of simply being clever, the meticulousness, the guesswork. But he hated the blackmail and the treachery, the deceit, the desperation, and the way one always stabbed the enemy in the back.

The platform was becoming more crowded. Godliman sat down while there was still room, and found himself leaning against a man in bus-driver's uniform. The man smiled and said: 'Oh to be in England, now that summer's here. Know who said that?'

'Now that April's there,' Godliman corrected him. 'It was Browning.'

'I heard it was Adolf Hitler,' the driver said. A woman next to him squealed with laughter, and he turned his attention to her. 'Did you hear what the evacuee said to the farmer's wife?'

Godliman tuned out and remembered an April when he had longed for England, crouching on a high branch of a plane tree, peering through a cold mist across a French valley behind the German lines. He could see nothing but vague dark shapes, even through his telescope, and he was about to slide down and walk a mile or so farther when three German soldiers came from nowhere to sit around the base of the tree and smoke. After a while they took out cards and began to play, and young Percival Godliman realized they had found a way of skiving off and were here for the day. He stayed in the tree, hardly moving, until he began to shiver and his muscles knotted with cramp and his bladder felt as if it would burst. Then he took out his revolver and shot the three of them, one after another, through the tops of their close-cropped heads. And three people, laughing and cursing and gambling their pay, had simply ceased to exist. It was the first time he killed, and all he could think was: Just because I had to pee.

Godliman shifted on the cold concrete of the station platform and let the memory fade away. There was a warm wind from the tunnel and a train came in. The people who got off found spaces and settled to wait. Godliman listened to the voices.

'Did you hear Churchill on the wireless? We was listening in at the Duke of Wellington. Old Jack Thornton cried. Silly old bugger . . .'

'From what I can gather Kathy's boy's in a stately home and got his own footman! My Alfie milks the cow . . .'

'Haven't had fillet steak on the menu for so long I've forgotton the bally taste . . . wine committee saw the war coming and bought in twenty thousand dozen, thank God . . .'

'Yes, a quiet wedding, but what's the point in waiting when you don't know what the next day's going to bring?'

'They call it Spring, Ma, he says to me, and they have one down here every year . . .'

'She's pregnant again, you know . . . yes, thirteen years since the last . . . I thought I'd found out what was causing it!'

'No, Peter never came back from Dunkirk . . .'

The bus driver offered him a cigarette. Godliman refused, and took out his pipe. Someone started to sing.

A blackout warden passing yelled
'Ma, pull down that blind—
Just look at what you're showing,' and we
Shouted 'Never mind.' Oh!
Knees up Mother Brown . . .

The song spread through the crowd until everyone was singing. Godliman joined in, knowing that this was a nation losing a war and singing to hide its fear, as a man will whistle past the graveyard at night; knowing that the sudden affection he felt for London and Londoners was an ephemeral sentiment, akin to mob hysteria; mistrusting the voice inside him which said 'This, this is what the war is about, this is what makes it worth fighting'; knowing but not caring, because for the first time in so many years he was feeling the sheer physical thrill of comradeship and he liked it.

When the all-clear sounded they went singing up the staircases and into the street, and Godliman found a phone box and called Colonel Terry to ask how soon he could start.

THREE

The small country church was old and very beautiful. A dry-stone wall enclosed a graveyard where wild flowers grew. The church itself had been there – well, bits of it had – the last time Britain was invaded, almost a millennium ago. The north wall of the nave, several feet thick and pierced with only two tiny windows, could remember that last invasion; it had been built when churches were places of physical as well as spiritual sanctuary, and the little round-headed windows were better for shooting arrows out of than for letting the Lord's sunshine in. Indeed, the Local Defence Volunteers had detailed plans for using the church if and when the current bunch of European thugs crossed the Channel.

But no jackboots sounded in the tiled choir in this August of 1940; not yet. The sun glowed through stained-glass windows which had survived Cromwell's iconoclasts and Henry VIII's greed, and the roof resounded to the notes of an organ which had yet to yield to woodworm and dry rot.

It was a lovely wedding. Lucy wore white, of course; and her five sisters were bridesmaids in apricot dresses. David wore the Mess uniform of a Flying Officer in the

Royal Air Force, all crisp and new for it was the first time he had put it on. They sang Psalm 23, The Lord's My Shepherd, to the tune *Crimond*.

Lucy's father looked proud, as a man will on the day his eldest and most beautiful daughter marries a fine boy in a uniform. He was a farmer, but it was a long time since he had sat on a tractor: he rented out his arable land and used the rent to raise racehorses, although this winter of course his pasture would go under the plough and potatoes would be planted. Although he was really more gentleman than farmer, he nevertheless had the open-air skin, the deep chest, and the big stubby hands of agricultural people. Most of the men on that side of the church bore him a resemblance: barrel-chested men, with weathered red faces, those not in tail coats favouring tweed suits and stout shoes.

The bridesmaids had something of that look, too; they were country girls. But the bride was like her mother. Her hair was a dark, dark red, long and thick, shining and glorious, and she had wide-apart amber eyes set in an oval face; and when she looked at the vicar with that clear, direct gaze and said 'I will' in that firm, clear voice, the vicar was startled and thought, 'By God she means it!' which was an odd thought for a vicar to have in the middle of a wedding.

The family on the other side of the nave had a certain look about them, too. David's father was a lawyer: his permanent frown was a professional affectation, and concealed a sunny nature. (He had been a Major in the Army in the last war, and thought all this business about the RAF and war in the air was a fad which would soon pass.) But nobody looked like him, not even his son who stood now at the altar promising to love his wife until death, which might not be far away, God forbid. No, they all looked like David's mother, who sat beside her husband now, with almost-black hair, dark skin and long, slender limbs.

David was the tallest of the lot. He had broken high-jump records last year at Cambridge University. He was rather too good-looking for a man – his face would have been feminine were it not for the dark, ineradicable shadow of a heavy beard. He shaved twice a day. He had long eyelashes, and he looked intelligent, as he was, and sensitive, which he was not.

It was idyllic: two happy, handsome people, children of solid, comfortably off, backbone-of-England type families, getting married in a country church in the finest summer weather Britain can offer.

When they were pronounced man and wife both mothers were dry-eyed, and both the fathers cried.

Kissing the bride was a barbarous custom, Lucy thought as yet another middle-aged pair of champagne-wet lips smeared her cheek. It was probably descended from even more barbarous customs in the Dark Ages, when every man in the tribe was allowed to – well, anyway, it was time we got properly civilized and dropped the whole business.

She had known she would not like this part of the

wedding. She liked champagne, but she was not crazy about chicken drumsticks or dollops of caviar on squares of cold toast, and as for the speeches and the photographs and the honeymoon jokes, well . . . But it could have been worse. If it had been peacetime Father would have hired the Albert Hall.

So far nine people had said, 'May all your troubles be little ones,' and one person, with scarcely more originality, had said, 'I want to see more than a fence running around your garden.' Lucy had shaken countless hands and pretended not to hear remarks like, 'I wouldn't mind being in David's pyjamas tonight.' David had made a speech in which he thanked Lucy's parents for giving him their daughter, as if she were an inanimate object to be gift-wrapped in white satin and presented to the most deserving applicant. Lucy's father had been crass enough to say that he was not losing a daughter but gaining a son. It was all hopelessly gaga, but one did it for one's parents.

A distant uncle loomed up from the direction of the bar, swaying slightly, and Lucy repressed a shudder. She introduced him to her husband. 'David, this is Uncle Norman.'

Uncle Norman pumped David's bony hand. 'Well, m'boy, when do you take up your commission?'

'Tomorrow, sir.'

'What, no honeymoon?'

'Just twenty-four hours.'

'But you've only just finished your training, so I gather.'

'Yes, but I could fly before, you know. I learned at Cambridge. Besides, with all this going on they can't spare pilots. I expect I shall be in the air tomorrow.'

Lucy said quietly: 'David, don't,' but she was ignored.

'What'll you fly?' Uncle Norman asked with schoolboy enthusiasm.

'Spitfire. I saw her yesterday. She's a lovely kite.' David had consciously adopted all the RAF slang, kites and crates and the drink and bandits at two o'clock. 'She's got eight guns, she does three hundred and fifty knots, and she'll turn around in a shoebox.'

'Marvellous, marvellous. You boys are certainly knocking the stuffing out of the Luftwaffe, what?'

'We got sixty yesterday for eleven of our own,' David said, as proudly as if he had shot them all down himself. 'The day before, when they had a go at Yorkshire, we sent the bally lot back to Norway with their tails between their legs – and we didn't lose a single kite!'

Uncle Norman gripped David's shoulder with tipsy fervour. 'Never,' he quoted pompously, 'was so much owed by so many to so few. Churchill said that the other day.'

David tried a modest grin. 'He must have been talking about the mess bills.'

Lucy hated the way they trivialized bloodshed and destruction. She said: 'David, we should go and change now.'

They went in separate cars to Lucy's home. Her mother helped her out of the wedding dress and said: 'Now, my dear, I don't quite know what you're expecting tonight, but you ought to know—'

'Oh, mother, don't be embarrassing,' Lucy interrupted. 'You're about ten years too late to tell me the facts of life. This *is* 1940, you know!'

Her mother coloured slightly. 'Very well, dear,' she said mildly. 'But if there is anything you want to talk about, later on . . .'

It occurred to Lucy that to say things like this cost her mother considerable effort, and she regretted her sharp reply. 'Thank you,' she said. She touched her mother's hand. 'I will.'

'I'll leave you to it, then. Call me if you want anything.' She kissed Lucy's cheek and went out.

Lucy sat at the dressing-table in her slip and began to brush her hair. She knew exactly what to expect tonight. She felt a faint glow of pleasure as she remembered.

It was a well-planned seduction, although at the time it did not occur to Lucy that David might have plotted every move beforehand.

It happened in June, a year after they had met at the Glad Rag Ball. They were seeing each other every week by this time, and David had spent part of the Easter vacation with Lucy's people. Mother and Father approved of him: he was handsome, clever and gentlemanly, and he came from precisely the same stratum of society as they did. Father thought he was a shade too opinionated, but Mother said the landed gentry had been saying that about undergraduates for six hundred years, and *she* thought David would be kind to his wife, which was the most important thing in the long run. So in June Lucy went to David's family home for a weekend.

The place was a Victorian copy of an eighteenth-century grange, a square-shaped house with nine bedrooms and a terrace with a vista. What impressed Lucy about it was the realization that the people who planted the garden must have known they would be long dead before it reached maturity. The atmosphere was very easy, and the two of them drank beer on the terrace in the afternoon sunshine. That was when David told her that he had been accepted for officer training in the RAF, along with four pals from the university flying club. He wanted to be a fighter pilot.

'I can fly all right,' he said, 'and they'll need people once this war gets going – they say it'll be won and lost in the air, this time.'

'Aren't you afraid?' she said quietly.

'Not a bit,' he said. Then he covered his eyes with his hand and said: 'Yes, I am.'

She thought he was very brave, and held his hand.

A little later they put on swimming costumes and went down to the lake. The water was clear and cool, but the sun was still strong and the air was warm. They splashed about gleefully, as if they knew this was the end of their childhood.

'Are you a good swimmer?' he asked her.

'Better than you!'

'All right. Race you to the island.'

She shaded her eyes to look into the sun. She held the pose for a minute, pretending she did not know how desirable she was in her wet swimsuit with her arms raised and her shoulders back. The island was a small patch of bushes and trees about three hundred yards away, in the centre of the lake.

She dropped her hands, shouted 'Go!', and struck out in a fast crawl.

David won, of course, with his long arms and legs. Lucy found herself in difficulty when she was still fifty yards from the island. She switched to breaststroke, but she was too exhausted even for that, and she had to roll over on to her back and float. David, who was already sitting on the bank blowing like a walrus, slipped back into the water and swam to meet her. He got behind her, held her beneath the arms in the correct lifesaving position, and pulled her slowly to the shore. His hands were just below her breasts.

'I'm enjoying this,' he said, and she giggled despite her breathlessness.

A few moments later he said: 'I suppose I might as well tell you.'

'What?' she panted.

'The lake is only four feet deep.'

'You rogue!' She wriggled out of his arms, spluttering and laughing, and found her footing.

He took her hand and led her out of the water and through the trees. He pointed to an old wooden rowing-boat, rotting upside-down beneath a hawthorn. 'When I was a boy I used to row out here in that, with one of Papa's pipes, a box of matches, and a pinch of tobacco in a twist of paper. This is where I used to smoke it.'

They were in a clearing, completely surrounded by

bushes. The turf underfoot was clean and springy. Lucy flopped on the ground.

'We'll swim back slowly,' David said.

'Let's not even talk about it just yet,' she replied.

He sat beside her and kissed her, then pushed her gently backwards until she was lying down. He stroked her hip and kissed her throat, and soon she stopped shivering. When he laid his hand gently, nervously, on the soft mound between her legs, she arched upwards, willing him to press harder. She pulled his face to hers and kissed him open-mouthed and wetly. His hands went to the straps of her swimsuit, and he pulled them down over her shoulders. She said: 'No.'

He buried his face between her breasts. 'Lucy, please.'

'No.'

He looked at her. 'It might be my last chance.'

She rolled away from him and stood up. Then, because of the war, and because of the pleading look on his flushed young face, and because of the glow inside her which would not go away, she took off her costume with one swift movement, and removed her swimming-cap so that her dark red hair shook out over her shoulders, and knelt in front of him, taking his face in her hands and guiding his lips to her breast.

She lost her virginity painlessly, enthusiastically, and only a little too quickly.

The spice of guilt made the memory more pleasant, not less. If it had been a well-planned seduction then she had been a willing, not to say eager, victim, especially at the end.

She began to dress in her going-away outfit. She had startled him a couple of times, that afternoon on the island: once when she wanted him to kiss her breasts, and again when she had guided him inside her with her hands. Apparently such things did not happen in the books he read. Like most of her friends, Lucy read D. H. Lawrence for information about sex. She believed in his choreography and mistrusted the noises-off: the things his people did to one another sounded nice, but not that nice; she was not expecting trumpets and thunderstorms and the clash of cymbals at her sexual awakening.

David was a little more ignorant than she; but he was gentle, and he took pleasure in her pleasure, and she was sure that was the important thing.

They had done it only once since the first time. Exactly a week before their wedding they had made love again, and it caused their first row.

This time it was at her parents' house, in the morning after everyone else had left. He came to her room in his dressing-gown and got into bed with her. She almost changed her mind about Lawrence's trumpets and cymbals. David got out of bed immediately afterwards.

'Don't go,' she said.

'Somebody might come in.'

'I'll chance it. Come back to bed.' She was warm and drowsy and comfortable, and she wanted him beside her.

He put on his dressing-gown. 'It makes me nervous.'

'You weren't nervous five minutes ago.' She reached for him. 'Lie with me. I want to get to know your body.'

'My God, you're brazen.'

She looked at him to see whether he was joking, and when she realized he was not, she became angry. '*Just* what the *hell* does *that* mean?'

'You're just not . . . ladylike!'

'What a *stupid* thing to say—'

'You act like a – a – tart.'

She flounced out of bed, naked and furious, her lovely breasts heaving with rage. 'Just how much do you know about tarts?'

'Nothing!'

'How much do you know about women?'

'I know how a virgin is supposed to behave!'

'I am . . . I was . . . until I met you . . .' She sat on the edge of the bed and burst into tears.

That was the end of the quarrel, of course. David put his arms around her and said: 'I'm sorry, sorry, sorry. You're the first one for me, too, and I don't know what to expect, and I feel confused . . . I mean, nobody tells you anything about this, do they?'

She snuffled and shook her head in agreement, and it occurred to her that what was *really* unnerving him was the knowledge that in eight days' time he had to take off in a flimsy aircraft and fight for his life above the clouds; so she forgave him, and he dried her tears, and they got back into bed and held each other tightly for courage.

Lucy told her friend Joanna about the row, saying it was over a dress David thought to be brazen. Joanna said that couples always quarrelled before the wedding, usually the night before: it was the last chance to test the strength of their love.

She was just about ready. She examined herself in a full-length mirror. Her suit was faintly military, with square shoulders and epaulettes, but the blouse beneath it was feminine, for balance. Her hair fell in sausage curls beneath a natty pill-box hat. It would not have been right to go away gorgeously dressed, not this year; but she felt she had achieved the kind of briskly practical, yet attractive, look which was rapidly becoming fashionable.

David was waiting for her in the hall. He kissed her and said: 'You look wonderful, Mrs Rose.'

They were driven back to the reception to say goodbye to everyone, before leaving to spend the night in London, at Claridge's; then David would drive on to Biggin Hill and Lucy would come home again. She was going to live with her parents: she had the use of a cottage for when David was on leave.

There was another half-hour of handshakes and kisses, then they went out to the car. Some of David's cousins had got at his open-top MG. There were tin cans and an old boot tied to the bumpers with string, the running-boards were awash with confetti, and 'Just Married' was scrawled all over the paintwork in bright red lipstick.

They drove away, smiling and waving, the guests filling the street behind them. A mile down the road they stopped and cleaned up the car.

It was dusk when they got going again. David's

headlights were fitted with blackout masks, but he drove very fast just the same. Lucy felt very happy.

David said: 'There's a bottle of bubbly in the glove box.'

Lucy opened the compartment and found the champagne and two glasses carefully wrapped in tissue paper. It was still quite cold. The cork came out with a loud pop and shot off into the night. David lit a cigarette while Lucy poured the wine.

'We're going to be late for supper,' he said.

'Who cares?' She handed him a glass.

She was too tired to drink, really. She became sleepy. The car seemed to be going terribly fast. She let David have most of the champagne. He began to whistle *St Louis Blues.*

Driving through England in the blackout was a weird experience. One missed lights which one hadn't realized were there before the war: lights in cottage porches and farmhouse windows, lights on cathedral spires and inn signs, and – most of all – the luminous glow, low in the distant sky, of the thousand lights of a nearby town. Even if one had been able to see, there were no signposts to look at: they had been removed to confuse the German parachutists who were expected any day. (Just a few days ago in the Midlands farmers had found parachutes, radios and maps; but since there were no footprints leading away from the objects, it had been concluded that no men had landed, and the whole thing was a feeble Nazi attempt to panic the population.) Anyway, David knew the way to London.

They climbed a long hill. The little sports car took it

nimbly. Lucy gazed through half-closed eyes at the blackness ahead. The downside of the hill was steep and winding. Lucy heard the distant roar of an approaching lorry.

The MG's tyres squealed as David raced around the bends. 'I think you're going too fast,' Lucy said mildly.

The back of the car skidded on a left-hander. David changed down, afraid to brake in case he skidded again. On either side, the hedgerows were dimly picked out by the shaded headlights. There was a sharp right-hand bend, and David lost the back again. The curve seemed to go on and on forever. The little car slid sideways and turned through 180 degrees, so that it was going backwards; then continued to turn in the same direction.

Lucy screamed: 'David!'

The moon came out suddenly, and they saw the lorry. It was struggling up the hill at a snail's pace, with thick smoke, made silvery by the moonlight, pouring from its snout-shaped bonnet. Lucy glimpsed the driver's face, even his cloth cap and his moustache; his mouth was open in terror as he stood on his brakes.

The car was travelling forward again now. There was just room to pass the lorry if David could regain control of the car. He heaved the steering wheel over and touched the accelerator. It was a mistake.

The car and the lorry collided head-on.

FOUR

Foreigners have spies: Britain has Military Intelligence. As if that were not euphemism enough, it is abbreviated to MI. In 1940, MI was part of the War Office. It was spreading like couch grass at the time – not surprisingly – and its different sections were known by numbers: MI9 ran the escape routes from prisoner-of-war camps through Occupied Europe to neutral countries; MI8 monitored enemy wireless traffic, and was of more value than six regiments; MI6 sent agents into France.

It was MI5 that Professor Percival Godliman joined in the autumn of 1940. He turned up at the War Office in Whitehall on a cold September morning after a night spent putting out fires all over the East End: the Blitz was at its height and he was an Auxiliary Fireman.

Military Intelligence was run by soldiers in peacetime, when – in Godliman's opinion – espionage made no difference to anything anyhow; but now, he found, it was populated by amateurs, and he was delighted to discover that he knew half the people in MI5. On his first day he met a barrister who was a member of his club, an art historian with whom he had been to college, an archivist from his own university, and his favourite writer of detective stories.

He was shown into Colonel Terry's office at ten a.m. Terry had been there for several hours: there were two empty cigarette packets in the waste-paper bin.

Godliman said: 'Should I call you "Sir" now?'

'There's not much bull around here, Percy. "Uncle Andrew" will do fine. Sit down.'

All the same, there was a briskness about Terry which had not been present when they had lunch at the Savoy. Godliman noticed that he did not smile, and his attention kept wandering to a pile of unread signals on the desk.

Terry looked at his watch and said: 'I'm going to put you in the picture, briefly – finish the lecture I started over lunch.'

Godliman smiled. 'This time I won't get up on my high horse.'

Terry lit another cigarette.

Canaris's spies in Britain were useless people (Terry resumed, as if their conversation had been interrupted five minutes rather than three months ago). Dorothy O'Grady was typical: we caught her cutting military telephone wires on the Isle of Wight. She was writing letters to Portugal in the kind of secret ink you buy in joke shops.

A new wave of spies began in September. Their task was to reconnoitre Britain in preparation for the invasion: to map beaches suitable for landings, fields and roads which could be used by troop-carrying gliders, tank traps and road blocks and barbed-wire obstacles.

They seem to have been badly selected, hastily mustered, inadequately trained and poorly equipped. Typical were the four who came over on the night of 2–3 September: Meier, Kieboom, Pons and Waldberg. Kieboom and Pons landed at dawn near Hythe, and were arrested by Private Tollervey of the Somerset Light Infantry, who came upon them in the sand-dunes tucking in to a dirty great *wurst.*

Waldberg actually managed to send a signal to Hamburg:

ARRIVED SAFELY. DOCUMENT DESTROYED. ENGLISH PATROL 200 METRES FROM COAST. BEACH WITH BROWN NETS AND RAILWAY SLEEPERS AT A DISTANCE OF 50 METRES. NO MINES. FEW SOLDIERS. UNFINISHED BLOCK-HOUSE. NEW ROAD. WALDBERG.

Clearly he did not know where he was, nor did he even have a code name. The quality of his briefing is indicated by the fact that he knew nothing of English licensing laws: he went into a pub at nine o'clock in the morning and asked for a quart of cider.

(Godliman laughed at this, and Terry said: 'Wait – it gets funnier.')

The landlord told Waldberg to come back at ten. He could spend the hour looking at the village church, he suggested. Amazingly, Waldberg was back at ten sharp, whereupon two policemen on bicycles arrested him.

('It's like a script for *It's That Man Again,*' said Godliman.)

Meier was found a few hours later. Eleven more

agents were picked up over the next few weeks, most of them within hours of landing on British soil. Almost all of them were destined for the scaffold.

('*Almost* all?' said Godliman. Terry said: 'Yes. A couple have been handed over to our section B-1(a). I'll come back to that in a minute.')

Others landed in Eire. One was Ernst Weber-Drohl, a well-known acrobat who had two illegitimate children in Ireland – he had toured music-halls there as 'The World's Strongest Man'. He was arrested by the Garda Siochania, fined three pounds, and turned over to B-1(a).

Another was Hermann Goetz, who parachuted into Ulster instead of Eire by mistake, was robbed by the IRA, swam the Boyne in his fur underwear, and eventually swallowed his suicide pill. He had a torch marked 'Made in Dresden'.

('If it's so easy to pick these bunglers up,' Terry said, 'why are we taking on brainy types like yourself to catch them? Two reasons. One: we've got no way of knowing how many we *haven't* picked up. Two: it's what we do with the ones we don't hang that matters. This is where B-1(a) comes in. But to explain that I have to go back to 1936.')

Alfred George Owens was an electrical engineer with a company that had a few government contracts. He visited Germany several times during the thirties, and voluntarily gave to the Admiralty odd bits of technical information he picked up there. Eventually Naval Intelligence passed him on to MI6 who began to develop him as an agent. The Abwehr recruited him at about the same time, as MI6 discovered when they intercepted a letter from him to a known German cover address. Clearly he was a man totally without loyalty: he just wanted to be a spy. We called him 'Snow'; the Germans called him 'Johnny'.

In January 1939 Snow got a letter containing (i) instructions for the use of a wireless transmitter and (ii) a ticket for the cloakroom at Victoria Station.

He was arrested the day after war broke out, and he and his transmitter (which he had picked up, in a suitcase, when he presented the cloakroom ticket) were locked up in Wandsworth Prison. He continued to communicate with Hamburg, but now all the messages were written by section B-1(a) of MI5.

The Abwehr put him in touch with two more German agents in England, whom we immediately nabbed. They also gave him a code and detailed wireless procedure, all of which was invaluable.

Snow was followed by Charlie, Rainbow, Summer, Biscuit, and eventually a small army of enemy spies, all in regular contact with Canaris, all apparently trusted by him, and all totally controlled by the British counter-intelligence apparatus.

At that point MI5 began dimly to glimpse an awesome and tantalizing prospect: with a bit of luck, *they could control and manipulate the entire German espionage network in Britain.*

'Turning agents into double agents instead of hanging them has two crucial advantages,' Terry wound up. 'Since the enemy thinks his spies are still active, he doesn't try to replace them with others who may not get caught. And, since *we* are supplying the information the spies tell their controllers, we can deceive the enemy and mislead his strategists.'

'It can't be that easy,' said Godliman.

'Certainly not.' Terry opened a window to let out the fug of cigarette and pipe smoke. 'To work, the system has to be very nearly total. If there is any substantial number of genuine agents here, their information will contradict that of the double agents and the Abwehr will smell a rat.'

'It sounds tremendously exciting,' Godliman said. His pipe had gone out.

Terry smiled for the first time that morning. 'The people here will tell you it's hard work – long hours, high tension, frustration – but yes, of course it's exciting.' He looked at his watch. 'Now I want you to meet a very bright young member of my staff. Let me walk you to his office.'

They went out of the room, up some stairs, and along several corridors. 'His name is Frederick Bloggs, and he gets annoyed if you make jokes about it,' Terry continued. 'We pinched him from Scotland Yard – he was an inspector with Special Branch. If you need arms and legs, use his. You'll rank above him, but I shouldn't make too much of that – we don't, here. I suppose I hardly need to say that to you.'

They entered a small, bare room which looked out on to a blank wall. There was no carpet. A photograph of a pretty girl hung on the wall, and there was a pair of handcuffs on the hat-stand.

Terry said: 'Frederick Bloggs, Percival Godliman. I'll leave you to it.'

The man behind the desk was blond, stocky and short – he must have been only just tall enough to get into the police force, Godliman thought. His tie was an eyesore, but he had a pleasant, open face and an attractive grin. His handshake was firm.

He said: 'Tell you what, Percy – I was just going to nip home for lunch – why don't you come along? The wife makes a lovely sausage and chips.' He had a broad cockney accent.

Sausage and chips was not Godliman's favourite meal, but he went along. They walked to Trafalgar Square and caught a bus to Hoxton. Bloggs said: 'I married a wonderful girl, but she can't cook for nuts. I have sausage and chips every day.'

East London was still smoking from the previous night's air raid. They passed groups of firemen and volunteers digging through rubble, playing hoses over dying fires, and clearing debris from the streets. They saw an old man carry a precious radio out of a half-ruined house.

Godliman made conversation. 'So we're to catch spies together.'

'We'll have a go, Perce.'

Bloggs's home was a three-bedroom semi in a street of exactly similar houses. The tiny front gardens were all being used to grow vegetables. Mrs Bloggs was the pretty girl in the photograph on the office wall. She looked tired. Bloggs said: 'She drives an ambulance during the raids, don't you, love?' He was proud of her. Her name was Christine.

She said: 'Every morning when I come home I wonder if the house will still be here.'

'Notice it's the house she's worried about, not me,' Bloggs said.

Godliman picked up a medal in a presentation case from the mantelpiece. 'How did you get this?'

Christine answered. 'He took a shotgun off a villain who was robbing a post office.'

'You're quite a pair,' Godliman said.

'You married, Percy?' Bloggs asked.

'I'm a widower.'

'Sorry.'

'My wife died of tuberculosis in 1930. We never had any children.'

'We're not having any yet,' Bloggs said. 'Not while the world's in this state.'

Christine said: 'Oh, Fred, he's not interested in that!' She went out to the kitchen.

They sat around a square table in the centre of the room to eat. Bloggs was touched by this couple and the domestic scene, and found himself thinking of his Eleanor. That was unusual: he had been immune to sentiment for some years. Perhaps the nerves were coming alive again, at last. War did funny things.

Christine's cooking was truly awful. The sausages were burned. Bloggs drowned his meal in tomato ketchup, and Godliman cheerfully followed suit.

When they got back to Whitehall Bloggs showed Godliman the file on unidentified enemy agents still thought to be operating in Britain.

There were three sources of information about such

people. The first was the immigration records of the Home Office. Passport control had long been an arm of Military Intelligence, and there was a list – going back to the last war – of aliens who had entered the country but had not left or been accounted for in other ways, such as death or naturalization. At the outbreak of war they had all gone before tribunals which classified them in three groups. At first only 'A' class aliens were interned; but by July of 1940, after some scaremongering by Fleet Street, the 'B' and 'C' classes were taken out of circulation. There was a small number of immigrants who could not be located, and it was a fair assumption that some of them were spies.

Their papers were in Bloggs's file.

The second source was wireless transmissions. Section C of MI8 scanned the airwaves nightly, recorded everything they did not know for certain to be ours, and passed it to the Government Code and Cypher School. This outfit, which had recently been moved from London's Berkeley Street to a country house at Bletchley Park, was not a school at all but a collection of chess champions, musicians, mathematicians and crossword-puzzle enthusiasts dedicated to the belief that if a man could invent a code a man could crack it. Signals originating in the UK which could not be accounted for by any of the Services were assumed to be messages from spies.

The decoded messages were in Bloggs's file.

Finally there were the double agents; but their value was largely hoped-for rather than actual. Messages to them from the Abwehr had warned of several incoming agents, and had given away one resident spy – Mrs Matilda Krafft of Bournemouth, who had sent money to Snow by post and was subsequently incarcerated in Holloway prison. But the doubles had not been able to reveal the identity or location of the kind of quietly effective professional spies who are most valuable to a secret intelligence service. No one doubted that there were such people. There were clues: someone, for example, had brought Snow's transmitter over from Germany and deposited it in the cloakroom at Victoria Station for him to collect. But either the Abwehr or the spies themselves were too cautious to be caught by the doubles.

However, the clues were in Bloggs's file.

Other sources were being developed: the boffins were working to improve methods of triangulation (the directional pin-pointing of radio transmitters); and MI6 were trying to rebuild the networks of agents in Europe which had sunk beneath the tidal wave of Hitler's armies.

What little information there was, was in Bloggs's file.

'It can be infuriating at times,' he told Godliman. 'Look at this.'

He took from the file a long radio intercept about British plans for an expeditionary force for Finland. 'This was picked up early in the year. The information is impeccable. They were trying to get a fix on him when he broke off in the middle, for no apparent reason – perhaps he was interrupted. He resumed a few minutes later, but he was off the air again before our boys had a chance to plug in.'

Godliman said: 'What's this – "Regards to Willi"?'

'Now, that's important,' said Bloggs. He was getting enthusiastic. 'Here's a scrap of another message, quite recent. Look – "Regards to Willi". This time there was a reply. He's addressed as "Die Nadel".'

'The Needle.'

'This bloke's a pro. Look at his messages: terse, economical, but detailed and completely unambiguous.'

Godliman studied the fragment of the second message. 'It appears to be about the effects of the bombing.'

'He's obviously toured the East End. A pro, a pro.'

'What else do we know about Die Nadel?'

Bloggs's expression of youthful eagerness collapsed comically. 'That's it, I'm afraid.'

'His code name is Die Nadel, he signs off "Regards to Willi", and he has good information – and that's it?'

' 'Fraid so.'

Godliman sat on the edge of the desk and stared out of the window. On the wall of the opposite building, underneath an ornate windowsill, he could see the nest of a house-marten. 'On that basis, what chance have we of catching him?'

Bloggs shrugged. 'On that basis, none at all.'

FIVE

It is for places like this that the word 'bleak' has been invented.

The island is a J-shaped lump of rock rising sullenly out of the North Sea. It lies on the map like the top half of a broken walking-stick; parallel with the equator but a long, long way north; its curved handle toward Aberdeen, its broken, jagged stump pointing threateningly at distant Denmark. It is ten miles long.

Around most of its coast the cliffs rise out of the cold sea without the courtesy of a beach. Angered by this rudeness the waves pound on the rock in impotent rage; a ten-thousand-year fit of bad temper which the island ignores with impunity.

In the cup of the J the sea is calmer, for there it has provided itself with a more pleasant reception. Its tides have thrown into that cup so much sand and seaweed, driftwood and pebbles and seashells, that there is now, between the foot of the cliff and the water's edge, a crescent of something closely resembling dry land, a more-or-less beach.

Each summer the vegetation at the top of the cliff drops a handful of seeds on to the beach, the way a rich man throws loose change to beggars. If the winter is mild and the spring comes early, a few of the seeds take feeble root; but they are never healthy enough to flower themselves and spread their own seeds, so the beach exists from year to year on handouts.

On the land itself, the proper land, held out of the sea's reach by the cliffs, green things do grow and multiply. The vegetation is mostly coarse grass, only just good enough to nourish the few bony sheep, but tough enough to bind the topsoil to the island's bedrock. There are some bushes, all thorny, which provide homes for rabbits; and a brave stand of conifers on the leeward slope of the hill at the eastern end.

The higher land is ruled by heather. Every few years the man – yes, there is a man here – the man sets fire to the heather, and then the grass will grow and the sheep can graze here too; but after a couple of years the heather comes back, God knows from where, and drives the sheep away until the man burns it again.

The rabbits are here because they were born here; the sheep are here because they were brought here; and the man is here to look after the sheep; but the birds are here because they like it. There are hundreds of thousands of them: long-legged rock pipits whistling *peep peep peep* as they soar and *pe-pe-pe-pe* as they dive like a Spitfire coming at a Messerschmitt out of the sun; corncrakes, which the man rarely sees, but he knows they are there because their bark keeps him awake at night; ravens and carrion crows and kittiwakes and *countless* gulls; and a pair of golden eagles which the man shoots at when he sees them, for he *knows* – regardless of what naturalists and experts from Edinburgh may tell him – that they *do* prey upon live lambs and not just the carcases of those already dead.

The island's most constant visitor is the wind. It comes mostly from the north-east, from *really* cold places where there are fiords and glaciers and icebergs; often bringing with it unwelcome gifts of snow and driving rain and cold, cold mist; sometimes arriving empty-handed, just to howl and whoop and raise hell, tearing up bushes and bending trees and whipping the intemperate ocean into fresh paroxysms of foam-flecked rage. It is tireless, this wind; and that is its mistake. If it came occasionally it could take the island by surprise and do some real damage; but because it is almost always here, the island has learned to live with it. The plants put down deep roots, and the rabbits hide far inside the thickets, and the trees grow up with their backs ready-bent for the flogging, and the birds nest on sheltered ledges, and the man's house is sturdy and squat, built with a craftsmanship that knows this wind of old.

This house is made of big grey stones and grey slates, the colour of the sea. It has small windows and close-fitting doors and a chimney in its pine end. It stands at the top of the hill at the eastern end of the island, close to the splintered stub of the broken walking-stick. It crowns the hill, defying the wind and the rain, not out of bravado but so that the man can see the sheep.

There is another house, very similar, ten miles away at the opposite end of the island near the more-or-less beach; but nobody lives there. There was once another man. He thought he knew better than the island; he thought he could grow oats and potatoes and keep a few cows. He battled for three years with the wind and the cold and the soil before he admitted he was wrong. When he had gone, nobody wanted his home.

This is a hard place. Only hard things survive here: hard rock, coarse grass, tough sheep, savage birds, sturdy houses and strong men. Hard things and cold things, and cruel and bitter and pointed things, rugged and slow-moving and determined things; things as cold and hard and ruthless as the island itself.

It is for places like this that the word 'bleak' has been invented.

'It's called Storm Island,' said Alfred Rose. 'I think you're going to like it.'

David and Lucy Rose sat in the prow of the fishing-boat and looked across the choppy water. It was a fine November day, cold and breezy yet clear and dry. A weak sun sparkled off the wavelets.

'I bought it in 1926,' Papa Rose continued, 'when we thought there was going to be a revolution and we'd need somewhere to hide from the working class. It's just the place for a convalescence.'

Lucy thought he was being suspiciously hearty, but she had to admit it looked lovely: all windblown and natural and fresh. And it made sense, this move. They had to get away from their parents and make a new start at being married; and there was no point in moving to a city to be bombed, when neither of them was really well enough to help; and then David's father had revealed that he owned an island off the coast of Scotland, and it seemed too good to be true.

'I own the sheep, too,' Papa Rose said. 'Shearers come over from the mainland each spring, and the wool brings in just about enough money to pay Tom McAvity's wages. Old Tom's the shepherd.'

'How old is he?' Lucy asked.

'Good Lord, he must be – oh, seventy?'

'I suppose he's eccentric.' The boat turned into the bay, and Lucy could see two small figures on the jetty: a man and a dog.

'Eccentric? No more than you'd be if you'd lived alone for twenty years. He talks to his dog.'

Lucy turned to the skipper of the small boat. 'How often do you call?'

'Once a fortnight, missus. I bring Tom's shopping, which isna much, and his mail, which is even less. You just give me your list, every other Monday, and if it can be bought in Aberdeen I'll bring it.'

He cut the motor and threw a rope to Tom. The dog barked and ran around in circles, beside himself with excitement. Lucy put one foot on the gunwale and sprang out on to the jetty.

Tom took her hand. He had a face of leather and a huge briar pipe with a lid. He was shorter than she, but wide, and he looked ridiculously healthy. He wore the hairiest tweed jacket she had ever seen, with a knitted sweater that must have been made by an elderly sister somewhere, plus a checked cap and army boots. His nose was huge, red and veined. 'Pleased to meet you,' he said politely, as if she was his ninth visitor today instead of the first human face he had seen in fourteen days.

'Here y'are, Tom,' said the skipper. He handed two cardboard boxes out of the boat. 'No eggs this time, but here's a letter from Devon.'

'It'll be from ma niece.'

Lucy thought: That explains the sweater.

David was still in the boat. The skipper stood behind him and said: 'Are you ready?'

Tom and Papa Rose leaned into the boat to assist, and the three of them lifted David in his wheelchair on to the jetty.

'If I don't go now I'll have to wait a fortnight for the next bus,' Papa Rose said with a smile. 'The house has been done up quite nicely, you'll see. All your stuff is in there. Tom will show you where everything is.' He kissed Lucy, squeezed David's shoulder, and shook Tom's hand. 'Have a few months of rest and togetherness, get completely fit, then come back: there are important war jobs for both of you.'

They would not be going back, Lucy knew; not before the end of the war: but she had not told anyone about that yet.

Papa got back into the boat. It wheeled away in a tight circle. Lucy waved until it disappeared around the headland.

Tom pushed the wheelchair, so Lucy took his groceries. Between the landward end of the jetty and the cliff top was a long, steep, narrow ramp rising high above the beach like a bridge. Lucy would have had trouble getting the wheelchair to the top, but Tom managed without apparent exertion.

The cottage was perfect.

It was small and grey, and sheltered from the wind by a little rise in the ground. All the woodwork was freshly painted, and a wild rose bush grew beside the doorstep. Curls of smoke rose from the chimney to be whipped away by the breeze. The tiny windows looked over the bay.

Lucy said: 'I love it!'

The interior had been cleaned and aired and painted, and there were thick rugs on the stone floors. It had four rooms: downstairs, a modernized kitchen and a living-room with a stone fireplace; upstairs, two bedrooms. One end of the house had been carefully remodelled to take modern plumbing, with a bathroom above and a kitchen extension below.

Their clothes were in the wardrobes. There were towels in the bathroom and food in the kitchen.

Tom said: 'There's something in the barn I've to show you.'

It was a shed, not a barn. It lay hidden behind the cottage, and inside it was a gleaming new jeep.

'Mr Rose says it's been specially adapted for young Mr Rose to drive,' Tom said. 'It's got automatic gears, and the throttle and brake are operated by hand. That's what he said.' He seemed to be repeating the words parrot-fashion, as if he had very little idea of what gears, brakes and throttles might be.

Lucy said: 'Isn't that super, David?'

'Top-hole. But where shall I go in it?'

Tom said: 'You're always welcome to visit me and share a pipe and a drop of whisky. I've been looking forward to having neighbours again.'

'Thank you,' said Lucy.

'This here's the generator,' Tom said, turning around and pointing. 'I've got one just the same. You put the fuel in here. It delivers alternating current.'

David said: 'That's unusual – small generators are usually direct current.'

'Aye. I don't really know the difference, but they tell me this is safer.'

'True. A shock from this would throw you across the room, but direct current would kill you.'

They went back to the cottage. Tom said: 'Well, you'll want to settle in, and I've sheep to tend, so I'll say good-day. Oh! I ought to tell you: in an emergency, I can contact the mainland by wireless radio.'

David was surprised. 'You've got a radio transmitter?'

'Aye,' Tom said proudly. 'I'm an enemy aircraft spotter in the Royal Observer Corps.'

'Ever spotted any?' David asked.

Lucy flashed her disapproval of the sarcasm in David's voice, but Tom seemed not to notice. 'Not yet,' he replied.

David said: 'Jolly good show.'

When Tom had gone Lucy said: 'He only wants to do his bit.'

'There are lots of us who *want* to do our bit,' David said bitterly. And that, Lucy reflected, was the trouble.

She dropped the subject, and wheeled her crippled husband into their new home.

When Lucy had been asked to visit the hospital psychologist, she had immediately assumed that David had brain damage. It was not so. 'All that's wrong with his head is a nasty bruise on the left temple,' the psychologist said. She went on: 'However, the loss of both his legs brings about a trauma, and there's no telling how it will affect his state of mind. Did he want very much to be a pilot?'

Lucy pondered. 'He was afraid, but I think he wanted it very badly, all the same.'

'Well, he'll need all the reassurance and support that you can give him. And patience, too: one thing we can predict is that he will be resentful and ill-tempered for a while. He needs love and rest.'

However, during their first few months on the island he seemed to want neither. He did not make love to her, perhaps because he was waiting until his injuries were fully healed. But he did not rest, either. He threw himself into the business of sheep farming, tearing about the island in his jeep with the wheelchair in the back. He built fences along the more treacherous cliffs, shot at the eagles, helped Tom train a new dog when Betsy began to go blind, and burned-off the heather; and in the spring he was out every night delivering lambs. One day he felled a great old pine tree near Tom's cottage, and spent a fortnight stripping it, hewing it into manageable logs, and carting them back to the house for firewood. He relished really hard manual labour. He learned to strap himself tightly to the chair to keep his body anchored while he wielded an axe or a mallet. He carved a pair of Indian clubs and exercised with them for hours when Tom could find nothing more for him to do. The muscles of his arms and back became grotesque, like those of men who win body-building contests.

He refused point-blank to wash dishes, cook food or clean the house.

Lucy was not unhappy. She had been afraid he might sit by the fire all day and brood over his bad luck. The way he worked was faintly worrying because it was so obsessive, but at least he was not vegetating.

She told him about the baby at Christmas.

In the morning she gave him a petrol-driven saw, and he gave her a bolt of silk. Tom came over for dinner, and they ate a wild goose he had shot. David drove the shepherd home after tea, and when he came back Lucy opened a bottle of brandy.

Then she said: 'I have another present for you, but you can't open it until May.'

He laughed. 'What on earth are you talking about? How much of that brandy did you drink while I was out?'

'I'm having a baby.'

He stared at her, and all the laughter went out of his face. 'Good God, that's all we bloody well need.'

'David!'

'Well, for God's sake . . . When the hell did it happen?'

'That's not too difficult to figure out, is it?' she said bitterly. 'It must have been a week before the wedding. It's a miracle it survived the crash.'

'Have you seen a doctor?'

'Huh – when?'

'So how do you know for sure?'

'Oh, David, don't be so boring. I know for sure because my periods have stopped and my nipples hurt and I throw up in the mornings and my waist is four inches bigger than it used to be. If you ever *looked* at me *you* would know for sure.'

'All right.'

'What's the matter with you? You're supposed to be thrilled!'

'Oh, sure. Perhaps we'll have a son, and then I can take him for walks and play football with him, and he'll grow up wanting to be like his father the war hero, a legless fucking joke!'

'Oh, David, David,' she whispered. She knelt in front of his wheelchair. 'David, don't think like that. He will respect you. He'll look up to you because you put your life together again, and because you can do the work of two men from your wheelchair, and because you carried your disability with courage and cheerfulness.'

'Don't be so damned condescending,' he snapped. 'You sound like a sanctimonious priest.'

She stood up. 'Well, don't act as if it's my fault. Men can take precautions too, you know.'

'You can't take precautions against invisible lorries in the blackout!'

That was a silly, feeble excuse, and they both knew it, so Lucy said nothing. The whole idea of Christmas seemed utterly trite now: the bits of coloured paper on the walls, and the tree in the corner, and the remains of a goose in the kitchen waiting to be thrown away – none of it had anything to do with her life. She began to wonder what she was doing on this bleak island with a man who seemed not to love her, having a baby he didn't want. Why shouldn't she – why not – well, she could . . . Then she realized she had nowhere else to go, nothing else to do with her life, nobody else to *be* other than Mrs David Rose.

Eventually David said: 'Well, I'm going to bed.' He wheeled himself to the hall and dragged himself out of the chair and up the stairs backwards. She heard him scrape across the floor, heard the bed creak as he hauled himself on to it, heard his clothes hit the corner of the room as he undressed, then heard the final groaning of the springs as he lay down and pulled the blankets up over his pyjamas.

And still she would not cry.

She looked at the brandy bottle and thought: If I drink all of this now, and have a bath, perhaps I won't be pregnant in the morning.

She thought about it for a long time, until she came to the conclusion that life without David and the island and the baby would be even worse because it would be empty.

So she did not cry, and she did not drink the brandy,

and she did not leave the island; but instead she went upstairs and got into bed, and lay awake beside her sleeping husband, listening to the wind and trying not to think, until the gulls began to call, and a grey rainy dawn crept over the North Sea and filled the little bedroom with a cold, cheerless, silver light, and then at last she went to sleep.

A kind of peace settled over her in the spring, as if all threats were postponed until after the baby was born. When the February snow had thawed she planted flowers and vegetables in the patch of ground between the kitchen door and the barn, not really believing they would grow. She cleaned the house thoroughly and told David that if he wanted it done again before August he would have to do it himself. She wrote to her mother and did a lot of knitting and ordered nappies by post. They suggested she go home to have the baby, but she knew that if she went she would never come back. She went for long walks over the moors, with a bird book under her arm, until her own weight became too much for her to carry very far. She kept the bottle of brandy in a cupboard David never used, and whenever she felt depressed she went to look at it and remind herself of what she had almost lost.

Three weeks before the baby was due, she got the boat into Aberdeen. David and Tom waved from the jetty. The sea was so rough that both she and the skipper were terrified she might give birth before they reached the mainland. She went into hospital in Aberdeen, and four weeks later brought the baby home on the same boat.

David knew none of it. He probably thought that women gave birth as easily as ewes. He was oblivious to the pain of contractions, and that awful, impossible stretching, and the soreness afterwards, and the bossy, know-all nurses who didn't want you to *touch* your baby because you weren't brisk and efficient and trained and *sterile* like they were; he just saw you go away pregnant and come back with a beautiful, white-wrapped, healthy baby boy and said: 'We'll call him Jonathan.'

They added Alfred for David's father, and Malcolm for Lucy's, and Thomas for old Tom, but they called the boy Jo, because he was too tiny for Jonathan, let alone Jonathan Alfred Malcolm Thomas Rose. David learned to give him his bottle and burp him and change his nappy, and he even dandled him in his lap occasionally, but his interest was distant, uninvolved. He had a problem-solving approach, like the nurses; it was not for him as it was for Lucy. Tom was closer to the baby than David. Lucy would not let him smoke in the room where the baby was, and the old boy would put his great briar pipe with the lid in his pocket for hours and gurgle at little Jo, or watch him kick his feet, or help Lucy bath him. Lucy suggested mildly that he might be neglecting the sheep. Tom said they did not need him to watch them feed – he would rather watch Jo feed. He carved a rattle out of driftwood and filled it with small round pebbles, and was overjoyed when Jo grabbed it and shook it, first time, without having to be shown how.

And still David and Lucy did not make love.

First there had been his injuries, and then she had been pregnant, and then she had been recovering from childbirth; but now the reasons had run out.

One night she said: 'I'm back to normal, now.'

'How do you mean?'

'After the baby. My body is normal. I've healed.'

'Oh, I see. That's good.' And he turned away.

She made sure to go up to bed with him so that he could watch her undress, but he always turned his back. As they lay there, dozing off, she would move so that her hand, or her thigh, or her breast, brushed against him, a casual but unmistakable invitation. There was no response.

She believed firmly that there was nothing wrong with her. She wasn't a nymphomaniac: she didn't simply want sex, she wanted sex with David. She was sure that, even if there had been another man under seventy on the island, she would not have been tempted. She wasn't a sex-starved tart, she was a love-starved wife.

The crunch came on one of those nights when they lay on their backs, side by side, both wide awake, listening to the wind outside and the small sounds of Jo from the next room. It seemed to Lucy that it was time he either did it or came right out and said why not; and that he was going to avoid the issue until she forced it; and that she might as well force it now as live in miserable incomprehension any longer.

So she brushed her arm across his thighs and opened her mouth to speak – and almost cried out with shock to discover that he had an erection. So he could do it!

And he wanted to, or why else – And her hand closed triumphantly around the evidence of his desire, and she shifted closer to him, and sighed: 'David—'

He said: 'Oh, for God's sake!' He gripped her wrist and thrust her hand away from him and turned on to his side.

But this time she was not going to accept his rebuff in modest silence. She said: 'David, why not?'

'Jesus, Christ!' He threw the blankets off, swung himself to the floor, grabbed the eiderdown with one hand, and dragged himself to the door.

Lucy sat up in bed and screamed at him: 'Why not?'

Jo began to cry.

David pulled up the empty legs of his cut-off pyjama trousers, pointed to the pursed white skin of his stumps, and said: 'That's why not! That's why not!'

He slithered downstairs to sleep on the sofa, and Lucy went into the next bedroom to comfort Jo.

It took a long time to lull him back to sleep, probably because she herself was so much in need of comfort. The baby tasted the tears on her cheeks, and she wondered if he had any inkling of their meaning: wouldn't tears be one of the first things a baby came to understand? She could not bring herself to sing to him, nor could she with any sincerity murmur that everything was all right; so she held him tight and rocked him, and when *he* had soothed *her* with his warmth and his clinging, he went to sleep in her arms.

She put him back in the cot and stood looking at him for a while. There was no point in going back to bed. She could hear David's deep-sleep snoring from the living-room – he had to take powerful pills, otherwise the old pain kept him awake. Lucy needed to get right away from him, where she could neither see nor hear him, where he couldn't find her for a few hours even if he wanted to. She put on trousers and a sweater, a heavy coat and boots, and crept downstairs and out into the night.

There was a swirling mist, damp and bitterly cold, the kind the island specialized in. She put up the collar of her coat, thought about going back inside for a scarf, and decided not to. She squelched along the muddy path, welcoming the bite of the fog in her throat, the small discomfort of the weather taking her mind off the larger hurt inside her.

She reached the cliff top and walked gingerly down the steep, narrow ramp, placing her feet carefully on the slippery boards. At the bottom she jumped off on to the sand and walked to the edge of the sea.

The wind and the water were carrying on their perpetual quarrel, the wind swooping down to tease the waves and the sea hissing and spitting as it crashed against the land, the two of them doomed to bicker forever because neither could be calm while the other was there, but neither had any place else to go.

Lucy walked along the hard sand, letting the noise and the weather fill her head, until the beach ended in a sharp point where the water met the cliff, when she turned and walked back. She paced the shore all night. Toward dawn a thought came to her, unbidden: It is his way of being strong.

As it was, the thought was not much help, holding its

meaning in a tightly clenched fist. But she worked on it for a while, and the fist opened to reveal what looked like a small pearl of wisdom nestling in its palm: for perhaps David's coldness to her was of one piece with his chopping down trees, and undressing himself, and driving the jeep, and throwing the Indian clubs, and coming to live on a cold cruel island in the North Sea . . .

What was it he had said? '. . . his father the war hero, a legless joke . . .' He had something to prove, something that would sound trite if it were put into words; something he could have done as a fighter pilot, but now had to do with trees and fences and Indian clubs and a wheelchair. They wouldn't let him take the test, and he wanted to be able to say: 'I could have passed it anyway, just *look* how I can suffer.'

It was cruelly, hopelessly, screamingly unjust: he had had the courage, and he had suffered the wounds, but he could take no pride in it. If a Messerschmitt had taken his legs the wheelchair would have been like a medal, a badge of courage. But now, all his life, he would have to say: 'It was during the war – but no, I never saw any action, this was a car crash, I did my training and I was going to fight, the very next day, I had seen my kite, she was a beauty, and I *would* have been brave, I know . . .'

Yes, it was his way of being strong. And perhaps she could be strong, too. She might find ways of patching up the wreck of her life so that it would sail again. David had once been good and kind and loving, and she might now learn to wait patiently while he battled to become the complete man he used to be. She could find new hopes, new things to live for. Other women had found the strength to cope with bereavement, and bombed-out houses, and husbands in prisoner-of-war camps.

She picked up a pebble, drew back her arm, and threw it out to sea with all her might. She did not see or hear it land: it might have gone on forever, circling the earth like a satellite in a space story.

She shouted: 'I can be strong, too!'

Then she turned around and started up the ramp to the cottage. It was almost time for Jo's first feed.

SIX

It looked like a mansion; and, up to a point, that was what it was: a large house, in its own grounds, in the leafy town of Wohldorf just outside North Hamburg. It might have been the home of a mine owner, or a successful importer, or an industrialist. It was in fact owned by the Abwehr.

It owed its fate to the weather – not here, but two hundred miles south-east in Berlin, where atmospheric conditions were unsuitable for wireless communication with England.

It was a mansion only down to ground level. Below that were two huge concrete shelters and several million Reichsmarks worth of radio equipment. The electronics system had been put together by one Major Werner Trautmann, and he did a good job. Each hall had twenty neat little soundproofed listening posts, occupied by radio operators who could recognize a spy by the way he tapped out his message, as easily as you can recognize your mother's handwriting on an envelope.

The receiving equipment was built with quality in mind, for the transmitters that were sending the messages had been designed for compactness rather than power. Most of them were the little suitcase sets called Klamotten which had been developed by Telefunken for Admiral Wilhelm Canaris, the head of the Abwehr.

On this night the airwaves were relatively quiet, so everyone knew when Die Nadel came through. The message was taken by one of the older operators. He tapped out an acknowledgement, transcribed the signal quickly, tore the sheet off his notepad and went to the phone. He read the message over the direct line to Abwehr headquarters at Sophien Terrace in Hamburg, then he came back to his booth for a smoke.

He offered a cigarette to the youngster in the next booth, and the two of them stood together for a few minutes, leaning against the wall and smoking.

The youngster said: 'Anything?'

The older man shrugged. 'There's always *something* when he calls. But not much, this time. The Luftwaffe missed St Paul's Cathedral again.'

'No reply for him?'

'We don't think he waits for replies. He's an independent bastard, that one. Always was. I trained him in wireless, you know: and once I'd finished he thought he knew it better than me.'

The youngster was awestruck. 'You've *met* Die Nadel?'

'Oh, yes,' said the old-timer, flicking ash.

'What's he like?'

'As a drinking companion, he's about as much fun as a dead fish. I think he likes women, on the quiet, but as for sinking a few steins with the boys – forget it. All the same, he's the best agent we've got.'

'Really?'

'Definitely. Some say the best spy ever. There's a story that he spent five years working his way up in the NKVD in Russia, and ended up one of Stalin's most trusted aides . . . I don't know whether it's true, but it's the kind of thing he'd do. A real pro. And the Führer knows it.'

'Hitler knows him?'

The older man nodded. 'At one time he wanted to see all Die Nadel's signals. I don't know if he still does. Not that it would make any difference to Die Nadel. Nothing impresses that man. You know something? He looks at everybody the same way: as if he's figuring out how he'll kill you if you make a wrong move.'

'I'm glad I didn't have to train him.'

'He learned quickly, I'll give him that.'

'Good pupil?'

'The best. He worked at it twenty-four hours a day, then when he'd mastered it, he wouldn't give me a good morning. It takes him all his time to remember to salute Canaris.'

'*Ach du meine Scheisse.*'

'Oh, yes. Didn't you know – he always signs off "Regards to Willi". That's how much he cares about rank.'

'No. Regards to Willi? *Ach du meine Scheisse.*'

They finished their cigarettes, dropped them on the floor, and trod them out. Then the older man picked up the stubs and pocketed them, because smoking was not really permitted in the dugout. The radios were still quiet.

'Yes, he won't use his code name,' the older man went on. 'Von Braun gave it to him, and he's never liked it. He's never liked Von Braun either. Do you remember the time – no, it was before you joined us – Braun told Nadel to go to the airfield in Farnborough, Kent. The message came back, quick as a flash: "There is no airfield at Farnborough, Kent. There is one at Farnborough, Hampshire. Fortunately the Luftwaffe's geography is better than yours, you cunt." Just like that.'

'I suppose it's understandable. When we make mistakes we put their lives at risk.'

The older man frowned. He was the one who delivered such judgements, and he did not like his audience to weigh in with opinions of its own. 'Perhaps,' he said grudgingly.

The youngster reverted to his original wide-eyed role. 'Why doesn't he like his code name?'

'He says it has a meaning, and a code word with a meaning can give a man away. Von Braun wouldn't listen.'

'A meaning? The Needle? What does it mean?'

But at that moment the old-timer's radio chirped, and he returned quickly to his station; so the youngster never did find out.

PART TWO

SEVEN

The message annoyed Faber, because it forced him to face issues which he had been avoiding.

Hamburg had made damn sure the message reached him. He had given his call-sign, and instead of the usual 'Acknowledge – proceed' they had sent back 'Make rendezvous one'.

He acknowledged the order, transmitted his report, and packed the wireless set back into its suitcase. Then he wheeled his bicycle out of Erith Marshes – his cover was that of a bird-watcher – and he got on the road to Blackheath. As he cycled back to his cramped two-room flatlet, he wondered whether to obey the order.

He had two reasons for disobedience: one professional, one personal.

The professional reason was that 'rendezvous one' was an old code, set up by Canaris back in 1937. It meant he was to go to the doorway of a certain shop between Leicester Square and Piccadilly Circus to meet another agent. The agents would recognize each other by the fact that they both carried a Bible. Then there was a patter:

'What is today's chapter?'

'One Kings thirteen.'

Then, if they were certain they were not being followed, they would agree that the chapter was 'most inspiring'. Otherwise one would say: 'I'm afraid I haven't read it yet.'

The shop doorway might not be there any more, but it was not that which troubled Faber. He thought Canaris had probably given the code to most of the bumbling amateurs who had crossed the Channel in 1940 and landed in the arms of MI5. Faber knew they had been caught because the hangings had been publicized, no doubt to reassure the public that something was being done about Fifth Columnists. They would certainly have given away secrets before they died, so the British now probably knew the old rendezvous code. If they had picked up the message from Hamburg, that shop doorway must by now be swarming with well-spoken young Englishmen carrying Bibles and practising saying 'Most inspiring' in a German accent.

The Abwehr had thrown professionalism to the wind, back in those heady days when the invasion seemed so close. Faber had not trusted Hamburg since. He would not tell them where he lived, he refused to communicate with their other agents in Britain, he varied the frequency he used for transmission without caring whether he trod all over someone else's signal.

If he had always obeyed his masters, he would not have survived so long.

At Woolwich Faber was joined by a mass of other cyclists, many of them women, as the workers came streaming out of the munitions factory at the end of the day shift. Their cheerful weariness reminded Faber of his personal reason for disobedience: he thought his side was losing the war.

They certainly were not winning. The Russians and the Americans had joined in, Africa was lost, the Italians had collapsed; the Allies must invade France this year, 1944.

Faber did not want to risk his life to no purpose.

He arrived home and put his bicycle away. While he was washing his face it dawned on him that, against all logic, he *wanted* to make the rendezvous.

It was a foolish risk, taken in a lost cause, but he was itching to get to it. And the simple reason was that he was unspeakably bored. The routine transmissions, the bird-watching, the bicycle, the boarding-house teas: it was four years since he had experienced anything remotely like action. He seemed to be in no danger whatsoever, and that made him jumpy, because he imagined invisible perils. He was happiest when every so often he could identify a threat and take steps to neutralize it.

Yes, he would make the rendezvous. But not in the way they expected.

There were still crowds in the West End of London, despite the war; Faber wondered whether it was the same in Berlin. He bought a Bible at Hatchard's bookshop in Piccadilly, and stuffed it into his inside coat pocket, out of sight. It was a mild, damp day, with intermittent drizzle, and Faber was carrying an umbrella.

This rendezvous was timed for either between nine and ten o'clock in the morning or between five and six in the afternoon, and the arrangement was that one went there every day until the other party turned up. If no contact was made for five successive days one went there on alternate days for a fortnight. After that one gave up.

Faber got to Leicester Square at ten past nine. The contact was there, in the tobacconist's doorway, with a blackbound Bible under his arm, pretending to shelter from the rain. Faber spotted him out of the corner of his eye and hurried past, head down. The man was youngish, with a blond moustache and a well-fed look. He wore a black double-breasted showerproof coat, and he was reading the *Daily Express* and chewing gum. He was not familiar.

When Faber walked by the second time on the opposite side of the street, he spotted the tail. A short, stocky man wearing the trench coat and trilby hat beloved of English plain-clothes policemen was standing just inside the foyer of an office building, looking through the glass doors across the street to the spy in the doorway.

There were two possibilities. If the agent did not know he had been rumbled, Faber had only to get him away from the rendezvous and lose the tail. However, the alternative was that the agent had been captured and the man in the doorway was a substitute, in which case neither he nor the tail must be allowed to see Faber's face.

Faber assumed the worst, then thought of a way to deal with it.

There was a telephone kiosk in the Square. Faber went inside and memorized the number. Then he found I Kings 13 in the Bible, tore out the page, and scribbled in the margin: 'Go to the phone box in the Square.'

He walked around the back streets behind the National Gallery until he found a small boy, aged about ten or eleven, sitting on a doorstep throwing stones at puddles.

Faber said: 'Do you know the tobacconist in the Square?'

The boy said: 'Yerst.'

'Do you like chewing-gum?'

'Yerst.'

Faber gave him the page torn from the Bible. 'There's a man in the doorway of the tobacconist's. If you give him this he'll give you some gum.'

'All right,' the boy said. He stood up. 'Is this geezer a Yank?'

Faber said: 'Yerst.'

The boy ran off. Faber followed him. As the boy approached the agent, Faber ducked into the doorway of the building opposite. The tail was still there, peering through the glass. Faber stood just outside the door, blocking the tail's view of the scene across the street, and opened his umbrella. He pretended to be struggling with it. He saw the agent give something to the boy and walk off. He ended his charade with the umbrella, and walked in the direction opposite to the way the agent had gone. He looked back over his shoulder to see the tail run into the street, looking for the vanished agent.

Faber stopped at the nearest call box and dialled the number of the kiosk in the Square. It took a few minutes to get through. At last a deep voice said: 'Hello?'

Faber said: 'What is today's chapter?'

'One Kings thirteen.'

'Most inspiring.'

'Yes, isn't it.'

The fool has no idea of the trouble he's in, Faber thought. Aloud he said: 'Well?'

'I must see you.'

'That is impossible.'

'But I must!' There was a note in the voice which Faber thought close to despair. 'The message comes from the very top – do you understand?'

Faber pretended to waver. 'All right, then. I will meet you in one week's time under the arch at Euston Station at nine a.m.'

'Can't you make it sooner?'

Faber hung up and stepped outside. Walking quickly, he rounded two corners and came within sight of the phone box in the Square. He saw the agent walking in the direction of Piccadilly. There was no sign of the tail. Faber followed the agent.

The man went into Piccadilly Circus underground station and bought a ticket to Stockwell. Faber immediately realized he could get there by a more direct route. He came out of the station, walked quickly to Leicester

Square, and got on a Northern Line train. The agent would have to change trains at Waterloo, whereas Faber's train was direct; so Faber would reach Stockwell first, or at the worst they would arrive on the same train.

In fact Faber had to wait outside the station at Stockwell for twenty-five minutes before the agent emerged. Faber followed him again. He went into a café.

There was absolutely nowhere nearby where a man could plausibly stand still for any length of time: no shop windows to gaze into, no benches to sit on or parks to walk around, no bus stops or taxi ranks or public buildings. It was a dreary, blank suburb. Faber had to walk up and down the street, always looking as if he were going somewhere, carrying on until he was just out of sight of the café then returning on the opposite side, while the agent sat in the warm, steamy café drinking tea and eating hot toast.

He came out after half an hour. Faber tailed him through a succession of residential streets. The agent knew where he was going, but was in no hurry: he walked like a man who is going home with nothing to do for the rest of the day. He did not look back, and Faber thought: Another amateur.

At last he went into a house – one of the poor, anonymous, inconspicuous lodging-houses used by spies everywhere. It had a dormer window in the roof: that would be the agent's room, high up for better wireless reception.

Faber walked past, scanning the opposite side of the

street. Yes – there. A movement behind an upstairs window, a glimpse of a jacket and tie, a watching face withdrawn: the opposition was here too. The agent must have gone to the rendezvous yesterday and allowed himself to be followed home by MI5 – unless, of course, he *was* MI5.

Faber turned the corner and walked down the next parallel street, counting the houses. Almost directly behind the place the agent had entered there was the bomb-damaged shell of what had been a pair of semi-detached houses. Good.

As he walked back to the station he felt a buzz of excitement. His step was springier, his heart beat a shade faster, and he looked around him with bright-eyed interest. It was good. The game was on.

He dressed in black that night: a woollen hat, a roll-neck sweater under a short leather flying jacket, trousers tucked into socks, rubber-soled shoes; all black. He would be almost invisible, for London, too, was blacked out.

He cycled through the quiet streets with dimmed lights, keeping off main roads. It was after midnight, and he saw no one. He left the bike a quarter of a mile away from his destination, padlocking it to the fence in a pub yard.

He went, not to the agent's house, but to the bombed-out shell in the next street. He picked his way carefully across the rubble in the front garden, entered the gaping doorway, and went through the house to the back. It was very dark. A thick screen of low cloud hid the moon and stars. Faber had to walk slowly with his hands in front of him.

He reached the end of the garden, jumped over the fence, and crossed the next two gardens. In one of the houses a dog barked for a minute.

The garden of the lodging-house was unkempt. Faber walked into a blackberry bush and stumbled. The thorns scratched his face. He ducked under a line of washing – there was enough light for him to see that.

He found the kitchen window and took from his pocket a small tool with a scoop-shaped blade. The putty around the glass was old and brittle, and already flaking away in places. After twenty minutes' silent work he took the pane out of the frame and laid it gently on the grass. He shone a torch through the empty hole to make sure there were no noisy obstacles in his way, then climbed in.

The darkened house smelled of boiled fish and disinfectant. Faber unlocked the back door – a precaution for fast escape – before entering the hall. He flashed his pencil torch on and off quickly, once. In that instant of light he took in a tiled hallway, a kidney table he must circumvent, a row of coats on hooks and a staircase, to the right, carpeted.

He climbed the stairs silently.

He was halfway across the landing to the second flight when he saw the light under the door. A split-second later there was an asthmatic cough and the sound of a toilet flushing. Faber reached the door in two strides and froze against the wall.

Light flooded the landing as the door opened. Faber slipped his stiletto out of his sleeve. The old man came out of the toilet and crossed the landing, leaving the light on. At his bedroom door he grunted, turned, and came back.

He must see me, Faber thought. He tightened his grip on the handle of his knife. The old man's half-open eyes were directed to the floor. He looked up as he reached for the light cord, and Faber almost killed him then – but the man fumbled for the switch, and Faber realized he was so sleepy he was practically sleepwalking.

The light died, the old man shuffled back to bed, and Faber breathed again.

There was only one door at the top of the second flight of stairs. Faber tried it gently. It was locked.

He took another tool from the pocket of his jacket. The noise of the cistern filling covered the sound of Faber picking the lock. He opened the door and listened.

He could hear deep, regular breathing. He stepped inside. The sound came from the opposite corner of the room. He could see nothing. He crossed the pitch-black room very slowly, feeling the air in front of him at each step, until he was beside the bed.

He had the torch in his left hand, the stiletto loose in his sleeve, and his right hand free. He switched on the torch and grabbed the sleeping man's throat in a strangling grip.

The agent's eyes snapped open, full of fear, but he could make no sound. Faber straddled the bed and sat on him. Then he whispered: 'One Kings thirteen,' and relaxed his grip.

'You!' the agent said. He peered into the torchlight, trying to see Faber's face. He rubbed his neck where Faber's hand had squeezed.

Faber hissed: 'Be still!' He shone the torch into the agent's eyes, and with his right hand drew the stiletto.

'Aren't you going to let me get up?'

'I prefer you in bed where you can do no more damage.'

'Damage? More damage?'

'You were watched in Leicester Square, you let me follow you here, and they are observing this house. Should I trust you to do anything?'

'My God, I'm sorry.'

'Why did they send you?'

'The message had to be delivered personally. The orders come from the Führer himself.' The agent stopped.

'Well? What orders?'

'I . . . have to be sure it is you.'

'How can you be sure?'

'I must see your face.'

Faber hesitated, then shone the torch at himself briefly. 'Satisfied?'

'Die Nadel,' the man breathed.

'And who are you?'

'Major Friedrich Kaldor, at your service, sir.'

'Then I should call you "Sir".'

'Oh, no, sir. You've been promoted twice in your absence. You are now a lieutenant-colonel.'

'Have they nothing better to do in Hamburg?'

'Aren't you pleased?'

'I should be pleased to go back and put Major von Braun on latrine duty.'

'May I get up, sir?'

'Certainly not. What if Major Kaldor is languishing in Wandsworth gaol, and you are a substitute, just waiting to give some kind of signal to your watching friends in the house opposite?'

'Very well.'

'So – what are these orders from Hitler himself?'

'Well, sir, the Reich believes there will be an invasion of France this year.'

'Brilliant, brilliant. Go on.'

'They believe that General Patton is massing the First United States Army Group in the part of England known as East Anglia. If that army is the invasion force, then it follows that they will attack via the Pas de Calais.'

'That makes sense. But I have seen no sign of this army of Patton's.'

'There is some doubt in the highest circles in Berlin. The Führer's astrologer—'

'What?'

'Yes, sir, he has an astrologer, who tells him to defend Normandy.'

'My God. Are things that bad there?'

'He gets plenty of earthbound advice, too. I personally believe he uses the astrologer as an excuse when he thinks the generals are wrong but he cannot fault their arguments.'

Faber sighed. He had been afraid of news like this. 'Go on.'

'Your assignment is to assess the strength of FUSAG: numbers of troops, artillery, air support—'

'I know how to measure armies, thank you.'

'Of course.' He paused. 'I am instructed to emphasize the importance of the mission, sir.'

'And you have done so. Tell me: are things that bad in Berlin?'

The agent hesitated, and said: 'No, sir. Morale is high, output of munitions increases every month, the people spit at the bombers of the RAF—'

'Never mind,' Faber interrupted him. 'I can get the propaganda from my radio.'

The younger man was silent.

Faber said: 'Do you have anything else to tell me? Officially, I mean.'

'Yes. For the duration of the assignment you have a special bolthole.'

'They *do* think it's important,' Faber said.

'You rendezvous with a U-boat in the North Sea, ten miles due east of a town called Aberdeen. Just call them in on your normal radio frequency and they will surface. As soon as you or I have told Hamburg that the orders have been passed from me to you, the route will be open. The boat will be there every Friday and Monday at six p.m. and will wait until six a.m.'

'Aberdeen is a big town. Do you have an exact map reference?'

'Yes.' The agent recited the numbers, and Faber memorized them.

'Is that everything, Major?'

'Yes, sir.'

'What do you plan to do about the gentlemen from MI5 in the house across the road?'

The agent shrugged. 'I shall have to give them the slip.'

Faber thought: It's no good. 'What are your orders for action after you have seen me? Do you have a bolthole?'

'No. I am to go to a place called Weymouth and steal a boat in which to return to France.'

That was no plan at all. So, Faber thought: Canaris knew how it would be. Very well.

He said: 'And if you are caught by the British, and tortured?'

'I have a suicide pill.'

'And you will use it?'

'Most certainly.'

Faber looked at him. 'I think you might,' he said. He placed his left hand on the agent's chest and put his weight on it, as if he were about to get off the bed. That way he was able to feel exactly where the rib cage ended and the soft belly began. He thrust the point of the stiletto in just under the ribs and stabbed upward to the heart.

The agent's eyes widened for a terror-stricken instant. A cry came to his throat but did not escape. His body convulsed. Faber pushed the stiletto an inch farther in. The eyes closed and the body went limp.

Faber said: 'You saw my face.'

EIGHT

'I think we've lost control of it,' said Percival Godliman.

Frederick Bloggs nodded agreement, and added: 'It's my fault.'

The boy looked weary, Godliman thought. He had had that look for almost a year, ever since the night they dragged the crushed remains of his wife from underneath the rubble of their bombed house in Hoxton.

'I'm not interested in apportioning blame,' Godliman said briskly. 'The fact is that something happened in Leicester Square those few seconds when you lost sight of Blondie.'

'Do you think the contact was made?'

'Possibly.'

'When we picked him up again back in Stockwell, I thought he had simply given up for the day.'

'If that were the case he would have made the rendezvous again yesterday and today.' Godliman was making patterns with matchsticks on his desk, an aid to thinking he had developed into a habit. 'Still no movement at the house?'

'Nothing. He's been in there for forty-eight hours.' Bloggs repeated: 'It's my fault.'

'Don't be a bore, old chap,' Godliman said. 'It was my decision to let him run, so that he would lead us to someone else; and I still think it was the right move.'

Bloggs sat motionless, his expression blank, his hands in the pockets of his raincoat. 'If the contact has been made, we shouldn't delay picking Blondie up and finding out what his mission was.'

'That way we lose whatever chance we have of following Blondie to somebody really dangerous.'

'Your decision.'

Godliman had made a church with his matches. He stared at it for a moment, then took a halfpenny from his pocket and tossed it. 'Tails,' he observed. 'Give him another twenty-four hours.'

The landlord was a middle-aged Irish Republican from Lisdoonvarna, County Clare, who harboured a secret hope that the Germans would win the war and thus free the Emerald Isle from English oppression forever. He limped arthritically around the old house, collecting his weekly rents, thinking how much he would be worth if those rents were allowed to rise to their true market value. He was not a rich man – he owned only two houses, this and the smaller one in which he lived. He was permanently bad-tempered.

On the first floor he tapped on the door of the old man. This tenant was always pleased to see him. He was probably pleased to see anybody. He said: 'Hello, Mr Riley, would you like a cup of tea?'

'No time today.'

'Oh, well.' The old man handed over the money. 'I expect you've seen the kitchen window.'

'No, I didn't go in there.'

'Oh! Well, there's a pane of glass out. I patched it over with blackout curtain, but of course there is a draught.'

'Who smashed it?' the landlord asked.

'Funny thing, it ain't broke. Just lying there on the grass. I expect the old putty just gave way. I'll mend it myself, if you can get hold of a bit of putty.'

You old fool, the landlord thought. Aloud he said: 'I don't suppose it occurred to you that you might have been burgled?'

The old man looked astonished. 'I never thought of that.'

'Nobody's missing any valuables?'

'Nobody's said so to me.'

The landlord went to the door. 'All right, I'll have a look when I go down.'

The old man followed him out. 'I don't think the new bloke is in, upstairs,' he said. 'I haven't heard a sound for a couple of days.'

The landlord was sniffing. 'Has he been cooking in his room?'

'I wouldn't know, Mr Riley.'

The two of them went up the stairs. The old man said: 'He's very quiet, if he is in there.'

'Whatever he's cooking, he'll have to stop. It smells bloody awful.'

The landlord knocked on the door. There was no answer. He opened it and went in, and the old man followed him.

'Well, well, well,' the old sergeant said heartily. 'I think you've got a dead one.'

He stood in the doorway, surveying the room. 'You touched anything, Paddy?'

'No,' the landlord replied. 'And the name's Mr Riley.'

The policeman ignored this. 'Not long dead, though. I've smelled worse.' His survey took in the old chest of drawers, the suitcase on the low table, the faded square of carpet, the dirty curtains on the dormer window, and the rumpled bed in the corner. There were no signs of a struggle.

He went over to the bed. The young man's face was peaceful, his hands clasped over his chest. 'I'd say heart attack, if he wasn't so young.' There was no empty sleeping-pill bottle to indicate suicide. He picked up the leather wallet on top of the chest and looked through its contents. There was an identity card and a ration book, and a fairly thick wad of notes. 'Papers in order and he ain't been robbed.'

'He's only been here a week or so,' the landlord ventured. 'I don't know much about him at all. He came from North Wales to work in a factory.'

The sergeant observed: 'If he was as healthy as he looked he'd be in the Army.' He opened the suitcase on the table. 'Bloody hell, what's this lot?'

The landlord and the old man had edged their way into the room now. The landlord said: 'It's a radio' at the same time as the old man said: 'He's bleeding.'

'Don't touch that body!' the sergeant said.

'He's had a knife in the guts,' the old man persisted.

The sergeant gingerly lifted one of the dead hands from the chest to reveal a small patch of dried blood. 'He *was* bleeding,' he said. 'Where's the nearest phone?'

'Five doors down,' the landlord told him.

'Lock this room and stay out until I get back.'

The sergeant left the house and knocked at the door of the neighbour with the phone. A woman opened it. 'Good morning, madam. May I use your telephone?'

'Come in.' She showed him the phone, on a stand in the hall. 'What's happened – anything exciting?'

'A tenant died in a lodging-house just up the road,' he told her as he dialled.

'Murdered?' she asked, wide-eyed.

'I leave that to the experts. Hello? Superintendent Jones, please. This is Canter.' He looked at the woman. 'Might I ask you just to pop in the kitchen while I talk to my governor?'

She went, disappointed.

'Hello, Super. This body's got a knife wound and a suitcase radio.'

'What's the address again, Sarge?'

Sergeant Canter told him.

'Yes, that's the one they've been watching. This is an MI5 job, Sarge. Go to number forty-two and tell the surveillance team what you've found. I'll get on to their chief. Off you go.'

Canter thanked the woman and crossed the road. He was quite thrilled: this was only his second murder in 31 years as a Metropolitan Policeman, and it turned out to involve espionage! He might make Inspector yet.

He knocked on the door of number forty-two. It opened, and two men stood there.

Sergeant Canter said: 'Are you the secret agents from MI5?'

Bloggs arrived at the same time as a Special Branch man, Detective-Inspector Harris, whom he had known in his Scotland Yard days. Canter showed them the body.

They stood still for a moment, looking at the peaceful young face with its blond moustache.

Harris said: 'Who is he?'

'Codename Blondie,' Bloggs told him. 'We think he came in by parachute a couple of weeks ago. We picked up a radio message to another agent arranging a rendezvous. We knew the code, so we were able to watch the rendezvous. We hoped Blondie would lead us to the resident agent, who would be a much more dangerous specimen.'

'So what happened here?'

'Buggered if I know.'

Harris looked at the wound in the agent's chest. 'Stiletto?'

'Something like that. A very neat job. Under the ribs and straight up into the heart. Quick.'

'There are worse ways to die.'

Sergeant Canter said: 'Would you like to see the method of entry?'

He led them downstairs to the kitchen. They looked at the window-frame and the unbroken pane of glass lying on the lawn.

Canter said: 'Also, the lock on the bedroom door had been picked.'

They sat down at the kitchen table, and Canter made tea. Bloggs said: 'It happened the night after I lost him in Leicester Square. I fouled it all up.'

Harris said: 'Nobody's perfect.'

They drank their tea in silence for a while. Harris said: 'How are things with you, anyway? You don't drop in at the Yard.'

'Busy.'

'How's Christine?'

'Killed in the bombing.'

Harris's eyes widened. 'You poor bastard.'

'You all right?'

'Lost my brother in North Africa. Did you ever meet Johnny?'

'No.'

'He was a lad. Drink? You've never seen anything like it. Spent so much on booze, he could never afford to get married – which is just as well, the way things turned out.'

'Most people have lost somebody.'

'If you're on your own, come round our place for dinner on Sunday.'

'Thanks, I work Sundays now.'

Harris nodded. 'Well, whenever you feel like it.'

A detective-constable poked his head around the door and addressed Harris. 'Can we start bagging-up the evidence, guv?'

Harris looked at Bloggs.

'I've finished,' Bloggs said.

'All right, son, carry on,' Harris told him.

Bloggs said: 'Suppose he made contact after I lost him, and arranged for the resident agent to come here. The resident may have suspected a trap – that would explain why he came in through the window and picked the lock.'

'It makes him a devilish suspicious bastard,' Harris observed.

'That might be why we've never caught him. Anyway, he gets into Blondie's room and wakes him up. Now he knows it isn't a trap, right?'

'Right.'

'So why does he kill Blondie?'

'Maybe they quarrelled.'

'There were no signs of a struggle.'

Harris frowned into his empty cup. 'Perhaps he twigged that Blondie was being watched, and he was afraid we'd pick the boy up and make him spill the beans.'

Bloggs said: 'That makes him a ruthless bastard.'

'That might be why we've never caught him.'

'Come in. Sit down. I've just had a call from MI6. Canaris has been fired.'

Bloggs went in, sat down, and said: 'Is that good news or bad?'

'Very bad,' said Godliman. 'It's happened at the worst possible moment.'

'Do I get told why?'

Godliman looked at him through narrow eyes, then said: 'I think you need to know. At this moment we have forty double-agents broadcasting to Hamburg false information about Allied plans for the invasion of France.'

Bloggs whistled. 'I didn't know it was quite that big. I suppose the doubles say we're going in at Cherbourg, but really it will be Calais, or vice versa.'

'Something like that. Apparently I don't need to know the details. Anyway they haven't told me. However, the whole thing is in danger. We knew Canaris; we knew we had him fooled; we could have gone on fooling him. A new broom may mistrust his predecessor's agents. There's more: we've had some defections from the other side, people who could have betrayed the Abwehr's people over here if they hadn't been betrayed already. It's another reason for the Germans to begin to suspect our doubles.

'Then there's the possibility of a leak. Literally thousands of people now know about the double-cross system. There are doubles in Iceland, Canada, and Ceylon. We ran a double-cross in the Middle East.

'And we made a bad mistake last year by repatriating a German called Erich Carl. We later learned he was an Abwehr agent – a real one – and that while he was in internment on the Isle of Man he may have learned about two doubles called Mutt and Jeff, and possibly a third called Tate.

'So we're skating on thin ice. If one decent Abwehr agent in Britain gets to know about Fortitude – that's the codename for the deception plan – the whole strategy will be endangered. Not to mince words, we could lose the fucking war.'

Bloggs suppressed a smile: he could remember a time when Professor Godliman did not know the meaning of such words.

The professor went on: 'The Twenty Committee has made it quite clear that they expect me to make sure there aren't any decent Abwehr agents in Britain.'

'Last week we would have been quite confident that there weren't,' Bloggs said.

'Now we know there's at least one.'

'And we let him slip through our fingers.'

'So now we have to find him again.'

'I don't know,' Bloggs said gloomily. 'We don't know what part of the country he's operating from, we haven't the faintest idea what he looks like. He's too crafty to be pinpointed by triangulation while he's transmitting – otherwise we would have nabbed him long ago. We don't even know his codename. So where do we start?'

'Unsolved crimes,' said Godliman. 'Look: a spy is bound to break the law. He forges papers, he steals petrol and ammunition, he evades checkpoints, he enters restricted areas, he takes photographs, and when people rumble him he kills them. The police are bound to get to know of some of these crimes, if the spy has been operating for any length of time. If we go through the unsolved crimes files since the war, we'll find traces.'

'Don't you realize that *most* crimes are unsolved?' Bloggs said incredulously. 'The files would fill the Albert Hall!'

Godliman shrugged. 'So, we narrow it down to London, and we start with murders.'

They found what they were looking for on the very first day of their search.

It happened to be Godliman who came across it, and at first he did not realize its significance.

It was the file on the murder of a Mrs Una Garden in Highgate in 1940. Her throat had been cut and she had been sexually molested, although not raped. She had been found in the bedroom of her lodger, with a considerable amount of alcohol in her bloodstream. The picture was fairly clear: she had had a tryst with the lodger, he had wanted to go farther than she was prepared to let him, they had quarrelled, he had killed her, and the murder had neutralized his libido. But the police had never found the lodger.

Godliman had been about to pass over the file: spies did not get involved in sexual assaults. But he was a meticulous man with records, so he read every word, and consequently discovered that the unfortunate Mrs Garden had received stiletto wounds in her back, as well as the fatal wound to her throat.

Godliman and Bloggs were on opposite sides of a wooden table in the records room at Old Scotland Yard. Godliman tossed the file across the table and said: 'I think this is it.'

Bloggs glanced through it and said: 'The stiletto.'

They signed for the file and walked the short distance to the War Office. When they returned to Godliman's room, there was a decoded signal on his desk. He read it casually, then thumped the table in excitement. 'It's him!'

Bloggs read: 'Orders received. Regards to Willi.'

'Remember him?' Godliman said. 'Die Nadel?'

'Yes,' Bloggs said hesitantly. 'The Needle. But there's not much information here.'

'Think, think! A stilletto is like a needle. It's the same man: the murder of Mrs Garden, all those signals in 1940 that we couldn't trace, the rendezvous with Blondie . . .'

'Possibly.' Bloggs looked thoughtful.

'I can prove it,' Godliman said. 'Remember the transmission about Finland that you showed me the first day I came here? The one which was interrupted?'

'Yes.' Bloggs went to the file to find it.

'If my memory serves me well, the date of that transmission is the same as the date of this murder . . . and I'll bet the time of death coincides with the interruption.'

Bloggs looked at the signal in the file. 'Right both times.'

'There!'

'He's been operating in London for at least five

years, and it's taken us until now to get on to him,' Bloggs reflected. 'He won't be easy to catch.'

Godliman suddenly looked wolfish. 'He may be clever, but he's not as clever as me,' he said tightly. 'I'm going to nail him to the fucking wall.'

Bloggs laughed out loud. 'My God, you've changed, Professor.'

Godliman said: 'Do you realize that's the first time you've laughed for a year?'

NINE

The supply boat rounded the headland and chugged into the bay at Storm Island under a blue sky. There were two women in it: one was the skipper's wife – he had been called up and now she ran the business – and the other was Lucy's mother.

Mother got out of the boat, wearing a utility suit – a mannish jacket and an above-the-knee skirt. Lucy hugged her mightily.

'Mother! What a surprise!'

'But I wrote to you.'

The letter was with the mail on the boat – Mother had forgotten that the post only came once a fortnight on Storm Island.

'Is this my grandson? Isn't he a big boy?'

Little Jo, almost three years old, turned bashful and hid behind Lucy's skirt. He was dark-haired, pretty, and tall for his age.

Mother said: 'Isn't he like his father!'

'Yes,' Lucy said. Her assent held a note of disapproval. 'You must be freezing – come up to the house. Where *did* you get that skirt?'

They picked up the groceries and began to walk up the ramp to the cliff top. Mother chattered as they went. 'It's the fashion, dear. It saves on material. But it isn't as cold as this on the mainland. Such a wind! I suppose it's all right to leave my case on the jetty – nobody to steal it! Jane is engaged to an American soldier – a white one, thank God. He comes from a place called Milwaukee, and he doesn't chew gum. Isn't that nice? I've only got four more daughters to marry off now. Your father is a Captain in the Home Guard, did I tell you? He's up half the night patrolling the common waiting for German parachutists. Uncle Stephen's warehouse was bombed – I don't know *what* he'll do, it's an Act of War or something—'

'Don't rush, Mother, you've got fourteen days to tell me the news.' Lucy laughed.

They reached the cottage. Mother said: 'Isn't this *lovely*?' They went in. 'I think this is just lovely.'

Lucy parked Mother at the kitchen table and made tea. 'Tom will get your case up. He'll be here for his lunch shortly.'

'The shepherd?'

'Yes.'

'Does he find things for David to do, then?'

Lucy laughed. 'It's the other way around. I'm sure he'll tell you all about it himself. You haven't told me why you're here.'

'My dear, it's about time I saw you. I know we're not supposed to make unnecessary journeys, but once in four years isn't extravagant, is it?'

They heard the jeep outside, and a moment later David wheeled himself in. He kissed his mother-in-law and introduced Tom.

Lucy said: 'Tom, you can earn your lunch today by bringing Mother's case up, as she carried your groceries.'

David was warming his hands at the stove. 'It's raw today.'

Mother said: 'You're really taking sheep-farming seriously, then?'

'The flock is double what it was three years ago,' David told her. 'My father never farmed this island seriously. I've fenced six miles of the cliff top, improved the grazing, and introduced modern breeding methods. Not only do we have more sheep, but each animal gives us more meat and wool.'

Mother said tentatively: 'I suppose Tom does the physical work and you give the orders.'

David laughed. 'Equal partners, Mother.'

They had hearts for lunch, and both men ate mountains of potatoes. Mother commented favourably on Jo's table manners. Afterwards David lit a cigarette and Tom stuffed his pipe.

Mother said: 'What I really want to know is when you're going to give me more grandchildren.' She smiled brightly.

There was a long silence.

'Well, I think it's wonderful, the way David copes,' said Mother.

Lucy said: 'Yes,' and again there was that note of disapproval.

They were walking along the cliff top. The wind had

dropped on the third day of Mother's visit, and it was mild enough to go out. They took Jo, dressed in a fisherman's sweater and a fur coat. They had stopped at the top of a rise to watch David, Tom and the dog herding sheep. Lucy could see in Mother's face an internal struggle as concern vied with discretion. She decided to save her mother the effort of asking.

'He doesn't love me,' she said.

Mother looked quickly to make sure Jo was out of earshot. 'I'm sure it's not that bad, dear. Different men show their love in diff—'

'Mother, we haven't been man and wife – properly – since we were married.'

'But . . .?' She indicated Jo with a nod.

'That was a week before the wedding.'

'Oh! Oh, dear.' She was shocked. 'Is it, you know, the accident?'

'Yes, but not in the way you mean. It's nothing physical. He just . . . won't.' Lucy was crying quietly, the tears trickling down her wind-browned cheeks.

'Have you talked about it?'

'I've tried. Mother, what shall I do?'

'Perhaps with time—'

'It's been almost four years!'

There was a pause. They began to walk on across the heather, into the weak afternoon sun. Jo chased gulls. Mother said: 'I almost left your father, once.'

It was Lucy's turn to be shocked. 'When?'

'It was soon after Jane was born. We weren't so well-off in those days, you know – Father was still working for his father, and there was a slump. I was expecting for the third time in three years, and it seemed that a life of having babies and making ends meet stretched out in front of me with nothing to relieve the monotony. Then I discovered he was seeing an old flame of his – Brenda Simmonds, you never knew her, she went to Basingstoke. Suddenly I asked myself what I was doing it for, and I couldn't think of a sensible answer.'

Lucy had dim, patchy memories of those days: her grandfather with a white moustache; her father, a more slender edition; extended-family meals in the great farmhouse kitchen; a lot of laughter and sunshine and animals. Even then her parents' marriage had seemed to represent solid contentment, happy permanence. She said: 'Why didn't you? Leave, I mean.'

'Oh, people just didn't, in those days. There wasn't all this divorce, and a woman couldn't get a job.'

'Women work at all sorts of things now.'

'They did in the last war, but everything changed afterwards with a bit of unemployment. I expect it will be the same this time. Men get their way, you know, generally speaking.'

'And you're glad you stayed.' It was not a question.

'People my age shouldn't make pronouncements about Life. But *my* life has been a matter of making-do, and the same goes for most of the women I know. Steadfastness always looks like a sacrifice, but usually it isn't. Anyway, I'm not going to give you advice. You wouldn't take it, and if you did you'd blame your problems on me, I expect.'

'Oh, Mother.' Lucy smiled.

Mother said: 'Shall we turn round? I think we've gone far enough for one day.'

In the kitchen one evening Lucy said to David: 'I'd like Mother to stay another two weeks, if she will.'

Mother was upstairs putting Jo to bed, telling him a story.

David said: 'Isn't a fortnight long enough for you to dissect my personality?'

'Don't be silly, David.'

He wheeled himself over to her chair. 'Are you telling me you don't talk about me?'

'Of course we talk about you – you're my husband.'

'What do you say to her, then?'

'Why are you so worried?' Lucy said, not without malice. 'What are you so ashamed of?'

'Damn you, I've nothing to be ashamed of. No one wants his personal life talked about by a pair of gossiping women.'

'We don't gossip about you.'

'What do you say?'

'Aren't you touchy!'

'Answer my question.'

'I say I want to leave you, and she tries to talk me out of it.'

He spun around and wheeled away. 'Tell her not to bother for my sake.'

She called: 'Do you mean that?'

He stopped. 'I don't need anybody, do you understand? I can manage alone. I'm self-sufficient.'

'And what about me?' she said quietly. 'Perhaps I need somebody.'

'What for?'

'To love me.'

Mother came in, and sensed the atmosphere. 'He's fast asleep,' she said. 'Dropped off before Cinderella got to the ball. I think I'll pack a few things, not to leave it all until tomorrow.' She went out again.

'Do you think it will ever change, David?' Lucy asked.

'I don't know what you mean.'

'Will we ever be . . . the way we were, before the wedding?'

'My legs won't grow back, if that's what you mean.'

'Oh, God, don't you know that doesn't bother me? I just want to be loved.'

David shrugged. 'That's your problem.' He went out before she started to cry.

Mother did not stay the second fortnight. Lucy walked with her down to the jetty the next day. It was raining hard, and they both wore mackintoshes. They stood in silence waiting for the boat, watching the rain pit the sea with tiny craters. Mother held Jo in her arms.

'Things will change, in time, you know,' she said. 'Four years is nothing in a marriage.'

Lucy said: 'I don't think he'll change, but there's not much I can do other than give it a chance. There's Jo, and the war, and David's disability – how can I leave?'

The boat arrived, and Lucy exchanged her mother for three boxes of groceries and five letters. The water was choppy. Mother sat in the boat's tiny cabin. They waved her around the headland. Lucy felt very lonely.

Jo began to cry. 'I don't want Gran to go away!'

'Nor do I,' said Lucy.

TEN

Godliman and Bloggs walked side by side along the pavement of a bomb-damaged London shopping street. They were a mismatched pair: the stooped, bird-like professor, with pebble-lensed spectacles and a pipe, not looking where he was going, taking short, scurrying steps; and the flatfooted youngster, blond and purposeful, in his detective's raincoat and melodramatic hat: a cartoon looking for a caption.

Godliman was saying: 'I think Die Nadel is well-connected.'

'Why?'

'The only way he could be so insubordinate with impunity. It's this "Regards to Willi" line. It must refer to Canaris.'

'You think he was pals with Canaris.'

'He's pals with somebody – perhaps someone more powerful than Canaris was.'

'I have the feeling this is leading somewhere.'

'People who are well-connected generally make those connections at school, or university, or staff college. Look at that.'

They were outside a shop which had a huge empty space where once there had been a plate-glass window. A rough sign, hand-painted and nailed to the window-frame, said: 'Even more open than usual.'

Bloggs laughed, and said: 'I saw one outside a bombed police station: "Be good. We are still open."'

'It's become a minor art form.'

They walked on. Bloggs said: 'So, what if Die Nadel did go to school with someone high in the Wermacht?'

'People always have their pictures taken at school. Midwinter down in the basement at Kensington – that house where MI6 used to be before the war – he's got a collection of thousands of photographs of German officers: school photos, binges in the Mess, passing-out parades, shaking hands with Adolf, newspaper pictures – everything.'

'I see,' Bloggs said. 'So if you're right, and Die Nadel has been through Germany's equivalent of Eton and Sandhurst, we've probably got a picture of him.'

'Almost certainly. Spies are notoriously camera-shy, but they don't become spies until they're well into adulthood. It will be a youthful Die Nadel that we find in Midwinter's files.'

They skirted a huge crater outside a barber's. The shop was intact, but the traditional red-and-white striped pole lay in shards on the pavement. The sign in the window said: 'We've had a close shave – come and get one yourself.'

Bloggs said: 'How will we recognize him? No one has ever seen him.'

'Yes, they have. At Mrs Garden's boarding-house in Highgate they know him quite well.'

The Victorian house stood on a hill overlooking London. It was built of red brick, and Bloggs thought it looked angry at the damage Hitler was doing to its city. It was high up; a good place from which to broadcast. Die Nadel would have lived on the top floor. Bloggs wondered what secrets the spy had transmitted to Hamburg from this place in the dark days of 1940. Map references for aircraft factories and steelworks, details of coastal defences, political gossip, gas masks and Anderson shelters and sandbags, British morale, bomb damage reports, 'Well done, boys, you got Christine Bloggs at last – ' Shut up.

The door was opened by an elderly man in a black jacket and striped trousers.

'Good morning. I'm Inspector Bloggs, from Scotland Yard. I'd like a word with the householder, please.'

Bloggs saw fear leap to the man's eyes, then a young woman appeared in the doorway and said: 'Come in, please.'

The tiled hall smelled of wax polish. Bloggs hung his hat and coat on a stand. The old man disappeared into the depths of the house, and the woman led Bloggs into a lounge. It was expensively furnished in a rich, old-fashioned way. There were bottles of whisky, gin and sherry on a trolley: all the bottles were unopened. The woman sat down on a floral armchair and crossed her legs.

Bloggs said: 'Why is the old man frightened of the police?'

'My father-in-law is a German Jew. He came here in 1935 to escape Hitler, and in 1940 you put him in a concentration camp. His wife killed herself at the prospect. He has just been released from the Isle of Man. He had a letter from the King, apologizing for the inconvenience to which he had been put.'

Bloggs said: 'We don't have concentration camps.'

'We invented them. In South Africa. Didn't you know? We go on about our history, but we forget bits. We're so good at blinding ourselves to unpleasant facts.'

'Perhaps it's just as well.'

'What?'

'In 1939 we blinded ourselves to the unpleasant fact that we couldn't win a war with Germany – and look what happened.'

'That's what my father-in-law says. He's not as cynical as I. What can we do to assist Scotland Yard?'

Bloggs had been enjoying the exchange, and now it was with reluctance that he turned his attention to work. 'It's about a murder that took place here four years ago.'

'So long!'

'Some new evidence may have come to light.'

'I know about it, of course. The previous owner was killed by a tenant. My husband bought the house from her executor – she had no heirs.'

'I want to trace the other people who were tenants at that time.'

'Yes.' The woman's hostility had gone, now, and her intelligent face showed the effort of recollection. 'When we arrived there were three who had been here before the murder: a retired naval officer, a salesman, and a young boy from Yorkshire. The boy joined the Army – he still writes to us. The salesman was called up, and he died at sea. I know because two of his five wives got in touch with us! And the Commander is still here.'

'Still here!' That was a piece of luck. 'I'd like to see him, please.'

'Surely.' She stood up. 'He's aged a lot. I'll take you to his room.'

They went up the carpeted stairs to the first floor. She said: 'While you're talking to him, I'll look up the last letter from the boy in the Army.' She knocked on the door. It was more than Bloggs's landlady would have done, he thought wryly.

A voice called: 'It's open,' and Bloggs went in.

The Commander sat in a chair by the window with a blanket over his knees. He wore a blazer, a collar and a tie, and spectacles. His hair was thin, his moustache grey, his skin loose and wrinkled over a face that might once have been strong. The room was the home of a man living on memories: there were paintings of sailing ships, a sextant and a telescope, and a photograph of himself as a boy aboard HMS *Winchester*.

'Look at this,' he said without turning around. 'Tell me why that chap isn't in the Navy.'

Bloggs crossed to the window. A horse-drawn baker's van was at the kerb outside the house, the elderly horse dipping into its nosebag while the deliveries were made. That 'chap' was a woman with short blonde hair in trousers. She had a magnificent bust. Bloggs laughed. 'It's a woman in trousers,' he said.

'Bless my soul, so it is!' The Commander turned around. 'Can't tell, these days, you know. Women in trousers!'

Bloggs introduced himself. 'We've reopened the case of a murder committed here in 1940. I believe you lived here at the same time as the main suspect, one Henry Faber.'

'Indeed! What can I do to help?'

'How well do you remember Faber?'

'Perfectly. Tall chap, dark hair, well-spoken, quiet. Rather shabby clothes – if you were the kind who judges by appearances, you might well mistake him. I didn't dislike him – wouldn't have minded getting to know him better, but he didn't want that. I suppose he was about your age.'

Bloggs suppressed a smile: he was used to people assuming he must be older simply because he was a detective.

The Commander added: 'I'm sure he didn't do it, you know. I know a bit about character – you can't command a ship without learning – and if that man was a sex maniac, I'm Hermann Goering.'

Bloggs suddenly connected the blonde in trousers with the mistake about his age, and the conclusion depressed him. He said: 'You know, you should always ask to see a policeman's warrant card.'

The Commander was slightly taken aback. 'All right, then, let's have it.'

Bloggs opened his wallet and folded it to display the picture of Christine. 'Here.'

The Commander studied it for a moment, then said: 'A very good likeness.'

Bloggs sighed. The old man was very nearly blind.

He stood up. 'That's all, for now,' he said. 'Thank you.'

'Any time. Whatever I can do to help. I'm not much value to England these days – you've got to be pretty useless to get invalided out of the Home Guard, you know.'

'Goodbye.' Bloggs went out.

The woman was in the hall downstairs. She handed Bloggs a letter. 'The address is a Forces box number,' she said. 'No doubt you'll be able to find out where he is.'

'You knew the Commander would be no use,' Bloggs said.

'I guessed not. But a visitor makes his day.' She opened the door.

On impulse, Bloggs said: 'Will you have dinner with me?'

A shadow crossed her face. 'My husband is still on the Isle of Man.'

'I'm sorry – I thought—'

'It's all right. I'm flattered.'

'I wanted to convince you we're not the Gestapo.'

'I know you're not. A woman alone just gets bitter.'

Bloggs said: 'I lost my wife in the bombing.'

'Then you know how it makes you hate.'

'Yes,' said Bloggs. 'It makes you hate.' He went down the steps. The door closed behind him. It had started to rain.

It had been raining then. Bloggs was late. He had been going over some new material with Godliman. Now he was hurrying, so that he would have half an hour with Christine before she went out to drive her ambulance. It was dark, and the raid had already started. The things Christine saw at night were so awful she had stopped talking about them.

Bloggs was proud of her, proud. The people she worked with said she was better than two men: she hurtled through blacked-out London, driving like a veteran, taking corners on two wheels, whistling and cracking jokes as the city turned to flame around her. Fearless, they called her. Bloggs knew better: she was terrified, but she would not let it show. He knew because he saw her eyes in the morning, when he got up and she went to bed; when her guard was down and it was over for a few hours. He knew it was not fearlessness but courage, and he was proud.

It was raining harder when he got off the bus. He pulled down his hat and put up his collar. At a kiosk he bought cigarettes for Christine: she had started smoking recently, like a lot of women. The shopkeeper would let him have only five, because of the shortage. He put them in a Woolworth's bakelite cigarette case.

A policeman stopped him and asked for his identity

card: another two minutes wasted. An ambulance passed him, similar to the one Christine drove; a requisitioned fruit lorry, painted grey.

He began to get nervous as he approached home. The explosions were sounding closer, and he could hear the aircraft clearly. The East End was in for another bruising tonight: he would sleep in the Morrison shelter. There was a big one, terribly close, and he quickened his step. He would eat his supper in the shelter, too.

He turned into his own street, saw the ambulances and the fire engines, and broke into a run.

The bomb had landed on his side of the street, around the middle. It must be close to his own home. Jesus in heaven, not us, no—

There had been a direct hit on the roof, and the house was literally flattened. He raced up to the crowd of people, neighbours and firemen and volunteers. 'Is my wife all right? Is she out? IS SHE IN THERE?'

A fireman looked at him with compassion. 'Nobody's come out of there, mate.'

Rescuers were picking over the rubble. Suddenly one of them shouted: 'Over here!' Then he said: 'Bugger me, it's Fearless Bloggs!'

Frederick dashed to where the man stood. Christine was underneath a huge chunk of brickwork. Her face was visible: the eyes were closed.

The rescuer called: 'Lifting gear, boys, sharp's the word.'

Christine moaned and stirred.

Bloggs said: 'She's alive!' He knelt down beside her

and got his hands under the edge of the lump of rubble.

The rescuer said: 'You won't shift that, son.'

The brickwork lifted.

The rescuer said: 'Strewth, you'll kill yourself,' and bent down to help.

When it was two feet off the ground they got their shoulders under it. The weight was off Christine now. A third man joined in, and a fourth. They all straightened up together.

Bloggs said: 'I'll lift her out.'

He crawled under the sloping roof of brick and cradled his wife in his arms.

Someone shouted: 'Fuck me it's slipping!'

Bloggs scurried out from under with Christine held tightly to his chest. As soon as he was clear the rescuers let go of the rubble and jumped away. It fell back to earth with a sickening thud; and when Bloggs realized that *that* had landed on Christine, he knew she was going to die.

He carried her to the ambulance, and it took off immediately. She opened her eyes again once, before she died, and said: 'You'll have to win the war without me, kiddo.'

More than a year later, as he walked downhill from Highgate into the bowl of London, with the rain on his face mingling with the tears again, he thought the woman in the spy's house had said a mighty truth: it makes you hate.

*

In war boys become men, and men become soldiers, and soldiers get promoted; and this is why Billy Parkin, aged 18, who should have been an apprentice in his father's tannery at Scarborough, was believed by the Army to be twenty-one, made up to sergeant, and given the job of leading his advance squad through a hot, dry forest toward a dusty whitewashed Italian village.

The Italians had surrendered but the Germans had not, and it was the Germans who were defending Italy against the combined British-American invasion. The Allies were going to Rome, and for Sergeant Parkin's squad it was a long walk.

They came out of the forest at the top of a hill, and lay flat on their bellies to look down on the village. Parkin got out his binoculars and said: 'What wouldn't I fookin give for a fookin cup of fookin tea.' He had taken to drinking, and cigarettes, and women, and his language was like that of soldiers everywhere. He no longer went to prayer meetings.

Some of these villages were defended and some were not. Parkin recognized that as sound tactics: you didn't know which were undefended, so you approached them all cautiously, and caution cost time.

The downside of the hill held little cover – just a few bushes – and the village began at its foot. There were a few white houses, a river with a wooden bridge, then more houses around a little piazza with a town hall and a clock tower. There was a clear line-of-sight from the tower to the bridge: if the enemy were here at all, he would be in the town hall. A few figures worked in the surrounding fields: God knew who they were. They might be genuine peasants, or any one of a host of factions: fascisti, mafia, corsos, partigianos, communisti . . . or even Germans. You didn't know whose side they would be on until the shooting started.

Parkin said: 'All right, Corporal.'

Corporal Watkins disappeared back into the forest and emerged, five minutes later, on the dirt road into the village, wearing a civilian hat and a filthy old blanket over his uniform. He stumbled, rather than walked, and over his shoulder was a bundle that could have been anything from a bag of onions to a dead rabbit. He reached the near edge of the village and vanished into the darkness of a low cottage.

After a moment he came out. Standing close to the wall, where he could not be seen from the village, he looked toward the soldiers on the hilltop and waved: one, two, three.

The squad scrambled down the hillside into the village.

Watkins said: 'All the houses empty, Sarge.'

Parkin nodded. It meant nothing.

They moved through the houses to the edge of the river. Parkin said: 'Your turn, Smiler. Swim the Mississippi here.'

Private 'Smiler' Hudson put his equipment in a neat pile, took off his helmet, boots and tunic, and slid into the narrow stream. He emerged on the far side, climbed the bank, and disappeared among the houses. This time there was a longer wait: more area to check. Finally Hudson walked back across the wooden bridge. 'If they're 'ere, they're 'iding,' he said.

He retrieved his gear and the squad crossed the bridge into the village. They kept to the sides of the street as they walked toward the piazza. A bird flew off a roof and startled Parkin. Some of the men kicked open a few doors as they passed. There was nobody.

They stood at the edge of the piazza. Parkin nodded at the town hall. 'Did you go inside the place, Smiler?'

'Yes, sir.'

'Looks like the village is ours, then.'

'Yes, sir.'

Parkin stepped forward to cross the piazza, and then the storm broke. There was a crash of rifles, and bullets hailed all around them. Someone screamed. Parkin was running, dodging, ducking. Watkins, in front of him, shouted with pain and clutched his leg: Parkin picked him up bodily. A bullet clanged off his tin hat. He raced for the nearest house, charged the door, and fell inside.

The shooting stopped. Parkin risked a peep outside. One man lay wounded in the piazza: Hudson. Rough justice. Hudson moved, and a solitary shot rang out. Then he was still. Parkin said: 'Fookin bastards.'

Watkins was doing something to his leg, cursing. Parkin said: 'Bullet still in there?'

Watkins yelled: 'Ouch!' then grinned and held something up. 'Not any more.'

Parkin looked outside again. 'They're in the clock tower,' he said. 'You wouldn't think there was room. Can't be many of them.'

'They can shoot, though.'

'Yes. They've got us pinned.' Parkin frowned. 'Got any fireworks?'

'Aye.'

'Let's have a look.' Parkin opened Watkins's pack and took out the dynamite. 'Here. Fix me a ten-second fuse.'

The others were in the house across the street. Parkin called out: 'Hey!'

A face appeared at the door. 'Sarge?'

'I'm going to throw a tomato. When I shout, give me covering fire.'

'Right.'

Parkin lit a cigarette. Watkins handed him a bundle of dynamite. Parkin shouted: 'Fire!' He lit the fuse with the cigarette, stepped into the street, drew back his arm, and threw the bomb at the clock tower. He ducked back into the house, the fire of his own men ringing in his ears. A bullet shaved the woodwork, and he caught a splinter under his chin. He heard the dynamite explode.

Before he could look, someone across the street shouted: 'Bull's-eye!'

Parkin stepped outside. The ancient clock tower had crumbled. A chime sounded incongruously as dust settled over the ruins.

Watkins said: 'You ever play cricket? That was a bloody good shot.'

Parkin walked to the centre of the piazza. There seemed to be enough human spare parts to make about three Germans. He said: 'The tower was pretty unsteady anyway. It would probably have fallen down if we'd all sneezed at it in unison.' He turned away. 'Another day, another dollar.' It was a phrase the Yanks used.

'Sarge? Radio.' It was the R/T operator.

Parkin walked back and took the handset from him. 'Sergeant Parkin.'

'Major Roberts. You're discharged from active duty as of now, Sergeant.'

'Why?' Parkin's first thought was that they had discovered his true age.

'The brass want you in London. Don't ask me why because I don't know. Leave your corporal in charge and make your way back to base. A car will meet you on the road.'

'Yes, sir.'

'The orders also say that on no account are you to risk your life. Got that?'

Parkin grinned, thinking of the clock tower and the dynamite. 'Got it.'

'All right. On your way. You lucky sod.'

Everyone had called him a boy, but they had known him before he joined the Army, Bloggs thought. There was no doubt he was a man now. He walked with confidence and grace, looked about him sharply, and was respectful without being ill-at-ease in the company of superior officers. Bloggs knew that he was lying about his age, not because of his looks or manner, but because of the small signs that appeared whenever age was mentioned – signs which Bloggs, an experienced interrogator, picked up out of habit.

He had been amused when they told him they wanted him to look at pictures. Now, in his third day in

Mr Midwinter's dusty Kensington vault, the amusement had gone and tedium had set in. What irritated him most was the no-smoking rule.

It was even more boring for Bloggs, who had to sit and watch him.

At one point Parkin said: 'You wouldn't call me back from Italy to help in a four-year-old murder case that could wait until after the war. Also, these pictures are mostly of German officers. If this case is something I should keep mum about, you'd better tell me.'

'It's something you should keep mum about,' said Bloggs.

Parkin went back to his pictures.

They were all old, mostly browned and fading. Many were out of books, magazines and newspapers. Sometimes Parkin picked up a magnifying glass Mr Midwinter had thoughtfully provided, to peer more closely at a tiny face in a group; and each time this happened Bloggs's heart raced, only to slow down when Parkin put the glass to one side and picked up the next photograph.

They went to a nearby pub for lunch. The ale was weak, like most wartime beer, but Bloggs still thought it wise to restrict young Parkin to two pints – on his own he would have sunk a gallon.

'Mr Faber was the quiet sort,' Parkin said. 'You wouldn't think he had it in him. Mind you, the landlady wasn't bad looking. And she wanted it. Looking back, I think I could have had her myself if I'd known how to go about it. There, I was, only – eighteen.'

They ate bread and cheese, and Parkin swallowed a

dozen pickled onions. When they went back, they stopped outside the house while Parkin smoked another cigarette.

'Mind you,' he said, 'he was a biggish chap, good-looking, well-spoken. We all thought he was nothing much because his clothes were poor, and he rode a bike, and he'd no money. I suppose it could have been a subtle kind of disguise.' His eyebrows were raised in a question.

'It could have been,' Bloggs said.

That afternoon Parkin found not one but three pictures of Faber.

One of them was only nine years old.

And Mr Midwinter had the negative.

Henrik Rudolph Hans von Muller-Guder ('Let's just call him Faber,' said Godliman with a laugh) was born on 26 May 1900 at a village called Oln in West Prussia. His father's family had been substantial landowners in the area for generations. His father was the second son; so was Henrik. All the second sons were Army officers. His mother, the daughter of a senior official of the Second Reich, was born and raised to be an aristocrat's wife, and that was what she was.

At the age of thirteen he went to the Karlsruhe cadet school in Baden; two years later he was transferred to the more prestigious Gross-Lichterfelde, near Berlin. Both places were hard, disciplinarian institutions where the minds of the pupils were improved with canes and cold baths and bad food. However, Henrik learned to speak English and French and studied history, and passed the Reifeprüfung with the highest mark recorded since the turn of the century. There were only three other points of note in his school career: one bitter winter he rebelled against authority to the extent of sneaking out of the school at night and walking 150 miles to his aunt's house; he broke the arm of his wrestling instructor during a practice bout; and he was flogged for insurbordination.

He served briefly as an ensign-cadet in the neutral zone of Friedrichsfeld, near Wesel, in 1920; did token officer training at the War School at Metz in 1921, and was commissioned Second Lieutenant in 1922.

('What was the phrase you used?' Godliman asked Bloggs. 'The German equivalent of Eton and Sandhurst.')

Over the next few years he did short tours of duty in half a dozen places, in the manner of one who is being groomed for the general staff. He continued to distinguish himself as an athlete, specializing in longer-distance running. He made no close friendships, never married, and refused to join the National Socialist party. His promotion to lieutenant was somewhat delayed by a vague incident involving the pregnancy of the daughter of a lieutenant-colonel in the Defence Ministry, but eventually came about in 1928. His habit of talking to superior officers as if they were equals came to be accepted as pardonable in one who was both a rising young officer and a Prussian aristocrat.

In the late twenties Admiral Wilhelm Canaris became friendly with Henrik's Uncle Otto, his father's elder brother, and spent several holidays at the family estate at Oln. In 1931 Adolf Hitler, not yet Chancellor of Germany, was a guest there.

In 1933 Henrik was promoted Captain, and went to Berlin for unspecified duties. This is the date of the last photograph.

About then, according to published information, he seems to have ceased to exist.

'We can conjecture the rest,' said Percival Godliman. 'The Abwehr trains him in wireless transmission, codes, map-making, burglary, blackmail, sabotage and silent killing. He comes to London in about 1937 with plenty of time to set himself up with a solid cover – perhaps two. His loner instincts are honed sharp by the spying game. When war breaks out, he considers himself licensed to kill.' He looked at the photograph on his desk. 'He's a handsome fellow.'

It was a picture of the running team of the 10th Hanoverian Jaeger Battalion. Faber was in the middle, holding a cup. He had a high forehead, with cropped hair; a long chin; and a small mouth decorated with a narrow moustache.

Godliman passed the picture to Billy Parkin. 'Has he changed much?'

'He looks a lot older, but that might be his . . . bearing.' He studied the photograph thoughtfully. 'His hair is longer now, and the moustache has gone.' He passed the picture back across the desk. 'But it's him, all right.'

'There are two more items in the file, both of them conjectural,' Godliman said. 'First, they say he may have gone into Intelligence in 1933 – that's the routine assumption when an officer's record just stops for no apparent reason. The second item is a rumour, unconfirmed by any reliable source, that he spent some years as a confidential advisor to Stalin, using the name Vasily Zankov.'

'That's incredible,' Bloggs said. 'I don't believe that.'

Godliman shrugged. '*Somebody* persuaded Stalin to execute the cream of his officer corps during the years Hitler rose to power.'

Bloggs shook his head, and changed the subject. 'Where do we go from here?'

Godliman considered. 'Let's have Sergeant Parkin transferred to us. He's the only man we know who has actually seen Die Nadel. Besides, he knows too much for us to risk him in the front line: he could get captured and interrogated, and give the game away. Next, make a first-class print of this photo, and have the hair thickened and the moustache obliterated by a re-touch artist. Then we can distribute copies.'

'Do we want to start a hue and cry?' Bloggs said doubtfully.

'No. For now, let's tread softly. If we put the thing in the newspapers he'll get to hear of it, and vanish. Just send the photo to police forces for the time being.'

'Is that all?'

'I think so. Unless you've got other ideas.'

Parkin cleared his throat. 'Sir?'

'Yes.'

'I really would prefer to go back to my unit. I'm not really the administrative type, if you know what I mean.'

'You're not being offered a choice, Sergeant. At this stage of the conflict, one Italian village more or less makes no difference – but this man Faber could lose us the war. As the Americans say, I'm not kidding.'

ELEVEN

Faber had gone fishing.

He was stretched out on the deck of a thirty-foot boat, enjoying the spring sunshine, moving along the canal at about three knots. One lazy hand held the tiller, the other rested on a rod which trailed its line in the water behind the boat.

He hadn't caught a thing all day.

As well as fishing, he was bird-watching – both out of interest (he was actually getting to know quite a lot about the damn birds) and as an excuse for carrying binoculars. Earlier today he had seen a kingfisher's nest.

The people at the boatyard in Norwich had been delighted to rent him the vessel for a fortnight. Business was bad: they had only two boats nowadays, and one of them had not been used since Dunkirk. Faber had haggled over the price, just for the sake of form. In the end they had thrown in a locker of tinned food.

He had bought bait in a shop nearby; the fishing tackle he had brought from London. They had observed that he had nice weather for it, and wished him good fishing. Nobody even asked to see his identity card.

So far, so good.

The difficult bit was to come. For assessing the strength of an army was difficult. First you had to find it.

In peacetime the Army would put up its own road signs to help you. Now they had taken down, not only their own but everyone else's road signs.

The simple solution would be to get in a car and follow the first military vehicle you saw until it stopped. However, Faber had no car; it was nearly impossible for a civilian to hire one; and even if you got one you couldn't get petrol for it. Besides, a civilian driving around the countryside following Army lorries and looking at Army camps was liable to be arrested.

Hence the boat.

Some years ago, before it had become illegal to sell maps, Faber had discovered that Britain had thousands of miles of inland waterways. The original network of rivers had been augmented during the nineteenth century by a spider-web of canals. In some areas there was almost as much waterway as there was road. Norfolk was one of these areas.

The boat had many advantages. On a road, a man was going somewhere: on a river he was just sailing. Sleeping in a parked car was conspicuous: sleeping in a moored boat was natural. The waterway was lonely. And who ever heard of a canal-block?

There were disadvantages. Airfields and barracks had to be near roads, but they were located without reference to access by water. Faber had to explore the countryside at night, leaving his moored boat and tramping the hillsides by moonlight, exhausting forty-mile round trips during which he could easily miss what he was looking for because of the darkness or because he simply did not have enough time to check every square mile of land.

When he returned, a couple of hours after dawn, he would sleep until midday then move on, stopping occasionally to climb a nearby hill and check the outlook. At locks, isolated farmhouses and riverside pubs he would talk to people, hoping for hints of a military presence. So far there had been none.

He was beginning to wonder whether he was in the right area. He had tried to put himself in General Patton's place, thinking: If I were planning to invade France east of the Seine from a base in eastern England, where would I locate that base? Norfolk was obvious: a vast expanse of lonely countryside, plenty of flat ground for aircraft, close to the sea for rapid departure. And the Wash was a natural place to gather a fleet of ships. However, his guesswork might be wrong for reasons unknown to him. Soon he would have to consider a rapid move across country to a new area: perhaps the Fens.

A lock appeared ahead of him, and he trimmed his sails to slow his pace. He glided gently into the lock and bumped softly against the gates. The lock-keeper's house was on the bank. Faber cupped his hands around his mouth and hallooed. Then he settled down to wait. He had learned that lock-keepers were a breed that could not be hurried. Moreover, it was tea-time, and at tea-time they could hardly be moved at all.

A woman came to the door of the house and beckoned. Faber waved back, then jumped on to the bank, tied up the boat, and went into the house. The lock-keeper was in his shirt-sleeves at the kitchen table. He said: 'Not in a hurry, are you?'

Faber smiled. 'Not at all.'

'Pour him a cup of tea, Mavis.'

'No, really,' Faber said politely.

'It's all right, we've just made a pot.'

'Thank you.' Faber sat down. The little kitchen was airy and clean, and his tea came in a pretty china cup.

'Fishing holiday?' the lock-keeper asked.

'Fishing and bird-watching,' Faber answered. 'I'm thinking of tying-up quite soon and spending a couple of days on land.'

'Oh, aye. Well, best keep to the far side of the canal, then. Restricted area this side.'

'Really? I didn't know there was Army land hereabouts.'

'Aye, it starts about half a mile from here. As to whether it's Army, I wouldn't know. They don't tell me.'

'Well, I suppose we don't need to know,' Faber said.

'Aye. Drink up, then, and I'll see you through the lock. Thanks for letting me finish my tea.'

They left the house, and Faber got into the boat and untied it. The gates behind him closed slowly, and then the keeper opened the sluices. The boat gradually sank with the level of the water in the lock, then the keeper opened the front gates.

Faber made sail and moved out. The lock-keeper waved.

He stopped again about four miles away and moored the boat to a stout tree on the bank. While he waited for night to fall he made a meal of tinned sausage-meat, dry biscuits, and bottled water. He dressed in his black clothes, put into a shoulder-bag his binoculars, camera, and copy of *Rare Birds of East Anglia,* pocketed his compass and picked up his torch. He was ready.

He doused the hurricane lamp, locked the cabin door, and jumped on to the bank. Consulting his compass by torchlight, he entered the belt of woodland alongside the canal.

He walked due south from his boat for about half a mile until he hit the fence. It was six feet high, chicken-wire, with coiled barbed wire on top. He backtracked into the wood and climbed a tall tree.

There was scattered cloud above. The moon showed through fitfully. Beyond the fence was open land, a gentle rise. Faber had done this sort of thing before, at Biggin Hill, Aldershot, and a host of military areas all over Southern England. There were two levels of security: a mobile patrol around the perimeter fence, and stationary sentries at the installations.

Both could be evaded by patience and caution.

Faber came down the tree and returned to the fence. He concealed himself behind a bush and settled down to wait.

He had to know when the mobile patrol passed this point. If they did not come until dawn, he would simply return the following night. If he was lucky, they would pass shortly. From the apparent size of the area under guard he guessed they would only make one complete tour of the fence each night.

He was lucky. Soon after ten o'clock he heard the tramp of feet, and three men marched by on the inside of the fence.

Five minutes later Faber crossed the fence.

He walked due south: when all directions are equal, a straight line is best. He did not use his flashlight. He kept close to hedges and trees when he could, and avoided high ground where he might be silhouetted against a sudden flash of moonlight. The sparse countryside was an abstract in black, grey and silver. The ground underfoot was a little soggy, as if there might be marshes nearby. A fox ran across a field in front of him, as fast as a greyhound, as graceful as a cat.

It was 11.30 p.m. when he came across the first indications of military activity – and very odd indications they were.

The moon came out and he saw, perhaps a quarter of a mile ahead, several rows of one-storey buildings laid out with the unmistakable precision of an Army barracks. He dropped to the ground immediately, but he was already doubting the reality of what he apparently saw; for there were no lights and no noise.

He lay still for ten minutes, to give explanations a chance to emerge, but nothing happened except that a badger lumbered into view, saw him, and made off.

Faber crawled forward.

As he got closer he realized that the barracks were

not just unoccupied, but unfinished. Most of them were little more than a roof supported by cornerposts. Some had one wall.

A sudden sound stopped him: a man's laugh. He lay still and watched. A match flared briefly and died, leaving two glowing red spots in one of the unfinished huts: guards.

Faber touched the stiletto in his sleeve, then began to crawl again, making for the side of the camp away from the sentries.

The half-built huts had no floors and no foundations. There were no construction vehicles around, no wheelbarrows, concrete mixers, shovels or piles of bricks. A mud track led away from the camp across the fields, but spring grass was growing in the ruts: it had not been used much lately.

It was as if someone had decided to billet ten thousand men here, then changed his mind a few weeks after building started.

Yet there was something about the place that did not quite fit that explanation.

Faber walked around softly, alert lest the sentries should take it into their heads to make a patrol. There was a group of military vehicles in the centre of the camp. They were old and rusting, and had been degutted – none had an engine or any interior components. But if one was going to cannibalize obsolete vehicles, why not take the shells for scrap?

Those huts which did have a wall were on the outermost rows, and their walls faced out. It was like a movie set, not a building site.

Faber decided he had learned all he could from this place. He walked to the east edge of the camp, then dropped to his hands and knees and crawled away until he was out of sight behind a hedge. Half a mile farther on, near the top of a rise, he looked back. Now it looked exactly like a barracks again.

The glimmer of an idea formed in his mind. He gave it time.

The land was still relatively flat, relieved only by gentle folds. There were patches of woodland and marshy scrub which Faber took advantage of. Once he had to detour around a lake, its surface a silver mirror under the moon. He heard the hoot of an owl, and looked in that direction to see a tumbledown barn in the distance.

Five miles on, he saw the airfield.

There were more planes here than he thought were possessed by the entire Royal Air Force. There were Pathfinders to drop flares, Lancasters and American B-17S for softening-up bombing, Hurricanes and Spitfires and Mosquitoes for reconnaissance and strafing: enough planes for an invasion.

Without exception their undercarriages had sunk into the soft earth, and they were up to their bellies in mud.

Once again there were no lights and no noise.

Faber followed the same procedure, crawling flat toward the planes until he located the guards. In the middle of the airfield was a small tent. The faint glow of a lamp shone through the canvas. Two men, perhaps three.

As Faber approached the planes they seemed to become flatter, as if they had all been squashed.

He reached the nearest and touched it in amazement. It was a piece of half-inch plywood, cut out in the outline of a Spitfire, painted with camouflage, and roped to the ground.

Every other plane was the same.

There were more than a thousand of them.

Faber got to his feet, watching the tent from the corner of his eye, ready to drop to the ground at the slightest sign of movement. He walked all around the phoney airfield, looking at the phoney fighters and bombers, connecting them with the movie-set barracks, reeling at the implications of what he had found.

He knew that if he continued to explore he would find more airfields like this, more half-built barracks. If he went to the Wash he would find a fleet of plywood destroyers and troop ships.

It was a vast, meticulous, costly, outrageous trick.

Of course, it could not possibly fool an onlooker for very long. But it was not designed to deceive observers on the ground.

It was meant to be seen from the air.

Even a low-flying reconnaissance plane equipped with the latest cameras and fast film would come back with pictures which indisputably showed an enormous concentration of men and machines.

No wonder the general staff were anticipating an invasion east of the Seine.

There would be other elements to the deception, he guessed. The British would refer to FUSAG in signals, using codes they knew to be broken. There would be phoney espionage reports channelled through the Spanish diplomatic bag to Hamburg. The possibilities were endless.

The British had had four years to arm themselves for this invasion. Most of the German army was fighting Russia. Once the Allies got a toehold on French soil, they would be unstoppable. The Germans' only chance was to catch them on the beaches and annihilate them as they came off the troop ships.

If they were waiting in the wrong place, they would lose that one chance.

The whole strategy was immediately clear. It was simple, and it was devastating.

Faber had to tell Hamburg.

He wondered whether they would believe him.

War strategy was rarely altered on the word of one man. His own standing was particularly high, but was it that high?

He needed to get proof, and then take it to Berlin.

He needed photographs.

He would take pictures of this gigantic dummy army, then he would go to Scotland and meet the U-boat, and he would deliver the pictures personally to the Führer. He could do no more.

For photography he needed light. He would have to wait until dawn. There had been a ruined barn a little way back: he could spend the rest of the night there.

He checked his compass and set off. The barn was farther than he thought, and the walk took him an hour. It was an old wooden building with holes in the roof. The rats had long ago deserted it for lack of food, but there were bats in the hayloft.

Faber lay down on some planks, but he could not sleep for the knowledge that he was now personally capable of altering the course of the greatest war in history.

Dawn was due at 05.21. At 04.20 Faber left the barn.

Although he had not slept, the two hours of immobility had rested his body and calmed his mind, and he was now in fine spirits. The cloud was clearing with a west wind, so although the moon had set there was starlight.

His timing was good. The sky was growing perceptibly brighter as he came in sight of the 'airfield'.

The sentries were still in their tent. With luck, they would be sleeping: Faber knew from his own experience of such duties that it was hardest to stay awake during the last few hours.

And if they did come out, he would just have to kill them.

He selected his position and loaded the Leica with a 36-frame roll of 35mm fast Agfa film. He hoped the film's light-sensitive chemicals had not spoiled, for it had been stored in his suitcase since before the war: you couldn't buy film in Britain nowadays. It should be all right, for he had kept it in a light-proof bag away from any heat.

When the red rim of the sun edged over the horizon he began shooting. He took a series of shots from different vantage points and various distances, finishing with a close-up of one dummy plane: the pictures would show both the illusion and the reality.

As he took the last he saw movement from the corner of his eye. He dropped flat and crawled under a plywood Mosquito. A soldier emerged from the tent, walked a few paces, and urinated on the ground. The man stretched and yawned, then lit a cigarette. He looked around the airfield, shivered, and returned to the tent.

Faber got up and ran.

A quarter of a mile away he looked back. The airfield was out of sight. He headed west, toward the barracks.

This would be more than an ordinary espionage coup. Hitler had had a life of being the only one in step. The man who brought the proof that, yet again, the Führer was right and all the experts were wrong, could look for more than a pat on the back. Faber knew that already Hitler rated him the Abwehr's best agent: this triumph would probably get him Canaris's job.

If he made it.

He increased his pace, jogging twenty yards, walking the next twenty, and jogging again, so that he reached the barracks by 06.30. It was bright daylight now, and he could not approach close, because these sentries were not in a tent, but in one of the wall-less huts, with a clear view all around them. He lay down by the hedge and took his pictures from a distance. Ordinary prints would just show a barracks, but big enlargements ought to reveal the details of the deception.

When he headed back toward the boat he had exposed thirty frames. Again he hurried, for he was now terribly conspicuous, a black-clad man carrying a canvas bag of equipment, jogging across the open fields of a restricted area.

He reached the fence an hour later, having seen nothing but wild geese. As he climbed over the wire, he felt a great release of tension. Inside the fence the balance of suspicion had been against him; outside it was in his favour. He could revert to his bird-watching, fishing, sailing role. The period of greatest risk was over.

He strolled through the belt of woodland, catching his breath and letting the strain of the night's work seep away. He would sail a few miles on, he decided, before mooring again to catch a few hours' sleep.

He reached the canal. It was over. The boat looked pretty in the morning sunshine. As soon as he was under way he would make some tea, then—

A man in uniform stepped out of the cabin of the boat and said: 'Well, well. And who might you be?'

Faber stood stock still, letting the icy calm and the old instincts come into play. The intruder wore the uniform of a captain in the Home Guard. He had some kind of handgun in a holster with a buttoned flap. He was tall and rangy, but he looked to be in his late fifties. White hair showed under his cap. He made no move to draw his gun. Faber took all this in as he said: 'You are on my boat, so I think it is I who should ask who you are.'

'Captain Stephen Langham, Home Guard.'

'James Baker.' Faber stayed on the bank. A captain did not patrol alone.

'And what are you doing?'

'I'm on holiday.'

'Where have you been?'

'Bird-watching.'

'Since before dawn? Cover him, Watson.'

A youngish man in denim uniform appeared on Faber's left, carrying a shotgun. Faber looked around. There was another man to his right and a fourth behind him.

The captain called: 'Which direction did he come from, Corporal?'

The reply came from the top of an oak tree. 'From the restricted area, sir.'

Faber was calculating odds. Four to one – until the corporal came down from the tree. They had only two guns: the shotgun and the captain's pistol. And they were amateurs. The boat would help, too.

He said: 'Restricted area? All I saw was a bit of fence. Look, do you mind pointing that blunderbuss away? It might go off.'

The captain said: 'Nobody goes bird-watching in the dark.'

'If you set up your hide under cover of darkness, you're concealed by the time the birds wake up. It's the accepted way to do it. Now look, the Home Guard is jolly patriotic and keen and all that, but let's not take it too far, what? Don't you just have to check my papers and file a report?'

The captain was looking a shade doubtful. 'What's in that canvas bag?'

'Binoculars, a camera, and a reference book.' Faber's hands went to the bag.

'No, you don't,' the captain said. 'Look inside it, Watson.'

There it was: the amateur's error.

Watson said: 'Hands up.'

Faber raised his hands above his head, his right hand close to the left sleeve of his jacket. Faber choreographed the next few seconds: there must be no gunfire.

Watson came up on Faber's left side, pointing the shotgun at him, and opened the flap of Faber's canvas bag. Faber drew the stiletto from his sleeve, moved inside Watson's guard, and plunged the knife downward into Watson's neck up to the hilt. Faber's other hand twisted the shotgun out of the young man's grasp.

The other two soldiers on the bank moved toward him, and the corporal began to crash down through the branches of the oak.

Faber tugged the stiletto out of Watson's neck as the man collapsed to the ground. The captain was fumbling at the flap of his holster. Faber leaped into the well of the boat. It rocked, sending the captain staggering. Faber struck at him with the knife, but the man was too far away for an accurate thrust. The point caught in the lapel of his uniform jacket, then jerked up, slashing his chin. His hand came away from the holster to clutch the wound.

Faber whipped around to face the bank. One of the soldiers jumped. Faber stepped forward and held his right arm out rigidly. The leaping soldier impaled himself on the eight-inch needle.

The impact knocked Faber off his feet, and he lost his grip on the stiletto. The soldier fell on top of the weapon. Faber got to his knees: there was no time to retrieve the stiletto, for the captain was opening his holster. Faber jumped at him, his hands going for the officer's face. The gun came out. Faber's thumbs gouged at the captain's eyes, and he screamed in pain and tried to push Faber's arms aside.

There was a thud as the fourth guardsman landed in the well of the boat. Faber turned from the captain, who would now be unable to see to fire his pistol even if he could get the safety off. The fourth man held a policeman's truncheon. He brought it down hard. Faber shifted to the right, so that the blow missed his head and caught his left shoulder. His left arm momentarily became paralysed. He chopped the man's neck with the side of his right hand, a powerful, accurate blow. Amazingly, the man survived it, and brought his truncheon up for a second swipe. Faber closed in. The feeling returned to his left arm, and it began to hurt mightily. He took the soldier's face in both his hands, pushed, twisted, and pushed again. There was a sharp crack as the man's neck broke. At the same instant the truncheon landed again, this time on Faber's head. He reeled away, dazed.

The captain bumped into him, still staggering. Faber pushed him. His cap went flying as he stumbled backward over the gunwale and fell into the canal with a huge splash.

The corporal jumped the last six feet from the oak tree on to the ground. Faber retrieved his stiletto from the impaled guard and leaped to the bank. Watson was still alive, but it would not be for long: blood was pumping out of the wound in his neck.

Faber and the corporal faced each other. The corporal had a gun.

He was utterly terrified. In the few seconds it had taken him to climb down the oak tree, this stranger had killed three of his mates and thrown the fourth into the canal. Horror shone from his eyes like torchlight.

Faber looked at the gun. It was *old* – it looked like a museum piece. If the corporal had any confidence in it, he would have fired it already.

The corporal took a step forward, and Faber noticed that he favoured his right leg – perhaps he had hurt it coming out of the tree. Faber stepped sideways, forcing the corporal to put his weight on the weak leg as he swung to keep his gun on target. Faber got the toe of his shoe under a stone and kicked upward. The corporal's eyes flicked to the stone, and Faber moved.

The corporal pulled the trigger, and nothing happened. The old gun had jammed. Even if it had fired, he would have missed Faber: his eyes were on the stone, he stumbled on the weak leg, and Faber had moved.

Faber killed him with the neck stab.

Only the captain was left.

Faber looked, to see the man clambering out of the water on the far bank. He found a stone and threw it.

It hit the captain's head, but the man heaved himself on to dry land and began to run.

Faber ran to the bank, dived in, swam a few strokes, and came up on the far side. The captain was a hundred yards away and running; but he was old. Faber gave chase. He gained steadily until he could hear the man's agonized, ragged breathing. The captain slowed, then collapsed into a bush.

Faber came up to him and turned him over.

The captain said: 'You're a . . . devil.'

'You saw my face,' Faber said, and killed him.

TWELVE

The Ju-52 trimotor transport plane with swastikas on the wings bumped to a halt on the rain-wet runway at Rastenburg in the East Prussian forest. A small man with big features – a large nose, a wide mouth, big ears – disembarked and walked quickly across the tarmac to a waiting Mercedes car.

As the car drove through the gloomy, damp forest, Field Marshal Erwin Rommel took off his cap and rubbed a nervous hand along his receding hairline. In a few weeks' time, he knew, another man would travel this route with a bomb in his briefcase – a bomb destined for the Führer himself. Meanwhile the fight must go on, so that the new leader of Germany – who might even be Rommel himself – could negotiate with the Allies from a strong position.

At the end of a ten-mile drive the car arrived at the Wolfsschanze, the Wolves' Lair, headquarters now for Hitler and the increasingly tight, neurotic circle of generals who surrounded him.

There was a steady drizzle, and raindrops dripped from the tall conifers in the compound. At the gate to Hitler's personal quarters, Rommel put on his cap and got out of the car. Oberführer Rattenhuber, the chief of the SS bodyguard, wordlessly held out his hand to receive Rommel's pistol.

The conference was to be held in the underground bunker, a cold, damp, airless shelter lined with concrete. Rommel went down the steps and entered. There were a dozen or so there already, waiting for the noon meeting: Himmler, Goering, von Ribbentrop, Keitel. Rommel nodded greetings and sat on a hard chair to wait.

They all stood when Hitler entered. He wore a grey tunic and black trousers, and he was becoming more and more stooped, Rommel observed. He walked straight to the far end of the bunker, where a large wall map of north-western Europe was tacked to the concrete. He looked tired and irritable. He spoke without preamble.

'There will be an Allied invasion of Europe. It will come this year. It will be launched from Britain, with English and American troops. They will land in France. We will destroy them at the high-water mark. On this there is no room for discussion.'

He looked around, as if daring his staff to contradict him. There was silence. Rommel shivered: the bunker was as cold as death.

'The question is: where will they land? Von Roenne – your report.'

Colonel Alexis von Roenne, who had taken over, effectively, from Canaris, got to his feet. A mere captain at the outbreak of war, he had distinguished himself with a superb report on the weaknesses of the French army – a report which had been called a decisive factor in the German victory. He had become chief of the army intelligence bureau in 1942, and that bureau had absorbed the Abwehr on the fall of Canaris. Rommel had heard that he was proud and outspoken, but able.

Roenne said: 'Our information is extensive, but by no means complete. The Allies' codename for the invasion is Overlord. Troop concentrations in Britain are as follows.' He picked up a pointer and crossed the room to the wall map. 'First: along the south coast. Second: here in the district known as East Anglia. Third: in Scotland. The East Anglian concentration is *by far* the greatest. We conclude that the invasion will be three-pronged. First: a diversionary attack on Normandy. Second: the main thrust, across the Straits of Dover to the Calais coast. Third: a flanking invasion from Scotland across the North Sea to Norway. All intelligence sources support this prognosis.' He sat down.

Hitler said: 'Comments?'

Rommel, who was Commander of Army Group B, which controlled the north coast of France, said: 'I can report one confirming sign: the Pas de Calais has received by far the greatest tonnage of bombs.'

Goering said: 'What intelligence sources support your prognosis, von Roenne?'

Roenne stood up again. 'There are three: air reconnaissance, monitoring of enemy wireless signals, and the reports of agents.' He sat down.

Hitler crossed his hands protectively in front of his genitals, a nervous habit which was a sign that he was about to make a speech. 'I shall now tell you,' he began, 'how I would be thinking if I were Winston Churchill. Two choices confront me: east of the Seine, or west of the Seine. East has one advantage: it is nearer. But in modern warfare there are only two distances – *within* fighter range and *outside* fighter range. *Both* of these choices are within fighter range. Therefore distance is not a consideration.

'West has a great port – Cherbourg – but east has none. And most important – east is more heavily fortified than west. The enemy too has air reconnaissance.

'So, I would choose west. And what would I do then? I would try to make the Germans think the opposite! I would send two bombers to the Pas de Calais for every one to Normandy. I would try to knock out every bridge over the Seine. I would put out misleading wireless signals, send false intelligence reports, dispose my troops in a misleading fashion. I would deceive fools like Rommel and von Roenne. I would hope to deceive the Führer himself!'

Goering spoke first after a lengthy silence. 'My Führer, I believe you flatter Churchill by crediting him with ingenuity equal to your own.'

There was a noticeable easing of tension in the uncomfortable bunker. Goering had said exactly the right thing, managing to voice his disagreement in the form of a compliment. The others followed him, each stating the case a little more strongly: the Allies would choose the shorter sea crossing for speed; the closer coast would allow the covering fighter aircraft to refuel and return in shorter time; the south-east was a better launch pad, with more estuaries and harbours; it was unlikely that all the intelligence reports would be unanimously wrong.

Hitler listened for half an hour, then held up his hand for silence. He picked up a yellowing sheaf of papers from the table and waved them. 'In 1941,' he said, 'I issued my directive *Construction of Coastal Defences,* in which I forecast that the decisive landing of the Allies would come at the protruding parts of Normandy and Brittany, where the excellent harbours would make ideal beachheads. That was what my intuition told me then, and that is what it tells me now!' A fleck of foam appeared on the Führer's lower lip.

Von Roenne spoke up. (He has more courage than I, Rommel thought.) 'My Führer, our investigations continue, quite naturally, and there is one particular line of inquiry which you should know about. I have in recent weeks sent an emissary to England to contact the agent known as Die Nadel.'

Hitler's eyes gleamed. 'Ah! I know the man. Carry on.'

'Die Nadel's orders are to assess the strength of the First United States Army Group under General Patton in East Anglia. If he finds that this has been exaggerated, we must surely reconsider our prognosis. If, however, he reports that the army is as strong as we presently believe, there can be little doubt that Calais is the target.'

Goering looked at von Roenne. 'Who is this Nadel?'

Hitler answered the question. 'The only decent agent Canaris ever recruited – because he recruited him at my behest,' he said. 'I know his family – a pillar of the Reich. Strong, loyal, upright Germans. And Die Nadel – a brilliant man, brilliant! I see all his reports. He has been in London since before the English started the war. Earlier than that, in Russia—'

Von Roenne interrupted: 'My Führer—'

Hitler glared at him, but he seemed to realize that the spy chief had been right to stop him. 'Well?'

Von Roenne said tentatively: 'Then you will accept Die Nadel's report?'

Hitler nodded. 'That man will discover the truth.'

PART THREE

THIRTEEN

Faber leaned against a tree, shivering, and threw up.

Then he considered whether he should bury the five dead men.

It would take between thirty and sixty minutes, he estimated, depending on how well he concealed the bodies. During that time he might be caught.

He had to weigh that risk against the precious hours he might gain by delaying the discovery of the deaths. The five men would be missed very soon: there would be a search under way by around nine o'clock. Assuming they were on a regular patrol, their route would be known. The searchers' first move would be to send a runner to cover the route. If the bodies were left as they were, he would see them and raise the alarm. Otherwise, he would report back and a full-scale search would be mounted, with bloodhounds and policemen beating the bushes. It might take them all day to discover the corpses. By that time Faber could be in London. It was important for him to be out of the area before they knew they were looking for a murderer. He decided to risk the additional hour.

He swam back across the canal with the elderly captain across his shoulder. He dumped him unceremoniously behind a bush. He retrieved the two bodies from the well of the boat and piled them on top of the captain. Then he added Watson and the corporal to the heap.

He had no spade, and he needed a big grave. He found a patch of loose earth a few yards into the wood. The ground there was slightly hollowed, to give him an advantage. He got a saucepan from the boat's tiny galley and began to dig.

For a couple of feet there was just leaf-mould, and the going was easy. Then he got down to clay, and digging became extremely difficult. In half an hour he had added only another eighteen inches of depth to the hole. It would have to do.

He carried the bodies to the hole one by one and threw them in. Then he took off his muddy, blood-stained clothes and dropped them on top. He covered the grave with loose earth and a layer of foliage ripped from nearby bushes and trees. It should be good enough to pass that first, superficial inspection.

He kicked earth over the patch of ground near the bank where the life-blood of Watson had poured out. There was blood in the boat, too, where the impaled soldier had lain. Faber found a rag and swabbed-down the deck.

Then he put on clean clothes, made sail, and moved off.

He did not fish or watch birds: this was no time for pleasant embellishments to his cover. Instead he piled-on the sail, putting as much distance as possible between himself and the grave. He had to get off the water and into some faster transport as soon as possible. He reflected, as he sailed, on the relative merits of catching a train or stealing a car. A car was faster, if one could be found to steal; but the search for it might start quite soon, regardless of whether the theft was connected with the missing Home Guard patrol. Finding a railway station might take a long time, but it seemed safer: if he were careful he could escape suspicion for most of the day.

He wondered what to do about the boat. Ideally he would scuttle it, but he might be seen doing so. If he left it in a harbour somewhere, or simply moored at the canalside, the police would connect it with the murders that much sooner; and that would tell them in which direction he was moving. He postponed the decision.

Unfortunately, he was not sure where he was. His map of England's waterways gave every bridge, harbour and lock; but it did not show railway lines. He calculated he was within an hour or two's walk of half a dozen villages, but a village did not necessarily mean a station.

In the end luck solved two problems at once: the canal went under a railway bridge.

He took his compass, the film from the camera, his wallet and his stiletto. All his other possessions would go down with the boat.

The towpath on both sides was shaded with trees, and there were no roads nearby. He furled the sails, dismantled the base of the mast, and laid the pole on the deck. Then he removed the bung-hole stopper from the keel and stepped on to the bank, holding the rope.

Gradually filling with water, the boat drifted under the bridge. Faber hauled on the rope to hold the vessel in position directly under the brick arch as it sank. The after-deck went under first, the prow followed, and finally the water of the canal closed over the roof of the cabin. There were a few bubbles, then nothing. The outline of the boat was hidden from a casual glance by the shadow of the bridge. Faber threw the rope in.

The railway line ran north-east to south-west. Faber climbed the embankment and walked south-west, which was the direction in which London lay. It was a two-line track, probably a rural branch line. There would be few trains, but they would stop at all stations.

The sun grew stronger as he walked, and the exertion made him hot. When he had buried his blood-stained black clothes he had put on a double-breasted blazer and heavy flannel trousers. Now he took off the blazer and slung it over his shoulder.

After forty minutes he heard a distant chuff-chuff-chuff, and hid in a bush beside the line. An old steam engine went slowly by, heading north-west, puffing great clouds of smoke and hauling a train of coal trucks. If one came by in the opposite direction, he could jump it. Should he? It would save him a long walk. On the other hand, he would get conspicuously dirty, and he might have trouble disembarking without being seen. No, it was safer to walk.

The line ran straight as an arrow across the flat countryside. Faber passed a farmer, ploughing a field with a tractor. There was no way to avoid being seen.

The farmer waved to him without stopping in his work. He was too far away to get a good sight of Faber's face.

He had walked about ten miles when he saw a station ahead. It was half a mile away, and all he could see was the rise of the platforms and a cluster of signals. He left the line and cut across the fields, keeping close to borders of trees, until he met a road.

Within a few minutes he entered the village. There was nothing to tell him its name. Now that the threat of invasion was a memory, signposts and place-names were being re-erected, but this village had not got around to it.

There was a Post Office, a Corn Store, and a pub called The Bull. A woman with a pram gave him a friendly 'Good morning!' as he passed the War Memorial. The little station basked sleepily in the spring sunshine. Faber went in.

A timetable was pasted to a notice-board. Faber stood in front of it. From behind the little ticket window a voice said: 'I shouldn't take any notice of that, if I were you. It's the biggest work of fiction since *The Forsyte Saga.*'

Faber had known the timetable would be out-of-date, but he had needed to establish whether the trains went to London. They did. He said: 'Any idea what time the next train leaves for Liverpool Street?'

The clerk laughed sarcastically. 'Some time today, if you're lucky.'

'I'll buy a ticket anyway. Single, please.'

'Five-and-fourpence. They say the Italian trains run on time,' the clerk said.

'Not any more,' Faber remarked. 'Anyway, I'd rather have bad trains and our politics.'

The man shot him a nervous look. 'You're right, of course. Do you want to wait in The Bull? You'll hear the train – or, if not, I'll send for you.'

Faber did not want more people to see his face. 'No, thanks, I'd only spend money.' He took his ticket and went on to the platform.

The clerk followed him a few minutes later, and sat on the bench beside him in the sunshine. He said: 'You in a hurry?'

Faber shook his head. 'I've written today off. I got up late, I quarrelled with the boss, and the lorry that gave me a lift broke down.'

'One of those days. Ah, well.' The clerk looked at his watch. 'She went up on time this morning, and what goes up must come down, they say. You might be lucky.' He went back into his office.

Faber was lucky. The train came twenty minutes later. It was crowded with farmers, families, businessmen and soldiers. Faber found a space on the floor close to a window. As the train lumbered away, he picked up a discarded two-day-old newspaper, borrowed a pencil, and started to do the crossword. He was proud of his ability to do crosswords in English: it was the acid test of fluency in a foreign language. After a while the motion of the train lulled him into a shallow sleep, and he dreamed.

*

It was a familiar dream, the dream of his arrival in London.

He had crossed from France, carrying a Belgian passport which said he was Jan van Gelder, a representative for Philips (which would explain his suitcase radio if the Customs opened it). His English then was fluent but not colloquial. The Customs had not bothered him: he was an ally. He had caught the train to London. In those days there had been plenty of empty seats in the carriages, and you could get a meal. Faber had dined on roast beef and Yorkshire pudding. It amused him. He had talked with a history student from Cardiff about the European political situation. The dream was like the reality until the train stopped at Waterloo. Then it turned into a nightmare.

The trouble started at the ticket barrier. Like all dreams it had its own weird illogicality. The document they queried was not his forged passport but his perfectly legitimate railway ticket. The collector said: 'This is an Abwehr ticket.'

'No, it is not,' said Faber, speaking with a ludicrously thick German accent. What had happened to his dainty English consonants? They would not come. 'I have it in Dover gekauft.' Damn, that did it.

But the ticket collector, who had turned into a London policeman complete with helmet, seemed to ignore the sudden lapse into German. He smiled politely and said: 'I'd better just check your Klamotte, sir.'

The station was crowded with people. Faber thought that if he could get into the crowd he might escape. He dropped the suitcase radio and fled, pushing his way through the crowd. Suddenly he realized he had left his trousers on the train, and there were swastikas on his socks. He would have to buy trousers at the very first shop, before people noticed the trouserless running man with Nazi hose – then someone in the crowd said: 'I've seen your face before,' and tripped him, and he fell with a bump and landed on the floor of the railway carriage where he had gone to sleep.

He blinked, yawned, and looked around him. He had a headache. For a moment he was filled with relief that it was all a dream, then he was amused by the ridiculousness of the symbolism – swastika socks, for God's sake!

A man in overalls beside him said: 'You had a good sleep.'

Faber looked up sharply. He was always afraid of talking in his sleep and giving himself away. He said: 'I had an unpleasant dream.' The man made no comment.

It was getting dark. He *had* slept for a long time. The carriage light came on suddenly, a single blue bulb, and someone drew the blinds. People's faces turned into pale, featureless ovals. The workman became talkative again. 'You missed the excitement,' he told Faber.

Faber frowned. 'What happened?' It was impossible he should have slept through some kind of police check.

'One of them Yank trains passed us. It was going about ten miles an hour, nigger driving it, ringing its bell, with a bloody great cow-catcher on the front! Talk about the Wild West.'

Faber smiled and thought back to the dream. In fact his arrival in London had been without incident. He had checked into an hotel at first, still using his Belgian cover. Within a week he had visited several country churchyards, taken the names of men his age from the gravestones, and applied for three duplicate birth certificates. Then he took lodgings and found humble work, using forged references from a non-existent Manchester firm. He had even got on to the electoral register in Highgate before the war. He voted Conservative. When rationing came in, the ration books were issued via householders to every person who had slept in the house on a particular night. Faber contrived to spend part of that night in each of three different houses, and so obtained papers for each of his personae. He burned the Belgian passport – in the unlikely event he should need a passport, he could get three British ones.

The train stopped, and from the noise outside the passengers guessed they had arrived. When Faber got out he realized how hungry and thirsty he was. His last meal had been sausage-meat, dry biscuits and bottled water, the day before. He went through the ticket barrier and found the station buffet. It was full of people, mostly soldiers, sleeping or trying to sleep at the tables. Faber asked for a cheese sandwich and a cup of tea.

'The food is reserved for servicemen,' said the woman behind the counter.

'Just the tea, then.'

'Got a cup?'

Faber was surprised. 'No, I haven't.'

'Neither have we, chum.'

Faber left in disgust. He contemplated going into the Great Eastern Hotel for dinner, but that would take time. He found a pub and drank two pints of weak beer, then bought a bag of chips at a fish-and-chip shop and ate them from the newspaper wrapping, standing on the pavement. They made him feel surprisingly full.

Now he had to find a chemist's shop and break in.

He wanted to develop his film, to make sure the pictures came out. He was not going to risk returning to Germany with a roll of spoiled, useless film. If the pictures were no good he would have to steal more film and go back. The thought was unbearable.

It would have to be a small independent shop, not a branch of a chain which would process film centrally. It must be in an area where the local people could afford cameras (or could have afforded them before the war). The part of East London in which Liverpool Street Station stood was no good. He decided to head toward Bloomsbury.

The moonlit streets were quiet. There had been no sirens so far tonight. Two Military Policemen stopped him in Chancery Lane and asked for his identity card. Faber pretended to be slightly drunk, and the MPs did not ask what he was doing out of doors.

He found the shop he was looking for at the north end of Southampton Row. There was a Kodak sign in the window. Surprisingly, the shop was open. He went in.

A stooped, irritable man with thinning hair and glasses stood behind the counter, wearing a white coat. He said: 'We're only open for doctors' prescriptions.'

'That's all right. I just want to ask whether you develop photographs.'

'Yes, if you come back tomorrow—'

'Do you do them on the premises?' Faber asked. 'I need them quickly, you see.'

'Yes, if you come back tomorrow—'

'Could I have the prints the same day? My brother's on leave, and he wants to take some back—'

'Twenty-four hours is the best we can do. Come back tomorrow.'

'Thank you, I will,' Faber lied. On his way out he noticed that the shop was due to close in ten minutes. He crossed the road and stood in the shadows, waiting.

Promptly at nine o'clock the pharmacist came out, locking the shop behind him, and walked off down the road. Faber went in the opposite direction and turned two corners.

There seemed to be no access to the back of the shop. That was something of a blow: Faber did not want to break in the front way, in case the unlocked door was noticed by a patrolling policeman while he was in there. He walked along the parallel street, looking for a way through. Apparently there was none. Yet there had to be a well of some kind at the back, for the two streets were too far apart for the buildings to be joined back-to-back.

Finally he came across a large old house with a nameplate marking it as a Hall of Residence for a nearby college. The front door was unlocked. Faber went in and walked quickly through to a communal kitchen. A lone girl sat at a table, drinking coffee and reading a book. Faber muttered: 'College blackout check.' She nodded and returned to her text. Faber went out of the back door.

He crossed a yard, bumping into a cluster of garbage cans on the way, and found a door to a lane. In seconds he was at the rear of the chemist's shop. This entrance was obviously never used. He clambered over some tyres and a discarded mattress, and threw his shoulder at the door. The rotten wood gave easily, and Faber was inside.

He found the darkroom and shut himself in. The light switch operated a dim red lamp in the ceiling. The place was quite well-equipped, with neatly labelled bottles of developing fluid, an enlarger, and even a dryer for prints.

Faber worked quickly but carefully, getting the temperature of the tanks exactly right, agitating the fluids to develop the film evenly, timing the processes by the hands of a large electric clock on the wall.

The negatives were perfect.

He let them dry, then fed them through the enlarger and made one complete set of ten-by-eight prints. He felt a sense of elation as he saw the images gradually appear in the bath of developer – God, he had done a good job!

There was now a major decision to be made.

The problem had been in his mind all day, and now that the pictures had come out he was forced to confront it.

What if he did not make it home?

The journey ahead of him was, to say the least, hazardous. He was confident of his own ability to make the rendezvous in spite of travel restrictions and coastal security; but he could not guarantee that the U-boat would be there; or that it would get back across the North Sea. Indeed, he might walk out of here and get run over by a bus.

The possibility that, having discovered the greatest secret of the war, he might die and his secret die with him, was too awful to contemplate.

He had to have a fall-back stratagem; a second method of ensuring that the evidence of the Allied deception reached the Abwehr. And that meant writing to Hamburg.

There was, of course, no postal service between England and Germany. Mail had to go via a neutral country. All such mail was sure to be censored. He could write in code, but there was no point: he had to send the pictures, for it was the evidence that counted.

There was a route, but it was an old one. At the Portuguese Embassy in London there was an official, sympathetic to Germany for political reasons and because he was well bribed, who would pass messages via the diplomatic bag to the German Embassy in Lisbon. The route had been opened early in 1939, and Faber had never used it except for one routine test communication Canaris had asked for.

It would have to do.

Faber felt irrationally angry. He *hated* to place his faith in others. This route might no longer be open, or it might be insecure; in which case the British could discover that he had found out their secret.

It was a fundamental rule of espionage that the opposition must not know which of their secrets you have found out; for if they do, the value of your discoveries is nullified. However, in this case that was not so; for what could the British do with their knowledge? They still had the problem of conquering France.

Faber's mind was clear. The balance of argument indisputably favoured entrusting his secret to the Portuguese Embassy contact.

Against all his instincts, he sat down to write a letter.

FOURTEEN

Frederick Bloggs had spent an unpleasant afternoon in the countryside.

When five worried wives had contacted their local police station to say their husbands had not come home, a rural constable had exercised his limited powers of deduction and concluded that a whole patrol of the Home Guard had gone missing. He was fairly sure they had simply got lost – they were all deaf, daft or senile, otherwise they would have been in the Army – but all the same he notified his Constabulary headquarters, just to cover himself. The operations-room sergeant who took the message realized at once that the missing men had been patrolling a particularly sensitive military area, and he notified his inspector, who notified Scotland Yard, who sent a Special Branch man down there and notified M15, who sent Bloggs.

The Special Branch man was Harris, who had been on the Stockwell murder. He and Bloggs met on the train, which was one of the Wild West locomotives lent to Britain by the Americans because of the shortage of trains. Harris repeated his invitation to Sunday dinner, and Bloggs told him again that he worked most Sundays.

When they got off the train they borrowed bicycles to ride along the canal towpath until they met up with the search party. Harris, ten years older than Bloggs and four stone heavier, found the ride a strain.

They met a section of the search party under a railway bridge. Harris welcomed the opportunity to get off the bicycle. 'What have you found?' he said. 'Bodies?'

'No, a boat,' said a policeman. 'Who are you?'

They introduced themselves. A constable stripped to his underwear was diving down to examine the vessel. He came up with a bung in his hand.

Bloggs looked at Harris. 'Deliberately scuttled?'

'Looks like it.' Harris turned to the diver. 'Notice anything else?'

'She hasn't been down there for long, she's in good condition, and the mast has been taken down, not broken.'

Harris said: 'That's a lot of information from a minute under water.'

'I'm a weekend sailor,' the diver said.

Harris and Bloggs mounted their cycles and moved on.

When they met up with the main party, the bodies had been found.

'Murdered, all five,' said the uniformed inspector in charge. 'Captain Langham, Corporal Lee, and Privates Watson, Dayton and Forbes. Dayton's neck was broken, the rest were killed with some kind of knife. Langham's body had been in the canal. All found together in a shallow grave. Bloody murder.' He was quite shaken.

Harris looked closely at the five bodies, laid out in a line. 'I've seen wounds like this before, Fred,' he said.

Bloggs looked closely. 'Jesus Christ, it's him.'

Harris nodded. 'Stiletto.'

The inspector said in astonishment: 'You know who did it?'

'We can guess,' Harris said. 'We think he's killed twice before. If it's the same man, we know *who* he is but not *where* he is.'

The inspector's eyes narrowed. 'What with the restricted area so close, and Special Branch and MI5 arriving on the scene so quick, is there anything else I need to know about this case?'

Harris answered: 'Just that you keep very quiet until your Chief Constable has talked to our people.'

' 'Nuff said.'

Bloggs asked. 'Anything else found, Inspector?'

'We're still combing the area, in ever-widening circles; but nothing so far. There were some clothes in the grave.' He pointed.

Bloggs touched them gingerly: black trousers, a black sweater, a short black leather jacket, RAF-style.

Harris said: 'Clothes for night work.'

'To fit a big man,' Bloggs added.

'How tall is your man?'

'Over six foot.'

The inspector said: 'Did you pass the men who found the sunken boat?'

'Yes.' Bloggs frowned. 'Where's the nearest lock?'

'Four miles upstream.'

'If our man was in a boat, the lock-keeper must have seen him, mustn't he?'

'Must have,' the inspector agreed.

Bloggs said: 'We'd better talk to him.' He returned to his cycle.

'Not another four miles,' Harris complained.

Bloggs said: 'Work off some of those Sunday dinners.'

The four-mile ride took them most of an hour, because the towpath was made for horses, not wheels, and it was uneven, muddy, and mined with loose boulders and tree roots. Harris was sweating and cursing by the time they reached the lock.

The lock-keeper was sitting outside his little house, smoking a pipe and enjoying the mild air of afternoon. He was a middle-aged man of slow speech and slower movements. He regarded the two cyclists with faint amusement.

Bloggs spoke, because Harris was out of breath. 'We're police officers,' he said.

'Is that so?' said the lock-keeper. 'What's the excitement?' He looked as excited as a cat in front of a fire.

Bloggs took the photograph of Die Nadel out of his wallet and gave it to the man. 'Have you ever seen him?'

The lock-keeper put the picture on his lap while he held a fresh match to his pipe. Then he studied the photograph for a while, and handed it back.

'Well?' Harris said.

'Aye.' The lock-keeper nodded slowly. 'He was here about this time yesterday. Came in for a cup of tea.

Nice enough chap. What's he done, shown a light after blackout?'

Bloggs sat down heavily. 'That clinches it,' he said.

Harris thought aloud. 'He moors the boat downstream from here, and goes into the restricted area after dark.' He spoke quietly, so that the lock-keeper should not hear. 'When he comes back, the Home Guard has his boat staked out. He deals with them, sails a bit farther to the railway, scuttles his boat and . . . hops a train?'

Bloggs said to the lock-keeper: 'The railway line that crosses the canal a few miles downstream – where does it go?'

'London.'

Bloggs said: 'Oh, shit.'

Bloggs got back to the War Office in Whitehall at midnight. Godliman and Parkin were there, waiting for him. Bloggs said: 'It's him, all right,' and told them the story.

Parkin was excited, Godliman just looked tense. When Bloggs had finished, Godliman said: 'So now he's back in London, and we're looking for a needle in a haystack again.' He was playing with matches, forming a picture with them on his desk. 'Do you know, every time I look at that photograph I get the feeling I've actually *met* the damn fellow.'

'Well, think! 'Bloggs said. 'Where?'

Godliman shook his head in frustration. 'It must have been only once, and somewhere strange. It's like a face I've seen in a lecture audience, or in the background at a cocktail party. A fleeting glimpse, a casual encounter – when I remember it probably won't do us any good.'

Parkin said: 'What's in that area?'

'I don't know, which means it's probably highly important,' Godliman said.

There was a silence. Parkin lit a cigarette with one of Godliman's matches. Bloggs looked up. 'We could print a million copies of his picture – give one to every policeman, ARP warden, member of the Home Guard, serviceman, railway porter; paste them up on hoardings and publish them in the papers . . .'

Godliman shook his head. 'Too risky. What if he's already talked to Hamburg about whatever he's seen? If we make a public fuss about the man they'll know that his information is good. We'd only be lending credence to him.'

'We've got to do something.'

'Surely. We will circulate his picture to police officers. We'll give his description to the press, and say he's just a straightforward murderer. We can give the details of the Highgate and Stockwell murders, without saying that security is involved.'

Parkin said: 'What you're saying is, we can fight with one hand tied behind our back.'

'For now, anyway.'

'I'll start the ball rolling with the Yard,' Bloggs said. He picked up the phone.

Godliman looked at his watch. 'There's not much

more we can do tonight, but I don't feel like going home. I shan't sleep.'

Parkin stood up. 'In that case I'm going to find a kettle and make some tea.' He went out.

The matches on Godliman's desk made a picture of a horse and carriage. He took away one of the horse's legs and lit his pipe with it. 'Have you got a girl, Fred?' he asked conversationally.

'No.'

'Not since—?'

'No.'

Godliman puffed at his pipe. 'There has to be an end to grief, you know.'

Bloggs made no reply.

Godliman said: 'Look, perhaps I shouldn't talk to you like a Dutch uncle. But I know how you feel – I've been through it myself. The only difference was that I didn't have anyone to blame.'

'You didn't remarry,' Bloggs said, not looking at Godliman.

'No. And I don't want you to make the same mistake. When you reach middle age, living alone can be very depressing.'

'Did I ever tell you, they called her Fearless Bloggs.'

'Yes, you did.'

Bloggs looked at Godliman at last. 'Tell me, where in the world will I find another girl like that?'

'Does she have to be a hero?'

'After Christine – yes.'

'England is full of heroes, Fred.'

At that moment Colonel Terry walked in.

Godliman said: 'Ah, Uncle Andrew—'

Terry interrupted: 'Don't get up. This is important. Listen carefully, because I have to give it to you fast. Bloggs, you need to know this, too. Whoever killed those five Home Guard has learned our most vital secret.

'Number one: our invasion force for Europe will land at Normandy. Number two: the Germans believe it will land at Calais. Number three: one of the most vital aspects of the deception is a very large phoney army, called the First United States Army Group, located in the restricted area those men were patrolling. That area contains dummy barracks, cardboard aircraft, rubber tanks – a huge toy army which looks real to the observers in the reconnaissance planes we've been letting through.'

Bloggs said: 'How come you're so sure the spy found out?'

Terry went to the door. 'Come in, Rodriguez.'

A tall, handsome man with jet-black hair and a long nose entered the room and nodded politely to Godliman and Bloggs. Terry said: 'Senhor Rodriguez is our man at the Portuguese Embassy. Tell them what happened, Rodriguez.'

The man stood by the door, holding his hat. 'A taxi came to the Embassy at about eleven o'clock. The passenger did not get out, but the driver came to the door with an envelope addressed to Francisco. The doorman called me, as he has been instructed to do, and I took possession of the envelope. I was in time to take the number of the cab.'

'I'm having the cabbie traced,' Terry said. 'All right, Rodriguez, you'd better get back. And thank you.'

The tall Portuguese left the room. Terry handed to Godliman a large yellow envelope, addressed to Manuel Francisco. Godliman opened it – it had already been unsealed – and withdrew a second envelope marked with a meaningless series of letters: presumably a code.

Within the inner envelope were several sheets of paper covered with handwriting and a set of ten-by-eight photographs. Godliman examined the letter. 'It looks like a very basic code,' he said.

'You don't need to read it,' Terry said impatiently. 'Look at the photographs.'

Godliman did so. There were about thirty of them, and he looked at each one before speaking. He handed them to Bloggs and said: 'This is a catastrophe.'

Bloggs glanced through the pictures then put them down.

Godliman said: 'This is only his back-up. He's still got the negatives, *and he's going somewhere with them.*'

The three men sat still in the little office, like a tableau. The only illumination came from a spotlight on Godliman's desk. With the cream walls, the blacked-out window, the spare furniture and the worn Civil Service carpet, they might have been anywhere in the world.

Terry said: 'I'm going to have to tell Churchill.'

The phone rang, and the Colonel picked it up. 'Yes. Good. Bring him here right away, please – but before you do, ask him where he dropped the passenger. What? Really? Thank you, get here fast.' He hung up. 'The taxi dropped our man at University College Hospital.'

Bloggs said: 'Perhaps he was injured in the fight with the Home Guard.'

Terry said: 'Where is that hospital?'

'About five minutes' walk from Euston Station,' Godliman said. 'Trains from Euston go to Holyhead, Liverpool, Glasgow . . . all places from which you can catch a ferry to Ireland.'

'Liverpool to Belfast,' Bloggs said. 'Then a car to the border and across into Eire, and a U-boat on the Atlantic coast. He wouldn't risk Holyhead-to-Dublin because of the passport control, and there would be no point in going beyond Liverpool to Glasgow.'

Godliman said: 'Fred, you'd better go to the station and show the picture of Faber around, see if anyone noticed him getting on a train. I'll phone the station and warn them you're coming, and at the same time find out which trains have left since about ten-thirty.'

Bloggs picked up his hat and coat. 'I'm on my way.'

Godliman lifted the phone. 'Yes, we're on our way.'

There were still plenty of people at Euston Station. Although in normal times the station closed around midnight, wartime delays were such that the last train often had not left before the earliest milk train of the morning arrived. The station concourse was a mass of kitbags and sleeping bodies.

Bloggs showed the picture to three railway policemen. None of them recognized the face. He tried ten women porters: nothing. He went to every ticket barrier. One of the guards said: 'We look at tickets, not faces.' He tried half a dozen passengers without result. Finally he went into the ticket office and showed the picture to each of the clerks.

A very fat, bald clerk with ill-fitting false teeth recognized the face. 'I play a game,' he told Bloggs. 'I try to spot something about a passenger that tells me why he's catching a train. Like, he might have a black tie for a funeral, or muddy boots means he's a farmer going home, or there might be a college scarf, or a white mark on a woman's finger where she's took off her wedding ring . . . know what I mean? This is a dull job – not that I'm complaining—'

'What did you notice about this chap?' Bloggs interrupted him.

'Nothing. That was it, see – I couldn't make him out at all. Almost like he was trying to be inconspicuous, know what I mean?'

'I know what you mean.' Bloggs paused. 'Now, I want you to think very carefully. Where was he going – can you remember?'

'Yes,' said the fat clerk. 'Inverness.'

'That doesn't mean he's going there,' said Godliman. 'He's a professional – he knows we can ask questions at railway stations. I expect he automatically buys a ticket for the wrong destination.' He looked at his watch. 'He must have caught the eleven forty-five. That train is now pulling into Stafford. I checked with the railway, they checked with the signalman,' he added by way of explanation. 'They're going to stop the train this side of Crewe. I've got a plane standing by to fly you two to Stoke-on-Trent.

'Parkin, you'll board the train where it's stopped, outside Crewe. You'll be dressed as a ticket inspector, and you'll look at every ticket – and every face – on that train. When you've spotted Faber, just stay close to him.

'Bloggs, you'll be waiting at the ticket barrier at Crewe, just in case Faber decides to hop off there. But he won't. You'll get on the train, and be first off at Liverpool, and waiting at the ticket barrier for Parkin and Faber to come off. Half the local constabulary will be there to back you up.'

'That's all very well if he doesn't recognize me,' Parkin said. 'What if he remembers my face from Highgate?'

Godliman opened a desk drawer, took out a pistol, and gave it to Parkin. 'If he recognizes you, shoot the bastard.'

Parkin pocketed the weapon without comment.

Godliman said: 'I want both of you to be quite clear on the importance of all this. If we don't catch this man, the invasion of Europe will have to be postponed – possibly for a year. In that year the balance of war could turn against us. The time may never be this right again.'

Bloggs said: 'Do we get told how long it is to D-Day?'

'All I know is that it's a matter of weeks.'

Parkin was thinking. 'It'll be June, then.'

Bloggs said: 'Shit.'

Godliman said: 'No comment.'

The phone rang and Godliman picked it up. After a moment he looked up. 'Your car's here.'

Bloggs and Parkin stood up.

Godliman said: 'Wait a minute.'

They stood by the door, looking at the professor. He was saying: 'Yes, sir. Certainly. I will. Goodbye, sir.'

Bloggs could not think of anyone Godliman called Sir. He said: 'Who was that?'

Godliman said: 'Churchill.'

'What did he have to say?' Parkin asked, awestruck.

Godliman said: 'He wishes you both good luck and Godspeed.'

FIFTEEN

The carriage was pitch dark. Faber thought of the jokes people made: 'Take your hand off my knee. No, not you, you.' The British would make jokes out of anything. Their railways were now worse than ever, but nobody complained any more because it was in a good cause. Faber preferred the dark: it was anonymous.

There had been singing, earlier on. Three sailors in the corridor had started it, and the whole carriage had joined in. They had been through *Be Like The Kettle And Sing, There'll Always Be An England* (followed by *Glasgow Belongs To Me* and *Land Of My Fathers* for ethnic balance), and appropriately, *Don't Get Around Much Any More.*

There had been an air-raid warning, and the train slowed to thirty miles an hour. They were all supposed to lie on the floor, but of course there was no room. An anonymous female voice had said: 'Oh, God, I'm frightened,' and a male voice, equally anonymous except that it was Cockney, had said: 'You're in the safest place, girl – they can't 'it a movin' target.' Then everyone laughed and nobody was scared any more. Someone opened a suitcase and passed around a packet of dried-egg sandwiches.

One of the sailors wanted to play cards.

'How can we play cards in the dark?'

'Feel the edges. All Harry's cards are marked.'

The train stopped unaccountably at about 4 a.m. A cultured voice – the dried-egg sandwich supplier, Faber thought – said: 'My guess is we're outside Crewe.'

'Knowing the railways, we could be anywhere from Bolton to Bournemouth,' said the Cockney.

The train jerked and moved off, and everyone cheered. Where, Faber wondered, was the caricature Englishman, with his icy reserve and his stiff upper lip? Not here.

A few minutes later a voice in the corridor said: 'Tickets, please.' Faber noted the Yorkshire accent: they were in the north now. He fumbled in his pockets for his ticket.

He had the corner seat, near the door, so he could see into the corridor. The inspector was shining a torch on to the tickets. Faber saw the man's silhouette in the reflected light. It looked vaguely familiar.

He settled back in his seat to wait. He remembered the nightmare: 'This is an Abwehr ticket' – and smiled in the dark.

Then he frowned. The train stops unaccountably; shortly afterwards a ticket inspection begins; the inspector's face is vaguely familiar . . . It might be nothing, but Faber stayed alive by worrying about things that *might* be nothing. He looked in the corridor again, but the man had entered a compartment.

The train stopped briefly – the station was Crewe, according to informed opinion in Faber's compartment – and moved off again.

Faber got another look at the inspector's face, and now he remembered. The boarding house in Highgate! The boy from Yorkshire who wanted to get into the Army!

Faber watched him carefully. His torch flashed across the face of every passenger. He was not just looking at the tickets.

No, Faber told himself, don't jump to conclusions. How could they possibly have got on to him? They could not have found out which train he was on, got hold of one of the few people in the world who knew what he looked like, and got the man on the train dressed as a ticket inspector in so short a time. It was unbelievable.

Parkin, that was his name. Billy Parkin. Somehow he looked a lot older now. He was coming closer.

It must be a look-alike – perhaps an elder brother. This had to be a coincidence.

Parkin entered the compartment next to Faber's. There was no time left.

Faber assumed the worst and prepared to deal with it.

He got up, left the compartment, and went along the corridor, picking his way over suitcases and kitbags and bodies, to the lavatory. It was vacant. He went in and locked the door.

He was only buying time – ticket inspectors did not fail to check the toilets. He sat on the seat and wondered how to get out of this. The train had speeded up, and was travelling too fast for him to jump off.

Besides, someone would see him go, and if they were really searching for him they would stop the train.

'All tickets, please.'

Parkin was getting close again.

Faber had an idea. The coupling between the carriages was a tiny space like an air-lock, enclosed by a bellows-like cover between the cars of the train, shut off at both ends by doors because of the noise and draughts. He left the lavatory, fought his way to the end of the carriage, opened the door, and stepped into the connecting passage. He closed the door behind him.

It was freezing cold, and the noise was terrific. Faber sat on the floor and curled up, pretending to sleep. Only a dead man could sleep here, but people did strange things on trains these days. He tried not to shiver.

The door opened behind him. 'Tickets, please.'

He ignored it. He heard the door close.

'Wake up, Sleeping Beauty.' The voice was unmistakable.

Faber pretended to stir, then got to his feet, keeping his back to Parkin. When he turned the stiletto was in his hand. He pushed Parkin up against the door, held the point of the knife at his throat, and said: 'Be still or I'll kill you.'

With his left hand he took Parkin's torch, and shone it into the young man's face. Parkin did not look as frightened as he ought to be.

Faber said: 'Well, well. Billy Parkin, who wanted to

join the Army, and ended up on the railways. Still, it's a uniform.'

Parkin said: 'You.'

'You know damn well it's me, little Billy Parkin. You were looking for me. Why?' He was doing his best to sound vicious.

'I don't know why I should be looking for you – I'm not a policeman.'

Faber jerked the knife melodramatically. 'Stop lying to me.'

'Honest, Mr Faber. Let me go – I promise I won't tell anyone I've seen you.'

Faber began to have doubts. Either Parkin was telling the truth, or he was overacting as much as Faber himself.

Parkin's body shifted, his right arm moving in the darkness. Faber grabbed the wrist in an iron grip. Parkin struggled for an instant, but Faber let the needle point of the stiletto sink a fraction of an inch into Parkin's throat, and the man was still. Faber found the pocket Parkin had been reaching for, and pulled out a gun.

'Ticket inspectors do not go armed,' he said. 'Who are you with, Parkin?'

'We all carry guns now – there's a lot of crime on trains because of the dark.'

Parkin was lying courageously and persistently. Faber decided that threats were not enough to loosen his tongue.

His movement was sudden, swift and accurate. The blade of the stiletto leaped in his fist. Its point entered a measured half-inch into Parkin's left eye and came out again.

Faber's hand covered Parkin's mouth. The muffled scream of agony was drowned by the noise of the train. Parkin's hands went to his ruined eye.

Faber pressed his advantage. 'Save yourself the other eye, Parkin. Who are you with?'

'Military Intelligence, oh God, please don't do it again.'

'Who? Menzies? Masterman?'

'Oh, God, it's Godliman, Percy Godliman.'

'Godliman!' Faber knew the name, but this was no time to search his memory for details. 'What have they got?'

'A picture – I picked you out from the files.'

'What picture? *What picture?*'

'A racing team – running – with a cup – the Army—'

Faber remembered. Christ, where had they got hold of that? It was his nightmare: *they had a picture.* People would know his face. His *face.*

He moved the knife closer to Parkin's right eye. 'How did you know where I was?'

'Don't do it, please – agent in the Portuguese Embassy intercepted your letter – took the cab's number – inquiries at Euston – please, not the other eye—' He covered both his eyes with his hands.

'What's the plan? Where is the trap?'

'Glasgow. They're waiting for you at Glasgow. The train will be emptied there.'

Faber lowered the knife to the level of Parkin's belly.

To distract him, he said: 'How many men?' Then he pushed hard, inward and upward to the heart.

Parkin's one eye stared in horror, and he did not die. It was the drawback to Faber's favoured method of killing. Normally the shock of the knife was enough to stop the heart. But if the heart was strong it did not always work – after all, surgeons sometimes stuck a hypodermic needle directly into the heart to inject adrenalin. If the heart continued to pump, the motion would work a hole around the blade, from which the blood would leak. It was just as fatal, but longer.

At last Parkin's body went limp. Faber held him against the wall for a moment, thinking. There had been something – a flicker of courage, the ghost of a smile – before the man died. It meant something. Such things always did.

He let the body fall to the floor, then arranged it in a sleeping position, with the wounds hidden from view. He kicked the railway cap into a corner. He cleaned his stiletto on Parkin's trousers, and wiped the ocular liquid from his hands. It had been a messy business.

He put the knife away in his sleeve and opened the door to the carriage. He made his way back to his compartment in the dark.

As he sat down the Cockney said: 'You took your time – is there a queue?'

Faber said: 'It must have been something I ate.'

'Probably a dried-egg sandwich.' The Cockney laughed.

Faber was thinking about Godliman. He knew the name – he could even put a vague face to it: a middle-aged, bespectacled face, with a pipe and an absent, professorial air. That was it – he was a professor.

It was coming back. In his first couple of years in London Faber had had little to do. The war had not yet started, and most people believed it would not come. (Faber was not among the optimists.) He had been able to do a little useful work – mostly checking and revising the Abwehr's out-of-date maps, plus general reports based on his own observations and his reading of the newspapers – but not much. To fill in time, to improve his English, and to flesh out his cover, he had gone sightseeing.

His purpose in visiting Canterbury Cathedral had been innocent, although he did buy an aerial view of the town and the cathedral which he sent back for the Luftwaffe – not that it did much good: they spent most of 1942 missing it. Faber had taken a whole day to see the building: reading the ancient initials carved in walls, distinguishing the different architectural styles, reading the guidebook line by line as he walked slowly around.

He had been in the south ambulatory of the choir, looking at the blind arcading, when he became conscious of another absorbed figure by his side; an older man. 'Fascinating, isn't it?' the man said; and Faber asked him what he meant.

'The one pointed arch in an arcade of round ones. No reason for it – that section obviously hasn't been rebuilt. For some reason, somebody just altered that one. I wonder why.'

Faber saw what he meant. The choir was Romanesque, the nave Gothic; yet here in the choir was a solitary Gothic arch. 'Perhaps,' he said, 'the monks demanded to see what the pointed arches would look like, and the architect did this to show them.'

The older man stared at him. 'What a splendid conjecture! Of course that's the reason. Are you an historian?'

Faber laughed. 'No, just a clerk and an occasional reader of history books.'

'People get doctorates for inspired guesses like that!'

'Are you? An historian, I mean.'

'Yes, for my sins.' He stuck out his hand. 'Percy Godliman.'

Was it possible, Faber thought as the train rattled on through Lancashire, that that unimpressive figure in a tweed suit could be the man who had discovered his identity? Spies generally claimed they were civil servants, or something equally vague; not historians – that lie could be too easily found out. Yet it was rumoured that Military Intelligence had been bolstered by a number of academics. Faber had imagined them to be young, fit, aggressive and bellicose as well as clever. Godliman was clever, but none of the rest. Unless he had changed.

Faber had seen him once again, although he had not spoken to him on the second occasion. After the brief encounter in the cathedral Faber had seen a notice advertising a public lecture on Henry II to be given by Professor Godliman at his college. He had gone along, out of curiosity. The talk had been erudite, lively and convincing. Godliman was still a faintly comic figure, prancing about behind the lectern, getting enthusiastic about his subject; but it was clear his mind was as sharp as a knife.

So that was the man who had discovered what Die Nadel looked like.

Jesus Christ, an *amateur.*

Well, he would make amateur mistakes. Sending Billy Parkin had been one: Faber had recognized the boy. Godliman should have sent someone Faber did not know. Parkin had a better chance of recognizing Faber, but no chance at all of surviving the encounter. A professional would have known that.

The train shuddered to a halt, and a muffled voice outside announced that this was Liverpool. Faber cursed under his breath: he should have been spending the time working out his next move, not remembering Percival Godliman.

They were waiting at Glasgow, Parkin had said before he died. Why Glasgow? Their inquiries at Euston would have told them he was going to Inverness. And if they suspected Inverness to be a red herring, they would have speculated that he was coming here, to Liverpool, for this was the nearest link point for an Irish ferry.

Faber hated snap decisions.

He had to get off the train, whatever.

He stood up, opened the door, stepped out, and headed for the ticket barrier.

He thought of something else. What was it that had flashed in Billy Parkin's eyes before he died? Not hatred, not fear, not pain – although all those had been present. It was more like . . . triumph.

Faber looked up, past the ticket collector, and understood.

Waiting on the other side, dressed in a hat and raincoat, was the blond young tail from Leicester Square.

Parkin, dying in agony and humiliation and betrayal, had deceived Faber at the last. The trap was here.

The man in the raincoat had not yet noticed Faber in the crowd. Faber turned and stepped back on to the train. Once inside, he pulled aside the blind and looked out. The tail was searching the faces in the crowd. He had not noticed the man who got back on the train.

Faber watched while the passengers filtered through the gate until the platform was empty. The blond man spoke urgently to the ticket collector, who shook his head in negation. The man seemed to insist. After a moment he waved to someone out of sight. A police officer emerged from the shadows and spoke to the collector. The platform guard joined the group, followed by a man in a civilian suit who was presumably a more senior railway official.

The engine driver and his fireman left the locomotive and went over to the barrier. There was more waving of arms and shaking of heads.

Finally the railwaymen shrugged, turned away, or rolled their eyes upward, all telegraphing surrender. The blond and the police officer summoned other policemen, and they moved determinedly on to the platform.

They were going to search the train.

All the railway officials, including the engine crew,

had disappeared in the opposite direction, no doubt to seek tea and sandwiches while the lunatics tried to search a jampacked train. That gave Faber an idea.

He opened the door and jumped out of the wrong side of the train, the side opposite the platform. Concealed from the police by the carriages, he ran along the tracks, stumbling on the sleepers and slipping on the gravel, toward the engine.

It had to be bad news, of course. From the moment he realized Billy Parkin was not going to saunter off that train, Frederick Bloggs knew that Die Nadel had slipped through their fingers again. As the uniformed police moved on to the train in pairs, two men to search each carriage, Bloggs thought of several possible explanations of Parkin's non-appearance; and all the explanations were depressing.

He turned up his coat collar and paced the draughty platform. He wanted very badly to catch Die Nadel: not just for the sake of the invasion – although that was reason enough, God knew – but for Percy Godliman, and for the five Home Guard, and for Christine.

He looked at his watch: four o'clock. Soon it would be day. Bloggs had been up all night, and he had not eaten since breakfast yesterday, but until now he had kept going on adrenalin. The failure of the trap – he was quite sure it *had* failed – drained him of energy. Hunger and fatigue caught up with him. He had to make a conscious effort not to daydream about hot food and a warm bed.

'Sir!' A policeman was leaning out of a carriage and waving at him. 'Sir!'

Bloggs walked toward him, then broke into a run. 'What have you found?'

'It might be your man Parkin.'

Bloggs climbed into the carriage. 'What do you mean, might be?'

'You'd better have a look.' The policeman opened the communicating door between the carriages and shone his torch inside.

It was Parkin; Bloggs could tell by the ticket-inspector's uniform. He was curled up on the floor. Bloggs took the policeman's torch, knelt down beside Parkin, and turned him over.

He saw Parkin's face, looked quickly away, and said: 'Oh, dear God.'

'I take it this is Parkin?' the policeman said.

Bloggs nodded. He got up, very slowly, without looking again at the body. 'We'll interview everybody in this carriage and the next,' he said. 'Anyone who saw or heard anything unusual will be detained for further questioning. Not that it will do us any good: the murderer must have jumped off the train before it got here.'

Bloggs went back out on to the platform. All the searchers had completed their tasks and were gathered in a group. He detailed six of them to help with the interviewing.

The police inspector said: 'Your villain's hopped it, then.'

'Almost certainly,' Bloggs agreed. 'You've looked in every toilet, and the guard's van?'

'Yes, and on top of the train and under it, and in the engine and the coal tender.'

A passenger got off the train and approached Bloggs and the inspector. He was a small man with a bad chest, and he wheezed badly. He said: 'Excuse me.'

'Yes, sir,' the inspector said.

The passenger said: 'I was wondering, are you looking for somebody?'

'Why do you ask?'

'Well, if you are, I was wondering, would he be a tall chap?'

The inspector said: 'Why do you ask?'

Bloggs interrupted impatiently. 'Yes, a tall man. Come on, spit it out.'

'Well, it's just that a tall chap got out the wrong side of the train.'

'When?'

'A minute or two after the train pulled into the station. He got on, like, then he got off, on the wrong side. Jumped down on to the track. Only he had no luggage, you see, which was another odd thing, and I just thought—'

The inspector said: 'Balls.'

'He must have spotted the trap,' Bloggs said. 'But how? He doesn't know my face, and your men were out of sight.'

'Something made him suspicious.'

'So he crossed the line to the next platform and went out that way. Wouldn't he have been seen?'

The inspector shrugged. 'Not too many people about, this late. And if he was seen he could just say he was too impatient to queue at the ticket barrier.'

'Didn't you have the other ticket barriers covered?'

'I didn't think of it.'

'Nor did I.'

'Well, we can search the surrounding area, and later on we can check various places in the city, and of course we'll watch the ferry—'

'Yes, please do,' Bloggs said.

But somehow he knew Faber would not be found.

It was more than an hour before the train started to move. Faber had cramp in his left calf and dust in his nose. He heard the footplatemen climb back into their cab, and caught snatches of conversation about a body being found on the train. There was a metallic rattle as the fireman shovelled coal, then the hiss of steam, a clanking of pistons, a jerk and a sigh of smoke as the train moved off. Gratefully, Faber shifted his position and indulged in a smothered sneeze. Then he felt better.

He was at the back of the coal tender, buried deep in the coal, where it would take a man with a shovel ten minutes' hard work to expose him. As he had hoped, the police search of the tender had consisted of one good long look and no more.

He wondered whether he could risk emerging now. It must be getting light: would he be visible from a bridge over the line? He thought not. His skin was now quite black, and in a moving train in the pale light of dawn he would just be a dark blur on a dark background. Yes, he would chance it. Slowly and carefully, he dug his way out of his grave of coal.

He breathed the cool air deeply. The coal was shovelled out of the tender via a small hole in the front end. Later, perhaps, the fireman would have to enter the tender, when the pile of fuel got lower. Faber was safe for now.

As the light strengthened he looked himself over. He was covered from head to toe in coal dust, like a miner coming up from the pit. Somehow he had to wash and change his clothes.

He chanced a peep over the side of the tender. The train was still in the suburbs, passing factories and warehouses and rows of grimy little houses. He had to think about his next move.

His original plan had been to get off the train at Glasgow and there catch another train to Dundee and up the east coast to Aberdeen. It was still possible for him to disembark at Glasgow. He could not get off at the station, of course, but he might jump off either just before or just after. However, there were risks in that. The train was sure to stop at intermediate stations between Liverpool and Glasgow, and at those stops Faber might be spotted. No, he had to get off the train soon and find other means of transport.

The ideal spot would be a lonely stretch of track just outside a city or village. It had to be lonely, for he must not be seen leaping from the coal tender; but it had to be fairly near houses so that he could steal clothes and a car. And it needed to be an uphill stretch of track, so that the train would be travelling slowly enough for him to jump.

Right now its speed was about forty miles an hour. Faber lay back on the coal to wait. He could not keep a permanent watch on the country through which he was passing, for fear of being seen. He decided he would look out whenever the train slowed down. Otherwise he would lie still.

After a few minutes he caught himself dropping off to sleep, despite the discomfort of his bed. He shifted his position and reclined on his elbows, so that if he did sleep he would fall and be wakened by the impact.

The train was gathering speed. Between London and Liverpool it had seemed to be stationary more than moving; now it steamed through the country at a fine pace. To complete his discomfort, it started to rain; a cold, steady drizzle that soaked right through his clothes and seemed to turn to ice on his skin. There was another reason for getting off the train: he could die of exposure before they reached Glasgow!

After half an hour at high speed he was contemplating killing the footplate crew and stopping the train himself. A signal box saved their lives. The train slowed suddenly as brakes were applied. It decelerated in stages: Faber guessed the track was marked with descending speed limits. He looked out. They were in the countryside again. He could see the reason for the slowdown – they were approaching a track junction, and the signals were against them.

Faber stayed in the tender while the train stood still. After five minutes it started up again. Faber scrambled up the side of the tender, perched on the edge for a moment, and jumped.

He landed on the embankment and lay, face down, in the overgrown weeds. When the train was out of earshot he got to his feet. The only sign of civilization nearby was the signal box, a two-storey wooden structure with large windows in the control room at the top, an outside staircase, and a door at ground-floor level. On the far side was a cinder track leading away.

Faber walked in a wide circle to approach the place from the back, where there were no windows. He entered a ground-floor door and found what he had been expecting: a toilet, a washbasin and a coat hanging on a peg.

He took off his soaking wet clothes, washed his hands and face, and rubbed himself vigorously all over with a grubby towel. The little cylindrical film can containing the negatives was still taped securely to his chest. He put his clothes back on, but substituted the signalman's overcoat for his own sopping wet jacket.

Now all he needed was transport. The signalman must have got here somehow. Faber went outside and found a bicycle padlocked to a rail on the other side of the little building. He snapped the little lock with the blade of his stiletto. Moving in a straight line away from the blank rear wall of the signal box, he wheeled the cycle until he was out of sight of the building. Then he cut across until he reached the cinder track, climbed on the cycle, and rode away.

SIXTEEN

Percival Godliman had brought a little camp bed from his home. He lay on it in his office, dressed in trousers and shirt, trying in vain to sleep. He had not suffered insomnia for almost forty years, since he took his final exams at university. He would gladly swap the anxieties of those days for the worries which kept him awake now.

He had been a different man then, he knew; not just younger, but also a lot less . . . abstracted. He had been outgoing, aggressive, ambitious: he planned to go into politics. He was not studious then – he had reason to be anxious about the exams.

His two mismatched enthusiasms in those days had been debating and ballroom dancing. He had spoken with distinction at the Oxford Union and had been pictured in *The Tatler* waltzing with debutantes. He was no great womanizer: he wanted sex with a woman he loved, not because he believed in any high-minded principle to that effect, but because that was the way he felt about it.

And so he had been a virgin until he met Eleanor, who was not one of the debutantes, but a brilliant graduate mathematician with grace and warmth and a father dying of lung disease after forty years as a collier. The young Percival had taken her to meet his people. His father was Lord Lieutenant of the county, and the house had seemed a mansion to Eleanor, but she had been natural and charming and not in the least awe-struck; and when Percy's mother had been disgracefully condescending to her at one point she had reacted with merciless wit, for which he loved her all the more.

He had taken his master's degree, then after the Great War he taught in a public school and stood in three by-elections. They were both disappointed when they discovered they could not have children; but they loved each other totally, and they were happy, and her death was the most appalling tragedy Godliman ever knew. It had ended his interest in the real world, and he had retreated into the Middle Ages.

It had drawn him and Bloggs together, this common bereavement. The war had brought Godliman back to life; revived in him those characteristics of dash and aggression and fervour which had made him a great speaker and teacher and the hope of the Liberal Party. He wished for something in Bloggs's life to rescue him from an existence of bitterness and introversion.

While he was in Godliman's thoughts, Bloggs phoned from Liverpool to say that Die Nadel had slipped through the net, and Parkin had been killed.

Godliman, sitting on the edge of the camp bed to speak on the phone, closed his eyes in despair. 'I should have put you on the train,' he murmured.

'Thanks!' Bloggs said.

'Only because he doesn't know your face.'

'I think he may,' Bloggs argued. 'We suspect he spotted the trap, and mine was the only face visible to him as he got off the train.'

'But where could he have seen you? Oh! No, surely . . . not Leicester Square?'

'I don't see how, but then . . . we always seem to underestimate him.'

'I wish he were on our side,' Godliman muttered. 'Have you got the ferry covered?'

'Yes.'

'He won't use it, of course – too obvious. He's more likely to steal a boat. On the other hand, he may still be heading for Inverness.'

'I've alerted the police up there.'

'Good. But look, I don't think we can make any assumptions about his destination. Let's keep an open mind.'

'Agreed.'

Godliman stood, picked up the phone, and began to pace the carpet. 'Also, don't assume it was he who got off the train on the wrong side. Work on the premise that he got off before, at, or after Liverpool.' Godliman's brain was in gear again, sorting permutations and possibilities. 'Let me talk to the Chief Superintendent.'

'He's here.'

There was a pause, then a new voice said: 'Chief Superintendent Anthony speaking.'

Godliman said: 'Do you agree with me that our man has got off this train somewhere in your area?'

'That seems likely, yes.'

'Good. Now the first thing he needs is transport – so I want you to get details of every car, boat, bicycle or donkey stolen within a hundred miles of Liverpool during the next twenty-four hours. Keep me informed, but give the information to Bloggs and work closely with him in following-up the leads.'

'Yes, sir.'

'Keep an eye on other crimes that might be committed by a fugitive – theft of food or clothing, unexplained assaults, identity card irregularities, and so on.'

'Right.'

'Now, Mr Anthony, you realize this man is more than just a mass murderer?'

'I assume so, sir, from the fact of your involvement. However, I don't know the details.'

'Nor shall you. Suffice it to say that this is a matter of national security so grave that the Prime Minister is in hourly contact with this office.'

'I understand. Uh, Mr Bloggs would like a word, sir.'

Bloggs came back on. 'Have you remembered how you know his face?'

'Oh, yes – but it's of no value, as I forecast. I met him by chance at Canterbury Cathedral, and we had a conversation about the architecture. All it tells us is that he's clever – he made some rather perceptive remarks, as I recall.'

'We knew he was clever.'

'Only too well.'

*

Chief Superintendent Anthony was a burly member of the middle class with a carefully softened Liverpool accent. He did not know whether to be peeved at the way MI5 ordered him about or thrilled at the chance to save England on his own manor.

Bloggs knew of the man's inner struggle – he met this sort of thing all the time when working with local police forces – and he knew how to tip the balance in his own favour. He said: 'I'm grateful for your helpfulness, Chief Superintendent. These things don't go unnoticed in Whitehall.'

'Only doing our duty,' Anthony said. He was not sure whether he was supposed to call Bloggs 'Sir'.

'Still, there's a big difference between reluctant assistance and willing help.'

'Yes. Well, it'll likely be a few hours before we pick up this man's scent again. Do you want to catch forty winks?'

'Yes,' Bloggs said gratefully. 'If you've got a chair in a corner somewhere . . .'

'Stay here,' Anthony said, indicating his office. 'I'll be down in the operations room. I'll wake you as soon as we've got something. Make yourself comfortable.'

Anthony went out, and Bloggs moved to an easy chair and sat back with his eyes closed. Immediately, he saw Godliman's face, as if projected on to the backs of his eyelids like a film, saying: 'There has to be an end to bereavement . . . I don't want you to make the same mistake.' Bloggs realized suddenly that he did not want the war to end, for that would make him face issues like the one Godliman had raised. The war made life simple, for he knew why he hated the enemy and he knew what he was supposed to do about it. Afterwards . . . the thought of another woman seemed disloyal, not just to Christine but, in some obscure way, to England.

He yawned and slumped farther into his seat, his thinking becoming woolly as sleep crept up on him. If Christine had died before the war, he would have felt very differently about remarrying. He had always been fond of her and respected her, of course; but after she took that ambulance job respect had turned to awe-struck admiration, and fondness turned to love. Then they had something special, something they knew other lovers did not share. Now, more than a year later, it would be easy for Bloggs to find another woman he could respect and be fond of, but he knew that would never be enough for him. An ordinary marriage, an ordinary woman, would always remind him that once he had possessed the ideal.

He stirred in his chair, trying to shake off imponderables so that he could sleep. England was full of heroes, Godliman had said. If Die Nadel got away England would be full of slaves. First things first . . .

Someone shook him. He was in a very deep sleep, dreaming that he was in a room with Die Nadel but could not pick him out because Die Nadel had blinded him with the stiletto. When he awoke he still thought he was blind because he could not see who was shaking him, until he realized he simply had his eyes closed. He opened them to see the large uniformed figure of Superintendent Anthony above him.

Bloggs raised himself to a more upright position and rubbed his eyes. 'Got something?' he asked.

'Lots of things,' Anthony said. 'Question is, which of 'em counts? Here's your breakfast.' He put a cup of tea and a biscuit on the desk and went to sit on the other side of it.

Bloggs left his easy chair and pulled a hard chair up to the desk. He sipped the tea. It was weak and very sweet. 'Let's get to it,' he said.

Anthony handed him a sheaf of five or six slips of paper.

Bloggs said: 'Don't tell me these are the only crimes in your area—'

'Of course not,' Anthony said. 'We're not interested in drunkenness, domestic disputes, blackout violations, traffic offences, or crimes for which arrests have already been made.'

'Sorry,' Bloggs said. 'I'm still waking up. Give me a chance to read these.'

There were three house burglaries. In two of them, valuables had been taken – jewellery in one case, furs in another. Bloggs said: 'He might steal valuables just to throw us off the scent. Mark these on the map, will you? They may show some pattern.' He handed the two slips back to Anthony. The third burglary had only just been reported, and no details were available. Anthony marked the location on the map.

A Food Office in Manchester had been robbed of

hundreds of ration books. Bloggs said: 'He doesn't need ration books – he needs food.' He set that one aside. There was a bicycle theft just outside Preston and a rape in Birkenhead. 'I don't think he's a rapist, but mark it anyway,' Bloggs told Anthony.

The bicycle theft and the third of the house burglaries were close together. Bloggs said: 'The signal box that the bike was stolen from – is that on the main line?'

'Yes, I think so,' Anthony said.

'Suppose Faber was hiding on that train and somehow we missed him. Would the signal box be the first place at which the train stopped after it left Liverpool?'

'It might be.'

Bloggs looked at the sheet of paper. 'An overcoat was stolen and a wet jacket left in its place.'

Anthony shrugged. 'Could mean anything.'

'No cars stolen?' Bloggs said sceptically.

'Nor boats, nor donkeys,' Anthony replied. 'We don't get many car thefts these days. Cars are easy to come by – it's petrol people steal.'

'I felt sure he'd steal a car in Liverpool,' Bloggs said. He thumped his knee in frustration. 'A bicycle isn't much use to him, surely.'

'I think we should follow it up, anyway,' Anthony pressed. 'It's our best lead.'

'All right. But meanwhile, double-check the burglaries to see whether food or clothing was pinched – the losers might not have noticed at first. Show Faber's picture to the rape victim, too. And keep checking all crimes. Can you fix me transport to Preston?'

'I'll get you a car,' Anthony said.

'How long will it take to get details of this third burglary?'

'They're probably interviewing at this minute,' Anthony said. 'By the time you reach the signal box I should have the complete picture.'

'Don't let them drag their feet.' Bloggs reached for his coat. 'I'll check with you the minute I get there.'

'Anthony? This is Bloggs. I'm at the signal box.'

'Don't waste any time there. The third burglary was your man.'

'Sure?'

'Unless there are two buggers running around threatening people with stiletto knives.'

'Who?'

'Two old ladies living alone in a little cottage.'

'Oh, God. Dead?'

'Not unless they died of excitement.'

'Eh?'

'Get over there. You'll see what I mean.'

'I'm on my way.'

It was the kind of cottage which is always inhabited by two elderly ladies living alone. It was small and square and old, and around the door grew a wild rose bush fertilized by thousands of pots of used tea leaves. Rows of vegetables sprouted tidily in a little front garden with a trimmed hedge. There were pink-and-white curtains at the leaded windows, and the gate creaked. The front door had been painted painstakingly by an amateur, and its knocker was made from a horse brass.

Bloggs's knock was answered by an octogenarian with a shotgun.

He said: 'Good morning. I'm from the police.'

'No, you're not,' she said. 'They've been already. Now get going before I blow your head off.'

Bloggs regarded her. She was less than five feet tall, with thick white hair in a bun and a pale, wrinkled face. Her hands were matchstick-thin, but her grasp on the shotgun was firm. The pocket of her apron was full of clothes-pegs. Bloggs looked down at her feet, and saw that she was wearing a man's working boots. He said: 'The police you saw this morning were local. I'm from Scotland Yard.'

'How do I know that?' she said.

Bloggs turned and called to his police driver. The constable got out of the car and came to the gate. Bloggs said to the old lady: 'Is the uniform enough to convince you?'

'All right,' she said, and stood aside for him to enter.

He stepped down into a low-ceilinged room with a tiled floor. The room was crammed with heavy, old furniture, and every surface was decorated with ornaments of china and glass. A small coal fire burned in the grate. The place smelled of lavender and cats.

A second old lady got out of a chair. She was like the first, but about twice as wide. Two cats spilled from her lap as she rose. She said: 'Hello, I'm Emma Parton, my sister is Jessie. Don't take any notice of that shotgun

– it's not loaded, thank God. Jessie loves drama. Will you sit down? You look so young to be a policeman. I'm surprised Scotland Yard is interested in our little robbery. Have you come from London this morning? Make the boy a cup of tea, Jessie.'

Bloggs sat down. 'If we're right about the identity of the burglar, he's a fugitive from justice,' he said.

'I told you! 'Jessie said. 'We might have been done in – slaughtered, in cold blood!'

'Don't be silly,' Emma said. She turned to Bloggs. 'He was such a nice man.'

'Tell me what happened,' Bloggs said.

'Well, I'd gone out the back,' Emma began. 'I was in the hen coop, hoping for some eggs. Jessie was in the kitchen—'

'He surprised me,' Jessie interrupted. 'I didn't have time to go for me gun.'

'You see too many cowboy films,' Emma admonished her.

'They're better than your love films – all tears and kisses—'

Bloggs took the picture of Faber from his wallet. 'Is this the man?'

Jessie scrutinized it. 'That's him.'

'Aren't you clever?' Emma marvelled.

'If we were clever we'd have caught him by now,' Bloggs said. 'What did he do?'

Jessie said: 'He held a knife to my throat and said: "One false move and I'll slit your gizzard." And he meant it.'

'Oh, Jessie, you told me he said: "I won't harm you if you do as I say." '

'Words to that effect, Emma!'

Bloggs said: 'What did he want?'

'Food, a bath, dry clothes and a car. Well, we gave him the eggs, of course. We found some clothes that belonged to Jessie's late husband Norman—'

'Would you describe them?'

'Yes. A blue donkey jacket, blue overalls, a check shirt. And he took poor Norman's car. I don't know how we'll be able to go to the pictures without it. That's our only vice, you know – the pictures.'

'What sort of car?'

'A Morris. Norman bought it in 1924. It's served us well, that little car.'

Jessie said: 'He didn't get his hot bath, though!'

'Well,' Emma said, 'I had to explain to him that two ladies living alone can hardly have a man taking a bath in their kitchen . . .' She blushed.

Jessie said: 'You'd rather have your throat slit than see a man in his combinations, wouldn't you, you silly fool.'

Bloggs said: 'What did he say when you refused?'

'He laughed,' Emma said. 'But I think he understood our position.'

Bloggs could not help but smile. 'I think you're very brave,' he said.

'I don't know about that, I'm sure.'

'So he left here in a 1924 Morris, wearing overalls and a blue jacket. What time was that?'

'About half-past nine.'

Bloggs absently stroked a marmalade cat. It blinked and purred. 'Was there much petrol in the car?'

'A couple of gallons – but he took our coupons.'

A thought struck Bloggs. 'How do you ladies qualify for a petrol ration?'

'Agricultural purposes,' Emma said defensively. She blushed.

Jessie snorted. 'And we're isolated, and we're elderly. Of course we qualify.'

'We always go to the corn stores at the same time as the pictures,' Emma added. 'We don't waste petrol.'

Bloggs smiled and held up a hand. 'All right, don't worry – rationing isn't my department anyway. How fast does the car go?'

Emma said: 'We never exceed thirty miles per hour.'

Bloggs looked at his watch. 'Even at that speed he could be seventy-five miles away by now.' He stood up. 'I must phone the details to Liverpool. You don't have a telephone, do you?'

'No.'

'What kind of Morris is it?'

'A Cowley. Norman used to call it a Bullnose.'

'Colour?'

'Grey.'

'Registration number?'

'MLN 29.'

Bloggs wrote it all down.

Emma said: 'Will we ever get our car back, do you think?'

'I expect so – but it may not be in very good

condition. When someone is driving a stolen car he generally doesn't take good care of it.' He walked to the door.

'I hope you catch him,' Emma called.

Jessie saw him out. She was still clutching the shotgun. At the door she caught Bloggs's sleeve and said in a stage whisper: 'Tell me – what is he? Escaped convict? Murderer? Rapist?'

Bloggs looked down at her. Her small green eyes were bright with excitement. She would believe anything he chose to tell her. He bent his head to speak quietly in her ear. 'Don't tell a soul,' he murmured, 'but he's a German spy.'

SEVENTEEN

Faber crossed the Sark Bridge and entered Scotland shortly after midday. He passed the Sark Toll Bar House, a low building with a signboard announcing that it was the first house in Scotland and a tablet above the door bearing some legend about marriages which he could not read. A quarter of a mile farther on he understood, when he entered the village of Gretna: he knew this was a place runaways came to get married.

The roads were still damp from the early rain, but the sun was drying them rapidly. Signposts and name-boards had been re-erected since the relaxation of invasion precautions, and Faber sped through a series of small lowland villages: Kirkpatrick, Kirtlebridge, Ecclefechan. The open countryside was pleasant, the green moors sparkling in the sunshine.

He had stopped for petrol in Carlisle. The pump attendant, a middle-aged woman in an oily apron, had not asked any awkward questions. Faber had filled the tank and the spare can fixed to the offside running-board.

He was very pleased with the little two-seater. It would still do fifty miles an hour, despite its age. The four-cylinder, 1548cc side-valve engine worked smoothly and tirelessly as he climbed and descended the Scottish hills. The leather-upholstered bench seat was comfortable. He squeezed the bulb horn to warn a straying sheep of his approach.

He went through the little market town of Lockerbie, crossed the River Annan by the picturesque Johnstone Bridge, and began the ascent to Beattock Summit. He found himself using the three-speed gearbox more and more.

He had decided not to take the most direct route to Aberdeen, via Edinburgh and the coast road. Much of Scotland's east coast, either side of the Firth of Forth, was a restricted area. Visitors were prohibited from a ten-mile-wide strip of land. Of course, the authorities could not seriously police such a long border. Nevertheless, Faber was less likely to be stopped and questioned while he stayed outside the security zone.

He would have to enter it eventually – later rather than sooner – and he turned his mind to the story he would tell if he were interrogated. Private motoring for pleasure had virtually ceased in the last couple of years because of the ever-stricter petrol rationing, and people who had cars for essential journeys were liable to be prosecuted for going a few yards off their necessary route for personal reasons. Faber had read of a famous impresario gaoled for using petrol supplied for agricultural purposes to take several actors from a theatre to the Savoy Hotel. Endless propaganda told people that a Lancaster bomber needed 2,000 gallons to get to the Ruhr. Nothing would please Faber more than to waste petrol which might otherwise be used to bomb his homeland, in normal circumstances; but to be stopped now, with the information he had taped to his chest, and arrested for a rationing violation would be an unbearable irony.

It was difficult. Most traffic was military, but he had no military papers. He could not claim to be delivering essential supplies because he had nothing in the car to deliver. He frowned. Who travelled, these days? Sailors on leave, officials, rare holidaymakers, skilled workmen . . . That was it. He would be an engineer, a specialist in some esoteric field like high-temperature gearbox oils, going to solve a manufacturing problem in a factory at Inverness. If he were asked which factory, he would say it was classified. (His fictitious destination had to be a long way from the real one so that he would never be questioned by someone who knew for certain there were no such factory.) He doubted whether consulting engineers ever wore overalls like the ones he had stolen from the elderly sisters – but anything was possible in wartime.

Having figured all that out, he felt he was reasonably safe from any random spot checks. The danger of being stopped by someone who was looking specifically for Henry Faber, fugitive spy, was another problem. They had that picture—

They knew his face. His face!

—and before long they would have a description of the car in which he was travelling. He did not think they would set up roadblocks, as they had no way of guessing where he was headed; but he was sure that every policeman in the land would be on the lookout for the grey Morris Cowley Bullnose, registration number MLN 29.

If he were spotted in the open country, he would not be captured immediately, for country policemen had bicycles, not cars. But the policeman would telephone his headquarters, and cars would be after Faber within minutes. If he saw a policeman, he decided, he would have to ditch this car, steal another, and divert from his planned route. However, in the sparsely populated Scottish lowlands there was a good chance he could get all the way to Aberdeen without passing a country policeman. The towns would be different. There, the danger of being chased by a police car was very great. He would be unlikely to escape: his car was old and relatively slow, and the police were generally good drivers. His best chance would be to get out of the vehicle and hope to lose himself in crowds or back streets. He contemplated ditching the car and stealing another each time he was forced to enter a major town. The problem there was that he would be leaving a trail a mile wide for MI5 to follow. Perhaps the best solution was a compromise: he would drive into the towns but try to use only the back streets. He looked at his watch. He would reach Glasgow around dusk, and thereafter he would benefit from the darkness.

Well, it was not satisfactory, but the only way to be totally safe was not to be a spy.

As he topped the one-thousand-feet-high Beattock Summit, it began to rain. Faber stopped the car and got out to raise the canvas roof. The air was oppressively warm. Faber looked up. The sky had clouded over very quickly. Thunder and lightning were promised.

As he drove on he discovered some of the little car's shortcomings. Wind and rain leaked in through several flaws in the canvas roof, and the small wiper sweeping the top half of the horizontally divided windscreen provided only a tunnel-like view of the road ahead. As the terrain became progressively more hilly, the engine note began to sound faintly ragged. It was hardly surprising: the twenty-year-old car was being pushed hard.

The shower ended. The threatened storm had not arrived, but the sky remained dark and the atmosphere forbidding.

Faber passed through Crawford, nestling in green hills; Abington, a church and a Post Office on the west bank of the River Clyde; and Lesmahagow, on the edge of a heathery moor.

Half an hour later he reached the outskirts of Glasgow. As soon as he entered the built-up area, he turned north off the main road, hoping to circumvent the city. He followed a succession of minor roads, crossing the major arteries into the city's east side, until he reached Cumbernauld Road, where he turned east again and sped out of the city.

It had been quicker than he expected. His luck was holding.

He was on the A80 road, passing factories, mines and farms. More Scots place-names drifted in and out of his consciousness: Millerston, Stepps, Muirhead, Mollinsburn, Condorrat.

His luck ran out between Cumbernauld and Stirling.

He was accelerating along a straight stretch of road, slightly downhill, with open fields on either side. As the speedometer needle touched forty-five there was a sudden, very loud noise from the engine; a heavy rattle, like the sound of a large chain pulling over a cog. He slowed to thirty, but the noise did not get perceptively quieter. Clearly some large and important piece of the mechanism had failed. Faber listened carefully. It was either a cracked ball-bearing in the transmission, or a hole in a big end. Certainly it was nothing so simple as a blocked carburettor or a dirty sparking-plug; nothing that could be repaired outside a workshop.

He pulled up and looked under the bonnet. There seemed to be a lot of oil everywhere, but otherwise he could see no clues. He got back behind the wheel and drove off. There was a definite loss of power, but the car would still go.

Three miles farther on, steam began to billow out of the radiator. Faber realized that the car would soon stop altogether. He looked for a place to dump it.

He found a mud track leading off the main road, presumably to a farm. One hundred yards from the road, the track curved behind a blackberry bush. Faber parked the car close to the bush and killed the engine. The hiss of escaping steam gradually subsided. He got out and locked the door. He felt a twinge of regret for Emma and Jessie, who would find it very difficult to get their car repaired before the end of the war.

He walked back to the main road. From there, the car could not be seen. It might be a day or even two before the abandoned vehicle aroused suspicion. By then, Faber thought, I may be in Berlin.

He began to walk. Sooner or later he would hit a town where he could steal another vehicle. He was doing well enough: it was less than twenty-four hours since he had left London, and he still had a whole day before the U-boat arrived at the rendezvous at six p.m. tomorrow.

The sun had set long ago, and now darkness fell suddenly. Faber could hardly see. Fortunately there was a painted white line down the middle of the road – a safety innovation made necessary by the blackout – and he was just about able to follow it. Because of the night silence he would hear an oncoming car in plenty of time.

In fact only one car passed him. He heard its deep-throated engine in the distance, and went off the road a few yards to lie out of sight until it had gone. It was a large car, a Vauxhall Ten, Faber guessed, and it was travelling at speed. He let it go by, then got up and resumed walking. Twenty minutes later he saw it again, parked by the roadside. He would have taken a detour across the field if he had noticed the car in time, but its light were off and its engine silent, and he almost bumped into it in the darkness.

Before he could consider what to do, a torch shone up toward him from under the car's bonnet, and a voice said: 'I say, is anybody there?'

Faber moved into the beam and said: 'Having trouble?'

'I'll say.'

The torch was pointed down, and as Faber moved closer he could see, by the reflected light, the moustached face of a middle-aged man in a double-breasted coat. In his other hand the man held, rather uncertainly, a large spanner; seeming unsure of what to do with it.

Faber looked at the engine. 'What's wrong?'

'Loss of power,' the man said, pronouncing it 'Lorse of par'. 'One moment she was going like a top, the next she started to hobble. I'm afraid I'm not much of a mechanic.' He shone the torch at Faber again. 'Are you?' he finished hopefully.

'Not exactly,' Faber said, 'but I know a disconnected lead when I see one.' He took the torch from the man, reached down into the engine, and plugged the stray lead back on to the cylinder head. 'Try her now.'

The man got into the car and started the engine. 'Perfect!' he shouted over the noise. 'You're a genius! Hop in.'

It crossed Faber's mind that this might be an elaborate MI5 trap, but he dismissed the thought: in the unlikely event they knew where he was, why should they tread softly? They could as easily send twenty policemen and a couple of armoured cars to pick him up.

He got in.

The driver pulled away and moved rapidly up through the gears until the car was travelling at a good speed. Faber made himself comfortable. The driver said: 'By the way, I'm Richard Porter.'

Faber thought quickly of the identity card in his wallet. 'James Baker.'

'How do you do. I must have passed you on the road back there – didn't see you.'

Faber realized the man was apologizing for not picking him up – everyone picked up hitch-hikers since the petrol shortage. 'It's okay,' Faber said. 'I was probably off the road, behind a bush, answering a call of nature. I did hear a car.'

'Have you come far?' Porter offered a cigar.

'It's good of you, but I don't smoke,' Faber said. 'Yes, I've come from London.'

'Hitch-hiked all the way?'

'No, my car broke down in Edinburgh. Apparently it requires a spare part which isn't in stock, so I had to leave it at the garage.'

'Hard luck. Well, I'm going to Aberdeen, so I can drop you anywhere along the way.'

Faber thought fast. This was a piece of good fortune. He closed his eyes and pictured the map of Scotland. 'That's marvellous,' he said. 'I'm going to Banff, so Aberdeen would be a great help. But I was planning to take the high road, because I didn't get myself a pass – is Aberdeen a Restricted Area?'

'Only the harbour,' Porter said. 'Anyway, you neen't worry about that sort of thing while you're in my car – I'm a JP and a member of the Watch Committee. How's that?'

Faber smiled in the darkness. It was his lucky day. 'Thank you,' he said. He decided to change the subject of the conversation. 'Is that a full-time job? Being a magistrate, I mean.'

Porter put a match to his cigar and puffed smoke.

'Not really. I'm semi-retired, y'know. Used to be a solicitor, until they discovered my weak heart.'

'Ah.' Faber tried to put some sympathy into his voice.

'Hope you don't mind the smoke?' Porter waved the fat cigar.

'Not a bit.'

'What takes you to Banff?'

'I'm an engineer. There's a problem in a factory . . . actually, the job is sort of classified.'

Porter held up his hand. 'Don't say another word. I understand.'

There was silence for a while. The car flashed through several towns. Porter obviously knew the road very well, to drive so fast in the blackout. The big car gobbled up the miles. Its smooth progress was soporific. Faber smothered a yawn.

'Damn, you must be tired,' Porter said. 'Silly of me. Don't be too polite to have a nap.'

'Thank you,' said Faber. 'I will.' He closed his eyes.

The motion of the car was like the rocking of a train, and Faber had his arrival nightmare again, only this time it was slightly different. Instead of dining on the train and talking politics with a fellow passenger, he was obliged for some unknown reason to travel in the coal tender, sitting on his suitcase radio with his back against the hard iron side of the truck. When the train arrived at Waterloo, everyone – including the disembarking passengers – was carrying a little duplicated photograph of Faber in the running team; and they were all looking at each other and comparing the faces they saw with the face in the picture. At the ticket barrier the collector took his shoulder and said: 'You're the man in the photo, aren't you?' Faber found himself dumb. All he could do was stare at the photograph and remember the way he had run to win that cup. God, how he had run: he had peaked a shade too early, started his final burst a quarter of a mile sooner than he had planned, and for the last 500 metres he wanted to die – and now perhaps he would die, because of that photograph in the ticket collector's hand . . . The collector was saying: 'Wake up! Wake up!' and suddenly Faber was back in Richard Porter's Vauxhall Ten, and it was Porter who was telling him to wake up.

His right hand was half way to his left sleeve, where the stiletto was sheathed, in the split-second before he remembered that as far as Porter was concerned James Baker was an innocent hitch-hiker. Then his hand dropped and he relaxed.

'You wake up like a soldier,' Porter said with amusement. 'This is Aberdeen.'

Faber noted that 'soldier' had been pronounced 'sol-juh', and recalled that Porter was a magistrate and a member of the police authority. He looked at the man in the dull light of early day: Porter had a red face and a waxed moustache, and his camel-coloured overcoat looked expensive. He was wealthy and powerful in this town, Faber guessed. If he were to disappear he would be missed almost immediately. Faber decided not to kill him.

Faber said: 'Good morning.'

He looked out of the window at the granite city.

They were moving slowly along the main street with shops on either side. There were several early workers about, all moving purposefully in the same direction: fishermen, Faber reckoned. It seemed a cold, windy place.

Porter said: 'Would you like to have a shave and a bit of breakfast before you continue your journey? You're welcome to come to my place.'

'You're very kind—'

'Not at all. If it weren't for you I should still be on the A80 at Stirling, waiting for a garage to open.'

'—but I won't, thank you. I want to get on with the journey.'

Porter did not insist, and Faber suspected that he was relieved not to have his offer taken up. The man said: 'In that case, I'll drop you at George Street – that's the start of the A96, and it's a straight road to Banff.' A moment later he stopped the car at a corner. 'Here you are.'

Faber opened the door. 'Thanks for the lift.'

'A pleasure.' Porter offered a handshake. 'Good luck!'

Faber got out and closed the door, and the car pulled away. He had nothing to fear from Porter, he thought; the man would go home and sleep all day, and by the time he realized he had helped a fugitive, it would be too late to do anything about it.

He watched the Vauxhall out of sight, then crossed the road and entered the promisingly named Market Street. Shortly he found himself in the docks and, following his nose, arrived at the fish market. He felt safely anonymous in the bustling, noisy, smelly market, where everyone was dressed in working clothes as he was. Wet fish and cheerful profanities flew through the air. Faber found it hard to understand the clipped, guttural accents. At a stall he bought hot, strong tea in a chipped half-pint mug and a large bread roll with a doorstep of white cheese.

He sat on a barrel to eat and drink. This evening would be the time to steal a boat. It was galling, to have to wait all day; and it left him with the problem of concealing himself for the next twelve hours; but he was too close now to take risks, and stealing a boat in broad daylight was much more risky than at the twilit end of the day.

He finished his breakfast and stood up. It would be a couple of hours before the rest of the city came to life. He would use the time to pick out a good hiding-place.

He made a circuit of the docks and the tidal harbour. The security was perfunctory, and he spotted several places where he could slip past the checkpoints. He worked his way around to the sandy beach, and set off along the two-mile esplanade. At its far end, a couple of pleasure yachts were moored at the mouth of the River Don. They would have suited Faber's purpose very well, but they would have no fuel.

A thick ceiling of cloud hid the sunrise. The air became very warm and thundery again. A few determined holidaymakers emerged from the seafront hotels and sat stubbornly on the beach, waiting for sunshine. Faber doubted they would get it today.

The beach might be the place to hide. The police would check the railway station and the bus depot, but they would not mount a full-scale search of the city. They might check a few hotels and guest-houses. It was unlikely they would approach everyone on the beach. He decided to spend the day in a deck-chair.

He bought a newspaper from a stall and hired a chair. He removed his shirt and put it back on over his overalls. He left his jacket off.

He would see a policeman, if one came, well before he reached the spot where Faber sat. There would be plenty of time to leave the beach and vanish into the streets.

He began to read the paper. There was a new Allied offensive in Italy, the newspaper rejoiced. Faber was sceptical. Anzio had been a shambles. The paper was badly printed and there were no photographs. He read that the police were searching for one Henry Faber, who had murdered two people in London with a stiletto . . .

A woman in a bathing suit walked by, looking hard at Faber. His heart missed a beat. Then he realized she was being flirtatious. For an instant he was tempted to speak to her. It had been so long . . . He shook himself mentally. Patience, patience. Tomorrow he would be home.

She was a small fishing boat, fifty or sixty feet long and broad in the beam, with an inboard motor. The aerial told of a powerful radio. Most of the deck was taken up with hatches to the small hold below. The cabin was aft, and only large enough to hold two men, standing, plus the dashboard and controls. The hull was clinker-built and newly caulked, and the paintwork looked fresh.

Two other boats in the harbour would have done as well, but Faber had stood on the quay and watched the crew of this one tie her up and refuel before they left for their homes.

He gave them a few minutes to get well away, then walked around the edge of the harbour and jumped on to the boat. She was called *Marie II.*

He found the wheel chained up. He sat on the floor of the little cabin, out of sight, and spent ten minutes picking the lock. Darkness was coming early because of the cloud layer which still blanketed the sky.

When he had freed the wheel he raised the small anchor, then sprang back on to the quay and untied the ropes. He returned to the cabin, primed the diesel engine, and pulled the starter. The motor coughed and died. He tried again. This time it roared to life. He began to manoeuvre out of the mooring.

He got clear of the other craft at the quayside and found the main channel out of the harbour, marked by buoys. He guessed that only boats of much deeper draught really needed to stick to the channel, but he saw no harm in being overcautious.

Once outside the harbour, he felt a stiff breeze, and hoped it was not a sign that the weather was about to break. The sea was surprisingly rough, and the stout little boat lifted high on the waves. Faber opened the throttle wide, consulted the dashboard compass, and set a course. He found some charts in a locker below the wheel. They looked old and little-used: no doubt the boat's skipper knew the local waters too well to need charts. Faber checked the map reference he had memorized that night in Stockwell, set a more exact course, and engaged the wheel-clamp.

The cabin windows were obscured by water. Faber could not tell whether it was rain or spray. The wind was slicing off the tops of the waves now. He poked his head out of the cabin door for a moment, and got his face thoroughly wet.

He switched on the radio. It hummed for a moment, then crackled. He moved the frequency control, wandering the airwaves, and picked up a few garbled messages. The set was working perfectly. He tuned to the U-boat's frequency, then switched off – it was too soon to make contact.

The waves increased in size as he progressed into deeper waters. Now the boat reared up like a bucking horse with each wave, then teetered momentarily at the top before plunging sickeningly down into the next trough. Faber stared blindly out of the cabin windows. Night had fallen, and he could see nothing at all. He felt faintly seasick.

Each time he convinced himself that the waves could not possibly get bigger, a new monster taller than the rest lifted the vessel toward the sky. They started to come closer together, so that the boat was always lying with its stern pointed either up at the sky or down at the sea bed. In a particularly deep trough the little boat was suddenly illuminated, as clearly as if it were day, by a flash of lightning. Faber saw a grey-green mountain of water descend on the prow and wash over the deck and the cabin where he stood. He could not tell whether the terrible crack which sounded a second afterwards was the thunderclap or the noise of the timbers of the boat breaking up. Frantically he searched the little cabin for a life jacket. There was none.

The lightning came repeatedly then. Faber held the locked wheel and braced his back against the cabin wall to stay upright. There was no point in operating the controls now – the boat would go where the sea threw it.

He kept telling himself that the boat must be built to withstand such sudden summer gales. He could not convince himself. Experienced fishermen probably would have seen the signs of such a storm, and refrained from leaving shore, knowing their vessel could not survive such weather.

He had no idea where he was, now. He might be almost back in Aberdeen, or he might be at his rendezvous. He sat on the cabin floor and switched on the radio. The wild rocking and shuddering made it difficult to operate the set. When it warmed up he experimented with the dials, and could pick up nothing. He turned the volume to maximum: still no sound.

The aerial must have been broken off its fixing on the cabin roof.

He switched to Transmit and repeated the simple message 'Come in, please,' several times; then left the set on Receive. He had little hope of his signal getting through.

He killed the engine to conserve fuel. He was going to have to ride out the storm – if he could – then find a way to repair or replace the aerial. He might need his fuel.

The boat slid terrifyingly sideways down the next big wave, and Faber realized he needed the engine power to ensure the vessel met waves head-on. He pulled the starter, but nothing happened. He tried several times, then gave up, cursing his foolishness for switching off.

The boat rolled so far on to its side that Faber fell and cracked his head on the wheel. He lay dazed on the cabin floor, expecting the vessel to turn turtle at any minute. Another wave crashed on the cabin, and this time the glass in the windows shattered. Suddenly Faber was under water. Certain the boat was sinking, he struggled to his feet, and broke surface. All the windows were out, but the vessel was still floating. He kicked open the cabin door, and the water gushed out. He clutched the wheel to prevent himself being washed into the sea.

Incredibly, the storm continued to get worse. One of Faber's last coherent thoughts was that these waters probably did not see such a storm more than once in a century. Then all his concentration and will were focused on the problem of keeping hold of the wheel. He should have tied himself to it, but now he did not dare to let go long enough to find a piece of rope. He lost all sense of up and down as the boat pitched and rolled on waves like cliffs. Gale force winds and thousands of gallons of water strained to pull him from his place. His feet slipped continually on the wet floor and walls, and the muscles of his arms burned with pain. He sucked air when he found his head above water, but otherwise held his breath. Many times he came close to blacking out. He vaguely realized that the flat roof of the cabin had disappeared.

He got brief, nightmarish glimpses of the sea whenever the lightning flashed. He was always surprised to see where the wave was: ahead, below, rearing up beside him, or completely out of sight. He discovered with a shock that he could not feel his hands, and looked down to see that they were still locked to the wheel, frozen in a grip like rigor mortis. There was a continuous roar in his ears, the wind indistinguishable from the thunder and the sea.

The power of intelligent thought slipped slowly away from him. In something that was less than a hallucination but more than a daydream, he saw the girl who had stared at him on the beach. She walked endlessly toward him over the bucking deck of the fishing boat, her swimsuit clinging to her body, always getting closer but never reaching him. He knew that, when she came within touching distance, he would take his dead hands from the wheel and reach for her, but he kept saying 'Not yet, not yet,' as she walked and smiled and swayed her hips. He was tempted to leave the wheel and close the gap himself, but something at the back of his mind told him that if he moved he would never reach her, so he waited and watched and smiled back at her from time to time, and even when he closed his eyes he could see her still.

He was slipping in and out of consciousness now.

His mind would drift away, the sea and the boat disappearing first, then the girl fading, until he would jerk awake to find that, incredibly, he was still standing, still holding the wheel, still alive; then for a while he would will himself to stay conscious, but eventually exhaustion would take over again.

In one of his last clear moments he noticed that the waves were moving in one direction, carrying the boat with them. Lightning flashed again, and he saw to one side a huge dark mass, an impossibly high wave – no, it was not a wave, it was a cliff . . . The realization that he was close to land was swamped by the fear of being hurled against the cliff and smashed. Stupidly, he pulled the starter, then hastily returned his hand to the wheel; but it would no longer grip.

A new wave lifted the boat and threw it down like a discarded toy. As he fell through the air, still clutching the wheel with one hand, Faber saw a pointed rock like a stiletto sticking up out of the trough of the wave. It seemed certain to impale the boat. But the hull of the little craft scraped the edge of the rock and was carried past.

The mountainous waves were breaking now. The next one was too much for the vessel's timbers. The boat hit the trough with a solid impact, and the sound of the hull splitting cracked the night like an explosion. Faber knew the boat was finished.

The water retreated, and Faber realized that the hull had broken because it had hit land. He stared in dumb astonishment as a new flash of lightning revealed a beach. The sea lifted the ruined boat off the sand as water crashed over the deck again, knocking Faber to the floor. But he had seen everything with daylight clarity in that moment. The beach was narrow, and the waves were breaking right up to the cliff. But there was a jetty, over to his right, and a bridge of some kind leading from the jetty to the cliff top. He knew that if he left the boat for the beach, the next wave would kill him with tons of water or break his head like an egg against the cliff. But if he could reach the jetty in between waves, he might scramble far enough up the bridge to be out of reach of the water.

He might survive yet.

The next wave split the deck open as if the seasoned wood were no stronger than a banana skin. The boat collapsed under Faber, and he found himself sucked backward by the receding surf. He scrambled upright, his legs like jelly beneath him, and broke into a run, splashing through the shallows toward the jetty. Running those few yards was the hardest thing he had ever done. He *wanted* to stumble, so that he could rest in the water and die; but he stayed upright, just as he had when he won the 5,000 metres race, until he crashed into one of the pillars of the jetty. He reached up and grabbed the boards with his hands, willing them to come back to life for a few seconds; and lifted himself until his chin was over the edge; then he swung his legs up and rolled over.

The wave came as he got to his knees. He threw himself forward. The wave carried him a few yards then flung him brutally against the wooden planking. He swallowed water and saw stars. When the weight lifted from his back he summoned the will to move. It would not come. He felt himself being dragged inexorably back. A sudden rage possessed him. He would not be beaten, not now! He screamed his hatred of the storm and the sea and the British and Percival Godliman, and suddenly he was on his feet and running, running, away from the sea and up the ramp, running with his eyes shut and his mouth open and madness in his heart, daring his lungs to burst and his bones to break; remembering, dimly, that he had called on this madness once before and almost died; running with no sense of destination, but knowing he would not stop until he lost his mind.

The ramp was long and steep. A strong man might have run all the way to the top, if he were in training and rested. An Olympic athlete, if he were tired, might have got half way. The average forty-year-old man would have managed a yard or two.

Faber made it to the top.

A yard from the end of the ramp he had a slight heart attack and lost consciousness, but his legs pumped twice more before he hit the sodden turf.

He never knew how long he lay there. When he opened his eyes the storm still raged, but day had broken, and he could see, a few yards away from him, a small cottage which looked inhabited.

He got to his knees and began the long crawl to the front door.

EIGHTEEN

The *U-505* wheeled in a tedious circle, her powerful diesels chugging slowly as she nosed through the depths like a grey, toothless shark. Lieutenant-Commander Werner Heer, her master, was drinking ersatz coffee and trying not to smoke any more cigarettes. It had been a long day and a long night. He disliked his assignment, for he was a fighting man and there was no fighting to be done; and he disliked the quiet Abwehr officer with sly blue eyes who was an unwelcome guest aboard the submarine.

The Intelligence man, Major Wohl, sat opposite the captain. The man never looked tired, damn him. Those blue eyes looked around, taking things in, but the expression in them never changed. His uniform never got rumpled, despite the rigours of underwater life; and he lit a new cigarette every twenty minutes, on the dot, and smoked it to a quarter-inch stub. Heer would have stopped smoking, just so that he could enforce regulations and prevent Wohl from enjoying tobacco, but Heer himself was too much of an addict.

Heer never liked Intelligence people, because he always had the feeling they were gathering intelligence on him. Nor did he like working with Abwehr. His vessel was made for battle, not for skulking around the British coast waiting to pick up secret agents. It seemed to him plain madness to put at risk a costly piece of fighting machinery, not to mention its skilled crew, for the sake of one man who might even fail to appear.

He emptied his cup and made a face. 'Damn coffee,' he said. 'It tastes vile.'

Wohl's expressionless gaze rested on him for a moment then moved away. He said nothing.

Heer shifted restlessly in his seat. On the bridge of a ship he would have paced up and down, but men on submarines learn to avoid unnecessary movement. He said: 'Your man won't come in this weather, you know.'

Wohl looked at his watch. 'We will wait until six a.m.,' he said calmly.

It was not an order, for Wohl could not give orders to Heer; but the bald statement of fact was still an insult to a superior officer. Heer said: 'Damn you, I'm the master of this vessel!'

'We will both follow our orders,' Wohl said. 'As you know, they originate from a very high authority indeed.'

Heer controlled his anger. The young whipper-snapper was right, of course. Heer would follow his orders. When they returned to port he would report Wohl for insubordination. Not that it would do much good: fifteen years in the Navy had taught Heer that headquarters people were a law unto themselves.

He said: 'If your man is fool enough to venture out tonight, he is certainly not seaman enough to survive.'

Wohl's only reply was the same blank gaze.

Heer called to the radio operator. 'Weissman?'

'Nothing, sir.'

Wohl said: 'I have an unpleasant feeling that the murmurs we heard a few hours ago were from him.'

'If they were, he was a long way from the rendezvous, sir,' the radio operator volunteered. 'To me it sounded more like lightning.'

Heer added: 'If it was not him, it was not him. If it was him, he is now drowned.' His tone was smug.

'You don't know the man,' Wohl said, and this time there was a trace of emotion in his voice.

Heer subsided into silence. The engine note altered slightly, and he thought he could distinguish a faint rattle. If it increased on the journey home he would have it looked at in port. He might do that anyway, just to avoid another voyage with the unspeakable Major Wohl.

A seaman looked in. 'Coffee, sir?'

Heer shook his head. 'If I drink any more I'll be pissing coffee.'

Wohl said: 'I will, please.' He took out a cigarette.

That made Heer look at his watch. It was ten past six. The subtle Major Wohl had delayed his six o'clock cigarette to keep the U-boat there a few extra minutes. Heer said: 'Set a course for home.'

'One moment,' Wohl said. 'I think we should take a look on the surface before we leave.'

'Don't be a fool,' Heer said. He knew he was on safe ground now. 'Do you realize what kind of storm is raging up there? We would not be able to open the hatch, and the periscope will show us nothing that is more than a few yards away.'

'How can you tell what the storm is like from this depth?'

'Experience,' Heer told him.

'Then at least send a signal to base, telling them that our man has not made contact. They may order us to stay here.'

Heer gave an exasperated sigh. 'It's not possible to make radio contact from this depth, not with base,' he said.

Wohl's calm was shattered at last. 'Commander Heer, I strongly recommend you surface and radio home before leaving this rendezvous. The man we are to pick up has information vital to the future of the Reich. The Führer himself is waiting for his report!'

Heer looked at him. 'Thank you for letting me have your opinion, Major,' he said. He turned away. 'Full ahead both!' he barked.

The sound of the twin diesels rose to a roar, and the U-boat began to pick up speed.

PART FOUR

NINETEEN

When Lucy woke up, the storm that had broken the evening before was still raging. She leaned over the edge of the bed, moving cautiously so that she would not disturb David, and picked up her wristwatch from the door. It was just after six. The wind was howling around the roof. David could sleep on: little work would be done today.

She wondered whether they had lost any slates off the roof during the night. She would need to check the loft. The job would have to wait until David was out, otherwise he would be angry that she had not asked him to do it.

She slipped out of bed. It was very cold. The warm weather of the last few days had been a phoney summer, the build-up to the storm. Now it was as cold as November. She pulled the flannel nightdress off over her head and quickly got into her underwear, trousers and sweater. David stirred. She looked at him: he turned over, but did not wake.

She crossed the tiny landing and looked into Jo's room. The three-year-old had graduated from a cot to a bed, and he often fell out during the night without waking. This morning he was on his bed, lying asleep on his back with his mouth wide open. Lucy smiled. He looked adorable when he was asleep.

She went quietly downstairs, wondering briefly why she had woken up so early. Perhaps Jo had made a noise, or maybe it was the storm.

She knelt in front of the fireplace, pushing back the sleeves of her sweater, and began to make the fire. As she swept out the grate she whistled a tune she had heard on the radio, *Is You Is Or Is You Ain't My Baby*? She raked the cold ashes, using the biggest lumps to form the base for today's fire. Dried bracken provided the tinder and wood and then coal went on top. Sometimes she just used wood, but coal was better in this weather. She held a page of newspaper across the fireplace for a few minutes to create an updraught in the chimney. When she removed it the wood was burning and the coal glowing red. She folded the paper and placed it under the coal scuttle for use tomorrow.

The blaze would soon warm the little house, but a hot cup of tea would help meanwhile. Lucy went into the kitchen and put the kettle on the electric cooker. She put two cups on a tray, then found David's cigarettes and an ashtray. She made the tea, filled the cups, and carried the tray through the hall to the stairs.

She had one foot on the lowest stair when she heard the tapping. She stopped, frowned, decided it was the wind rattling something, and took another step. The sound came again. It was like someone knocking on the front door.

That was ridiculous, of course. There was no one to

knock on the front door – only Tom, and he always came to the kitchen door and never knocked.

The tapping came again.

Just to assuage her curiosity, she came down the stairs and, balancing the tea tray on one hand, opened the front door.

She dropped the tray in shock. The man fell into the hall, knocking her over. Lucy screamed.

She was frightened only for a moment. The stranger lay prone beside her on the hall floor, plainly incapable of attacking anyone. His clothes were soaking wet, and his hands and face were stone-white with cold.

Lucy got to her feet. David slid down the stairs on his bottom, saying: 'What is it? What is it?'

'Him,' Lucy said, and pointed.

David arrived at the foot of the stairs, clad in pyjamas, and hauled himself into his wheelchair. 'I don't see what there is to scream about,' he said. He wheeled himself closer and peered at the man on the floor.

'I'm sorry. He startled me.' She bent over and, taking the man by his upper arms, dragged him into the living-room. David followed. Lucy laid the man in front of the fire.

David stared pensively at the unconscious body. 'Where the devil did he come from?' he wondered.

'He must be a shipwrecked sailor.'

'Of course.'

But he was wearing the clothes of a workman, not a sailor, Lucy noticed. She studied him. He was quite a big man, longer than the six-foot hearth-rug, and heavy around the neck and shoulders. His face was strong and fine-boned, with a high forehead and a long jaw. He might be handsome, she thought, if he were not such a ghastly colour.

The stranger stirred and opened his eyes. At first he looked terribly frightened, like a little boy waking in strange surroundings; but, very quickly, his expression became relaxed, and he looked about him sharply, his gaze resting briefly on Lucy, David, the window, the door, and the fire.

Lucy said: 'We must get him out of these clothes. Fetch a pair of pyjamas and a robe, David.'

David wheeled himself out, and Lucy knelt beside the stranger. She took off his boots and socks first. There almost seemed to be a hint of amusement in his eyes as he watched her. But when she reached for his jacket he crossed his arms protectively over his chest.

'You'll die of pneumonia if you keep these clothes on,' she said in her best bedside manner. 'Let me take them off.'

The stranger said: 'I really don't think we know each other well enough – after all, we haven't been introduced.'

It was the first time he had spoken. His voice was so confident, his words so formal, that the contrast with his terrible appearance made Lucy laugh out loud. 'You're shy?' she said.

'I just think a man should preserve an air of mystery.' He was grinning broadly, but his smile collapsed suddenly and his eyes closed in pain.

David came back in with clean nightclothes over his arm. 'You two seem to be getting on remarkably well already,' he said.

'You'll have to undress him,' Lucy said. 'He won't let me.'

David's look was unreadable.

The stranger said: 'I'll manage on my own, thanks – if it's not too awfully ungracious of me.'

'Suit yourself,' David said. He dumped the clothes on a chair and wheeled out.

'I'll make some more tea,' Lucy said as she followed. She closed the living-room door behind her.

In the kitchen, David was already filling the kettle, a lighted cigarette dangling from his lips. Lucy quickly cleared up the broken china in the hall then joined him.

David said: 'Five minutes ago I wasn't at all sure the chap was alive – and now he's dressing himself.'

Lucy busied herself with a teapot. 'Perhaps he was shamming.'

'The prospect of being undressed by you certainly brought about a rapid recovery.'

'I can't believe anyone could be that shy.'

'Your own deficiency in that area may lead you to underestimate its power in others.'

Lucy rattled cups. 'You don't usually get all bitter and twisted until after breakfast. Besides, how can an area be powerful?'

'Semantics is always your last line of defence.' David doused the butt of his cigarette in a pool of water in the sink.

Lucy poured boiling water into the teapot. 'Let's not quarrel today – we've got something more interesting to do, for a change.' She picked up the tray and walked into the living-room.

The stranger was buttoning his pyjama jacket. He turned his back to her as she walked in. She put the tray down and poured tea. When she turned back he was wearing David's robe.

'You're very kind,' he said. His gaze was direct.

He really didn't seem the shy type, Lucy thought. However, he was some years older than she – about forty, she guessed. That might account for it. He was looking less of a castaway every minute.

'Sit close to the fire,' she told him. She handed him a cup of tea.

'I'm not sure I can manage the saucer,' he said. 'My fingers aren't functioning.' He took the cup from her stiff-handed, holding it between both palms, and carried it carefully to his lips.

David came in and offered him a cigarette. He declined.

The stranger emptied the cup. 'Where am I?' he asked.

David said: 'This place is called Storm Island.'

The man showed a trace of relief. 'I thought I might have been blown back to the mainland.'

David spread his hands to the fire to warm his fingers. 'You were probably swept into the bay,' he said. 'Things usually are. That's how the beach was formed.'

Jo came in, bleary-eyed, trailing a one-armed panda

as big as himself. When he saw the stranger he ran to Lucy and hid his face.

'I've frightened your little girl,' the man smiled.

'He's a boy. I must cut his hair.' Lucy lifted Jo on to her lap.

'I'm sorry.' The stranger's eyes closed again, and he swayed in his seat.

Lucy stood up, dumping Jo on the sofa. 'We must put the poor man to bed, David.'

'Just a minute,' David said. He wheeled himself closer to the man. 'Might there be any other survivors?' he asked.

The man's face looked up. 'I was alone,' he muttered. He was very nearly all in.

'David—' Lucy began.

'One more question: Did you notify the coastguard of your route?'

'What does it matter?' Lucy said.

'It matters because, if he did, there may be men out there risking their lives looking for him, and we can let them know he's safe.'

The man said slowly: 'I . . . did . . . not.'

'That's enough,' Lucy told David. She knelt in front of the man. 'Can you make it upstairs?'

He nodded and got slowly to his feet.

Lucy looped his arm over her shoulders and began to walk him out. 'I'll put him in Jo's bed,' she said.

They took the stairs one at a time, pausing on each. When they reached the top, the little colour that the fire had restored to the man's face had drained away again. Lucy led him into the smaller bedroom. He collapsed on to the bed.

Lucy arranged the blankets over him, tucked him in, and left the room, closing the door quietly.

Relief washed over Faber in a tidal wave. For the last few minutes, the effort of self-control had been superhuman. He felt limp, defeated and ill.

After the front door had opened, he had allowed himself to collapse for a while. The danger had come when the beautiful girl had started to undress him, and he had remembered the can of film taped to his chest. Dealing with that had restored his alertness for a while. He had also been afraid they might call for an ambulance, but that had not been mentioned: perhaps the island was too small to have a hospital. At least he was not on the mainland – there, it would have been impossible to prevent the reporting of the shipwreck. However, the trend of the husband's questions had indicated that no report would be made immediately.

Faber had no energy to speculate about perils farther in the future. He seemed to be safe for the time being, and that was as far as he could go. In the meantime he was warm and dry and alive, and the bed was soft.

He turned over, reconnoitring the room: door, window, chimney. The habit of caution survived everything but death itself. The walls were pink, as if the couple had hoped for a baby girl. There was a train set and a great many picture books on the floor. It was a safe, domestic place; a home. He was a wolf in a sheep fold, but a lame wolf.

He closed his eyes. Despite his exhaustion, he had to

force himself to relax, muscle by muscle. Gradually his head emptied of thought, and he slept.

Lucy tasted the porridge, and added another pinch of salt. They had got to like it the way Tom made it, the Scots way, without sugar. She would never go back to making sweet porridge, even when sugar became plentiful and unrationed again. It was funny how you got used to things when you had to: brown bread and margarine and salt porridge.

She ladled it out and the family sat down to breakfast. Jo had lots of milk to cool his. David ate vast quantities these days, without getting fat: it was the outdoor life. She looked at his hands, on the table. They were rough, and permanently brown, the hands of a manual worker. She had noticed the stranger's hands. His fingers were long, the skin white under the blood and the bruising. He was unused to the abrasive work of crewing a boat.

Lucy said: 'You won't get much done today. The storm looks like staying.'

'Makes no difference,' David grunted. 'Sheep still have to be cared for, whatever the weather.'

'Where will you be?'

'Tom's end. I'll go up there in the jeep.'

Jo said: 'Can I come?'

'Not today,' Lucy told him. 'It's too wet and cold.'

'But I don't like the man.'

Lucy smiled. 'Don't be silly. He won't do us any harm. He's almost too ill to move.'

'Who is he?'

'We don't know his name. He's been shipwrecked, and we have to look after him until he's well enough to go back to the mainland. He's a very nice man.'

'Is he my uncle?'

'Just a stranger, Jo. Eat up.'

Jo looked disappointed. He had met an uncle once. In his mind uncles were people who gave out candy, which he liked, and money, which he had no use for.

David finished his breakfast and put on his mackintosh. It was a tent-shaped garment, with sleeves and a hole for his head, and it covered most of his wheelchair as well as him. He put a sou'wester on his head and tied it under his chin. He kissed Jo and said goodbye to Lucy.

A minute or two later she heard the jeep start up. She went to the window to watch David drive off into the rain. The rear wheels of the vehicle slithered about in the mud. He would have to take care.

She turned to Jo. He said: 'This is a dog.' He was making a picture on the tablecloth with porridge and milk.

Lucy slapped his hand, saying: 'What a horrid mess!' The boy's face took on a grim, sulky look, and Lucy thought how much he resembled his father. They had the same dark skin and nearly black hair, and they both had a way of withdrawing when they were cross. But Jo laughed a lot – he had inherited something from Lucy's side of the family, thank God.

Jo mistook her contemplative stare for anger, and said: 'I'm sorry.'

She washed him at the kitchen sink, then cleared away the breakfast things, thinking about the stranger upstairs. Now that the immediate crisis was past, and she knew the man was not going to die, she was consumed with curiosity about him. Who was he? Where was he from? What had he been doing in the storm? Did he have a family? Why did he have workman's clothes, a clerk's hands, and a Home Counties accent? It was rather exciting.

It occurred to her that, if she had lived anywhere else, she would not have accepted his sudden appearance so readily. He might, she supposed, be a deserter, or a criminal, or even an escaped prisoner-of-war. But one forgot, living on the island, that other human beings could be threatening instead of companionable. It was so nice to see a new face that to harbour suspicions seemed ungrateful. Maybe – unpleasant thought – she more than most people was ready to welcome an attractive man . . . She pushed the thought out of her mind.

Silly, silly. He was so tired and ill that he could not possibly threaten anyone. Even on the mainland, who could have refused to take him in, bedraggled and unconscious? When he felt better they could question him, and if his account of how he got here was less than plausible, they could radio the mainland from Tom's cottage.

When she had washed up she crept upstairs to peep at him. He slept facing the door, and when she looked in his eyes opened instantly. Again there was that initial, split-second flash of fear.

'It's all right,' Lucy whispered. 'Just making sure you're okay.'

He closed his eyes without speaking.

She went downstairs again. She dressed herself and Jo in oilskins and wellington boots, and they went out. The rain was still coming down in torrents and the wind was terrific. She glanced up at the roof: they had lost some slates. Leaning into the wind, she headed for the cliff top.

She held Jo's hand tightly – he might quite easily be blown away. Two minutes later she was wishing she had stayed indoors. Rain came in under her raincoat collar and over the tops of her boots, and she was soaked. Jo must be too, but now that they were wet they might as well stay wet for a few minutes more. Lucy wanted to go to the beach.

However, when they reached the top of the ramp she realized it was impossible. The narrow wooden walkway was slippery with rain, and in this wind she might lose her balance and fall off, to plunge sixty feet to the beach below. She had to content herself with looking.

It was quite a sight.

Vast waves, each the size of a small house, were rolling in rapidly, close on each other's heels. Crossing the beach the wave would rise even higher, its crest curling in a question mark, then throw itself against the foot of the cliff in a rage. Spray rose over the cliff top in sheets, causing Lucy to step back hurriedly and Jo to squeal with delight. Lucy could hear her son's laughter only because he had jumped into her arms, and his mouth was now close to her ear: the noise of the wind and the sea drowned more distant sounds.

There was something terribly thrilling in watching the elements spit and sway and roar in fury, in standing fractionally too close to the cliff edge, feeling threatened and safe at the same time, shivering with cold and yet perspiring in fear. It was thrilling, and there were few thrills in Lucy's life.

She was about to go back, mindful of Jo's health, when she saw the boat.

It was not a boat any more, of course; that was what was so shocking about it. All that was left were the huge timbers of the deck and the keel. They were scattered on the rocks below the cliffs like a dropped handful of matches. It had been a *big* boat, Lucy realized. One man might have piloted it alone, but not easily. And the damage the sea had wrought on man's craftsmanship was awesome. It was hard to spot two bits of wood still joined together.

How, in Heaven's name, had the stranger come out of it alive?

She shuddered when she thought of what those waves and those rocks might have done to a human body. Jo caught her sudden change of mood, and said into her ear: 'Go home, now.' She turned quickly away from the sea and hurried back along the muddy path to the cottage.

Back inside, they took off their wet coats, hats and boots, and hung them in the kitchen to dry. Lucy went upstairs and looked in on the stranger again. This time he did not open his eyes. He seemed to be sleeping very peacefully, yet she had a feeling that he had awakened and recognized her tread on the stairs, and closed his eyes again before she opened the door.

She ran a hot bath. She and the boy were soaked to the skin. She undressed Jo and put him in the tub, then – on impulse – took off her own clothes and got in with him. The heat was blissful. She closed her eyes and relaxed. This was good, too: to be in a house, feeling warm, while the storm beat impotently at the strong stone walls.

Life had turned interesting, all of a sudden. In one night there had come a storm, a shipwreck and a mystery man; this after three years of tedium. She hoped the stranger would wake up soon, so that she could find out all about him.

It was time she started cooking lunch for the men. She had some breast of lamb to make a stew. She got out of the bath and towelled herself gently. Jo was playing with his bath toy, a much-chewed rubber cat. Lucy looked at herself in the mirror, examining the stretch-marks on her belly left by pregnancy. They were fading, slowly, but they would never completely disappear. An all-over suntan would help, though. She smiled to herself, thinking: Fat chance of that! Besides, who was interested in her tummy? Nobody but herself.

Jo said: 'Can I stay in a minute more?' It was a phrase he used, 'a minute more', and it could mean anything up to half a day.

Lucy said: 'Just while I get dressed.' She hung the towel on a rail and moved toward the door.

The stranger stood in the doorway, looking at her.

They stared at each other. It was odd – Lucy thought later – that she felt not a bit afraid. It was the way he looked at her: there was no threat in his expression, no lewdness, no smirk, no lust. He was not looking at her pubis, or even her breasts, but at her face – into her eyes. She gazed back, a little shocked but not embarrassed, with just a tiny part of her mind wondering why she did not squeal, cover herself with her hands, and slam the door on him.

Something did come into his eyes, at last – perhaps she was imagining it, but she saw admiration, and a faint twinkle of honest humour, and a trace of sadness – and then the spell was broken, and he turned away and went back into his bedroom, closing the door. A moment later Lucy heard the springs creak as his weight settled on the bed.

And for no good reason at all she felt dreadfully guilty.

TWENTY

By this time Percival Godliman had pulled out all the stops.

Every policeman in the UK had a copy of the photograph of Faber, and about half of them were engaged full-time in the search. In the cities they were checking hotels and guest-houses, railway stations and bus terminals, cafés and shopping centres; and the bridges, arches, and bombed lots where the derelict hang out. In the country they were looking in barns and silos, empty cottages and ruined castles, thickets and clearings and cornfields. They were showing the photograph to ticket clerks, petrol station staff, ferry hands and toll collectors. All the passenger ports and airfields were covered, with the picture pinned behind a board at every Passport Control desk.

The police thought they were looking for a straightforward murderer.

The cop on the street knew that the man in the picture had killed two people with a knife in London. Senior officers knew a bit more: that one of the murders had been a sexual assault, another apparently motiveless, and a third – which their men were not to know of – was an unexplained but bloody attack on a soldier on the Euston-to-Liverpool train. Only chief constables, and a few officers at Scotland Yard, realized that the soldier had been on temporary attachment to MI5 and that all the murders were connected with Security.

The newspapers, too, thought it was just an ordinary murder hunt. The day after Godliman had released details, most of the papers had carried the story in their later editions – the first editions, bound for Scotland, Ulster and North Wales, had missed it, so they had carried a shortened version a day later. The Stockwell victim had been identified as a labourer, and given a false name and a vague London background. Godliman's press release had connected that murder with the death of Mrs Una Garden in 1940, but had been vague about the nature of the link. The murder weapon was said to be a stiletto.

The two Liverpool newspapers heard very quickly of the body on the train, and both wondered whether the London knife murderer was responsible. Both made enquiries with the Liverpool police. The editors of both papers received phone calls from the Chief Constable. Neither paper carried the story.

A total of one hundred and fifty-seven tall dark men were arrested on suspicion of being Faber. All but twenty-nine of them were able to prove that they could not possibly have committed the murders. Interviewers from MI5 talked to the twenty-nine. Twenty-seven called in parents, relatives and neighbours who affirmed that they had been born in Britain and had been living there during the twenties, when Faber had been in Germany.

The last two were brought to London and interviewed again, this time by Godliman. Both were bachelors, living alone, with no surviving relatives, leading a transient existence.

The first was a well-dressed, confident man who claimed implausibly that his way of life was to travel the country taking odd jobs as a manual labourer. Godliman explained that he was looking for a German spy, and that he – unlike the police – had the power to incarcerate anyone for the duration of the war, and no questions asked. Furthermore, he went on, he was not in the least interested in capturing ordinary criminals, and any information given him here at the War Office was strictly confidential, and would go no further.

The prisoner promptly confessed to being a confidence trickster and gave the addresses of nineteen elderly ladies whom he had cheated out of their old jewellery during the past three weeks. Godliman turned him over to the police.

He felt no obligation to be honest with a professional liar.

The last suspect also cracked under Godliman's treatment. His secret was that he was not a bachelor at all, not by a long way. He had a wife in Brighton. And in Solihull, Birmingham. And in Colchester, Newbury and Exeter. All five were able to produce marriage certificates later that day. The bigamist went to gaol to await trial.

Godliman slept in his office while the hunt went on.

*

Bristol, Temple Meads, railway station:

'Good morning, Miss. Would you look at this, please?'

'Hey, girls – the bobby's going to show us his snaps!'

'Now, don't muck about, just tell me if you've seen him.'

'Ooh, ain't he handsome! I wish I had!'

'You wouldn't if you knew what he'd done. Would you all take a look, please?'

'Never seen him.'

'Me neither.'

'Not me.'

'No.'

'When you catch him, ask him if he wants to meet a nice young Bristol girl.'

'You girls – I don't know . . . Just because they give you a pair of trousers and a porter's job, you think you're supposed to act like men . . .'

The Woolwich Ferry:

'Filthy day, Constable.'

'Morning, Captain. I expect it's worse on the high seas.'

'Can I help you? Or are you just crossing the river?'

'I want you to look at a face, Captain.'

'Let me put my specs on. Oh, don't worry, I can see to guide the ship. It's close things I need the glasses for, Now then . . .'

'Ring any bells?'

'Sorry, Constable. Means nothing to me.'

'Well, let me know if you see him.'

'Certainly.'

'Bon voyage.'

Number thirty-five Leak Street, London E1:

'Sergeant Riley – what a nice surprise!'

'Never mind the lip, Mabel. Who've you got here?'

'All respectable guests, Sergeant; you know me.'

'I know you, all right. That's why I'm here. Would any of your nice respectable guests happen to be on the trot?'

'Since when have you been recruiting for the Army?'

'I'm not, Mabel, I'm looking for a villain, and if he's here, he's probably told you he's on the trot.'

'Look, Jack – if I tell you there's nobody here I don't know, will you go away and stop pestering me?'

'Why should I trust you?'

'Because of 1936.'

'You were better looking then, Mabel.'

'So were you, Jack.'

'You win . . . Take a butcher's at this. If chummy comes in here, send word, okay?'

'Promise.'

'Don't waste any time about it, either.'

'All right!'

'Mabel . . . he knifed a woman your age. I'm just marking your cards.'

'I know. Thanks.'

'Ta-ta.'

'Take care, Jacko.'

Bill's Café, on the A30 near Bagshot:

'Tea, please, Bill. Two sugars.'

'Good morning, Constable Pearson. Filthy day.'

'What's on that plate, Bill – pebbles from Portsmouth?'

'Buttered buns, as well you know.'

'Oh! I'll have two, then. Thanks . . . Now then, lads! Anyone who wants his lorry checked from top to bottom can leave right away . . . That's better. Take a look at this picture, please.'

'What are you after him for, Constable – cycling without lights?'

'Never mind the jokes, Harry – pass the picture round. Anybody given a lift to that bloke?'

'Not me.'

'No.'

'Sorry, Constable.'

'Never clapped eyes on him.'

'Thank you, lads. If you see him, report it. Cheerio.'

'Constable?'

'Yes, Bill?'

'You haven't paid for the buns.'

'I'm confiscating them as evidence. Cheerio.'

Smethwick's Garage, Carlisle:

'Morning, Missus. When you've got a minute . . .'

'Be right with you, officer. Just let me attend to this

gentleman . . . Twelve and sixpence, please, sir. Thank you. Goodbye . . .'

'How's business?'

'Terrible, as usual. What can I do for you?'

'Can we go in the office for a minute?'

'Aye, come on . . . Now, then.'

'Take a look at this picture and tell me whether you've served that man with petrol recently.'

'Well, it shouldn't be too difficult. It's not as if we get hordes of customers passing through . . . ooh! D'you know, I think I have served him!'

'When?'

'Day before yesterday, in the morning.'

'How sure are you?'

'Well . . . he was older than the picture, but I'm pretty sure.'

'What was he driving?'

'A grey car. I'm no good on makes, this is my husband's business really, but he's in the Navy now.'

'Well, what did it look like? Sports car? Limousine?'

'It was the old sort, with a canvas roof that comes up. A two-seater. Sporty. It had a spare petrol tank bolted to the running-board, and I filled that, too.'

'Do you remember what he was wearing?'

'Not really. Working clothes, I think.'

'A tall man?'

'Yes, taller than you.'

'By the heck, I think it's him! Have you got a telephone . . .?'

*

William Duncan was twenty-five years old, five-feet-ten, weighed a trim 150 pounds, and was in first-class health. His open-air life and total lack of interest in tobacco, drink, late nights and loose living kept him that way. Yet he was not in the Armed Services.

He had seemed to be a normal child, if a little backward, until the age of eight, when his mind simply stopped developing. There had been no trauma that anyone knew about, no physical damage to account for sudden breakdown. Indeed, it was some years before anyone noticed that there was anything wrong, for at the age of ten he was no more than a little backward, and at twelve he was just dim-witted; but by fifteen he was obviously simple, and by eighteen he was known as Daft Willie.

His parents both belonged to an obscure Fundamentalist religious group whose members were not allowed to marry outside the Church (which may or may not have had something to do with Willie's daftness). They prayed for him, of course; but they also took him to a specialist in Stirling. The doctor, an elderly man, did several tests and then told them, over the tops of his gold-rimmed half-glasses, that the boy had a mental age of eight and his mind would grow no older, ever. They continued to pray for him, but they suspected that the Lord had sent this to try them, so they made sure that Willie was Saved and looked forward to the day when they would meet him again in the Glory and he would be healed. Meanwhile, he needed a job.

An eight-year-old can herd cows, but herding cows is nevertheless a job, so Daft Willie became a cowherd.

And it was while herding cows that he saw the car for the first time.

He assumed there were lovers in it.

Willie knew about lovers. That is to say, he knew that lovers existed, and that they did unmentionable things to one another in dark places like copses and cinemas and cars; and that one did not speak of them. So he hurried the cows quickly past the bush beside which was parked the 1924 Morris Cowley Bullnose two-seater (he knew about cars, too, like any eight-year-old) and tried very hard not to look inside it in case he should behold sin.

He took his little herd into the cowshed for milking, went by a roundabout route to his home, ate supper, read a chapter from Leviticus to his father – aloud, painstakingly – then went to bed to dream about lovers.

The car was still there on the evening of the next day.

For all his innocence, Willie knew that lovers did not do whatever it was that they did to one another for twenty-four hours at a stretch.

This time he went right up to the car and looked inside. It was empty. The ground beneath the engine was black and sticky with oil. Willie devised a new explanation: the car had broken down and had been abandoned by its driver. It did not occur to him to wonder why it had been semi-concealed in a bush.

When he arrived at the cowshed he told the farmer what he had seen. 'There's a broken-down car on the path up by the main road.'

The farmer was a big man with heavy sand-coloured eyebrows which drew together when he was thinking. 'Was there nobody about?'

'No – and it was there yesterday.'

'Why did you not tell me yesterday, then?'

Willie blushed. 'I thought it was maybe . . . lovers.'

'Och! 'The farmer realized that Willie was not being coy, but was genuinely embarrassed. He patted the boy's shoulder. 'Well, away home and leave it to me to deal with.'

After the milking the farmer went to look for himself. It did occur to him to wonder why the car was semi-concealed. He had heard about the London stiletto murderer; and while he did not jump to the conclusion that the car had been abandoned by the killer, all the same he thought there might be a connection between the car and some crime or other. So after supper he sent his eldest son into the village on horseback to telephone the police in Stirling.

The police arrived before his son got back from the phone. There were at least a dozen of them, every one apparently a non-stop tea drinker. The farmer and his wife were up half the night looking after them.

Daft Willie was summoned to tell his story again, repeating that he had first seen the car the previous evening, blushing again when he explained that he had assumed it contained lovers.

All in all, it was the most exciting night of the war.

*

That evening Percival Godliman, facing his fourth consecutive night in the office, went home to bathe, change, and pack a suitcase.

He had a service flat in a block in Chelsea. It was small, though plenty big enough for a single man, and it was clean and tidy except for the study, which the cleaner was not allowed to enter and in consequence was littered with books and papers. The furniture was all pre-war, of course, but it was rather well-chosen, and the flat had a comfortable air. There were leather club chairs and a gramophone in the living-room, and the kitchen was full of hardly used labour-saving devices.

While his bath was filling he smoked a cigarette – he had taken to them lately, a pipe was so much fuss – and looked at his most valuable possession, a grimly fantastic medieval scene which was probably by Hieronymous Bosch. It was a family heirloom and Godliman had never sold it, even when he needed the money, because he liked it.

In the bath he thought about Barbara Dickens and her son, Peter. He had not told anyone about her, not even Bloggs, although he had been about to mention her during their conversation about remarrying, but Colonel Terry had interrupted. She was a widow: her husband had been killed in action at the very beginning of the war. Godliman did not know how old she was, but she looked about forty, which was young for the mother of a twenty-two-year-old boy. She worked on translations of intercepted enemy signals, and she was bright, amusing, and very attractive. She was also rich. Godliman had taken her to dinner, three times, before the present crisis blew up. He thought she was in love with him.

She had contrived a meeting between Godliman and her son Peter, who was a captain. Godliman liked the boy. But he knew something which neither Barbara nor her son was aware of: Peter was going to Normandy.

Which was all the more reason to catch Die Nadel.

He got out of the bath and took a long, careful shave, thinking: Am I in love with her? He was not sure what love ought to feel like in middle age. Not, surely, the burning passion of youth. Affection, admiration, tenderness, and a trace of uncertain lust? If they amounted to love, he loved her.

And he needed to share his life, now. For years he had wanted only solitude and his research. Now the camaraderie of Military Intelligence was sucking him in: the parties, the all-night sessions when something big broke, the spirit of dedicated amateurism, the frantic pleasure-seeking of people to whom death is always close and never predictable – all these had infected him. It would vanish after the war, he knew; but other things would remain: the need to talk to someone close about his disappointment and his triumphs, the need to touch someone else at night, the need to say: 'There! Look at that! Isn't it fine?'

War was gruelling and oppressive and frustrating and uncomfortable, but one had friends. If peace brought back loneliness, Godliman thought he would be unhappy.

Right now the feel of clean underwear and a crisply ironed shirt was the height of luxury. He put more fresh clothes in a case, then sat down to enjoy a glass of whisky before returning to the office. The military chauffeur in the commandeered Daimler outside could wait a little longer.

He was filling a pipe when the phone rang. He put down the pipe and lit a cigarette instead.

His phone was connected to the War Office switchboard. The telephonist told him that a Chief Superintendent Dalkeith was calling from Stirling.

He waited for the click of the connection, and said: 'Godliman speaking.'

'We've found your Morris Cowley,' Dalkeith said without preamble.

'Where?'

'On the A80 just south of Stirling.'

'Empty?'

'Aye, broken down. It's been there at least twenty-four hours. It was driven a few yards off the main road and hidden in a bush. A half-witted farm boy found it.'

'Is there a bus stop or railway station within walking distance of the spot?'

'No.'

Godliman grunted. 'So it's likely our man had to walk or hitch-hike after leaving the car.'

'Aye.'

'In that case, will you ask around—'

'We're already trying to find out whether anyone local saw him or gave him a lift.'

'Good. Let me know . . . Meanwhile, I'll pass the news to the Yard. Thank you, Dalkeith.'

'We'll keep in touch. Goodbye, sir.'

Godliman put the phone on the hook and went into his study. He sat down with an atlas open to the road map of northern Britain. London, Liverpool, Carlisle, Stirling . . . Faber was heading for north-east Scotland.

Godliman wondered whether he should reconsider the theory that Faber was trying to get out. The best way out was west, via neutral Eire. Scotland's east coast, however, was the scene of military activity of various kinds. Was it possible that Faber had the nerve to continue his reconnaissance, knowing that MI5 was on his tail? It was possible, Godliman decided – he knew Faber had a lot of guts – but nevertheless unlikely. Nothing the man might discover in Scotland could be as important as the information he already had.

Therefore Faber was getting out via the east coast. Godliman ran over the methods of escape which were open to the spy: a light plane, landing on a lonely moor; a one-man voyage across the North Sea in a stolen vessel; a rendezvous with a U-boat off the coast; a passage in a merchant ship via a neutral country to the Baltic, disembarking in Sweden and crossing the border to occupied Norway . . . there were many ways.

The Yard must be told of the latest development. They would ask all Scots police forces to try to find someone who had picked up a hitch-hiker outside Stirling. Godliman returned to the living-room to phone, but the instrument rang before he got there. He picked it up.

'Godliman speaking.'

'A Mr Richard Porter is calling from Aberdeen.'

'Oh!' Godliman had been expecting Bloggs to check in from Carlisle. 'Put him on, please. Hello? Godliman speaking.'

'Ah, Richard Porter here. I'm on the local Watch Committee up here.'

'Yes, what can I do for you?'

'Well, actually, old boy, it's terribly embarrassing.'

Godliman controlled his impatience. 'Go on.'

'This chappie you're looking for – knife murders and so on. Well, I'm pretty sure I gave the bally fellow a lift in my own car.'

Godliman gripped the receiver more tightly. 'When?'

'Night before last. My car broke down on the A80 just outside Stirling. Middle of the bally night. Along comes this chappie, on foot, and mends it, just like that. So naturally—'

'Where did you drop him?'

'Right here in Aberdeen. Said he was going on to Banff. Thing is, I slept most of yesterday, so it wasn't until this afternoon—'

'Don't reproach yourself, Mr Porter. Thank you for calling.'

'Well, goodbye.'

Godliman jiggled the receiver and the War Office telephonist came back on the line.

Godliman said: 'Get Mr Bloggs for me, would you? He's in Carlisle.'

'He's holding on for you right now, sir.'

'Good!'

'Hello, Percy. What news?'

'We're on his trail again, Fred. He abandoned the Morris just outside Stirling and hitched a lift to Aberdeen.'

'Aberdeen!'

'He must be trying to get out through the east door.'

'When did he reach Aberdeen?'

'Probably early yesterday morning.'

'In that case he won't have had time to get out, unless he was very quick indeed. They're having the worst storm in living memory up here. It started last night and it's still going on. No ships are going out and it's certainly too rough to land a plane.'

'Good! Get up there as fast as you can. I'll start the local police moving in the meantime. Call me when you reach Aberdeen.'

'I'm on my way.'

'Fred?'

'Yes?'

'We'll catch the bastard yet.'

Fred was still laughing as Godliman hung up.

TWENTY-ONE

When Faber woke up it was almost dark. Through the bedroom window he could see the last streaks of grey being inked out of the sky by the encroaching night. The storm had not eased: rain drummed on the roof and overflowed from a gutter, and the wind howled and gusted tirelessly.

He switched on the little lamp beside the bed. The effort tired him, and he slumped back on to the pillow. It frightened him, to be this weak. Those who believe that Might is Right must always be mighty, and Faber was sufficiently self-aware to know the implications of his own ethics. Fear was never far from the surface of his emotions: perhaps that was why he had survived so long. He was chronically incapable of feeling safe. He understood, in that vague way in which we understand the most fundamental things about ourselves, that his insecurity was the reason he chose the profession of spy: it was the only walk of life which permitted him instantly to kill anyone who posed him the slightest threat. The fear of being weak was part of the syndrome which included his obsessive independence, his insecurity, and his contempt for his military superiors.

He lay on the child's bed in the pink-walled bedroom

and inventoried his body. He seemed to be bruised just about everywhere, but apparently nothing was broken. He did not feel feverish: his constitution had withstood bronchial infection despite the night on the boat. There was just the weakness. He suspected it was more than exhaustion. He remembered a moment, as he had reached the top of the ramp, when he had thought he was going to die; and he wondered whether he had inflicted upon himself some permanent damage with that last mindbending uphill dash.

He checked his possessions, too. The can of photographic negatives was still taped to his chest, the stiletto was strapped to his left arm, and his papers and money were in the jacket pocket of his borrowed pyjamas.

He pushed the blankets aside and swung himself into a sitting position with his feet on the floor. A moment of dizziness came and went. He stood up. It was important not to permit oneself the psychological attitudes of the invalid. He put on the dressing-gown and went into the bathroom.

When he returned his own clothes were at the foot of the bed, clean and pressed: underwear, overalls, and shirt. Suddenly he remembered getting up some time during the morning and seeing the woman naked in the bathroom: it had been an odd scene, and he was not sure what it meant. She was very beautiful, he recalled.

He dressed slowly. He would have liked a shave, but he decided to ask his host's permission before borrowing the blade on the bathroom shelf: some men were as possessive of their razors as they were of their wives.

However, he did take the liberty of using the child's plastic comb he found in the top drawer of the chest.

He looked into the mirror without pride. He had no conceit. He knew that some women found him attractive, and others did not; and he assumed this was so for most men. Of course, he had had more women than most men, but he attributed this to his appetite, not to his looks. His reflection told him he was presentable, and that was all he needed to know.

Satisfied, he left the bedroom and went slowly down the stairs. Again he felt a wave of weakness; again he willed himself to overcome it, gripping the banister rail and placing one foot deliberately before the other until he reached the ground floor.

He paused outside the living-room door and, hearing no noise, went on to the kitchen. He knocked and went in. The young couple were at the table, finishing supper.

The woman stood up when he entered. 'You got up!' she said. 'Are you sure you should?'

Faber permitted himself to be led to a chair. 'Thank you,' he said. 'You really mustn't encourage me to pretend to be ill.'

'I don't think you realize what a terrible experience you've been through,' she said. 'Do you feel like food?'

'I'm imposing on you—'

'Not at all. Don't be silly. I kept some soup hot for you.'

Faber said: 'You're so kind, and I don't even know your names.'

'David and Lucy Rose.' She ladled soup into a bowl

and placed it on the table in front of him. 'Cut some bread, David, would you?'

'I'm Henry Baker.' Faber did not know why he had said that: he had no papers in that name. Henry Faber was the man the police were hunting, so he should have used his James Baker identity; but somehow he wanted this woman to call him Henry, the nearest English equivalent of his real name, Henrik. Perhaps it did not matter – he could always say his name was James but he had always been called Henry.

He took a sip of the soup, and suddenly he was ravenously hungry. He ate it all quickly, then the bread. When he had finished, Lucy laughed. She looked lovely when she laughed: her mouth opened wide, showing lots of even white teeth, and her eyes crinkled merrily at the corners.

'More?' she offered.

'Thank you very much.'

'I can see it doing you good. The colour is coming back to your cheeks.'

Faber realized he felt physically better. He ate his second helping more slowly, out of courtesy rather than repletion.

David said: 'How did you happen to be out in this storm?' It was the first time he had spoken.

Lucy said: 'Don't badger him, David.'

'It's all right,' Faber said. 'I was foolish, that's all. This is the first fishing holiday I've been able to have since before the war, and I just refused to let the weather spoil it. Are you a fisherman?'

David shook his head. 'Sheep farmer.'

'Do you have many employees?'

'Just one, old Tom.'

'I suppose there are other sheep farms on the island.'

'No. We live at this end, Tom lives at the other end, and in between there's nothing but sheep.'

Faber nodded slowly. This was good – very good. A woman, a cripple, a child and an old man could not constitute an obstacle. And he was feeling much stronger already.

Faber said: 'How do you contact the mainland?'

'There's a boat once a fortnight. It's due this Monday, but it won't come if the storm keeps up. There's a radio transmitter in Tom's cottage, but we can only use that in emergencies. If I thought people might be searching for you, or if you needed urgent medical help, I should use it. But as things are I don't feel it's necessary. There's little point: nobody can come to fetch you off the island until the storm clears, and when that happens the boat will come anyway.'

'Of course.' Faber concealed his delight. The problem of how to contact the U-boat on Monday had been nagging at the back of his mind. He had seen an ordinary wireless set in the Roses' living-room, and he would, in a pinch, have been able to rig up a transmitter from that. But the fact that Tom had a proper radio made everything so much easier.

Faber said: 'What does Tom need a transmitter for?'

'He's a member of the Royal Observer Corps. Aberdeen was bombed in July 1940. There was no air-raid warning. Consequently there were fifty casualties. That was when they recruited Tom. It's a good thing his hearing is better than his eyesight.'

'I suppose the bombers come from Norway.'

'I suppose so.'

Lucy stood up. 'Let's go into the other room.'

The two men followed her. Faber felt no weakness, no dizziness. He held the living-room door for David, who wheeled himself close to the fire. Lucy offered Faber brandy. He declined. She poured for her husband and herself.

Faber sat back and studied the couple. Lucy's looks were really quite striking: she had an oval face, wide-set eyes of an unusual, cat-like amber colour, and a lot of rich, dark-red hair. Under the mannish fisherman's sweater and baggy trousers there was the suggestion of a very fine, fullish figure. If she were to curl her hair and put on silk stockings and a cocktail dress she might be very glamorous. David was also good-looking – almost pretty, except for the shadow of a very dark beard. His hair was nearly black and his skin looked Mediterranean. He would have been tall, if he had had legs in proportion to his arms. Faber suspected that those arms might be powerful, muscled from years of pushing the wheels of the chair to get from A to B.

Yes, they were an attractive couple – but there was something badly wrong between them. Faber was no expert on marriage, but his training in interrogation techniques had taught him to read the silent language of the body – to know, from small gestures, when someone was frightened, confident, hiding something, or lying. Lucy and David rarely looked at one another, and never touched. They spoke to him more than to each other. They circled one another, like turkeys trying to keep in front of them a few square feet of vacant portable territory. The tension between them was enormous. They were like Churchill and Stalin, obliged temporarily to fight side by side, fiercely suppressing a deeper enmity. Faber wondered what awful trauma lay at the back of their hatred.

This cosy little house must be an emotional pressure-cooker, despite its rugs and its bright paintwork, its floral armchairs and blazing fires and framed water-colours. To live alone, with only an old man and a child for company, with this thing between them . . . it reminded him of a play he had seen in London, by an American called Tennessee something.

Abruptly, David swallowed his drink and said: 'I must turn in. My back's playing up.'

Faber got to his feet and said: 'I'm sorry – I've been keeping you up.'

David waved him down. 'Not at all. You've been asleep all day – you won't want to go back to bed right away. Besides, Lucy would like to chat, I'm sure. It's just that I mistreat my back – backs were designed to share the load with the legs, you know.'

Lucy said: 'You'd better take two pills tonight, then.' She took a bottle from the top shelf of the bookcase, shook out two tablets, and gave them to her husband.

He swallowed them dry. 'I'll say goodnight.' He wheeled himself out.

'Goodnight, David.'

'Goodnight, Mr Rose.'

After a moment Faber heard David dragging himself up the stairs, and wondered just how he did it.

Lucy spoke, as if to cover the sound of David. 'Where do you live, Mr Baker?'

'Please call me Henry. I live in London.'

'I haven't been to London for years. There's probably not much of it left.'

'It's changed, but not as much as you might think. When were you last there?'

'Nineteen-forty.' She poured herself another brandy. 'Since we came here, I've only been off the island once, and that was to have the baby. One can't travel much these days, can one?'

'What made you come here?'

'Um.' She sat down, sipped her drink, and looked into the fire.

'Perhaps I shouldn't—'

'It's all right. We had an accident the day we got married. That's how David lost his legs. He'd been training as a fighter pilot . . . we both wanted to run away, I think. I believe it was a mistake, but it seemed like a good idea at the time.'

'It has allowed his resentment to incubate.'

She shot him a sharp look. 'You're a perceptive man.'

'It's obvious.' He spoke very quietly. 'You don't deserve such unhappiness.'

She blinked several times. 'You see too much.'

'It's not difficult. Why do you continue, if it's not working?'

'I don't know what to tell you. Do you want clichés? The vows of marriage, the child, the war . . . If there's another answer, I can't find words for it.'

'Guilt,' Faber said. 'But you're thinking of leaving him, aren't you?'

She stared at him, slowly shaking her head with incredulity. 'How do you know so much?'

'You've lost the art of dissembling in four years on this island. Besides, these things are so much simpler from the outside.'

'Have you ever been married?'

'No. That's what I mean.'

'Why not? I think you ought to be.'

It was Faber's turn to look pensively into the fire. Why not, indeed? His stock answer – to himself – was his profession. But he could not tell her that, and anyway it was too glib. He said suddenly: 'I don't trust myself to love anyone that much.' The words had come out without forethought, and he wondered whether they were true. A moment later he wondered how Lucy had got past his guard, when he had thought he was disarming her.

Neither of them spoke for a while. The fire was dying. A few stray raindrops found their way down the chimney and hissed in the cooling coals. The storm showed no sign of letting up. Faber found himself thinking of the last woman he had had. What was her name? Gertrude. It was seven years ago, but he could picture her now, in the flickering fire: a round German face, fair hair, green eyes, beautiful breasts, much-too-wide hips, fat legs, bad feet; the conversational style of an express train, a wild, inexhaustible enthusiasm for sex . . . She had flattered him, admiring his mind (she said) and adoring his body (she had no need to tell him). She wrote lyrics for popular songs, and read them to him in a poor basement flat in Berlin: it was not a lucrative profession. He visualized her in that untidy bedroom, lying naked, urging him to do more bizarre and erotic things with her: to hurt her, to touch himself, to lie completely still while she made love to him . . . He shook his head slightly to brush away the memories. He had not thought like that in all the years he had been celibate. Such visions were disturbing. He looked at Lucy.

'You were far away,' she said with a smile.

'Memories,' he said. 'This talk of love . . .'

'I shouldn't burden you.'

'You're not.'

'Good memories?'

'Very good. And yours? You were thinking, too.'

She smiled again. 'I was in the future, not the past.'

'What do you see there?'

She seemed about to answer, then changed her mind. It happened twice. There were signs of tension about her eyes.

'I see you finding another man,' Faber said. As he spoke he was thinking: Why am I doing this? 'He is a weaker man than David, and less handsome; but it is for his weakness that you love him. He is clever, but not rich; compassionate without being sentimental; tender, caring, loving. He—'

The brandy glass in her hand shattered under the

pressure of her grip. The fragments fell into her lap and on to the carpet, and she ignored them. Faber crossed to her chair and knelt in front of her. Her thumb was bleeding. He took her hand.

'You've hurt yourself.'

She looked at him. She was crying.

'I'm sorry,' he said.

The cut was superficial. She took a handkerchief from her trousers pocket and staunched the blood. Faber released her hand and began to pick up the pieces of broken glass, wishing he had kissed her when he had the chance. He put the shards on the chimney-breast.

'I didn't mean to upset you,' he said.

She took away the handkerchief and looked at her thumb. It was still bleeding.

'A little bandage,' he suggested.

'In the kitchen.'

He found a roll of bandage, a pair of scissors, and a safety pin. He filled a small bowl with hot water and returned to the living-room.

In his absence she had somehow obliterated the evidence of tears on her face. She sat passively, limp, while he bathed her thumb in the hot water, dried it, and fixed a small strip of bandage over the cut. She looked all the time at his face, not at his hands; but her expression was unreadable.

He finished the job and stood back abruptly. This was silly: he had taken the thing too far. It was time to disengage. He said: 'I think I'd better go to bed.'

She nodded.

'I'm sorry—'

'Stop apologizing,' she told him. 'It doesn't suit you.'

Her tone was harsh. He guessed that she, too, felt the thing had got out of hand.

'Are you staying up?' he asked.

She shook her head.

'Well . . .' He walked to the door and held it for her.

She avoided his eyes as she passed him. He followed her through the hall and up the stairs. As he watched her climb, he could not help imagining her in other clothes, her hips swaying gently underneath some silky material, long legs clad in stockings instead of worsted grey trousers, high-heeled dress shoes instead of worn felt slippers.

At the top of the stairs, on the tiny landing, she turned and whispered: 'Goodnight.'

He said: 'Goodnight, Lucy.'

She looked at him for a moment. He reached for her hand, but she foresaw his intention and turned quickly away, entering her bedroom and closing the door without a backward look, leaving him standing there with his hand out and his mouth open, wondering what was in her mind and – more to the point – what was in his.

TWENTY-TWO

Bloggs drove dangerously fast through the night in a commandeered Sunbeam Talbot with a souped-up engine. The hilly, winding Scottish roads were slick with rain and, in a few low places, two or three inches deep in water. The rain drove across the windscreen in sheets. On the more exposed hilltops the gale-force winds threatened to blow the car off the road and into the soggy turf alongside. For mile after mile, Bloggs sat forward in the seat, peering through the small area of glass that was cleared by the wiper, straining his eyes to make out the shape of the road in front as the headlights battled with the obscuring rain. Just north of Edinburgh he ran over three rabbits, feeling the sickening bump as the tyres squashed their small furry bodies. He did not slow the car, but for a while afterwards he wondered whether rabbits normally came out at night.

The strain gave him a headache, and his sitting position made his back hurt. He also felt hungry. He opened the window for a cold breeze to keep him awake, but so much water came in that he was forced to close it again immediately. He thought about Die Nadel, or Faber or whatever he was calling himself now:

a smiling young man in running-shorts holding a trophy. Well, Faber was winning this race. He was forty-eight hours ahead and he had the advantage that only he knew the route that had to be followed. Bloggs would have enjoyed a contest with that man, if the stakes had not been so high, so bloody high.

He wondered what he would do if he ever came face to face with the man. I'd shoot the bugger out of hand, he thought, before he killed me. Faber was a pro, and you couldn't mess with that type. Most spies were amateurs: frustrated revolutionaries of the left or right, people who wanted the imaginary glamour of espionage, greedy men or lovesick women, or blackmail victims. The few professionals were very dangerous indeed, because they knew that the professionals they were up against were not merciful men.

Dawn was still an hour or two away when Bloggs drove into Aberdeen. Never in his life had he been so grateful for street lights, dimmed and masked though they were. He had no idea where the police station was, and there was no one on the streets to give him directions, so he drove around the town until he saw the familiar blue lamp (also dimmed).

He parked the car and dashed through the rain into the building. He was expected. Godliman had been on the phone, and Godliman was now very senior indeed. Bloggs was shown into the office of Alan Kincaid, a Detective-Chief-Inspector in his middle fifties. There were three other officers in the room: Bloggs shook their hands and instantly forgot their names.

Kincaid said: 'You made bloody good time from Carlisle.'

'Nearly killed myself doing it,' Bloggs replied. He sat down. 'If you can rustle up a sandwich . . .'

'Of course.' Kincaid leaned his head out of the door and shouted something. 'It'll be here in two shakes,' he told Bloggs.

The office had off-white walls, a plank floor, and plain hard furniture: a desk, a few chairs and a filing cabinet. It was totally unrelieved: no pictures, no ornaments, no personal touches of any kind. There was a tray of dirty cups on the floor, and the air was thick with smoke. It smelled like somewhere men had been working all night.

Kincaid had a small moustache, thin grey hair, and spectacles. A big, intelligent-looking man in shirtsleeves and braces, he was the kind of policeman that – Bloggs thought – made up the backbone of the British police force. He spoke with a local accent, a sign that, like Bloggs, he had come up through the ranks – though from his age it was clear that his rise had been slower than Bloggs's.

Bloggs said: 'How much do you know of what this is all about?'

'Not much,' Kincaid said. 'But your governor, Godliman, did say that the London murders are the least of this man's crimes. We also know which department you're with, so we can put two and two together and conclude that Faber is a very dangerous spy.'

'That's about it,' Bloggs said.

Kincaid nodded.

'What have you done so far?' Bloggs asked.

Kincaid put his feet on his desk. 'He arrived here two days ago, yes?'

'Yes.'

'That was when we started looking for him. We had the pictures – I assume every force in the country got them.'

'Yes.'

'We checked the hotels and lodging houses, the station and the bus depot. We did it quite thoroughly, although at the time we didn't know he had come here. Needless to say, we had no results. We're checking again, of course; but my opinion is that he probably left Aberdeen immediately.'

A woman police constable came in with a cup of tea and a very thick cheese sandwich. Bloggs thanked her and set about the sandwich greedily.

Kincaid went on: 'We had a man at the railway station before the first train left in the morning. Ditto for the bus depot. So, if he left the town, either he stole a car or he hitched a ride. We've had no stolen cars reported.'

'Damn,' Bloggs said through a mouthful of wholemeal bread. He swallowed. 'That makes it about as difficult as it can be to trace him.'

'No doubt that's why he chose to hitch-hike.'

'He might have gone by sea.'

'Of the boats that left the harbour that day, none was big enough to stow away on. Since then, of course, nothing's gone out because of the storm.'

'Stolen boats?'

'None reported.'

Bloggs shrugged. 'If there's no prospect of going out, the owners might not come to the harbour – in which case the theft of a boat might go unnoticed until the storm ends.'

One of the officers in the room said: 'We missed that one, Chief.'

'We did,' Kincaid said.

Bloggs said: 'Perhaps the harbourmaster could look around all the regular moorings—'

'I'm with you,' Kincaid said. He was already dialling. After a moment he spoke into the phone. 'Captain Douglas? Kincaid. Aye, I know civilized people sleep at this hour. You haven't heard the worst – I want you to take a walk in the rain. Aye, you heard me right . . .'

The other policemen started to laugh.

Kincaid put his hand over the mouthpiece and said: 'You know what they say about seamen's language? It's true.' He spoke into the phone again. 'Go round all the regular moorings and make a note of any vessels not in their usual spot. Ignoring those you know to be legitimately out of port, give me the names and addresses – and phone numbers if you have them – of the owners. Aye. Aye, I know . . . I'll make it a double. All right, a bottle. And a good morning to you too, old friend.' He hung up.

Bloggs smiled. 'Salty?'

'If I did what he suggested I do with my truncheon, I'd never be able to sit down again.' Kincaid became serious. 'It'll take him about half an hour, then we'll need a couple of hours to check all the addresses.

It's worth doing, although I still think he hitched a ride.'

'So do I,' Bloggs said.

The door opened, and a middle-aged man in civilian clothes walked in. Kincaid and his officers stood up, and Bloggs followed suit.

Kincaid said: 'Good morning, sir. This is Mr Bloggs. Mr Bloggs, Richard Porter.'

They shook hands. Porter had a red face and a carefully cultivated moustache. He wore a double-breasted, camel-coloured overcoat. He said: 'How do you do. I'm the blighter that gave your chappie a lift to Aberdeen. Most embarrassing.' He had no local accent.

Bloggs said: 'How do you do.' On first acquaintance Porter seemed to be exactly the kind of silly ass who would give a spy a lift half across the country. However, Bloggs knew the type: the air of empty-headed heartiness might well mask a shrewd mind. He asked: 'What made you realize that the man you'd picked up was the . . . the stiletto murderer?'

'I heard about the abandoned Morris. I picked him up at that very spot.'

'You've seen the picture?'

'Yes. Of course, I didn't get a good look at the chappie, because it was dark for most of the journey. But I saw enough of him, in the light of the torch when we were under the bonnet, and afterwards when we entered Aberdeen – it was dawn by then. If I'd only seen the picture, I'd say it *could* have been him. Given the spot at which I picked him up, so near to where the Morris was found, I say it *was* him.'

'I agree,' Bloggs said. He thought for a moment, wondering what useful information he could get out of this man. 'How did Faber impress you?' he asked eventually.

Porter said promptly: 'He struck me as exhausted, nervous and determined, in that order. Also, he was no Scotsman.'

'How would you describe his accent?'

'Neutral. No trace of the Hun in his voice . . . except perhaps in retrospect, and that might be my imagination. The accent – minor public school, Home Counties. Jarred with his clothes, if you know what I mean. He was wearing overalls. Another thing I didn't remark until afterwards.'

Kincaid interrupted to offer tea. Everyone accepted. The policeman went to the door.

Bloggs had decided that Porter was less foolish than he looked. 'What did you talk about?'

'Oh, nothing much.'

'But you were together for hours—'

'He slept most of the way. He mended the car – it was only a disconnected lead, but I'm afraid I'm hopeless with machines – then he told me his own car had broken down in Edinburgh, and he was going to Banff. Said he didn't really want to go through Aberdeen, as he didn't have a Restricted Area Pass. I'm afraid I . . . I told him not to worry about that. Said I'd vouch for him if we were stopped. Makes one feel such a bloody fool, you know – but I felt I owed him a favour. He had got me out of a bit of a hole, y'know.'

Kincaid said: 'Nobody's blaming you, sir.'

Bloggs was, but he did not say so. Instead he said: 'There are very few people who have met Faber and can tell us what he's like. Can you think hard and tell me what kind of a man you took him to be?'

'He woke up like a soldier,' Porter said. 'He was courteous, and seemed intelligent. Firm handshake. I take notice of handshakes.'

'Anything else? Think very hard.'

'Something else about when he woke up . . .' Porter's florid face creased up in a frown. 'His right hand went to his left forearm, like this.' He demonstrated.

'That's something,' Bloggs said. 'That'll be where he keeps the knife. A sleeve-sheath.'

'Nothing else, I'm afraid.'

'And he said he was going to Banff. That means he's not.'

'Really?'

'Spies always lie, on principle. I'll bet you told him where you were going before he told you where he was going.'

'I believe I did.' Porter nodded thoughtfully. 'Well, well.'

'Either Aberdeen was his destination, or he went south after you dropped him. Since he said he was going north, he probably didn't go north.'

Kincaid said: 'That kind of second-guessing could get out of hand.'

'Sometimes it does,' Bloggs grinned. 'Did you tell him that you're a magistrate?'

'Yes.'

'That's why he didn't kill you.'

'What? Good Lord! What do you mean?'

'He knew you'd be missed.'

'Good Lord!' Porter repeated. He had gone slightly pale. The idea that he might actually have been killed clearly had not occurred to him.

The door opened again. The man who walked in said: 'I've got your information, and I hope it was fucken worth it.'

Bloggs grinned. This was, undoubtedly, the harbour-master: a short man with cropped white hair, smoking a large pipe and wearing a blazer with brass buttons.

Kincaid said: 'Come in, Captain. How did you get so wet? You shouldn't go out in the rain.'

'Fuck off,' the Captain said. Bloggs was not sure how much of his anger was real: very little of it, to judge by the delighted expressions on the other faces in the room.

Porter said: 'Morning, Captain.'

'Good morning, Your Worship,' the Captain said.

Kincaid said: 'What have you got?'

The Captain took off his cap and shook drops of rain from its crown. 'The *Marie II* has gone missing,' he said. 'I saw her come in on the afternoon the storm began. I didn't see her go out, but I know she shouldn't have sailed again that day. However, it seems she did.'

'Who owns her?'

'Tam Halfpenny. I telephoned him. He left her in her mooring that day and hasn't seen her since.'

Bloggs said: 'What kind of vessel is she?'

'A small fishing boat, sixty feet and broad in the beam. Stout little craft. Inboard motor. No particular style – the fishermen round here don't follow the pattern book when they build boats.'

'Let me ask you a very important question,' Bloggs said. 'Could that boat have survived the storm?'

The Captain paused in the act of putting a match to his pipe. After a moment he said: 'With a very skilful sailor at the helm – maybe. Maybe not.'

'How far might he have got before the storm broke?'

'Not far – a few miles. The *Marie II* was not tied up until evening.'

Bloggs stood up, walked around his chair, and sat down again. 'So where is he now?'

'At the bottom of the sea, in all probability, the bloody fool.' The Captain's statement was not without relish.

Bloggs could take no satisfaction in the likelihood that Faber was dead. It was too inconclusive. The discontent spread to his body, and he felt restless, itchy, and frustrated. He scratched his chin: he needed a shave. 'I'll believe it when I see it,' he said.

'You won't.'

'Save your lugubrious guesswork,' Bloggs said sharply. 'I want information, not pessimism.' The other men in the room suddenly remembered that, despite his youth, he was the senior officer there. 'Let's rehearse the possibilities. One: he left Aberdeen by land and someone else stole the *Marie II.* In that case he has probably reached his destination by now, but he won't have left the country because of the storm. We already have all the other police forces looking for him, and that's all we can do about number one.

'Two: he's still in Aberdeen. Again, we have this possibility covered: we're still looking for him.

'Three: he left Aberdeen by sea. I think we're agreed this is the strongest option. Let's break it down. Three A: he transferred to another vessel – probably a U-boat – before the storm broke. We don't think he had time, but he might've. Three B: he found shelter somewhere, or was shipwrecked somewhere – mainland or island. Three C: he died.

'If he caught a U-boat, we've had it. We've lost. There's nothing more we can do. So let's forget that one. If he found shelter, or was shipwrecked, we'll find evidence sooner or later – either the *Marie II*, or bits of it. We can search the coastline right away and survey the sea as soon as the weather clears sufficiently for us to get a plane up. If he's gone to the bottom of the ocean we may still find bits of the boat floating.

'So we have three courses of action to take. We continue the searches already going on; we mount a new search of the coastline, working north and south from Aberdeen; and we prepare for an air-sea search the minute the weather improves.'

Bloggs had begun to pace up and down as he spoke, thinking on his feet. He stopped now, and looked around. 'Comments, queries and suggestions?'

The late hour had got to all of them. Bloggs's sudden access of energy jerked them out of a creeping lethargy. One leaned forward, rubbing his hands; another tied his shoelaces; a third put his jacket on. They wanted to go to work. There were no questions.

'All right,' said Bloggs. 'Let's win the war.'

TWENTY-THREE

Faber was awake. His body probably needed sleep, despite the fact that he had spent the day in bed; but his mind was hyperactive, turning over possibilities, sketching scenarios, thinking about women and about home.

Now that he was so close to getting out, his memories of home became quite painfully sweet. He thought of quite silly things, like sausages fat enough to eat in slices, and motor cars on the right-hand side of the road, and *really* tall trees, and most of all his own language – words with guts and precision, hard consonants and pure vowels and the verb at the end of the sentence where it ought to be, finality and meaning in the same climactic terminal.

Thoughts of climaxes brought Gertrude to mind again: her face beneath his, make-up washed away by his kisses, eyes closing tight in pleasure then opening again to look with delight into his, mouth stretched wide in a permanent gasp, saying '*Ja, Liebling, ja . . .*'

It was silly. He had led the life of a monk for seven years, but she had no reason to do the same. She would have had a dozen men since Faber. She might even be dead, bombed by the RAF or murdered by the maniacs because her nose was half an inch too long or run over by a motor car in the blackout. Anyway, she would hardly remember him. He would probably never see her again. But she was a symbol.

He did not normally permit himself the indulgence of sentiment. There was in his nature a very cold streak, and he cultivated it because it protected him. Now, however, he was within an inch of success, and he felt free, not to relax his vigilance, but to fantasize a little.

The storm was his safeguard while it continued. He would simply contact the U-boat with Tom's radio on Monday, and its captain would send a dinghy into the bay as soon as the weather cleared. However, if the storm ended before Monday, there was a slight complication: the supply boat. David and Lucy would naturally expect him to take the boat back to the mainland.

Lucy came into his thoughts in vivid, full-colour visions which he could not quite control. He saw her striking amber eyes watching him as he made a bandage for her thumb; her outline walking up the stairs in front of him clad in shapeless man's clothing; her heavy breasts, perfectly round, as she stood naked in the bathroom: and as the visions developed from memory into fantasy she leaned over the bandage and kissed his mouth, turned back on the stairs and took him in her arms, stepped out of the bathroom and placed his hands on her breasts.

He turned restessly in the little bed, cursing the imagination which sent him dreams the like of which he had not suffered since his schooldays. At that time, before he had experienced the reality of sex, he had constructed elaborate sexual scenarios featuring the older women with whom he came into daily contact: the starchy Matron; Professor Nagel's dark, thin, intellectual wife; the shopkeeper in the village who wore red lipstick and talked to her husband with contempt. Sometimes he put all three of them into one orgiastic fantasy. When at the age of fifteen he had seduced a housemaid's daughter in the twilight of a West Prussian forest, he abandoned the imaginary orgies because they were so much better than the disappointing real thing. Young Henrik had been greatly puzzled by this: where was the blinding ecstasy, the sensation of soaring through the air like a bird, the mystical fusion of two bodies into one? The fantasies became painful, reminding him of his failure to make them real. Later, of course, the reality improved, and Henrik formed the view that ecstasy comes not from a man's pleasure in a woman, but from their pleasure in each other. He had voiced that opinion to his elder brother, who seemed to think it banal, a truism rather than a discovery; and before long Henrik saw it that way too.

He became a good lover, eventually. He found sex interesting, as well as physically pleasant. He was never a great seducer, for the thrill of conquest was not what he wanted. But he was expert at giving and receiving sexual gratification, without the expert's illusion that technique is all. For some women he was a highly desirable man, and the fact that he did not know this only served to make him even more attractive.

He tried to remember how many women he had had: Anna, Gretchen, Ingrid, the American girl, those two whores in Stuttgart . . . he could not recall them all, but there could not have been more than about twenty.

None of them, he thought, had been quite as beautiful as Lucy. He gave an exasperated sigh: he had let this woman get to him, just because he was close to home and had been so careful for so long. He was annoyed with himself. It was undisciplined: one should not relax until the assignment was over, and this was not over, not quite.

There was the problem of the supply boat. Several solutions came to mind: perhaps the most promising was to incapacitate the island's inhabitants, meet the boat himself, and send the boatman away with a cock-and-bull story. He could say he was visiting them, had come out on another boat; that he was a relative, or a bird-watcher . . . anything. It was too small a problem to engage his full attention at present. Later, when and if the weather improved, he would work something out.

He had no serious problems. A lonely island, miles off the coast, with four inhabitants – it was an ideal hideout. From now on, leaving Britain was going to be as easy as breaking out of a baby's playpen. When he thought of the situations he had already come through, the people he had killed – the five Home Guard men, the Yorkshire lad on the train, the Abwehr messenger – he considered himself now to be sitting pretty.

An old man, a cripple, a woman and a child . . . Killing them would be so simple.

*

Lucy, too, lay awake. She was listening. There was a lot to hear. The weather was an orchestra, rain drumming on the roof, wind fluting in the eaves of the cottage, sea performing glissandi with the beach. The old house talked, too, creaking in its joints as it suffered the buffeting of the storm. Within the room there were more sounds: David's slow, regular breathing, threatening but never quite achieving a snore as he slept deeply under the influence of the double dose of soporific; and the quicker, shallow breaths of Jo, sprawled comfortably across a camp bed beside the far wall.

The noise is keeping me awake, Lucy thought; then immediately: Who am I trying to fool? Her wakefulness was caused by Henry, who had looked at her naked body, and had touched her hands gently as he bandaged her thumb, and who now lay in bed in the next room, probably fast asleep.

He had not told her much about himself, she realized: only that he was unmarried. She did not know where he had been born – his accent gave no clue. He had not even hinted at what he did for a living, though she imagined he must be a professional man, perhaps a dentist or a soldier. He was not dull enough to be a solicitor, too intelligent to be a journalist, and doctors could never keep their profession secret for longer than five minutes. He was not rich enough to be a barrister, too self-effacing to be an actor. She would bet on the Army.

Did he live alone, she wondered? Or with his mother? Or a woman? What did he wear when he wasn't fishing? She would like to see him in a dark blue suit, double-breasted, with a white handkerchief in the top pocket. Did he have a motor car? Yes, he would; something rather unusual, and quite new. He probably drove very fast.

That thought brought back memories of David's two-seater, and she closed her eyes tightly to shut out the nightmare images. Think of something else, think of something *else.*

She thought of Henry again, and realized an odd thing: she wanted to make love to him.

It was a peculiar wish; the kind of wish that, in her scheme of things, afflicted men but not women. A woman might meet a man briefly and find him attractive, want to get to know him better, even begin to fall in love with him; but she did not feel an immediate physical desire, not unless she was . . . abnormal.

She told herself that this was ridiculous; that what she needed was to make love with her husband, not to copulate with the first eligible man who came along. She told herself she was not that kind.

All the same, it was pleasant to speculate. David and Jo were fast asleep: there was nothing to stop her getting out of bed, crossing the landing, entering his room, sliding into bed next to him . . .

Nothing to stop her, except character, good breeding, and a respectable upbringing.

If she were going to do it with anybody, she would do it with someone like Henry. He would be kind, and gentle, and considerate; he would not despise her for offering herself like a Soho streetwalker.

She turned over in the bed, smiling at her own foolishness: for how could she possibly know whether he would despise her? She had known him only for a day, and he had spent most of that day asleep.

Still, it would be nice to have him look at her again, his expression of admiration tinged with some kind of amusement. It would be nice to feel his hands, to touch his body, to squeeze against the warmth of his skin.

She realized that her body was responding to the images in her mind. She felt the urge to touch herself, and resisted it, as she had done for four years. At least I haven't dried up, like an old crone, she thought.

She moved her legs, and sighed as a warm sensation spread through her loins. This was getting unreasonable. It was time to go to sleep. There was just no way she would make love to Henry, or to anyone else, tonight.

With that thought she got out of bed and went to the door.

Faber heard a footfall on the landing, and he reacted automatically.

His mind cleared instantly of the idle, lascivious thoughts with which it had been occupied. He swung his legs to the floor and slid out from under the bedclothes in a single, fluid movement; then silently crossed the room to stand beside the window in the darkest corner, the stiletto knife in his hand.

He heard the door open, heard the intruder step inside, heard the door close again. At that point he started to think, for an assassin would have left the door open for a quick getaway, and it occurred to him that there were a hundred reasons why it was impossible that an assassin should have found him here.

He ignored the thought, for he had survived this long by catering for the one-in-a-thousand chance. The wind dropped momentarily, and he heard an indrawn breath, a faint gasp, from beside his bed, enabling him to locate the intruder's exact position. He sprang.

He had her on the bed, face down, with his knife at her throat and his knee in the small of her back, before he realized that the intruder was a woman. A split-second later he guessed her identity. He eased his grip, reached out to the bedside table, and switched on the light.

Her face was pale in the dim glow of the lamp.

Faber sheathed the knife before she could see it. He took his weight off her body. 'I'm awfully sorry,' he said.

She turned on to her back and looked up at him as he straddled her. She began to giggle.

Faber added: 'I thought you were a burglar.'

'And where would a burglar come from?' she laughed. The colour rushed back to her cheeks in a blush.

She was wearing a very loose, old-fashioned flannel nightgown which covered her from her throat to her ankles. Her dark-red hair spread across Faber's pillow in disarray. Her eyes seemed very large, and her lips were moist.

'You are remarkably beautiful,' Faber said quietly.

She closed her eyes.

Faber bent over her and kissed her mouth. Her lips parted immediately, and she returned his kiss hungrily. With his fingertips he stroked her shoulders, her neck and her ears. She moved beneath him.

He wanted to kiss her for a long time, to explore her mouth and savour the intimacy; but he realized that she had no time for tenderness. She reached inside his pyjama trousers and squeezed. She moaned softly and began to breathe hard.

Still kissing her, Faber reached for the light and killed it. He pulled away from her and took off his pyjama jacket. Quickly, so that she would not wonder what he was doing, he tugged at the can stuck to his chest, ignoring the sting as the sticky tape was jerked away from his skin. He slid the photographs under the bed. He also unbuttoned the sheath on his left forearm and dropped that.

He pushed the skirt of her nightdress up to her waist. She wore nothing underneath.

'Quickly,' she said. 'Quickly.'

Faber lowered his body to hers.

Lucy did not feel the least bit guilty afterwards. She just felt content, satisfied, replete. She had had what she wanted, and she was glad. She lay still, eyes closed, stroking the bristly hair at the back of Henry's neck, enjoying the rough tickling sensation on her hands.

After a while she said: 'I was in such a rush . . .'

'It's not over yet,' he murmured.

She frowned in the dark. 'Didn't you . . . ?'

'No, I didn't. You hardly did.'

She smiled. 'I beg to differ.'

He turned on the light and looked at her. 'We'll see.'

He slipped down the bed, his torso between her thighs, and kissed her belly. His tongue flicked in and out of her navel. It was quite nice. Then his head went lower. Surely, she thought, he doesn't want to kiss me *there*. He did. And he did more than kiss. His lips pulled at the soft folds of her skin. She was paralysed by shock as his tongue began to probe in the crevices and then, as he parted her lips with his fingers, to thrust deep inside her.

Finally his restless tongue found a tiny, sensitive place, so small she had not known it existed, so sensitive that his touch was almost painful at first. She forgot her shock as she was overwhelmed by the most piercing sensation she had ever experienced. Unable to restrain herself, she moved her hips up and down, faster and faster, rubbing her slippery flesh over his mouth, his chin, his nose, his forehead; totally absorbed in her own pleasure. The thrill built and built, like feedback in a microphone, feeding upon itself, until she felt utterly possessed by joy and opened her mouth to scream, whereupon Henry clapped his hand over her face to quiet her; but she screamed in her throat as the climax went on and on, ending in something that felt like an explosion and left her so drained that she thought she would never get up.

Her mind seemed to go blank for a while. She knew

vaguely that Henry still lay between her legs, his bristly cheek against the soft inside of her thigh, his lips moving gently, affectionately.

Eventually she said: 'Now I *know* what Lawrence means.'

He lifted his head. 'I don't understand.'

She sighed. 'I didn't realize it could be like that. It was lovely.'

'*Was?*'

'Oh, God, I've no more energy . . .'

He changed position, kneeling astride her chest, and she realized what he wanted her to do, and for the second time she was frozen by shock: it was just too *big* . . . but suddenly she *wanted* to do it, she *needed* to take him into her mouth; so she lifted her head, and her lips closed around him, and he gave a soft groan.

He held her head in his hands, moving it to and fro, moaning quietly. She looked at his face. He was staring wild-eyed at her, drinking in the sight of what she was doing. She wondered what she would do when he . . . *came* . . . and she decided she didn't care, because everything else had been so good with him that she knew she would enjoy even that.

But it was not to be. When she thought he was on the point of losing control he stopped, moved away, lay on top of her, and entered her again. This time it was very slow and relaxed, like the rhythm of the sea on the beach; until he put his hands under her hips and grasped the globes of her bottom, and she looked at his face and knew that now, now he was ready to shed his self-control and lose himself in her. That excited her more than anything, so that when at last he arched his back, his face screwed up into a mask of pain, and groaned deep in his chest, she wrapped her legs around his waist and abandoned herself to ecstasy; and then, after so long, she heard the trumpets and thunder-storms and the clash of cymbals that Lawrence had promised.

They were quiet for a long time. Lucy felt warm, as if she were glowing; she had never felt so warm in all her time on the island. When their breathing subsided she could hear the storm outside. Henry was heavy on top of her, but she did not want him to move: she liked his weight, and the faint tang of perspiration from his white skin. From time to time he moved his head to brush his lips against her cheek.

He was the perfect man to have an affair with. He knew more about her body than she did. His own body was very beautiful: broad and muscular at the shoulders, narrow at the waist and hips, with long, strong, hairy legs. She thought he had some scars: she was not sure. Strong, gentle and handsome: perfect. Yet she knew she would never fall in love with him, never want to run away with him and marry him. Deep inside him, she sensed, there was something very cold and hard, some part of him that was committed elsewhere, a readiness to abandon commonplace emotions for some higher duty. He would never belong to any woman, for he had some other ultimate loyalty – like a painter's art, a businessman's greed, a patriot's country, a socialist's revolution. She would have to hold him at arm's length, and use him cautiously, like an addictive drug.

Not that she would have time to get hooked: he would be gone in little more than a day.

She stirred at last, and immediately he rolled off her and on to his back. She lifted herself on one elbow and looked at his naked body. Yes, he did have scars: a long one on his chest, and a small mark like a star – it might have been a burn – on his hip. She rubbed his chest with the palm of her hand.

'It's not very ladylike,' she said, 'but I want to say thank you.'

He reached out to touch her cheek, and smiled. 'You're very ladylike.'

'You don't know what you've done. You've—'

He put a finger over her lips. 'I know what I've done.'

She bit his finger, then put his hand on her breast. He felt for her nipple. She said: 'Please do it again.'

'I don't think I can,' he said.

But he did.

She left him a couple of hours after dawn. There was a small noise from the other bedroom, and she seemed suddenly to remember that she had a husband and a son in the house. Faber wanted to tell her that it didn't matter, that neither he nor she had the least reason to care what the husband knew or thought; but he held his tongue and let her go. She kissed him once more, very wetly; then she stood up, smoothed her rumpled nightgown over her body, and tiptoed out. He watched her fondly.

She's quite something, he thought. He lay on his back and looked at the ceiling. She was quite naive, and very inexperienced, but all the same she had been very good. I could fall in love with her, he thought.

He got up and retrieved the film can and the knife in its sheath from under the bed. He wondered whether to keep them on his person. He might want to make love to her in the day . . . He decided to wear the knife – he would feel undressed without it – and leave the can somewhere. He put it on top of the chest-of-drawers and covered it with his papers and his wallet. He knew that he was breaking all the rules; but this was sure to be his last assignment, and he felt entitled to enjoy a woman. It would hardly matter if someone saw the pictures – what could they do?

He lay down on the bed, then got up again. Years of training would not let him take risks. He put the can and his papers into the pocket of his jacket. Now he could relax.

He heard the child's voice, then Lucy's tread as she went down the stairs, and then David dragging himself to the bathroom. He would have to get up and have breakfast with the household. He did not want to sleep now, anyway.

He stood at the rain-streaked window, watching the weather rage, until he heard the bathroom door open. Then he put on his pyjama jacket and went in to shave. He used David's razor, without permission.

It did not seem to matter now.

TWENTY-FOUR

Erwin Rommel knew from the start that he was going to quarrel with Heinz Guderian.

General Guderian was exactly the kind of aristocratic Prussian officer Rommel hated. He had known him for some time. They had both, in their early days, commanded the Goslar Jaeger Battalion, and they had met again during the Polish campaign. When Rommel left Africa he had recommended Guderian to succeed him, knowing the battle was lost: the manoeuvre was a failure because at that time Guderian had been out of favour with Hitler and the recommendation was rejected out of hand.

The General was, Rommel felt, the kind of man who put a silk handkerchief on his knee to protect the crease in his trousers as he sat drinking in the Herrenklub. He was an officer because his father had been an officer and his grandfather had been rich. Rommel, the schoolteacher's son who had risen from Lieutenant-Colonel to Field Marshal in only four years, despised the military caste of which he had never been a member.

Now he stared across the table at the General, who was sipping brandy appropriated from the French

Rothschilds. Guderian and his sidekick, General von Geyr, had come to Rommel's headquarters at La Roche Guyon in Northern France to tell him how to deploy his troops. Rommel's reactions to such visits ranged from impatience to fury. In his view the General Staff were there to provide reliable intelligence and regular supplies, and he knew from his experience in Africa that they were incompetent at both tasks.

Guderian had a cropped, fair moustache, and the corners of his eyes were heavily wrinkled so that he always appeared to be grinning at you. He was tall and handsome, which did nothing to endear him to the short, ugly, balding Rommel. He seemed relaxed, and any German general who could relax at this stage of the war was surely a fool. The meal they had just finished – local veal and wine from farther south – was no excuse.

Rommel looked out of the window and watched the rain dripping from the lime trees into the courtyard while he waited for Guderian to begin the discussion. When eventually he spoke, it was clear the General had been thinking about the best way to make his point, and had decided to approach it sideways.

'In Turkey,' he began, 'the British 9th and 10th armies, with the Turkish army, are grouping at the border with Greece. In Yugoslavia, the partisans are also concentrating. The French in Algeria are preparing to invade the Riviera. The Russians appear to be mounting an amphibious invasion of Sweden. In Italy, the Allies are ready to march on Rome.

'There are smaller signals: a general kidnapped in

Crete; an Intelligence officer murdered at Lyon; a radar post attacked at Rhodes; an aircraft sabotaged with abrasive grease and destroyed at Athens; a commando raid on Sagvaag; an explosion in the oxygen factory at Boulogne-sur-Seine; a train derailed in the Ardennes; a petrol dump fired at Boussens . . . I could go on.

'The picture is clear. In occupied territories, there is ever-increasing sabotage and treachery; on our borders, everywhere we see preparations for invasion. None of us doubts that there will be a major Allied offensive this summer; and we can be equally sure that all this skirmishing is intended to confuse us about where the attack will come.'

The General paused. The lecture, delivered in schoolmaster style, was irritating Rommel, and he took the opportunity to interrupt. 'This is why we have a General Staff: to digest such information, produce appreciations of enemy activity, and forecast his future moves.'

Guderian smiled indulgently. 'We must also be aware of the limitations of such crystal-gazing. You have your ideas about where the attack will come, I'm sure: we all do. Our strategy must take into account the possibility that our guesses are wrong.'

Rommel now saw where the General's roundabout argument was leading, and he suppressed the urge to shout his disagreement before the conclusion was stated.

'You have four armoured divisions under your command,' Guderian continued. 'The 2nd Panzers at Amiens; the 116th at Rouen; the 21st at Caen; and the

2nd SS at Toulouse. General von Geyr has already proposed to you that these should be grouped well back from the coast, all together, ready for fast retaliation at any point. Indeed, this stratagem is a principle of OKW policy. Nevertheless, you have not only resisted von Geyr's suggestion, but have in fact moved the 21st right up to the Atlantic coast.'

'And the other three must be moved to the coast as soon as possible,' Rommel burst out. 'When will you people learn? *The Allies rule the air.* Once the invasion is launched there will be no further major movements of armour. Mobile operations are no longer possible. If your precious panzers are in Paris when the Allies land on the coast, they will *stay* in Paris – pinned down by the RAF – until the Allies march along the Boulevard St Michel. I *know* – they've done it to me. Twice!' He paused to draw breath. 'To group our armour as a mobile reserve is to render it useless. There will be no counter-attack. The invasion must be met on the beaches, when it is most vulnerable, and pushed back into the sea.'

The flush receded from his face as he began to expound his own defensive strategy. 'I have created underwater obstacles, strengthened the Atlantic Wall, laid minefields, and driven stakes into every meadow that might be used to land airplanes behind our lines. All my troops are engaged in digging defences whenever they're not actually training.

'My armoured divisions must be moved to the coast. The OKW reserve should be redeployed in France. The 9th and 10th SS divisions have to be brought back from the Eastern Front. Our whole strategy must be to prevent the Allies from securing a beachhead, for once they achieve that, the battle is lost . . . perhaps even the war.'

Guderian leaned forward, his eyes narrowing in that infuriating half-grin. 'You want us to defend the European coastline from Tromso in Norway all around the Iberian Peninsula to Rome. From where shall we get the armies?'

'That question should have been asked in 1938,' Rommel muttered.

There was an embarrassed silence after this remark, which was all the more shocking coming from the notoriously apolitical Rommel.

Von Geyr broke the spell. 'Where do *you* believe the attack will come, Field-Marshal?'

Rommel considered. 'Until recently I was convinced of the Pas de Calais theory. However, last time I was with the Führer I was impressed by his arguments in favour of Normandy. I am also impressed by his instinct, and its record of accuracy. Therefore I believe our panzers should be deployed primarily along the Normandy coast, with perhaps one division at the mouth of the Somme – this last supported by forces outside my group.'

Guderian shook his head solemnly. 'No, no, no. It's far too risky.'

'I'm prepared to take this argument to Hitler himself,' Rommel threatened.

'Then that's what you must do,' Guderian said resignedly, 'for I shan't assent to your plan, unless . . .'

'Well?' Rommel was surprised that the General's position might be qualified.

Guderian shifted in his seat, reluctant to give a concession to so obdurate an antagonist as Rommel. 'You may know that the Führer is waiting for a report from an unusually effective agent in England.'

'I remember,' Rommel nodded. 'Die Nadel.'

'Yes. He has been assigned to assess the strength of the First United States Army Group under Patton's command in the eastern part of England. If he finds – as I am certain he will – that that army is large, strong, and ready to move, then I shall continue to oppose you. However, if he finds that FUSAG is a bluff – a small army masquerading as an invasion force – then I shall concede that you are right, and you shall have your panzers. Will you accept that compromise?'

Rommel bowed his large head in assent. 'It all depends on Die Nadel, then.'

'It all depends on Die Nadel.'

PART FIVE

TWENTY-FIVE

The cottage was terribly small, Lucy realized quite suddenly. As she went about her morning chores – lighting the stove, making porridge, tidying up, dressing Jo – the walls seemed to press in on her claustrophobically. After all, it was only four rooms, linked by a little passage with a staircase; you couldn't move without bumping into someone else. If you stood still and listened you could hear what everyone was doing: Henry running water into the wash-basin, David sliding down the stairs, Jo chastising his teddy-bear in the living-room. Lucy would have liked some time on her own before meeting people: time to let the events of the night settle into her memory, recede from the forefront of her thoughts, so that she could act normally without a conscious effort.

She guessed she was not going to be good at deception. It did not come naturally to her. She had no experience of it. She tried to think of another occasion in her life when she had deceived someone close to her, and she could not. It was not that she lived by very high principles – the *thought* of lying did not trouble her. It was just that she had never had reason for dishonesty. Does that mean, she wondered, that I've led a sheltered life?

David and Jo sat down at the kitchen table and began to eat. David was silent, Jo talked non-stop just for the pleasure of making words. Lucy did not want food.

'Aren't you eating?' David said casually.

'I've had some.' There – her first lie. It wasn't so bad.

The storm made the claustrophobia worse. The rain was so heavy that Lucy could hardly see the barn from the kitchen window. One felt even more shut-in when to open a door or window was a major operation. The low, steel-grey sky and the wisps of mist created a permanent twilight. In the garden, the rain ran in rivers between the rows of potato plants, and the herb patch was a shallow pond. The sparrow's nest under the outhouse roof had been washed away, and the birds flitted in and out of the eaves, panicking.

Lucy heard Henry coming down the stairs, and she felt better. For some reason, she was quite sure that he was very good at deception.

'Good morning!' Faber said heartily. David, sitting at the table in his wheelchair, looked up and smiled. Lucy busied herself at the stove. There was guilt written all over her face. Faber groaned inwardly, but David did not seem to notice her expression. Faber began to think that David was an oaf.

Lucy said: 'Sit down and have some breakfast, Henry.'

'Thank you very much.'

David said: 'Can't offer to take you to church, I'm

afraid. Hymn-singing on the wireless is the best we can do.'

Faber realized it was Sunday. 'Are you churchgoing people?'

'No,' David said. 'You?'

'No.'

'Sunday is much the same as any other day for farmers,' David continued. 'I'll be driving over to the other end of the island to see my shepherd. You could come, if you feel up to it.'

'I'd like to,' Faber told him. It would give him a chance to reconnoitre. He would need to know the way to the cottage with the transmitter. 'Would you like me to drive you?'

David looked at him sharply. 'I can manage quite well.' There was a strained moment of silence. 'In this weather, the road is just a memory. We'll be a lot safer with me at the wheel.'

'Of course.' Faber began to eat.

'It makes no difference to me,' David persisted. 'I don't want you to come if you think it would be too much—'

'Really, I'd be glad to.'

'Did you sleep all right? It didn't occur to me you might still be tired. I hope Lucy didn't keep you up late.'

Faber willed himself not to look at Lucy. Out of the corner of his eye he could see that she was blushing to the roots of her hair. 'I slept all day yesterday,' he said, trying to fix David's eyes with his own.

It was no use. David was looking at his wife. She

turned her back. The trace of a frown creased his forehead, and then just for a moment, his jaw dropped open in a classic expression of surprise.

Faber was mildly annoyed. David would be hostile now, and antagonism was half way to suspicion. It was not dangerous, but it might be tiresome.

The husband recovered his composure quickly. He pushed his chair away from the table and wheeled himself to the back door. 'I'll get the jeep out of the barn,' he muttered. He took an oilskin off a hook and put it over his head, then opened the door and rolled out.

In the few moments the door was open, the storm blew into the little kitchen, leaving the floor wet and the people cold. When it shut, Lucy shivered and began to mop the water from the tiles.

Faber reached out and touched her arm.

'Don't,' she said, jerking her head toward Jo in warning.

'You're being silly,' Faber told her.

'I think he knows,' she said.

'But, if you reflect for a minute, you don't really care whether he knows or not, do you?'

She considered. 'I'm not supposed to.'

Faber shrugged. The jeep's horn sounded impatiently outside. Lucy handed him an oilskin and a pair of wellington boots.

'Don't talk about me,' she said.

Faber put on the waterproof clothes and went to the front door. Lucy followed him, closing the kitchen door on Jo.

With his hand on the latch, Faber turned and kissed her.

She kissed him back, forcefully, then turned and went into the kitchen.

Faber dashed through the rain, across a sea of mud, and jumped into the jeep beside David. He pulled away immediately.

The vehicle had been specially adapted for the legless man to drive. It had a hand throttle, automatic gearshift, and a handle on the rim of the wheel to enable the driver to steer one-handed. The folded-up wheelchair slid into a special compartment behind the driver's seat. There was a shotgun in a rack above the windscreen.

David drove competently. He had been right about the road: it was no more than a strip of heath worn bare by the jeep's tyres. The rain pooled in the deep ruts. The car slithered about in the mud. David seemed to enjoy it. There was a cigarette between his lips, and he wore an incongruous air of bravado. Perhaps this was his substitute for flying.

'What do you do when you're not fishing?' he said around the cigarette.

'Civil servant,' Faber told him.

'What sort of work?'

'Finance. I'm just a cog in the machine.'

'Treasury, eh?'

'Mainly.'

Even that asinine answer did not stop David's questioning. 'Interesting work?' he persisted.

'Fairly.' Faber summoned up the energy to invent a

story. 'I know a bit about how much a given piece of engineering ought to cost, and I spend most of my time making sure the taxpayer isn't being overcharged.'

'Any particular sort of engineering?'

'Everything from paper clips to aircraft engines.'

'Ah, well. We all contribute to the war effort in our own way.'

It was a snide remark, and David would naturally have no idea why Faber did not resent it. 'I'm too old to fight,' Faber said mildly.

'Were you in the first lot?'

'Too young.'

'A lucky escape.'

'Doubtless.'

The track ran quite close to the cliff edge, but David did not slow down. It crossed Faber's mind that he might want to kill them both. He reached for a grab handle.

'Am I going too fast for you?' David asked.

'You seem to know the road,' Faber replied.

'You looked frightened,' David said.

Faber ignored that, and David slowed down a little, apparently satisfied that he had made some kind of point.

The island was fairly flat, and bare, Faber observed. The ground rose and fell slightly, but as yet he had seen no hills. The vegetation was mostly grass, with some ferns and bushes, but few trees: there was little protection from the weather. David Rose's sheep must be hardy, he thought.

'Are you married?' David asked suddenly.

'No.'

'Wise man.'

'Oh, I don't know.'

'I'll bet you put yourself about a bit up in London,' David leered.

Faber had never liked the nudging, contemptuous way some men talked about women. He said sharply: 'I should think you're extremely fortunate to have Lucy.'

'Oh, would you.'

'Yes.'

'Nothing like variety, though, eh?'

Faber thought: What the devil is he getting at? He said: 'I haven't had the chance to discover the merits of monogamy.'

'Quite.'

Faber thought: *He* doesn't know what he's getting at, either. He decided to say no more, since everything he said was fuel to the fire.

'I must say, you don't *look* like a Government accountant. Where's the rolled umbrella and the bowler hat?'

Faber tried a thin smile.

'And you seem quite fit for a pen-pusher.'

'I ride a bicycle.'

'You must be quite tough, to have survived that wreck.'

'Thank you.'

'You don't *look* too old to be in the Army, either.'

Faber turned his gaze on David. 'What are you driving at, David?' he asked calmly.

'We're there,' David said.

Faber looked out of the windscreen and saw a

cottage very similar to Lucy's, with stone walls, a slate roof, and small windows. It stood at the top of a hill, the only hill Faber had seen on the island, and not much of a hill at that. The house had a squat, resilient look about it. Climbing up to it, the jeep skirted a small stand of pine and fir trees. Faber wondered why the cottage had not been built in the shelter of the trees.

Beside the house was a hawthorn tree in bedraggled blossom. David stopped the car. Faber watched him unfold the wheelchair and ease himself out of the driving seat into the chair: he would have resented an offer of help.

They entered the house by a plank door with no lock. They were greeted in the hall by a black-and-white collie, a small, broad-headed dog who wagged his tail but did not bark. The layout of the cottage was identical with that of Lucy's, but the atmosphere was different: this place was bare, cheerless, and none too clean.

David led the way into the kitchen. The shepherd sat by an old-fashioned wood-burning kitchen range, warming his hands. He stood up.

David said: 'Henry, this is Tom McAvity.'

'Pleased to meet you,' Tom said formally.

Faber shook his hand. He was a short man, and broad, with a face like an old tan suitcase. He was wearing a cloth cap and smoking a very large briar pipe with a lid. His grip was firm, and the skin of his hand felt like sandpaper. He had a very big nose. Faber had to concentrate hard to understand what he was saying: his Scots accent was very broad.

'I hope I'm not going to be in the way,' Faber said. 'I only came along for the ride.'

David wheeled himself up to the table. 'I don't suppose we'll do much this morning, Tom – just take a look around.'

'Aye. We'll have some tay before we go, though.'

Tom poured strong tea into three mugs, and added a shot of whisky to each. The three men sat and sipped it in silence, David smoking a cigarette and Tom drawing gently at his pipe, and Faber felt certain that the other two spent a great deal of time together in this way, smoking and warming their hands and saying nothing.

When they had finished their tea Tom put the mugs in the shallow stone sink and they went out in the jeep. Faber sat in the back. David drove slowly this time, and the dog, which was called Bob, loped alongside, keeping pace without apparent effort. It was obvious that David knew the terrain very well, for he steered confidently across the open grassland without once getting bogged down in swampy ground. The sheep looked very sorry for themselves. With their fleeces sopping wet, they huddled in hollows, or close to bramble bushes, or on the leeward slopes, too dispirited to graze. Even the lambs were subdued, hiding beneath their mothers.

Faber was watching the dog when it stopped, listened for a moment, and then raced off at a tangent.

Tom had been watching, too. 'Bob's found something,' he said.

The jeep followed the dog for a quarter of a mile. When they stopped Faber could hear the sea: they were close to the island's northern edge. The dog was standing at the brink of a small gully. When the men got out of the car they could hear what the dog had heard: the bleating of a sheep in distress. They went to the edge of the gully and looked down.

The animal lay on its side about twenty feet down, balanced precariously on the steeply sloping bank. It held one foreleg at an awkward angle. Tom went down to it, treading cautiously, and examined the leg.

'Mutton tonight,' he called.

David got the gun from the jeep and slid it down to him. Tom put the sheep out of its misery.

'Do you want to rope it up?' David called.

'Aye – unless Henry wants to come and give me a hand.'

'Surely,' Faber said. He picked his way down to where Tom stood. They took a leg each and dragged the dead animal back up the slope. Faber's oilskin caught on a thorny bush, and he almost fell before he tugged the material free with a loud ripping sound.

They threw the sheep into the jeep and drove on. Faber felt very wet, and he realized he had torn away most of the back of the oilskin. 'I'm afraid I've ruined this garment,' he said.

'All in a good cause,' Tom told him.

Soon they returned to Tom's cottage. Faber took off

the oilskin and his wet donkey jacket, and Tom put the jacket over the stove to dry. Then each went to the outhouse – Tom's cottage did not have the modern plumbing that had been added to Lucy's – and Tom made more tea.

'She's the first we've lost this year,' David said.

'Aye.'

'We'll fence the gully this summer.'

'Aye.'

Faber sensed a change in the atmosphere: it was not the same as it had been two or three hours earlier. They sat, drinking and smoking as before, but David seemed restless. Twice Faber caught the man staring at him, deep in thought.

Eventually David said: 'We'll leave you to butcher the ewe, Tom.'

'Aye.'

David and Faber left. Tom did not get up, but the dog saw them to the door.

Before starting the jeep David took the shotgun from its rack above the windscreen, reloaded it, and put it back.

On the way home he underwent another change of mood and became chatty. 'I used to fly Spitfires, you know. Lovely kites. Four guns in each wing – American Brownings, they were, firing one thousand two hundred and sixty rounds a minute. The Jerries prefer cannon, of course – their Me 109s only have two machine guns. A cannon does more damage, but our Brownings are faster, and more accurate.'

'Really?' Faber said politely.

'They put cannon in the Hurricanes later, but it was the Spitfire that won the Battle of Britain.'

Faber found his boastfulness irritating. He said: 'How many enemy aircraft did you shoot down?'

'I lost my legs while I was training,' David said.

Faber stole a glance at his face: it was a mask of repressed fury.

David said: 'No, I haven't killed a single German, yet.'

It was an unmistakable signal. Faber suddenly became very alert. He had no idea what David might have deduced or discovered, but there could be no doubt that the man knew something was up. Faber turned slightly sideways to face David, braced himself with his foot against the transmission tunnel on the floor, and rested his right hand lightly on his left forearm. He waited for David's next move.

'Are you interested in aircraft?' David asked.

'No.' Faber's voice was flat.

'It's become a national pastime, I gather – aircraft spotting. Like bird-watching. People buy books on aircraft identification. Spend whole afternoons on their backs, looking at the sky through telescopes. I thought you might be an enthusiast.'

'Why?'

'Pardon?'

'What made you think I might be an enthusiast?'

'Oh, I don't know.' David stopped the jeep to light a cigarette. They were at the island's mid-point, five miles from Tom's cottage with another five miles to go to

Lucy's. David dropped the match on the floor. 'Perhaps it was the photographs that fell out of your jacket pocket—'

As he spoke, he tossed the lighted cigarette at Faber's face, and reached for the gun above the windscreen.

TWENTY-SIX

Sid Cripps looked out of the window and cursed under his breath. The meadow was full of American tanks – at least eighty of them. He realized there was a war on, and all that, but if only they'd asked him he would have offered them another field, where the grass was not so lush. By now the caterpillar tracks would have chewed up his best grazing.

He pulled on his boots and went out. There were some Yank soldiers in the field, and he wondered whether they had noticed the bull. When he got to the stile he stopped and scratched his head. There was something very funny going on.

The tanks had *not* chewed up his grass. They had left no tracks. But the American soldiers were *making* tank tracks with a tool something like a harrow.

While Sid was trying to figure it all out, the bull noticed the tanks. It stared at them for a while, then pawed the ground and lumbered into a run. It was going to charge a tank.

'Daft bugger, you'll break your head,' Sid muttered.

The soldiers were watching the bull, too. They seemed to think it was funny.

The bull ran full-tilt into the tank, its horns piercing the armour-plated side of the vehicle. Sid hoped fervently that British tanks were stronger than the American ones.

There was a loud hissing noise as the bull worked its horns free. The tank collapsed like a deflated balloon. The American soldiers fell about laughing.

Sid Cripps scratched his head again. It was all very strange.

Percival Godliman walked quickly across Parliament Square, carrying an umbrella. He wore a dark striped suit under his raincoat, and his black shoes were highly polished – at least, they had been until he stepped out into the rain – for it was not every day, come to that it was not every year, that he had a private audience with Churchill.

A career soldier would have been nervous at going with such bad news to see the supreme commander of the nation's armed forces. Godliman was not nervous, for a distinguished historian has nothing to fear from soldiers and politicians, not unless his view of history is a good deal more radical than Godliman's was. Not nervous, then; but he was worried.

He was thinking about the effort, the forethought, the care, the money and the manpower that had gone into the creation of the totally phoney First United States Army Group stationed in East Anglia: the four hundred landing ships, made of canvas and scaffolding floated on oil drums, which thronged the harbours and estuaries; the carefully manufactured inflatable dummies of tanks, artillery, trucks, half-tracks and even ammunition dumps; the complaints planted in the correspondence columns of the local newspapers about the decline in moral standards since the arrival of thousands of American troops in the area; the phoney oil dock at Dover, designed by Britain's most distinguished architect and built – out of cardboard and old sewage pipes – by craftsmen borrowed from film studios; the carefully faked reports transmitted to Hamburg by German agents who had been 'turned' by the XX Committee; and the incessant radio chatter, broadcast solely for the benefit of the German listening posts, consisting of messages compiled by professional writers of fiction, and including such gems as 'I/5th Queen's Royal Regiment report a number of civilian women, presumably unauthorized, in the baggage train. What are we going to do with them – take them to Calais?'

A lot had been achieved. The signs were that the Germans had fallen for it. And now the whole elaborate deception had been placed in jeopardy because of one spy – a spy Godliman had failed to catch.

His short, birdlike paces measured the Westminster pavement to the small doorway at No 2, Great George Street. The armed guard standing beside the wall of sandbags examined his pass and waved him in. He crossed the lobby and went down the stairs to Churchill's underground headquarters.

It was like going below decks on a battleship. Protected from bombs by a four-foot-thick ceiling of reinforced concrete, the command post featured steel bulkhead doors and roof props of ancient timber. As

Godliman entered the map room a cluster of youngish people with solemn faces emerged from the conference room beyond. An aide followed them a moment later, and spotted Godliman.

'You're very punctual, sir,' the aide said. 'He's ready for you.'

Godliman stepped into the small, comfortable conference room. There were rugs on the floor and a portrait of the King on the wall. An electric fan stirred the tobacco smoke in the air. Churchill sat at the head of an old, mirror-smooth table in the centre of which was a statuette of a faun – the emblem of Churchill's own deception outfit, the London Controlling Section.

Godliman decided not to salute.

Churchill said: 'Sit down, Professor.'

Godliman suddenly realized that Churchill was not a big man – but he *sat* like a big man: shoulders hunched, elbows on the arms of his chair, chin lowered, legs apart. Instead of the famous siren suit he was wearing a solicitor's black-and-stripes – short black jacket and striped grey trousers – with a spotted blue bow tie and a brilliant-white shirt. Despite his stocky frame and his paunch, the hand holding the fountain pen was delicate, thin-fingered. His complexion was baby-pink. The other hand held a cigar, and on the table beside the papers stood a glass containing what looked like whisky.

He was making notes in the margin of a typewritten report, and as he scribbled he muttered occasionally. Godliman was not in the least awed by the great man. As a peacetime statesman Churchill had been, in Godliman's view, a disaster. However, the man had the qualities of a great warrior chieftain, and Godliman respected him for that. (Years later, Churchill modestly denied having been the British lion, saying that he had merely been privileged to give the roar: Godliman thought that assessment was just about right.)

He looked up abruptly and said: 'I suppose there's no doubt this damned spy has discovered what we're up to?'

'None whatsoever, sir,' Godliman said.

'You think he's got away?'

'We chased him to Aberdeen. It's almost certain that he left there two nights ago in a stolen boat – presumably for a rendezvous in the North Sea. However, he can't have been far out of port when the storm blew up. He may have met the U-boat before the storm hit, but it's unlikely. In all probability he drowned. I'm sorry we can't offer more definite information.'

'So am I,' Churchill said. Suddenly he seemed angry, though not with Godliman. He got out of his chair and went over to the clock on the wall, staring as if mesmerized at the inscription *Victoria RI, Ministry of Works, 1889.* Then, as if he had forgotten that Godliman was there, he began to pace up and down alongside the table, muttering to himself. Godliman was able to make out the words, and what he heard astonished him. The great man was mumbling: 'This stocky figure, with a slight stoop, striding up and down, suddenly unconscious of any presence beyond his own thoughts . . .' It was as if Churchill were acting out a Hollywood screenplay which he wrote as he went along.

The performance ended as abruptly as it had begun,

and if the man knew he had been behaving eccentrically, he gave no sign of it. He sat down, handed Godliman a sheet of paper, and said: 'This is the German order of battle as of last week.'

Godliman read:

Russian front:	*122*	*infantry divisions*
	25	*panzer divisions*
	17	*miscellaneous divisions*
Italy & Balkans:	*37*	*infantry divisions*
	9	*panzer divisions*
	4	*miscellaneous divisions*
Western front:	*64*	*infantry divisions*
	12	*panzer divisions*
	12	*miscellaneous divisions*
Germany:	*3*	*infantry divisions*
	1	*panzer division*
	4	*miscellaneous divisions*

Churchill said: 'Of those twelve panzer divisions in the west, only *one* is actually on the Normandy coast. The great SS divisions, *Das Reich* and *Adolf Hitler*, are at Toulouse and Brussels respectively and show no signs of moving. What does all this tell you, Professor?'

'Our deception and cover plans seem to have been successful,' Godliman answered.

'Totally!' Churchill barked. 'They are confused and uncertain, and their best guesses about our intentions are wildly wrong. And yet!' He paused for effect. 'And yet, despite all that, General Walter Bedell Smith – Ike's Chief of Staff – tells me that . . .' He picked up another piece of paper from the table and read it aloud. 'Our chances of holding the beachhead, particularly after the Germans get their buildup, are only fifty-fifty.'

He put his cigar down, and his voice became quite soft. 'It will be June the fifth – possibly the sixth or the seventh. The tides are right . . . it has been decided. The build-up of troops in the West Country has already begun. The convoys are even now making their way along the country roads of England. It has taken the total military and industrial might of the whole English-speaking world – the greatest civilization since the Roman Empire – four years to win this fifty-fifty chance. If this spy gets out, we lose even that.'

He stared at Godliman for a moment, then he picked up his pen with a frail white hand. 'Don't bring me probabilities, Professor,' he said. 'Bring me the body of Die Nadel.'

He looked down and began to write. After a moment Percival Godliman got up and quietly left the room.

TWENTY-SEVEN

Cigarette tobacco burns at eight hundred degrees centigrade. However, the coal at the end of the cigarette is normally surrounded by a thin layer of ash. To cause a burn, the cigarette has to be pressed against the skin for the better part of a second: a glancing touch will hardly be felt. This applies even to the eyes, for blinking is the fastest involuntary reaction of the human body. Only amateurs throw cigarettes. Professionals – there are just a few people in the world for whom hand-to-hand fighting is a professional skill – ignore them.

Faber ignored the lighted cigarette that David Rose threw at him. He did right, for the cigarette glanced off his forehead and fell to the metal floor of the jeep. Then he made a grab for David's gun, and this was an error. He should have drawn his stiletto and stabbed David: for although David *might* have shot him first, he had never before pointed a gun at a human being, let alone killed somebody; so he would almost certainly have hesitated, and in that moment Faber could have killed him.

The mistake cost dear.

David had both hands on the midsection of the gun

– left hand on the barrel, right hand around the breech – and had pulled the weapon about six inches from its rack when Faber got a one-handed grip on the muzzle. David tugged the gun toward himself, but for a moment Faber's grasp held, and the gun pointed at the windscreen.

Faber was a strong man, but David was exceptionally strong. His shoulders, arms and wrists had moved his body and his wheelchair for four years, and the muscles had become abnormally developed. Furthermore, he had both hands on the gun in front of him, and Faber was holding on with one hand at an awkward angle. David tugged again, more determinedly this time, and the muzzle slipped from Faber's grasp.

At that instant, with the shotgun pointed at his belly and David's finger curling around the trigger, Faber felt very close to death.

He jerked upwards, catapulting himself out of his seat. His head hit the canvas roof of the jeep as the gun exploded with a crash that numbed the ears and produced a physical pain behind the eyes. The window by the passenger seat shattered into innumerable small pieces and the rain blew in through the empty frame. Faber twisted his body and fell back, not on to his own seat, but across David. He got both hands to David's throat and squeezed with his thumbs.

David tried to bring the gun around between their bodies to fire the other barrel, but the weapon was too big. Faber looked into his eyes, and saw . . . what was it? Exhilaration! Of course – at last the man had a chance to fight for his country. Then his expression changed as his body felt the lack of oxygen and he began to fight for breath.

David released his grip on the gun and brought both elbows back as far as he could, then punched Faber's lower ribs with a powerful double jab.

The pain was excruciating, and Faber screwed up his face in anguish, but he held his grip on David's throat. He knew he could withstand David's punches longer than David could hold his breath.

David must have had the same thought. He crossed his forearms between their bodies and pushed Faber away; then, when the gap was a few inches wide, he brought his hands up in an upward-and-outward blow against Faber's arms, breaking the stranglehold. He bunched his right fist and swung downwards with a mighty but unscientific punch which landed on Faber's cheekbone and brought water to his eyes.

Faber replied with a series of body jabs; David continued to bruise his face. They were too close together to do real damage to each other in a short time, but David's greater strength began to tell.

Grimly, Faber realized that David had shrewdly picked the time and place for the fight: he had had the advantages of surprise, the gun, and the confined space in which his muscle counted for much and Faber's better balance and greater manoeuvrability counted for little.

Faber shifted his weight slightly and his hip came into contact with the gearshift, throwing the transmission into forward. The engine was still running, and the car jerked, putting him off balance. David took the opportunity to release a long straight left which – more by luck than judgement – caught Faber full on the chin and threw him clear across the cab of the jeep. His head cracked against the A-post, he slumped with his shoulder on the door handle, the door opened, and he fell out of the car in a backward somersault to land on his face in the mud.

For a moment he was too dazed to move. When he opened his eyes he could see nothing but flashes of blue lightning against a misty red background. He heard the engine of the jeep racing. He shook his head, desperately trying to clear the fireworks from his vision, and struggled on to his hands and knees. The sound of the jeep receded and came closer again. He turned his head toward the noise, and as the colours in front of his eyes dissolved and disappeared, he saw the vehicle bearing down on him at high speed.

David was going to run him over.

With the front bumper less than a yard from his face he hurled himself sideways. He felt a blast of wind. A fender struck his outflung foot as the jeep roared past, its heavy-gauge tyres tearing up the spongy turf and spitting mud. He rolled over twice in the wet grass, then got to one knee. His foot hurt. He watched the jeep turn in a tight circle and come for him again.

He could see David's face through the windscreen. The young man was leaning forward, hunched over the steering wheel, his lips drawn back over his teeth in a savage, almost maniacal grin. He seemed to be imagining himself in the cockpit of a Spitfire, coming down out of the sun at an enemy plane with all eight Browning machine-guns blazing 1,260 rounds per minute.

Faber moved toward the cliff edge. The jeep gathered speed. Faber knew that, for a moment, he was incapable of running. He looked over the cliff: it was a rocky, almost vertical slope to the angry sea a hundred feet below. The jeep was coming straight down the cliff's edge toward him. Frantically, Faber looked up and down for a ledge, or even a foothold. There was none.

The jeep was four or five yards away, travelling at something like forty miles per hour. Its wheels were less than two feet from the cliff's edge. Faber dropped flat and swung his legs out into space, supporting his weight on his forearms as he hung on the brink.

The wheels passed him within inches. A few yards farther on, one tyre actually slipped over the edge. For a moment Faber thought the whole vehicle would slide over and fall into the sea below, but the other three wheels dragged the jeep to safety.

The ground under Faber's arms shifted. The vibration of the jeep's passing had loosened the earth. He felt himself slip a fraction. One hundred feet below, a raging sea boiled among the rocks. Faber stretched one arm to its farthest extent and dug his fingers deep into the soft ground. He felt a nail tear, and ignored it. He repeated the process with his other arm. With two hands anchored in the earth he pulled himself upward. It was agonizingly slow, but eventually his head drew level with his hands, his hips reached firm ground, and he was able to swivel around and roll away from the edge.

The jeep was turning again. Faber ran toward it. His foot was painful, but not broken. David accelerated for another pass. Faber turned and ran at right angles to the jeep's direction, forcing David to turn the wheel and consequently slow down.

Faber could not keep this up much longer. He was certain to tire before David. This had to be the last pass.

He ran faster. David steered an interception course, headed for a point in front of Faber. Faber doubled back, and the jeep zigzagged. It was now quite close. Faber broke into a sprint, his course compelling David to drive in a tight circle. The jeep was getting slower and Faber was getting closer. There were only a few yards between them when David realized what Faber was up to. He steered away, but it was too late. Faber raced to the jeep's side and threw himself upwards, landing face down on top of the canvas roof.

He lay there for a few seconds, catching his breath. His injured foot felt as if it was being held in a fire, and his lungs ached painfully.

The jeep was still moving. Faber drew the stiletto from its sheath under his sleeve and cut a long, jagged tear in the canvas roof. The material flapped downwards and Faber found himself staring at the back of David's head.

David looked up and back. A look of utter astonishment crossed his face. Faber drew back his arm for a knife thrust.

David jammed the throttle open and heaved the wheel around. The jeep leaped forward and lifted on two wheels as it screeched around in a tight curve. Faber struggled to stay on. The jeep, gathering speed still, crashed down on to four wheels then lifted again. It teetered precariously for a few yards, then the wheels slipped on the sodden ground and the vehicle toppled on to its side with a grinding crash.

Faber was thrown several yards and landed awkwardly. The breath was knocked out of him by the impact. It was several seconds before he could move.

The jeep's crazy course had taken it perilously close to the cliff once more.

Faber saw his knife in the grass a few yards away. He picked it up, then turned to the jeep.

Somehow, David had got himself and his wheelchair out through the ripped roof, and he was now sitting in the chair and pushing himself away along the cliff edge. Faber had to acknowledge his courage.

All the same, he had to die.

Faber ran after him. David must have heard the footsteps, for just before Faber caught up the chair stopped dead and spun around; and Faber glimpsed a heavy spanner in David's hand.

Faber crashed into the wheelchair, overturning it. His last thought was that both men and the chair might end up in the sea below – then the spanner hit the back of his head and he blacked out.

When he came to, the wheelchair lay beside him, but David was nowhere to be seen. He stood up and looked around in dazed puzzlement.

'Here! '

The voice came from over the cliff. David must have been flung from the chair and slid over the edge. Faber crawled to the cliff and looked over.

David had one hand around the stem of a bush which grew just under the lip of the cliff. The other hand was jammed into a small crevice in the rock. He hung suspended, just as Faber had a few minutes earlier. His bravado had gone, and there was naked terror in his eyes.

'Pull me up, for God's sake,' he shouted hoarsely.

Faber leaned closer. 'How did you know about the pictures?' he said.

'Help me, please!'

'Tell me about the pictures.'

'Oh, God.' David made a mighty effort to concentrate. 'When you went to Tom's outhouse you left your jacket drying in the kitchen. Tom went upstairs for more whisky, and I went through your pockets. I found the negatives.'

'And that was evidence enough for you to try to kill me?' Faber said wonderingly.

'That, and what you did with my wife in my house. No Englishman would behave like that.'

Faber could not help laughing. 'Where are the negatives now?'

'In my pocket.'

'Give them to me, and I'll pull you up.'

'You'll have to take them – I can't let go.'

Faber lay flat on his stomach and reached down, under David's oilskin, to the breast pocket of his jacket. He gave a sigh of satisfaction as his fingers touched the film can and withdrew it. He looked at the films: they all seemed to be there. He put the can in the pocket of his jacket, buttoned the flap, and reached down to David again.

He took hold of the bush David was clinging to and uprooted it with a savage jerk.

David screamed: 'No!' He scrabbled desperately for grip as his other hand slipped inexorably out of the crack in the rock.

'It's not fair!' he screamed. Then his hand came away from the crevice.

He seemed to hang in mid-air: then he dropped, faster and faster, bouncing twice against the cliff on his way down, until he hit the water with a huge splash.

Faber watched for a while to make sure he did not come up again. 'Not fair?' he murmured to himself. 'Not fair? Don't you know there's a war on?'

He looked down at the sea for some minutes. Once he thought he saw a flash of yellow oilskin on the surface, but it was gone before he could focus on it. There was just the sea and the rocks.

Suddenly he felt terribly tired. His injuries penetrated his consciousness one by one: the damaged foot, the bump on his head, the bruises all over his face. David Rose had been a fool, a braggart and a poor husband, and he had died screaming for mercy; but he had been a brave man too, and he had died for his country – he had got his wish.

Faber wondered whether his own death would be as good.

At last he turned away from the cliff edge and walked back toward the overturned jeep.

TWENTY-EIGHT

Percival Godliman felt refreshed, determined, even inspired.

When he reflected on it, this made him uncomfortable. Pep-talks are for the rank-and-file, and intellectuals believe themselves immune from inspirational speeches. Yet, although he knew that the great man's performance had been carefully scripted, the crescendos and diminuendos of the speech predetermined like a symphony, nevertheless it had worked on him, as effectively as if he had been the captain of the school cricket team hearing last-minute exhortations from the games master.

He got back to his office itching to do *something.*

He dropped his brolly in the umbrella-stand, hung up his wet raincoat, and looked at himself in the mirror on the inside of the cupboard door. Without doubt something had happened to his face since he became one of England's spycatchers. The other day he had come across a photograph of himself taken in 1937, with a group of students at a seminar in Oxford. In those days he actually looked older than he did now: pale skin, wispy hair, the patchy shave and ill-fitting clothes of a retired man. The wispy hair had gone: he was now bald except for a monkish fringe. His clothes were those of a business executive, not a teacher. It seemed to him – he might, he supposed, have been imagining it – that the set of his jaw was firmer, his eyes were brighter, and he took more care shaving.

He sat down behind his desk and lit a cigarette. *That* innovation was not welcome: he had developed a cough, tried to give it up, and discovered that he had become addicted. But almost everybody smoked in wartime Britain, even some of the women. Well, they were doing men's jobs – they were entitled to masculine vices. The smoke caught in Godliman's throat, making him cough. He put the cigarette out in the tin-lid he used for an ashtray (crockery was scarce).

The trouble with being inspired to perform the impossible, he reflected, was that the inspiration gave you no clues to the practical means. He recalled his college thesis, about the travels of an obscure medieval monk called Thomas of the Tree. Godliman had set himself the minor but difficult task of plotting the monk's itinerary over a five-year period. There had been a baffling gap of eight months when he had been either in Paris or Canterbury, but Godliman had been unable to determine which, and this had threatened the value of the whole project. The records he was using simply did not contain the information. If the monk's stay had gone unrecorded, then there was no way to find out where he had been, and that was that. With the optimism of youth, young Godliman had refused to believe that the information was just not there, and he had worked on the assumption that *somewhere* there had to be a record of how Thomas had spent those months – despite the well-known fact that almost everything that happened in the Middle Ages went unrecorded. If Thomas was not in Paris or Canterbury he must have been in transit between the two, Godliman had argued; and then he had found shipping records in an Amsterdam museum which showed that Thomas had boarded a vessel bound for Dover which got blown off course and was eventually wrecked on the Irish coast. This model piece of historical research had got Godliman his professorship.

He might try applying that kind of thinking to the problem of what had happened to Faber.

It was most likely that Faber had drowned. If he had not, then he was probably in Germany by now. Neither of those possibilities presented any course of action that Godliman could follow, so they should be discounted. He must assume that Faber was alive and had reached land somewhere.

He left his office and went down one flight of stairs to the map room. His uncle, Colonel Terry, was there, standing in front of the map of Europe with a cigarette between his lips, thinking. Godliman realized that this was a familiar sight in the War Office these days: senior men gazing entranced at maps, silently making their own computations of whether the war would be won or lost. He guessed it was because all the plans had been made, the vast machine had been set in motion, and for those who made the big decisions there was nothing to do but wait and see if they had been right.

Terry saw him come in, and said: 'How did you get on with the great man?'

'He was drinking whisky,' Godliman said.

'He drinks all day, but it never seems to make any difference to him,' Terry said. 'What did he say?'

'He wants Die Nadel's head on a platter.' Godliman crossed the room to the wall map of Great Britain and put a finger on Aberdeen. 'If you were sending a U-boat in to pick up a fugitive spy, what would you think was the nearest the sub could safely come to the coast?'

Terry stood beside him and looked at the map. 'I wouldn't want to come closer than the three-mile limit. But for preference, I'd stop ten miles out.'

'Right.' Godliman drew two pencil lines parallel to the coast, three miles and ten miles out respectively. 'Now, if you were an amateur sailor setting out from Aberdeen in a smallish fishing boat, how far would you go before you began to get nervous?'

'You mean, what's a reasonable distance to travel in such a boat?'

'Indeed.'

Terry shrugged. 'Ask the Navy. I'd say fifteen or twenty miles.'

'I agree.' Godliman drew an arc of twenty miles radius with its centre on Aberdeen. 'Now: if Faber is alive, he's either back on the mainland or somewhere within this space.' He indicated the area bounded by the parallel lines and the arc.

'There's no land in that area.'

'Have we got a bigger map?'

Terry pulled open a drawer and got out a large-scale

map of Scotland. He spread it on top of the chest. Godliman copied the pencil marks from the smaller map on to the larger.

There was still no land within the area.

'But look,' Godliman said. Just to the east of the ten-mile limit was a long, narrow island.

Terry peered closer. 'Storm Island,' he read. 'How apt.'

Godliman snapped his fingers. 'I'll bet that's where he is.'

'Can you send someone there?'

'When the storm clears. Bloggs is up there: I'll get a plane laid on for him. He can take off the minute the weather improves.' He went to the door.

'Good luck!' Terry called after him.

Godliman ran up the stairs to the next floor and entered his office. He picked up the phone. 'Get Mr Bloggs in Aberdeen, please.'

While he waited he doodled on his blotter, drawing the island. It was shaped like the top half of a walking-stick, with the crook at the western end. It must have been about ten miles long, and perhaps a mile wide. He wondered what sort of place it was: was it a barren lump of rock, or a thriving community of crofters? If Faber was there he might still be able to contact his U-boat: Bloggs would have to get to the island before the submarine. It would be difficult.

'I have Mr Bloggs,' the switchboard girl said.

'Fred?'

'Hello, Percy.'

'I think he's on an island called Storm Island.'

'No, he's not,' Bloggs said. 'We've just arrested him.'

The stiletto was nine inches long, with an engraved handle and a stubby little crosspiece. Its needle-like point was extremely sharp. Bloggs thought it looked like a highly efficient killing instrument. It had recently been polished.

Bloggs and Detective-Chief-Inspector Kincaid stood looking at it, neither man wanting to touch it.

'He was trying to catch a bus to Edinburgh,' Kincaid said. 'A PC spotted him at the ticket office and asked for his identification. He dropped his suitcase and ran away. A woman bus-conductor hit him over the head with her ticket machine. He took ten minutes to come around.'

'Let's have a look at him,' Bloggs said.

They went down the corridor to the cells. 'This one,' Kincaid said.

Bloggs looked through the judas. The man sat on a stool in the far corner of the cell with his back against the wall. His legs were crossed, his eyes closed, his hands in his pockets. 'He's been in cells before,' Bloggs remarked. The man was tall, with a long, handsome face and dark hair. It could have been the man in the photograph, but it was hard to be certain.

'Want to go in?' Kincaid asked.

'In a minute. What was in his suitcase, apart from the stiletto?'

'The tools of a burglar's trade. Quite a lot of money

in small notes. A pistol and some ammunition. Black clothes and crepe-soled shoes. Two hundred Lucky Strike cigarettes.'

'No photographs?'

Kincaid shook his head.

'Balls,' Bloggs said feelingly.

'Papers identify him as Peter Fredericks, of Wembley, Middlesex. Says he's an unemployed toolmaker looking for work.'

'Toolmaker?' Bloggs said sceptically. 'There hasn't been an unemployed toolmaker in Britain in the last four years. You'd think a spy would know that. Still . . .'

Kincaid asked: 'Shall I start the questioning, or will you?'

'You.'

Kincaid opened the door and Bloggs followed him in. The man in the corner opened his eyes incuriously. He did not alter his position.

Kincaid sat at a small, plain table. Bloggs leaned against the wall.

Kincaid said: 'What's your real name?'

'Peter Fredericks.'

'What are you doing so far from home?'

'Looking for work.'

'Why aren't you in the Army?'

'Weak heart.'

'Where have you been for the last few days?'

'Here, in Aberdeen. Before that Dundee, before that Perth.'

'When did you arrive in Aberdeen?'

'The day before yesterday.'

Kincaid glanced at Bloggs, who nodded. Kincaid said: 'Your story is silly. Toolmakers don't need to look for work. The country hasn't got enough of them. You'd better tell the truth.'

'I'm telling the truth.'

Bloggs took all the loose change out of his pocket and tied it up in his handkerchief. He stood watching, saying nothing, swinging the little bundle in his right hand.

'Where are the photographs?' Kincaid said.

The man's expression did not change. 'I don't know what you're talking about.'

Kincaid shrugged, and looked at Bloggs.

Bloggs said: 'On your feet.'

'Pardon?' the man said.

'On your FEET!' Bloggs bawled.

The man stood up casually.

'Forward!'

He took two steps up to the table.

'Name?'

'Peter Fredericks.'

Bloggs came off the wall and hit the man with the weighted handkerchief. The blow caught him accurately on the bridge of the nose, and he cried out. His hands went to his face.

'Stand to attention!' Bloggs shouted. 'Name!'

The man stood upright, let his hands fall to his sides, and whispered: 'Peter Fredericks.'

Bloggs hit him again in exactly the same place. This time he went down on one knee, and his eyes watered.

'Where are the photographs?' Bloggs screamed.

The man shook his head dumbly.

Bloggs pulled him to his feet, kneed him in the groin, and punched his stomach. 'What did you do with the negatives?'

The man fell to the floor and threw up. Bloggs kicked his face. There was a sharp crack, as if something had broken. 'What about the U-boat? Where is the rendezvous? What is the signal?'

Kincaid grabbed Bloggs from behind. 'That's enough, Bloggs,' he said. 'This is my station, and I can only turn a blind eye for so long, you know.'

Bloggs rounded on him. 'We're not dealing with a case of petty housebreaking, Kincaid – this man is jeopardizing the whole war effort.' He wagged a finger under the detective's nose. 'Just remember: I'm MI5, and I'll do what I fucking well like in your station. If the prisoner dies, I'll take responsibility.' He turned back to the man on the floor.

The man was staring at Bloggs and Kincaid. His face, covered with blood, showed an expression of incredulity. 'What are you talking about?' he said weakly. 'What is this?'

Bloggs hauled him to his feet again. 'You are Henrik Rudolph Hans von Muller-Guder, born at Oln on 26 May 1900; also known as Henry Faber; a lieutenant-colonel in German Intelligence. Within three months you will be hanged for espionage, unless you turn out to be more useful to us dead than alive. You'd better start making yourself useful, Colonel Muller-Guder.'

'No,' the man said. 'No, no! I'm a thief, not a spy. Please!' He cowered away from Bloggs's upraised fist. 'I can prove it.'

Bloggs hit him again, and Kincaid intervened for the second time. 'Wait,' the detective said. 'All right, Fredericks – if that's your name – prove you're a thief.'

'I done three houses in Jubilee Crescent last week,' the man gasped. 'I took about five hundred quid from one and some jewellery from the next one – diamond rings and some pearls – and I never got nothing from the other one because of the dog . . . you must know I'm telling the truth, they must have reported it, didn't they? Oh, Jesus—'

Kincaid looked at Bloggs. 'All those burglaries took place.'

'He could have read about them in the newspapers.'

'The third one wasn't reported.'

'Perhaps he did them – he could still be a spy. Spies can steal.'

'But this was last week – your man was in London, wasn't he?'

Bloggs was silent for a moment. Then he said: 'Well, fuck it,' and walked out.

Peter Fredericks looked up at Kincaid through a mask of blood. 'Who's he, the bleedin' Gestapo?' he said.

Kincaid stared at him thoughtfully. 'Be glad you're not really the man he's looking for.'

*

'Well?' Godliman said into the phone.

'False alarm.' Bloggs's voice was scratchy and distorted over the long-distance line. 'A small-time housebreaker who happens to carry a stiletto and look like Faber.'

'Back to square one,' Godliman said. 'Damn.'

'You said something about an island.'

'Yes. Storm Island – it's about ten miles off the coast, due east of Aberdeen. You'll find it on a large-scale map.'

'What makes you sure he's there?'

'I'm not sure; not at all. We still have to cover every other possibility – other towns, the coast, everything. But if he did steal that boat, the . . . ?'

'*Marie II.*'

'Yes. If he did steal it, his rendezvous was probably in the area of this island; and if I'm right about *that*, then he's either drowned or shipwrecked on the island.'

'Okay, that makes sense.'

'What's the weather like up there?'

'No change.'

'Could you reach the island in a big ship?'

Bloggs grunted. 'I suppose you can ride any storm if your ship's big enough. But this island won't have much of a dock, will it?'

'You'd better find out. However, I expect you're right. Now listen: there's an RAF fighter base near Edinburgh. By the time you get there, I'll have an amphibious plane standing by. You take off the minute the storm begins to clear. Have the local coastguard ready to move at a moment's notice, too – I'm not sure who'll get there first.'

'Mm.' Bloggs sounded dubious. 'If the U-boat is also waiting for the storm to clear, it will get there first.'

'You're right.' Godliman lit a cigarette, fumbling for inspiration. 'Well, we can get a Navy corvette to circle the island and listen for Faber's radio signal. When the storm clears it can land a boat on the island. Yes, that's a good idea.'

'What about some fighters?'

'Yes. Although like you, they'll have to wait until the weather breaks.'

'It can't go on much longer.'

'What do the Scottish meteorologists say?'

'Another day of it, at least.'

'Damn.'

'It doesn't make much difference,' Bloggs said. 'All the time we're grounded he's bottled up.'

'If he's there at all.'

'Yes.'

'All right,' Godliman said. 'We'll have a corvette, the coastguard, some fighters and an amphibian.'

'And me.'

'You'd better get on your way. Call me from Rosyth. Take care.'

'Cheerio.'

Godliman hung up. His cigarette, neglected in the ashtray, had burned down to a tiny stub. He lit another, then picked up the phone again and began organizing.

TWENTY-NINE

Lying on its side, the jeep looked powerful but helpless, like a wounded elephant. The engine had stalled. Faber gave it a hefty push and it toppled majestically on to all four wheels. It had survived the fight relatively undamaged. The canvas roof was destroyed, of course: the rip Faber's knife had made had become a long tear running from one side to the other. The offside front wing, which had ploughed into the earth and stopped the vehicle, was crumpled. The headlight on that side had smashed. The window on the same side had been broken by the shot from the gun. The windscreen was miraculously intact.

Faber climbed into the driving seat, put the gearshift into neutral, and tried the starter. It kicked over and died. He tried again, and the engine fired. He sighed with relief: he could not have faced a long walk just then.

He sat in the car for a while, inventorying his wounds. He touched his right ankle gingerly: it was swelling massively. Perhaps he had cracked a bone. It was as well that the jeep was designed to be driven by a man with no legs, for Faber could not have pressed a brake pedal. The lump on the back of his head felt huge, the size of a golf ball; and when he touched it his hand came away sticky with blood. He examined his face in the driving mirror. It was a mass of small cuts and big bruises, like the face of the loser at the end of a boxing match.

He had abandoned his oilskin back at the cottage, so his jacket and overalls were soggy with rain and smeared with mud. He needed to get warm and dry very soon.

He gripped the steering wheel, and a burning pain shot through his hand: he had forgotten the torn fingernail. He looked at it. It was the nastiest of his injuries. He would have to drive one-handed.

He pulled away slowly and found what he guessed was the road. There was no danger of getting lost on this island – all he had to do was follow the cliff-edge until he came to Lucy's cottage.

He needed to invent a lie to explain to Lucy what had become of her husband. He might, of course, tell her the truth: there was nothing she could do about it. However, if she became awkward he might have to kill her; and there had grown within him an aversion to killing Lucy. Driving slowly along the cliff-top through the pouring rain and howling wind, he marvelled at this new thing inside him, this scruple. It was the first time he had ever felt reluctance to kill. It was not that he was amoral: quite the contrary. He had made up his mind that the killing he did was on the same moral level as death on the battlefield, and his emotions followed his intellect. He always had the physical reaction, the vomiting, after he killed, but that was something incomprehensible which he ignored.

So why did he not want to kill Lucy?

The feeling was on a par with the affection which drove him to send the Luftwaffe erroneous directions to St Paul's Cathedral: a compulsion to protect a thing of beauty. She was a remarkable creation, as full of loveliness and subtlety as a work of art. Faber could live with himself as a killer, but not as an iconoclast. It was, he recognized as soon as the thought occurred to him, a peculiar way to be. But then, spies were peculiar people.

He thought of some of the spies who had been recruited by the Abwehr at the same time as he: Otto, the Nordic giant who made delicate paper sculptures in the Japanese fashion and hated women; Friedrich, the sly little mathematical genius who jumped at shadows and went into a five-day depression if he lost a game of chess; Helmut, who liked to read books about slavery in America and had soon joined the SS . . . all different, all peculiar. If they had anything more specific in common, he did not know what it was.

He seemed to be driving more and more slowly, and the rain and mist became more impenetrable. He began to worry about the cliff-edge on his left-hand side. He felt very hot, but suffered spasms of shivering. He realized he had been speaking aloud about Otto and Friedrich and Helmut; and he recognized the signs of delirium. He made an effort to think of nothing but the problem of keeping the jeep on a straight course.

The noise of the wind took on some kind of rhythm, becoming hypnotic. Once he found himself stationary, staring out over the sea, and had no idea how long he had stopped.

It seemed hours later that Lucy's cottage came into view. He steered toward it, thinking: I must remember to put the brake on before I hit the wall. There was a figure standing in the doorway, looking at him through the rain. He had to stay in control of himself long enough to tell her the lie. He had to remember, had to remember . . .

It was late afternoon by the time the jeep came back. Lucy was worried about what had happened to the men, and at the same time angry with them for not coming home for the lunch she had prepared. As the day waned she had spent more and more time at the windows, looking out for them.

When the jeep came down the slight slope to the cottage, it was clear something was wrong. It was moving terribly slowly, weaving all over the track, and there was only one person in it. It came closer, and she saw that the front was dented and the headlamp smashed.

'Oh, God,' she murmured.

The vehicle shuddered to a halt in front of the cottage, and she saw that the figure inside was Henry. He made no move to get out. Lucy ran out into the rain and opened the driver's door.

Henry sat there with his head back and his eyes half-closed. His hand was on the brake. His face was bloody and bruised.

Lucy said: 'What happened? *What happened?*'

Henry's hand slipped off the brake, and the jeep moved forward. Lucy leaned across him and slipped the gearshift into neutral.

Henry said: 'Left David at Tom's cottage . . . had crash on way back . . .' The words seemed to cost him a great effort.

Now that she knew what had happened, Lucy's panic subsided. 'Come inside,' she said sharply. The urgency in her voice got through to Henry. He turned toward her, put his foot on the running board to step down, and promptly fell to the ground. Lucy saw that his ankle was swollen like a balloon.

She got her hands under his shoulders and pulled him upright, saying: 'Put your weight on the other foot and lean on me.' She got his right arm around her neck and half-carried him inside.

Jo watched wide-eyed as she helped Henry into the living-room and got him on to the sofa. He lay back with his eyes shut. His clothes were soaked and muddy.

Lucy said: 'Jo, go upstairs and get your pyjamas on, please.'

'But I haven't had my story. Is *he* dead?'

'He's not dead, but he's had a car crash, and you can't have a story tonight. Go on.'

The child made a complaining sound, and Lucy looked threateningly at him. He went.

Lucy got the big scissors out of her sewing basket

and cut Henry's clothes away: first the jacket, then the overalls, then the shirt. She frowned in puzzlement when she saw the knife in its sheath strapped to his left forearm: she guessed it was a special implement for cleaning fish, or something. When she tried to take it off, Henry pushed her hand away. She shrugged, and turned her attention to his boots. The left one came off easily, and its sock; but he cried out in pain when she touched the right.

'It must come off,' she told him. 'You'll have to be brave.'

A funny kind of smile came over his face, then, and he nodded assent. She cut the laces, took the shoe gently but firmly in both hands, and pulled it off. This time he made no sound. She cut the elastic in the sock and pulled that off too.

Jo came in and said: 'He's in his pants!'

'His clothes are all wet.' She kissed the boy goodnight. 'Put yourself to bed, darling. I'll tuck you up later.'

'Kiss teddy, then.'

'Goodnight, teddy.'

Jo went out. Lucy looked back to Henry. His eyes were open, and he was smiling. He said: 'Kiss Henry, then.'

She leaned over him and kissed his battered face. Then, carefully, she cut away his underpants.

The heat from the fire would quickly dry his naked skin. She went into the kitchen and filled a bowl with warm water and a little antiseptic to bathe his wounds.

She found a roll of cotton wool and returned to the living-room.

'This is the second time you've turned up on the doorstep half dead,' she said as she set about her task.

'The usual signal,' Henry said.

'What?'

'Waiting at Calais for a phantom army.'

'Henry, what are you talking about?'

'Every Friday and Monday.'

She realized he was delirious. 'Don't try to talk,' she said. She lifted his head slightly to clean away the dried blood from around the bump.

Suddenly he sat upright, looked fiercely at her, and said: 'What day is it? What day is it?'

'It's Sunday, relax.'

'Okay.'

He was quiet after that, and he let her remove the knife. She bathed his face, bandaged his finger where he had lost the nail, and put a dressing on his ankle. When she had finished she stood looking at him for a while. He seemed to be sleeping. She touched the long scar on his chest, and the star-shaped mark on his hip. The star was a birthmark, she decided.

She went through his pockets before throwing the lacerated clothes away. There wasn't much: some moncy, his papers, a leather wallet and a film can. She put them all in a little pile on the mantelpiece beside his fish knife. He would havc to have some of David's clothes.

She left him and went upstairs to see Jo. The boy was

asleep, lying on his teddy bear, with his arms outflung. She kissed his soft cheek and tucked him in. She went outside and put the jeep in the barn.

She made herself a drink in the kitchen then sat watching Henry, wishing he would wake up and make love to her again.

It was almost midnight when he awoke. He opened his eyes, and his face showed the series of expressions which were now familiar to her: first the fear, then the wary survey of the room, then the relaxation. On impulse, she asked him: 'What are you afraid of, Henry?'

'I don't know what you mean.'

'You always look frightened when you wake up.'

'I don't know.' He shrugged, and the movement seemed to hurt. 'God, I'm battered.'

'Do you want to tell me what happened?'

'Yes, if you'll give me a small amount of brandy.'

She got the brandy out of the cupboard. 'You can have some of David's clothes.'

'In a minute . . . unless you're embarrassed.'

She handed him the glass, smiling. 'I'm afraid I'm enjoying it.'

'What happened to my clothes?'

'I had to cut them off you. I've thrown them away.'

'Not my papers, I hope.' He smiled, but there was some other emotion just below the surface.

'On the mantelpiece.' She pointed. 'I suppose that knife is for cleaning fish, or something.'

His right hand went to his left forearm, where the sheath had been. 'Something like that,' he said. He seemed uneasy for a moment, then relaxed with an effort and sipped his drink. 'That's good.'

After a moment she said: 'Well?'

'What?'

'How did you manage to lose my husband and crash my jeep?'

'David decided to stay over at Tom's for the night. Some of the sheep got into trouble in a place they called the Gully—'

'I know it.'

'—and six or seven of them were injured. They're all in Tom's kitchen, being bandaged up and making a frightful row. Anyway, David suggested I came back to tell you he would be staying. I don't really know how I managed to crash. The car is unfamiliar, there's no real road, I hit something and went into a skid, and the jeep ended up on its side. The details . . .' he shrugged.

'You must have been going quite fast – you were in an awful mess when you got here.'

'I suppose I rattled around inside the jeep a bit. Banged my head, twisted my ankle . . .'

'Lost a fingernail, bashed your face, and almost caught pneumonia. You must be accident-prone.'

He swung his legs to the floor, stood up, and went to the mantelpiece.

Lucy said: 'Your powers of recuperation are incredible.'

He was strapping the knife to his arm. 'We fishermen are very healthy. What about those clothes?'

She got up and stood close to him. 'What do you need clothes for? It's bedtime.'

He drew her to him, pressing her against his naked body, and kissed her hard. She stroked his thighs.

After a while he broke away from her. He picked up his things from the mantelpiece, took her hand, then, hobbling, he led her upstairs to bed.

THIRTY

The wide, white autobahn snaked through the Bavarian valley up into the mountains. In the leather rear seat of the staff Mercedes, Field Marshal Gerd von Rundstedt was still and weary. Aged sixtynine, he knew he was too fond of champagne and not fond enough of Hitler. His thin, lugubrious face reflected a career longer and more erratic than that of any of Hitler's other officers: he had been dismissed in disgrace more times than he could remember, but the Führer always asked him to come back.

As the car passed through the sixteenth-century village of Berchtesgaden, he wondered why he always returned to his command when Hitler forgave him. Money meant nothing to him: he had already achieved the highest possible rank; decorations were valueless in the Third Reich; and he believed that it was not possible to win honour in this war.

It was Rundstedt who had first called Hitler 'the Bohemian corporal'. The little man knew nothing of the German military tradition, nor – despite his flashes of inspiration – of military strategy. If he had, he would not have started this war, for it was unwinnable. Rundstedt was Germany's finest soldier, and he had proved it in Poland, France and Russia; but he had no hope of victory.

All the same, he would have nothing to do with the small group of generals who – he knew – were plotting to overthrow Hitler. He turned a blind eye to them, but the *Fahneneid*, the blood oath of the German warrior, was too strong within him to permit him to join the conspiracy. And that, he supposed, was why he continued to serve the Reich. Right or wrong, his country was in danger, and he had no option but to protect it. I'm like an old cavalry horse, he thought: if I stayed at home I should feel ashamed.

He commanded five armies on the Western front, now. A million and a half men were under him. They were not as strong as they might be – some divisions were little better than rest homes for invalids from the Russian front, there was a shortage of armour, and there were many non-German conscripts among the other ranks – but Rundstedt could still keep the Allies out of France if he deployed his forces shrewdly.

It was that deployment that he must now discuss with Hitler.

The car climbed the Kehlsteinstrasse until the road ended at a vast bronze door in the side of the Kehlstein Mountain. An SS guard touched a button, the door hummed open, and the car entered a long marble tunnel lit by bronze lanterns. At the far end of the tunnel the driver stopped the car, and Rundstedt walked to the elevator and sat in one of its leather seats for the four-hundred-foot ascent to the Adlerhorst, the Eagle's Nest.

In the anteroom Rattenhuber took his pistol and left him to wait. He stared unappreciatively at Hitler's porcelain and went over in his mind the words he would say.

A few moments later the blond bodyguard returned to usher him into the conference room.

The place made him think of an eighteenth-century palace. The walls were covered with oil paintings and tapestries, and there was a bust of Wagner and a huge clock with a bronze eagle on its top. The view from the side window was truly remarkable: one could see the hills of Salzburg and the peak of the Untersberg, the mountain where the body of the Emperor Frederick Barbarossa waited, according to legend, to rise from the grave and save the Fatherland. Inside the room, seated in the peculiarly rustic chairs, were Hitler and just three of his staff: Admiral Theodor Krancke, the naval commander in the west; General Alfred Jodl, chief of staff; and Admiral Karl Jesko von Puttkamer, Hitler's aide-de-camp.

Rundstedt saluted and was motioned to a chair. A footman brought a plate of caviar sandwiches and a glass of champagne. Hitler stood at the large window, looking out, with his hands clasped behind his back. Without turning, he said abruptly: 'Rundstedt has changed his mind. He now agrees with Rommel that the Allies will invade Normandy. This is what my instinct has all along told me. Krancke, however, still favours Calais. Rundstedt, tell Krancke how you arrived at your conclusion.'

Rundstedt swallowed a mouthful and coughed into

his hand. Damn, Hitler had no manners: didn't even give a chap a chance to catch his breath. 'There are two things: one new piece of information and one new line of reasoning,' Rundstedt began. 'First, the information. The latest summaries of Allied bombing in France show without doubt that their principal aim is to destroy every bridge across the River Seine. Now, if they land at Calais the Seine is irrelevant to the battle; but if they land in Normandy all our reserves have to cross the Seine to reach the zone of conflict.

'Second, the reasoning. I have given some thought to how I would invade France if I were commanding the Allied forces. My conclusion is that the first goal must be to establish a bridgehead through which men and supplies can be funnelled at speed. The initial thrust must therefore come in the region of a large and roomy harbour. The natural choice is Cherbourg.

'Both the bombing pattern and the strategic requirements point to Normandy,' he finished. He picked up his glass and emptied it, and the footman came forward to refill it.

Jodl said: 'All our intelligence points to Calais—'

'And we have just executed the head of the Abwehr as a traitor,' Hitler interrupted. 'Krancke, are you convinced?'

'My Führer, I am not,' the Admiral said. 'I, too, have considered how I would conduct the invasion if I were on the other side – but I have brought into the reasoning a number of factors of a nautical nature of which Rundstedt may not have been aware. I believe they will attack under cover of darkness, by moonlight, at full tide to sail over Rommel's underwater obstacles, and away from cliffs, rocky waters and strong currents. Normandy? Never.'

Hitler shook his head in disgusted disagreement. Jodl said: 'There is another small piece of information which I find significant. The Guards Armoured Division has been transferred from the north of England to Hove, on the south-east coast, to join the First United States Army Group under General Patton. We learned this from wireless surveillance – there was a baggage mix-up en route, one unit had another's silver cutlery, and the fools have been quarrelling about it over the radio. This is a crack British division, very blue-blooded, commanded by General Sir Allan Henry Shafto Adair. I feel sure they will not be far from the centre of the battle when it comes.'

Hitler's hands moved nervously, and his face twitched in an agony of indecision. 'Generals!' he barked at them. 'Either I get conflicting advice, or no advice at all! I have to tell you everything – everything!'

With characteristic boldness, Rundstedt plunged on. 'My Führer, you have four superb panzer divisions doing nothing here in Germany. If I am right, they will never get to Normandy in time to repel the invasion. I beg you, order them to France and put them under Rommel's command. If we are wrong, and the invasion begins at Calais, they will still be close enough to enter the battle at an early stage.'

'I don't know – I don't know!' Hitler's eyes widened, and Rundstedt wondered if he had pushed too hard – again.

Puttkamer spoke for the first time. 'My Führer, today is Sunday.'

'Well?'

'Tomorrow night the U-boat may pick up the spy, Die Nadel.'

'Ah, yes! Someone I can trust.'

'Of course, he can report by radio at any time. However, there may be some reason for him to avoid the radio; in which case he would bring his information personally. Given this possibility, you may like to consider postponing your decision for twenty-four hours, in case he does contact us, one way or the other, today or tomorrow.'

Rundstedt said: 'There isn't time to postpone decisions. Both air attacks and sabotage activities have increased dramatically. The invasion may come any day.'

'I disagree,' Krancke said. 'The weather conditions will not be right until early June.'

'That is not very far away!'

'Enough!' Hitler shouted. 'I have made up my mind. My panzers stay in Germany – for now. On Tuesday, when we have heard from Die Nadel, I will reconsider the disposition of these forces. If his information favours Normandy – as I believe it will – I will move the panzers.'

Rundstedt said softly: 'And if he does not report?'

'If he does not report, I shall reconsider just the same.'

Rundstedt bowed assent. 'With your permission, I shall return to my command.'

'Very well.'

Rundstedt got to his feet, saluted and went out. In the copper-lined elevator, falling four hundred feet to the underground garage, he felt his stomach turn over, and wondered whether the sensation was caused by the speed of descent or by the thought that the destiny of his country lay in the hands of a single, lonely spy.

PART SIX

THIRTY-ONE

Lucy woke up slowly. She rose gradually, languidly, from the warm void of deep sleep, up through layers of unconsciousness, perceiving the world piece by isolated piece: first the warm, hard male body beside her; then the strangeness of the little bed; the noise of the storm outside, as angry and tireless as yesterday and the day before; the faint smell of the man's skin; her arm across his chest, her leg thrown across his as if to keep him there, her breasts pressed against his side; the light of day beating against her eyelids; the regular, light breathing that blew softly across her face; and then, all at once like the solution to a puzzle, the realization that she was flagrantly and adulterously lying with a man she had met only forty-eight hours before, and that they were naked in bed in her husband's house.

She opened her eyes and saw Jo.

He was standing beside the bed in his rumpled pyjamas, hair tousled, a battered rag doll under his arm, sucking his thumb and staring wide-eyed at his mummy and the strange man cuddling each other in his, Jo's, bed. Lucy could not read his expression, for at this time of day he stared wide-eyed at most things, as if all the world was new and marvellous every morning. She stared back at him in silence, not knowing what to say.

Then Henry's deep voice said: 'Good morning.'

Jo took his thumb out of his mouth, said: 'Good morning,' turned around and went out of the bedroom.

Lucy said: 'Damn, damn, damn.'

Henry slid down in the bed until his face was level with hers, and kissed her. His hand went between her thighs and held her possessively.

She pushed him away. 'For God's sake, stop.'

'Why?'

'Jo's seen us!'

'So what?'

'He can talk, you know. Sooner or later he'll say something to David. What am I going to do?'

'Do nothing. So David finds out. Does it matter?'

'Of course it matters.'

'I don't see why. He has wronged you, and this is the consequence. You shouldn't feel guilty.'

Lucy suddenly realized that Henry simply had no conception of the complex tangle of loyalties and obligations that constituted a marriage. She said: 'It's not *that* simple.'

She got out of bed and crossed the landing to her own bedroom. She slipped into knickers, trousers and a sweater, then remembered she had destroyed all Henry's clothes and had to lend him some of David's. She found underwear and socks, a knitted shirt and a V-necked pullover, and finally – right at the bottom of a trunk – one pair of trousers that were not cut off at the knee and sewn up. All the while Jo watched her in silence.

She took the clothes into the other bedroom. Henry had gone into the bathroom to shave. She called through the door: 'Your clothes are on the bed.'

She went downstairs, lit the stove in the kitchen, and put a saucepan of water on to heat. She decided to have boiled eggs for breakfast. She washed Jo's face at the kitchen sink, combed his hair, and dressed him quickly. 'You're very quiet this morning,' she said brightly. He made no reply.

Henry came down and sat at the table, as naturally as if he had been doing it every morning for years. Lucy felt very weird, seeing him there in David's clothes, handing him a breakfast egg, putting a rack of toast on the table in front of him.

Jo said suddenly: 'Is my daddy dead?'

Henry gave the boy a queer look and said nothing.

Lucy said: 'Don't be silly. He's at Tom's house.'

Jo ignored her and spoke to Henry. 'You've got my daddy's clothes, *and* you've got my mummy. Are you going to be my daddy now?'

Lucy muttered: 'Out of the mouth of babes and sucklings . . .'

Henry said: 'Didn't you see my clothes last night?'

Jo nodded.

'Well, then, you know why I had to borrow some of your daddy's clothes. I'll give them back to him when I get some more of my own.'

'Will you give my mummy back?'

'Of course.'

Lucy said: 'Eat your egg, Jo.'

The child tucked into his breakfast, apparently satisfied. Lucy was gazing out of the kitchen window. 'The boat won't come today,' she said.

'Are you glad?' Henry asked her.

She looked at him. 'I don't know.'

Lucy did not feel hungry. She drank a cup of tea while Jo and Henry ate. Afterwards, Jo went upstairs to play and Henry cleared the table. As he stacked crockery in the sink he said: 'Are you afraid David will hurt you, physically?'

She shook her head in negation.

'You should forget him,' Henry went on. 'You were planning to leave him anyway. Why should it concern you whether he finds out or not?'

'He's my *husband*,' she said. 'That counts for something. The kind of husband he's been . . . all that . . . doesn't give me the right to humiliate him.'

'I think it gives you the right not to care whether he's humiliated or not.'

'It's not a question that can be settled logically. It's just the way I *feel*.'

He made a giving-up gesture with his arms. 'I'd better drive over to Tom's and find out whether your *husband* wants to come back. Where are my boots?'

'In the living-room. I'll get you a jacket.' She went upstairs and got David's old hacking jacket out of the wardrobe. It was a fine grey-green tweed, very elegant with a nipped-in waist and slanted pocket flaps. Lucy had put leather patches on the elbows to preserve it: you couldn't buy clothes like this any more. She took it down to the living-room, where Henry was putting his boots on. He had laced the left one, and was gingerly inserting his injured right foot into the other. Lucy knelt to help him.

'The swelling has gone down,' she said.

'The damn thing still hurts.'

They got the boot on, but left it untied and took the lace out. Henry stood up experimentally.

'It's okay,' he said.

Lucy helped him into the jacket. It was a little tight across the shoulders. 'We haven't got another oilskin,' she said.

'Then I'll get wet.' He pulled her to him and kissed her roughly. She put her arms around him and held tightly for a moment.

'Drive more carefully today,' she said.

He smiled and nodded, kissed her again – briefly this time – and went out. She watched him limp across to the barn, and stood at the window while he started the jeep and drove away, up the slight rise and out of sight. When he had gone she felt relieved, but somehow empty.

She began to put the house straight, making beds and washing dishes, cleaning and tidying; but she could summon up no enthusiasm for the task. She was restless. She worried at the problem of what to do with her life, following old arguments around in familiar circles, unable to put her mind to anything else. She found the cottage claustrophobic instead of snug. There was a big world out there somewhere, a world of war and heroism, full of colour and passion and people, millions of people; she wanted to be out there in the midst of it, to meet new minds and see cities and hear music. She turned on the radio: a futile gesture, for the news broadcast made her feel more isolated, not less. There was a battle report from Italy, the rationing regulations had been eased a little, the London stiletto murderer was still at large, Roosevelt had made a speech. Sandy Macpherson began to play a theatre organ, and Lucy switched off. None of it touched her, for she did not live in that world.

She wanted to scream.

She had to get out of the house, despite the weather. It would be only a symbolic escape, for the stone walls of the cottage were not what imprisoned her; but the symbol was better than nothing. She collected Jo from upstairs, separating him with some difficulty from a regiment of toy soldiers, and wrapped him up in waterproof clothing.

'Why are we going out?' he asked.

'To see if the boat comes.'

'You said it won't come today.'

'Just in case.'

They put bright yellow sou'westers on their heads, lacing them under their chins, and stepped outside the door.

The wind was like a physical blow, unbalancing Lucy so that she staggered. In seconds her face was as wet as if she had dipped it in a bowl, and the ends of hair protruding from under her hat lay limp and clinging on her cheeks and the shoulders of her oilskin. Jo screamed with delight and jumped in a puddle.

They walked along the cliff-top to the head of the bay, and looked down at the huge North Sea rollers hurling themselves to destruction against the cliffs and on the beach. The storm had uprooted underwater vegetation from God-only-knew what depth and flung it in heaps on the sand and rocks. Mother and son became absorbed in the ceaselessly shifting patterns of the waves. They had done this before: the sea had a hypnotic effect on both of them, and Lucy was never quite sure, afterwards, how long they had spent silently watching.

The spell was broken this time by something she saw. At first there was only a flash of colour in the trough of a wave, so fleeting that she was not certain what colour it had been, so small and far away that she immediately doubted whether she had seen it at all. She looked for it, but did not see it again, and her gaze drifted back to the bay and the little jetty, on which flotsam gathered in drifts only to be swept away by the next big wave. After the storm, on the first fine day, she and Jo would go beachcombing to see what treasures the sea had disgorged, and come back with oddly coloured rocks, bits of wood of mystifying origin, huge seashells and twisted fragments of rusted metal.

She saw the flash of colour again, much nearer, and this time it stayed within sight for a few seconds. It was bright yellow, the colour of all their oilskins. She peered at it through the sheets of rain, but could not identify its shape before it disappeared again. But the current was bringing it closer, as it brought everything to the bay, depositing its rubbish on the sand like a man emptying his trouser pockets on to a table.

It *was* an oilskin: she could see that when the sea lifted it on the crest of a wave and showed it to her for the third and final time. Henry had come back without his, yesterday, but how had it got into the sea? The wave broke over the jetty and flung the object on the wet wooden boards of the ramp, and Lucy realized it was not Henry's oilskin, for the owner was still inside it. Her gasp of horror was whipped away by the wind so that not even she could hear it. Who was he? Where had he come from? Another shipwreck?

It occurred to her that he might still be alive. She must go and see. She bent and shouted in Jo's ear: 'Stay here – keep still – don't move.' Then she ran down the ramp.

Half way down she heard footsteps behind her: Jo was following. The ramp was narrow and slippery, quite dangerous. She stopped, turned, and scooped the child up in her arms, saying: 'You naughty boy, I told you to wait!' She looked from the body below to the safety of the clifftop, dithered for a moment in painful indecision, discerned that the sea would wash the body away at any moment, and proceeded downward, carrying Jo.

A smaller wave covered the body, and when the water receded Lucy was close enough to see that it was a man, and that it had been in the sea long enough for the water to swell and distort the features. That meant he was dead. She could therefore do nothing for him, and she was not going to risk her life and her son's to preserve a corpse. She was about to turn back when something about the bloated face struck her as familiar. She stared at it, uncomprehending, trying to fit the features to something in her memory; and then, quite abruptly, she saw the face for what it was, and sheer, paralysing terror gripped her, and it seemed that her heart stopped, and she whispered: 'No, David, no!'

Oblivious now to the danger she walked forward. Another lesser wave broke around her knees, filling her wellington boots with foamy salt water, but she did not notice. Jo twisted in her arms to face forward, but she screamed 'Don't look!' in his ear and pushed his face into her shoulder. He began to cry.

She knelt beside the body and touched the horrible face with her hand. It was David. There was no doubt. He was dead, and had been for some time. Moved by some deep instinct to make absolutely certain, she lifted the skirt of the oilskin and looked at the stumps of his legs.

It was impossible to take in the fact of the death. She had, in a way, been wishing him dead; but her feelings about him were confused by guilt and the fear of being found out in infidelity. Grief, horror, liberation, relief: they fluttered in her mind like birds, none of them willing to settle.

She would have stayed there, motionless, but the next wave was a big one. Its force knocked her flying, and she took a great gulp of sea water. Somehow she managed to keep Jo in her grasp and stay on the ramp;

and when the surf settled she got to her feet and ran up out of the greedy reach of the ocean.

She walked all the way to the cliff-top without looking back. When she came within sight of the cottage, she saw the jeep standing outside. Henry was back.

Still carrying Jo, she broke into a stumbling run, desperate to share her hurt with Henry, to feel his arms around her and have him comfort her. Her breath came in ragged sobs, and tears mixed invisibly with the rain on her face. She went to the back of the cottage, burst into the kitchen, and dumped Jo urgently on the floor.

Henry said: 'David decided to stay over at Tom's another day.'

She stared at him, her mind an incredulous blank; and then, in a flash of intuition, she understood everything.

Henry had killed David.

The conclusion came first, like a punch in the stomach, winding her; the reasons followed a split-second later. The shipwreck, the odd-shaped knife he was so attached to, the crashed jeep, the news bulletin about the London stiletto murderer: suddenly everything fitted together, a box of jigsaw pieces thrown in the air and landing, improbably, fully assembled.

'Don't look so surprised,' Henry said with a smile. 'They've got a lot of work to do over there, and I didn't encourage him to come back.'

Tom. She had to go to Tom. He would know what to do; he would protect her and Jo until the police came; he had a dog and a gun.

Her fear was interrupted by a shaft of sadness, of sorrow for the Henry she had believed in, had almost loved; for clearly he did not exist – she had imagined him. Instead of a warm, strong, affectionate man, she saw in front of her a monster who sat and smiled and calmly gave her invented messages from the husband he had murdered.

She suppressed a shudder. Taking Jo's hand, she walked out of the kitchen, along the hall, and out of the front door. She got into the jeep, sat Jo beside her, and started the engine.

But Henry was there, resting his foot casually on the running-board, and holding David's shotgun, saying: 'Where are you going?'

Her heart sank. If she drove away now he might shoot – what instinct had warned him to take the gun into the house this time? – and while she herself might chance it, she could not endanger Jo. She said: 'Just putting the jeep away.'

'You need Jo's help for that?'

'He likes the ride. Don't cross-examine me!'

Henry shrugged, and stepped back.

She looked at him for a moment, wearing David's hacking jacket and holding David's gun so casually, and wondered whether he really would shoot her if she simply drove away. Then she recalled the vein of ice she had sensed within him right from the start, and knew that that ultimate commitment, that ruthlessness, would permit him to do anything.

With an awful feeling of weariness, she surrendered. She threw the jeep into reverse and backed into the barn. She switched off, got out, and walked with Jo back into the cottage. She had no idea what she would say to Henry, what she would do in his presence, how she would hide her knowledge – if, indeed she had not already betrayed it.

She had no plans.

But she had left the barn door open.

THIRTY-TWO

'That's the place, Number One,' the captain said, and lowered his telescope.

The first lieutenant peered out through the rain and the spray. 'Not quite the ideal holiday resort, what, sir? Jolly stark, I should say.'

'Indeed.' The captain was an old-fashioned naval officer with a grizzled beard who had been at sea during the first war with Germany. However, he had learned to overlook his first lieutenant's foppish conversational style, for the boy had turned out – against all expectations – to be a perfectly good sailor.

The 'boy', who was past thirty and an old salt by this war's standards, had no idea of the magnanimity from which he benefited. He held on to a rail and braced himself as the corvette mounted the steep side of a wave, righted itself at the crest, and dived into the trough 'Now that we're here, sir, what do we do?'

'Circle the island.'

'Very good, sir.'

'And keep our eyes open for a U-boat.'

'We're not likely to get one anywhere near the surface in this weather – and if we did, we couldn't see it unless it came within spitting distance.'

'The storm will blow itself out tonight – tomorrow at the latest.' The captain began stuffing tobacco into a pipe.

'Do you think so?'

'I'm sure.'

'Nautical instinct, I suppose?'

The captain grunted. 'That, and the weather forecast.'

The corvette rounded a headland, and they saw a small bay with a jetty. Above it, on the cliff top, was a little cottage standing small and square, hunched against the wind.

The captain pointed. 'We'll land a party there as soon as we can.'

The first lieutenant nodded. 'All the same . . .'

'Well?'

'Each circuit of the island will take us about an hour, I should say.'

'So?'

'So, unless we're jolly lucky and happen to be in exactly the right place at exactly the right time . . .'

'The U-boat will surface, take on its passenger, and submerge again without us even seeing the ripples,' the captain finished.

'Yes.'

The captain lit his pipe with an expertise which spoke of long experience of lighting pipes in heavy seas. He puffed a few times, then inhaled a lungful of smoke. 'Ours not to reason why,' he said, and blew smoke through his nostrils.

'A rather unfortunate quotation, sir.'

'Why?'

'It refers to the notorious charge of the Light Brigade.'

'Good God! I never knew that.' The captain puffed contentedly. 'What it must be to be educated.'

There was another little cottage at the eastern end of the island. The captain scrutinized it through his telescope, and observed that it had a large, professional-looking radio aerial. 'Sparks!' he called. 'See if you can raise that cottage. Try the Royal Observer Corps's frequency.'

'Aye, aye, sir.'

When the cottage had passed out of sight, the radio operator called: 'No response, sir.'

'All right, Sparks,' the captain said. 'It wasn't important.'

The crew of the coastguard cutter sat below decks in Aberdeen Harbour, playing pontoon for halfpennies and musing on the feeble-mindedness which seemed invariably to accompany high rank.

'Twist,' said Jack Smith, who was more Scots than his name.

Albert 'Slim' Parish, a fat Londoner far from home, dealt him a jack.

'Bust,' Smith said.

Slim raked in his stake. 'A penny-ha'penny,' he said in mock wonder. 'I only hope I live to spend it.'

Smith rubbed condensation off the inside of a port-hole and peered out at the boats bobbing up and down in the harbour. 'The way the skipper's panicking,' he observed, 'you'd think we were going to bloody Berlin, not Storm Island.'

'Didn't you know? We're the spearhead of the Allied invasion.' Slim turned over a ten, dealt himself a king, and said: 'Pay twenty-ones.'

Smith said: 'What is this guy, anyway – a deserter? If you ask me, it's a job for the military police, not us.'

Slim shuffled the pack. 'I'll tell you what he is: an escaped prisoner-of-war.'

There was a chorus of disbelieving jeers.

'All right, don't listen to me. But when we pick him up, just take note of his accent.' He put the cards down. 'Listen: what boats go to Storm Island?'

'Only the grocer,' someone said.

'So, if he's a deserter, the only way he can get back to the mainland is on the grocer's boat. So, the Military Police just have to wait for Charlie's regular trip to the island, and pick the deserter up when he steps off the boat at this end. There's no reason for us to be sitting here, waiting to weigh anchor and shoot over there at the speed of light the minute the weather clears, unless . . .' He paused melodramatically. 'Unless he's got some other means of getting off the island.'

'Like what?'

'A U-boat.'

'Bollocks,' Smith said contemptuously. The others merely laughed.

Slim dealt another hand. Smith won this time, but everyone else lost. 'I'm a shilling up,' Slim said. 'I think

I'll retire to that nice little cottage in Devon. We won't catch him, of course.'

'The deserter?'

'The prisoner-of-war.'

'Why not?'

Slim tapped his head. 'Use your noddle. When the storm clears, we'll be here and the U-boat will be at the bottom of the bay in the island. So who'll get there first? The Jerries.'

'So why are we doing it?' Smith said.

'Because the people who are giving the orders are not as sharp as yours truly, Albert Parish. You may laugh!' He dealt another hand. 'Place your bets. You'll see I'm right. What's that, Smithie, a penny? Gorblimey, don't go mad. I tell you what, I'll give odds of five to one we come back from Storm Island empty-handed. Any takers? What if I say ten to one? Eh? Ten to one?'

'No takers,' said Smith. 'Deal the cards.'

Slim dealt the cards.

Squadron-Leader Peterkin Blenkinsop (he had tried to shorten Peterkin to Peter, but somehow the men always found out) stood ramrod-straight in front of the map and addressed the room. 'We fly in formations of three,' he began. 'The first three will take off as soon as weather permits. Our target—' he touched the map with a pointer. '—is here. Storm Island. On arrival, we will circle for twenty minutes at low altitudes, looking for U-boats. After twenty minutes, we return to base.'

He paused. 'Those of you with a logical turn of mind will by now have deduced that, to achieve continuous cover, the second formation of three aircraft must take off precisely twenty minutes after the first, and so on. Any questions?'

Flying-Officer Longman said: 'Sir?'

'Longman?'

'What do we do if we see this U-boat?'

'Strafe it, of course. Drop a few grenades. Cause trouble.'

'But we're flying fighters, sir – there's not much we can do to stop a U-boat. That's a job for battleships, isn't it?'

Blenkinsop sighed. 'As usual, those of you who can think of better ways to win the war are invited to write directly to Mr Winston Churchill, number ten Downing Street, London South-West-One. Now, are there any questions, as opposed to fat-headed criticisms?'

There were no questions.

The later years of the war had produced a different kind of RAF officer, Bloggs mused. He sat on a soft chair in the scramble room, close to the fire, listening to the rain drumming on the tin roof, and intermittently dozing. The Battle of Britain pilots had seemed incorrigibly cheerful, with their undergraduate slang, their perpetual drinking, their tirelessness, and their cavalier disregard of the flaming death they faced every day. That schoolboy heroism had not been enough to carry them through subsequent years, as the war dragged on in places far from home, and the emphasis shifted from the dashing individuality of aerial dogfighting to the mechanical drudgery of bombing missions. They still drank and talked in jargon, but they appeared older, harder, more cynical: there was nothing in them now of *Tom Brown's Schooldays.* Bloggs recalled what he had done to that poor common-or-garden housebreaker in the police cells at Aberdeen, and he thought: It's happened to us all.

They were very quiet. They sat all around him: some dozing, like himself; others reading books or playing board games. A bespectacled navigator in a corner was learning Russian.

As Bloggs surveyed the room with half-closed eyes, another pilot came in, and he thought immediately that this one had not been aged by the war. He had a wide grin and a fresh face that looked as if it hardly needed shaving more than once a week. He wore his jacket open and carried his helmet. He made a beeline for Bloggs.

'Detective-Inspector Bloggs?'

'That's me.'

'Jolly good show. I'm your pilot. Charles Calder.'

'Fine.' Bloggs shook hands.

'The kite's all ready, and the engine's as sweet as a bird. She's an amphibian, I suppose you know.'

'Yes.'

'Jolly good show. We'll land on the sea, taxi in to about ten yards from the shore, and put you off in a dinghy.'

'Then you wait for me to come back.'

'Indeed. Well, all we need now is the weather.'

'Yes. Look, Charles, I've been chasing this bloke all over the country for six days and nights, so I'm catching up on my sleep while I've got the chance. You won't mind.'

'Of course not!' The pilot sat down and produced a thick book from under his jacket. 'Catching up on my education,' he said. '*War and Peace.*'

Bloggs said: 'Jolly good show,' and closed his eyes.

Percival Godliman and his uncle, Colonel Terry, sat side by side in the map room, drinking coffee and tapping the ash of their cigarettes into a fire bucket on the floor between them. Godliman was repeating himself.

'I can't think of anything more we can do,' he said.

'So you said.'

'The corvette is already there, and the fighters are only a few minutes away, so the sub will come under fire as soon as she shows herself above the surface.'

'If she's seen.'

'The corvette will land a party as soon as possible. Bloggs will be there soon after that, and the coastguard will bring up the rear.'

'And none of them can be sure to get there in time.'

'I know,' Godliman said wearily. 'We've done all we can, but is it enough?'

Terry lit another cigarette. 'What about the inhabitants of the island?'

'Oh, yes. There are only two houses there. There's a

sheep farmer and his wife in one – they have a young child – and an old shepherd lives in the other. The shepherd's got a radio – Royal Observer Corps – but we can't raise him: he probably keeps the set switched to Transmit. He's old.'

'The farmer sounds promising,' Terry said. 'If he's a bright fellow he might stop your spy.'

Godliman shook his head. 'The poor chap's in a wheelchair.'

'Dear God, we don't get any luck, do we?'

'No,' said Godliman. 'Die Nadel gets all the luck there is.'

THIRTY-THREE

Lucy was becoming quite calm. The feeling crept over her gradually, like the icy spread of an anaesthetic, deadening her emotions and sharpening her wits. The times when she was momentarily paralysed by the thought that she was sharing a house with a murderer became fewer, and she was possessed by a cool-headed watchfulness that surprised her.

As she went about the household chores, sweeping around Henry as he sat in the living-room reading a novel, she wondered how much he had noticed of the change in her feelings. He was very observant: he did not miss much, and there had been a definite wariness, if not outright suspicion, in that confrontation over the jeep. He must have known she was shaken by something. On the other hand, she had been upset before he left, because Jo had discovered them in bed together: he might think that that was all that had been wrong.

She had the strangest feeling that he knew exactly what was in her mind, but he preferred to pretend that everything was all right.

She hung her laundry on a clothes-horse in the kitchen to dry. 'I'm sorry about this,' she said, 'but I can't wait forever for the rain to stop.'

He looked uninterestedly at the clothes and said: 'That's all right.' He went back into the living-room.

Scattered among the wet garments was a complete set of clean, dry clothes for Lucy.

For lunch she made a vegetable pie using an austerity recipe. She called Jo and Henry to the table and served up.

David's gun was propped in a corner of the kitchen. Lucy said: 'I don't like having a loaded gun in the house, Henry.'

'I'll take it outside after lunch,' he said. 'The pie is good.'

'I don't like it,' Jo said.

Lucy picked up the gun and put it on top of the Welsh dresser. 'I suppose it's all right as long as it's out of Jo's reach.'

Jo said: 'When I grow up I'm going to shoot Germans.'

'This afternoon I want you to have a sleep,' Lucy told him. She went into the living-room and took one of David's sleeping pills from the bottle in the cupboard. Two of the pills were a heavy dose for a 160-pound man, she reasoned, therefore one quarter of one pill should be just enough to make a 50-pound boy sleep in the afternoon. She put the pill on her chopping-block and halved it, then halved it again. She put a quarter on a spoon, crushed it with the back of another spoon, and stirred the powder into a small glass of milk. She gave the glass to Jo and said: 'I want you to drink every last drop.'

Henry watched the whole thing without comment.

After lunch she settled Jo on the sofa with a pile of books. He could not read, of course; but he had heard the stories read aloud so many times that he knew them by heart, and he could turn the pages of the books, looking at the pictures and reciting from memory the words on the page.

'Would you like some coffee?' she asked Henry.

'Real coffee?' he said, surprised.

'I've got a little hoard.'

'Yes, please!'

He watched her making it. She wondered if he was afraid she might try to give him sleeping pills, too. She could hear Jo's voice from the next room:

'What I said was, "Is anybody at home?"' called out Pooh very loudly.

'No!' said a voice . . .

– and he laughed heartily, as he always did at that joke. Oh, God, Lucy thought: don't let Jo be hurt.

She poured the coffee and sat opposite Henry. He reached across the table and held her hand. They sat in silence, sipping coffee and listening to the rain and Jo's voice.

'How long does getting thin take?' asked Pooh anxiously.

'About a week, I should think.'

'But I can't stay here for a week!'

He began to sound sleepy, and then he stopped. Lucy went and covered him with a blanket. She picked up the book, which had slipped from his fingers to the floor. It had been hers when she was a child, and she, too, knew the stories by heart. The flyleaf was inscribed in her mother's copperplate: 'To Lucy, aged four, with love from Mother and Father.' She put the book on the sideboard.

She went back into the kitchen. 'He's asleep.'

'And . . . ?'

She held out her hand. Henry took it. She tugged gently. He stood up. She led him upstairs and into the bedroom. She closed the door, then pulled her sweater off over her head.

For a moment he stood still, looking at her breasts. Then he began to undress.

As she got into the bed, she thought: Give me strength. This was the part that she dreaded, the part she was not sure she could manage: pretending to enjoy his body, when really all she could feel was fear, loathing, and guilt.

He got into bed and embraced her.

In a little while she found she did not have to pretend after all.

For a few seconds she lay in the crook of his arm, wondering how it was that a man could kill so coldly and love so warmly.

But what she said was: 'Would you like a cup of tea?'

He grinned. 'No, thank you.'

'Well, I would.' She extricated herself and got up. When he moved, she put her hand on his flat belly and said: 'No, you stay there. I'll bring the tea up. I haven't finished with you.'

He grinned again. 'You're really making up for your four wasted years.'

As soon as she was outside the room the smile dropped from her face like a mask. Her heart pounded in her chest as she went quickly, naked, down the stairs. In the kitchen she banged the kettle on the stove and rattled some china for realism. Then she began to put on the clothes she had left hidden in the wet laundry. Her hands were shaking so much that she could hardly button the trousers.

She heard the bed creak upstairs, and she stood frozen to the spot, listening, thinking: Stay there! Stay there! But he was only shifting his position.

She was ready. She went into the living-room. Jo was in a deep sleep, grinding his teeth. Dear God, don't let him wake up, Lucy prayed. She picked him up. He muttered in his sleep, something about Christopher Robin, and Lucy closed her eyes tightly and *willed* him to be quiet.

She wrapped the blanket around him securely. She went back into the kitchen and reached up to the top of the Welsh dresser for the gun. It slipped from her grasp and fell to the shelf, smashing a plate and two cups. The crash was deafening. She stood rooted to the spot.

'What happened?' Henry called from upstairs.

'I dropped a cup,' she shouted. She could not suppress the tremor in her voice.

The bed creaked again, and there was a footfall on the floor above her. But it was now too late for her to turn back. She picked up the gun, opened the back door, and, clutching Jo to her, ran across to the barn.

On the way she had a moment of panic: had she left the keys in the jeep? Surely she had: she always did.

She slipped in the wet mud and fell to her knees. She burst into tears. For a second she was tempted to stay there, and let him catch her and kill her as he had killed her husband; then she remembered the child in her arms, and she got up and ran on.

She entered the barn and opened the passenger door of the jeep. She put Jo on the seat. He slipped sideways. Lucy sobbed: 'Oh, God!' She pulled Jo upright, and this time he stayed that way. She ran around to the other side of the jeep and got in, dropping the gun on to the floor between her legs.

She turned the starter.

It coughed and died.

'Please, *please*!'

She turned it again.

The engine roared into life.

Henry came out of the back door at a run.

Lucy raced the engine and threw the gearshift into forward. The jeep leaped out of the barn. She rammed the throttle open.

The wheels spun in the mud for a second, then bit again. The jeep gathered speed with agonizing languor. She steered away from Henry. He chased the vehicle, barefoot in the mud.

She realized he was gaining on her.

She pushed the hand-throttle with all her might, almost snapping the thin lever. She wanted to scream with frustration. Henry was only a yard or so away, almost level with her, running like an athlete, his arms going like pistons, his bare feet pounding the turf, his cheeks blowing, his naked chest heaving.

The engine screamed, and there was a jerk as the automatic transmission changed up, then a new surge of power.

Lucy looked sideways again. Henry seemed to see that he had almost lost her. He flung himself forward through the air in a dive. He got a grip on the door handle with his left hand, and brought the right hand across. Pulled by the jeep, he ran alongside for a few paces, his feet hardly touching the ground. Lucy stared at his face, so close to hers: it was red with effort, twisted in pain; the cords of his powerful neck bulged with the strain.

Suddenly she knew what she had to do.

She took her hand off the wheel, reached through the open window, and poked him viciously in the eye with a long-nailed forefinger.

He let go and fell away, his hands covering his face.

The distance between him and the jeep increased rapidly.

Lucy realized she was crying like a baby.

Two miles from her cottage she saw the wheelchair.

It stood on the cliff top like a memorial, its metal frame and big rubber tyres impervious to the incessant rain. Lucy approached it from a slight dip, and saw its black outline framed by the slate-grey sky and the boiling sea. It had a wounded look, like the hole left by an uprooted tree or a house with broken windows; as if its passenger had been wrenched from it.

She recalled the first time she had seen it, in the hospital. It had stood beside David's bed, new and shiny, and he had swung himself into it expertly and swished up and down the ward, showing off. 'She's light as a feather – made of aircraft alloy,' he had said with brittle enthusiasm, and sped off between the rows of beds. He had stopped at the far end of the ward with his back to her, and after a minute she went up behind him and saw that he was weeping. She had knelt in front of him and held his hands, saying nothing.

It was the last time she had been able to comfort him.

There on the cliff-top, the rain and the salt wind would soon blemish the alloy, and eventually it would rust and crumble, its rubber perished, its leather seat rotted away.

Lucy drove past without slowing.

Three miles farther on, when she was half way between the two cottages, she ran out of petrol.

She fought down the panic and tried to think rationally as the jeep shuddered to a halt.

People walked at four miles an hour, she remembered reading somewhere. Henry was athletic, but he had hurt his ankle, and even though it seemed to have healed rapidly, the running he had done after the jeep must have hurt it. Therefore she must be a good hour ahead of him.

(She had no doubt he *would* come after her: he knew as well as she did that there was a wireless transmitter in Tom's cottage.)

She had plenty of time. In the back of the jeep was a half-gallon can of fuel for just such occasions as this. She got out of the car, fumbled the can out of the back, and opened the petrol cap.

Then she thought again, and the inspiration that came to her surprised her by its fiendishness.

She replaced the petrol cap and went to the front of the car. She checked that the ignition was off and opened the bonnet. She was no mechanic, but she could identify the distributor cap and trace the leads to the engine. She lodged the petrol can securely beside the wheel arch and took off its cap.

There was a plug spanner in the tool kit. She took out a plug, checked again that the ignition was off, and put the plug in the mouth of the petrol can, securing it there with tape. Then she closed the bonnet.

When Henry came along he was certain to try to start the jeep. He would switch on, the starter motor would turn, the plug would spark and the half-gallon of petrol would explode.

She was not sure how much damage it would do, but she could be certain it would be no help.

An hour later she was regretting her cleverness.

Trudging through the mud, soaked to the skin, with the sleeping child a dead weight over her shoulder, she wanted nothing more than to lie down and die. The booby-trap seemed, on reflection, dubious and risky: petrol would burn, not explode; if there was not enough air in the mouth of the can it might not even ignite; worst of all, Henry might suspect a trap, look under the bonnet, dismantle the bomb, pour the petrol into the tank and drive after her.

She contemplated stopping for a rest, but decided that if she sat down she might never get up again.

She should have been in sight of Tom's house by now. She could not possibly have got lost – even if she had not walked this path a dozen times before, the whole island just was not big enough to get lost on.

She recognized a thicket where she and Jo had once seen a fox. She must be about a mile from the shepherd's home. She could have seen it, but for the rain.

She shifted Jo to the other shoulder, switched the shotgun from one hand to the other, and forced herself to continue putting one foot in front of the other.

When at last the cottage became visible through the sheeting rain she could have cried with relief. She was nearer than she thought – perhaps a quarter of a mile.

Suddenly Jo seemed lighter, and although the last stretch was uphill – the only hill on the island – she seemed to cover it in no time at all.

'Tom!' she called as she approached the front door, 'Tom, oh, Tom!'

She heard the answering bark of Bob.

She went in by the front door. 'Tom, quickly!' Bob dodged excitedly about her ankles, barking furiously. Tom could not be far away – he was probably in the outhouse. Lucy went upstairs and laid Jo on Tom's bed.

The wireless was in the bedroom, a complex-looking construction of wires and dials and knobs. There was something that looked like a Morse key: she touched it experimentally, and it gave a beep. A thought came to her from the depths of her memory – something from a schoolgirl thriller – the Morse code for SOS. She touched the key again: three short, three long, three short.

Where was Tom?

She heard a noise, and rushed to the window.

The jeep was making its way up the hill to the house.

Henry had found the booby-trap, and used the petrol to fill the tank.

Where was Tom?

She rushed out of the bedroom, intending to go and bang on the outhouse door. At the head of the stairs she paused. Bob was standing in the open doorway of the other bedroom, the empty one.

'Come here, Bob,' she said. The dog stood his ground, barking. She went to him and bent to pick him up.

Then she saw Tom.

He lay on his back, on the bare floorboards of the vacant bedroom, his eyes staring sightlessly at the ceiling, his cap upside-down on the floor behind his head. His jacket was open, and there was a small spot of blood on the shirt underneath. Close to his hand was a crate of whisky, and Lucy found herself thinking wildly, irrelevantly: I didn't know he drank that much.

She felt his pulse.

He was dead.

Think, *think*!

Yesterday Henry had returned to Lucy's cottage

battered, as if he had been in a fight. That must have been when he killed David. Today he had come here, to Tom's cottage, 'to fetch David' he had said. But he had known David was not there. So why had he made the journey?

Obviously, to kill Tom.

What drove him? What purpose burned inside him so fiercely that he would get in a car, drive ten miles, stick a knife into an old man, and drive back as calm and quiet and composed as if he had been out to take the air? Lucy shuddered.

Now she was on her own.

She took hold of the dog by its collar and dragged it away from the body of its master. On impulse, she returned and buttoned the jacket over the small stiletto wound which had killed the shepherd. Then she closed the door on the corpse. She said to the dog: 'He's dead, but I need you.'

She returned to the front bedroom and looked out of the window.

The jeep drew up in front of the house and stopped; and Henry got out.

THIRTY-FOUR

Lucy's distress call was heard by the corvette.

'Captain, sir,' said Sparks, 'I just picked up an SOS from the island.'

The captain frowned. 'Nothing we can do until we can land a boat,' he said. 'Did they say anything else?'

'Not a thing, sir. It wasn't even repeated.'

The captain thought a little more. 'Nothing we can do,' he said again. 'Send a signal to the mainland, reporting it. And keep listening.'

'Aye, aye, sir.'

It was also picked up by an M18 listening post on top of a Scottish mountain. The R/T operator, a young man with abdominal wounds who had been invalided out of the RAF and had only six months to live, was trying to pick up German Navy signals from Norway, and he ignored the SOS. However, he went off duty five minutes later, and he mentioned it casually to his Commanding Officer.

'It was only broadcast once,' he said. 'Probably a

fishing vessel off the Scottish coast – there might well be the odd small ship in trouble, in this weather.'

'Leave it with me,' the CO said. 'I'll give the Navy a buzz. And I suppose I'd better inform Whitehall. Protocol, y'know.'

'Thank you, sir.'

At the Royal Observer Corps station there was something of a panic. Of course, SOS was not the signal an observer was *supposed* to give when he sighted enemy aircraft, but they knew that Tom was old, and who could say what he might send if he got excited? So the air-raid sirens were sounded, and all other posts were alerted, and anti-aircraft guns were rolled out all over the east coast of Scotland, and the radio operator tried frantically to raise Tom.

No German bombers came, of course; and the War Office wanted to know why a full alert had been sounded when there was nothing in the sky but a few bedraggled geese?

So they were told.

The Coastguard heard it, too.

They would have responded to it, if it had been on the correct frequency, and if they had been able to establish the position of the transmitter, and if that position had been within reasonable distance of the coast.

As it was they guessed, from the fact that the signal

came over on the Observer Corps frequency, that it originated from Old Tom; and they were already doing all they could about *that* situation, whatever the hell that situation was.

When the news reached the below-deck card game on the cutter in the harbour at Aberdeen, Slim dealt another hand of pontoon and said: 'I'll tell you what's happened. Old Tom's caught the prisoner-of-war and he's sitting on his head waiting for the Army to arrive and take the bugger away.'

'Bollocks,' said Smith, and there was general agreement with that sentiment.

And the *U-505* heard it.

She was still more than thirty nautical miles away from Storm Island, but Weissman was roaming the dial to see what he could pick up – and hoping, improbably, to hear Glenn Miller records from the American Forces Network in Britain – and his tuner happened to be on the right wavelength at the right time. He passed the information to Lieutenant-Commander Heer, adding: 'It was not on our man's frequency.'

Major Wohl, who was still around and as irritating as ever, said: 'Then it means nothing.'

Heer did not miss the opportunity to correct him. 'It means *something*,' he said. 'It means that there may be some activity on the surface when we go up.'

'But this is unlikely to trouble us.'

'Most unlikely,' Heer agreed.

'Then it is meaningless.'

'It is *probably* meaningless.'

They argued about it all the way to the island.

So it was that within the space of five minutes the Navy, the Royal Observer Corps, M18 and the Coastguard all phoned Godliman to tell him about the SOS. And Godliman phoned Bloggs.

Bloggs had finally fallen into a deep sleep in front of the fire in the scramble room. The shrill ring of the telephone startled him, and he leaped to his feet, thinking that the planes were about to take off.

A pilot picked it up, said 'Yes' into it twice, and handed it to Bloggs. 'A Mr Godliman for you.'

Bloggs said: 'Hello, Percy.'

'Fred, somebody on the island just broadcast an SOS.'

Bloggs shook his head to clear the last remaining clouds of sleep. 'Who?'

'We don't know. There was just the one signal, not repeated, and they don't seem to be receiving at all.'

'Still, there's not much doubt now.'

'No. Everything ready up there?'

'All except the weather.'

'Good luck.'

'Thanks.'

Bloggs hung up and turned to the young pilot who was still reading *War and Peace*. 'Good news,' he told him. 'The bastard's definitely on the island.'

'Jolly good show,' said the pilot.

THIRTY-FIVE

Henry closed the door of the jeep and began walking quite slowly toward the house. He was wearing David's hacking jacket again. There was mud all over his trousers, where he had fallen, and his hair was plastered wetly against his skull. He was limping slightly on his right foot.

Lucy backed away from the window and ran out of the bedroom and down the stairs. The shotgun was on the floor in the hall, where she had dropped it. She picked it up. Suddenly it felt very heavy. She had never actually fired a gun, and she had no idea how to check whether this one was loaded. She could figure it out, given time; but there was no time.

She took a deep breath and flung open the front door. 'Stop!' she shouted. Her voice was pitched higher than she had intended, and it sounded shrill and hysterical.

Henry smiled pleasantly and kept on walking.

Lucy pointed the gun at him, holding the barrel with her left hand and the breech with her right. Her finger was on the trigger. 'I'll kill you!' she yelled.

'Don't be silly, Lucy,' he said mildly. 'How could you hurt me? After all the things we've done together? Haven't we loved each other, a little . . . ?'

It was true. She had told herself she could not fall in love with him, and that was true too; but she *had* felt *something* for him, and if it was not love, it was something very like.

'You knew about me this afternoon,' he said, and now he was thirty yards away, 'but it made no difference to you then, did it?'

That was true. For a moment, she saw in her mind's eye a vivid picture of herself sitting astride him, holding his sensitive hands to her breasts, and then she realized what he was doing—

'We can work something out, Lucy, we can still have each other—'

– and she pulled the trigger.

There was an ear-splitting crash, and the weapon jumped in her hands like a live thing, its butt bruising her hip with the recoil. She almost dropped it in shock. She had never imagined that firing a gun would feel like that. She was quite deaf for a moment.

The shot went high over Henry's head, but all the same he ducked, turned, and ran zig-zagging back to the jeep. Lucy was tempted to fire again, but she stopped herself just in time, realizing that if he knew both barrels had been emptied there would be nothing to stop him turning and coming back.

He flung open the door of the jeep, leaped in, and shot off down the hill.

Lucy knew he would be back.

Suddenly she felt happy, almost gay. She had won the first round – she had driven him off – and she was a woman!

But he would be back.

Still, she had the upper hand. She was indoors, and she had the gun. And she had time to prepare.

Prepare. She must be ready for him. Next time he would be more subtle. He would surely try to creep up on her.

She hoped he would wait until dark, for that would give her time.

First she had to reload the gun.

She went into the kitchen. Tom kept everything in his kitchen – food, coal, tools, stores – and he had a gun like David's. She knew the two firearms were the same, for David had examined Tom's then sent away for one exactly like it. The two men had enjoyed long discussions about weaponry.

She found Tom's gun and a box of ammunition. She put the two guns and the box on the kitchen table.

Machines were simple, she was convinced: it was apprehension, not stupidity, which made women fumble when faced with a piece of engineering.

She fiddled with David's gun, keeping the barrel pointed away from herself, until it came open at the breech. Then she worked out what she had done to open it, and practised doing it again a couple of times.

It was incredibly simple.

She loaded both guns. Then, to make sure she had done everything correctly, she pointed Tom's gun at the kitchen wall and pulled the trigger.

There was a shower of plaster, Bob barked like a maniac, and she bruised her hip and deafened herself again. But she was armed.

She must remember to pull the triggers gently so as not to jerk the gun and spoil her aim. Men probably got taught that kind of thing in the Army.

What to do next? She should make it difficult for Henry to get into the house.

Neither of the doors had locks, of course: if a house was burgled on this island, one would know that the culprit lived in the other house. Lucy rummaged in Tom's tool box and found a shiny, sharp-bladed axe. She stood on the stairs and began to hack away at the bannister.

The work made her arms ache, but in five minutes she had six short lengths of stout, seasoned oak. She found a hammer and some nails, and fixed the oak bars across the front and back doors, three bars to each door, four nails to each bar. When it was done her wrists were agony and the hammer felt as heavy as lead, but she was not finished.

She got another handful of the shiny, four-inch nails, and went around every window in the house, nailing them shut. She realized, with a sense of discovery, why men always put nails in their mouths: it was because you needed both hands for the work and if you put them in your pocket they stuck into your skin.

By the time she had finished it was dark. She left the lights off.

He could still get into the house, of course; but he could not get in quietly. He would have to break something and give himself away – and then she would be ready with the guns.

She went upstairs, carrying both guns, to check on

Jo. He was still asleep, wrapped in his blanket, on Tom's bed. Lucy struck a match to look at his face. The sleeping pill must have really knocked him out, but he was an average sort of colour, his temperature seemed normal, and he was breathing easily. 'Just stay that way, little boy,' Lucy whispered. The sudden access of tenderness left her feeling more savage toward Henry.

She patrolled the house restlessly for a while, peering through the windows into the darkness, the dog following her everywhere. She took to carrying just one of the guns, leaving the other at the head of the stairs; but she hooked the axe into the belt of her trousers.

She remembered the radio, and tapped out her SOS several more times. She had no idea whether anybody was listening, or even whether the radio was working. She knew no more Morse, so she could not broadcast anything else.

It occurred to her that Tom probably did not know Morse code. Surely he must have a book somewhere? If only she could tell someone what was happening here! She searched the house, using dozens of matches, feeling terrified every time she lit one within sight of a downstairs window; but she found nothing.

All right, perhaps he *did* know Morse.

On the other hand, why should he need it? He only had to tell the mainland that there were enemy aircraft approaching, and there was no reason why that information shouldn't go over the air . . . what was the phrase David had used? . . . *en clair*.

She went back to the bedroom and looked again at

the wireless set. To one side of the main cabinet, hidden from her previous cursory glance, was a microphone.

If she could talk to them, they could talk to her.

The sound of another human voice – a normal, sane, mainland voice – suddenly seemed the most desirable thing in the world.

She picked up the microphone and began to experiment with the switches.

Bob growled softly.

She put the mike down and reached out her hand toward the dog in the darkness. 'What is it, Bob?'

He growled again. She could feel his ears standing stiffly upright. She was terribly afraid: the confidence won by confronting Henry with the gun, by learning how to reload, by barricading the doors and nailing down the windows . . . all evaporated at one growl from an alert dog.

'Downstairs,' she whispered. 'Quietly.'

She held his collar and let him lead her down the stairs. In the darkness she felt for the bannister, forgetting that she had chopped it up for barricades, and she almost overbalanced. She regained her equilibrium and sucked at a splinter in her finger.

The dog hesitated in the hall, then growled more loudly and tugged her toward the kitchen. She picked him up and held his muzzle shut to silence him. Then she crept through the doorway.

She looked in the direction of the window, but there was nothing in front of her eyes other than velvet blackness.

She listened. The window creaked: at first almost inaudibly, then louder. He was trying to get in. Bob rumbled threateningly, deep in his throat, but seemed to understand the sudden squeeze she gave his muzzle.

The night became quieter. Lucy realized the storm was easing, almost imperceptibly. Henry seemed to have given up on the kitchen window. She moved to the living-room.

She heard the same creak of old wood resisting pressure. Now Henry seemed more determined: there were three muffled bumps, as if he were tapping the window-frame with the cushioned heel of his hand.

Lucy put the dog down and hefted the shotgun. It might almost have been imagination, but she could just make out the window as a square of grey in the blank darkness. If he got the window open, she would fire immediately.

There was a much harder bang. Bob lost control and gave a loud bark. She heard a scuffling noise outside.

Then came the voice.

'Lucy?'

She bit her lip.

'Lucy?'

He was using the voice he used in bed: deep, soft, and intimate.

'Lucy, can you hear me? Don't be afraid. I don't want to hurt you. Talk to me, please.'

She had to fight the urge to pull both triggers there and then, just to silence that awful sound and repress the memories it brought to her unwilling consciousness.

'Lucy, my darling . . .' She thought she heard a muffled sob. 'Lucy, he attacked me – I had to kill him . . . I killed for my country, you shouldn't hate me for that.'

She could not understand that. It sounded mad. Could he be insane, and have hidden it for two intimate days? He had seemed saner than most people – and yet he had murdered before . . . unless he was a victim of injustice . . . Damn. She was softening up, and that must be exactly what he wanted.

She had an idea.

'Lucy, just speak to me . . .'

His voice faded as she tip-toed into the kitchen. Bob would warn her if Henry did anything more than talk. She fumbled in Tom's tool-box and found a pair of pliers. She went to the kitchen window and found with her fingertips the heads of the three nails she had hammered there. Carefully, as quietly as possible, she drew them out. The job demanded all her strength.

When they were out she went back into the living-room to listen.

' . . . don't obstruct me, and I'll leave you . . .'

As silently as she could she lifted the kitchen window open. She crept into the living-room, picked the dog up, and returned yet again to the kitchen.

' . . . hurt you, last thing in the world . . .'

She stroked the dog once or twice, and murmured: 'I wouldn't do this if I didn't have to, boy.' Then she pushed him out of the window.

She closed it rapidly, found a nail, and hammered it in at a new spot with three sharp blows.

She dropped the hammer, picked up the gun, and ran into the front room to stand close to the window, pressing herself up against the wall.

'. . . give you one last chance – ah!'

There was a rush of small feet; a blood-curdling bark Lucy had never heard from a sheepdog before; a scuffling sound; and the noise of a big man falling. She could hear Henry's breathing, gasping, grunting; then another flurry of canine paws; a shout of pain; a curse in a foreign language; another bark. She wished she could see what was happening.

The noises became muffled and more distant, then suddenly ceased. Lucy waited, pressed against the wall next to the window, straining her ears. She wanted to go and check on Jo, wanted to try the radio again, wanted to cough; but she did not dare to move. Bloodthirsty visions of what Bob might have done to Henry passed in and out of her mind, and she yearned to hear the dog snuffling at the door.

She looked at the window. Then she *realized* she was looking at the window: she could see, not just a square patch of faintly lighter grey, but the wooden crosspiece of the frame. It was still night, but only just: she knew that if she looked outside the sky would be faintly diffused with a just-perceptible light, instead of being impenetrably black. Dawn would come at any minute. Then she would be able to see the furniture in the room, and Henry would no longer be able to surprise her in the darkness—

There was a crash of breaking glass inches away from her face. She jumped. She felt a small sharp pain in her cheek, touched the spot, and knew that she had been cut by a flying shard. She hefted the shotgun, waiting for Henry to come through the window; but nothing happened. It was not until a minute or two had passed that she wondered what had broken the window.

She peered at the floor. Among the pieces of broken glass was a large dark shape. She found she could see it better if she looked to one side of it rather than directly at it. When she did that, she was able to make out the familiar shape of the dog.

She closed her eyes, then looked away. She was unable to feel any emotion at all at the death of the faithful sheepdog. Her heart had been numbed by all the danger and death that had gone before: first David, then Tom, then the endless screaming tension of the all-night siege . . . All she felt was hunger. All day yesterday she had been too nervous to eat, which meant it was thirty-six hours since her last meal. Now, incongruously, ridiculously, she found herself longing for a cheese sandwich.

Something else was coming through the window.

She saw it out of the corner of her eye, then turned her head to look directly at it.

It was Henry's hand.

She stared at it, mesmerized: a long-fingered hand, without rings, white under the dirt, with cared-for nails and a band-aid around the tip of the index finger; a hand that had touched her intimately, had played her body like a harp, and thrust a knife into the heart of an old shepherd.

The hand broke away a piece of glass, then another,

enlarging the hole in the pane. Then it reached right through, up to the elbow, and fumbled along the windowsill, searching for a catch to unfasten.

Trying to be utterly silent, with painful slowness, Lucy shifted the gun to her left hand, and with her right took the axe from her belt, lifted it high above her head, and brought it down with all her might on Henry's hand.

He must have sensed it, or heard the rush of wind, or seen a blur of ghostly movement behind the window; for he moved sharply a split-second before the blow landed.

The axe thudded into the wood of the windowsill, sticking there. For a fraction of an instant Lucy thought she had missed: then, from outside, there came a scream of pain and loss, and she saw beside the axe blade, lying on the varnished wood like caterpillars, two severed fingers.

She heard the sound of feet running away.

Lucy threw up.

The exhaustion hit her then, closely followed by a surge of self-pity. She had suffered enough, surely to God, had she not? There were policemen and soldiers in the world to deal with situations like this – nobody could expect an ordinary housewife and mother to keep a killer at bay indefinitely. Who could blame her if she gave up now? Who could honestly say they would have done better, lasted longer, stayed brave and resolute and resourceful for another minute?

She was finished. *They* would have to take over: the outside world, the policemen and soldiers, whoever was at the other end of that radio link. She could do no more.

She tore her eyes away from the grotesque objects on the windowsill and went wearily up the stairs. She picked up the second gun and took both weapons into the bedroom with her.

Jo was still asleep, bless him. He had hardly moved all night, utterly oblivious to the apocalypse going on around him. She could tell, somehow, that he was not sleeping so deeply now: something about the look on his face and the way he breathed let her know that he would wake soon and want his breakfast.

She longed for that simple life, now: getting up in the morning, making breakfast, dressing Jo, doing simple, tedious, *safe* household chores like washing and cleaning and cutting herbs from the garden and making pots of tea. It seemed incredible that she had been so dissatisfied with David's lovelessness, the long boring evenings, the endless bleak landscape of turf and heather and rain.

It would never come back, that life.

She had wanted excitement, cities, music, people, ideas. Now the desire for those things had left her, and she could not understand how she had ever wanted them. Peace was all a human being ought to ask for, it seemed to her.

She sat in front of the radio and studied its switches and dials. She would do this one thing, then she would rest. She made a tremendous effort and forced herself to think analytically for a little longer. There were not *so* many possible combinations of switch and dial. She found a knob with two settings, turned it, and tapped the Morse key. There was no sound. Perhaps that meant the microphone was now in circuit.

She pulled it to her and spoke into it. 'Hello, hello, is there anybody there? Hello?'

There was a switch which had 'Transmit' above it and 'Receive' below. It was turned to 'Transmit'. If the world was to talk back to her, obviously she had to throw the switch to 'Receive'.

She said: 'Hello, is anybody listening?' and threw the switch to 'Receive'.

Nothing.

Then: 'Come in, Storm Island, receiving you loud and clear.'

It was a man's voice. He sounded young and strong, capable and confident and reassuring and alive and *normal.*

'Come in, Storm Island, we've been trying to raise you all night . . . where the devil have you *been?*'

Lucy switched to 'Transmit', tried to speak, and burst into tears.

THIRTY-SIX

Percival Godliman had a headache from too many cigarettes and too little sleep. He had taken a little whisky to help him through the long, worried night in his office, and that had been a mistake. Everything oppressed him: the weather, his office, his job, the war. For the first time since he had become a spycatcher he found himself longing for dusty libraries, illegible manuscripts, and medieval Latin.

Colonel Terry walked in with two cups of tea on a tray. 'Nobody around here sleeps,' he said cheerfully. He sat down. 'Ship's biscuit?' He offered Godliman a plate.

Godliman refused the biscuit and drank the tea. It gave him a temporary lift.

'I just had a call from the man with the fat cigar,' Terry said. 'He's keeping the night vigil with us.'

'I can't imagine why,' Godliman said sourly.

'He's worried.'

The phone rang.

'Godliman.'

'I have the Royal Observer Corps in Aberdeen for you, sir.'

'Yes.'

A new voice came on, the voice of a young man. 'Royal Observer Corps, Aberdeen, here, sir.'

'Yes.'

'Is that Mr Godliman?'

'*Yes.*' Dear God, these military types took their time.

'We've raised Storm Island at last, sir.'

'Thank God!'

'It's not our regular observer. In fact it's a woman.'

'What did she say?'

'Nothing, yet, sir.'

'What do you *mean*?' Godliman fought down the angry impatience that rose inside him.

'She's just . . . well, crying, sir.'

'Oh.' Godliman hesitated. 'Can you connect me to her?'

'Yes. Hold on.' There was a pause punctuated by several clicks and a hum. Then Godliman heard the sound of a woman weeping.

He said: 'Hello, can you hear me?'

The weeping went on.

The young man came back on the line to say: 'She won't be able to hear you until she switches to "Receive", sir – ah, she's done it. Go ahead.'

Godliman said: 'Hello, young lady. When I've finished speaking I'll say "Over", then you switch to "Transmit" to speak to me and *you* say "Over" when *you* have finished. Do you understand? Over.'

The woman's voice came on. 'Oh, thank God for somebody sane. Yes, I understand. Over.'

'Now, then,' Godliman said gently, 'tell me what's been happening there. Over.'

'A man was shipwrecked here two – no, three days ago. I think he's the stiletto murderer from London. He killed my husband and our shepherd, and now he's outside the house, and I've got my little boy here . . . I've nailed the windows shut, and fired at him with a shotgun, and barred the doors, and set the dog on him but he killed the dog, and I hit him with the axe when he tried to get in through the window and *I can't do it any more so please come and save me* . . . Over.'

Godliman put his hand over the phone. His face was white. 'You poor woman,' he breathed. But when he spoke to her, he was brisk. 'You must hold on a little longer,' he began. 'There are sailors and coastguards and policemen and all sorts of people on their way to you, but they can't land until the storm ends. Now, there's something I want you to do, and I can't tell you why you must do it because the wrong people may be listening to us, but I can tell you that it is *absolutely essential.* Are you hearing me clearly? Over.'

'Yes, go on. Over.'

'You must destroy your radio. Over.'

'Oh, no, please . . . must I?'

'Yes,' Godliman said, then he realized she was still transmitting.

'I don't . . . I can't . . .' Then there was a scream.

Godliman said: 'Hello, Aberdeen, what's happening?'

The young man came on. 'The set's still transmitting, sir, but she's not speaking. We can't hear anything.'

'She screamed.'

'Yes, we got that.'

'Damn.' Godliman thought for a minute. 'What's the weather like up there?'

'It's raining, sir.' The young man sounded puzzled.

'I'm not making conversation, lad,' Godliman snapped. 'Is there any sign of the storm letting up?'

'It has eased a little in the last few minutes, sir.'

'Good. Get back to me the instant that woman comes back on air.'

'Very good, sir.'

Godliman said to Terry: 'God only knows what that girl's going through up there.' He jiggled the cradle of the phone.

The Colonel crossed his legs. 'If only she would smash up the radio, then . . .'

'Then we don't care if he kills her?'

'You said it.'

Godliman spoke into the phone. 'Get me Bloggs at Rosyth.'

Bloggs woke up with a start, and listened. Outside, it was dawn. Everyone in the scramble hut was listening, too. They could hear nothing. That was what they were listening to: the silence.

The rain had stopped drumming on the tin roof.

Bloggs went to the window. The sky was grey with a band of white on the eastern horizon. The wind had dropped suddenly, and the rain had become a light drizzle.

The pilots started putting on jackets and helmets, lacing boots, lighting last cigarettes.

A klaxon sounded, and a voice boomed out over the airfield: 'Scramble! Scramble!'

The phone rang. The pilots ignored it and piled out through the door. Bloggs picked it up. 'Yes?'

'Percy here, Fred. We just contacted the island. He's killed the two men. The woman's holding him off at the moment, but she won't last much longer.'

Bloggs said: 'The rain has stopped. We're taking off now.'

'Make it fast, Fred. Goodbye.'

Bloggs hung up and looked around for his pilot. Charles Calder had fallen asleep over *War and Peace.* Bloggs shook him roughly. 'Wake up, you dozy bastard, wake up!'

He opened his eyes.

Bloggs could have hit him. 'Wake up, come on, we're going, the storm's ended!'

The pilot jumped to his feet. 'Jolly good show,' he said.

He ran out of the door and Bloggs followed him.

The lifeboat dropped into the water with a crack like a pistol and a wide, V-shaped splash. The sea was far from calm, but here in the partial shelter of the bay there was no risk to a stout boat in the hands of experienced sailors.

The captain said: 'Carry on, Number One.'

The first lieutenant was standing at the rail with three ratings. He wore a pistol in a waterproof holster. He said: 'Let's go, chaps.'

The four men scrambled down the ladders and into the boat. The first mate sat in the stern and the three sailors broke out the oars and began to row.

For a few moments the captain watched their steady progress toward the jetty. Then he returned to the bridge and gave orders for the corvette to continue circling the island.

The shrill ringing of a bell broke up the card game on the cutter.

Slim said: 'I thought something was different. We aren't going up and down so much. Almost motionless, really. Makes me quite seasick.'

Nobody was listening: the crew were hurrying to their stations, some of them fastening life-jackets as they went.

The engines fired with a roar, and the vessel began to tremble faintly but perceptibly.

Up on deck, Smith stood in the prow, enjoying the fresh air and the spray on his face after a day and a night below.

As the cutter left the harbour Slim joined him.

'Here we go again,' Slim said.

'I knew the bell was going to ring then,' Smith said. 'You know why?'

'Tell me.'

'Know what I had in my hand? Ace and a king.'

'Banker's pontoon,' said Slim. 'Well I never.'

*

Lieutenant-Commander Werner Heer looked at his watch and said: 'Thirty minutes.'

Major Wohl nodded impassively. 'What is the weather like?' he asked.

'The storm has ended,' Heer said reluctantly. He would have preferred to keep that information to himself.

'Then we should surface.'

'If your man were there, he would send us a signal.'

'The war is not won by hypothesis, Captain,' said Wohl. 'I firmly suggest that we surface.'

There had been a blazing row, while the U-boat was in dock, between Heer's superior officer and Wohl's; and Wohl's had won. Heer was still captain of the ship, but he had been told in no uncertain terms that he had better have a damned good reason next time he ignored one of Major Wohl's firm suggestions.

'We will surface at six o'clock exactly,' he said.

Wohl nodded again and looked away.

THIRTY-SEVEN

The sound of breaking glass, then an explosion like an incendiary bomb:

Whooomph!

Lucy dropped the microphone. Something was happening downstairs. She picked up a shotgun and ran down.

The living-room was ablaze. The fire centred on a broken jar on the floor. Henry had made some kind of bomb with the petrol from the jeep. The flames were spreading hungrily across Tom's threadbare carpet and licking up over the loose covers of his ancient three-piece suite. A feather-filled cushion caught, and the fire reached up toward the ceiling.

Lucy picked up the cushion and flung it through the broken window, singeing her hand. She tore her coat off and threw it on the carpet, stamping on it. She picked it up again and draped it over the floral settee. She was winning—

There was another crash of glass.

It came from upstairs.

Lucy screamed: 'Jo!'

She dropped the coat and raced up the stairs and into the front bedroom.

Henry was sitting on the bed with Jo on his lap. The child was awake, sucking his thumb, wearing his wide-eyed morning look. Henry was stroking his tousled hair.

Henry said: 'Throw the gun on the bed, Lucy.'

Her shoulders sagged in defeat, and she did as he said. 'You climbed the wall and got through the window,' she said dully.

Henry dumped Jo off his lap. 'Go to Mummy.'

Jo ran to her and she lifted him up.

Henry picked up both guns and went to the radio. He was holding his right hand under his left armpit, and there was a great red bloodstain on his jacket. He sat down. 'You hurt me,' he said. Then he turned his attention to the transmitter.

Suddenly it spoke. 'Come in, Storm Island.'

Henry picked up the microphone. 'Hello?'

'Just a minute.'

There was a pause, then another voice came on. Lucy recognized it as the man in London who had told her to destroy the radio. He would be disappointed in her. It said: 'Hello, this is Godliman again. Can you hear me? Over.'

Henry said: 'Yes, I can hear you, Professor. Seen any good cathedrals lately?'

'Is that . . .'

'Yes.' Henry smiled. 'How do you do.' Then the smile left his face abruptly, as if playtime was over, and he turned the frequency dial of the radio.

Lucy turned and left the room. It was over, and she had lost. She walked listlessly down the stairs and into the kitchen. There was nothing for her to do but wait for him to kill her. She could not run away – she did not have the energy, and he obviously knew it.

She looked out of the window. The storm had ended. The howling gale had dropped to a stiff breeze, there was no rain, and the eastern sky was bright with the promise of sunshine. The sea—

She frowned, and looked again.

Yes, it *was* a submarine.

Destroy the radio, the Professor had said.

Last night Henry had cursed in a foreign language.

'*I did it for my country,*' he had said.

And, in his delirium: *Waiting at Calais for a phantom army.*

Destroy the radio.

Why would a man take a wallet of photographic negatives on a fishing trip?

She had known all along he was not insane.

The submarine was a German U-boat, Henry was an enemy agent, and he was at this very second trying to contact the vessel by radio.

Destroy the radio.

She knew what she had to do. She had no right to give up, now that she understood; for it was not only her life that was at stake. She had to do this one last thing for David and for all the other young men who had died in the war.

She knew what she had to do. She was not afraid of the pain – it would be *very* painful, she knew, and might well kill her – but she had known the pain of childbirth, and it could not be worse than that.

She knew what she had to do. She would have liked to put Jo somewhere else, where he could not see it; but there was no time for that, for Henry would find his frequency at any second, and then it might be too late.

She knew what she had to do. She had to destroy the radio, but the radio was upstairs with Henry, and he had both the guns and he *would* kill her.

She knew what she had to do.

She placed one of Tom's kitchen chairs in the centre of the room, stood on it, reached up and unscrewed the light bulb.

She got off the chair, went to the door, and threw the switch.

'Are you changing the bulb?' Jo said.

Lucy climbed on the chair, hesitated for a moment, then thrust three fingers into the live socket.

There was a bang, an instant of agony, and then unconsciousness.

Faber heard the bang. He had found the right frequency on the transmitter, had thrown the switch to 'Transmit', and had picked up the microphone. He was about to speak when the noise came. Immediately afterwards the lights on the dials of the wireless set went out.

His face suffused with anger. She had short-circuited the electricity supply to the whole house. He had not credited her with that much ingenuity.

He should have killed her before. What the hell was wrong with him? He had never hesitated, not ever, until he met this woman.

He picked up one of the guns and went downstairs.

The child was crying. Lucy lay in the kitchen doorway, out cold. Faber took in the empty light socket with the chair beneath it. He frowned in amazement.

She had done it with her *hand.*

Faber said: 'Jesus Christ Almighty.'

Lucy's eyes opened. She hurt all over.

Henry was standing over her with the gun in his hands. He said: 'Why did you use your hand? Why not a screwdriver?'

She said: 'I didn't know you could do it with a screwdriver.'

He shook his head in incredulity. 'You are a truly astonishing woman,' he said. He lifted the gun, aimed it at her, and lowered it again. '*Damn* you!'

His gaze went to the window, and he started.

'You saw it,' he said.

She nodded.

He stood tense for a moment, then he went to the door. Finding it nailed shut, he smashed the window with the butt of his gun and climbed out.

Lucy got to her feet. Jo threw his arms around her legs. She did not feel strong enough to pick him up. She staggered to the window and looked out.

Henry was running toward the cliff. The U-boat was still there, perhaps half a mile offshore. Henry reached the cliff edge and crawled over. He was going to try to swim to the submarine.

Lucy had to stop him.

Dear God, no more, she prayed.

She climbed through the window, blotting out the cries of her son, and ran after Henry.

When she reached the cliff edge she lay down and looked over. He was about half way between her and the sea. He looked up and saw her, froze for a moment, and then began to move faster, dangerously fast.

Her first thought was to climb down after him. But what would she do then? Even if she caught him, she could not stop him.

The ground beneath her shifted slightly. She scrambled back, afraid it would give way and throw her down the cliff.

That gave her an idea.

She thumped on the rocky ground with both fists. It seemed to shake a little more, and a crack appeared. She got one hand over the edge and thrust the other into the crack. A piece of earthy chalk the size of a watermelon came away in her hands.

She looked over the edge and sighted Henry.

She took careful aim and dropped the stone.

It seemed to fall very slowly. He saw it coming, and covered his head with his arm. It looked as if it would miss him.

The rock passed within a couple of inches of his head, and hit his left shoulder. He was holding on with his left hand. He seemed to loosen his grip. He balanced precariously for a moment. The right hand, the injured one, scrabbled for a hold. Then he appeared to lean out, away from the face of the rock, arms windmilling, until his feet slipped from their narrow ledge and he was suddenly in mid-air, suspended; and finally he dropped like a stone to the rocks below.

He made no sound.

He landed on a flat rock that jutted above the surface of the water. The noise his body made hitting the rock was sickening. He lay there on his back like a broken doll, arms outflung, head at an impossible angle.

Something vile seeped out from inside him on to the stone, and Lucy turned away.

She had killed him.

Everything happened at once, then.

There was a roaring sound from the sky and three aircraft with RAF circles on their wings flew out of the clouds and dipped low over the U-boat, their guns blazing.

Four sailors came up the hill toward the house at a jog-trot, one of them shouting 'Left-right-left-right-left-right.'

Another plane landed on the sea, a dinghy emerged, and a man in a life-jacket began to row toward the cliff.

A small ship came around the headland and steamed aggressively toward the U-boat.

The U-boat submerged.

The dinghy bumped into the rocks at the foot of the cliff, and the man got out and examined the body of Henry.

A boat she recognized as the coastguard cutter appeared.

One of the sailors came up to her and said: 'Are you all right, love? Only there's a little girl in the cottage crying for her mummy.'

'It's a boy,' Lucy said. 'I must cut his hair.' And for no reason at all she smiled.

Bloggs steered the dinghy toward the body at the foot of the cliff. The boat bumped against the rock, and he scrambled out and on to the flat surface.

It was Die Nadel.

He was very dead. His skull had smashed like a glass goblet when he hit the rock. Looking more closely, Bloggs could see that the man had been somewhat battered even before the fall: his right hand was mutilated and there was something wrong with his ankle.

Bloggs searched the body. The stiletto was where he had guessed it might be: in a sheath strapped to the left forearm. In the inside pocket of the expensive-looking, bloodstained jacket, Bloggs found a wallet, papers, money, and a little film can containing twenty-four 35mm photographic negatives. He held them up to the strengthening light: they were the negatives of the prints found in the envelopes Faber had sent to the Portuguese Embassy.

The sailors on the cliff top threw down a rope. Bloggs put Faber's possessions into his own pockets, then tied the rope around the corpse. They hauled it up, then sent the rope down for Bloggs.

When he got to the top one of the sailors said: 'You left his brains on the rock, but never mind.'

The sub-lieutenant introduced himself, and they walked across to the little cottage on top of the hill.

'We haven't touched anything, for fear of destroying evidence,' the senior sailor said.

'Don't worry too much,' Bloggs told him. 'There won't be a prosecution.'

They had to enter the house through the broken kitchen window. The woman was sitting at a table, with the child on her lap. Bloggs smiled at her. He could not think of anything to say.

He looked quickly around the little cottage. It was a battlefield. He saw the nailed-up windows, the barred doors, the remains of the fire, the dog with its throat cut, the shotguns, the broken bannister, and the axe embedded in the windowsill beside two severed fingers.

He thought: What kind of woman is she?

He set the sailors to work: one to tidy the house and unbar the doors and windows; another to mend the blown fuse; a third to make tea.

He sat down in front of the woman and looked at her. She was dressed in ill-fitting, mannish clothes; her hair was wet; her face was dirty. Despite all that she was remarkably beautiful, with lovely amber eyes in an oval face.

Bloggs smiled at the child and spoke very gently to the woman. 'What you've done is enormously important to the war,' he said. 'One of these days I'll explain just how important it is. But for now, I have to ask you two questions. Is that, okay?'

Her eyes focused on him, and after a moment she nodded.

'Did the man Faber succeed in contacting the U-boat by radio?'

The woman just looked blank.

Bloggs found a toffee in his trousers pocket. 'Can I give the boy a sweet?' he asked. 'He looks hungry.'

'Thank you,' she said.

'Now: did Faber contact the U-boat?'

'His name was Henry Baker,' she said.

'Ah. Well, did he?'

'No. I short-circuited the electricity.'

'That was smart,' Bloggs said. 'How did you do it?'

She pointed at the empty light socket above them.

'Screwdriver, eh?'

'No.' She smiled thinly. 'I wasn't that smart. Fingers.'

He gave her a look of horror. The thought of deliberately . . . He shook himself. It was ghastly. He put it out of his mind. 'Right. Do you think anyone on the U-boat could have seen him coming down the cliff?'

The effort of concentration showed on her face. 'Nobody came out of the hatch,' she said. 'Could they have seen him through their periscope?'

'No,' he said confidently. 'This is good news. It means they don't know he's been captured and . . . neutralized. Anyway . . .' He changed the subject hastily. 'You've been through as much as men on the front line are expected to suffer. We're going to get you and the boy to a hospital on the mainland.'

'Yes,' she said.

Bloggs addressed the senior sailor. 'Is there any form of transport around?'

'Yes – a jeep down in that little stand of trees.'

'Good. Will you drive these two over to the jetty and get them on to your boat?'

'Surely.'

'Treat them gently.'

'Of course.'

Bloggs turned to the woman again. He felt an overwhelming surge of affection and admiration for her. She looked frail and helpless, now: but he knew she was brave and strong as well as beautiful. Impulsively, he took her hand. 'When you've been in hospital a day or two, you'll begin to feel terribly depressed. That's a sign you're getting better. I won't be far away, and the doctors will tell me. I'll want to talk to you some more. But not before you feel like it. Okay?'

At last she smiled at him, and it felt like the warmth of a fire. 'You're kind,' she said.

She stood up and carried her child out of the house.

'Kind?' Bloggs muttered to himself. 'God's truth, what a woman.'

He went upstairs to the radio and tuned it to the Royal Observer Corps frequency.

'Storm Island calling, over.'

'Come in, Storm Island.'

'Patch me through to London.'

'Hold on.' There was a long pause, then a familiar voice. 'Godliman.'

'Percy. We caught the . . . smuggler. He's dead.'

'Marvellous, marvellous.' There was triumph in Godliman's voice. 'Did he manage to contact his partner?'

'Almost certainly not.'

'Well done, well done!'

'Don't congratulate me,' Bloggs said. 'By the time I got here it was all over bar the tidying up.'

'Who killed him, then?'

'The woman.'

'Well, I'm damned. What's she like?'

Bloggs grinned. 'She's a hero, Percy.'

Godliman laughed aloud. 'I think I know what you mean.'

THIRTY-EIGHT

Hitler stood at the panoramic window, looking out at the mountains. He wore his dove-grey uniform, and he looked tired and depressed. He had called his physician during the night.

Admiral Puttkamer saluted and said: 'Good morning, my Führer.'

Hitler turned and peered closely at his aide-de-camp. Those beady eyes never failed to unnerve Puttkamer. Hitler said: 'Was Die Nadel picked up?'

'No.' There was some trouble at the rendezvous – the English police were chasing smugglers. It appears Die Nadel was not there, anyway. He sent a wireless message a few minutes ago.' He proffered a sheet of paper.

Hitler took it from him, put on his spectacles, and began to read:

YOUR RENDEZVOUS INSECURE YOU CUNTS I AM WOUNDED AND TRANSMITTING LEFT HANDED FIRST UNITED STATES ARMY GROUP ASSEMBLED EAST ANGLIA UNDER PATTON ORDER OF BATTLE AS FOLLOWS TWENTYONE INFANTRY DIVISIONS FIVE ARMOURED DIVISIONS APPROXIMATELY FIVE THOUSAND AIRCRAFT PLUS REQUISITE TROOP

SHIPS IN THE WASH FUSAG WILL ATTACK CALAIS JUNE FIFTEENTH REGARDS TO WILLI

Hitler handed the message back to Puttkamer and sighed. 'So it's Calais after all.'

'Can we be sure of this man?' the aide asked.

'Absolutely.' Hitler turned and walked across the room to a chair. His movements were stiff, and he seemed in pain. 'He is a loyal German. I know his family.'

'But your instinct . . .'

'Ach . . . I said I would trust this man's report, and so I shall.' He made a gesture of dismissal. 'Tell Rommel and Rundstedt they can't have their panzers. And send in that damned doctor.'

Puttkamer saluted again and went out to relay the orders.

EPILOGUE

THIRTY-NINE

When Germany defeated England in the quarter-final of the 1970 World Cup soccer tournament Grandpa was furious.

He sat in front of the colour television set and muttered through his beard at the screen. 'Cunning!' he told the assorted experts who were now dissecting the game. 'Cunning and stealth! That's the way to defeat the Hun!'

He would not be mollified until his grandchildren arrived. Jo's white Jaguar drew up on the drive of the modest three-bedroom house, and little David rushed in to sit on Grandpa's lap and pull his beard. The rest of the family followed more sedately: Rebecca, David's little sister; then Jo's wife Ann; then Jo himself, prosperous-looking in a suede jacket. Grandma came out of the kitchen to greet them.

Jo said: 'Did you watch the football, Pop?'

'Terrible,' Grandpa said. 'We were rubbish.' Since he retired from the Force and had more leisure time, he had taken an interest in sport.

Jo scratched his moustache. 'The Germans were better,' he said. 'They play good football. We can't win it every time.'

'Don't talk to me about bloody Germans,' Grandpa said.

Jo grinned. 'I do a lot of business with Germany.'

Grandma's voice came from the kitchen. 'Don't start him off, Jo!' She pretended to be going deaf, but there was not much she missed.

'I know,' Grandpa said. 'Forgive and forget, and drive round in a bloody Audi.'

'Good cars.'

'Cunning and stealth, that's the way to defeat the Hun,' Grandpa repeated. He addressed the grandson on his lap, who was not really his grandson, since Jo was not his son. 'That's the way we beat them in the war, Davy – we tricked them.'

'How did you trick them?' David asked, with the child's assumption that his forebears did everything in history.

'Well, see, we made them think—' Grandpa's voice became low and conspiratorial, and the child giggled in anticipation. 'We made them think we were going to attack Calais—'

'That's in France, not Germany.'

'Yes, but the Germans were all over France, then. The Froggies didn't defend themselves as well as we did.'

Jo said: 'Nothing to do with the fact that we're an island, of course.'

Ann shushed him. 'Let Grandpa tell his war stories.'

'Anyway,' Grandpa continued, 'we made them think we were going to attack Calais, so they put all their tanks and soldiers there.' He used a cushion to represent France, an ashtray for the Germans, and a penknife for the Allies. '*But* we attacked Normandy, and there was nobody there but old Rommel and a few pop-guns! Cunning and stealth, see?'

'Didn't they find out about the trick?' David asked.

'They *nearly* did. In fact, there was one spy who found out. Now not many people know that, but I know because I was a spycatcher in the war.'

'What happened to the spy?'

'We killed him before he could tell.'

'Did you kill him, Grandpa?'

'No – Grandma did.'

David's eyes widened. '*Grandma* killed him?'

Grandma came in carrying a teapot, and said: 'Fred Bloggs, are you frightening the children?'

'Why shouldn't they know?' he groused. 'She's got a medal, you know. She won't tell me where she keeps it because she doesn't like me showing it to visitors.'

Grandma was pouring tea. 'It's all over now, and best forgotten, just as Jo says. Anyway, not much good came out of it.' She handed a cup and saucer to Grandpa.

He took her arm and held her there. '*Some* good came out of it,' he said. His voice was suddenly quite gentle, all the elderly grumpiness gone. 'I met a hero, and married her.'

They looked at each other for a moment. Her beautiful hair was pepper-and-salt now, and she wore it in a bun. She was heavier than she used to be. For years her clothes had always been fashionable and glamorous, but she no longer had the figure for haute couture.

But her eyes were still the same: large and amber, and remarkably beautiful.

Those eyes looked back at him, now, and they both were very still, remembering the way it had been.

Then David jumped off his grandpa's lap and knocked the cup of tea to the floor, and the spell was broken.

The Pillars of the Earth

Critical acclaim for the worldwide bestselling epic
The Pillars of the Earth, ***voted into the BBC's top 100 of Britain's favourite novels***

'Enormous and brilliant . . . this mammoth tale seems to touch all human emotion – love and hate, loyalty and treachery, hope and despair. See for yourself. This is truly a novel to get lost in'
Cosmopolitan

'A highly enjoyable tale . . . this book evokes its period brilliantly'
Sunday Times

'A historical saga of such breadth and density . . . Follett succeeds brilliantly in combining hugeness and detail to create a novel imbued with the rawness, violence and blind faith of the era'
Sunday Express

extracts reading groups
competitions books new
discounts extracts
competitions
books new
events books
extracts
new reading groups
interviews
events extracts
discounts
new books events
events new
discounts extracts discounts
www.panmacmillan.com
extracts events reading groups
competitions books extracts new

THE SPIRE

Richard North Patterson is the bestselling author of *Eclipse*, *Exile*, *The Race* and fourteen other critically acclaimed novels. Formerly a trial lawyer, he was the SEC liaison to the Watergate special prosecutor and has served on the boards of several Washington advocacy groups. He lives in San Francisco and on Martha's Vineyard with his wife, Dr Nancy Clair.

Praise for Richard North Patterson's fiction

'An astonishing book, a hugely entertaining human drama'
Bill Clinton

'Easily the most compelling novel about US politics since *Primary Colors*'
Spectator

'A grippingly believable portrayal of the nitty-gritty of American politics'
Sunday Times

'Every now and then – but a lot more rarely than that implies – you come across a thriller so important that it absolutely demands to be read. This is one'
The Times

'Richard North Patterson has combined the legal and political thriller genres with this gripping tale'
Daily Telegraph

ALSO BY RICHARD NORTH PATTERSON

In the Name of Honour
Eclipse
The Race
Exile
Conviction
Balance of Power
Protect and Defend
Dark Lady
No Safe Place
Silent Witness
The Final Judgment
Eyes of a Child
Degree of Guilt
Private Screening
Escape the Night
The Outside Man
The Lasko Tangent

THE SPIRE

A Novel

RICHARD NORTH
PATTERSON

PAN BOOKS

First published 2009 by Henry Holt and Company, New York

First published in Great Britain 2010 by Macmillan

This edition published 2010 by Pan Books
an imprint of Pan Macmillan, a division of Macmillan Publishers Limited
Pan Macmillan, 20 New Wharf Road, London N1 9RR
Basingstoke and Oxford
Associated companies throughout the world
www.panmacmillan.com

ISBN 978-1-4472-0878-5

1 3 5 7 9 8 6 4 2

A CIP catalogue record for this book is available from the British Library.

Typeset by Intype Libra Ltd, London
Printed in the UK by CPI Mackays, Chatham ME5 8TD

For Justin Feldman and Linda Fairstein

PROLOGUE

THE OFFER

SIXTEEN YEARS AFTER THE MURDER OF ANGELA HALL had precipitated the decline of Caldwell College, Mark Darrow returned to campus, standing in the shadow of the Spire.

Darrow had come at the urgent request of Dr. Lionel Farr, his professor and mentor, one of the seminal figures in Caldwell's history and in Darrow's life. It was the end of the spring semester and blossoming dogwood trees, set between generous oaks, brightened the landscape with pink. Even here, Darrow could detect Farr's influence; since becoming provost, Lionel Farr had overseen the planting of pine trees and neatly tended gardens, giving the foliage both variety and order. But the buildings spaced throughout had no particular theme: the oldest–elaborate brownstones with Gothic steeples and towers–were mixed with square, staid structures from the late nineteenth century and newer buildings in a variety of architectural styles, some more nondescript than others. As a student, Darrow had found this hodgepodge engaging, a stone-and-brick record of the growth of Caldwell College over time. Though the campus would never resemble that of a picture-book college, these structures had housed generations of students and nurtured much learning–including, as Darrow gratefully remembered, his own.

The current students looked much like Darrow's

classmates had all those years ago. With the subdued, somewhat dazed look of college kids facing finals, they wandered past him, taking little notice, Darrow reflected wryly, of the former campus legend, now a late-thirtyish lawyer in a business suit, headed for his meeting with the presidential search committee of a small Ohio school in crisis. Then Darrow looked up at the Spire, recalling the most vivid hours of his youth, and all trace of humor vanished.

Erected two decades before the Civil War by the school's founder, the Reverend Charles Caldwell, the tower remained as Caldwell had intended: the epicenter of campus, with four brick pathways radiating outward like spokes, the other buildings set at an appropriate, almost reverent distance. At its base was chiseled, CHRIST, THE CHIEF CORNERSTONE. From there, at Caldwell's insistence, over two hundred feet of sandstone rose above everything but sky.

The founder's aspirations had been realized–the Spire dominated both the landscape and the psyche of Caldwell College. Its image graced the yearbook, the alumni magazine, the school's letterhead, and, for over 160 years, had decorated every diploma issued to a graduate of Caldwell. Part of Darrow's fraternity initiation had been to memorize *Webster's* definition of a spire: "a structure that tapers to a point at the top, as in a steeple." Just below the steeple, in a space with four long openings, the great bell of the college hung, its deep resonant clang reserved for moments of celebration or sadness. The lawn beneath the Spire was the scene of graduations, weddings, pep rallies, and memorial services. In the week before Caldwell's annual football grudge match with its hated rival, Ohio Lutheran, students guarded it at night from vandals: by long tradition, the Spire was where, if Caldwell emerged triumphant, the celebration would begin. It was on such a Saturday in November that a twenty-one-year-old Mark Darrow had ascended the Spire for the first and only time, never imagining that, within hours, this memory, and this place, would turn dark for all the years that followed.

A scant hour before, Mark had thrown the last of four touchdown passes, sealing Ohio Lutheran's defeat; Coach Fiske, whose privilege this was, had designated Mark to ring the bell atop the Spire. Very rarely was a student admitted to the bell tower–the Spire's oaken door had been padlocked since 1938, when a drunken celebrant had fallen from the Spire to his death. The new president, Clark Durbin, had opened the door for Mark and passed him the ceremonial bronze axe with the chip in its blade, the spoils of Caldwell's victory. Then Mark stepped inside.

Alone, he paused inside the shadowy tower, filled with awe and reluctance. Since early childhood, Mark had loathed confined spaces; the absence of light frightened and depressed him. The winding staircase, dark and dank and steep, led, in Mark's imagination, to a chamber suitable to druids or high priests. Battling claustrophobia, conscious of his responsibility to commence the celebration, Mark started climbing. He felt his chest tighten, a nameless terror choking his breathing. As a distraction, he counted each stone step to confirm that–as his fraternity had also required him to remember–the Spire had 207 steps, each one foot high.

Reaching the top at last, Mark opened its door. The square chamber was bare, its mortared stone walls adding to its severity. Hanging over him was a massive brass bell. Mark's other aversion was heights: though the four long openings of the tower began at his waist, he approached the one he had chosen gingerly, as though some invisible hand might send him hurtling into space. But as he surveyed the throng below, a surge of triumph overcame his fear.

The lawn was covered with students, many of whom had already embarked on an alcohol-fueled bacchanalia that, for some, might last until dawn. Among them stood Lionel Farr, his wife, Anne, and their twelve-year-old daughter, Taylor, who had waited with the others for Mark to appear. Mark spotted them and then, for Farr more than anyone, he brandished the axe, his grin of triumph spreading as Taylor waved back with an adolescent's adoration. Seeing him, the crowd let loose with a deep-throated roar. Then, heart pounding, Mark reached for the heavy iron chain . . .

Staring up at the tower, Darrow could still hear the deep tolling whose echo had nearly deafened him. But now there were spotlights placed around the Spire, so that darkness never came here. This, too, was the work of Lionel Farr.

THE MOMENTS BEFORE he had first met Farr—an encounter that changed his life forever—were also imprinted in Darrow's memory.

He had been a seventeen-year-old in a small Ohio town, a star football player but a middling student. With no real family or any future he could see, he hoped only to wrest one timeless moment from a high school athlete's transient glory. His chance came down to the last play of his final game as quarterback of the Wayne Generals. The air was crisp, carrying the smell of popcorn and burnt leaves; the field, a bowl of light in the darkness, reverberated with the enthusiasm of a football town of seventeen thousand, perhaps half of them here huddled against the cold, screaming and stomping the wooden bleachers with booted feet, the small minority of blacks quieter and seated in their own clusters. There were six yards to go, four seconds left, three points between Wayne and its first defeat in an otherwise perfect season. The Generals broke the huddle, seven linemen in blue jerseys loping toward the line of scrimmage, their shadows moving alongside, as Mark, two running backs, and a flanker spread out behind them. Opposite them was the Cloverdale defense, eleven boys in green uniforms, their four defensive backs–poised to thwart a pass or run–portraits of taut alertness.

For an instant Mark took it all in–the light and darkness, the primal roar of the crowd, the illuminated clock frozen at 0:04. Pulsing with adrenaline, he positioned himself, setting his hands between the center's legs, conscious of his halfback, George Garrison, slightly behind and to the right. Time slowed for Mark; the cadence of his voice seemed to come from somewhere else.

The ball snapped into his hands.

Spinning, Mark slid the ball into George's stomach, then withdrew it as George, the decoy, hit the line as though determined to break through. Alone, Mark sprinted toward the sideline with the ball. Two linebackers ran parallel, barring his path to the end zone while his own blockers fanned in front of him. Without seeming to look, Mark saw the flanker, Steve Tillman, suddenly break toward the center of the field, two feet ahead of the back assigned to cover him.

At once Mark decided. Stopping abruptly, he threw the ball, praying that Steve would reach it before it fell to earth. Desperately, Steve leaped, feet leaving the grass as he stretched, arms extended, grasping at the ball. Then he clasped it, clutching it to his stomach as he landed near the goal line amid the crowd's thin cry of uncertainty, awaiting the referee's signal that Steve had either reached it or fallen short, the difference between victory and defeat.

Mark's heart raced. Then, gazing down at Steve, the referee thrust both hands into the air.

Tears came to Mark's eyes, a swift surge of joy and loss. This was it, he was certain: the last clear triumph of his life.

The first teammate to reach him, George Garrison, hugged him, his round black face alight. But when Steve Tillman wedged between them, George turned away. "You're the best," Steve said. When Mark reached out for George, he was gone.

The next half hour was a blur–the screaming crowd; the shouted questions from sports reporters; the celebration in the locker room, joyous yet shadowed by the seniors' awareness, so vivid in Mark's mind, that this was the end, deepened by his own deflating knowledge that he had no plan or even hope for where his life might take him now. When he emerged into the chill night with Steve, his sole vision of the future was to take Steve's station wagon and, armed with beer and whiskey, meet two girls at the reservoir.

A man stood in their path, hands thrust into his pockets. "Mark?"

Mark paused, impatient to be on his way, regarding the stranger with mild annoyance. "I'm Lionel Farr," the man said in a voice of calm authority. "I teach at Caldwell College."

Though Mark had met other professors at Caldwell–all of them parents of his classmates–Farr looked like none of them. An inch or two taller than Mark, Farr had strong features and the erect posture of an athlete or a soldier. Unlike most of the townspeople, he was bareheaded;

instead of a jacket, he wore an olive wool coat, belted at the waist, adding to his martial air. Nodding to Steve, Farr asked Mark, "Can we talk for a moment?"

Shooting a glance at his friend, who was obviously mystified, Mark saw George Garrison leaving with a pretty classmate, Angela Hall. He thought to call out to them; then, not knowing the black girl, and aware of Steve and George's aversion to each other, he stifled the thought. "I'll meet you at the car," he told Steve.

Steve walked away, casting a last look of bemusement toward his friend. Turning to Farr, Mark said, "What is it?"

The brusque inquiry evoked the trace of a smile. "I've been watching you all season," Farr responded. "You have great presence of mind and understand the game. You could play football in college."

Mark shook his head. "Too small, too slow."

Farr continued to look amused. "I didn't mean at Ohio State. The right college–Division III-A, where small but slow has a chance to survive."

Mark shook his head, feeling the obscure resentment of someone being baited. "Those schools don't give scholarships. For grades, maybe, but not football."

"What *are* your college plans?"

Mark looked down. "I don't know. Money's a problem." He hesitated. "So's my transcript."

Farr waited until Mark met his eyes. "I understand. I know something about your life, Mark. The money and grades seem to be related."

Instinctively, Mark bridled at this intimation of sympathy.

"I have friends at the high school," Farr added mildly. "I hope you don't mind that I did a little checking."

In the semidarkness, Mark studied the professor's face. "It sort of depends on the reason."

Despite Mark's curtness, Farr looked unfazed. "A good one, I think. But this isn't the time and place to discuss it. My wife and I would like you to come for dinner."

Mark was unsettled. He did not know this man at all, let alone what this was about. Seeing Mark's reluctance, Farr continued, "Why don't we say Monday. You can come to my four o'clock class, then home with me. A small taste of college life."

Bereft of words, Mark responded to the stranger's understated but palpable force of personality. "I guess so. Sure."

"Good. I'll call the Tillmans with directions."

With this last suggestion that Farr was uncomfortably conversant with Mark's life, Farr extended his hand.

As though responding to an order, Mark took it.

YEARS LATER, MARK Darrow wondered if his interest in justice and morality, the seeds of his law career, had wakened that next Monday in Farr's four o'clock seminar.

Mark did not know the campus; for him it existed as a rarefied world, in which young people smarter and more privileged than him engaged in a mysterious rite of passage, learning punctuated by drunken parties. "Brundage Hall is behind the Spire," Dr. Farr had told him, and so he made his way toward the tower, which before he had only glimpsed above the trees that shrouded the campus. He took one path, then another, until the campus opened to the large grassy circle at its heart. Positioned at the center of the circle, the Spire was austere but strangely powerful: weathered and stained by time, it was topped by a graceful steeple so high that Mark had to lean back to see it. Hurrying past, he managed to find Farr's class.

Dressed in boots, khakis, and a wool fisherman's

sweater, Farr paused momentarily in his lecture, nodding briefly to Mark as he found a desk in one corner of the musty classroom. Turning back to the dozen or so students clustered near the front, Farr said, "Friedrich Nietzsche was hardly the first philosopher to challenge the concept of objective morality. Who were his most convincing predecessors?"

Several hands shot up; Farr pointed to a bearded, red-haired kid in an army jacket. "Callicles and Thrasymachus," he answered, "in Plato's dialogues. Both argued that the idea of 'justice' is a sham, a subjective means of social control, and that therefore a wise man subverts 'justice' to his own ends."

"Then what makes Nietzsche distinctive?"

The redhead answered swiftly, eagerly: "He attacked two thousand years of Western thought, where philosophers promoted 'morality' as a kind of social glue."

Farr nodded. After barely a minute, Mark had grasped how completely he commanded the classroom, how intensely the students wanted his approval or, at least, to interest him. "So if moralists are charlatans or fools, Mr. Clyde, what did Nietzsche think was at the root of our foolishness?"

"Religion," a pudgy student in wire-rimmed glasses responded. "The Christians and Jews were weak; the Romans who ruled them were strong. Therefore these religions used the idea of morality as a defense against the Romans, who, by accepting 'morality,' would be more likely to allow them to survive."

"If," Farr asked, "our most sacred moral precepts–even the Ten Commandments–are merely a tactical invention of the weak, what does that imply?"

Mark felt the desire to object–he had learned the Ten Commandments in Sunday school, and the subordination of self from a string of coaches. "Racism," a dark-haired female student said sharply. "If Jews are weak, and morality a fantasy they invented to survive, there's no reason not to exterminate them."

Farr gave her an arid smile. "To be fair, Nietzsche also says some rather nasty things about Christians, Germans, and his fellow philosophers."

"But he *can* be read to justify evil." Glancing at her notes, the young woman read, "'As the wicked enjoy a hundred kinds of happiness of which the virtuous have no inkling, so do they possess a hundred kinds of beauty.' Hitler would have agreed."

Farr eyed her narrowly, his leonine head still, as though deciding whether to play this out. "What is Nietzsche positing about man's inherent nature?"

"It suggests that we have within us the desire to be cruel and the need to dominate."

Farr cocked his head. "Let's put that to the test, Ms. Rosenberg. Suppose you ordered one of your classmates whipped or beaten. How would you feel?"

I couldn't do that, Mark thought automatically. The young woman answered promptly, "I'd feel guilty."

Farr's cool blue eyes glinted. "To Nietzsche, justice is merely a mechanism through which the state exerts its will, dressing it up in moral sentiments to disguise its exercise of power. What does this do to the concept of guilt?"

The woman hesitated. "That it only exists in our own minds," a clean-cut blond man interjected. "Nietzsche suggests that guilt is a mechanism of social control, keeping us from exercising our own free will."

Once again, Farr nodded briskly. Mark felt the relationship between teacher and class as an organic entity, in which, directed by Farr, minds fed upon one another.

As the debate continued, Mark was surprised to

discover that he grasped its core: Does whoever is in authority make the rules to suit themselves, or are some rules a simple matter of right and wrong? "For our next discussion," Farr concluded, "I ask you to consider your own nature. Do you refrain from theft or rape or murder because you're afraid of getting caught or because you'd feel guilty? And, if so, is your guilt based on anything more than what you've been trained to feel?" A smile played on Farr's lips. "I expect an answer from each of you by Thursday."

With that, the students began slowly filing out, as though still pondering the question. Picking up a trim leather briefcase, Farr asked in a tone of mild inquiry, "Do *you* have an answer, Mark?"

Looking up at the keen face of this professor, Mark felt the same need to please him he had seen in the others, even as he tried to find the bones of a response. Instinctively, he said, "I don't think the rules were just made up. If there weren't any, we'd all end up killing each other. You can't always count on being the strongest."

Farr laughed softly. "I should introduce you to Thomas Hobbes. We can talk about *him* on the way home."

A FEW MINUTES later, Mark entered yet another world.

The Farrs' home, a rambling red-brick structure located on a tree-lined street, was strikingly different from the shotgun ranch house Mark had lived in for most of his seventeen years. It dated back to the 1850s, Farr explained. Lovingly restored, the living room featured a hardwood floor covered by rich-looking Oriental rugs; shelves filled with hardcover books; and paintings that, because they resembled nothing in life, Mark assumed to be modern art. But perhaps most striking was Anne Farr, extending her hand with a smile at once gracious and reserved, her jet-black hair showing the first few strands of gray, her handsome, chiseled face so pale Mark thought of porcelain, her eastern accent suggesting what people called good breeding. "Excuse me while I see to dinner," she told him pleasantly. "You two just enjoy yourselves."

Looking around, Mark noticed a sunroom containing white wicker furniture and a slender young girl seated at an easel. He could see only her back; dark-haired like her mother, she painted with total concentration, applying a new brushstroke so carefully her hand barely seemed to move. Noticing Mark's curiosity, Lionel Farr led him to the sunroom, speaking gently as though not to break the girl's spell.

"Taylor," Farr ventured, then added with pleasant irony, "this is Mr. Darrow."

The girl turned. Mark guessed that she was seven or eight; blue-eyed and grave, she regarded him in preternatural silence, as though assessing how she should feel about this stranger. If Anne Farr was still a beauty, someday this child would become one. "My name's Mark," he amended with a smile.

Silent, she continued her deep appraisal of him. Awkwardly, Mark asked, "Do you paint a lot?"

"Yes," she answered with surprising directness. "But I'm not very good."

Her painting was a child's landscape. Though the sky was pale blue, its sun was partially obscured by clouds. Beneath it, the figure of a girl stood in shadow, gazing down at a patch of sunlit grass. "Looks to me like you're good," Mark said.

This induced her first smile, skeptical but pleased, even as her serious eyes still focused on Mark's face. "It *is* good," her father offered. "We'll let you finish it, Taylor."

Farr led Mark to a book-lined study with two leather

chairs, a rolltop desk, and an antique world globe featuring countries that no longer existed. For Mark, the life of privilege this suggested was as alien—though more refined—as what he saw on *Beverly Hills 90210*. "Taylor's like her mother," Farr was remarking. "Somewhat reserved, and very artistic. Anne paints as well, though her real forte is poetry."

Mark could not think of a response. Then his eye caught an oil painting of an officer he guessed might be from the Revolutionary War and, near that, a map of Vietnam. "That's General Wayne," Farr said of the painting, "'Mad Anthony'—the man who gave your football team its name. He cleared the Indian confederacy out of Ohio, gaining a reputation for military genius and a mercurial temper. I don't know that he was mad, though sometimes genius and madness feed upon each other."

Mark turned to the map. "Were you there?"

"Vietnam? Yes. I was an officer in the Special Forces."

Mark thrust his hands in his pockets. "What was it like?"

He felt Farr weigh his answer. "Suffice it to say I learned things there that West Point hadn't prepared me for, including what men are capable of doing when there's no constraint on their impulses or desire. Which, I suppose, was the point of today's lecture."

Mark turned to him. "I wish I knew more about that philosopher."

"Not all my students find Nietzsche uplifting." He waved Mark to a leather chair, settling into his own. "Nevertheless, it's important to examine the choices you make, and the freedom you feel to choose. Do you know anything about Jean-Paul Sartre?"

"Not really, no."

Translated, Mark's answer meant "Never heard of him."

Nodding benignly, Farr continued: "Sartre contends that the human condition is one of absolute freedom. His argument is that we're free to make choices that reflect our authentic self. So let me ask you this, Mark: If you could define yourself, who and what would you choose to be?"

The abrupt shift to the personal made Mark fidget. "I haven't really thought about it," he confessed. "I mean, what's the point?"

Farr's face seemed to harden. "What do *you* think it is? From your test scores, you're far brighter than your grades suggest."

Mark felt defensive and exposed. "Why not just call me an underachiever."

Farr looked unfazed. "Because I think that's oversimplified. Tell me how you came to live with Steve Tillman's family."

Mark had sensed that Farr already knew. "It's simple," he said in a flat tone. "My mother's been put away–she's a drunk, and she's crazy. My dad's just a drunk. Being with them was like living alone, only worse."

Farr nodded, seemingly less in sympathy than in acknowledgment of a truth. "It must be difficult not to feel cheated."

"Mostly I don't give a damn." Feeling Farr's probing gaze, Mark felt himself speak against his will. "Sometimes I got pissed off at them. I still can."

"Understandably. But your problem is that the world doesn't care. The only person you're hurting is yourself."

Mark heard a knock. Anne Farr leaned in, looking from her husband to Mark. "I hope I'm not interrupting. But I thought you two might like your dinner warm."

The dining room was as elegant and subdued as the living room was bright. Taylor was lighting candles, the only source of illumination. "We do this every night,"

Anne explained. "In Boston, where I grew up, my parents made a ritual of it. Candlelight slowed us down, my father said, gave us time to talk."

Over dinner, fish in a surprisingly tasty sauce, Mark sensed that he was expected to converse. Groping for a subject, he asked about Anne's poetry. She was published in literary magazines, he discovered, too obscure for him to know. "I'm sorry," he apologized. "The only ones I read are *Sports Illustrated* and *Field and Stream*."

Farr laughed. "Anne and Taylor are the aesthetes in the family. There's more beauty in one of Taylor's paintings, or a line of Anne's poetry, than in the entire book I'm writing now."

Mark had never known anyone who had written a book. "About Nietzsche?"

Farr smiled. "Yet again. But it's more a psychological study, relating his life to his beliefs–the why of them, I suppose. Including the idea that a man's supposedly objective beliefs are so often a product of his needs."

Anne Farr appraised her husband with a neutral expression. "You do believe that, don't you."

Her husband's smile faded. "Yes. Unfortunately, perhaps."

Quiet, Taylor watched them. Noting this, Mark turned to Taylor and asked about her painting. Somewhat wistfully, the girl said, "I know what's beautiful. But I can't paint it in real life."

"You will someday," Mark assured her. "When I was seven, I couldn't throw a football."

"Can you now?"

Mark smiled. "A little."

After dessert, a caramel flan, Mark offered to help clear the table. "The women can tackle it," Farr said dryly. "Let's finish our discussion."

Settling back in the den, Farr said, "From our talk on Friday, I assume you'd continue playing football if you could."

Despite their courtesy, Mark realized how much at sea he felt in the Farrs' household. Hesitant, he answered, "Sports is the only place I feel at home."

"You can find others, Mark. But first you have to change your destiny. For so many kids in Wayne, life after high school means a job making auto parts, or copper fittings, or maybe helping to fabricate Sky Climbers to wash the windows of buildings in big cities most of them will never see. I assume you must want more than that."

Once again, Mark felt on edge, grasping for the threads of a response. "Maybe go to community college. I thought someday I might want to coach."

Farr shook his head. "I was watching you in class today. A full scholarship to Caldwell College would open worlds you've never imagined."

Mark struggled to absorb this. It took a moment for him to realize how long he had been silent. "Sorry. I mean, how could that happen?"

"I'm the chairman of Caldwell's scholarship committee. You certainly qualify financially. If you can get your grades up this semester, I'm sure the committee would take notice. We want to reach more kids who lack opportunities."

Mark still could find no words. "Amazing," he finally murmured.

"You don't know *how* amazing," Farr said firmly. "A solid education. A chance to play sports, and then to do far more than that–become a lawyer, a teacher, a business leader, or anything your gifts entitle you to do. You'd graduate debt-free. All it will take to begin your change of destiny is two months of working harder at high school than you've ever worked before. From what I can see, you have it in you." Farr paused for emphasis. "If *you* think you do."

Mark imagined explaining this to Steve.

"What is it?" Farr asked.

Mark struggled to crystallize his thoughts. "I was thinking about the Tillmans–I mean, they took me in. Steve's almost as poor as I am, and he's got better grades."

Farr smiled fractionally–it did not seem in his nature, Mark realized, to exhibit unambiguous good cheer. "If you're asking whether we can extend similar largesse to your friend, I think Mr. Tillman may lack your potential. But I'll see about him."

Abruptly, Farr stood. "You should go home, and I've got work to do. It's become my job to read books to Taylor. She chooses rather precocious ones, I'm afraid."

Mark trailed Farr to the living room. Anne Farr sat on the couch, sipping wine. It struck Mark that she had an ethereal quality, and that, although lovely, she did not appear strong or healthy–unlike his mother, who, drunk or sober, sane or crazy, would burn fiercely until the end. Smiling, Anne said, "Please come again, Mark. Lionel suffers from a surplus of females."

"Thanks," Mark said, then added, "I only counted two of you."

Anne's smile became ambiguous. "Even so."

As they walked to the door, Mark saw Taylor in the living room, studying her painting as if she had not captured what she imagined–or could not. Suddenly conscious of his gaze, she turned, studying Mark with the same quiet gravity. Farr waited until Mark faced him again. "I thought you might ask about Steve Tillman. If I try to help him, Mark, do we have a deal?"

For an instant, Mark felt himself standing on the edge

of the unknown. Then, drawn by the sudden promise of hope and the force of Farr's personality, he answered, "If you can help me go to school here, I'll do whatever it takes."

EVER SINCE THAT day, Mark Darrow had done exactly that. But he had not risen by his efforts alone. Lionel Farr had touched the scales of his life, and every privilege he had stemmed from that. Farr had not ordained his tragedies, only his successes.

Two weeks before his return to Caldwell, Farr had telephoned Darrow and asked if he could come by Darrow's law office in Boston. Farr had not explained himself, and Darrow had not requested him to. Awaiting Farr with curiosity, Darrow had gazed out the window of his corner office in the Prudential Center, rewarded by a panoramic view of the Public Garden and the Boston Common. Five months prior, Darrow had won a $120 million verdict in a financial fraud case stemming from the subprime mortgage meltdown, adding to a fortune already swollen beyond his wildest imaginings. On his desk the bones and sinews of a complex shareholder suit —financial statements; an expert deposition in which Darrow had eviscerated an arrogant investment banker— were neatly arranged before him. But as Darrow recalled his last visit with Farr, his eye turned, as it so often did, to the photograph of his wife.

Dark and pretty, Lee stood at the bottom of a ski slope, flushed from a breakneck run, her grin of triumph cracking clean and white and sharp. In the photo she was twenty-eight; in Darrow's mind, she was forever twenty-nine, in the fifth month of her pregnancy, waving to him through the window of the taxi that began her final trip to Iowa.

In the two years since, Mark Darrow had turned thirty-eight. He had not seen Farr since Lee's memorial service.

Even among the throng of friends and relatives and Lee's colleagues from MSNBC and the *Boston Globe* who'd crowded the darkened church, Farr had stood out: at sixty-five, he was tall and astonishingly fit, with thick gray-blond hair and the erect posture of the Special Forces officer he had been before he had resigned his commission to pursue a doctorate in philosophy at Yale. That day he had been a quiet presence, offering a few words of sustenance to help Darrow endure this bleakest of winter afternoons. But Farr had lingered for two days after the service, until Darrow had fulfilled his obligations to Lee's parents, then taken him to dinner at the Federalist.

For Darrow, their reunion was shadowed by the day thirteen years before when, in a strange reversal of roles, the young Mark Darrow had called on the newly widowed Farr. Then Mark had managed only to recite a few words of concern for his mentor and his daughter, Taylor; years later, Farr offered him a stiff martini and companionable semisilence until—amid the elegantly appointed room, the quiet talk and laughter of couples taking their normal life for granted—Darrow had asked simply, "What do I do now?"

Sipping his scotch, Farr studied Mark across the table. They were similar enough in appearance that, at times, people mistook them for father and son: Farr's blue eyes retained the clarity of youth, and his still aquiline nose and seamed face, though betraying his years, showed no trace of dissolution. Answering Darrow, his features seemed graven with his own hard memories. "What I did, I suppose. Each day I picked out a task or two, and tried to perform it like the doing mattered. Teaching helped; I had an audience whose faces revealed how I'd done. So did being a parent, though there I functioned far less well." He grimaced. "Perhaps I was better at performing for students than consoling a young daughter shattered by her mother's death. But each morning I tried to look no further than the day ahead.

"There was no bright line, no turning point. More a slow acceptance of what could not be helped, and the realization over time that a greater portion of any given day held a measure of happiness—or, more realistically given who I am, satisfaction. I had my work, however cerebral and self-contained; you have yours, more engrossing in that it's filled with challenges and surprises and because, when you're ready, it will present you with new people to know." Farr gave a brief, reflective smile. "Eventually the life that goes on all around you, indifferent to your sadness, will sweep you up again. For better or worse there's a certain Viking hardiness in our natures, an appetite for more."

Darrow caught Farr's tacit suggestion: however unthinkable now, there would be women—then *a* woman—beyond Lee Hatton. "I've lost a wife," Darrow answered, "and an unborn child. How does one come back from that?" He paused, then added softly, "Anne died thirteen years ago, Lionel. You're still alone."

Farr seemed to look inward. "Perhaps Anne, not solitude, was my anomaly." He shrugged the remark away. "In any case, I was at a different stage of life than you, more than a decade older, with a daughter who needed whatever solace I could muster. As you'll recall, Caldwell College is a bit out of the way, and Wayne, Ohio, hardly a magnet for the bright, attractive young people who flock to Boston." He held up a hand. "Not that it matters in the face of such a profound loss. I'm simply offering my excuses. It would be tasteless to say more beyond the obvious—that you're young, successful, and live in a vibrant city among close friends. For which I, to whom you mean a great deal, am profoundly grateful."

Darrow stared at his half-empty martini glass. Then Farr reached across the table, grasping Darrow's forearm in a gesture of solidarity and consolation. Darrow was touched—Lionel Farr was not given to overt gestures of affection. Which had made his response to Lee's death all the more telling: though it was seldom expressed, since their first meeting, a great portion of Farr's empathy and respect, so sparely given, had resided with Mark Darrow.

Between that dinner and Farr's unexplained reappearance in Boston, Darrow had forced himself to live each day as if it mattered. But even after two years, his life seemed to matter less. Making money—if it had ever been—was no longer Darrow's purpose.

His intercom buzzed, announcing Lionel Farr, and then Rebecca, his assistant, opened the door to wave Farr inside.

Standing, Darrow embraced him. Then he leaned back, giving his mentor a look of mock appraisal. "You look pretty good, Lionel. I could still pick you out of a lineup."

Farr grimaced, a pantomime of doubt. In truth, Darrow saw a change; though still fit and handsome as he entered his late sixties, Farr looked more tired than Darrow could remember, the flesh beneath his eyes appearing slack and a little bruised. They sat in Darrow's wing chairs, Farr appraising the younger man with affectionate curiosity.

"So," Farr inquired after a time, "how are you?"

Darrow shrugged. "All right. I'm still living out the clichés of grief: anger, pain, acceptance. Some days are okay. Then, on a random morning, I'll wake up and, for a moment, Lee's still alive. I reach across the bed, touching where she used to sleep, and feel her loss all over again. I suppose someday that will stop."

Farr nodded in sympathy. "Eventually. Does your work help at all?"

"Sometimes." Keen to change the subject, and curious about the unstated reason for Farr's visit, Darrow asked, "How's your life as provost?"

Farr gathered his thoughts. "Troubled, as is the school. You remember the impact of Angela Hall's murder: we experienced it as no one else could have—except, perhaps, Steve Tillman. When I recall the loss of a young woman with so much promise, murdered in such a terrible way, I still feel disbelief.

"But what remains is the impact on Caldwell College. Sixteen years later, it still lingers: however unfair to the school, the perception of a murder tinged with race caused a falloff in applications, donations, minority students, and—as a result—the quality of the student body. For a short but crucial period, our endowment dipped, limiting our ability to give the kind of scholarships you and Angela received. We've never really recovered."

Darrow was surprised. "I thought the place had stabilized."

"In a fashion," Farr answered sardonically. "We've achieved a slower but steady decline. You'll recall that you turned down an appointment to the board of trustees, enabling you to preserve your sense of optimism. But the precise rate of decline hardly matters now, for reasons you must keep in strictest confidence."

A bit stung, Darrow answered, "Who would I tell?"

" 'Who would give a damn' do you mean? Both of us, I hope." Farr stood, reminding Darrow of how restless he could be. "Mind if we take a walk, Mark? It's been years since I strolled through Boston."

It was a fine spring day, breezy but sunny. Passing the pond in the Public Garden, filled with tourists in swan boats, they stopped at a food stand to buy Polish dogs smothered in grilled onions. Sitting on a park bench, Farr observed, "I always liked this city. You chose well, Mark."

Finishing his hot dog, Darrow saw a nun glance at them, smiling to herself–even now Darrow could be taken for Farr's son. Still, the resemblance was not precise. Even before Farr's hair grayed, Darrow's had been blonder; his face, however well proportioned, lacked Farr's striking angularity, the look of warriors; though obviously fit, little about Darrow, now prone to cuff links and Savile Row suits, suggested the Spartan bearing of a soldier. But the most striking difference was in their smiles. Orthodontics, Darrow's mother's last sacrifice before descending into schizophrenia, had purchased what Lee once called his killer smile, which before her death had marked the chief difference between Darrow and Farr. Farr's smile, when it came, was less a show of teeth than a manifestation of his pervasive sense of irony.

"So," Darrow said. "Caldwell."

They began walking again. "Put simply," Farr responded, "nine hundred thousand dollars of endowment money has vanished."

Darrow turned to him. "How is that possible?"

Farr looked off into the distance, as though pondering the question. "Deciphering financial chicanery isn't my specialty. But as provost, I'm obliged to try. From what I know, the signs point to our president. You'll recall Clark Durbin."

"Durbin?" In his astonishment, Darrow almost laughed. "The man's a classic academic–remember how you had to prop him up after I found her body? I can imagine him writing a paper about embezzlement, complete with footnotes. But not stealing."

"Clark's weak." Farr's voice was etched with disdain. "Faced with hardship, the weak step out of character–or, perhaps, discover it. Clark's wife is an invalid, and his son's a drug addict who needed extensive treatment; heroin, as I observed in Vietnam, grips a man by the throat. Add that Clark has the investment skills common to many of my colleagues: none."

"So how did a man who can't pick stocks develop a talent for theft?"

Farr stopped to contemplate a dog chasing a Frisbee thrown by his youthful master, the animal's stubby legs leaving him endlessly short of the red plastic disk. "That dog," he observed, "will have a coronary. It's the downside of trying too hard to please. As for Clark, our board has an investments committee, with your old friend Joe Betts as chairman."

"Joe?" Darrow felt his amazement growing. "In college, his idea of high finance was sending his bloated credit card bills home to Dad."

"People change," Farr responded. "As you'd be the first to acknowledge. Joe Betts is now a partner in a respected investment advisory firm that oversees our endowment. Durbin was on Joe's committee, each of whose members was entitled to direct transfer of endowment funds beneath one million dollars.

"The funds in question were certificates of deposit. What seems to have happened is that Durbin e-mailed Joe's firm, directing that the CDs be transferred to a bank account in the name of Caldwell College, set up by Clark himself. From which, at his direction, the money was transferred to a bank account in Geneva–"

"Then you can forget it," Darrow said flatly. "The Swiss are a black hole."

Farr nodded. "In theory, everyone on the investment committee is suspect. But Durbin sent the e-mail, and his signature is on the papers used to open the bank account in Wayne that received the money."

"Are there other possibilities?"

Farr shrugged. "The other person seemingly involved is Joe himself, who transferred the money based on Durbin's e-mail. But it's hard to see how Joe could send that e-mail to himself, or gain access to Durbin's computer. It all comes back to Clark."

Pausing, Darrow watched a young couple walking hand in hand, careless of anything but each other. "Still, nine hundred thousand isn't that much. How large is our endowment?"

"Less than seventy million. The timing of Angela's death killed a capital campaign we desperately needed. And historically the school has never done well with its money–until the last few years, our investment committee might as well have put it under a mattress. We got heavily into equities just in time for the dot-com meltdown, then the near collapse of our financial system–too heavily, it turns out. By the time Joe's firm took over, we'd lost over a third of our endowment. And now this." Farr shook his head in disgust. "Stupidity and criminality are a lethal combination. Piety is even worse: church-related schools, I'm finding, don't have the financial safeguards they should–they were founded on notions of man's goodness. What pure-hearted Christian would suspect Clark Durbin of being a crook?"

"Or just clever enough to be a fool," Darrow answered. "Embezzlement's a dead-end crime: sooner or later, the thief always gets caught." He faced Farr again. "If it's money you need, I can make up the nine hundred thousand. More, if you like."

Farr smiled faintly. "Who would have ever thought, Mark? I guess lawyering *does* pay better than coaching, your original ambition. But, with deepest thanks, the missing money is not Caldwell's problem. It's reputation.

"As the events surrounding Angela's death suggested, reputation, once lost, is hard to regain–especially among the donors we need to survive. We were planning a hundred-million-dollar capital campaign when the board got wind of this. All that's needed for disaster to strike, I've realized, is for Caldwell to dream up a new fund-raising effort." Farr's voice softened. "Clark's embezzlement has become an existential threat. How do you ask people for money when they don't believe you can safeguard what you have?"

Darrow stopped, hands in his pockets, facing Farr. "You've just redefined your problem, Lionel. It's public relations. How much does the media know?"

"Nothing, yet. *That* problem is still hanging over us."

"Then if you've come to me for advice, I've got some. I assume the board is hiring a forensic accountant to sort out how Durbin's supposed to have done this."

"As we speak."

"Have them draw up a new system of financial controls, to assure the alumni–and the media–that nothing like this can ever happen again." Squinting into the afternoon sun, Darrow put on his sunglasses. "The next thing is to engage an outside public relations firm. You'll need to write this story before somebody else does."

Farr folded his arms. "The board's current hope," he responded in a dubious tone, "is to keep this quiet until we find out all the details. There's some thought that Clark will help us retrieve the money in return for a low-key resignation because of 'health.' Durbin has reason to cooperate–if he refuses, and this leaks out, some on our board want to press criminal charges. I doubt a mild-mannered heterosexual like Clark will want to make the kind of 'special friends' he'll encounter in state prison."

Reflexively, Darrow thought of Steve Tillman. "At least Durbin won't have spent his life there."

From the glint in Farr's eyes, Darrow saw that he'd grasped the reference. "True enough. But let's hope, for Clark's sake, that one prisoner from our community is enough."

"Whatever the case," Darrow said, "get all the facts, then make a complete disclosure. Dribbling out partial information is almost as bad as stonewalling." He looked at his mentor keenly. "But you know all this, I'm sure. So tell me what else I can do."

Farr was silent for a moment. "That depends, I suppose, on how you feel about your current life. And what plans you have for the future."

Darrow slowly shook his head. "I can't help but think about the first time you asked me that question. My answer's much the same: I don't really know. Before she died, Lee and I talked about what we'd do if she got tired of chasing after campaigns. But all that was complicated by the idea of starting a family . . ."

His voice trailed off. "What about the law?" Farr asked.

Darrow shrugged. "I'm a very good trial lawyer, no doubt. I've proven that. But there are other talented lawyers who can bring these cases, and I can't tell myself that I'm doing God's work. My dilemma is that it's easier to feel restless in the present than to define a different future." Giving Farr a fleeting smile, he finished: "It's like you said when we first met. I'm lacking in direction. But if you still want me to join the board, I will."

Briefly, Farr paused. The look in his eyes struck Darrow as speculative. "Actually, I want you to consider becoming president of Caldwell College."

This time Darrow did laugh. Removing his sunglasses, he said, "You're joking."

"Hardly."

"Then you should be. I've got no academic credentials; no administrative experience; no background with an educational institution of any kind. I haven't even kept up with the school. I've already offered the only thing I'm good for–money."

Farr folded his arms. Fleetingly, Darrow imagined how they looked to others: two men in business suits in the middle of the Public Garden, talking quietly but forcefully about something very serious. "If your model of a college president is someone like Clark Durbin," Farr said bluntly, "God help us. That's the last thing we need. Even colleges that aren't in trouble are making nontraditional hires: Oberlin just hired Michigan's outside lawyer, and the Stanford Business School's run by a former CEO."

"That makes a kind of sense," Darrow said. "This doesn't."

"No?" Farr countered dryly. "You spent five years prosecuting criminal cases–including homicides–and eight more years untangling every financial scam known to man. Given Caldwell's recent history, some might say you're perfect."

"*That's* pretty sad."

"But true. More fundamentally, you embody the best of Caldwell College: a small-town boy who made good through attending a school that stresses teaching instead of research. To be plain, you're here because of Caldwell."

"And you," Darrow answered softly. "I'm well aware of that."

"As the alumni are of you. You're an athletic hero, enshrined in our Sports Hall of Fame. You're a graduate of Yale Law, a nationally renowned lawyer. You've been on the cover of *U.S. News*, the *ABA Journal*, *American Lawyer*, and–three times already–our alumni magazine." Farr spoke with quiet urgency now, brooking no interruption. "You're young, attractive, and gifted with considerable charisma. You know the school. And what the school needs is a leader with élan and a sense of humor, the vitality to lift our morale, redefine our message, refocus Caldwell on its future, and, in a year or so, help restart the capital campaign required for us to *have* a future.

"For you, the job wouldn't be a stepping stone to somewhere better. You'd be saying you believe in Caldwell College–that if you invest, others should."

Darrow held up his hand. "You need more than a symbol. You need someone with qualifications."

"The first qualification is judgment, which you have. Critical for the fix we're in, you're not remote, authoritarian, or rigid–in fact, you've always been adaptable, the quickest study I know. You won't have to learn the culture of Caldwell or the town." Farr's tone became emphatic. "With you as president, we can address our problems squarely. You're more than just a symbol, Mark. You're a human Hail Mary, a concrete sign that Caldwell can rise again. Anyone else is second best."

Stunned, Darrow felt a surge of doubt, the stubborn urge to dissent. " 'Anyone,' Lionel? What about you?"

"The board will make me interim president, if that's necessary. But I'm too old to do what's needed. We need a fresh face, one that doesn't look like a relief map of Afghanistan." Seeing Darrow smile, Farr added swiftly, "If you wish it, I'll stay on as provost–for any president, a good relationship with the provost matters. I can walk you through the budget, issues regarding the faculty and board, where the figurative bodies are buried. Whatever you need to ensure that you do well."

"You talk like all you need is my consent. Don't you have a search committee?"

"To be sure, and you'd have to meet with them. But I'm not here on some frolic of my own. There's substantial support for this idea–starting with Joe Betts, who seems to recall you more admiringly than you remember him."

"We were friends," Darrow demurred. "With a reservation here or there, I liked Joe, whatever his role in Steve Tillman's trial. But Joe no more knows me in the present than I know him."

"He thinks otherwise. So do I. By your senior year, your essential character was apparent. You were, and are, a leader."

"Of what, precisely? The football team?"

Farr looked nettled. "Don't be obtuse. People were drawn to you; you had a gift for empathy rare in someone your age. You can't be in the dark about why you've done so well with juries." Farr softened his speech. "Even the timing is right. It's April–if you start in June, you'll have two months of paid rehearsals before the students arrive. During which you can focus on our alumni."

Darrow smiled at this. "As usual, you've thought of everything. Except whether the timing's right for *me*."

Farr's face clouded briefly. "Only you can say for sure." Glancing at his watch, he said, "It's past four-thirty. Suppose I buy you a drink at the Ritz Carlton."

"Won't help, and the Ritz is now the Taj, a cog in the global economy. But sure–the bar's the same, and it still makes a good martini."

Silent, they walked across the gardens in lengthening shadows, crossing Arlington Street to enter the hotel. The first-floor bar faced back toward the gardens; its paneled walls, leather chairs, and oil paintings of hunting scenes reminded Darrow faintly of Farr's study. With a look of satisfaction, Farr sat across from him at a marble table by the window and ordered dry martinis for them both. Farr permitted Darrow a first bracing sip before saying, "About your timing, I *do* have thoughts."

"So do I. My life in Wayne, Ohio, seems like a thousand years ago. And as you confessed after Lee's memorial service, the dating pool is not exactly infinite."

Farr raised his eyebrows. "At last, you refer to a personal life. Is there one?"

Darrow pondered this. "Call it a half life. On a good day, three-quarters."

"There's a woman, then?"

"Plural." For a moment, Darrow fell quiet. "Physically, I function well enough. But my emotional equipment feels a little stuck."

Farr contemplated the table, considering his next words. "Forgive me if this sounds tactless. But it seems you're free to leave Boston without uprooting anyone, including yourself. This may be your time for something new."

Darrow smiled a little. "Whose idea *was* this, Lionel?"

Farr gave him an ironic smile of his own. "Mine. But the last idea I had about your life turned out pretty well."

"Except when it didn't," Darrow answered mildly. But that was not Farr's doing. In all but one respect–that which had come to matter most–Darrow was the luckiest man he knew. His debt to Caldwell College, it seemed, was indistinguishable from his debt to Lionel Farr.

As if reading his thoughts, Farr spoke quietly: "There's no place where you could make such a difference. In a few years, you could give our college what it needs. Perhaps you need that as well."

Darrow sorted through the jumble of his thoughts, the minefield of memory. The apogee of his young life, and his greatest trauma until Lee's death, had occurred at Caldwell College in the space of sixteen hours. Perhaps that was why he had never returned. "Do you ever visit Steve Tillman?" Darrow asked.

This seemingly irrelevant question would have puzzled anyone but Farr. "On rare occasions. These days we struggle for subjects. As you'd expect, it's very sad."

Despite his own guilt, Darrow heard no rebuke. The two men lapsed into silence.

Darrow finished his martini, feeling its initial jolt filter slowly through his system. "Give me a day or two, Lionel. You took me by surprise, and there's a lot for me to sift through. And remember."

Farr's eyes held understanding and compassion. "Perhaps more than anyone, I know. That morning we stood at the Spire, looking down at her, is something no one could forget. Certainly not the two of us."

PART I
THE SHADOW

1

Sixteen years later, Darrow's memory of that terrible night and morning remained as fresh as yesterday, as disorienting as the aftershock of a nightmare.

Moments after ringing the great brass bell, he had descended from the Spire, less triumphant than grateful for his release from its stifling gloom. For a while he was caught up in the jubilation of the crowd. Then he headed for a celebration at the Delta Beta Epsilon house, his pleasure fading into a slightly melancholy sense of life's transience.

What the campus called fraternity row was, in fact, a grassy oval, surrounded by red-brick houses. Sheltered by trees, each house varied in style: one had filigreed balconies reminiscent of a New Orleans mansion; another reflected the Georgian revival; two had pillars that evoked southern plantations; still another, the greatest departure, resembled a suburban ranch house. The DBE house was a mixture of styles. Three stories high, it had a small portico at one side as its entrance, and steps in the rear that rose from a parking lot to a generous porch. At the front were six tall windows through which brothers congregating in the living room could monitor the abode of their fiercest adversaries, the SAEs, whose stone lions, situated by the front steps like sentries, stared fiercely across the oval.

For Mark, the sight of the lions summoned a memory shared by only one other person. After the Ohio Lutheran game two years before, he and Steve Tillman, armed with tear gas canisters, had gassed the second floor of the Sigma Alpha Epsilon house at four A.M. This act of daring, attributed in legend to suspects as varied as students from Ohio Lutheran and a local motorcycle gang, had caused a cluster of SAEs to flee the house, weeping and vomiting, as the two adrenalized perpetrators watched from DBE's darkened living room. Reaching the house, Mark wondered what memories *this* night would bring.

On the lawn, Mark passed a band of would-be athletes–his fraternity brothers, fueled by beer–playing a desultory game of touch football. Declining their shouted invitation to join them with a wave and a smile, Mark entered the house. Though it was not yet six o'clock, the sound system was pumping out Pearl Jam, and revelers were gathering in the living room and library–so called because, although no one ever used it for studying, its shelves of athletic trophies were interspersed with leather-bound books no one ever opened. Avoiding notice, Mark climbed the scuffed linoleum stairs to the second floor, still in search of his best friend.

Like Mark and several other football players, Steve had a room in the stadium itself. Mark had not found him there. As a junior, Steve had ripped up his knee in this emblematic game, leaving him with a permanent limp and no physical outlet for his competitive nature; the pain of no longer playing, Mark knew, sometimes caused Steve to separate himself. But Steve was one reason Mark had no date this year, just as on the same night one year ago he had postponed his date to go with Steve to the hospital. Out of friendship and solidarity, Mark had resolved to spend this special Saturday with his friend.

On the second floor, Mark went from room to room, looking into each cramped living space. Most were empty;

none held Steve. Instead, sticking his head into Jerry Feldman's room, Mark found Joe Betts, a fellow denizen of the football stadium, sipping from a whiskey bottle as he watched a video.

"Seen Steve?" Mark inquired.

"Nope," Joe answered with indifference, riveted by the video.

Mark hesitated, mentally taking Joe's emotional temperature. Tall and rangy, Joe had been a decent enough flanker before dropping football altogether. Whereas Mark and Steve had strained to make the most of whatever ability they had, Joe's self-indulgence and aversion to training was so marked that Coach Fiske had given him a choice: work harder or leave. Joe had left. Now Joe looked a little soft, the outlines of his handsome face more indistinct, though his round glasses and swept-back hair still lent him an air of eastern prep school panache. That he had started in on whiskey was not a good sign. Otherwise contained and somewhat aloof, when drunk Joe could be mercurial and foul-tempered, prone to outbursts that ripened into fights. Mark sometimes wondered what psychic trip wires lurked inside Joe Betts; in three years of college, Mark had grasped that his own wounds were not unique, and that he often understood very little about the inner recesses of people he considered his friends. Drawn by Joe's fixation on the screen, Mark stepped inside.

The tape was a sex video. The naked female, a sturdy blond, looked somehow familiar. "Tonya Harding," Joe said in a tone of satisfaction and contempt. "Trailer trash turned Olympic skater. Seems like her career's gone downhill since her ex-husband hired that douche bag to kneecap Nancy Kerrigan."

Mark eyed the screen. "Downhill's one thing," he observed. "This is more like free fall."

Joe shrugged, still watching the screen. "Her husband videotaped it, then decided he was Steven Spielberg. You and I are the incidental beneficiaries."

"She's all yours, man. I need to find Steve."

Joe flushed, as though Mark had insulted him. "*I'd* fuck her," he said with unsettling vehemence. "I'd fuck anything right now."

Mark flashed on Joe's girlfriend, Laurie, an attractive but reticent blond whose attachment to Joe, given his volatility, had always puzzled Mark. Mildly, he said, "I thought you had that covered."

Joe's eyes narrowed. "Think harder."

Mark sensed that he had touched a nerve. "See you downstairs," he said, and left.

On the door of the stairwell was posted a list of duties for freshmen—cleaning bathrooms and scrubbing floors—the aim of which, a hygienic DBE house, was largely aspirational. Opening the door, Mark found Steve Tillman seated on the steps, beer in hand. Above them, an anonymous whoop of laughter issued from the third floor.

Surprised, Mark asked, "What the hell are you doing *here*?"

"I love the view." A shadow crossed Steve's open midwestern face. "Nice game."

This sounded sincere. But Mark understood Steve's clouded expression. Their trajectories had crossed: after Lionel Farr's challenge, Mark had finished high school with straight A's and, as though the scales had fallen from his eyes, had worked hard to continue the pattern at Caldwell. Once a better student than Mark, Steve—as Farr had guessed—found college academics more difficult. When his knee had gone, it seemed, so had Steve's sense of self; ever since, he had been mired in the C range, hoping for the career to which Mark had once aspired, that of high school coach. Now, aided by Farr, Mark was set on getting into Yale Law School, and it was Steve who had no vision of the future. Sometimes Mark imagined that they had traded places the night Farr first set Mark on his path, leaving Steve Tillman an afterthought.

Awkwardly, Mark said, "Wish I'd thrown those touchdown passes to you. If I hadn't played with you in high school, I wouldn't have been out there today."

Steve drained his beer. "You ran with it, chief. Not your fault no one shredded your knee." He stared at the cinder-block stairwell. "Shouldn't you be at the party?"

Mark shrugged. "I'll get there. It hit me today that *my* career's ending, too, like I thought it would in high school. No more football, just life. I wanted to hang with you awhile."

For a moment, Steve bit his lip, struggling with some unspoken feeling. Then he summoned a grin. "Tell you what," he said. "You have a beer, and I'll have another beer, and together we can work up a few minutes of real sentiment."

Mark looked into Steve's face. Beneath the short haircut, the same as in high school, was a face less bright, eyes less innocent. Sitting beside him, Mark answered, "Maybe we can fill up a whole hour."

So they sat as Steve killed most of the six-pack, reminiscing. At length, Steve placed a hand on Mark's shoulder. "You're my best friend," he confessed in a somewhat slurry voice. "Maybe the best I'll ever have."

"Keep drinking, pal. I get better."

"Nope," Steve said with sudden resolve. "We could drink all night, and you'd never be a woman. Let's go downstairs and see what our future holds."

2

In the living room, Mark paused with Steve, taking in the scene.

The night was building. Some couples had gathered in front of the stone fireplace engraved with the DBE insignia, drinking and watching the fire; others crowded together on the couches, their gestures animated by alcohol and adrenaline. On the front lawn Tim Fedak and Skip Ellis had rigged up a catapult with steel rods and surgical hose, and had begun launching water balloons at the SAE house, the rubbery spheroids traveling in an arc of impressive distance and velocity. "Those fucking balloons will kill someone," Steve opined. "Unless the SAEs kill those guys first."

Mark shrugged. "Either way it's no great loss. Let's go find the party."

Heading for the stairs to the basement, Mark spotted Carl Hall sliding through the front door. A slender young black man, Carl had wary eyes that constantly assessed his surroundings, making him seem older than he was. But even in high school, Carl had always struck Mark as a guy who would not live to see old age; his vocation–drug dealer–and a certain slippery quality suggested to Mark that someday one of his commercial calculations, skewed by self-interest, would prove fatal. Nodding toward Carl, Mark inquired of Steve, "You ask him here?"

"Nope. Only his sister." Steve frowned. "He shouldn't be at this party. If Scotty invited him, it's a bad move."

The disapproving reference to Jackie Scott, a basketball star who was the only black fraternity brother, evoked Mark's sympathy: Scotty lived in a twilight zone, perched uncomfortably between his white peer group and his connections to Wayne's black community, the nearest thing to the neighborhood from which he had come. "No matter," Mark answered. "No one's getting busted tonight. 'Zero tolerance' means 'Don't snort coke in Clark Durbin's driveway.' "

Steve gave a delayed but knowing laugh. In all the time they'd been there, the college had never enforced its drug and alcohol policy–draconian in theory–preferring ignorance to raids and spot inspections. Whatever surprises happened at the party, they would not involve the campus cops. As Carl Hall slipped into the basement, the two friends followed.

The room was dark, the lights dimmed so low that Mark could see only shadowy forms. Tom Petty's "Don't Back Down" blasted from the sound system–sooner or later, Mark could expect to hear the Smashing Pumpkins, the Gin Blossoms, Green Day, the Beastie Boys, and, inevitably, Kurt Cobain fronting Nirvana. A few of the shadows were dancing; others were drinking from paper cups full of beer or liquor; a guy and girl were sharing a joint next to an anonymous couple making out in a corner of the room. "Right on schedule," Steve murmured.

Glancing around, Mark spotted a form he thought was Carl Hall facing the chubby outline of a guy who must be one of his customers. Instinctively, Mark felt less sanguine than he had sounded to Steve. By coming, Carl had crossed a line, undefined but real, introducing an element of unpredictability into an already combustible environment.

"Mark," Shawn Hale's voice called out. "Hey, man."

Someone started clapping. Before Mark knew it, Shawn, Charlie Ware, and Jim Neeley had picked him up, one leg on Charlie's shoulder, the other on Shawn's, and were carrying him through the crush of bodies, yelling "Ice Man . . . Ice Man . . . Ice Man" in a tribute to his coolheadedness against Ohio Lutheran. Some at the party cheered; others took no notice. Pleased but embarrassed, Mark jerked Shawn by the hair. "Put me down," he shouted above the din, "before you three clowns drop me."

Shawn said something to the others. Abruptly, they tossed Mark to the floor. Stumbling forward, he found himself facing Angela Hall.

Carl's twin sister was alone, her eyes half slits, dancing with no one. It was strange, Mark thought—though they had gone to high school together, then college, until three weeks ago his only impression of Angela had been that she was shy. But until three weeks ago, when Steve had asked Mark to come along, he had never been to the Alibi Club.

THE CLUB WAS in the black section of Wayne, on the corner of a randomly zoned street that included a small grocery, a beauty shop, a shabby apartment building, and wooden houses and duplexes in various states of repair. Though near the border of Colored Town—as Wayne's older whites often called it—the street was a few blocks from fraternity row, marking an uneasy intersection of cultures where underage college kids sought out the Alibi Club for drinks and the drugs they could buy from Carl Hall, the son of the club's owner.

A neatly maintained red-brick structure, the club had a

blinking neon sign that beckoned customers at night, its reflection flashing in the windows on the second floor, where the proprietress lived with her family. Though its primary clientele was black, the shadowy convergence of race and class served the community as well as the college: since high school, Steve Tillman, like other whites, had come here for what he could not get elsewhere. Though this was unspoken, the police treated the Alibi Club as they did the campus: short of murder, they left it alone.

What rules the club had–its own–were strictly enforced by a three-hundred-pound black man named Hugo. On the evening Steve first took Mark there, Hugo was at the door, his broad, impassive face revealing nothing as he nodded them inside.

The room was dark and smoky. An old jukebox blared soul music; black working-class men hunched at the bar; black couples sat at tables; a pair of white college kids huddled in one corner, drinking what looked like screwdrivers and keeping to themselves. When Steve went to the end of the bar, Mark took the stool beside him, noting the incongruity of two young white faces in the mirror fronted by rows of liquor bottles. Then he saw Angela Hall serving drinks at the other end.

She held herself tall, suggesting pride and a certain distance. As far as he could remember, they had never spoken. He knew only that her father was dead–much like Mark, she had fended for herself. They had both been in one of Farr's philosophy classes; she had impressed Mark as smart and conscientious, though on occasion, exposed by Farr's sharp questions, she seemed to have fallen behind.

Now Mark took in how pretty she was. Spotting Steve, she gave him a smile that, while fleeting, seemed friendly enough. Casually, Steve waved.

The brief interaction made Mark curious. "Thought you didn't like black folks."

"Times change." Gazing at Angela, Steve added softly, "Who wouldn't like that?"

Angela came up to them. "Hey," she said to Steve.

"Hey, yourself. How's life?"

Angela laughed ruefully. "What life? I go to class, I tend Mom's bar, I go upstairs to the flat I got born in and crack the books until my eyes close. Not exactly *Melrose Place*–which, by the way, I don't have time to watch."

"Life's tough," Steve allowed. "Maybe I should take you away from all this."

Her smile was at once flirtatious and amused. "Like to a movie, you mean? I'll be waiting by the phone." She glanced at Mark. "So what do you guys want?"

"Two beers," Steve answered. "Is Carl around?"

Displeasure seemed to surface in her eyes, and then they fixed on the door. With quiet distaste, she said, "Speak of the devil."

Mark turned. Gliding through the door, Carl stopped to look around. He summoned an expression of mild surprise at the sight of Steve Tillman, then came over to the bar. Ignoring his sister, he asked Steve, "Passing the time with Princess Angela?"

There was an edge in his voice, though Mark could not tell whether it was for Angela or Steve. "Yup," Steve said evenly. "Waiting for you to show up. You guessed right again last Sunday–your goddamn Pittsburgh Steelers beat the spread."

Her face closing, Angela turned away. She surely recognized, as Mark did, the charade through which Carl sold pot and powder cocaine to his Caldwell clientele. They gave him money in advance, paying off a fictitious "bet"; a day or so later they found a bag behind some musty tome in a corner of the public library, or beneath the rear seat of an unlocked car. But at the Alibi Club Carl was, at worst, a bookie.

Steve passed him a wad of bills. "Got a second?" he asked.

Carl glanced mistrustfully at Mark. "Let's grab a table."

Steve put a hand on Mark's shoulder, excusing himself. Mark nodded his understanding: in Carl's mind, Mark was a potential witness, a needless risk to a business built on subterfuge and discretion. When Angela brought back two beers, Mark was sitting alone. The dislike she clearly felt for her twin brother had left her silent.

Awkwardly, Mark said, "I'm Mark Darrow, by the way."

Angela laughed at this. "The whole damn campus knows who you are. Even the people you never talk to—in college *or* in high school."

Embarrassed, Mark said, "So let's talk now."

Angela put her hands on her hips, a mocking gesture. "Concerning what?"

"How about what you're studying so hard for. Seems like you've got a plan besides running Mom's bar."

She paused to look at him, and then her expression became serious. "My plan—if you really want to know—is to put this whole period of my life in the rearview mirror. Right along with Wayne, Ohio."

"And go where?"

"Same place you are, I guess. The best law school that'll pay me to show up. Which narrows the field a little." Picking up a cloth, she began wiping the bar. "So what kind of law are you thinking about?"

Mark shrugged. "Not sure yet. Maybe criminal, I guess. And you?"

Still wiping, Angela said, "Not that—I've seen enough

criminals to last a lifetime. Corporate law, I'm thinking. Or maybe teach if I do well enough."

Though quiet, her voice held a determination close to longing, the sense—or hope—that she was bigger than the life she had been given. At once Mark intuited how alone she must feel. "I'll be rooting for you," he said. "Maybe Yale has scholarships for both of us."

Glancing up, Angela gave him a wry smile. "Aren't you worried that being white is a competitive disadvantage?"

"Is it? I hadn't noticed."

"You'll get by." Her smile softened a little. "Good luck to us both."

Steve came back, glancing from Mark to Angela. "Thanks for keeping my buddy company," he told her.

Mark wondered if he imagined something proprietary in Steve's tone, or at least familiar, suggesting more than a barroom friendship. Angela shrugged, briefly meeting Mark's eyes. "He's really not so bad," she told Steve, and went back to tending bar.

NOW SHE SMILED at Mark again. "Congratulations," she said above the din of the party. "Big day for you, seems like."

She was holding a drink and her voice seemed thick, her balance compromised. Though Mark did not really know her, this surprised him. Gesturing at the crowd, he said, "In fifteen minutes, they'll forget me."

She took a deep swallow of liquor. "In fifteen minutes," she countered, "they'll probably forget everything. Like I mean to."

Troubled, Mark sensed that she had come here to lose herself. "You with anyone?" he asked.

Blinking, she looked at him more closely. "Steve

invited me, whatever that means. Other than that, I'm with no one in particular."

Mark hesitated. "Neither am I. If you need someone to get you home, I'm here."

"Tonight? You're supposed to be celebrating."

"True. You'd be saving me a hangover."

The look she gave him combined a question and a challenge. Defensively, she said, "Are you saying I should leave now?"

Mark shoved his hands in his pockets. "I'm wondering, that's all."

She shook her head, moving close to him. Softly, she said, "Gonna be a long night for me, I think." She gave him a quick, darting kiss on the lips. "You're kind of sweet, Mark Darrow."

Surprised, Mark thought he saw tears in her eyes. Then she turned, wandering aimlessly into the crowd, alone.

MARK WENT TO the makeshift bar in the corner, pouring himself a Jack Daniel's on ice. He felt a hand on his shoulder.

Turning, he expected to see a friend, perhaps to hear a few drunken words of praise. Instead Carl Hall demanded in a hostile tone, "You get off on fucking around with black girls like Tillman does?"

Mark felt a flash of temper. Removing Carl's hand from his shoulder, he said, "If you mean your sister, that's not what's going on."

"Looked like that. In fact, looks like you want to fuck her."

Mark stared at him. "This can't be some sort of principle for you. You've never had any."

Hall's eyes flashed. "Look," Mark said more evenly,

"Angela's already over the line. If you care about her at all, take her home. Might be a good idea for both of you."

Hall stood taller. "Don't like me at *your* house, white boy?"

"That's not it," Mark answered. "I don't like you anywhere. So you'd better back off right now."

Carl gave him a measured look, as though assessing the difference in their strength and will. Then he turned abruptly, vanishing as his sister had.

3

For an hour or so, Mark drank and danced with whoever came along.

In the dark he felt an odd detachment, the numb whiskey glow spreading through his limbs as the forms and faces in front of him kept changing. Then the newest face became Joe Betts's girlfriend. "Hey, Laurie," he said with foolish surprise. "It's you."

He waited for the smile he could expect from Laurie Shilts. Instead, she shook her head, speaking quietly beneath the cacophony of the party. "This isn't any good."

"The party?"

"Everything."

With fraternal affection, Mark pulled her closer. Her small, pretty face looked pained; the cheek beneath her right eye looked bruised and puffy. Silent, she leaned her head against his shoulder.

"Maybe we should talk," Mark suggested.

Laurie's laugh was mirthless. "Here?"

Without speaking, Mark took her hand, leading her to the back of the room. He pushed open the stainless steel doors to the kitchen, where, six nights a week, their cook prepared meals for sixty brothers. As the doors closed behind them, partially sealing off the sound, Mark switched on the lights.

Laurie winced at the new brightness. She looked small,

diminished, her blond shag straggly. The bruise beneath her eye was a faint blue-purple.

Disturbed, Mark motioned her to one of the stools in front of the oversized sink where, for most of his sophomore year, he had earned money by peeling potatoes or washing iron pots. They sat next to each other, quiet for a time.

"I came looking for him," she said in a monotone. "So stupid—he was already drunk. I was stupid for staying with him so long."

Her blue-green eyes looked at once miserable and angry. Uncertain of how to respond, Mark said, "Joe's okay when he's not drinking."

Laurie crossed her arms. "So which Joe's the real one?" she asked bitterly. "Both of them, actually—they're the same fucking guy. Drinking just rips the surface off his anger." Her voice faltered. "You don't really know him, Mark. Deep down, Joe hates women."

Despite his own haziness, a memory came to Mark. It had been late Saturday night exactly a year ago, the end of a long evening during which he had gone with Steve to the hospital, spent time at the party with his date, and then, devastated by Steve's injury, wound up drinking with Joe on the front lawn of the DBE house, their backs against an oak tree. Sipping from his silver flask, Joe had said, "Keeps the cold away, doesn't it."

"Yup."

"Only problem is, it makes me think about dear old Dad."

His tone wavered between sardonic and sentimental. Two months before, Joe's father had dropped dead from a massive heart attack. Mark assumed that the sentiment was for his father, its acrid undertone a drunken attempt at emotional distance. "Yeah," Mark commiserated. "That must be hard."

"You've got no idea, Mark." Joe's voice softened. "I loved him, and I hated him."

Mark turned his head, face against the rough bark of the oak. "How's that?"

Joe took a deeper swallow. "Jekyll-Hyde, man–Jekyll and fucking Hyde. Used to get drunk and beat the shit out of my mother. Next day he'd sit around all quiet and ashamed. You never heard a house so filled with silence."

Surprised, Mark thought of his own parents–that one got drunk had inspired the other to follow. "Maybe she should've gotten him to stop."

Joe's bark of laughter held disdain. "Too weak. Her father was just like mine, a red-faced drunk who no doubt beat up Grandma. Deep down I think Mom wanted that–my old man was what she thought a man should be. At least that's what all the textbooks say." He took a deep swallow of bourbon. "Who gives a shit now, right? The bastard's dead, and Mom can blubber over his memory in peace. It's done . . ."

Now, facing Laurie, Mark believed that it was not. "Did you ever ask Joe not to drink?"

Briefly, Laurie's crescent eyes shut. "Try 'beg.' "

"What happened?"

"I picked the wrong time. More and more with him, there's *no* right time. I found that out again tonight." Her voice, though soft, had new intensity and clarity. "Joe's got bigger problems than drinking. Way bigger. This is about my own survival."

Mark hesitated. Glancing at her cheek, he asked, "Want to tell me about it?"

Laurie looked slowly around the bright industrial kitchen, as though rediscovering her surroundings and herself. "No," she said firmly. "I need to go back to the dorm, start respecting myself. My new plan is to forget Joe Betts and everything that's happened."

Mark pondered his obligations. "Can I do anything?"

Looking at the whiskey in his cup, Laurie's laugh was free of rancor. "Tonight? Maybe we can find some better time." Her voice softened. "But you're a good listener, Mark. Drunk or sober."

"Seems like this is my night for it." Looking at her, he saw a small, cute girl with a bruise beneath her cheek, carrying a memory not easily erased. "I'm sorry, Laurie."

Laurie grimaced. "I'll be fine. It's Joe's next girl you should worry about."

Touching his arm, she left. Alone on the stool, Mark watched the metal doors swing in her wake.

He supposed the only cure for how depressed he felt was whiskey.

ANOTHER HOUR LATER, taking his own advice, Mark sat in the living room drinking whiskey with Rusty Clark.

A slight redhead with the countenance of a shrewd but amiable badger, Rusty was feeling valedictory. Gazing at his gin and tonic, Rusty gestured at the couples by the fireplace. "Tonight it hit me that we're leaving in six months. We may never see these people again."

Mark laughed thickly. "I'm not sure we're seeing them now."

Rusty gave him a faux-sententious look. "Aren't you feeling a little nostalgic?"

Mark shrugged. "A few hours ago I was. Now I feel like it's getting to be time to go."

Rusty nodded solemnly. "To law school, right?"

"For sure. I can make a living defending drunks. They're a recipe for trouble."

Rusty raised his cup. "Maybe *I* should go. Got a truckload of clients right here."

"They're leaving, remember? You'll never see them again."

"True." Rusty thought for a moment. "There's always the good citizens of Wayne."

Mark turned to him. "Don't get stuck, Rusty. It's time for us to bail."

On a nearby couch, Bobby Gardner took his date's hand, pulling her upstairs. Watching, Rusty said, "I always thought I'd meet someone here. Maybe settle down."

Mark took a swallow of whiskey. "You sound like you're about to die. We're twenty-fucking-one."

Rusty looked offended. "Easy for you to say–you run through girls like potato chips."

"Mixed metaphor, Rusty. I can feel the crumbs between my toes."

"Come on, man. You know what I mean."

Mark reflected. What he could not say to Rusty was that, in great measure because of Lionel Farr, his idea of himself had changed. Whoever he would become, he knew he was not yet there; he should wait for the woman the future Mark Darrow would know was right. Nor was he inclined to reveal that his parents, who had married right out of high school, had poisoned the ideal of young love. Even drunk, Mark knew that he was better at listening than self-revelation. "Yeah," he temporized for Rusty's sake. "I know what you mean. I just haven't found her yet."

Mollified, Rusty settled back on the couch. Mark realized that he had drunk too much already–the room was starting to cxpand and contract; voiccs bcyond Rusty's seemed to come from a great distance. "Well," Rusty announced, "look at *this*."

Turning, Mark saw what this comment was about: Steve Tillman had emerged from the basement with Angela Hall, his arm around her waist. At the top of the stairs they paused, kissing. "True love strikes," Rusty said. "Aren't you sorry you're such a cynic?"

Mark found the sight jarring—not because of Steve or Angela but because of what he knew to be, at least until now, Steve's small-town disdain for blacks. His face close to Angela's, Steve whispered something. Then he turned, heading for the first-floor bathroom, his limp briefly becoming a stagger. In the tone of a TV color commentator, Rusty opined, "Looks pretty fucked up to *me,* sports fans."

Gazing at Angela, Mark did not answer. Alone, she faced the living room; spotting Mark, she gave him a small wave and a smile, fey and wistful and embarrassed. This is what the night had brought, her expression said; the idea that whatever might follow was a premeditated act of carelessness, somehow sad, penetrated Mark's fog. It crossed his mind that this night might be—perhaps should be—the last epic drunk of his life. Then Joe Betts came reeling up the stairs.

When Mark glanced over, Rusty was smiling to himself, gone to another place. But Mark was at once alert: Joe's expression was purposeful and closed to reason, and his eyes were fixed on Angela.

She stood with her back to him, gazing at the tile floor. When Joe put his arm around her, she started. Joe pulled her closer, his face flushed with alcohol and desire.

Steadying himself, Mark rose.

Joe turned Angela's face to him. As Mark started forward, Steve emerged from the bathroom, stopping at the sight of Joe. "What the fuck you doing?" he demanded.

Joe spun, eyes widening with surprise. Three feet separated them when Joe raised his fist at Steve. "*No,*" Angela cried out.

Startled, Steve teetered back as Joe's roundhouse swing struck him on the arm. Swiftly Mark stepped between them, grabbing Joe by the shirt collar and staring into his eyes. Joe's breath was rank with whiskey, his gaze wild and opaque. "Stop," Mark told him in a low, savage voice. "You've seen this movie before, remember?"

Joe stiffened, his body taut with fury. Heart racing, Mark snapped to Steve, "Get out of here. Angela, too."

Steve hesitated, then stepped forward, grasping Angela's hand. Struggling, Joe grabbed Mark's wrists. "*Look at me,*" Mark ordered.

Joe did. Mark heard the door open, felt the cool night air before Steve slammed the door behind them. Feeling Joe's fingers tighten, Mark jerked him upright. "Stay right here, Joe," he said more softly. "I've got the next dance."

For a few precious seconds more, Joe froze, forehead shining with sweat. Then he wrenched himself away and hurried toward the door.

Mark went after him. As Joe ran toward the parking lot, Mark saw the red taillights of Steve's Camaro careen into the night. He felt himself expel a breath. When he looked for Joe again, he saw no one.

Coming from behind him, Carl Hall's voice was etched with anger. "Guess your buddy wins the prize. Maybe you two can share her."

Mark turned and stared at Carl. "Too bad she's not an only child, Carl. Just the only one smart enough to leave."

Without awaiting an answer, Mark brushed past him. Rusty was standing in the doorway. "Night like this," he said, "no one should be driving." His face clouded. "Never seen Joe *that* bad before."

Mark thought of Laurie Shilts. "Maybe we haven't been looking."

They went back to the living room. Already the couples remaining, dulled by drink, seemed to have forgotten the incident. His face brightening, Rusty saw Tim Fedak and Skip Ellis, coinventors of the DBE catapult.

Turning to Mark, Rusty announced, "I've got a plan. Hang here."

Rusty hurried over to Tim and Skip. As their heads came together, Tim's eyes widened with delight, and Skip began laughing and nodding. "You got to hear this," Rusty called to Mark.

When Mark came over, Rusty convened them in a mock huddle, their faces nearly touching. "Here's the play," Rusty said. "Joe's car is still here. He shouldn't touch the wheel tonight, okay? So we go to the parking lot, lift his Miata, and carry it back up here. He's way too drunk to drive back down the steps."

"You're putting it where?" Mark asked.

Rusty pointed toward the library. "There."

Mark felt the beginning of awe, the germination of another piece of DBE lore. "You're serious."

"We *all* are," Tim replied. "You the quarterback, or not?"

Mark laughed. "For one last play."

With purposeful strides, the four friends went outside, threw open the double doors leading to the living room, and took the steps down to the parking lot. Joe's Miata awaited them, conveniently parked at the foot of the steps.

The cool night air brushed Mark's face. "Think we can carry it?" Skip asked.

Rusty smiled. "C'mon, man. It's fucking tinfoil."

The strongest of the quartet, Mark and Tim took the front bumper, preparing to back up the steps. Knees bent,

Skip and Rusty put their hands beneath the rear. As if calling signals, Mark barked, "Hut one . . . hut two . . . hut three."

Muscles straining, the brothers slowly lifted the car. Elated, they started up the steps, their effort punctuated by grunts and muttered encouragement. As they reached the porch, onlookers gathered in the doorway. "Make way," Rusty called out in martial tones. "We bring you the spoils of victory."

Laughing, the revelers stood aside; some, catching the spirit, moved the couches to clear a space in the living room. What Rusty proclaimed as "Team Betts" deposited Joe's Miata with great ceremony, as though unfurling the flag at Iwo Jima or toppling the statue of a dictator. "Aren't we going to the library?" Mark asked.

"Got to clear the road." Rusty reached into the Miata, producing Joe's car keys. "It's your day, Mark. You get to drive."

Rusty was not usually a leader–it struck Mark that, for him, inspiring this teamwork meant more than the perpetration of a prank. "Whatever you say, Captain. From this night on your name will forever live in legend."

With pleased solemnity, Rusty issued directions. As Tim and Skip pulled the library table to one corner, Rusty handed Mark the keys.

Sitting inside, Mark turned the ignition far enough to put Joe's top down, then started the motor. To cheers and applause, Mark slowly drove the Miata through the open double doors, into the library.

He killed the engine, then sat there, mildly astounded. Rusty handed him a cup of whiskey on ice. "Why don't you try out the sound system," he suggested.

Mark took a deep, harsh swallow of whiskey, then reached into the glove compartment for a tape. It was Bon

Jovi, a favorite. Surrounded by friends, Mark leaned his head back, listening to the music as he slowly closed his eyes.

WHEN MARK AWAKENED, the library was dark.

He felt sick. His head pounded, and his mind filled with rueful self-recrimination. The illuminated clock in Joe's Miata read 3:04.

He needed to get back to his room. But he lived in the bowels of the stadium, a good three-quarters of a mile away. Too far to walk at night–too far, period.

Still drunk, he reached for Joe's car phone.

Steve owed him, he reasoned–Mark had saved him from certain death at the hands of Joe Betts. Early-morning taxi service was not too much to ask.

With a trembling hand, he punched in the number to Steve's room.

The phone rang once, then twice. At fourteen rings Mark hung up. "Wake up, you sonofobitch," he murmured.

Nothing.

Mark dialed again, counting to fifteen rings.

Slowly, he replaced the phone. Never again, he promised himself. Then he shut his eyes once more.

4

When Mark awoke again, his skull throbbed and his mouth tasted sour. The stale air smelled of beer and whiskey and cigarette smoke, the faint pungent whiff of marijuana. Adjusting to the dark, his eyes were slits. He could not remember feeling so stupid.

The clock in Joe's car read 5:43. Soon dawn would break, providing enough light for him to stagger home. He craved fresh air and his own bed.

Slowly, Mark extracted himself from the Miata.

The living room was empty except for a body sprawled on the couch. Rusty Clark. Passing through, Mark cautiously opened the side door, as though expecting to find himself in a foreign country. He took one deep breath of chill morning air and started on his way.

The first thick ribbon of orange-gray dawn appeared above the trees outlined in the semidark. In the distance, Mark discerned the steeple atop the Spire.

He headed there. Between the fraternities and campus, a gently sloping walkway flanked by trees and gardens passed modern buildings constructed of red brick–the library, the student theater, the alumni center, and, newest and most impressive, the architecturally striking student union, a steel-and-glass marvel that was the pride of Caldwell. But as with most other paths at the college, this one led to the Spire, towering above all else. As the sky lightened, the steeple emerged more clearly, creating the illusion that it was moving toward him from above the trees. There was a dusting of frost on the ground.

At the foot of the pathway, a black metal clock, eight feet high, told Mark that it was now 6:07. Passing it, Mark entered the main campus, demarked by a sandstone gateway. For the next few minutes he wended his way through the buildings, varied in size and style, that housed his classes in English, history, philosophy, and science. At midday, he promised himself, he would go for a very long run and afterward, head cleared, resume his pursuit of a place at Yale Law School. Then he reached the lawn surrounding the Spire.

He paused there, recalling the tumult he had inspired hours before, the primal roar of the crowd as he'd brandished the bronze axe. Now the site of the Spire was so quiet and empty that it evoked a vanished civilization. Gazing up at the steeple, he remembered the harsh severity of the bell tower, his brief attack of vertigo. With a sense of awe, he again approached the tower.

He stopped abruptly.

A dark form lay on the grass. Completely still, it was too long and angular to be anything but a person. He stepped forward, wondering if someone had passed out here, deeply afraid that this was something worse.

It was a woman. Arms outflung, her body faced the sky. A terrible sense of familiarity hit him as he moved closer.

He stopped abruptly, sickened.

Angela Hall lay at the foot of the Spire like a sacrifice on an altar. She stared up at him, her eyes too fixed to be alive. Her lips were parted in an expression of pain or anger, exposing her white teeth.

A cry of animal anguish issued from Mark's throat. He forced himself to kneel, touching her wrist. It was not as cold as he had imagined or as warm as he had hoped.

Feeling this contact like an electric shock, he fought back the reflex to vomit.

Mark stood. There was no telephone, he realized, no way of calling for help. Instinctively he began running across the lawn, heading for the one house he knew near campus, Lionel Farr's.

Again and again he rang the doorbell, jabbing the button as though willing Farr to answer. At last, minutes later, someone jerked open the door.

It was Farr, his strong face lined with sleep, his eyes keen with a displeasure that changed to surprise. He was still adjusting his sweater, and his gray-blond hair was mussed. "For God's sake, Mark. What is it?"

Mark's throat was parched. "Angela Hall. I found her near the Spire." Voice catching, he finished: "I think she's dead."

For an instant, Farr's eyes froze. Then he snapped, "Wait here."

Mark stood on the porch, shaken yet relieved. Farr hurried through the door. "I've called the police," he said. "We'll meet them there."

Together they rushed down the street toward the Spire. Between breaths, Mark said, "I saw her last night."

Loping beside him, Farr asked sharply, "Where?"

"The DBE house."

"Tell me."

As they entered the campus, Mark began a hasty outline of the party.

"She left with Steve?" Farr interrupted.

"Yes."

They reached the grass, Mark hoping against hope that this was a dream. The landscape was empty but for Angela.

Slowing, Farr approached her. His military posture

vanished. Kneeling beside the body, he looked into her face, his eyes narrowing in scrutiny until, briefly, they shut. "She's been strangled."

"Strangled?" Mark repeated.

"Look at her eyes," Farr responded softly.

Mark forced himself to do that. There were red pinpoints in the whites of her sightless eyes. In a monotone, he said, "I should have taken her home."

Farr turned. Following his gaze, Mark saw two uniformed policemen running toward the Spire. "Whatever happened," Farr said with quiet urgency, "tell them everything . . ."

"What about Steve?"

"Everything, dammit. You can't know who it helps or hurts. But concealment helps no one–especially you."

One of the policemen was George Garrison–his high school teammate and Angela's friend. Staring at Angela, George slumped. "Sweet Lord," he said to the body. "What happened to you, baby?" It was not the voice of a cop.

When Mark looked up at him, George was staring back. The other cop, white and older, put his hand on George's shoulder. Then he spoke to Mark and Farr. "The detectives are coming," he told them. "I want you over on that bench."

The next several minutes were a blur. Seated at the edge of the grass, Mark and Lionel Farr watched the police tape off the grass around the Spire. A photographer and videocam operator focused on Angela; a youngish blond woman carefully examined her body; two plainclothes detectives took notes. Mark tried to remember whether he had seen, or only now imagined, a bruise on Angela's face.

At length the two detectives walked toward the bench.

"Tell them everything," Farr repeated. "Leave nothing out."

The older, red-headed detective identified himself as Fred Bender; the bulky man with a worn, sad face was Jack Muhlberg. Standing over them, Muhlberg said evenly, "So what happened here?"

With quiet efficiency, Farr traced their movements from Mark's arrival at his door. The detective pointed to a nearby garden. "Let's talk over here," he told Farr.

They left Mark alone. Disbelieving, he watched men in white jackets examine the ground near Angela's body. The morning sun, he noticed, was turning the frost to dew.

If only.

If only Steve had not invited her. If only she had left before. If only Steve had not left with her. Mark could not decipher cause and effect, only its rudiments. He kept seeing Joe's glazed eyes, Steve's taillights swerving into the night, Angela's wistful smile. Somewhere between that moment and dawn, tragedy had waited for her.

The two detectives returned with Farr. "Okay, Mark," Muhlberg said. "We'll need to go over just what happened." Turning to Farr, he added, "You can leave now, Professor."

"I'd like to stay."

Bender shook his head. "That's not how we do things."

"Is Mark in custody?"

Glancing at Muhlberg, Bender said, "Of course not."

Farr crossed his arms. "Then you should understand that he's much more than a student to me. It comes down to this: either I stay, or I'm hiring him a lawyer. Your choice."

Muhlberg looked nettled. "How do you feel, Mark?"

Mark sorted out his thoughts. "Professor Farr said to tell you everything. I'd like him here with me."

When Bender turned to him, Muhlberg shrugged in resignation. Silent, Mark saw George Garrison watching over his murdered friend. He stood so still he could have been in a trance.

"Okay, Mark," Bender said briskly, and the questioning began.

THE TWO DETECTIVES were dogged and thorough. Reluctantly, Mark described the night: drinking with Steve, encountering Angela, confronting Carl, breaking up the fight between Steve and Joe. Under persistent questioning, Mark explained his relationship to each. "Before you found her," Muhlberg asked again, "when did you last see Angela alive?"

It dawned on Mark that he was a suspect. "When she left with Steve," he answered tiredly. "Just like I told you before."

"Where does Steve live?"

"Where I do. We both have rooms in the football stadium."

The two detectives glanced at each other. "Can you tell us anything else?" Muhlberg asked.

For an instant, Mark hesitated. "Yeah. You should talk to Laurie Shilts, Joe's girlfriend. She was at the party, too."

Muhlberg sat beside him. "I thought Joe went after Angela."

"They'd broken up, Laurie told me."

"Did she say why?"

"You'd have to ask her." Mark stared straight ahead. "All I know for sure is they'd had a fight."

Bender wrote this down. Moving forward, Farr asked, "Can Mark go now?"

Nodding, Muhlberg gazed at Mark. "Do us a favor," he said, "and also yourself. Don't talk about this to anyone.

I know these kids are your friends. But we need to get their independent memories."

Silent, Mark nodded. To his surprise, Muhlberg put a hand on his shoulder. "You were a great quarterback, Mark. I always liked watching you play."

"I always liked playing," Mark answered.

THE TWO DETECTIVES left.

"I don't care what they say," Mark told Farr. "I've got to find Steve."

"That would be a mistake," Farr said firmly. "It's also too late. I'm sure they've already gone to his room. All you'd do is walk in on them and make yourself look bad."

Mark felt the enormity of events crashing down on him, the world as he knew it spinning out of control. "Then what do I do now?"

"Stay out of trouble." Farr's taut voice brooked no dissent. "I have to tell Clark Durbin, and you're coming with me."

5

THEY RUSHED TO DURBIN'S HOUSE ON FOOT. STILL disoriented, unsure of his role here, Mark sensed that Farr meant to keep him close, away from Steve or Joe or the police. His face careworn, Farr said little. Only when they approached the door of the president's house did he pause, saying softly and sadly, "That beautiful girl." Then he stood taller, fully himself, and rapped the brass door knocker.

Opening the door, Durbin looked from Farr to Darrow, his reflexive half smile at odds with his expression of puzzlement. "There's been a terrible tragedy," Farr said in a low voice. "Angela Hall, a black scholarship student. Mark found her at the Spire, strangled. The police are already there."

Durbin stared at Mark, lips parting slightly. He had been president for three months. Yesterday at the Spire, when Mark had met him for the first time, his fleeting impression had been of a slight dark-haired man in his forties with a ready smile and warm blue eyes who gave off a jittery energy. Now his body seemed to sag; in his slack expression and softening chin, Mark saw only shock. For an instant, Mark compared his reaction to Farr's—Durbin seemed momentarily paralyzed.

"Come in," he said haltingly. "Please."

Mark followed Farr inside. The one-story house was modern and light, with an open floor plan and tall windows that looked out on a patio and garden. Durbin waved them to a couch, sitting across from them with his hands clasped, his expression more focused. "A student's lost her life," he said. "That's the worst thing that can hit any school. I need to hear everything you know."

Farr took a moment to gather himself. "That's why I'm here. Not many–if any–people know. By this afternoon everyone will. No matter the shock, you'll have to move quickly. But it's worth taking an hour now to design the best response." Farr nodded toward Mark. "From what I understand, this tragedy may have started with a party at the DBE house. Mark was there. He has a story to tell you that may bear on what you should do."

Surprised, Mark stared at Farr. "Go ahead," Durbin urged Mark. "Please."

Facing him, Mark outlined the events, culminating in Angela's departure with Steve. He could not shake the sense of betraying his friend. But Durbin listened closely, his expression open and even kind. "Thank you, Mark," he said, then turned to Farr. "Obviously, I need to address the school right away. The students will need a sense of calmness."

"That's only part of it," Farr ventured. "The police know all this from Mark–no doubt they're questioning Steve Tillman right now. Inevitably, this story will be tinged with drugs, alcohol, and overtones of racism. It heightens the risk of frightening our students and our applicants, including minorities. How you react in the next twenty-four hours, and then the next few days, will help determine how bad that gets." Farr leaned forward, saying gently, "I've had a few more minutes to think about this. May I offer some suggestions?"

To Mark, Durbin appeared freshly appalled by what he faced. "Please."

"First, call an all-school meeting for seven o'clock tonight–use the school's voice-mail system. Between then and now, phone Angela's mother to express our grief and ask what we can do. Call any leader of the black community you can find. Also our board chair and general counsel–you'll need their advice, and there'll be hell to pay if you don't take it. Especially about preventing a racial or town-gown conflict."

Durbin held up his hand. Walking to a desk, he took out a legal pad and pen. Sitting again, he asked, "How do you see this all-school meeting?"

"The purpose–as you say–is to calm the campus. Offer the students grief counseling. Announce a memorial service for Angela, and a day of reflection in our classrooms on what this tragedy means to Caldwell. Invite student leaders in for meetings–including leaders of minority groups."

"What about campus safety?" Durbin cut in. "I should hire more security guards."

"Agreed," Farr responded with quiet force. "But by itself that suggests that this place is dangerous. Have your VP for student affairs gather the statistics on previous campus crime rates–I've been here almost twenty years now, and I can assure you that it's pretty low. At tonight's meeting, tell the students that."

Durbin shook his head. "That would sound like I'm saying there's nothing to worry about. Plainly, there is."

"Then why not announce a new campus safety program–tonight. A buddy system where students are encouraged to walk together. A ride system for women walking back to their dorms or sorority houses at night. Telephones every fifty yards or so, connecting students to the campus police. A new lighting system to illuminate the campus after dark." Farr paused for emphasis. "Let them know that you won't rest until you're certain—and *they're* certain—that this will never happen again."

As Mark listened, it struck him that Farr's professorial persona was falling away, exposing the military officer he once had been, quick-thinking and decisive under stress. Durbin scribbled a few more notes, then looked up at Mark. "I can't imagine how you must feel, Mark. Still, I'd appreciate any thoughts you have."

For a moment, Mark studied a patch of sunlight on Durbin's tan carpet. "Okay," he said finally. "Don't just have this meeting. You should also go where we live—you, or the deans, or maybe some professors. Give every student you can find someone they can talk to. A lot of the guys I know won't relate to some psychologist they've never met."

Slowly, Durbin nodded. "Good advice."

"Also," Farr added, "you should announce another student forum in one week's time, to tell them what you've learned and whatever else you're doing. It's no good that you're in charge unless the students, board, faculty, alumni, and community know that. For the sake of us all, it's imperative that you emerge from this tragedy as the leader Caldwell needs."

To Mark, Farr's implicit warning was unmistakable. Whatever else Durbin did in the future no longer mattered—his presidency would be judged, favorably or not, based on how he handled Angela's murder. "I need to get our board chair on campus," Durbin said to Farr. "Also Ernie Sims—it might be good to remind everyone that our thirty-person board actually includes an African-American. As soon as possible, the three of us should visit Angela's family."

"If you like," Farr offered, "I'll go with you. I'm the head of the committee that gave Angela her scholarship.

More than that, I'm the only one of us who actually knew her." A look of sadness crossed Farr's face. "Consoling her family is the hardest job we'll have, and one of the most critical. For the sake of Angela's mother, we can't seem distant from her dead daughter. And to be brutally practical, we don't want her suing the school."

Once again, Mark absorbed Farr's ability to anticipate potential consequences. "We'll need more outreach to the black community as a whole," Durbin said. "The town seems pretty segregated, and we can't let the blacks in Wayne fester in their own resentment and isolation."

Durbin was right, Mark knew. Blacks seldom went downtown; even at the high school, black and white kids rarely socialized. Racial attitudes, even if unspoken, were often adversarial. Uncomfortably, Mark thought of Steve Tillman and his casual, if infrequent disparagement of black classmates. "True enough," Farr was saying. "Then there's our alumni. As you well know, their donations help fund this place. You've got to reassure them quickly." Farr's tone became grim. "A big problem with *that* is the media. A white-on-black murder, if that's what we have, will be catnip for them."

Durbin frowned at this. "I'll get our public relations people on this right away."

"It's over their heads, Clark. Hire an outside PR firm with experience in crisis management. We need to bombard the media and our funders with Caldwell's story–the low crime rate, the new campus safety program, how we've gotten our own kids through this, how much we welcome minorities." Farr's tone was pointed. "They should also provide talking points for our admissions people. You can take it to the bank that our applications will drop. What we have is not just murder, but a combustible mix of race and drugs and alcohol."

"There we can point to our substance abuse policy," Durbin said. "It's one of the first things I asked about in the interview process."

"Did they mention that our policy is bullshit?" Farr inclined his head toward Mark. "Any student can tell you that this place is awash in alcohol and drugs, including the DBE house. I should know: I'm on the student-faculty disciplinary committee, and every so often some drunk or drugged-out kid destroys a dorm room or precipitates a charge of date rape. That's the only time we stop pretending there's no problem." He turned to Mark. "You said Angela's brother was at the party. He deals drugs out of the Alibi Club, right?"

Mark hesitated. "Yeah, he does."

"Not much we can do about *that,*" Farr told Durbin. "Angela's mother owns the place. That leaves the fraternities."

"That's tougher, Lionel. A lot of the alumni I'm meeting feel like their fraternity was the heart of their experience at Caldwell."

"And a lot of them are morons," Farr responded. "Here's what I'd recommend. Conduct a full investigation of that party. Warn the presidents of every fraternity that their parties are no longer off-limits to school authorities. If fraternities tolerate drugs or underage drinking, it's not the particular student who'll go–it's the fraternity. Any kid caught once with drugs will get compulsory drug and alcohol counseling; twice, they'll be suspended; three times, they'll be expelled. Make sure they know what date rape is, and that any assault on a woman, of any kind, will be dealt with harshly.

"It's clear and it's fair, Clark. More alumni will praise you than resent you. Ask the ones who complain if they care more about the idiots in their old fraternity than about the reputation of the school and the safety of its students." Farr's tone was quiet but firm. "Tell them your job is to make Caldwell College the safest place on earth. Then do it."

Durbin frowned. "I came here to raise money from them, not to beat them over the head. This is my first presidency; fund-raising's my skill set. The board hired me to launch a new capital campaign and beef up our endowment."

"You can't right now," Farr said with muted impatience. "Not for at least a year. It's not just that there's been a murder after a fraternity party. In all likelihood, Angela Hall was strangled by a student at this college."

Durbin raised his eyebrows. "Specifically, Steve Tillman?"

At once, Mark began to fear that Steve might be railroaded to save the school. "Perhaps," Farr answered. "If so, it's possible that sex–consensual or nonconsensual–may become part of the mix. I know one thing for sure: if any student is charged, we have to expel them. Neither the school nor its students can live with anything less."

Abruptly, Durbin stood. "I need to get started. For the next few hours, Lionel, I want you at my side."

Farr nodded. "Of course. Just let me talk with Mark for a minute."

"Please." Facing Mark, Durbin said, "You've been through a lot since yesterday, when we first met. I know you have Professor Farr to lean on. But if there's anything I can do for you, at any hour, just call."

Even through his fog, Mark felt this man's essential goodness. "Thank you, sir. I will."

Farr touched his arm. "I'll walk out with you."

The two of them stopped on the front porch. In the driveway, a pale, uncoordinated-looking boy of about twelve was shooting baskets without much skill, oblivious to all that had happened. Mark turned to Farr and saw that his eyes suddenly looked tired and deeply sad. "It's hard to believe," he murmured, shaking his head. "She was full of promise, full of plans. I had so much hope for her." Looking intently at Mark, he asked, "Are *you* all right?"

Mark tried to imagine the next hours and days. "I guess so. But there's no way Steve could have done this. I'm starting to get scared for him."

"I know," Farr responded gently. "But there's no help for that now–or for any of it. There hasn't been, ever since you found her."

Slowly, Mark nodded. Farr placed a hand on his shoulder. "There's one more thing," he admonished quietly. "No one should know about this meeting. Whatever Clark Durbin does should be seen as his initiative. He's the president, and now it's his time to be a leader."

6

Filled with dread, Mark walked slowly across the campus to the football stadium.

A quiet gathering of students ringed the Spire, cordoned off by yellow tape. Mark kept his head down, avoiding eye contact with anyone he passed. Within hours, he had gone from hungover to adrenalized to how he felt now–stunned and disoriented and filled with disbelief, yet constantly seeing Angela's stricken face. He felt a deep sadness for Angela, and a deep worry about the meaning of what he had witnessed the night before. His only hope now was that this tragedy, whatever its cause, would not touch Steve Tillman.

Like Mark's own, Steve's room was on the first floor of the worn gray football stadium, a relic of the twenties. But the entrance to Steve's dimly lit corridor was marked with yellow tape saying crime scene. From inside echoed male voices, too authoritative to come from students. Mark felt a nightmare closing around him.

He needed air. Caught between the need to find Steve and the desire to be alone, he chose a place where he and Steve sometimes went–a section of bleachers on the fifty-yard line where, concealed by night, he would sit with Steve while his friend smoked pot. These sessions were more common, Mark reflected, since Steve had torn up his knee and, it seemed, plunged into despondency. Now Mark hoped that this had not awakened something worse.

The afternoon was darker than the morning. The sun had been extinguished by the lowering lead-gray sky common to Ohio as fall deepened into winter, and though it was not raining, the air felt cold and damp. As Mark stared at the empty field, the noise and sweat and exhilaration of yesterday's game felt like a barely remembered dream. A white hot dog wrapper skittered across the field.

Mark sat there, grateful for solitude. Then he heard heavy thudding footsteps on the wooden stands, suggesting a limp, and turned to see Steve Tillman.

Steve's face was pale, his brown hair matted and askew. His gaze held a hint of pain and puzzlement commingled with dissociation. Then he said, "I guess you've heard."

Mark's own voice sounded foreign to him. "I found her."

Steve stared at him. "You told them about me."

"I had to," Mark said in weary protest. "At least about the party."

Steve shoved his hands in his pockets. After a moment, he nodded.

"What happened?" Mark asked.

He meant between Steve and Angela. But instead Steve answered, "The cops came to my room. I was so fucked up, I couldn't really say what happened, I'm not sure I *know* what happened."

"What did the cops ask?"

As Steve began talking, Mark envisioned the scene, a narrative of innocence and surprise he did not know whether to believe.

SOMETIME DURING THE the early morning hours, Steve had passed out. He awoke to a knocking on his door, then a male voice calling his name.

Eyes opening, he looked around his room in a fog. His

bedside lamp was knocked over, its base shattered into pieces. There were drink glasses on the tile floor, a bottle of rum, empty Coke cans. His sheets, a tangled mess, were strewn across and beside the bed.

"Steve Tillman?" the rough voice queried.

Judging from the light behind the curtains, it was day. "Wait a minute," Steve shouted back.

He was naked. Grabbing boxer shorts and a T-shirt, he struggled to put them on. When he opened the door, Steve saw two grim-faced men he knew were not from the school.

"You're Steve?" the red-haired guy said.

"Yeah."

Swiftly, the man's eyes took in the mess that was Steve's room. "I'm Detective Bender, Steve, and this is Detective Muhlberg. Can we talk with you for a minute?"

There was cocaine hidden in his drawer, Steve realized, bought from Carl Hall. "Let me get dressed," Steve said hastily. "I'll meet you outside."

The cop's voice was softer now. "It might be better if we talked in private."

Steve looked at the other guy, Muhlberg. "We need your help," Muhlberg told him. "A female student's been murdered."

Steve felt pinpricks on his skin, then a numbness that made his limbs feel heavy. "Who?"

"Her name was Angela Hall."

Steve sat down on the bed.

Muhlberg pulled up the desk chair, stationing himself in front of Steve. His sad eyes filled with sympathy. "I know this must be a shock, Steve."

Steve was aware of Bender looking around his room. "She's dead?" Steve heard himself say.

"Strangled, seems like."

"Where?"

"We don't know where, Steve. That's what we're trying to find out." Muhlberg's voice was reasonable, unthreatening. "We're talking to people who knew her. You were with her at the DBE house, right?"

Steve hesitated. Cautiously, he answered, "Right."

Haltingly, Steve let them extract his story–drinking beer; meeting Angela; switching to whiskey; the near fight with Joe Betts; heading with Angela for his dorm room.

Muhlberg wrote it all down. "What happened then?" he asked.

"I COULDN'T REMEMBER," Steve told Mark now.

Sitting in the bleachers, Mark felt his disbelief become fear. "What do you mean?"

"I was too fucked up. I think maybe I did a line of coke, drank some rum." Steve began rubbing his temples, elbows resting on his knees. "It's like I have these images, but I can't be sure they're real. You know those lights that flash at parties?"

"Strobe lights?"

"It's like that. There's light for a second, and you can see–then it's dark. Remembering her is like that." He covered his face, fingers splayed. "I can't believe she's dead, Mark."

Mark inhaled, the nausea of the previous night returning. "What *do* you remember?"

Softly, Steve answered, "I think we must have had sex."

AS HIS FRIEND spoke, Mark tried to link the scattered images Steve evoked.

A flash of light, Angela undressing. Slim hips. Full breasts. Nipples with dark brown areolas.

Another flash. She slid down her panties, exposing the tangle of her fur as she looked into his eyes.

The light came back on. She had turned to show him her firm round buttocks.

Do you want me?

Steve pulled her to the bed, something crashing in the darkness. The scent of her skin suffused his senses . . .

I have to go.

Steve struggled to comprehend this. *Leave?*

I have to.

MARK STRUGGLED TO imagine this. But it made no sense.

Filled with doubts, he asked, "Did you leave with her?"

Steve shook his head. "No way."

I tried to call you, Mark wanted to say. *From the house, at three in the morning.* Instead, he asked, "Did you go anywhere at all?"

Steve looked over at him. His pale face had turned blotchy, his expression suddenly guarded. "When?"

"Anytime that night."

"I must have been passed out." Steve shook his head, as though in wonder at the wreckage of his memory. "I can't bring anything back. I don't know, man. I don't get what's happening at all."

Mark tried to sort out his thoughts. "After you left the party, did you see Joe?"

"Nope." Steve's tone was faintly hostile. "They asked me *that,* too."

Mark looked out at the football field. The sky was lower yet; in an hour or so, he guessed, the gray would darken with impending night. Facing Steve, he asked, "Got a place to sleep tonight?"

"I'm going to my folks'." Steve shook his head again.

"They don't even know about this. When those cops took me to the station, they kept me too busy to call."

Mark's foreboding deepened. "What did they do?"

"They swabbed my mouth, scraped under my fingernails, drew some blood." His voice became resentful. "Then they ordered me to strip, and took pictures of me buck naked. Hope *those* don't get out."

"What else?"

Steve gazed out at the empty field. "They asked me if I'd hit her. I said I didn't do that kind of shit to women."

But Joe Betts might, Mark thought. His mind a kaleidoscope of confusion, he tried to remember whether Angela's face was bruised. Then he imagined Steve's parents–his plain, perpetually mystified mother; his bluff, kind father–struggling to absorb what might be happening. "Want me to go home with you?" Mark asked.

Steve grimaced. "Don't think so, man. This one I'd better do alone."

He stood, his bad knee buckling slightly. Turning, Steve asked, "You look at something for me?"

"Sure."

He pulled up his sweatshirt, exposing his pale back. "See anything?"

The red scratches on Steve's back resembled welts. Quietly, Mark said, "You've got some scratches, pal. Bad ones."

Slowly, heavily, Steve sat down again. "Yeah," he mumbled. "It feels like that."

Mark lapsed into silence. "Maybe I fucked her," Steve said. "But that doesn't mean I killed her."

To this remark, disturbing in so many ways, Mark had nothing to say.

7

In the days that followed, Steve was barely seen on campus.

For Mark, time was a blur–the all-campus meeting, President Durbin announcing the measures Farr had crafted for him; nights of sleeplessness; bleak dinners at the DBE house; the refuge of an evening at the Farrs'; a memorial service for Angela held in the chapel of College Hall. Mark managed to avoid Joe Betts. Then on Thursday afternoon, when they emerged from a history class devoted to discussing what–if anything–the murder revealed about Caldwell College, Joe caught up with him.

"Hear you were the driver," Joe said in a sardonic tone.

Mark shrugged. "It was a selfless act, Joe. You didn't need to be driving."

To Mark's surprise, Joe did not protest. They headed across campus, pausing at the green around the Spire.

A crowd had gathered, alien to Caldwell–some white but mostly black, carrying signs demanding JUSTICE FOR ANGELA, with reporters and video cameras interspersed among them. Though Mark had lived here all his life, many of the demonstrators were strangers to him. An imposing black man in a clerical collar addressed them. "We come here today," he said, "to demand that Caldwell College search its soul. It is not enough for a school to say that it welcomes students of color. Caldwell College must create an environment where our young women leave the school in a cap and gown, not a coffin."

Applause burst from the crowd. Accompanied by Farr, Clark Durbin made his way toward the speaker. Farr placed a hand on the clergyman's shoulder, speaking to him quietly. Nodding, the minister passed the microphone to Durbin.

Though Durbin tried to stand taller, the reverend towered over him, and the president's voice was high and reedy. "You have come," he said, "to challenge our consciences. I welcome that, and make two promises. First, we will ensure that this is a safe place for students of all origins, offering those opportunities that our society all too often forecloses. As of next fall, the Angela Hall Memorial Scholarship program will offer four years at Caldwell College–free tuition and room and board–to worthy minority students."

At the tepid applause, Durbin raised a hand. "I recognize that we gave such an opportunity to Angela. I recognize that we failed her." His voice grew firmer. "It will never happen again. And we will do everything we can to help the authorities find the perpetrator of this loathsome crime–whoever and wherever they may be."

The applause, deeper now, mingled with an outcry of a crowd in search of justice. As a black-and-white placard of Angela's high school graduation picture thrust from their midst, a pleasant-looking man took the microphone from Durbin.

Dressed in a suit and tie, he had a ruddy complexion and russet hair and projected an air of calm. "I'm Dave Farragher," he said, "the prosecutor for Wayne County. I've come to assure you that we are working night and day to solve this terrible murder." He paused, his gaze sweeping the crowd, focused on the video cameras. "We expect to have an announcement soon–"

For four days, the authorities had said nothing. Now Mark felt an invisible web enveloping Steve Tillman. Unable to repress the thought, he murmured to Joe, "I think Steve's in trouble."

"I know he is." When Joe turned toward him, his eyes held a pleading look Mark had never seen before. "Let's get out of here, okay?"

JOE SUGGESTED THE Carriage House, a wood-paneled restaurant-bar long favored by students and locals that provided booths where patrons could talk in relative privacy. He sat across from Mark with slumped shoulders and a look of troubled abstraction, as though burdened by the weight of his own thoughts. When Mark ordered a beer, Joe asked the waitress for a Diet Coke on ice.

"No beer?" Mark asked.

He meant it as a casual remark. But Joe stared at the table. "I don't feel like it. I may never feel like it again." He looked up at Mark. "I'm an asshole when I drink."

Joe's expression, more often cynical or superior, was so vulnerable that his practiced veneer of prep school toughness vanished. He seemed to expect a response. "Sometimes," Mark agreed.

Joe nodded slowly. Cautiously, he asked. "How was I at that party?"

Mark eyed him with puzzled skepticism. "You don't remember?"

Joe winced. Removing his glasses, he wiped the lenses with a paper napkin, as though to improve his vision. "Kind of." He met Mark's eyes again. "I shouldn't drink at all, should I?"

Weighing his response, Mark reflected on the mercurial

relationship among Joe's personae: the supercilious but amusing child of privilege; the wounded son of an angry father; the abrasive, abusive drunk. Why, Mark wondered, were he and Joe so different when both their childhoods had been train wrecks? Maybe it was innate; maybe it was that Mark had Lionel Farr. Or maybe it was that his own parents, unlike Joe's, were equals in their irrationality and rage. "When you don't drink," Mark responded evenly, "you're a good guy. When you do, you're more than an asshole–you're dangerous. I don't know you anymore." Mark paused, then decided to take a chance. "Maybe I'm meeting your father, Joe. The guy who kicked the shit out of Mom."

Eyes closing, Joe became very still. Mark felt his friend withdrawing to another place–some bad memory or deep within his most hidden thoughts. Then he opened his eyes again. Softly, he said, "I don't want to know that person anymore."

The statement sounded literal, the expression of a strong desire–even a need–to exorcise something within himself that Joe despised and feared. Mark felt a troubling shadow pass between them, his own unease about what lay beneath his friend's confession. Then Joe said with quiet fervor, "I need to make someone a promise, Mark. I've chosen you."

Mark cocked his head. "Not Laurie?"

A flicker of emotion–perhaps fear, perhaps shame–crossed Joe's face. "Too late." He put his hand on Mark's wrist, as though establishing a bond. "My old man's dead now. From now until I die, I'm never taking another drink."

"I believe you."

In truth, Mark was not sure. But Joe gave him a look of deep relief, as though Mark had absolved him. "Thanks, man. I mean it. I know the last few days have been hard for you."

Now it was Mark who stared at the table. At length he said, "I keep remembering her face." He paused, then finished in a monotone: "I'd never seen anyone dead before. All I can think is that no one should die that way."

Joe grimaced. "She looked bad, I guess."

"Yeah."

Through his own discomfort, Mark wondered what lay behind the question–compassion, morbid curiosity, or something deeper. Then Joe asked, "The night she died, when was the last time you saw Tillman?"

Mark met his eyes again. "When he left with her."

"What did *I* do?"

"You ran after them. After they got in Steve's car, you just disappeared."

Joe contemplated the remnants of his Coke. "I guess I went back to the dorm. I was asleep when the cops started pounding on the door."

"That's what Steve says, too."

Joe touched his eyes. "There's something else about that night," he said at last.

Once more, Mark felt pinpricks on his skin. "About Steve?"

"Yeah. I saw him."

"With Angela?"

Joe shook his head. "In the middle of the night, I woke up feeling like I was about to puke. So I went to the window and cracked it open, trying to suck in air."

Mark tried to envision this. Joe's room was on the second floor, a level above Mark's and Steve's. Save for lights at the entry to the dorm section, the stadium at night was dark. "And?" Mark prodded.

"Steve was outside." Joe's eyes narrowed, as though

refocusing his memory. "It was only a second or two. But I could see it was him, passing through the light as he came toward the stadium. No one else limps like that." His face became grim. "I heard his key, the downstairs door opening, then closing."

Mark tried to gauge the importance of this. "Could you tell where he was coming from?"

"He was outside, that's all. Like I said, it was only a few seconds."

"Do you know what time it was?"

"Yeah, 'cause I remember looking at the clock. It was a little after three."

From the reluctance in his voice, Mark knew that Joe understood the danger inherent in his story—were Steve outside the stadium, he could have left with Angela, potentially placing him near the Spire. Then what neither Joe nor the police knew hit Mark with a jolt. At 3:04, Mark had called Steve's room, then called again; for whatever reason, his friend had not answered.

A flush was spreading across Joe's face. "Thing is, I told the cops about it."

Mark stared at him. In a pleading tone, Joe said, "Don't tell anyone at the house, okay? They'll feel like I ratted Steve out. But you just don't lie to those guys."

Unless you had good reason to lie, Mark thought. But now he had an uneasy conscience of his own: uncertain of its meaning, certain only of the damage it might do, he could not bring himself to tell anyone about his phone call.

"I won't tell anyone," Mark promised.

Joe seemed both somber and relieved. "Let's go up to the house," he said abruptly. "We're almost late for dinner."

*

WITH THE HELP of their fraternity brothers, Joe had liberated his Miata from the library. Silent, they drove from downtown Wayne to the DBE house, parking close to the rear steps, where, in what Mark thought of as a more innocent time, he and three inebriated friends had lifted Joe's convertible.

Sliding out of the passenger seat, Mark saw the back doors of their fraternity house open.

Framed in the doorway, Steve Tillman was flanked by two policemen, one at each elbow. Steve's hands were cuffed behind him. Stunned, Mark saw that one of the cops was their former teammate George Garrison, Angela's high school friend.

At the head of the steps, Steve stumbled, his damaged knee buckling. When he saw Mark, his mouth twisted in an odd, chagrined smile, as though he had been busted with a nickel bag of pot. On the other side of the car, Joe softly murmured, "Jesus . . ."

Mark wanted to say something. Instead, he froze, paralyzed by confusion and what he had learned from Joe. With the force of a blow, Mark understood that their lives had changed in a profound and frightening way.

The police trundled Steve into a squad car. Without speaking to Joe, Mark hurried off to the only place he could go for help.

HE ARRIVED AT Lionel Farr's out of breath, pursued by his memory of running there only days before. To his surprise, Taylor answered the door.

Unlike most adolescents, she seemed to be skipping the gawky stage: at eleven, Taylor was part child, part the dark-haired beauty prefigured by her mother. But already she had the preternatural seriousness, sometimes disconcerting to Mark, of an adult guarding her private thoughts.

Anne had dryly remarked that Taylor reserved her brightest smiles for Mark, practicing for when boys her age became halfway human, and sometimes it seemed so. But tonight the girl simply stared at him, her eyes so filled with sorrow that he guessed she must know why he had come.

"Is your dad home?" he asked.

Reluctantly, Taylor opened the door, inching aside.

Farr sat beside his wife in the living room. Though Anne greeted him pleasantly, her voice was soft, her face ashen. Farr looked tired; all the energy and resolve Mark had seen since Angela's death seemed to have drained from him. In a voice more weary than welcoming, he asked, "What is it, Mark?"

"They've arrested Steve."

Anne looked down. Standing, Farr touched her shoulder, an overt gesture of tenderness Mark had seldom seen from him. "Let's talk in the den," Farr said.

WHEN FARR SAT across from him, Mark thought briefly of his first dinner here, the night that had changed his life. But now Farr's manner was far less expansive. Bluntly, he said, "You must have felt as if you were walking into a séance. The trouble is that Anne's not well."

Despite his own anxiety, Mark was startled. "Is she okay?"

"In a manner of speaking. At least for now." Farr's voice softened. "Anne has a heart condition. It's something all three of us live with, though Taylor is simply afraid of her mother dying. Sometimes Anne's blood pressure drops so precipitously that she passes out. In truth, that's one of her lesser problems. But today Taylor found Anne on the kitchen floor and thought that she was dead."

This explained Taylor's greeting, Mark thought—in fact, it might explain much more about her. "So," Farr said in a flat voice, "they've decided Steve's the one. I know how that must upset you."

Mark felt deflated. "I think he needs a lawyer."

"I'm quite sure he does." Watching Mark's face, Farr inquired, "Are you so sure he didn't kill her? I learned long ago how little we know about others, even those we're certain we know well. You also know nothing about what may have happened between those two. People can do strange things when liquor unleashes their darker natures."

Mark felt himself resist this. "That's not Steve."

"Then who did this?" Farr parried. "Murder by strangulation is not an impulsive act. It took someone a long time to suffocate her like that."

Farr's voice betrayed an undertone of anger. Chastened, Mark realized that Farr had felt closer to Angela than to Steve, and had admired her far more. It was even possible, Mark thought, that his own presence reminded Farr of why Steve had been given a scholarship, and that, with Angela dead, Farr bitterly regretted his role. "Steve's my friend," Mark said. "His parents took me in. I've got to help him somehow."

Farr regarded him closely. "Discussing this is difficult," he said at length, "given my relationship to the school and my feelings about Angela. But if Steve's a murderer, it's quite certain he was impaired. That's the basis for *some* sort of defense. I suppose it's even possible that he's innocent."

Mark felt the whipsaw of his own doubt, the secret lodged within him. He waited for Farr to speak again. "I know a decent lawyer in town," Farr continued. "Griffin Nordlinger. I expect he might do better than some overworked state public defender from who knows where. At least Griff might be good for some advice. I'll see if he'll agree to visit your friend."

The new reality hit Mark: Steve was in jail now, his expulsion from Caldwell certain. It felt like another death.

CROSSING THE DARKENED campus, Mark reached the stadium filled with apprehension and despair.

He found Joe in the recreation room, watching a local TV station. Dave Farragher spoke from behind a podium. "With this arrest," the prosecutor said firmly, "our community and the college can start to feel safe again."

Standing to one side, Mark regarded Joe's face in profile. Neither acknowledged the other's presence.

8

"Keep moving forward," Farr urged Mark more than once. "All you control is whether you do your damnedest to get into Yale Law School. Don't let Angela's murder kill your dreams as well."

Days became weeks, then months. Mark studied relentlessly. He rarely dated, and avoided parties altogether. He told no one about Joe's story, or the phone calls Steve had failed to answer. He learned nothing more about the case against his friend.

The trial was set for September, four months after the graduation ceremonies that would no longer include Steve Tillman or Angela Hall. Mark never discussed the impending trial with Joe Betts; they seldom spoke at all. For Mark, except for his studies, college was done. His main activity beyond class was visiting Steve at the county jail.

Separated by Plexiglas, they met every Sunday, speaking through miniature microphones. Mark offered encouragement; sometimes they reminisced. But Steve's lawyer, Griffin Nordlinger, had forbidden him to discuss the charges in any detail. Perhaps he could not have, Mark thought; unless Steve was lying, he seemed to live in a fugue state, unable to recall or reconstruct the events that now controlled his fate. He seemed crushed by the fear of never being free. "Just think," Steve murmured. "That may be the last time I ever touch a woman, and I can barely remember it."

Mark did not know how to respond. Once again, he thought of his three o'clock phone calls.

Winter passed; spring came. And then, in April, Mark's senior year became cemented in his mind as the year of death.

IT WAS A week before Mark expected to hear from Yale. He walked into Lionel Farr's nine o'clock Philosophy of Mind class, a choice driven less by its subject matter than by a desire to experience, for one final time, the stimulation that had first drawn him to Caldwell. But another professor, Michael Dunn, appeared–Farr had been called home abruptly, interrupting his eight o'clock class. Anne was dead; Farr's classes were canceled until further notice.

Mark waited until late afternoon, thinking of Farr and Taylor, struggling to accept that Anne had died. Then he went to their home unannounced, hoping that Farr would not take it amiss.

Farr himself answered. His gaze was spectral, although he managed to summon a wispy smile. His voice was unusually gentle. "Hello, Mark. It's good of you to come."

Awkwardly standing on the porch, Mark shifted his weight from one foot to the other. "I'm just worried about you, that's all. And Taylor."

"Her mother would thank you for that." Pain surfaced in his eyes. "Taylor found her, Mark. Her deepest fear became real."

The image of Taylor discovering Anne sent a frisson through Mark. He tried to imagine how she must feel, a twelve-year-old girl facing life without her mother. "Is there anything I can do?" he finally asked. "Maybe in a couple of days, I can take Taylor somewhere."

Farr placed a hand on his shoulder. "Thank you, Mark. Right now she's sedated, or I'd let you see her–she's very fond of you. But her grandparents are coming to help care for her."

Slowly, Mark nodded. "I only wish there was some way I could help. All three of you mean a lot to me."

"And you to us." Farr's grip on Mark's shoulder tightened, then relaxed. "There'll be a memorial service, I'm sure. We'll hope to see you then."

THEY HELD THE service in the shadow of the Spire.

Perhaps this was Farr's true memorial to Anne, Mark reflected, allowing her death to rededicate this site through a commemoration that, however premature, had occurred in the natural order of things. The day was breezy and pleasant; the lawn chairs were filled with family and faculty and students, a scattering of friends from Wayne and elsewhere. Sitting with Joe Betts and Rusty Clark, Mark was glad of this. But the Episcopal service performed by the school chaplain, while consistent with Anne's eastern heritage, came to Mark as a meaningless drone, divorced from life on earth or the woman who no longer lived here.

"I am the resurrection and the life; he that believeth in me, though he were dead, yet shall he live . . ."

Farr sat with Anne's parents, two dignified and stoic New Englanders. Anne's mother held her granddaughter's hand. Taylor looked blank, as though she, like her mother, had gone elsewhere. The chaplain's litany continued.

"I know that my redeemer liveth, and that he shall stand at the latter day upon the earth; and though this body be destroyed, yet shall I see God . . ."

Mark closed his eyes.

At last Farr spoke for himself and Taylor. The woman he described was articulate and graceful, her voice the music of their household, her love the touchstone of their lives. He spoke of Anne's countless acts of kindness, performed with a tact and lightness that called no attention to itself and asked for nothing in return. It struck Mark as true to his sense of her: though her sensitivity was plain to see, there were few light anecdotes to share. He, with so few good memories of family, wondered what Taylor would remember.

Still she stared ahead, as though she were alone.

After the service Mark spoke to Farr, who embraced him, then to Anne's father and mother, to whom, clearly, he was just another stranger in a pageant that filled them with unspoken horror, two parents who had outlived their only child. But when Mark paused in front of Taylor, her stoic mask dissolved. Silent tears ran down her face.

Instinctively, Mark held her. When at last he drew back, Taylor's eyes locked his with something akin to desperation. "I missed you," she whispered.

"I'm sorry." He clasped both of her hands in his. "You still have your dad, Taylor. You can lean on him now. That's what he wants you to do."

For a moment, she looked as though she had not heard him. Then she squeezed his hands, keeping him there an extra moment before her grandmother introduced her to a woman she did not know. As Mark moved on, Taylor turned back to look at him.

That afternoon, as on every Sunday, Mark went to see Steve Tillman.

9

WHEN YALE LAW ACCEPTED HIM, MARK WAS LESS elated than relieved. He was moving on–life beyond Caldwell was tangible now. His graduation a month later was not so much a culmination as a way station. Though Farr congratulated him warmly, the ceremony reminded Mark that, unlike his classmates, he had no family to inflate the moment; nor, given their own pain, could he have asked Steve's parents to come. Tactfully alluding to Angela Hall, Clark Durbin said nothing about the person Mark missed most keenly, his closest friend.

He spent his final summer in Wayne working construction, losing himself in the doing of tasks, the oddly pleasant ache of joints and muscles. On the Sunday before he left for Yale, Mark paid Steve a final visit.

Steve gazed at him through the Plexiglas. "So you're off to law school," he said.

Mark felt a stab of guilt. "Yeah."

"You're on your way, pal." Steve's lips compressed. "My lawyer thinks *I'm* going to the pen."

"Did he say that?"

Doubt and anger surfaced in Steve's eyes. "Not exactly. But he asked me to think about involuntary manslaughter–letting the jury consider that along with a murder charge. If I was too drunk to know what I was doing, Griff says, maybe I can get off with ten years."

Mark wondered if Steve was asking for advice. He had

none to give. Something about Griffin Nordlinger bothered Mark—an air of distraction, a sense of always running behind, combined with Mark's knowledge that the lawyer's bills were likely to cost Steve's parents the only home they had ever owned. But in the last few weeks Mark had heard vague rumors of another witness who bolstered the prosecution's case. Mark was bedeviled by the thought that this person might help corroborate Joe Betts's story, making Steve's failure to answer Mark's phone calls seem more damning. Cautiously, Mark asked, "What did you tell him?"

Steve's mouth set in a stubborn line. "Going for involuntary manslaughter would be like saying I killed her but can't remember. Who'd believe that? They'd just convict me of murder." His tone was at once pleading and insistent. "I may not remember things, but alcohol and a little coke didn't turn me into some other person. Besides, I liked her."

Once more, Mark had a terrible sense of randomness, a death at once tragic and banal. "Can you remember *anything* else about what happened?"

"No." Reading the doubt in Mark's eyes, Steve snapped, "If you don't believe me, don't come back for the trial."

Mark did not have a choice. Farragher might want him to testify about the party; Nordlinger would call him as a character witness. Quietly, Mark answered, "I'll be there for you."

Tears surfaced in Steve's eyes. Mark had known him since they were twelve; now he could not console him, or even hug him. Briefly, Steve leaned his forehead against the Plexiglas. Then he straightened again, summoning a strained smile for his friend.

"Do good at Yale," he told Mark.

*

On the night before Mark left, Lionel Farr took him to dinner at the Carriage House.

Mark had little to say. After a while, Farr observed, "You don't seem very excited, Mark. I gather Tillman still weighs on your mind."

Mark nodded. "I'm feeling like I should stay here," he admitted. "Hardly anyone visits him now."

Farr put down his scotch. "And postpone Yale? Or, worse yet, *lose* Yale?" His face hardened. "I refuse to let you throw your life away because Steve ruined his. Not to mention taking someone else's life."

Mark bridled at his mentor's certainty. "I'm not sure he did."

"That's what trials are for, Mark." Farr modulated his tone. "Your boyhood friend did a foolish thing, perhaps a terrible thing. He's got an able lawyer. It's not your fault you saw him leave that party with Angela."

"Maybe not. But I started this by telling the police that. They came down on Steve before he knew what hit him."

Narrow-eyed, Farr looked off into the middle distance. "I don't know if this helps," he said at length, "but I've spoken to Dave Farragher. He won't need your testimony at the trial. So that part, at least, won't be on your conscience. You needn't come back at all."

Mark shook his head. "I will, though. Griff Nordlinger wants me to be a character witness."

"To say what?"

"That Steve's truthful. That I've never seen him act violent, or even be angry enough to hit someone."

"Is that so?"

"I've known him half my life." Mark felt the burden of his secret overtake him. "There's something else, though. Something I haven't told anyone."

He felt Farr appraising him closely. "Then maybe you

should tell *me,* Mark. Better now than when Farragher cross-examines you."

Mark paused a final moment. Then, haltingly, he told Farr about the two phone calls.

Listening, Farr steepled his fingers, placing them to his lips. Then he looked around, as though concerned that the other diners–couples and college students and families with kids–might overhear. "Let me make sure I get this," he responded quietly. "Joe Betts will testify that he saw Steve returning to his room at three A.M. or so. Farragher could use this secret you've been keeping–that Steve didn't answer when you called him–to help confirm Betts's story. The implication for you is this: you think Steve may be guilty but don't want to help convict him. You also don't want to lie on the witness stand–for the sake of your own integrity, and because you don't want to commit perjury to protect someone who may have murdered an admirable girl. Does that cover it?"

"Yes," Mark answered miserably.

"Then there's only one solution, however imperfect. Don't go anywhere near that trial."

Mark gazed past Farr, torn between the desire to stand by Steve and the need not to seal his friend's fate or lie on the witness stand. "Do I have a choice?" he asked.

"I'll talk to Griff Nordlinger." Farr's tone became both kind and weary. "However *I* feel about this information, I doubt Griff will want you back here."

Awash with both relief and a sense of betrayal, Mark felt himself separating from Steve Tillman, even as he felt guilty about making Farr complicit in his secret. When their steaks arrived, Mark did not pick up his fork. "Eat something," Farr said mildly. "You've got a long drive to New Haven tomorrow."

Mark began cutting a piece of meat. It struck him that

he had asked nothing about Farr's life. "I still don't know how *you* are," Mark said simply.

Farr smiled faintly. "Keeping busy, at least. It seems that Clark Durbin and the board want me to consider becoming provost of Caldwell College."

The idea of Farr not teaching seemed unfathomable. "You wouldn't be a professor?"

"Maybe I'd teach a class. But there seems to be a feeling, shared by Clark, that I helped keep the school going in the wake of Angela's murder."

"Not a feeling. You did."

Farr shrugged. "Whether that's true or not, it's difficult to say no. Especially given that taking on a new challenge would be helpful to me personally. To understate things, Anne's death lingers."

Mark sipped his beer, watching a family in an adjacent booth, two parents and three kids cheerful in one another's company. "What about for Taylor?" he asked.

Farr frowned. "That's my one reservation. Taylor can't seem to reconcile herself to Anne's absence. She's become withdrawn, almost angry." Pausing, Farr issued an uncharacteristic sigh. "These things take time, I know. But I'm worried about our future as father and daughter, so I don't want to lose myself in work."

Mark felt sadness for them both. "Is there anything I can do?"

"No, thank you. The question is what *I* do."

The statement had a dismissive sound. Farr lapsed into silence, seemingly lost in his own thoughts. Then he said softly, "About this other thing, Mark: I'll take care of it. But let's not talk of it again, between us or to anyone else. For both our sakes."

Once more, Mark felt that he had led this man, who

had done so much for him, into a moral gray zone. Nodding his assent, he tried to focus on his steak.

After dinner, they stood outside the restaurant as twilight descended, deepening the valedictory mood Mark felt enveloping them both. Farr was too much a man of his generation to hug Mark. Instead, he shook his hand, bracing Mark's arm as he did. Realizing how much he had depended on Lionel Farr, Mark suddenly felt alone. "I'll miss you," he said simply.

Farr shook his head. "There's so much ahead for you now. Standing here, I think of the night I first approached you." He paused, his voice rough with banked emotion. "I can't express how proud I am of you, and how proud you should be of yourself. Take what you've achieved and make your place in the world. Leave the past behind."

Mark tried, and occasionally, over the next few months, he succeeded. In mid-October, as he prepared for midterms, Steve Tillman was convicted of first-degree murder and sentenced to life without parole.

PART II

THE RETURN

1

On the first Saturday in June, hours after his return as the seventeenth president of Caldwell College, Mark Darrow called on Lionel Farr at home.

He had shipped his possessions ahead and driven from Boston to Wayne in his Porsche convertible. Reaching central Ohio, he found the countryside just as he recalled it, green and flat for miles on end, with a gentle roll now and then. But, he noted wryly, he had long since become a creature of urban culture, somehow surprised to pass more cemeteries than hybrid cars. The people of Wayne believed in tradition–they buried, rather than cremated, their dead. Darrow's mother was one; he supposed he should visit her.

The president's house–where he and Farr had met with Clark Durbin, now his predecessor–felt strange to him. Driving to Farr's, Darrow put the top down, a favorite indulgence when he and Lee had taken weekend trips to Cape Cod. The feel of the air–warm, a touch muggy–brought back his youth; the sight of Farr's house infused old memories, both pleasant and painful, with a startling immediacy. As he stepped from the car, Darrow felt a curious dislocation, as though he were the unsettled youth he once had been rather than the presumptive savior of Caldwell College. Resolving to act his current age, Darrow knocked on the door.

To his surprise, it was opened by a young woman in her twenties. Framed by raven hair, her chiseled face was at once aristocratic and startlingly beautiful, with deep blue eyes that gave an impression of wariness, intelligence, and, as she studied him, amusement. Darrow had the odd sense that he knew her, though surely they had never met: hers was a face he would not forget.

"Hello, Mark," she said. "I'd still recognize you anywhere."

Darrow stared at her, then emitted a startled laugh. "You're supposed to be eleven."

"Twelve," Taylor Farr corrected him. "Except that I'm actually twenty-eight."

"And living here again?"

She led him inside. "Visiting," she answered. "I'm taking the summer off from teaching classes at NYU to work on my PhD dissertation."

He followed her through the living room. "In what discipline?"

"Art history." She smiled at him over her shoulder. "As an artist, I was always long on theory."

Darrow realized how little he knew about what had become of her. Farr's comments about Taylor, sparing and detached, had suggested an unspoken estrangement. "So what's it like being back?"

Turning, she paused in the living room, her expression openly curious. "I was going to ask you that."

After a moment's hesitation, he decided to acknowledge their shared history. "Weird, at times. When I first came back to campus, I found myself standing in the shadow of the Spire."

Her blue eyes seemed to darken. "That was the last place I saw you, remember? You were very kind to a twelve-year-old girl in pain."

"I liked you, Taylor. And I'd had my own experiences with pain."

Taylor seemed to study him. "And more since then, I know. I'm so sorry about your wife."

"Thank you." He put his hands in his pockets. "It seems that Lee's death changed things for me. After everything that happened my senior year, I planned never to come back here. But now Caldwell has a need, and maybe I do, too."

Taylor simply nodded. In her silence, Darrow felt disconcerted by their moment of near intimacy. But he supposed it was not surprising that he and Lionel Farr's daughter should retain a kinship. "I know my father needs you," she said. "He's in his study, more eager to see you than he'll admit."

She led him there. She was taller than her mother, Darrow noticed, though she had the same grace of movement, the indefinable air of separateness. Softly knocking, she opened the door to Farr's study.

Caldwell's provost rose from his familiar chair to shake Darrow's hand. "I see you've remet Taylor."

"Uh huh." Glancing at Taylor, he said, "I recognized her right away. Hasn't changed a bit."

"But she has, of course. Taylor's become her mother." Giving Taylor a brief smile, Farr added, "That's a considerable compliment. But Taylor has talents all her own."

Taylor's smile was somewhat arid. "If you're going to talk like I'm not here," she told both men, "I'll make it easier by leaving." To Darrow, she said, "Do you need anything?"

"No. Thank you."

Briefly, she met his eyes. "Then just say good-bye before you go."

She left, closing the door behind her. Farr gazed after her. "She does resemble Anne, don't you think?"

Sitting, Darrow shook his head. "Actually, Lionel, she looks more like you than Anne, though the results are better than I'd have expected. She also *seems* more like you."

Farr raised his eyebrows. "How so?"

"More edge." Darrow hesitated. "Taylor also strikes me as more present. Anne as I remember her was kind but subdued."

"She wasn't well." A look of reflection crossed Farr's face. "As for Taylor, Anne's death seems to have created a wall between us that still exists. The tacit silence builds, and what we do say to each other leaves many things unsaid. I've often felt that our idea of family is a myth, the reality of which is bound to disappoint. As a father, I suppose I disappoint myself."

"Have you disappointed Taylor?"

"I'm afraid to ask. But a decade-plus of absence–physical and emotional–made that plain enough. This may be our last chance. That's why, despite any awkwardness, I'm glad to have her back." Farr leaned forward, speaking with more cheer. "I'm also glad to have *you* back, Mark."

Darrow smiled at this. "The least I could do."

"Oh, it's something." Farr gave a rueful wince, wrinkling the corners of his eyes. "The fig leaf of 'health' we used to cover Clark's resignation is in shreds. During your trip out, someone leaked word of the embezzlement. As of this morning, the media carried the story of our missing near million all over Ohio. I'm already hearing from alumni, and our board chair, Ray Carrick, is apoplectic."

Darrow's shrug was philosophical. "It was bound to get

out sometime. The real problem is that we've lost control of the story. Do you know who leaked it?"

"No. But a good guess is any board member who wants Clark Durbin pilloried." Farr sat back. "This leak puts Durbin on the hot seat, and you along with him. Welcome back to Caldwell, Mark."

"This is why you hired me, isn't it? Tell me what else I'm facing the next few days, and then we'll think through this embezzlement."

Briefly standing, Farr reached into his rolltop desk and handed Darrow two stapled pages. "As we discussed, I've prepared a schedule for the next three weeks. Why don't we look at it now?"

Darrow scanned the pages. "You'll see," Farr told him, "that you've got meetings with key donors in New York, Cleveland, and Chicago, as well as alumni events in each city. When you're on campus, you'll meet with our CFO, the finance committee, and the investment committee, headed by Joe Betts."

"That reunion should be jolly," Darrow said. "In light of the embezzlement."

"Yes. You'll find Joe's feeling a little raw. Ditto with the faculty. Some have great ambitions for expanding our curriculum and won't be happy that Durbin's now-public defalcation may derail yet another capital campaign. Which is why," Farr added pointedly, "throwing Durbin to the wolves—or, more specifically, to Dave Farragher—would provide the discontented a welcome distraction from whatever cuts you're forced to make. There are times when your new job requires a certain ruthlessness."

"Much like my old one," Darrow answered crisply. "But before I castrate someone, I prefer the reasons to be my own. I'll decide about prosecuting Durbin when I know more."

Farr gave him a cool look of amusement and surprise. "Fair enough. Just remember that a part of this job is political awareness. Clark's no longer popular."

"I'll keep that in mind," Darrow responded amiably.

Farr paused a moment. "Turning back to the schedule, you'll also see meetings with community leaders."

Darrow read the names, stopping at the police chief. "Is that *the* George Garrison?"

"I'm only aware of one."

Darrow laughed in surprise. "That *is* progress."

Farr nodded. "Since Angela's death, black-white relations have changed a bit. Whites became more aware; blacks felt that justice was done, by the police and by Dave Farragher. That's the only good that came from that tragedy–an absence of more harm."

"Except to Steve."

"Is punishment for committing murder 'harm'?" Farr hesitated, then asked in a neutral tone, "When was the last time you saw him?"

"You know when it was," Darrow said more sharply than he wished. "Ten years ago, just after both his parents died. After that I stopped coming back at all."

"For which no one can blame you," Farr said calmly. "Especially if they knew about your phone calls to Steve that night. It's well to remember that the jury convicted Steve without that, and that you might feel even worse if they'd acquitted him. I know *I* would."

At this, the first mention of their shared secret since he'd departed for Yale, Darrow fell silent. At length he said, "Let's discuss our division of labor. I've done considerable reading about why college presidents succeed or fail–especially people who, like me, have no actual qualifications for the job. One major ingredient is a successful partnership with the provost."

As though relieved at the change of subject, Farr nodded his affirmation. "I suggest that you focus on the externals: alumni, the board, public relations, fund-raising, and the general infusion of inspiration and vision. I'll deal with the plumbing: curriculum, personnel, appointments, tenure, the physical plant, and student life." He held up a hand. "Which is not to say that you should allow me carte blanche. But I know the culture and politics of this place, the pitfalls and personalities–to borrow an unpleasant metaphor, where the bodies are buried."

"I appreciate that. And I could certainly use the help."

"A word then about our students and faculty. Kids come here with more psychological, familial, and personal problems than they once did–"

"More than me?" Darrow interjected with a smile.

"More and different. These days, we don't turn away students with learning problems–we try to work with them. And though we're tougher about enforcement, all these issues are still exacerbated by drug and alcohol abuse. So just be warned about that."

"And the faculty? Are all of *them* screwed up, too?"

Farr gave a short laugh. "Just more steroidal. During Clark Durbin's tenure, there was an enhancement of faculty power over academic matters, to some degree at the president's expense–"

"But not the provost's expense, I assume."

"No," Farr acknowledged. "As a former faculty member, I'll concede this was largely my doing, and it enhanced my own authority as well. But my reason was a sound one–the faculty are the experts in these areas, and honoring that attracts better faculty. That's one area in which Caldwell's grown stronger."

Darrow absorbed this, unsurprised. Farr was a natural

leader, born to fill vacuums or–if need be–create them; Durbin was not. And Darrow was not Clark Durbin. But this, Darrow decided, was an issue for another day. "Is there anything else I should know?"

"Perhaps something you should consider. I'm sure you're accustomed to acting quickly and decisively. But if you're not facing a crisis, strike a balance between decisiveness and diplomacy.

"As provost, I learned patience. It takes time to win the trust of a community. The quality of one's decisions isn't enough–in any given case, the board, faculty, or alumni need to feel they're included. That means listening a lot, and discerning friends from enemies–aware that on any given issue, friends can become enemies overnight." Farr smiled. "Fortunately for you, academia's not your life; nor is money of any concern. Everyone knows that we need you way more than you need us. It's just better if you don't rub people's faces in it. Make your moves in a deliberative way."

"Good advice," Darrow answered. "Which brings me back to the embezzlement and Durbin. Where does that stand?"

Farr sat back in his chair. "As I told you, the board's hired an excellent forensic accountant–his investigation is well under way. As you suggested, new safeguards are already being crafted. "Embezzlement isn't pretty, but at least it's not the murder of a student. The accounting details are in good hands, and we've hired an outside PR firm. Your major worry *is* public relations: assuring alumni that this will never happen again and deciding what to do with Durbin."

Darrow nodded. "Still, I'd like to meet with this accountant. When alumni ask questions, I'll need command of detail."

"That makes sense. Conveniently, he'll be here on Monday, along with Joe Betts. I'll make sure they see you."

"Good." Darrow stood. "I'd better get settled in. Durbin's old house is filled with my boxes. Where *is* Clark, by the way?"

Farr grimaced. "Living in a furnished apartment, consulting with lawyers while awaiting his fate. A melancholy outcome to a career."

"And a surprising one, I still think." Darrow paused. "The schedule is fine, by the way. Go ahead and set it up."

Farr nodded. "I'll see you Monday, then. Your first official day as president."

They shook hands warmly. "Don't bother to walk me out," Darrow said. "I promised Taylor I'd come find her."

She was in the sunroom, a stack of papers on her lap. When she looked up, Darrow said, "As I remember, this is where you used to paint."

Smiling, she put the papers aside. "I'm working on another thing of beauty—my dissertation." She stood, walking him to the door. "Did you two have a satisfying summit conference?"

"Of course. The renaissance of Caldwell College has begun."

"Just in time," she said in a tone that contained good-humored mockery with truth. "Thank God you're here."

"I suppose." Darrow paused at the door. "But except for Lionel, I barely know anyone now. Do you?"

She shook her head. "I've spent the last fourteen years avoiding that. The center of our life in Wayne is the same man—your friend, my father."

Darrow considered this. "Then maybe we should expand our social circle. Can I buy you dinner Monday night?"

Despite her poise, Taylor looked pleased. "Think I'm old enough now?"

"Yup. Unless you think I'm *too* old."

"Not yet," Taylor answered philanthropically. "I'll make reservations at the Carriage House. Some things don't change; it's still the only place in town."

THAT NIGHT, UNABLE to sleep, Darrow listened to the distant sound of a train whistle.

This, too, had not changed. In high school, bereft of family, he had lain awake in the bedroom he shared with Steve, listening to the same whistle. It had become the symbol of the larger world, life bypassing Wayne, Ohio. But now he was back.

Tomorrow he would visit his friend.

2

Once again, Darrow faced a Plexiglas shield. The shield had a small oval with metal grids through which they might speak. A door on the prisoner's side opened, and then Steve walked toward him.

The first thing Darrow noticed was that his limp remained. As Steve sat on his side of the Plexiglas, his eyes seemed to drill into Darrow's core. His skull was shaved, his face hard. In his jumpsuit he looked fit and well muscled, as though he had channeled his energy and anger into making himself invulnerable. He looked so alien that Darrow cringed inside.

Some of this must have shown in his eyes. With their faces two feet apart, the smile he gave Darrow was sardonic and unwelcoming. "Think you'd have recognized me, Mark?"

The question mingled accusation with curiosity, making Darrow feel more defensive. "Only by the surroundings," he answered. "How are you, Steve?"

"Better off than my parents. That jury sentenced them to die of shame and misery. I'm merely in prison for life, still wondering what happened to me."

His speech and phrasing seemed more studied than that of the small-town boy Darrow had grown up with, his emotional range flatter, yet suffused with subterranean anger. Awkwardly, Darrow asked, "How do you cope?"

"Exercise. And reading. You name it: history, politics,

philosophy, anything but prison novels. My professors would be amazed—right now I'm into the new translation of *War and Peace*. But my favorites are books on repressed or recovered memory." His eyes bored into Darrow's. "So why did you show up now? Curiosity?"

Darrow chose not to answer. "I'm back in Wayne. They've made me president of Caldwell."

Steve flashed a wolfish smile. "So I hear. You buy them a building or something?"

"They didn't have the bargaining power."

"Guess not. Lionel and the rest must be pretty desperate these days. First Angela; now Durbin's fingers in the cash box. That day you won the Lutheran game was the end of our Age of Innocence." The mirthless smile returned. "Yeah, I even read Edith Wharton."

Darrow had a profound sense of a life wasted. He took in the tile floors and cinder-block walls, yellow under the light from fluorescent tubes.

"Books keep me from going insane," Steve continued. "And memories. Sometimes I relive college a week at a time, from freshman year until that night, remembering what it felt like to be free. Except now that kid I was seems like a blind man, headed for some terrible moment hidden in the ambush of time." His voice softened. "Sixteen years now, and I still don't know what happened between Angela and me. I've filled notebook after notebook with scribbles about that night—scraps of memory that might have happened, but I'm not sure of; images I might have imagined because I'm so fucking desperate to know. It's like strip-mining a played-out vein of coal. Nothing left but dust."

To Darrow it sounded hauntingly like the truth. Either Steve was a gifted liar and always had been, or he was tormented by the fear that he had killed someone, or he was innocent. Of these, the hardest to imagine was a murderer so drunk that he had strangled Angela to death, then awakened wondering what had happened. Buffeted by doubts, Mark could not resist asking, "Do you remember leaving the dorm in the middle of the night?"

"No," Steve answered tersely. "You'd have to ask Joe about that. He fucked me over at the trial."

Darrow had a piercing memory of hearing Joe's story, coupled with his own foreboding about phone calls Steve did not answer. "How, exactly?"

Anger and confusion clashed in Steve's eyes. "According to Joe, he had to lean out the window to keep from puking. I happened–just happened–to be strolling back from the general direction of the Spire. I didn't see him; he didn't say a word to me. Only to the cops." Steve's voice became quietly caustic. "You should have seen him on the witness stand, so hangdog, so sorry to testify that he couldn't even look at me. I barely recognized the arrogant prick you and I used to live with. Hope Mr. Prep School's not still suffering too much."

Darrow felt more disquiet: he, too, held a potential piece of evidence, perhaps corroborating Joe's story. "Joe couldn't have convicted you by himself," Darrow said. "What else was there?"

Steve tilted his head, staring at Darrow through the Plexiglas. "Why all the questions?"

Darrow did not care to answer. "Maybe habit," he finally said. "I spent the first five years after Yale as a prosecutor. Asking questions becomes a reflex; if you're any good, so does doubt. Sometimes lawyers or cops who want an outcome arrange the facts to fit what's convenient to believe."

"I certainly was convenient," Steve said with corrosive sarcasm. "Not just for the prosecutor, but for Caldwell College. Once they put me away, the campus was safe. You could send your daughter there knowing I couldn't choke her to death."

Darrow could find no adequate response. Finally, he said, "Is anyone still working on your case?"

"On what, exactly? That I sort of remember Angela saying she had to leave? What kind of sense does *that* make?" Steve's tone was suffused with pain. "I'll tell you what makes no sense to me. That I'm a murderer but don't remember being one. That I'd want to hurt a woman, let alone kill a woman I liked enough to sleep with."

Mark thought of Angela at the party, seemingly bent on losing herself. "You both were drunk. The next day, you said you could barely remember whether you'd had sex with her or not."

Tillman stared at him. "I liked her sober, Mark."

"So did I." Saying this, Darrow felt twisted up inside. "I should have stayed in touch, Steve. I haven't known how to deal with everything that happened. Including my own role."

Steve's gaze was unyielding. "That's a lot of guilt to carry. Wondering if you failed me, then wondering if I strangled her. I can't imagine how hard it must be for you to wonder if I might be innocent."

Again, Darrow chose not to respond. "Maybe you don't want to see me," he said at length. "But if you don't mind, I'll come back next Sunday. Maybe there's something I can bring."

Steve gave him a crooked smile. "They don't usually let you 'bring' stuff. Just your own psychic baggage."

Darrow's own smile was strained. "Sixteen years, and you've become portentous."

"And you've got a truckload of new baggage. The price of freedom, I guess." Steve's voice became less biting. "Sorry about your wife–I saw the reports on television.

Locked up here, you forget that life outside this place has moments of darkness."

"More than a moment." Darrow hesitated, then said, "Our time ran out. Sometimes people forget that all of us live a few feet, or a few seconds, from tragedy–some random accident that just misses us without our even knowing. I should have a wife and a two-year-old son. Instead Lee hit a patch of ice she could have missed."

After a moment, Steve nodded. "I think that's what happened to me, Mark. I only wish I knew."

THAT NIGHT DARROW stood in the semidarkness of what had been Clark Durbin's home. It needed more lighting; the furniture was sterile; the representational art on the walls was at odds with the decor and Darrow's tastes. But then, it wasn't his home. It was still the place where Lionel Farr had prepared Durbin to cope with Angela Hall's murder. Coupled with the arrest of Steve Tillman, that crucial hour had enabled Durbin to survive so that, sixteen years later, he could bring Caldwell to the brink of permanent decline again.

Darrow thought of Steve's fate, then Durbin's; in each case, their guilt in some way served to insulate Caldwell from further damage. It had been hard to imagine his friend a murderer; now, if one believed the available evidence, Durbin was a thief. It was another humbling example, Darrow supposed, of the mysteries of character –how little you understood the people you thought you knew unless, by chance, you happened on some unguarded window on their lives. For a moment he wished Lee were here. Then he remembered that, in ways that shamed him now, he had not truly known her either.

Darrow went to the bedroom and unpacked another box.

3

Darrow's first day as president of Caldwell College began quietly.

He walked from his residence to College Hall, the site of his office, a 160-year-old Gothic brownstone with a steeple far more modest than the Spire. The morning was already warm, and summer students were heading to early classes in T-shirts and jeans or shorts, among them a few kids from India or the Far East, a much rarer sight when Darrow himself had attended Caldwell. With a sense of mild wonder at his return, Darrow climbed the steps to the front entrance.

Inside, the floors were marble, the hallways hushed and shadowy, the wood-paneled walls darkly stained. Along the spacious corridor leading to Darrow's new office were oil paintings of the past presidents of Caldwell College—save Clark Durbin—beginning with the Reverend Caldwell himself, whose deep-set brown eyes stared at Darrow with a fierce and unbending rectitude. Darrow remembered these portraits well; it struck him that, if he helped save the school, his own would hang here long after he was dead. He found the thought amusing and more than a little jarring.

Feeling like an impostor, he proceeded to the president's suite. He greeted his assistant, Lisa Forbes, then stepped into his office and shut the door. Instantly the spacious room felt sealed off, its decor—a Louis XIV desk, leather chairs and couch, an oil painting of the Spire—like a movie set waiting to be occupied. In fifteen minutes, when Joe Betts appeared, Darrow's history at Caldwell would resume. He used the time to carefully consider his approach to this most delicate of subjects, the embezzlement that had triggered his return.

WHEN THE DOOR opened, Lisa ushered in the forensic accountant hired to investigate Durbin's theft, followed by Joseph C. Betts III—as the day's schedule had listed him—chair of the investment committee of Caldwell's board of trustees.

Joe stopped in the doorway, eyeing Darrow with mock astonishment. "Oh my God," he said. "He's b-a-a-ack."

Darrow emitted the appropriate laugh. "Just like Freddy Krueger."

Crossing the room, Joe gave him a quick embrace. "It's terrific to find you in this office, man. Truly." Turning to his companion, he said, "Mark, I'd like you to meet Greg Fox, financial bloodhound par excellence."

Darrow took in Fox, a small, neatly dressed man in his forties with salt-and-pepper hair, black eyes, and a shrewd expression that suggested quiet confidence. Shaking his hand, Darrow said, "Thanks for coming. I hear you do terrific work."

Smiling, Fox took a chair beside Joe, enabling Darrow to take a closer look at his old friend. Joe looked youthful and healthy, his face virtually unlined, with modish swept-back hair, horn-rimmed glasses, and a jovial demeanor somewhat at odds with his watchful eyes. He seemed the epitome of an East Coast financial adviser, sound as a pre–9/11 dollar, save that Darrow caught—or imagined—a glimmer of the uneasy college student beneath. "Is it true,"

Darrow asked him in a parody of amazement, "that some misguided woman actually agreed to marry you?"

It was not, Darrow realized at once, the most artful thing to say: for an instant Joe's face darkened, as though Darrow were reopening old wounds. But he answered lightly enough. "Not only to marry, but to procreate. We have a boy and a girl—both blond-haired paradigms of brilliance. Clearly Katie's kids. All I did was light the match."

Greg Fox, Mark noticed, took in this badinage with smiling but careful attention, as though listening for distant signals on a crystal set. "Congratulations," Mark told Joe. "As Somerset Maugham once said, 'Luck is a talent.'" He smiled again. "It's really great to see you, Joe."

"Likewise," Joe rejoined dryly. "As the spider said to the fly."

At once Darrow became serious. To both Joe and the accountant, Mark said, "Dealing with this embezzlement is critical. I'm grateful for all you're doing."

Joe's eyes narrowed slightly, as though Darrow had rebuked him. "I'm just trying to help fix what I helped screw up. If I hadn't been so trusting, Clark couldn't have stolen close to a million bucks."

Glancing at Fox, Darrow shook his head. "*I'd* have trusted Durbin, Joe—certainly about money. But I'd still like your take on how it all happened."

"Stupidity," Joe said with a grimace. "Greg can give you an outline. More, if you like."

Darrow shook his head. "For now the Cliffs Notes version's fine."

Fox glanced from Joe to Darrow. "Okay," he said briskly. "Caldwell's board has a five-man investment committee. Including Joe, all the outside members—Ed Rardin, Paul Johns, and John Stewart—are well-off and financially sophisticated." Fox's midwestern twang sharpened. "The fifth member was Clark Durbin.

"Each member of the committee had the authority to direct transactions under one million dollars—"

"Obviously a mistake," Darrow interjected.

"Which we're correcting," Joe said swiftly. "Going forward, we'll require the written authorization of three committee members, a majority."

"In any event," Fox told Darrow, "we had nine hundred thousand dollars sitting at Joe's firm, Buckeye Capital in Columbus. Durbin e-mailed Joe, directing that he transfer the proceeds to the Wayne County Bank, where Clark had opened an account in the name of Caldwell College. His signature is on all the papers."

"I sent an e-mail back to Clark," Joe put in, "confirming his instructions and copying the bank. It all checked out."

Darrow nodded. "And from there, it appears, Durbin transferred the nine hundred thousand to an account in Switzerland. Cutting off our ability to get the cash back, or even find out where it went."

"Exactly," Fox responded. "As I expect you also know, the only entity that can persuade the Swiss to lift their veil of secrecy is the U.S. government. In our case, Uncle Sam won't even try. The money's not enough to care about, and our government reserves its leverage for tracking transfers by known terrorists."

Joe shook his head in disgust. "Durbin turned out to be smarter than I'd ever have imagined."

"To a point," Darrow said. "I gather our auditors tumbled to this soon enough."

"Routinely," Fox confirmed, "and inevitably. They tried to verify the amount of the CDs at Joe's firm and wound up tracing the money all the way to Switzerland. At which point they contacted the audit committee of the board."

Darrow considered this. "What's so jarring is that Durbin was clever in the service of a stupid crime. Embezzlers always get caught; the only difference here is that most crooks steal money in small amounts, hoping to escape detection–at least for as long as possible. Stealing a larger amount of money, as Durbin did, exponentially accelerates the timetable for getting caught. Unless the embezzler disappears."

"He was desperate," Joe said simply. "His kid was a junkie; his wife has Lou Gehrig's disease; his own investments went south. Serial disasters caused Durbin to look into his character and find a thief." Joe's voice softened. "Then he looked at me and must have seen a fool."

"You'd be surprised," Fox told both men in a mollifying tone. "At small schools like Caldwell, people know each other over long periods of time. So trust builds up. That explains the lax policy on transfers of money–which, I might add, was known to every member of the committee. The only reason Joe became the fall guy is that his investment firm served as advisers to the school. So Joe was sitting on the money Durbin wanted."

"At my suggestion," Joe told Darrow hastily, "we've decided that no member of the committee should profit in any way from Caldwell's investments."

"All good," Darrow concurred. "By the time your work is through, I'm confident that what Durbin did would be impossible. What still troubles me is accepting that he did this in the first place."

Joe shook his head. "Why, Mark? It's Occam's razor–sometimes the simplest explanation is the right one."

Still unsatisfied, Darrow turned to Fox. "Up until a few weeks ago, my job was trying financial fraud cases. Mind if I have one of my old experts take a look at what happened here?"

For an instant Fox looked mildly annoyed; then his expression eased. "Sure," he answered. "As I always say, two heads are better than one. As long as they're not on the same body."

Darrow smiled at this. "Then I won't take more of your time."

Both men stood, Darrow shaking Fox's hand. With a final thanks, Darrow walked Fox to the door, closing it behind him.

Joe stood with his hands in his pockets. "Not that you weren't gracious, Mark. But Greg's top-flight, and you may have stepped on his pride a little. Sure you need to bring in your own expert?"

Darrow nodded. "Maybe you're right, Joe. I'll ponder it." He waved Joe to the couch, sitting companionably at the other end. "So tell me how you've been."

"Good." Nodding in self-affirmation, Joe said, "Really good, actually. In college, I never thought marriage could be this great. As you'll recall, my parents' marriage sure as hell wasn't."

"How *is* your mom?"

"Good enough. In her mind, my dad's become a saint. I guess it helps that he's still dead." A moment's unease crossed Joe's face. "About Lee, I don't know what to say. I can't even say that I know how you feel. Only that I feel for you."

Darrow mustered a smile. "That's all anyone can say, Joe. In a very real sense, we all go through life alone. Although some days alone is lonely any way you slice it."

Joe nodded in commiseration. "So what's it like for you, being back?"

"A lot of different things–I guess you could say it's

complicated." He looked at Joe more closely. "Yesterday I went to visit Steve."

Joe blinked. "In the pen? How was he?"

"Different. Extremely buff, not to mention an eclectic reader. Also highly articulate."

"You're joking, right?"

Darrow shook his head. "Not at all. Steve's a stellar example of what can happen if you take an inherently good mind and eliminate all distractions."

Joe looked away. After a moment, he said, "I guess you know about the trial."

"Of course."

Joe nodded to himself, eyes still averted. "Did my name come up?"

Mark weighed his response. "It did. Steve has a point of view, and he's had sixteen years to perfect it." More quietly, he added, "Whatever you saw that night couldn't be helped, Joe. No reasonable person could expect you to lie on the witness stand."

Joe looked up. "Did Steve talk about that?"

"Only that he doesn't remember being outside the dorm. But then he claims not to remember much about Angela, either. Including whether he strangled her."

"That's bullshit," Joe said with sudden harshness. "Either he killed her or he didn't. But he sure as hell didn't forget about it."

"Yeah. That's what I think, too."

Joe seemed to ponder this. Then he stood, mustering a reasonable facsimile of the smile he had entered with. "It really is wonderful to see you, Mark. And even better that you're doing this for the school."

Darrow shrugged. "I owe this place," he answered. "I only hope I can give Caldwell what it deserves."

*

Alone, Darrow considered the last hour, then called Mike Riley, the forensic accountant he had used in Boston.

"Mark," Riley said in a jocular tone, "I thought you'd returned to the Poison Ivy League."

"Fucking Harvard snob," Darrow said. "Though it pains me, I'd like a moment of your time. The halls of ivy are crawling with crooks."

"Explain, please."

Darrow summarized the meeting. "So what bothers you?" Riley asked. "That a gentleman and scholar can open up a Swiss account? Or steal that much money without any sensible exit strategy?"

"Maybe both–I'm not quite sure yet. It's more a feeling I have."

"You've had them before," Riley answered. "Now and then you were even right. Problem is, I'm a little busy. Can't this wait two, three weeks?"

"Sure. The money's gone."

Riley laughed. "Okay, then. I've always wanted to visit Wayne, Ohio."

Hanging up, Darrow glanced at his schedule. Thanks to Lionel Farr, for the rest of the day there was barely time to breathe, let alone think. Ruefully, he recalled that the Reverend Caldwell had believed in total immersion baptism.

When Darrow emerged from his office, his watch read seven o'clock, and he was running late for dinner with Taylor Farr. The evening was still light, the air muggy. Darrow put his top down, smiling at this gesture to his Porsche-less youth.

The main drag of Wayne, Scioto Street, bisected the town's commercial area. Downtown seemed much as it had been when Darrow left: two-story buildings that housed a hardware store, a haberdashery, a barbershop, and offices for real estate agents, accountants, lawyers, and insurance salesmen. Except for an outdoor café, a novelty, haute-bourgeois chic still seemed alien to Wayne. But the parking meters, Darrow noticed when he stopped, remained a bargain–four quarters bought two hours, ample time for dinner at the Carriage House.

The restaurant was at the end of the block. Two cars away, a slender black man with thinning hair stood by a silver Mercedes, sticking quarters into the meter. Turning, he examined Darrow with cool but ostentatious interest. "Well," he said in a silken voice, "Mark Darrow himself. And still the hero, seems like."

It took Darrow a moment to be certain. He glanced at the quarter between the man's fingers. "And you're still dealing in cash, seems like."

Carl Hall emitted a short laugh. Nodding toward Darrow's Porsche, he said, "Nice ride."

"Yours, too. So what are you up to, Carl?"

Hall gave him a complacent smile. "This and that. You know how it is."

"I certainly remember." Darrow waited for a moment. "I remember a lot of things, in fact. Yesterday I went to see Steve Tillman."

Hall's smile turned canine, more a show of teeth. "As they say, that's mighty white of you."

Casually, Darrow propped his arm on a parking meter. "He still insists he didn't kill her, Carl. That Angela told him she had to leave."

"Sure, at two in the morning. Must have had an appointment to get those white teeth cleaned."

Darrow repressed his visceral dislike. He waited for an elderly couple to pass them on the sidewalk, then asked in a tone of mild curiosity, "Did your sister have a relationship?"

Hall scrutinized Darrow more closely. "A secret boyfriend, you mean?"

"If you do."

"How would I know? The princess and I weren't that close."

Scumbag, Darrow thought. "Funny," he told Hall. "You had enough brotherly feeling to warn me off her at the party."

"That was about *you,*" Hall shot back. "I never minded taking money from white college boys. But I didn't like you people fucking my black sisters, related or not."

Darrow stared at him. "Fucking's not killing."

"Your buddy," Hall said flatly, "was a racist. Ask any black kid who went to high school with him. Surprised *you* missed it, actually. Assuming you did." He shook his head in weary scorn. "Stupid white men have been abusing black women since time began–that's how Angela's skin became that tawny shade you boys prefer. Tillman just took things one step further. So live with it, Mr. President."

Abruptly, Hall turned and walked away

4

WALKING INTO THE CARRIAGE HOUSE, DARROW entered a time warp, a place unchanged since he was in college. The commodious bar had three shelves filled with wine, liquor bottles, and painted signs touting extinct beers; the two rows of wooden booths still featured Tiffany lampshades overhead and sports memorabilia decorating the walls–jerseys, pennants, pictures, and framed articles capturing athletic triumphs. The place was packed with couples, old and young, and families across the generations; one long table included a pregnant woman, her husband, three restless kids, and a weary but patient grandmother. A man Darrow did not know waved in recognition, as though he had watched Darrow play football a week before. Friendly and unpretentious, the atmosphere suggested ordinary people going about their lives, uninterested in the concerns of Darrow's friends in Boston, who were so often focused on politics, travel, the arts, or vacation homes. Searching for Taylor, Darrow spotted Dave Farragher sitting with his wife and decided not to approach him.

Taylor occupied a booth near the back of the room. She wore blue jeans and a red silk blouse, which, Darrow thought, suited her color well. Approaching, he saw that she sat beneath a picture of the young Mark Darrow, thrusting the ceremonial bronze axe from the steeple of the Spire. He sat across from Taylor, glancing at his own image. "I can't seem to escape myself."

Taylor considered the photograph. "I remember that moment exactly–my parents and I were so excited for you. Looking at this picture now, I wish that were all I remembered."

"So do I."

She faced him, her expression pensive. "The owner meant well, seating us here. But you and I have a unique relationship to the Spire. For you, it's Angela; for me, my mother. I wouldn't mind crossing the campus someday and seeing that thing gone."

"No chance of that. There'd be an alumni revolt." He resolved to lighten her mood. "Nice blouse, by the way."

Taylor smiled. "If you see me again, you'll see *it* again. Part-time college instructors lack extensive wardrobes–the rewards of academic life are purer than that." She raised her eyebrows. "How was *your* first day in academia?"

"Terrific," he answered dryly. "The faculty's nervous; the alumni restive; and my predecessor–so it appears–was a criminal. A less optimistic man would say Caldwell's in trouble."

"So my father says. What will you do about it?"

"What I'd like is to start an endowment drive. But I can't just say to alumni, 'The last guy stole your money, so give me some more.' So I'm hitting the road, hoping to change the conversation from 'How the hell did this happen?' to 'How can I invest in Caldwell and its dynamic new leader?' " Darrow glanced at a waitress, drawing her attention. "In the meanwhile," he concluded, "I've hired a consultant to help me assess the priorities of the school. Before I try to raise a hundred million dollars, I need a fresh vision of what Caldwell can be."

The waitress, a wiry middle-aged blond with a nice

smile but tired eyes, took their drink orders. It gave Darrow time to absorb once more how attractive Taylor was. When the waitress left, Taylor said, "It sounds like a lot of work. Does Caldwell really mean that much to you?"

Darrow considered his answer. Abruptly he decided to give this woman the truth as best he knew it. "When I left here," he acknowledged, "I meant to leave this place behind. Not just Caldwell, but the town. My family life was miserable; I'd grown up wanting to escape but never believing that I would." He paused, parsing his complex thoughts. "It's strange. I walked in here tonight and remembered all that's good about this town: that most people are friendly and straightforward; that they're bonded by clubs or civic groups or church; that they connect with one another in a way lost to e-commuters and the residents of gated communities; that despite their blind spots—race being one—they tend to be generous to anyone they actually know. And yet I also had this spasm of fear: that somehow I'd reverted, and was coming back for good.

"But the reason I left is the reason I returned. Caldwell—and your father—changed my life. If I'd turned him down, it would be like denying the central fact of my existence: the act of generosity that made me whoever I am now."

Abruptly, Darrow felt as though he had said too much. But Taylor regarded him with a look of sympathy and reflection. "Was it hard to leave Boston?" she asked.

Their drinks arrived. Darrow sipped his whiskey, pondering how much more to say to a woman he barely knew but for whom, given their shared history, he felt an affinity. At length he said, "Like Caldwell, Boston has its ghosts. Suddenly what remained felt empty."

Taylor regarded the table, as though considering what to say. Then she looked up at him again. "When I read that your wife had died, I thought about writing you. But it seemed gratuitous, a condolence note from someone who remembered you more clearly than I'm certain you remembered me. I imagined my note being more puzzling than consoling. So I didn't."

"I wouldn't have minded, actually. Now and then I've wondered about what became of you. How is it for *you,* being back?"

Taylor tasted her gimlet. "Funny," she answered. "Dad's still a stranger, although I feel him trying. And for some odd reason I don't sleep well in that house. But then I haven't had much practice since I was fourteen."

"Fourteen?"

Taylor nodded. "I went away to the Trumble School, in Connecticut. My grandfather Taylor went there—my uncle, too. So my grandparents offered to pay my way." Taylor paused, her eyes pensive. "They seemed to sense that my dad and I were both adrift. He didn't know what to do with me; worse, I think I resented him—terrible as this is to say—for being the parent who survived. Looking back, my grandparents were giving us both some breathing space. But when I left, I left for good."

When the waitress returned, they paused to order dinner. Picking up the conversation, Darrow thought of Joe Betts. "What was Trumble like?" he asked. "I always imagined prep school as a gilded prison."

Taylor laughed. "Oh, there's a little of that. Sometimes I think parents pay schools like Trumble a ridiculous amount of money to warehouse the puberty-maddened, imposing rules that Mom and Dad would never dream of trying. Imagine your mom conducting room inspections."

"I can't."

Registering his sardonic tone, Taylor smiled faintly. "No, I guess not. But add to that hall monitors who called you out for wearing headphones, sign-in sheets for breakfast, and a schedule where every hour from seven A.M. to nine at night was planned." She laughed softly at herself. "I make it sound like Alcatraz. The fact is, Trumble was good for me, and mostly I adored it. Suddenly I had friends from everywhere—my three closest girlfriends were from Ghana, Hong Kong, and Spanish Harlem. Our classmates called us the 'four corners of the world,' which we wore as a badge of pride." Taylor's expression grew reflective. "I missed my mom, of course. There were so many times I wanted to talk with her about friends or boys or social pressures or dreams about the future, and I couldn't. But no one had a mom on-site. Instead, my friends became like a second family."

Thinking of Steve Tillman, Darrow nodded. "As a teenager I remember feeling like we were a secret society, conspiring against clueless adults."

Taylor smiled in recognition. "The four of us certainly had our secrets. When Lupe, from Harlem, was the first to sleep with a guy, the rest of us knew within hours. But no one else did, ever—except for all the people *his* friends told, of course."

Darrow cocked his head. "I'm curious about the logistics. Where did Lupe go to pull this off?"

Taylor grinned. "Sedgwick Chapel—the holiest of holies on the Trumble campus, laden with history: graduations, memorial services, addresses by storied alumni. No student was supposed to have a key, but someone always did. I've often thought the richest part of chapel lore was its unofficial history. Which no one ever acknowledged."

Darrow glanced at the photograph. "Sounds something like the Spire."

"I suppose so. But nothing died in Sedgwick except virtue, and most of us were dying to be rid of it." Taylor's expression grew serious. "Trumble was where I learned to cope with whatever happened to me. I left there as an adult, more or less."

It struck Darrow that Taylor, weaned from family, in some ways had become even more of a loner than the girl he remembered. "After prep school," he asked, "how were things with Lionel?"

"Much the same. Even at Trumble, I spent summers as a camp counselor, or with my grandparents on Martha's Vineyard. Same thing when I went on to Williams. During my junior year, my grandfather Taylor died, then Grandmother six months later. So I decided to leave the country altogether."

Their steaks arrived, pronged with small plastic signs that said, CERTIFIED ANGUS BEEF and promised that both were cooked medium rare. Darrow smiled at this. "The Carriage House," he told her, "has the virtue of being utterly resistant to fashion. It's been open for half a century now. In London or San Francisco, restaurants open and close in a year."

Taylor cut a decorous sliver of steak. "Have you spent much time in London?"

"A little." He hesitated. "That and Paris were Lee's favorite cities. We split our honeymoon between them."

Taylor took this in. "I lived in London for almost three years, taking a crash course in art dealering at Sotheby's, then getting my master's at the Courtauld Institute. It's probably the city I know best."

"Did you like it?"

"Quite a bit," she answered. "In fact, I thought about staying. But the best doctorate program anywhere is at NYU. So I went there, and learned to love the West Village. Now I need time off to finish my dissertation. So here I am, in Wayne."

"So here we both are–you living with your dad, me in what I still think of as Clark Durbin's house."

"The President's House," Taylor amended. "What's that like?"

"Not exactly to my taste. It feels a little like one of those furnished apartments that serve as a halfway house for husbands whose wives have thrown them out." He sipped his drink. "Perhaps it's my state of mind. In my former life we had a town house near the Common, filled with things we'd chosen over time. To me home is something organic. This is a place to sleep."

Taylor gave him a curious look. "Do you still own the town house?"

"Uh-huh. But it's begun to feel like a remnant of some other life. There's too much of Lee there, and it seems empty without her." Embarrassed, he stopped himself. "God, I'm sounding sorry for myself. Lord knows why I'm subjecting you to this–I'm generally pretty okay."

Taylor shook her head. "You don't sound sorry for yourself, Mark. Just honest."

Darrow shrugged. "Then you can take it as an inverted compliment. I don't much like talking about myself."

Taylor smiled a little. "As I remember you at my parents' dinner table, you never did. Sort of like me. I guess we've been saving it up."

They finished dinner, chatting easily. Leaving the restaurant, Darrow was conscious of heads turning–perhaps for both of them; no doubt for Taylor Farr.

He walked Taylor to her car. They faced each other in the twilight. "I've been thinking," she told him. "Maybe you should do something to the President's House."

"Such as."

"Change it a little, or a lot." Her tone became wry. "At your own expense, of course–I gather you can afford it.

But it's no good being in new surroundings if they depress you."

Darrow considered this. "That's not a bad idea, actually. Except for the time it would take." He tilted his head in inquiry. "Think you could advise me?"

Taylor laughed. "About what? Just like I'm not an artist, I'm not an interior designer. Besides, my specialty is postmodern art–any suggestion I made would terrify you. By the time I finished, you'd be sleepless, too, just knowing what horrors were lurking in your living room."

Darrow shrugged. "At least I'd be entertained."

She looked at him, her smile lingering. "You're serious."

"Completely. I'm curious about whatever you'd come up with. Besides–as you pointed out when we met again–you're not twelve anymore." Though still light, his tone softened. "Truth to tell, I enjoyed myself tonight."

Slowly, Taylor nodded. "So did I, Mark. If you want my advice, just call me."

5

By Thursday evening, Darrow had spoken to alumni groups in Cleveland, Chicago, and New York. What daunted him was being introduced as the savior of Caldwell College; what pleased him was that, when he finished, the applause was louder than before he had begun. Besides the embezzlement and, in one case, the lingering effect of Angela Hall's murder, alumni concerns varied: in New York, the penultimate question was how Caldwell could let Huntley Stadium become so shabby; the last question, more to Darrow's liking, was, "Describe how you envision Caldwell College in five years' time."

"With a new football stadium," Darrow deadpanned. When the laughter died, he said, "New facilities will help us attract the best faculty and students. But what concerns me even more is where our students come from."

Pausing, his gaze swept the crowd, three hundred alumni assembled for dinner in a hotel ballroom. "Look around you," he suggested. "We're mostly white and uniformly prosperous." Darrow flashed a smile. "Mind you, I've got nothing against rich white people, and neither did the search committee. But the years since I graduated—thanks, I might add, to our school's generosity—have marked a decline of opportunity, not only for minorities but for middle-class kids squeezed out by rising tuition. Too many other Americans, fortunate themselves, have begun to live in gated communities of the mind, where no one asks them to care about people outside their own direct experience."

The audience was quiet now. Sensing their discomfort, Darrow continued firmly: "The Hall tragedy diminished what I want Caldwell to offer–excellence in education for students whose only barrier to college is money. *That* will make our school a place that enriches our country by expanding its promise. *That's* the heart of *my* vision for Caldwell College, and *that's* the effort I will ask you to support . . ."

To Darrow's surprise, the alumni gave him a standing ovation.

IN THE TAXI to the airport, Darrow's cell phone rang. "I'm calling about Pamela Hartman," Lionel Farr said without preface, "an associate professor of history. Her husband killed himself tonight."

"Good God," Darrow said reflexively. "Does anyone know why?"

"He lost his job." Farr sounded weary. "But who knows why anyone takes their own life. This man left Pam with two young kids."

Darrow realized that a woman he did not know, suddenly a widow, would need his consolation and support. "How's she doing?"

"Not well. Apparently her husband kept things buttoned up tight. Right up until he shot himself."

Darrow thought swiftly. "Let me know whatever she needs from us," he instructed. "If she wants to take a leave from teaching, we'll make the necessary arrangements. As soon as she's ready, I'll go see her."

Darrow stared out the window at the darkness. Remembering the call from Iowa telling him that Lee was dead, he felt this woman's grief and pain and, he imagined, guilt. Then he recalled Clark Durbin's kindness to him on the day of Angela's death. For the first time, he fully accepted that he was president of Caldwell College.

ON FRIDAY MORNING Darrow called on Professor Hartman. Then he drove to Huntley Stadium, the scene of his athletic triumphs, the place where he had once lived with Steve Tillman and Joe Betts. Farr was already there, gazing through the iron gateway from the parking lot to the football stadium. When Darrow approached, Farr asked, "How was Pam?"

"She still doesn't believe it. Part of her won't for a very long time."

"I know," Farr answered softly. "We both do."

The two men fell quiet. The weather was gentle enough, Darrow reflected, unlike the raw gray day after Angela's death, when he and Steve had sat in the bleachers. But even in sunlight, the stadium looked dingy, its walls darkened and eroded by time and wind and dampness. The stands were worn, the field patchy. "At the time I thought it was a dumb question," Darrow said, "But that alumnus who asked me that was right. This place is a dump."

Farr smiled a little. "It always was. You were just too young to notice. For you, Huntley was the Garden of Eden. And why not?"

They began to walk toward the center of campus. Turning back to look at the stadium, Darrow asked, "What about the wing where I used to live?"

"Padlocked. It's a storage area now. No one's lived there since you graduated."

Silent, Darrow gazed up at the window that had once admitted light into his room and, next door, the window through which Joe Betts—at least by his account—had seen

Steve Tillman returning from the direction of the Spire. Glancing at Farr, Darrow asked, "Have time to walk with me awhile?"

The main campus was empty save for a man and woman heading for the science lab. The walkway they followed was flanked by the safety measures Farr had suggested to Clark Durbin: lights every fifty yards or so and, along the way, telephones connected to the campus police. Darrow was silent until they reached the grass surrounding the Spire. Then he turned, gazing back at the stadium. "How far would you say it is from Huntley to the Spire?"

Farr glanced back at the tower, then toward the stadium, blue eyes crinkling at the corners. It was the look of eagles; at that moment Darrow pictured the combat officer Farr once had been. "Two hundred yards," Farr estimated. "Give or take."

"Do you know if Steve's lawyer asked for the jury to come out here?"

"No. I don't."

Darrow gazed at the grass where he had found Angela, watching the play of light and shadow cast by swiftly moving clouds. "There are two possibilities," he said at last. "Either Steve killed her near the Spire or he carried her body two hundred yards, dumping it in the heart of campus. Neither makes much sense to me. Especially the latter."

Farr considered this. "It doesn't seem logical, does it? Of course, drunks aren't always rational. And assuming he killed Angela in his room, even a drunk would know her body couldn't stay there."

"True," Darrow conceded. "But Steve had a car that year. Why not throw her body in the river? Why walk all that way, with a bum knee, and risk letting someone see him?"

Farr looked at Darrow keenly. "You're asking the wrong man. But for the sake of argument, consider the hour. As you know all too well, the party action had moved to the fraternity houses." Farr paused a moment. "The time for kids from Ohio Lutheran to vandalize the Spire had passed, so no one would be guarding it. By two A.M. on a deserted campus, Steve would know that the pedestrian traffic was nil. Better to leave her here than get snagged for drunk driving with a corpse in his trunk."

Darrow faced the provost. "Fair enough," he said. "But did Steve Tillman ever strike you as capable of strangling Angela to death?"

Farr grimaced at the question. "Put that way, no. But who does? Certainly not anyone you've ever imagined you knew."

Briefly, Darrow thought of Joe Betts at the party, the puffy discoloration on his girlfriend's face. "There's a deeper reason," Farr went on, "why your question has no meaning to me."

"Vietnam?"

Farr studied the same swath of grass. "When we found her, I knew at once that she'd been strangled. That wasn't a guess. In my last year of service, our unit had what one might call unusual assignments. Perhaps made easier by latent–or not so latent–prejudice against an Asian populace where we couldn't tell enemy from friend.

"After that, I was never quite the same. Vietnam became a great silence; perhaps that's what Taylor senses in me. As did her mother." Farr straightened his shoulders, as though sloughing off the past. "That's done. But it left me with one advantage, if you care to call it that. You've never been forced to confront the full range of what you–or anyone you know–is capable of doing. I have."

Darrow had no response. More quietly, Farr said, "Follow your curiosity, Mark–I'm not trying to dissuade you. Exorcise Angela, if you can. But don't be disappointed by whatever you may find."

6

At noon, Darrow left the campus. Later that day, his tasks involved Caldwell's budget: discussing potential cuts with Farr and the vice president of finance, followed by a meeting with faculty department heads, accustomed to their prerogatives, to broach the same subject as tactfully as he could. But his immediate mission was external—speaking to the Wayne Chamber of Commerce about his plans for the school.

He found himself facing almost a hundred citizens, mostly men, after a generous introduction by the mayor. Scanning the faces, he saw Dave Farragher, George Garrison, and, to his pleasure and surprise, a prosperous-looking man who could only be Rusty Clark. The welcoming ovation gratified Darrow as well—remembering him as an athlete, the town took satisfaction in his success and pride in his return. His speech was an appreciation of what Caldwell and Wayne had given him, sincere in what it expressed and artful in what it chose to omit. Its focal point, a promise to give deserving local students the same chance Darrow himself had received, drew warm applause.

Afterward, he sought out Rusty, who, he discovered, was practicing law in town. "Who knew?" Darrow said of them both, and made plans to meet Rusty for breakfast. Shaking more hands, he suddenly faced George Garrison.

In the uniform of Wayne's chief of police, Garrison looked bulkier. His perfunctory smile accompanied a look of shrewd appraisal that lent maturity to his still-youthful face. "Good speech," Garrison told him. "You've come a long way since we pulled out that last game."

"Seems like we both have." Darrow glanced around. "I'd like a moment, if you have one. Can you walk with me to the parking lot?"

Garrison checked his watch. "I can spare a moment," he answered. "After all, I'm the chief."

THEY STOPPED BY Garrison's squad car. "So," the chief said, "life's been good for you. At least mostly."

"Mostly. And for you. You're pretty young to be chief."

Garrison gave him the same measured smile. "And you're pretty young to be president of anything. As for me, the mayor seems to think I've got more to offer than just police work. I'm a big believer in community relations, and our black and white communities still need some relating."

It was strange, Darrow thought: in the social pattern of Wayne, he and Garrison had lived parallel lives, been classmates and teammates without knowing each other well. The last time Darrow had seen him—as a young cop, standing over the body of a murdered girl he had known far better than Darrow had—underscored their separateness. Now both had new and demanding jobs, entrusted to them, at least in part, because of what they symbolized. Curious, Darrow asked, "What's it like to be a cop in the town where you grew up?"

Garrison shrugged. "You know this place. The black folks live on the southeast side, the middle-class whites in the northwest, blue-collar whites in between. Only the Hispanics are new, and they keep to themselves, too. A lot of them are illegals and don't want anything to do with the police." Garrison's tone was dispassionate. "In certain ways the separation helps—you don't get a lot of overt conflict. The problem is that blacks and whites and Hispanics don't talk to one another much, even when they need to. That makes my life as chief a little harder."

"Was it hard for you to get the job?"

Garrison considered his answer. "What was hard, at first, was being the only black guy on the force. Bust a drunken white guy and he'd call me 'nigger,' trying to get a rise. Older white folks forgot my name and left messages for 'the colored officer.' As for blacks, a fair number treated my questions like accusations; kids didn't wave when I drove through the old 'hood; when I arrested some badass, no matter for what, it was like he couldn't believe a brother was doing this to him. But my colleagues were always pretty good—we're mostly college graduates, even if some of us went at night, and all of us went through psychological testing before they hired us. We've even got a woman now. All in all, the people on the force seem to accept me fine. But among my own, I still tread a little lighter."

In sixteen years, Darrow reflected, George Garrison seemed to have become a solid man—philosophical, pragmatic, measured, and observant. Perhaps those qualities had always been there and the young Mark Darrow had seen them less clearly. Casually, Darrow asked, "Ever go by the Alibi Club?"

Garrison looked at him harder; to Darrow, the quiet stare suggested that they were edging toward more difficult subjects. In the same even tone, the chief said, "Now and then. Mrs. Hall's attitude is still that the club takes care of its own problems until there's something they can't handle. Not much of that. You remember Hugo."

Darrow smiled. "The doorman. He was big enough to block the sun."

"Yeah. Second year on the job they sent me out there to bust him for a stack of parking tickets he'd never paid." Garrison shook his head. "No way I wanted to do that at the club. So I just told Hugo he ought to come on down in the next week or so, pay those suckers off. For a while he just looks at me, sitting in that chair like a potentate receiving an ambassador from China. Then he nods and tells me he appreciates my attitude.

"A couple of days later, he paid off the tickets. Ever since, if I have to go to the club, Hugo says, 'I got your back, boy.' No more 'I smell bacon' from the guys drinking at the bar–on account of Hugo, everyone's real polite." His tone became pointed. "It helps that anyone who knows Mrs. Hall also knows that after Angela died, I was there for her. Carl wasn't much use."

Darrow nodded. "So," Garrison said, "you just wondering about life in Wayne, or is there something more particular?"

Darrow considered his answer. "I ran into Carl the other day, which piqued my curiosity. What's with Carl's Mercedes?"

Garrison's smile was no smile at all. "Carl," he answered, "is chief executive officer of a small but successful business."

"The same business?"

"More or less. Also the same clientele, including kids from Caldwell with just enough brains to know that the college still protects its own." Once more Garrison spoke with a slight edge. "Kind of like the kids at the last party Angela ever went to. Only change is her brother's product line. Back then it was weed and powder cocaine; now Carl's branched off into heroin. The irony here, in terms of Caldwell, is that we think Carl was the one selling smack to Clark Durbin's boy."

"A sad case," Darrow remarked. "Not to mention expensive–Clark's rehab bills for his son ran over a hundred thousand."

Garrison nodded. "I heard. Guess that was part of why his fingers got so light."

"So people think. You ever try to shut Carl down?"

"If we could, we would. But Carl's still smart. He communicates by prepaid cell phones, uses different stash houses to conceal his drugs. Living in a small town, he's got a nose for narcs or anyone wearing a wire. Plus he gets his heroin through illegals, who can't drop the dime on him without getting deported." Garrison eyed the asphalt at their feet. "Truth is, Carl's not exactly a law enforcement priority."

"Why's that?"

"We don't have unlimited manpower. So we care less about the drugs than the trouble they cause for law-abiding citizens." Garrison looked up again. "That's why we focus on crystal meth and crack cocaine, drugs that make users crazy and violent–we don't want them raping, mugging, and killing innocent folks at random. So we keep after the scum that sells that shit. That's another way Carl's smart: the product he peddles doesn't cause his clients to kill anyone. Except maybe themselves."

Darrow considered this. "I'd think running a cash business would create a problem for him. That's how the feds got Al Capone–not murder but tax evasion. I guess Carl must launder his profits through the Alibi Club."

"That's what we assume. You can also bet he's put that Mercedes in someone else's name." Garrison scowled. "In recent years, it seems like Carl's expanded his operation a whole lot: buying more, selling more–heroin, especially. The guy who runs the county's drug task force thinks Carl got financing from somewhere. But no one has the time or resources to try and nail that down."

"A shame."

"I suppose. But so many things are." Garrison's expression seemed to harden. "I'm standing here, looking at you. Do you know what I see? Not the quarterback for the Wayne Generals or even the president of Caldwell College. I see you standing over her body. Then I look at you again, and all I see is Tillman."

Darrow met his gaze. "That was a bad morning, after a bad night. Lives changed."

"Especially hers." Garrison's tone was quiet. "Except for my wife, she was the sweetest and smartest girl I ever knew. Leaving out lethal injection, your friend got what he deserved."

Darrow shoved his hands into his pockets. "I went to see him last Sunday. I'm not so sure he's glad to be alive."

"Then I guess I'm glad he is."

"Are you *that* sure he killed her?"

Garrison's eyes widened in a pantomime of astonishment. "Guess no one told you about the trial."

"Not in detail, no."

"That's where they present evidence," Garrison said caustically. "Sort of like they taught you about in law school. According to the *evidence,* Steve Tillman was a murderer with a mile-wide streak of racism."

"Steve was thoughtless," Darrow retorted. "He said cruel or stupid things by rote, like a lot of people in Wayne. None of whom are murderers."

"Most of whom," Garrison shot back, "probably don't have weird pathologies about sex between blacks and whites." He paused, then spoke more calmly. "After you found Angela, the force kept me out of it—didn't want me involved in a case where I'd gone out with the victim, even if it was only high school. But there was plenty of evidence on how Tillman felt toward *us* without me telling the jury about the date I *didn't* have. The one with your buddy's kid sister."

"Mary?"

"You never heard about that? That surprises me some, seeing how you lived with him. But then maybe Tillman's racist talk was all white noise to you." Garrison paused, then spoke with the same weary patience. "Senior year, I asked Mary out. She said yes—we liked each other, so why not? Then Steve pulled me aside after practice and said, 'Keep your black hands off my sister.' He looked and sounded like whatever he imagined us doing made him sick.

"Mary never went out with me—after that, she couldn't. But that didn't keep Tillman from wanting Angela." Garrison's voice was softer yet. "Maybe after sex, he felt so sick that he had to kill her. All I know is that he did. Funny he can't remember."

"What Steve says he can't remember," Darrow answered, "is whatever happened in that room. Do *you* know for sure? I don't. But I *did* know Steve, and I *did* see him with Angela. And I'm pretty damned sure that sexual revulsion was *not* Steve's motive."

"No one knows," Garrison said flatly. "And who cares now? You don't need a motive to prove murder."

"It's just more satisfying that way," Darrow answered. "I wasn't looking to pick a quarrel, George. But my feelings about this are more complicated than yours. If I knew for sure Steve killed her, then I could accept where he is."

Garrison put his hands on his hips. "Then let me tell you a story. A couple of years ago, at the high school, a white teacher started sleeping with a seventeen-year-old black girl. When the school found out, the girl claimed that he'd coerced her into sex in exchange for grades.

"Maybe it happened that way, maybe it didn't. But both blacks and whites got mighty riled. The man ended up losing his job, his wife, and his kid." Garrison's gaze was steady. "Suppose Tillman raped Angela. What would have happened to him if she'd lived to tell someone? Like with that teacher, nothing good."

"*Did* he rape her?"

Garrison scowled. "There's rape, and there's rape. No one but Angela could say exactly what this was. But she couldn't, could she?"

Darrow had no answer. "Look," Garrison said. "I wish you luck with being president. I'm sure you wish me luck being chief. I never thought you were a bad guy, and now we've both got our jobs to do, problems in the here and now. Why don't we leave the past where it was."

Darrow nodded. Wayne's chief of police extended his hand, shaking Darrow's, and then they went their separate ways.

7

I

On Sunday morning, Darrow decided to walk the residential part of campus, toward fraternity row.

It was ten o'clock, and the slanting sunlight, warm and moist on his skin, presaged a hot, cloudless day. Taking a brick pathway past a colonial-style dormitory dating from the 1870s, Darrow had a sharp, sudden memory: a bright spring day, its warmth lingering into early evening, the light sound of women's voices through a window as he passed this very dorm. Even then he had marked the moment, combining the irretrievable preciousness of a time soon to be lost with the promise of a future still ahead–in which a woman yet unknown to him might be taking a path that would someday merge with his. So much had happened since, for good or ill. But it was no use, at thirty-eight, to mourn his youth: he was still young, and he could hope that the best moments of his life waited for him yet.

He tried to date the memory. Surely it had been late May, or perhaps even early June. Since that time, the school year had been shortened, cutting off the weeks to which the moment belonged. No doubt it made sense, from Caldwell's perspective, to charge more tuition for less schooling. But the young Mark Darrow had savored the arrival of spring on campus: the greening of trees and the bright flowering of dogwoods; the careless interplay of young men and women outdoors as their clothing became lighter; a sense of awakening on campus that felt almost sensual. A long time ago, Darrow thought.

FRATERNITY ROW WAS also much as Darrow recalled it; the trees around the grassy oval were somewhat fuller, the large brick houses sixteen years deeper into their aura of solidity and permanence. But while the SAE house across the street was, like most others, reasonably well maintained, the DBE house evoked the House of Usher: the white paint on the wooden trim was peeling; the scabrous lawn was pocked with crabgrass; and the screen of an upstairs window was askew, like an idiot's glasses. Even had Darrow not suspected the cause, the portrait of decline was plain enough.

In summer, the house would be manned by a skeleton crew of students. Chary of what he might find, Darrow walked inside.

The living room was empty, the furniture worn. Darrow could have sworn that he had sat on that same couch when Steve and Joe had fought over Angela. For a moment Angela's tipsy, poignant glance at him seemed as fresh as yesterday. As he gazed at the library, another flashback struck him: awakening in Joe's Miata, blinking at the dial of its clock, and then, on the car phone, vainly trying to call Steve. His thoughts from that time, a sort of stupefied irritation, struck him as innocent compared to the guilt and uncertainty their memory surfaced now.

Darrow went downstairs to the basement.

There should have been ten tables, accommodating sixty or so college boys for dinner on any given night. But now there were only four. The tiles, worn and scuffed with dirt, were certainly the same tiles he had stood on when he and Angela had exchanged their final words.

If you need someone to get you home, he'd said, *I'm here.*

She had shaken her head, moving close to him. *Gonna be a long night for me, I think.* Then she had given him a brief kiss on the lips. *You're kind of sweet, Mark Darrow.*

Standing there alone, Darrow shook his head.

Crossing the room, he peered into the kitchen. Laurie Shilts appeared in his mind, barely twenty-one. *You don't really know him, Mark. Deep down, Joe hates women.*

Briefly, Darrow closed his eyes. He tried to imagine Angela Hall, perhaps with the sheets pulled up around her, telling Steve that she had to leave. But he could not summon the image; it was not his memory. Nor, perhaps, was it Steve's.

Darrow went back upstairs.

He stopped in the stairwell where he and Steve had drunk beer on the night of the party. It had still hurt Steve to walk; the knee injury had banished him from football one year before. And yet if he had strangled Angela in his room, Steve must have carried the dead weight of her body at least two lengths of a football field.

Surely Steve's lawyer had focused on this incongruity. And yet a jury had found him guilty.

To George Garrison, and perhaps to the jury, Steve had been a racist. Maybe this was so. But his attitudes had always struck Darrow as rote village bigotry, more reflexive than embedded in Steve's psyche. Garrison saw him differently. No doubt George had the right; most people changed with the eyes of the beholder. But few changed so completely or so tragically.

Entering the second floor, Darrow glanced into the room where Joe had watched the video of Tonya Harding. To his surprise, it was occupied by a bulky kid watching ESPN. With a one-day growth of beard and what looked like barbecue sauce smeared on his T-shirt, he seemed in roughly the same state of disrepair as the house itself. He eyed the trim stranger in sport coat and blue jeans with a look of torpid wariness.

"Sorry to bother you," Darrow said. "But I used to live here. I guess that makes us fraternity brothers."

It took the kid a few seconds to compute this. "You're President Darrow."

Darrow smiled. "So they tell me."

The boy got to his feet and shook Darrow's hand. "I'm Skip Penton," he said, summoning a sheepish grin. "I'm president of the DBEs."

"How's it going?"

The grin became a skeptical smile. "You can't tell?"

"I can guess. The house looks kind of sad."

"No help for it. When you guys were here, how many brothers in the chapter?"

"Sixty-plus."

Skip grimaced. "We're down to twenty-one. After that black girl was killed, everything changed. And when that guy Tillman was found guilty of murder, it sunk our reputation."

"Not to mention Steve's," Darrow answered mildly. "What happened was bad all the way around. Angela Hall was a good person, and Steve was my closest friend."

Skip seemed to consider his response. His tone mingled apology with grievance. "Whoever's fault it was, we suffered for it. The school watches us like hawks. Except for hard-core loyalists like my dad, the alumni punted us too, like we were a pack of drunken, drug-crazed, racist murderers. Even on the weekend of the Lutheran game, they never come here anymore."

So this, too, had become part of house lore, repeated by its oral historians like the epic achievements of its athletes, or the famous "Nude Olympics" party of '67, after which, it was said, three female guests turned up pregnant. But Darrow knew other stories, far more common but less often told, of loyalty and kindness and friendships made for life, like those he had once imagined having with Steve Tillman or Joe Betts—the good qualities encouraged, the frailties tolerated unless they needed to be addressed. And one of Darrow's more recent memories involved the numerous and desperate appeals for help from chapter presidents, the latest being Skip's letter, which Darrow had chosen to ignore. "How's your maintenance budget?" Darrow asked.

"A lot like the school's. Only worse."

Ruefully, Darrow laughed. Then he took his checkbook from his coat pocket and, leaning on the desk, scrawled out a check for twenty thousand dollars before handing it to Skip. "This should cover painting, landscaping, and new furniture on the first floor. When I come back here this fall, I want to see them all."

Skip gaped at the check, then at Darrow. "I don't know what to say."

"Nothing," he answered. "It's an anonymous gift. But it might help with fraternity rush, or when you invite alumni back over Lutheran weekend to see the improvements you've made. If they think other alums are supporting you, *they* might."

Leaving, Darrow checked his watch. In an hour, Sunday visiting time would commence at the penitentiary in Lucasville.

FACING HIM THROUGH the Plexiglas, Steve looked mildly surprised. "You came back."

Darrow's smile felt synthetic. "I said I would. This may sound strange, but I've never shaken what happened. Especially to you."

Steve's laugh was a derisive bark. "Then this is a new record for delayed reactions."

"I keep getting reminded." Darrow looked into Steve's eyes. "I saw George Garrison the other day. He's chief of police now."

Steve's reaction was contradictory–a sardonic smile, a guilty flicker in his eyes. "So I heard. Seems like everyone's moving up but me. George isn't exactly a fan of mine, is he?"

"Not exactly. Before he thought you were a murderer, he just thought you were a racist prick."

"Guilty," Steve said with sudden softness. "At least on the 'racist prick' count. In high school, we had a little incident."

"Over your kid sister?"

"Yeah." Steve looked down. "As best I remember, I told George I didn't want him trying to stick his black dick into Mary."

Darrow winced inside. "George left that part out. But it helps explain why *he* remembers the moment so clearly. Also why he thinks you might be a psychopath when it comes to interracial sex."

Steve's head jerked up. "So how does Sigmund Freud Garrison square that with me and Angela doing it? That I'm a racist *and* a hypocrite?"

"*And* fucked up. In George's estimate, you turned on yourself. And her."

"Jesus fucking Christ." Steve's voice became a whisper. "It's like a curse, man. It never expires."

Darrow watched his face. "I don't follow."

Steve's eyes misted. "What I'd said to George about my sister. I told Angela about it. She was tending bar and I was drinking–"

"You must have been, to bring it up. Especially there."

Through the grid, Darrow could hear Steve exhale. "It was something I'd begun feeling shitty about. So I told her what I'd said to George, kind of like an apology."

"What did she say?"

"That George had told her about it, years before. And that maybe I should be apologizing to him." Steve shook his head. "For a minute, I thought she was pissed off–like she was my all-purpose black confessor, stuck listening to a stupid white boy purge his conscience of bigotry. Then she admitted she'd ripped into George for asking out a white girl. 'I wonder if it's something we learn,' she told me, 'or it's just hardwired in the species. Either way it's pretty sad.'

"She went to serve drinks at the other end of the bar. I just sat there for a while, thinking. That's when we started to be friends."

Gazing at Steve, Darrow pondered the story. It might not be true; Steve had had sixteen years to invent, or even imagine, a redemptive tale. But the story accounted for the casual friendliness between Steve and Angela–perhaps hinting at more–at the Alibi Club when Angela and Darrow had first spoken. It also explained why Steve had invited her to the party, and why she had felt inclined to leave with him. And it turned George Garrison's theory of Steve's psychology inside out.

Thought you didn't like black folks, Darrow had said to Steve.

Times change. Gazing at Angela, Steve had added softly, *Who wouldn't like that?*

"I was over that crap," Steve said now. "But they wouldn't *let* me be over it."

"When?"

"At the trial." Steve's voice filled with anger. "What was Caldwell College supposed to be *for*? Making you think, right? Being challenged by people like Lionel Farr to question your assumptions and prejudices." Steve's voice thickened. "Part of my deal with Angela was about that—wanting to learn more about her, find out what her life was like. I think that's why she went with me that night, when we'd never been alone before. I wanted to *know* her, not strangle her." His voice steadied. "I even think that's why Farr comes to see me once in a blue moon. Caldwell—Durbin and Farr—may have thought it was convenient for me to be a sacrificial lamb. But I think deep down Farr sees that giving me a scholarship to Caldwell made me a better person, and that now I've been thrown away."

Darrow wondered. Farr was too deeply skeptical of human nature and, it seemed clear, of Steve's innocence. In Darrow's estimation, Farr had helped Steve find a lawyer only because Darrow had asked; if, after the trial, Farr had shown Steve kindness, it was because—despite his deeper fondness for Angela—Farr knew that men were too complex to be defined by the worst moment in their lives. But all Darrow said was "Farr's a good man, Steve. I'm sorry I'm not a better one."

Steve simply nodded.

8

DARROW BEGAN HIS SECOND WEEK AS PRESIDENT BY meeting Rusty Clark for breakfast at the Bluebird Grill.

The first to arrive, Darrow took one of three booths at the rear, surveying the once-familiar setting. To accommodate more customers, the wooden counters were configured around two T-shaped spaces in which waitresses served breakfasts or lunches to diners on both sides. All were white. Most of the men wore jackets and baseball caps with the logos of local employers; the women tended toward pantsuits and short hair, often stiffly lacquered. In the eyes of some women, Darrow detected a vaguely fretful, worried look, reminding him that surrounding Caldwell College sat a small midwestern town where jobs were limited and paychecks finite. Most of the diners seemed to know one another; they chatted sporadically, laconically, their speech uninflected. Eyeing that morning's specials, scrawled in Magic Marker on a board over the open grill, Darrow saw Rusty hurrying through the door.

His college friend waved, giving Darrow a wide smile that seemed to melt away years. "Had to drop my oldest boy at school," Rusty explained as he slid into the booth. "Takes after his old man–slow to wake up. By ten or so he'll resemble human life."

Darrow laughed. "How many do you have?"

Rusty whipped out his wallet, displaying a picture of a

pert, pretty woman with a red-haired boy and two strawberry-blond girls flashing smiles just like Rusty's.

"These aren't children," Darrow adjudged. "They're clones."

Rusty chuckled with pleasure. "At least I know they're mine. Meg says that all she did was perform a storage function."

"Other than that and tolerating you, what else does Meg do?"

"Teaches English at the high school–she loves the kids and likes her colleagues. And I've cobbled together a decent practice out of what happens in a place like Wayne: death, divorce, real estate transactions, and petty crime. Together we'll get our kids through college without going into hock. Some days it's a mini–rat race, but life's turned out okay." He smiled again. "Remember Tim Fedak?"

"How could I not? He helped us stick Betts's Miata in the library."

Rusty seemed momentarily sobered by the underside of memory. "So he did. Anyhow, Tim's into real estate development around here. His family, mine, and two other couples with kids take a group vacation every year at a small lake in northern Michigan–the kids fish, swim, and water-ski while we cook steaks and keep them all from drowning. With any luck, someday us and our kids will be trekking up with *their* kids. We grandparents will be happy, and our children can do the cooking."

Smiling, Darrow absorbed his friend's contentment. If Rusty was spared life's random tragedies, Darrow had little doubt, the future would unfold much as he intended: marital fidelity, attentive parenting, deepening roots in a chosen place and time. Though he envied Rusty what fate had taken from him–a wife and child–Darrow knew that he had become incapable of choosing a course so circumscribed; for him, and for Lee before she died, hell was knowing with utter certainty what one's path would be. But it pleased him that Rusty was realizing his fondest hopes. "I'd say you were lucky," Darrow told him. "But as Lionel Farr once told me, luck is a talent."

Nodding, Rusty acknowledged the compliment. "I figured out what I wanted and went for it. So did you." He paused, adding quietly, "What happened to you surely wasn't fair."

Perhaps not, Mark thought—too often, the consequence of not fully comprehending someone close to you far exceeds the sin. But he had never expressed to anyone his fear that Lee's accident was not, in one sense, accidental. "My life has its fair share of compensations," he answered. "Certainly compared to Steve's."

Rusty studied the table. "I keep thinking I should visit him," he said at length. "But I've been thinking that for almost fifteen years. I can't get past what Steve's inside for."

The plump young waitress arrived. Rusty ordered scrambled eggs; Darrow, English muffins. "Sorry," the waitress told Darrow. "We don't have those. Only toast."

When Rusty smiled at Darrow's look of perplexity, Darrow realized, yet again, how far he had journeyed from Boston. After Darrow ordered wheat toast, Rusty asked, "Have *you* seen Steve yet?"

Darrow took a sip of coffee. "Twice."

"Does he still 'think' he's innocent?"

"So he says. You know the story. He's never had a better one."

"He never had a *good* one. The racial thing didn't help him, either."

Once again, Darrow felt a lingering guilt about avoid-

said, "Heart attack on a plate. How do people in t[illegible]
ever become old?"

Rusty patted his stomach. "Prepaid quadruple b[illegible]
My insurance guy is working on a plan."

Darrow smiled at this. "As near as you could tell,"
asked, "what was Nordlinger's reputation?"

"For high-end criminal work? I don't think he had one." Rusty took a bite of his eggs. "To be fair, Steve didn't give a lawyer much to work with."

"Ever think about how *you* might have defended him?"

"You mean if they'd held a gun to my head?" Distractedly, Rusty moved his eggs around the plate. "I'd go into every aspect of his relationship to Angela. Then I'd scour his memory of the day she died, hour by hour, and whatever the cops did with him after that–interrogation, tests, any clue to what he was up against." He looked up at Darrow. "You can't assume the police are rubes–they're smart and highly trained. Like the lawyers, all they lack is murder cases to practice on."

"So the next step is replicating what the cops did?"

"Exactly. Interview everyone at the party–you, me, Carl Hall, anyone else who saw anything at all. Including Joe Betts. *Especially* Joe, even if he hadn't turned out to be Farragher's star witness." For a split second, Rusty hesitated. "You knew him better than I did. Was he doing coke that night?"

"I don't think he needed to be. That night seems to be why Joe quit drinking."

"Whatever it was, I didn't want to be anywhere near him." Rusty took a quick gulp of coffee. "Speaking as a lawyer, you'd want to find out what *Joe's* thing about Angela was, and what he did after he left the party. Not to mention whether he saw what he *says* he saw on a pitch-black night–including inconsistencies, or any reason he'd want to nail Steve." Abruptly Rusty's voice softened. "I'm just thinking like a defense lawyer. Joe is make-or-break—his story is either true, or a mistake, or a setup."

"Then one more thing," Darrow added quietly. "He's also your alternative suspect."

Rusty focused on his eggs. "I'd sure like to have a motive, Mark. Jealousy seems like a stretch to me."

"So what was Steve's motive? Even drunks and bigots have a sense of self-preservation. Why kill her when you'd be such an obvious suspect?"

Rusty looked up. Quietly, he said, "She's stayed with you, hasn't she?"

"Her face has. It wasn't a drive-by shooting, Rusty. This was personal."

Rusty took his last bite of sausage. After a time, he said, "Steve didn't seem like that, did he?"

"Not to me." Darrow hesitated. "Even now, that bothers me. Especially after seeing him again."

"So, as a lawyer, a big question is whether you'd have put him on the stand. That's what Nordlinger did. It's also what a good lawyer *should* do, if he can. I've never believed that relying on the presumption of innocence and a defendant's right to silence cuts it with a jury."

"I agree. But the downside would have been leaving Steve wide open to whatever Farragher's got. If you make the wrong decision, he's done." Signaling the waitress for more coffee, Darrow turned back to Rusty. "What are the chances of looking at the transcript of Steve's trial?"

"You personally?" Rusty asked in a tone of surprise. "If you wanted to, you could—Ohio has an open-records law for old files. The practical problem is what kind of shape they're in. The last old files I dug up had been stored in an attic infested with hungry rats and sparrows—they'd converted the most critical papers into pellets and bird poop. Hopefully Steve's files aren't as appetizing."

"What about files from the autopsy and forensics?"

"Those should be fine. Our coroner's just a functionary. When an autopsy is called for, he farms it out to the ME in Columbus. Same with the crime lab. The Bureau of Criminal Investigation stores the records."

When the waitress brought the check, Darrow grabbed it before Rusty could. "This is on me," Darrow said. "I could use a favor, though. If I become a paying client, think you could copy Steve's files?"

"Sure, at cost. But not without Dave Farragher knowing who wanted them."

Darrow shrugged. "That's okay."

Rusty gave him a dubious look. "Is it? You've just come back here, and you've got big problems at the school. For years Farragher served on Caldwell's board of trustees, and he's still got lots of friends there. I can imagine someone asking why you're wasting time reading the transcript of a fifteen-year-old murder case."

"Who would care that much?"

"Farragher. Our local congressman's about to pack it in, and Dave wants to take his place." Rusty frowned. "That was the biggest case Dave ever had. The only thing between him and Congress might be for someone to suggest that he convicted an innocent man."

"I'm not suggesting anything, Rusty. I'm just curious about how and why Steve got convicted. Maybe the only way to ease my mind is to read the trial transcript."

Rusty glanced at his watch. "Up to you, pal." He paused again, then added, "If you're poking around, the police chief's where you can do some business."

"Garrison? You didn't go to high school here. He despises Steve."

"Maybe so. But George has graduated, all the way to chief of police." Rusty leaned forward. "Farragher pushed a white guy for the chief's job, a Republican friend of his—pushed him hard, in fact. But the mayor chose George. So there's no love lost between our chief and our county prosecutor; Farragher's still a threat to George's job, and George still has something to prove. Undoing Farragher's finest hour would not break George's heart."

"Small towns," Darrow said with a smile. "All I want is a look at those files. I'm a long way from threatening anyone's ambitions."

Rusty stood. "Including your own, I hope. For a lot of us, Caldwell College is a very special place. We've got a stake in your success."

"I'll remember that," Darrow promised.

9

THE MAJOR EVENT ON DARROW'S SCHEDULE THAT day was a midmorning meeting with Ray Carrick, the chairman of Caldwell's board of trustees. Darrow intended to spend the preceding two hours reviewing budget projections, calling prominent alumni, and scanning plans for a new science building–which, although badly needed, would require $20 million Caldwell did not have. Then a sharp knock punctuated his thoughts, and Lionel Farr leaned through his office door. In a tone drenched with irony, Farr said, "As Sartre once remarked, 'Hell is other people.'"

"Which people?" Darrow inquired.

"In this case, your faculty. A potential charge of sexual harassment."

Grimacing, Darrow waved him to a chair. "What's the genesis?"

"Stupidity. You took a history course from Tom Craig, right?"

"Uh-huh. A good professor, I thought."

"He still is. Also easily bored. So he decided that sleeping with a student might, as it were, help him fill the void." Farr's tone held weary exasperation. "The *wrong* student–a young woman from India of considerable volatility, spiked by cultural misunderstanding. Whatever the reason, Ms. Kashfi imagined that Tom planned to leave his wife."

"Which he didn't."

"Of course not. So our student showed up at Tom's house two days ago, threatening Anita with bodily harm. Dr. Craig has become a bystander–for Anita, the price of marital peace is having Ms. Kashfi deported."

"Is she crazy?"

Farr emitted a mirthless laugh. "For my money, they both are. But now we own the problem."

Darrow sighed in irritation. "Ms. Kashfi requires counseling, not expulsion–let alone deportation. As for Craig, any time a professor's screwing a student you're risking angry parents, potential lawsuits, and the possibility of trading grades for sex. Not to mention an erosion of student respect for the faculty and damage to Caldwell's reputation. So what *is* our policy on faculty-student involvements?"

"There is none," Farr conceded. "We have 'guidelines.' In all of these cases, you're dealing with two people who are over the age of consent–"

"Granted," Darrow cut in. "But also with a power differential ripe for abuse. Describe these so-called guidelines."

"We strongly discourage romantic relationships between faculty and students, listing all the reasons you suggest." Pausing, Farr added dryly, "In reality, we're asking for a modicum of judgment and discretion among consenting adults. For faculty, the unwritten message seems to be 'It's okay to marry a student, but please don't date them first.' At least not where anyone can see you."

Darrow shook his head. "That's like sitting on nitroglycerin. As we both know all too well, people kill each other over sex. What if Ms. Kashfi had shown up at midnight and Anita Craig had put a bullet through her brain? Or vice versa? And even short of murder, the whole thing reeks.

"Bring our general counsel in. We need to craft a stronger policy, clearly understood. Our faculty should know that I'll go after anyone guilty of abusing their power over students–if I could, I'd bar these relationships outright. But if any professor still insists on dating a student, we should require them to disclose that to their department head *and* to you, and to refrain from teaching anyone they're involved with. If they don't, I'll do my damnedest to get rid of them."

"The faculty may bridle, Mark. Some will call it an invasion of privacy."

"No doubt. But it would cut down on the threat of lawsuits and put the fear of God in married faculty that their spouses will find out." Darrow's own voice held a trace of sarcasm. "I'll solicit faculty responses, of course–I'm sensitive to their prerogatives, and I'll hate cutting down their dating pool. But reasonable professors will understand, and the rest will be wary of making themselves conspicuous. Especially if we cite Tom Craig's embarrassment as a teachable moment."

Farr smiled a little. "I'll call our general counsel, Mr. President. Are you ready to face the chairman of our board?"

THE SPIRE WAS Ray Carrick's favorite place on campus, and so his tour of Caldwell's facilities ended in its shadow. He walked between Farr and Darrow, his paunch preceding him, his movements ponderous and heavy-shouldered. He had the self-satisfied countenance of a provincial worthy with, in Darrow's estimation, the sensibility to match: tough, shrewd, reliable, loyal, and wholly unoriginal. In better times, Darrow judged, he would have been a proper steward of Caldwell's affairs. But becoming a leading business magnate in a central Ohio town had dulled Carrick's self-perception and inflated his self-regard. Though no friction had developed between Caldwell's new president and its board chair, Farr had counseled Darrow to treat Ray Carrick with care.

Now Carrick turned from the Spire, facing Darrow. "We need money," he summarized peremptorily. "The science building's outmoded, and so's our field house. As for Huntley Stadium, it looks more like a soccer stadium in downtown Baghdad."

Darrow smiled. "Never seen one, Ray. But I'll take your word."

Carrick's mouth clamped down. "It's no joke, Mark—we've got to get cracking on a big endowment drive. Why do you want to cancel our feasibility study? Walter Berg's all ready to go."

"No doubt. But I don't want to pay Walter's consulting firm a hundred grand to tell me what I already know—that we can't raise a hundred million until the alumni believe that I've straightened this place out." Glancing at Farr, Darrow finished: "Lionel and I have talked about this. In the short term, the best way to engage our alumni is to ask them not for money but ideas. If I can enlist them in defining our needs and goals, they'll pony up when I ask them to."

Carrick turned to Farr. "Mark's right," Farr said simply. "For the next year or two we just have to keep the school afloat."

Carrick crossed his arms, eyeing the grass at their feet and then Mark Darrow. "You say the alumni need to know you're cleaning things up. Isn't the best way to ask Dave Farragher to indict Clark Durbin? Let's place the blame where it belongs and put the Durbin era behind us."

"Perhaps. But I don't want to do that yet, Ray."

"Why not?" Carrick asked with palpable annoyance. "Most folks on the board see this as a moral issue. If Durbin won't cooperate by helping us trace the money, then he deserves a stretch in jail. Give the bastard a choice, I say. Where's the virtue in shilly-shallying when a man we trusted turns out to be a crook?"

"Because Durbin's not the problem anymore. Assuring alumni that another embezzlement won't happen *is,* and I've begun to do that. As for Durbin," Darrow continued in the same calm tone, "he's not running off to Paraguay. Within a month the accountant I'm bringing in can help us decide what to do with him."

Carrick's eyebrows shot up. "What about Joe Betts's man? Doesn't he already have this buttoned up?"

"Fox is good," Darrow answered. "So's my guy. I want him to look at this without preconceptions."

"Durbin stole the money," Carrick snapped. "Isn't it obvious?"

"It seems so. But there are a couple of things about the embezzlement I'd like to nail down. After that we can consider the benefits of prosecuting Durbin or letting him go quietly." To placate Carrick, Darrow added, "You're right about the money–assuming there's any left. If Durbin's guilty, we can give him some hard choices."

With a dubious expression, Carrick turned to Farr. "What do *you* think, Lionel?"

Farr inclined his head toward Darrow. "That we hired Mark to make these calls. Besides, he knows more about financial chicanery than both of us combined. If there's something here that bothers him, I think we'd do well to listen."

Carrick wheeled on Darrow. "*Is* there, Mark?"

Darrow found himself cornered. "I can't tell you, exactly. Maybe *that's* what troubles me. It's too neat."

Carrick gave a snort–half laugh, half resignation. Then he turned again, gazing at the base of the Spire. "Such a tragedy," he said with surprising quiet. "All our troubles started *here,* when Tillman killed that black girl. To associate a murder with such a special place makes it that much sadder."

Darrow thought of Taylor Farr. "The other day," he told Carrick, "someone asked if we'd consider tearing the Spire down."

Carrick gave him a hard sideways look. "Over my dead body, Mark. Over my dead body."

"That," Farr ventured mildly, "is an unfortunate turn of phrase."

Carrick shook his head. "Damn Steve Tillman," he said to Farr with muted vehemence. "I wish you'd never given him that scholarship."

"So do I, Ray. But that's how we got Mark."

This exchange, Darrow discovered, touched the nerve ends of his guilt and obligation. Facing Darrow, Carrick said softly, "So it was, and I'm glad for that. Once you finish those alumni calls, Mark, let me know how they went."

The two men shook hands. Extending his hand to Farr, Carrick said with genuine warmth, "Thank you, Lionel. Without you, I don't know where we'd be."

Shaking Carrick's hand, Farr smiled. "You have no idea, Ray. But neither do I."

Carrick chuckled, and headed off for the parking lot.

Darrow and Farr watched him go. "Thanks," Darrow said. "It's clear you've got more credibility than I do."

"More years, anyhow." Farr turned to him. "You know how Ray is. He's smart enough to know you're smarter, and spoiled enough not to enjoy it. Mind if I reiterate a word of advice?"

"Of course not."

"Don't alienate him over Durbin. Do whatever you need to feel more comfortable, then move as quickly as you can. As a practical matter, feeding him Clark Durbin will buy you Ray's goodwill on bigger issues. It's the kind of callous act that makes a leader great."

Darrow laughed softly. "I'll remember that, Chairman Mao."

Darrow placed alumni calls through lunch, then used the afternoon to catch up with his schedule. A little after five o'clock he stuffed the budget figures in his briefcase, pledging to revisit them before he went to sleep, and left his office for the day.

The police station was new since Darrow had graduated, a two-story building constructed of red brick, its modernity suggesting that Wayne was now on the cutting edge of law enforcement. Darrow went to a reception area protected by bulletproof glass and, reminded of his visits to Steve Tillman, spoke through a grid to the receptionist. A moment later George Garrison leaned through a metal door. "Come on back," he said.

Darrow followed him to his corner office. One bookshelf was filed with tomes on criminology; on another, next to George's college diploma and certificates of completion from advanced policing courses, was a picture of a smiling, round-faced woman and two bright-eyed kids. Families everywhere, Darrow thought.

"Have a seat," Garrison said brusquely. "To what do I owe the pleasure?"

"A couple of things. For openers, I went to see Steve again."

Garrison's face turned opaque. "And?"

"He told me about the incident involving you and his sister. He also claims that he told Angela about it shortly before the murder, apparently by way of apology."

"*That's* what you came to tell me?" Garrison paused, then muted his tone of incredulity. "You don't just 'get over' a prejudice so deeply ingrained. Even by your account, Angela was Tillman's one black 'friend,' and his idea of racial amity was fucking. God knows what happened between them in that room."

Darrow shifted in his chair. "Maybe so. But murder's an extreme form of prejudice. Did your investigation come up with any other instance where Steve became violent—whether with women, blacks, or otherwise?"

"Not that I know of," Garrison said. "But suppose you believe, like Tillman says, that Angela left his room alive. Then who killed her? Someone lurking by the Spire at two A.M.? A random murderer walking across a deserted campus, looking for some equally random victim to strangle but not rape or rob? Some drunk who had the sudden inspiration to kill the first woman he saw?" Once more, Garrison modulated his tone. "Why don't you ask Fred Bender. Should be easy enough—in case you've missed it, Fred became Caldwell's chief of security. He'll know who the suspects were, if any."

"What about Griff Nordlinger?" Darrow asked. "I'd ask *him,* but he seems to have disappeared."

"All the way to heaven. Nordlinger died in Phoenix, several years ago."

"Of what?"

"Heart attack, I think. The man had worked his ticker overtime." Garrison seemed to sit more heavily. "A couple of years after the trial, I busted him for possession of cocaine. By then—or so his ex-wife said—he had a wicked cross-addiction to powder cocaine and whiskey. Nordlinger was finished as a lawyer–I had him ready to flip, name Carl Hall as his supplier. But instead of pressing charges, the chief let Griff's daughter hustle him off to rehab in Arizona. Not my call–I wanted Carl pretty bad. Needless to say, Nordlinger never came back to Wayne."

Darrow parsed the implications of this. "During Steve's trial, was Nordlinger screwed up?"

"Thought you'd ask that," Garrison answered with a trace of asperity. "As far as I recall, no one ever said so during the trial. In Tillman's case, I doubt it would have mattered. Anything else you want to know?"

"One thing. Who performed the autopsy on Angela? All I remember is that she was blond."

Garrison nodded. "That would be Carly Simmons."

"Know where I can find her?"

"Yeah. She lives here in the county, out by Cahaba Road." Garrison leaned forward, gazing at Darrow across the desk. "I don't know what you're up to, Mark. But I don't have the time or the manpower to excavate the past. Or, in Tillman's case, a reason. So the next time we discuss him, it'll be because you've got something real to say."

Darrow thanked him. Leaving, he walked swiftly to the parking lot, hoping to beat Taylor to his door.

10

Taylor Farr, Darrow noted, was a punctual woman—at six-thirty she arrived at his door, wearing jeans and a sweater and carrying a thick black binder. Pointing at the binder, Darrow asked, "Is that my homework?"

"More or less," she said briskly. "A survey of post-modern art, culled from the Internet and screened through my quirky sensibilities. But after you called me, I tried to be gentle. There may be something in here that you actually like."

"It's fat enough." Motioning her inside, Darrow said, "Ready to inspect the chamber of horrors?"

She walked past him into the living room, her swift, graceful strides reminding him of both an athlete and a runway model. From the back he watched her look from piece to piece: the pastel watercolor portraying spring; a winsome girl with saucer eyes; the nondescript Swedish modern furniture; the dining room table of blond wood; the glass coffee-table top set on the lacquered stump of a redwood tree; and, over the fireplace, an oil painting of the Reverend Charles Caldwell, his forbidding mien meant to signal rectitude but, to Darrow, more evocative of a hanging judge. She studied the Reverend Caldwell for a good while, her long raven hair tilting with the angle of her head.

"Well?" Darrow asked.

Taylor did not turn. "I'm speechless."

"Try."

Facing him, she knit her brow in mock concentration. "'Dreadful'? No. What word means both 'depressing' and 'horrifying'? The art's insipid, the furniture sterile, and nothing goes together. You're living in the Museum of Modern Dreck." Waving a hand at the Reverend Caldwell, she said, "Then there's him. If you look at him too long, you'll never have sex again. And if you *stay* here too long, you'll kill yourself."

"The thought's occurred to me," Darrow answered solemnly. "Tell me, are art historians always this scathing? Or is this lacerating commentary inspired by my decor?"

Taylor laughed. "Both. There's no art historian typology, really. But all of us tend to be passionate about art, and more than usually opinionated." Placing her binder on the coffee table, she added, "We're also trained to see things, though I think some of that's inherent. Even as a kid, I saw that what I drew wasn't as good as what I could perceive in someone else's work."

"I liked what you painted."

Taylor smiled up at him. "That's because you're inherently nice. You'd have said something kind if I'd painted a lopsided dollhouse with smoke coming out the chimney. But I wasn't an artist, like my mother; I was an interpreter and describer, like my father. Sometimes I think we're too much alike."

For an instant, Darrow thought of Taylor at eight or nine. The image he retained was of a lovely child, serious and very observant, who seemed to harbor more thoughts than she cared to express. "You're certainly less quiet than you were," Darrow remarked lightly. "And very clear about what you think. That's Lionel as I know him."

Taylor's smile was fainter. "So's the quiet. Beneath what my father chooses to express is a bottomless well of silence. I try to guess his thoughts and feelings, and all too often draw a blank. Perhaps he's lonely, an introvert by nature."

Though Darrow shared this sense of Lionel Farr, he had come to accept it as a given. "I've sometimes thought that," he responded. "Though I'm sure it's more perplexing in a parent than a provost. Would you care for some wine, by the way?"

"Yes, thanks. A white, if you have one open."

Darrow went to the kitchen. When he returned, Taylor was flipping pages in her binder, her concentration total. It gave him a moment to consider, once again, the evolution of child to adult. The child Taylor's beauty had a porcelain quality, contained within itself; the woman radiated a more vibrant beauty, a presence that filled a room even when, as now, she was silent.

He sat beside her, placing two glasses on the table. "So," he asked, "you think you're more like Lionel than your mother?"

Taylor took a sip of wine. "I guess I'd *like* to be my mother's daughter, if only because I remember feeling so loved by her. But my dad's a strong personality, and the genetic lottery has whims of its own." She smiled again. "One thing for sure–we both have way too many books. In my case, big ones, filled with paintings. Half my income is spent hauling tomes from place to place."

"Where do you want to end up?"

"I'm not sure yet. It seems like I've got two choices: teaching or a curatorship–the collection side of the museum world."

"Not running an art gallery?"

"God, no," Taylor answered with a laugh. "My senior year at Williams, they took us around to visit people who owned galleries. I met a bunch of glamorous women wearing expensive jewelry and Hermès scarves, more absorbed in bling than scholarship. It was like visiting a club where I could never belong." Her tone became self-mocking. "I'm way too *serious* a person, Mark. I need to work for a museum with a sense of adventure, or teach in a good school in a good city with smart students and colleagues, where I can further refine my extraordinary gifts. With all respect to your new position, I'd go mad in Wayne, Ohio."

"So what constitutes a good city?"

"New York, definitely. There's more *there* there–art, music, theater, varied ethnic influences, and every species of humanity you can think of. Assuming I can afford it."

"What about Boston?"

"It's not a *terrible* city," Taylor allowed. A mischievous smile played on her lips. "On the downside, it's painfully provincial–too many overeducated people with too little to do, except obsessing over the Red Sox and worshipping their ancestors. Plus it's jam-packed with racists, too muggy in the summer, and five degrees too cold in January."

Though intended to tease him, Darrow realized, the description had a certain jaundiced accuracy. "Picky," he said.

"Oh, I'd *look* at Boston, if the job were right. There are some very good schools there. And if the Museum of Fine Arts ever got serious about contemporary works . . ." She stopped, laughing at herself. "As if it's *my* choice. Right now, the only job I have is helping you attack this aesthetic nightmare. Care to look at what I've brought?"

"Sure." Darrow hesitated, then asked, "Are you hungry? I used to know a place that delivers Chinese food."

"In Wayne?" Her voice softened. "I'll stop being a critic, Mark. I'm always up for experiments."

*

LEAFING THROUGH THE pages, they nibbled passable chow mein and snow peas and started a new bottle of sauvignon blanc. To Mark's relief, he liked much of what Taylor had selected as examples of what he might look for: a chromagraphic print by Andreas Gursky of a bank tower at night; an installation by James Turrell, a field of colored light so cleverly designed that its elements looked like phantom shapes; a piece composed of Ektacolor prints by Richard Prince, four beautiful but strikingly different women, their heads tilted in the same direction to appraise some unseen object; a gelatin-silver print by James Casebere; and, though perhaps too challenging to live with, eight black-and-white photographs by the German Anselm Kiefer, together forming a stark portrait of stone and gnarled trees disturbingly evocative of Nazi art. Taken together, Taylor's compilation bespoke a keen eye, considerable aesthetic judgment, and, flattering to Darrow, a great deal of time and thought. Finishing, he imagined himself embarking on a new project with a curiosity and enthusiasm he had not felt since Lee's death.

"Can you leave this here?" he asked. "I'd like to look it over some more."

"Of course. That's why I put it together."

Darrow closed the book. "Thank you, Taylor—really. It's enjoyable to think about redesigning a space again."

Taylor sipped her wine. "What was your town house in Boston like?"

"As light as we could make it, and filled with modern art." He touched the notebook. "Though *not* this modern. Among other things, we had a Vasarely, an Agam, and a Dalí print. But our criteria was less the artist than how we felt about the piece."

"Did you have an art consultant?"

"No. Lee and I made it our project. Fortunately, we had similar tastes—bright colors, bold images, abstract forms. No paintings of horses, hunting parties, dilapidated barns, or pastoral New England. Half the fun was looking at a space and imagining the right piece for it; the other half was finding it. By the end, every object in the house came with its own story."

The smile Taylor gave him seemed reflective, even wistful. "Is that why you didn't bring anything with you? Even photographs?"

"I left in a hurry. I figured there would be time to settle in later." He took another sip of wine, then decided to give Taylor a deeper version of the truth. "To a degree I didn't fully appreciate, at least until now, the town house became the museum of our marriage. But I couldn't seem to change anything, because I couldn't ask Lee about it." He gazed into his wine glass, speaking quietly. "Even her closet stayed the same. Shortly after the first anniversary of her death, I made myself give her clothes to charity. It felt weird, like I was losing another piece of her. I remember staring at the empty closet and not knowing what to do."

Pausing, Darrow felt the ache of memory. Softly, Taylor said, "I'm sorry."

"For asking? Don't be. I never say these things, and maybe I should. Perhaps it would help to talk about her to another human being."

He felt Taylor watching his face. "I remember her, actually."

Darrow looked up at her. "How?"

"Since college, I've been an election junkie. Lee was on MSNBC a lot—I remember thinking how smart she was, with a wicked, almost subversive sense of humor. Not to mention that she was *really* pretty. Anyone would have been drawn to her."

"Oh, they were. The night we met–at a cocktail party, of all things–I had loads of competition."

Taylor smiled at this. "But you won out, of course."

"I had certain natural advantages. Lee and I were both self-invented: kids from small towns whose parents never got past high school, and whose families were utterly dysfunctional." Darrow poured more wine. "Lee was from Virginia, the smartest kid around. Her dad sold insurance; her mother kept the books; Lee worked in the office after school. When she left for the University of Virginia, she never looked back. Ever."

"And you were like that, too."

"Uh-huh, especially after what happened at Caldwell. Both of us hell-bent on the future. We never took success for granted, because we'd never had a lot. That made us different from almost everyone around us–on an almost instinctive level, we got each other." Darrow looked down again. "For Lee, her career was more than an identity. It was the thing that kept her from being like her alcoholic father or, worse, a mother so scarred and narrow that what she felt for Lee was jealousy."

Taylor considered that. "She hardly looked like a woman in danger of regressing."

"No way. Still, on one level I could understand her–as I said, I still have the superstitious sense that I'll become who I was before Lionel changed everything. But Lee had a depth of fear beyond anything she could express, or I could fathom. The idea of becoming her mother tied her in a psychic knot." Almost against his will, Darrow felt himself edging closer to the source of his unspoken pain. "The decision to become pregnant was extremely hard for Lee. But she knew how much I wanted to give a child the love and security I'd never had." His voice softened. "Up to the day she died, I worried that she'd just given in. But I never asked. I was too afraid of the answer, and what it might cause her to do."

All at once, Darrow knew that finishing the story would be too hard. He felt Taylor appraising him and then, without words, deciding not to press him. "Lately," she said, "I've thought about having kids. In a wholly abstract sort of way."

Relieved, Darrow turned to her. "What did you conclude?"

"That I want them. It came to me when I realized that the guy I was involved with imagined being the only child of our marriage. I'd like to be a mother, as good as I believe my mother was. But for the right reasons."

"Which are?"

In Taylor's silence, Darrow watched her framing the answer with care. "For me, parenting can't be a means of making up to myself for what I missed, using my child as a surrogate. There's too much narcissism in the way some people parent, and I don't want to become an obsessive mother. Moms or dads like that too often warp their children, or force them to fill parental needs in some fairly unhealthy ways." After taking a sip of wine, she finished quietly: "The gap between the myth of what family should be and the sad reality of what it often is can be pretty hard on everyone."

Perhaps Taylor was talking about her own family, or the better family she hoped to have. But, however tactfully, she had also held Darrow's own image of fatherhood to the light. He felt torn between the desire to say something and uncertainty about what he wished to say. Then Taylor checked her watch. "I forgot this was a school night, Mark. It's getting late for both of us."

Darrow felt a stab of disappointment. Awkwardly, he said, "I hope we're not finished."

She gave him a swift, sidelong glance. "With your surroundings? We've barely started."

Darrow walked her to the door. "This weekend," he ventured, "why don't we do something?"

Taylor looked amused. "Something? Whatever it is, I'm willing to discuss it."

Later, falling into bed, Darrow felt restless. Then he remembered finding the package Rusty Clark's assistant had left on his doorstep, a partial transcript of Steve Tillman's trial. Turning on the light, he began reading.

11

THE NEXT MORNING, DARROW MET WITH THE PUBLIC relations expert hired to deal with the embezzlement. It was brief and efficient: all statements by the school would come from Darrow himself, whose focus on imposing strict accounting controls seemed to placate restive alumni. But the next meeting, with Provost Farr and faculty department heads, was longer.

It was the last such gathering before the faculty went off for their various summer studies, trips abroad, or retreats to produce works of scholarship. As a group, Darrow had discovered, the heads represented the usual mix of personalities–wry, enthusiastic, detached, rancorous, intemperate, and ingratiating. Though most accepted his proposal to restrict faculty-student dating, their other complaints were many. Some lobbied to improve the lives of students; others, to assert the primacy of their departments in the battle over Caldwell's slim resources. There was not enough money to satisfy them all–or any of them. Instead Darrow solicited a written summary of their departments' needs and ambitions, promising that, in due course, he would consider these in framing an endowment plan–which, however, must also finance his aim to recruit disadvantaged students. They departed in various states of hope and discontent. It was, Farr told him afterward, the best Darrow could hope for.

His workday ended with a conference call from Joe

Betts and Greg Fox, scheduled at Joe's urgent request. With evident satisfaction, Fox reported the discovery of a second account in the name of Caldwell College, opened at the local branch of the First Columbus Bank, for which the signature card bore Clark Durbin's name. "What's different here," Fox explained, "is that the money didn't *leave* for Switzerland–it came back."

"How much?" Darrow asked.

"Fifty thousand dollars, transferred three months ago."

"This clinches it," Joe Betts's voice broke in. "Durbin laundered the money through Switzerland and sent it back to himself in Wayne."

"It seems circular to me," Darrow said. "Why would Durbin do that?"

"Concealment," Joe answered promptly. "He was trying to make it harder to trace the flow of cash. This is the last piece of evidence we need to prosecute."

Darrow scribbled two words on his notepad: "Why Columbus?" Then he asked, "What do you think, Greg?"

"I'm with Joe," Fox answered crisply. "Durbin outsmarted himself. Most embezzlers do."

"True enough," Darrow answered. "I'll let Mike Riley know about this. He'll be in touch with you soon."

"Your guy?" Joe's voice rose slightly. "Do we really need him after this? Seems like a waste of time and money."

"Time, maybe. Not money. I'll pay him myself."

After a moment's silence, Fox allowed a note of strained patience to seep into his voice. "I'll be waiting for his call."

Hanging up, Darrow scribbled, "Missing: $850,000." Then he left a voice message with Mike Riley in Boston, and hurried out the door.

IT WAS A soft summer evening, lightly humid, and the rolling landscape outside Wayne evoked a slice of

Darrow's teenage years: aimless drives with friends, radio blaring, cold six-packs of beer hidden in the trunk while they searched for a place to drink it. But the once-verdant farmland was now dotted with pseudobaronial homes, their acreage demarked by rustic fences—the retreats of Columbus-based businessmen like Joe Betts, designed to suggest the horse country of Kentucky. Only Carly Simmons's place had been there twenty years ago: a rambling white nineteenth-century farmhouse, with a barn that still displayed a worn advertisement for Red Man chewing tobacco, its yellow letters peeling, its fierce-looking Indian head fading into commercial history. The sight made Darrow smile.

Simmons waited in a fenced-off area in front of the barn, throwing a wooden stick to a black terrier who returned it eagerly and repeatedly. As the wheels of Darrow's Porsche crunched the gravel driveway, Simmons turned and waved by way of greeting. Even after sixteen years she looked familiar, though the blond woman who'd once knelt by Angela's body was stockier now, her curls tipped with gray. Her ruddy face flushed from exercise, she gave him a firm handshake.

"So you're president of Caldwell," she said without preface.

"Yup."

"A lot to do, I imagine." Her tone flattened out. "You also found her body, I remember."

Darrow nodded. "It's something you don't forget. Now that I'm back, I've started thinking about all the things I still don't know."

"Don't blame you," Simmons said matter-of-factly. "It was one of my first cases, and it sticks in the mind. Partly because of the victim, partly because I pretzeled myself to get things right."

The statement was factual, and undefensive. But her large brown eyes seemed to examine him closely. "So," she finished, "you're back, and now you're nagged by unanswered questions. What do you want to know?"

"Several things," Darrow said, "in no particular order. For example, how drunk was Angela before she died?"

The terrier nudged Simmons's leg, stick between its teeth. Reaching down, Simmons retrieved the piece of wood and threw it toward the fence. "Drunk enough," she answered. "It's hard to be precise. But tests on the two glasses we found in Steve's room showed they'd both kept on drinking. Though from the toxicology report, Angela had begun to metabolize the alcohol before she died."

Darrow watched the dog scamper for the stick, tail bobbing. "What does that tell you?"

The lines at the corners of Simmons's eyes deepened slightly. "That she'd stopped consuming alcohol. Also, possibly, that she'd had some form of physical activity."

"Like walking?"

"Maybe. Or sex."

"How drunk was Steve?"

Simmons smiled faintly. "That was kind of critical, given his story. You don't black out on a couple of Miller Lites. Let alone suffer gaps in memory." She paused, ordering her thoughts. "By his own account, Tillman was a seasoned drinker, much more so than she was. That means he metabolized alcohol more quickly.

"By the time we took his blood sample, maybe nine hours later, he was a hair below the legal limit of .08 blood alcohol concentration. Once you stop drinking, you drop about .0125 every hour. So put Tillman up around 2.0 at the height of his intoxication."

"That's pretty drunk."

Simmons nodded. "I can't tell you at what point the

kid's lights would start going out. But yeah, that's pretty drunk. Not to mention he'd done some coke."

"So we've got a drunk with a bum knee lugging a dead body around campus."

Simmons threw the stick again. "So they say. Maybe the coke jacked him up. I don't try the cases; I just do the corpses."

"Any chance she was strangled near the Spire?"

The question made her turn, eyes focused on the question. "Are you familiar with the concept of lividity?"

"Uh-huh. Once the heart stops pumping, gravity governs the flow of blood. Depending on the position of the body, blood flows to its lowest point." Darrow shoved his hands into his pockets. "I found Angela lying face-up. So the blood should have gravitated to her back."

"Which it did."

"Nowhere else?"

Simmons slowly shook her head. "I checked her fingers and toes. No lividity."

"What did *that* suggest?"

Crossing her arms, Simmons ignored the dog at her feet. "There are two possibilities. The first is that the killer carried Angela to where you found her quickly enough that the blood didn't flow to her extremities. The second is that she was strangled much closer to the Spire."

Darrow felt his instincts quicken. "So there's no medical evidence affirmatively suggesting that she was carried there?"

Simmons shook her head again. "I can't rule that out. Nor can I rule it in."

Watching the terrier paw Simmons's pant leg for attention, Darrow tried to organize his thoughts. "What about time of death?" he asked.

Simmons threw the stick again. "That's more art than

science. We go on body temperature. But there's all sorts of variables: ambient air temperature, moving air currents, type of clothing, how long the body had been outside. Angela was slender, causing her body to cool more quickly. But she was wearing a heavy coat. So it was hard to be exact."

Listening to the vicissitudes of science, Darrow remembered Angela herself–her face at the party so human and vulnerable, in death a mask of agony.

"The range we settled on," Simmons continued, "was that she'd been dead from six to twelve hours. But my best estimate was she'd died between two and three A.M. Which, as it turned out, was more or less consistent with the trial testimony."

"From Joe Betts, you mean?"

"Yeah, and that waitress."

"What waitress?" Darrow asked in surprise.

Simmons threw the stick still farther, grunting with exertion. "I forget her name–she worked the night shift at Donut King. As best I recall, she was taking a shortcut across campus. She claimed to have seen the outline of a man beneath the Spire laying down what looked like a body."

"What time was it?"

"Shortly after three A.M., I think she said."

Darrow struggled to reorganize the puzzle pieces to accommodate a new one. Joe Betts claimed to have seen Steve outside the dorm around three o'clock; apparently the waitress believed that an unidentified man had deposited Angela's body a few minutes later. But, despite this contradiction, both accounts suggested that Angela had been carried to the Spire. At length, Darrow asked bluntly, "Was Angela raped?"

Simmons pursed her lips. "There was evidence

consistent with rape. That the sperm was Tillman's only proved they'd had sex. Ditto that both their pubic areas contained each other's hair. But there were scratches on his back, and skin under her fingernails—Tillman's, according to the DNA. Add the contusion on her cheek and you can come up with a sexual assault."

"What about forcible penetration?"

"There weren't any vaginal tears. That doesn't mean the sex was consensual. Angela wasn't a virgin, it's clear. And she could have given in to avoid a beating, or just passed out. That's still rape. But you just can't know."

"Yeah. I keep hearing that."

Kneeling, Simmons took the stick from the terrier's mouth, ruffling the fur on its neck. "Enough, Diablo. You're wearing me out." She stood again, gazing at the landscape in the gently slanting light. Evenly, she said, "We didn't have all the medical evidence we might want. But there was an absence of any evidence helpful to Tillman. There was no one else's DNA on Angela's body. I tried to get something off her neck—the murderer's fingerprint, or even DNA from the moisture on his fingers. Either one could have further inculpated Tillman or, conceivably, exculpated him. But those were long shots, and neither panned out." She gave a fatalistic shrug. "So we lived with what we had. With the witnesses, it turned out to be enough."

Darrow absorbed this in silence. After a moment, Simmons faced him again. "There's something else you should think about," she said. "Ever try to strangle someone?"

"I've considered it once or twice."

Simmons's expression became grim. "It's an extremely unpleasant act—for both the victim and the murderer. To asphyxiate another human being by strangulation takes about three minutes. The killer doesn't just need to be strong–he needs to be determined. Whoever decided that Angela Hall needed killing remained firm in his intentions despite ample opportunity to reconsider. Even a drunk had time for second thoughts." Finishing, Simmons spoke coolly and incisively: "What that means, Mr. Darrow, is that first-degree murder was the appropriate verdict. This was an intentional homicide, carried out by someone who wanted to make sure this young woman never saw another day, or spoke another word. The murderer was either very cold-blooded or very angry. Maybe both."

Darrow thanked her.

Driving to his empty residence, he watched the blue-gray of twilight envelop the horizon. He already knew what part of the trial transcript he would read.

12

In the morning, Darrow tried to set aside what he had discovered in the trial transcript. He began his workday by reviewing Joe Betts's plan to tighten Caldwell's financial safeguards; with one addition, which Darrow scrawled in the margins, it seemed prudent and comprehensive. Then he prepared to meet with Fred Bender, now Caldwell's head of security, by scanning the campus safety program—which, he knew, tracked what Farr had suggested to Clark Durbin on the morning of Angela's murder. Finishing, Darrow reflected that both plans, sound in themselves, existed to prevent disasters that had already occurred.

The next problem on his desk, though new, had been exacerbated by the old ones. The campus employees no one thought much about—the maintenance crew, cafeteria workers, and distributors of campus mail—were seeking a raise they clearly deserved; Caldwell had little money to give them. Picking up the phone, Darrow asked Farr what the employees might accept.

"Whatever we give them," Farr answered bluntly. "The job market's brutal; their skills minimal; the economic trends Darwinian, winnowing out the less gifted or educated. Your faculty—which also deserves more money—knows that. So does our board of trustees. Give them a choice between a happy maintenance staff or renovating a building, bricks and mortar will win every time."

"Maybe so," Darrow said. "But why should I choose *for* them? If they want to screw these people, let them say so."

"Why expend your political capital on mere charity?" Farr replied sardonically. "Especially when you're telling the board to put off a new capital campaign. Besides which, as of an hour ago, you can't afford an act of human kindness."

"Because?"

"A leaky pipe in the IT center has caused the supports to rot. Which means, I'm afraid, moving our entire computer system, at considerable expense, infuriating whatever department whose office space you jam it into. And, of course, the board will blame our maintenance crew, however underpaid and understaffed they happen to be. George Armstrong Custer himself wouldn't ask Ray Carrick to approve a raise."

The sense of choicelessness, Darrow found, deepened the depression seeping into his brain. "First things first, then. We'd better solve the IT problem."

As though registering Darrow's mood, Farr said equably, "It's four-thirty now. Why not come for a drink at six. We can figure this out then."

Why not? Darrow thought. A martini could not hurt, and he would not mind seeing Taylor. "By six," he responded dryly, "I'll expect you to have answers for all our problems."

WHEN DARROW ARRIVED, Taylor was nowhere in sight.

The evening was warm and breezy. Ties loosened, Darrow and Farr sat in the intricately landscaped backyard, Anne Farr's legacy—Farr drinking Scotch, Darrow a martini. By the second drink, the two men had moved the IT center to the basement of the old art building and resolved to defer any pay increases with a promise of better raises in better times. Sipping his martini, Darrow paused a moment, then spoke to the roots of his disquiet. "The last couple of nights," he told Farr, "I've been reading Steve Tillman's trial transcript."

Farr's eyebrows shot up. "Oh?"

"Call it a professional compulsion. Now that I'm back, I can't help thinking about how Steve got where he is."

Farr studied him. "Reach any conclusions?"

"No. But I have some distinct impressions."

"Such as?"

As Darrow ordered his thoughts, the door from the sunroom opened and Taylor Farr stepped onto the brick patio, miming shock at the sight of sunlight. "I've been locked up with my dissertation all day," she announced. "Hibernation isn't meant for summer." Turning to Darrow, she said, "Hello, Mark. Hope you've taken the Reverend Caldwell off your wall."

"I'm giving him to you," Darrow answered her. "As thanks for all the advice you gave me the other night."

Taylor laughed. Farr looked from Darrow to his daughter, eyes keen and head slightly tilted, as if listening to notes no one else could hear. After a moment, he asked, "Care for a drink, Taylor?"

"White wine, thanks. I'll get it myself."

As she left, Farr resumed his appraisal of Darrow. "You said you had 'impressions.'"

"Several. What they add up to is whether Steve should have been convicted at all."

Farr cradled his drink, unsipped for the last few moments. "The jury thought so. Frankly, so did I. The evidence seemed good enough."

Taylor emerged with a glass of wine. Gauging the two men's expressions, she sat at the edge of the wooden table, watching them in silence. "Maybe in the abstract," Darrow was saying to Farr. "The key witnesses against Steve were the two homicide cops, principally Fred Bender; Carly Simmons, the pathologist; a waitress returning home from the doughnut shop; and, critically, Joe Betts."

"There were also Steve's own statements to the police," Farr amended.

"True, and they weren't helpful to him. But the essence of the case was this: Angela left the party with Steve. They went to his room. They drank some more and had sex, leaving scratches on Steve's back and, perhaps, a bruise on Angela's face. To the police, that suggested rape, as did the fact that the room was disordered and Steve's bedside lamp knocked over.

"Two witnesses strung these pieces together. The waitress claimed to have seen a man about Steve's size and build setting down a body near the Spire around three A.M. But Joe Betts was the clincher: by swearing he saw Steve returning to his room from the direction of the Spire, he made Steve out to be a liar–and therefore a murderer. Without Joe, Steve might well have walked."

Still quiet, Taylor looked from Darrow to her father. "But there *was* Joe," Farr proferred mildly. "The only alternatives are that *he* was lying or that Steve didn't remember leaving his room. The latter's not plausible."

"Assuming he'd returned from carrying a body. Suppose he was just a drunk in search of fresh air–which was Joe's stated reason for sticking his head out the window."

Left unanswered were the implications of Farr's first alternative. Carefully, Farr asked, "Who else do you suppose wanted to kill Angela?"

"That *is* the question," Darrow concurred, "as Dave Farragher emphasized in his closing argument. 'Don't leave your common sense at home,' he told the jury. 'Do you really believe Angela just wandered away and was strangled at random?' "

Narrow-eyed, Farr put down his tumbler, contemplating its contents. "Perhaps I'm out of my depth. But I was there, and I watched the jury's faces. For me, the key was when Dave said something like 'Sometime during your deliberations, I want you to remain silent for one hundred and eighty seconds, the time it took the murderer to choke the life from Angela Hall. Then ask yourself these questions: Was her death the product of a momentary impulse or was the murderer implacably determined to kill her? And would a murder so deliberate, so remorseless, so angry, and so intimate be committed by a stranger?' What's *your* answer, Mark?"

Darrow felt Taylor watching him closely, her own mind at work. "If *that's* the question, Lionel, my answer is clearly no."

Farr nodded briskly. "Meaning that whoever strangled Angela knew her and was driven by what seemed to him—and it's fair to assume it was a him, given the strength it took—an extremely powerful motive. Who else but Steve Tillman?"

Darrow chose not to answer. During his silence, Taylor looked at the two men's empty glasses. "Can I offer either of you a refill?" she asked. "Perhaps some wine?"

Intent now, Darrow shook his head, glancing at Farr.

"No," Farr said curtly. "Thank you."

After giving her father a swift glance, Taylor turned to Mark. "What *did* the defense lawyer do?" she asked.

"Nothing good," Darrow replied. "If Nordlinger did any pretrial investigation, it isn't evident from the transcript. When he called on Steve in his own defense, Steve wasn't prepared for what happened to him."

"Which was?"

"Accusations of racism," Darrow said crisply. "Farragher went after all the times in high school someone heard him say 'nigger.' He also forced Steve to admit that he had confronted George Garrison about asking out his sister."

Taylor finished her wine. "Not pretty. But that doesn't make Tillman a murderer."

"Exactly. If it did, back in the nineties a chunk of our population would have been on death row. At the least, Nordlinger should have objected like crazy."

"On what grounds?" Farr inquired. "That there's a difference between racial animus and murder? Or that wanting to sleep with a black woman is the opposite of wanting to kill her?"

"The legal frame," Darrow answered, "is that racist statements are more 'prejudicial than probative'–they create bias against Steve without providing any evidence of murder. I knew *that* much before I passed the bar."

Farr sat back, emitting a barely audible sigh. "You drive me to a painful admission. During the trial, Griff Nordlinger didn't look right to me–I thought he might be sick, literally. Months later I heard that his marriage was falling apart, and that the cause might be some serious substance abuse. If I'd suspected that Griff might have been impaired, I never would have suggested he take Steve's case. But by then the trial was over.

"On appeal, the public defender's office replaced Griff. I told myself his problems didn't matter–or, if they did, that the appellate courts would consider them. And I believed then, as I do now, that Steve Tillman strangled Angela." He glanced at Taylor, and his voice went softer still. "Racism makes savagery more thinkable. So do cocaine and alcohol–beyond question, Steve had overindulged in both. If he was guilty, I concluded, Griff's overindulgence was beside the point."

Uncharacteristically, Farr sounded pained. Choosing silence, Darrow felt Taylor watching his face. "If *you* had been Steve's lawyer," she asked him, "how would you have defended him?"

It was the same question Darrow had asked himself. Mindful of Farr's sensitivities, he organized his thoughts. "It's not an easy case," he acknowledged. "There are only so many defenses: 'somebody else did it'; 'I did it, but I'm insane'; 'I did it for a good reason'; or, as Nordlinger tried, 'reasonable doubt.' I would have combined 'reasonable doubt' with 'somebody else did it.'

"You'd start by attacking the physical evidence. There's no doubt Steve and Angela had sex. But she had no vaginal tears, and the scratches she left on his back might simply have reflected Angela's involvement in the moment."

A corner of Taylor's mouth twitched. "Is that often your experience?"

Darrow smiled faintly. "As to Steve's messy room, my experience–and I'm sure yours–is that college boys have messy rooms and drunks knock over lamps. The physical evidence, by itself, does nothing to establish murder."

"What about the bruise on Angela's face?"

"That's more problematic, I'll admit. But how did she get it? She could have bumped into a wall."

"Or Tillman could have hit her," Taylor interrupted coolly. "As a prelude to rape. And what about the witnesses?"

In the enveloping dusk, Darrow noted, Farr had dropped out of the conversation, watching the exchange between Darrow and his daughter. "Contrary to popular belief," Darrow answered, "eyewitness testimony is pretty unreliable. And what did the witnesses actually say? The waitress merely claimed she saw a shadowy figure of about Steve's size and stature–which, as it happens, could also describe the two men on either side of you.

"Only Joe Betts claims to have actually seen Steve. But Joe was neither reliable nor unbiased–he was as drunk as Steve, and they'd fought over Angela just hours before. Even if you believe Joe's story, placing Steve outside the dorm doesn't put his fingers around Angela's throat." After glancing at Farr to underscore his point, Darrow again faced Taylor. "Let me ask you this: If Steve Tillman raped Angela in his dorm room–given the freezing night, the only location that makes sense–what does it tell you that she was found by the Spire, fully dressed?"

"That Steve carried her there–"

"Despite his leg and his condition?"

Taylor gave him a mock-patient look. "What I was going to say, before being interrupted, is that what's strange to me is the 'dressed' part."

Darrow smiled again. "Why's that?"

"Because it suggests that she dressed herself following sex, perhaps a rape. Which means that Steve didn't kill her during, or immediately after, whatever happened in his bed."

Beside her gifts in her chosen field, Darrow was perceiving, Taylor had Farr's talent for linear thought–though not a lawyer, she had swiftly integrated the known facts with the probabilities of human nature. "Or," Darrow added, "that she was dressed when they had sex."

"Then why the scratches on his back? If it was consensual, they'd both be naked. And if it was rape, why would he undress?"

Darrow had considered this. "There's a grim alternative–that Steve forced her to undress, raped her, then strangled her. After which he dressed her body and carried it to the Spire."

Taylor shook her head. "Unlikely. Dressing a corpse can't be easy. It also suggests a cold-blooded guy with real presence of mind. That doesn't sound like a drunk to me." Taylor's face closed. "I can't tell you about the scratches. But like most women, I've been in a couple of scary situations with a guy who couldn't hear no. I've sometimes wondered what I'd have done if things had spun out of control."

Darrow brushed away this unwelcome image. "What did you conclude?"

"That I might have given in, however much I hated it, rather than have someone beat me up or tear my vagina to shreds. She also might have passed out before penetration." She turned to Farr. "Sorry, Dad. But the lack of vaginal injury tells me nothing."

Both Farr and Darrow fell quiet again. "After all this it may seem odd," Taylor told them, "but I'm getting hungry. You must be, too. Mind if I order a pizza?"

Farr looked distracted, as though lost in the exchange between Darrow and Taylor. "Pizza's fine," he said. "Mark?"

"Anything you want," Darrow told Taylor. "Vegetarian's okay with me."

Taylor flashed a smile. "That's very thoughtful. But I'm a carnivore, remember? On our first 'date' we both ate steak."

Standing, Taylor went back into the house. Darrow followed her with his eyes, then became aware that Farr was watching him watch his daughter, his own expression thoughtful and enigmatic.

*

After lighting a candle, Taylor poured three glasses of chardonnay, then distributed slices of pepperoni pizza. "So," she asked Darrow, "what did the prosecutor say Steve's motive was?"

"He didn't," Darrow said. "Your dad makes a good argument that people in extremity are capable of the worst. But the Steve Tillman I knew was never abusive to women or aggressive toward anyone off the football field. And Farragher found no one to say otherwise. That makes strangling Angela a pretty startling anomaly.

"You asked how I would have defended Steve. After raising reasonable doubt, I'd have hammered on motive, then tried to find an alternative suspect. If Nordlinger had done that with any plausibility, my guess is that they'd have acquitted Steve."

Farr did not touch his pizza. "What I keep returning to," he said slowly, "is that two courts of appeals upheld the guilty verdict."

"True," Darrow answered. "But Nordlinger lost the appeal by screwing up the trial. Appellate courts don't reopen the evidence. They just review the record before them–in this case, one made by a skilled prosecutor and a lousy defense lawyer, perhaps an impaired one. And judges don't like finding lawyers inadequate. Even–and this is an actual death-penalty appeal in Texas–a drunk who slept through his client's trial. If there *was* enough evidence to keep Steve in jail, they don't care what the trial was like. And there was enough evidence–barely."

Farr stared at the flickering candle. "Then perhaps there's nothing for it," he said at length. "I'm sorry, Mark. But I can't help thinking about all you're facing in the here and now, and all the board and alumni expect you to do for Caldwell. If they sense you've been distracted from that, they'll never understand the reason."

Darrow felt nettled, perhaps because he saw the truth of this. “I don’t expect them to,” he answered. “And they won’t have to. I’ll do the job I came to do. But two years ago, Lionel, life conspired to give me some spare time. So instead of reading bedtime stories to a two-year-old boy, I’m reading trial transcripts.

“I was once a criminal lawyer, and Steve Tillman was once my friend. Knowing he’ll die in prison after a trial like this one gives me a restless conscience.”

Taylor, Darrow noticed, had become pensive. She remained so throughout dinner.

13

IN THE EARLY-MORNING LIGHT, DARROW STOOD BY his mother's untended grave.

Oak Hill Cemetery was quiet. A few robins chirped; the damp overgrown grass had a fresh day's sheen of newness. NEILA DARROW, the headstone read, WIFE OF GEORGE, MOTHER OF MARK. No one knew George Darrow's whereabouts. Steve Tillman's parents had paid for the marker; they knew better than to make more elaborate claims.

"Well," Darrow said softly. "I'm back."

But she would not have known him. Even in his teens she barely did; the insanity that enveloped her made her perceptions a distorted mirror. And the Mark Darrow gazing at her worn headstone was, as he had acknowledged to Taylor, his own invention—even Darrow's erudition of speech, a departure from his plainspoken youth, was derived from listening to Lionel Farr, and summer nights spent reading the books Farr suggested. Neila had given him life and, Darrow profoundly hoped, little else: her last years had frightened him almost as much as how she had chosen to end them. Surely he had transcended her madness, her terrible dissociation from others.

But only Neila had a son.

Enough, he told himself. The past was done. He would spend this day, then whatever days fate gave him, as best he could.

He went to meet Fred Bender.

*

SITTING BESIDE BENDER on the bench where they had first met, Darrow had the ironic perception that—despite his credo, and by his own acts—his past had resumed tugging at his present.

Bender smoked a Camel. His once-red hair was steel gray; the mottled skin of his face was so close to the bone that it evoked a mummy. But the seen-it-all cop's eyes staring from this weathered carapace remained a clear and lucid blue.

"President Darrow," he commented wryly. "Who knew."

"Who indeed. It's 'Mark,' by the way. Like on the day you questioned me."

Bender took a drag, then exhaled. "A long time now."

"A long, safe time. Thanks to you, in part."

As two female students passed by, laughing, Bender watched with the air of a silent guardian. "More thanks to Lionel Farr. The campus security plan he designed has stood the test of years. Phones every hundred yards, a buddy system, and monitors at campus entry points."

"The technology's different," Darrow pointed out.

"True. Now we use computers to warn students of any problems and remind them of what they shouldn't do—drinking too much or tearing up their dorms. But we still deal with our issues in-house. Parents don't send their kids here so we can turn them over to the Wayne police." He gave a faintly sarcastic laugh. "No matter how many FBI training courses Garrison sends them to.

"What's different is that Caldwell's stopped being a sanctuary for bad behavior. Angela Hall's murder started with drugs and alcohol. Now we bust kids for public intoxication, conduct periodic sweeps for drugs, monitor fraternity parties, discipline underage kids for going to places like the Alibi Club, and let outsiders like Carl Hall know that they're not welcome here. All that's Lionel's doing–the Hall murder hit him hard. I just oversee things."

Darrow gazed up at the Spire. "How'd you come to take the job?" he inquired. "With all that Lionel's done, seems like Caldwell might be too quiet."

Bender took a ravenous puff, flicking ashes off his sport coat. "After the Tillman trial was done, he approached me about coming here. Farr's pitch was pretty much the same, I guess, as the one he just gave you–you can have all the systems you want in place, but it's people who inspire confidence. Even with the school's fiscal crunch, he dangled more money than I was making, then sold the idea to Durbin." He paused, adding softly, "Who knew about *him,* either.

"Anyhow, I came here. Since then we've had a couple of assaults, a few brawls, and our share of petty theft. But no rapes in sixteen years. And, thank God, no murders."

"Seems like Lionel and you made my job a little easier."

Bender shrugged. "Lionel Farr is a leader. Guess he's been one since he left West Point. Hope you can do as well."

Darrow found that Bender's awe of Farr both nettled and amused him. "That's what I'm praying for," he answered mildly. "I still can't walk on water, but I'm learning how to skate."

Eyeing Darrow anew, Bender gave a hollow chuckle. "Somehow I think you'll do just fine. So what else can I do for you?"

Fred Bender was no fool, Darrow reminded himself. "I know it's ancient history. But Steve Tillman was my closest friend, and being here brings all that back. Especially because I helped put him where he is–"

"Tillman," Bender interrupted harshly, "put himself

there—not you, and not us. We just followed his bread crumbs."

"Mind if we talk about that?"

"You're the boss. Anything in particular?"

"Several things. I'm curious about what you did after you questioned me."

Bender ground out the cigarette butt on the sidewalk, then tossed it into a metal trash bin, a smoker retrained. "We started wondering about you—it wouldn't be the first time the real killer dropped the dime on somebody else. So we sent George Garrison to the DBE house to ask about what you did the night before." He paused, then added with satiric wonder, "George Garrison as chief is another 'who knew.' But George more or less cleared you. By then we'd been to Tillman's room."

As though reverting in time, Darrow felt events closing around his friend. "How was he?"

Bender lit another cigarette. "Seemed pretty fucked up. His room sure was—broken lamp, sheets half off his bed, drink glasses on the floor, a trace of white powder on his desk. With the naked eye I could see come stains on the mattress, a couple of dark hairs on the pillow that didn't look like his. Even before we brought in the forensics people, you could feel that something might have happened in that room."

Darrow tried to envision this. "Think we can take a look?"

Bender appraised him, then shrugged. "Why not—I've got the keys. The walk will give me time to finish off my smoke."

DARROW AND BENDER stood at the base of the football field. Inserting a key, Bender gave the door a savage jerk, and then Darrow stepped into his own past.

The entryway was barren, the lights dim, the tile as scuffed and worn as he remembered. Turning to his right, he walked through the bleak corridor toward Steve Tillman's room, as the young Mark Darrow had countless times before.

The door was unlocked. Pushing it open, Darrow found–in place of the bed and desk and posters summoned by his mind's eye–a storeroom jammed with ancient audiovisual equipment. Memory plays tricks, Darrow reflected–the room was smaller than he remembered. Stale air filled his nostrils. Darrow's stomach felt sour.

"Different," Bender observed. "No one's lived here since she died here."

The thought haunted him, Darrow found. Drawing a breath, he sat on a giant loudspeaker that lay sideways, gazing through the open door. Arms folded, Bender leaned against the cinder-block wall. "Bring back memories?"

"I'm more interested in yours. Remind me of what the crime lab found."

"A lot of what I already knew. The sperm was Tillman's; the hairs, Angela's. Two glasses contained traces of rum and Coke; the powder turned out to be cocaine."

"What about fingerprints?"

"Yup. His and hers, each on one of the glasses."

Pensive, Darrow tried to imagine Steve and Angela's drunken arrival and, crediting Steve's story, her mystifying departure. Once more his eyes lit on the doorway. "What about on the doors?" he asked. "Both to the dorm and to Steve's room. On the outside *and* the inside."

Bender's eyes glinted. "Let me see if I follow you. The lab might well find Tillman's prints on both sides of those doors or doorknobs–after all, he came and went all the time. But not Angela. Her prints on the inside of either door might suggest she'd left here still alive. You're wondering if we thought of that, and what we might have found."

"All these years, Fred, and you're still ahead of me."

Bender smiled without humor. "Yes, we thought of that. And no, she left no prints on the inside of either door. Finding prints is hit or miss. But we found no evidence that she'd left this room alive. Unless you count Tillman's illogical story."

"You said he was 'fucked up.' Does that mean disoriented?"

"Maybe that. He still seemed drunk to me, like he couldn't compute what was happening. His account was Swiss cheese–he claimed to remember almost nothing. But he had a small-town boy's manner: open, respectful of authority, hoping you'd like him. You didn't want to believe how things were beginning to look for him."

"But you *did* believe it."

Bender's eyes narrowed slightly. "In other words, did we consider other suspects or just take the easy way out."

"Not my question," Darrow answered. "All I know is that Angela was killed on Saturday and Farragher charged Steve with murder the following Thursday."

"That's Farragher. For our part we worked around the clock, interviewing anyone who might know anything at all–Angela's friends, the other kids at the party, her mother, her scumbag of a brother. Joe Betts, you already know about.

"Our big focus was Angela Hall herself. You had to figure she'd been strangled for a reason. So we went all over her life and anything she'd left behind–her room, her calendar, her medical records, her checkbook. We even tracked down an old boyfriend whose name we found on a postcard, and delved into their sex life." He took out the pack of cigarettes. "Before you ask, she left no scratches on his back. Or so he claimed."

Bender, Darrow saw, could track his thoughts with ease. "What about her academics?" Darrow asked. "Any changes?"

"We looked for that, too. We checked out her files and talked to her professors for the last couple of semesters—including Farr, who also ran the committee that reauthorized her scholarship every year. We found no sign of trouble, and nobody thought different. In fact, I seem to recall her grades were on the rise."

Stymied, Darrow sifted his impressions of Angela. "At the party, she seemed troubled to me—like drinking was an act of self-obliteration. Was there a hint of any new problems in her life?"

For an instant, Bender hesitated. "We couldn't be sure. Her mother said she'd started going out in the middle of the night—one A.M., two A.M. College kids do that. But this was new for her, Mom said, and Angela wouldn't tell her where or why."

Darrow felt his nerve ends tingle. "Did you ever figure it out?"

Bender frowned. "No. We looked for suggestions of a drug problem, or even that she'd turned to hooking. No evidence of either—she seemed like a different proposition than her brother."

"And yet she'd started leaving at nights, and never saying why. Did you ever find anyone who'd admitted seeing her?"

"Nobody. That seemed to haunt her mother." Reaching into the pack of Camels, Bender began fidgeting with an unlit cigarette. "According to Mom, when Angela was younger she'd kept a diary hidden beneath her mattress.

Her mother thought that she still did, though she swore she'd never read it. That was hard to believe—my wife sure as hell would have. But the woman was absolutely torn up—if she'd read the diary, she kept saying, maybe she could have saved her daughter."

"Based on what?"

"Grief and helplessness. Anyhow, we never found a diary. Wish we had. But we couldn't chase after something that might never have existed—or if it did, might not have told us anything of value. Whichever one, sure as hell the murderer didn't make it disappear."

"Did you ask her brother about it?"

"Yup. He gave us nothing: no diary, no boyfriends, except maybe Tillman. We had to lean on him about his drug dealing to even get him to talk about his murdered sister. All we got was what we already knew: that Carl was a greedy little shit. Which he still is, only now he's a prosperous little shit." Bender's lips compressed. "Too bad. What with his dislike of whites and his connections with bad people, I thought *he* might have something to do with her murder. That would have suited me fine."

Darrow considered this. "Where'd Carl go after the party?"

"Home, he said. To bed. We never found out different."

"Just like Joe Betts," Darrow observed. "That's how he got to be a witness. While we're here, mind if we look at his room?"

For a moment, Bender watched Darrow's eyes. Then he shrugged. "Why not," he answered. "If we open that window, I can smoke this cigarette."

14

DARROW AND BENDER LEANED OUT THE WINDOW OF Joe Betts's old room on the second floor, Bender smoking, Darrow watching a few summer students, clad in shorts and T-shirts, taking the pathways that radiated from the Spire. Shadowed by trees, its base was barely visible—the distance, Farr had calculated, was roughly two hundred yards. Darrow tried to imagine the scene on the night of Angela's murder.

"Exactly where," he asked Bender, "did Joe say he saw Steve?"

Bender pointed to a spot a few feet from the entrance. Gazing down, Darrow observed, "Seems like you'd mostly see the top of someone's head. There weren't any outdoor lights then, right?"

"Just by the door itself."

"And the moon?"

"Full." Bender took a drag, exhaling the smoke away from Darrow. "Muhlberg and I tried it two nights later, and I could make out who he was. It helped that I knew him. But Betts knew Tillman, too."

Darrow turned to him. "But if Steve was close enough to identify, Joe couldn't know which direction he was coming from—let alone that he was returning from the Spire. For all Joe knew, Steve could have been outside throwing up."

"No upchuck in the grass," Bender said tersely. "Or

footprints we could trace to anyone—the ground was semi-frozen. As I said, we were thorough."

"But thanks to Joe you had your murderer?"

Bender did not react to this. Instead, he asked, "Back then, how well did you know Joe Betts?"

"Pretty well."

"Did you like him?"

Darrow parsed his feelings, then and now, conscious of their implications. "It depended on the moment. And whether he'd been drinking."

Bender flicked an ash. "Really? Betts was more or less sober when we found him. And I still thought he was a dick."

Surprised, Darrow asked, "How so?"

"He had attitude—not like Tillman at all. Betts was an East Coast kid, a preppy out of some rich suburb in Connecticut. We still get them at Caldwell—too lazy as students to make the Ivy League, thinking they're above whatever team they're playing on." Bender's tone was flat. "That was Joe Betts—he thought just getting born had made him better than anyone. That was his attitude toward us."

"Still, he gave you Tillman."

With a thin smile, Bender rejoined, "At first he gave us nothing. Based on what you'd told us, we started by asking him about the party. He refused to talk. Next thing we knew, his uncle had the kid lawyered up—a criminal defense specialist out of Columbus, expensive and smart. The lawyer kept him on ice for twenty-four hours, refusing to let us take a polygraph or meet with Betts at all.

"Finally, we let it drop to your old coach that Betts was looking good for the crime—a little psychology, to loosen Betts up. Like we knew he would, Coach Fiske passed the word. That was when Betts and his lawyer decided to give up Tillman."

Darrow recalled Joe's confession the day of Steve's arrest; Joe had told him none of this. "Didn't that make you skeptical?"

Bender laughed softly. "Back then everything about Joe Betts made me skeptical. Especially when he claimed to have stonewalled us just to keep from getting his friend Tillman in trouble. But his story cemented a decent circumstantial case. The question for us–and Farragher–was whether to believe it."

"Which you did," Darrow said.

"Not at first. We'd checked out *his* life, too–he was a bad drunk, it was pretty clear, and he'd just broken up with his girlfriend. Fighting with Tillman over Angela Hall made him the leading alternative; his story might have been intended to frame Steve for a murder Betts had committed." Bender took another puff. "Thing is, we never found anything tying Joe to the murder. No witness, no physical evidence. Nothing to say that he didn't walk back to his dorm room, like he told us, to try and sleep it off."

"Did anyone see him come in?"

"No. But as far as we could tell, no one saw him anywhere at all. We know he wasn't with Angela. Tillman was."

Darrow cocked his head. "What did Laurie Shilts tell you?"

"Joe's girlfriend? Nothing much. According to her, their breakup was nothing dramatic–she couldn't see a future, I guess you'd say."

"That's a way of putting it. Happen to notice a bruise on her cheek?"

"No." Bender turned to him, openly curious. "I remember she was wearing a lot of makeup."

"Maybe that day."

"So you're telling me Betts hit her?" Bender asked bluntly. "Just like we figure the murderer hit Angela."

Darrow fell quiet, reflecting on his moments with Laurie. *Deep down,* she had told him, *Joe hates women.* "Laurie never said," he answered. "But that was my impression."

For a time, Bender appraised him keenly. "You had more on your mind than we knew, didn't you?"

Remembering his calls to Steve, Darrow felt his unease deepen. "Maybe so. But I didn't know what it meant, or anything about Joe's story. Since then I've gotten better at stringing things together."

"So it seems."

Beneath Bender's tone, though mild, Darrow heard a note of accusation. Quietly, he asked, "What do you know about Joe's father?"

"Only that he was dead." Bender's voice became weary. "I guess you're also going to tell me the old man beat Joe's mother."

"According to Joe. No reason to lie about that."

"*That* would have been of interest. You and I both know that men who abuse women often learned from Dad." After stubbing his cigarette out on the windowsill, Bender put it in the pocket of his sport coat. "But if it makes you feel better, in the end none of this would have mattered. We had nothing on Betts except the fight over Angela Hall. The only DNA we could get from her body belonged to Tillman. When the crime lab scoured Betts's room and found nothing, the one surprise was how neat it was.

"As a suspect, Betts looked better than he turned out to be—at least based on what we could find. And what would his motive have been? He'd have to have been so pissed off about what happened at the party that, four hours later, he followed Angela when she left the dorm and strangled her near the Spire. Even if you can imagine that, there's no evidence that it happened. That leaves Tillman."

Darrow found himself gazing at the Spire, burnished in the sunlight above the trees. "Maybe it does. But the scenario I still have trouble with is that Steve Tillman strangled her, dressed her, and then decided to deposit her body at the foot of the most iconic structure on Caldwell's campus."

Turning, Bender had a small, grim smile. "Who's to say he dressed her? You and I will never know what happened in that room. But, if you're interested, I can tell you what I think went on between the two of them."

Darrow felt a new tautness, interest combined with dread. "Sure."

"It's simple enough. Tillman and the girl were drinking and making out, both hotted up. Tillman had a little coke, and began wanting something more. Angela wasn't so up for that. But Tillman just had to fuck her, no matter how. When she resisted, he lost it. That was when he hit her."

Bender, Darrow realized, had thought about this long and hard; like Darrow himself, he needed a story that made sense and that, at least, conformed to the physical evidence. "So she gave in," Darrow said.

"A fateful choice," Bender answered softly. "Tillman made her undress, then used his finger to make her wet enough to enter, leaving no injuries. When he was done, she dressed herself. But Angela never left the room alive."

"You think she threatened to report him."

"Uh-huh. Everything we know says she was a strong-willed girl with real pride, nobody's victim. And she was too drunk or angry to realize that a guy capable of rape and battery might take the final step. But Tillman knew enough to understand that he could spend a stretch in prison, and was coked up enough for rage to overtake his reason." Bender took another puff, eyes narrow, as though reenvisioning the murder. "All your friend knew was not to let her talk. Three minutes later, she couldn't."

Silent, Darrow reviewed Bender's thesis. "If Angela let him penetrate her, why the scratches on Steve's back?"

"Maybe she changed her mind, or wanted to leave her mark." Pausing, Bender fished out another cigarette. "Nothing's perfect. Including the logic of a homicide involving two drunken kids."

"There's also this," Darrow rejoined. "Joe didn't have a car that night; he left on foot, and then we clever fraternity boys parked his Miata in the library. But Steve *did* have a car. Does illogic also cover a drunk with a trick knee carrying a corpse two hundred yards to a very public space–instead of dumping her in his trunk and throwing her in the river? Or dumping her body in a place–the old lime pit, for example–where you might never find her?"

Bender seemed unruffled. "No clue–Tillman sure didn't tell us. Maybe he thought she'd leave traces in his car. All we know is what he did with her."

"How do you know *what* he did? How did he carry her, for one thing? Did the forensic people find any drag marks on her heels?"

"No. But if he carried her over his shoulder, there wouldn't be."

"In which case," Darrow rejoined, "you'd think there might be traces of her saliva on his clothes. Were there any?"

Momentarily quiet, Bender considered the implications of the question. "Corpses drool," he said. "Maybe just not this one. At least not that the crime lab found."

"In other words, there's no evidence at all that Steve carried her to the Spire. All we know is that I found her there."

"Not all. Pat Flynn—the waitress from the Donut King—saw the guy who carried her there. She swore he was about Tillman's height and build."

"That could have been me, Fred. Or anyone." Darrow hesitated. "Does Pat still live in Wayne?"

"Yup. Same life, same job. Donut King's still there."

For a long time, Bender said nothing more. "Since you came back," he finally asked Darrow, "have you run into Joe Betts?"

"Once."

"Last few years, I've met him a couple of different times. By appearance, I could have picked him out of a lineup. But he seems like a different guy, and not just because he's sober." He turned to Darrow. "A decent guy, wouldn't you say?"

Darrow hesitated. "Yeah," he answered. "I would."

WALKING WITH DARROW back to his office, Bender paused at the foot of the Spire for a final smoke. For Darrow, the site evoked many things. But what he recalled now was stopping with Joe Betts to watch the rally where Dave Farragher had pledged before a swarm of TV cameras to solve the murder of Angela Hall.

"Tell me about Farragher," Darrow said.

Bender weighed the question. "At the time of the murder, he was still pretty new in the job—had only been prosecutor for three years. But he'd been an assistant prosecutor, known for being sharp. Legally and politically."

"Which mattered most?"

"In this case, both. Dave was up for reelection, so he

was on the hot seat. No point indicting someone if you may well lose at trial, or just turn out to be wrong. Dave needed to be right."

"Within three days?"

"A fair question," Bender conceded. "Dave was under a lot of pressure, including from the black community, as well as from the college. And the media. You didn't need to be as smart as Dave to know this one was make-or-break, the biggest case he might ever see." Briefly, Bender interrupted himself by coughing. "No one thought his vision of the future ended with county prosecutor. Some folks used to call him 'Governor' behind his back. Only two things could derail him for sure—some sort of scandal or fucking up this case. He needed a conviction."

"So when did he decide that he could win a case against Steve?"

"When Muhlberg and I brought him Joe Betts's story. 'That makes Tillman a liar,' I recall him saying. 'If I can prove to the jury he lied about something that important, that could seal a conviction.' " Bender finished his cigarette. "I wasn't there when he met with Betts. But whatever Joe said was enough to convince Farragher that Tillman was the one. A few hours later, Dave had him arrested."

This was another detail, Darrow remembered, that Joe had not revealed to him. He felt Bender watching his face. "Look," the detective said evenly. "I know this is complicated for you. You found her body. Steve Tillman was your best friend, and you also knew Joe Betts pretty well. Looking back at it, I imagine you're remembering a lot of things, and maybe feeling some sort of guilt you can't quite put a name to.

"But this is a classic cold case, with gaps no one can fill in. The passage of fifteen years has made it worse."

Dropping the cigarette in the grass, Bender ground it with his shoe. "The real problem is Angela Hall. She's what I'd call a legitimate victim—not some gangbanger anyone might have shot, where there are a lot of potential witnesses. Or suspects.

"People like Angela aren't courting death. With victims like her, often there's no witnesses except the killer. So you work with what you've got. And you learn to accept that that's probably all you'll ever have."

"Not easy."

Stooping, Bender picked up the butt, then faced Darrow. "Believe me," he said quietly, "I wish I had all the answers. This was the last case of my career. No one wants to end with an unsolved homicide. But no cop wants to die still wondering about his biggest success."

Bender put the dead cigarette in his pocket. Alone, Darrow went back to his office.

15

Darrow capped a review of Caldwell's finance by taking Joe Betts to dinner.

The venue was the Carriage House. As before, the owner seated Darrow in the booth below his photograph—the much younger Mark Darrow brandished the ceremonial axe from atop the Spire. "This seems to have become my table," Darrow remarked.

Eyeing the picture, Joe shook his head. "That was a moment. Too bad the day didn't end there."

The waitress took their drink orders. "Just give me Château Perrier," Joe told her amiably. "I hear May 2009 was a good month."

When the waitress left, Darrow said, "You really *did* give it up, didn't you?"

"Cold turkey," Joe answered. "After that night, I didn't need a twelve-step program. I *knew*."

He looked unsettled by the memory. "That was years ago," Darrow said. "You've done well, Joe. Certainly for Caldwell—given the times, our portfolio could have taken a far bigger beating than it has."

Joe grimaced. "Not many good places to put our money, what with the housing bubble and the rest. My great achievement was not losing more. Compared to letting Durbin embezzle close to a million bucks, I guess that's a point of pride."

Joe might have changed, Darrow thought, but not

entirely; beneath the smooth exterior, he sensed the touchiness and insecurity Joe had tried to conceal in college. "No one figured Clark Durbin for a crook," Darrow responded. "The flaw was in the system, and your proposals for fixing it are sound. Once we get them in place, it'll close the books on this whole sad episode."

"We'll close the books, Mark, when we throw the book at Durbin. You ready to do that yet?"

Darrow sipped his martini. "Not quite. I still want my guy Mike Riley to take a look at this. Call me thorough."

To Darrow's surprise, Joe flushed with anger. "That's not diligence, for Chrissakes–that's necrophilia. Especially after we found the account where Durbin transferred money back from Switzerland. I'm with Ray Carrick: nailing Durbin to the mast is what the alumni need to see. New financial controls are good and well, but they don't satisfy the viscera."

"Whose viscera?" Darrow asked mildly. "I've been called a lot of things, but 'corpse fucker' is pretty novel."

Joe managed a sour smile. "Okay," he acknowledged. "The Durbin thing is personal to me. I feel like a buffoon, and now it's like you're second-guessing Greg Fox and me. For no reason either of us can detect except that you can."

"I'm way too busy for petty shows of authority," Darrow answered firmly. "So bear with me. I owe a debt to Caldwell College, and have ever since Lionel got me in. That's why I came back despite all the reasons I had to stay away."

Taking off his horn-rimmed glasses, Betts wiped both lenses with a napkin, removing spots only he could see. "I know that, Mark. Believe me." He paused a moment. "Have you gone to see Steve again?"

"Yeah. It's becoming a regular stop."

"Anything new?"

"Not much happening at the pen–or many distractions, either. Prison seems to breed a certain monomania. It's fair to say he still blames you for his misery."

Joe put his glasses back on, fiddling with one of the stems. "That's pretty misdirected, wouldn't *you* say?"

Darrow shrugged. "I guess that depends on whether he killed her. Steve still swears she walked out alive and that he never left the dorm." He hesitated, then asked mildly, "Any chance at all the guy you saw was someone else?"

Joe's jaw set, defensiveness flashing in his eyes. "No matter what had happened between Steve and me, I wouldn't put a friend in jail unless I *knew*. Even if I hadn't glimpsed his face, the guy *limped*. I'd have known Steve Tillman if he'd been walking with fifteen other guys."

After a moment, Darrow nodded. In a tone of idle curiosity, he asked, "Do you remember what he was wearing?"

"Not really, no."

"Did you happen to notice the time?"

Joe was quiet for a moment, brow slightly furrowed. "I thought it was around three o'clock, but can't remember why. Leaning out that window, I still felt pretty fucked up."

Darrow thought quickly of his own memory, still undisclosed, that he had tried to reach Steve Tillman after three o'clock. Joe's sense of time, were his story true, would put Steve back in his dorm room an hour before. But the significance of this–if any–was unclear. "Between the party and whenever you spotted him," Darrow inquired, "did you see Steve or Angela at all?"

"You mean after he drove off with her? No." Joe bit his lip. "The mood I was in, if I'd known they were screwing one floor below, I might have busted in on them. Would have been better if I had–Angela Hall might still be alive."

Joe's voice softened. "As it was, all I did was go home and puke in the upstairs john. I remember being on my hands and knees, grabbing both sides of the commode, then staggering up to look in the mirror. I hated what I saw there–not just how I looked, but who I was."

"A bad night, Joe."

Summoning a look of candor, Joe met Darrow's eyes. "No," he answered. "A bad *guy*. I'd lost my girlfriend. I'd fought with Steve. I'd made a fool of myself in public. All I wanted was to get off the earth somehow–not just leave the night behind; leave *myself* behind. Other than my own face, the last thing I wanted to see was those two cops, wanting to go through what I'd done, over and over. I didn't tell them about Steve until I had to."

The latent ambiguity in this last statement left Darrow quiet. Joe's expression became pleading. "I'm different now, Mark. My whole life is different. My career's good. Katie and I are good, and we've got two great kids. Now I'm on Caldwell's board, and I like to think, despite this screwup, that I'm repaying my own debt to the school." He paused, then added in a lower voice, "I didn't become my old man, after all. The guy you saw that night isn't me anymore. He's as dead as Angela Hall."

Darrow had a deep sense of sadness. He remembered Steve Tillman saying much the same thing after his arrest– "That's not me." Except that Joe Betts was disowning the person he had been, not the act for which Tillman was imprisoned. Beneath Joe's plea, Darrow felt the man's fierce desire never to reprise memories that, whatever his reason, frightened him too deeply to conceal.

"I understand," Darrow said gently. "Do you happen to have a picture of Katie and the kids?"

With evident relief, Joe pulled a picture from his wallet, sliding it across the table. In her tennis dress, Katie Betts looked athletic and well-groomed, a classic blond from some wealthy precinct of Connecticut. Standing beside her, a bright-eyed boy and his gap-toothed sister were laughing at something off-camera.

"Nice," Darrow affirmed. "I envy you, Joe."

DARROW LEFT THE Carriage House a little after nine o'clock. He stood on the sidewalk, breathing in the lightly humid air and recalling the summer evenings he had savored before his senior year at Caldwell transformed his memory. Reaching back in time, he located Donut King in his mental map of the past.

It was next to the Greyhound bus station, a one-story building with the same red neon sign. As he entered he saw, sitting at the counter, a man in a windbreaker and another in the jacket of a bowling team drinking fruit drinks, a new offering since Darrow had last come here after his high school prom. But the place still smelled like the glazed doughnuts he no longer allowed himself to eat.

A waitress in her fifties, peroxide-blond hair tightly curled, greeted him with a smile that lit her gaunt face. "You're Mark Darrow," she said.

Darrow smiled. "Guilty. And you are . . ."

"Pat Flynn. What can I get you?"

"Black coffee. Wish I had room for a doughnut–after twenty years, I can still taste them."

Flynn laughed. "I've been here so long I smell like one. But they're still good. Sure I can't tempt you?"

Darrow grinned. "'You're a long time dead,' somebody once told me. So, sure."

She returned with coffee and a doughnut. "You've still got that same smile," she informed him. "Guess you're back to clean up this latest mess."

"That's the idea. Really, *this* mess isn't that bad."

At once Flynn became somber. "You mean no one died this time."

"Yeah." Darrow took a sip of coffee. "That can't have been easy for you, Pat."

She looked unsettled for a moment, and then the expression passed—Wayne was a small town, her role in Steve's trial common knowledge. "All I said is what I saw. It wasn't my place to say what it meant." More sadly, she added, "Still, I remember Steve Tillman coming in here a few times. Always polite. Always friendly, the last person you'd imagine doing what he did. But that's probably what all those dead girls thought about Ted Bundy, right up until his mask slipped."

Darrow eyed his doughnut. "You just don't know, I guess. Anyhow, you never told them it was Steve."

"God, no. At the time, I wasn't quite sure what I'd seen. It was all, like they say, circumstantial." Her mouth formed a wispy smile. "Guess I watch too much Court TV. But his frat buddy's the one who nailed him. I couldn't have picked the guy I saw out of a two-man lineup."

"How'd you even happen to be there?"

"It was late, past three o'clock, and I was so tired I could hardly see straight. My car was in the shop, so I decided to take a shortcut home." She poured Darrow a refill of coffee. "I'd done that a couple of times before—to me it was better than walking through deserted streets. Anyone you'd meet might be out for no good reason, whereas—or so I thought—the campus would be empty. Dumb, huh?"

"Not that anyone would have thought." Darrow sipped his coffee. "Where were you when you saw him?"

"Near College Hall, a fair distance from the Spire. There weren't any lights there. But the moon was full, as I recall, and there weren't any trees nearby to block the light. When I saw him, I just froze–half scared, half just surprised. At first I couldn't see her at all."

"How do you mean?"

"He had his back to me. So I couldn't tell *what* he was doing."

Darrow put the cup down. "I'm trying to envision this. If you were by Caldwell Chapel, and he had his back to you, then he must have been more or less facing in the direction of Steve Tillman's dorm."

Flynn squinted, searching her memory. "I guess so, yeah."

"Which was closer to you, the Spire or the man you saw?"

"The Spire."

"So he had his back to the Spire and was facing toward the dorm."

"Uh-huh." Her eyes became wary. "He wasn't coming *from* the dorm, if that's what you mean."

Darrow gave her an easy smile. "I'm not sure what I mean. *You* watch too much Court TV; *I've* spent too much time in courtrooms."

Flynn's face relaxed. "No, this is interesting. Thinking back, I don't believe Steve Tillman's lawyer asked me about all this."

Nordlinger had not, Darrow knew. "Could you make out what this guy was wearing?"

"Some sort of overcoat, I thought. Seemed like I could only see his legs below the knee."

"When did you first realize that he was carrying a body?"

Flynn glanced at her two other customers, assuring herself that they were content. "He turned sideways, sort of looking around. That was when I saw that he was cradling something–maybe a sack, is what I thought. Then he started to lay it down, and her arm sort of dangled." Her voice turned thin. "That was spooky. I thought maybe the person was drunk. But when he laid her down, she didn't move at all. The guy just hurried off, like he was afraid of being seen."

"Could you tell in which direction?"

"No. Like I said, except for the moon it was dark. He disappeared in seconds." She shook her head. "I still didn't know what I'd seen. But it really creeped me out."

Darrow nodded in sympathy. "Other than thinking he wore a coat, what do you remember about him?"

"That he was tall, and pretty slim, it seemed. Nothing else to remember. I couldn't have told you his age, or whether he was black or white or Asian or had landed in Roswell, New Mexico."

"Or if he was wearing glasses?"

"Nope. The police asked me that. If I couldn't see his face, I sure couldn't make out glasses."

"Guess not." Darrow feigned thought, as though something had just occurred to him. "Was there anything funny about how he walked?"

"How do you mean?"

"A limp, maybe."

Flynn considered this. "Not that I remember. Of course, his legs were mostly covered. Mainly, though, I just wanted to get out of there. So I did."

"Yeah. I would have, too."

Slowly, Flynn nodded, and then eyed his plate. "You going to eat your doughnut? Or you want a bag for that?"

Darrow smiled. "How about a bag?" he said. "I'll enjoy having it for breakfast."

16

It was close to eleven when Darrow left the Donut King–time, he supposed, for the normal thirty-eight-year-old college president to go home to his empty bed. Instead, still arranging and rearranging facts–the compulsion of an ex-lawyer and Steve Tillman's onetime friend–he found himself heading for the Alibi Club.

The neighborhood had not changed much: as with the rest of Wayne, on the southeast side the global economy was, at most, a rumor. As he approached the club, a clump of young men on a corner eyed his Porsche with envy and suspicion. Parking on the half-empty street, Darrow approached the door of the Alibi Club, feeling that he was about to turn back time.

Hugo sat on his stool by the door, more massive than ever, his close-cropped hair turned white. His eyes widened at the sight of the newcomer, his mouth forming a grim smile of displeasure before he curtly nodded Darrow inside.

In the darkness, the first thing that hit Darrow was the pulse of rap music. He half-expected to spot some white kids at the bar, where he once had perched, chatting with Angela, while Steve scored pot from her brother. Instead, the patrons appeared older–men and a few women drinking whiskey or beer and listening to a rapper who, if Darrow's ear was good, might be Kanye West. The smell of cigarettes and beer evoked the DBE party on the night of Angela's death; like prosperity, the anti-smoking movement had bypassed the neighborhood. But Farr's campus control measures had clearly worked—the club was no longer a haven for underage would-be alcoholics from Caldwell College. Darrow was the only white man in the place.

An older woman tended bar. Though Darrow had never seen Angela's mother, he could not have mistaken her—slender, she had a faded version of Angela's prettiness and grace. As with many black women in middle age, her eyes were older than her face, staring at Darrow with hostile weariness from a lineless mask. She held his gaze until he felt impelled to take a seat at the bar.

As he did, two men at the other end shot him a glance. The woman approached him, looking hard into Darrow's face. "So," she said curtly. "Do ghosts drink liquor?"

Darrow did not respond to this. "Hello, Mrs. Hall."

She laid her hands flat on the bar. "You're the last person I'd expect to see here."

Darrow nodded slightly. "If that dredges up hard feelings, I apologize."

"Hard memories," she said coldly. "You were one of the last to see my daughter alive, the first to see her dead. Except for your friend. I don't need you to remind me of how she looked when he got through."

Darrow weighed his response. "I can't claim to know how you feel, Mrs. Hall. But Angela and I were becoming friends. How she died still makes no sense to me."

She stared at him, repelling sympathy. "Do you want a drink, or not?"

"Cutty Sark, neat." Darrow was glad he had not eaten the doughnut.

After a time, she brought him his scotch, then watched him take a sip. "*What* made no sense?" she demanded.

"Something feels like it's missing." Darrow hesitated. "The night I saw her, she was drinking to get drunk. I didn't know her that well, but it bothered me enough to offer to drive her home."

Her voice softened slightly. "Lord knows I wish you had."

"She didn't want to go. It was like she was on a mission that night, but wouldn't talk about it."

"Maybe you're seeing a mystery where there was no mystery." Maggie Hall looked around herself, then back at Darrow, a sudden film appearing in her eyes. "Maybe, for once, my daughter wanted to escape. That's nothing to die over."

Darrow cocked his head. "Escape from what, Mrs. Hall?"

"From being so *good* all the time. If you knew her at all, you must know that much–working to meet expenses, studying late at night to keep from losing her scholarship, always scared to death of failure."

"Or just driven to succeed. I know she was set on going to a good law school."

Maggie Hall's eyes grew distant. "That was always her dream. Angela was the child with dreams."

The last was spoken with deep sadness, perhaps a hint of disdain for the child who had survived. Softly, Darrow said, "Still, working like that had been her life for all four years. Did something happen to make that harder?"

She gave him a probing look. "Maybe my girl just wore out. Why does any of this matter to you now?"

"Because I became part of it, and it's still with me." He took another swallow of scotch. "I guess you know they made me president of Caldwell."

"Who doesn't? It's like the pope showed up, except you're not wearing a dress."

Darrow knew better than to smile. "Fred Bender's our chief of security. The other day, I asked him about Angela. Fred gave me the sense that her life had changed in her last few months."

The woman's face closed. Relinquishing secrets about a child was hard, Darrow surmised–even a dead child. Maggie Hall had spoken to Bender in anguish and then, perhaps, with Angela buried and Steve convicted, reinterred her daughter in memory as the near-perfect striver. Now Darrow was digging her up.

"What good is this?" Maggie Hall said flatly. "She's dead."

"The reason still matters," Darrow answered. "After law school, I spent time prosecuting homicide cases. I can't help thinking about Angela. How she died and where I found her aren't quite adding up for me."

In a guarded tone, Hall said, "I don't follow."

"Steve Tillman still says Angela told him she needed to go somewhere–"

"What *would* he say?" Hall snapped. "It was two o'clock in the morning. Think my girl was going to the movies?"

"I understand your feelings about Steve. But suppose, just for a moment, that he was telling the truth. You told Fred Bender that Angela had started disappearing at night–that you didn't know where, and it wasn't like her."

Staring at the lacquered bar, Hall briefly closed her eyes. "I thought maybe it was to sleep with someone. A new guy called for her a couple of times–sounded like a white college boy, but he wouldn't leave his name or number."

Surprised, Darrow asked, "Do you think it was Steve?"

"I didn't know. But I asked her about it, the whole business of sneaking out," she said in a muted tone. "Angela got real angry. Her late father hadn't left us anything, she said, and I wasn't *paying* for anything. So I had no right to ask about her life, or how she made her way in the world."

"Did she often get that angry?"

"This was more like being defensive," Hall answered in a parched voice, "like I'd said out loud she was selling herself. So I asked her if she was.

"The girl just stared at me. 'You don't understand me at all,' she said. 'You don't understand my life at all.'" Hall's tone became harsher. "I wanted to bury the hurt of what she said, and the trial helped me do that. Or I think I'd have died from the hole in my heart."

Darrow wondered what right he had to strip-mine this woman's pain. But in the brutal logic of the law, someone should have done it long ago—certainly Steve Tillman's lawyer. "Fred Bender said you thought she was keeping a diary. I guess you don't know what happened to it, or what was in it."

Hall shook her head, either in affirmation or refusal to speak. After a moment, she said, "Finish your drink, Mr. Darrow. And please don't come back here again."

Darrow nodded. Maggie Hall's decision not to spy on her daughter, he supposed, had become her deepest wound: she was afraid that by shrinking from the truth she had caused Angela's death. Only Steve Tillman's guilt could salve her own.

Darrow paid for the drink and left.

17

Looking ahead to Friday night, Taylor proposed to provide their dinner. She enjoyed cooking, she explained, and they had largely exhausted Wayne's cuisine. All she needed was to borrow Darrow's kitchen. "With all respect," she told him, "I don't want your provost hovering around."

Laughing, Darrow said that was fine. He found himself looking forward to the evening.

The day was crystalline—electric-blue sky, a light pleasant breeze, little dampness in the air. Taylor called him in midafternoon, suggesting a change of plans. "Would you mind going to the riverbank?" she asked. "I haven't been there for a very long time."

Something in her tone suggested that this was more than a whim spurred by lovely weather. "Sure," Darrow said. "Do you want me to pick up something?"

"Maybe some wine," she answered. "I'll pull together a gourmet picnic from the heartland."

For whatever reason, she sounded preoccupied. "I'll bring a nice bottle," he said.

Darrow picked her up in his convertible. As they drove up Scioto Street with the top down, he was suddenly aware of the impression—or misimpression—they might make: the president of Caldwell and his provost's daughter cruising through town, wind blowing her raven hair. "I think maybe I should garage the car," Darrow remarked. "It's beginning to feel a little ostentatious."

Smiling, Taylor did not answer. After a time she said, "I should give you directions."

"I know the way. I used to go out there all the time."

"Up to no good, I suppose."

Darrow grinned. "Depends on your point of view."

"I can imagine. But if you don't mind not reliving your off-the-field highlights, there's a place I'd like us to go."

As they sped through the sloping countryside, nearing the river, Taylor became quieter. "You okay?" he asked.

She turned to him. "This is going to sound kind of weird. We're going where my parents used to take me when I was young, to swim and picnic. But the last time I went there was with my father, to scatter my mother's ashes. I've never been able to go back."

Darrow thought of visiting his mother's grave. "Memories have their undertow," he said. "Sometimes it's best to face them."

Taylor gave him a pensive look. Perhaps, Darrow realized, she thought he was remembering his wife. But, this time, he had not been.

FLANKED BY TREES and grassy banks, the Miami River resembled a wide creek, perhaps a hundred feet across, its waters so serene and still that they barely created a ripple. At once Darrow thought of riverbank parties, fraternity raft races, dope and beer and sex at night in the grass. But Taylor's images, it seemed, began with the dawn of her memory.

They sat on a blanket in the light of summer's longest evening, drinking red Tuscan wine from plastic glasses. "At first," Taylor told him, "my dad would carry me in on his shoulders. When I was five, he gave me swimming lessons–sometimes a bit impatiently, like I was in boot camp for kindergartners. But I learned to swim, and not to be afraid. Fear, he always insisted, should be mastered."

Darrow tried to imagine Lionel Farr as the father of a little girl. "Did your mother swim as well?"

"She watched us, mainly. Often she'd write poetry or something in a journal she kept; other times she painted. Sometimes I'd see her smiling at me." Taylor's face clouded. "Most of these memories are from when I was six or seven. I don't remember her coming here much after that. Maybe it was her heart."

"Was that always a problem?"

Taylor spread pesto on two crackers and put them on Darrow's paper plate. "I don't really know. What I recall so vividly is finding her on the kitchen floor, unconscious, blood coming from her nose. My dad stayed calm–by the time the doctor arrived, she'd recovered." Taylor gazed out at the water. "Both my parents tried to reassure me. But every day until she died I worried that I'd lose her."

Darrow watched her face, filling with remembrance of a child's fears. "I came over that night, remember?"

"Did you?" Turning, Taylor smiled a little. "I don't recall that, so I *must* have been devastated. When I was young, you showing up was a real highlight."

Though she said this lightly, Darrow sensed she was not joking. "I didn't know I'd made such an impression."

"Part of it was your smile." Saying this, Taylor's own faint smile lingered. "That, and the way you talked with me, and listened."

Recalling her own vulnerability, Darrow reflected, seemed to soften her a little. "I remember everything about that day," he told her. "I came to tell your dad that Steve Tillman had been arrested."

Taylor shook her head. "Something so important to you, and for me it's like you were never there. The only other part I remember is sitting in the living room, the two of them trying to reassure me. My mother had a heart condition, she explained–sometimes her blood pressure would drop suddenly and she'd just pass out. There was medication for it; I needn't worry. I fought back tears: somehow it was important to show them–him, really–that I wasn't afraid. Then my mother promised that she'd always be there for me."

Her deep blue eyes, though directed at Darrow, seemed focused on the past. "But you didn't believe her."

"No. Her promise scared me more than anything else they'd said. That was when I knew she wasn't like other moms, that she might leave me in an instant. After that, whenever I'd come back from school, I'd go through the house, heart in my throat, until I found her. When I did, she'd smile–in a sad and knowing kind of way, I think now–and give me a hug."

To fear losing a mother, Darrow reflected, must have been haunting for a girl that young. He wondered whether Taylor's fear had been more long-standing and intuitive, preceding her discovery of Anne lying unconscious on the kitchen floor. That might explain the solemnity of the lovely child he remembered and, perhaps, her retreat into painting and drawing. "She hugged me every day," Taylor concluded simply. "Five months' worth of hugs, and she was gone."

Darrow nodded. "I went to class that morning, and Lionel wasn't there. You found her, didn't you?"

"Yes." Taylor paused, as though summoning the will to

say more. When she did, her words were so vivid that Darrow, listening, could imagine how she felt.

IT WAS A bright spring morning, a little before eight o'clock. That semester her father taught an early class, so Anne drove Taylor to school. But on this day her mother did not seem to have awakened.

Tentative, Taylor walked down the hallway to Anne's bedroom. Her parents had begun sleeping apart–her father was a restless sleeper, Anne had told her recently, with dreams that seemed to surface from the murky void of Vietnam. Leaning her face against the bedroom door, Taylor heard no stirring. She knocked on the door, and still there was no sound.

Taylor steeled herself, then cracked open the bedroom door.

She half-expected–deeply hoped–to find her mother stirring. Instead, Anne lay on top of the covers, still and very pale. Something about the cast of her face did not resemble sleep; it was as though, Taylor thought, her soul had left behind a shell.

Taylor could not touch her. Turning, she rushed out the door and ran toward the campus, heart pounding wildly, tears streaming down her face. She arrived at her father's classroom out of breath.

He saw her standing in the doorway and knew at once what must have happened.

Calmly, Farr faced his students and explained that he had to leave. Then he took her by the hand, his grip firm, and hurried across the campus, urging Taylor to run with him as fast as she could.

Reaching the house, he paused briefly at the door, then pushed it open. "Where is she?" he asked.

Mute, Taylor pointed toward Anne's bedroom. Her father swiftly climbed the stairs, Taylor following.

The bedroom door was open. Her father knelt by the bed, feeling for Anne Farr's pulse. Briefly, Taylor saw his eyes shut, and then he turned to her.

"She's gone," he told her gently.

LISTENING, DARROW REMEMBERED Farr kneeling by a murdered girl, the beginning of a terrible, tragic year. Now he wondered if Farr had thought of Angela Hall as he pronounced his own wife dead.

"I remember him calling the doctor," Taylor finished. "After that it's all a blur. Except that I still recall, very distinctly, how kind you were to me at her memorial service. I didn't want to let you go."

"I wish I could have helped more."

Taylor gazed out at the water. "I don't know what else you could have done. I went into a kind of fugue state, as though I were sedated. My next clear memory is when we came here with my mother's ashes." She turned to Darrow again, as if returning to the present. "I hope you don't mind my bringing you here. But I needed to come, and not with my father. I guess this is what you get to do for me, after fifteen years."

"A long time," Darrow said softly.

"Right now," she answered, "it's yesterday."

THE AFTERNOON HER father chose was sunny and mild; the trees were budding with new growth, and slanting sun lightened the blue-brown waters. When Taylor could not bring herself to open the urn that held her mother's ashes, Farr took it from her hands.

"This was always her wish," he explained. "Ever since she learned that her time with us might be too short. Your mother loved beauty–lived for it, really, when she wasn't living for you. When her heart began to fail, she told me that she wanted to be part of nature in a place we three had shared. A place where we could remember her fondest memories."

Taylor had no reason to dispute this. Nor could she imagine her mother trapped in a box, with six feet of earth between her and the light she so loved. Complying with her father's instructions, Taylor helped him scatter her mother's ashes on the glistening surface of the river, watching the gray and silver remnants recede from sight. Suddenly, Taylor was bereft: her mother had vanished from this place, and from her life. There was nowhere she could whisper secrets to her, even if her mother could not answer.

She looked up at her father. His smile, meant to be of comfort, made her feel angry and alone.

"Even then," Taylor told Darrow, "I knew it was unfair. He must have been hurting too, and he tried to give me solace. But he couldn't.

"Certainly, I was no comfort to him. For me he was Lionel Farr, the Special Forces officer and great professor. *She* was my mother."

Darrow found the story painful. He imagined two people, isolated by their own sorrow, without the gift to reach for each other. "How was Lionel as a father?" he asked.

Distractedly, Taylor sipped her wine. "In many ways, a stranger. *You* knew him better, I think. You were almost an adult, and I imagine he saw you as a quasi son he could launch into the world, a living reflection of himself.

"I don't mean that as harshly as it sounds–in the best

of parents, love can't be separated from ego. But I was her daughter, not his son. I could never crack his code."

"Because you were a girl?"

"That's part of it, I think–he didn't know what to do with me." She paused, recrossing her legs, moving a little closer to Darrow. "He'd come of age in the fifties, then entered the most masculine environment there was–West Point. In those days, men not only weren't taught to understand women, they didn't think it was possible. Even a wife or a daughter."

"Maybe so," Darrow said. "But don't think my relationship with Lionel was warm and fuzzy–he's more a combat leader than a therapist. Not that there haven't been moments. When Lee was killed, he shared his feelings about your mother, as one man who'd lost his wife to another. And in college he always made sure I had enough money, like the time he got me a job taking around prospective students. But our relationship was about mentoring and exhortation, making sure I realized whatever potential I had." Darrow's voice softened. "I owe who I am to Lionel. But there were a few important things I had to learn on my own."

Taylor surprised him by smiling. "Like listening to girls?"

Darrow laughed. "And old friends."

Taylor shook her head. "I think you care about people, period. I also think you'd rather listen to others than talk about yourself. It's partly a strategy of avoidance."

The comment was so accurate that it took Darrow by surprise. "Am I that obvious?"

"Maybe to me," Taylor said. "But my course in Mark Darrow studies began when you were seventeen. You've changed a lot, and very little."

"That *is* disheartening," Darrow replied. "And more than a little scary. You were seven, Taylor."

"And very perceptive," she said briskly. "Then, and now. Which is why I'd guess that working with my father is not exactly problem-free."

This time surprise made Darrow laugh. "Not *too* problematic. But for someone in my position, Lionel has the faults of his virtues."

Taylor gave him a keen look of interest. "Such as?"

Darrow had meant to reveal these thoughts to no one. But Taylor's directness, and perhaps the wine, made elaboration tempting–especially given her insight into Lionel Farr. "In confidence?" he asked.

"Of course," Taylor said with some impatience. "In case you haven't grasped this, I've said more to you in one night than to my father in either millennium."

"Okay." Pausing, Darrow organized his thoughts. "As you suggest, your dad is a classic 'guy'–give him a problem, and he'll fix it; give him a void, and he'll fill it. Because he's also a born leader, regardless of whatever role he's in.

"In a crisis, he thinks faster and better than anyone. When Angela Hall was murdered, Lionel had the instincts Clark Durbin lacked. In a very real way your father cemented Durbin's presidency, as surely as he made me who I am. So in return for Lionel propping him up, Durbin turned over the internal management of the school.

"All in all, your dad is a man of prodigious gifts–that Caldwell's still afloat is mainly due to him. But Lionel amasses power like a magnet draws iron filings. Add his considerable force of personality, and people are very disinclined to tell him no. *That,* I realize more and more, is how I became president."

"You didn't sense that all along?"

"Of course I did. But it seems more troubling now that I'm here. One example is the faculty—their power's too entrenched, and their sway over hiring, tenure, and curriculum reflect Lionel's own prerogatives. In some very important ways, Clark Durbin became a figurehead. Which suited your dad just fine, I think, right up to the moment a chunk of Caldwell's money disappeared."

Listening closely, Taylor frowned. "But you're a wholly different proposition than Durbin. My father may be willful, Mark. But he also can be quite subtle, and he's certainly no fool."

"Never that," Darrow agreed. "But extremely confident in his own vision. So sometimes he doesn't see other people as clearly as he usually does. I've noticed a couple instances of that, one regarding a female foreign student who was sleeping with her professor. To me, it was a delicate situation, and Lionel's touch a little off."

Taylor poured them more wine. "That's the old adage," she remarked. "My father can read the notes, but can't always hear the music. And I believe he knows it. That was part of our problem, I think. It may also be why he never married again."

Darrow scrutinized her, curious. "How are the two of you doing?"

Taylor shrugged. "Now that I'm an adult, I don't think I was always fair to him. Part of growing up is perceiving that Dad and Mom aren't Adam and Eve—that your parents had parents too. One reason I came back is to see if I could make things better."

"Are they?"

For a moment, Taylor was quiet, gazing at the tranquil river as its color dulled in the fading light. "A little. Maybe

I'm just more accepting. Which would certainly be suitable for a twenty-eight-year-old."

To Darrow, this sounded more aspirational than heartfelt. Watching her face in profile, he found himself hoping that, before Taylor left, he could help bridge the lingering divide between two people he cared about.

The thought brought him up short. He had cared about Lionel Farr for over half his life, perhaps even loved him. Now—he did not know quite when—he had begun to care for Lionel's daughter. No doubt this connection was rooted in their past. But perhaps, he suddenly realized, there were reasons still to be discovered.

For a long time, neither spoke at all. Then, without wholly understanding the impulse, Darrow took Taylor's hand.

She did not turn. Her only acknowledgment that anything had happened was the slightest tightening of her fingers around his. Quietly, she requested, "Tell me about your mother."

The inquiry surprised him. Instinctively, Darrow had expected her to ask about his wife. But in Taylor, he had begun to understand, sensitivity followed perception.

"Not much to tell," Darrow answered. "She was a woman of moods—all mutable, many frightening. When you're a kid, it's hard learning to be scared of the person every instinct says should be your protector.

"I wanted to love her, but I couldn't. When they locked her in the asylum, I was relieved; when she killed herself, I felt nothing at all. Later on I learned that she came from a dynasty of schizophrenics, and understood how damaged she must have been. But the damage made her impossible to love."

Taylor absorbed this. "That must be hard, Mark. Even now."

"Not really. I moved on–I started my own life, began looking forward to a family of my own, nothing like the one I came from. I still try not to think about her much. Her legacy, if there is one, is that I try to do my best to see people whole, for who they are and what they've been through. Especially those who matter to me."

Taylor asked nothing more. After a time, she moved closer. Darrow could smell her hair, fresh and lightly scented. Suddenly he felt the pulse in his own throat.

Tentative, he turned her face to his. Her eyes were open, their expression both expectant and surprised. "What . . ." she began to ask.

Darrow kissed her. Pressing against him, Taylor's lips were soft and warm.

After a moment she broke the kiss, resting her forehead against his. "As I was saying," she murmured.

Darrow's skin still tingled. "Yes?"

He sensed her reluctance to speak. "Before tonight, you acted like I was still a child. Then I revert to childhood, talking about my mother–and now this. Is being a child-woman what you want from me?"

Though the wariness of her question startled him, it spoke to her honesty, her desire for this in others. "No," he answered firmly. "That's the opposite of how I've come to see you. I may be ten years older, but I'm way too young to be your father."

She rested her arms on his shoulders. Softly, she asked, "Then where do you think we're going with this?"

Darrow hesitated. "Home, I thought."

"Home?"

He sensed a smile in her voice. "My place," he answered. "Our original destination, if you'll recall."

As she drew back, looking into his face, Darrow

detected a disbelief and wonder that seemed to match his own. "That was before you kissed me."

Darrow kissed her again, slowly and deeply. "Okay," Taylor said with a modest sigh. "Really, it was about time."

IN THE LIGHT and shadow of his bedroom, Darrow undressed her. What he could see of her body was as beautiful as her face.

Holding hands, they walked to his bed.

They touched each other, filled with desire, yet both wishing not to hurry. In time his mouth found all of her.

"Now," she whispered.

Darrow slipped inside her, still aware of her responses, yet lost in the moment. Only at the edge of consciousness did he sense something within her that Taylor still held back. Then he felt her shudder, heard the cry she repressed.

Briefly, Darrow wondered at this. Then he gave himself up to wanting her.

Afterward, they lay close together in the dark, feeling the dampness of their skin, the depth of what they felt. Darrow touched her face. "Are you okay with this?" he asked.

"More than okay." Her voice lowered. "I hope you'll give me time."

Darrow felt surprised. "I didn't know I was holding tryouts."

"It's not you," she demurred. "Definitely not you. But I've always been slow to trust, and sometimes it follows me to bed. I wish I could tell you why. But I worry about losing myself, or giving any man too much power over me."

"I don't want that. Or need it."

Taylor took his hand. "I think I know that about you. But then, in a way, I've known you for a very long time."

"Maybe so," Darrow said lightly. "But I'm sure *this* didn't occur to either of us. At least I hope not."

"When I was seven? Hardly–I didn't even know that I had a crush on you. But I did think you were the most beautiful person I'd ever seen." Taylor laughed at herself. "The first time I saw you again, I *still* thought that. Think that makes me shallow?"

"Then so am I. Even when you were a child, I thought you were very pretty. But looking at you now, you damn near take my breath away. Except you've no doubt heard similar things too often to trust them, either."

He felt Taylor's mood turn serious again. "I've just never been sure it mattered much. Especially at times like this one."

Darrow hesitated. Then, by instinct, he spoke aloud another thought that took him by surprise. "Then try this instead, Taylor. You're the first woman since Lee died who can make me forget her. Not just tonight. For moments at a time, I'm simply *with* you. That's a bigger gift to me than you can ever know."

Taylor moved closer, breasts touching his chest. "Then I guess I'll stay."

"Was there a question?"

"Several." Taylor paused again. "Like my father, sometimes I have nightmares. I don't want to wake you up."

She was serious, Darrow realized. "Nightmares about what?"

"The usual panoply, I suppose. Fears, random scraps from the subconscious, the dregs of one's imagination. It really doesn't matter."

But it did to Taylor, Darrow sensed. "I want you to stay," he affirmed. "Including for breakfast. That way you won't pass your father as he's going out the door for our squash game."

Taylor summoned a theatrical moan of horror. "God," she said. "That's absolutely Greek."

"I agree. So let's deal with it later."

Taylor gave him the complicit kiss of a co-conspirator. Later, Darrow lay awake, absorbing what had happened to them. Taylor slept through the night.

18

In at 10:00 a.m., Darrow and Lionel Farr played squash at Caldwell's gym.

They had never played before. The game was Farr's idea: no quarter was given or sought; neither man liked to lose, Farr even less than Darrow. Punctuated by the quick, hollow thud of their tennis shoes, the green ball ricocheted off the white walls, pursued by an echo, a rubberized whine that carried into the next hit. Though swifter and younger, Darrow was less experienced; Farr's grim determination was aided by the guile of a veteran who had mastered the tactics and geometry of the nearly claustrophobic rectangle. For an hour they fought for dominance, playing with a trapped intensity until Darrow felt propelled by reserves of adrenaline, half conscious. On the final point, Farr slashed a wickedly angled shot to Darrow's right. With an instinct driven by the harsh lessons of the last hour, Darrow, anticipating this, lunged, skidding on his chest as he stretched to hit the rubber ball with a desperate flick of his wrist. The ball looped off the front wall just beyond Farr's reach. Darrow's point, Darrow's game.

Breathing deeply, Farr watched the ball dying in small bounces at his feet with a last rubbery whimper. Grimacing in disgust, he told Darrow, "You'll never do that again."

Sprawled on the wooden floor, Darrow laughed. "I'm

never playing you again. To quote the immortal Rocky, 'No rematches.' "

"Unacceptable," Farr said curtly. "For someone who barely edged a man in late middle age–on a lucky shot, at that–you're far too pleased with yourself."

"No triumph too small," Darrow responded dryly.

Farr managed a sour smile.

There was no one waiting for the court. The two men sat, backs against the wall, drinking from bottles of mineral water. In a serious tone, Farr said, "There's something we should talk about."

The subject, Darrow guessed, might well be Taylor. "What is it?"

"The latest student contretemps–allegations of date rape, to be precise."

Shaking his head, Darrow turned to his erstwhile competitor. "What are the specifics?"

"They're fairly unsympathetic. Three nights ago, it seems, an inebriated sorority girl invited two guys back to her dorm room for a three-way. Both admit being quite enthusiastic–"

"Jesus," Darrow interjected. "Don't our summer students ever go to class? Or even to sleep?"

"Apparently not. As far as I can sort this out, one boy penetrated her to climax. Before the other could follow suit, her friends burst in and broke things up.

"That was Wednesday. Yesterday, our venturesome young lady charged the one who *didn't* penetrate her with rape, claiming that he'd intimidated her. I don't see that as likely, but she's becoming quite belligerent." Farr's tone became astringent. "No doubt some of this indignation reflects her assertion that the guy in question ripped her forty-dollar underwear.

"Grounds for moral outrage these days, I'm sure.

Whatever the case, I get to deal with this farce. As provost, I'm the final arbiter in charges involving student conduct."

"A neutral arbiter, I'm sure."

"Naturally," Farr responded with weary disgust. "However unsympathetic the complainant, or incredible her charges."

"Maybe on the surface," Darrow cautioned. "Likely this woman's claims are meant to cover her own embarrassment. But, if not, she may have been too drunk to report this right away." He paused a moment. "As both of us are well aware, in cases like this it's hard to ever know."

"Not every case is Angela Hall, Mark."

Darrow turned to him. "Nonetheless, I don't want to hang these guys for something too ambiguous to resolve. But we need to hear this woman out."

"Of course," Farr answered crisply. "But there's no guarantee she won't go running to Dave Farragher. Absent his involvement, I'll give our newly vehement complainant a hearing so dispassionate and thorough that your law professors at Yale would be proud."

"I never doubted it." Pausing, Darrow wiped the sweat off his forehead. "Speaking of Farragher, he called me at home this morning. Now that I've settled in, he said, he'd like to buy me a drink. You wouldn't happen to know what might have spurred this."

Farr sipped some mineral water, gazing at the opposite wall. "I think I do, actually. I imagine you do, too."

Darrow turned to him again. More sharply than intended, he asked, "'Think,' Lionel? Or know."

Farr kept his own voice casual. "Ray Carrick called me yesterday. To paraphrase his bluster, he wonders why you're more concerned with exhuming a sixteen-year-old corpse than with prosecuting Clark Durbin for stealing Caldwell's money."

Darrow was irritated. "Setting aside Ray's characterization, who told him that I was?"

"It seems Dave Farragher's tumbled to your bedside reading. As you well know, once you asked for the transcript, Dave was bound to hear about it. What you may not have known is that Ray is one of Farragher's closest friends."

"Terrific."

Farr placed a hand on Darrow's shoulder. "Caldwell's small, and so is Wayne. So's the core group of men who run our board of trustees." His tone became avuncular. "For all our sakes, it's not the time for your interest in the Hall case to become a focus of their attention. Please treat Farragher with the exquisite tact you'd have me lavish on our female complainant. Like her, Dave may feel a little aggrieved. Perhaps for better reasons."

Unsettled, Darrow wondered whether Farr's involvement in this matter ended with Carrick's phone call. "Is there anything else I should know?" he asked.

For a moment, Farr was quiet. "Nothing important, Mark. Once you consider your options, you'll know what to do."

IN THE EVENT, Darrow's hour with Farragher was mainly pleasant; Dave Farragher was an amiable man, with a ready smile and a forthright air, burnished by fifteen years spent shrewdly tending the political capital engendered by the conviction of Steve Tillman. The venue, Wayne's country club, was unpretentious and relaxed, a rambling white wooden structure from the twenties where everyone knew everyone else. Sitting near the bar, for a half hour the two men talked about predictable subjects—how much Farragher admired Darrow's athletic and professional successes; how the community and college had changed and not changed; the shock of Clark Durbin's misconduct, now so evident; the resulting challenges Darrow faced as president. Only during the second drink did Farragher mention the murder of Angela Hall.

"Look," he concluded with an air of puzzlement. "I know Steve Tillman was your closest friend. But what in particular has caught your eye? You're a smart guy, Mark, and I'm wondering if there's anything I missed."

With his ruddy, open face and clear blue eyes, Farragher was a portrait of candor. But the question was so disingenuous that Darrow repressed a smile. Amiably, he answered, "I don't think you missed a thing, Dave."

A flicker of relief showed in Farragher's eyes. "Really?"

"Really. In fact, there are two things I don't doubt at all. That you and the police were extremely thorough, and that you're a way better lawyer than Griff Nordlinger."

Farragher chuckled briefly. "You give me too much credit."

"Not at all," Darrow assured him. "In fact, if Nordlinger had been the prosecutor and you'd been Steve's defense lawyer, I think he might have walked."

Farragher picked up his scotch, then put it down unsipped. "The court of appeals," he responded, "upheld Steve's conviction. So did the Ohio Supreme Court. Both rejected inadequacy of counsel as grounds for a reversal.

"I know what you're thinking–that doesn't make Griff adequate. But the case against Tillman was there, and the appellate courts so found."

Darrow nodded. "I've read both opinions. But, as a practical matter, why do *you* think the jurors found Steve guilty?"

The thrust of the question, directed at third parties, seemed to make Farragher relax again. "You can tick them off," he said. "Tillman and Angela Hall had sex. There were scratches on his back, a bruise on her face. If you believed Joe Betts–and the jury did–Steve lied to them on the witness stand.

"Add to that the absence of any other plausible suspect. Disparage Griff as you will, but there was nothing anyone could pin on Betts–or, for that matter, Carl Hall. Nor, despite her nocturnal wanderings, could any of us locate a boyfriend in Angela's recent life; at best, her mother remembered an anonymous white guy calling once or twice. No one found *him,* either."

"And the diary?"

Farragher spread his hands. "Who's to say it ever existed? And if it did, who in the world could have taken it from under her mattress?"

"An excellent question," Darrow concurred mildly.

"*We* thought so." Farragher took a gulp of scotch. "Believe me, we didn't stop investigating just because we'd arrested Tillman. We even checked out whether there were any known stalkers in the area, although the idea that someone like that would be on campus at three A.M. was pretty far-fetched. Nothing.

"In the end, Griff had no alternative killer. There was none. The jury had no choice but to return a guilty verdict." Farragher looked squarely into Darrow's face. "As for me, I wouldn't have brought the case unless I was morally certain that Tillman strangled Angela Hall. Why, only *he* knows for sure."

Darrow held his gaze. "As I recall, you gave the jury a couple of possibilities to ponder. One was that, in high school, Steve had broadcast his racial bias. You pretty much clobbered him with that on cross."

"Tillman was a bigot," Farragher said crisply. "And Angela *was* black."

"And Griff Nordlinger opened all that up by putting

Steve on the witness stand, then not objecting to your questions."

"I don't know that he *could* have objected. Once Tillman claimed to have cared so much about Angela, he opened up questions of credibility. I'd have been derelict not to bring out Tillman's racism." Farragher shrugged dismissively. "I'm sure the jury viewed all that as secondary. On closing argument, Griff argued quite vigorously that we'd never offered a motive."

Darrow sipped his martini. In an even tone, he observed, "Still, you had the last word on rebuttal, including with respect to motive. That was the first time you floated Fred Bender's theory—that Steve strangled Angela Hall to stop her from reporting a rape. Maybe I missed something. But I couldn't find any evidence in the transcript to support that. And the suggestion itself is lethal. Had you been Nordlinger, you'd have asked for a mistrial." Matter-of-factly, Darrow finished: "Which makes my original point, I think. From beginning to end, you were a whole lot sharper."

Though blandly delivered, the double-edged compliment induced in Farragher a somewhat cornered look. "My statement on rebuttal implied facts that *were* before the jury—that Angela was a proud and assertive woman committed to women's rights." Farragher paused a moment, then added in a straightforward manner, "You were once a prosecutor, Mark. In a situation like that, wouldn't *you* have been tempted to do the same?"

"That's hard for me to say, Dave. I never faced a defense counsel quite that bad." Darrow finished his drink. "A cynical colleague once said that a trial is where twelve people gather after a performance to vote for who they thought was the best lawyer. If so, you won."

Farragher regarded him with a quizzical smile. "Seems

like we'll just have to agree to disagree. I wish you luck at Caldwell, Mark."

They parted with a civil handshake.

19

On Sunday morning, Darrow and Taylor played tennis.

At Darrow's invitation, Taylor drove them in his Porsche. On the way to the municipal courts, Darrow asked, "What is it with the Farrs and smacking balls with rackets?"

Taylor kept her eyes on the road, a smile playing on her lips. "I heard you played squash with Dad. How was it?"

"Brutal. Even worse was that I won. He's not a happy loser."

Taylor's enigmatic smile lingered. "How well I know it. When *I* beat him, he sulked for half a day. I'm hoping you're a better sport."

Darrow stared at her. She did not seem to be joking.

They parked beside an empty court. Taylor hopped out and walked ahead of him, eager to get started, long legs moving in swift, confident strides. She did not appear to have an ounce of body fat.

Standing at the service line, she said, "Want to hit some practice serves?"

"Sure. You first."

Darrow went to the opposite side, crouching behind the service box. Eyes narrowing in concentration, Taylor tossed the ball in the air and then, stretching her five feet eight inches until she stood on the tips of her toes, extended the racket high above her head and uncoiled a swing so smooth and powerful that the ball became a blur, skidding past Darrow before he could even react.

"Guess I'm ready," she said laconically. "Your turn."

Darrow walked to the net. "Anything more you'd like to tell me, Taylor?"

Unable to contain herself, she grinned. "Okay, I was captain of the women's tennis team at Trumble. I also played at Williams–which is probably why they let me in. So please don't be too hard on yourself."

Darrow lasted two sets. Though fit, he was untutored; despite a little rustiness, Taylor covered the court like a greyhound, swift of foot and eye, settling into a rhythm, one smooth stroke after another speeding the ball to where Darrow was not. By the end of the second set–another 6–2 loss for Darrow–he was winded. Taylor met him at the net, the light of not-so-innocent triumph in her eyes. "You did great," she told him generously. "It's probably just the difference in our ages."

Darrow laughed. "You're certainly a gracious winner. I can guess who first taught you how to play."

"Of course he did. Those were among our better moments, at least after I could hit with him–silent communication, like a dad and son playing catch. And my dad was a good teacher. But I could never shake the feeling that he wished I were a boy."

"That would have been a waste," Darrow answered with a smile. "Think he knows what's going on?"

"With us? I'm not sure. But if we continue like we did the other night, he will."

Within this comment, Darrow sensed, lurked a question about their relationship and one unspoken aspect of it: in other circumstances, that Farr was Darrow's provost would be inherently problematic. Tilting his head, Darrow asked, "What would you like to do tonight?"

Taylor bit her lip in pretended thought. "Well," she said at length, "I suppose I could always shower at the museum of bad taste you call home–there's a change of clothes in my duffel bag. What do *you* want to do?"

Leaning across the net, Darrow kissed her. "I was hoping for a rematch," he told her.

As SHE STEPPED into the shower after him, Darrow gazed at her in open appreciation. Everything about her, he thought, was beautiful: her face, her elegant neck, rounded breasts with brown areolas, flat stomach, womanly hips that tapered from the black fur in the midst to long, slender legs. An athlete, he thought again, or a runway model–both and neither. She was uniquely Taylor Farr.

She looked into his face, not shy. "Have you never showered with a girl before?"

Not since Lee, he thought. "It's as I said, Taylor. Sometimes you don't leave room for anyone else."

"For me," she answered simply, "there's no one else in the way."

After the shower, they slipped into bed.

The sheets felt crisp and cool, Taylor's skin warm. Darrow's lips found her stomach, her nipples, the hollow of her neck. He could feel her breath catch, hear the soft murmur of desire in her throat. When at last he entered her, she spoke his name.

After that, the only sounds were not speech but guides to the movements of their bodies, synchronized by instinct until both shuddered as one. Eyes opening, Taylor looked up into his face. "Mark Darrow," she murmured. "So nice of you to find me after I grew up."

QUIET, TAYLOR LAY in his arms.

As he held her, Darrow found himself remembering

doing this with Lee, lazy Sunday mornings at their town house in Boston. He felt a moment of confusion: the tug of past loyalties, eroding the sweetness of this moment with Taylor; and yet the sense that, by replicating an act of tenderness he had once shared with his wife—and, at last, by wishing to—he was slipping further away from the past. "What are you thinking?" Taylor asked.

"Many things. Including about you. I was also remembering Boston, and the place I used to live."

"And where all your things still are."

Not just his things, Darrow thought; as Taylor's remark implied, the house was filled with memories. He supposed that was why he never brought another woman there. "Speaking of Boston," Taylor told him, "I had some news yesterday. The Museum of Fine Arts has offered me an interview. Seems they're developing an interest in post-modernism, after all."

Darrow was surprised. He propped his elbow on the pillow, cradling his head in his hand. "I thought you didn't like Boston."

Taylor smiled. "Now that there's some interest there, I've decided I just don't *know* Boston. So I told them I'd come in."

"When are you going?"

"I'm not sure yet. We're still working that out."

Darrow thought for a moment. "Why don't we go together. My former partners want me to consult on a couple of cases I turned over, and I owe my town house an inspection. If you like, I can try to fit my dates with yours."

Taylor gave him an inquiring look. "Is that something you really want to do?"

"Sure," Darrow said, even as he realized that they might

be crossing another bridge. "I can show you around a little. It might be fun for us to get away from Wayne."

Taylor kissed him. "As long as you can find us a place to stay."

THAT AFTERNOON, AS was now his custom, Darrow visited Steve Tillman at the penitentiary. Speaking through the slits in the Plexiglas, Steve asked sardonically, "So how was *your* week?"

Darrow did not blink. "Fine, Steve. And yours?"

Steve gave him a crooked smile. "They're great believers in structure here. We're a 'special needs' community—surprises might unsettle the student body. As usual, I've been using my leisure time to read."

"Anything in particular?"

"My current area of concentration," Steve said with mock gravity, "is twentieth-century Europe. Specifically, the rise of the Nazis in Weimar Germany. The topics include the role of World War I, the Versailles Treaty, inflation, economic collapse, and, of course, anti-Semitism. Hanging over all this, naturally, is the specter of the Holocaust—the central question being 'Why Germany?' A lot for me to think about, wouldn't you say?"

However ironic, this disquisition was so unlike anything that might have issued from his college friend that, again, Darrow was overcome by a sense of waste. "Actually, I've been thinking a lot about the Hall case."

Steve stared at him. "I *always* do, Mark. For you, it's optional." He paused, then spoke more evenly. "Don't think I held a grudge about what you told the police. That part you couldn't help. What sticks in my craw is that you just disappeared—fewer visits, then letters, then fewer letters, then nothing. You did a very thorough job of moving on. Maybe that's what you're best at."

Stung, Darrow tried to distance himself from his own emotions. "Sometimes I wish I were better at it. But about drifting away from you, no excuses. Except maybe for the last couple of years, when it felt like I was seeing the world through a very thick pane of glass."

"Like Plexiglas?" Steve gibed. "From where I sit, you seem pretty okay to me. Better than you did when you first showed up."

Darrow waited a moment. "Let me ask you something, Steve. Do you know anything about Angela keeping a diary?"

"No. What was in it?"

"I don't know. But her mother says she kept one. If so, it's disappeared. Which is also what Angela herself began doing, late at night, in the weeks before she died. Was any of that time spent with you?"

Steve inhaled, eyes fixed on Darrow. "Mark," he said slowly, "I don't have a fucking clue about any of this. If Angela and I had been screwing in the dorm, you'd have known about it."

"Yeah, I guess so."

"Guess?" Steve's laugh, though brief, held a hint of humor. "How many times were both of us in and out of each other's rooms? Remember when I walked in on you and Connie Coolman?"

Darrow smiled. "That *was* a bad night–for Connie, and for me. She was so embarrassed she completely lost interest."

"Connie was always old-fashioned. Guess she didn't count on *two* guys seeing her naked." Steve's expression darkened. "Wish you'd barged in the night I was with

Angela. By now all three of us might have been able to laugh about it."

The sad image silenced Darrow for a moment. "Before that night," he asked, "had you ever called Angela at home?"

"No. I don't think I even had her number."

"Then how did you ask her to the party?"

"I was at the club when she was tending bar. I had a couple of drinks, and it began to seem like a good idea." Steve looked down. "This may sound pathetic, but I still didn't know her all that well. I don't even know what I had in mind. We just seemed to like each other."

Darrow nodded. "That fall, I don't remember you going out with anyone. Were you?"

"No," Steve answered curtly. "Maybe you've forgotten, what with all you've had to think about in life. But I spent a whole damn year brooding over Laurie Shilts dumping me for that asshole Betts. If anyone held a grudge, it should have been me."

At once Darrow remembered this: the hurt of losing Laurie had compounded the wound inflicted by the sudden end of Steve's football career, accelerating his downward spiral. "Have any idea why Joe was so pissed off that night?"

"About me and Angela? Betts didn't need a reason. It only took a drink or two to release his inner jerk."

"Did they have some sort of relationship?"

"Not that I know about. Betts was still with Laurie, remember? I couldn't figure out why he wanted Angela. Except maybe that she was with me."

"Maybe so. But I ran into Laurie that night, Steve. She and Joe had just broken up."

"No shit? Did she say why?"

Darrow hesitated. "Not directly. But for her part, Laurie was very clear that she and Joe were through."

Intent, Steve pondered this. "Then maybe it *was* about Angela. Guess you'd have to ask Laurie. Any idea where she is?"

"No. But I could find out easily enough. To escape our development office, you have to enter the witness protection program."

Steve did not smile. "If you find her," he said softly, "tell Laurie I said hi."

To Darrow, the statement was at once wistful and bitter. "I know you've gone over this a thousand times," he said. "But do you have any idea at all why Joe said he'd seen you outside the dorm?"

"Besides that he's spiteful enough to lie?" Steve's voice became hard. "I've thought about that for fifteen years—my brilliant lawyer made quite a point of asking who would have killed her, then carried her body all the way to the Spire. But he never gave the jury an answer. Thanks to him, I've had the time to develop one on my own. Joe Betts."

Though Darrow had been expecting this, hearing it spoken aloud was jarring. "It's a theory," he allowed. "But Joe would have had to maintain an insane level of anger for several hours, wait for her outside the dorm, then strangle her. That's obsessive to the point of madness. It also raises the question of where you imagine Angela was going."

A new brightness made Steve's eyes glint. "Still, I can see I'm not alone. You've thought about it, too. So who strikes you as likeliest to kill a woman? Betts or me?"

Darrow did not answer. "Is there any way that you could be innocent and Joe still be telling the truth?"

"How? Because I blacked out, and sort of sleepwalked

out of the dorm? Or maybe wanted a gulp of air at the same time Betts did? Or maybe I followed Angela in a drunken stupor to the Spire, changed my mind about killing her, then left before somebody else did. And then literally forgot about it." Steve shook his head in seeming bewilderment. "Of course, I forgot a lot of things that night. The last thing I remember, or *believe* I remember, is Angela saying she had to leave. And what sense does that make?"

"I don't know. There are a few things about this no one can make sense of."

"One person can," Steve said succinctly. "The guy who actually killed her. *He* knows everything. Including why he did it."

That night, alone again, Darrow pondered this. He could not seem to sleep.

20

The first telephone call of Darrow's workday surprised him.

"Mark," the 'thin voice said, "this is Clark Durbin."

"Hello, Clark," Darrow said phlegmatically, then waited for whatever might come next.

Faced with Darrow's coolness, Durbin sounded shaky. "I wanted to congratulate you. I mean, you're my successor. It feels odd we haven't talked."

"Not so odd," Darrow answered in an even tone. "You're accused of stealing nearly a million dollars. That's why I'm here. Given that, I have a say in whether you're indicted. It's not as though you're passing me the baton so I can run a victory lap."

A brief silence ensued. "That's why I need to talk to you," Durbin said.

The simple statement held a pleading note. "Under the circumstances," Darrow said, "I can't meet with you alone. There can't be any misunderstanding of what either of us may say."

Durbin exhaled. "All right."

Darrow glanced at his calendar. "I've got an hour free at ten. Meet me at my office–I'll ask Lionel to join us. Bring a lawyer, if you like. In fact, I'd advise it."

"All right," Durbin repeated. He sounded like a beaten man.

Hanging up, Darrow called Farr. "Durbin wants to meet with me," he said.

"No surprise," Farr said with an edge of disdain. "He's been insisting, however incongruously, on his innocence. You're a new audience, potentially the difference between jail and mere penury. No doubt he wants to appeal to whatever quantum of mercy you haven't lavished on Steve Tillman. The only question is whether he'll try to make you feel like you're about to execute Bambi, or whether he'll float all the sympathetic reasons he chose to steal our money. Perhaps he was drunk."

The remarks were so caustic and so comprehensive that Darrow laughed aloud. "Ten o'clock," he said. "My office. After that you can tell me which president of Caldwell is the bigger fool."

TO DARROW'S SURPRISE, Durbin came alone.

Darrow sat behind his desk; Durbin, in one of two wing chairs facing him. Farr settled in the other, studying Durbin while the former president focused on his successor. Always slight, Durbin looked diminished, his hair dyed an unconvincing black, heightening the contrast with his thin but sagging face. With a tepid smile, Durbin said, "I can't help but think about the first time the three of us met together. Strange, isn't it?"

Darrow thought so, too. Then, he had been hardly more than a boy, sickened and confused, grateful for Durbin's kindness; now, at least in theory, he was the most powerful man in the room, Durbin his supplicant. "Well," Darrow said, "at least this time no one's dead. But the school's been shafted. If you were me, what would *you* do about you?"

Darrow caught the flicker of Farr's arid smile, perhaps at the toughness of his protégé, perhaps because the reversal of fortune was so complete. But the chill look in Farr's blue eyes suggested that he was not amused by the subject of the meeting—or, Darrow surmised, by the fact that it was he who had once saved Durbin's presidency. Still watching Darrow, Durbin leaned slightly forward, fingers steepled in a precatory gesture. "No matter what you have been led to think," he said slowly, "I did not do this."

"Clark," Darrow answered softly, "there's a paper trail that followed you here. The orders are from your e-mail. Money went to your bank accounts—"

"I didn't send those e-mails," Durbin interrupted. "I didn't open those accounts—"

"Don't bullshit me," Darrow cut in. "For that to be true, some mastermind would have had to know where Caldwell had parked nine hundred thousand dollars in CDs, used your personal computer to ask Joe Betts to transfer them, and forged your signature for two different banks, all in an elaborate effort to frame you. Got anyone in mind?"

Durbin ignored his sarcasm. Stubbornly, he said, "It would have had to be someone on the investment committee."

"That certainly narrows down our list of suspects, doesn't it? Aside from you, that leaves Ed Rardin, Paul Johns, John Stewart—and Joe, of course. None of whom live in Wayne. Which one had access to your computer?"

Durbin seemed to rock in his chair. "None that I know of. But they were often here."

"Let's skip over that, then—as well as the slander inherent in suggesting that one of four honorable and wealthy men is a crook. Who among them has the skill to forge your signature?"

Durbin grimaced. Tightly, he said, "Someone could have traced it."

Farr, Darrow saw, was staring at the rug, as though he could no longer stand to look at Durbin. "Clark," Darrow said with renewed gentleness, "your investments went bad. Your son was in rehab for heroin addiction. Your wife was terribly sick. You needed money."

Durbin shook his head. "I'm not a thief, Mark. If I were, I wouldn't be that stupid."

Darrow gave him the glacial stare he had perfected in the courtroom. "Desperate men do stupid things. You had no other source of money. In my experience, embezzlers imagine they can cover themselves before they're caught, often by moving around more cash. This embezzler was smart enough to game the system—which, as you pointed out, suggests an insider, someone with access to the information held within the investment committee. Which gets me back to the question you can't answer: which one had a key to your office?"

"I don't know."

"Then I can't help you. So help yourself, Clark. Tell us where the last eight hundred and fifty thousand went."

Durbin stared at him, his expression slack. "I don't know *where* the money is."

"Too bad," Darrow said in a pitiless tone. "Should you remember, please come back. Bring a lawyer with you next time, and do be quick about it. After this morning's performance, I'm an hour closer to calling up Dave Farragher."

Mechanically, Durbin rose, not trying to shake hands. "By the way," Darrow inquired casually, "who was supplying your kid with smack?"

Durbin's eyes were moist. "I don't know that, either. But maybe it was Carl Hall. Ironic, isn't it."

Still sitting, Darrow shrugged.

Farr stood, opening the door for Durbin. As Durbin paused there, looking back at Darrow, Farr placed a hand on his shoulder, a gesture that, to Darrow, combined a fleeting compassion with a reminder to leave. Somehow this moment reminded Darrow that, just yesterday, he had heard another plea of innocence. Perhaps there was nothing else Steve Tillman or Clark Durbin could have said.

Farr closed the door behind Durbin. "Human wreckage," he remarked, then looked at Darrow intently. "I haven't seen that side of you."

"A professional necessity. If Durbin's smart, he'll drop the fantasy that he's somehow getting away with this." Darrow waved Farr to his chair. "Can you stick around a minute? There's something else we need to talk about."

Farr sat back down. "Concerning?"

Darrow paused a moment. "Taylor," he answered. "We've been spending time together."

Farr's expression was neutral. "So I understand. I'm pleased you've become friends."

"We're certainly friends. But this may have a little more texture."

Farr raised his eyebrows. "How so?"

Darrow considered how to answer. "When I'm with Taylor, I don't think about Lee. For the first time in a long while, a greater part of me is living in the present."

Farr seemed to look inward, as though monitoring his own reactions. "Can I ask how far this has gone? Emotionally, I mean."

"It's still very new. But we're going to Boston together." Darrow waited until Farr met his eyes. "This isn't the Dark Ages. In any other situation, I wouldn't owe Taylor's father an explanation. But it's you, and you're the provost—

college presidents generally don't pursue their provost's daughter. I'm not sure if the fact that this involves you and me makes it better, or more awkward."

Farr smiled slightly. "Some sort of incest taboo, you mean?"

"Jesus, Lionel. That *is* weird."

"Excuse my wan attempt to make light of this." Farr paused, seeming to gather his thoughts. "Given our relationship, the idea that you, as president, are involved with my twenty-eight-year-old daughter doesn't qualify as a scandal. The main complication for me is that I care for you both–I want both of you happy, and neither of you hurt. The chances are good that one of you will be; that's the inevitable outcome of almost every romantic relationship between a man and a woman. And either outcome would be hurtful to me. So forgive me for having mixed feelings."

Darrow felt deflated. "You mentioned happiness. The only way to get there is by assuming the risk."

Farr studied him. "Then how do you assess the risk with Taylor?"

"To her? Or to me?"

"Both."

Darrow leaned back. "For myself, all I can say is that I feel more open. Even before I had to deal with Lee's death, I never found it that easy. I very much want to see where this goes."

"And Taylor?"

"I'm not sure yet. There are remarkable elements to her personality."

Farr nodded. "I agree. Like her mother, Taylor has many gifts. But I also worry that she has a tendency toward melancholy that perhaps you've yet to see." Pausing, Farr added quietly, "Also like her mother."

Darrow managed a smile he did not feel. "Are you warning me off?"

Farr frowned in thought. "Merely cautioning you. For your own sake, but also for Taylor's. I believe that life has made both of you more vulnerable to hurt than others might be."

Darrow watched him. As remarkable as the conversation was, he sensed that there was a second conversation hidden beneath the first, the words to which remained unspoken. "Is that all there is?"

Farr looked down, studying a patch of sunlight on Darrow's Persian rug. "Perhaps not," he said at last. "Perhaps, in a non-Oedipal way, I'm a little stung–or at least saddened–that your new relationship with Taylor may be stronger than my own. I hope that's not affecting me. But self-knowledge is, at best, imperfect. Never more so than when the entire truth about oneself may be less attractive than one hopes."

Darrow felt a wave of sympathy. Though armored in his confidence and reputation, Farr might well be lonelier than he allowed. "That's only human, Lionel. Thanks for being honest."

Smiling, Farr stood. "Then I've fulfilled my obligations–as provost, father, and friend. Should you and Taylor defy the odds, nothing would please me more."

Darrow nodded. "I know that."

Farr looked relieved. "Then go with God, my son. And do go over those budget figures I prepared."

When Farr left, Darrow gazed at the door, lost in thought. Then he picked up the phone and called Mike Riley in Boston.

"I'm coming to town," he told the accountant. "Can you make time to see me?"

"Always. You still grappling with this embezzlement?"

"Yes. Durbin came to see me today, to assert his innocence. It was fairly pathetic. He tried to blame some unnamed person on the investment committee, as I'd guessed he might. So I challenged his suggestion with several questions, none of which he could answer."

"Did you expect him to?"

"Of course not. But I thought you might be able to do better."

Riley chuckled. "Still not quite convinced he did it, are you?"

"Not quite yet. I'll put all my questions in an e-mail. If I give you a couple of days, can you look over all the documents and tell me what you think?"

"Sure. What brings you back to Boston, by the way?"

"The hope of better meals."

"You might try San Francisco," Riley said, and got off.

Pensive, Darrow placed another call. "This is nice," Taylor said cheerfully. "I woke up this morning, and there was nothing to look forward to but my thesis. What made you think to call?"

"I've been bonding with your dad," Darrow informed her. "I told him. He seems to be feeling a little tender, even threatened. Like he's become the odd man out."

Taylor was quiet. "Do you find that a little curious?" she inquired coolly.

Against his will, Darrow heard Farr say, *She has a tendency toward melancholy.* And then heard Taylor telling him, *I worry about losing myself, or giving any man too much power over me.* In a casual tone, he answered, "I think he means well. But Lionel's a complicated person. As are we all, I suppose."

"Him most of all," Taylor responded in the same voice. "Don't worry, I'll tread lightly with him. In the end, we're all he has."

21

On Wednesday evening, Darrow spoke to a hundred alumni at a hotel ballroom in Columbus. "Almost everyone," he told them, "had a professor who influenced the course of your life, like Lionel Farr did mine. That's why you're here; it's why I'm here. So my first mission as president of Caldwell is to earn your trust. My second mission–which I hope becomes yours–will be to ensure that Caldwell has the resources to build state-of-the-art facilities, endow chairs for the most gifted teachers, and fund scholarships for any deserving student who entrusts us with her future.

"Next year I'll be back with a blueprint for this endeavor. If you'll give me your help, together we'll build a Caldwell College that offers the next generation of alumni even more than it gave us."

The crowd's applause was warm, its questions respectful. But, as at several recent events, the good feeling was punctured by an aggressive businessman who asserted that *his* trust was contingent on the prosecution of Clark Durbin. Deflecting the question, Darrow guessed that these challenges–similar in wording–reflected a pressure campaign orchestrated from within the board of trustees. Whoever it was, they meant for Darrow to yield Durbin on their timetable.

Afterward, Darrow mingled with the group, connecting stories with names and faces and, he hoped, lodging each detail in his memory bank. Then a bleached blond about his age approached him with a smile at once bright and tentative, as though worried she would evoke no response. "Mark, I'm Laurie," she said. "Laurie Shilts. Would you have recognized me?"

Fifteen years and twenty pounds added up to "maybe not"—at least if Darrow had not asked alumni relations to ensure that Laurie was coming. But the blue-green eyes were still those of the sad and angry girl with a dull bruise on her face, telling him at the fateful party about breaking up with Joe Betts. Kissing her on the cheek, he said, "With those eyes? Always."

She drew back, examining him with the proprietary expression of a fond old friend. "Imagine this—you as the president of Caldwell."

Darrow grinned. "'The Decline of the West,'" he said lightly. "Can I buy you a drink? Meet me at the bar in fifteen minutes, and we'll review the last fifteen years."

Laurie's smile contained a dollop of flirtation. "Better late than never," she said.

It was a half hour before Darrow entered the bar, delayed by several pledges of increased support for Caldwell. By the time he sat with Laurie at a small but unsteady wooden table, she had a glass of white wine in front of her, and a flush to her cheeks that suggested this was not her first. Signaling the waitress, Darrow ordered a glass of cabernet.

Laurie summoned a smile of knowing sadness. "So how *are* you, Mark?"

He could not miss the allusion to Lee. "I'm okay. As I guess you know, I lost my wife."

She touched his hand. "I do know. And I'm sorry."

Darrow shrugged. "A lot's happened to all of us since we left Caldwell."

Laurie sipped her wine, pensive now. "A lot happened before we left."

"I remember," Darrow said quietly. "What I don't have a clue about is the rest of your life."

With a faintly rueful laugh, Laurie said, "Oh, that."

"That. So start anywhere you like–job, married or single, kids, where you live, hobbies, criminal record, bizarre quirks you're concealing from your neighbors."

In truth, Laurie's alumni file had already told him much of this. Leaning forward, she said, "Let's skip the fetishes and the conditions of my parole. My ex-husband was–and is–a drunk. So I'm a single mom with a twelve-year-old daughter."

"Twelve?"

"I started making mistakes early." Quickly, Laurie amended this: "Or *continued* making them. Not Chloe–her dad, the deadbeat. It's not easy raising an adolescent girl alone, especially on a teacher's salary."

"I can imagine. Which grade?"

"Ninth-grade English in a nice suburban high school filled with largely uncurious white kids. They're probably not so different than me at that age, though I find that more depressing than comforting." Her smile resembled a grimace. "The prospering classes move there to escape. I guess it's some comfort that their kids are smoking pot with their socioeconomic peer group. But why should I complain? The school's safe, and so's my job."

"And Chloe?"

"She's bright and pretty–actually, she's beginning to look like my old yearbook pictures, back in more innocent times." Laurie frowned. "But she's getting a case of the sullens–if my teenage self is any guide, she'll spend the next six years despising me, all the more so because I'm the only parental game in town." Her voice softened. "It's sad for both of us, I guess. For a long time she was my only company–I leaned on her more than I should have. No boundaries, as they say.

"But now she makes me feel lonely. I guess that's what girls and their moms endure on the way to becoming human again." Laurie summoned a falsely bright smile. "Tales of a Mundane Life. I shouldn't squander the chance to see you on feeling sorry for myself."

Darrow shook his head in demurral. "Sometimes being alone is hard."

She gave him a solicitous look. "For everyone. On the surface, you still seem like the golden boy, so good-looking that I was always surprised by how nice you were. But maybe that helps you cover pain. Even back in college."

"Maybe so. Things happen all your life that no one else can fix." Then Darrow thought of Farr and Taylor, and wondered if this was true.

Laurie's gaze became open, curious. "But you're okay now?"

"Better. Part of that is the Caldwell job. It's a daily challenge, and it keeps me busy and engaged–there's nowhere for a college president to hide."

"It seems like you really care about Caldwell, Mark."

"I do. I just hibernated for sixteen years."

Laurie sipped her wine. "I don't blame you."

To Darrow, this sounded more like a shared emotion than sympathy. "It was tough on all of us, Laurie. We weren't prepared for what happened."

She put a curled finger to her lips. "I still think about that party, talking with you. It was only a few hours later . . ." Her voice trailed off, and then she gave him a sideways look. "Do you ever see Joe?"

"Quite a bit, lately."

"How is he?"

"Pretty good, I think. As far as I can tell, he's got a stable marriage and two nice kids." Darrow paused, looking at her. "It probably helps that he sticks to sparkling water."

Laurie bit her lip, nodding toward her empty glass. "I don't, clearly."

Darrow felt caught between the desire to keep her talking and misgivings just as deep. "So let's have one more for the road," he said, and hated the sound of that.

Laurie nodded. As Darrow caught the waitress's eye, she said, "I'm a friendly drunk, you'll be glad to know. Not like Joe."

"Yeah. I remember how he was."

"Maybe so," Laurie responded with a somber tone. "But not as well as I do."

When the wine arrived, Darrow took a sip. "I also remember," he ventured, "Joe talking about his father getting drunk and beating on his mother."

Laurie's mouth twisted in a smile that made her appear both hard and tired. "He never said that to me. But everyone needs a role model, I guess."

Darrow met her eyes, feeling torn between acceptance and dread. "Joe hit you?"

"Not in the beginning." She shook her head, as though to clear it. "This is pretty hard to talk about. I never really have—for a whole set of reasons, I guess. Is this anything you really want to know?"

"Yes. At least if you'd like to tell me."

The fleeting look she gave him was both grateful and reluctant. "When I first left Steve for Joe," she said at length, "he was gentle. But part of the attraction was that

Joe was wounded–I believed that beneath the spoiled rich kid was a boy who'd been hurt. I was the girl who could help him heal." As she paused, Darrow noted the slight slur in her voice merging with a delay in choosing words. "One night he got really drunk at a party, and he said he wanted to 'fuck' me right away. So he bent me over a chair in someone else's room, all the time saying disgusting things. It felt more like rape than sex." Briefly her eyes closed. "He kept asking if he was better than Steve. And bigger."

Darrow felt uneasy. "Yeah," he said with gentle irony. "It's the fear that haunts us all."

"You're not like that," Laurie said emphatically. "Steve wasn't either." Abruptly she paused, the flush of her cheeks deepening. "At least not with me. When I dumped him, he was angry, but I never thought he'd hit me–not once. Instead he just felt terrible."

Darrow paused. Quietly, he said, "So Steve tells me."

She looked up again. "You saw him, too?"

"Yeah. He's changed a lot–bitter, but also thoughtful. There's more to Steve than most people got."

"Not me. I always knew that Steve saw and felt more than he said–like you, I guess. When I was with Joe, sometimes, I wondered why I'd left Steve. My ex-husband is the answer. Meet a prick, and I still imagine seeing a wounded boy."

Weighing how much to press her, Darrow looked around them. The crowd in the bar, commercial travelers in the final stages of enforced conviviality, was dwindling. "That night," he said, "I thought Joe might have hit you."

As though remembering, Laurie touched her face. "He had. But it happened the night before."

"*What* happened, exactly?"

"It wasn't the first time. He'd get drunk. Then suddenly

he'd be jealous of Steve, like alcohol flipped a switch in his brain–I think he even scared himself a little. My father used to say, Never be with a man who scares you. That night was when I got scared for good."

The quiet fervor with which she pronounced this intimated something left unsaid. Softly, Darrow asked, "What was different?"

As Laurie drained her wine, Darrow signaled for another. A long silence ensued, Darrow waiting her out. In a monotone, Laurie said, "I've never told this to anyone."

"Then maybe it's time."

Laurie averted her eyes. When the chardonnay arrived, she took a quick swallow. "I was alone in his room, studying. I didn't expect him for an hour. So I did what a lot of other girls would do–started going through my boyfriend's drawers. The first two drawers only told me what I already knew–college boys are slobs."

She stopped abruptly, fingers twisting a strand of frosted hair. "And then?" Darrow asked.

"I opened the last drawer." Her voice became pinched. "It was filled with magazines. Pornography."

She looked so disturbed that Darrow hesitated. "And that was what scared you?"

Laurie's expression became self-questioning. "Was I scared then? Or just disgusted? I can't put myself back there when so much has happened. I just stared at the magazines, one after the other, until all I could hear was the way he talked when he was inside me." Her voice softened. "Except I couldn't have been in the pictures."

Puzzled, Darrow watched her. "Because?"

"Because I wasn't black." Laurie's throat twitched. "It was like something from a slave-ship fantasy, white men degrading black women in chains, sodomizing or whipping them. When I felt myself wanting to vomit, I closed the drawer.

"Joe came back an hour later, drunk. He wanted me. I told him no—because of how he was, and because of the pictures. His eyes got wild, and he asked if I still wanted to do it with Steve. I was so disgusted I said, 'Only when I want to feel like a woman.' Then he hit me across the face."

"What did you do?"

"I said I never wanted to see him again." She paused again, looking up at Darrow. "He started to cry, almost sob. Then he said in this kind of whisper, 'Tell anyone about this, and I'll kill you.' "

Darrow felt a chill. "So you didn't."

"No." Laurie took a sip of wine, unable to look at Darrow. "I was like Joe. Too ashamed for people to know what he was like, or the things I let him do."

Darrow tried to find something to say. Finally, he said, "I think I understand."

Laurie shook her head, rejecting easy comfort. "After you found Angela Hall, I thought about telling someone. But then it turned out she was with Steve."

Darrow was silent until she met his gaze again. "So you didn't have to say anything about Joe hitting you."

"Yes," she answered dully. "Or those pictures."

So the police had missed it, Darrow thought, as had Steve Tillman's lawyer. Both, it seemed clear, should have scoured Joe Betts's life much harder. How many people, he wondered now, had been served by Steve's guilt—if only to salve their conscience or put unspoken misgivings about Angela's murder safely behind them. He understood Laurie Shilts well enough: she had never wished to speak of these things, just as part of Darrow wished that he had never heard them. But now he bore the weight of knowing. Gently, he said, "In the end, it only mattered to you."

She gave him the bleakest of smiles. "You're such a good guy, Mark. You always were."

A useful attribute, Darrow thought uncomfortably, if you wanted to manipulate someone. "So tell me," she continued in a throatier voice, "does a nice guy like you have anyone now? I hope that's not a tasteless question."

Darrow smiled, shaking his head. "After two years, a fair one. The answer is maybe. But I don't know whether it's real yet, or how long it can last. She and I are in very different places."

Saying this, he realized that he had spoken of Taylor to no one save her father. Hearing himself say the last phrase aloud, he realized how true it was.

Perhaps it showed on his face. "Only time will tell," Laurie said. "Sorry if I unloaded on you."

Darrow heard the regret in her voice, perhaps the fear of making herself less attractive. "It's been really nice to see you," he assured her. "If you ever need to talk, just call me."

Hope and doubt mingled in her eyes. "Better go now, huh? It's a school day for us both."

Standing, she teetered for an instant. "Let me get you a cab," Darrow said.

Laurie steadied herself. "Am I really that bad off?"

The bar was empty now, Darrow noticed. "No," he answered. "But I had a bad experience with this once, and you've got Chloe to look after. Call me overresponsible."

She took his arm, grateful to depend on him but still working out the logistics. "Tomorrow I have to drive her to school."

"Don't worry," Darrow said firmly. "I'll send a car for you and Chloe in the morning, and another one after school's out. You can tell anyone who cares that you've got car trouble, and a paranoid new boyfriend."

Laurie smiled. "That would keep them guessing, wouldn't it?"

Darrow walked her outside and hailed a cab. As she got in, Laurie kissed him on the cheek.

Darrow stood there for a time. It was just as well, he supposed, that Taylor was not sleeping over. He had far too much to think about.

22

Darrow barely slept. Late the next morning, after several more hours of thought, he decided to telephone Carl Hall.

To Darrow's surprise, given that Hall conducted his business by cell phone, the number was listed. To his greater surprise, Hall answered. "This is Mark Darrow," Darrow said without preface. "We need to talk."

Warily, Hall asked, "About what?"

"I'll save that for later. Alone, and in person."

The attenuated quiet that followed, Darrow knew, could be professional caution or something more. "Give me a clue," Hall demanded. "I don't want to be wasting my time."

Darrow thought quickly. "Among other things, your sister."

Hall's voice became quieter, less derisive. "What about her?"

Darrow decided to take a chance. "You can talk to me, Carl. Or I can go to Garrison."

"I guess you know where I live," Hall said at length.

"I can find it."

"Tonight then. Say ten o'clock."

Hall hung up.

Darrow sat at his desk, motionless, wondering what mistake he might have made, what secret Angela's brother might harbor. All he knew was that Carl Hall had one.

*

DARROW SPENT THE day on autopilot. He met with the chairs of the English and history departments about their needs; wrested more time from Ray Carrick, albeit with increasing difficulty, to dispose of Clark Durbin; importuned a wealthy but irate alumna not to strike Caldwell from her will; began recruiting a committee of alumni, faculty, and board members to address Caldwell's goals and more sharply define the school's identity; spoke to a specialist in minority recruitment; coordinated with Taylor to find dates for their trip to Boston; then asked the alumni relations director to schedule meetings during those days with prominent alumni. After normal working hours he reviewed potential budget cuts over dinner with Josh Daily, Caldwell's chief financial officer, and Joe Betts, who also suggested ways of further protecting Caldwell's endowment from adverse market conditions. Pushing his disquiet to the edges of his consciousness, Darrow did not mention Laurie Shilts. By the time he reached home, it was well past eight o'clock, and the house felt more lonely than normal. Contrary to his usual custom, he did not watch the news.

Something was badly wrong, he believed, and had been for sixteen years. Whatever that was, Darrow had the sense–more intuitive than reasoned–that it shadowed Caldwell still. But until he learned more, he could trust no one with his thoughts, not even Farr or Garrison. Neither man, he was sure, would feel this unease as keenly as he; both might reasonably question his preoccupation with Angela Hall's murder and–given Caldwell's very real problems–Darrow's judgment in stepping outside his role. He could not yet put a name to his suspicions, or risk his own or another person's reputation by accusing someone other than Steve Tillman.

He sat in the living room, glancing at his watch, turning facts and surmises over in his mind, arranging and rearranging them in a kaleidoscope of possibilities. The ones that troubled him most were those he could least afford to speak aloud.

At nine forty-five, Darrow left the house.

CARL HALL LIVED in a ranch-style home surrounded by several acres of fallow land, sequestered at the end of a cul-de-sac on the outer reaches of Wayne. Everything about it served the interests of a man running an illegal business: the gravel drive was long, and the house itself, shrouded by trees, could not be seen from the road. At night, Hall's normal business hours, a visitor could come and go without being identified. But as Darrow parked near the house, his footsteps crunching gravel, it struck him that for a man in a dangerous business this solitude could be a problem, depriving Hall of the protections offered by living on an urban block. No doubt Hall had weapons.

There were no lights on inside the house. Perhaps this was defensive; perhaps not. But Darrow felt pinpricks on the back of his neck. More clearly now, he saw the risk inherent in having told no one of this visit to an isolated place. If the threat he posed to Hall was greater than he knew, Hall might well make him disappear. Darrow did not like the stillness all around him, the darkness of the house itself.

He stepped up to the porch and stopped. Eyes adjusting to the thin moonlight, he found the doorbell. The ring inside chimed through what must have been an open window.

Nothing. Darrow tried again. Aside from the bell, the only sound he heard was the chirping of crickets.

He pressed the door latch with his thumb. To his

surprise, the door was unlocked. Carefully, Darrow slipped into the dark inside, the door still open behind him.

"Carl?" he said quietly. His own voice sounded forlorn to him, hollow in the darkened space.

Still he heard no sound. Instinct told him to leave; nothing–at least nothing good–would come of staying. But he could not seem to move. Still facing a room too dark for sight, he felt for a wall switch by the door.

Finding one, he hesitated, stopped by fears he could not define. Then he chose to flick the switch.

He stood in the entry to a half-furnished living room. Carl Hall sat slumped in an overstuffed chair, as if asleep. For an instant, he reminded Darrow of his own father, save for the absence of an alcoholic's ragged snores.

Darrow felt his skin crawl. "Carl?" he said again, then recognized how foolish this was.

He stepped forward, softly, as though concerned with startling his host. But Darrow was acquainted with the dead: first Angela Hall; then murder victims at crime scenes; last, the body of his pregnant wife, lying in an Iowa morgue. In every case there was a terrible difference between slumber and death. Hall's lips were parted and his eyes wide, as though surprised by his own fate. On the arm of his chair was a hypodermic needle.

Darrow felt the shock wearing off. Unlike other deaths, Carl Hall's evoked no sadness or pity. What seeped through Darrow was a deepening fear of the unknown.

He took out his cell phone and, with a calm that surprised him, called George Garrison at home. "George," he began, "I'm at Carl Hall's house. I think you'd better come."

THE POLICE ARRIVED, then the team of specialists familiar to Darrow since he had found the body of Angela

Hall. "First Angela," Garrison murmured. "Now Carl. Only their mother left."

For a time Garrison left Darrow with a detective. Standing outside the house, Darrow heard Garrison directing the others. Then the chief joined Darrow and the detective, his eyes keen in an emotionless face. "Let's hear it," he demanded of Darrow. "Starting with why you're here at all."

Darrow gave them the minimum: facts stripped of surmise; nothing about anyone but Hall. "You know I've been looking at Angela's murder," he told Garrison. "Carl's role seems pivotal. His own sister–who he lives with–is murdered, but Hall won't talk to the police until Fred Bender leans on him, and even then he tells Fred nothing. His mother says a white guy called for Angela; Hall doesn't know who. His mother says Angela kept a diary; the diary's missing, and Hall claims not to know it ever existed. Angela starts disappearing at night; Hall says he doesn't know why or where. I think he was lying about it all."

In an even tone, Garrison inquired, "Why would he do that?"

"Because he had something to lose by talking or to gain by keeping quiet."

"But you don't know what the 'something' is."

"Look," Darrow said, "every problem Caldwell has seems to involve Hall. Angela was murdered after a party; Carl was at the party. Griff Nordlinger tanked Steve's defense because of a cocaine problem; you think Hall was Nordlinger's supplier. Ditto Clark Durbin's son, only the drug was heroin. Part of Durbin's motive for embezzlement, the story goes, was to pay for his son's rehab."

"Carl sells drugs," Garrison said with muted impatience. "Carl likes money."

"So why is he dead?"

His eyes slits, Garrison examined the ground, as though debating whether to answer. "Looks like he died from a heroin overdose. We found the makings for an injection in the kitchen."

"Why would Carl use his own product? He'd know too well what it does." When Garrison said nothing, Darrow added, "I couldn't see track marks on his arm."

Garrison shoved his hands into his pockets. "You can also smoke the stuff. Or snort it."

"Then why change delivery systems? Because he'd started worrying about lung cancer?" Darrow softened his voice. "I'll make you a bet, George. Once toxicology runs their tests, they'll tell you that there's no other sign Carl was using, and that he died from an overdose massive enough to kill a basketball team. If so, there's a good chance someone murdered him."

Garrison glanced at the detective, scribbling notes at Darrow's side. "With Carl's cooperation?" Garrison said curtly. "Why not suicide?"

"Because Carl lacked the requisite self-awareness."

To Darrow's surprise, Garrison laughed softly. "That's another problem—people liked Carl a whole lot less than he liked himself. Anyone might have decided to kill him—a rival dealer or a customer wanting drugs."

"Maybe so. But they'd have put a bullet through his brain."

The front door opened as two paramedics carried Hall, shrouded on a stretcher, to an ambulance waiting in the driveway. Darrow and the police chief watched until the doors of the ambulance slammed shut, echoing in the night.

"I walked right through an unlocked door," Darrow said. "Any sign of a robbery or break-in?"

Garrison exhaled. "No. Guess that means that Hall let somebody shoot him up, after he was nice enough to let him–or them–in through the front door."

"He *knew* him, George," Darrow said urgently. "Bear with me. I called Hall this morning, threatening to go to you. He sounded worried; he couldn't know how little I knew. Suppose he told somebody I was coming–someone who knew everything I don't, and couldn't let anyone else find out. If so, you won't find his fingerprints."

The detective glanced at Garrison. "Of course not," the chief said flatly. "Or any evidence that he exists. Be nice if you'd give this nameless ghost a motive."

Darrow tried to remain unfazed. "I can't. But do me a favor and I'll give you my best guess."

In the moonlight, Darrow saw Garrison's hard stare of distrust. "What's the favor?"

"Keep my name out of this, for now. For Caldwell's sake, and also mine. There's no good explanation for me meeting a drug dealer."

"That's why you shouldn't have," Garrison snapped. "Bad judgment; tough luck. You should have called me."

"Maybe so. But you get nothing from making me look bad."

Garrison shrugged in indifference, moving his heavy shoulders. Tiredly, he said, "What's your guess?"

"It's possible Hall killed his sister, though I can never work out why. But if Carl didn't kill her–and Steve Tillman didn't–then Carl knew who did." Darrow's voice gained force. "I think Carl was blackmailing someone. Look for the diary, and for secret bank accounts or anywhere else where Carl might hide money."

Garrison stared at Darrow. "You should have called me," he repeated softly.

"Would you have listened?"

Garrison fell silent. "I'll cover you for now," he finally said. "As a favor to an old teammate. Unlike Tillman, you were never a prick."

Darrow left without mentioning Joe Betts.

PART III

THE SPIRE

1

For days Darrow went about his life, busy on the surface, preoccupied beneath it. No one but the police–and, perhaps, a murderer–knew his secret.

He made speeches, chaired meetings, pushed his new committee into life. He saw Taylor often, enjoying each new intimacy of thought and feeling, yet fighting back the knowledge–most intense when he was with her–of concealing that which consumed him. His interactions with Joe Betts were shadowed by things he did not wish to know, suspicions he did not wish to have. He visited Steve Tillman, saying nothing new about the case. The principal salve to his conscience was that he had placed the matter in Garrison's hands. But even there he had hidden much. For now he would wait to see what Garrison did, then decide what else to do.

The character of Joe Betts preoccupied him. Abusing Laurie Shilts and obsessing about black women did not in themselves implicate him in Angela's murder. But Joe could have been the caller mentioned by Angela's mother. Nor had he any corroboration for his assertion that, in the last hours of Angela's life, he was alone in his dorm room. It was disturbingly convenient that, by Joe's account, he had awakened just in time to become the witness who put Steve Tillman in prison.

That was Darrow's dilemma. For now, he was caught between his belief that Steve might be innocent and the reluctance to accuse a prominent member of Caldwell's board, a man with a seemingly sound marriage and blameless life, of an ugly murder. Especially when one basis for the accusation, Laurie's account, might change that life for good.

At several points Darrow was tempted to confide in Lionel Farr. The closest he came was when Farr, remarking on newspaper accounts of Carl Hall's death, expressed puzzlement that "a man who lived off other people's misery would inflict it on himself." Given his own misgivings, the remark deepened Darrow's unease. Joe Betts had been in Wayne on the night of Hall's death. But though Darrow tried to envision Joe with a needle in his hand, he could not easily imagine the mechanisms of a murder by heroin injection. More than anything, this was what kept him from confiding in Farr a theory so lurid yet so speculative that it could transform Farr's concept either of Joe or of Darrow himself.

Eleven days into Darrow's paralysis, Garrison called him. "I want to see you," the chief said brusquely. It was not a request.

THEY MET IN Garrison's office, alone. Garrison closed the door behind him.

At once, Darrow feared that his role in Hall's death was about to become public. The chief sat behind his desk, his gaze penetrating and cool. "Well?" Darrow said.

"We've got things to talk about. Some of which you can't tell a living soul." Sitting back, Garrison regarded Darrow in momentary silence. "You were right about Hall's death. There's no evidence that he used heroin before that night–no tracks, no sign in his blood or tissues. The dose he took would kill anyone. An experienced user would know better, and so would Hall."

Though unsurprising, the revelation heightened Darrow's unease. "We pretty much knew that."

Eyes hooded, Garrison continued: "There were also abrasions on Carl's wrists, bruises on his ankles. It's possible that his arms and legs were bound or handcuffed at the time he was injected."

Absorbing this, Darrow asked, "How would that have happened?"

"If it did? Someone could have held a gun to his head and made him shackle himself. But that's only a guess—not many folks carry handcuffs around with them." Garrison paused, then continued in a lower register: "The point is that we can't rule out your idea that someone killed him. And that Hall knew the man who did."

Quiet, Darrow gazed out Garrison's window. The day was sunny; traffic moved at its normal pace, people going about their lives. But Darrow felt his world changing. Facing Garrison, he said, "You've got no reason to tell me this. There's something else."

After a moment, Garrison nodded. "We found a safe deposit box. Inside was a bag of diamonds worth over half a million dollars."

"So that's how Carl converted drug money."

"Maybe. But Carl knew how to launder money through the Alibi Club. Plus, from the record of entry for the box, he'd apparently begun depositing diamonds thirteen years ago and stopped five years later. Pretty rich for a guy whose drug business was small-time way back then."

Absently, Darrow touched the knot in his tie. "Same question, George. Why are you telling me all this?"

Still watching Darrow, Garrison opened his desk drawer. He took out a single piece of paper and slid it across the desk. Glancing down, Darrow saw a typed schedule, showing numerous transfers of money into seven different bank accounts for businesses Darrow did not recognize. "What is this?" Darrow asked.

"Keep reading."

As Darrow did, a pattern emerged. The transfers had occurred within the last year. By Darrow's swift calculation, that total exceeded six hundred thousand dollars, all in amounts less than ten thousand. "What this suggests to me," he said at length, "is an effort to avoid transfers above the threshold that triggers an automatic inquiry by federal bank authorities." Looking up at Garrison, he asked, "Who's the signatory on these accounts?"

"Carl Hall."

Edgy, Darrow scoured the schedule again. "All these transfers," he said slowly, "happened after Caldwell's money disappeared."

A glint appeared in Garrison's eyes. "You'd be the one to know. No one from the college has taken the embezzlement to Farragher. At least not formally."

Darrow did not respond to this. "Who transferred the money to Hall?" he asked.

"The Security Bank of Geneva. Familiar?"

It was a different bank, Darrow recognized at once, than the one that had transferred money to an account in Clark Durbin's name—the last piece of evidence in the case against him. "Only by name," he said. "It's also a dead end. A Swiss bank will never disclose whoever controls this account. Only Carl could have told you what this means."

Garrison sat back. "Any idea what Carl might have to do with Durbin?"

"Other than that Hall supplied Durbin's son with heroin? That's the only connection I can make between Hall and Caldwell College—except for Angela's murder, which happened sixteen years ago. I can't get to why

Durbin would be siphoning Caldwell's money to Carl Hall."

Garrison propped his chin on folded hands. "What about Durbin's son?"

Darrow shook his head. "He would've had to use his dad's computer to e-mail Joe Betts, then forge Durbin's name to open bank accounts. Pretty sophisticated for a twenty-something drug addict. Beyond that, you'd also need an inside knowledge of Caldwell's financial system.

"Obviously, the members of Caldwell's investment committee had that, including Durbin. So maybe Durbin's kid went through his father's files. But he would have had to figure out that Joe Betts's firm had $900,000 in CDs, and that his father had authority to move it by sending Joe an e-mail. Which gets us back to the question of why Durbin—or Durbin's kid or anyone else at Caldwell—would embezzle money to pay off Carl Hall."

Garrison fixed him with a gelid stare. "Remember what you told Hall you wanted to talk about?"

"Angela."

"Angela," Garrison repeated softly. "I think you know things you're still not saying. Just like you seem to know everyone involved, back from college days." He reached into the drawer again. "I want you to read something. You can't tell anyone you've seen it, and I don't think you'll want to. But after you're through maybe you'll want to tell me more."

Standing, Garrison placed a sheaf of Xeroxed pages, bound by a rubber band, in Darrow's lap. "Take your time," he said.

Without saying more, Garrison closed the office door behind him.

Removing the rubber band, Darrow felt a jolt. In his

hands was what appeared to be a journal, written in a clearly feminine hand.

Alone, Darrow began reading. The nightmare began on the second page: an account of bondage and sexual sadism, supposedly inflicted on the writer by a male figure known only as "HE." Briefly, Darrow paused, touching his half-closed eyes.

The woman's tormentor, if he existed in life, was a man of considerable inventiveness. His techniques were varied, all calculated to produce humiliation without leaving a mark; all, in the diary's account, excited him in proportion to their debasement of the victim. But HE remained nameless, more a force of domination than a man with human characteristics and emotions, so defined by his obsessions that Darrow wondered if he was reading an elaborate exercise in sadomasochistic fantasy. The voice of the narrator was detached; it resembled the accounts of rape victims Darrow had heard as a prosecutor, wherein the woman, helpless during the act, has willed her conscious mind to go elsewhere. Yet the details were quite specific, meticulously recorded in the toneless voice of a concentration camp survivor, too resigned to inhumanity to respond with outrage.

On the last page, the only words she had written were: "There is such darkness in the chamber of stone."

Shaken, for some moments Darrow sat alone in the silent office. His thoughts kept returning to Laurie Shilts, the magazines she'd found in Joe Betts's drawer–which, for Laurie, had exposed Joe's deepest self, transmuting sympathy to fear.

The door opened, startling Darrow.

Garrison stood there, reading Darrow's face. "We found that in Carl's safe," he said. "We don't know what happened to the original."

Slowly, Darrow nodded. “Is this her handwriting?”

“Yeah. When we showed it to her mother, she just shriveled up.”

Darrow waited for a question that never came. “It could all be fabricated,” he said. “There’s plenty of literary precedent for that.”

Garrison laughed without humor. “So that’s what this is. Something Angela wrote for fun.”

“There’s only one alternative: that HE was a real person.”

Garrison crossed his arms. “Then maybe Carl was blackmailing him, just like you said. So HE bought him off with Caldwell’s money, to hide that he was a murderer. If that’s right, the question is why HE killed her.”

It was odd, Darrow realized, to feel more horror in Garrison’s office than standing over Carl Hall’s body. “The diary tells us almost nothing,” he replied, “except about this man’s pathology. There’s no person in those pages. Maybe HE was angry. Maybe HE went too far. Or maybe, as Fred Bender believed about Steve Tillman, HE killed Angela to prevent exposure.”

Garrison gazed down at Darrow. “So tell me this: If the man used Caldwell’s money, who could he be?”

After a moment, Darrow stood. “I’ll think about that very hard, George. For Angela’s sake, and Steve’s.”

2

On the flight to Boston, Darrow and Taylor were companionable but quiet. No doubt, Darrow thought, Taylor was contemplating her interview. Unable to shake the images conjured by Angela's diary, Darrow pondered the psychic landscape–real or imagined–that had produced the faceless HE. For the next four days, he promised himself, he would focus on Taylor as much as he could.

The days would be full. They had dinner reservations, tickets to a Red Sox–Yankees game, plans for walks through Darrow's favorite parts of the city. But he, like Taylor, had work. Aside from meetings with his partners and selected Caldwell alumni, Darrow had two appointments he had mentioned to no one. His forensic accountant, Mike Riley, had analyzed the transfer of money to Hall's bank accounts and, more critically, would try to answer Darrow's questions. Of more speculative value was a meeting with the psychiatrist whose skill and rigor had helped Darrow after Lee's death.

When Darrow turned to her again, Taylor was asleep.

He studied her, pensive. After some misgivings, he had proposed staying at his town house. A shadow had crossed her face. "Will that be all right?" she had asked.

"I think it's time," Darrow had answered simply.

That night, Taylor had awakened from a nightmare she

chose not to describe. The next morning, after she left, Darrow called his housekeeper in Boston.

DARROW AND LEE had lived in a handsome three-story brownstone on the first block of Commonwealth Avenue, near the Public Garden. Standing on the sidewalk, Taylor gazed at the town house. "You must be glad to see it," she said. "The location is lovely."

"I just hope you approve of the decor."

She gave him a sideways look, smiling a little. "Compared to where you're camping out?"

They entered the house. Stopping in the living room, Taylor took it all in–fourteen-foot ceilings, crown moldings, a large stone fireplace, and hardwood floors, brightened by Chinese carpets and bold modern art on the walls, accented by the black grand piano only Lee had played. Taylor admired the piano for a moment, then followed Darrow upstairs.

The rooms–a library, a master suite and two guest rooms, offices for Lee and Darrow, the exercise room where both had worked out–had been, as much as practical, scrubbed clean of any trace of her. Putting their suitcases in a guest room, Darrow wondered if Taylor sensed this.

"I like what you've done," she told him. "Instead of filling a hundred-and-fifty-year-old house with antiques, like you were communing with somebody's ancestors, you made it your own. You'll be pleased to know," she added wryly, "that I even like the art."

"That *is* a relief."

They descended the spiral staircase to the living room. Pausing by the piano, she rested a fingernail on the black enamel, tracing a line that bisected a light sprinkling of dust. Without turning, Taylor said quietly, "You needn't have done that."

"Done what?"

Facing him, Taylor answered, "Remove her pictures."

Darrow tried to smile. "Are you some kind of witch?"

"I hope not. Maybe I'm more sensitive to my surroundings than most, to spaces where something's missing." Her tone was even. "I can still feel her, Mark. I don't need to be part of an exorcism."

Darrow felt at sea. "Maybe we should go to a hotel."

"That's not what I'm saying," Taylor replied. "She's part of your life, and you love this house. So why pretend?"

Briefly, Darrow spread his hands, a gesture ending in a helpless shrug. "You're the first woman I've brought here, Taylor."

"Somehow I'd guessed that." Moving closer, she touched his wrist. "Living in my father's house, and remembering my mother, is much harder. This is something I'll get used to."

"Will you?"

"Yes." Briefly, Taylor smiled. "Of course, I'm looking forward to dinner out. The wine will help, too."

"Then you can choose it," Darrow promised.

TAYLOR CHOSE MEURSAULT. It was clear she liked the Federalist; they relaxed into dinner, talking easily again. It struck Darrow that he had dined here with her father, two days after Lee's memorial service. Farr had gently implied that, in time, there would be another woman for Darrow. Now Lionel's daughter sat across the table.

After dinner, Taylor and Darrow walked through the Common and the Public Garden. Dusk had fallen; the swan boats on the duck pond became shadows in the fading light, and an evening breeze stirred the branches of the willows. Away from Wayne and Caldwell, Darrow felt lighter. "Truth to tell," he said, "I sometimes think about selling it."

"The house? Setting aside that I feel like a trespasser, it really is very nice."

Abruptly, Darrow realized that he did not yet wish to go back. They sat beneath a willow, gazing at the first faint moonlight on the pond. Sensing his mood, Taylor let him be.

"About the photographs of Lee," he said at length. "That was also for me."

She turned to him, head tilted. "Yes?"

Darrow drew a breath. "When I look at them, I don't just feel sad. I feel angry, and guilty."

"Because she died?"

"Because of how she died, and why." Darrow felt repressed emotions coming to the surface. "Lee was the most engaging person I never completely knew. She grew up with an alcoholic father and a mother who took her own misery out on Lee. The result was a childhood almost as bleak as mine.

"Lee's reaction was to become completely driven—always in motion, never looking back. She was as perceptive about the politicians she covered as she was scared of looking at herself, especially when the truth was hard." Darrow turned, gazing at the pond. "In the context of our marriage, one of the hard truths about Lee is that she never wanted kids."

Taylor was quiet for a moment. "But she was pregnant when she died."

"She was also drunk," Darrow said flatly. "Not just a little, but a lot, driving faster than she should have. And it was dark. So she hit that patch of ice and lost control."

Taylor touched his hand. "I'm sorry, Mark."

"So am I," he said with quiet bitterness. "Also about the seat belt she wasn't wearing when the car flipped. One act of carelessness after another, resulting in two deaths–hers, and the son I very much wanted.

"I knew Lee didn't, without her ever saying so. She'd learned too well from her mother that kids were a form of enslavement." Darrow's voice softened. "Of course, I overlooked that. And Lee, being who she was, enabled me. Perhaps she loved me enough to violate her own instincts. But once she was pregnant, I could feel how much she hated it."

He felt Taylor watching him. "Had drinking always been a problem?"

"No. Living with an alcoholic father terrified her. Even before the pregnancy, Lee didn't drink much. Except on the night she died."

Softly, Taylor asked. "What happened that night?"

Darrow hesitated. "The facts are pretty banal," he began. "She was drinking with the press pack at a hangout near where the candidate she was covering had camped out for the night. Lee was more vivacious than normal–almost manic, I'm told. And she was with old friends, the ones who must have sensed how much she feared what motherhood would do to her career." Darrow's tone flattened. "Maybe she wanted to escape being pregnant; maybe she was running from our marriage. Whatever, she broke her rule about abstaining during pregnancy. She had a drink and just kept on going."

"And no one tried to stop her?"

"Not that anyone's willing to say. But Lee's biggest mistake was driving. Or maybe it was becoming pregnant." Darrow's voice lowered again. "We'd never really talked about that. If we had, I'd have promised to do more than my fair share of parenting.

"That would have been okay. Instead, Lee died, and I hated her for it, and still loved her. As screwed up as this may sound, I've even wondered if I helped kill her." Darrow exhaled. "So there it is. And here *I* am, awash in self-pity."

After a moment, Taylor said gently, "And you never talked to anyone about all this?"

"No one. Somehow I couldn't. Except the psychiatrist I found to keep myself sane."

"Did that help?"

"Some. Our friends tried to help, too–it wasn't their fault they didn't know. The same with the women I eventually started seeing." Darrow studied the swan boats, silver in the moonlight. "Maybe I'm like Lee. It's hard for me to lean on anyone. Except, at times, your father."

"But not about this. Or anything like this."

"No."

"Yet it's okay for people to lean on you," Taylor responded softly. "Like the night I talked about my mother–too much, I thought–and you were so sensitive to how I felt. Just as you were when I was twelve."

A catch in his throat took Darrow by surprise. "Maybe I knew something."

"Maybe I did, too."

Tears surfaced in his eyes. As he fought them back, Taylor leaned her forehead against his. After a time, she said, "Let's go home, Mark."

THEY TRIED TO sleep. Neither did. Late at night, they found each other. It was sweet and intense.

In the morning, as Taylor slept, Darrow went downstairs to make them coffee. The house seemed different, he realized. He liked knowing she was here.

3

The next morning Darrow met with his ex-partners, while Taylor window-shopped on Newbury Street, "practicing for when I have a job." After lunch together, Taylor went to her interview, Darrow to the psychiatrist who had once helped him.

Jerry Seitz was a lean, bright-eyed man in his mid-forties whose attentive stillness seemed imposed on a naturally energetic nature. Darrow and Lee had known him socially. Before turning to Seitz in the aftermath of her death, Darrow had seen in him an ingenuous sweetness, almost a naïveté, which did not square with his profession. But within the confines of his office, Seitz was incisive and bracingly direct. Darrow liked him a great deal.

For the first time in a year, they faced each other in Seitz's sparely appointed office. "So," Seitz inquired bluntly, "are you still blaming yourself for Lee's death? Or have you managed to accept that Lee also fell short in your marriage?"

Darrow shifted in his chair. "I understand that Lee had her own difficulties. But the accident kept us from facing up to things." He stopped, shaking his head. "You knew her, Jerry. If she'd missed that patch of ice, would we have made it?"

Leaning forward, Seitz clasped his hands, weighing his

answer as he looked into Darrow's face. "Maybe. I know you would have tried, Mark–awfully hard."

"And Lee?"

Seitz gave the slightest of shrugs. "Would have done the best she could. But I always felt that more of the burden would have fallen on you."

Darrow absorbed this. "I'll never really know, will I? I was talking about that just last night."

Seitz's eyebrows shot up. "That's new for you, isn't it?"

"One could say that."

"Who is she?"

Despite himself, Darrow laughed. "My provost's daughter. She came here with me."

Seitz's eyes lit with interest. "Is this serious?"

"It could be. But she's twenty-eight–looking for her first full-time job, completing her PhD dissertation, and intent on living in a major city when I've just moved to the place she never felt at home. Those are pretty serious impediments."

"So what is it about her?"

Darrow smiled a little. "As near as I can tell in a month's time? Everything else."

Still watching Darrow, Seitz smiled too, signaling encouragement. "If she's the right one, Mark, see if you can make things work. It says something that you've opened up to her." His smile vanishing, Seitz picked up a piece of paper from the table beside his chair. "On to a grimmer subject. I took detailed notes on what you told me about this diary. You're right that the whole thing could be fiction–the abstract quality of the narrative might suggest that. Still, you've asked me to assume it's real. So let's reprise the rules."

"All right."

"First, you want me to speculate on the character of the

narrator and the man she chose to call HE. Second, you asked me to assume that HE killed her." Seitz briefly checked his notes. "Finally, you're trying to compare HE with a man you *know* to be real: a former classmate who was frequently inebriated, physically abusive to women, and obsessed with bondage involving African-American females. But who also, by your account, gave up drinking shortly after the strangulation of our narrator, and since then has led an ostensibly productive life that includes a highly successful career and a wife and kids he appears to cherish. Does that about cover it?"

"Pretty much."

Seitz puffed his cheeks. "This isn't psychology, Mark—it's more like divination. We should be doing this in a bar. But I'll try."

"All I can ask, Jerry."

"Though we know nothing else about him, the acts Angela ascribes to HE are clearly aberrant. Equally apparent, this man feels a deep contempt for women, however well masked in his so-called normal life. A common background begins with a hard-handed father who exploited a codependent mother. These guys often hate their fathers but also despise their mothers, for being weak."

"That's my old classmate, Jerry. Or so he told me in college."

"Interesting. The next step is that the son adopts the contempt of his father toward his mother, while Mom, replicating the pattern, placates him." Seitz grimaced. "In an adolescent boy there tends to be an erotic element in his subjugation of Mom—her submission begins feeling sexual to him. And because he hates his father, he begins to compete with Dad for power.

"This can get pretty tangled. When he was sixteen, a

patient of mine came home from a date and found his mother in a negligee, drunk. So he pulled up her negligee and fucked her. She responded, and he liked cuckolding Dad. But he and Mom never spoke of it again. Perverse enough for you?"

"It'll do."

Seitz cocked his head. "By the way, what do you know about your classmate's wife?"

"Never met her. As near as I can tell, her role is to be wife and mother."

"Well, maybe they're the Cleaver family. Of course, you just can't know what happens once the kids are in bed. So I'll move on to the difference between a sociopath and a psychopath."

"Think HE is one or the other?"

"Only one of them," Seitz said succinctly. "As a lawyer, no doubt you've met your share of sociopaths—superficially charming but wholly lacking in empathy. For a sociopath, the only function of other people is to fulfill their own needs. If you're perceptive, they're pretty easy to spot. Most critical here is that they tend to be non-violent—their sense of caution is too great."

"That would be Carl Hall, actually."

"Which brings me to the psychopath." Seitz's voice softened. "Psychopaths are very special people."

Beneath Seitz's words Darrow heard a warning. "In what way?"

"To begin, they're pretty rare. Like sociopaths, they tend to grow up in an abusive and hostile environment." Seitz paused, then added quietly, "So did you, I know. But psychopaths experience other people solely as objects. And they have absolute mastery over emotions that most of us can't control."

"Such as?"

"Fear. Put an ordinary person in a frightening situation—say, someone draws a knife—and their heart rate jumps. But a psychopath's anxiety level actually *decreases*. They thrive on danger, and tend to be absolutely fearless."

Imagining HE as a real person, Darrow felt uneasy. "How do they relate to women?"

"For a psychopath, sex is power. He needs and despises women at the same time. So he seeks out submissive women—perhaps prostitutes." Again, Seitz paused. "As the diary also suggests, he can get off on the thrill of it, until the need for sexual dominance becomes an addiction."

"What about their willingness to kill?"

"It's often very high. That, too, typically originates with a harsh father. But because a psychopath feels neither anxiety nor guilt, he can kill without remorse. And once he does, he can go to bed and never lose a minute's sleep." Seitz looked hard at Darrow. "By nature, psychopaths aren't anxious people. They don't tend to act on impulse. Instead, they're typically brilliant planners, meticulous in what they do. The man who murdered Angela Hall and her brother—assuming it's the same man, and that Hall was, in fact, murdered—may well be a psychopath. All he'd require is a reason that compels him."

"Would blackmail do?"

Seitz nodded. "Blackmail," he said gravely, "would do very well."

Reflective, Darrow sat back, steepling his fingers to his lips. "It was after Angela's murder that Joe Betts became sober. Maybe he was reacting to being dumped by his college girlfriend. In either case, that doesn't feel consistent with what you're saying."

Seitz tilted his head, as though examining Darrow's question with a jeweler's eye. "If your classmate was moved by shame or conscience, I'd agree. But simple self-preservation is sufficient for a psychopath. Pretending to honor the rules can enable them to conceal who they are. Given the proper motivation, psychopaths are capable of incredible self-control, even over their own deepest desires. Often for years at a time."

Darrow felt a nascent sense of dread. "You're saying HE could have lived a seemingly normal life after murdering Angela Hall. Including succeeding in a demanding career, as Joe Betts has."

"Sure," Seitz responded with an ironic smile. "In the annals of psychopaths, success as a financial adviser is pretty small potatoes. Consider Hitler and Stalin, both paragons of the breed. We remember them as mass murderers. But both also managed to outmaneuver their rivals–and, indeed, entire countries–until they dominated a fair share of the world."

"They were also obviously nuts."

"A lot of people didn't think so. And their form of insanity helped them." Seitz got up, cracking his window to admit a measure of fresh air from another sunlit day. "For one thing, they loved power and had a talent for exploitation–show weakness, and they'd only become more cruel. The only people they respected were those who shared their ruthlessness and lack of fear.

"For them, a couple of murders and a little embezzlement would have been light work. Yet they were often brilliant at reading other people. Neither felt any sentiment that would interfere with their insight and discernment. Faced with Hitler, Neville Chamberlain never had a prayer."

"Ruthlessness is one thing," Darrow retorted. "Charm is another. Sociopaths have that."

"So can psychopaths. And their confidence–concealed arrogance, really–inspires trust in them." Seitz slowed his speech for emphasis. "Stalin and Hitler survived in a much harsher environment than Wayne or the financial services industry."

Darrow fell quiet. After a time, he said, "I'm trying to square this with Joe Betts. For that matter, with his present family life as he presents it."

Seitz pondered this. "The man you describe is engaging, and capable enough to be a great financial success at a very young age. So much so that Caldwell made him a trustee in his mid-thirties, then asked him to oversee the school's investments.

"What you can't know is what he's like to be around in his most unguarded hours. As you concede, you don't know Betts's wife at all. But if she's perceptive, a spouse may realize there's something off. Best to have a wife who's somewhat otherworldly and trusting. Family members see more than the rest of us."

Darrow was still for a time, staring at a watercolor he did not truly see. "Outside the family circle, would HE have any weakness?"

"Arrogance. Psychopaths tend to have superior intelligence. They also know it. So every success they have in getting away with something increases their feeling of omnipotence." Seitz's tone became clipped. "As I noted, they excel at reading other people. But, because they can, they tend to underrate those around them and overrate themselves. They get caught, if at all, when they finally encounter someone as smart as they are."

Darrow took this in. "Tell me about Angela Hall."

"Sure," Seitz said promptly. "Unlike HE, we know Angela was real. What we don't know is whether the narrator in the diary is Angela or a surrogate for fantasies she never actually experienced. But a fair chunk of the populace gets a rush from a modest amount of pain, as long as it's not too dangerous. So in 'normal' S&M, there are rules.

"The problem for our narrator is that HE seems to have no rules. His pleasure comes not just from scaring, but from hurting. Thus his entwinement with her becomes more dangerous, his techniques ever more sadistic."

Darrow nodded. "At the beginning of her diary," he said, "the game seems somewhat manageable. What I was feeling was a process of seduction–Angela could take it, perhaps even be intrigued by it. But by the end, beneath her tone of eerie dispassion, she sounded frightened to me.

"My problem is that I knew her–or thought I did. I know we flatter ourselves by thinking that we understand people based on seeing a tiny fraction of their lives, that which they allow us to see. But the Angela I perceived wouldn't have signed on for this. At least not voluntarily."

"What do you know about *her* family?"

"Nothing."

"So for all you know," Seitz said pointedly, "Dad beat Mom. Like spousal abusers, their victims tend to replicate what they grew up with."

"Suppose that doesn't apply here?"

Seitz shrugged. "You know the alternatives. One, she liked it. Two, HE had some kind of leverage. Three, HE paid her."

Darrow sat back. "Joe had no leverage I can think of. If Joe was HE, they either met each other's needs or he was paying her. God knows Joe was rich enough. But the cops found no sign that Angela was getting money from anything but work."

"What about those diamonds?"

"Those were her brother's–" Darrow stopped himself. "Let me think about that."

"Let's return to Betts. How well does what I've told you fit?"

Darrow organized his thoughts. "Some pieces do. The abusive dad, contempt for women, hitting his girlfriend, an interest in S&M involving black females. And Joe was always smart enough and–at least when he was sober–personable.

"But could he have done all this? Beneath the arrogance you describe, Joe seems vulnerable and insecure. That's what I still struggle with."

Seitz nodded. "Anything else?"

"Your point about dormancy is important–the idea that a psychopath, if faced with danger, might have sufficient self-control to swear off S&M for years. Or, equally, important, alcohol . . ."

"That would especially be true," Seitz asked, "if he'd killed someone while drunk–either in a rage, or because he didn't know how to stop. He might well not kill again until Carl Hall threatened to strip the cover off his Norman Rockwell existence." Seitz paused, then admonished Darrow: "As you know better than anyone, *facts* are what you need here. The best you can do is take what I've given you and use it as a guide. Never forgetting that all our theorizing could be a pile of garbage."

Despite the darkness of his mood, Darrow smiled a little. "I'll still pay your bill, Jerry. But there is one thing I'm certain of. The personality you describe is *not* Steve Tillman."

4

Darrow and Taylor dined at Excelsior enjoying a table by the window overlooking the Public Garden. Over cocktails, Taylor described her interview.

"They're very serious," she said, her tone sober and a bit surprised. "The museum wants to expand its collection of contemporary art, and they have the resources to do it."

"And they also seem serious about you?"

"Definitely. I don't have a lot of experience with interviews like this, but they were very thorough and interested in probing my ideas." She smiled, acknowledging a pride she could not contain. "In fact, they asked me to come back tomorrow, to meet with the head curator."

That she would be leaving Wayne, Darrow told himself, was inevitable; whatever his real feelings, his role was to be pleased for her. "If they offer you a job, would you take it?"

Taylor bit her lip, her look of pleasure succeeded by perplexity. "I wasn't expecting to make a decision this soon–either about a job or a city I barely know. But jobs like this are hard to find."

"Can you hold them off for a while?"

Taylor shook her head. "Not if they want me. They'd like someone to start tomorrow, if they could, and they're interviewing other candidates."

Darrow gazed out at the greenery of the Public Garden,

his eyes following a young couple holding hands as they walked a meandering pathway. "Sometimes," he observed, "it's easier when decisions get made for you. It's far more difficult when *you* have to make them, not knowing what else may be out there."

Taylor gave him a curious look. "What was it like to live in Boston?"

The question made Darrow feel oddly glum. "As a single person? Fine, I guess—there's enough to do. Compared to a lot of cities, Boston's a magnet for young people. It's where I met Lee." Darrow gave her a somewhat rueful smile. "It seems like we're headed in different directions. Thanks to your dad, I'm a citizen of Wayne, Ohio."

Catching his mood, Taylor covered his hand. "If you hadn't come to Caldwell, Mark, we wouldn't know each other at all. At least not in this way."

Darrow tried to make his smile less equivocal. "I'd have missed that," he said.

THE THOUGHT OF separation, Darrow realized, brought new sensuality to their lovemaking, the sweet but sad awareness that, next month or the month after, they would be unable to reach for each other in the middle of the night. Though he told himself it was childish, he could not help but feel cheated. They had really just begun.

Lying beside her, he pondered this deep into the night. "What are you thinking?" she whispered.

He turned his face to her. "How did you know I was awake?"

"Because you breathe more deeply when you're sleeping."

She slept less well than he did, Darrow was learning, often restless until early morning. "I was thinking about you," he said. "Hoping this job prospect turns out however it's supposed to."

That seemed to make her thoughtful. Softly, she said, "I'll miss you, too."

They remained quiet until Darrow drifted off. As he did, he remembered Lee saying that most men were like Norsemen–they could eat well, make love with gusto, then fall into a dreamless sleep, untroubled by their own stirrings.

Suddenly, Darrow started awake.

It took a moment to orient himself. Then he realized that Taylor was sitting on the edge of the bed, still naked, her face in her hands. Placing his hands on her shoulders, he felt her flinch, heard a stifled sob.

"Taylor," he said with quiet urgency. "What is it?"

For a long time, she did not answer. "The same dream," she murmured. "Ever since I was twelve."

"What happens?"

She did not turn. "I find my mother dead. I try to get her to talk to me, and she can't."

He rested his chin on her shoulder, his face against hers. "Is that how it happened?"

"I don't think so–not the talking part. But I've had the dream so long I don't even know what's real." She paused, then said with muted despair, "I thought I'd finally outrun it."

"How do you mean?"

She turned sideways, staring out into the darkness. "The last year, at NYU, it seemed to have gone away. Returning to Wayne revived it." Her voice held a note of self-contempt. "It's just so arrested. It's like I'm twelve again, stuck in the worst part of my life."

"Did you ever go to a therapist?"

"At twelve? I wouldn't have known how to ask, and

then I went to prep school." She turned, speaking softly. "What's there to explain, really? I lost my mother in adolescence, when I had no equipment for dealing with it, no one I could bring myself to talk with. Instead I ran away to Trumble, trying to shut off all my feelings. But they just migrated to my dream life. Living in the house where I found her body is bringing it all back."

She sounded close to devastated. "Be kind to yourself," Darrow said. "You lost the parent you loved most at the time you were least prepared. If you need help, Taylor, why not get some?"

She said nothing. But afterward, neither slept.

The next morning, over breakfast in his kitchen, Taylor remained silent. She did not finish her cereal, or even seem to know he was there. It was as if she were walled off.

She has a tendency toward melancholy, Farr had told him. Darrow did not know quite what to do.

Gazing at the table, Taylor said tonelessly, "I still have an interview, don't I."

MIKE RAILEY'S OFFICE was jammed with manila folders in stacks, tomes on finance, and manuals on forensic accounting. Small, dark, fidgety, and often amused, Riley defied Darrow's image of a certified public accountant. He was also brilliant.

Sitting in front of Riley's cluttered desk, Darrow inquired, "Where's your pocket protector?"

"Lame," Riley replied. "Especially from a recovering lawyer who needs my help."

"So you believe what everyone else does?" Darrow said. "That Durbin is a crook?"

"He may be," Riley answered. "Just not indubitably."

"Explain."

"First, the facts inculpating Durbin look pretty

persuasive. He was on the investment committee, his e-mail address is on the directive to Joe Betts, and what appears to be his signature is on the bank account where the proceeds went. As well as on the second account that received fifty thousand dollars wired from a Swiss bank."

Darrow took a swallow of black coffee. "What else?"

"There are still some holes." Riley spoke more slowly now. "The missing piece in the chain of evidence is that we don't know who controls the Swiss account. Obviously, the Swiss will never tell us. A new piece, also unexplained, is why over six hundred thousand came back to Carl Hall from another bank in Switzerland, and what, if anything, that has to do with Caldwell College. Given that the transfers to Hall happened *after* the embezzlement may suggest that the same person transferred money from one Swiss bank to the other. But that leaves us to wonder why Durbin would siphon money to Hall." He gave Darrow an arid smile. "That Carl died from a shitload of heroin is also inconvenient."

"Which brings us to my alternate theory," Darrow rejoined. "Blackmail, with the embezzler using Caldwell's money to pay off Hall."

Riley took out the schedule of transfers that Garrison had given Darrow. "What's interesting about these transfers is that they suggest a certain level of sophistication. Whoever moved the money understood that individual transfers of over ten thousand to or from a Swiss bank would trigger a federal inquiry."

Darrow looked at him keenly. "Anyone in the financial services industry would know that. Certainly anyone on Caldwell's investment committee. Except, perhaps, Clark Durbin."

Picking up a pen, Riley held it to his lips. "And so, you ask, could someone like Betts have framed Durbin?"

Darrow nodded. "You know the problem, Mike. Who else but Durbin would have access to his computer and e-mail account, plus the ability to 'forge' Durbin's name? No one believes Clark when he says it wasn't him."

"I don't believe him," Riley said flatly. "Or disbelieve him. Ever hear of 'spoofing'?"

"No."

"Not many people have. In brief, it's a very clever technique through which, by changing the settings on your PC, you can send an e-mail using someone else's address." Riley looked at Darrow keenly. "Someone *could* have done that to Durbin."

"What about Betts's reply? I've seen the e-mail trail; Joe e-mailed Durbin in response."

"Sure. But the sender of the original e-mail, by rigging his computer, can ensure that the reply goes to his PC. In my scenario, Durbin would never receive it." His eyes were bright with interest. "That would work particularly well, I suppose, if Betts were replying to himself."

Darrow reflected. "But anyone with inside knowledge could have done it?"

Riley grinned. "Anyone in central Ohio," he corrected. "I had my IT guy take a look at this. He tells me that's where Durbin's e-mail to Betts originated. Aside from Durbin, who on the investment committee lives in central Ohio?"

Darrow felt his instincts quicken. "Betts," he answered promptly. "And Ed Rardin. But our investigators obtained access to the PCs of everyone on the committee."

Riley waved a dismissive hand. "Of course they did. But that proves nothing if a member of the committee used a separate computer with a false account. Which is exactly what he would have done."

"What about Durbin's signatures?"

"I showed the copies you sent me to a handwriting expert." Riley gave a fatalistic shrug. "Inconclusive, he says. If someone forged Durbin's name, he varied the script enough that he must have been working from multiple examples of Durbin's real signature—no one signs his name the same way twice. But my expert also thought the pen tracks appeared heavier than Durbin's normal script, creating the possibility that someone was imitating Durbin's signature with painstaking deliberation. Bottom line, he isn't sure."

Pensive, Darrow eyed the Harvard coffee mug where Riley kept his pens and pencils. "So where are we?"

"Limbo. I can't tell you that any of this happened. I'm just saying it *could* have." He flashed a brief but jaunty smile. "Bring your laptop with you?"

"Sure."

"When you get home, open up your e-mail. Check out what pops up."

"I'll do that," Darrow said, and left.

WHEN HE ARRIVED home, the house was quiet, and Taylor had not returned.

Restless, he went upstairs to his office and opened his e-mail. Amid the cluster from Caldwell was one from Mike Riley. Opening it, he found a separate e-mail to Riley from Darrow's own address. "Mike," it began, "this will explain how I stole Caldwell's money. Being a lawyer, theft comes easy. I first learned by sending bills to clients."

Caught between amusement and unease, Darrow replied, "Lawyers also sue people. Please look up 'libel' in the dictionary."

Which, if Joe Betts knew what Darrow was doing, Joe might also suggest.

*

When Taylor came through the door, Darrow was dressed for the Red Sox game. Though she looked tired, she seemed to have recovered her aplomb. "So?" he asked.

"So I'm sorry for the morning's séance."

"I liked the quiet," he said lightly. "How was your second interview?"

"Depends on your point of view." Taylor's smile was tentative. "They offered me the position, Mark. For better or worse, no one's making this decision for me."

Despite himself, Darrow was surprised. "This is major," he said. "Shall we skip the game and talk this over?"

Taylor shook her head. "I'd really like to go–we can always talk between innings. After all, I've got a whole week to decide."

They drove to Fenway Park, Taylor describing the offer and her impression of the curator. "It all sounds good," Darrow said as they arrived.

"If I let this go," Taylor responded, "I may regret it. But I also regret that it comes too soon. As they say, I'm torn."

The night was balmy, perfect for baseball. They sat between home and first base, three rows back, gazing in a direct line at the pitcher's mound and, beyond that, the left-field wall known as the Green Monster. "I love baseball," Taylor said. "The people, the smell of beer and hot dogs . . ."

"What about the game?"

"Especially the game," Taylor said. "It's performance art–there's a beautiful geometry to how it's played, the lines and angles. Every game is a creation, different than whatever came before. But there's a wonderful history, passed through generations." She smiled a little. "I never saw Ted Williams play. But my father could describe his swing so perfectly, I felt as if I had."

Once again, Darrow had the sad sense of potential

lost—a father and daughter who, their lives altered by the same event, were unable to transcend it. "I have no memories like that," he said. "My father and I never played a game, or went to one. He just disappeared one day, leaving nothing behind. I don't even know if he's alive." And when his mother died, Darrow thought but did not say, all he had felt was emptiness.

Taylor glanced at him. Judging from his expression, she realized that he had said this less from personal sadness than to make a modest point about Farr. She chose to focus on the game.

It was unusually well played, a pitcher's battle between Josh Beckett and C. C. Sabathia in which, with the game tied 1–1 in the eighth inning, both pitchers finally yielded to the bullpen. "Why don't we do this," Darrow proposed. "If the Red Sox win, you take the job and never look back."

Taylor smiled. "That would be a relief, actually. Let the gods of baseball decide."

In the ninth, Alex Rodriguez put the Yankees ahead with a shot over the Green Monster. Taylor bit her lip. "Guess they want me in New York."

"Give Boston a chance," Darrow said.

The Red Sox got through the rest of the top of the ninth with no further damage. With one out in the bottom of the ninth, Dustin Pedroia singled. Then, with two outs, David Ortiz hit a towering home run off Mariano Rivera that won the game for Boston. Amid the tumult, Darrow gave Taylor a hug. "Seems like they're excited for you."

Taylor leaned back, her smile uncertain. "Want the decision back?" Darrow asked.

"No." Taylor kissed him. "It's a perfect job for me. I'm just thinking how much I'll miss you."

5

THERE WERE CERTAIN MORNINGS, DARROW THOUGHT, when the world at first light seemed as fresh and new and awesome as creation.

This Monday morning was one. Walking from the President's House to his appointment with Lionel Farr, he crossed the gentle hillock between two older red-brick dormitories, taking in the scent of flowers, the deep greenness of oak trees, the seeming closeness of an unsullied blue sky, the glistening wet remnants on the grass from an overnight thunderstorm that, with the stiff breezes that followed, seemed to have purified nature. Light and landscape had always affected Darrow's moods: dank, dark enclosures depressed him; a mountain vista or a pristine beach or even a bright morning like this could exhilarate him. He had learned to savor such moments. And so, instead of meeting in his office, he had suggested to Farr that they walk there together.

Farr was waiting outside his house. Casually dressed for summer in slacks and a polo shirt, at first sighting the provost looked much younger than he was, his gray-blond hair still thick, his stomach flat, his profile clean. Even at a closer range that revealed the deep lines on his skin, the angles of his face seemed hewn from granite, the light blue eyes penetrating and clear. Lionel Farr would not slide gently into his dotage; he would fight against old age until he exhausted his last resources. But today the sight of him, usually welcome, jolted Darrow from his reveries. The conversation he intended would be difficult, its outcome unclear. Darrow had no script for this.

They headed toward College Hall, two men of roughly the same height and build, walking with the same easy rhythm. "How was Boston?" Farr inquired.

"Fine. What does Taylor say?"

Farr gave him a brief, sideways look. "Taylor," he said carefully, "can be a woman of shifting moods, somewhat difficult to read. At least for me. But she seemed a bit preoccupied, I thought." He paused, then added with an undertone of regret, "I'm in the odd position of asking Caldwell's president how my daughter's doing."

Taylor, Darrow realized at once, had said nothing about her job offer. "If you're asking how we are," Darrow said, "the answer's that we're still quite new. And running out of time."

The words seemed stiffer than Darrow had intended. "I don't mean to pry," Farr responded with parental dignity. "But I care for you both. I think you know that. Perhaps, at some point, Taylor will, too."

Darrow turned to him, trying to refine his sense that Farr was obscurely wounded. "I think she does, Lionel. But her mother's death seems to have been a fault line in both your lives. She's lived with her own thoughts for a very long time."

He could not find his balance this morning, Darrow reflected; he had said more than he had meant to. Quiet, Farr seemed to withdraw a little. "Anne was fragile," he said at length. "Not just physically, but emotionally. In some ways, so is Taylor–it's as if she believes that I could somehow have protected the mother she loved from the ravages of heart disease. It's a child's way of looking at the world."

The comment nettled Darrow. "That's a little harsh, Lionel."

"Perhaps so. But I think Taylor sees her mother as the princess in the tower, a helpless woman allowed to die. In the mythology, I'm less a human being than a marble statue, with the emotions to match." Farr's voice softened. "Anne's death devastated us both. The added price I paid with Taylor was my recompense for surviving. I, not Anne, was supposed to die."

The statement stunned Darrow. "For God's sake, Lionel."

They had reached the edge of fraternity row, the head of the walkway leading to the main campus. Abruptly, Farr stopped, looking not at Darrow but at the steeple of the Spire. "No doubt you think I'm being melodramatic."

"No," Darrow said bluntly. "Hurt, and a little resentful."

Farr's eyes narrowed, and then he nodded slowly. "Fifteen years of distance can do that. I have no doubt that had Anne lived, Taylor would not have left so soon, or remained alienated for so long. I still believe that as she got older, I might have done better as a father. Things could have been quite different."

"She did come back, after all."

"I know that," Farr said at length. "Perhaps some good will come of it–whether for Taylor and me or for the two of you." He faced Darrow, his expression somber. "You know she won't stay here, Mark. Not just because of work, or even the place itself. In her heart she believes that Anne depended on me too much. I hope you understand that Taylor is determined to control her own psychic space, to have a piece of her life that is hers alone."

"I don't expect anything else," Darrow said. "And don't want it. When the summer's done, Taylor has to move on."

"Which may not be bad for either of you," Farr responded. "In your case it will give you the time to better comprehend Taylor–both her strengths and her vulnerabilities." Farr's smile, faint and fleeting, seemed directed at himself. "I know I sound like the pompous father in *Love Story.* But if you and Taylor are meant to be more than you are now, it will stand the test of time and distance."

Darrow tried to untangle his own reaction, a shifting compound of irritation, sadness, and amusement. "Worse than *Love Story,*" he said dryly. "Nonetheless, I'll hold the thought."

Farr laughed softly, and they began walking again. "There was something else," Farr prodded. "You wanted to speak in confidence."

"I do." Though Darrow had gone over what he meant to say–editing and rearranging the sequence of his explanation–he found that starting did not come easy. "Mind if we sit somewhere?"

They found a stone bench in a manicured garden, incongruously Asian in character, between the library and the student union. At this hour, a little before eight, few summer students were ambitious enough to surface; effectively deserted, the site afforded Darrow the privacy he needed and yet kept him from feeling claustrophobic. The subject was bad enough.

"There's no good place to begin this," Darrow said. "So I'll start with the most recent events. There's a fair chance that most of Caldwell's stolen money was siphoned to Carl Hall."

Farr raised his head slightly, as though looking at Darrow from a new angle. Something about his pupils reminded Darrow of drill bits. "Go on."

Succinctly, Darrow outlined Garrison's schedule of

Hall's transactions: the timing and disbursements of money; their connection to a Swiss bank; their apparent structuring to avoid federal oversight. The skepticism in Farr's gaze seemed to border on antagonism. "The man was a drug dealer," he said curtly. "I assume you've given this information to Joe Betts and Greg Fox."

"Not yet."

"And why not, for the love of God?"

Darrow tried to remain calm. "I'll get to that," he said. "In the meanwhile, please withhold judgment. You can have a coronary once I'm done."

Farr inhaled slowly. "All right," he said in a neutral voice. "Tell me why the police entrusted you with this delicate information."

"Several reasons. One is that I found Hall's body."

Farr's smile, a rare show of teeth, held more anger than his hardened tone. "Of course. What better job for the president of Caldwell College."

"Part of my job," Darrow snapped, "is being smarter than the people you and Carrick chose to investigate this mess. I wish *that* part were harder."

The fury and frustration in Darrow's tone seemed to give Farr pause. In a frosty voice, he said, "Please justify that statement."

"Joe and Fox are masters of the obvious. 'Obviously,' Durbin embezzled money—after all, he sent an e-mail to Joe Betts, then signed his own name to bank accounts. 'Obviously,' Durbin's not only a criminal but criminally stupid. But the fact is—and I have an expert to confirm it—that a reasonably savvy person could have replicated Durbin's e-mail and forged his signature, leaving Durbin none the wiser. If you don't know you stole the money, it's hard to cover your tracks."

Farr crossed his arms. His voice soft and ironic, he asked, "So who did steal it, Mark?"

"Someone on the investment committee."

Briefly, Farr closed his eyes. With the same quiet, he said, "We're talking about business leaders of considerable wealth and unquestioned probity. I may be cynical about human nature, but your thesis borders on hallucinatory. Pass over whether any of them have the inventiveness you posit. What could possibly motivate one of those men to steal nine hundred thousand dollars, then try to ruin Clark Durbin's life, at considerable risk to their own?"

"Blackmail."

Farr propped his elbows on his knees, staring at the garden. "Let me grasp this. A black drug dealer from the southeast side of Wayne was blackmailing a prominent white alumnus. Makes perfect sense. Just tell me what connects two such disparate men."

Darrow steeled himself. "That's one reason I went to see Hall. After I found his body, the police located a safe deposit box in Carl's name. Inside was a small bag of diamonds, and a Xerox copy of a diary written by Angela Hall."

"Angela kept a diary?"

"Yes. It's not very pleasant to read. Or to describe."

In unsparing detail, Darrow did. The blood drained from Farr's face, making him look older. Tonelessly, he said, "Pray God this was an experiment in creative writing and that those things never happened to her."

"And if they did?"

"It defies every notion I had of this young woman." As he considered Darrow's words, the grooves in Farr's face seemed to deepen. "From what you say, the man she calls HE seems barely real."

"His perversions sound real enough." Darrow paused.

"A couple of months before she died, Angela began disappearing at night. No one knows where she went. But her mother believes *that* was when she began this particular diary. After she was murdered, it disappeared."

"From which you posit . . ."

"That Angela went out to meet the man called HE. After she died, Carl stole her diary. That was his tool of blackmail."

Farr gazed straight ahead. "By your own account, the diary gives no clue to the man's identity. Even were he real, how would Carl know?"

"I don't have any idea. But I believe that Carl *did* know, and therefore knew that the same man might well have killed her. That's why HE murdered Carl."

Farr's mind moved quickly now, following the rules of Darrow's logic. "Making HE a member of our investment committee."

"Yes." Darrow paused and took a breath. "Joe Betts."

To Darrow's surprise, Farr was expressionless. "For which accusation, I assume, your reasons go back sixteen years. Joe was at the party. Joe and Tillman fought over Angela. No one saw Joe during the hours when Angela died. But Joe claimed to see Tillman returning from the Spire, sealing Steve's conviction." He turned to Darrow. "We've always known these things. But what on earth makes you think Joe was capable of the practices depicted in Angela's diary?"

"Joe hit his college girlfriend," Darrow answered softly. "He also collected pornography involving black women and sadomasochism."

Farr pinched the bridge of his nose, rubbing it as though trying to erase a headache. "And you know this because–"

"Joe's ex-girlfriend told me."

"When?"

"About two weeks ago."

Turning again, Farr examined Darrow steadily. "You have been busy, haven't you?"

"Yes. Sorry it's so inconvenient."

"This is no time for petulance. Tell me why Angela wished to satisfy Joe's desires."

Darrow shook his head. "I don't know."

"He wasn't paying her?"

"Not that I know about."

Farr grimaced. "Outside the fateful party, do we know if Betts and Angela Hall had any relationship at all?"

Darrow hesitated. "Her mother remembers a youthful-sounding white guy calling Angela at home . . ."

"But not Joe."

"She just doesn't know." Once again, Darrow marshaled his arguments. "We know Steve had sex with her. But everything else, factually and psychologically, makes Joe as plausible a murderer as Steve Tillman. We know Steve didn't shoot up Carl Hall. Throw in the diary and the embezzlement, and a web starts tightening around Joe Betts."

Farr looked around, as though fearful that they might be overhead. "So what you're asking me to believe is that, by whatever means, a financial adviser from Columbus subdued Carl Hall inside his home on the outskirts of Wayne, prepared a heroin injection that–for reasons not apparent to me–he knew was lethal, and then put Carl to sleep like a terminally ill house pet."

"Essentially, yes."

"Your theory is a house of cards," Farr said tightly. "Change a single fact or eliminate one assumption, and the whole thing collapses. You become, if not the biggest fool in Caldwell's history, one of the most arrogant and presumptuous. The man who smeared an innocent man with wild accusations in order to save a guilty friend." Farr paused, then continued in a tone of deliberate calm: "We'll pass over all the leaps in logic. I won't ask you to decipher the baroque description of 'darkness in the chamber of stone.' We'll even forget the incongruity of converting a member of Caldwell's investment committee into a forger, a specialist in computer fakery, a sado-masochist, and an expert in preparing and administering heroin, all packaged in a man as nerveless as a brain surgeon. Just tell me why the 'blackmail' commenced only in the last year."

Farr's self-control, Darrow found, was more daunting than his anger. "It didn't start this year," he answered. "Hall opened the safe deposit box over a decade ago, and converting cash to diamonds is a classic technique for laundering money. I'm assuming that's how the payments began–"

"When Joe was barely out of school? Where did he get the money?"

"Inheritance, I'm guessing. His father died in our junior year."

Farr scowled. "At least you have him using his own money. So why would he risk embezzling Caldwell's investment funds?"

"I don't know. Maybe Joe no longer has the money we think he does. Or, after he got married, perhaps his wife started keeping an eye on their finances."

The day was becoming warmer, Darrow realized. He could see the dampness on Farr's forehead, feel it on his own. "Then take your central assumption," Farr countered, "that Betts killed Hall. Were that disproven, would you agree that your entire theory evanesces?"

"It wouldn't help," Darrow acknowledged. "But Joe was

here in Wayne that night. We had a meeting to discuss our finances."

"Which ended when?"

Darrow tried to remember. "A little before eight, I think."

"What time did you find Hall?"

"Around ten."

"So sometime between eight and ten, you posit, Joe drove across town to Hall's, then subdued and killed him. All while escaping detection." Farr put his hand on Darrow's shoulder. "Let me propose an alternative theory. It would have taken less than an hour for Joe to drive back to Columbus. By nine o'clock, rather than killing Carl, Joe was watching the Disney Channel with his kids. Why don't you ask his wife?" Farr's tone became softer yet. "Of course, she might wonder why you care."

Darrow was silent. "Depending on her answer," Farr said, "your theory could be in deep trouble. I hope you've not been so careless as to share it with anyone else."

Darrow shook his head. "No. Not even the police."

Farr looked into Darrow's eyes. "Well, at least you retained the judgment to tell me. So, for all our sakes, hear me well.

"I understand why Tillman's conviction troubles you. But there's no way for you to know what really happened that night. Just as there's little reason to believe–and no way to prove–that Carl Hall's possibly accidental death relates to the college's sad history. My ultimate question is this: Why do you insist that Durbin's apparent theft must connect to Angela's murder?" Farr's grip on Darrow's shoulder tightened. "Take this fantasy to Chief Garrison, if you must. *He* can blow it up. But once you do that, you may destroy your presidency and, given all that's happened, jeopardize Caldwell College itself.

"That's not what you came here for, Mark. Angela Hall's dead; the money's gone. Your sole responsibility is to secure our future. Just as, after Angela's death, I did everything in my power to keep this school alive."

Darrow met his eyes. "I care about Caldwell, too. Perhaps as much as you."

Farr released his shoulder. "This isn't just about Caldwell," he said quietly. "You and Taylor are the most important people I have left. For either of you to suffer for this is more than I can bear. Please, tread lightly."

Slowly, Darrow nodded. "I will."

6

SHORTLY AFTER LUNCH, DARROW RECEIVED A CALL from Ray Carrick. Without preface, Carrick demanded, "When are we turning Durbin over to Dave Farragher?"

"When I know everything I need to know," Darrow answered simply.

"What else is there to know?" Carrick said with weary disgust. His voice became flinty. "At this point, Mark, you can either prosecute Durbin or explain why not. The governance committee of the board is meeting next Monday. We look forward to hearing from you."

Still raw from his confrontation with Lionel Farr, Darrow briefly wondered if his provost had telephoned Carrick, agreeing on a strategy to force his hand. Perhaps this was paranoid. But whatever the case, Darrow was trapped—he could not explain himself fully without accusing Joe Betts, and Carrick had given him one week. "Then I'll look forward to seeing you," Darrow said.

This reply, temperate but uncowed, induced in Carrick a momentary silence. "While we're on the phone," Darrow continued, "is there anything else you want to talk about?"

The question seemed to catch Carrick off guard. "Yes," he said defensively. "This whole business with the Tillman case—poking around in Farragher's files. We didn't hire you to do Dave's job."

Darrow held his temper. "They're not Dave's files," he replied. "They're public. Steve Tillman was my friend.

One reason he's in jail is that everybody did their job except the lawyer who was defending him. If that bothers me enough to take a second look, that's my privilege as a citizen. I'm sure you agree that the man serving life for murdering a Caldwell student should actually have killed her."

"Dave Farragher has no doubt," Carrick said testily.

"He mentioned that–as I think you know." Darrow softened his tone. "I hope this isn't an issue for the board, Ray. But if it is, we can make it a subject of Monday's meeting as well."

Carrick's silence made it clear that he had heard Darrow's message: Darrow was willing to risk a public confrontation that, perhaps, could spin out of Carrick's control. "I'll reflect on that," Carrick said slowly.

Darrow wondered again whether, by private agreement, Farr was using Carrick to protect Darrow from his own excesses. But he felt Ray Carrick becoming his adversary. "I'd be happy to discuss this further, Ray," Darrow said in his most amiable tone. "On the phone or over lunch. I'd hate for us to misunderstand each other."

"So would I, Mark. If you have anything else to tell me, please do."

Very soon, Darrow knew, he would have to stand on something more concrete than his authority as Caldwell's president. "I will, Ray."

Hanging up, Darrow wondered what else he could learn in seven days.

LATE THAT AFTERNOON, Darrow called Joe Betts's office.

As he expected, Joe's assistant answered the phone. "Hi, Mr. Darrow. Looking for Joe?"

"You, actually." He sat back in his chair. "I'm trying to

put together my expense reports, and I think I've scrambled some dates. Including a dinner with Joe."

"I'm sure I can help," Julie said with maternal good cheer. "I'm used to looking after boys."

"No doubt. Specifically, I'm showing a meeting with Joe at eight o'clock on the twenty-fifth. But that somehow doesn't seem right to me. Mind checking Joe's calendar?"

"Just a minute."

Waiting, Darrow calculated how to maneuver the conversation. At length Julie came back on the line. "The twenty-fifth's right. But Joe's calendar shows six o'clock, not eight."

"Bizarre," Darrow said, his voice puzzled. "It couldn't have been eight o'clock?"

"I don't think so. I'm showing that he drove to Cleveland that night, for a client meeting early the next morning." She gave the knowing but affectionate chuckle of an assistant attuned to her employer's eccentricities. "Joe doesn't schedule things late—he's a stickler for his full eight hours of sleep, especially on the road. I keep telling him to pack his fluffy pillow."

It was possible, Darrow saw at once, for Joe to have murdered Carl Hall before driving to Cleveland. As Farr had suggested, all that would require was some very surprising skills and the nerve of an assassin. "Thanks for the help," Darrow told Julie.

"You're welcome." Swiftly, she added, "Hold on, Mr. Darrow." There was a brief pause, then Julie explained, "Joe was passing by. When he heard it was you, he wanted to say hello."

Darrow hesitated. "Great. Please put him on."

"Hey, Mark," Joe said cheerfully, "Guess you need Julie to tell you where you've been."

"Yup. And all I need now is for her to tell me where I'm going."

"All of us could use that." Betts's voice changed pitch. "Anything new that I should know about?"

"Nothing in particular."

Joe hesitated. "Ray Carrick called me today, checking on the whole Durbin fiasco. He was wondering if we'd learned anything new that would keep us from seeking prosecution."

"Why am I not surprised?"

"So do we? You were going to see your forensics guy, I know. Ray seems to want this buttoned up."

"We're all on the same page, Joe." Darrow's tone became placating. "It's been three weeks since I told Durbin that he should come to Jesus. His time is running out."

The brief silence that followed suggested that Betts had caught Darrow's evasion. "And your guy in Boston," he prodded.

"Can't say that Durbin didn't do it."

The small equivocation seemed to unsettle Joe still more. "So I guess you've got nothing more to tell governance next Monday."

Darrow gave a short laugh. "News travels fast. Ray's not bashful, is he?"

"Not when something sticks in his craw. And Durbin does." Joe's tone became sympathetic. "This may be a time to give Ray what he wants. Still, if you think prosecuting Clark would hurt Caldwell more than help us, I'm more open to that argument. For whatever my opinion might be worth to Ray."

Darrow noted this change of attitude. Suspicion followed at once: if Joe had murdered Carl Hall, perhaps he no longer wanted the police or prosecutor to dig more deeply into the embezzlement. If so, Joe and Darrow were both ensnared in the crosscurrents of what might be an agreement between Farr and Carrick to prosecute Clark Durbin. But Darrow's confrontation with Farr had jarred him—he had a shade less confidence in the logic of his intuitions, and his interpretations of behaviors with multiple explanations.

"I'll let you know," Darrow said easily. "There's a decent argument that indicting Durbin would shake loose where the money went."

"It could," Joe agreed. "Or we could shut this down and let Clark just go quietly. You have to weigh recovering the money against ongoing negative publicity if Durbin goes to trial. For Caldwell's sake, I'm now willing to swallow my pride."

"Thanks, Joe. And I'm sorry to have bothered Julie."

"No problem," Joe said amiably. "Except on weekends, that was my only dinner out the entire month."

"Even with clients? You're leading a quiet life, Joe."

"By design. Dinner with Katie and the kids is pretty close to sacred." Joe's voice became serious. "In college, I told you about the old man. He'd come home on the train from Wall Street, spending a good hour in the bar car. I don't know who was more scared when Dad came through the door—Mother or my sisters and me.

"It stays with you, Mark. Once the kids were born, Katie and I agreed that dinner would be a time for us and the kids to enjoy each other, talk about the day, or just hear what's on everyone's mind. I can't change my childhood, but I can make theirs different."

However gratuitous in context, Joe's tribute to family life sounded heartfelt. Joe might be sincere or an extremely practiced actor—in either case, he very much wanted Darrow to know how completely he had changed, and how much his family relied on him. "As I said before," Darrow said, "I envy you."

"It'll come," Joe said almost gently. "Someday."

Deeply reflective, Darrow said good-bye.

Turning, he gazed out the window at the tree-shaded lawn in front of College Hall, recalling, as he did, walking with Joe across this lawn on the day of Joe's confession. HE was a psychopath, Jerry Seitz had surmised–amoral, adaptive, attuned to danger, gifted at outwitting others, able to restrain his deepest desires in order to survive. If Joe was guilty, these were among his attributes. In that case, Joe's claim of familial closeness was a complete and utter fraud.

Darrow tried to untangle his thoughts, let them lead wherever they would. But they kept gravitating to Laurie Shilts, the bondage magazine, the pathology detailed in Angela's diary. *There is such darkness in the chamber of stone.*

It was early evening, Darrow realized. He picked up the telephone and called Fred Bender's office.

The chief of security was in. "Mind if I walk over?" Darrow asked.

"Sure," Bender said laconically. "Been wanting to discuss our budget."

WHEN DARROW ARRIVED, Bender was leaning against the building near the doorway, smoking a Camel. Darrow joined him, looking across campus toward the sandstone base of the Spire.

"I've been thinking about our conversation," Darrow said.

"About Steve Tillman?" Bender moved his shoulders. "So have I, to no great purpose. What's bothering you now?"

"It's more a question. Back at the time of Angela's murder, who had access to the Spire?"

Bender gave him a curious glance. "Far as I know, things were pretty much the same as they are now. And had been ever since some drunken fool took a swan dive from the bell tower." Bender took a drag on his cigarette. "Security is supposed to have the only keys. But the president, administrators, trustees, and faculty members can borrow one to show alumni or special guests–anyone dumb enough to risk a heart attack by climbing a couple hundred steps."

"I recall each step," Darrow said with a smile.

"I bet you do. The day you climbed there, Durbin got a key from security to open the door himself. By tradition, that's the president's job whenever we beat Ohio Lutheran."

Darrow nodded. Facing him, Bender said, "I guess you're wondering if someone got inside there the night Angela Hall was murdered."

Darrow kept his face blank. "I've been grasping for a reason why I found her near the Spire."

Bender gave him a skeptical smile. "It's like a prison in there. Who'd want to be inside the Spire at night? Anyhow, once you came back down, Durbin locked it and gave the key back to security."

"You asked him?"

"Yeah. You weren't in any shape to notice, but it was locked when we showed up in response to Lionel's call."

A fragment of memory surfaced in Darrow's mind: Taylor's amusing account of how a prep school friend lost her virginity in the chapel, supposedly sacrosanct, when her boyfriend managed to obtain a key. "Were students ever allowed to borrow a key?" he asked.

"Not without an authorized person." Puffing his

cigarette, Bender added with a note of humor, "I don't claim it never happened. If there's one thing I've learned, it's to respect the enterprise of college students in the face of adult obstacles."

Darrow nodded. "I remember well."

Bender's eyes grew serious. Softly, he said, "Can't say we asked Tillman if he had a duplicate key. Or, for that matter, Joe Betts. If that's what you mean."

"I don't know what I mean, Fred."

Bender finished his cigarette. Glancing at his watch, he said, "Quitting time."

"For both of us," Darrow said. "Thanks."

He started back to his office. Over his shoulder, Bender said, "About the budget. You going to give me the extra man I need?"

Turning, Darrow smiled, giving a careless wave of the hand. "Anything you want, Fred. Fuck the English Department."

Bender emitted a skeptical laugh, and ground out the Camel with the heel of his shoe.

7

In place of an elaborate dinner, Taylor and Darrow prepared a picnic of red wine, Gruyère cheese, bruschetta, and cold shrimp. They ate at a wrought iron table behind the President's House, the twilight gathering around them.

"You look tired," Taylor said.

And also preoccupied, Darrow reflected, with both the burden of his secrets and the strain of withholding them from Taylor. "I've got a lot on my mind, I guess."

"Care to talk about it?"

"Maybe later. I'm curious about your final answer to the museum."

Taylor's brow knit, her expression becoming abstracted. "I'm accepting the position tomorrow," she said. "Or the next day. The salary's decent and the acquisition budget is more than that. Having sniffed around in the last couple of days, I can't see anything else where I'd have this kind of autonomy."

"Then congratulations," Darrow said, raising his glass. "When do you plan to start?"

Taylor touched her glass to his, looking more serious than pleased. "I'll try to get another six weeks here, to finish my dissertation." She sipped her wine, adding, "And to spend more time with you while I can."

Despite his worries, Darrow felt relieved. "I thought you couldn't wait to blow this particular pop stand."

"In most ways, I can't. Wayne isn't a good place for me." She hesitated, the doubt on her face replaced by candor. "We haven't had much time together, and I'm not sure what either of us is ready for. But I like you very much, Mark–more, at this stage, than I've ever cared for anyone." As though to cover her embarrassment, Taylor finished lightly: "Of course, you had a head start on anyone else. You're the only guy I had a crush on even before I knew what sex was."

Darrow laughed. "We met when you were seven, Taylor. I had to wait for you to catch up."

Taylor's smile did not quite reach her eyes. "So how do you feel about long-distance relationships?"

Darrow pondered the question. "Lee and I had one, every election cycle. Maybe she needed that. I didn't, really." Reading the disappointment on Taylor's face, Darrow took her hand. "I wasn't looking for someone who lived in another city. But the way I feel about you may end up mattering far more."

Taylor tilted her head. "It might be hard–me in Boston, you here, both of us with demanding jobs."

Still holding her hand, Darrow shrugged. "We're two smart people who seem to be able to talk pretty openly. I've already had one career, and I'm into my second. Launching yours is pretty important. We'll figure out what's right to do."

"Then I guess we're taking this as it comes."

"Starting now," Darrow said. "Have your dad's permission for an overnight?"

Taylor rolled her eyes. "That's still a little strange," she answered, then continued in a musing tone: "When I came back to Wayne, I thought Dad and I might become closer. Instead there's this weird constraint between us, partly because of what's happening with me and you.

Sometimes I feel guilty, as though the energy I should be putting into healing my relationship with my father is going to you instead." She managed a smile. "I guess the truth is that you're just easier."

Darrow felt regret that this three-sided relationship had become more complex than he wished. "At one point," he replied, "I had this illusion that I might help things. In the end, I hope I can."

"I hope so, too."

Dusk had come, Darrow noticed, and with it a surprising coolness in the air. "So things are no better between Lionel and you?"

"A little, I suppose–I think he appreciates that I came home. But there's something Olympian about my father, a distance."

"That's not just with you, Taylor. Lionel is a man of his time–even with the people who most admire him, and that's pretty much everyone around the place."

A corner of Taylor's mouth turned down, lending her expression a trace of sadness and frustration. "But shouldn't it be different with a daughter who's also an adult?" Taylor's voice sharpened with annoyance. "He still treats me like a child, Mark, sometimes even in the smallest ways. The other day, I found him struggling with something on his computer. It's painfully obvious that the Internet is like a foreign country to him. But he absolutely refused to let me touch his dinosaur of a laptop."

Darrow smiled, recalling the many times when some contemporary had complained that a personal computer had reduced a parent to their babbling infant. "Once a child," he said, "always a child. And never more so than when a parent resents you for knowing more than they do."

Taylor did not smile. "Maybe so. But he was that way

with my mother, I've begun to remember. Like he couldn't trust anyone but himself to do things right."

"Maybe that's one reason you've been so slow to trust."

"With men? I admitted that, didn't I." Taylor thought for a moment. "Maybe it's my father. But probably that's too simple. I loved my mother completely. But I realize now I never wanted to be as passive as I thought she was." Taylor shook her head, as if to clear away confusion. "Maybe she was just worn out, from a heart that had never worked right. A child's perspective is skewed by the limits of a child's perceptions."

"Speaking for my own childhood," Darrow agreed, "that's true enough. To me, my parents weren't human. Even now, it's hard to sort them out." He paused, then added simply, "At least Lionel's still alive. The two of you have time yet."

Taylor gazed at him, and then her expression softened. "Whatever else, I like the way *we* are. You and me."

"Does that mean you're staying over?"

Leaning across the table, Taylor kissed him. "Of course."

THEY LAY TOGETHER in the dark. The shared warmth of lovemaking and the comfortable talk that often followed had begun to feel familiar to him.

"You never told me about your day," she said.

Darrow composed his thoughts. "It's not so much about today. Or any particular day. It's much bigger than that, and much more draining."

"Can you talk about it?"

"I'm not sure." Darrow paused, then repeated softly, "I'm just not sure."

Something in his tone caused Taylor to sit up, leaning

on her elbow as she looked at him. "You've been holding something back, haven't you? I could feel it in Boston."

"I had no choice, Taylor. For many reasons."

"Is this about Steve Tillman?"

Darrow weighed his answer. "And Angela Hall. And several other things, all of them pretty volatile. I don't want you to become part of this."

"You're sounding like my father." She caught herself, then said more evenly, "Maybe that's not fair, either. Even lovers are entitled to zones of privacy. I know I have mine. But, spoken or not, they still affect the other person."

"Like your nightmares, you mean."

"Exactly like them. You may not always know what they're about, Mark. But they're still with us, as you're well aware."

Darrow fell silent. Though he could not see her expression, he could read it in Taylor's voice–serious, intent, unwilling to let this go yet. "So I've begun to tell you things," she continued. "That's not easy for me. But I felt that you wouldn't exploit my candor, and that what goes on with me really matters to you. So, okay, this isn't a transaction. But what goes on with you really matters to me, too."

Darrow tried to unravel the mix of fact, intuition, and suspicion that ate at him. "Some things I'm not free to reveal, Taylor. Others could badly damage at least one man's reputation. But here's the essence: I don't think Steve killed Angela, in part because I believe the same man killed her brother."

He felt Taylor sitting up straighter. "Carl died from an overdose, I thought."

"True. But I don't think Carl did that to himself."

"Then you believe Angela's murderer is still out there."

"He may be, yes."

Taylor absorbed this. "How much have you told my father?"

"Most of it." Darrow hesitated. "A lot of this bears on Caldwell, in the present as well as the past."

"What *can* you tell me, Mark?"

Darrow hesitated. "Angela kept a diary," he said. "After she died, no one could find it. Now it turns out that Carl made a copy. The contents were pretty disturbing."

"How?"

"It suggests that she may have been involved in a fairly pathological relationship with an unnamed man. If he's real, he may know more about her murder than anyone still alive. The last page ends abruptly, and quite strangely. A single sentence: 'There is such darkness in the chamber of stone.'" Darrow paused. "I can't make sense of it. But I've started relating it to the Spire, maybe because I found her body there. Of course, I've never forgotten climbing to the top on the day she died."

"I remember, too. I was standing between my father and mother, looking up at you."

"I'd rather have been where you were. I'm pretty claustrophobic and don't much like heights. The stairway was so dark and gloomy I half-expected to encounter druid priests." He touched her arm. "But enough about the Spire. About my worries, I've told you all I can. At least for now."

Taylor did not answer. She lay on her back, staring into the darkness, toward the ceiling. "What is it?" Darrow asked.

Taylor's voice was muted. "I was recalling childhood fears. At some point I became terrified of the Spire."

Darrow rolled onto his side. "Because of Angela?"

"Before then," Taylor said softly. "Don't ask me to explain it. Maybe it's a child's imagination. For better or worse, I had quite a vivid one, and frightening fairy tales often feature stone towers."

She asked him no more questions. Nor, Darrow sensed, did she wish to talk. He held her until he fell asleep.

Suddenly he awakened. Crying out, Taylor struggled in his arms, trying to break free. "Taylor," he said urgently. "It's me–Mark."

She twitched and then was still. He felt new dampness on her skin. "You all right?" he whispered.

She seemed to shiver. "Just hold me."

For the moment, Darrow realized, that was all he could do.

8

For the next few hours, Darrow kept his thoughts to himself. When Taylor left, still preoccupied, Darrow called his assistant, asking her to clear his schedule and then track down every file concerning Angela Hall's time at Caldwell and to deliver it to his home. "Do it yourself," he told her. "It's absolutely critical that nobody else know about this. No one at all."

After hanging up, he telephoned George Garrison. "Got anything for me?" Garrison asked bluntly.

Once again, Darrow thought of all he was concealing. "I was hoping you did."

Garrison grunted, refusing to answer. "Why do I feel like you're still playing games with me?"

Darrow considered the risks of antagonizing a policeman who could, whenever he chose, place him at the scene of Carl Hall's death. "What I'm sitting on," Darrow said slowly, "is theory, not facts. If my theory's wrong, it could be very damaging to Caldwell, and at least one innocent person. I'd like to feel more certain about this before I come to you."

"If you even think you know something new about Angela or Carl," Garrison said, "*we* should sort it out. How you 'feel' about that isn't my priority."

His time was running out, Darrow knew. "Watching out for Caldwell is one of mine," he answered. "Just give me until Monday. Six more days isn't a lot to ask."

*

STEVE TILLMAN STUDIED Darrow through the Plexiglas window. "I wasn't expecting you," he said. "They don't make it easy to visit on short notice."

"This wouldn't keep."

Something in Darrow's voice caused Steve's gaze to harden. "I guess this isn't a cheer-up-the-prisoner visit."

Darrow watched his face. "There's something I've never told you—or the police. The reason I avoided your trial."

Surprise stole through Steve's eyes. With unconvincing sarcasm, he said, "At last I get to know."

"Yes. Then I want the truth from you."

"About what?"

"The night Angela was murdered," Darrow said flatly. "I called you from the fraternity house at about three A.M. That's roughly when the waitress saw someone laying Angela's body by the Spire. The same time, basically, that Joe claims to have seen you outside the dorm. You didn't answer the phone."

The smile Steve deployed at last was a movement of lips. "And *you* didn't tell anyone."

"Only Lionel Farr."

To Darrow's surprise, Steve laughed aloud. "So you and *Lionel* covered for me?"

"Lionel thought you were guilty," Darrow said succinctly. "He stayed quiet for my sake, and helped keep me away from the trial."

"What did *you* think?"

"I didn't know. But I couldn't be part of putting you away for life. Tell me where you were that night."

Steve's bitter smile returned. "Maybe you should have asked me then."

"I'm asking now."

Steve shrugged. "If I don't remember screwing Angela,

why would I remember that? I was pretty fucked up that night. Maybe I was just passed out."

Darrow leaned closer. His face and Steve's, now inches apart, were separated by Plexiglas. Under his breath, Darrow said, "Bullshit."

Steve's smile vanished. "The phone was right by your bed," Darrow went on. "I called twice–fourteen rings, then fifteen. Anyone but a dead man would have answered."

Given Steve's blood alcohol level, Darrow was not sure of this. But Steve's gaze broke. "Like I said, maybe I went outside to breathe."

"But that's not *really* what you said, is it. What you keep on telling me was what a fucking liar Joe Betts was." Darrow's tone became cutting. "You're the liar, Steve. You were outside the room."

A vein in his friend's temple throbbed. "Maybe I was," he allowed. "Even then I couldn't tell real from unreal."

"So why accuse Joe?" Darrow snapped.

"Because I didn't kill her." Briefly Steve's eyes shut. "At least I know why you didn't visit all those years."

"That's not the reason."

"Well now you've got a good one. Please don't feel obligated."

Darrow stood. Softly, he said, "But I am, pal. We're not done yet."

DARROW DROVE HOME, doubt and depression seeping through him.

On the way, the only call he took was from Lisa, his assistant. Retrieving Angela Hall's records, she wanted him to know, had required a trip to a storage facility on the outskirts of Columbus. But the files would be inside his door when he got home.

They were. Opening the package, Darrow found Angela's application to Caldwell, memos of scholarship committee meetings, transcripts of grades, and the beginnings of graduate school applications prematurely interrupted–a draft letter of recommendation, a list of prospective law schools. Feeling spent, Darrow spread the files on his dining room table.

He had no idea what he was looking for. From his first conversation with Fred Bender, Darrow knew that he would not find obvious signs of emotional problems–behavioral issues or plummeting grades. Sorting the files, he tried to clear his mind.

Angela's first year, he discovered, was like that of many freshmen. A stellar student at Wayne High, she had struggled to maintain the 3.0 GPA necessary to retain her scholarship. Like Darrow, she had difficulty with the required science and math courses; unlike Darrow, her expository writing, though adequate for high school, had necessitated extra work at Caldwell. Nor had her choice of a prospective major, political science, seemed to suit her. None of this surprised him. Nor had it alienated the scholarship committee headed by Lionel Farr. Instead, the committee had allowed her to achieve the minimum grade point average by taking, without charge, a summer school classics course known as an easy mark.

For a moment, Darrow paused, imagining the challenges she'd faced.

Money was a constant problem. Unlike the full scholarship Lionel Farr had obtained for him, Angela's package covered tuition but not room and board. Darrow was not forced to work during the school year; Angela was compelled to, and the thinness of her resources required her to live at home. The necessity of a scholarship, and her trouble in maintaining a 3.0 average while working, had her dangling over a precipice as she entered her sophomore year.

Scanning her transcript for the fall semester, Darrow felt an odd relief. Three B's and an A in Farr's entry-level philosophy course had left Angela with some margin for error. The second semester enhanced this—along with two B's in basic courses she had received a B plus and an A minus in two philosophy classes, the latter taught by Lionel Farr. Darrow wondered if Farr, a stickler for high standards but a man with his own sense of justice, had, as with Darrow himself, responded to Angela's effort and ambition by reading her exam papers with a merciful eye. By the end of sophomore year, Angela had made Farr her academic adviser and had switched her major to philosophy.

This, too, evoked a memory in Darrow. Finding a kindred spirit in the head of the history department, he had switched his major from economics and made Dr. Silberstein his adviser, taking every possible course from him. Only an honest self-evaluation—and Charlie Silberstein's amusing but caustic description of academic life—had helped dissuade Darrow from considering a career in academia to parallel that of Farr, still his principal mentor. Farr's own judgment had proven definitive: "You're not cut out for our cloistered world, Mark. You have the mind and instincts of a lawyer."

Darrow closed the folder. He was tired, he realized, his concentration wandering. After brewing a strong cup of French roast, he turned to Angela's junior year.

From its beginning, she blossomed as a student. Her skills in composition improved exponentially: an A in an expository writing class was accompanied by a B plus in advanced Spanish and two A's in philosophy courses—one based on a take-home essay exam; the other, taught by

Farr, on a rigorous final exam concerning Friedrich Nietzsche, a topic with which Darrow was all too familiar. Angela's second semester, almost as strong, was topped by another A, in Farr's Philosophy of the Enlightenment class. By the end of the spring semester her GPA was just shy of 3.5.

Her reward, as Darrow now recalled, was a summer job as Farr's research assistant. From the file, her contribution to his scholarship was unknown. Darrow smiled at this a little: that same summer Farr had helped secure Darrow a job at the admissions department–the compensation for which, combined with modest work hours, had allowed him to do some remedial carousing.

Reaching for the last folder, he reflected that, on paper, Angela was still alive.

The thought renewed his sadness and foreboding. When was it, Darrow wondered now, that Angela Hall had first met Steve Tillman? Or, for that matter, Joe Betts? In the fall, he supposed, the period of her unexplained disappearances, when it seemed she had begun her final diary.

By this time Angela's path toward a scholarship at an elite law school was becoming clear. She had conquered her writing difficulties; dramatically raised her academic performance despite working at the Alibi Club; and secured an assistantship with a respected professor–who, as he had for Darrow, would no doubt write a forceful recommendation to the law school of her choice. There seemed to be little in Angela's way: no medical issues, visits to the school psychologist, or other hints of stress. All that remained was for her to nail the fall semester. Knowing that the transcript in the last file would be blank, Darrow hesitated to open it.

Nonetheless, he did. The courses she had chosen,

including a senior seminar from Farr, would likely have raised her average still higher. Reading Farr's draft letter of recommendation–as laudatory as that he had written for Darrow, but distinctive in its endorsement of Angela's character and abilities–Darrow could feel still more the depth of his mentor's sadness at her murder.

Closing the file, Darrow's hand froze.

For a moment, losing all sense of time, he sat still. Against his will, the pattern of his thoughts began to rearrange itself.

Keep an open mind, Farr had once admonished him, long ago. *Don't impose your own narrative on the world all around you.*

Rearranging Angela's files, Darrow started from the beginning, again, this time inverting the prism he had brought to them before. In the interstices of fact, he realized, he had woven a story of Angela's progress that paralleled his own. But a different story, far more troubling, might be hidden by the first.

That story, were it true, had not ended with her death.

The telephone startled Darrow. He hesitated, then went to the kitchen and answered.

"So I accepted the job," Taylor informed him.

It took a moment for Darrow to focus. "How does it feel?"

"Great. They seemed absolutely ecstatic." Her voice softened. "This will be good, Mark. I'm sure of it."

In the future, perhaps, but in the present, Darrow reflected, he was parting from Taylor much too soon. "Then I'll take you out to celebrate," he proposed.

"Are you sure? I was so caught up in my own news I didn't even ask why you're out today."

"Just working at home." He paused, then added softly, "I feel like I need to see you."

Taylor was quiet. "Is everything okay?"

"I'll meet you at the Carriage House. Seven o'clock."

Saying good-bye, Darrow paused in the kitchen doorway, staring at the files on the table. For an odd moment he thought of the bones of some prehistoric animal through which, using facts and guesswork, archaeologists summoned a living thing from the dead past. Darrow loathed what he had conjured, and himself for his worst thoughts. But his new story of Angela Hall, imagined or real, was too deeply embedded in his own past, and in the present of Caldwell College.

Reaching into his coat pocket, Darrow retrieved his cell phone.

His law school roommate, David Rotner, had been the best man at his wedding. David's ambitions had taken him to Washington, as deputy to the general counsel of the Defense Department. Whenever they managed to get together, once or twice a year, Darrow asked Rotner where Bin Laden resided now.

After dialing the number, he waited, as always, to be transferred at least twice. To his surprise, he found Rotner within two minutes.

"Is this about Bin Laden?" his old roommate inquired. "If so, I can reassure you that Caldwell College is well down on his list."

Darrow managed to laugh. "But not on yours, I hope. I'm calling to ask a favor."

"Which is?"

For an instant, Darrow paused. "I need you to tell me how to access the files of a former army officer."

"How former?"

"He would have left the military in the early seventies."

Rotner thought. "There's a depository of records at Fort

Benjamin Harrison, in Indiana. Likely that's where they are. Who is this guy?"

"A Special Forces officer who served in Vietnam. I'd like to know what he did there. Including whether, for some reason or another, he got involved in moving money around."

"Vietnam," Rotner answered, "got pretty funky. But what's all that to you?"

"He's affiliated with Caldwell. Among other problems we've had a major embezzlement. My predecessor looks good for that. But there are two other people, at least in theory, who could have done it if they had the skills. This man's one."

"Then why not leave this to the authorities, whoever they might be?"

"Too sensitive."

"That's a problem. Any prosecutor would have an easier time getting this file than you would. When do you need it?"

Darrow hesitated. "By the end of this week."

Rotner laughed. "This is the federal government, Mark. Not to mention that there's a separate bureaucracy for requests like this. Try the end of this *year*."

"No time for that." Darrow began pacing. "Suppose you wanted to see this thing tomorrow. Could you?"

"If I was really curious and really lucky? Maybe. But I'm not the secretary of defense." In a tone of caution, Rotner inquired, "What are you asking me to do?"

"To look at his records, then tell me whether there's anything of interest. This is very serious, David, and not just to me. Or else I'd never ask."

"I can look at them," Rotner finally replied. "But I can't describe the contents. All I can do is tell you whether they're worth a written request."

Darrow rubbed his temples. “Then that's all I can ask.” He paused, then said quietly, “The man's name is Lionel Farr.”

9

Despite Taylor's news, both Darrow and she were listless at dinner. On the drive home, she asked, "What's making you so quiet?"

Darrow pulled into the driveway. "A lot of things," he answered. "You, for one. You don't seem all that happy."

"I've been thinking about Angela's diary," she said simply. "You called it 'pathological.' But you've told me almost nothing. Mark, please–I need to know what's bothering you so much."

They sat in the car in front of the darkened house, silent for a time. "By itself," Darrow answered, "the diary doesn't prove a thing. Not even whether the man she describes is real."

"And if he is?"

Darrow did not answer. In a low voice, she repeated her request: "Please tell me about the diary."

Gazing into the darkness, he tried to untangle the reasons he wished to tell her yet feared to do so. At length he turned and faced her directly. "If you want me to," he said.

For the next few minutes, Darrow described the diary in detail–its specificity, its flatness of tone, its depiction of ritual subjugation slipping out of control. Taylor leaned her head back against the car seat, her eyes half-closed, until his narrative was done.

"I think it's real," she said simply. "Angela didn't just make it up."

"How do you know that?"

"If this were some writing exercise, she'd describe her own feelings. Instead she's removed herself." Taylor faced him again. "She was traumatized, Mark."

Darrow thought of Angela on the night of the party—her drinking, her edge of desperation, her refusal of a ride home, the tears in her eyes when she gave him an impulsive hug. *Gonna be a long night for me, I think.*

"Is there something else?" Taylor asked.

As best he could, Darrow reprised this memory. Finishing, he asked, "What do you make of all that?"

Taylor's voice remained quiet, her manner contained. "The same thing you do, I imagine. Angela may not have expected to die. But that night she was afraid of something, or someone. I'm not even sure that what happened to her was wholly a surprise."

By silent consent, they went inside. But, as on the morning in Boston after her nightmare, part of her seemed absent. Alone, she went to his bedroom.

He found her there, naked, sitting on the edge of his bed with her arms crossed. Lying beside her, Darrow touched Taylor's shoulder. "It's not you," she said. "Maybe I'm just tired."

Darrow turned out the light. After a time she slid into bed with him, their bodies apart. All that he knew was that Angela's diary had taken her somewhere he could not reach.

To his surprise, she slept. Darrow did not. Lying awake, he felt her restless stirrings, heard small cries that were not words escape her lips.

IN THE MIDDLE of the night, Taylor shuddered. Only when Darrow heard her stifling sobs did he know she was awake.

Darrow put his arms around her. She lay there, silent.

He reached for the bedside lamp.

The light made her flinch. Then she turned on her back, eyes open, as though reorienting herself. A strand of hair stuck to her dampened skin. "The dream?" Darrow asked.

Her lips parting slightly, she gazed up at the ceiling. "A part I've never told you."

"Maybe it would be better if you did."

"Better?" she asked softly.

"What could be worse?"

He felt her shiver. In a monotone, Taylor described the dream.

HER PARENTS WERE in their bedroom. She did not know how old she was; dreams have their own logic. But, in life, it would have been before her mother slept in a separate room.

Her parents' voices, though raised, were too muffled for Taylor to understand. She pressed her face against the door. Then her mother spoke in voice so intense, and so unlike her, that Taylor could hear. "We're done. Look for your ideal woman somewhere else."

Taylor turned and walked away so softly that her footsteps made no sound, certain only that her parents were not as she hoped, but as she feared.

"I DON'T KNOW what it means," she told Darrow now. "If anything."

"How do you know it's a dream and not a memory?"

She turned, looking wordlessly into his eyes.

"You said they started sleeping apart." Darrow took her hand. "You were a child, Taylor. There are whole pieces of childhood I simply don't remember. When you've got no other means of escaping, dissociation provides one."

"Do you ever dream?"

"Not if I can help it." His tone softened. "My parents are both gone. There's no one living to remind me."

Taylor said nothing. Reaching across his body, she turned out the light.

When she slipped out of bed into the darkness, Darrow did not follow for a time.

He found her on his couch, a blanket draped around her. Darrow sat beside her.

"I don't think it's a dream," she said.

"The argument?"

"No." Her eyes narrowed with the effort to remember. "Something else. In memory, it's the last time the three of us went to the riverbank."

Her mother was painting, her father reading pages from his manuscript on Friedrich Nietzsche. Though that spring was unseasonably warm, the water was still too chilly for swimming. Alone on a blanket, Taylor read a Nancy Drew book, restive because the mystery seemed transparent. She looked up, intending to complain to her mother.

Her father stood behind her mother, staring at the painting. His expression was dark. Seeming to ignore him, her mother added brushstrokes. Her eyes were grave, the half smile on her face oddly bitter. Taylor had never seen this look before.

"What was the painting?" Darrow asked.

"A tower. The only one I'd ever seen."

In Darrow's silence, Taylor pulled the blanket tight around her shoulders. "I could swear the painting was real, Mark. But I never saw it again."

"When was this, do you think?"

Taylor shook her head. "I can't tell. But in my mind, it's days before she died. Maybe that's part of my aversion to the Spire."

Darrow asked nothing more. At last they both slept.

In the morning, leaving, Taylor smiled sadly. "This must be like living with the insane," she said.

"No," he answered. "My mother was insane. I can tell the difference."

Trying to work, Darrow could not concentrate. He made the scheduled telephone calls to alumni. Though his mind drifted, he was grateful for the distraction from his own thoughts. Pleading the press of work, he canceled a meeting with Lionel Farr.

Instead, he called Carly Simmons, the medical examiner in the Angela Hall case. Simmons was not in; all he could do was leave his number. By midafternoon, Simmons still had not responded.

When his telephone rang, Darrow snatched at it.

The caller was not Simmons but David Rotner. "I've got the file," Rotner said at once.

He sounded somber. Surprised, Darrow asked, "And?"

"There's nothing to suggest that Farr was laundering money," Rotner said. "Though the last outfit he served in was run by the CIA. As you probably know, the agency moved money around in all sorts of ways. But your man's specialty was on the operational side."

"Meaning?"

"I told you what my constraints are." Rotner's voice lowered. "All I can say is that you'd find the files interesting. But there's nothing here that makes him an embezzler."

Sitting in his chair, Darrow gazed out at the rolling grounds. "What about a double murderer?"

For a moment Rotner was silent. "Why do you ask that?"

"It's nothing I can be sure of. But a second murder–if it is one–happened about three weeks ago."

"Then you've got me in a bind, Mark."

"How so?"

"Because you're one of my closest friends, and I'm not supposed to tell you a fucking thing." His tone became emphatic. "But I will say this: based on these records and what you just told me, you may be dealing with a very singular personality. I strongly suggest that some appropriate person request them."

Darrow made himself stay calm. "I don't have time for that, David."

For a moment Rotner said nothing. At length, he asked, "Have you ever heard of the Phoenix program?"

"No."

"It was a very special, very secret operation during Vietnam. Under the auspices of the CIA, Special Forces personnel carried out targeted assassinations of Viet Cong, alleged VC agents or sympathizers who gave them information. Your man was in the program."

Darrow felt his nerves come alive. "How were these killings done?"

"As I understand it, the techniques varied. A bullet in the head, or maybe a slit throat if silence was important."

"What about pumping someone full of heroin?"

"No idea. But it could have happened. It might make for a quiet death, and Vietnam was awash in smack." Rotner sounded defensive. "The work was dirty, dangerous, and stressful. Our guys got through it by believing that they were protecting their fellow soldiers, the mission, and our country, maybe even Vietnam itself. That's how they stayed sane."

"Did Farr remain sane?"

"The question you need to ask, Mark, is who he was going in."

"What do you mean?"

"Dammit, Mark." Rotner paused, then said with resignation, "Your guy exceeded orders. He seemed to like his work too much."

Darrow felt caged. "Meaning?"

"They'd go into a village at night to kill a VC agent. The orders would be specific to that person–you'd have to put in an application for a particular target and have it approved up the line. It was *not* a hunting license–neither the army nor CIA nor the guys doing it saw this as a form of recreation or a license for mass murder. The idea was to create fear, not hatred.

"Farr was different. Tell him to kill a VC and somehow the target's entire family would end up dead. The army concluded that Farr was a liability."

An image of Farr in Vietnam, those years he would never speak of, made Darrow feel queasy. "You mean they thought he was insane."

"They believed," Rotner answered flatly, "that Farr was dangerous. Let someone damaged step outside normal societal boundaries and it might be hard to bring him back. For many in the Phoenix program, Vietnam was a nightmare. But a man like Farr might believe it was the rest of us who were living in a fairy tale."

"Did anyone use the word 'psychopath'?"

"The Special Forces never wanted guys like that, and they screened their candidates with care." Rotner paused, then added, "Still, it's always possible for a psychopath to slip through, especially someone with a very high IQ.

Witness Jeffrey MacDonald, the Special Forces doctor convicted of killing his wife and kids, then planting evidence that they were murdered by intruders. My understanding of psychopaths is that the moral dimensions of murder don't occur to them at all. What was scary about Macdonald was that he was so smart and so persuasive, he damn near got away with it."

Darrow stared at the papers on his desk: budget figures, the draft of a speech–the stuff of normal life. "Was that why Farr left the military?"

"Not exactly." Rotner hesitated. "There was also the murder of a prostitute in Saigon."

Head bent, Darrow rubbed the bridge of his nose. "What were the circumstances?"

"The killer tied this woman to her bed. The evidence suggested she was strangled during sex." Rotner tried to keep his voice neutral. "The woman who ran the brothel identified a photograph of Farr. So did a friend of the dead girl's."

For what seemed to him a long time, Darrow was quiet. "Mark?" Rotner asked.

"I was wondering why Farr wasn't prosecuted."

"The army was set to bring charges. Then both women retracted their stories. It seemed clear they'd been intimidated, but neither would say so. Without them a court-martial was pointless." Rotner's tone contained a quiet awe. "The army threatened Farr with prosecution anyhow, hoping to compel his resignation. Farr called their bluff. What's plain is that the man had the nerve of a cat burglar, completely without fear.

"In the end, all the army could do was arrange an administrative separation, effectively burying the reasons. The only trace of what must have happened is the file on my desk. To the rest of the world, Lionel Farr was just a war-weary soldier, like so many others in those times."

"He's not like the others," Darrow said quietly. "He's much more remarkable."

"And much more dangerous," Rotner said. "According to these files, he must be in his sixties. But he's not someone who's passive when cornered. Be cautious, Mark."

Darrow promised he would.

FOR THE NEXT few minutes, Darrow thought of many things: the moment when Farr offered to change his life, Farr kneeling beside Angela's body, Farr helping Durbin take charge of Caldwell's response, Farr promising his help on the day the police arrested Steve Tillman. But Darrow's mind kept returning to Taylor, both the child and the woman.

Picking up the telephone, he called Carly Simmons again. "Got your message," she said brusquely. "But the dead have their ways of demanding my attention. You'd think they'd be more patient than the living."

On another day, Darrow might have laughed. "I'll make it quick," he said in an apologetic tone. "Fifteen years ago, would an unattended death in Wayne County have automatically triggered an autopsy?"

"Automatically?" Simmons sounded mildly amused. "We certainly autopsied Angela Hall."

"This isn't about Angela. My question pertains to a woman in her mid-forties with a history of heart disease."

"You've sure got a wide-ranging curiosity," Simmons said dryly. "In the case you describe, it depends. Back then the old doctor who'd come out and sign the death certificate, Rodney Harrison, might not have called for an autopsy. Especially if he knew the woman and her history and nothing seemed amiss."

Darrow's mouth felt dry. "One last question. If you wanted to kill someone in her sleep and leave no trace, how would you do it?"

"Last time *I* did that," Simmons replied in a quietly caustic tone, "I used a pillow. Of course, an autopsy would give you the cause of death. But there's a good chance nothing would be apparent to the naked eye." More sharply, she said, "Mind telling me what *this* is all about?"

"I will," Darrow promised. "Just not yet."

"Then let me get back to my corpses, Mr. Darrow. They're generally more informative."

Darrow thanked her. Without putting down the telephone, he called Taylor on her cell. "Where are you?" he asked.

Taylor sounded puzzled. "My dad's house. Working on my dissertation."

"Stay there," he said. "I'm coming over."

10

Taylor met him at the door, her face drawn from lack of sleep. Her voice anxious, she asked, "What's wrong, Mark?"

He brushed past her, tense as she, glancing around the living room. "Where's Lionel?"

"At work." She paused. "It's not even four o'clock."

He turned to her. "I want you out of here. Pack up what you need."

She folded her arms, visibly striving for a deliberate calm, her eyes flecked with doubt and worry. "Tell me what's going on."

"Later."

"Now," she said tightly. "Is this about my father?"

Darrow made himself pause, searching for words. "And your mother," he said. "Do you remember if she had an autopsy?"

Taylor stared at him. She could not seem to move. "Why are you asking?"

Silent, Darrow placed his hands on her shoulders. For a moment, she looked into his face. Then, haltingly at first, Taylor began speaking.

The white-haired doctor stood with her father by her mother's bed, touching Anne Farr's wrist. Taylor watched from the doorway, gazing at her mother's lifeless face, a ghastly yellow in the light through her bedroom window. In a dispassionate tone, the old man said, "I'm sorry, Lionel. But Anne appears to have died quite peacefully. I guess her heart just gave out."

"So it seems. Taylor found her like this."

Neither man, Taylor realized, had noticed her. "Dear God," Dr. Harrison said in a sorrowful wheeze. "That must have been hard for her."

"It's what we always feared," her father responded. "But this came too soon. We're not ready, Taylor and I."

"At least she has you." The doctor placed a consoling hand on her father's shoulder. "Are you curious about the precise cause of death? If so, we can perform an autopsy."

It took a moment for her father to answer. "If you feel compelled to do it, Rodney."

"And otherwise?"

Turning, her father spoke in a voice thick with grief. "She's dead, for God's sake. Will carving up Anne's body bring her back to life? We both know her heart betrayed her." His speech slowed. "Forgive me. But remembering her like this is hard enough. I don't want to think about an autopsy."

Awkwardly, Dr. Harrison patted his shoulder. "I understand."

"Good," her father answered. "As you say, there's Taylor to think of now."

TAYLOR LOOKED AT Darrow, the cloud of anguish darkening her eyes. Darrow felt the entire foundation of his life being upended by the same man, her father. "Your dreams are about something," he told her. "I'm not sure they're dreams at all."

Taylor shook her head, less in denial, Darrow perceived, than dismay at what she had never acknowledged. He spoke with gentle urgency. "You were a child, Taylor, unable to face your doubts, and without anyone to hear them. All you could do was repress your deepest fears, then run away as far as you could go. At least until now." He paused, then added quietly, "I think your mother knew what he'd done—or believed she did. That's what you've been sensing."

To his surprise, Taylor backed away, saying in a cool, clear voice, "Dreams aren't proof, Mark. Tell me what else you know."

"There's no time for this—"

Her eyes filled with pain and rage. "Tell me, dammit."

"All right," he said. "The money embezzled from Caldwell went to bank accounts controlled by Carl Hall. Somehow Carl knew that your father was the man in Angela's diary. Lionel used the weakness in Caldwell's financial system to pay off Carl and frame Clark Durbin by fabricating his e-mail—"

"How?" Taylor interrupted. "When it comes to computers, my father struggles just to cope."

"Or so he's made us think. It seems he's very good at that."

Taylor took this in, her gaze intense with thought. Briefly, she shut her eyes. Then she seemed to stand straighter, controlling her emotions with an act of will. With icy calm, she said, "We have to check his office, Mark."

Darrow stared at her. Moments before, she had confronted her own suspicion that one parent had murdered the other, which must have been lodged in her subconscious since adolescence. Now, eerily, she had begun to function as her father did in moments of crisis or danger—detached from her own emotions, thinking swiftly, so devoid of doubt or fear that it sharpened

Darrow's edginess. "We need to get out of here," he said. "Go to the police."

"And tell them what?" Taylor stared into Darrow's eyes, speaking with the same dispassion. "I finally know why he keeps his study locked. I also know where he keeps his keys. If we don't look, he'll destroy whatever's there. Just like he cremated my mother's body."

Turning, she went to her father's bedroom. Darrow followed and found her reaching into a small drawer in a rolltop desk. She held up a set of keys. "When I was a child," Taylor said, "this was where he hid things. He never knew I saw him."

This enmity, Darrow realized, was years deep, practiced by two quiet adversaries. "How do you know what these open?" he asked her.

"One day my laptop shut down. He wasn't home, and I needed to check my e-mail on his computer. He never knew I'd violated his sanctuary." Swiftly, Taylor walked to his study. "How many men, I wonder, lock their study at home to keep their family out."

Darrow stared at the dead bolt. "I don't remember seeing this."

"You didn't," Taylor answered tersely. "He installed it the day after we scattered her ashes. It was one of the things we never spoke of."

Though made gloomier by the absence of light, the office was familiar: the map of Vietnam, the oil painting of Mad Anthony Wayne, the leather chair where Farr had sat when he offered the teenage Darrow a new vision of his future. The sense of trespass caused Darrow to pause. He watched Taylor pull out her father's desk chair and log in to Farr's laptop. "You won't find anything," Darrow said. "To imitate Durbin's e-mail, he'd have needed a different computer."

Glancing up, Taylor handed him the keys. "Then look in his drawers."

These, too, had locks. Finding the key, Darrow unlocked three drawers. Two were empty save for writing utensils and printing paper; the third was stuffed with bank records and extra checks. Wedged into the fourth was a small laptop. Darrow remembered a report prepared by Greg Fox and Joe Betts; Farr's spare computer, he realized, was identical to the one Clark Durbin had used as president of Caldwell. Glancing up, he discovered that Taylor was watching him.

"We should take that," she said. "Someone can look it over later."

"Then let's go. I don't want you anywhere near here, Taylor. Let Garrison do the rest."

"What will you tell him? If I understand what you've told me, my father set all this up perfectly, including Swiss bank accounts. Then he murdered the only witness."

"That's my point."

"And mine. If dreams and instincts and pages from a diary added up to anything, you'd have already gone to the police." With the same frightening calm, Taylor refocused on her father's laptop. "There's a reason he didn't want me touching this."

Darrow glanced at his watch. It was nearly five o'clock. "What time does he come home?"

"Usually around six." Taylor tapped the keyboard, summoning her father's files–research papers, records of bills, student essays. "When I began my dissertation," she told Darrow, "I was absolutely paranoid that someone might steal from it. So I encrypted it with a password: 'Anne,' after my mother. No one could have guessed it unless they knew me very well."

She could have been discussing the last novel she had

read or her favorite restaurant in the West Village. Only the way she held her head, still and focused on the screen, betrayed her feelings. Quietly, she said, "He must have hidden a file using a separate password."

Watching her, Darrow flashed on his first financial fraud case. The chief financial officer of a major company had mapped out the falsification of profits on his home computer, in a file entitled "Liberal Accounting Adjustments." The man was more arrogant than inventive; too accustomed to believing himself smarter than his adversaries, he thought himself impervious. In this he had been wrong. The password he had chosen, the name of his graduate school, had embarrassed Wharton deeply when Darrow revealed it in court. Taylor looked up. "I just tried to open a file called 'Family Pictures,'" she told him. "But the computer is asking me for a password. Any ideas?"

"No."

"We both know things about him," Taylor insisted. "What password would he use?"

"Try 'Nietzsche.'"

Swiftly, Taylor did this. "No," she told him.

She tried several others. Edgy, Darrow went to the entrance of the study, half-expecting Farr. Darrow had betrayed his thoughts, though not quite all, to a man with a feral sense of danger. He thought of all the ways Farr had covered himself, even within his own family, in part to keep his daughter's doubts at bay. An ambiguous but disturbing image came to Darrow: Anne Farr painting beside the river; Lionel Farr staring at a depiction of the Spire that Taylor had never seen again.

Over his shoulder, Darrow said, "Try 'Spire.'"

He walked into the living room. Opening the front door, he stood on the porch and looked up and down the street. Though blocks away, neither of the two men he saw on foot had Farr's erect posture or martial stride. How many times, Darrow wondered, had the sight of those things made him smile? With a leaden feeling, he closed the door, carrying the burden of his fears and memories to Farr's office.

Taylor had turned from the screen.

In profile, her skin was unnaturally pale. She did not move. All that distinguished her from a mannequin was the single tear running down her face.

"What is it?" Darrow asked, and then looked at the screen.

Her back to a dark stone wall, Angela Hall stared back at him, naked but for the leather straps that bound her wrists and ankles. Stunned, Darrow placed his hand on Taylor's shoulder and felt the tremor running through her. With unearthly quiet, she said, "Imagine calling this file 'Family Pictures.' "

His hand resting on her shoulder, Darrow clicked to another photograph, then several more. Her face frozen when it was not turned away, Angela was captured in different poses. The photographs suggested varied possibilities. But their common theme was exposure and helplessness–the man behind the camera could tell her to perform the act suggested and Angela could not resist. The photographs could have illustrated her diary.

Darrow clicked again.

The next set of photographs was of a young white woman he did not know. From the length and style of her hair, Darrow guessed, she had entered Caldwell before him. He supposed that she, like Angela, might have majored in philosophy.

Darrow stopped clicking.

"Keep going," Taylor said in an ashen voice.

She had turned to the screen, the streaks of wetness on

her face glistening in its gray-blue glow. "No," he answered.

Reaching past him, Taylor clicked the mouse. Rather than looking at the screen, Darrow watched his lover's face.

Her expression, he thought now, was like Angela's: oddly stoic, eyes frozen in shock. Suddenly she flinched, crying out, then bent forward with her eyes shut.

Darrow faced the screen. Naked, Anne Farr hung by the wrists from the chain of the Spire's bell. The bell was behind her head; had Farr pushed her, Darrow thought, it might have rung.

Darrow shut off the computer.

Resting his face against the crown of Taylor's head, he murmured, "Take both laptops, Taylor. That's all that's left for you to do."

There was nothing else to say, Darrow knew, or the time to say it. Taylor seemed to grasp this. After a moment, she raised her head to look at him.

"Go to the police station," Darrow directed. "Tell Garrison what we found."

Moving slowly, Taylor unplugged the laptop. Her voice muted, she said, "Where will you be?"

Darrow did not respond. Instead, he picked up Farr's desk phone and dialed a number he knew from memory.

On the third ring, Farr answered his private line. "It's Mark," Darrow said. "I need to see you."

For an instant, Farr did not respond. "Concerning what?"

"Family pictures. The ones on your computer."

As Darrow absorbed Farr's profound silence, Taylor's eyes widened in fear. "So this is what we've come to," Farr said at length.

"Yes."

"Then I'll meet you at the Spire, Mark."

Abruptly, Farr hung up.

Taylor grabbed the lapels of Darrow's suit coat. "We know what he is," she said in desperation. "Please, don't do this."

"I have to," Darrow answered. "Because of all he is to me."

11

When Darrow reached the Spire, the oaken door at its base was ajar.

He stopped, afraid of what might follow if he entered, dreading the claustrophobia that had enveloped him in the tower sixteen years before. Farr would know this; he knew Mark Darrow well. Breathing deeply, Darrow filled his lungs and then crossed the threshold.

The dank smell of moist sandstone flooded his nostrils. The winding stairs above him, lit dimly by lamps placed too wide apart, disappeared in shadows. Darrow began climbing, his loathing of close spaces tightening around him like a vise. This time, he could not distract himself by counting the steps. This time, Farr awaited him.

As he climbed the Spire, Darrow thought of finding Angela Hall's body. From the moment a stunned Mark Darrow had run to him for help, Farr had taken control, improvising with what Darrow now understood was a psychopath's nerveless brilliance. Perceiving that Darrow's account of the party led directly to Steve Tillman, Farr had prevented Darrow from warning Steve by taking him to Durbin's home. There Farr had taken charge of Caldwell's response, making himself as indispensable to Durbin as he was above suspicion. When Steve was arrested and Mark had asked for his help, Farr had sent Steve to a lawyer he knew to be incompetent. The last piece of Farr's lightning adaptations was the sacrifice of Mark's closest friend to a life in prison.

Briefly Darrow paused in the darkness, recalling the night Farr had first approached him. Moments before that, he had thrown the winning touchdown pass to Steve; barking signals, Mark had shut down his emotions, banishing all thought except to execute this play. The crowd noise had vanished; the task before him became no more daunting than a video game. Mark had first done this as a boy, shutting out his mother's frightening shifts of mood, the sudden violence of his alcoholic father. Perhaps that was why his coach had called him the "mentally toughest guy around." Except, perhaps, for the man at the top of the Spire.

He was not quite ready, Darrow realized. In his reasoning mind he understood who Farr had been in secret. Murder was nothing to him. And yet this same man had saved Darrow from a life so dreary that it frightened him to recall. He could not make two decades of affection vanish in an hour.

Darrow kept climbing. The only sound he heard was the echo of his footsteps. He must not think of Taylor, or anything outside the Spire.

Why had Farr chosen this place, Darrow wondered. He kept expecting the provost to appear on the darkened steps above him. Surely he was near the top; the sound of Darrow's breathing, more labored now, whispered against the stone. But there was no way of knowing where Farr was–the staircase kept winding upward, vanishing from sight. Darrow bent in a semicrouch, preparing to dodge or leap.

He suddenly stopped, the pit of his stomach hollow. At the top of the staircase he saw the door to the bell tower, slightly open. Farr had entered Angela Hall's "chamber of stone."

Darrow climbed the final steps. As before, his footfalls caused a thudding echo; the element of surprise belonged to Farr alone, a man who seemed to have retained his assassin's skills.

Abruptly, Darrow pushed open the door.

He saw nothing but the brass bell and the chain from which Anne Farr had been suspended. Edging forward, Darrow looked to each side. The door shut softly behind him.

Flinching, he heard Farr's mirthless laugh.

Darrow turned to face him.

Farr stood beside the door, his blue eyes glinting with keen appraisal. But for this, he looked disconcertingly the same. Something in Darrow's expression caused him to smile slightly.

"You were expecting me to start speaking in tongues?" Farr inquired sarcastically. "Or perhaps a disjointed rant?"

He was utterly calm, Darrow realized. Mildly, Farr asked, "Are you afraid, Mark?"

Darrow found his voice. "You murdered at least four people."

"Four?"

"I'm counting the prostitute in Vietnam."

The trace of amusement vanished from Farr's eyes, replaced by heightened attention. "I've underrated you, it seems."

Once more, Darrow willed himself to feel nothing. "Maybe so. I'm the one you left whole."

"Unlike Taylor, you mean."

Darrow nodded. "At least she's still alive. You must have always watched her, wondering if you'd be forced to choose between her life and yours."

Farr stepped closer to Darrow, grasping the chain of the bell. Then he leaned against its metallic mass in a pose of relaxation that, to Darrow, seemed explosive in its stillness. "When did you divine all this, Mark?"

Darrow did not move. "I'm not here to impress you. I came to tell you that it's over, and that killing me is pointless. I want you to come down with me."

Farr's eyes became a chill blue. "Then persuade me. Enthrall me with all you know."

"What's to say, Lionel? You're a sexual psychopath. The rest followed."

Farr's expression became blank, almost bored. "Spare me the lecture on pathology. If we're both to leave here alive, I want facts, not stereotypes."

The explicit threat was so casually delivered that it made Darrow's skin clammy. Against his will, he absorbed the gloomy shadows, the heavy bell, the dingy stones against which Angela had died. The sole light came from the four openings in the stone–through one of which, decades ago, a young man had fallen to his death. Finding his voice again, Darrow said, "Angela, then."

"Yes," Farr concurred. "Angela."

"A bit at a time, you brought her close–saving her scholarship, taking a professorial interest, giving her grades she feared she hadn't earned, reviewing her papers, then making revisions until she was no longer sure whose work it was. Pretending to help her, you eroded her sense of self. Whether or not she needed you to succeed, she came to believe she did. Helping her financially was part of the endgame. That, and the draft letter of recommendation you dangled."

Watching Farr's expression, keen with interest, Darrow stopped there. "Go on," Farr demanded.

This, too, was a game, Darrow realized, its stakes

obscure but perhaps lethal. He shrugged his assent, continuing with a casualness he did not feel: "Your psychic stalking had worked before. Whatever her reasons, Angela let you bring her here, becoming little more than robotic as she submitted to what you needed." Darrow's voice became cutting. "She wrote the diary to record what you were doing to her. By its end, she loathed you as deeply as you deserved."

Behind Farr's opaque mask, Darrow sensed an anger he was fighting to control. "Is that what you think?"

"*You* read the diary," Darrow retorted. "You killed Carl for it. Angela was so young, Lionel. Before you found her, she was filled with hope. Maybe that came back to her. Maybe sleeping with Steve Tillman, even drunk, made her skin crawl at the thought of you. When she left his room to come here, she was done with you." Darrow softened his voice. "Fred Bender thought Steve killed her because she threatened to charge him with rape. Right theory, wrong man. Angela threatened to expose you to Clark Durbin. So you beat her, then strangled her to death where we're standing now.

"After you carried her body down, the waitress saw you laying it on the ground. Even then, you'd had the presence of mind to lock the door behind you. No one but Carl Hall and Taylor's mother ever imagined what had happened in this place."

Farr's glacial eyes remained on Darrow's face. "Are you expecting me to comment? Or are you simply trying to dazzle me?"

The questions jarred loose Darrow's anger. "We're talking about murder and sadomasochism. If you still imagine I'm who you need me to be, you're a fool."

A flush appeared on Farr's cheekbones. "It's not that easy to insult me, Mark. Your story's incomplete."

"So's your comprehension," Darrow responded. "DNA lasts the longest in dark places. I'm sure there's a genetic trace of both of you still here."

Farr's eyes narrowed. "And Carl?"

"Gazed into his sister's coffin and saw dollars. I imagine he'd followed her here, no doubt on an earlier night, and seen you leaving. After her murder he came to you, asking to be paid." Darrow paused. "You couldn't risk a double murder that soon. Worse, you were married to a woman who was afraid you'd strangled Angela Hall. When Anne painted the Spire, you knew."

Eyes cool, Farr shook his head, miming disapproval. "Your tale's becoming gothic."

"Gothic novels don't turn on life insurance policies. Anne had one, I suspect, to help cover Taylor's education. You killed her for the proceeds, eliminating the threat that she'd expose you and giving you money to buy off Carl Hall. But transfers of cash create a paper trail. Diamonds don't."

A moment's surprise surfaced in Farr's eyes. "Tell me the rest, Mark."

"The other problem was Taylor. She loved her mother, and she was as sensitive and intuitive as she was bright. I wonder which of you frightened the other more–the remote father or the haunted child who knew in her subconscious that something wasn't right. I suppose Taylor's fortunate she didn't 'drown.'"

Farr crossed his arms, his face now pale in the fading light. "At least it's fortunate for you. Or was."

Darrow did not respond to this. "If you were to let Taylor live," he went on, "you needed to separate her from her memories. But you had no money to send her away. So Anne's parents paid for her education, and gave her a second home until they died. Only Carl was still in Wayne."

The remark evoked in Farr a smile of contempt. "Yes, Carl. As Heraclitus once said, 'Character is fate.' "

"Carl's *and* yours. He kept wanting more money, and was too street-smart for you to kill easily—especially because he kept to a neighborhood where a white college professor would be conspicuous." Pausing, Darrow watched Farr closely, both men tense and alert. "Over time, you must have become quite desperate. Then you saw an opportunity to embezzle money and frame a man with severe financial problems, including a son whose heroin addiction was conveniently fed by Carl Hall. Everything Joe Betts could have done to implicate Durbin, you did. And everyone believed it. Which brings the story back to me."

Farr's expression changed again, betraying the faintest regret. "That was unfortunate for us both, wasn't it."

"Certainly for you," Darrow retorted. "Your chief concern was that Caldwell's next president be as malleable as Durbin. You couldn't count on controlling a stranger, or even remaining as provost. I was young, presentable, well-known to the board and alumni, and, most ironic of all, sophisticated in criminal and financial fraud cases." Darrow spoke quietly, reining in his anger. "But I had another qualification no other candidate could match: the admiration and affection you'd imbued me with since I was seventeen. You saw me as the person least likely to suspect you, the one you could deflect from any area of danger.

"That was a miscalculation, Lionel—quite a bad one. Not just because I was also the most likely to sense that something was wrong. You still can't believe that anyone else is as smart as you, can you?"

Farr gave the brass bell a shove, propelling it toward Darrow. "You did alter the balance of things, Mark. You got a man killed."

"Carl got Carl killed," Darrow said flatly. "He became too greedy and told himself you were too old to be a threat to him. He didn't know you'd murdered people as a vocation. Once you grasped my doubts about where Caldwell's money went, you couldn't risk letting him live.

"That left only Taylor. You never expected that she'd return. And the last thing you wanted was for me to spend much time with her." Darrow's voice softened again. "Maybe she suspected you, Lionel. But maybe she just hoped to know you better. Thanks to me, she does."

"Meaning?"

"She took your 'family pictures' to Garrison. You couldn't be more finished."

Farr shoved the bell again, swinging it closer to Darrow's face. "When I snatched you off the football field," Farr told him, "I chose well. It was almost like choosing my own son." His voice became oddly gentle. "You claim there's little point in killing you. Instead, you've persuaded me you shouldn't live. If you're the one who's ruined me, why give you the pleasure of watching me come to an inglorious end? One victory celebration in the Spire is enough for a man's lifetime." Pausing, Farr shook his head. "The sad part is that I loved you. More than anything, that's why I brought you back. Now both of us are finished."

Shaken, Darrow backed away from the swinging bell. "What about Taylor, Lionel?"

Farr smiled in disbelief. "Even if you lived, do you imagine your relationship could possibly survive this?"

"If how I feel counts for anything, it will. Taylor's the one woman you didn't destroy."

"Do you really think so?" Suddenly Farr gave the bell a violent shove toward Darrow. Reeling backward, Darrow reached for the wall, trying to brace himself. To his horror, he found himself framed against an opening in the tower.

Farr came swiftly toward him. Frozen, Darrow crouched as Farr grasped his shoulders with both hands. Swinging behind them, the bell tolled sonorously.

Farr looked deeply into his eyes, as though trying to hold a memory. In a tone tinged with regret, he said, "Good-bye, Mark."

Darrow wrenched from his grasp and staggered sideways.

Farr let him go, staring at him with the thinnest of smiles. Softly, Farr said, "You still don't understand."

The bell kept tolling. As it echoed through the tower, Darrow watched Farr move to the opening, turn, and sit on the ledge. For a last moment he gazed back at Darrow. Then Farr closed his eyes and toppled backward into space.

Shocked, Darrow stared at the opening, seconds before filled by his friend and mentor. Then, despite his fear of heights, he willed himself to peer down at the grass below.

Farr lay on the grass, his body crumpled. Much as Darrow had knelt over Angela, Taylor knelt beside him now, her raven hair almost touching her father's face. Only then did she look up toward Darrow.

12

Taylor had her father cremated. She let the crematorium dispose of his ashes as they chose.

The museum gave her an extra month. She would visit friends in the East, she told Darrow—she could not stay in Wayne. Darrow understood this. She had suffered the greater loss; he would have to deal with his own confusion and grief alone. For now, it was enough that Taylor had survived.

There was much for Darrow to do. At his direction, Joe Betts and the investment committee filed a claim against Carl Hall's estate. Assisted by George Garrison, Dave Farragher petitioned for Steve Tillman's release; days later, Farragher postponed his run for Congress. When his friend was released, Darrow drove him away from the prison.

Though Steve thanked him, he said little about Farr. The whiplash of his emotions, combined with sudden freedom, had left him troubled and confused. "What will I do now?" he asked Darrow.

"There's a room at my place," Darrow said. "Seems only fair."

Steve managed to smile. "Football season's starting," Darrow told him. "Caldwell needs a receivers coach. If you want the job, it'll give you some time to sort this out."

Steve considered this. "I haven't seen a game in sixteen years."

"Nothing's changed. Our team is still white; the receivers are still slow. You'll catch up."

At length, Steve nodded. His reactions seemed delayed, Darrow realized, as though he could not trust his own perceptions of reality. "Then I guess I'll take it," Steve finally said.

The next day, over lunch, Darrow described Steve's state of mind to Garrison. "If I'd come to you before," Darrow added, "I'd have accused the wrong man. There's been enough of that."

Garrison sat back, hands folded across his stomach, his expression curious and not unkind. "Lionel Farr," he said. "How are *you* dealing with that?"

Darrow shrugged. "It's taking a while. But Farr made me responsible for Caldwell's future. That tends to get me through the day."

But not the nights. A few evenings a week, less often than he wished, Darrow called Taylor. Their conversations were halting; it was as though Taylor, like Steve, had been paralyzed by Lionel Farr's death. "I can help you through this," Darrow told her once.

"Can you?"

There was neither challenge nor hope in her voice, only a dispassionate curiosity that Darrow found disheartening. He said good-bye that night without knowing what else to say.

That weekend he flew to Boston and sat down with Jerry Seitz.

For several hours Darrow told him about Taylor and his own relationship to Farr. "This man didn't make you," Seitz responded. "Maybe Caldwell did. But you made yourself a very different man. That's why you were finally able to see him as he truly was."

Darrow was quiet for a time. "Farr killed himself, Jerry,

instead of trying to throw me off the Spire. Explain *that* to me."

Seitz shook his head. "I'm not a mind reader. But he didn't kill Taylor, either. One could argue that he kept you alive for her."

"Do you believe that?"

Seitz gave a short laugh. "Not really. Nor do I think for a moment that what he felt for her–or you–was 'love' as most of us define it. No doubt he saw himself in you, his quasi son; no doubt the admiration you gave him was a source of considerable pleasure. Still, even psychopaths have a subconscious. Maybe he wanted to be a better father than the one he had."

"I don't know anything about that."

"He'd never tell you." The light of new thought appeared in Seitz's eyes. "Know what I think, Mark? Farr admired you. In your own way, you can be very cold-blooded. Maybe Farr saw in you someone almost as smart and ruthless as he."

Darrow's own smile was bleak. "Are you saying that to make me feel better?"

"Don't worry, Mark. You can turn that side of you on and off like a switch. You've learned to use it only when you need to. At your worst, you can never be as subarctic as Lionel Farr." He paused. "The ultimate reason for Farr's suicide, I think, is that he refused to let you win."

The thought chilled Darrow; he still could not shake the image of Farr's ruined body, Taylor kneeling over him. "What did the Spire mean to him, I wonder."

"God knows. Theories abound–maybe he wanted to appropriate Caldwell's most important symbol. I don't need to dwell on the sexual imagery. But the Spire became his private realm; no one could stop him there. In terms of the subconscious, it's also a place where a man can fall from the greatest heights. In the end, that's literally what Farr chose for himself."

Darrow became quiet. "Farr's dead," he said at length. "I can deal with that at leisure. But Taylor is still alive."

"Give her time, Mark."

"I know that. But how much time?"

"Whatever she needs." Seitz's tone was quiet and compassionate. "You have to face that it may not work out with Taylor. Before this happened, she admitted to her own issues with trust. Knowing that your father killed your mother has to be deeply traumatic, and you're at the core of it.

"Maybe she'll get through this once she sorts it out some more. Maybe you can help her. But she'll always be more than a little cautious."

Darrow nodded. Since Farr's death, Taylor and he had barely touched each other.

This conversation, with its unanswered questions and sorrowful doubts, followed him back to Wayne, and into a meeting with Ray Carrick and the governance committee of the board of trustees.

In the wake of Farr's death, Darrow and Carrick had agreed that, because of Darrow's own involvement, Carrick would speak on behalf of Caldwell. The statement, largely drafted by Darrow, had traced Farr's role in Angela's death and the embezzlement, absolving Clark Durbin of wrongdoing. Carrick had added his own coda: "The shadow on our school is lifted. It was the work of a single man, and that man is gone from our community. Caldwell's healing can now begin." Darrow thought this utter horseshit.

It was in this mood that he faced the committee, knowing that he, like Farr before him, had become indispensable. Looking at Ray Carrick, Darrow informed them that—were he to remain here—he intended to demolish the Spire. "There's been too much idolatry," he said. "This school was never about a stone tower, any more than it was about its provost. The heart of Caldwell's campus should look to the future, not the past."

Darrow glanced at each trustee, five men and a woman. No one—including Carrick—challenged him. "Good," Darrow said. "I think we can also agree that we need more women on the board. But that's for the fall meeting. The immediate problem is to find a new provost. I have one."

Surprised, Carrick asked, "Who?"

"Clark Durbin."

"*Durbin?*" Carrick repeated with astonishment.

"Yes. Once we get used to the idea that he's not a crook, Clark makes perfect sense. He knows the school, the faculty always liked him, and he's a good fund-raiser. From my perspective, another advantage is that he lacks Lionel's belief that a provost should run the school." Darrow looked at Carrick, adding, in a sardonic tone, "Besides, it'll keep Clark from suing us for firing him without just cause. If *I* were Clark, I would."

"Would he even take it?"

Darrow smiled. "He says he would. I could certainly use his help. Are we agreed?"

Carrick hesitated. At the other end of the conference table, Joe Betts leaned forward to speak. "We all owe you a lot, Mark. A mistake is a mistake, and we made a big one. I, for one, don't want to lose you. You're the guy who saved our ass."

Without destroying your reputation, Darrow thought, or your marriage. "Thank you," Darrow said simply. "But there's still a lot ahead of us. At least for the next three years, I'll do my best."

Carrick looked from Darrow to Betts, once a reliable

ally. The balance of power was shifting; if Carrick did not like it, Darrow thought, he damn well could pretend.

"Three years?" Carrie Goode inquired.

Darrow nodded. "That's the most I can promise. Three years is enough time to launch a capital campaign, get the school in order, and find the long-term leader Caldwell needs. After that, I hope to have a different life."

A day later, Taylor called him.

THEY MET IN Boston.

Over dinner and long into the night, they merely talked, describing as best they could what each had gone through, without speaking of the future. To Darrow, Taylor's intentions were opaque. Though they slept beside each other, sometimes touching, they did not make love.

In the morning, they sat on the brick patio of Darrow's town house. Once Darrow and Lee had enjoyed this, heedless of what awaited them. Now Darrow was acutely aware of not knowing if what he wanted could still exist.

"I haven't wanted to ask about Caldwell," Taylor said. "How is that now?"

"All right." Darrow hesitated. "Next week they're tearing down the Spire."

For a moment, her eyes were haunted and deeply sad. "That's the easy part," she answered.

She said nothing more. In their silence, Darrow felt Taylor studying him. There was a new clarity in her eyes, as though she had awakened to find him sitting there. "What are you thinking, Mark?"

He smiled a little. "I was thinking about you. That happens fairly often."

"I know. And I'm sorry."

Darrow felt a stab of dismay. "Sorry?"

"I know how I've been," she said quietly. "At least you know my excuse."

"I do know." Darrow hesitated. "This hasn't been easy for me, either. But the fact that Lionel wasn't my father lends me a certain clarity."

"About what?"

"You." Darrow felt his caution overcome by emotions he could no longer defer. "I don't want to lose you, Taylor."

Silent, she watched him, her expression wary yet not closed. Darrow's words came swiftly: "I'm not a mystic, so I don't know how to explain this. But I think we were meant to be together from the beginning. Even when I was in college and what's happened between us now was unimaginable.

"I think you feel it, too. To let Lionel destroy us gives him too much power. Maybe looking at me forces you to remember him. If so, at least that's better than nightmares and repression." He forced himself to speak more gently. "Together, you and I can face whatever happened. Who else could understand each other as well as you and I do?"

Doubt surfaced in Taylor's eyes. "I really mean that much to you?"

"More than I can express." Darrow drew a breath, deciding to take his time. "I'm in love with you, Taylor. When we're in the same space, no matter what you're doing, I feel at peace. I've never had that before. Without you, I don't think I ever will. And I don't think losing me would be any good for you, either.

"You want kids. I want *our* kids. Together we can give them what we never had. We can do that because of all we've learned. And because we can tell each other and our children the truth as best we know it." Darrow took her hand. "I've got three years at Caldwell, and then I'm done.

We don't have to wait. America still makes airplanes, and I still have a home in Boston. Our life can be what we choose; you'll have the career you want. All I know is that the life we can have together will be much richer than the lives we'd lead apart."

Taylor tilted her head, the slightest smile at the corner of her lips. "That's more than I've heard you say at one time since I was seven. Are you quite sure you're done?"

Darrow watched her, caught between a feeling of release and a deep fear of losing her. "Only for the moment."

Head bowed, Taylor touched her eyes. "I'm not sure how to answer."

"You can start by looking at me."

"Another willful man," she murmured, and then raised her gaze to his. "This is hard, Mark. It *will* be hard, at least for a while."

"I know that," Darrow answered. "All we can do is try."

To his surprise, Taylor kissed him. "Then let's go inside," she said.

AFTERWORD AND ACKNOWLEDGMENTS

One of the deepest pleasures of writing *The Spire* was returning, after over a decade away, to writing a psychological suspense novel intensely focused on characters, story, and setting. So I'm grateful to all those who helped me along the way.

Among them were old and new friends affiliated with my undergraduate school, Ohio Wesleyan University, and the small town in which it is located, Delaware–both of which supplied considerable atmosphere without the dire history. Interim President David Robbins helped me grasp Darrow's challenges and Lionel Farr's duties, while Dr. Carl Pinkele lent a faculty perspective. Dr. Erin Flynn gave me advice on Farr's philosophy class, while Dr. Carol Neuman de Vegvar lent Taylor Farr a background in art history. Two college friends who became prominent lawyers in Delaware, Dan Bennington and Tony Heald, conspired with me to bring the Tillman case to life, and Delaware County Prosecutor Dave Yost cordially shared a prosecutor's perspective. I'm also very grateful to Chief of Police Russ Martin and Officer Sean Sneed, who helped me imagine the investigation, as well as the challenges facing Chief George Garrison. Finally, thanks to all the members of the wonderful Ohio Wesleyan community–students, alumni, faculty, administrators, and board members—with whom I so enjoyed working during my tenure as a trustee.

Others helped me create the world of *The Spire*. My friend Derek Bok, former president of Harvard, was generous with his advice, as was Bob Edgar, president of Common Cause. Invaluable insight into the Tillman case came from prosecutor Al Giannini, defense lawyer Jim Collins, homicide inspector Joe Toomey, and forensic pathologist Terri Haddix. My son, Brooke, and daughter, Katie, shared some anecdotes from college and prep school that I was happy to learn after the fact. Retired General Hugh Shelton was kind enough to impart some needed military background. Dale Walker explained to a computer illiterate how Darrow and Taylor might get into Farr's PC. Researcher Cristin Williams helped reconstruct the cultural background of Darrow's college years. And, as always, my friend Bob Tyrer helped me investigate varied areas of ignorance.

Psychiatry and forensic accounting are worlds unto themselves. Dr. Rodney Shapiro gave me a fascinating insight into the psychological possibilities presented by Lionel Farr. Several members of the splendid firm of Deloitte & Touche helped me create the accounting scenario: Pat Brady, Karen Kennard, Richard Miller, and Rick Potocek. Similarly generous were Jeff Raymon and Elliot Rosenfield of the firm that bears their names, as well as Ted Bunn and Bryan St. Germain, who otherwise spend some of their time protecting me from the vagarics of the stock market.

As always, I owe a great debt to my figurative board of directors: my assistant, Alison Porter Thomas; my agent, Fred Hill; my editor, John Sterling; my splendid copy editor, Bonnie Thompson; and my wife and discerning reader, Dr. Nancy Clair.

Finally, there are my cherished friends–and one of our favorite couples–Justin Feldman and Linda Fairstein. For several years now, the four of us have enjoyed long and wonderful evenings together. Justin has been a constant source of friendship, warmth, humor, and advice–as well as some of the best legal and political anecdotes ever told. As for Linda, it is not enough that she, as a lawyer, helped establish the Manhattan DA's Sex Crimes Unit, or that she has since written numerous engrossing and best-selling novels. Linda also wrote the vows for our wedding this summer, which–thanks to her and Justin's generosity–took place on the grounds of their beautiful home on Martha's Vineyard. For all of that, and more, Nancy and I dedicate this book to them.